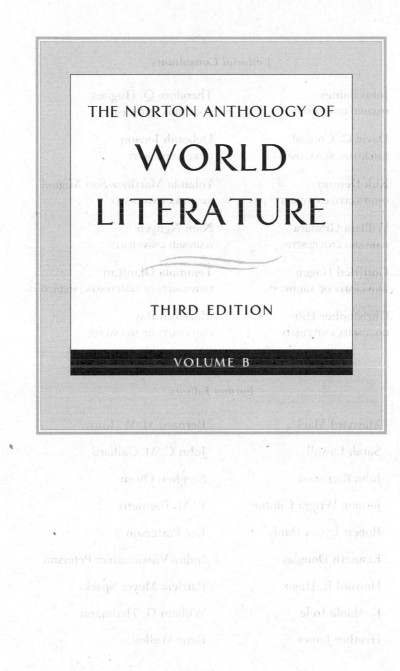

THE NORTON ANTHOLOGY OF

WORLD

LITERATURE

THIRD EDITION

VOLUME B

THE NORTON ANTHOLOGY OF

WORLD
LITERATURE

THIRD EDITION

MARTIN PUCHNER, *General Editor*
HARVARD UNIVERSITY

SUZANNE AKBARI
UNIVERSITY OF TORONTO

WIEBKE DENECKE
BOSTON UNIVERSITY

VINAY DHARWADKER
UNIVERSITY OF WISCONSIN, MADISON

BARBARA FUCHS
UNIVERSITY OF CALIFORNIA, LOS ANGELES

CAROLINE LEVINE
UNIVERSITY OF WISCONSIN, MADISON

PERICLES LEWIS
YALE UNIVERSITY

EMILY WILSON
UNIVERSITY OF PENNSYLVANIA

VOLUME B

W. W. NORTON & COMPANY | New York · London

W. W. Norton & Company has been independent since its founding in 1923, when William Warder Norton and Mary D. Herter Norton first published lectures delivered at the People's Institute, the adult education division of New York City's Cooper Union. The firm soon expanded its program beyond the Institute, publishing books by celebrated academics from America and abroad. By midcentury, the two major pillars of Norton's publishing program—trade books and college texts—were firmly established. In the 1950s, the Norton family transferred control of the company to its employees, and today—with a staff of four hundred and a comparable number of trade, college, and professional titles published each year—W. W. Norton & Company stands as the largest and oldest publishing house owned wholly by its employees.

Editor: Peter Simon
Assistant Editor: Conor Sullivan
Managing Editor, College: Marian Johnson
Manuscript Editors: Barney Latimer, Alice Falk, Katharine Ings, Michael Fleming, Susan Joseph, Pamela Lawson, Diane Cipollone
Electronic Media Editor: Eileen Connell
Print Ancillary Editor: Laura Musich
Editorial Assistant, Media: Jennifer Barnhardt
Marketing Manager, Literature: Kimberly Bowers
Senior Production Manager, College: Benjamin Reynolds
Photo Editor: Patricia Marx
Permissions Manager: Megan Jackson
Permissions Clearing: Margaret Gorenstein
Text Design: Jo Anne Metsch
Art Director: Rubina Yeh
Cartographer: Adrian Kitzinger
Composition: Jouve North America, Brattleboro, VT
Manufacturing: R. R. Donnelley & Sons—Crawfordsville, IN

The text of this book is composed in Fairfield Medium with the display set in Aperto.

Library of Congress Cataloging-in-Publication Data

The Norton anthology of world literature / Martin Puchner, general editor . . . [et al.].—3rd ed.
   p. cm.
   "Volume B."
   Includes bibliographical references and index.
   ISBN 978-0-393-91329-3 (v. A : pbk.)—**ISBN 978-0-393-91330-9 (v. B : pbk.)**—
ISBN 978-0-393-91331-6 (v. C : pbk.)—ISBN 978-0-393-91332-3 (v. D : pbk.)—
ISBN 978-0-393-91333-0 (v. E : pbk.)—ISBN 978-0-393-91334-7 (v. F : pbk.) 1. Literature—
Collections. I. Puchner, Martin, 1969– II. Norton anthology of world masterpieces
   PN6014.N66 2012
   808.8—dc23

                               2011047211

W. W. Norton & Company, Inc., 500 Fifth Avenue, New York, NY 10110-0017
wwnorton.com
W. W. Norton & Company Ltd., Castle House, 75/76 Wells Street, London W1T 3QT

5 6 7 8 9 0

Contents

IV. JAPAN'S CLASSICAL AGE   1073

Preface

In 1665, a Turkish nobleman traveled from his native Istanbul to Europe and recorded with disarming honesty his encounter with an alien civilization. Over the course of his life, Evliya Çelebi would crisscross the Ottoman Empire from Egypt all the way to inner Asia, filling volume after volume with his reports of the cities, peoples, and legends he came across. This was his first journey to Vienna, a longtime foe of the Ottoman Empire. Full of confidence about the superiority of his own culture, Evliya was nevertheless impressed by Vienna's technical and cultural achievements. One episode from his *Travels*, a charming moment of self-deprecation, tells us how, during his tour of Vienna's inner city, Evliya sees what he believes to be "captives from the nation of Muhammad" sitting in front of various shops, toiling away at mind-numbing, repetitive tasks. Feeling pity for them, he offers them some coins, only to find that they are in fact mechanical automatons. Embarrassed and amazed at the same time, Evliya ends this tale by embracing the pleasure of seeing something new: "This was a marvelous and wonderful adventure indeed!"

Throughout his travels, Evliya remained good-humored about such disorienting experiences, and he maintained an open mind as he compared the cultural achievements of his home with those of Vienna. The crowning achievement of Vienna is the cathedral, which towers over the rest of the city. But Evliya found that it couldn't compare with the architectural wonders of Istanbul's great mosques. As soon as he was taken to the library, however, he was awestruck: "There are God knows how many books in the mosques of Sultan Barqūq and Sultan Faraj in Cairo, and in the mosques of [Sultan Mehmed] The Conqueror and Sultan Süleyman and Sultan Bāyezīd and the New Mosque, but in this St. Stephen's Monastery in Vienna there are even more." He admired the sheer diversity and volume of books: "As many nations and different languages as there are, of all their authors and writers in their languages there are many times a hundred thousand books here." He was drawn, naturally enough, to the books that make visible the contours and riches of the world: atlases, maps, and illustrated books. An experienced travel writer, he nonetheless struggled to keep his equilibrium, saying finally that he was simply "stunned."

Opening *The Norton Anthology of World Literature* for the first time, a reader may feel as overwhelmed by its selection of authors and works (from "as many different languages as there are") as Evliya was by the cathedral library. For most students, the world literature course is a semester- or year-long encounter with the unknown—a challenging and rewarding journey, not a stroll down familiar, well-worn paths. Secure in their knowledge of the culture of their upbringing, and perhaps even proud of its accomplishments, most students will discover in world literature a bewildering variety of similarly rich and admirable cultures about which they know little, or nothing. Setting off on an imaginative journey in an unfamiliar text, readers may ask themselves questions similar to those a traveler in a strange land might ponder: How should I orient myself in this unfamiliar culture? What am I not seeing that someone raised in this culture would recognize right away? What can I learn here? How can I relate to the people I meet? Students might imagine the perils of the encounter, wondering if they will embarrass themselves in the process, or simply find themselves "stunned" by the sheer number of things they do not know.

But as much as they may feel anxiety at the prospect of world literature, students may also feel, as Evliya did, excitement at the discovery of something new, the exhilaration of having their horizons expanded. This, after all, is why Evliya traveled in the first place. Travel, for him, became almost an addiction. He sought again and again the rush of the unknown, the experience of being stunned, the feeling of marveling over cultural achievements from across the world. Clearly Evliya would have liked to linger in the cathedral library and immerse himself in its treasures. This experience is precisely what *The Norton Anthology of World Literature* offers to you and your students.

As editors of the Third Edition, we celebrate the excitement of world literature, but we also acknowledge that the encounter with the literary unknown is a source of anxiety. From the beginning of our collaboration, we have set out to make the journey more enticing and less intimidating for our readers.

First, we have made the introductory matter clearer and more informative by shortening headnotes and by following a consistent pattern of presentation, beginning with the author's biography, then moving to the cultural context, and ending with a brief introduction to the work itself. The goal of this approach is to provide students with just enough information to prepare them for their own reading of the work, but not so much information that their sense of discovery is numbed.

The mere presentation of an anthology—page after page of unbroken text—can feel overwhelming to anyone, but especially to an inexperienced student of literature. To alleviate this feeling, and to provide contextual information that words might not be able to convey, we have added hundreds of images and other forms of visual support to the anthology. Most of these images are integrated into the introductions to each major section of the anthology, providing context and visual interest. More than fifty of these images are featured in six newly conceived color inserts that offer pictures of various media, utensils, tools, technologies, and types of writing, as well as scenes of writing and reading from different epochs. The result is a rich visual overview of the material and cultural importance of writing and texts. Recognizing the importance of geography to many of the works in the anthology, the editors have revised the map program so that it complements the literature more directly. Each of the twenty-six maps has been redrawn to help readers orient themselves in the many corners of the world to which this anthology will take them. Finally, newly redesigned timelines at the end of each volume help students see at a glance the temporal relationships among literary works and historical events. Taken together, all of these visual elements make the anthology not only more inviting but also more informative than ever before.

The goal of making world literature a pleasurable adventure also guided our selection of translations. World literature gained its power from the way it reflected and shaped the imagination of peoples, and from the way it circulated outside its original context. For this, it depends on translation. While purists sometimes insist on studying literature only in the original language, a dogma that radically shrinks what one can read, world literature not only relies on translation but actually thrives on it. Translation is a necessity, the only thing that enables a worldwide circulation of literature. It also is an art. One need only think of the way in which translations of the Bible shaped the history of Latin or English. Translations are re-creations of works for new readers. Our edition pays keen attention to translation, and we feature dozens of new translations that make classical texts newly readable and capture the originals in compelling ways. With each choice of translation, we sought a version that would spark a sense of wonder while still being accessible to a contemporary reader. Many of the anthology's most fundamental classics—from *Gilgamesh*, Homer's epics, the Greek dramatists, Virgil, the Bible, the *Bhagavad-Gītā*, and the Qur'an to *The Canterbury Tales*, *The Tale of Genji*, Goethe's *Faust*, Ibsen's *Hedda Gabler*, and Kafka's *Metamorphosis*— are presented in new translations that are both exciting works in English and skillful echoes of the spirit and flavor of the original. In some cases, we commissioned new translations—for instance, for the work of the South Asian poet Kabir, rendered beautifully by our South Asian editor and prize-winning translator Vinay Dharwadker, and for a portion of Çelebi's travels to Vienna by our Ottoman expert Gottfried Hagen that has never before been translated into English.

Finally, the editors decided to make some of the guiding themes of the world literature course, and this anthology, more visible. Experienced teachers know about these major themes and use them to create linked reading assignments, and the anthology has long touched on these topics, but with the Third Edition, these themes rise to the surface, giving all readers a clearer sense of the ties that bind diverse works together. Following is discussion of each of these organizing themes.

Contact and Culture

Again and again, literature evokes journeys away from home and out into the world, bringing its protagonists—and thus its readers—into contact with peoples who are different from them. Such contact, and the cross-pollination it fosters, was crucial for the formation of cultures. The earliest civilizations— the civilizations that invented writing and hence literature—sprang up where they did because they were located along strategic trading and migration routes. Contact was not just something that happened between fully formed cultures, but something that made these cultures possible in the first place.

Committed to presenting the anthology's riches in a way that conveys this central fact of world literature, we have created new sections that encompass broad contact zones—areas of intense trade in peoples, goods, art, and ideas. The largest such zone is centered on the Mediterranean basin and reaches as far as the Fertile Crescent. It is in this large area that the earliest literatures emerged and intermingled. For the Mediterranean Sea was not just a hostile environment that could derail a journey home, as it did for Odysseus, who took ten years to find his way back to Greece from the Trojan War in Asia Minor; it was a connecting tissue as well, allowing for intense contact around its harbors. Medieval maps of the Mediterranean pay tribute to this fact: so-called portolan charts show a veritable mesh of lines connecting hundreds of ports. In the reorganized Mediterranean sections in volumes A and B, we have placed together texts from this broad region, the location of intense conflict as well as friendly exchange, rather than isolating them from each other. In a similar manner, the two major traditions of East Asia, China and Japan, are now presented in the context of the larger region, which means that for the first time the anthology includes texts from Vietnam and Korea.

One of the many ways that human beings have bound themselves to each other and have attempted to bridge cultural and geographic distances is through religion. As a form of cultural exchange, and an inspiration for cultural conflict, religion is an important part of the deep history of contact and encounter presented in the anthology, and the editors have taken every opportunity to call attention to this fact. This is nowhere more visible than in a new section in volume C called "Encounters with Islam," which follows the cultural influence of Islam beyond its point of origin in Arabia and Persia. Here we draw together works from western Africa, Asia Minor, and South Asia, each of them blending the ideas and values of Islam with indigenous folk traditions to create new forms of cultural expression. The original oral stories of the extraordinary Mali epic *Sunjata* (in a newly established version and translation) incorporate elements of Islam much the way the Anglo-Saxon epic *Beowulf* incorporates elements of Christianity. The early Turkish epic *The Book of Dede Korkut* similarly blends Islamic thought and expression with the cultural traditions of the pre-Islamic nomadic tribes whose stories make up the bulk of the book. In a different way, the encounter of Islam with other cultures emerges at the eastern end of its sphere of influence, in South Asia, where a multireligious culture absorbs and transforms Islamic material, as in the philosophical poems of Tukaram and Kabir (both presented in new selections and translations). Evliya Çelebi, with his journey to Vienna, belongs to this larger history as well, giving us another lens through which to view the encounter of Islam and Christianity that is dramatized by so many writers elsewhere in the anthology (most notably, in the *Song of Roland*).

The new emphasis on contact and encounter is expressed not just in the overall organization of the anthology and the selection of material; it is also made visible in clusters of texts on the theme of travel and conquest, giving students access to documents related to travel, contact, trade, and conflict. The greatest story of encounter between peoples to be told in the first half of the anthology is the encounter of Europe (and thus of Eurasia) with the Americas. To tell this story properly, the editors decided to eliminate the old dividing line between the European Renaissance and the New World that had prevailed in previous editions and instead created one broad cultural sphere that combines the two. A (newly expanded) cluster within this section gathers texts immediately relevant to this encounter, vividly chronicling all of its willful violence and its unintended consequences in the "New" World. This section also reveals the ways in which the European discovery of the Americas wrought violence in Europe. Old certainties and authorities overthrown, new worlds imagined, the very concept of being human revised—nothing that happened in the European Renaissance was untouched by the New World. Rarely had contact between two geographic zones had more consequences: henceforth, the Americas would be an important part of the story of Europe.

For a few centuries European empires dominated global politics and economics and accelerated the pace of globalization by laying down worldwide trade routes and communication networks, but old empires, such as China, continued to be influential as well. A new section called "At the Crossroads of Empire" in volume E gathers literature produced in Vietnam, India, and China as Asian and European empires met and collided, vying for control not only of trade routes and raw materials but also of ideas and values. The writers included here felt the pressures of ancient traditions and new imperial powers and resisted both, crafting brave and imaginative responses to repressive conditions. Another new section, "Realism across the World," traces perhaps the first truly global artistic movement, one that found expression in France, Britain, Russia, Brazil, and Japan. And it was not just an effect of European dominance. Representing the daily experiences of people living in gritty urban poverty, for example, the Japanese writer Higuchi Ichiyō developed her own realism without ever having read a European novel.

In the twentieth century, the pace of cultural exchange and contact, so much swifter than in preceding centuries, transformed most literary movements, from modernism to postcolonialism, into truly global phenomena. At the end of the final volume, we encounter Elizabeth Costello, the title character in J. M. Coetzee's novel. A writer herself, Costello has been asked to give lectures on a cruise ship; mobile and deracinated, she and a colleague deliver lectures on the novel in Africa, including the role of geography and oral literature. The scene captures many themes of world literature—and serves as an image of our present stage of globalization. World literature is a story about the relation between the world and literature, and we tell this story partly by paying attention to this geographic dimension.

Travel

The accounts of Evliya Çelebi and other explorers are intriguing because they recount real journeys and real people. But travel has also inspired a rich array of fictional fabulation. This theme lived in past editions of the anthology, as indeed it does in nearly any world literature course in which Homer's *Odyssey*, Chaucer's *Canterbury Tales*, Cervantes' *Don Quixote*, Swift's *Gulliver's Travels*, and many other touchstones of the world literature canon are read. To further develop this theme in the Third Edition, the editors have added several new texts with travel at their center. Among them is the first and most influential Spanish picaresque novel, *Lazarillo de Tormes*, a fast-paced story that shows how fortune has her way with the low-born hero. Lazarillo's resilience and native smarts help him move from master to master, serving a priest, a friar, a chaplain, and an archbishop, all of whom seek to exploit him. The great Vietnamese epic *The Tale of Kiều*, another new selection, features an even greater survival artist. In this tale the heroine, repeatedly abducted and pressed into prostitution and marriage, survives because of her impeccable stoicism, which she maintains in the face of a life that seems shaped by cruel accidents and ill fortune. Even as these tales delight in adventures and highlight the qualities that allow their heroes to survive them, they are invested in something else: the sheer movement from one place to the next. Travel narratives are relentlessly driven forward, stopping in each locale for only the duration of an adventure before forcing their heroes to resume their wanderings. Through such restless wandering, travel literature, both factual and fiction, crisscrosses the world and thereby incorporates it into literature.

Worlds of the Imagination

Literature not only moves us to remote corners of the world and across landscapes; it also presents us with whole imagined worlds to which we as readers can travel. The construction of literary, clearly made-up worlds has always been a theme of world literature, which has suggested answers to fundamental questions, including how the world came into being. The Mayan epic *Popol Vuh*, featured in volume C, develops one of the most elaborate creation myths, including several attempts at creating humans (only the fourth is successful). In the same volume, Milton retells the biblical story of the Fall, but he also depicts the creation of new worlds, including earth, in a manner that is influenced by the discovery of the New World in the Western Hemisphere. For this new edition, the editors have decided to underline this theme, which also celebrates the world-creating power of language and literature, by placing a new cluster of creation myths, called "Creation and the Cosmos," at the very beginning of the anthology. The myths in this cluster resonate throughout the history of world literature, providing imaginative touchstones for later authors (such as Virgil, John Mandeville, Dante, and Goethe) to adapt and use in their own imaginative world-creation.

But world-creation, as highlighted in the new cluster, not only operates on a grand scale. It also occurs at moments when literature restricts itself to small, enclosed universes that are observed with minute attention. The great eighteenth-century Chinese novel *The Story of the Stone* by Cao Xuequin (presented in a new selection) withdraws to a family compound, whose walls it almost never leaves, to depict life in all its subtlety within this restricted space for several thousand pages. Sometimes we are invited into the even more circumscribed space of the narrator's own head, where we encounter strange and surreal worlds, as in the great modernist and postmodernist fictions from Franz Kafka and Jorge Luis Borges. By providing a thematic through-line, the new edition of the anthology reveals the myriad ways in which authors not only seek to explain our world but also compete with it by imagining new and different ones.

Genres

Over the millennia, literature has developed a set of rules and conventions that authors work with and against as they make decisions about subject matter, style, and form. These rules help us distinguish between different types of literature—that is, different genres. The broad view of literature afforded by the anthology, across both space and time, is particularly capable of showing how genres emerge and are transformed as they are used by different writers and for different purposes. The new edition of the anthology underscores this crucial dimension of literature by tracking the movement of genres—of, for example, the frame-tale narration from South Asia to northern Europe. To help readers recognize this theme, we have created ways of making genre visible. Lyric poetry is found everywhere in the anthology, from the foundational poetry anthologies of China to modern experiments, but it is the focus of specially designed clusters that cast light on medieval lyric; on how Petrarch's invention, the sonnet, is adopted by other writers; or, to turn to one of the world's most successful poetic genres, on the haiku. By the same token, a cluster on manifestos highlights modernism's most characteristic invention, with its shrill demands and aggressive layout. Among the genres, drama is perhaps the most difficult to grapple with because it is so closely entangled with theatrical performance. You don't understand a play unless you understand what kind of theater it was intended for, how it was performed, and how audiences watched it. To capture this dimension, we have grouped two of the most prominent regional drama traditions—Greek theater and East Asian drama—in their own sections.

Oral Literature

The relation of the spoken word to literature is perhaps the most important theme that emerges from these pages. All literature goes back to oral storytelling—all the foundational epics, from South Asia via Greece and Africa to Central America, are deeply rooted in oral storytelling; poetry's rhythms are best appreciated when heard; and drama, a form that comes alive in performance, continues to be engaged with an oral tradition. Throughout the anthology, we connect works to the oral traditions from which they sprang and remind readers that writing has coexisted with oral storytelling since the invention of the former. A new and important cluster in volume E on oral literature foregrounds this theme and showcases the nineteenth-century interest in oral traditions such as fairy and folk tales and slave stories. At the same time, this cluster, and the anthology as a whole, shows the importance of gaining literacy.

Varieties of Literature

In presenting everything from the earliest literatures to a (much-expanded) selection of contemporary literature reaching to the early twenty-first century, and from oral storytelling to literary experiments of the avant-garde, the anthology confronts us with the question not just of world literature, but of literature as such. We call attention to the changing nature of literature with new thematic clusters on literature in the early volumes, to give students and teachers access to how early writers from different cultures thought about literature. But the changing role and nature of literature are visible in the anthology as a whole. The world of Greek myth is seen by almost everyone as literary, even though it arose from ritual practices that are different from what we associate with literature. But this is even more the case with other texts, such as the Qur'an or the Bible, which still function as religious texts for many, while others appreciate them primarily or exclusively as literature. Some texts, such as those by Laozi (new addition) or Plato (in a new and expanded selection) or Kant (new addition) belong in philosophy, while others, such as the Declaration of Independence (new addition), are primarily political documents. Our modern conception of literature as imaginative literature, as fiction, is very recent, about two hundred years old. In this Third Edition, we have opted for a much-expanded conception of literature that includes creation myths, wisdom literature, religious texts, philosophy, political writing, and fairy tales in addition to plays, poems, and narrative fiction. This answers to an older definition of literature as writing of high quality. There are many texts of philosophy, or religion, or politics that are not remarkable or influential for their literary qualities and that would therefore have no place in an anthology of world literature. But the works presented here do: in addition to or as part of their other functions, they have acquired the status of literature.

This brings us to the last and perhaps most important question: When we study the world, why study it through its literature? Hasn't literature lost some of its luster for us, we who are faced with so many competing media and art forms? Like no other art form or medium, literature offers us a deep history of human thinking. As our illustration program shows, writing was invented not for the composition of literature, but for much more mundane purposes, such as the recording of ownership, contracts, or astronomical observations. But literature is writing's most glorious side-product. Because language expresses human consciousness, no other art form can capture the human past with the precision and scope of literature. Language shapes our thinking, and literature, the highest expression of language, plays an important role in that process, pushing the boundaries of what we can think, and how we think it. The other great advantage of literature is that it can be reactivated with each reading. The great architectural monuments of the past are now in ruins. Literature, too, often has to be excavated, as with many classical texts. But once a text has been found or reconstructed it can be experienced as if for the first time by new readers. Even though many of the literary texts collected in this anthology are at first strange, because they originated so very long ago, they still speak to today's readers with great eloquence and freshness.

Because works of world literature are alive today, they continue to elicit strong emotions and investments. The epic *Rāmāyana*, for example, plays an important role in the politics of India, where it has been used to bolster Hindu nationalism, just as the *Bhagavad-Gītā*, here in a new translation, continues to be a moral touchstone in the ethical deliberation about war. Saddam Hussein wrote an updated version of the *Epic of Gilgamesh*. And the three religions of the book, Judaism, Christianity, and Islam, make our selections from their scriptures a more than historical exercise. China has recently elevated the sayings of Confucius, whose influence on Chinese attitudes about the state had waned in the twentieth century, creating Confucius Institutes all over the world to promote Chinese culture in what is now called New Confucianism. The debates about the role of the church and secularism, which we highlight through a new cluster and selections in all volumes, have become newly important in current deliberations on the relation between church and state. World literature is never neutral. We know its relevance precisely by the controversies it inspires.

Going back to the earliest moments of cultural contact and moving forward to the global flows of the twenty-first century, *The Norton Anthology of World Literature* attempts to provide a deep history. But it is a special type of history: a literary one. World literature is grounded in the history of the world, but it is also the history of imagining this world; it is a history not just of what happened, but also of how humans imagined their place in the midst of history. We, the editors of this Third Edition, can think of no better way to prepare young people for a global future than through a deep and meaningful exploration of world literature. Evliya Çelebi sums up his exploration of Vienna as a "marvelous and wonderful adventure"—we hope that readers will feel the same about the adventure in reading made possible by this anthology and will return to it for the rest of their lives.

About the Third Edition

New Selections and Translations

This Third Edition represents a thoroughgoing, top-to-bottom revision of the anthology that altered nearly every section in important ways. Following is a list of the new sections and works, in order:

VOLUME A

A new cluster, "Creation and the Cosmos," and a new grouping, "Ancient Egyptian Literature" • Benjamin Foster's translation of *Gilgamesh* • Selections from chapters 12, 17, 28, 29, 31, and 50 of Genesis, and from chapters 19 and 20 of Exodus • All selections from Genesis, Exodus, and Job are newly featured in Robert Alter's translation, and chapter 25 of Genesis (Jacob spurning his birthright) is presented in a graphic visualization by R. Crumb based on Alter's translation • Homer's *Iliad* and *Odyssey* are now featured in Stanley Lombardo's highly regarded translations • A selection of Aesop's *Fables* • A new selection and a new translation of Sappho's lyrics • A new grouping, "Ancient Athenian Drama," gathers together the three major Greek tragedians and Aristophanes • New translations of *Oedipus the King*, *Antigone* (both by Robert Bagg), *Medea* (by Diane Arnson Svarlien), and *Lysistrata* (by Sarah Ruden) • A new cluster, "Travel and Conquest" • Plato's *Symposium* • A new selection of Catullus's poems, in a new translation by Peter Green • *The Aeneid* is now featured in Robert Fagles's career-topping translation • New selections from book 1 of Ovid's *Metamorphoses* join the previous selection, now featured in Charles Martin's recent translation • A new cluster, "Speech, Writing, Poetry," features ancient Egyptian writings on writing • A new tale from the Indian *Jātaka* • New selections from the Chinese *Classic of Poetry* • Confucius's *Analects* now in a new translation by Simon Leys • *Daodejing* • New selections from the Chinese *Songs of the South* • Chinese historian Sima Qian • A new cluster, "Speech, Writing, and Poetry in Early China," features selections by Confucius, Zhuangzi, and Han Feizi.

VOLUME B

Selections from the Christian Bible now featured in a new translation by Richmond Lattimore • A selection from book 3 of Apuleius's *The Golden Ass* • Selections from the Qur'an now featured in Abdel Haleem's translation • A new selection from Abolqasem Ferdowsi's *Shahnameh*, in a new translation by Dick Davis • Avicenna • Petrus Alfonsi • Additional material from Marie de France's *Lais*, in a translation by Robert Hanning and Joan Ferrante • An expanded selection of poems fills out the "Medieval Lyrics" cluster • Dante's *Divine Comedy* now featured in Mark Musa's translation • The Ethiopian

Kebra Nagast • An expanded selection from Boccaccio's *Decameron*, in a new translation by Wayne Rebhorn • A new translation by Sheila Fisher of Chaucer's *Canterbury Tales* • *Sir Gawain and the Green Knight* now featured in a new translation by Simon Armitage • Christine de Pizan's *Book of the City of Ladies* • A new cluster, "Travel and Encounter," features selections from Marco Polo, Ibn Battuta, and John Mandeville • New selections in fresh translations of classical Tamil and Sanskrit lyric poetry • New selections and translations of Chinese lyric poetry • A new cluster, "Literature about Literature," in the Medieval Chinese Literature section • Refreshed selections and new translations of lyric poetry in "Japan's Classical Age" • Selection from Ki No Tsurayuki's *Tosa Diary* • A new translation by Meredith McKinney of Sei Shōnagon's *Pillow Book* • A new, expanded selection from, and a new translation of, Murasaki Shikibu's *The Tale of Genji* • New selections from *The Tales of the Heike*, in Burton Watson's newly included translation.

VOLUME C

A new translation by David C. Conrad of the West African epic *Sunjata* • *The Book of Dede Korkut* • A new selection from Evliya Çelebi's *The Book of Travels*, never before translated into English, now in Gottfried Hagen's translation • New selection of Indian lyric poetry by Basavaṇṇā, Mahādevīyakkā, Kabir, Mīrabāī, and Tukaram, in fresh new translations • Two new clusters, "Humanism and the Rediscovery of the Classical Past" and "Petrarch and the Love Lyric," open the new section "Europe and the New World" • Sir Thomas More's *Utopia* in its entirety • Story 10 newly added to the selection of Marguerite de Navarre's *Heptameron* • *Lazarillo de Tormes* included in its entirety • A new cluster, "The Encounter of Europe and the New World" • Lope de Vega's *Fuenteovejuna* now featured in Gregary Racz's recent translation • A new cluster, "God, Church, and Self."

VOLUME D

A new section, "East Asian Drama," brings together four examples of Asian drama from the fourteenth through nineteenth centuries, including Zeami's *Atsumori*, Kong Shangren's *The Peach Blossom Fan* (in a new translation by Stephen Owen), and two newly included works: Chikamatsu's *Love Suicides at Amijima* and the Korean drama *Song of Ch'un-hyang* • A new cluster, "What Is Enlightenment?" • Molière's *Tartuffe* now featured in a new translation by Constance Congdon and Virginia Scott • Aphra Behn's *Oroonoko; or, The Royal Slave*, complete • New selections by Sor Juana Inés de la Cruz, in a new translation by Electa Arenal and Amanda Powell • An expanded, refreshed selection from Cao Xueqin's *The Story of the Stone*, part of which is now featured in John Minford's translation • Ihara Saikaku's *Life of a Sensuous Woman* • A new cluster, "The World of Haiku," features work by Kitamura Kigin, Matsuo Bashō, Morikawa Kyoriku, and Yosa Buson.

VOLUME E

A new cluster, "Revolutionary Contexts," features selections from the Declaration of Independence, the Declaration of the Rights of Man and of the Citizen, and the Declaration of Sentiments from the Seneca Falls convention, as well as pieces by Olympe de Gouges, Edmund Burke, Jean-Jacques Dessalines, William Wordsworth, and Simón Bólivar • New selection from book 2 of Rousseau's *Confessions* • Olaudah Equiano's *Interesting Narrative* • Goethe's *Faust* now featured in Martin Greenberg's translation • Selections from Domingo Sarmiento's *Facundo* • A new grouping, "Romantic Poets and Their Successors," features a generous sampling of lyric poetry from the period, including new poems by Anna Laetitia Barbauld, William Wordsworth, Samuel Taylor Coleridge, Anna Bunina, Andrés Bello, John Keats, Heinrich Heine, Elizabeth Barrett Browning, Tennyson, Robert Browning, Walt Whitman, Christina Rossetti, Rosalía de Castro, and José Martí, as well as an exciting new translation of Arthur Rimbaud's *Illuminations* by John Ashbery • From Vietnam, Nguyễn Du's *The Tale of Kiều* • A new selection and all new translations of Ghalib's poetry by Vinay Dharwadker • Liu E's *The Travels of Lao Can* • Two pieces by Pandita Ramabai • Flaubert's *A Simple Heart* • Ibsen's *Hedda Gabler*, now featured in a new translation by Rick Davis and Brian Johnston • Machado de Assis's *The Rod of Justice* • Chekhov's *The Cherry Orchard*, now featured in a new translation by Paul Schmidt • Tagore's *Kabuliwala* • Higuchi Ichiyō's *Separate Ways* • A new cluster, "Orature," with German, English, Irish, and Hawaiian folktales; Anansi stories from Ghana, Jamaica, and the United States; as well as slave songs, stories, and spirituals, Malagasy wisdom poetry, and the Navajo Night Chant.

VOLUME F

Joseph Conrad's *Heart of Darkness* • Tanizaki's *The Tattooer* • Selection from Marcel Proust's *Remembrance of Things Past* now featured in Lydia Davis's critically acclaimed translation • Franz Kafka's *The Metamorphosis* now featured in Michael Hofmann's translation • Lu Xun, *Medicine* • Akutagawa's *In a Bamboo Grove* • Kawabata's *The Izu Dancer* • Chapter 1 of Woolf's *A Room of One's Own* newly added to the selections from chapters 2 and 3 • Two new Faulkner stories: "Spotted Horses" and "Barn Burning" • Kushi Fusako, *Memoirs of a Declining Ryukyuan Woman* • Lao She, *An Old and Established Name* • Ch'ae Man-Sik, *My Innocent Uncle* • Zhang Ailing's *Sealed Off* • Constantine Cavafy • Octavio Paz • A new cluster, "Manifestos" • Julio Cortazár • Tadeusz Borowski's *This Way for the Gas, Ladies and Gentlemen*, in a new translation by Barbara Vedder • Paul Celan • Saadat Hasan Manto • James Baldwin • Vladimir Nabokov • Tayeb Salih • Chinua Achebe's *Chike's School Days* • Carlos Fuentes • Mahmoud Darwish • Seamus Heaney • Ama Ata Aidoo • V. S. Naipaul • Ngugi Wa Thiong'o • Bessie Head • Ōe Kenzaburō • Salman Rushdie • Mahasweta Devi's *Giribala* • Hanan Al-Shaykh • Toni Morrison • Mo Yan • Niyi Osundare • Nguyen Huy Thiep • Isabel Allende • Chu T'ien-Hsin • Junot Díaz • Roberto Bolaño • J. M. Coetzee • Orhan Pamuk.

Supplements for Instructors and Students

Norton is pleased to provide instructors and students with several supplements to make the study and teaching of world literature an even more interesting and rewarding experience:

Instructor Resource Folder

A new Instructor Resource Folder features images and video clips that allow instructors to enhance their lectures with some of the sights and sounds of world literature and its contexts.

Instructor Course Guide

Teaching with The Norton Anthology of World Literature: *A Guide for Instructors* provides teaching plans, suggestions for in-class activities, discussion topics and writing projects, and extensive lists of scholarly and media resources.

Coursepacks

Available in a variety of formats, Norton coursepacks bring digital resources into a new or existing online course. Coursepacks are free to instructors, easy to download and install, and available in a variety of formats, including Blackboard, Desire2Learn, Angel, and Moodle.

StudySpace (*wwnorton.com/nawol*)

This free student companion site features a variety of complementary materials to help students read and study world literature. Among them are reading-comprehension quizzes, quick-reference summaries of the anthology's introductions, review quizzes, an audio glossary to help students pronunce names and terms, tours of some of the world's important cultural landmarks, timelines, maps, and other contextual materials.

Writing about World Literature

Written by Karen Gocsik, Executive Director of the Writing Program at Dartmouth College, in collaboration with faculty in the world literature program at the University of Nevada, Las Vegas, *Writing about World Literature* provides course-specific guidance for writing papers and essay exams in the world literature course.

For more information about any of these supplements, instructors should contact their local Norton representative.

Acknowledgments

The editors would like to thank the following people, who have provided invaluable assistance by giving us sage advice, important encouragement, and help with the preparation of the manuscript: Sara Akbari, Alannah de Barra, Wendy Belcher, Jodi Bilinkoff, Freya Brackett, Psyche Brackett, Michaela Bronstein, Amanda Claybaugh, Rachel Carroll, Lewis Cook, David Damrosch, Dick Davis, Amanda Detry, Anthony Domestico, Merve Emre, Maria Fackler, Guillermina de Ferrari, Karina Galperín, Stanton B. Garner, Kimberly Dara Gordon, Elyse Graham, Stephen Greenblatt, Sara Guyer, Langdon Hammer, Iain Higgins, Mohja Kahf, Peter Kornicki, Paul Kroll, Lydia Liu, Bala Venkat Mani, Ann Matter, Barry McCrea, Alexandra McCullough-Garcia, Rachel McGuiness, Jon McKenzie, Mary Mullen, Djibril Tamsir Niane, Felicity Nussbaum, Andy Orchard, John Peters, Daniel Taro Poch, Daniel Potts, Megan Quigley, Imogen Roth, Catherine de Rose, Ellen Sapega, Jesse Schotter, Stephen Scully, Brian Stock, Tomi Suzuki, Joshua Taft, Sara Torres, Lisa Voigt, Kristen Wanner, and Emily Weissbourd.

All the editors would like to thank the wonderful people at Norton, principally our editor Pete Simon, the driving force behind this whole undertaking, as well as Marian Johnson (Managing Editor, College), Alice Falk, Michael Fleming, Katharine Ings, Susan Joseph, Barney Latimer, and Diane Cipollone (Copyeditors), Conor Sullivan (Assistant Editor), Megan Jackson (College Permissions Manager), Margaret Gorenstein (Permissions), Patricia Marx (Art Research Director), Debra Morton Hoyt (Art Director; cover design), Rubina Yeh (Design Director), Jo Anne Metsch (Designer; interior text design), Adrian Kitzinger (cartography), Agnieszka Gasparska (timeline design), Eileen Connell, (Media Editor), Jennifer Barnhardt (Editorial Assistant, Media), Laura Musich (Associate Editor; Instructor's Guide), Benjamin Reynolds (Production Manager), and Kim Bowers (Marketing Manager, Literature) and Ashley Cain (Humanities Sales Specialist).

This anthology represents a collaboration not only among the editors and their close advisors, but also among the thousands of instructors who teach from the anthology and provide valuable and constructive guidance to the publisher and editors. *The Norton Anthology of World Literature* is as much their book as it is ours, and we are grateful to everyone who has cared enough about this anthology to help make it better. We're especially grateful to the more than five hundred professors of world literature who responded to an online survey in early 2008, whom we have listed below. Thank you all.

Michel Aaij (Auburn University Montgomery); Sandra Acres (Mississippi Gulf Coast Community College); Larry Adams (University of North Alabama); Mary Adams (Western Carolina University); Stephen Adams (Westfield State

College); Roberta Adams (Roger Williams University); Kirk Adams (Tarrant County College); Kathleen Aguero (Pine Manor College); Richard Albright (Harrisburg Area Community College); Deborah Albritton (Jefferson Davis Community College); Todd Aldridge (Auburn University); Judith Allen-Leventhal (College of Southern Maryland); Carolyn Amory (Binghamton University); Kenneth Anania (Massasoit Community College); Phillip Anderson (University of Central Arkansas); Walter Anderson (University of Arkansas at Little Rock); Vivienne Anderson (North Carolina Wesleyan College); Susan Andrade (University of Pittsburgh); Kit Andrews (Western Oregon University); Joe Antinarella (Tidewater Community College); Nancy Applegate (Georgia Highlands College); Sona Aronian (University of Rhode Island); Sona Aronian (University of Rhode Island); Eugene Arva (University of Miami); M. G. Aune (California University of Pennsylvania); Carolyn Ayers (Saint Mary's University of Minnesota); Diana Badur (Black Hawk College); Susan Bagby (Longwood University); Maryam Barrie (Washtenaw Community College); Maria Baskin (Alamance Community College); Samantha Batten (Auburn University); Charles Beach (Nyack College); Michael Beard (University of North Dakota); Bridget Beaver (Connors State College); James Bednarz (C. W. Post College); Khani Begum (Bowling Green State University); Albert Bekus (Austin Peay State University); Lynne Belcher (Southern Arkansas University); Karen Bell (Delta State University); Elisabeth Ly Bell (University of Rhode Island); Angela Belli (St. John's University); Leo Benardo (Baruch College); Paula Berggren (Baruch College, CUNY); Frank Bergmann (Utica College); Nancy Blomgren (Volunteer State Community College); Scott Boltwood (Emory & Henry College); Ashley Bonds (Copiah-Lincoln Community College); Thomas Bonner (Xavier University of Louisiana); Debbie Boyd (East Central Community College); Norman Boyer (Saint Xavier University); Nodya Boyko (Auburn University); Robert Brandon (Rockingham Community College); Alan Brasher (East Georgia College); Harry Brent (Baruch College); Charles Bressler (Indiana Wesleyan University); Katherine Brewer; Mary Ruth Brindley (Mississippi Delta Community College); Mamye Britt (Georgia Perimeter College); Gloria Brooks (Tyler Junior College); Monika Brown (University of North Carolina–Pembroke); Greg Bryant (Highland Community College); Austin Busch (SUNY Brockport); Barbara Cade (Texas College); Karen Caig (University of Arkansas Community College at Morrilton); Jonizo Cain-Calloway (Del Mar College); Mark Calkins (San Francisco State University); Catherine Calloway (Arkansas State University); Mechel Camp (Jackson State Community College); Robert Canary (University of Wisconsin–Parkside); Stephen Canham (University of Hawaii at Manoa); Marian Carcache (Auburn University); Alfred Carson (Kennesaw State University); Farrah Cato (University of Central Florida); Biling Chen (University of Central Arkansas); Larry Chilton (Blinn College); Eric Chock (University of Hawaii at West Oahu); Cheryl Clark (Miami Dade College–Wolfson Campus); Sarah Beth Clark (Holmes Community College); Jim Cody (Brookdale Community College); Carol Colatrella (Georgia Institute of Technology); Janelle Collins (Arkansas State University); Theresa Collins (St. John's University); Susan Comfort (Indiana University of Pennsylvania); Kenneth Cook (National Park Community College); Angie Cook (Cisco Junior College); Yvonne Cooper (Pierce College); Brenda Cornell (Central Texas College); Judith Cortelloni (Lincoln College); Robert Cosgrove (Saddleback College); Rosemary Cox (Georgia Perimeter College);

Daniel Cozart (Georgia Perimeter College); Brenda Craven (Fort Hays State University); Susan Crisafulli (Franklin College); Janice Crosby (Southern University); Randall Crump (Kennesaw State University); Catherine Cucinella (California State University San Marcos); T. Allen Culpepper (Manatee Community College–Venice); Rodger Cunningham (Alice Lloyd College); Lynne Dahmen (Purdue University); Patsy J. Daniels (Jackson State University); James Davis (Troy University); Evan Davis (Southwestern Oregon Community College); Margaret Dean (Eastern Kentucky University); JoEllen DeLucia (John Jay College, CUNY); Hivren Demir-Atay (Binghamton University); Rae Ann DeRosse (University of North Carolina–Greensboro); Anna Crowe Dewart (College of Coastal Georgia); Joan Digby (C. W. Post Campus Long Island University); Diana Dominguez (University of Texas at Brownsville); Dee Douglas-Jones (Winston-Salem State University); Jeremy Downes (Auburn University); Denell Downum (Suffolk University); Sharon Drake (Texarkana College); Damian Dressick (Robert Morris University); Clyburn Duder (Concordia University Texas); Dawn Duncan (Concordia College); Kendall Dunkelberg (Mississippi University for Women); Janet Eber (County College of Morris); Emmanuel Egar (University of Arkansas at Pine Bluff); David Eggebrecht (Concordia University of Wisconsin); Sarah Eichelman (Walters State Community College); Hank Eidson (Georgia Perimeter College); Monia Eisenbraun (Oglala Lakota College/Cheyenne-Eagle Butte High School); Dave Elias (Eastern Kentucky University); Chris Ellery (Angelo State University); Christina Elvidge (Marywood University); Ernest Enchelmayer (Arkansas Tech University); Niko Endres (Western Kentucky University); Kathrynn Engberg (Alabama A&M University); Chad Engbers (Calvin College); Edward Eriksson (Suffolk Community College); Donna Estill (Alabama Southern Community College); Andrew Ettin (Wake Forest University); Jim Everett (Mississippi College); Gene Fant (Union University); Nathan Faries (University of Dubuque); Martin Fashbaugh (Auburn University); Donald J. Fay (Kennesaw State University); Meribeth Fell (College of Coastal Georgia); David Fell (Carroll Community College); Jill Ferguson (San Francisco Conservatory of Music); Susan French Ferguson (Mountain View Comumunity College); Robyn Ferret (Cascadia Community College); Colin Fewer (Purdue Calumet); Hannah Fischthal (St. John's University); Jim Fisher (Peninsula College); Gene Fitzgerald (University of Utah); Monika Fleming (Edgecombe Community College); Phyllis Fleming (Patrick Henry Community College); Francis Fletcher (Folsom Lake College); Denise Folwell (Montgomery College); Ulanda Forbess (North Lake College); Robert Forman (St. John's University); Suzanne Forster (University of Alaska–Anchorage); Patricia Fountain (Coastal Carolina Community College); Kathleen Fowler (Surry Community College); Sheela Free (San Bernardino Valley College); Lea Fridman (Kingsborough Community College); David Galef (Montclair State University); Paul Gallipeo (Adirondack Community College); Jan Gane (University of North Carolina–Pembroke); Jennifer Garlen (University of Alabama–Huntsville); Anita Garner (University of North Alabama); Elizabeth Gassel (Darton College); Patricia Gaston (West Virginia University, Parkersburg); Marge Geiger (Cuyahoga Community College); Laura Getty (North Georgia College & State University); Amy Getty (Grand View College); Leah Ghiradella (Middlesex County College); Dick Gibson (Jacksonville University); Teresa Gibson (University of Texas–Brownsville); Wayne Gilbert (Community College of Aurora); Sandra Giles (Abraham Baldwin Agricultural College); Pamela Gist (Cedar Valley College); Suzanne Gitonga (North Lake College); James Glickman (Community College of Rhode Island); R. James Goldstein (Auburn University); Jennifer Golz (Tennessee Tech University); Marian Goodin (North Central Missouri College); Susan Gorman (Massachusetts College of Pharmacy and Health Sciences); Anissa Graham (University of North Alabama); Eric Gray (St. Gregory's University); Geoffrey Green (San Francisco State University); Russell Greer (Texas Woman's University); Charles Grey (Albany State University); Frank Gruber (Bergen Community College); Alfonso Guerriero Jr. (Baruch College, CUNY); Letizia Guglielmo (Kennesaw State University); Nira Gupta-Casale (Kean University); Gary Gutchess (SUNY Tompkins Cortland Community College); William Hagen (Oklahoma Baptist University); John Hagge (Iowa State University); Julia Hall (Henderson State University); Margaret Hallissy (C. W. Post Campus Long Island University); Laura Hammons (Hinds Community College); Nancy Hancock (Austin Peay State University); Carol Harding (Western Oregon University); Cynthia Hardy (University of Alaska–Fairbanks); Steven Harthorn (Williams Baptist College); Stanley Hauer (University of Southern Mississippi); Leean Hawkins (National Park Community College); Kayla Haynie (Harding University); Maysa Hayward (Ocean County College); Karen Head (Georgia Institute of Technology); Sandra Kay Heck (Walters State Community College); Frances Helphinstine (Morehead State University); Karen Henck (Eastern Nazarene College); Betty Fleming Hendricks (University of Arkansas); Yndaleci Hinojosa (Northwest Vista College); Richard Hishmeh (Palomar College); Ruth Hoberman (Eastern Illinois University); Rebecca Hogan (University of Wisconsin–Whitewater); Mark Holland (East Tennessee State University); John Holmes (Virginia State University); Sandra Holstein (Southern Oregon University); Fran Holt (Georgia Perimeter College–Clarkston); William Hood (North Central Texas College); Glenn Hopp (Howard Payne University); George Horneker (Arkansas State University); Barbara Howard (Central Bible College); Pamela Howell (Midland College); Melissa Hull (Tennessee State University); Barbara Hunt (Columbus State University); Leeann Hunter (University of South Florida); Gill Hunter (Eastern Kentucky University); Helen Huntley (California Baptist University); Luis Iglesias (University of Southern Mississippi); Judith Irvine (Georgia State University); Miglena Ivanova (Coastal Carolina University); Kern Jackson (University of South Alabama); Kenneth Jackson (Yale University); M. W. Jackson (St. Bonaventure University); Robb Jackson (Texas A&M University–Corpus Christi); Karen Jacobsen (Valdosta State University); Maggie Jaffe (San Diego State University); Robert Jakubovic (Raymond Walters College); Stokes James (University of Wisconsin–Stevens Point); Beverly Jamison (South Carolina State University); Ymitri Jayasundera-Mathison (Prairie View A&M University); Katarzyna Jerzak (University of Georgia); Alice Jewell (Harding University); Elizabeth Jones (Auburn University); Jeff Jones (University of Idaho); Dan Jones (Walters State Community College); Mary Kaiser (Jefferson State Community College); James Keller (Middlesex County College); Jill Keller (Middlesex Community College); Tim Kelley (Northwest-Shoals Community College); Andrew Kelley (Jackson State Community College); Hans Kellner (North Carolina State); Brian Kennedy (Pasadena City College); Shirin Khanmohamadi (San Francisco State University); Jeremy Kiene (McDaniel College); Mary Catherine Kiliany (Robert Morris University); Sue Kim (University of Alabama–Birmingham); Pam Kingsbury (University of North Alabama); Sharon Kinoshita (University of California, Santa Cruz); Lydia Kualapai (Schreiner University); Rita Kumar (University of Cincinnati); Roger Ladd (University of North Carolina–Pembroke); Daniel Lane (Norwich University); Erica Lara (Southwest Texas Junior College); Leah Larson (Our Lady of the Lake University); Dana Lauro (Ocean County College); Shanon Lawson (Pikes Peak Community College); Michael Leddy (Eastern Illinois University); Eric Leuschner (Fort Hays State University); Patricia Licklider (John Jay College, CUNY); Pamela Light (Rochester College); Alison Ligon (Morehouse College); Linda Linzey (Southeastern University); Thomas Lisk (North Carolina State University); Matthew Livesey (University of Wisconsin–Stout); Vickie Lloyd (University of Arkansas Community College at Hope); Judy Lloyd (Southside Virginia Community College); Mary Long (Ouachita Baptist University); Rick Lott (Arkansas State University); Scott Lucas (The Citadel); Katrine Lvovskaya (Rutgers University); Carolin Lynn (Mercyhurst College); Susan Lyons (University of Connecticut—Avery Point); William Thomas MacCary (Hofstra University); Richard Mace (Pace University); Peter Marbais (Mount Olive College); Lacy Marschalk (Auburn University); Seth Martin (Harrisburg Area Community College–Lancaster); Carter Mathes (Rutgers University); Rebecca Mathews (University of Connecticut); Marsha Mathews (Dalton State College); Darren Mathews (Grambling State University); Corine Mathis (Auburn University); Ken McAferty (Pensacola State College); Jeff McAlpine (Clackamas Community College); Kelli McBride (Seminole State College); Kay McClellan (South Plains College); Michael McClung (Northwest-Shoals Community College); Michael McClure (Virginia State University); Jennifer McCune (University of Central Arkansas); Kathleen McDonald (Norwich University); Charles McDonnell (Piedmont Technical College); Nancy McGee (Macomb Community College); Gregory McNamara (Clayton State University); Abby Mendelson (Point Park University); Ken Meyers (Wilson Community College); Barbara Mezeske (Hope College); Brett Millan (South Texas College); Sheila Miller (Hinds Community College); David Miller (Mississippi College); Matt Miller (University of South Carolina–Aiken); Yvonne Milspaw (Harrisburg Area Community College); Ruth Misheloff (Baruch College); Lamata Mitchell (Rock Valley College); D'Juana Montgomery (Southwestern Assemblies of God University); Lorne Mook (Taylor University); Renee Moore (Mississippi Delta Community College); Dan Morgan (Scott Community College); Samantha Morgan-Curtis (Tennessee State University); Beth Morley (Collin College); Vicki Moulson (College of the Albemarle); L. Carl Nadeau (University of Saint Francis); Wayne Narey (Arkansas State University); LeAnn Nash (Texas A&M University–Commerce); Leanne Nayden (University of Evansville); Jim Neilson (Wake Technical Community College); Jeff Nelson (University of Alabama–Huntsville); Mary Nelson (Dallas Baptist University); Deborah Nester (Northwest Florida State College); William Netherton (Amarillo College); William Newman (Perimeter College); Adele Newson-Horst (Missouri State University); George Nicholas (Benedictine College); Dana Nichols (Gainesville State College); Mark Nicoll-Johnson (Merced College); John Mark Nielsen (Dana College); Michael Nifong (Georgia College & State University); Laura Noell (North Virginia Community College); Bonnie Noonan (Xavier University of Louisiana); Patricia Noone (College of

Mount Saint Vincent); Paralee Norman (Northwestern State University–Leesville); Frank Novak (Pepperdine University); Kevin O'Brien (Chapman University); Sarah Odishoo (Columbia College Chicago); Samuel Olorounto (New River Community College); Jamili Omar (Lone Star College–CyFair); Michael Orlofsky (Troy University); Priscilla Orr (Sussex County Community College); Jim Owen (Columbus State University); Darlene Pagan (Pacific University); Yolanda Page (University of Arkansas–Pine Bluff); Lori Paige (Westfield State College); Linda Palumbo (Cerritos College); Joseph Parry (Brigham Young University); Carla Patterson (Georgia Highlands College); Andra Pavuls (Davenport University); Sunita Peacock (Slippery Rock University); Velvet Pearson (Long Beach City College); Joe Pellegrino (Georgia Southern University); Sonali Perera (Rutgers University); Clem Perez (St. Philip's College); Caesar Perkowski (Gordon College); Gerald Perkus (Collin College); John Peters (University of North Texas); Lesley Peterson (University of North Alabama); Judy Peterson (John Tyler Community College); Sandra Petree (Northwestern Oklahoma State University); Angela Pettit (Tarrant County College NE); Michell Phifer (University of Texas–Arlington); Ziva Piltch (Rockland Community College); Nancy Popkin (Harris-Stowe State University); Marlana Portolano (Towson University); Rhonda Powers (Auburn University); Lisa Propst (University of West Georgia); Melody Pugh (Wheaton College); Jonathan Purkiss (Pulaski Technical College); Patrick Quinn (College of Southern Nevada); Peter Rabinowitz (Hamilton College); Evan Radcliffe (Villanova University); Jody Ragsdale (Northeast Alabama Community College); Ken Raines (Eastern Arizona College); Gita Rajan (Fairfield University); Elizabeth Rambo (Campbell University); Richard Ramsey (Indiana University–Purdue University Fort Wayne); Jonathan Randle (Mississippi College); Amy Randolph (Waynesburg University); Rodney Rather (Tarrant County College Northwest); Helaine Razovsky (Northwestern State University); Rachel Reed (Auburn University); Karin Rhodes (Salem State College); Donald R. Riccomini (Santa Clara University); Christina Roberts (Otero Junior College); Paula Robison (Temple University); Jean Roelke (University of North Texas); Barrie Rosen (St. John's University); James Rosenberg (Point Park University); Sherry Rosenthal (College of Southern Nevada); Daniel Ross (Columbus State University); Maria Rouphail (North Carolina State University); Lance Rubin (Arapahoe Community College); Mary Ann Rygiel (Auburn University); Geoffrey Sadock (Bergen Community College); Allen Salerno (Auburn University); Mike Sanders (Kent State University); Deborah Scally (Richland College); Margaret Scanlan (Indiana University South Bend); Michael Schaefer (University of Central Arkansas); Tracy Schaelen (Southwestern College); Daniel Schenker (University of Alabama–Huntsville); Robyn Schiffman (Fairleigh Dickinson University); Roger Schmidt (Idaho State University); Robert Schmidt (Tarrant County College–Northwest Campus); Adrianne Schot (Weatherford College); Pamela Schuman (Brookhaven College); Sharon Seals (Ouachita Technical College); Su Senapati (Abraham Baldwin Agricultural College); Phyllis Senfleben (North Shore Community College); Theda Shapiro (University of California–Riverside); Mary Sheldon (Washburn University); Donald Shull (Freed-Hardeman University); Ellen Shull (Palo Alto College); Conrad Shumaker (University of Central Arkansas); Sara Shumaker (University of Central Arkansas); Dave Shuping (Spartanburg Methodist College); Horacio Sierra (University of Florida); Scott Simkins (Auburn University); Bruce

Simon (SUNY Fredonia); LaRue Sloan (University of Louisiana–Monroe); Peter Smeraldo (Caldwell College); Renee Smith (Lamar University); Victoria Smith (Texas State University); Connie Smith (College of St. Joseph); Grant Smith (Eastern Washington University); Mary Karen Solomon (Coloardo NW Community College); Micheline Soong (Hawaii Pacific University); Leah Souffrant (Baruch College, CUNY); Cindy Spangler (Faulkner University); Charlotte Speer (Bevill State Community College); John Staines (John Jay College, CUNY); Tanja Stampfl (Louisiana State University); Scott Starbuck (San Diego Mesa College); Kathryn Stasio (Saint Leo University); Joyce Stavick (North Georgia College & State University); Judith Steele (Mid-America Christian University); Stephanie Stephens (Howard College); Rachel Sternberg (Case Western Reserve University); Holly Sterner (College of Coastal Georgia); Karen Stewart (Norwich University); Sioux Stoeckle (Palo Verde College); Ron Stormer (Culver-Stockton College); Frank Stringfellow (University of Miami); Ayse Stromsdorfer (Soldan I. S. H. S.); Ashley Strong-Green (Paine College); James Sullivan (Illinois Central College); Zohreh Sullivan (University of Illinois); Richard Sullivan (Worcester State College); Duke Sutherland (Mississippi Gulf Coast Community College/Jackson County Campus); Maureen Sutton (Kean University); Marianne Szlyk (Montgomery College); Rebecca Taksel (Point Park University); Robert Tally (Texas State University); Tim Tarkington (Georgia Perimeter College); Patricia Taylor (Western Kentucky University); Mary Ann Taylor (Mountain View College); Susan Tekulve (Converse College); Stephen Teller (Pittsburgh State University); Stephen Thomas (Community College of Denver); Freddy Thomas (Virginia State University); Andy Thomason (Lindenwood University); Diane Thompson (Northern Virginia Community College); C. H. Thornton (Northwest-Shoals Community College); Elizabeth Thornton (Georgia Perimeter); Burt Thorp (University of North Dakota); Willie Todd (Clark Atlanta University); Martin Trapp (Northwestern Michigan College); Brenda Tuberville (University of Texas–Tyler); William Tucker (Olney Central College); Martha Turner (Troy University); Joya Uraizee (Saint Louis University); Randal Urwiller (Texas College); Emily Uzendoski (Central Community College–Columbus Campus); Kenneth Van Dover (Lincoln University); Kay Walter (University of Arkansas–Monticello); Cassandra Ward-Shah (West Chester University); Gina Weaver (Southern Nazarene University); Cathy Webb (Meridian Community College); Eric Weil (Elizabeth City State University); Marian Wernicke (Pensacola Junior College); Robert West (Mississippi State University); Cindy Wheeler (Georgia Highlands College); Chuck Whitchurch (Golden West College); Julianne White (Arizona State University); Denise White (Kennesaw State University); Amy White (Lee University); Patricia White (Norwich University); Gwen Whitehead (Lamar State College–Orange); Terri Whitney (North Shore Community College); Tamora Whitney (Creighton University); Stewart Whittemore (Auburn University); Johannes Wich-Schwarz (Maryville University); Charles Wilkinson (Southwest Tennessee Community College); Donald Williams (Toccoa Falls College); Rick Williams (Rogue Community College); Lea Williams (Norwich University); Susan Willis (Auburn University–Montgomery); Sharon Wilson (University of Northern Colorado); J. D. Wireman (Indiana State University); Rachel Wiren (Baptist Bible College); Bertha Wise (Oklahoma City Community College); Sallie Wolf (Arapahoe Community College); Rebecca Wong (James Madison University); Donna

Woodford-Gormley (New Mexico Highlands University); Paul Woodruff (University of Texas–Austin); William Woods (Wichita State University); Marjorie Woods (University of Texas–Austin); Valorie Worthy (Ohio University); Wei Yan (Darton College); Teresa Young (Philander Smith College); Darcy Zabel (Friends University); Michelle Zenor (Lon Morris College); and Jacqueline Zubeck (College of Mount Saint Vincent).

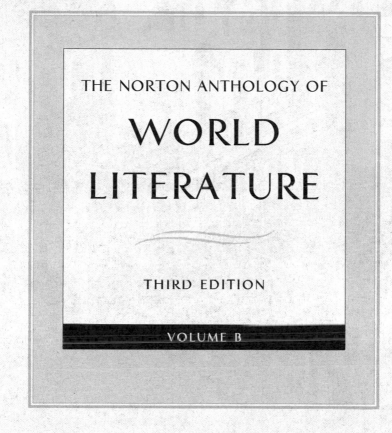

THE NORTON ANTHOLOGY OF

WORLD
LITERATURE

THIRD EDITION

VOLUME B

I

Circling the Mediterranean: Europe and the Islamic World

he word "Mediterranean" comes from Latin, meaning "in the middle of the lands." From antiquity through the Middle Ages, the centrally located Mediterranean Sea—also called by those who lived along its shores *Mare nostrum,* or "our sea"—facilitated trade and exchange. Not only commodities but also stories and songs continually circulated from place to place, crisscrossing the water to link nations in Europe, North Africa, and the Near and Middle East. Port cities all around the Mediterranean were sites of particularly intense cultural and economic interaction, collectively making up a single complex web that knit together distant lands.

While earlier generations of historians have tended to see the diverse cultures of the Mediterranean region in monolithic terms, conceiving of an Islamic world and a Christian world that were fundamentally opposed, more recent research has unearthed the intimate links between the various cultures of the region. There was both a great deal of interaction *between* the cultural spheres conventionally marked as "Europe" and "the Islamic world" and, on the other hand, a great deal of diversity *within* each one of these apparently undifferentiated units. "Europe," as a multinational concept, almost never appeared during the Middle Ages; people referred to themselves as

A fourteenth-century image of the Venetian trader Marco Polo, embarking from Venice.

3

"English," "Franks," "Normans," and "Lombards," not as "Europeans." "The Islamic world" was similarly divided by rival efforts to lead the Muslim community in the caliphates of Damascus, Baghdad, and Cairo, as well as by the Mongol invasions of the thirteenth century. The opposition of "the Islamic world" and "Europe" is a modern invention: it was not the way medieval people described themselves or the world they lived in.

The false division between Europe and the Islamic world enabled a misleading view of history in which Christian Europe was seen as the sole heir to a rich legacy of Greco-Roman philosophy and literature, uncontaminated by Arabic or Persian influences—an uninterrupted cultural bloodline, so to speak, reaching back from Aquinas to **Aristotle**, from **Dante** to **Virgil**. Nothing could be further from the truth. The Arabic translations of ancient Greek philoso-phy and science that made the work of **Plato**, Aristotle, and Ptolemy available to Europeans as they slowly emerged from a long period of intellectual dormancy were not just passive vessels that transmitted ancient knowledge to an awakening Europe on the cusp of the Renaissance: on the contrary, the cultural ferment of the Islamic world was an essential element in the emergence of the early modern West. The story of premodern history and literature is, therefore, above all a story of connections, interaction, and mutual influence.

CHRISTIANITY AND PLATONISM

By the year 100, broad changes were under way in the lands circling the Mediterranean Sea. The Roman Empire, which had reached its pinnacle of cultural and military supremacy during the

This image, from an illuminated thirteenth-century Arabic manuscript, depicts the Greek philosopher Socrates discoursing with his students.

reign of Augustus Caesar, had expanded to the point that unrest in the eastern provinces was a perpetual worry. In the Roman-ruled province of Judea (roughly, modern Israel), the suppression by the civil authorities of a loosely organized rebellion culminated in the destruction of Jerusalem and scattering (or "diaspora") of the Jewish community in 70 C.E. Those exiled from the region included the Jewish followers of James and John who had embraced the message of the gospel, as well as those mixed Jewish and Gentile communities that took up the intensely hellenized brand of Christianity developed by Paul and his followers, which drew on the philosophy of Plato as well as of mystical Neoplatonists such as Plotinus and Porphyry. Not until about three centuries later would this heterogeneous collection of new religious orientations become codified as a single Christian doctrine, encapsulated in Jerome's production of the Latin (or "Vulgate") **Bible** and in **Augustine**'s masterful synthesis of Christian doctrine and Greek philosophy.

Augustine's autobiography, the *Confessions*, pays tribute to the theologian's engagement with the philosophy and literature of the Roman world: he paraphrases Seneca and Cicero, and movingly describes the tears he shed while reading Virgil's account of Dido in the *Aeneid*. These moments illustrate the imaginative pull of classical literature, which persisted during the period of Christianity's emergence. The values of Rome, its celebration of the arts and worldly pleasures, were very much at odds with a Christian ethic that demanded a rejection of the things of this world. Music, art, and poetry were to be avoided, unless they were explicitly in the service of God: liturgical music, as part of the act of communal worship, along with painted images of the crucified Christ, the Virgin Mary, and apostles, became increasingly important in early Christianity, while the classical principles of poetic composi-

tion were applied to new types of writing such as religious hymns and saints' lives. Writers found that poetry could be made to serve Christ, in the same way that figurative parables could disseminate the eternal truths of scripture. Jesus had told illustrative anecdotes, such as the parable of the Sower or the parable of the Wise and Foolish Virgins: preachers therefore believed that they too were authorized to use fictions, as long as the effort was wholly in the service of the Lord and not intended to seduce the soul with bodily pleasures.

The yearning for a mystical faith that would provide a sense of purpose was ubiquitous in the late Roman Empire, as can be seen, for example, in the devotion to the cult of Isis described so vividly by **Apuleius**. Christianity was just one of a number of religious cults that had fashioned a kind of cultural compromise with the philosophical orientation of the period; but it thrived as no other religion did, ultimately becoming the state religion of the Roman Empire under the rule of Constantine in the fourth century. While the Italian city of Rome remained the seat of imperial power in the West, the capital city of Byzantium (modern Istanbul, in Turkey) represented Rome in the East. Renamed "Constantinople" (Constantine's city) by the Christian emperor of Rome, the city would be simply known as "al-Rum" (Rome) to speakers of Arabic and Persian. An empire stretched so widely that it had two capitals, one in the West and one in the East, was ripe for dissolution: sooner or later in the history of every empire, things fall apart. The waves of invasion of Italy by Germanic tribes came to a head in the fifth century, when Rome endured a series of weak rulers. The eastern Roman capital of Constantinople, by contrast, remained intact until the end of the Middle Ages, though during that time its character had changed very substantially from what it had been in the age of the Caesars. Both Augustine

HANACTACIC

This Byzantine mosaic in the monastery church in Hosios Loukas, Greece, depicts Christ saving Adam, Eve, King David, and King Solomon, who had been confined in limbo.

and Boethius, writing in the fifth and sixth centuries, bear witness to the decay of Rome—and to the birth of something entirely new, as a Christian culture, various and diffuse, rose out of the ashes of empire.

The diaspora—literally, "scattering" (Greek)—of Jews from Jerusalem in 70 C.E. not only facilitated the spread of Christianity throughout the Roman Empire but also created a new cultural environment that would lead to the development of rabbinic Judaism. The simultaneous emergence of rabbinic Judaism and Christianity can be described as a kind of twin birth, both of them formed in the crucible of Roman aggression in the first century. Beyond the physical experience of exile, the figurative concept of diaspora—like the ancient paradigm of the mass movement of people described in Exodus, which recounts the migration of the Jewish nation from Egypt to the promised land

after many years of exile—provided an enormously powerful model for thinking about the movement of peoples in the early Middle Ages. Whereas the Jewish people were thought to be consigned to a permanent state of diaspora, endlessly wandering in the desert of the wide world, other communities sometimes claimed for themselves the role of the "true Israel": for medieval Christians, thinking of themselves as the true Israel meant identifying themselves as a chosen people. But their promised land was not to be found on the earth—it was the Heavenly Jerusalem, whose pleasures would be enjoyed only in the afterlife. National histories, too, made the history of the Jewish people into a template for their own myths of origin: this can be seen in medieval chronicles that liken accounts of the Trojans, who fled the ruins of Troy to found the great city of Rome, to accounts of the Jews in the diaspora. A similar national myth of origins can be found in the East African **Kebra Nagast**, which draws on the founding stories of the Jewish peoples to claim for Ethiopian Christians a place in the same lineage, identifying their rulers as the offspring of Solomon and Sheba and asserting that they preserved the original ark of the covenant in Ethiopia.

THE SPREAD OF ISLAM

Like the emergence of Christianity in the wake of the Jewish diaspora, the dissemination of the **Qur'an** by Muhammad and his followers in the seventh century and the subsequent formation of an Islamic community had a dramatic effect on the development of Mediterranean culture. In his account of Muhammad's life, the early biographer **Ibn Ishaq** describes a community struggling to form itself not only in accord with the explicit dictates found in its holy book, the Qur'an, but also in conformity with the exemplary life led by its prophet, Muhammad. These two models, the revealed book and the life perfectly led, were the religious guidelines of an empire that grew almost overnight to dominate large swathes of the Middle East and North Africa: in 750, little more than a century after Muhammad began delivering the Qur'an in 610, Islamic rule extended westward through Spain into southern France and eastward through Persia (modern Iran) into India. The spread of Islam took place not only through cultural and religious means but also through direct military conquest, such as the assault on the Byzantine Christian empire that culminated in the Battle of Yarmūk in 636: after that time, the southern regions of Anatolia (modern Turkey) and virtually the whole of the Levant (modern Near East) were under the control of the armies of Islam. In spite of its military successes and dynamic expansion, this new empire was far from mono-

lithic: after the fall of the Umayyad caliphate (literally, "headship") that had been based in Damascus, the Abbasid caliphate was established at Baghdad, where it endured for more than five hundred years until the Mongol invasions from Central Asia in the mid-thirteenth century. Even after their fall from power in the East, however, the Umayyads retained control in the West, where they continued to rule the Spanish provinces they had named "al-Andalus."

In addition to the political divisions centered on the caliphates, religious divisions also cut across the nations gathered under Islamic rule. The most important of these is the division of Sunni from Shi'a Islam: the former centers on a strict conformity to the exemplary life of the Prophet Muhammad and a literal reading of the Holy Book; the latter instead prescribes a special veneration of the family of the Prophet, especially his daughter Fatima, her husband (who was also the Prophet's cousin) Ali, and their sons Hasan and Hussain. The highly emotional, affective quality of Shi'a Islam is expressed in devotional stories and plays chronicling the martyrdom of the members of the Prophet's family, as well as in the later medieval emergence of Sufi mysticism; the mystics used figurative poetic language to convey the soul's experience of the divine. Both Shi'a veneration of the family of the Prophet and Sufi poetic expressions of religious devotion were regarded with suspicion wherever Sunni practice was the norm; the literature of Shi'a and Sufi piety, however, has continued to be widely popular not only in the Arabic and Persian-speaking populations of the Near and Middle East but also—in translation—throughout the world.

Divisions, both political and religious, persisted throughout the lands of medieval Islam: in response to the alienation of the Shi'a community by the Abbasids who ruled from Baghdad, a separate Fatimid caliphate that was Shi'a in orientation arose in Cairo.

North Sea

Atlantic Ocean

Rhine

Elbe

Oder

Vistula

Dneiper

Dneister

FRANCE

Loire

ALPS

CARPATHIAN MTNS

Black

Rhône

Milan

Lombardy

Pavia

Danube

Provence

Ravenna

Marseille

Adriatic Sea

Macedonia

Thrace

Constantinople
(Byzantium)

Douro

PYRENEES

Corsica

Rome

Thessaly

Troy

Saragossa

Ebro

Ostia

Tuz

AL-ANDALUS

Tagus

Toledo

Tyrrhenian Sea

Sardinia

G
R
E
E
C
E

Aegean Sea

Konya

Hypata

UMAYYAD CALIPHATE

Thebes

Athens

ASIA

Cordoba

Mediterranean

Palermo

TAURUS

Granada

Sea

Sicily

Malta

Rhodes

Hippo

Carthage

Crete

Cyprus

Madaurus

Thagaste

KINGDOM OF FEZ

Kairouan

Fez

HAMMADIDS

HIGH ATLAS MOUNTAINS

ZIRIDS

AFRICA

Alexandria

Cairo

EGYPT

FATIMID CALIPHATE

Nile

EUROPE, NORTH AFRICA, ARABIA, ASIA MINOR & WESTERN CENTRAL ASIA
ca. 750–1200

Tropic of Cancer

0   200   400   600   800 kilometers
0   100   200   300   400   500 miles

Limits of the Byzantine Empire
as of 750

Sunni Muslim state
between 900–1200

Seljuk Empire in 1100

Shiite Muslim state
between 900–1200

Lake Balkash

Volga

Aral
Sea

QARAKHANIDS

Oxus

• Samarkand

• Bukhara

Caspian
Sea

K H O R A S A N

• Balkh

• Merv

Helmand

• Kabul

Sea

Nishapur • • Tus

• Ghazna

Lahore

A S I A

M I N O R

GHAZNAVID EMPIRE

Mosul •

• Hamadan

• Aleppo

Euphrates

Tigris

BUYID SULTANATE

P E R S I A

Indus

I N D I A

Tyre •
• Damascus

• Baghdad

Babylon •

• Nazareth

• Shiraz

• Jerusalem
• Bethlehem
Gaza

Sinai

Persian Gulf

A R A B I A

Arabian Sea

• Medina

Red Sea

• Mecca

I n d i a n   O c e a n

Axum •

• Aden

E T H I O P I A

A twelfth-century copy of a ninth-century Arabic manuscript by Hunayn Ibn Ishaq on the anatomy of the eye. Ibn Ishaq wrote a wide variety of medical and scientific treatises under the patronage of the Abbasid caliphate.

Internal squabbling finally gave way to utter chaos with the invasion of the Mongols in the early thirteenth century and their seizure of Baghdad in 1258. The Mongols soon converted to Islam, following the same pattern of rule through assimilation that led to their long domination of East Asia, centered on the powerful regional force of China. Successive Islamic dynasties ended, at last, when the Ottomans invaded and consolidated their power in the eastern Mediterranean with the conquest of Constantinople in 1453. The Ottomans remained in a position of strength in the region: their siege of Vienna in 1683 was an assault on the gates of early modern Europe, and they went on to establish diplomatic relations with several European nations.

Regardless of where the dominant caliphate was based—Damascus, Baghdad, or Cairo—the various nations yoked under Islamic rule shared one crucial element: the Arabic language. It served not only as the standard language of administration but also as the language of religious observance (all Muslims were urged to memorize the Qur'an, at least short sections that could be recited within the daily prayers), as well as the common vernacular that straddled national borders. Arabic was the standard language of conversation, administration, and poetic composition not only for Muslims but also for Christians and Jews who lived in regions under Islamic rule, such as al-Andalus. In this way, the Arabic language served to unify diverse populations, in much the same way as Greek had done in the ancient eastern Mediterranean and Latin would do in medieval Europe. Poetic traditions in Arabia before the revelation of the Qur'an had placed special value on recitation and the musical quality of verse, its rhythmic repetitions and use of end rhyme. Because the Qur'an itself conformed to many of these pre-Islamic norms, it became a standard model for poetic excellence while maintaining its preeminent theological value.

As Islamic influence spread further eastward, the historically powerful and culturally dominant civilization of Persia came within its orbit. The effect was transformative, both for Persian culture, which developed a particularly rich strand of mystical Islam, and for Islamic culture more broadly, which assimilated much of the poetic richness offered by Persian literature. Even though Arabic quickly became the language of administration and religion in Persia, the Persian language remained predominant in poetry and common in both philosophy and the natural sciences. In addition, the complex and vivid mythology of the indigenous religion of Persia, Zoroastrianism, persisted well after the advent of Islamic rule, as can be seen in the **Shahnameh** or *Book of Kings*, the national epic composed by **Ferdowsi**. Persian influence continued to be felt throughout the Islamic world, especially after the Mongol invasions and the establishment of Ottoman rule at Constantinople (renamed Istanbul). The Ottomans held Persian language, art, and poetics in high esteem, and imported painters as well as writers to serve their imperial court. Finally, the marriage of religious devotion and an exquisite poetic sensibility, so finely expressed in the lyrics of **Attar**, **Rumi**, and **Hafez**, would come to be a crucial part of the literary legacy of Islam, widely disseminated not only among the community of Muslim readers but also among the diverse modern audiences of world literature.

In addition to the intersection of poetics and theology, an extraordinarily productive feature of medieval culture was the intersection of poetics and philosophy, in the Latin Christian realm as well as in the Islamic world. Just as Augustine integrated Christian doctrine with Platonic philosophy in his theological writings, so too the Persian philosopher-poet **Avicenna** integrated the Islamic narrative of miraculous ascent into the heavens with a Platonic vision of the cosmos and its relationship to the individual soul in his *Mi'raj-nameh*. In these strikingly parallel cases, Platonic philosophy supplied the means to express a religious worldview that focuses particularly—whether in Christian or in Islamic terms—on how the individual soul can come to experience the divine presence. Versions of the *mi'raj*, or miraculous night journey, of the Prophet Muhammad first appeared in conservative, highly traditional Sunni accounts of the early history of Islam. Later versions of the mi'raj, such as that attributed to Avicenna, began to interpret the literal journey metaphorically or even mystically, understanding the singular ascent of the Prophet as a model for the journey that every soul must make toward God. By the thirteenth century, versions of the mi'raj had

been produced in al-Andalus, including one translated into Castilian at the order of the Spanish ruler Alfonso the Wise. This text, known as the *Libro della Scala* (or *Book of the Ladder*) was widely disseminated, providing a vision of the layered heavens that would inspire European Christian writers, including Dante.

The influence of Islamic literature was felt not only through the exalted union of philosophy and theology with poetics but also on a more mundane, vernacular level. The vibrant tradition of frame-tale narratives, in which an outer layer organizes a series of nested narratives that are contained within the frame like the layers of an onion, had a long history in the Mediterranean region: writers as early as **Ovid** and **Apuleius**, in the first and second centuries, had relied on nested narratives. But with the arrival of more elaborate frame-tale models—especially *Kalila wa Dimna*, a series of animal fables based on the Indian *Pañcatantra*—the genre took off in Persian and Arabic literatures. Perhaps the best known example of the frame tale, *The Thousand and One Nights*, survives in its earliest versions in the Persian language; these were soon supplemented by a range of retellings in Arabic. The *Nights* circulated about the Mediterranean, with bits and pieces of it finding its way into other collections and its frame-tale form serving as the inspiration for many European manifestations of the genre, including **Boccaccio's** *Decameron* and **Chaucer's** *Canterbury Tales*.

THE INVENTION OF THE WEST

For writers in the Islamic world, "the West" (*al-maghrib*) was the northern coast of Africa and al-Andalus, a region that was recognized as at once part of the Islamic sphere of influence and yet culturally and regionally distinctive.

EUROPE
ca. 1300

| 0 | 200 | 400 | 600 | 800 | kilometers |
| 0 | 100 | 200 | 300 | 400 | 500 | miles |

FINNS

Novgorod

ESTONIANS

Baltic Sea

LETTS

TEUTONIC ORDER

(3)

RUSSIANS

LITHUANIANS

POLES

Vistula

General directions of the expansion of Latin Christendom
from the 7th to the 15th centuries—

(1) through the Spanish Reconquista

(2) through the Norman conquest of Sicily

(3) through migration and conquest in eastern and northern Europe

(4) through the Crusades

Kiev

Dnieper

Approximate line of
division between Roman
Catholics and Orthodox
Christians in the 14th century

Approximate line of division
between Christendom and
the Muslim world in 1300

Volga

(3)

SLOVAKS

Dneister

Prut

MAGYARS

CARPATHIAN MOUNTAINS

Danube

Black Sea

BULGARS

Trebizond

BYZANTINE EMPIRE

Constantinople

S E L J U K   S T A T E S

A S I A   M I N O R

MESOPOTAMIA

Tigris

Chios

Smyrna (Izmir)

CAPPADOCIA

Athens

Chiarenza

Aegean Sea

Morea

Aegina

TAURUS MOUNTAINS

Aleppo

Euphrates

Antioch

Sea

Rhodes

Paphos

Cyprus

CRUSADER STATES

Damascus

Crete

(4)

Syrian Desert

Jerusalem

Alexandria

MUMLAKS

The so-called Hereford Mappamundi, ca. 1300. Jerusalem sits at the center of this medieval map; Asia occupies most of the top half; and Europe is in the lower-left quadrant.

The idea of the West as a synonym for Christian Europe—which seems so natural and familiar to modern readers—did not even begin to emerge until the late Middle Ages. Medieval inhabitants of Europe instead categorized themselves in different ways: in terms of their ethnic origin or "nation," in terms of their primary language, and—above all—in terms of their religion. Unlike in the areas under Islamic rule, where Jews and Christians were tolerated albeit subject to special taxation and restrictions (so-called *dhimmi* rule), in Christian Europe Jews were only sporadically tolerated, and Muslims were virtually unknown. We can thus infer that Europe exhibited much more religious homogeneity, at least until the first glimmerings of early Protestant reform impulses in the late fourteenth century. Uniformity of religion was further strengthened by uniformity of language, as Latin was used not only for all religious but also all political and administrative purposes, just as Arabic was in the Islamic world. Indeed, Latin's cultural hold was stronger: medieval Christians used it exclusively to compose their philosophical and scientific works, while both Arabic and Per-

sian functioned as languages of literature and learning for Muslims. Beginning in the ninth century, however, and with increasing frequency from the twelfth century onward, vernacular languages such as English, French, German, Italian, and Spanish became more common vehicles for poetic composition.

Medieval people defined themselves first of all by their religious orientation and next by ethnic origin, relying not at all on the categories familiar to modern readers. This perspective on the place of the self in the world is well illustrated on the medieval world maps, or *mappaemundi*, that were used not as practical guides to navigation but rather as abstract overviews of both the literal shape of the world and its metaphorical meaning. Accordingly, such maps conventionally place Jerusalem at the exact center, marking the site of Christ's crucifixion as the fixed point about which the whole world revolves. The mappamundi itself is almost always oriented toward the east (Latin *oriens*), rather than toward the north as on modern maps, so that its easternmost point, the Garden of Eden, appears—appropriately—as both the beginning of space and the beginning of time. Asia, Europe, and

A detail from a page of the Luttrell Psalter (ca. 1300) depicts Richard I and Saladin jousting during the Third Crusade. Saladin is drawn with a grotesque blue face—a rendering that makes it all the easier for the psalter's Christian readers to see the conflict as a clearly defined battle between good and evil.

Africa, the three known continents, are depicted symmetrically on the map. Asia takes up twice as much space as the other two, dominating the top half of the world sphere; Europe is tucked away at the lower left; and "the West" (Latin *occidens*) lies, rather forlornly, at the bottom.

The medieval map, with its deeply religious imaginative geography and central focus on Jerusalem, illuminates the ways in which the repeated cycles of European warfare around the Mediterranean and into the Middle East—called "Crusades," after the cross (Latin *crux*) sewn by the warriors onto their garments—functioned not just as actual military campaigns but also as symbolic assaults designed to reclaim control of the spiritual homeland of the medieval Christian. The First Crusade, launched in 1095, included a violent assault on Jerusalem that ended with the slaughter of most of the city's inhabitants and the establishment of the "Latin Kingdom of Jerusalem": a significant outpost of Europeans occupying Jerusalem itself together with additional European fortifications in adjoining towns along the coast (most importantly Acre, which remained in European hands until 1291). Although expeditions continued to be launched intermittently until the end of the Middle Ages—including the dramatic

Third Crusade, which united the English army of Richard the Lion-Hearted with the armies of Philip of France and Frederick Barbarossa of Germany—no later military successes matched those of the First Crusade that began them all. The Crusades functioned mainly as opportunities for economic development and international cooperation among the nations of Europe, helping to unify these disparate Christian nations through their shared opposition to the Muslim enemy. The passions stirred by this effort to stimulate political unity through religious fervor came at a high price: with each successive call to crusade, violent attacks were made on the only locally available non-Christian populations within the cities of Europe—that is, the Jews. Anti-Muslim violence in the form of crusade was therefore closely linked with the persecution of Jews and the early emergence of anti-Semitism.

The opposition of Christian and non-Christian, so fundamental to the ideology of crusade, permeates the epic literature of the Middle Ages. It is especially visible in the poetry of the eleventh century, such as the **Song of Roland**, which is often described as the national epic of France: "Christian" and "pagan" are set against one another throughout the work, as the conflict is cast as white versus black, right versus wrong. The ultimate triumph of the Christian forces of

Charlemagne over the Muslims at Saragossa literally takes place in medieval Spain; metaphorically, however, the victory of Christian over pagan is presented as a template for all holy war—including the First Crusade, which was being launched at the very moment that *Roland* (originally an oral poem) was committed to the page.

The epic genre began to emerge, originally in oral form and subsequently in written texts, by the ninth century. Like the Persian *Shahnameh* of Ferdowsi, the Anglo-Saxon **Beowulf** describes a shadowy era in which myth and history are intertwined; both works also have a similar complicated relationship to the religions that had become obligatory in their cultures but were anachronisms in the mythic worlds that they evoked. For Ferdowsi, Islam was an overlay that covered over but did not obscure the indigenous Persian myth that animates the epic of kings; for the anonymous author of *Beowulf*, Christianity is likewise an innovation applied as a veneer, here on a pagan Germanic past. The Germanic notion of *wyrd* or fate is aligned, by the *Beowulf*-poet, with Christian notions of divine providence, but it remains clear that the two concepts are far from identical. Epic, whether in England or in Persia, thus creates a sense of national identity by evoking a common historical origin, but it also grafts upon the rootstock of native myth new forms of identity—especially religious forms imported from outside the borders of the nation.

Epic is often opposed to romance: the former is portrayed as a masculine genre dedicated to the deeds of knights and the matter of war, the latter as a feminine genre that focuses on the relations of the lady and her lover, confined to the domestic sphere of the court. However, both genres, which rose to prominence in the twelfth century, share the idealized image of the knight: if he expresses his chivalry on the field of battle, the work is epic, but if his prowess is displayed in the private space of the bedchamber, the work is romance. The romances of Chrétien de Troyes, like the shorter romance works or **lais** of his predecessor, **Marie de France**, highlight this idealized role of the knight, which is also seen in the later medieval English, German, and Italian romances that were adapted from French originals. The French origins of the romance genre are also closely tied to the emergence of French as a literary language. Latin was unquestionably the primary language of scholarly learning, whether theological, philosophical, or scientific, but vernacular or spoken languages increasingly came to be the first choice for poetic composition. In the twelfth century, French was the first of the European languages to be elevated in this way; by the fourteenth century, other vernaculars had also begun to be widely used. Explicitly, in his treatise on languages (*De vulgari eloquentia*), and implicitly, in his **Divine Comedy**, Dante Alighieri stakes a claim for the local Florentine dialect of Italian as the "most illustrious vernacular," while Chaucer will make similar claims for English in his *Canterbury Tales*.

In spite of this ongoing shift, Latin experienced an important revival in the fourteenth century. Paradoxically at just the moment when literature in the vernacular was reaching new levels of sophistication with works such as Boccaccio's *Decameron* and Chaucer's *Canterbury Tales*, classical forms of Latin were being championed in humanistic circles under the guiding hand of **Petrarch**. Ambivalence about the competing claims of a revived classical Latin, on the one hand, and the potent spontaneity of the vernacular, on the other hand, is evident in the work of Petrarch himself: the author of several Latin treatises and a powerful advocate for classical scholarship, his exquisite lyrics in Italian would exert a powerful influence on the rise of Renaissance lyric not only in Italy but also in France and England. This paradox is reflected in modern scholarship, which tends to label Petrarch, who wrote in the early fourteenth century, as a "Renaissance" poet and his friend and disciple Boccaccio, who wrote in the mid-fourteenth century, as a "medieval" writer. The example of these two contemporaries illustrates the ways in which period divisions, like geographical divisions, sometimes obscure the profound continuities that underlie literary history.

Though Boccaccio wrote his masterwork, the *Decameron*, in Italian, he also composed (at the encouragement of Petrarch) several treatises in Latin. Chaucer did not write in Latin, but he shared Boccaccio's consciousness of the importance of the legacy of Roman antiquity and Latin literature; he produced several English translations of Latin works, including Boethius's *Consolation of Philosophy*. In late medieval French circles too, as illustrated in the mythographic works of **Christine de Pizan** written under the influence of Boccaccio, the Greco-Roman past loomed large. In all three of these major writers, the yearning for a revival of classical antiquity reveals the extent to which the wholehearted embrace of the ancient past that we tend to associate exclusively with the Renaissance was amply foreshadowed in the work of at least some late medieval authors, especially those whose perspective was particularly cosmopolitan, rooted in the experience of the city as a cultural, economic, linguistic, and—above all—literary crossroads.

While we can read Boccaccio, Chaucer, and Christine de Pizan in the context of the emergence of Latin humanism, they can also be seen as central participants in the late medieval European flowering of the frame-tale genre. Transmitted from India to Persia and then disseminated throughout the Islamic world

and across the Mediterranean, frame-tale narratives such as the *Thousand and One Nights* were widely popular, both in written and in oral form. One of the first medieval examples of the genre to cross over from the Islamic world into Europe is the twelfth-century **Disciplina Clericalis** (*Scholar's Guide*) of **Petrus Alfonsi**, an Andalusi Jew who had converted to Christianity and spent the later part of his life in England and northern France. His own experience of moving between cultures, religious communities, and linguistic groups bears a striking resemblance to the frame-tale genre itself, which shows an almost uncanny ability to slip through the borders that separate national literatures. Petrus Alfonsi's work is just one of the first in a long series of frame-tale narratives, including Marie de France's *Lais* and the work of Boccaccio and Chaucer, and it is ample testimony to the cultural flux so strongly expressed in medieval Spain, and more broadly throughout the Mediterranean world.

The age of Boccaccio and Chaucer also witnessed the rise of yet one more genre centered on the crossing of cultural boundaries: the travel narrative. Early in the thirteenth century **Marco Polo** had already committed to paper an account of his journeys along the Silk Road as far as the east coast of China, but it was not until the fourteenth century that travel literature won general popularity with the wide diffusion of such works as *The Book of John Mandeville*, which begins with a conventional pilgrimage itinerary to Jerusalem but then goes on to a wildly speculative journey through Asia in search of Prester John's Land. Columbus carried copies of both Marco Polo and Mandeville on his journey in search of a westward passage to the Indies, where he stumbled across a new land that would alter the shape of the old world maps and offer new horizons for conquest, thus bringing the medieval age to a close.

THE CHRISTIAN BIBLE
THE NEW TESTAMENT GOSPELS
ca. first century C.E.

For some readers, the Bible is to be read as sacred history and divine revelation, as a book whose truth is grounded by religious faith. For others, it is a rich trove of cultural history, sometimes supported by archaeology and other corroborating evidence, sometimes not. Beginning in the nineteenth century, however, readers started to also think of the Bible as a work of literature, analyzing it in terms of genre and poetics and comparing it to other literary works written around the same time. The Gospels of Matthew, Mark, and Luke, for instance, all of which retell the life of Jesus, can be read as examples of Greco-Roman biography as practiced around the Mediterranean during the first century C.E. The metaphorical language of the Gospel of John reflects the strong influence of Platonic philosophy on Jewish communities within the Roman Empire. This literary approach to the Bible has inspired recent generations of modern intellectuals, writers, and artists—sometimes from a devout perspective, sometimes not. Yet it is crucial to realize that considering the Christian Bible as literature is not a modern novelty: over the past two thousand years, poets have constantly quoted and paraphrased the Gospels in order to enrich their own work with the resonant, messianic tone and powerful turns of phrase that appear in what is arguably the single most influential text of world literature.

CHRISTIAN CULTURE IN THE ROMAN EMPIRE

Jesus was born in the town of Bethlehem, a town located in the province of Judea in the eastern part of the Roman Empire. While Latin was the language mainly used in Rome itself, in far-off Judea the language of administration was Greek. For most local inhabitants, however, the vernacular was Aramaic, a language related to Hebrew but sufficiently different from it that Aramaic speakers would not necessarily have understood Hebrew. The polyglot nature of the region was mirrored in the wide range of ethnicities and religious orientations found there. Judea and the surrounding lands had formerly been part of the vast empire established by Alexander the Great, under whose influence the local Jewish population—especially the more affluent and educated classes—had embraced Greek literature and philosophy. This religious and cultural ferment gave rise to a variety of religious groups; some became marginalized and died out, but others (including Christianity and rabbinic Judaism) would live on.

From Roman administrative records, we know that there was a historical Jesus, a disruptive rabble-rouser who attracted the attention of the local authorities and was ultimately executed. Yet the Jesus of the gospel accounts is something far more complex, more a phenomenon than a man. It is clear that the events of his life rapidly led to the establishment of not just a single community but a number of communities organized around the symbolic significance that could be assigned to this man, his words, and his deeds. These included both Jewish communities, for whom Jesus was to be identified with the long-awaited Messiah, and non-Jewish (or "Gentile") communities around the Mediterranean Sea. The dating system we use today reflects the fundamental break in time that early Christians believed had taken place. Dates in the Roman Empire were ordinarily based on the number of the year in the reign of the individual ruler, but Christians viewed Jesus as a divine lord whose authority surmounted that of any earthly kingdom or empire. Consequently, they began to number the years "A.D."—that is, *Anno Domini*, or "In the year of the Lord." Today, we more often use the more inclusive abbreviation C.E. for the Common Era, but we continue to number years from the birth of Jesus—a practice that reflects the early Christians' profound sense of a temporal rupture, the belief that a new age had dawned.

WORK

Together with the Gospel of Mark, the three books of the Bible excerpted here—the Gospels of Matthew, Luke, and John—form the core of the collection of twenty-seven books that Christians call the New Testament. This label, taken with the "Old Testament," encapsulates the Christian perspective on the relationship of Jesus' mission to the history of the Jewish people recounted in the **Hebrew Bible**, comprising the Pentateuch (the first five books, or Torah), the books of prophets and history, and the poetic books. For Christians, the old covenant established by God with Abraham and, after the flood, reestablished with Noah was merely a prefiguration, the first stage of a process that would be fulfilled only with the advent of Jesus and subsequent rise of Christianity. In some ways, this perspective honors and elevates the role of the Jewish people; in other ways, it denigrates Judaism, relegating it to a subordinate position in the divine plan for humanity.

Although the Gospels present themselves as eyewitness testimony to events in the life of Jesus, they were actually committed to written form decades after his death. The earliest of them, the Gospel of Mark, probably dates to about 70 C.E.; the latest, the Gospel of John, dates to about 100 C.E. The sequence of four gospels was established relatively early on, as was the authoritativeness of their testimony. The second-century theologian Irenaeus of Lyons declared that there are only four gospels, just as there are only four corners of the earth, and four winds in the heavens. This declaration served to exclude the many alternative accounts of the life of Jesus that were also in circulation, and to give a more specific structure to the teachings of Jesus and his authorized followers; the final result was a codified form of the New Testament and, ultimately, Christian theology. The Gospels of Matthew, Mark, and Luke are called the Synoptic Gospels, because they give a panorama or overview (synopsis) of the life of Jesus, all telling the same story but from rather distinctive perspectives. The Gospel of John also recounts the life of Jesus, but with a very different narrative line and a deep concern to integrate Platonic philosophy and mysticism into the expression of divinity in the person of Jesus Christ, identified as the Word of God.

The Synoptic Gospels have a number of episodes in common, of which the most important are the Sermon on the Mount, the Last Supper, and the crucifixion and resurrection of Jesus. Yet each of the three gospels also has its own individual character: Luke tells us the most about the childhood and parentage of Jesus, and his work is closely related to the noncanonical tradition of "infancy gospels"—stories about the life of Jesus as a child that survive in Arabic as well as in Greek and Syriac versions. Mark provides the tightest and most focused account, placing special emphasis on the death of Jesus and recounting his biography in simpler, more primitive language. Mark appears to be addressing a Gentile audience, and his gospel is sometimes associated with the early foundation of Christian communities in Rome or, at least, in the regions of the Roman Empire lying to the west of Judea. Matthew, conversely, clearly directs his biography at an audience that is quite familiar with the Hebrew Bible: he gives a very detailed account of Jesus' preaching mission and his role as the long-awaited Messiah. Matthew exhibits a special interest in the ways in which Jewish history is fulfilled in the coming of Jesus Christ, and in the ways in which the old covenant established between God and man is renewed in and superseded by the new covenant established with the sacrifice of Christ in the crucifixion.

Matthew also displays a central concern with the ways in which Jesus preached, especially his use of parables: little stories that reveal profound spiritual truths through metaphorical, even allegorical language. The excerpts presented here include parables of Jesus as recounted both by Matthew and by Luke, passages of the Gospels that are among those with the most profound literary influence on writers throughout the Middle Ages. The figurative, philosophical language of the Gospel of John would also go on to be highly influential, disseminated through a wide range of poetic evocations of the divine nature. John's account of the birth of Christ, excerpted here, seemingly describes the same transformative event narrated in the infancy chapters of Luke. Yet the two accounts could not be more different, as they represent two totally different perspectives on the nature of Jesus Christ, understood as that deepest of all paradoxes, the being who is at once both God and man. For John, Christ is the Word through which God creates all things, a mediator between matter and spirit, the temporal and the eternal. For Luke, he is Jesus of Nazareth, whose divine nature smoothly coexists with his human status, rooted in the cultural norms and social structures of first-century Judea.

The Gospels as we have them today reflect a complex and intertwined linguistic history: Jesus and his apostles would have spoken Aramaic, which we hear when Jesus cries out on the crucifix, "Eli, eli, lama sabachthani?" ("My God, my God, why have you forsaken me?" [Matthew 27.46]). However, the Gospels were written down in koine Greek, the vernacular that was the lingua franca of the eastern Mediterranean. This was a language meant to travel, and so the Gospels did: they were swiftly passed on in both oral and written form across the Mediterranean Sea, through Asia, Europe, and northern Africa. Latin translations of the Gospels soon began to be produced, and in 382 Pope Damasus asked the theologian Jerome to prepare a full, authorized translation into Latin. This version, known as the Vulgate, would become the standard version of the Bible read for more than a thousand years in the West, until new versions of the sacred text began to be produced at the dawn of the Reformation. Over the five hundred years since then, translations of the Bible have multiplied exponentially, as every spoken language has produced its own version of holy scripture. Most recently, modern writers and artists have moved the Bible into new formats such as the graphic novel, used by devout Christians to educate their children and enjoyed by a wide range of nonreligious readers.

THE BIBLE: THE NEW TESTAMENT GOSPELS[1]

Luke 2

[The Birth and Youth of Jesus]

It happened in those days that a decree went forth from Augustus Caesar[2] that all the world should be enrolled in a census. This was the first census, when Quirinius was governor of Syria. And all went to be enrolled, each to his own city. And Joseph also went up from Galilee,[3] from the city of Nazareth, to Judaea, to the city of David[4] which is called Bethlehem, because he was of the house and family of David; to be enrolled with Mary his promised wife, who was pregnant. And it happened that while they were there her time was completed, and she bore a son, her first-born, and she wrapped him in swaddling clothes and laid him in a manger, because there was no room for them in the inn. And there were shepherds in that region, camping out at night and keeping guard over their flock. And an angel of the Lord stood before them, and the glory of the Lord shone about them, and they were afraid with a great fear. The angel said to them: Do not be afraid; behold, I tell you good news, great joy which shall be for all the people; because this day there has been born for you in the city of David a savior who is Christ the Lord. And here is a sign for you; you will find a baby wrapped in swaddling clothes and lying in a manger. And suddenly with the angel there was a multitude of the heavenly host, praising God and saying: Glory to God in the highest and peace on earth among men of good will. And it happened that after the angels had gone off from them into the sky, the shepherds began saying to each other: Let us go to Bethlehem and see this thing which has happened, which the Lord made known to us; and they went, hastening, and found Mary and Joseph, and the baby lying in the manger; and when they had seen, they spread the news about what had been told them concerning this baby. And all who heard wondered at what had been told them by the shepherds; and Mary kept in mind all these sayings as she pondered them in her heart. And the shepherds returned, glorifying and praising God over all they had heard and seen, as it had been told them.

And when eight days were past, for his circumcision, his name was called Jesus, as it was named by the angel before he was conceived in the womb.

And when the days for their purification[5] according to the Law of Moses had been completed, they took him up to Jerusalem to set him before the Lord, as it has been written in the Law of the Lord: Every male child who opens the womb shall be called sacred to the Lord; and to give sacrifice as it is stated in the Law of the Lord, a pair of turtle doves or two young pigeons. And behold, there was a man in Jerusalem whose name was Simeon, and this man was righteous and virtuous and looked forward to the consolation of Israel, and the Holy Spirit was upon him; and it had been prophesied to him by the Holy Spirit that he should not look upon his death until he had looked on the Lord's Anointed. And in the

---

1. Translated by Richmond Lattimore.
2. Gaius Julius Caesar (63 B.C.E.–14 C.E.), who took the title Augustus as the first Roman emperor.
3. The region surrounding the Sea of Galilee, in the Roman province of Judea (modern Israel).

4. Second king of Israel, according to the Hebrew Bible; he was anointed king in Bethlehem, his traditional birthplace.
5. The ritual cleansing following childbirth (prescribed in Leviticus 12).

spirit he went into the temple; and as his parents brought in the child Jesus so that they could do for him what was customary according to the law, Simeon himself took him in his arms and blessed God and said: Now, Lord, you release your slave, in peace, according to your word; because my eyes have looked on your salvation, what you made ready in the presence of all the peoples; a light for the revelation to the Gentiles, and the glory of your people, Israel. And his father and his mother were in wonder at what was being said about him. And Simeon blessed them and said to Mary his mother: Behold, he is appointed for the fall and the rise of many in Israel; and as a sign which is disputed; and through your soul also will pass the sword; so that the reasonings of many hearts may be revealed. And there was Anna, a prophetess, the daughter of Phanuel, of the tribe of Asher. And she was well advanced in years, having lived with her husband seven years from the time of her maidenhood, and now she was eighty-four years a widow. And she did not leave the temple, serving night and day with fastings and prayers. And at this same time she came near and gave thanks to God and spoke of the child to those who looked forward to the deliverance of Jerusalem.

And when they had done everything according to the Law of the Lord, they went back to Galilee, to their own city, Nazareth.

And the child grew in stature and strength as he was filled with wisdom, and the grace of God was upon him.

Now his parents used to journey every year to Jerusalem for the feast of the Passover.[6] And when he was twelve years old, when they went up according to their custom for the festival and had completed their days there, on their return the boy Jesus stayed behind in Jerusalem, and his parents did not know it. And supposing that he was in their company they went a day's journey and then looked for him among their relatives and friends, and when they did not find him they turned back to Jerusalem in search of him. And it happened that after three days they found him in the temple sitting in the midst of the masters, listening to them and asking them questions. And all who heard him were amazed at his intelligence and his answers. And they were astonished at seeing him, and his mother said to him: Child, why did you do this to us? See, your father and I have been looking for you, in distress. He said to them: But why were you looking for me? Did you not know that I must be in my father's house? And they did not understand what he had said to them. And he returned with them and came to Nazareth, and was in their charge. And his mother kept all his sayings in her heart. And Jesus advanced in wisdom and stature, and in the favor of God and men.

6. The holiday (Heb. *Pesach*) commemorating the liberation of the people of Israel, led by Moses, from bondage in Egypt.

Matthew 5–7

[*The Sermon on the Mount*]

And seeing the multitudes he went up onto the mountain, and when he was seated, his disciples came to him, and he opened his mouth and taught them, saying:

Blessed are the poor in spirit, because theirs is the Kingdom of Heaven.

Blessed are they who sorrow, because they shall be comforted.

Blessed are the gentle, because they shall inherit the earth.

Blessed are they who are hungry and thirsty for righteousness, because they shall be fed.

Blessed are they who have pity, because they shall be pitied.

Blessed are the pure in heart, because they shall see God.

Blessed are the peacemakers, because they shall be called the sons of God.

Blessed are they who are persecuted for their righteousness, because theirs is the Kingdom of Heaven.

Blessed are you when they shall revile you and persecute you and speak every evil thing of you, lying, because of me. Rejoice and be glad, because your reward in heaven is great, for thus did they persecute the prophets before you.

You are the salt of the earth; but if the salt loses its power, with what shall it be salted? It is good for nothing but to be thrown away and trampled by men. You are the light of the world. A city cannot be hidden when it is set on top of a hill. Nor do men light a lamp and set it under a basket, but they set it on a stand, and it gives its light to all in the house. So let your light shine before men, so that they may see your good works and glorify your father in heaven.

Do not think that I have come to destroy the law[1] and the prophets. I have not come to destroy but to complete. Indeed, I say to you, until the sky and the earth are gone, not one iota or one end of a letter must go from the law, until all is done. He who breaks one of the least of these commandments and teaches men accordingly shall be called the least in the Kingdom of Heaven; he who performs and teaches these commandments shall be called great in the Kingdom of Heaven. For I tell you, if your righteousness is not more abundant than that of the scribes and the Pharisees,[2] you may not enter the Kingdom of Heaven.

You have heard that it was said to the ancients: You shall not murder. He who murders shall be liable to judgment. I say to you that any man who is angry with his brother shall be liable to judgment; and he who says to his brother, fool, shall be liable before the council; and he who says to his brother, sinner, shall be liable to Gehenna.[3] If then you bring your gift to the altar, and there remember that your brother has some grievance against you, leave your gift before the altar, and go first and be reconciled with your brother, and then go and offer your gift. Be quick to be conciliatory with your adversary at law when you are in the street with him, for fear your adversary may turn you over to the judge, and the judge to the officer, and you be thrown into prison. Truly I tell you, you cannot come out of there until you pay the last penny.

---

1. That is, the Torah, the five books of the law that begin the Hebrew Bible.

2. A major Jewish sect that emphasized strict observance of Jewish law; they were instrumental in the development of rabbinic Judaism.

3. Hell (Heb. *gehinnom*); figurative use of the name of a valley outside Jerusalem where children were sacrificed to pagan gods.

You have heard that it has been said: You shall not commit adultery. I tell you that any man who looks at a woman so as to desire her has already committed adultery with her in his heart. If your right eye makes you go amiss, take it out and cast it from you; it is better that one part of you should be lost instead of your whole body being cast into Gehenna. And if your right hand makes you go amiss, cut it off and cast it from you; it is better that one part of you should be lost instead of your whole body going to Gehenna. It has been said: If a man puts away his wife, let him give her a contract of divorce. I tell you that any man who puts away his wife, except for the reason of harlotry, is making her the victim of adultery; and any man who marries a wife who has been divorced is committing adultery. Again, you have heard that it has been said to the ancients: You shall not swear falsely, but you shall make good your oaths to the Lord. I tell you not to swear at all: not by heaven, because it is the throne of God; not by the earth, because it is the footstool for his feet; not by Jerusalem, because it is the city of the great king; not by your own head, because you cannot make one hair of it white or black. Let your speech be yes yes, no no; more than that comes from the evil one.

You have heard that it has been said: An eye for an eye and a tooth for a tooth. I tell you not to resist the wicked man; but if one strikes you on the right cheek, turn the other one to him also; and if a man wishes to go to law with you and take your tunic, give him your cloak also, and if one makes you his porter for a mile, go with him for two. Give to him who asks, and do not turn away one who wishes to borrow from you. You have heard that it has been said: You shall love your neighbor and hate your enemy. I tell you, love your enemies and pray for those who persecute you, so that you may be sons of your father who is in heaven, because he makes his sun rise on the evil and the good, and rains on the just and the unjust. For if you love those who love you, what reward do you have? Do not even the tax collectors do the same? And if you greet only your brothers, what do you do that is more than others do? Do not even the pagans do the same? Be perfect as your father in heaven is perfect.

Take care not to practice your righteousness publicly before men so as to be seen by them; if you do, you shall have no recompense from your father in heaven. Then when you do charity, do not have a trumpet blown before you, as the hypocrites do in the synagogues and the streets, so that men may think well of them. Truly I tell you, they have their due reward. But when you do charity, let your left hand not know what your right hand is doing, so that your charity may be in secret; and your father, who sees what is secret, will reward you. And when you pray, you must not be like the hypocrites, who love to stand up in the synagogues and the corners of the squares to pray, so that they may be seen by men. Truly I tell you, they have their due reward. But when you pray, go into your inner room and close the door and pray to your father, who is in secret; and your father, who sees what is secret, will reward you. When you pray, do not babble as the pagans do; for they think that by saying much they will be heard. Do not then be like them; for your father knows what you need before you ask him. Pray thus, then:[4] Our father in heaven, may your name be hallowed, may your kingdom come, may your will be done, as in heaven, so upon

---

4. The following verses, commonly known as the Lord's Prayer, are central to Christian religious practice.

earth. Give us today our sufficient bread, and forgive us our debts, as we also have forgiven our debtors. And do not bring us into temptation, but deliver us from evil. For if you forgive men their offenses, your heavenly father will forgive you; but if you do not forgive men, neither will your father forgive you your offenses. And when you fast, do not scowl like the hypocrites; for they make ugly faces so that men can see that they are fasting. Truly I tell you, they have their due reward. But when you fast, anoint your head and wash your face, so that you may not show as fasting to men, but to your father, in secret; and your father, who sees what is secret, will reward you.

Do not store up your treasures on earth, where the moth and rust destroy them, and where burglars dig through and steal them; but store up your treasures in heaven, where neither moth nor rust destroys them, and where burglars do not dig through or steal; for where your treasure is, there also will be your heart. The lamp of the body is the eye. Thus if your eye is clear, your whole body is full of light; but if your eye is soiled, your whole body is dark. If the light in you is darkness, how dark it is. No man can serve two masters. For either he will hate the one and love the other, or he will cling to one and despise the other; you cannot serve God and mammon.[5] Therefore I tell you, do not take thought for your life, what you will eat, or for your body, what you will wear. Is not your life more than its food and your body more than its clothing? Consider the birds of the sky, that they do not sow or harvest or collect for their granaries, and your heavenly father feeds them. Are you not preferred above them? Which of you by taking thought can add one cubit to his growth? And why do you take thought about clothing? Study the lilies in the field, how they grow. They do not toil or spin; yet I tell you, not even Solomon[6] in all his glory was clothed like one of these. But if God so clothes the grass of the field, which grows today and tomorrow is thrown in the oven, will he not much more clothe you, you men of little faith? Do not then worry and say: What shall we eat? Or: What shall we drink? Or: What shall we wear? For all this the Gentiles study. Your father in heaven knows that you need all these things. But seek out first his kingdom and his justice, and all these things shall be given to you. Do not then take thought of tomorrow; tomorrow will take care of itself, sufficient to the day is its own evil.

Do not judge, so you may not be judged. You shall be judged by that judgment by which you judge, and your measure will be made by the measure by which you measure. Why do you look at the straw which is in the eye of your brother, and not see the log which is in your eye? Or how will you say to your brother: Let me take the straw out of your eye, and behold, the log is in your eye. You hypocrite, first take the log out of your eye, and then you will see to take the straw out of the eye of your brother. Do not give what is sacred to the dogs, and do not cast your pearls before swine, lest they trample them under their feet and turn and rend you. Ask, and it shall be given you; seek, and you shall find; knock, and the door will be opened for you. Everyone who asks receives, and he who seeks finds, and for him who knocks the door will be opened. Or what man is there among you, whose son shall ask him for bread, that will give him a stone?

5. Wealth (an Aramaic word transliterated into Greek); the personification of Mammon as a god became a common trope in later Christian literature.

6. King of Israel and son of David, famed for his wisdom and for building the First Temple in Jerusalem.

Or ask him for fish, that will give him a snake? If then you, who are corrupt, know how to give good gifts to your children, by how much more your father who is in heaven will give good things to those who ask him. Whatever you wish men to do to you, so do to them. For this is the law and the prophets.

Go in through the narrow gate; because wide and spacious is the road that leads to destruction, and there are many who go in through it; because narrow is the gate and cramped the road that leads to life, and few are they who find it. Beware of the false prophets, who come to you in sheep's clothing, but inside they are ravening wolves. From their fruits you will know them. Do men gather grapes from thorns or figs from thistles? Thus every good tree produces good fruits, but the rotten tree produces bad fruits. A good tree cannot bear bad fruits, and a rotten tree cannot bear good fruits. Every tree that does not produce good fruit is cut out and thrown in the fire. So from their fruits you will know them. Not everyone who says to me Lord Lord will come into the Kingdom of Heaven, but he who does the will of my father in heaven. Many will say to me on that day: Lord, Lord, did we not prophesy in your name, and in your name did we not cast out demons, and in your name did we not assume great powers? And then I shall admit to them: I never knew you. Go from me, for you do what is against the law.

Every man who hears what I say and does what I say shall be like the prudent man who built his house upon the rock. And the rain fell and the rivers came and the winds blew and dashed against that house, and it did not fall, for it was founded upon the rock. And every man who hears what I say and does not do what I say will be like the reckless man who built his house on the sand. And the rain fell and the rivers came and the winds blew and battered that house, and it fell, and that was a great fall.

And it happened that when Jesus had ended these words, the multitudes were astonished at his teaching, for he taught them as one who has authority, and not like their own scribes.

Luke 15

[Parables]

All the tax collectors and the sinners kept coming around him, to listen to him. And the Pharisees and the scribes muttered, saying: This man receives sinners and eats with them. But he told them this parable, saying: Which man among you who has a hundred sheep and has lost one of them will not leave the ninety-nine in the wilds and go after the lost one until he finds it? And when he does find it, he sets it on his shoulders, rejoicing, and goes to his house and invites in his friends and his neighbors, saying to them: Rejoice with me, because I found my sheep which was lost. I tell you that thus there will be joy in heaven over one sinner who repents, rather than over ninety-nine righteous ones who have no need of repentance. Or what woman who has ten drachmas,[1] if she loses one drachma, does not light the lamp and sweep the house and search diligently until she finds it? And finding it she invites in her friends

1. Greek silver coins, each roughly equivalent in value to a manual laborer's wages for one day.

and neighbors, saying: Rejoice with me, because I found the drachma I lost. Such, I tell you, is the joy among the angels of God over one sinner who repents.

And he said: There was a man who had two sons. And the younger of them said to his father: Father, give me my appropriate share of the property. And the father divided his substance between them. And not many days afterward the younger son gathered everything together and left the country for a distant land, and there he squandered his substance in riotous living. And after he had spent everything, there was a severe famine in that country, and he began to be in need. And he went and attached himself to one of the citizens of that country, who sent him out into the fields to feed the pigs. And he longed to be nourished on the nuts that the pigs ate, and no one would give to him. And he went and said to himself: How many hired servants of my father have plenty of bread while I am dying of hunger here. I will rise up and go to my father and say to him: Father, I have sinned against heaven and in your sight, I am no longer worthy to be called your son. Make me like one of your hired servants. And he rose up and went to his father. And when he was still a long way off, his father saw him and was moved and ran and fell on his neck and kissed him. The son said to him: Father, I have sinned against heaven and in your sight, I am no longer worthy to be called your son. But his father said to his slaves: Quick, bring the best clothing and put it on him, and have a ring for his hand and shoes for his feet, and bring the fatted calf, slaughter him, and let us eat and make merry because this man, my son, was a dead man and came to life, he was lost and he has been found. And they began to make merry. His older son was out on the estate, and as he came nearer to the house he heard music and dancing, and he called over one of the servants and asked what was going on. He told him: Your brother is here, and your father slaughtered the fatted calf, because he got him back in good health. He was angry and did not want to go in. But his father came out and entreated him. But he answered and said to his father: Look, all these years I have been your slave and never neglected an order of yours, but you never gave me a kid so that I could make merry with my friends. But when this son of yours comes back, the one who ate up your livelihood in the company of whores, you slaughtered the fatted calf for him. But he said to him: My child, you are always with me, and all that is mine is yours; but we had to make merry and rejoice, because your brother was a dead man and came to life, he was lost and has been found.

From Matthew 13

[Why Jesus Teaches in Parables]

On that day Jesus went out of the house and sat beside the sea; and a great multitude gathered before him, so that he went aboard a ship and sat there, and all the multitude stood on the shore. And he talked to them, speaking mostly in parables: Behold, a sower went out to sow. And as he sowed, some of the grain fell beside the way, and birds came and ate it. Some fell on stony ground where there was not much soil, and it shot up quickly because there was no depth of soil, but when the sun came up it was parched, and because it had no roots it dried away. Some fell among thorns, and the thorns grew up and stifled it. But some fell upon the good soil and bore fruit, some a hundred-fold, some sixtyfold, some thirtyfold. He who has ears, let him hear. Then his disciples came to him and said: Why do you talk to them in parables? He answered them and said: Because it is given to you to understand the secrets of the Kingdom of Heaven, but to them it is not given. When a man has, he shall be given, and it will be more than he needs; but when he has not, even what he has shall be taken away from him. Therefore I talk to them in parables, because they have sight but do not see, and hearing but do not hear or understand. And for them is fulfilled the prophecy of Isaiah,[1] saying: With your hearing you shall hear and not understand, and you shall use your sight and look but not see. For the heart of this people is stiffened, and they hear with difficulty, and they have closed their eyes; so that they may never see with their eyes, or hear with their ears and with their hearts understand and turn back, so that I can heal them.

Blessed are your eyes because they see, and your ears because they hear. Truly I tell you that many prophets and good men have longed to see what you see, and not seen it, and to hear what you hear, and not heard it. Hear, then, the parable of the sower. To every man who hears the word of the Kingdom and does not understand it, the evil one comes and seizes what has been sown in his heart. This is the seed sown by the way. The seed sown on the stony ground is the man who hears the word and immediately accepts it with joy; but he has no root in himself, and he is a man of the moment, and when there comes affliction and persecution, because of the word, he does not stand fast. The seed sown among thorns is the man who hears the word, and concern for the world and the beguilement of riches stifle the word, and he bears no fruit. And the seed sown on the good soil is the man who hears the word and understands it, who bears fruit and makes it, one a hundredfold, one sixtyfold, and one thirtyfold.

He set before them another parable, saying: The Kingdom of Heaven is like a man who sowed good seed in his field. And while the people were asleep, his enemy came and sowed darnel in with the grain, and went away. When the plants grew and produced a crop, the darnel was seen. Then the slaves of the master came to him and said: Master, did you not sow good grain in your field? Where does the darnel come from? He said to them: A man who is my enemy did it. His slaves said: Do you wish us to go out and gather it? But he said: No, for fear that when you gather the darnel you may pull up the grain with it. Let them both grow until harvest time, and in the time of harvest I shall say to the harvesters: First gather the darnel, and bind it in sheaves for burning, but store the grain in my granary.

He set before them another parable, saying: The Kingdom of Heaven is like a grain of mustard, which a man took and sowed in his field; which is the smallest of all seeds, but when it grows, it is the largest of the greens and grows into a tree, so that the birds of the air come and nest in its branches.

He told them another parable: The Kingdom of Heaven is like leaven, which a woman took and buried in three measures of dough, so that it all rose.

All this Jesus told the multitudes in parables, and he did not talk to them except in parables; so as to fulfill the word spoken by the prophet, saying: I will open my mouth in parables, and pour out what has been hidden since the creation. Then he sent away the multitudes and went to the house. And his

1. See Isaiah 6.9–10.

disciples came to him and said: Make plain to us the parable of the darnel in the field. He answered them and said: The sower of the good seed is the son of man; the field is the world; the good seed is the sons of the Kingdom; the darnel is the sons of the evil one, and the enemy who sowed it is the devil; the harvest time is the end of the world, and the harvesters are angels. Then as the darnel is gathered and burned in the fire, so it is at the end of the world. The son of man will send out his angels, and they will gather from his Kingdom all that misleads, and the people who do what is not lawful, and cast them in the furnace of fire; and there will be weeping and gnashing of teeth. Then the righteous men will shine forth like the sun in the Kingdom of their father. He who has ears, let him hear. The Kingdom of Heaven is like a treasure hidden in the field, which a man found and hid, and for joy of it he goes and sells all he has and buys that field. Again, the Kingdom of Heaven is like a trader looking for fine pearls; he found one of great value, and went and sold all he had and bought it. Again, the Kingdom of Heaven is like a dragnet cast into the sea and netting every kind of fish; and when it is full they draw it out and sit on the beach and gather the good ones in baskets, but the bad they throw away. So will it be at the end of the world. The angels will go out and separate the bad from the midst of the righteous, and cast them in the furnace of fire; and there will be weeping and gnashing of teeth. Do you understand all this? They said to him: Yes. And he said to them: Therefore every scribe who is learned in the Kingdom of Heaven is like a man who is master of a house, who issues from his storehouse what is new and what is old.

Matthew 27–28

[Crucifixion and Resurrection]

When morning came, all the high priests and elders of the people held a meeting against Jesus, to have him killed. And they bound him and took him away and gave him over to Pilate the governor.[1]

   Then when Judas, who had betrayed him, saw that he had been condemned, he repented and proffered the thirty pieces of silver back to the high priests and the elders, saying: I did wrong to betray innocent blood. They said: What is that to us? You look to it. And he threw down the silver pieces in the temple and went away, and when he was alone he hanged himself. The high priests took up the silver pieces and said: We cannot put them in the treasury, since it is blood money. Then they took counsel together and with the money they bought the potter's field[2] to bury strangers in. Therefore that field has been called the Field of Blood, to this day. Then was fulfilled the word spoken by Jeremiah the prophet,[3] saying: I took the thirty pieces of silver, the price of him on whom a price was set, whom they priced from among the sons of Israel, and I gave the money for the field of the potter, as my Lord commanded me.

1. Pontius Pilate, imperial adminstrator of the Roman province of Judea (26–36 C.E.).
2. A place where clay was dug to make pottery; after the Gospels, a common term for a burying place for the poor.

3. Alluding perhaps to the purchase of a field in Jeremiah 32, or to the potter of Jeremiah 18–19 (though the citation is to Zechariah 11.13).

Now Jesus stood before the governor; and the governor questioned him, saying: Are you the King of the Jews? Jesus answered: It is you who say it. And while he was being accused by the high priests and the elders he made no answer. Then Pilate said to him: Do you not hear all their testimony against you? And he made no answer to a single word, so that the governor was greatly amazed.

For the festival, the governor was accustomed to release one prisoner for the multitude, whichever one they wished. And they had at that time a notorious man, who was called Barabbas.[4] Now as they were assembled Pilate said to them: Which one do you wish me to release for you, Barabbas, or Jesus, who is called Christ? For he knew that it was through malice that they had turned him over. Now as he was sitting on the platform, his wife sent him a message, saying: Let there be nothing between you and this just man; for I have suffered much today because of a dream about him. But the high priests and the elders persuaded the crowd to ask for Barabbas and destroy Jesus. Then the governor spoke forth and said to them: Which of the two shall I give you? They answered: Barabbas. Pilate said to them: What then shall I do with Jesus, who is called Christ? They all said: Let him be crucified. But Pilate said: Why? What harm has he done? But they screamed all the more, saying: Let him be crucified. And Pilate, seeing that he was doing no good and that the disorder was growing, took water and washed his hands before the crowd, saying: I am innocent of the blood of this man. You see to it. And all the people answered and said: His blood is upon us and upon our children. Then Pilate gave them Barabbas, but he had Jesus flogged, and gave him over to be crucified.

Then the soldiers of the governor took Jesus to the residence, and drew up all their battalion around him. And they stripped him and put a red mantle about him, and wove a wreath of thorns and put it on his head, and put a reed in his right hand, and knelt before him and mocked him, saying: Hail, King of the Jews. And they spat upon him and took the reed and beat him on the head. And after they had mocked him, they took off the mantle and put his own clothes on him, and led him away to be crucified. And as they went out they found a man of Cyrene, named Simon. They impressed him for carrying the cross.

Then they came to a place called Golgotha, which means the place of the skull, and gave him wine mixed with gall to drink. When he tasted it he would not drink it. Then they crucified him, and divided up his clothes, casting lots, and sat there and watched him. Over his head they put the label giving the charge against him, where it was written: This is Jesus, the King of the Jews. Then there were crucified with him two robbers, one on his right and one on his left. And those who passed by blasphemed against him, wagging their heads, and saying: You who tear down the temple and rebuild it in three days, save yourself, and come down from the cross, if you are the son of God. So too the high priests, mocking him along with the scribes and the elders, said: He saved others, he cannot save himself. He is King of Israel, let him come down from the cross and we will believe in him. He trusted in God, let him save him now, if he will; for he said: I am the son of God. And the robbers who were crucified with him spoke abusively to him in the same way.

---

4. Bar-Abbas, meaning "son of Abbas" (literally, "son of the Father"). John 18.40 calls Barabbas a "bandit" (*lēstēs*), a term often applied to the Jewish revolutionaries who defied Roman rule (Mark 15.7 refers to his involvement in "sedition").

But from the sixth hour there was darkness over all the earth until the ninth hour. But about the ninth hour Jesus cried out in a great voice, saying: *Elei elei lema sabachthanei?*[5] Which is: My God, my God, why have you forsaken me? But some of those who were standing there heard and said: This man calls to Elijah.[6] And at once one of them ran and took a sponge, soaked it in vinegar and put it on the end of a reed, and gave it to him to drink. But the rest said: Let us see if Elijah comes to save him.

Then Jesus cried out again in a great voice, and gave up his life. And behold, the veil of the temple[7] was split in two from top to bottom, and the earth was shaken, and the rocks were split, and the tombs opened and many bodies of the holy sleepers rose up; and after his resurrection they came out of their tombs and went into the holy city, and were seen by many. But the company commander and those with him who kept guard over Jesus, when they saw the earthquake and the things that happened, were greatly afraid, saying: In truth this was the son of God. And there were many women watching from a distance there, who had followed Jesus from Galilee, waiting on him. Among them were Mary the Magdalene, and Mary the mother of James and Joseph, and the mother of the sons of Zebedee.

When it was evening, there came a rich man of Arimathaea, Joseph by name, who also had been a disciple of Jesus. This man went to Pilate and asked for the body of Jesus. Then Pilate ordered that it be given up to him. And Joseph took the body and wrapped it in clean linen, and laid it in his new tomb, which he had cut in the rock, and rolled a great stone before the door of the tomb, and went away. But Mary the Magdalene and the other Mary were there, sitting before the tomb. On the next day, which is the day after the Day of Preparation, the high priests and the Pharisees gathered in the presence of Pilate, and said: Lord, we have remembered how that impostor said while he was still alive: After three days I shall rise up. Give orders, then, that the tomb be secured until after the third day, for fear his disciples may come and steal him away and say to the people: He rose from the dead. And that will be the ultimate deception, worse than the former one. Pilate said to them: You have a guard. Go and secure it as best you can. And they went and secured the tomb, sealing it with the help of the guard.

Late on the sabbath, as the light grew toward the first day after the sabbath, Mary the Magdalene and the other Mary came to visit the tomb. And behold, there was a great earthquake, for the angel of the Lord came down from heaven and approached the stone and rolled it away and was sitting on it. His look was like lightning, and his clothing white as snow. And those who were on guard were shaken with fear of him and became like dead men. But the angel spoke forth and said to the women: Do not you fear; for I know that you look for Jesus, who was crucified. He is not here. For he rose up, as he said. Come here, and look at the place where he lay. Then go quickly and tell his disciples that he has risen from the dead, and behold, he goes before you into Galilee. There you will see him. See; I have told you. And quickly leaving the tomb, in fear and great

---

5. These words are in Aramaic, a Semitic language commonly spoken in the region (closely related to Hebrew and Syriac); the rest of the gospel is in vernacular Greek.
6. The prophet who was bodily taken up to heaven in a chariot of fire (2 Kings 2.8–11);

his return was prophesied to herald the coming of the Messiah (Malachi 3.1; 4:5).
7. The veil covering the door of the inner sanctuary of the Temple (Exodus 26.31–34), where God was said to appear (Leviticus 16.2).

joy, they ran to tell the news to his disciples. And behold, Jesus met them, saying: I give you greeting. They came up to him and took his feet and worshipped him. Then Jesus said to them: Do not fear. Go and tell my brothers to go into Galilee, and there they will see me. And as they went on their way, behold, some of the guards went into the city and reported to the high priests all that had happened. And they met with the elders and took counsel together, and gave the soldiers a quantity of money, saying: Say that the disciples came in the night and stole him away while we were sleeping. And if this is heard in the house of the governor, we shall reason with him, and make it so that you have nothing to fear. And they took the money and did as they were instructed. And this is the story that has been spread about among the Jews, to this day.

Then the eleven disciples went on into Galilee, to the mountain where Jesus had given them instructions to go; and when they saw him, they worshipped him; but some doubted. And Jesus came up to them and talked with them, saying: All authority has been given to me, in heaven and on earth. Go out, therefore, and instruct all the nations, baptizing them in the name of the Father and the Son and the Holy Spirit, teaching them to observe all that I have taught you. And behold, I am with you, all the days until the end of the world.

John 1

[The Word]

In the beginning was the word, and the word was with God, and the word was God. He was in the beginning, with God. Everything came about through him, and without him not one thing came about. What came about in him was life, and the life was the light of mankind; and the light shines in the darkness, and the darkness did not understand it.

There was a man sent from God; his name was John. This man came for testimony, to testify concerning the light, so that all should believe through him. He was not the light, but was to testify concerning the light. The light was the true light, which illuminates every person who comes into the world. He was in the world, and the world came about through him, and the world did not know him. He went to his own and his own people did not accept him. Those who accepted him, he gave them power to become children of God, to those who believed in his name, who were born not from blood or from the will of the flesh or from the will of man, but from God.

And the word became flesh and lived among us, and we have seen his glory, glory as of a single son from his father, full of grace and truth. John bears witness concerning him, and he cried out, saying (for it was he who was speaking): He who is coming after me was before me, because he was there before I was; because we have all received from his fullness, and grace for grace. Because the law was given through Moses; the grace and the truth came through Jesus Christ. No one has ever seen God; the only-born God who is in the bosom of his father, it is he who told of him.

And this is the testimony of John, when the Jews sent priests and Levites[1] from Jerusalem to ask him: Who are you? And he confessed, and made no

---

1. Members of the tribe of Levi (one of the sons of Jacob), who formed a hereditary subordinate priesthood (see Numbers 18.1–6).

denial, but confessed: I am not the Christ. And they asked him: What then? Are you Elijah? And he said: I am not. Are you the prophet? And he answered: No. Then they said to him: Who are you? So that we can give an answer to those who sent us. What do you say about yourself? He said: I am the voice of one crying in the desert: Make straight the way of the Lord; as Isaiah the prophet said. Now they had been sent by the Pharisees. And they questioned him and said to him: Why then do you baptize, if you are not the Christ, or Elijah or the prophet? John answered them saying: I baptize with water; but in your midst stands one whom you do not know, who is coming after me, and I am not fit to untie the fastening of his shoe. All this happened in Bethany beyond the Jordan,[2] where John was baptizing.

The next day he saw Jesus coming toward him and said: See, the lamb of God who takes away the sinfulness of the world. This is the one of whom I said: A man is coming after me who was before me, because he was there before I was. And I did not know him. But so that he might be made known to Israel, this was why I came baptizing with water. And John bore witness, saying: I have seen the Spirit descending like a dove from the sky, and it remained upon him; and I did not know him, but the one who sent me to baptize with water was the one who said to me: That one, on whom you see the Spirit descending and remaining upon him, is the one who baptizes with the Holy Spirit. And I have seen, and I have borne witness that this is the son of God.

The next day John was standing with two of his disciples, and he saw Jesus walking about and said: See, the lamb of God. His two disciples heard what he said and followed Jesus. Jesus turned about and saw them following him and said. What are you seeking? They said to him: Rabbi (which translated means master), where are you staying? He said to them: Come and see. So they came, and saw where he was staying, and stayed with him for that day. It was about the tenth hour. Andrew, one of the two who heard Jesus and followed him, was the brother of Simon Peter. He went first and found his brother Simon and said to him: We have found the Messiah (which is, translated, the Christ). He took him to Jesus. Jesus looked at him and said: You are Simon, the son of John. You shall be called Cephas[3] (which means Peter).

The next day Jesus wished to go out to Galilee. And he found Philip and said to him: Follow me. Philip was from Bethsaida, the city of Andrew and Peter. Philip found Nathanael and said to him: We have found the one of whom Moses wrote in the law, and the prophets: Jesus the son of Joseph, from Nazareth. And Nathanael said to him: Can anything good come from Nazareth? Philip said to him: Come and see. Jesus saw Nathanael coming toward him and said of him: See, a true son of Israel, in whom there is no guile. Nathanael said to him: How is it that you know me? Jesus answered and said to him: I saw you when you were under the fig tree, before Philip called you. Nathanael answered: Master, you are the son of God, you are the King of Israel. Jesus answered and said to him: Because I told you I saw you under the fig tree, you believe? You will see greater things than that. And he said to him: Truly truly I tell you, you will see the heaven open and the angels of God ascending and descending to the son of man.[4]

---

2. The river that forms the border between modern Israel and, to the east, Jordan and Syria.
3. Kêfâ (Aramaic), meaning "rock" or "stone" (Greek petros).
4. Compare Jacob's vision of the ladder at Bethel (Genesis 28.10–17).

APULEIUS

ca. 125–ca. 180

The Golden Ass is a wildly miscellaneous stew of elements. It is a novel, but has stories embedded within it, like a frame-tale narrative; it features processions and theatrical settings, as does a play, but also has a dreamlike, almost hallucinatory quality. The work's alternative title, *Metamorphoses*, points to the main literary model for this work: the human and animal transformations in the **Metamorphoses** of **Ovid**. But while the Roman poet features the classical gods, such as Jupiter and Apollo, Apuleius introduces us to the exotic cult of Isis, which originated in Egypt, and the dangerous allure of witchcraft. We follow our hero, Lucius, through a series of erotic encounters, comic catastrophes, and exotic transformations and finally—like Lucius—we reflect on what lessons might be learned from a life so extravagantly led.

We have two sources of information about Apuleius: what he tells himself in his four surviving works, and what his African countryman **Augustine** wrote about him (rather disapprovingly) two centuries later. Apuleius was born in Madaurus (near modern Mdaourouch, in Algeria), the same town where Augustine would be educated before moving on to Carthage and Rome. The Roman provinces that made up Apuleius's Africa were in a state of cultural flux; Carthaginian culture strongly persisted and the Punic language remained in use, while the greater Roman Empire still was a political and economic power. Madaurus was a city of four languages: the local vernaculars of Punic and Libyan plus Latin and Greek, the administrative and elite languages of the empire. Apuleius says he spoke Greek as a mother tongue,

though he also pursued it at an advanced level during his study abroad in Athens, and his novel is composed in remarkably eloquent Latin. In one sense, Apuleius is a product of Roman culture, although he lived in the provinces; yet Apuleius himself makes much of his African background and takes a native pride in the region. Born to a family of wealth and status, with a father who, as a *duumvir* (colonial magistrate), held the highest political office in the region and who left his two sons a vast fortune, Apuleius was lavishly educated, first in Carthage and then in Athens and Rome. His travels and education identify him clearly as a member of the cosmopolitan Roman Empire.

Although we do not know when Apuleius wrote *The Golden Ass*, we do have a firm date for one of his other works, the *Apology*: Apuleius delivered this defense orally at his trial in 158, after he was charged with practicing black magic in order to seduce his wealthy older wife, Pudentilla, and then poisoning her son (and Apuleius's former best friend) Pontianus. Apuleius was acquitted and went on to serve as orator and politician at Carthage. The author of a huge number of works, though only four survive, he wrote in many genres, including speeches, novels, poems, philosophical dialogues, and histories; the subjects of his prose treatises ranged from arithmetic to love to zoology. His capacious and synthetic mind enabled Apuleius to collate and disseminate a huge array of information, as well as to compose the most extraordinarily heterogeneous literary work of the premodern age.

The *Apology* is useful in providing not only information about Apuleius's life and times but also an intriguing context for reading *The Golden Ass*, whose narrator Lucius also experiences a traumatic court trial, is drawn in by the appeal of transgressive romantic liaisons, and discovers the dangers of magic. The eleven books of *The Golden Ass* take the reader on a whirlwind of adventure. At times Lucius is trapped in the position of a slave, his position hopeless; then a sudden reversal of fortune sets him free and another cycle of wild adventure begins. The excerpts provided here center on Lucius's magical transformation, which takes place during his stay at the city of Hypata in Thessaly (Greece). At the marketplace, Lucius meets an old family friend, Byrrhaena, who warns him about his host, Milo, and the secret powers of seduction possessed by Pamphile, Milo's wife. More intrigued than alarmed, Lucius decides to try to learn more about Pamphile with the aid of her equally attractive maid, Photis—with disastrous and comic results.

The style of *The Golden Ass* is highly episodic, as our hero undergoes a series of adventures—some sordid, some titillating. He is a young man of privileged background and limited experience, and his transformation into a beast of burden leads him to experience the underbelly of society as lived in the eastern cities of the Roman Empire. Lucius meets thieves and beggars, prostitutes and slave women, and while in their company he hears the everyday comic and scurrilous tales that were fundamental to the oral culture of the second century—a culture that is largely invisible to modern readers, because ancient writers tended to stick to more elevated subject matter. Though *The Golden Ass* is based on an earlier Greek novel by one Lucius of Patras (perhaps Lucian of Samosata), Apuleius does much more than simply translate the story into Latin. He reduces the Greek cultural framework significantly, placing his narrator instead in the heterogeneous world of the Roman Empire as he moves through Asia Minor (modern Turkey), Greece, Egypt, and Italy. Beyond adding a great deal of local detail about daily life in various cultural centers, Apuleius creates an entirely new ending set not in Greece but in Rome. Yet this is an Orientalized Rome, where the narrator becomes a devotee of the religion of Isis, an Egyptian goddess whose cult had taken hold in the imperial center.

The Golden Ass was popular in its own time, circulating especially in North Africa and the eastern Mediterranean, where it was read eagerly by the student populations that Augustine describes with such contempt in his *City of God* and *Confessions*. Interest in it reawakened in the Renaissance, reflected in the hybrid jackass-man Nick Bottom in **Shakespeare**'s *Midsummer Night's Dream*, and its influence has persisted in modernist fiction, including the hideously transformed Gregor Samsa of Franz Kafka's *Metamorphosis* and the hapless companions of the hero, turned into donkeys, in Carlo Collodi's novel *The Adventures of Pinocchio*.

From The Golden Ass[1]

FROM BOOK 2

[*Lucius in Hypata*]

As soon as the darkness was dispelled and a new sun ushered in the day, I rose from my couch the moment I awoke from sleep, for I was generally buoyed up, and most eager to discover the weird and wonderful features of the place. I recalled that I was in the heart of Thessaly,[2] the source of those spells of the magic art which are famed by common consent through the entire world. I remembered too that the tale recounted by Aristomenes, that best of companions,[3] had its origin in this city. So in expectation and enthusiasm alike I was quite alert, and I studied each feature with some care. I did not believe that anything which I gazed on in the city was merely what it was, but that every single object had been transformed into a different shape by some muttered and deadly incantation. I thought that the stones which caused me to trip were petrified persons, that the birds which I could hear were feathered humans, that the trees enclosing the city-limits were people who had likewise sprouted foliage, that the waters of the fountains were issuing from human bodies. I imagined that at any moment the statues and portraits would parade about, that the walls would speak, that oxen and other cattle would prophesy, that the very sky and the sun's orb would suddenly proclaim an oracular message.

In this trance, or rather hypnosis, induced by such tortured longing, I went round examining everything, but without finding a suggestion or even a trace of what I passionately sought. I wandered from door to door like a man seeking some extravagant and dissolute diversion, and all unknowing I suddenly found myself at the food-market. I caught sight of a woman walking through it, surrounded by a sizeable retinue, and I quickened my step and overtook her. Her jewellery was gold-inlaid and her clothes gold-embroidered, undoubtedly signalling that she was an upper-class matron. Walking close to her side was a man of advanced years. As soon as he set eyes on me he exclaimed: 'Heavens, it's Lucius!' and he gave me a kiss of greeting. At once he whispered something in the lady's ear which I could not overhear. 'This is your aunt,' he said. 'You must approach her yourself, and greet her.' 'I'm shy of doing that', I said, 'for I do not know her.' Whereupon I blushed all over, and kept my distance with my head bowed.

The lady then turned to stare at me. 'My goodness,' she said, 'he has the manners of a gentleman. He gets them from his mother Salvia who is a model of goodness. And damn me if his appearance generally isn't just right! He is tall, but not lofty; he's slim, but there is spunk there; his colour is moderately ruddy, his hair is blonde but not foppish; his green eyes have a watchful look, quick to focus, sharp as an eagle's. His face looks healthy from every angle, and his walk is pleasing and natural.'

Then she added: 'Lucius, these hands of mine reared you. That was as it should be, for not only am I your mother's blood relation, but we were brought up together. We are both descended from Plutarch's household, we had the same wet-nurse, and we grew up together as inseparable sisters. The one thing

1. Translated by P. G. Walsh.
2. A region of northern Greece, traditionally associated with sorcery.
3. Met by Lucius in book 1.

that distinguishes us is our social standing. She contracted marriage with a prominent public figure, whereas I married a private citizen. I'm called Byrrhena; you may recall the name through mention of it among those who brought you up. So don't be shy of accepting our hospitality; in fact our house is yours.'

These remarks of hers had given me time to disguise my blushes, and I spoke up in reply. 'Dear aunt,' I said, 'I could hardly bid my host Milo goodbye without his feeling aggrieved. I shall make every effort to do what I can, short of breaching my obligation to him. Whenever any occasion for a journey this way arises in future, I shall always lodge with you.' In the course of these and similar exchanges, the short journey we had made on foot brought us to Byrrhena's house.

The reception-area was very fine. Pillars stood at each corner, supporting statues representing the goddess Victory. In these representations, her wings were outspread but motionless, and her dewy feet stood on tiptoe on the slippery surface of a revolving sphere, momentarily joined to it but giving the impression of imminent flight. But the notable feature was Parian marble chiselled into the likeness of Diana,[4] which occupied the centre of the whole atrium, and was raised off the ground. The statue gleamed spectacularly; with her garment breeze-blown, her lively figure was hastening forward as if to confront the incomer with the august majesty of her godhead. Hounds, likewise executed in marble, escorted the goddess on both flanks. Their eyes were threatening, their ears pricked up, their nostrils flaring, their maws savage. If barking sounded loudly from anywhere near at hand, you would think that it issued from those mouths of marble. But the highest feat of craftsmanship achieved by that genius of a sculptor was that the hounds were rearing breast-high, and their hind legs were braking while their forelegs were in rapid motion.

To the rear of the goddess rose a rock forming a cave. Out of the stone sprouted moss, green plants, foliage and brushwood; vines on one side were set off against miniature trees on the other. Within the cave the reflection of the statue shone out because of the smooth brightness of the marble. Apples and grapes hung from the lower edge of the rock; their highly artistic finish, depicted with a skill rivalling nature's, made them lifelike, so that you could imagine that some of them could be plucked for eating once the maturing autumn endowed them with the colour of ripeness. If you bent low and gazed into the water which skirted the goddess's feet as it lapped in gentle waves, you would think that the bunches of grapes hanging from the rock possessed the faculty of movement as well as other lifelike qualities. In the middle of the marble foliage a statue of Actaeon[5] was visible, fashioned in marble and reflected in the water; his neck craned forward as he gazed with curiosity towards the goddess. He was already animal-like, on the point of becoming a stag as he waited for Diana to take her bath.

As I repeatedly ran my eye over this scene with intense delight, Byrrhena remarked: 'All that you see is yours.' After saying this, she had a private word with all the others, and asked them to leave us. When they had all been sent away, she said to me: 'Dearest Lucius, I swear by the goddess here; I am troubled and

---

4. Roman goddess of virginity, the moon, and the hunt (and thus often depicted with her hunting dogs).
5. In Greek myth, a hunter who saw Diana/ Artemis bathing in the woods; after the furious goddess transformed him into a stag, he was devoured by his own hunting dogs (see Ovid, *Metamorphoses* 3.138–52).

fearful for you. Since you are my cherished son, I should like to give you warning well in advance. Watch out for yourself. Take stringent precautions against the wicked arts and evil enticements of the notorious Pamphile, the wife of Milo, who you say is your host. She is reputed to be a witch of the first rank, a specialist in all forms of necromancy. She has only to breathe on twigs, pebbles, and common objects of that kind, and she can plunge all this light of day which descends from the starry heavens into the lowest depths of Tartarus,[6] reducing it to the chaos of old. Then as soon as she catches sight of any handsome young man, she is captivated by his charms, and at once focuses her eyes and her attention on him. She sows the seeds of allurements, dominates his will, and proceeds to imprison him in eternal bonds of deep love. If those who are less amenable prove worthless to her because they scorn her, she transforms them in a trice into stones or cattle or any animal you can think of, while others she utterly destroys. These are the fears I have for you, and I think that you should be on your guard against them, for she is constantly ablaze with desire, and your youth and handsome bearing make you a suitable target for her.' These were the troubled thoughts which Byrrhena shared with me.

But I was already disposed to curiosity, and as soon as I heard mention of the art of magic which I had always prayed for, so far from taking precautions against Pamphile, I was eager even without compulsion to undergo such schooling willingly, and to pay a heavy price for it. In short, I was all for taking a running jump and landing myself headlong in those murky depths. So with lunatic haste I freed myself from Byrrhena's detaining hand as if from a confining chain, and bade her a hasty farewell. I then flew off at top speed to Milo's lodging. As I redoubled my steps like one demented, I said to myself: 'Lucius, look alive, and keep your wits about you. This is the chance you were praying for. You will be able to achieve that long-standing ambition of yours, and obtain your heart's content of wonderful stories. Dismiss your childish fears, come to grips with the issue at close quarters and without cowardice. You must steer clear of any love-relationship with your hostess, and scrupulously respect the good Milo's marriage-bed. Make a bee-line instead for the maidservant Photis. She is attractive, she has amusing ways, and she is quite sharp. Last night when you retired to sleep, she genially escorted you to your room, fussed over you in getting you to your bed, tucked you in quite affectionately, kissed your forehead, and showed by her face her unwillingness to leave. In fact she kept halting and looking back. So even though it has its hazards, Photis must be your target. The best of luck in your endeavours.'

These were the arguments occupying my mind as I made for Milo's door. I voted with my feet, as the expression goes. I found neither Milo nor his wife at home, but only my dear Photis. She was cooking minced pork for stuffing, and slices of meat, and some very spicy sausage of which I had already caught a whiff. She was wearing an elegant linen dress, with a bright red belt fastened up supporting her breasts. As she turned the casserole-dish round and round with her petal-like fingers, and shook it repeatedly in its circular motion, she simultaneously rotated her body. Her hips moved lightly in rhythm, and as she wiggled her supple spine, her person rippled most attractively. I was spellbound at the sight, and stood there lost in admiration. The parts of me that

6. In classical myth, the part of the underworld in which the wicked are punished.

were asleep before now stood to attention. Finally I managed to speak to her; 'My dear Photis,' I said, 'how lusciously and attractively you wiggle that wee pot, and your bottom with it! That's a succulent dish you have in readiness there! How lucky a fellow would be if you let him stick his finger in—he'd be on top of the world!'

That pert and witty girl at once replied: 'Keep clear, poor boy, keep clear as far as possible from this stove of mine. If once my little flame shoots out and as much as sears you, you will be all ablaze inside, and I'll be the only one who can put your fire out. The spices which I incorporate are sweet. I'm an expert at pleasurably shaking a bed as well as a pot.'

With these words she looked me in the eye, and grinned. I did not leave her presence until I had carefully studied all the features of her appearance. Of her other charms I need say nothing, for it has always been my one obsession first to examine a person's head of hair thoroughly and openly outside, and then to take pleasure in it privately indoors. I have a secure and well-established justification for preferring this criterion of beauty. First comes the fact that the head is the outstanding part of the body; it is exposed and prominent, and is the first feature to meet the eye. Secondly, whereas the other physical parts are made attractive by the gay colour of bright clothing, it is the head's own natural sheen which achieves this. Lastly, most women when they wish to demonstrate their personal attractions disrobe and remove all their clothes in their eagerness to show off their naked beauty, seeking to please the eye more with the rosy blush of their skin than with the golden colour of their dress. But if you were to scalp some lady of outstanding beauty, and thus rob her face of its natural adornment—this is a sacrilegious suggestion, and I pray that so grisly an illustration of my point may never materialize—it would not matter if she came down from heaven, or rose from the sea, or was sprung from the waves. In other words, it would not matter if she were Venus[7] herself, flanked by a whole choir of Graces, accompanied by the entire body of Cupids, wearing that belt of hers around her waist, diffusing the scent of cinnamon and bedewing the air with balsam; if she appeared without her hair, she would not give pleasure even to her Vulcan.

How enchanting is a woman's hair when its pleasing colour and glossy sheen shines out! When it faces the sun's rays, it is enlivened and flashes fire, or gently reflects the sunlight. Sometimes it offers contrasting pleasures by varying its appearance. Hair with a golden glow subsides into the soft shaded colour of honey. Hair which is raven-black seeks to rival the ultramarine necks of doves. Hair oiled with drops of Arabian perfume, parted with the fine teeth of a sharp comb, and gathered at the back, serves as a mirror when it confronts the lover's eyes, and affords him a more flattering reflection. Sometimes numerous strands are combined to form a thick wedge on top of the head, or they flow down the back, extending in a long plait. Such in fact is the lofty status of a woman's hair that she can appear before us adorned with gold, fine clothes, jewellery and the rest of her finery, but unless she has ordered her hair she cannot be regarded as well-groomed.

My Photis, however, had not fussed over hers, and yet its tousled arrangement lent her added charm. Her abundant hair had been let hang soft and free

---

7. The beautiful Roman goddess of love, mother of Cupid (Eros, god of love) and wife of Vulcan, god of the forge; she was closely associated with the Graces, personifications of grace and beauty.

down from her head over her neck, and having rested briefly on the golden border of her dress, it had finally been gathered and fastened in a knot on top of her head.

I could no longer endure the fierce torture of my extreme pleasure. I leaned over her, and implanted the sweetest of honeyed kisses where her hair reached the crown of her head. She then twisted her neck to face me, and gave me a sidelong look with devouring eyes. 'Hey there, schoolboy,' she said, 'the savoury dish you're sampling is bitter as well as sweet. Just watch out; that honey which tastes so sweet may bring on a lengthy attack of bitter bile.'

'How can you say that, light of my life?' I asked. 'I am ready to be laid and grilled on this fire of yours, once you have roused me with one little kiss.' As I spoke I grasped her tightly in my arms, and started to kiss her. In a moment she was as abandoned as I was, as she rose to the same heat of passion. With unrestrained desire she showed her longing for me; the breath from her open lips was like cinnamon, and the thrust of her tongue was like nectar as it met mine. I said to her: 'This is killing me! Indeed, I'm already dead unless you take pity on me.' She gave me another long kiss, and answered: 'Don't worry. That longing which we share makes me your slave, and our pleasure will be postponed no longer. As soon as the first lamp is lit, I'll be in your bedroom. So be off with you, and make your preparations. I shall engage you in an all-night battle with the strength of passion.'

FROM **BOOK 3**

[*Metamorphosis*]

Eventually my Photis came in, after having seen her mistress to bed. Her demeanour was quite different from before, for she did not look cheerful, nor was her conversation spiced with wit. She wore a sombre look, wrinkling her face into a frown.

At last she spoke hesitantly and timidly. 'I have to confess', she said, 'that I caused this discomfiture of yours.' As she spoke, she produced a strap from under her dress, and handed it to me. 'Take your revenge, I beg you,' she said, 'on a woman who has betrayed you, or exact some punishment even greater than this. But I implore you not to imagine that I deliberately planned this painful treatment for you. God forbid that you should suffer even the slightest vexation on my account. If anything untoward threatens you, I pray that my life-blood may avert it. It was because of a mischance that befell me, when ordered to perform a different task, that the damage was inflicted on you.'

Impelled by my habitual curiosity and eager to have the hidden cause of the incident of the previous night revealed, I then replied: 'This is a wicked and most presumptuous strap, since you have allotted it the task of beating you. I shall destroy it by cutting it up or by slashing it to pieces rather than have it touch your skin, which is soft as down and white as milk. But tell me truthfully: what action of yours was attended by the perversity of savage Fortune, and resulted in my downfall? I swear by that head of yours which is so dear to me that I can believe no one, and you least of all, in the suggestion that you laid any plan for my undoing. In any case, a chance happening, or even a detrimental occurrence, cannot convert innocent intentions into guilty deeds.' As I finished speaking, I thirstily applied my mouth to the moist and trembling eyes of my Photis, which were languid with uncontrolled desire, and were now half-closed as I pressed hungry kisses upon them.

Her high spirits now restored, 'Please wait a moment,' she said, 'until I carefully close the bedroom door. I don't wish to commit a grievous error by carelessly and sacrilegiously letting my tongue run free.' As she spoke, she thrust home the bolts and fastened the hook securely. Then she came back to me, and took my neck in both her hands. In a low and quite restrained voice, she said: 'I am fearful and mortally terrified of revealing the secrets of this house, and of exposing the hidden mysteries wrought by my mistress. But I have considerable trust in you and your learning. In addition to the noble distinction of your birth and your outstanding intellect, you have been initiated into several sacred cults, and you are certainly aware of the need for the sacred confidentiality of silence. So all that I entrust to the sanctuary of your pious heart you must for ever enclose and guard within its confines, and thus repay the ingenuous trust of my revelations with the steadfast security of your silence. The love which holds me fast to you compels me to reveal to you things which I alone know. You are now to gain acquaintance with the entire nature of our household, with the wondrous and secret spells of my mistress. To these the spirits hearken and the elements are enslaved, and by them the stars are dislocated and the divine powers harnessed. But for no purpose does my mistress have recourse to the power of this art so much as when she eyes with pleasure some young man of elegant appearance, and indeed this is a frequent practice of hers.

'At the moment she is passionately obsessed with a young and extremely handsome Boeotian,[8] and she eagerly deploys every device and every technique of her art. Only this evening I heard her with my own ears threatening the sun itself with cloud cover and unbroken darkness because it had not retired from the sky quickly enough, and had yielded to nightfall too late for her to practise the enticements of magic. Yesterday, when she was on her way back from the baths, she happened to catch sight of the young man sitting in the barber's, and she ordered me to remove secretly his hair which had been snipped off by the scissors and was lying on the floor. As I was carefully and unobtrusively gathering it, the barber caught me at it. Now we in this city have a bad name for practising the art of sorcery, so he grabbed me brusquely and rebuked me. "You brazen hussy, is there no end to your repeatedly stealing the hair of eligible young men? If you don't finally stop this criminal practice, I'll have you up at once before the magistrates." He followed up his words with action; he thrust his hands between my breasts, felt around, and angrily extracted some hair which I had already hidden there. I was extremely concerned at this turn of events, remembering my mistress's usual temper. She often gets quite annoyed if she is frustrated in this way, and she takes it out on me most savagely. I actually thought of running away from her, but the thought of you at once caused me to reject the idea.

'I was just returning dispirited and afraid to go back empty-handed from the barber's, when I saw a man paring some goatskins with scissors. Once I watched the skins inflated, tightly tied, and hanging up, and the hair from them lying on the ground and of the same blonde colour as that of the young Boeotian, I abstracted a quantity of it and passed it to my mistress, concealing

8. A native of Boeotia, a region of central Greece northwest of Athens.

its true provenance. So it was that in the first hours of darkness, before you returned from your dinner, my mistress Pamphile in a fit of ecstatic madness climbed up towards the overlapping roof. On the far side of the house there is an area which is uncovered and exposed to the elements. It commands every view on the eastern side, as well as those in other directions. So it is especially convenient for those magical arts of hers, and she practises them there in secret. First of all she fitted out her infernal laboratory with the usual supplies, including every kind of aromatic plant, metal strips inscribed with unintelligible letters, the surviving remains of ill-omened birds, and a fairly large collection of corpses' limbs, earlier mourned over by relatives and in some cases even buried. Noses and fingers were in a heap in one place, and in another, nails from the gibbet to which there still clung flesh from the men hanged there. In yet another place the blood of slaughtered men was kept, and also gnawed skulls, torn from the fangs of wild beasts.

'Then, after chanting spells over quivering entrails, she poured propitiating offerings of various liquids—now spring-water, now cow's milk, now mountain-honey; she also poured out mead. She twisted and entwined the locks of hair with each other, and placed them on live coals to be burnt with a variety of fragrant plants. Immediately, through this combination of the irresistible power of her magic lore and the hidden energy of the harnessed deities, the bodies from which the hair was crackling and smoking acquired human breath, and were able to feel and walk. They headed for the place to which the stench from the hair they had shed led them, and thus they took the place of the Boeotian youth in barging at the doors, in their attempt to gain entrance. At that moment you appeared on the scene, drunk with wine and deceived by the darkness of the sightless night. You drew your short sword, and armed yourself for the role of the mad Ajax.[9] But whereas he inflicted violence on living cattle and lacerated whole herds, you much more courageously dealt the death-blow to three inflated goat-skins. Thus you laid low the enemy without shedding a drop of blood, so that I can embrace not a homicide but an utricide.'[1]

This elegant remark of Photis made me smile, and I responded in the same joking spirit. 'Well then,' I said, 'I can regard this as the first trophy won by my valour, in the tradition of Hercules' twelve labours,[2] for I can equate the body of Geryon which was in triplicate, or the three-formed shape of Cerberus, with the like number of skins that I slew. But to obtain as you desire my forgiveness willingly for the entire error by which you involved me in such great distress, you must grant me the favour which is my dearest wish. Let me watch your mistress when she sets in train some application of her supernatural art. Let me see her when she summons the gods, or at any rate when she changes her shape. I am all agog to witness magic from close up. Mind you, you yourself do not seem to be a novice wholly innocent of such things. I have come to be quite convinced

---

9. One of the greatest Greek warriors at Troy. Driven mad by Athena, he killed animals, believing that he was attacking the Greek leaders who had refused to give him the armor of the dead Achilles; returned to sanity, he killed himself in shame.
1. A skin-slayer; in Latin, a *uter* is a bag or bottle made of animal hide.

2. The tasks undertaken by the greatest hero of classical mythology as part of his purification after he killed his wife and children in a fit of madness; they included stealing the cattle of Geryon, who had the bodies of three men joined at the waist, and capturing Cerberus, the monstrous three-headed dog of the lord of the underworld.

of this, for your flashing eyes and rosy cheeks, your shining hair, your kisses with parted lips, and your fragrant breasts hold me fast as your willing slave and bondsman, whereas previously I always spurned the embraces of matrons. So now I have no thought of returning home or planning my departure there; there is nothing which I count better than spending a night with you.'

'Lucius,' she replied, 'I should dearly love to grant your wish, but her surly disposition aside, Pamphile invariably seeks solitude and likes to perform such secret rites when no one else is present. However, I shall put your wish before my personal danger. I shall watch out for a favourable occasion, and carefully arrange what you seek. My only stipulation, as I said at the beginning, is that you must promise to maintain silence in this momentous matter.'

As we chatted away, our desire for each other roused the minds and bodies of both of us. We threw off the clothes we wore until we were wholly naked, and enjoyed a wild love-orgy. When I was wearied with her feminine generosity, Photis offered me a boy's pleasure. Finally this period of wakefulness caused our eyes to droop; sleep invaded them, and held us fast until it was broad daylight.

After we had spent a few nights in such pleasurable pursuits, one day Photis came hurrying to me trembling with excitement. Her mistress, she said, was having no success in her love-affair by other means, and so she intended on the following night to invest herself with a bird's plumage, and to join her beloved by taking wing. I should accordingly be ready to observe with due circumspection this astonishing feat. So just as darkness fell, Photis led me silently on tiptoe to that upper chamber, and instructed me to witness what was happening there through a chink in the door.

Pamphile first divested herself of all her clothing. She then opened a small casket and took from it several small boxes. She removed the lid from one of these, and extracted ointment from it. This she rubbed for some time between her hands, and then smeared it all over herself from the tips of her toes to the crown of her head. She next held a long and private conversation with the lamp, and proceeded to flap her arms and legs with a trembling motion. As she gently moved them up and down, soft feathers began to sprout on them, and sturdy wings began to grow. Her nose became curved and hard, and her nails became talons. In this way Pamphile became an owl; she uttered a plaintive squawk as she tried out her new identity by gradually forsaking the ground. Soon she rose aloft, and with the full power of her wings quitted the house.

This was how Pamphile deliberately changed her shape by employing techniques of magic. I too was spellbound, but not through any incantation. I was rooted to the ground with astonishment at this event, and I seemed to have become something other than Lucius. In this state of ecstasy and riveted mindlessness, I was acting out a waking dream, and accordingly I rubbed my eyes repeatedly in an effort to discover whether I was awake. Finally I returned to awareness of my surroundings, and seizing Photis' hand I placed it on my eyes. 'While the chance allows,' I begged her, 'do please allow me one great and unprecedented boon bestowed by your affection. Get me, my honey-sweet, a little ointment from that same box—by those dear breasts of yours I beg you. Bind me as your slave for ever by a favour which I can never repay, and in this way ensure that I shall become a winged Cupid,[3] drawing close to my Venus.'

---

3. Cupid was conventionally depicted with wings.

'Is that what you're after, my foxy lover?' she asked. 'Are you trying to force me to apply an axe to my own limbs? When you are in that vulnerable state, I can scarcely keep you safe from those two-legged Thessalian wolves! And where shall I seek you, when shall I see you, once you become a bird?'

'The gods preserve me from perpetrating such an outrage,' I replied. 'Even if I were to fly through the entire heavens on the soaring wings of an eagle, as the appointed messenger or happy squire of highest Jove,[4] would I not sweep down from time to time from the enjoyment of such distinction on the wing to this fond nest of mine? I swear by this sweet knot that binds your hair and has enmeshed my heart, there is no other girl I prefer to my dear Photis. A second thought comes to my mind: once I have smeared myself and have become a bird like that, I shall have to keep a safe distance from all habitations. What a handsome and amusing lover I should make for matrons to enjoy when I'm an owl! If those night-birds do get inside a house, the residents, as we see, take care to catch them and nail them to their doors, to expiate by their sufferings the threatened destruction to the household occasioned by their ill-omened flight. But I almost forgot to ask: what word or action do I need to discard those feathers and to return to my being Lucius?' 'You have no worries in ensuring that,' she answered, 'for my mistress has shown me each and every substance that can restore to human form those who have adopted such shapes. Do not imagine that she did this out of mere goodwill; it was so that I could aid her with an efficacious remedy on her return. Observe with what cheap and everyday herbs such a great transformation is achieved. You wash yourself with water in which a sprig of dill and some bay-leaves have been steeped, and drink some of it.'

She made this claim repeatedly, and then with great apprehension she crept into the chamber, and took a box from the casket. First I hugged and kissed it, and prayed that it would bring me happy flying hours. Then I hastily tore off all my clothes, dipped my hands eagerly into the box, drew out a good quantity of the ointment, and rubbed all my limbs with it. I then flapped my arms up and down, imitating the movements of a bird. But no down and no sign of feathers appeared. Instead, the hair on my body was becoming coarse bristles, and my tender skin was hardening into hide. There were no longer five fingers at the extremities of my hands, for each was compressed into one hoof. From the base of my spine protruded an enormous tail. My face became misshapen, my mouth widened, my nostrils flared open, my lips became pendulous, and my ears huge and bristly. The sole consolation I could see in this wretched transformation was the swelling of my penis—though now I could not embrace Photis.

As I helplessly surveyed the entire length of my body, and came to the realization that I was not a bird but an ass, I tried to complain at what Photis had done to me. But I was now deprived of the human faculties of gesture and speech; all I could do by way of silent reproach was to droop my lower lip, and with tearful eyes give her a sidelong look. As soon as she saw what I had become, she beat her brow with remorseful hands and cried: 'That's the end of poor me! In my panic and haste I made a mistake; those look-alike boxes deceived me. But the saving grace is that the remedy for this transformation is quite easy and available. Just chew some roses, and you will stop being an ass and at once become my Lucius again.'

4. Another name for Jupiter, whose bird was the eagle.

AUGUSTINE
354–430

When Augustine lay dying in August of 430, Vandal armies were besieging the African city of Hippo (modern Annaba, Algeria), where Augustine was the spiritual leader of a vibrant community of Christians living under the rule of the Roman Empire. Within weeks, Hippo would fall; the great city of Rome itself would be captured within thirty years. Born into the culture of antiquity but laying the foundations for the medieval millennium that was just about to begin, Augustine stands with one foot in each world. His monumental autobiography, the *Confessions*, constantly draws on the rich literature of the Roman orators and prose writers, especially Cicero. Yet it also reaches forward, innovatively exploring the ways in which the reader—like Augustine himself—might find that the Word of God has all along been lodged within his innermost soul.

LIFE AND TIMES

Augustine was a native of the northern African regions that were part of the Roman Empire. Yet the empire was in a gradual state of collapse throughout Augustine's lifetime: strong military leaders were running the government in all but name from 395 onward, and the final Roman emperor would be deposed by rebellious mercenary troops in 476. It was a transitional period—a time of great instability and, simultaneously, cultural and religious ferment. Mystery and cult religions were particularly popular, as witnessed by Augustine's account of his years with the Manichaeans; **Apuleius** also captures this milieu in his description of the devotees of Isis

in *The Golden Ass*. Despite the instability and uncertainty of the period, the administrative and economic structures of the empire were still healthy enough to ease travel between its various parts, allowing Augustine to journey throughout northern Africa and Italy.

Augustine spent his early years in Africa, where there were several provincial cities of substantial size. Born at Thagaste (modern Souk-Ahras, Algeria), he had his first schooling at the nearby town of Madaurus and, later, at the sophisticated cultural capital of Carthage. There, Augustine became intrigued by Manichaeanism, a dualistic religion that resembled early Christianity in emphasizing the life of the mind and the drive toward increasing spiritual purity, though the two religions differed very significantly in their views of the nature of God. Augustine quickly rose to the top of his profession as an educator and public speaker, teaching grammar at his birthplace of Thagaste and, later, rhetoric at Carthage. These provincial successes impelled him to Rome, where he established a school of rhetoric; he was then invited to come to Milan, which had become a capital of the Western Roman Empire, to take on the chair of rhetoric and such duties as writing honorific speeches to be presented at court. At Milan, Augustine entered into a very sophisticated intellectual community, where he became deeply involved in Neoplatonism both as a philosophy and as a quasi-religious form of mysticism. He also came to know Ambrose, the bishop of Milan. At the time, Augustine says, he told himself that he was attending Ambrose's sermons simply to judge his excellence as a public speaker. In fact, Augustine was becoming increasingly drawn to Christianity, a religion to which his mother, Monica, had vainly tried to introduce him since he was a young child.

The bond between Augustine and Ambrose was strengthened enormously by Monica, who had followed her son to Milan and become close to Ambrose; the bishop reciprocated, constantly telling his friend Augustine what a treasure he had in his faithful and devout mother. The *Confessions* shows that Monica played a major role in her son's spiritual growth, which culminated in Augustine's conversion and baptism on Easter 386, at age thirty-two. This was a moment of complete change for Augustine, not just spiritually but also practically: he gave up his chair in rhetoric at the imperial court of Milan, withdrew from his engagement to marry, and went with his mother to the port of Ostia to return to Africa. But before they could sail from Italy, Monica died, as did Augustine's son, Adeodatus, who had been born in Carthage to Augustine's longtime mistress, traveled to Italy with Augustine, and undergone baptism alongside his father. Alone back in Thagaste, Augustine surrounded himself with spiritual brothers—members of the growing Christian community in the region—and transformed his family home into a monastery. When he paid a visit to a friend at Hippo in 391, Augustine found that his reputation as a spiritual leader had preceded him. The community at Hippo begged Augustine to remain with them, and he was ordained a priest at their request. By 396, he was bishop of Hippo, a position he held until his death.

WORK

Augustine probably began work on the *Confessions* in 397, when he was forty-three years old. He seems to have been suffering from a terrible case of writer's block, with several half-finished pieces of work on hand. The experience of writing the *Confessions* apparently cured it, for almost immediately after completing it Augustine went on to produce an extraordinarily large number of works. The *Confessions* is, as the name suggests, autobiographical, the story of one man's life in his own words. But it is also confessional in the sense of being a full account of one's sins; a story addressed first of all to God, the hearer who is able to forgive the transgressions that Augustine recounts. At the same time, the *Confessions* has a secondary addressee, as Augustine himself acknowledges: other would-be Christians who might be able to trace the path of their own spiritual journey as a result of having read about the struggles of another. Of the thirteen books of the *Confessions*, only the first nine are autobiographical, covering the period from Augustine's early childhood memories to his stay in Ostia in 387, as he waits for the boat that would take him home. The autobiographical genre, almost without precedent in this period, is perhaps Augustine's greatest literary legacy. We hear nothing from Augustine about his later years in Africa; instead, the final books of the *Confessions* are an analysis of the account of creation in Genesis, along with a sustained meditation on the nature of time and memory. The overall effect of the *Confessions* is to turn the reader inward, away from the individual journey of Augustine and toward the collective journey of humanity toward the divine.

Surprisingly for a book dedicated to the relationship of the soul to God, the most moving parts of the *Confessions* focus on Augustine's relationship to other human beings—not just his mother, Monica, who was so instrumental to Augustine's conversion to Christianity, but also his beloved son, Adeodatus, and the unnamed mistress who was Augustine's companion from age seventeen (when he first went to Carthage) until his mother persuaded him to enter into an arranged marriage in 385, shortly before his conversion. This woman, whom Augustine simply calls "the One," faithfully followed him on his journeys, first to Rome and then to Milan. When Augustine finally renounced his relationship with her, she returned to Africa, "swearing that she would never know another man." All of these human relationships, however passionate, are in the end subsumed within Augustine's all-consuming relationship with God. He addresses God familiarly throughout the *Confessions*, as if he were an intimate friend who knew all Augustine's secrets, but who also had the terrifying capacity to destroy, inspiring both adoration and fear.

Augustine writes frankly about his self-fashioning within the various communities to which he belonged, from his involvement in a gang of undisciplined youths to his immersion in the Manichaean community at Carthage, his time among the Neoplatonists in Milan, and his final place of rest among the Christian community at Hippo. His journey is, at a deep level, a search for the self, which he comes to find only after long struggle, and only through the companionship of others. Augustine comes home first spiritually, with a conversion inspired by the supernatural voice of a child, and then physically, sailing from Ostia to Thagaste, where he will make a new spiritual home filled with Christian believers among the bricks and mortar of his childhood house. Desire and longing structure the narrative of the *Confessions*, from Augustine's heady days in Carthage, at the theater by day and in the arms of his mistress by night, to his patient vigil at the port of Ostia, consumed at once by sorrow for the death of Monica and joy in his discovery of Christ. Caught between his love for human beings and his longing for the divine, Augustine is never more present to us than when, shortly before his conversion, he cries out to God, "Make me chaste—but not yet." Augustine's painstaking examination of his innermost self, racked with contradictions and unexplained desires, had a profound influence not only on the medieval Christians who sought, like Augustine, to purge their souls of sin but also on the secular self-examination of early modern writers such as **Montaigne** and **Rousseau**.

From Confessions[1]

FROM BOOK I

[Childhood]

What have I to say to Thee, God, save that I know not where I came from, when I came into this life-in-death—or should I call it death-in-life? I do not know. I only know that the gifts Your mercy had provided sustained me from the first moment: not that I remember it but so I have heard from the parents of my flesh, the father from whom, and the mother in whom, You fashioned me in time.

Thus for my sustenance and my delight I had woman's milk: yet it was not my mother or my nurses who stored their breasts for me: it was Yourself, using them to give me the food of my infancy, according to Your ordinance and the riches set by You at every level of creation. It was by Your gift that I desired what You gave and no more, by Your gift that those who suckled me willed to give me what You had given them: for it was by the love implanted in them by

1. Translated by F. J. Sheed.

You that they gave so willingly that milk which by Your gift flowed in the breasts. It was a good for them that I received good from them, though I received it not *from* them but only through them: since all good things are from You, O God, and *from God is all my health*.[2] But this I have learnt since: You have made it abundantly clear by all that I have seen You give, within me and about me. For at that time I knew how to suck, to lie quiet when I was content, to cry when I was in pain: and that was all I knew.

Later I added smiling to the things I could do, first in sleep, then awake. This again I have on the word of others, for naturally I do not remember; in any event, I believe it, for I have seen other infants do the same. And gradually I began to notice where I was, and the will grew in me to make my wants known to those who might satisfy them; but I could not, for my wants were within me and those others were outside: nor had they any faculty enabling them to enter into my mind. So I would fling my arms and legs about and utter sounds, making the few gestures in my power—these being as apt to express my wishes as I could make them: but they were not very apt. And when I did not get what I wanted, either because my wishes were not clear or the things not good for me, I was in a rage—with my parents as though I had a right to their submission, with free human beings as though they had been bound to serve me; and I took my revenge in screams. That infants are like this, I have learnt from watching other infants; and that I was like it myself I have learnt more clearly from these other infants, who did not know me, than from my nurses who did.

* * *

From infancy I came to boyhood, or rather it came to me, taking the place of infancy. Yet infancy did not go: for where was it to go to? Simply it was no longer there. For now I was not an infant, without speech, but a boy, speaking. This I remember; and I have since discovered by observation how I learned to speak. I did not learn by elders teaching me words in any systematic way, as I was soon after taught to read and write. But of my own motion, using the mind which You, my God, gave me, I strove with cries and various sounds and much moving of my limbs to utter the feelings of my heart—all this in order to get my own way. Now I did not always manage to express the right meanings to the right people. So I began to reflect [I observed that][3] my elders would make some particular sound, and as they made it would point at or move towards some particular thing: and from this I came to realize that the thing was called by the sound they made when they wished to draw my attention to it. That they intended this was clear from the motions of their body, by a kind of natural language common to all races which consists in facial expressions, glances of the eye, gestures, and the tones by which the voice expresses the mind's state— for example whether things are to be sought, kept, thrown away, or avoided. So, as I heard the same words again and again properly used in different phrases, I came gradually to grasp what things they signified; and forcing my mouth to the same sounds, I began to use them to express my own wishes. Thus I learnt to convey what I meant to those about me; and so took another long step along the stormy way of human life in society, while I was still subject to the authority of my parents and at the beck and call of my elders.

2. Throughout the *Confessions* Augustine quotes liberally from the Bible; the quotations are set off in italics. When a quotation bears on Augustine's situation, it is annotated.
3. Words in brackets are the translator's.

O God, my God, what emptiness and mockeries did I now experience: for it was impressed upon me as right and proper in a boy to obey those who taught me, that I might get on in the world and excel in the handling of words[4] to gain honor among men and deceitful riches. I, poor wretch, could not see the use of the things I was sent to school to learn; but if I proved idle in learning, I was soundly beaten. For this procedure seemed wise to our ancestors: and many, passing the same way in days past, had built a sorrowful road by which we too must go, with multiplication of grief and toil upon the sons of Adam.

Yet, Lord, I observed men praying to You: and I learnt to do likewise, thinking of You (to the best of my understanding) as some great being who, though unseen, could hear and help me. As a boy I fell into the way of calling upon You, my Help and my Refuge; and in those prayers I broke the strings of my tongue—praying to You, small as I was but with no small energy, that I might not be beaten at school.[5] And when You did not hear me (*not as giving me over to folly*), my elders and even my parents, who certainly wished me no harm, treated my stripes as a huge joke, which they were very far from being to me. Surely, Lord, there is no one so steeled in mind or cleaving to You so close—or even so insensitive, for that might have the same effect—as to make light of the racks and hooks and other torture instruments[6] (from which in all lands men pray so fervently to be saved) while truly loving those who are in such bitter fear of them. Yet my parents seemed to be amused at the torments inflicted upon me as a boy by my masters, though I was no less afraid of my punishments or zealous in my prayers to You for deliverance. But in spite of my terrors I still did wrong, by writing or reading or studying less than my set tasks. It was not, Lord, that I lacked mind or memory, for You had given me as much of these as my age required; but the one thing I revelled in was play; and for this I was punished by men who after all were doing exactly the same things themselves. But the idling of men is called business; the idling of boys, though exactly like, is punished by those same men: and no one pities either boys or men. Perhaps an unbiased observer would hold that I was rightly punished as a boy for playing with a ball: because this hindered my progress in studies—studies which would give me the opportunity as a man to play at things more degraded. And what difference was there between me and the master who flogged me? For if on some trifling point he had the worst of the argument with some fellow-master, he was more torn with angry vanity than I when I was beaten in a game of ball.

* * *

But to continue with my boyhood, which was in less peril of sin than my adolescence. I disliked learning and hated to be forced to it. But I *was* forced to it, so that good was done to me though it was not my doing. Short of being driven to it, I certainly would not have learned. But no one does well against his will, even if the thing he does is a good thing to do. Nor did those who forced me do well: it was by You, O God, that well was done. Those others had no deeper vision of the use to which I might put all they forced me to learn, but to sate the insatiable desire of man for wealth that is but penury and glory that is but shame.

---

4. The study of rhetoric, which was the passport to eminence in public life.
5. Augustine recognizes the necessity of this rigorous training; that he never forgot its harshness is clear from his remark in the *City*
of God (21.14): "If a choice were given him between suffering death and living his early years over again, who would not shudder and choose death?"
6. The instruments of public execution.

But You, Lord, *by Whom the very hairs of our head are numbered*,[7] used for my good the error of those who urged me to study; but my own error, in that I had no will to learn, you used for my punishment—a punishment richly deserved by one so small a boy and so great a sinner. Thus, You brought good for me out of those who did ill, and justly punished me for the ill I did myself. So You have ordained and so it is: that every disorder of the soul is its own punishment.

To this day I do not quite see why I so hated the Greek tongue[8] that I was made to learn as a small boy. For I really liked Latin—not the rudiments that we got from our first teachers but the literature that we came to be taught later. For the rudiments—reading and writing and figuring—I found as hard and hateful as Greek. Yet this too could come only from sin and the vanity of life, because *I was flesh, and a wind that goes away and returns not*. For those first lessons were the surer. I acquired the power I still have to read what I find written and to write what I want to express; whereas in the studies that came later I was forced to memorize the wanderings of Aeneas[9]—whoever he was— while forgetting my own wanderings; and to weep for the death of Dido[1] who killed herself for love, while bearing dry-eyed my own pitiful state, in that among these studies I was becoming dead to You, O God, my life.

Nothing could be more pitiful than a pitiable creature who does not see to pity himself, and weeps for the death that Dido suffered through love of Aeneas and not for the death he suffers himself through not loving You, O God, Light of my heart, Bread of my soul, Power wedded to my mind and the depths of my thought. I did not love You and I went away from You in fornication:[2] and all around me in my fornication echoed applauding cries "Well done! Well done!" *For the friendship of this world is fornication against Thee:* and the world cries "Well done" so loudly that one is ashamed of unmanliness not to do it. And for this I did not grieve; but I grieved for Dido, slain as she sought by the sword an end to her woe,[3] while I too followed after the lowest of Your creatures, forsaking You, earth going unto earth. And if I were kept from reading, I grieved at not reading the tales that caused me such grief. This sort of folly is held nobler and richer than the studies by which we learn to read and write!

But now let my God cry aloud in my soul, and let Your truth assure me that it is not so: the earlier study is the better. I would more willingly forget the wanderings of Aeneas and all such things than how to write and read. Over the entrance of these grammar schools hangs a curtain:[4] but this should be seen not as lending honor to the mysteries, but as a cloak to the errors taught within. Let not those masters—who have now lost their terrors for me—cry out against me, because I confess to You, my God, the desire of my soul, and find soul's rest in blaming my evil ways that I may love Your holy ways. Let not the buyers or sell-

---

7. Who knows and attends to the smallest detail of each life (compare Matthew 10.30).
8. Important not only for gaining knowledge of Greek literature but also because it was the official language of the Eastern Roman Empire. Augustine never really mastered Greek, though his remark elsewhere that he had acquired so little Greek that it amounted to practically none is overmodest.
9. Virgil's *Aeneid* 3.
1. Queen of Carthage whose unrequited love for the Trojan warrior Aeneas ended in her

untimely death; Aeneas was obliged to pursue his destiny to be the founding father of Rome (Virgil, *Aeneid*, esp. book 4).
2. Here, metaphorically.
3. Virgil, *Aeneid* 6.457.
4. In Augustine's time, school entrances were covered by veils with an attendant standing by to make sure that only those who paid tution were admitted; the veil was also a symbol of the hidden knowledge that lay across the threshold.

ers of book-learning cry out against me. If I ask them whether it is true, as the poet says, that Aeneas ever went to Carthage, the more ignorant will have to answer that they do not know, the more scholarly that he certainly did not. But if I ask with what letters the name Aeneas is spelt, all whose schooling has gone so far will answer correctly, according to the convention men have agreed upon for the use of letters. Or again, were I to ask which loss would be more damaging to human life—the loss from men's memory of reading and writing or the loss of these poetic imaginings—there can be no question what anyone would answer who had not lost his own memory. Therefore as a boy I did wrong in liking the empty studies more than the useful—or rather in loving the empty and hating the useful. For one and one make two, two and two make four, I found a loathsome refrain; but such empty unrealities as the Wooden Horse with its armed men, and Troy on fire, and Creusa's Ghost, were sheer delight.[5]

* * *

Give me leave, O my God, to speak of my mind, Your gift, and of the follies in which I wasted it. It chanced that a task was set me, a task which I did not like but had to do. There was the promise of glory if I won, the fear of ignominy, and a flogging as well, if I lost. It was to declaim the words uttered by Juno in her rage and grief when she could not keep the Trojan prince from coming to Italy.[6] I had learnt that Juno had never said these words, but we were compelled to err in the footsteps of the poet who had invented them: and it was our duty to paraphrase in prose what he had said in verse. In this exercise that boy won most applause in whom the passions of grief and rage were expressed most powerfully and in the language most adequate to the majesty of the personage represented.

What could all this mean to me, O My true Life, My God? Why was there more applause for the performance I gave than for so many classmates of my own age? Was not the whole business so much smoke and wind? Surely some other matter could have been found to exercise mind and tongue. Thy praises, Lord, might have upheld the fresh young shoot of my heart, so that it might not have been whirled away by empty trifles, defiled, a prey to the spirits of the air. For there is more than one way of sacrificing to the fallen angels. * * *

FROM BOOK II

[The Pear Tree]

I propose now to set down my past wickedness and the carnal corruptions of my soul, not for love of them but that I may love Thee, O my God. I do it for love of Thy love, passing again in the bitterness of remembrance over my most evil ways that Thou mayest thereby grow ever lovelier to me, O Loveliness that dost not deceive, Loveliness happy and abiding: and I collect my self out of

5. While at a feast held in his honor by Dido, Aeneas tells the story of the fall of Troy and his escape from the burning city, during which he lost his wife, Creusa (Virgil, *Aeneid*, book 2, esp. 2.772).
6. Augustine was assigned the task of delivering a prose paraphrase of Juno's angry speech in *Aeneid* 1. In it she complains that her ene-mies, the Trojans under Aeneas, are on their way to their destined goal in Italy in spite of her resolution to prevent them. Rhetorical exercises such as this were common in the schools, because they served the double purpose of teaching both literature and rhetorical composition.

that broken state in which my very being was torn asunder because I was turned away from Thee, the One, and wasted myself upon the many.

Arrived now at adolescence I burned for all the satisfactions of hell, and I sank to the animal in a succession of dark lusts: *my beauty consumed away,* and I stank in Thine eyes, yet was pleasing in my own and anxious to please the eyes of men.

My one delight was to love and to be loved. But in this I did not keep the measure of mind to mind, which is the luminous line of friendship; but from the muddy concupiscence of the flesh and the hot imagination of puberty mists steamed up to becloud and darken my heart so that I could not distinguish the white light of love from the fog of lust. Both love and lust boiled within me, and swept my youthful immaturity over the precipice of evil desires to leave me half drowned in a whirlpool of abominable sins. Your wrath had grown mighty against me and I knew it not. I had grown deaf from the clanking of the chain of my mortality, the punishment for the pride of my soul: and I departed further from You, and You left me to myself: and I was tossed about and wasted and poured out and boiling over in my fornications: and You were silent, O my late-won Joy. You were silent, and I, arrogant and depressed, weary and restless, wandered further and further from You into more and more sins which could bear no fruit save sorrows.

* * *

Where then was I, and how far from the delights of Your house, in that sixteenth year of my life in this world, when the madness of lust—needing no licence from human shamelessness, receiving no licence from Your laws—took complete control of me, and I surrendered wholly to it? My family took no care to save me from this moral destruction by marriage: their only concern was that I should learn to make as fine and persuasive speeches as possible.

* * *

Your law, O Lord, punishes theft; and this law is so written in the hearts of men that not even the breaking of it blots it out: for no thief bears calmly being stolen from—not even if he is rich and the other steals through want. Yet I chose to steal, and not because want drove me to it—unless a want of justice and contempt for it and an excess for iniquity. For I stole things which I already had in plenty and of better quality. Nor had I any desire to enjoy the things I stole, but only the stealing of them and the sin. There was a pear tree near our vineyard, heavy with fruit, but fruit that was not particularly tempting either to look at or to taste. A group of young blackguards, and I among them, went out to knock down the pears and carry them off late one night, for it was our bad habit to carry on our games in the streets till very late. We carried off an immense load of pears, not to eat—for we barely tasted them before throwing them to the hogs. Our only pleasure in doing it was that it was forbidden. Such was my heart, O God, such was my heart: yet in the depth of the abyss You had pity on it. Let that heart now tell You what it sought when I was thus evil for no object, having no cause for wrongdoing save my wrongness. The malice of the act was base and I loved it—that is to say I loved my own undoing, I loved the evil in me—not the thing for which I did the evil, simply the evil: my soul was depraved, and hurled itself down from security in You into utter destruction, seeking no profit from wickedness but only to be wicked.

There is an appeal to the eye in beautiful things, in gold and silver and all such; the sense of touch has its own powerful pleasures; and the other senses find qualities in things suited to them. Worldly success has its glory, and the power to command and to overcome: and from this springs the thirst for revenge. But in our quest of all these things, we must not depart from You, Lord, or deviate from Your Law. This life we live here below has its own attractiveness, grounded in the measure of beauty it has and its harmony with the beauty of all lesser things. The bond of human friendship is admirable, holding many souls as one. Yet in the enjoyment of all such things we commit sin if through immoderate inclination to them—for though they are good, they are of the lowest order of good—things higher and better are forgotten, even You, O Lord our God, and Your Truth and Your Law. These lower things have their delights but not such as my God has, for He made them all: *and in Him doth the righteous delight, and He is the joy of the upright of heart.*

Now when we ask why this or that particular evil act was done, it is normal to assume that it could not have been done save through the desire of gaining or the fear of losing some one of these lower goods. For they have their own charm and their own beauty, though compared with the higher values of heaven they are poor and mean enough. Such a man has committed a murder. Why? He wanted the other man's wife or his property; or he had chosen robbery as a means of livelihood; or he feared to lose this or that through his victim's act; or he had been wronged and was aflame for vengeance. Would any man commit a murder for no cause, for the sheer delight of murdering? The thing would be incredible. There is of course the case of the man [Catiline] who was said[7] to be so stupidly and savagely cruel that he practised cruelty and evil even when he had nothing to gain by them. But even there a cause was stated—he did it, he said, lest through idleness his hand or his resolution should grow slack. And why did he want to prevent that? So that one day by the multiplication of his crimes the city should be his, and he would have gained honors and authority and riches, and would no longer be in fear of the law or in the difficulties that want of money and the awareness of his crimes had brought him. So that not even Catiline loved his crimes as crimes: he loved some other thing which was his reason for committing them.

What was it then that in my wretched folly I loved in you, O theft of mine, deed wrought in that dark night when I was sixteen? For you were not lovely: you were a theft. Or are you anything at all, that I should talk with you? The pears that we stole were beautiful for they were created by Thee, Thou most Beautiful of all, Creator of all, Thou good God, my Sovereign and true Good. The pears were beautiful but it was not pears that my empty soul desired. For I had any number of better pears of my own, and plucked those only that I might steal. For once I had gathered them I threw them away, tasting only my own sin and savouring that with delight; for if I took so much as a bite of any one of those pears, it was the sin that sweetened it. And now, Lord my God, I ask what was it that attracted me in that theft, for there was no beauty in it to attract. I do not mean merely that it lacked the beauty that there is in justice and prudence, or in the mind of man or his senses and vegetative life: or even so much as the beauty and glory of the stars in the heavens, or of earth and sea

7. By the Roman historian Sallust (*Catiline 16*). Cataline was a Roman politician whose conspiracy against the state was foiled by the consul Cicero in 63 B.C.E.

with their oncoming of new life to replace the generations that pass. It had not even that false show or shadow of beauty by which sin tempts us.

[For there *is* a certain show of beauty in sin.] Thus pride wears the mask of loftiness of spirit, although You alone, O God, are high over all. Ambition seeks honor and glory, although You alone are to be honored before all and glorious forever. By cruelty the great seek to be feared, yet who is to be feared but God alone: from His power what can be wrested away, or when or where or how or by whom? The caresses by which the lustful seduce are a seeking for love: but nothing is more caressing than Your charity, nor is anything more healthfully loved than Your supremely lovely, supremely luminous Truth. Curiosity may be regarded as a desire for knowledge, whereas You supremely know all things. Ignorance and sheer stupidity hide under the names of simplicity and innocence: yet no being has simplicity like to Yours: and none is more innocent than You, for it is their own deeds that harm the wicked. Sloth pretends that it wants quietude: but what sure rest is there save the Lord? Luxuriousness would be called abundance and completeness; but You are the fullness and inexhaustible abundance of incorruptible delight. Wastefulness is a parody of generosity: but You are the infinitely generous giver of all good. Avarice wants to possess overmuch: but You possess all. Enviousness claims that it strives to excel: but what can excel before You? Anger clamors for just vengeance: but whose vengeance is so just as Yours? Fear is the recoil from a new and sudden threat to something one holds dear, and a cautious regard for one's own safety: but nothing new or sudden can happen to You, nothing can threaten Your hold upon things loved, and where is safety secure save in You? Grief pines at the loss of things in which desire delighted: for it wills to be like to You from whom nothing can be taken away.

Thus the soul is guilty of fornication when she turns from You and seeks from any other source what she will nowhere find pure and without taint unless she returns to You. Thus even those who go from You and stand up against You are still perversely imitating You. But by the mere fact of their imitation, they declare that You are the creator of all that is, and that there is nowhere for them to go where You are not.

So once again what did I enjoy in that theft of mine? Of what excellence of my Lord was I making perverse and vicious imitation? Perhaps it was the thrill of acting against Your law—at least in appearance, since I had no power to do so in fact, the delight a prisoner might have in making some small gesture of liberty—getting a deceptive sense of omnipotence from doing something forbidden without immediate punishment. I was that slave, who fled from his Lord and pursued his Lord's shadow. O rottenness, O monstrousness of life and abyss of death! Could you find pleasure only in what was forbidden, and only because it was forbidden? * * *

FROM **BOOK III**

[Student at Carthage]

I came to Carthage[8] where a cauldron of illicit loves leapt and boiled about me. I was not yet in love, but I was in love with love, and from the very depth of my need hated myself for not more keenly feeling the need. I sought some object

---

8. The capital city of the province, where Augustine went to study rhetoric.

to love, since I was thus in love with loving; and I hated security and a life with no snares for my feet. For within I was hungry, all for the want of that spiritual food which is Thyself, my God; yet [though I was hungry for want of it] I did not hunger for it: I had no desire whatever for incorruptible food, not because I had it in abundance but the emptier I was, the more I hated the thought of it. Because of all this my soul was sick, and broke out in sores, whose itch I agonized to scratch with the rub of carnal things—carnal, yet if there were no soul in them, they would not be objects of love. My longing then was to love and to be loved, but most when I obtained the enjoyment of the body of the person who loved me.

Thus I polluted the stream of friendship with the filth of unclean desire and sullied its limpidity with the hell of lust. And vile and unclean as I was, so great was my vanity that I was bent upon passing for clean and courtly. And I did fall in love, simply from wanting to. O my God, my Mercy, with how much bitterness didst Thou in Thy goodness sprinkle the delights of that time! I was loved, and our love came to the bond of consummation: I wore my chains with bliss but with torment too, for I was scourged with the red hot rods of jealousy, with suspicions and fears and tempers and quarrels.

I developed a passion for stage plays, with the mirror they held up to my own miseries and the fuel they poured on my flame. How is it that a man wants to be made sad by the sight of tragic sufferings that he could not bear in his own person? Yet the spectator does want to feel sorrow, and it is actually his feeling of sorrow that he enjoys. Surely this is the most wretched lunacy? For the more a man feels such sufferings in himself, the more he is moved by the sight of them on the stage. Now when a man suffers himself, it is called misery; when he suffers in the suffering of another, it is called pity. But how can the unreal sufferings of the stage possibly move pity? The spectator is not moved to aid the sufferer but merely to be sorry for him; and the more the author of these fictions makes the audience grieve, the better they like him. If the tragic sorrows of the characters—whether historical or entirely fictitious—be so poorly represented that the spectator is not moved to tears, he leaves the theatre unsatisfied and full of complaints; if he is moved to tears, he stays to the end, fascinated and revelling in it. So that tears and sorrow, it would seem, are things to be sought. Yet surely every man prefers to be joyful. May it be that whereas no one wants to be miserable, there is real pleasure in pitying others—and we love their sorrows because without them we should have nothing to pity?

* * *

Those of my occupations at that time which were held as reputable[9] were directed towards the study of the law, in which I meant to excel—and the less honest I was, the more famous I should be. The very limit of human blindness is to glory in being blind. By this time I was a leader in the School of Rhetoric and I enjoyed this high station and was arrogant and swollen with importance: though You know, O Lord, that I was far quieter in my behavior and had no share in the riotousness of the eversores—the Overturners[1]—for this blackguardly

9. That is, his rhetorical studies.
1. *Eversores* is the Latin word that means "overturners": a group of students who prided

themselves on their wild actions and lack of discipline.

diabolical name they wore as the very badge of sophistication. Yet I was much in their company and much ashamed of the sense of shame that kept me from being like them. I was with them and I did for the most part enjoy their companionship, though I abominated the acts that were their specialty—as when they made a butt of some hapless newcomer, assailing him with really cruel mockery for no reason whatever, save the malicious pleasure they got from it. There was something very like the action of devils in their behavior. They were rightly called Overturners, since they had themselves been first overturned and perverted, tricked by those same devils who were secretly mocking them in the very acts by which they amused themselves in mocking and making fools of others.

With these men as companions of my immaturity, I was studying the books of eloquence; for in eloquence it was my ambition to shine, all from a damnable vaingloriousness and for the satisfaction of human vanity. Following the normal order of study I had come to a book of one Cicero,[2] whose tongue[3] practically everyone admires, though not his heart. That particular book is called *Hortensius*[4] and contains an exhortation to philosophy. Quite definitely it changed the direction of my mind, altered my prayers to You, O Lord, and gave me a new purpose and ambition. Suddenly all the vanity I had hoped in I saw as worthless, and with an incredible intensity of desire I longed after immortal wisdom. I had begun that journey upwards by which I was to return to You. My father was now dead two years; I was eighteen and was receiving money from my mother for the continuance of my study of eloquence. But I used that book not for the sharpening of my tongue; what won me in it was what it said, not the excellence of its phrasing.

* * *

So I resolved to make some study of the Sacred Scriptures and find what kind of books they were. But what I came upon was something not grasped by the proud, not revealed either to children, something utterly humble in the hearing but sublime in the doing, and shrouded deep in mystery. And I was not of the nature to enter into it or bend my neck to follow it. When I first read those Scriptures, I did not feel in the least what I have just said; they seemed to me unworthy to be compared with the majesty of Cicero. My conceit was repelled by their simplicity, and I had not the mind to penetrate into their depths. They were indeed of a nature to grow in Your little ones.[5] But I could not bear to be a little one; I was only swollen with pride, but to myself I seemed a very big man. * * *

---

2. Marcus Tullius Cicero (106–43 B.C.E.), Roman philosopher, politican, and lawyer. Augustine's admiration of Cicero is obvious; calling him "a certain Cicero" is a rhetorical convention; Augustine uses the same phrase to refer to the Apostle Paul.
3. Style.
4. Cicero's *Hortensius,* written in 45 B.C.E. and now lost, was an analysis of the sources of happiness, which Cicero concluded lay in the pursuit of wisdom.
5. Refers not only to the rhetorical simplicity of Jesus' teachings but also to his interest in teaching children; compare Matthew 19.14: "For of such is the kingdom of heaven."

[Augustine Leaves Carthage for Rome]

It was by Your action upon me that I was moved to go to Rome and teach there what I had taught in Carthage. How I was persuaded to this, I shall not omit to confess to you, because therein Your most profound depths and Your mercy ever present towards us are to be meditated upon and uttered forth. My reason for going to Rome was not the greater earnings and higher dignity promised by the friends who urged me to go—though at that time, these considerations certainly influenced my mind: the principal and practically conclusive reason, was that I had heard that youths there pursued their studies more quietly and were kept within a stricter limit of discipline. For instance, they were not allowed to come rushing insolently and at will into the school of one who was not their own master, nor indeed to enter it at all unless he permitted.

At Carthage the licence of the students is gross and beyond all measure. They break in impudently and like a pack of madmen play havoc with the order which the master has established for the good of his pupils. They commit many outrages, extraordinarily stupid acts, deserving the punishment of the law if custom did not protect them. Their state is the more hopeless because what they do is supposed to be sanctioned, though by Your eternal law it could never be sanctioned; and they think they do these things unpunished, when the very blindness in which they do them is their punishment, so that they suffer things incomparably worse than they do. When I was a student I would not have such habits in myself, but when I became a teacher I had to endure them in others; and so I decided to go to a place where, as I had been told by all who knew, such things were not done. But You, O my Hope and my Portion in the land of the living, forced me to change countries for my soul's salvation: You pricked me with such goads at Carthage as drove me out of it, and You set before me certain attractions by which I might be drawn to Rome—in either case using men who loved this life of death, one set doing lunatic things, the other promising vain things: and to reform my ways You secretly used their perversity and my own. For those who had disturbed my peace were blind in the frenzy of their viciousness, and those who urged me to go elsewhere savoured of earth. While I, detesting my real misery in the one place, hoped for an unreal happiness in the other.

Why I left the one country and went to the other, You Knew, O God, but You did not tell either me or my mother. She indeed was in dreadful grief at my going and followed me right to the seacoast.[6] There she clung to me passionately, determined that I should either go back home with her or take her to Rome with me, but I deceived her with the pretence that I had a friend whom I did not want to leave until he had sailed off with a fair wind. Thus I lied to my mother, and such a mother; and so got away from her. But this also You have mercifully forgiven me, bringing me from the waters of that sea, filled as I was with execrable uncleanness, unto the water of Your grace; so that when I was washed clean,[7] the floods that poured from my mother's eyes, the tears with

6. Here, Monica and Augustine are in the roles of Dido and Aeneas; see Virgil, *Aeneid*, book 4.
7. Ritual of immersion in water to signify the cleansing of the soul from sin; in Augustine's day, baptism was often put off until death was near, even by relatively observant Christians.

which daily she watered the ground towards which she bent her face in prayer for me, should cease to flow. She would not return home without me, but I managed with some difficulty to persuade her to spend the night in a place near the ship where there was an oratory in memory of St. Cyprian.[8] That night I stole away without her: she remained praying and weeping. And what was she praying for, O my God, with all those tears but that You should not allow me to sail! But You saw deeper and granted the essential of her prayer: You did not do what she was at that moment asking, that You might do the thing she was always asking. The wind blew and filled our sails and the shore dropped from our sight. And the next morning she was frantic with grief and filled Your ears with her moaning and complaints because You seemed to treat her tears so lightly, when in fact You were using my own desires to snatch me away for the healing of those desires, and were justly punishing her own too earthly affection for me with the scourge of grief. For she loved to have me with her, as is the way of mothers but far more than most mothers; and she did not realize what joys you would bring her from my going away. She did not realize it, and so she wept and lamented, and by the torments she suffered showed the heritage of Eve in her, seeking with sorrow what in sorrow she had brought forth. But when she had poured out all her accusation at my cruel deception, she turned once more to prayer to You for me. She went home and I to Rome. * * *

FROM BOOK VI

[Earthly Love]

By this time my mother had come to me, following me over sea and land with the courage of piety and relying upon You in all perils. For they were in danger from a storm, and she reassured even the sailors—by whom travelers newly ventured upon the deep are ordinarily reassured—promising them safe arrival because thus You had promised her in a vision. She found me in a perilous state through my deep despair of ever discovering the truth. But even when I told her that if I was not yet a Catholic Christian, I was no longer a Manichean,[9] she was not greatly exultant as at some unlooked-for good news, because she had already received assurance upon that part of my misery; she bewailed me as one dead certainly, but certainly to be raised again by You, offering me in her mind as one stretched out dead, that You might say to the widow's son: *"Young man, I say to thee arise"*:[1] and he should sit up and begin to speak and You should give him to his mother.

* * *

Great effort was made to get me married. I proposed, the girl was promised me. My mother played a great part in the matter for she wanted to have me married

---

8. Bishop of Carthage, local martyr, and saint who was especially popular among North African Christians.
9. Augustine had for nine years been a member of this religious sect, which followed the teaching of the Babylonian mystic Mani (216–277). The Manicheans believed that the world was a battleground for the forces of good and

evil; redemption in a future life would come to the elect, who renounced worldly occupations and possessions and practiced a severe asceticism (including abstention from meat). Augustine's mother, Monica, was a Christian, and lamented her son's Manichean beliefs.
1. Luke 7.14, recounting one of Christ's miracles.

and then cleansed with the saving waters of baptism,[2] rejoicing to see me grow every day more fitted for baptism and feeling that her prayers and Your promises were to be fulfilled in my faith. By my request and her own desire she begged You daily with the uttermost intensity of her heart to show her in a vision something of my future marriage, but You would never do it. She did indeed see certain vain fantasies, under the pressure of her mind's preoccupation with the matter; and she told them to me, not, however, with the confidence she always had when You had shown things to her, but as if she set small store by them; for she said that there was a certain unanalyzable savor, not to be expressed in words, by which she could distinguish between what You revealed and the dreams of her own spirit. Still she pushed on with the matter of my marriage, and the girl was asked for. She was still two years short of the age for marriage but I liked her and agreed to wait.[3]

There was a group of us friends who had much serious discussion together, concerning the cares and troubles of human life which we found so hard to endure. We had almost decided to seek a life of peace, away from the throng of men. This peace we hoped to attain by putting together whatever we could manage to get, and making one common household for all of us: so that in the clear trust of friendship, things should not belong to this or that individual, but one thing should be made of all our possessions, and belong wholly to each one of us, and everybody own everything. It seemed that there might be perhaps ten men in this fellowship. Among us there were some very rich men, especially Romanianus, our fellow townsman, who had been a close friend of mine from childhood and had been brought to the court in Milan by the press of some very urgent business. He was strongest of all for the idea and he had considerable influence in persuasion because his wealth was much greater than anyone else's. We agreed that two officers should be chosen every year to handle the details of our life together, leaving the rest undisturbed. But then we began to wonder whether our wives would agree, for some of us already had wives and I meant to have one. So the whole plan, which we had built up so neatly, fell to pieces in our hands and was simply dropped. We returned to our old sighing and groaning and treading of this world's broad and beaten ways:[4] for many thoughts were in our hearts, but *Thy counsel standeth forever.* And out of Thy counsel didst Thou deride ours and didst prepare Thine own things for us, meaning to *give us meat in due season and to open Thy hands and fill our souls with Thy blessing.*

Meanwhile my sins were multiplied. She with whom I had lived so long was torn from my side as a hindrance to my forthcoming marriage.[5] My heart which had held her very dear was broken and wounded and shed blood. She went back to Africa, swearing that she would never know another man, and left with me the natural son I had had of her. But I in my unhappiness could not,

---

2. He could not be baptized while living in sin with his mistress, a liaison that resulted in the birth of a son, Adeodatus, who later accompanied Augustine to Italy.

3. Under Roman law, the minimum age for marriage was twelve, so the girl that Monica arranged for Augustine to marry must have been about ten. Augustine was in his early

thirties at the time.

4. Compare Matthew 7.13: "Broad is the way that leadeth to destruction," that is, to damnation.

5. This woman had been Augustine's companion since he was seventeen and had accompanied him from Carthage to Rome.

for all my manhood, imitate her resolve. I was unable to bear the delay of two years which must pass before I was to get the girl I had asked for in marriage. In fact it was not really marriage that I wanted. I was simply a slave to lust. So I took another woman, not of course as a wife; and thus my soul's disease was nourished and kept alive as vigorously as ever, indeed worse than ever, that it might reach the realm of matrimony in the company of its ancient habit. Nor was the wound healed that had been made by the cutting off of my former mistress. For there was first burning and bitter grief; and after that it festered, and as the pain grew duller it only grew more hopeless. * * *

FROM BOOK VIII

[Conversion]

* * * Thus I was sick at heart and in torment, accusing myself with a new intensity of bitterness, twisting and turning in my chain in the hope that it might be utterly broken, for what held me was so small a thing! But it still held me. And You stood in the secret places of my soul, O Lord, in the harshness of Your mercy redoubling the scourges of fear[6] and shame lest I should give way again and that small slight tie which remained should not be broken but should grow again to full strength and bind me closer even than before. For I kept saying within myself: "Let it be now, let it be now," and by the mere words I had begun to move toward the resolution. I almost made it, yet I did not quite make it. But I did not fall back into my original state, but as it were stood near to get my breath. And I tried again and I was almost there, and now I could all but touch it and hold it: yet I was not quite there, I did not touch it or hold it. I still shrank from dying unto death and living unto life. The lower condition which had grown habitual was more powerful than the better condition which I had not tried. The nearer the point of time came in which I was to become different, the more it struck me with horror; but it did not force me utterly back nor turn me utterly away, but held me there between the two.

Those trifles of all trifles, and vanities of vanities, my one-time mistresses, held me back, plucking at my garment of flesh and murmuring softly: "Are you sending us away?" And "From this moment shall we not be with you, now or forever?" And "From this moment shall this or that not be allowed you, now or forever?" What were they suggesting to me in the phrase I have written "this or that," what were they suggesting to me, O my God? Do you in your mercy keep from the soul of Your servant the vileness and uncleanness they were suggesting. And now I began to hear them not half so loud; they no longer stood against me face to face, but were softly muttering behind my back and, as I tried to depart, plucking stealthily at me to make me look behind. Yet even that was enough, so hesitating was I, to keep me from snatching myself free, from shaking them off and leaping upwards on the way I was called: for the strong force of habit said to me: "Do you think you can live without them?"

But by this time its voice was growing fainter. In the direction toward which I had turned my face and was quivering in fear of going, I could see the austere beauty of Continence,[7] serene and indeed joyous but not evilly, honorably

6. Virgil, *Aeneid* 5.547.
7. Self-control or abstinence, especially with

regard to sexuality; here personified as a woman.

soliciting me to come to her and not linger, stretching forth loving hands to receive and embrace me, hands full of multitudes of good examples. With her I saw such hosts of young men and maidens, a multitude of youth and of every age, gray widows and women grown old in virginity, and in them all Continence herself, not barren but the fruitful mother of children, her joys, by You, Lord, her Spouse. And she smiled upon me and her smile gave courage as if she were saying: "Can you not do what these men have done, what these women have done? Or could men or women have done such in themselves, and not in the Lord their God? The Lord their God gave me to them. Why do you stand upon yourself and so not stand at all? Cast yourself upon Him and be not afraid; He will not draw away and let you fall. Cast yourself without fear, He will receive you and heal you."

Yet I was still ashamed, for I could still hear the murmuring of those vanities, and I still hung hesitant. And again it was as if she said: "Stop your ears against your unclean members, that they may be mortified. They tell you of delights, but not of such delights as the law of the Lord your God tells." This was the controversy raging in my heart, a controversy about myself against myself. And Alypius[8] stayed by my side and awaited in silence the issue of such agitation as he had never seen in me.

When my most searching scrutiny had drawn up all my vileness from the secret depths of my soul and heaped it in my heart's sight, a mighty storm arose in me, bringing a mighty rain of tears. That I might give way to my tears and lamentations, I rose from Alypius: for it struck me that solitude was more suited to the business of weeping. I went far enough from him to prevent his presence from being an embarrassment to me. So I felt, and he realized it. I suppose I had said something and the sound of my voice was heavy with tears. I arose, but he remained where we had been sitting, still in utter amazement. I flung myself down somehow under a certain fig tree and no longer tried to check my tears, which poured forth from my eyes in a flood, *an acceptable sacrifice to Thee.* And much I said not in these words but to this effect: "*And Thou, O Lord, how long? How long, Lord; wilt Thou be angry forever? Remember not our former iniquities.*"[9] For I felt that I was still bound by them. And I continued my miserable complaining: "How long, how long shall I go on saying tomorrow and again tomorrow? Why not now, why not have an end to my uncleanness this very hour?"

Such things I said, weeping in the most bitter sorrow of my heart. And suddenly I heard a voice from some nearby house, a boy's voice or a girl's voice, I do not know: but it was a sort of singsong, repeated again and again. "Take and read, take and read." I ceased weeping and immediately began to search my mind most carefully as to whether children were accustomed to chant these words in any kind of game, and I could not remember that I had ever heard any such thing. Damming back the flood of my tears I arose, interpreting the incident as quite certainly a divine command to open my book of Scripture and read the passage at which I should open. For it was part of what I had been

---

8. A student of Augustine's at Carthage; he had joined the Manichees with Augustine, followed him to Rome and Milan, and now shared his desires and doubts. Alypius finally became a bishop in North Africa in 394.
9. Compare Psalm 79.5–8; Augustine compares his spiritual despair with that of captive and subjected Israel.

told about Anthony,[1] that from the Gospel which he happened to be reading he had felt that he was being admonished as though what he read was spoken directly to himself: *Go, sell what thou hast and give to the poor and thou shalt have treasure in heaven; and come follow Me.*[2] By this experience he had been in that instant converted to You. So I was moved to return to the place where Alypius was sitting, for I had put down the Apostle's[3] book there when I arose. I snatched it up, opened it and in silence read the passage upon which my eyes first fell: *Not in rioting and drunkenness, not in chambering and impurities, not in contention and envy, but put ye on the Lord Jesus Christ and make not provision for the flesh in its concupiscences.* [Romans 13.13.] I had no wish to read further, and no need. For in that instant, with the very ending of the sentence, it was as though a light of utter confidence shone in all my heart, and all the darkness of uncertainty vanished away. Then leaving my finger in the place or marking it by some other sign, I closed the book and in complete calm told the whole thing to Alypius and he similarly told me what had been going on in himself, of which I knew nothing. He asked to see what I had read. I showed him, and he looked further than I had read. I had not known what followed. And this is what followed: *"Now him that is weak in faith, take unto you."* He applied this to himself and told me so. And he was confirmed by this message, and with no troubled wavering gave himself to God's goodwill and purpose—a purpose indeed most suited to his character, for in these matters he had been immeasurably better than I.

Then we went in to my mother and told her, to her great joy. We related how it had come about: she was filled with triumphant exultation, and praised You who are mighty beyond what we ask or conceive: for she saw that You had given her more than with all her pitiful weeping she had ever asked. For You converted me to Yourself so that I no longer sought a wife nor any of this world's promises, but stood upon that same rule of faith in which You had shown me to her so many years before.[4] Thus You changed her mourning into joy, a joy far richer than she had thought to wish, a joy much dearer and purer than she had thought to find in grandchildren of my flesh.

FROM BOOK IX

[Death of His Mother]

We kept together, meaning to live together in our devout purpose. We thought deeply as to the place in which we might serve You most usefully. As a result we started back for Africa. And when we had come as far as Ostia[5] on the Tiber, my mother died. I pass over many things, for I must make haste. Do You, O my God, accept my confessions and my gratitude for countless things of which I say

---

1. St. Anthony the Great, also called Anthony of the Desert (ca. 251–356), a Coptic Christian saint whose biography by Athanasius of Alexandria was widely circulated throughout the Mediterranean and was credited with many conversions.
2. Luke 18.22.
3. The Apostle Paul; Augustine is reading his letter to the Romans.

4. At Carthage, when Augustine was still a Manichee, Monica had dreamed that she was standing on a wooden ruler weeping for her son and then saw that he was standing on the same ruler as herself.
5. On the southwest coast of Italy; it was the port of Rome and the point of departure for Africa.

nothing. But I will not omit anything my mind brings forth concerning her, Your servant, who brought me forth—brought me forth in the flesh to this temporal light, and in her heart to light eternal. Not of her gifts do I speak but of Your gifts in her. For she did not bring herself into the world or educate herself in the world: it was You who created her, nor did her father or mother know what kind of being was to come forth from them. It was the scepter of Your Christ, the discipline of your Only-Begotten, that brought her up in holy fear, in a Catholic family which was a worthy member of Your church. Yet it was not the devotion of her mother in her upbringing that she talked most of, but of a certain aged servant, who had indeed carried my mother's father on her back when he was a baby, as little ones are accustomed to be carried on the backs of older girls. Because of this, because also of her age and her admirable character, she was very much respected by her master and mistress in their Christian household. As a result she was given charge of her master's daughters. This charge she fulfilled most conscientiously, checking them sharply when necessary with holy severity and teaching them soberly and prudently. Thus, except at the times when they ate—and that most temperately—at their parents' table, she would not let them even drink water, no matter how tormenting their thirst. By this she prevented the forming of a bad habit, and she used to remark very sensibly: "Now you drink water because you are not allowed to have wine: but when you are married, and thus mistresses of food-stores and wine-cellars, you will despise water, but the habit of drinking will still remain." By this kind of teaching and the authority of her commands she moderated the greediness that goes with childhood and brought the little girls' thirst to such a control that they no longer wanted what they ought not to have.

Yet, as Your servant told me, her son, there did steal upon my mother an inclination to wine. For when, in the usual way, she was sent by her parents, as a well-behaved child, to draw wine from the barrel, she would dip the cup in, but before pouring the wine from the cup into the flagon, she would sip a little with the very tip of her lips, only a little because she did not yet like the taste sufficiently to take more. Indeed she did it not out of any craving for wine, but rather from the excess of childhood's high spirits, which tend to boil over in absurdities, and are usually kept in check by the authority of elders. And so, adding to that daily drop a little more from day to day—for he that despises small things, falls little by little—she fell into the habit, so that she would drink off greedily cups almost full of wine. Where then was that wise old woman with her forceful prohibitions? Could anything avail against the evil in us, unless Your healing, O Lord, watched over us? When our father and mother and nurses are absent, You are present, who created us, who call us, who can use those placed over us for some good unto the salvation of our souls. What did You do then, O my God? How did You cure her, and bring her to health? From another soul you drew a harsh and cutting sarcasm, as though bringing forth a surgeon's knife from Your secret store, and with one blow amputated that sore place. A maidservant with whom she was accustomed to go to the cellar, one day fell into a quarrel with her small mistress when no one else chanced to be about, and hurled at her the most biting insult possible, calling her a drunkard. My mother was pierced to the quick, saw her fault in its true wickedness, and instantly condemned it and gave it up. Just as the flattery of a friend can pervert, so the insult of an enemy can sometimes correct. Nor do

You, O God, reward men according to what You do by means of them, but according to what they themselves intended. For the girl being in a temper wanted to enrage her young mistress, not to amend her, for she did it when no one else was there, either because the time and place happened to be thus when the quarrel arose, or because she was afraid that elders[6] would be angry because she had not told it sooner. But You, O Lord, Ruler of heavenly things and earthly, who turn to Your own purposes the very depths of rivers as they run and order the turbulence of the flow of time, did by the folly of one mind bring sanity to another; thus reminding us not to attribute it to our own power if another is amended by our word, even if we meant to amend him.

My mother, then, was modestly and soberly brought up, being rather made obedient to her parents by You than to You by her parents. When she reached the age for marriage, and was bestowed upon a husband, she served him as her lord. She used all her effort to win him to You, preaching You to him by her character, by which You made her beautiful to her husband, respected and loved by him and admirable in his sight. For she bore his acts of unfaithfulness quietly, and never had any jealous scene with her husband about them. She awaited Your mercy upon him, that he might grow chaste through faith in You. And as a matter of fact, though generous beyond measure, he had a very hot temper. But she knew that a woman must not resist a husband in anger, by deed or even by word. Only, when she saw him calm again and quiet, she would take the opportunity to give him an explanation of her actions, if it happened that he had been roused to anger unreasonably. The result was that whereas many matrons with much milder husbands carried the marks of blows to disfigure their faces, and would all get together to complain of the way their husbands behaved, my mother—talking lightly but meaning it seriously—advised them against their tongues: saying that from the day they heard the matrimonial contract read to them they should regard it as an instrument by which they became servants; and from that time they should be mindful of their condition and not set themselves up against their masters. And they often expressed amazement—for they knew how violent a husband she had to live with—that it had never been heard, and there was no mark to show, that Patricius[7] had beaten his wife or that there had been any family quarrel between them for so much as a single day. And when her friends asked her the reason, she taught them her rule, which was as I have just said. Those who followed it, found it good and thanked her; those who did not, went on being bullied and beaten.

Her mother-in-law began by being angry with her because of the whispers of malicious servants. But my mother won her completely by the respect she showed, and her unfailing patience and mildness. She ended by going to her son, telling him of the tales the servants had bandied about to the destruction of peace in the family between herself and her daughter-in-law, and asking him to punish them for it. So he, out of obedience to his mother and in the interests of order in the household and peace among his womenfolk, had the servants beaten whose names he had been given, as she had asked when giving them. To which she added the promise that anyone must expect a similar reward from her own hands who should think to please her by speaking ill of

---

6. Leaders of the church.   7. Augustine's father.

her daughter-in-law. And as no one had the courage to do so, they lived together with the most notable degree of kindness and harmony.

This great gift also, O my God, my Mercy, You gave to Your good servant, in whose womb You created me, that she showed herself, wherever possible, a peacemaker between people quarreling and minds at discord. For swelling and undigested discord often belches forth bitter words when in the venom of intimate conversation with a present friend hatred at its rawest is breathed out upon an absent enemy. But when my mother heard bitter things said by each of the other, she never said anything to either about the other save what would help to reconcile them. This might seem a small virtue, if I had not had the sorrow of seeing for myself so many people who—as if by some horrible widespreading infection of sin—not only tell angry people the things their enemies said in anger, but even add things that were never said at all. Whereas, on the contrary, ordinary humanity would seem to require not merely that we refrain from exciting or increasing wrath among men by evil speaking, but that we study to extinguish wrath by kind speaking. Such a one was she: and You were the master who taught her most secretly in the school of her heart.

The upshot was that toward the very end of his life she won her husband to You; and once he was a Christian she no longer had to complain of the things she had had to bear with before he was a Christian. Further, she was a servant of Your servants. Such of them as knew her praised and honored and loved You, O God, in her; for they felt Your presence in her heart, showing itself in the fruit of her holy conversation. She had been *the wife of one husband, had requited her parents, had governed her house* piously, *was well reported of for good works. She had brought up her children,*[8] being in labor of them as often as she saw them swerving away from You. Finally of all of us Your servants, O Lord—since by Your gift You suffer us to speak—who before her death were living together[9] after receiving the grace of baptism, she took as much care as if she had been the mother of us all, and served us as if she had been the daughter of us all.

When the day was approaching on which she was to depart this life—a day that You knew though we did not—it came about, as I believe by Your secret arrangement, that she and I stood alone leaning in a window, which looked inwards to the garden within the house where we were staying, at Ostia on the Tiber; for there we were away from everybody, resting for the sea voyage from the weariness of our long journey by land. There we talked together, she and I alone, in deep joy; and *forgetting the things that were behind and looking forward to those that were before,* we were discussing in the presence of Truth, which You are, what the eternal life of the saints could be like, *which eye has not seen nor ear heard, nor has it entered into the heart of man.* But with the mouth of our heart we panted for the high waters of Your fountain, the fountain of the life which is with You: that being sprinkled from that fountain according to our capacity, we might in some sense meditate upon so great a matter.

And our conversation had brought us to this point, that any pleasure whatsoever of the bodily senses, in any brightness whatsoever of corporeal light, seemed to us not worthy of comparison with the pleasure of that eternal Light,

8. Augustine is paraphrasing Paul's description of the duties of a widow, given in 1 Timothy 5.

9. Augustine and his fellow converts.

not worthy even of mention. Rising as our love flamed upward towards that Selfsame,[1] we passed in review the various levels of bodily things, up to the heavens themselves, whence sun and moon and stars shine upon this earth. And higher still we soared, thinking in our minds and speaking and marveling at Your works: and so we came to our own souls, and went beyond them to come at last to that region of richness unending, where You feed Israel forever with the food of truth:[2] and there life is that Wisdom by which all things are made, both the things that have been and the things that are yet to be. But this Wisdom itself is not made: it is as it has ever been, and so it shall be forever: indeed "has ever been" and "shall be forever" have no place in it, but it simply is, for it is eternal: whereas "to have been" and "to be going to be" are not eternal. And while we were thus talking of His Wisdom and panting for it, with all the effort of our heart we did for one instant attain to touch it; then sighing, and leaving the first fruits of our spirit bound to it, we returned to the sound of our own tongue, in which a word has both beginning and ending. For what is like to your Word, Our Lord, who abides in Himself forever, yet grows not old and makes all things new!

So we said: If to any man the tumult of the flesh grew silent, silent the images of earth and sea and air: and if the heavens grew silent, and the very soul grew silent to herself and by not thinking of self mounted beyond self: if all dreams and imagined visions grew silent, and every tongue and every sign and whatsoever is transient—for indeed if any man could hear them, he should hear them saying with one voice: We did not make ourselves, but He made us who abides forever: but if, having uttered this and so set us to listening to Him who made them, they all grew silent, and in their silence He alone spoke to us, not by them but by Himself: so that we should hear His word, not by any tongue of flesh nor the voice of an angel nor the sound of thunder nor in the darkness of a parable,[3] but that we should hear Himself whom in all these things we love, should hear Himself and not them: just as we two had but now reached forth and in a flash of the mind attained to touch the eternal Wisdom which abides over all: and if this could continue, and all other visions so different be quite taken away, and this one should so ravish and absorb and wrap the beholder in inward joys that his life should eternally be such as that one moment of understanding for which we had been sighing—would not this be: *Enter Thou into the joy of Thy Lord?* But when shall it be? Shall it be when *we shall all rise again* and *shall not all be changed?*[4]

Such thoughts I uttered, though not in that order or in those actual words; but You know, O Lord, that on that day when we talked of these things the world with all its delights seemed cheap to us in comparison with what we talked of. And my mother said: "Son, for my own part I no longer find joy in anything in this world. What I am still to do here and why I am here I know

---

1. Reality, the divine principle. This ecstasy of Augustine and Monica is throughout described in philosophical terms, in which God is Wisdom.
2. Reference to the manna that fed the Israelites in the desert during their flight from Egypt; see Exodus 16.11–35.
3. Compare Luke 8.10: "Unto you it is given to know the mysteries of the kingdom of God: but to others in parables; that seeing they might not see, and hearing they might not understand."
4. Compare 1 Corinthians 15.52: "the trumpet shall sound, and the dead shall be raised incorruptible, and we shall be changed," referring to the Last Judgment.

not, now that I no longer hope for anything from this world. One thing there was, for which I desired to remain still a little longer in this life, that I should see you a Catholic Christian before I died. This God has granted me in superabundance, in that I now see you His servant to the contempt of all worldly happiness. What then am I doing here?"

What answer I made, I do not clearly remember; within five days or not much longer she fell into a fever. And in her sickness, she one day fainted away and for the moment lost consciousness. We ran to her but she quickly returned to consciousness, and seeing my brother and me standing by her she said as one wondering: "Where was I?" Then looking closely upon us as we stood wordless in our grief, she said: "Here you will bury your mother." I stayed silent and checked my weeping. But my brother said something to the effect that he would be happier if she were to die in her own land and not in a strange country. But as she heard this she looked at him anxiously, restraining him with her eye because he savored of earthly things, and then she looked at me and said: "See the way he talks." And then she said to us both: "Lay this body wherever it may be. Let no care of it disturb you: this only I ask of you that you should remember me at the altar of the Lord wherever you may be." And when she had uttered this wish in such words as she could manage, she fell silent as her sickness took hold of her more strongly.

But as I considered Your gifts, O unseen God, which You send into the hearts of Your faithful to the springing up of such wonderful fruits, I was glad and gave thanks to You, remembering what I had previously known of the care as to her burial which had always troubled her: for she had arranged to be buried by the body of her husband. Because they had lived together in such harmony, she had wished—so little is the human mind capable of rising to the divine—that it should be granted her, as an addition to her happiness and as something to be spoken of among men, that after her pilgrimage beyond the sea the earthly part of man and wife should lie together under the same earth. Just when this vain desire had begun to vanish from her heart through the fullness of Your goodness, I did not know; but I was pleased and surprised that it had now so clearly vanished: though indeed in the conversation we had had together at the window, when she said: "What am I still doing here?" there had appeared no desire to die in her own land. Further I heard afterwards that in the time we were at Ostia, she had talked one day to some of my friends, as a mother talking to her children, of the contempt of this life and of the attraction of death. I was not there at the time. They marveled at such courage in a woman—but it was You who had given it to her—and asked if she was not afraid to leave her body so far from her own city. But she said: "Nothing is far from God, and I have no fear that He will not know at the end of the world from what place He is to raise me up." And so on the ninth day of her illness, in the fifty-sixth year of her life and the thirty-third of mine, that devout and holy soul was released from the body.

I closed her eyes; and an immeasurable sorrow flowed into my heart and would have overflowed in tears. But my eyes under the mind's strong constraint held back their flow and I stood dry-eyed. In that struggle it went very ill with me. As she breathed her last, the child Adeodatus[5] broke out into lamentation and we all checked him and brought him to silence. But in this very fact the

5. Augustine's son, Monica's grandson, then about fifteen or sixteen years old.

childish element in me, which was breaking out into tears, was checked and brought to silence by the manlier voice of my mind. For we felt that it was not fitting that her funeral should be solemnized with moaning and weeping and lamentation, for so it is normal to weep when death is seen as sheer misery or as complete extinction. But she had not died miserably, nor did she wholly die. Of the one thing we were sure by reason of her character, of the other by the reality of our faith.

What then was it that grieved my heart so deeply? Only the newness of the wound, in finding the custom I had so loved of living with her suddenly snapped short. It was a joy to me to have this one testimony from her: when her illness was close to its end, meeting with expressions of endearment such services as I rendered, she called me a dutiful loving son, and said in the great affection of her love that she had never heard from my mouth any harsh or reproachful word addressed to herself. But what possible comparison was there, O my God who made us, between the honor I showed her and the service she had rendered me?

Because I had now lost the great comfort of her, my soul was wounded and my very life torn asunder, for it had been one life made of hers and mine together. When the boy had been quieted and ceased weeping, Evodius took up the psalter and began to chant—with the whole house making the responses— the psalm *Mercy and judgment I will sing to Thee, O Lord.*[6] And when they heard what was being done, many of the brethren and religious women came to us; those whose office it was were making arrangement for the burial, while, in another part of the house where it could properly be done I discoursed, with friends who did not wish to leave me by myself, upon matters suitable for that time. Thus I used truth as a kind of fomentation[7] to bring relief to my torment, a torment known to You, but not known to those others: so that listening closely to me they thought that I lacked all feeling of grief. But in Your ears, where none of them could hear, I accused the emotion in me as weakness; and I held in the flood of my grief. It was for the moment a little diminished, but returned with fresh violence, not with any pouring of tears or change of countenance: but I knew what I was crushing down in my heart. I was very much ashamed that these human emotions could have such power over me—though it belongs to the due order and the lot of our earthly condition that they should come to us—and I felt a new grief at my grief and so was afflicted with a two-fold sorrow.

When the body was taken to burial, I went and returned without tears. During the prayers which we poured forth to you when the sacrifice of our redemption[8] was offered for her—while the body, as the custom there is, lay by the grave before it was actually buried—during those prayers I did not weep. Yet all that day I was heavy with grief within and in the trouble of my mind I begged of You in my own fashion to heal my pain; but You would not—I imagine because You meant to impress upon my memory by this proof how strongly the bond of habit holds the mind even when it no longer feeds upon deception. The idea came to me to go and bathe, for I had heard that the bath—which the Greeks call βαλανεῖον[9]—is so called because it drives anxiety from the mind.

---

6. Compare Psalm 101.1.
7. Soothing dressing for a wound.
8. Perhaps a communion service.

9. Augustine evidently derives *balaneion* ("bath") from the words *ballō* ("cast away") and *ania* ("sorrow").

And this also I acknowledge to Your mercy, O Father of orphans, that I bathed and was the same man after as before. The bitterness of grief had not sweated out of my heart. Then I fell asleep, and woke again to find my grief not a little relieved. And as I was in bed and no one about, I said over those true verses that Your servant Ambrose[1] wrote of You:

> God, the creator of all things
> and ruler of the heavens
> you who clothe the day with the glory of light,
> and the night with the gift of sleep,
>
> so that rest may relax the limbs
> and restore them for the day's work
> relieve the fatigue of the mind
> and dispel anxiety and grief (Latin).

And then little by little I began to recover my former feeling about Your handmaid, remembering how loving and devout was her conversation with You, how pleasant and considerate her conversation with me, of which I was thus suddenly deprived. And I found solace in weeping in Your sight both about her and for her, about myself and for myself. I no longer tried to check my tears, but let them flow as they would, making them a pillow for my heart: and it rested upon them, for it was Your ears that heard my weeping, and not the ears of a man, who would have misunderstood my tears and despised them. But now, O Lord, I confess it to You in writing, let him read it who will and interpret it as he will: and if he sees it as sin that for so small a portion of an hour I wept for my mother, now dead and departed from my sight, who had wept so many years for me that I should live ever in Your sight—let him not scorn me but rather, if he is a man of great charity, let him weep for my sins to You, the Father of all the brethren of Your Christ.

Now that my heart is healed of that wound, in which there was perhaps too much of earthly affection, I pour forth to You, O our God, tears of a very different sort for Your handmaid—tears that flow from a spirit shaken by the thought of the perils there are for every soul that dies in Adam.[2] For though she had been made alive in Christ, and while still in the body had so lived that Your name was glorified in her faith and her character, yet I dare not say that from the moment of her regeneration in baptism no word issued from her mouth contrary to Your Command. Your Son, who is Truth, has said: *Whosoever shall say to his brother, Thou fool, shall be in danger of hell fire;*[3] and it would go ill with the most praiseworthy life lived by men, if You were to examine it with Your mercy laid aside! But because You do not enquire too fiercely into our sins, we have hope and confidence of a place with You. Yet if a man reckons up before You the merits he truly has, what is he reckoning except Your own gifts? If only men would know themselves to be but men, so that he that glories would glory in the Lord!

1. Ambrose (ca. 337–397), bishop of Milan and mentor to Augustine, was the author of many theological works as well as poetic hymns.
2. That is, with the curse of Adam not nullified through baptism in Jesus Christ and conformity with his teachings.
3. From Matthew 5.22, Jesus' Sermon on the Mount. He is preaching a more severe moral code than the traditional one that whoever kills shall be liable to judgment.

Thus, my Glory and my Life, God of my heart, leaving aside for this time her good deeds, for which I give thanks to Thee in joy, I now pray to Thee for my mother's sins. Grant my prayer through the true Medicine of our wounds,[4] who hung upon the cross and who now sitting at Thy right hand makes intercession for us. I know that she dealt mercifully, and from her heart forgave those who trespassed against her: do Thou also forgive such trespasses as she may have been guilty of in all the years since her baptism, forgive them, Lord, forgive them, I beseech Thee: enter not into judgment with her. Let Thy mercy be exalted above Thy justice for Thy words are true and Thou hast promised that the merciful shall obtain mercy. That they should be merciful is Thy gift who *hast mercy on whom Thou wilt, and wilt have compassion on whom Thou wilt.*

And I believe that Thou hast already done what I am now asking; but be not offended, Lord, at the things my mouth would utter. For on that day when her death was so close, she was not concerned that her body should be sumptuously wrapped or embalmed with spices, nor with any thought of choosing a monument or even for burial in her own country. Of such things she gave us no command, but only desired to be remembered at Thy altar, which she had served without ever missing so much as a day, on which she knew that the holy Victim was offered; *by whom the handwriting is blotted out of the decree that was contrary to us,*[5] by which offering too the enemy was overcome who, reckoning our sins and seeking what may be laid to our charge, found nothing in Him, in whom we are conquerors. Who shall restore to Him his innocent blood? Who shall give Him back the price by which He purchased us and so take us from Him? To this sacrament of our redemption Thy handmaid had bound her soul by the bond of faith. Let none wrest her from Thy protection; let neither the lion nor the dragon[6] bar her way by force or craft. For she will not answer that she owes nothing, lest she should be contradicted and confuted by that cunning accuser: but she will answer that her debts have been remitted by Him, to whom no one can hand back the price which He paid for us, though He owed it not.

So let her rest in peace, together with her husband, for she had no other before nor after him, but served him, in patience bringing forth fruit for Thee, and winning him likewise for Thee. And inspire, O my Lord my God, inspire Thy servants my brethren, Thy sons my masters, whom I serve with heart and voice and pen, that as many of them as read this may remember at Thy altar Thy servant Monica, with Patricius, her husband, by whose bodies Thou didst bring me into this life, though how I know not.[7] May they with loving mind remember these who were my parents in this transitory light, my brethren who serve Thee as our Father in our Catholic mother, and those who are to be fellow citizens with me in the eternal Jerusalem,[8] which Thy people sigh for in their pilgrimage from birth until they come there: so that what my mother at her end asked of me may be fulfilled more richly in the prayers of so many gained for her by my Confessions than by my prayers alone.

*   *   *

4. Jesus.
5. An allusion to Christ's redemption of humanity from the curse of Adam through the Crucifixion.
6. Compare Psalm 91.13: "Thou shalt tread upon the lion and the adder: the young lion and the dragon shalt thou trample under feet, which invokes God's protection of the godly."
7. Augustine does not understand the seemingly miraculous process by which the fetus grows in the womb.
8. That is, heaven.

THE QUR'AN

610–632

The word *qur'an* literally means "the recitation." For Muslims, the Qur'an is not so much a book as a living and vibrant act of speech that has been passed down through an unbroken chain of human beings from the time of Muhammad, who with his companions in seventh-century Arabia formed the first community of Muslims. At the same time, the Qur'an is also conceived of as a book: not a literal object on the shelf but a divine work that exists only in the heavenly realm of paradise. Any physical copy of the Arabic text is thought of as a pale reflection of that ideal book, a tool to enable the reader to memorize and then recite the Qur'anic text. As divine speech, moreover, the Qur'an can never be rendered perfectly in the medium of the human voice, a deficiency that testifies to its fundamental inimitability, or *i'jaz*. In accord with this view of the nature of the Qur'an, no translation into any other language is thought of as actually being the holy book itself. The most that any translation can be, for the believer, is an aid to understanding the original.

The Qur'an presents itself as the last of a sequence of revealed holy books, including the Torah (in Arabic, Tawrat), the Psalms (Zabur), and the Gospels (Injil). Similarly, Muhammad is presented as one in a lineage of prophets (that is, those who have received communications directly from God) that begins with the first man, Adam. Earlier holy books each have an associated prophet: for the Torah, Moses; for the Psalms, David; and for the Gospels, Jesus and also Mary—who, despite being female, is also recognized as part of the prophetic lineage. Indeed, a minority of classical Muslim scholars, including Ibn Hazm (d. 1065), considered her to be a prophet outright. Stories and characters from Jewish and Christian scripture reappear in the Qur'an, as seen in the chapters (or suras) on Jonah, Joseph, and Mary. When hearing these verses, the earliest converts to Islam, drawn from the local Christian and Jewish communities located in Arabia, would have marveled at the different perspective brought to bear on familiar stories by this new revelation. The Qur'an recognizes the followers of other monotheistic religions, such as Jews and Christians, as "people of the Book"—those who follow the word of God as revealed by his prophets. From the point of view of Islam, the people of the Book who lived before the revelation of the Qur'an were also followers of *islam*, in the literal sense of "submission" to God's will. Those who continued to reverence their own, pre-Islamic holy books, such as Jews and Christians, could be tolerated within the Muslim community, but this inclusiveness of monotheism had its limits. Muslims generally viewed their Prophet as the last of his kind, "the seal of prophets," and the Qur'an as the last holy book that would ever be revealed to humanity. The Torah and the Gospels, while divine in their inspiration, had become corrupt over time. Only through submission to the divine will as revealed in the Qur'an, Muslims believed, could the faithful be sure they would enter into paradise and avoid the punishments of hell.

Only from the nineteenth century on has the **Bible** begun to be read as a work of literature as well as a divinely inspired text, and so too this dual focus on the Qur'an has been recent. From the Middle Ages to the twenty-first century,

Western readers of the Qur'an have all too often condemned what they saw as its theological deviance and narrative incoherence. As a result, Muslims have hesitated to offer up the Qur'an for study within the framework of literary history or to allow it to move beyond the conservative framework of faith-based perspectives. This attitude has begun to change, however, because of innovative approaches to Qur'anic interpretation on the part of Muslim communities and an increasing willingness to place the Qur'an into dialogue with other sacred scriptures. The Qur'an itself invites comparison with other literary traditions— most explicitly, the rich traditions of oral poetry found in pre-Islamic Arabia. In that context, it appears as a marvel of literature whose divine inspiration is manifest in the form of lyrical chant and resonant verse. Reading the Qur'an on the page, in translation, weakly conveys its virtue, which can be appreciated only in the musical oral recitation (*tajwid*) that reveals the rhythmic quality of the verse and the haunting repetition of syllables at the ends of successive lines. It is possible to get a sense of this music in the repeated refrain of the sura "The Lord of Mercy" ("Ar Rahman"), translated below.

The Qur'an is divided into 144 suras, some of which are quite short; others are very long, resembling a biblical book in form. Each sura is made up of a number of verses (*ayat*; singular *aya*). The Qur'an is also conventionally divided up into thirty sections (*ajza*; singular *juz'*) of roughly equal length to facilitate recitation of the entire work over the period of one month. Because of the emphasis placed on its oral recitation, which must be performed as part of the five daily prayers, Muslims begin to memorize the Qur'an at a young age; they start with the introductory sura, "The Opening" ("Al Fatiha"), and continue on with the short Meccan suras that are concentrated near the end of the Qur'an, including "Purity"

("Al Ikhlas"). Instead of being arranged in the order that Muhammad received them, the suras are arranged as Muhammad said he had been instructed by God. Some of the suras were revealed at Mecca, when the Muslim community was starting to develop, and others at Medina, where the persecuted community took refuge; the two types tend to differ not only in length but also in subject matter and in tone. Instead of being carefully separated, however, the Meccan and Medinan suras are intermingled, and many of the Meccan suras dating from early in Muhammad's prophetic mission appear near the end of the text. The effect is one of fragments arranged in a mosaic—yet that mosaic has a very clearly defined form, delineated by strands running throughout. The repetition of phrases and motifs across suras, often from different periods, creates a pattern as intricate as a woven tapestry.

With the exception of "The Feast" and "The Lord of Mercy," which were revealed at Medina, the excerpts reproduced here are Meccan suras, which tend to be relatively short. Our aim was to provide entire chapters rather than abbreviated selections, so that the highly structured nature of the suras could be grasped. The tightly ordered form illustrated on the level of the individual sura is also evident more generally in the Qur'an, in which the parts all contribute to make up the whole, but each part can also stand for the whole. Several of the suras are known by another name, reflecting this part–whole relationship: "The Opening," which is the first sura, is also known as "The Mother of the Book," while sura "Yasin" is sometimes called "The Heart of the Qur'an." One of the last suras, "Purity," was described by Muhammad himself as being "one-third of the Qur'an," because its highly condensed verses on the unity of God encapsulate the very core of Islamic theology. Other suras, such as "Jonah," "Joseph," and "Mary," illuminate the extent to which the Qur'an is intertwined with Jewish and Christian faith traditions. These connections can also be seen in one of the Medinan suras excerpted here, "The Feast," which begins with a description of allowed and prohibited foods that recalls the intricate rules laid down in Leviticus, thus elaborating one important area of common practice shared by Judaism and Islam. Yet the table, an image that is central to "The Feast," represents more than just a literal piece of furniture. It is also the figurative table shared by the people of the Book, given form in the table spread with food that Jesus presides over at the Last Supper. In the latter part of the sura, Jesus thanks God for what he has already given and asks for something more for the table: "Send down to us a feast from heaven. . . . Provide for us: You are the best provider." God replies, "I will send it down to you." This final gift for the table is understood as being the Prophet Muhammad, or even the Qur'an itself.

The Qur'an was received by Muhammad through the mediation of the angel Gabriel (Jibreel) over a period of about twenty-three years, beginning when he was forty years old and ending with his death in 632. During that time, the Qur'an existed as an oral recitation, repeated both by Muhammad himself and by the growing community of Muslims. After Muhammad's death, the community recognized the need to record the oral text to ensure that errors not creep into the recitation. The closest companions of Muhammad, under the supervision of the first caliph (or ruler) of the Muslim community, Abu Bakr, assembled the Qur'an in written form. The third caliph, Uthman, supervised the finalized version of the text, which was completed in 651, and then ordered all imperfect copies to be destroyed. It is this version of the Qur'an that we read today. Translations began to be produced almost immediately, beginning with a rendering of "The Opening" into the Persian language by Salman, one of the companions of the Prophet Muhammad. A full Persian translation of the Qur'an was made in the ninth century, attesting to the rapid embrace of Islam by the inhabitants of Persia (modern Iran). As is the case today, these translations were not made with the purpose of substituting Qur'anic verses in the local vernacular for the Arabic originals during prayer; instead, they were aids to understanding intended to enable fuller assimilation of the Arabic scripture within a new culture. Western audiences started to read the Qur'an in the Middle Ages, beginning with Robert of Ketton's Latin translation in 1143. The Qur'an is never accompanied by pictorial illustrations, in keeping with the Islamic practice of iconoclasm (the prohibition of any representation of living things, thereby avoiding the temptation of idolatry). It is, however, often rendered in elaborate calligraphy, a style of writing so ornate that it becomes art, fusing word with image in the aural masterpiece that is the Qur'an.

FROM THE QUR'AN[1]

1. The Opening

In the name of God, the Lord of Mercy, the Giver of Mercy! Praise belongs to God, Lord of the Worlds, the Lord of Mercy, the Giver of Mercy, Master of the Day of Judgement. It is You we worship; it is You we ask for help. Guide us to the straight path: the path of those You have blessed, those who incur no anger and who have not gone astray.

5. The Feast

In the name of God, the Lord of Mercy, the Giver of Mercy

You who believe, fulfil your obligations. Livestock animals are lawful as food for you, with the exception of what is about to be announced to you. You are forbidden to kill game while you are on pilgrimage—God commands what He will, so, you who believe, do not violate the sanctity of God's rites, the Sacred Month, the offerings, their garlands, nor those going to the Sacred House[2] to seek the bounty and pleasure of their Lord—but when you have completed the rites of pilgrimage you may hunt. Do not let your hatred for the people who barred you from the Sacred Mosque induce you to break the law: help one another to do what is right and good; do not help one another towards sin and hostility. Be mindful of God, for His punishment is severe.

You are forbidden to eat carrion; blood; pig's meat; any animal over which any name other than God's has been invoked; any animal strangled, or victim of a violent blow or a fall, or gored or savaged by a beast of prey, unless you still slaughter it [in the correct manner]; or anything sacrificed on idolatrous altars. You are also forbidden to allot shares [of meat] by drawing marked arrows[3]—a heinous practice—today the disbelievers have lost all hope that you will give up your religion. Do not fear them: fear Me. Today I have perfected your religion for you, completed My blessing upon you, and chosen as your religion *islam*: [total devotion to God]; but if any of you is forced by hunger to eat forbidden food, with no intention of doing wrong, then God is most forgiving and merciful.

They ask you, Prophet, what is lawful for them. Say, 'All good things are lawful for you.' [This includes] what you have taught your birds and beasts of prey to catch, teaching them as God has taught you, so eat what they catch for you, but first pronounce God's name over it. Be mindful of God: He is swift to take account. Today all good things have been made lawful for you. The food of the People of the Book[4] is lawful for you as your food is lawful for them. So are chaste, believing, women as well as chaste women of the people who were

1. Translated by M. A. S. Abdel Haleem; the bracketed material in the text is his.
2. The Ka'aba, central point of the pilgrimage to Mecca that takes place during "the Sacred Month" of the hajj. According to the Qur'an it was originally established by Abraham as a place to worship the one true God, and Muslims always face it when they pray.
3. That is, casting lots by a method commonly used in pre-Islamic Arabia to make decisions or select an individual.
4. The Jews.

given the Scripture before you, as long as you have given them their bride-gifts and married them, not taking them as lovers or secret mistresses. The deeds of anyone who rejects faith will come to nothing, and in the Hereafter he will be one of the losers.

You who believe, when you are about to pray, wash your faces and your hands up to the elbows, wipe your heads, wash your feet up to the ankles and, if required,[5] wash your whole body. If any of you is sick or on a journey, or has just relieved himself, or had intimate contact with a woman, and can find no water, then take some clean sand and wipe your face and hands with it. God does not wish to place any burden on you: He only wishes to cleanse you and perfect His blessing on you, so that you may be thankful. Remember God's blessing on you and the pledge with which you were bound when you said, 'We hear and we obey.' Be mindful of God: God has full knowledge of the secrets of the heart.

You who believe, be steadfast in your devotion to God and bear witness impartially: do not let hatred of others lead you away from justice, but adhere to justice, for that is closer to awareness of God. Be mindful of God: God is well aware of all that you do. God has promised forgiveness and a rich reward to those who have faith and do good works; those who reject faith and deny Our revelations will inhabit the blazing Fire.

You who believe, remember God's blessing on you when a certain people were about to raise their hands against you and He restrained them. Be mindful of God: let the believers put their trust in Him.

God took a pledge from the Children of Israel. We made twelve leaders arise among them, and God said, 'I am with you: if you keep up the prayer, pay the prescribed alms, believe in My messengers and support them, and lend God a good loan, I will wipe out your sins and admit you into Gardens[6] graced with flowing streams. Any of you who now ignore this [pledge] will be far from the right path.' But they broke their pledge, so We distanced them [from Us] and hardened their hearts. They distort the meaning of [revealed] words and have forgotten some of what they were told to remember: you [Prophet] will always find treachery in all but a few of them. Overlook this and pardon them: God loves those who do good. We also took a pledge from those who say, 'We are Christians,' but they too forgot some of what they were told to remember, so We stirred up enmity and hatred among them until the Day of Resurrection, when God will tell them what they have done.

People of the Book,[7] Our Messenger has come to make clear to you much of what you have kept hidden of the Scripture, and to overlook much [you have done]. A light has now come to you from God, and a Scripture making things clear, with which God guides to the ways of peace those who follow what pleases Him, bringing them from darkness out into light, by His will, and guiding them to a straight path. Those who say, 'God is the Messiah,[8] the son of Mary,' are defying the truth. Say, 'If it had been God's will, could anyone have prevented Him from destroying the Messiah, son of Mary, together with his

---

5. For example, if unclean from sexual intercourse or menstruation.
6. The heavenly paradise, depicted in the Qur'an as a garden.

7. Here, the Jews and the Christians.
8. In Jewish belief, the promised redeemer who will come at the end of time; in Christian belief, that redeemer is identified with Jesus Christ.

mother and everyone else on earth? Control of the heavens and earth and all that is between them belongs to God: He creates whatever He will. God has power over everything.' The Jews and the Christians say, 'We are the children of God and His beloved ones.' Say, 'Then why does He punish you for your sins? You are merely human beings, part of His creation: He forgives whoever He will and punishes whoever He will. Control of the heavens and earth and all that is between them belongs to Him: all journeys lead to Him.' People of the Book, Our Messenger comes to you now, after a break in the sequence of messengers, to make things clear for you in case you should say, 'No one has come to give us good news or to warn us.' So someone has come to you, to give you good news and warn you: God has the power to do all things.

Moses said to his people, 'My people, remember God's blessing on you: how He raised prophets among you and appointed kings for you and gave you what he had not given to any other people. My people, go into the holy land which God has ordained for you—do not turn back or you will be the losers.' They said, 'Moses, there is a fearsome people in this land. We will not go there until they leave. If they leave, then we will enter.' Yet two men whom God had blessed among those who were afraid said, 'Go in to them through the gate and when you go in you will overcome them. If you are true believers, put your trust in God.' They said, 'Moses, we will never enter while they are still there, so you and your Lord go in and fight, and we will stay here.' He said, 'Lord, I have authority over no one except myself and my brother: judge between the two of us and these disobedient people.' God said, 'The land is forbidden to them for forty years: they will wander the earth aimlessly. Do not grieve over those who disobey.'[9]

[Prophet], tell them the truth about the story of Adam's two sons:[1] each of them offered a sacrifice, and it was accepted from one and not the other. One said, 'I will kill you,' but the other said, 'God only accepts the sacrifice of those who are mindful of Him. If you raise your hand to kill me, I will not raise mine to kill you. I fear God, the Lord of all worlds, and I would rather you were burdened with my sins as well as yours and became an inhabitant of the Fire: such is the evildoers' reward.' But his soul prompted him to kill his brother: he killed him and became one of the losers. God sent a raven to scratch up the ground and show him how to cover his brother's corpse and he said, 'Woe is me! Could I not have been like this raven and covered up my brother's body?' He became remorseful. On account of [his deed], We decreed to the Children of Israel that if anyone kills a person—unless in retribution for murder or spreading corruption in the land—it is as if he kills all mankind, while if any saves a life it is as if he saves the lives of all mankind. Our messengers came to them with clear signs, but many of them continued to commit excesses in the land. Those who wage war against God and His Messenger and strive to spread corruption in the land should be punished by death, crucifixion, the amputation of an alternate hand and foot, or banishment from the land: a disgrace for them in this world, and then a terrible punishment in the Hereafter, unless they repent before you overpower them—in that case bear in mind that God is forgiving and merciful.

9. Compare Numbers 13.1–14.35.　　　　　1. Cain and Abel; see Genesis 4.1–15.

You who believe, be mindful of God, seek ways to come closer to Him and strive for His cause, so that you may prosper. If the disbelievers possessed all that is in the earth and twice as much again and offered it to ransom themselves from torment on the Day of Resurrection, it would not be accepted from them—they will have a painful torment. They will wish to come out of the Fire but they will be unable to do so: theirs will be a lasting torment.

Cut off the hands of thieves, whether they are man or woman, as punishment for what they have done—a deterrent from God: God is almighty and wise. But if anyone repents after his wrongdoing and makes amends, God will accept his repentance: God is most forgiving, most merciful. Do you [Prophet] not know that control of the heavens and earth belongs solely to God? He punishes whoever He will and forgives whoever He will: God has power over everything.

Messenger, do not be grieved by those who race to surpass one another in disbelief—those who say with their mouths, 'We believe,' but have no faith in their hearts, and the Jews who listen eagerly to lies and to those who have not even met you, who distort the meanings of [revealed] words and say [to each other], 'If you are given this ruling, accept it, but if you are not, then beware!'—if God intends some people to be so misguided, you will be powerless against God on their behalf. These are the ones whose hearts God does not intend to cleanse—a disgrace for them in this world, and then a heavy punishment in the Hereafter—they listen eagerly to lies and consume what is unlawful. If they come to you [Prophet] for judgement, you can either judge between them, or decline—if you decline, they will not harm you in any way, but if you do judge between them, judge justly: God loves the just—but why do they come to you for judgement when they have the Torah[2] with God's judgement, and even then still turn away? These are not believers. We revealed the Torah with guidance and light, and the prophets, who had submitted to God, judged according to it for the Jews. So did the rabbis and the scholars in accordance with that part of God's Scripture which they were entrusted to preserve, and to which they were witnesses. So [rabbis and scholars] do not fear people, fear Me; do not barter away My messages for a small price; those who do not judge according to what God has sent down are rejecting [God's teachings]. In the Torah We prescribed for them a life for a life, an eye for an eye, a nose for a nose, an ear for an ear, a tooth for a tooth, an equal wound for a wound:[3] if anyone forgoes this out of charity, it will serve as atonement for his bad deeds. Those who do not judge according to what God has revealed are doing grave wrong.

We sent Jesus, son of Mary, in their footsteps, to confirm the Torah that had been sent before him: We gave him the Gospel with guidance, light, and confirmation of the Torah already revealed—a guide and lesson for those who take heed of God. So let the followers of the Gospel judge according to what God has sent down in it. Those who do not judge according to what God has revealed are lawbreakers.

We sent to you [Muhammad] the Scripture with the truth, confirming the Scriptures that came before it, and with final authority over them: so judge between them according to what God has sent down. Do not follow their

---

2. The first five books of the Hebrew Bible (literally, "law" [Heb.]), traditionally ascribed to Moses.

3. See Leviticus 24.19–21; Deuteronomy 19.21.

whims, which deviate from the truth that has come to you. We have assigned a
law and a path to each of you. If God had so willed, He would have made you
one community, but He wanted to test you through that which He has given
you, so race to do good, you will all return to God and He will make clear to
you the matters you differed about. So [Prophet] judge between them according to what God has sent down. Do not follow their whims, and take good care
that they do not tempt you away from any of what God has sent down to you.
If they turn away, remember that God intends to punish them for some of the
sins they have committed, a great many people are lawbreakers. Do they want
judgement according to the time of pagan ignorance? Is there any better judge
than God for those of firm faith?

You who believe, do not take the Jews and Christians as allies, they are allies
only to each other. Anyone who takes them as an ally becomes one of them—
God does not guide such wrongdoers—yet you [Prophet] will see the perverse
at heart rushing to them for protection, saying, 'We are afraid fortune may turn
against us.' But God may well bring about a triumph or some other event of
His own making: then they will rue the secrets they harboured in their hearts,
and the believers will say, 'Are these the men who swore by God using their
strongest oaths that they were with you?' All they did was in vain: they have lost
everything.

You who believe, if any of you go back on your faith, God will soon replace
you with people He loves and who love Him, people who are humble towards
the believers, hard on the disbelievers, and who strive in God's way without
fearing anyone's reproach. Such is God's favour. He grants it to whoever He
will. God has endless bounty and knowledge. Your true allies are God, His
Messenger, and the believers—those who keep up the prayer, pay the prescribed alms, and bow down in worship. Those who turn for protection to God,
His Messenger, and the believers [are God's party]: God's party is sure to
triumph.

You who believe, do not take as allies those who ridicule your religion and
make fun of it—whether people who were given the Scripture before you, or
disbelievers—and be mindful of God if you are true believers. When you make
the call to prayer, they ridicule it and make fun of it: this is because they are
people who do not reason. Say [Prophet], 'People of the Book, do you resent us
for any reason other than the fact that we believe in God, in what has been
sent down to us, and in what was sent before us, while most of you are disobedient?' Say, 'Shall I tell you who deserves a worse punishment from God than
[the one you wish upon] us? Those God distanced from Himself, was angry
with, and condemned as apes and pigs, and those who worship idols: they are
worse in rank and have strayed further from the right path.

When they come to you [believers], they say, 'We believe,' but they come
disbelieving and leave disbelieving—God knows best what they are hiding. You
[Prophet] see many of them rushing into sin and hostility and consuming what
is unlawful. How evil their practices are! Why do their rabbis and scholars not
forbid them to speak sinfully and consume what is unlawful? How evil their
deeds are! The Jews have said, 'God is tight-fisted,' but it is they who are tight-
fisted, and they are rejected for what they have said. Truly, God's hands are
open wide: He gives as He pleases. What has been sent down to you from your
Lord is sure to increase insolence and defiance in many of them. We have

sown enmity and hatred amongst them till the Day of Resurrection. Whenever they kindle the fire of war, God will put it out. They try to spread corruption in the land, but God does not love those who corrupt. If only the People of the Book would believe and be mindful of God, We would take away their sins and bring them into the Gardens of Delight. If they had upheld the Torah and the Gospel and what was sent down to them from their Lord, they would have been given abundance from above and from below: some of them are on the right course, but many of them do evil.

Messenger, proclaim everything that has been sent down to you from your Lord—if you do not, then you will not have communicated His message—and God will protect you from people. God does not guide those who defy Him. Say, 'People of the Book, you have no true basis [for your religion] unless you uphold the Torah, the Gospel, and that which has been sent down to you from your Lord,' but what has been sent down to you [Prophet] from your Lord is sure to increase many of them in their insolence and defiance: do not worry about those who defy [God]. For the [Muslim] believers, the Jews, the Sabians,[4] and the Christians—those who believe in God and the Last Day and do good deeds—there is no fear: they will not grieve.

We took a pledge from the Children of Israel, and sent messengers to them. Whenever a messenger brought them anything they did not like, they accused some of lying and put others to death; they thought no harm could come to them and so became blind and deaf [to God]. God turned to them in mercy but many of them again became blind and deaf: God is fully aware of their actions. Those who say, 'God is the Messiah, son of Mary,' have defied God. The Messiah himself said, 'Children of Israel, worship God, my Lord and your Lord.' If anyone associates others with God, God will forbid him from the Garden, and Hell will be his home. No one will help such evildoers.

Those people who say that God is the third of three are defying [the truth]: there is only One God. If they persist in what they are saying, a painful punishment will afflict those of them who persist. Why do they not turn to God and ask His forgiveness, when God is most forgiving, most merciful? The Messiah, son of Mary, was only a messenger; other messengers had come and gone before him; his mother was a virtuous woman; both ate food [like other mortals]. See how clear We make these signs for them; see how deluded they are. Say, 'How can you worship something other than God, that has no power to do you harm or good? God alone is the All Hearing and All Knowing.' Say, 'People of the Book, do not overstep the bounds of truth in your religion and do not follow the whims of those who went astray before you—they led many others astray and themselves continue to stray from the even path.'

Those Children of Israel who defied [God] were rejected through the words of David,[5] and Jesus, son of Mary, because they disobeyed, they persistently overstepped the limits, they did not forbid each other to do wrong. How vile their deeds were! You [Prophet] see many of them allying themselves with the disbelievers. How terrible is what their souls have stored up for them: God is

4. Apparently a monotheistic group in Iraq who especially venerated the Psalms; they, too, were people of the Book.
5. Second king of Israel, according to the Hebrew Bible (see Samuel, 1 Kings, and 1 Chronicles); the model for later monarchs, despite his moral lapses, he is traditionally credited with authorship of the Psalms.

angry with them and they will remain tormented. If they had believed in God, in the Prophet, and in what was sent down to him, they would never have allied themselves with the disbelievers, but most of them are rebels.

You [Prophet] are sure to find that the most hostile to the believers are the Jews and those who associate other deities with God; you are sure to find that the closest in affection towards the believers are those who say, 'We are Christians,' for there are among them people devoted to learning and ascetics. These people are not given to arrogance, and when they listen to what has been sent down to the Messenger, you will see their eyes overflowing with tears because they recognize the Truth [in it]. They say, 'Our Lord, we believe, so count us amongst the witnesses. Why should we not believe in God and in the Truth that has come down to us, when we long for our Lord to include us in the company of the righteous?' For saying this, God has rewarded them with Gardens graced with flowing streams, and there they will stay: that is the reward of those who do good. Those who reject the truth and deny Our messages will be the inhabitants of Hellfire.

You who believe, do not forbid the good things God has made lawful to you—do not exceed the limits: God does not love those who exceed the limits—but eat the lawful and good things that God provides for you. Be mindful of God, in whom you believe. God does not take you [to task] for what is thoughtless in your oaths, only for your binding oaths: the atonement for breaking an oath is to feed ten poor people with food equivalent to what you would normally give your own families, or to clothe them, or to set free a slave—if a person cannot find the means, he should fast for three days. This is the atonement for breaking your oaths—keep your oaths. In this way God makes clear His revelations to you, so that you may be thankful.

You who believe, intoxicants and gambling, idolatrous practices, and [divining with] arrows are repugnant acts—Satan's doing—shun them so that you may prosper. With intoxicants and gambling, Satan seeks only to incite enmity and hatred among you, and to stop you remembering God and prayer. Will you not give them up? Obey God, obey the Messenger, and always be on your guard: if you pay no heed, bear in mind that the sole duty of Our Messenger is to deliver the message clearly. Those who believe and do good deeds will not be blamed for what they may have consumed [in the past] as long as they are mindful of God, believe and do good deeds, then are mindful of God and believe, then are mindful of God and do good deeds: God loves those who do good deeds.

You who believe, God is sure to test you with game within reach of your hands and spears, to find out who fears Him even though they cannot see Him: from now on, anyone who transgresses will have a painful punishment. You who believe, do not kill game while you are in the state of consecration [for pilgrimage]. If someone does so intentionally the penalty is an offering of a domestic animal brought to the Ka'ba[6] equivalent—as judged by two just men among you—to the one he has killed; alternatively, he may atone by feeding the needy or by fasting an equivalent number of days, so that he may taste the full gravity of his deed. God forgives what is past, but if anyone re-offends, God will exact the penalty from him: God is mighty, and capable of exacting the penalty. It is permitted for you to catch and eat seafood—an enjoyment for you and the

6. Also "Ka'aba"; see p. 74, n. 2.

traveller—but hunting game is forbidden while you are in the state of consecration [for pilgrimage]. Be mindful of God to whom you will be gathered.

God has made the Ka'ba—the Sacred House—a means of support for people, and the Sacred Months, the animals for sacrifice and their garlands: all this. Know that God has knowledge of all that is in the heavens and earth and that He is fully aware of all things. Know too that God is severe in punishment yet most forgiving and merciful. The Messenger's duty is only to deliver the message: God knows what you reveal and what you conceal.

Say [Prophet], 'Bad cannot be likened to good, though you may be dazzled by how abundant the bad is. Be mindful of God, people of understanding, so that you may prosper.' You who believe, do not ask about matters which, if made known to you, might make things difficult for you—if you ask about them while the Qur'an is being revealed, they will be made known to you—for God has kept silent about them: God is most forgiving and forbearing. Before you, some people asked about things, then ignored [the answers]. God did not institute the dedication of such things as *bahira, sa'iba, wasila,* or *ham*[7] to idols; but the disbelievers invent lies about God. Most of them do not use reason: when it is said to them, 'Come to what God has sent down, and to the Messenger,' they say, 'What we inherited from our forefathers is good enough for us,' even though their forefathers knew nothing and were not guided. You who believe, you are responsible for your own souls; if anyone else goes astray it will not harm you so long as you follow the guidance; you will all return to God, and He will make you realize what you have done.

You who believe, when death approaches any of you, let two just men from among you act as witnesses to the making of a bequest, or two men from another people if you are journeying in the land when death approaches. Keep the two witnesses back after prayer, if you have any doubts, and make them both swear by God, 'We will not sell our testimony for any price, even if a close relative is involved. We will not hide God's testimony, for then we should be doing wrong.' If it is discovered that these two are guilty [of perjury], two of those whose rights have been usurped have a better right to bear witness in their place. Let them swear by God, 'Our testimony is truer than theirs. We have said nothing but the truth, for that would make us wrongdoers': that will make it more likely they will give true and proper testimony, or fear that their oaths might be refuted by others afterwards. Be mindful of God and listen; God does not guide those who break His laws.

On the Day when God assembles all the messengers and asks, 'What response did you receive?' they will say, 'We do not have that knowledge: You alone know things that cannot be seen,' Then God will say, 'Jesus, son of Mary! Remember My favour to you and to your mother: how I strengthened you with the holy spirit, so that you spoke to people in your infancy and as a grown man; how I taught you the Scripture and wisdom, the Torah and the Gospel; how, by My leave, you fashioned the shape of a bird out of clay, breathed into it, and it became, by My leave, a bird; how, by My leave, you healed the blind person and the leper; how, by My leave, you brought the dead back to life; how I restrained the Children of Israel from [harming] you when you brought them clear signs,

7. Different classes of animals consecrated to idols in pre-Islamic Arabia.

and those of them who disbelieved said, "This is clearly nothing but sorcery";[8] and how I inspired the disciples to believe in Me and My messengers—they said, "We believe and bear witness that we devote ourselves [to God]."'

When the disciples said, 'Jesus, son of Mary, can your Lord send down a feast to us from heaven?' he said, 'Beware of God if you are true believers.' They said, 'We wish to eat from it; to have our hearts reassured; to know that you have told us the truth; and to be witnesses of it.' Jesus, son of Mary, said, 'Lord, send down to us a feast from heaven so that we can have a festival—the first and last of us—and a sign from You. Provide for us: You are the best provider.' God said, 'I will send it down to you, but anyone who disbelieves after this will be punished with a punishment that I will not inflict on anyone else in the world.'

When God says, 'Jesus, son of Mary, did you say to people, "Take me and my mother as two gods alongside God"?' he will say, 'May You be exalted! I would never say what I had no right to say—if I had said such a thing You would have known it: You know all that is within me, though I do not know what is within You, You alone have full knowledge of things unseen—I told them only what You commanded me to: "Worship God, my Lord and your Lord." I was a witness over them during my time among them. Ever since You took my soul, You alone have been the watcher over them: You are witness to all things and if You punish them, they are Your servants; if You forgive them, You are the Almighty, the Wise.' God will say, 'This is a Day when the truthful will benefit from their truthfulness. They will have Gardens graced with flowing streams, there to remain for ever. God is pleased with them and they with Him: that is the supreme triumph.' Control of the heavens and earth and everything in them belongs to God: He has power over all things.

10. Jonah

In the name of God, the Lord of Mercy, the Giver of Mercy

Alif Lam Ra[1]

These are the verses of the wise Book. Is it so surprising to people that We have revealed to a man from among them that he should warn people, and give glad news to those who believe, that they are on a sure footing with their Lord? [Yet] those who disbelieve say, 'This man is clearly a sorcerer.'

Your Lord is God who created the heavens and earth in six Days, then established Himself on the Throne, governing everything; there is no one that can intercede with Him, unless He has first given permission: this is God your Lord so worship Him. How can you not take heed? It is to Him you shall all return—that is a true promise from God. It was He who created [you] in the first place, and He will do so again, so that He may justly reward those who believe and do good deeds. But the disbelievers will have a drink of scalding water, and agonizing torment, because they persistently disbelieved.

---

8. This account of Jesus' miracles is similar to that found in apocryphal Christian accounts of his childhood (the so-called infancy gospels).

1. Letters of the Arabic alphabet; their meaning in this context is unclear.

It is He who made the sun a shining radiance and the moon a light, determining phases for it so that you might know the number of years and how to calculate time. God did not create all these without a true purpose; He explains His signs to those who understand. In the succession of night and day, and in what God created in the heavens and earth, there truly are signs for those who are aware of Him. Those who do not expect to meet Us and are pleased with the life of this world, contenting themselves with it and paying no heed to Our signs, shall have the Fire for their home because of what they used to do. But as for those who believe and do good deeds, their Lord will guide them because of their faith. Streams will flow at their feet in the Gardens of Bliss. Their prayer in them will be, 'Glory be to You, God!' their greeting, 'Peace,' and the last part of their prayer, 'Praise be to God, Lord of the Worlds.'[2]

If God were to hasten on for people the harm [they have earned] as they wish to hasten on the good, their time would already be up. But We leave those who do not expect to meet Us to wander blindly in their excesses. When trouble befalls man he cries out to Us, whether lying on his side, sitting, or standing, but as soon as We relieve him of his trouble he goes on his way as if he had never cried out to Us to remove his trouble. In this way the deeds of such heedless people are made attractive to them. Before you people, We destroyed whole generations when they did evil—their messengers brought them clear signs but they refused to believe. This is how We repay the guilty. Later We made you their successors in the land, to see how you would behave.

When Our clear revelations are recited to them, those who do not expect to meet with Us say, 'Bring [us] a different Qur'an, or change it.' [Prophet], say, 'It is not for me to change it of my own accord; I only follow what is revealed to me, for I fear the torment of an awesome Day, if I were to disobey my Lord.' Say, 'If God had so willed, I would not have recited it to you, nor would He have made it known to you. I lived a whole lifetime among you before it came to me. How can you not use your reason?'

Who could be more wicked than someone who invents lies against God or denies His revelations? The guilty will never prosper. They worship alongside God things that can neither harm not benefit them, and say, 'These are our intercessors with God.' Say, 'Do you think you can tell God about something He knows not to exist in the heavens or earth? Glory be to Him! He is far above the partner-gods they associate with Him! All people were originally one single community, but later they differed. If it had not been for a word from your Lord, the preordained judgement would already have been passed between them regarding their differences. They say, 'Why has no miraculous sign been sent down to him from his Lord?' Say [Prophet], 'Only God knows the unseen, so wait—I too am waiting.' No sooner do We let people taste some mercy after some hardship has afflicted them, than they begin to scheme against Our revelations. Say, 'God schemes even faster.' Our messengers[3] record all your scheming.

It is He who enables you to travel on land and sea until, when you are sailing on ships and rejoicing in the favouring wind, a storm arrives: waves come at those on board from all sides and they feel there is no escape. Then they pray to God, professing sincere devotion to Him, 'If You save us from this we shall

2. This phrase, taken from "The Opening," is repeated several times in each one of the five prescribed daily prayers.

3. That is, angels (in Greek, *angeloi*).

be truly thankful.' Yet no sooner does He save them than, back on land, they behave outrageously against all that is right. People! Your outrageous behaviour only works against yourselves. Take your little enjoyment in this present life; in the end you will return to Us and We shall confront you with everything you have done.

The life of this world is like this: rain that We send down from the sky is absorbed by the plants of the earth, from which humans and animals eat. But when the earth has taken on its finest appearance, and adorns itself, and its people think they have power over it, then the fate We commanded comes to it, by night or by day, and We reduce it to stubble, as if it had not flourished just the day before. This is the way We explain the revelations for those who reflect.

But God invites [everyone] to the Home of Peace, and guides whoever He will to a straight path. Those who did well will have the best reward and more besides. Neither darkness nor shame will cover their faces: these are the companions in Paradise, and there they will remain. As for those who did evil, each evil deed will be requited by its equal and humiliation will cover them—no one will protect them against God—as though their faces were covered with veils cut from the darkness of the night. These are the inmates of the Fire, and there they shall remain.

On the Day We gather them all together, We shall say to those who associate partners with God, 'Stay in your place, you and your partner-gods.' Then We shall separate them, and their partner-gods will say, 'It was not us you worshipped—God is witness enough between us and you—we had no idea that you worshipped us.' Every soul will realize, then and there, what it did in the past. They will be returned to God, their rightful Lord, and their invented [gods] will desert them.

Say [Prophet], 'Who provides for you from the sky and the earth? Who controls hearing and sight? Who brings forth the living from the dead and the dead from the living, and who governs everything?' They are sure to say, 'God.' Then say, 'So why do you not take heed of Him? That is God, your Lord, the Truth. Apart from the Truth, what is there except error? So how is it that you are dissuaded?' In this way, your Lord's word about those who defy [the Truth] has been proved—they do not believe. Ask them, 'Can any of your partner-gods originate creation, then bring it back to life again in the end?' Say, 'It is God that originates creation, and then brings it back to life, so how can you be misled?' Say, 'Can any of your partner-gods show the way to the Truth?' Say, 'God shows the way to the Truth. Is someone who shows the way to the Truth more worthy to be followed, or someone who cannot find the way unless he himself is shown? What is the matter with you? How do you judge?' Most of them follow nothing but assumptions, but assumptions can be of no value at all against the Truth: God is well aware of what they do.

Nor could this Qur'an have been devised by anyone other than God. It is a confirmation of what was revealed before it and an explanation of the Scripture—let there be no doubt about it—it is from the Lord of the Worlds. Or do they say, 'He has devised it'? Say, 'Then produce a sura like it, and call on anyone you can beside God if you are telling the truth.'[4] But they are denying what

---

4. This challenge is based on literary merit: the Qur'an dares any poet to match the eloquence of a single sura.

they cannot comprehend—its prophecy has yet to be fulfilled for them. In the same way, those before them refused to believe—see what was the end of those evildoers!

Some of them believe in it, and some do not: your Lord knows best those who cause corruption. If they do not believe you, [Prophet], say, 'I act for myself, and you for yourselves. You are not responsible for my actions nor am I responsible for yours.' Some of them do listen to you: but can you make the deaf hear if they will not use their minds? Some of them look at you: but can you guide the blind if they will not see? God does not wrong people at all—it is they who wrong themselves.

On the Day He gathers them together, it will be as if they have stayed [in the world] no longer than a single hour, and they will recognize one another. Those who denied the meeting with God will be the losers, for they did not follow the right guidance. Whether We let you [Prophet] see some of the punishment We have threatened them with, or cause you to die [first], they will return to Us: God is witness to what they do. Every community is sent a messenger, and when their messenger comes, they will be judged justly; they will not be wronged. They ask, 'When will this promise be fulfilled, if what you say is true?' Say [Prophet], 'I cannot control any harm or benefit that comes to me, except as God wills. There is an appointed term for every community, and when it is reached they can neither delay not hasten it, even for a moment.' Say, 'Think: if His punishment were to come to you, during the night or day, what part of it would the guilty wish to hasten? Will you believe in it, when it actually happens?' It will be said, 'Now [you believe], when [before] you sought to hasten it?' It will be said to the evildoers, 'Taste lasting punishment. Why should you be rewarded for anything but what you did?'

They ask you [Prophet], 'Is it true?' Say, 'Yes, by my Lord, it is true, and you cannot escape it.' Every soul that has done evil, if it possessed all that is on the earth, would gladly offer it as ransom. When they see the punishment, they will repent in secret, but they will be judged with justice and will not be wronged. It is to God that everything in the heavens and the earth truly belongs: God's promise is true, but most people do not realize it. It is He who gives life and takes it, and you will all be returned to Him.

People, a teaching from your Lord has come to you, a healing for what is in [your] hearts, and guidance and mercy for the believers. Say [Prophet], 'In God's grace and mercy let them rejoice: these are better than all they accumulate.' Say, 'Think about the provision God has sent down for you, some of which you have made unlawful and some lawful.' Say, 'Has God given you permission [to do this], or are you inventing lies about God?' What will those people who invent lies about Him think on the Day of Resurrection? God is bountiful towards people, but most of them do not give thanks.

In whatever matter you [Prophet] may be engaged and whatever part of the Qur'an you are reciting, whatever work you [people] are doing, we witness you when you are engaged in it. Not even the weight of a speck of dust in the earth or sky escapes your Lord, nor anything lesser or greater: it is all written in a clear record. But for those who are on God's side there is no fear, nor shall they grieve. For those who believe and are conscious of God, for them there is good news in this life and in the Hereafter—there is no changing the promises of God—that is truly the supreme triumph. Do not let their words grieve you

[Prophet]. Power belongs entirely to God; He hears all and knows all; indeed, all who are in the heavens and on the earth belong to Him. Those who call upon others beside God are not really following partner-gods; they are only following assumptions and telling lies. It is He who made the night so that you can rest in it and the daylight so that you can see—there truly are signs in this for those who hear.

They say, 'God has children!' May He be exalted! He is the Self-Sufficient One; everything in the heavens and the earth belongs to Him. You have no authority to say this. How dare you say things about God without any knowledge? Say [Prophet], 'Those who invent lies about God will not prosper.' They may have a little enjoyment in this world, but then they will return to Us. Then We shall make them taste severe punishment for persisting in blasphemy.

Tell them the story of Noah.[5] He said to his people, 'My people, if my presence among you and my reminding you of God's signs is too much for you, then I put my trust in God. Agree on your course of action, you and your partner-gods—do not be hesitant or secretive about it—then carry out your decision on me and give me no respite. But if you turn away, I have asked no reward from you; my reward is with God alone, and I am commanded to be one of those who devote themselves to Him.' But they rejected him. We saved him and those with him on the Ark and let them survive; and We drowned those who denied Our revelations—see what was the end of those who were forewarned!

Then, after him, We sent messengers to their peoples bringing them clear signs. But they would not believe in anything they had already rejected: in this way We seal the hearts of those who are full of hostility. After them We sent Moses and Aaron with Our signs to Pharaoh[6] and his leading supporters, but they acted arrogantly—they were wicked people. When the truth came to them from Us, they said, 'This is blatant sorcery.' Moses said, 'Is this what you say about the Truth when it comes to you? Is this sorcery? Sorcerers never prosper.' They said, 'Have you come to turn us away from the faith we found our fathers following, so that you and your brother can gain greatness in this land? We will never believe in you.' And Pharaoh said, 'Bring me every learned sorcerer.' When the sorcerers came, Moses said to them, 'Throw down whatever you have.' When they did so, Moses said, 'Everything you have brought is sorcery and God will show it to be false. God does not make the work of mischief-makers right; He will uphold the Truth with His words, even if the evildoers hate it.' But no one believed in Moses except a few of his own people, for fear that Pharaoh and their leaders would persecute them: Pharaoh was domineering in the land and prone to excess.

Moses said, 'My people, if you have faith in God and are devoted to Him, put your trust in Him.' They said, 'We have put our trust in God. Lord! Do not make us an object of persecution for the oppressors. Save us, in Your mercy, from those who reject [Your message].' We revealed to Moses and his brother: 'House your people in Egypt and make these houses places of worship; keep up the prayer; give good news to the believers!' And Moses said, 'Our Lord, You have given Pharaoh and his chiefs splendour and wealth in this present life and here they are, Lord, leading others astray from Your path. Our Lord, obliterate

5. Compare Genesis 5.28–9.29.   6. Compare Exodus 6.26–14.31.

their wealth and harden their hearts so that they do not believe until they see the agonizing torment.' God said, 'Your prayers are answered, so stay on the right course, and do not follow the path of those who do not know.'

We took the Children of Israel across the sea. Pharaoh and his troops pursued them in arrogance and aggression. But as he was drowning he cried, 'I believe there is no God except the one the Children of Israel believe in. I submit to Him.' 'Now? When you had always been a rebel, and a troublemaker! Today We shall save only your corpse as a sign to all posterity. A great many people fail to heed Our signs.' We settled the Children of Israel in a good place and provided good things as sustenance for them. It was only after knowledge had come to them that they began to differ among themselves. Your Lord will judge between them on the Day of Resurrection regarding their differences.

So if you [Prophet] are in doubt about what We have revealed to you, ask those who have been reading the scriptures before you. The Truth has come to you from your Lord, so be in no doubt and do not deny God's signs—then you would become one of the losers. Those against whom your Lord's sentence is passed will not believe, even if every sign comes to them, until they see the agonizing torment. If only a single town had believed and benefited from its belief! Only Jonah's people did so, and when they believed, We relieved them of the punishment of disgrace in the life of this world, and let them enjoy life for a time. Had your Lord willed, all the people on earth would have believed. So can you [Prophet] compel people to believe? No soul can believe except by God's will, and He brings disgrace on those who do not use their reason. Say, 'Look at what is in the heavens and on the earth.' But what use are signs and warnings to people who will not believe? What are they waiting for but the punishment that came to those before them? Say, 'Wait then, I am waiting too.' In the end We shall save Our messengers and the believers. We take it upon Ourself to save the believers.

[Prophet] say, 'People, even if you are in doubt about my religion, I do not worship those you worship other than God, but I worship God who will cause you to die, and I am commanded to be a believer.' [Prophet], set your face towards religion as a man of pure faith. Do not be one of those who join partners with God; do not pray to any other [god] that can neither benefit nor harm you: if you do, you will be one of the evildoers. If God inflicts harm on you, no one can remove it but Him, and if He intends good for you, no one can turn His bounty away; He grants His bounty to any of His servants He will. He is the Most Forgiving, the Most Merciful. Say, 'People, the Truth has come to you from your Lord. Whoever follows the right path follows it for his own good, and whoever strays does so to his own loss: I am not your guardian.' [Prophet], follow what is being revealed to you, and be steadfast until God gives His judgement, for He is the Best of Judges.

12. Joseph

In the name of God, the Lord of Mercy, the Giver of Mercy

Alif Lam Ra

These are the verses of the Scripture that makes things clear—We have sent it down as an Arabic Qur'an so that you [people] may understand.

We tell you [Prophet] the best of stories in revealing this Qur'an to you. Before this you were one of those who knew nothing about them. Joseph said to his father,[1] 'Father, I dreamed of eleven stars and the sun and the moon: I saw them all bow down before me,' and he replied, 'My son, tell your brothers nothing of this dream, or they may plot to harm you—Satan is man's sworn enemy. This is about how your Lord will choose you, teach you to interpret dreams, and perfect His blessing on you and the House of Jacob, just as He perfected it earlier on your forefathers Abraham and Isaac:[2] your Lord is all knowing and wise.'

There are lessons in the story of Joseph and his brothers for all who seek them. The brothers said [to each other], 'Although we are many, Joseph and his brother are dearer to our father than we are—our father is clearly in the wrong.' [One of them said], 'Kill Joseph or banish him to another land, and your father's attention will be free to turn to you. After that you can be righteous.' [Another of them] said, 'Do not kill Joseph, but, if you must, throw him into the hidden depths of a well where some caravan may pick him up.'

They said to their father, 'Why do you not trust us with Joseph? We wish him well. Send him with us tomorrow and he will enjoy himself and play—we will take good care of him.' He replied, 'The thought of you taking him away with you worries me: I am afraid a wolf may eat him when you are not paying attention.' They said, 'If a wolf were to eat him when there are so many of us, we would truly be losers!'

Then they took him away with them, resolved upon throwing him into the hidden depths of a well—We inspired him, saying, 'You will tell them of all this [at a time] when they do not realize [who you are]!'—and at nightfall they returned to their father weeping. They said, 'We went off racing one another, leaving Joseph behind with our things, and a wolf ate him. You will not believe us, though we are telling the truth!' and they showed him his shirt, deceptively stained with blood. He cried, 'No! Your souls have prompted you to do wrong! But it is best to be patient: from God alone I seek help to bear what you are saying.'

Some travellers came by. They sent someone to draw water and he let down his bucket. 'Good news!' he exclaimed. 'Here is a boy!' They hid him like a piece of merchandise—God was well aware of what they did—and then sold him for a small price, for a few pieces of silver: so little did they value him.

The Egyptian who bought him said to his wife, 'Look after him well! He may be useful to us, or we may adopt him as a son.' In this way We settled Joseph in that land and later taught him how to interpret dreams: God always prevails in His purpose, though most people do not realize it.

---

1. Compare Genesis 37.9–11.
2. Isaac is Jacob's father, and Abraham is his grandfather; all three are recognized as prophets in Islam.

When he reached maturity, We gave him judgement and knowledge: this is how We reward those who do good. The woman in whose house he was living tried to seduce him:[3] she bolted the doors and said, 'Come to me,' and he replied, 'God forbid! My master has been good to me; wrongdoers never prosper.' She made for him, and he would have succumbed to her if he had not seen evidence of his Lord—We did this in order to keep evil and indecency away from him, for he was truly one of Our chosen servants. They raced for the door—she tore his shirt from behind—and at the door they met her husband. She said, 'What, other than prison or painful punishment, should be the reward of someone who tried to dishonour your wife?' but he said, 'She tried to seduce me.' A member of her household suggested, 'If his shirt is torn at the front, then it is she who is telling the truth and he who is lying, but if it is torn at the back, then she is lying and he is telling the truth.' When the husband saw that the shirt was torn at the back, he said, 'This is another instance of women's treachery: your treachery is truly great. Joseph, overlook this; but you [wife], ask forgiveness for your sin—you have done wrong.'

Some women of the city said, 'The governor's wife is trying to seduce her slave! Love for him consumes her heart! It is clear to us that she has gone astray.' When she heard their malicious talk, she prepared a banquet and sent for them, giving each of them a knife. She said to Joseph, 'Come out and show yourself to them!' and when the women saw him, they were stunned by his beauty, and cut their hands, exclaiming, 'Great God! He cannot be mortal! He must be a precious angel!' She said, 'This is the one you blamed me for. I tried to seduce him and he wanted to remain chaste, but if he does not do what I command now, he will be put in prison and degraded.' Joseph said, 'My Lord! I would prefer prison to what these women are calling me to do. If You do not protect me from their treachery, I shall yield to them and do wrong,' and his Lord answered his prayer and protected him from their treachery—He is the All Hearing, the All Knowing.

In the end they thought it best, after seeing all the signs of his innocence, that they should imprison him for a while. Two young men went into prison alongside him. One of them said, 'I dreamed that I was pressing grapes'; the other said, 'I dreamed that I was carrying bread on my head and that the birds were eating it.' [They said], 'Tell us what this means—we can see that you are a knowledgeable man.'

He said, 'I can tell you what this means before any meal arrives: this is part of what my Lord has taught me. I reject the faith of those who disbelieve in God and deny the life to come, and I follow the faith of my forefathers Abraham, Isaac, and Jacob. Because of God's grace to us and to all mankind, we would never worship anything beside God, but most people are ungrateful. Fellow prisoners, would many diverse gods be better than God the One, the All Powerful? [No indeed!] All those you worship instead of Him are mere names you and your forefathers have invented, names for which God has sent down no sanction. Authority belongs to God alone, and He orders you to worship none but Him: this is the true faith, though most people do not realize it. Fellow prisoners, one of you will serve his master with wine; the other will be crucified and the birds will peck at his head. That is the end of the matter on

---

3. Compare Genesis 39.7–41.45.

which you asked my opinion.' Joseph said to the one he knew would be saved, 'Mention me to your master,' but Satan made him forget to do this, and so Joseph remained in prison for a number of years.

The king said, 'I dreamed about seven fat cows being eaten by seven lean ones; seven green ears of corn and [seven] others withered. Counsellors, if you can interpret dreams, tell me the meaning of my dream.' They said, 'These are confusing dreams and we are not skilled at dream-interpretation,' but the prisoner who had been freed at last remembered [Joseph] and said, 'I shall tell you what this means. Give me leave to go.'

'Truthful Joseph! Tell us the meaning of seven fat cows being eaten by seven lean ones, seven green ears of corn and [seven] others withered, then I can return to the people to inform them.' Joseph said, 'You will sow for seven consecutive years as usual. Store all that you reap, left in the ear, apart from the little you eat. After that will come seven years of hardship which will consume all but a little of what you stored up for them; after that will come a year when the people will have abundant rain and will press grapes.'

The king said, 'Bring him to me,' but when the messenger came to fetch Joseph, he said, 'Go back to your master and ask him about what happened to those women who cut their hands—my Lord knows all about their treachery.' The king asked the women, 'What happened when you tried to seduce Joseph?' They said, 'God forbid! We know nothing bad of him!' and the governor's wife said, 'Now the truth is out: it was I who tried to seduce him—he is an honest man.' [Joseph said, 'This was] for my master to know that I did not betray him behind his back: God does not guide the mischief of the treacherous. I do not pretend to be blameless, for man's very soul incites him to evil unless my Lord shows mercy: He is most forgiving, most merciful.'

The king said, 'Bring him to me: I will have him serve me personally,' and then, once he had spoken with him, 'From now on you will have our trust and favour.' Joseph said, 'Put me in charge of the nation's storehouses: I shall manage them prudently and carefully.' In this way We settled Joseph in that land to live wherever he wished: We grant Our mercy to whoever We will and do not fail to reward those who do good. The reward of the Hereafter is best for those who believe and are mindful of God.

Joseph's brothers came[4] and presented themselves before him. He recognized them—though they did not recognize him—and once he had given them their provisions, he said, 'Bring me the brother [you left with] your father![5] Have you not seen me giving generous measure and being the best of hosts? You will have no more corn from me if you do not bring him to me, and you will not be permitted to approach me.' They said, 'We shall do all we can to persuade his father to send him with us, indeed we shall.' Joseph said to his servants, 'Put their [traded] goods back into their saddlebags, so that they may recognize them when they go back to their family, and [be eager to] return.'

When they returned to their father, they said, 'Father, we have been denied any more corn, but send our brother back with us and we shall be given another measure. We shall guard him carefully.' He said, 'Am I to entrust him to you as I did his brother before? God is the best guardian and the Most Merciful of the

---

4. Compare Genesis 42.3–46.7.
5. Benjamin, Joseph's full brother; his other brothers had different mothers.

merciful.' Then, when they opened their packs, they discovered that their goods had been returned to them and they said, 'Father! We need no more [goods to barter]: look, our goods have been returned to us. We shall get corn for our household; we shall keep our brother safe; we shall be entitled to another camel-load of grain—an extra measure so easily achieved!' He said, 'I will never send him with you, not unless you swear by God that you will bring him back to me if that is humanly possible.' Then, when they had given him their pledge, he said, 'Our words are entrusted to God.' He said, 'My sons, do not enter all by one gate—use different gates. But I cannot help you against the will of God: all power is in God's hands. I trust in Him; let everyone put their trust in Him,' and, when they entered as their father had told them, it did not help them against the will of God, it merely satisfied a wish of Jacob's. He knew well what We had taught him, though most people do not.

Then, when they presented themselves before Joseph, he drew his brother apart and said, 'I am your brother, so do not be saddened by their past actions,' and, once he had given them their provisions, he placed the drinking-cup in his brother's pack. A man called out, 'People of the caravan! You are thieves!' and they turned and said, 'What have you lost?' They replied, 'The king's drinking-cup is missing,' and, 'Whoever returns it will get a camel-load [of grain],' and, 'I give you my word.' They said, 'By God! You must know that we did not come to make mischief in your land: we are no thieves.' They asked them, 'And if we find that you are lying, what penalty shall we apply to you?' and they answered, 'The penalty will be [the enslavement of] the person in whose bag the cup is found: this is how we punish wrongdoers.' [Joseph] began by searching their bags, then his brother's, and he pulled it out from his brother's bag.

In this way We devised a plan for Joseph—if God had not willed it so, he could not have detained his brother as a penalty under the king's law—We raise the rank of whoever We will. Above everyone who has knowledge there is the One who is all knowing.

[His brothers] said, 'If he is a thief then his brother was a thief before him,' but Joseph kept his secrets and did not reveal anything to them. He said, 'You are in a far worse situation. God knows best the truth of what you claim.' They said, 'Mighty governor, he has an elderly father. Take one of us in his place. We can see that you are a very good man.' He replied, 'God forbid that we should take anyone other than the person on whom we found our property: that would be unjust of us.' When they lost hope of [persuading] him, they withdrew to confer with each other: the eldest of them said, 'Do you not remember that your father took a solemn pledge from you in the name of God and before that you failed in your duty with regard to Joseph? I will not leave this land until my father gives me leave or God decides for me—He is the best decider—so go back to your father and say, "Your son stole. We can only tell you what we saw. How could we guard against the unforeseen? Ask in the town where we have been; ask the people of the caravan we travelled with: we are telling the truth."'

Their father said, 'No! Your souls have prompted you to do wrong! But it is best to be patient: may God bring all of them back to me—He alone is the All Knowing, the All Wise,' and he turned away from them, saying, 'Alas for Joseph!' His eyes went white with grief and he was filled with sorrow. They said, 'By God! You will ruin your health if you do not stop thinking of Joseph, or even die.' He said, 'I plead my grief and sorrow before God. I have knowledge from God that you do not have. My sons, go and seek news of Joseph and his brother and do not despair of God's mercy—only disbelievers despair of God's mercy.'

Then, when they presented themselves before Joseph, they said, 'Mighty governor, misfortune has afflicted us and our family. We have brought only a little merchandise, but give us full measure. Be charitable to us: God rewards the charitable.' He said, 'Do you now realize what you did to Joseph and his brother when you were ignorant?' and they cried, 'Could it be that you are Joseph?' He said, 'I am Joseph. This is my brother. God has been gracious to us: God does not deny anyone who is mindful of God and steadfast in adversity the rewards of those who do good.' They said, 'By God! God really did favour you over all of us and we were in the wrong!' but he said, 'You will hear no reproaches today. May God forgive you: He is the Most Merciful of the merciful. Take my shirt and lay it over my father's face: he will recover his sight. Then bring your whole family back to me.'

Later, when the caravan departed, their father said, 'You may think I am senile but I can smell Joseph,' but [people] said, 'By God! You are still lost in that old illusion of yours!' Then, when the bearer of good news came and placed the shirt on to Jacob's face, his eyesight returned and he said, 'Did I not tell you that I have knowledge from God that you do not have?' The [brothers] said, 'Father, ask God to forgive our sins—we were truly in the wrong.' He replied, 'I shall ask my Lord to forgive you: He is the Most Forgiving, the Most Merciful.'

Later, when they presented themselves before Joseph, he drew his parents to him—he said, 'Welcome to Egypt: you will all be safe here, God willing'—and took them up to [his] throne. They all bowed down before him and he said, 'Father, this is the fulfilment of that dream I had long ago. My Lord has made it come true and has been gracious to me—He released me from prison and He brought you here from the desert—after Satan sowed discord between me and my brothers. My Lord is most subtle in achieving what He will; He is the All Knowing, the Truly Wise. My Lord! You have given me authority; You have taught me something about the interpretation of dreams; Creator of the heavens and the earth, You are my protector in this world and in the Hereafter. Let me die in true devotion to You. Join me with the righteous.'

This account is part of what was beyond your knowledge [Muhammad]. We revealed it to you: you were not present with Joseph's brothers when they made their treacherous plans. However eagerly you may want them to, most men will not believe. You ask no reward from them for this: it is a reminder for all people and there are many signs in the heavens and the earth that they pass by and give no heed to—most of them will only believe in God while also joining others with Him. Are they so sure that an overwhelming punishment from God will not fall on them, or that the Last Hour will not come upon them suddenly when they least expect it? Say, 'This is my way: based on clear evidence, I, and all who follow me, call [people] to God—glory be to God!—I do not join others with Him.'

All the messengers We sent before you [Muhammad] were men to whom We made revelations, men chosen from the people of their towns. Have the [disbelievers] not travelled through the land and seen the end of those who went before them? For those who are mindful of God, the Home in the Hereafter is better. Do you [people] not use your reason? When the messengers lost all hope and realized that they had been dismissed as liars, Our help came to them: We saved whoever We pleased, but Our punishment will not be turned away from guilty people. There is a lesson in the stories of such people for those who understand. This revelation is no fabrication: it is a confirmation of the truth of what was sent before it; an explanation of everything; a guide and a blessing for those who believe.

19. Mary

In the name of God, the Lord of Mercy, the Giver of Mercy

Kaf Ha Ya 'Ayn Sad

This is an account of your Lord's grace towards His servant, Zachariah,[1] when he called to his Lord secretly, saying, 'Lord, my bones have weakened and my hair is ashen grey, but never, Lord, have I ever prayed to You in vain: I fear [what] my kinsmen [will do] when I am gone, for my wife is barren, so grant me a successor—a gift from You—to be my heir and the heir of the family of Jacob. Lord, make him well pleasing [to You].' 'Zachariah, We bring you good news of a son whose name will be John—We have chosen this name for no one before him.' He said, 'Lord, how can I have a son when my wife is barren, and I am old and frail?' He said, 'This is what your Lord has said: "It is easy for Me: I created you, though you were nothing before."'

He said, 'Give me a sign, Lord.' He said, 'Your sign is that you will not [be able to] speak to anyone for three full [days and] nights.' He went out of the sanctuary to his people and signalled to them to praise God morning and evening.

[We said], 'John, hold on to the Scripture firmly.' While he was still a boy, We granted him wisdom, tenderness from Us, and purity. He was devout, kind to his parents, not domineering or rebellious. Peace was on him the day he was born, the day he died, and it will be on him the day he is raised to life again.

Mention in the Qur'an the story of Mary. She withdrew from her family to a place to the east and secluded herself away; We sent Our Spirit to appear before her in the form of a perfected man. She said, 'I seek the Lord of Mercy's protection against you: if you have any fear of Him [do not approach]!' but he said, 'I am but a Messenger from your Lord, [come] to announce to you the gift of a pure son.' She said, 'How can I have a son when no man has touched me? I have not been unchaste,' and he said, 'This is what your Lord said: "It is easy for Me—We shall make him a sign to all people, a blessing from Us."' And so it was ordained: she conceived him. She withdrew to a distant place and, when the pains of childbirth drove her to [cling to] the trunk of a palm tree, she exclaimed, 'I wish I had been dead and forgotten long before all this!' but a voice cried to her from below, 'Do not worry: your Lord has provided a stream at your feet and, if you shake the trunk of the palm tree towards you, it will deliver fresh ripe dates for you, so eat, drink, be glad, and say to anyone you may see: "I have vowed to the Lord of Mercy to abstain from conversation, and I will not talk to anyone today."'

She went back to her people carrying the child, and they said, 'Mary! You have done something terrible! Sister of Aaron! Your father was not an evil man;

---

1. Compare Luke 1.5–64.

your mother was not unchaste!' She pointed at him. They said, 'How can we converse with an infant?' [But] he said: 'I am a servant of God. He has granted me the Scripture; made me a prophet; made me blessed wherever I may be. He commanded me to pray, to give alms as long as I live, to cherish my mother. He did not make me domineering or graceless. Peace was on me the day I was born, and will be on me the day I die and the day I am raised to life again.' Such was Jesus, son of Mary.

[This is] a statement of the Truth about which they are in doubt: it would not befit God to have a child. He is far above that: when He decrees something, He says only, 'Be,' and it is. 'God is my Lord and your Lord, so serve Him: that is a straight path.' But factions have differed among themselves. What suffering will come to those who obscure the truth when a dreadful Day arrives! How sharp of hearing, how sharp of sight they will be when they come to Us, although now they are clearly off course! Warn them [Muhammad] of the Day of Remorse when the matter will be decided, for they are heedless and do not believe. It is We who will inherit the earth and all who are on it: they will all be returned to Us.

Mention too, in the Qur'an, the story of Abraham. He was a man of truth, a prophet. He said to his father, 'Father, why do you worship something that can neither hear nor see nor benefit you in any way? Father, knowledge that has not reached you has come to me, so follow me: I will guide you to an even path. Father, do not worship Satan—Satan has rebelled against the Lord of Mercy. Father, I fear that a punishment from the Lord of Mercy may afflict you and that you may become Satan's companion [in Hell].' His father answered, 'Abraham, do you reject my gods? I will stone you if you do not stop this. Keep out of my way!' Abraham said, 'Peace be with you: I will beg my Lord to forgive you—He is always gracious to me—but for now I will leave you, and the idols you all pray to, and I will pray to my Lord and trust that my prayer will not be in vain.' When he left his people and those they served beside God, We granted him Isaac and Jacob and made them both prophets: We granted Our grace to all of them, and gave them a noble reputation.

Mention too, in the Qur'an, the story of Moses. He was specially chosen, a messenger and a prophet: We called to him from the right-hand side of the mountain and brought him close to Us in secret communion; out of Our grace We granted him his brother Aaron as a prophet. Mention too, in the Qur'an, the story of Ishmael.[2] He was true to his promise, a messenger and a prophet. He commanded his household to pray and give alms, and his Lord was well pleased with him. Mention too, in the Qur'an, the story of Idris.[3] He was a man of truth, a prophet. We raised him to a high position.

These were the prophets God blessed—from the seed of Adam, of those We carried in the Ark with Noah, from the seed of Abraham and Israel—and those We guided and chose. When the revelations of the Lord of Mercy were recited to them, they fell to their knees and wept, but there came after them generations who neglected prayer and were driven by their own desires. These will come face to face with their evil, but those who repent, who believe, who do righteous deeds, will enter Paradise. They will not be wronged in the least:

---

2. The first son of Abraham, the older half-brother of Isaac.
3. Unlike the earlier prophets mentioned,

Idris appears in neither the Hebrew Bible nor the Gospels.

they will enter the Gardens of Lasting Bliss, promised by the Lord of Mercy to His servants—it is not yet seen but truly His promise will be fulfilled. There they will hear only peaceful talk, nothing bad; there they will be given provision morning and evening. That is the Garden We shall give as their own to those of Our servants who were devout.

[Gabriel[4] said], 'We only descend [with revelation] at your Lord's command—everything before us, everything behind us, everything in between, all belongs to Him—your Lord is never forgetful. He is Lord of the heavens and earth and everything in between so worship Him: be steadfast in worshipping Him. Do you know of anyone equal to Him?'

Man says, 'What? Once I am dead, will I be brought back to life?' but does man not remember that We created him when he was nothing before? By your Lord [Prophet] We shall gather them and the devils together and set them on their knees around Hell; We shall seize out of each group those who were most disobedient towards the Lord of Mercy—We know best who most deserves to burn in Hell—but every single one of you will approach it, a decree from your Lord which must be fulfilled. We shall save the devout and leave the evildoers there on their knees.

When Our revelations are recited to them in all their clarity, [all that] the disbelievers say to the believers [is], 'Which side is better situated? Which side has the better following?' We have destroyed many a generation before them who surpassed them in riches and outward glitter! Say [Prophet], 'The Lord of Mercy lengthens [the lives] of the misguided, until, when they are confronted with what they have been warned about—either the punishment [in this life] or the Hour [of Judgement]—they realize who is worse situated and who has the weakest forces.' But God gives more guidance to those who are guided, and good deeds of lasting merit are best and most rewarding in your Lord's sight. Have you considered the man who rejects Our revelation, who says, 'I will certainly be given wealth and children'? Has he penetrated the unknown or received a pledge to that effect from the Lord of Mercy? No! We shall certainly record what he says and prolong his punishment: We shall inherit from him all that he speaks of and he will come to Us all alone.

They have taken other gods beside God to give them strength, but these gods will reject their worship and will even turn against them. Have you [Prophet] not seen how We send devils to incite the disbelievers to sin? There is no need for you to be impatient concerning them: We are counting down their [allotted] time. On the Day We gather the righteous as an honoured company before the Lord of Mercy and drive the sinful like a thirsty herd into Hell, no one will have power to intercede except for those who have permission from the Lord of Mercy.

The disbelievers say, 'The Lord of Mercy has offspring.'[5] How terrible is this thing you assert: it almost causes the heavens to be torn apart, the earth to split asunder, the mountains to crumble to pieces, that they attribute offspring to the Lord of Mercy. It does not befit the Lord of Mercy [to have offspring]: there is no one in the heavens or earth who will not come to the Lord of Mercy

---

4. In Christian tradition, an angel important as the messenger who came to Mary to announce that she would give birth to Jesus (Luke 1.26; cf. 1.19); in Islamic tradition, the messenger who delivers the Qur'an to Muhammad.

5. A reference not to the Christian belief that Jesus is the Son of God—a view criticized elsewhere in the Qur'an—but to the belief in pre-Islamic Arabia that the angels were the daughters of God.

as a servant—He has counted them all: He has numbered them exactly—and they will each return to Him on the Day of Resurrection all alone.

But the Lord of Mercy will give love to those who believe and do righteous deeds: We have made it easy, in your own language [Prophet], so that you may bring glad news to the righteous and warnings to a stubborn people. How many generations We have destroyed before them! Do you perceive a single one of them now, or hear as much as a whisper?

55. The Lord of Mercy

In the name of God, the Lord of Mercy, the Giver of Mercy

It is the Lord of Mercy who taught the Qur'an. He created man and taught him to communicate. The sun and the moon follow their calculated courses; the plants and the trees submit[1] to His designs; He has raised up the sky. He has set the balance so that you may not exceed in the balance: weigh with justice and do not fall short in the balance. He set down the Earth for His creatures, with its fruits, its palm trees with sheathed clusters, its husked grain, its fragrant plants. Which, then, of your Lord's blessings do you both deny?[2]

He created mankind out of dried clay, like pottery, the jinn out of smokeless fire. Which, then, of your Lord's blessings do you both deny?

He is Lord of the two risings and Lord of the two settings.[3] Which, then, of your Lord's blessings do you both deny?

He released the two bodies of [fresh and salt] water. They meet, yet there is a barrier between them they do not cross. Which, then, of your Lord's blessings do you both deny?

Pearls come forth from them: large ones, and small, brilliant ones. Which, then, of your Lord's blessings do you both deny?

His are the moving ships that float, high as mountains, on the sea. Which, then, of your Lord's blessings do you both deny?

Everyone on earth perishes; all that remains is the Face of your Lord, full of majesty, bestowing honour. Which, then, of your Lord's blessings do you both deny?

Everyone in heaven and earth entreats Him; every day He is at work. Which, then, of your Lord's blessings do you both deny?

We shall attend to you two huge armies [of jinn and mankind]. Which, then, of your Lord's blessings do you both deny?

Jinn and mankind, if you can pass beyond the regions of heaven and earth, then do so: you will not pass without Our authority. Which, then, of your Lord's blessings do you both deny?

A flash of fire and smoke will be released upon you and no one will come to your aid. Which, then, of your Lord's blessings do you both deny?

When the sky is torn apart and turns crimson, like red hide. Which, then, of your Lord's blessings do you both deny?

On that Day neither mankind nor jinn will be asked about their sins. Which, then, of your Lord's blessings do you both deny?

1. Literally, to bow down or submit (sajada).
2. "Both" is usually interpreted as humans and jinn (supernatural creatures also constrained by divine law).

3. The rising of the sun and the moon, or perhaps the farthest points of sunrise and sunset in summer and winter; an image of opposition and symmetry.

The guilty will be known by their mark and will be seized by their foreheads and their feet. Which, then, of your Lord's blessings do you both deny?

This is the Hell the guilty deny, but they will go round between its flames and scalding water. Which, then, of your Lord's blessings do you both deny?

For those who fear [the time when they will] stand before their Lord there are two gardens. Which, then, of your Lord's blessings do you both deny?

With shading branches. Which, then, of your Lord's blessings do you both deny?

With a pair of flowing springs. Which, then, of your Lord's blessings do you both deny?

With every kind of fruit in pairs. Which, then, of your Lord's blessings do you both deny?

They will sit on couches upholstered with brocade, the fruit of both gardens within easy reach. Which, then, of your Lord's blessings do you both deny?

There will be maidens restraining their glances, untouched beforehand by man or jinn. Which, then, of your Lord's blessings do you both deny?

Like rubies and brilliant pearls. Which, then, of your Lord's blessings do you both deny?

Shall the reward of good be anything but good? Which, then, of your Lord's blessings do you both deny?

There are two other gardens below these two.[4] Which, then, of your Lord's blessings do you both deny?

Both of deepest green. Which, then, of your Lord's blessings do you both deny?

With a pair of gushing springs. Which, then, of your Lord's blessings do you both deny?

With fruits—date palms and pomegranate trees. Which, then, of your Lord's blessings do you both deny?

There are good-natured, beautiful maidens. Which, then, of your Lord's blessings do you both deny?

Dark-eyed, sheltered in pavilions. Which, then, of your Lord's blessings do you both deny?

Untouched beforehand by man or jinn. Which, then, of your Lord's blessings do you both deny?

They will all sit on green cushions and fine carpets. Which, then, of your Lord's blessings do you both deny? Blessed is the name of your Lord, full of majesty, bestowing honour.

112. Purity [of Faith]

In the name of God, the Lord of Mercy, the Giver of Mercy

Say, 'He is God the One, God the eternal.[1] He begot no one nor was He begotten. No one is comparable to Him.'

---

4. The Islamic paradise has several ranks or levels, into which believers are to be placed after death according to their degree of merit; compare Dante's Paradiso for an adaptation of the structure of the Islamic paradise within a Christian framework.

1. The word here translated as "eternal" (samad) is sometimes rendered "self-sufficient" or "self-contained."

IBN ISHAQ

704–767

Already during the lifetime of Muhammad, oral traditions concerning his life were being eagerly transmitted among members of the newly formed Islamic community. Not until about a century later, however, were these traditions gathered together into a single narrative: Ibn Ishaq's *Path of the Prophet of God*. The term *sira* in Ibn Ishaq's title, usually translated as "life" or "biography" (as in the translation excerpted below, *The Biography of the Prophet*), literally means "path," a word that more accurately captures the purpose of the account. The Prophet's path is the road that every Muslim must try to travel, living an upright and faithful life and following (in the words of the opening chapter of the **Qur'an**) "the straight path" (*sira*). Yet the *Path of the Prophet of God* also has a second function, as it narrates not just the life of one person—the Prophet Muhammad—but also the life of the community, illustrating how its numbers grew and how conversion was able to bring widely disparate peoples into the capacious fold of Islam.

Muhammad ibn Ishaq ibn Yasar, usually known as Ibn Ishaq ("son of Isaac"), was the grandson of a slave who, upon conversion to Islam, became a free man. He wrote several works, but only the *Path* has survived—and only indirectly. One of Ibn Ishaq's pupils wrote an adaptation of the *Path*, now also lost, that was reedited in the ninth century by Ibn Hisham (d. 833). A second version of the *Path*, produced by another pupil of Ibn Ishaq, survives in extracts quoted in the universal history completed around 915 by at-Tabari. The two versions largely coincide, though a number of

episodes in at-Tabari's are missing from Ibn Hisham's. The *Path* is of interest on a number of levels—historical, devotional, and literary. For our purposes, the work is most remarkable as an instance of a very special mode of biography. It seeks to narrate the life not just of a famous or great man, but of *the* man: that is, Muhammad seen in his role not as deliverer of the Qur'an but as the exemplar for every human being.

At the time of Muhammad's death, the Muslim community—originally organized tightly around family and tribal loyalties—had expanded to cover almost all of the Arabian Peninsula and was on the verge of exploding outward into the great civilizations of Persia and Egypt. As it grew increasingly diverse, it needed a language in which to express the openness of Islam to all of humanity. Ibn Ishaq's *Path of the Prophet of God* provided exactly this language, offering a number of models of conversion ranging from members of Muhammad's own family to individuals born in lands distant from Mecca or Medina. The narrative of Salman the Persian, which appears early in the *Path*, makes clear the ways in which a person far removed from the tribes of Arabia can not only become a member of the Muslim community but actually be accepted into the household of Muhammad himself. In a famous hadith or traditional saying, Muhammad is said to have intervened when the Muslims of Mecca and the Muslims of Medina argued over who could claim Salman as their own adopted fellow, declaring, "He is one of us, one of the People of the House (Ahl al-Bayt)."

The story of Salman the Persian has two messages. It both makes clear the openness of the Muslim community to foreigners and emphasizes the superiority of Islam to the monotheistic religions that had come before it, including Zoroastrianism, the national religion of Persia (modern Iran), as well as Judaism and Christianity. The other conversion stories narrated in the *Path* have similarly complex messages. The story of the first convert to Islam, Muhammad's wife Khadijah, is significant in highlighting the role of women in the initial reception of the divine message. Much as the Gospels' account of the resurrection of Jesus stresses the faithful female disciples who wait outside the tomb, so too Ibn Ishaq's *Path* emphasizes the role of a woman in beginning the process of conversion within the community. Other notable converts include Ali, the first male to embrace Islam, who was Muhammad's cousin and then son-in-law, following his marriage to the Prophet's daughter Fatimah. Muhammad had brought up Ali in his own household, just as Ali's father had brought up Muhammad. The story of Ali's conversion thus provides a striking counterbalance to the story of Salman the Persian: one man coming from the very heart of the new Islamic community, one searching across several lands until finally arriving at his spiritual destination in Mecca. Together, the two accounts would help fuel the rapid rise of Islam within the kingdom of Persia, where the figure of Salman the Persian was immediately revered and the Shi'a branch of Islam, with its special devotion to Ali, would soon rise to prominence.

For the community of Muslims, the Qur'an was a complete guide, but the text was hard to understand and often obscure in its meaning. The life of the Prophet therefore became a kind of manual to the practical experience of life as a Muslim. One could not go wrong as long as one followed carefully in the footsteps of the Prophet, imitating his behaviors great and small and also imitating the behavior of those followers whom Muhammad had praised. The structure of the *Path*, as far as we can reconstruct it from its two surviving versions, seems to have been organically modeled on the lived experience of Muhammad. It opens with his genealogy, which begins with Adam as the first man and the first prophet, and closes with his interment. This structure makes the work into a kind of microcosm of the story of humanity, starting in Eden and ending in the grave. In keeping with the complexity of the *Path*, Ibn Ishaq's description of Muhammad's burial has two purposes, one practical and one literary. It provides a concrete guide to carrying out Islamic funeral rituals, which require burial to take place swiftly and prohibit excessive displays of mourning. But it also makes room for the continued support of the strong pre-Islamic traditions of Arabic poetry, for it includes the verses uttered at the burial ceremony by Hassan ibn Thabit, a Muslim from Medina. Poetry was now integrated within the Muslim community not just through the literary excellence of the Qur'an itself but also in the flowers of literature that would commemorate the seal of prophets, Muhammad.

From The Biography of the Prophet[1]

How Salman[2] Became a Muslim

Asim ibn Umar ibn Qatada al-Ansari told me, on the authority of Mahmud ibn Labid from Abdullah ibn Abbas as follows:[3] Salman said while I listened to his words: "I am a Persian from Ispahan[4] from a village called Jayy. My father was the principal landowner in his village and I was dearer to him than the whole world. His love for me went to such lengths that he shut me in his house as though I were a slave girl. I was such a zealous Magian[5] that I became keeper of the sacred fire, replenishing it and not letting it go out for a moment. Now my father owned a large farm, and one day when he could not attend to his farm he told me to go to it and learn about it, giving me certain instructions. 'Do not let yourself be detained,' he said, 'because you are more important to me than my farm and worrying about you will prevent me going about my business.' So I started out for the farm, and when I passed by a Christian church I heard the voices of the men praying. I knew nothing about them because my father kept me shut up in his house. When I heard their voices I went to see what they were doing; their prayers pleased me and I felt drawn to their worship and thought that it was better than our religion, and I decided that I would not leave them until sunset. So I did not go to the farm. When I asked them where their religion originated, they said 'Syria.' I returned to my father who had sent after me because anxiety on my account had interrupted all his work. He asked me where I had been and reproached me for not obeying his instructions. I told him that I had passed by some men who were praying in their church and was so pleased with what I saw of their religion that I stayed with them until sunset. He said, 'My son, there is no good in that religion; the religion of your fathers is better than that.' 'No,' I said, 'It is better than our religion.' My father was afraid of what I would do, so he bound me in fetters and imprisoned me in his house.

"I sent to the Christians and asked them if they would tell me when a caravan of Christian merchants came from Syria. They told me, and I said to them: 'When they have finished their business and want to go back to their own country, ask them if they will take me.' They did so and I cast off the fetters from my feet and went with them to Syria. Arrived there I asked for the most learned person in their religion and they directed me to the bishop. I went to him and told him that I liked his religion and should like to be with him and serve him in his church, to learn from him and to pray with him. He invited me to come in and I did so. Now he was a bad man who used to command people to give alms and induced them to do so and when they brought him money he put it in his own coffers and did not give it to the poor, until he had collected seven jars of gold and silver. I conceived a violent hatred for the man when I saw what he was doing. Sometime later when he died and the Christians came together to bury him I told them that he was a bad man who exhorted them and persuaded them to give alms, and when they brought money put it in his

---

1. Translated by Alfred Guillaume.
2. The first Persian convert to Islam and a major figure in the early history of the religion.
3. By including the names of all those who had passed a story down to him, the author

both asserts and demonstrates the truth of the account.
4. A large city in central Iran.
5. That is, Zoroastrian, a follower of Zoroastrianism, the principal religion of pre-Islamic Iran.

coffers and gave nothing to the poor. They asked how I could possibly know this, so I led them to his treasure and when I showed them the place they brought out seven jars full of gold and silver. As soon as they saw them they said, 'By God, we will never bury the fellow,' so they crucified him and stoned him and appointed another in his place.

"I have never seen any non-Muslim whom I consider more virtuous, more ascetic, more devoted to the next life, and more consistent night and day than he.[6] I loved him as I had never loved anyone before. I stayed with him a long time until when he was about to die I told him how I loved him and asked him to whom he would confide me and what orders he would give me now that he was about to die. He said, 'My dear son, I do not know anyone who is as I am. Men have died and have either altered or abandoned most of their true religion, except a man in Mausil;[7] he follows my faith, so join yourself to him.' So when he died and was buried, I attached myself to the bishop of Mausil telling him that so-and-so had confided me to him when he died and told me that he followed the same path. I stayed with him and found him just as he had been described, but it was not long before he died and I asked him to do for me what his predecessor had done. He replied that he knew of only one man, in Nasibin,[8] who followed the same path and he recommended me to go to him.[9]

"I stayed with this good man in Nasibin for some time and when he died he recommended me to go to a colleague in Ammuriya.[1] I stayed with him for some time and labored until I possessed some cows and a small flock of sheep; then when he was about to die I asked him to recommend me to someone else. He told me that he knew of no one who followed his way of life, but that a prophet was about to arise who would be sent with the religion of Abraham; he would come forth in Arabia and would migrate to a country between two lava belts, between which were palms. He has unmistakable marks. He will eat what is given to him but not things given as alms. Between his shoulders is the seal of prophecy. 'If you are able to go to that country, do so.' Then he died and was buried and I stayed in Ammuriya as long as God willed. Then a party of Kalbite[2] merchants passed by and I asked them to take me to Arabia and I would give them those cows and sheep of mine. They accepted the offer and took me with them until we reached Wadil-Qura,[3] when they sold me to a Jew as a slave. I saw the palm-trees and I hoped that this would be the town which my master had described to me, for I was not certain. Then a cousin of his from Bani Qurayza[4] of Medina came and bought me and carried me away to Medina, and, by God, as soon as I saw it I recognized it from my master's description. I dwelt there and the apostle of God[5] was sent and lived in Mecca; but I did not hear him mentioned because I was fully occupied as a slave. Then he migrated to Medina and as I was in the top of a palm-tree belonging to my master, carrying out my work while my master sat below, suddenly a cousin of

6. The new bishop.
7. A city in northern Iraq.
8. A town in upper Mesopotamia, now part of Turkey.
9. I have abbreviated the repetitive style of the narrative, which is that of popular stories all the world over. The same words, and the same details, occur in each paragraph with the change of names: Mausil, Nasibin, Ammuriya,

leading up to the obvious climax, Muhammad [translator's note].
1. A region in southwestern Turkey, ancient Amorium.
2. From the Bani Kalb, an Arab tribe.
3. A village in northwestern Arabia.
4. A Jewish tribe.
5. Muhammad.

his came up to him and said: 'God smite the Bani Qayla![6] They are gathering at this moment in Quba[7] round a man who has come to them from Mecca today asserting that he is a prophet.'

"When I heard this I was seized with trembling, so that I thought I should fall on my master; so I came down from the palm and began to say to his cousin, 'What did you say? What did you say?' My master was angered and gave me a smart blow, saying, 'What do you mean by this? Get back to your work.' I said, 'Never mind, I only wanted to find out the truth of his report.' Now I had a little food which I had gathered, and I took it that evening to the apostle of God who was in Quba and said, 'I have heard that you are an honest man and that your companions are strangers in want; here is something for alms, for I think that you have more right to it than others.' So I gave it to him. The apostle said to his companions, 'Eat!' but he did not hold out his own hand and did not eat. I said to myself, 'That is one'; then I left him and collected some food and the apostle went to Medina. Then I brought it to him and said, 'I see that you do not eat food given as alms, here is a present which I freely give you.' The apostle ate it and gave his companions some. I said, 'That's two'; then I came to the apostle when he was in Baqiu-l-Gharqad[8] where he had followed the bier of one of his companions. Now I had two cloaks, and as he was sitting with his companions, I saluted him and went round to look at his back so that I could see whether the seal which my master had described to me was there. When the apostle saw me looking at his back he knew that I was trying to find out the truth of what had been described to me, so he threw off his cloak laying bare his back and I looked at the seal and recognized it. Then I bent over him kissing him and weeping. The apostle said, 'Come here'; so I came and sat before him and told him my story as I have told you, O ibn Abbas.[9] The apostle wanted his companions to hear my story." Then servitude occupied Salman so that he could not be at Badr and Uhud[1] with the apostle.

Salman continued: "Then the apostle said to me, 'Write an agreement'; so I wrote to my master agreeing to plant three hundred palm-trees for him, digging out the base, and to pay forty okes[2] of gold. The apostle called on his companions to help me, which they did; one with thirty little palms, another with twenty, another with fifteen, and another with ten, each helping as much as he could until the three hundred were complete. The apostle told me to go and dig the holes for them, saying that when I had done so he would put them in with his own hand. Helped by my companions I dug the holes and came and told him; so we all went out together, and as we brought him the palm shoots he planted them with his own hand; and by God, not one of them died. Thus I had delivered the palm-trees, but the money was still owing. Now the apostle had been given a piece of gold as large as a hen's egg from one of the mines and he summoned me and told me to take it and pay my debt with it. 'How far will this relieve me of my debt, O Apostle of God?' I said. 'Take it,' he replied, 'for God will pay your debt with it.' So I took it and weighed it out to them, and by God, it weighed forty okes, and so I paid my debt with it and Salman was free. I took part with the Apostle in the battle of the Ditch as a free man and thereafter I was at every other battle."

6. A tribe.
7. Near Medina.
8. Medina's cemetery, outside the town.
9. The last person in the chain of transmission before Ibn Ishaq.

1. Sites of two famous battles between Muhammad's followers and the people of Mecca.
2. A measurement of weight; one "oke" is roughly equivalent to one ounce.

Yazid ibn Abu Habib from a man of Abdul-Qays from Salman told me[3] that the latter said: "When I said, 'How far will this relieve me of my debt?' the apostle took it and turned it over upon his tongue, then he said, 'Take it and pay them in full'; so I paid them in full, forty okes."

Asim ibn Umar ibn Qatada on the authority of a trustworthy informant from Umar ibn Abdul-Aziz ibn Marwan said that he was told that Salman the Persian told the apostle that his master in Ammuriya told him to go to a certain place in Syria where there was a man who lived between two thickets. "Every year as he used to go from one to the other, the sick used to stand in his way and everyone he prayed for was healed. He said, 'Ask him about this religion which you seek, for he can tell you of it.' So I went on until I came to the place I had been told of, and I found that people had gathered there with their sick until he came out to them that night passing from one thicket to the other. The people came to him with their sick and everyone he prayed for was healed. They prevented me from getting to him so that I could not approach him until he entered the thicket he was making for, but I took hold of his shoulder. He asked me who I was as he turned to me and I said, 'God have mercy on you, tell me about the Hanifiya,[4] the religion of Abraham.' He replied, 'You are asking about something men do not inquire of today; the time has come near when a prophet will be sent with this religion from the people of the *haram*.[5] Go to him, for he will bring you to it.'" Then he went into the thicket. The apostle said to Salman, "If you have told me the truth, you met Jesus the son of Mary."

* * *

The Beginning of the Sending Down of the Quran

The apostle began to receive revelations in the month of Ramadan.[6] In the words of God, "The month of Ramadan in which the Quran was brought down as a guidance to men, and proofs of guidance and a decisive criterion." And again, "Verily we have sent it down on the night of destiny, and what has shown you what the night of destiny is? The night of destiny is better than a thousand months. In it the angels and the spirit descend by their Lord's permission with every matter. It is peace until the rise of dawn." Again, "by the perspicuous book, verily we have sent it down in a blessed night. Verily, we were warning. In it every wise matter is decided as a command from us. Verily we sent it down." And again, "Had you believed in God and what we sent down to Our servant on the day of decision, the day on which the two parties met," i.e. the meeting of the apostle with the polytheists in Badr. Abu Jafar Muhammad ibn Ali ibn al-Husayn told me that the apostle of God met the polytheists in Badr on the morning of Friday, the 17th of Ramadan.

Then revelation came fully to the apostle while he was believing in Him and in the truth of His message. He received it willingly, and took upon himself what it entailed whether of man's goodwill or anger. Prophecy is a troublesome burden—only strong, resolute messengers can bear it by God's help and grace,

---

3. In other words, Ibn Ishaq heard this thirdhand.
4. The name by which Islam was first known: "those who follow the original true [monotheistic] religion."

5. The sacred shrine in Mecca.
6. The ninth month in the Arabian calendar; in Islam, it became the month of obligatory fasting.

because of the opposition which they meet from men in conveying God's message. The apostle carried out God's orders in spite of the opposition and ill treatment which he met with.

Khadija,[7] Daughter of Khuwaylid, Accepts Islam

Khadija believed in him and accepted as true what he brought from God, and helped him in his work. She was the first to believe in God and His apostle, and in the truth of his message. By her God lightened the burden of His prophet. He never met with contradiction and charges of falsehood, which saddened him, but God comforted him by her when he went home. She strengthened him, lightened his burden, proclaimed his truth, and belittled men's opposition. May God Almighty have mercy upon her!

Hisham ibn Urwa told me on the authority of his father Urwa ibn al-Zubayr from Abdullah ibn Jafar ibn Abu Talib that the apostle said, "I was commanded to give Khadija the good news of a house of *qasab*[8] wherein would be no clamour and no toil."

Then revelations stopped for a time so that the apostle of God was distressed and grieved. Then Gabriel brought him the Sura of the Morning, in which his Lord, who had so honoured him, swore that He had not forsaken him, and did not hate him. God said, "By the morning and the night when it is still, thy Lord hath not forsaken nor hated thee," meaning that He not left you and forsaken you, nor hated you after having loved you. "And verily, the latter end is better for you than the beginning," i.e. What I have for you when you return to Me is better than the honour which I have given you in the world. "And your Lord will give you and will satisfy you," i.e. of victory in this world and reward in the next. "Did he not find you an orphan and give you refuge, going astray and guided you, found you poor and made you rich?" God thus told him of how He had begun to honour him in his earthly life, and of His kindness to him as an orphan poor and wandering astray, and of His delivering him from all that by His compassion.

"Do not oppress the orphan and do not repel the beggar." That is, do not be a tyrant or proud or harsh or mean towards the weakest of God's creatures.

"Speak of the kindness of thy Lord," i.e. tell about the kindness of God in giving you prophecy, mention it and call men to it.

So the apostle began to mention secretly God's kindness to him and to his servants in the matter of prophecy to everyone among his people whom he could trust.

* * *

From Ali ibn Abu Talib,[9] the First Male to Accept Islam

Ali was the first male to believe in the apostle of God, to pray with him and to believe in his divine message, when he was a boy of ten. God favored him in that he was brought up in the care of the apostle before Islam began.

Abdullah ibn Abu Najih on the authority of Mujahid ibn Jabr Abul-Hajjaj told me that God showed His favor and goodwill towards him when a grievous

---

7. Muhammad's first wife.
8. Hollowed pearl.
9. "Ali the son of the father of Talib." Muslims

are often known as the father, or mother, of their first child, especially a son.

famine overtook Quraysh.[1] Now Abu Talib had a large family, and the prophet approached his uncle, Al-Abbas, who was one of the richest of Bani Hashim,[2] suggesting that in view of his large family and the famine which affected everyone, they should go together and offer to relieve him of the burden of some of his family. Al-Abbas agreed, and so they went to Abu Talib offering to relieve him from his responsibility of two boys until conditions improved. Abu Talib said, "Do what you like so long as you leave me Aqil." So the apostle took Ali and kept him with him and Al-Abbas took Jafar. Ali continued to be with the apostle until God sent him forth as a prophet. Ali followed him, believed him, and declared his truth, while Jafar remained with Al-Abbas until he became a Muslim and was independent of him.

A traditionist mentioned that when the time of prayer came the apostle used to go out to the glens of Mecca accompanied by Ali, who went unbeknown to his father, and his uncles and the rest of his people. There they used to pray the ritual prayers, and return at nightfall. This went on as long as God intended that it should, until one day Abu Talib came upon them while they were praying, and said to the apostle, "O nephew, what is this religion which I see you practicing?" He replied, "O uncle, this is the religion of God, His angels, His apostles, and the religion of our father Abraham." Or, as he said, "God has sent me as an apostle to mankind, and you, my uncle, most deserve that I should teach you the truth and call you to guidance, and you are the most worthy to respond and help me," or words to that effect. His uncle replied, "I cannot give up the religion of my fathers which they followed, but by God you shall never meet with anything to distress you so long as I live." They mention that he said to Ali, "My boy, what is this religion of yours?" He answered, "I believe in God and in the apostle of God, and I declare that what he has brought is true, and I pray to God with him and follow him." They allege that he said, "He would not call you to anything but what is good so stick to him."

Zayd, the freedman of the apostle, was the first male to accept Islam after Ali. The Abu Bahr ibn Abu Quhafa,[3] whose name was Atiq, became a Muslim. * * * When he became a Muslim, he showed his faith openly and called others to God and his apostle. He was a man whose society was desired, well liked and of easy manners. He knew more about the genealogy of Quraysh than anyone else and of their faults and merits. He was a merchant of high character and kindliness. His people used to come to him to discuss many matters with him because of his wide knowledge, his experience in commerce, and his sociable nature. He began to call to God and to Islam all whom he trusted of those who came to him and sat with him.

* * *

[The Burial Preparations]

On the same authority I was told that the last injunction the apostle gave was in his words "Let not two religions be left in the Arabian peninsula." The apostle died on the 12th Rabi-ul-awwal on the very day that he came to Medina

1. Muhammad's tribe, from which all caliphs must come.
2. A tribe.
3. A leader of the Quraysh who became the first caliph.

as an emigrant, having completed exactly twelve years in his migration. When the apostle was dead the Muslims were sore stricken. I have heard that Aisha used to say, "When the apostle died the Arabs apostatized and Christianity and Judaism raised their heads and disaffection appeared. The Muslims became as sheep exposed to rain on a winter's night through the loss of their prophet until God united them under Abu Bakr."

Hassan said mourning the apostle:

> Tell the poor that plenty has left them
> With the prophet who departed from them this morning.
> Who was it who has a saddle and a camel for me,
> My family's sustenance when rain fails?
> Or with whom can we argue without anxiety   5
> When the tongue runs away with a man?
> He was the light and the brilliance we followed.
> He was sight and hearing second only to God.
> The day they laid him in the grave
> And cast the earth upon him   10
> Would that God had not left one of us
> And neither man nor woman had survived him!

* * *

Hassan also said:

> I swear that no man is more careful than I
> In swearing an oath true and without falsehood.
> By God, no woman has conceived and given birth
> To one like the apostle the prophet and guide of his people;
> Nor has God created among his creatures   5
> One more faithful to his sojourner or his promise
> Than he who was the source of our light,
> Blessed in his deeds, just, and upright.
> Your wives stripped the tents in mourning
> And did not strike the pegs behind the curtains.   10
> Like nuns they put on garments of hair
> Certain of misery after happiness.
> O best of men, I was as it were in a river
> Without which I have become lonely in my thirst.

BEOWULF

ninth century

Surviving in a single tattered manuscript, its edges burned by fire, *Beowulf* provides a startlingly vivid glimpse into the early medieval past. Written in Old English, with a vocabulary that would have seemed old-fashioned even to its very first audience, the poem recalls a heroic age in which monsters stalked men by night, dragons guarded hoards of precious gems and heirloom swords, and heroes carried out great deeds of warfare that would later be commemorated by song and feasting. The bonds of family and clan give shape to the world of Beowulf and his companions, leading sometimes to the formation of new alliances, sometimes to the violent conflict of blood feud that lasted for generations. Like much Old English poetry, the poem is fundamentally elegiac, celebrating the beauty and mourning the disappearance of a culture that, by the year 1000, had already become part of the past.

The sole surviving copy of *Beowulf* can be dated with some certainty to the years around 1000, a time of rich flowering of Anglo-Saxon literature and learning, expressed in both Old English and Anglo-Latin poetry. Yet this time was also the end of an era, just a few generations before English society would be completely transformed by the Norman Conquest of 1066. The poem thus sums up a particular form of English culture that would very soon vanish. Among the other works included in the manuscript containing *Beowulf* are saints' lives and exotic tales of the Orient: despite their varied genres, all are unified by a common theme of monsters and heroes. The three monsters of *Beowulf*—Grendel, Grendel's mother, and the dragon—and the superhuman hero who fights against them appear beside other examples of nonhuman nature, from the so-called monstrous races encountered by Alexander the Great in the extreme reaches of India to the dog-headed (or "cynocephalic") Saint Christopher. Read in this context, the poem sheds light on the nature of medieval English culture, especially on its ability to integrate pagan Germanic history within the framework of the Christian Middle Ages.

While we can date the manuscript of *Beowulf* to the years around 1000, the poem itself is almost certainly much older—a judgment based on the poem's old-fashioned vocabulary and certain genealogical allusions as well as the manuscript itself, whose copying errors suggest that a long history of transmission lies behind it. Yet the poem in its oral form is even older, drawing on a rich stock of myth and legend that was surely familiar among the northern Germanic peoples who inhabited the regions now known as Scandinavia, the Low Countries, and the British Isles. Those who read *Beowulf* or heard it recited in the eleventh century would have likely recognized allusions to ancient blood feuds and tribal clashes that are only dimly comprehensible to modern readers. The poem appears to be set in the sixth century (in particular, we can date the death of Beowulf's lord, Hygelac, to around 520), and so the story would already have seemed like ancient history to the poem's earliest hearers. To the eleventh-century reader, the events of the poem are thus doubly removed into the past. Like **Homer's *Iliad***, whose written text codifies a much older oral form of the poem, *Beowulf* emerges as a written work of literature only at the end of generations of transmission as song.

Although we are accustomed to thinking of *Beowulf* as an "English" poem, its subject matter is not English people at all: Beowulf himself is a member of the tribe of the Geats, who live in the south of what is now Sweden, and he goes to serve in the court of Hrothgar, king of the Danes. In the period that the poem is set, England was only beginning to be settled by Germanic tribes, which had first invaded the island around 450. For the medieval English person reading the poem around 1000, therefore, the subject matter of the poem would have been at once strange and familiar— made up of persons and places that were remote in space and time from current-day England, but connected to the poem's audience by lines of heritage and descent. This simultaneous sense of strangeness and familiarity would have been heightened by *Beowulf*'s treatment of religion. While the readers and hearers of the poem, beginning in the ninth century and almost certainly earlier, would have brought a Christian perspective to the poem, the characters clearly belong to a pre-Christian world where *wyrd* (fate) governs the events that unfold in the lives of man. Yet the text is careful to maintain ambiguity regarding the role of Christianity in the world of the poem: the monstrous Grendel is said to be one of "Cain's clan," and is thus identified as an outcast from humanity in specifically biblical terms.

Grendel is only the first of three monsters that the hero Beowulf must confront. The initial single combat against this man-beast is quickly succeeded by a similar battle—this time carried out in the watery deeps of a distant wasteland— against Grendel's mother, an even more loathsome creature. After these successes, Beowulf's heroism is acclaimed, he is richly rewarded, and he returns to his own Geatish homeland to eventually

become ruler of his people. Only decades later, in that homeland, does the third episode of combat take place, which pits Beowulf against a fierce dragon guarding a buried hoard of gems and shining weapons. Once again he enters battle alone, but before the struggle ends he is aided by his kinsman and companion Wiglaf. These clashes are among the most gripping scenes of the poem. First the hero wrestles with a dreadful monster who bites through his victim's bones, drinks his blood, and swallows his flesh in great chunks, consuming him "hand and foot." The horror of the confrontation with Grendel's vengeful mother is still greater: she is a "swamp-thing from hell." In Beowulf's final monstrous encounter, the dragon "billowed and spewed" venomous fire, at once burning and poisoning his victim.

Yet Beowulf's horrific enemies are more complex than they might first appear: Grendel is both monster and man, one of the family of Cain. Like Cain himself, he is said to be "God-cursed," and his status as an outcast, cut off from the community of men, makes him seem curiously forlorn, "spurned and joyless." Although he is undoubtedly a monster, Grendel shows human emotions; he is whipped into a blind and jealous fury against those able to enjoy the bonds of family and tribe, who sleep blissfully in the communal space of Heorot's great hall. Similarly, Grendel's mother is driven not just by her monstrous nature but also by a maternal desire to avenge the death of her son— and according to the codes of Germanic tribal society, revenge was an entirely appropriate motive. Even the fight with the dragon is not cast in simple terms: when Beowulf enters his cavernous lair, it is the hero—not the monster—who is identified as the invader, and the dragon is called the "hordweard," or guardian of the hoard. Although one is a man and one is a beast, both are said to be clad in armor, the hero bearing his shield and helm, the dragon his "enameled scales." As the line that separates human from nonhuman is blurred, every violent clash, whether man against man or man against monster, is couched in terms of equivalence and balance.

As vivid as these encounters are, the poem also has an important second level, concerned with the interpersonal ties of kinship and tribe, as well as the voluntary relationship of lord and warrior. We see Beowulf take on a series of roles within this social system. He begins among the Geats as a strong fighter of somewhat marginal status as a nephew of the king, Hygelac; he then is adopted with great honor into the household of Hrothgar, king of the Danes, after defeating Grendel and his mother; and finally Beowulf becomes ruler of the Geats, when Hygelac dies without a male heir. Beowulf appears first as a warrior in the service of his lord, and later as himself a lord—in the language of the poem, a "giver of rings" as well as one who receives them. The relationship of king and warrior is reciprocal, as the warrior provides service while his lord offers protection and distributes wealth, often in the form of armbands or neck torques ("rings"). Yet perhaps the most valuable gift that the lord grants is entrance into the community itself: in *Beowulf*, as in Old English poetry more generally, no burden is heavier than involuntary solitude. The warm bonds of fellowship nurture the warrior, and to be cut off from them is unimaginably bitter. Such isolation afflicts Grendel, as we have seen, and is memorably evoked in the poem's description of how the dragon's golden hoard came into being. It was the accumulated treasure of a long-ago people, the poet says, buried for safekeeping by the last of their line: "Death had come / and taken them all," leaving just one man "deserted and alone, lamenting his unhappiness / day and night." For the despairing

survivor, there is "No trembling harp, / no tuned timber, no tumbling hawk / swerving through the hall." Bereft of the joys of the hall, the only man left alive can do little more than mourn as he waits for death.

The hall offers both the most secure and stable environment that a warrior can possibly inhabit and the culture's greatest point of vulnerability. Beowulf is given the opportunity to display his heroic nature in combat with Grendel because of the need to defend Heorot, the great hall of Hrothgar: the accursed monster has been sneaking into the hall by night, seizing and devouring warriors one by one. The threat is not simply to the lives of Hrothgar's men but to the very basis of the community, as the Danish warriors are reduced to fearful individuals, each concerned for his own life. The great hall of Heorot is a place of communal gathering and feasting, of goodwill and social bonds, where oaths of loyalty are sworn and golden rings are distributed, where heroic deeds are sung and the genealogies of kings recounted. Yet this idyllic space, representing the unity of the king and his people, is only temporary, for the danger posed to Heorot is not erased by the death of Grendel: other threats are darkly foreshadowed in the poem through allusions to the fate of the Danes after Hrothgar's reign ended. For the poem's medieval audiences, these passing references brought to mind the full story of the tragic downfall of Hrothgar's house and the burning of Heorot.

Swords and other weaponry appear throughout the poem, not just as tools of the warfare that punctuates the narrative at regular intervals but as a kind of social glue that links the community of warriors both in the present and across time and space. As treasures are shared, kings disburse weapons along with golden rings, items that are as precious for their ability to create interpersonal connections as for their physical material. Hrothgar's queen, Wealhtheow, rewards Beowulf with a golden collar that marks a new bond of affinity between the Geatish hero and the ruling house of the Danes, accompanying the sumptuous gift with the request that Beowulf do his best to support her young son in the future. The ring thus carries both material and social value, marking a bond of loyalty between persons and groups. Similarly, Hrothgar later rewards Beowulf with magnificent armor, which Beowulf goes on to deliver to his own Geatish lord, Hygelac, just as he also gives to Hygelac's queen, Hygd, the neck ring bestowed on him by Wealhtheow. Beowulf's gifts unite the Danes and the Geats and thereby redouble his own honor. And the connections formed by heirloom weapons can extend far into the past. As Beowulf prepares to battle Grendel's mother, the Danish warrior Unferth lends him "a rare and ancient sword," and he in turn leaves his own weapon, a "sharp-honed, wave-sheened wonder-blade," with the Dane, who may keep it if he fails to return. In the muddy pool where Beowulf defeats Grendel's mother, he finds another blade, whose gold hilt is inscribed with "rune-markings" telling the name of the one "for whom the sword had first been made." This sword, "from the days of the giants," passes through time, wielded by men and by monsters, until it finally comes into the hands of Beowulf, who in turn delivers its remnants to the Danish king Hrothgar. The chain of descent confers glory on the hero, and unites the community of warriors across the ages.

Each of these three ancient swords is described as an heirloom or "ealde lafe": literally, an "old thing that is left," a remainder of past glory. The weapon is thus an instrument of warfare and a symbol of continuity, linking past, present, and future as successive men bear it. Such work of commemoration suffuses the poem, perhaps nowhere more movingly than in the songs of heroes that punctuate the communal celebrations and feasting held in Heorot. Like the "ealde lafe," the heroic song recalls figures of the past and makes them live again as the warriors listen and join in the imagined community of the tribal nation and the symbolic space of the hall. After the defeat of Grendel, Hrothgar's minstrel sings a song of the Frisian king Finn and his Danish wife Hildeburh. The story is tragic, telling of the feud that destroyed their family, but the shared experience of the minstrel's music and tale brings Hrothgar's court together—a sense of community reawakened, perhaps, for the medieval audiences who heard *Beowulf* performed for them.

The translation here, by Seamus Heaney, seeks to reproduce the rhythmic quality of the Old English line—made up of two half-lines, each containing two beats. Coupled with the alliteration (repeated initial consonant sounds) that is prevalent in Old English poetry, the line produces a strong sense of rhythm, a recurrent thrumming sound that gives the poem its songlike quality, impossible to ignore even in written form. To give a clearer sense of the sound of the original work, reproduced at the top of page 112 are the closing lines (2262–69) of the lament of the last survivor, who long ago buried the hoard of treasure guarded by the dragon that is Beowulf's last and most dangerous enemy. Below these lines is a very literal, rhythmic translation that conveys the lines' aural quality more emphatically than does Heaney's version.

TRIBES AND GENEALOGIES

1. The Danes (Bright-, Half-, Ring-, Spear-, North-, East-, South-, West-Danes; Shieldings, Honor-, Victor-, War-Shieldings: Ing's friends).

2. The Geats (Sea-, War-, Weather-Geats).

3. The Swedes

*The daughter of Hygelac who was given to Eofor may have been born to him by a former wife, older than Hygd.

4. Miscellaneous.

A. The Half-Danes (also called Shieldings) involved in the fight at Finnsburg may represent a different tribe from the Danes described above. Their king Hoc had a son, Hnaef, who succeeded him, and a daughter Hildeburh, who married Finn, king of the Jutes.

B. The Jutes, or Frisians, are represented as enemies of the Danes in the fight at Finnsburg and as allies of the Franks at the time Hygelac the Geat made the attack in which he lost his life and from which Beowulf swam home. Also allied with the Franks at this time were the Hetware.

C. The Heatho-Bards (i.e., "Battle-Bards") are represented as inveterate enemies of the Danes. Their king Froda had been killed in an attack on the Danes, and Hrothgar's attempt to make peace with them by marrying his daughter Freawaru to Froda's son Ingeld failed when the latter attacked Heorot. The attack was repulsed, although Heorot was burned.

gomen gleobeames,
geond sæl swingeð,
burhstede beateð.
fela feorhcynna
Swa giomormod
an æfter eallum,
dæges ond nihtes,
hran æt heortan.

that joyful singing wood,
shoot through the hall,
beat his feet in the yard.
sent out of this world
So, sad in spirit,
one left after all were gone,
through both day and night,
touched his heart.

"Næs hearpan wyn,
ne god hafoc
ne se swifta mearh
Bealocwealm hafað
forð onsended."
giohtho mænde,
unbliðe hwearf
oððæt deaðes wylm

"There is no delight in the harp,
nor does the fine hawk
nor does the swift steed
Baleful death has
too many of our kind."
he lamented his loss,
unhappily went on
until death's wave

(trans. Suzanne Akbari)

Beowulf[1]

[Prologue: The Rise of the Danish Nation]

So. The Spear-Danes in days gone by
and the kings who ruled them had courage and greatness.
We have heard of those princes' heroic campaigns.
    There was Shield Sheafson,[2] scourge of many tribes,
a wrecker of mead-benches, rampaging among foes.   5
This terror of the hall-troops had come far.
A foundling to start with, he would flourish later on
as his powers waxed and his worth was proved.
In the end each clan on the outlying coasts
beyond the whale-road had to yield to him   10
and begin to pay tribute. That was one good king.
    Afterward a boy-child was born to Shield,
a cub in the yard, a comfort sent
by God to that nation. He knew what they had tholed,[3]
the long times and troubles they'd come through   15
without a leader; so the Lord of Life,
the glorious Almighty, made this man renowned.
Shield had fathered a famous son:
Beow's name was known through the north.
And a young prince must be prudent like that,   20

1. Translated by Seamus Heaney.
2. Translates *Scyld Scefing*, which probably means "son of Sheaf." Scyld's origins are mysterious.
3. An Anglo-Saxon word that means "suf-
fered, endured" and that survives in the translator's native land of Northern Ireland. In using this word, he also maintains an alliterative pattern similar to the original ("that . . . they . . . tholed").

giving freely while his father lives
so that afterward in age when fighting starts
steadfast companions will stand by him
and hold the line. Behavior that's admired
is the path to power among people everywhere.   25

    Shield was still thriving when his time came
and he crossed over into the Lord's keeping.
His warrior band did what he bade them
when he laid down the law among the Danes:
they shouldered him out to the sea's flood,   30
the chief they revered who had long ruled them.
A ring-whorled prow rode in the harbor,
ice-clad, outbound, a craft for a prince.
They stretched their beloved lord in his boat,
laid out by the mast, amidships,   35
the great ring-giver. Far-fetched treasures
were piled upon him, and precious gear.
I never heard before of a ship so well furbished
with battle-tackle, bladed weapons
and coats of mail. The massed treasure   40
was loaded on top of him: it would travel far
on out into the ocean's sway.
They decked his body no less bountifully
with offerings than those first ones did
who cast him away when he was a child   45
and launched him alone out over the waves.[4]
And they set a gold standard up
high above his head and let him drift
to wind and tide, bewailing him
and mourning their loss. No man can tell,   50
no wise man in hall or weathered veteran
knows for certain who salvaged that load.

    Then it fell to Beow to keep the forts.
He was well regarded and ruled the Danes
for a long time after his father took leave   55
of his life on earth. And then his heir,
the great Halfdane, held sway
for as long as he lived, their elder and warlord.
He was four times a father, this fighter prince:
one by one they entered the world,   60
Heorogar, Hrothgar, the good Halga,
and a daughter,[5] I have heard, who was Onela's queen,
a balm in bed to the battle-scarred Swede.

    The fortunes of war favored Hrothgar.
Friends and kinsmen flocked to his ranks,   65
young followers, a force that grew
to be a mighty army. So his mind turned

---

4. Since Shield arrived with nothing, this sentence is a litotes or understatement, a characteristic of the laconic style of old Germanic poetry.

5. The text is faulty here, and the name of Halfdane's daughter has been lost. Halfdane: according to another source, Halfdane's mother was Swedish; hence his name.

to hall-building: he handed down orders
for men to work on a great mead-hall
meant to be a wonder of the world forever; 70
it would be his throne-room and there he would dispense
his God-given goods to young and old—
but not the common land or people's lives.[6]
Far and wide through the world, I have heard,
orders for work to adorn that wallstead 75
were sent to many peoples. And soon it stood there
finished and ready, in full view,
the hall of halls. Heorot[7] was the name
he had settled on it, whose utterance was law.
Nor did he renege, but doled out rings 80
and torques[8] at the table. The hall towered,
its gables wide and high and awaiting
a barbarous burning.[9] That doom abided,
but in time it would come: the killer instinct
unleashed among in-laws, the blood-lust rampant. 85

[Heorot Is Attacked]

Then a powerful demon, a prowler through the dark,
nursed a hard grievance. It harrowed him
to hear the din of the loud banquet
every day in the hall, the harp being struck
and the clear song of a skilled poet 90
telling with mastery of man's beginnings,
how the Almighty had made the earth
a gleaming plain girdled with waters;
in His splendor He set the sun and the moon
to be earth's lamplight, lanterns for men, 95
and filled the broad lap of the world
with branches and leaves; and quickened life
in every other thing that moved.
    So times were pleasant for the people there
until finally one, a fiend out of hell,
began to work his evil in the world. 100
Grendel was the name of this grim demon
haunting the marches, marauding round the heath
and the desolate fens; he had dwelt for a time
in misery among the banished monsters,
Cain's clan, whom the Creator had outlawed 105
and condemned as outcasts.[1] For the killing of Abel

---

6. Apparently, slaves, along with pastureland used by all, were not in the king's power to give away.
7. That is, "hart," a symbol of royalty.
8. Golden bands worn around the neck.
9. The destruction by fire of Heorot—when the Heatho-Bard Ingeld attacked his father-in-law, Hrothgar—occurred at a later time than that of the poem's action. For a more detailed account of this feud and of Hrothgar's hope that it could be settled by the marriage of his daughter to Ingeld, see lines 2020–69.
1. Genesis 4.9–12.

the Eternal Lord had exacted a price:
Cain got no good from committing that murder
because the Almighty made him anathema 110
and out of the curse of his exile there sprang
ogres and elves and evil phantoms
and the giants too who strove with God
time and again until He gave them their reward.[2]

So, after nightfall, Grendel set out 115
for the lofty house, to see how the Ring-Danes
were settling into it after their drink,
and there he came upon them, a company of the best
asleep from their feasting, insensible to pain
and human sorrow. Suddenly then 120
the God-cursed brute was creating havoc:
greedy and grim, he grabbed thirty men
from their resting places and rushed to his lair,
flushed up and inflamed from the raid,
blundering back with the butchered corpses. 125
  Then as dawn brightened and the day broke,
Grendel's powers of destruction were plain:
their wassail was over, they wept to heaven
and mourned under morning. Their mighty prince,
the storied leader, sat stricken and helpless, 130
humiliated by the loss of his guard,
bewildered and stunned, staring aghast
at the demon's trail, in deep distress.
He was numb with grief, but got no respite
for one night later merciless Grendel 135
struck again with more gruesome murders.
Malignant by nature, he never showed remorse.
It was easy then to meet with a man
shifting himself to a safer distance
to bed in the bothies,[3] for who could be blind 140
to the evidence of his eyes, the obviousness
of the hall-watcher's hate? Whoever escaped
kept a weather-eye open and moved away.
  So Grendel ruled in defiance of right,
one against all, until the greatest house 145
in the world stood empty, a deserted wallstead.
For twelve winters, seasons of woe,
the lord of the Shieldings[4] suffered under
his load of sorrow; and so, before long,
the news was known over the whole world. 150
Sad lays were sung about the beset king,

---

2. The poet is thinking here of Genesis 6.2–8, where the Latin Bible in use at the time refers to giants mating with women who were understood to be the descendants of Cain and thereby creating the wicked race that God destroyed with the flood.
3. Outlying buildings; the word is current in Northern Ireland.
4. Hrothgar; as descendants of Shield, the Danes are called Shieldings.

the vicious raids and ravages of Grendel,
his long and unrelenting feud,
nothing but war; how he would never
parley or make peace with any Dane   155
nor stop his death-dealing nor pay the death-price.[5]
No counselor could ever expect
fair reparation from those rabid hands.
All were endangered; young and old
were hunted down by that dark death-shadow 160
who lurked and swooped in the long nights
on the misty moors; nobody knows
where these reavers from hell roam on their errands.

      So Grendel waged his lonely war,
inflicting constant cruelties on the people, 165
atrocious hurt. He took over Heorot,
haunted the glittering hall after dark,
but the throne itself, the treasure-seat,
he was kept from approaching; he was the Lord's outcast.

      These were hard times, heartbreaking   170
for the prince of the Shieldings; powerful counselors,
the highest in the land, would lend advice,
plotting how best the bold defenders
might resist and beat off sudden attacks.
Sometimes at pagan shrines they vowed   175
offerings to idols, swore oaths
that the killer of souls might come to their aid
and save the people.[6] That was their way,
their heathenish hope; deep in their hearts
they remembered hell. The Almighty Judge   180
of good deeds and bad, the Lord God,
Head of the Heavens and High King of the World,
was unknown to them. Oh, cursed is he
who in time of trouble has to thrust his soul
in the fire's embrace, forfeiting help;   185
he has nowhere to turn. But blessed is he
who after death can approach the Lord
and find friendship in the Father's embrace.

[The Hero Comes to Heorot]

      So that troubled time continued, woe
that never stopped, steady affliction   190
for Halfdane's son, too hard an ordeal.

---

5. According to Germanic law, a slayer could achieve peace with his victim's kinsmen only by paying them *wergild* ("man-price") as compensation for the slain man.
6. The poet interprets the heathen gods to whom the Danes make offerings as different incarnations of Satan. Naturally, the pagan Danes do not think of their gods in these biblical terms, but as the poet makes clear in the following lines, they have no other recourse.

There was panic after dark, people endured
raids in the night, riven by the terror.
    When he heard about Grendel, Hygelac's thane
was on home ground, over in Geatland.   195
There was no one else like him alive.
In his day, he was the mightiest man on earth,
highborn and powerful. He ordered a boat
that would ply the waves. He announced his plan:
to sail the swan's road[7] and seek out that king,   200
the famous prince who needed defenders.
Nobody tried to keep him from going,
no elder denied him, dear as he was to them.
Instead, they inspected omens and spurred
his ambition to go, whilst he moved about   205
like the leader he was, enlisting men,
the best he could find; with fourteen others
the warrior boarded the boat as captain,
a canny pilot along coast and currents.
    Time went by, the boat was on water,   210
in close under the cliffs.
Men climbed eagerly up the gangplank,
sand churned in surf, warriors loaded
a cargo of weapons, shining war-gear
in the vessel's hold, then heaved out,   215
away with a will in their wood-wreathed ship.
Over the waves, with the wind behind her
and foam at her neck, she flew like a bird
until her curved prow had covered the distance,
and on the following day, at the due hour,   220
those seafarers sighted land,
sunlit cliffs, sheer crags
and looming headlands, the landfall they sought.
It was the end of their voyage and the Geats vaulted
over the side, out on to the sand,   225
and moored their ship. There was a clash of mail
and a thresh of gear. They thanked God
for that easy crossing on a calm sea.
    When the watchman on the wall, the Shieldings' lookout
whose job it was to guard the sea-cliffs,   230
saw shields glittering on the gangplank
and battle-equipment being unloaded
he had to find out who and what
the arrivals were. So he rode to the shore,
this horseman of Hrothgar's, and challenged them   235
in formal terms, flourishing his spear:

---

7. That is, the sea. This is an example of a "kenning," a metaphoric phrase that is used to describe a common object. These kennings are very common throughout Anglo-Saxon poetry. See, for another instance, line 258, where the poet describes a man's capacity for speech as his "word-hoard."

"What kind of men are you who arrive
rigged out for combat in your coats of mail,
sailing here over the sea-lanes
in your steep-hulled boat? I have been stationed   240
as lookout on this coast for a long time.
My job is to watch the waves for raiders,
any danger to the Danish shore.
Never before has a force under arms
disembarked so openly—not bothering to ask   245
if the sentries allowed them safe passage
or the clan had consented. Nor have I seen
a mightier man-at-arms on this earth
than the one standing here: unless I am mistaken,
he is truly noble. This is no mere   250
hanger-on in a hero's armor.
So now, before you fare inland
as interlopers, I have to be informed
about who you are and where you hail from.
Outsiders from across the water,   255
I say it again: the sooner you tell
where you come from and why, the better."
     The leader of the troop unlocked his word-hoard;
the distinguished one delivered this answer:
"We belong by birth to the Geat people   260
and owe allegiance to Lord Hygelac.
In his day, my father was a famous man,
a noble warrior-lord named Ecgtheow.
He outlasted many a long winter
and went on his way. All over the world   265
men wise in counsel continue to remember him.
We come in good faith to find your lord
and nation's shield, the son of Halfdane.
Give us the right advice and direction.
We have arrived here on a great errand   270
to the lord of the Danes, and I believe therefore
there should be nothing hidden or withheld between us.
So tell us if what we have heard is true
about this threat, whatever it is,
this danger abroad in the dark nights,   275
this corpse-maker mongering death
in the Shieldings' country. I come to proffer
my wholehearted help and counsel.
I can show the wise Hrothgar a way
to defeat his enemy and find respite—   280
if any respite is to reach him, ever.
I can calm the turmoil and terror in his mind.
Otherwise, he must endure woes
and live with grief for as long as his hall
stands at the horizon on its high ground."   285
     Undaunted, sitting astride his horse,

the coast-guard answered: "Anyone with gumption
and a sharp mind will take the measure
of two things: what's said and what's done.
I believe what you have told me, that you are a troop   290
loyal to our king. So come ahead
with your arms and your gear, and I will guide you.
What's more, I'll order my own comrades
on their word of honor to watch your boat
down there on the strand—keep her safe   295
in her fresh tar, until the time comes
for her curved prow to preen on the waves
and bear this hero back to Geatland.
May one so valiant and venturesome
come unharmed through the clash of battle."   300
      So they went on their way. The ship rode the water,
broad-beamed, bound by its hawser
and anchored fast. Boar-shapes[8] flashed
above their cheek-guards, the brightly forged
work of goldsmiths, watching over   305
those stern-faced men. They marched in step,
hurrying on till the timbered hall
rose before them, radiant with gold.
Nobody on earth knew of another
building like it. Majesty lodged there,   310
its light shone over many lands.
So their gallant escort guided them
to that dazzling stronghold and indicated
the shortest way to it; then the noble warrior
wheeled on his horse and spoke these words: 315
"It is time for me to go. May the Almighty
Father keep you and in His kindness
watch over your exploits. I'm away to the sea,
back on alert against enemy raiders."
      It was a paved track, a path that kept them   320
in marching order. Their mail-shirts glinted,
hard and hand-linked; the high-gloss iron
of their armor rang. So they duly arrived
in their grim war-graith[9] and gear at the hall,
and, weary from the sea, stacked wide shields   325
of the toughest hardwood against the wall,
then collapsed on the benches; battle-dress
and weapons clashed. They collected their spears
in a seafarers' stook,[1] a stand of grayish
tapering ash. And the troops themselves   330
were as good as their weapons.

---

8. Images of boars—a cult animal among the
Germanic tribes and sacred to the god Freyr—
were fixed atop helmets in the belief that they
would provide protection from enemy blows.

9. "Graith" is an archaic word for equipment
or armor.
1. An archaic word for a pile or mass.

Then a proud warrior
questioned the men concerning their origins:
"Where do you come from, carrying these
decorated shields and shirts of mail,
these cheek-hinged helmets and javelins?   335
I am Hrothgar's herald and officer.
I have never seen so impressive or large
an assembly of strangers. Stoutness of heart,
bravery not banishment, must have brought you to Hrothgar."

    The man whose name was known for courage,   340
the Geat leader, resolute in his helmet,
answered in return: "We are retainers
from Hygelac's band. Beowulf is my name.
If your lord and master, the most renowned
son of Halfdane, will hear me out   345
and graciously allow me to greet him in person,
I am ready and willing to report my errand."

    Wulfgar replied, a Wendel[2] chief
renowned as a warrior, well known for his wisdom
and the temper of his mind: "I will take this message,   350
in accordance with your wish, to our noble king,
our dear lord, friend of the Danes,
the giver of rings. I will go and ask him
about your coming here, then hurry back
with whatever reply it pleases him to give."   355

    With that he turned to where Hrothgar sat,
an old man among retainers;
the valiant follower stood foursquare
in front of his king: he knew the courtesies.
Wulfgar addressed his dear lord: 360
"People from Geatland have put ashore.
They have sailed far over the wide sea.
They call the chief in charge of their band
by the name of Beowulf. They beg, my lord,
an audience with you, exchange of words   365
and formal greeting. Most gracious Hrothgar,
do not refuse them, but grant them a reply.
From their arms and appointment, they appear well born
and worthy of respect, especially the one
who has led them this far: he is formidable indeed."   370

    Hrothgar, protector of Shieldings, replied:
"I used to know him when he was a young boy.
His father before him was called Ecgtheow.
Hrethel the Geat[3] gave Ecgtheow

---

2. The Wendels or Vandals are another Germanic nation; it is not unusual for people to be members of nations different from the ones in which they reside. Hence Beowulf himself is both a Geat and a Waegmunding.

3. The leader of the Geats prior to his son Hygelac, who is the current leader. Note that Ecgtheow's marriage to Hrethel's daughter makes Beowulf part of the royal line.

his daughter in marriage. This man is their son, 375
here to follow up an old friendship.
A crew of seamen who sailed for me once
with a gift-cargo across to Geatland
returned with marvelous tales about him:
a thane,[4] they declared, with the strength of thirty 380
in the grip of each hand. Now Holy God
has, in His goodness, guided him here
to the West-Danes, to defend us from Grendel.
This is my hope; and for his heroism
I will recompense him with a rich treasure. 385
Go immediately, bid him and the Geats
he has in attendance to assemble and enter.
Say, moreover, when you speak to them,
they are welcome to Denmark."
                        At the door of the hall,
Wulfgar duly delivered the message: 390
"My lord, the conquering king of the Danes,
bids me announce that he knows your ancestry;
also that he welcomes you here to Heorot
and salutes your arrival from across the sea.
You are free now to move forward 395
to meet Hrothgar in helmets and armor,
but shields must stay here and spears be stacked
until the outcome of the audience is clear."
    The hero arose, surrounded closely
by his powerful thanes. A party remained 400
under orders to keep watch on the arms;
the rest proceeded, led by their prince
under Heorot's roof. And standing on the hearth
in webbed links that the smith had woven,
the fine-forged mesh of his gleaming mail-shirt, 405
resolute in his helmet, Beowulf spoke:
"Greetings to Hrothgar. I am Hygelac's kinsman,
one of his hall-troop. When I was younger,
I had great triumphs. Then news of Grendel,
hard to ignore, reached me at home: 410
sailors brought stories of the plight you suffer
in this legendary hall, how it lies deserted,
empty and useless once the evening light
hides itself under heaven's dome.
So every elder and experienced councilman 415
among my people supported my resolve
to come here to you, King Hrothgar,
because all knew of my awesome strength.
They had seen me boltered[5] in the blood of enemies
when I battled and bound five beasts, 420

---

4. That is, a warrior in the service of a lord   5. Clotted, sticky—a Northern Irish term.
like Hrethel or Hrothgar himself.

raided a troll-nest and in the night-sea
slaughtered sea-brutes. I have suffered extremes
and avenged the Geats (their enemies brought it
upon themselves; I devastated them).
Now I mean to be a match for Grendel,   425
settle the outcome in single combat.
And so, my request, O king of Bright-Danes,
dear prince of the Shieldings, friend of the people
and their ring of defense, my one request
is that you won't refuse me, who have come this far,   430
the privilege of purifying Heorot,
with my own men to help me, and nobody else.
I have heard moreover that the monster scorns
in his reckless way to use weapons;
therefore, to heighten Hygelac's fame   435
and gladden his heart, I hereby renounce
sword and the shelter of the broad shield,
the heavy war-board: hand-to-hand
is how it will be, a life-and-death
fight with the fiend. Whichever one death fells   440
must deem it a just judgment by God.
If Grendel wins, it will be a gruesome day;
he will glut himself on the Geats in the war-hall,
swoop without fear on that flower of manhood
as on others before. Then my face won't be there   445
to be covered in death: he will carry me away
as he goes to ground, gorged and bloodied;
he will run gloating with my raw corpse
and feed on it alone, in a cruel frenzy
fouling his moor-nest. No need then   450
to lament for long or lay out my body:
if the battle takes me, send back
this breast-webbing that Weland[6] fashioned
and Hrethel gave me, to Lord Hygelac.
Fate goes ever as fate must."   455

    Hrothgar, the helmet of Shieldings, spoke:
"Beowulf, my friend, you have traveled here
to favor us with help and to fight for us.
There was a feud one time, begun by your father.
With his own hands he had killed Heatholaf   460
who was a Wulfing;[7] so war was looming
and his people, in fear of it, forced him to leave.
He came away then over rolling waves
to the South-Danes here, the sons of honor.
I was then in the first flush of kingship,   465
establishing my sway over the rich strongholds
of this heroic land. Heorogar,

---

6. The blacksmith of the Norse gods.   7. The Wulfings are another Germanic nation.

my older brother and the better man,
also a son of Halfdane's, had died.
Finally I healed the feud by paying: 470
I shipped a treasure-trove to the Wulfings,
and Ecgtheow acknowledged me with oaths of allegiance.
    "It bothers me to have to burden anyone
with all the grief that Grendel has caused
and the havoc he has wreaked upon us in Heorot, 475
our humiliations. My household-guard
are on the wane, fate sweeps them away
into Grendel's clutches—but God can easily
halt these raids and harrowing attacks!
    "Time and again, when the goblets passed 480
and seasoned fighters got flushed with beer
they would pledge themselves to protect Heorot
and wait for Grendel with their whetted swords.
But when dawn broke and day crept in
over each empty, blood-spattered bench, 485
the floor of the mead-hall where they had feasted
would be slick with slaughter. And so they died,
faithful retainers, and my following dwindled.
Now take your place at the table, relish
the triumph of heroes to your heart's content." 490

[Feast at Heorot]

    Then a bench was cleared in that banquet hall
so the Geats could have room to be together
and the party sat, proud in their bearing,
strong and stalwart. An attendant stood by
with a decorated pitcher, pouring bright 495
helpings of mead. And the minstrel sang,
filling Heorot with his head-clearing voice,
gladdening that great rally of Geats and Danes.
    From where he crouched at the king's feet,
Unferth, a son of Ecglaf's, spoke 500
contrary words.[8] Beowulf's coming,
his sea-braving, made him sick with envy:
he could not brook or abide the fact
that anyone else alive under heaven
might enjoy greater regard than he did: 505
"Are you the Beowulf who took on Breca
in a swimming match[9] on the open sea,
risking the water just to prove that you could win?
It was sheer vanity made you venture out

8. Unferth is Hrothgar's *thyle*, a kind of
licensed spokesman who here engages Beowulf
in a traditional "flytting" or verbal combat; see
the note to line 1457. Ecglaf appears in the
poem only as the father of Unferth.

9. The original Anglo-Saxon describing this
contest can be interpreted in such a way that
Breca and Beowulf are competing not in swimming but in rowing, which is more plausible.

on the main deep. And no matter who tried,   510
friend or foe, to deflect the pair of you,
neither would back down: the sea-test obsessed you.
You waded in, embracing water,
taking its measure, mastering currents,
riding on the swell. The ocean swayed,   515
winter went wild in the waves, but you vied
for seven nights; and then he outswam you,
came ashore the stronger contender.
He was cast up safe and sound one morning
among the Heatho-Reams,[1] then made his way   520
to where he belonged in Bronding[2] country,
home again, sure of his ground
in strongroom and bawn.[3] So Breca made good
his boast upon you and was proved right.
No matter, therefore, how you may have fared   525
in every bout and battle until now,
this time you'll be worsted; no one has ever
outlasted an entire night against Grendel."
    Beowulf, Ecgtheow's son, replied:
"Well, friend Unferth, you have had your say   530
about Breca and me. But it was mostly beer
that was doing the talking. The truth is this:
when the going was heavy in those high waves,
I was the strongest swimmer of all.
We'd been children together and we grew up   535
daring ourselves to outdo each other,
boasting and urging each other to risk
our lives on the sea. And so it turned out.
Each of us swam holding a sword,
a naked, hard-proofed blade for protection   540
against the whale-beasts. But Breca could never
move out farther or faster from me
than I could manage to move from him.
Shoulder to shoulder, we struggled on
for five nights, until the long flow   545
and pitch of the waves, the perishing cold,
night falling and winds from the north
drove us apart. The deep boiled up
and its wallowing sent the sea-brutes wild.
My armor helped me to hold out;   550
my hard-ringed chain-mail, hand-forged and linked,
a fine, close-fitting filigree of gold,
kept me safe when some ocean creature
pulled me to the bottom. Pinioned fast
and swathed in its grip, I was granted one   555

---

1. A people of southern Norway.
2. The Brondings are the nation to which Breca belonged, but nothing is known of their territory.

3. Fortified outwork of a court or castle. The word was used by English planters in Ulster to describe fortified dwellings they erected on lands confiscated from the Irish [translator's note].

final chance: my sword plunged
and the ordeal was over. Through my own hands,
the fury of battle had finished off the sea-beast.

"Time and again, foul things attacked me,
lurking and stalking, but I lashed out,   560
gave as good as I got with my sword.
My flesh was not for feasting on,
there would be no monsters gnawing and gloating
over their banquet at the bottom of the sea.
Instead, in the morning, mangled and sleeping   565
the sleep of the sword, they slopped and floated
like the ocean's leavings. From now on
sailors would be safe, the deep-sea raids
were over for good. Light came from the east,
bright guarantee of God, and the waves   570
went quiet; I could see headlands
and buffeted cliffs. Often, for undaunted courage,
fate spares the man it has not already marked.
However it occurred, my sword had killed
nine sea-monsters. Such night dangers   575
and hard ordeals I have never heard of
nor of a man more desolate in surging waves.
But worn out as I was, I survived,
came through with my life. The ocean lifted
and laid me ashore, I landed safe   580
on the coast of Finland.
                    Now I cannot recall
any fight you entered, Unferth,
that bears comparison. I don't boast when I say
that neither you nor Breca were ever much
celebrated for swordsmanship   585
or for facing danger on the field of battle.
You killed your own kith and kin,
so for all your cleverness and quick tongue,
you will suffer damnation in the depths of hell.[4]
The fact is, Unferth, if you were truly   590
as keen or courageous as you claim to be
Grendel would never have got away with
such unchecked atrocity, attacks on your king,
havoc in Heorot and horrors everywhere.
But he knows he need never be in dread   595
of your blade making a mizzle[5] of his blood
or of vengeance arriving ever from this quarter—
from the Victory-Shieldings, the shoulderers of the spear.
He knows he can trample down you Danes
to his heart's content, humiliate and murder   600

---

4. The manuscript is damaged here, and the word "hell" may well be "hall": "You will suffer condemnation in the hall" is an acceptable translation of the line.

5. That is, drizzle.

without fear of reprisal. But he will find me different.
I will show him how Geats shape to kill
in the heat of battle. Then whoever wants to
may go bravely to mead,[6] when the morning light,
scarfed in sun-dazzle, shines forth from the south   605
and brings another daybreak to the world."
    Then the gray-haired treasure-giver was glad;
far-famed in battle, the prince of Bright-Danes
and keeper of his people counted on Beowulf,
on the warrior's steadfastness and his word.   610
So the laughter started, the din got louder
and the crowd was happy. Wealhtheow came in,
Hrothgar's queen, observing the courtesies.
Adorned in her gold, she graciously saluted
the men in the hall, then handed the cup   615
first to Hrothgar, their homeland's guardian,
urging him to drink deep and enjoy it
because he was dear to them. And he drank it down
like the warlord he was, with festive cheer.
So the Helming woman went on her rounds,   620
queenly and dignified, decked out in rings,
offering the goblet to all ranks,
treating the household and the assembled troop,
until it was Beowulf's turn to take it from her hand.
With measured words she welcomed the Geat   625
and thanked God for granting her wish
that a deliverer she could believe in would arrive
to ease their afflictions. He accepted the cup,
a daunting man, dangerous in action
and eager for it always. He addressed Wealhtheow;   630
Beowulf, son of Ecgtheow, said:
"I had a fixed purpose when I put to sea.
As I sat in the boat with my band of men,
I meant to perform to the uttermost
what your people wanted or perish in the attempt,   635
in the fiend's clutches. And I shall fulfill that purpose,
prove myself with a proud deed
or meet my death here in the mead-hall."
This formal boast by Beowulf the Geat
pleased the lady well and she went to sit   640
by Hrothgar, regal and arrayed with gold.
    Then it was like old times in the echoing hall,
proud talk and the people happy,
loud and excited; until soon enough
Halfdane's heir had to be away   645
to his night's rest. He realized
that the demon was going to descend on the hall,
that he had plotted all day, from dawn-light

---

6. An alcoholic drink made by fermenting honey and adding water.

until darkness gathered again over the world
and stealthy night-shapes came stealing forth   650
under the cloud-murk. The company stood
as the two leaders took leave of each other:
Hrothgar wished Beowulf health and good luck,
named him hall-warden and announced as follows:
"Never, since my hand could hold a shield   655
have I entrusted or given control
of the Danes' hall to anyone but you.
Ward and guard it, for it is the greatest of houses.
Be on your mettle now, keep in mind your fame,
beware of the enemy. There's nothing you wish for   660
that won't be yours if you win through alive."

[The Fight with Grendel]

Hrothgar departed then with his house-guard.
The lord of the Shieldings, their shelter in war,
left the mead-hall to lie with Wealhtheow,
his queen and bedmate. The King of Glory   665
(as people learned) had posted a lookout
who was a match for Grendel, a guard against monsters,
special protection to the Danish prince.
And the Geat placed complete trust
in his strength of limb and the Lord's favor.   670
   He began to remove his iron breast-mail,
took off the helmet and handed his attendant
the patterned sword, a smith's masterpiece,
ordering him to keep the equipment guarded.
And before he bedded down, Beowulf,   675
that prince of goodness, proudly asserted:
"When it comes to fighting, I count myself
as dangerous any day as Grendel.
So it won't be a cutting edge I'll wield
to mow him down, easily as I might.   680
He has no idea of the arts of war,
of shield or sword-play, although he does possess
a wild strength. No weapons, therefore,
for either this night: unarmed he shall face me
if face me he dares. And may the Divine Lord   685
in His wisdom grant the glory of victory
to whichever side He sees fit."
   Then down the brave man lay with his bolster
under his head and his whole company
of sea-rovers at rest beside him.   690
None of them expected he would ever see
his homeland again or get back
to his native place and the people who reared him.
They knew too well the way it was before,
how often the Danes had fallen prey   695
to death in the mead-hall. But the Lord was weaving

a victory on His war-loom for the Weather-Geats.
Through the strength of one they all prevailed;
they would crush their enemy and come through
in triumph and gladness. The truth is clear: 700
Almighty God rules over mankind
and always has.

                 Then out of the night
came the shadow-stalker, stealthy and swift.
The hall-guards were slack, asleep at their posts,
all except one; it was widely understood   705
that as long as God disallowed it,
the fiend could not bear them to his shadow-bourne.
One man, however, was in fighting mood,
awake and on edge, spoiling for action.

   In off the moors, down through the mist-bands   710
God-cursed Grendel came greedily loping.
The bane of the race of men roamed forth,
hunting for a prey in the high hall.
Under the cloud-murk he moved toward it
until it shone above him, a sheer keep   715
of fortified gold. Nor was that the first time
he had scouted the grounds of Hrothgar's dwelling—
although never in his life, before or since,
did he find harder fortune or hall-defenders.
Spurned and joyless, he journeyed on ahead   720
and arrived at the bawn. The iron-braced door
turned on its hinge when his hands touched it.
Then his rage boiled over, he ripped open
the mouth of the building, maddening for blood,
pacing the length of the patterned floor   725
with his loathsome tread, while a baleful light,
flame more than light, flared from his eyes.
He saw many men in the mansion, sleeping,
a ranked company of kinsmen and warriors
quartered together. And his glee was demonic,   730
picturing the mayhem: before morning
he would rip life from limb and devour them,
feed on their flesh; but his fate that night
was due to change, his days of ravening
had come to an end.

                 Mighty and canny,   735
Hygelac's kinsman was keenly watching
for the first move the monster would make.
Nor did the creature keep him waiting
but struck suddenly and started in;
he grabbed and mauled a man on his bench,   740
bit into his bone-lappings,[7] bolted down his blood
and gorged on him in lumps, leaving the body

---

7. That is, joints.

utterly lifeless, eaten up
hand and foot. Venturing closer,
his talon was raised to attack Beowulf   745
where he lay on the bed, he was bearing in
with open claw when the alert hero's
comeback and armlock forestalled him utterly.
The captain of evil discovered himself
in a handgrip harder than anything   750
he had ever encountered in any man
on the face of the earth. Every bone in his body
quailed and recoiled, but he could not escape.
He was desperate to flee to his den and hide
with the devil's litter, for in all his days   755
he had never been clamped or cornered like this.
Then Hygelac's trusty retainer recalled
his bedtime speech, sprang to his feet
and got a firm hold. Fingers were bursting,
the monster back-tracking, the man overpowering.   760
The dread of the land was desperate to escape,
to take a roundabout road and flee
to his lair in the fens. The latching power
in his fingers weakened; it was the worst trip
the terror-monger had taken to Heorot.   765
And now the timbers trembled and sang,
a hall-session[8] that harrowed every Dane
inside the stockade: stumbling in fury,
the two contenders crashed through the building.
The hall clattered and hammered, but somehow   770
survived the onslaught and kept standing:
it was handsomely structured, a sturdy frame
braced with the best of blacksmith's work
inside and out. The story goes
that as the pair struggled, mead-benches were smashed   775
and sprung off the floor, gold fittings and all.
Before then, no Shielding elder would believe
there was any power or person upon earth
capable of wrecking their horn-rigged hall
unless the burning embrace of a fire   780
engulf it in flame. Then an extraordinary
wail arose, and bewildering fear
came over the Danes. Everyone felt it
who heard that cry as it echoed off the wall,
a God-cursed scream and strain of catastrophe,   785
the howl of the loser, the lament of the hell-serf
keening his wound. He was overwhelmed,

8. In Hiberno-English the word "session" (*seissiún* in Irish) can mean a gathering where musicians and singers perform for their own enjoyment [translator's note]. In other words, the poet is making a laconic joke, since the main function of the hall is celebration and singing.

manacled tight by the man who of all men
was foremost and strongest in the days of this life.
   But the earl-troop's leader was not inclined   790
to allow his caller to depart alive:
he did not consider that life of much account
to anyone anywhere. Time and again,
Beowulf's warriors worked to defend
their lord's life, laying about them   795
as best they could, with their ancestral blades.
Stalwart in action, they kept striking out
on every side, seeking to cut
straight to the soul. When they joined the struggle
there was something they could not have known at the time,   800
that no blade on earth, no blacksmith's art
could ever damage their demon opponent.
He had conjured the harm from the cutting edge
of every weapon.[9] But his going away
out of this world and the days of his life   805
would be agony to him, and his alien spirit
would travel far into fiends' keeping.
   Then he who had harrowed the hearts of men
with pain and affliction in former times
and had given offense also to God   810
found that his bodily powers failed him.
Hygelac's kinsman kept him helplessly
locked in a handgrip. As long as either lived,
he was hateful to the other. The monster's whole
body was in pain; a tremendous wound   815
appeared on his shoulder. Sinews split
and the bone-lappings burst. Beowulf was granted
the glory of winning; Grendel was driven
under the fen-banks, fatally hurt,
to his desolate lair. His days were numbered,   820
the end of his life was coming over him,
he knew it for certain; and one bloody clash
had fulfilled the dearest wishes of the Danes.
The man who had lately landed among them,
proud and sure, had purged the hall,   825
kept it from harm; he was happy with his nightwork
and the courage he had shown. The Geat captain
had boldly fulfilled his boast to the Danes:
he had healed and relieved a huge distress,
unremitting humiliations,   830
the hard fate they'd been forced to undergo,
no small affliction. Clear proof of this
could be seen in the hand the hero displayed
high up near the roof: the whole of Grendel's
shoulder and arm, his awesome grasp.   835

9. Grendel is magically protected from weapons.

[Celebration at Heorot]

Then morning came and many a warrior
gathered, as I've heard, around the gift-hall,
clan-chiefs flocking from far and near
down wide-ranging roads, wondering greatly
at the monster's footprints. His fatal departure   840
was regretted by no one who witnessed his trail,
the ignominious marks of his flight
where he'd skulked away, exhausted in spirit
and beaten in battle, bloodying the path,
hauling his doom to the demons' mere.[1]   845
The bloodshot water wallowed and surged,
there were loathsome upthrows and overturnings
of waves and gore and wound-slurry.
With his death upon him, he had dived deep
into his marsh-den, drowned out his life   850
and his heathen soul; hell claimed him there.
Then away they rode, the old retainers
with many a young man following after,
a troop on horseback, in high spirits
on their bay steeds. Beowulf's doings   855
were praised over and over again.
Nowhere, they said, north or south
between the two seas or under the tall sky
on the broad earth was there anyone better
to raise a shield or to rule a kingdom.   860
Yet there was no laying of blame on their lord,
the noble Hrothgar; he was a good king.
    At times the war-band broke into a gallop,
letting their chestnut horses race
wherever they found the going good   865
on those well-known tracks. Meanwhile, a thane
of the king's household, a carrier of tales,
a traditional singer deeply schooled
in the lore of the past, linked a new theme
to a strict meter.[2] The man started   870
to recite with skill, rehearsing Beowulf's
triumphs and feats in well-fashioned lines,
entwining his words.
                        He told what he'd heard
repeated in songs about Sigemund's exploits,[3]
all of those many feats and marvels,   875
the struggles and wanderings of Waels's son,
things unknown to anyone

1. A lake or pool.
2. The singer or *scop* composes extemporaneously in alliterative verse.
3. According to Norse legend, Sigemund, the son of Waels (or Volsung, as he is known in Norse), slept with his sister Sigurth, who bore a son named Fitela; Fitela was thus also Sigemund's nephew, as he is described here. The singer here contrasts Sigemund's bravery in killing a dragon with the defeat of the Danish king Heremod, who could not protect his people. For more on Heremod as a bad king, see lines 1709–22.

except to Fitela, feuds and foul doings
confided by uncle to nephew when he felt
the urge to speak of them: always they had been   880
partners in the fight, friends in need.
They killed giants, their conquering swords
had brought them down.
                            After his death
Sigemund's glory   grew and grew
because of his courage   when he killed the dragon,   885
the guardian of the hoard.   Under gray stone
he had dared to enter   all by himself
to face the worst   without Fitela.
But it came to pass   that his sword plunged
right through   those radiant scales   890
and drove into the wall.   The dragon died of it.
His daring had given him   total possession
of the treasure-hoard,   his to dispose of
however he liked.   He loaded a boat:
Waels's son   weighted her hold   895
with dazzling spoils.   The hot dragon melted.
   Sigemund's name   was known everywhere.
He was utterly valiant   and venturesome,
a fence round his fighters   and flourished therefore
after King Heremod's   prowess declined   900
and his campaigns slowed down.   The king was betrayed,
ambushed in Jutland,   overpowered
and done away with.   The waves of his grief
had beaten him down,   made him a burden,
a source of anxiety   to his own nobles: 905
that expedition   was often condemned
in those earlier times   by experienced men,
men who relied   on his lordship for redress,
who presumed that the part   of a prince was to thrive
on his father's throne   and defend the nation,   910
the Shielding land   where they lived and belonged,
its holdings and strongholds.   Such was Beowulf
in the affection of his friends   and of everyone alive.
But evil entered   into Heremod.
   Meanwhile, the Danes kept racing their mounts   915
down sandy lanes. The light of day
broke and kept brightening. Bands of retainers
galloped in excitement to the gabled hall
to see the marvel; and the king himself,
guardian of the ring-hoard, goodness in person,   920
walked in majesty from the women's quarters
with a numerous train, attended by his queen
and her crowd of maidens, across to the mead-hall.
   When Hrothgar arrived at the hall, he spoke,
standing on the steps, under the steep eaves,   925
gazing toward the roofwork and Grendel's talon:
"First and foremost, let the Almighty Father

be thanked for this sight. I suffered a long
harrowing by Grendel. But the Heavenly Shepherd
can work His wonders always and everywhere.   930
Not long since, it seemed I would never
be granted the slightest solace or relief
from any of my burdens: the best of houses
glittered and reeked and ran with blood.
This one worry outweighed all others—   935
a constant distress to counselors entrusted
with defending the people's forts from assault
by monsters and demons. But now a man,
with the Lord's assistance, has accomplished something
none of us could manage before now   940
for all our efforts. Whoever she was
who brought forth this flower of manhood,
if she is still alive, that woman can say
that in her labor the Lord of Ages
bestowed a grace on her. So now, Beowulf,   945
I adopt you in my heart as a dear son.
Nourish and maintain this new connection,
you noblest of men; there'll be nothing you'll want for,
no worldly goods that won't be yours.
I have often honored smaller achievements,   950
recognized warriors not nearly as worthy,
lavished rewards on the less deserving.
But you have made yourself immortal
by your glorious action. May the God of Ages
continue to keep and requite you well."   955
    Beowulf, son of Ecgtheow, spoke:
"We have gone through with a glorious endeavor
and been much favored in this fight we dared
against the unknown. Nevertheless,
if you could have seen the monster himself   960
where he lay beaten, I would have been better pleased.
My plan was to pounce, pin him down
in a tight grip and grapple him to death—
have him panting for life, powerless and clasped
in my bare hands, his body in thrall.   965
But I couldn't stop him from slipping my hold.
The Lord allowed it, my lock on him
wasn't strong enough; he struggled fiercely
and broke and ran. Yet he bought his freedom
at a high price, for he left his hand   970
and arm and shoulder to show he had been here,
a cold comfort for having come among us.
And now he won't be long for this world.
He has done his worst but the wound will end him.
He is hasped and hooped and hirpling[4] with pain,   975

---

4. That is, limping.

limping and looped in it. Like a man outlawed
for wickedness, he must await
the mighty judgment of God in majesty."
There was less tampering and big talk then
from Unferth the boaster, less of his blather   980
as the hall-thanes eyed the awful proof
of the hero's prowess, the splayed hand
up under the eaves. Every nail,
claw-scale and spur, every spike
and welt on the hand of that heathen brute   985
was like barbed steel. Everybody said
there was no honed iron hard enough
to pierce him through, no time-proofed blade
that could cut his brutal, blood-caked claw.
Then the order was given for all hands   990
to help to refurbish Heorot immediately:
men and women thronging the wine-hall,
getting it ready. Gold thread shone
in the wall-hangings, woven scenes
that attracted and held the eye's attention.   995
But iron-braced as the inside of it had been,
that bright room lay in ruins now.
The very doors had been dragged from their hinges.
Only the roof remained unscathed
by the time the guilt-fouled fiend turned tail   1000
in despair of his life. But death is not easily
escaped from by anyone:
all of us with souls, earth-dwellers
and children of men, must make our way
to a destination already ordained   1005
where the body, after the banqueting,
sleeps on its deathbed.
                        Then the due time arrived
for Halfdane's son to proceed to the hall.
The king himself would sit down to feast.
No group ever gathered in greater numbers   1010
or better order around their ring-giver.
The benches filled with famous men
who fell to with relish; round upon round
of mead was passed; those powerful kinsmen,
Hrothgar and Hrothulf, were in high spirits   1015
in the raftered hall. Inside Heorot
there was nothing but friendship. The Shielding nation
was not yet familiar with feud and betrayal.[5]
Then Halfdane's son presented Beowulf

---

5. The poet here refers to the later history of
the Danes, when after Hrothgar's death his
nephew Hrothulf drove his son Hrethric from
the throne. For Wealhtheow's fear that this
betrayal will indeed come to pass, see lines
1168–90.

with a gold standard as a victory gift,   1020
an embroidered banner; also breast-mail
and a helmet; and a sword carried high,
that was both precious object and token of honor.
So Beowulf drank his drink, at ease;
it was hardly a shame to be showered with such gifts   1025
in front of the hall-troops. There haven't been many
moments, I am sure, when men exchanged
four such treasures at so friendly a sitting.
An embossed ridge, a band lapped with wire
arched over the helmet: head-protection   1030
to keep the keen-ground cutting edge
from damaging it when danger threatened
and the man was battling behind his shield.
Next the king ordered eight horses
with gold bridles to be brought through the yard   1035
into the hall. The harness of one
included a saddle of sumptuous design,
the battle-seat where the son of Halfdane
rode when he wished to join the sword-play:
wherever the killing and carnage were the worst,   1040
he would be to the fore, fighting hard.
Then the Danish prince, descendant of Ing,[6]
handed over both the arms and the horses,
urging Beowulf to use them well.
And so their leader, the lord and guard   1045
of coffer and strongroom, with customary grace
bestowed upon Beowulf both sets of gifts.
A fair witness can see how well each one behaved.
    The chieftain went on to reward the others:
each man on the bench who had sailed with Beowulf   1050
and risked the voyage received a bounty,
some treasured possession. And compensation,
a price in gold, was settled for the Geat
Grendel had cruelly killed earlier—
as he would have killed more, had not mindful God   1055
and one man's daring prevented that doom.
Past and present, God's will prevails.
Hence, understanding is always best
and a prudent mind. Whoever remains
for long here in this earthly life   1060
will enjoy and endure more than enough.
    They sang then and played to please the hero,
words and music for their warrior prince,
harp tunes and tales of adventure:
there were high times on the hall benches,   1065
and the king's poet performed his part
with the saga of Finn and his sons, unfolding

6. A Germanic deity and the protector of the Danes.

the tale of the fierce attack in Friesland
where Hnaef, king of the Danes, met death.[7]

Hildeburh
              had little cause
to credit the Jutes:
              son and brother,
she lost them both
              on the battlefield.
She, bereft
              and blameless, they
foredoomed, cut down
              and spear-gored. She,
the woman in shock,
              waylaid by grief,   1075
Hoc's daughter—
              how could she not
lament her fate
              when morning came
and the light broke
              on her murdered dears?
And so farewell
              delight on earth,
war carried away
              Finn's troop of thanes   1080
all but a few.
              How then could Finn
hold the line
              or fight on
to the end with Hengest,
              how save
the rump of his force
              from that enemy chief?
So a truce was offered
              as follows: first   1085
separate quarters
              to be cleared for the Danes,
hall and throne
              to be shared with the Frisians.
Then, second:
              every day
at the dole-out of gifts
              Finn, son of Focwald,

7. This song recounts the fight at Finnsburg
between the Dane Hengest and the Jute (or Frisian) Finn. The poet begins with the bereft
Hildeburh, daughter of the Danish king Hoc
and wife of the Jute Finn, whose unnamed son
and brother Hnaef have already been killed in
the first battle with Finn. He then tells how
Hengest, the new leader of the Danes, is offered
a truce by the weakened Finn, how together they
cremate their dead, following which Hengest
and the remaining Danes spend the winter with
Finn and the Jutes. But with the coming of
spring, the feud breaks out again and Finn and
the Jutes are slaughtered by Hengest with the
help of two other Danes, Guthlaf and Oslaf.

should honor the Danes,
                  bestow with an even   1090
hand to Hengest
                  and Hengest's men
the wrought-gold rings,
                  bounty to match
the measure he gave
                  his own Frisians—
to keep morale
                  in the beer-hall high.
Both sides then
                  sealed their agreement.   1095
With oaths to Hengest
                  Finn swore
openly, solemnly,
                  that the battle survivors
would be guaranteed
                  honor and status.
No infringement
                  by word or deed,
no provocation
                  would be permitted.   1100
Their own ring-giver
                  after all
was dead and gone,
                  they were leaderless,
in forced allegiance
                  to his murderer.
So if any Frisian
                  stirred up bad blood
with insinuations
                  or taunts about this,   1105
the blade of the sword
                  would arbitrate it.
A funeral pyre
                  was then prepared,
effulgent gold
                  brought out from the hoard.
The pride and prince
                  of the Shieldings lay
awaiting the flame.
                  Everywhere   1110
there were blood-plastered
                  coats of mail.
The pyre was heaped
                  with boar-shaped helmets
forged in gold,
                  with the gashed corpses
of wellborn Danes—
                  many had fallen.
Then Hildeburh

ordered her own   1115
son's body
              be burnt with Hnaef's
the flesh on his bones
                   to sputter and blaze
beside his uncle's.
              The woman wailed
and sang keens,
              the warrior went up.[8]
Carcass flame
              swirled and fumed,   1120
they stood round the burial
                   mound and howled
as heads melted,
                   crusted gashes
spattered and ran
                   bloody matter.
The glutton element
                   flamed and consumed
the dead of both sides.
                   Their great days were gone.   1125
Warriors scattered
              to homes and forts
all over Friesland,
              fewer now, feeling
loss of friends.
              Hengest stayed,
lived out that whole
              resentful, blood-sullen
winter with Finn,
              homesick and helpless.   1130
No ring-whorled prow
                   could up then
and away on the sea.
                   Wind and water
raged with storms,
                   wave and shingle
were shackled in ice
                   until another year
appeared in the yard
                   as it does to this day,   1135
the seasons constant,
                   the wonder of light
coming over us.
              Then winter was gone,
earth's lap grew lovely,
                   longing woke
in the cooped-up exile

8. The warrior (Hildeburh's son) either goes up on the pyre or goes up in smoke. "Keens": an
Irish word for funeral laments.

                         for a voyage home—
but more for vengeance,
                    some way of bringing   1140
things to a head:
               his sword arm hankered
to greet the Jutes.
                 So he did not balk
once Hunlafing[9]
                 placed on his lap
Dazzle-the-Duel,
                 the best sword of all,
whose edges Jutes
               knew only too well.   1145
Thus blood was spilled,
                       the gallant Finn
slain in his home
                 after Guthlaf and Oslaf[1]
back from their voyage
                   made old accusation:
the brutal ambush,
                 the fate they had suffered,
all blamed on Finn.
                   The wildness in them   1150
had to brim over.
                 The hall ran red
with blood of enemies.
                     Finn was cut down,
the queen brought away
                     and everything
the Shieldings could find
                     inside Finn's walls—
the Frisian king's
                 gold collars and gemstones—   1155
swept off to the ship.
                   Over sea-lanes then
back to Daneland
               the warrior troop
bore that lady home.

            The poem was over,
the poet had performed, a pleasant murmur
started on the benches, stewards did the rounds   1160
with wine in splendid jugs, and Wealhtheow came to sit
in her gold crown between two good men,
uncle and nephew, each one of whom
still trusted the other;[2] and the forthright Unferth,

---

9. A Danish follower of Hengest.
1. Danes who seem to have gone home in
order to bring reinforcements to Hengest. But
it is possible that these two have been with
Hengest all along and that "their voyage" is an
unrelated journey.
2. See p. 134, n. 5.

admired by all for his mind and courage   1165
although under a cloud for killing his brothers,
reclined near the king.
          The queen spoke:
"Enjoy this drink, my most generous lord;
raise up your goblet, entertain the Geats
duly and gently, discourse with them,   1170
be open-handed, happy and fond.
Relish their company, but recollect as well
all of the boons that have been bestowed on you.
The bright court of Heorot has been cleansed
and now the word is that you want to adopt   1175
this warrior as a son. So, while you may,
bask in your fortune, and then bequeath
kingdom and nation to your kith and kin,
before your decease. I am certain of Hrothulf.
He is noble and will use the young ones well.   1180
He will not let you down. Should you die before him,
he will treat our children truly and fairly.
He will honor, I am sure, our two sons,
repay them in kind, when he recollects
all the good things we gave him once,   1185
the favor and respect he found in his childhood."
She turned then to the bench where her boys sat,
Hrethric and Hrothmund, with other nobles' sons,
all the youth together; and that good man,
Beowulf the Geat, sat between the brothers.   1190
    The cup was carried to him, kind words
spoken in welcome and a wealth of wrought gold
graciously bestowed: two arm bangles,
a mail-shirt and rings, and the most resplendent
torque of gold I ever heard tell of   1195
anywhere on earth or under heaven.
There was no hoard like it since Hama snatched
the Brosings' neck-chain and bore it away
with its gems and settings to his shining fort,
away from Eormenric's wiles and hatred,   1200
and thereby ensured his eternal reward.[3]
Hygelac the Geat, grandson of Swerting,
wore this neck-ring on his last raid;[4]
at bay under his banner, he defended the booty,
treasure he had won. Fate swept him away   1205
because of his proud need to provoke
a feud with the Frisians. He fell beneath his shield,
in the same gem-crusted, kingly gear

---

3. The legend alluded to here seems to be that Hama stole the golden necklace of the Brosings from Eormenric (a historical figure, the king of the Ostrogoths, who died ca. 375), and then gave it to the goddess Freya.

4. The poet here refers to the death of Hygelac while raiding the Frisian territory of the Franks. This raid and Hygelac's death are recorded by the historian Gregory of Tours (d. 594) as having taken place about 520.

he had worn when he crossed the frothing wave-vat.
So the dead king fell into Frankish hands.   1210
They took his breast-mail, also his neck-torque,
and punier warriors plundered the slain
when the carnage ended; Geat corpses
covered the field.
        Applause filled the hall.
Then Wealhtheow pronounced in the presence of the company: 1215
"Take delight in this torque, dear Beowulf,
wear it for luck and wear also this mail
from our people's armory: may you prosper in them!
Be acclaimed for strength, for kindly guidance
to these two boys, and your bounty will be sure.   1220
You have won renown: you are known to all men
far and near, now and forever.
Your sway is wide as the wind's home,
as the sea around cliffs. And so, my prince,
I wish you a lifetime's luck and blessings   1225
to enjoy this treasure. Treat my sons
with tender care, be strong and kind.
Here each comrade is true to the other,
loyal to lord, loving in spirit.
The thanes have one purpose, the people are ready: 1230
having drunk and pledged, the ranks do as I bid."
    She moved then to her place. Men were drinking wine
at that rare feast; how could they know fate,
the grim shape of things to come,
the threat looming over many thanes   1235
as night approached and King Hrothgar prepared
to retire to his quarters? Retainers in great numbers
were posted on guard as so often in the past.
Benches were pushed back, bedding gear and bolsters
spread across the floor, and one man   1240
lay down to his rest, already marked for death.
At their heads they placed their polished timber
battle-shields; and on the bench above them,
each man's kit was kept to hand:
a towering war-helmet, webbed mail-shirt   1245
and great-shafted spear. It was their habit
always and everywhere to be ready for action,
at home or in the camp, in whatever case
and at whatever time the need arose
to rally round their lord. They were a right people.   1250

[Another Attack]

    They went to sleep. And one paid dearly
for his night's ease, as had happened to them often,
ever since Grendel occupied the gold-hall,
committing evil until the end came,
death after his crimes. Then it became clear,   1255

obvious to everyone once the fight was over,
that an avenger lurked and was still alive,
grimly biding time. Grendel's mother,
monstrous hell-bride, brooded on her wrongs.
She had been forced down into fearful waters,   1260
the cold depths, after Cain had killed
his father's son, felled his own
brother with a sword. Branded an outlaw,
marked by having murdered, he moved into the wilds,
shunned company and joy. And from Cain there sprang   1265
misbegotten spirits, among them Grendel,
the banished and accursed, due to come to grips
with that watcher in Heorot waiting to do battle.
The monster wrenched and wrestled with him,
but Beowulf was mindful of his mighty strength,   1270
the wondrous gifts God had showered on him:
he relied for help on the Lord of All,
on His care and favor. So he overcame the foe,
brought down the hell-brute. Broken and bowed,
outcast from all sweetness, the enemy of mankind   1275
made for his death-den. But now his mother
had sallied forth on a savage journey,
grief-racked and ravenous, desperate for revenge.
   She came to Heorot. There, inside the hall,
Danes lay asleep, earls who would soon endure   1280
a great reversal, once Grendel's mother
attacked and entered. Her onslaught was less
only by as much as an amazon warrior's
strength is less than an armed man's
when the hefted sword, its hammered edge   1285
and gleaming blade slathered in blood,
razes the sturdy boar-ridge off a helmet.
Then in the hall, hard-honed swords
were grabbed from the bench, many a broad shield
lifted and braced; there was little thought of helmets   1290
or woven mail when they woke in terror.
   The hell-dam was in panic, desperate to get out,
in mortal terror the moment she was found.
She had pounced and taken one of the retainers
in a tight hold, then headed for the fen.   1295
To Hrothgar, this man was the most beloved
of the friends he trusted between the two seas.
She had done away with a great warrior,
ambushed him at rest.
                         Beowulf was elsewhere.
Earlier, after the award of the treasure,   1300
the Geat had been given another lodging.
   There was uproar in Heorot. She had snatched their trophy,
Grendel's bloodied hand. It was a fresh blow
to the afflicted bawn. The bargain was hard,

both parties having to pay 1305
with the lives of friends. And the old lord,
the gray-haired warrior, was heartsore and weary
when he heard the news: his highest-placed adviser,
his dearest companion, was dead and gone.

Beowulf was quickly brought to the chamber: 1310
the winner of fights, the arch-warrior,
came first-footing in with his fellow troops
to where the king in his wisdom waited,
still wondering whether Almighty God
would ever turn the tide of his misfortunes. 1315
So Beowulf entered with his band in attendance
and the wooden floorboards banged and rang
as he advanced, hurrying to address
the prince of the Ingwins,[5] asking if he'd rested
since the urgent summons had come as a surprise. 1320

Then Hrothgar, the Shieldings' helmet, spoke:
"Rest? What is rest? Sorrow has returned.
Alas for the Danes! Aeschere is dead.
He was Yrmenlaf's elder brother
and a soul-mate to me, a true mentor, 1325
my right-hand man when the ranks clashed
and our boar-crests had to take a battering
in the line of action. Aeschere was everything
the world admires in a wise man and a friend.
Then this roaming killer came in a fury 1330
and slaughtered him in Heorot. Where she is hiding,
glutting on the corpse and glorying in her escape,
I cannot tell; she has taken up the feud
because of last night, when you killed Grendel,
wrestled and racked him in ruinous combat 1335
since for too long he had terrorized us
with his depredations. He died in battle,
paid with his life; and now this powerful
other one arrives, this force for evil
driven to avenge her kinsman's death. 1340
Or so it seems to thanes in their grief,
in the anguish every thane endures
at the loss of a ring-giver, now that the hand
that bestowed so richly has been stilled in death.

"I have heard it said by my people in hall, 1345
counselors who live in the upland country,
that they have seen two such creatures
prowling the moors, huge marauders
from some other world. One of these things,
as far as anyone ever can discern, 1350
looks like a woman; the other, warped
in the shape of a man, moves beyond the pale

5. The friends of the god Ing—that is, the Danes. See p. 135, n. 6.

bigger than any man, an unnatural birth
called Grendel by the country people
in former days. They are fatherless creatures,   1355
and their whole ancestry is hidden in a past
of demons and ghosts.[6] They dwell apart
among wolves on the hills, on windswept crags
and treacherous keshes, where cold streams
pour down the mountain and disappear   1360
under mist and moorland.

                  A few miles from here
a frost-stiffened wood waits and keeps watch
above a mere; the overhanging bank
is a maze of tree-roots mirrored in its surface.
At night there, something uncanny happens: 1365
the water burns. And the mere bottom
has never been sounded by the sons of men.
On its bank, the heather-stepper halts:
the hart in flight from pursuing hounds
will turn to face them with firm-set horns   1370
and die in the wood rather than dive
beneath its surface. That is no good place.
When wind blows up and stormy weather
makes clouds scud and the skies weep,
out of its depths a dirty surge   1375
is pitched toward the heavens. Now help depends
again on you and on you alone.
The gap of danger where the demon waits
is still unknown to you. Seek it if you dare.
I will compensate you for settling the feud   1380
as I did the last time with lavish wealth,
coffers of coiled gold, if you come back."

[Beowulf Fights Grendel's Mother]

Beowulf, son of Ecgtheow, spoke:
"Wise sir, do not grieve. It is always better
to avenge dear ones than to indulge in mourning.   1385
For every one of us, living in this world
means waiting for our end. Let whoever can
win glory before death. When a warrior is gone,
that will be his best and only bulwark.
So arise, my lord, and let us immediately   1390
set forth on the trail of this troll-dam.
I guarantee you: she will not get away,
not to dens under ground nor upland groves
nor the ocean floor. She'll have nowhere to flee to.
Endure your troubles today. Bear up   1395
and be the man I expect you to be."

6. Note that Hrothgar doesn't know of the biblical genealogy of Grendel and his mother that the
poet has given us in lines 102–14.

With that the old lord sprang to his feet
and praised God for Beowulf's pledge.
Then a bit and halter were brought for his horse
with the plaited mane. The wise king mounted   1400
the royal saddle and rode out in style
with a force of shield-bearers. The forest paths
were marked all over with the monster's tracks,
her trail on the ground wherever she had gone
across the dark moors, dragging away   1405
the body of that thane, Hrothgar's best
counselor and overseer of the country.
So the noble prince proceeded undismayed
up fells and screes, along narrow footpaths
and ways where they were forced into single file,   1410
ledges on cliffs above lairs of water-monsters.
He went in front with a few men,
good judges of the lie of the land,
and suddenly discovered the dismal wood,
mountain trees growing out at an angle   1415
above gray stones: the bloodshot water
surged underneath. It was a sore blow
to all of the Danes, friends of the Shieldings,
a hurt to each and every one
of that noble company when they came upon   1420
Aeschere's head at the foot of the cliff.
     Everybody gazed as the hot gore
kept wallowing up and an urgent war horn
repeated its notes: the whole party
sat down to watch. The water was infested   1425
with all kinds of reptiles. There were writhing sea-dragons
and monsters slouching on slopes by the cliff,
serpents and wild things such as those that often
surface at dawn to roam the sail-road
and doom the voyage. Down they plunged,   1430
lashing in anger at the loud call
of the battle-bugle. An arrow from the bow
of the Geat chief got one of them
as he surged to the surface: the seasoned shaft
stuck deep in his flank and his freedom in the water 1435
got less and less. It was his last swim.
He was swiftly overwhelmed in the shallows,
prodded by barbed boar-spears,
cornered, beaten, pulled up on the bank,
a strange lake-birth, a loathsome catch   1440
men gazed at in awe.
                    Beowulf got ready,
donned his war-gear, indifferent to death;
his mighty, hand-forged, fine-webbed mail
would soon meet with the menace underwater.
It would keep the bone-cage of his body safe: 1445

no enemy's clasp could crush him in it,
no vicious armlock choke his life out.
To guard his head he had a glittering helmet
that was due to be muddied on the mere bottom
and blurred in the upswirl. It was of beaten gold,   1450
princely headgear hooped and hasped
by a weapon-smith who had worked wonders
in days gone by and adorned it with boar-shapes;
since then it had resisted every sword.
And another item lent by Unferth   1455
at that moment of need was of no small importance:
the brehon[7] handed him a hilted weapon,
a rare and ancient sword named Hrunting.
The iron blade with its ill-boding patterns
had been tempered in blood. It had never failed   1460
the hand of anyone who hefted it in battle,
anyone who had fought and faced the worst
in the gap of danger. This was not the first time
it had been called to perform heroic feats.
     When he lent that blade to the better swordsman,   1465
Unferth, the strong-built son of Ecglaf,
could hardly have remembered the ranting speech
he had made in his cups. He was not man enough
to face the turmoil of a fight under water
and the risk to his life. So there he lost   1470
fame and repute. It was different for the other
rigged out in his gear, ready to do battle.
     Beowulf, son of Ecgtheow, spoke:
"Wisest of kings, now that I have come
to the point of action, I ask you to recall   1475
what we said earlier: that you, son of Halfdane
and gold-friend to retainers, that you, if I should fall
and suffer death while serving your cause,
would act like a father to me afterward.
If this combat kills me, take care   1480
of my young company, my comrades in arms.
And be sure also, my beloved Hrothgar,
to send Hygelac the treasures I received.
Let the lord of the Geats gaze on that gold,
let Hrethel's son take note of it and see   1485
that I found a ring-giver of rare magnificence
and enjoyed the good of his generosity.
And Unferth is to have what I inherited:
to that far-famed man I bequeath my own
sharp-honed, wave-sheened wonder-blade.   1490
With Hrunting I shall gain glory or die."
     After these words, the prince of the Weather-Geats

7. One of an ancient class of lawyers in Ireland [translator's note]. The word is used to translate
the Anglo-Saxon *thyle*.

was impatient to be away and plunged suddenly:
without more ado, he dived into the heaving
depths of the lake. It was the best part of a day   1495
before he could see the solid bottom.

    Quickly the one who haunted those waters,
who had scavenged and gone her gluttonous rounds
for a hundred seasons, sensed a human
observing her outlandish lair from above.   1500
So she lunged and clutched and managed to catch him
in her brutal grip; but his body, for all that,
remained unscathed: the mesh of the chain-mail
saved him on the outside. Her savage talons
failed to rip the web of his war-shirt.   1505
Then once she touched bottom, that wolfish swimmer
carried the ring-mailed prince to her court
so that for all his courage he could never use
the weapons he carried; and a bewildering horde
came at him from the depths, droves of sea-beasts   1510
who attacked with tusks and tore at his chain-mail
in a ghastly onslaught. The gallant man
could see he had entered some hellish turn-hole
and yet the water there did not work against him
because the hall-roofing held off   1515
the force of the current; then he saw firelight,
a gleam and flare-up, a glimmer of brightness.

    The hero observed that swamp thing from hell,
the tarn-hag[8] in all her terrible strength,
then heaved his war-sword and swung his arm: 1520
the decorated blade came down ringing
and singing on her head. But he soon found
his battle-torch extinguished; the shining blade
refused to bite. It spared her and failed
the man in his need. It had gone through many   1525
a hand-to-hand fight, had hewed the armor
and helmets of the doomed, but here at last
the fabulous powers of that heirloom failed.

    Hygelac's kinsman kept thinking about
his name and fame: he never lost heart.   1530
Then, in a fury, he flung his sword away.
The keen, inlaid, worm-loop-patterned steel
was hurled to the ground: he would have to rely
on the might of his arm. So must a man do
who intends to gain enduring glory   1535
in a combat. Life doesn't cost him a thought.
Then the prince of War-Geats, warming to this fight
with Grendel's mother, gripped her shoulder
and laid about him in a battle frenzy:
he pitched his killer opponent to the floor   1540

---

8. A "tarn" is a small lake.

but she rose quickly and retaliated,
grappled him tightly in her grim embrace.
The sure-footed fighter felt daunted,
the strongest of warriors stumbled and fell.
So she pounced upon him and pulled out   1545
a broad, whetted knife: now she would avenge
her only child. But the mesh of chain-mail
on Beowulf's shoulder shielded his life,
turned the edge and tip of the blade.
The son of Ecgtheow would have surely perished   1550
and the Geats lost their warrior under the wide earth
had the strong links and locks of his war-gear
not helped to save him: holy God
decided the victory. It was easy for the Lord,
the Ruler of Heaven, to redress the balance   1555
once Beowulf got back up on his feet.
   Then he saw a blade that boded well,
a sword in her armory, an ancient heirloom
from the days of the giants, an ideal weapon,
one that any warrior would envy,   1560
but so huge and heavy of itself
only Beowulf could wield it in a battle.
So the Shieldings' hero hard-pressed and enraged,
took a firm hold of the hilt and swung
the blade in an arc, a resolute blow   1565
that bit deep into her neck-bone
and severed it entirely, toppling the doomed
house of her flesh; she fell to the floor.
The sword dripped blood, the swordsman was elated.
   A light appeared and the place brightened   1570
the way the sky does when heaven's candle
is shining clearly. He inspected the vault:
with sword held high, its hilt raised
to guard and threaten, Hygelac's thane
scouted by the wall in Grendel's wake.   1575
Now the weapon was to prove its worth.
The warrior determined to take revenge
for every gross act Grendel had committed—
and not only for that one occasion
when he'd come to slaughter the sleeping troops,   1580
fifteen of Hrothgar's house-guards
surprised on their benches and ruthlessly devoured,
and as many again carried away,
a brutal plunder. Beowulf in his fury
now settled that score: he saw the monster   1585
in his resting place, war-weary and wrecked,
a lifeless corpse, a casualty
of the battle in Heorot. The body gaped
at the stroke dealt to it after death:
Beowulf cut the corpse's head off.   1590
   Immediately the counselors keeping a lookout
with Hrothgar, watching the lake water,

saw a heave-up and surge of waves
and blood in the backwash. They bowed gray heads,
spoke in their sage, experienced way   1595
about the good warrior, how they never again
expected to see that prince returning
in triumph to their king. It was clear to many
that the wolf of the deep had destroyed him forever.

    The ninth hour of the day arrived.   1600
The brave Shieldings abandoned the cliff-top
and the king went home; but sick at heart,
staring at the mere, the strangers held on.
They wished, without hope, to behold their lord,
Beowulf himself.

              Meanwhile, the sword   1605
began to wilt into gory icicles
to slather and thaw. It was a wonderful thing,
the way it all melted as ice melts
when the Father eases the fetters off the frost
and unravels the water-ropes, He who wields power   1610
over time and tide: He is the true Lord.

    The Geat captain saw treasure in abundance
but carried no spoils from those quarters
except for the head and the inlaid hilt
embossed with jewels; its blade had melted   1615
and the scrollwork on it burned, so scalding was the blood
of the poisonous fiend who had perished there.
Then away he swam, the one who had survived
the fall of his enemies, flailing to the surface.
The wide water, the waves and pools,   1620
were no longer infested once the wandering fiend
let go of her life and this unreliable world.

    The seafarers' leader made for land,
resolutely swimming, delighted with his prize,
the mighty load he was lugging to the surface.   1625
His thanes advanced in a troop to meet him,
thanking God and taking great delight
in seeing their prince back safe and sound.
Quickly the hero's helmet and mail-shirt
were loosed and unlaced. The lake settled,   1630
clouds darkened above the bloodshot depths.

    With high hearts they headed away
along footpaths and trails through the fields,
roads that they knew, each of them wrestling
with the head they were carrying from the lakeside cliff,   1635
men kingly in their courage and capable
of difficult work. It was a task for four
to hoist Grendel's head on a spear
and bear it under strain to the bright hall.
But soon enough they neared the place,   1640
fourteen Geats in fine fettle,
striding across the outlying ground
in a delighted throng around their leader.

In he came then, the thanes' commander,
the arch-warrior, to address Hrothgar: 1645
his courage was proven, his glory was secure.
Grendel's head was hauled by the hair,
dragged across the floor where the people were drinking,
a horror for both queen and company to behold.
They stared in awe. It was an astonishing sight.   1650

[Another Celebration at Heorot]

Beowulf, son of Ecgtheow, spoke:
"So, son of Halfdane, prince of the Shieldings,
we are glad to bring this booty from the lake.
It is a token of triumph and we tender it to you.
I barely survived the battle under water.   1655
It was hard-fought, a desperate affair
that could have gone badly; if God had not helped me,
the outcome would have been quick and fatal.
Although Hrunting is hard-edged,
I could never bring it to bear in battle.   1660
But the Lord of Men allowed me to behold—
for He often helps the unbefriended—
an ancient sword shining on the wall,
a weapon made for giants, there for the wielding.
Then my moment came in the combat and I struck   1665
the dwellers in that den. Next thing the damascened[9]
sword blade melted; it bloated and it burned
in their rushing blood. I have wrested the hilt
from the enemies' hand, avenged the evil
done to the Danes; it is what was due.   1670
And this I pledge, O prince of the Shieldings:
you can sleep secure with your company of troops
in Heorot Hall. Never need you fear
for a single thane of your sept[1] or nation,
young warriors or old, that laying waste of life   1675
that you and your people endured of yore."
    Then the gold hilt was handed over
to the old lord, a relic from long ago
for the venerable ruler. That rare smithwork
was passed on to the prince of the Danes   1680
when those devils perished; once death removed
that murdering, guilt-steeped, God-cursed fiend,
eliminating his unholy life
and his mother's as well, it was willed to that king
who of all the lavish gift-lords of the north   1685
was the best regarded between the two seas.
    Hrothgar spoke; he examined the hilt,
that relic of old times. It was engraved all over

---

9. Ornamented with inlaid designs.   1. An Irish term meaning a clan or division of a
                                                  tribe.

and showed how war first came into the world
and the flood destroyed the tribe of giants. 1690
They suffered a terrible severance from the Lord;
the Almighty made the waters rise,
drowned them in the deluge for retribution.
In pure gold inlay on the sword-guards
there were rune-markings correctly incised, 1695
stating and recording for whom the sword
had been first made and ornamented
with its scrollworked hilt. Then everyone hushed
as the son of Halfdane spoke this wisdom:
"A protector of his people, pledged to uphold 1700
truth and justice and to respect tradition,
is entitled to affirm that this man
was born to distinction. Beowulf, my friend,
your fame has gone far and wide,
you are known everywhere. In all things you are even-tempered, 1705
prudent and resolute. So I stand firm by the promise of friendship
we exchanged before. Forever you will be
your people's mainstay and your own warriors'
helping hand.
      Heremod was different,
the way he behaved to Ecgwela's sons.[2] 1710
His rise in the world brought little joy
to the Danish people, only death and destruction.
He vented his rage on men he caroused with,
killed his own comrades, a pariah king
who cut himself off from his own kind, 1715
even though Almighty God had made him
eminent and powerful and marked him from the start
for a happy life. But a change happened,
he grew bloodthirsty, gave no more rings
to honor the Danes. He suffered in the end 1720
for having plagued his people for so long:
his life lost happiness.
      So learn from this
and understand true values. I who tell you
have wintered into wisdom.
      It is a great wonder
how Almighty God in His magnificence 1725
favors our race with rank and scope
and the gift of wisdom; His sway is wide.
Sometimes He allows the mind of a man
of distinguished birth to follow its bent,
grants him fulfillment and felicity on earth 1730
and forts to command in his own country.
He permits him to lord it in many lands
until the man in his unthinkingness

---

2. That is, the Danes. Ecgwela was evidently a former king of the Danes.

forgets that it will ever end for him.
He indulges his desires; illness and old age   1735
mean nothing to him; his mind is untroubled
by envy or malice or the thought of enemies
with their hate-honed swords. The whole world
conforms to his will, he is kept from the worst
until an element of overweening   1740
enters him and takes hold
while the soul's guard, its sentry, drowses,
grown too distracted. A killer stalks him,
an archer who draws a deadly bow.
And then the man is hit in the heart,   1745
the arrow flies beneath his defenses,
the devious promptings of the demon start.
His old possessions seem paltry to him now.
He covets and resents; dishonors custom
and bestows no gold; and because of good things   1750
that the Heavenly Powers gave him in the past
he ignores the shape of things to come.
Then finally the end arrives
when the body he was lent collapses and falls
prey to its death; ancestral possessions   1755
and the goods he hoarded are inherited by another
who lets them go with a liberal hand.
    "O flower of warriors, beware of that trap.
Choose, dear Beowulf, the better part,
eternal rewards. Do not give way to pride.   1760
For a brief while your strength is in bloom
but it fades quickly; and soon there will follow
illness or the sword to lay you low,
or a sudden fire or surge of water
or jabbing blade or javelin from the air   1765
or repellent age. Your piercing eye
will dim and darken; and death will arrive,
dear warrior, to sweep you away.
    "Just so I ruled the Ring-Danes' country
for fifty years, defended them in wartime   1770
with spear and sword against constant assaults
by many tribes: I came to believe
my enemies had faded from the face of the earth.
Still, what happened was a hard reversal
from bliss to grief. Grendel struck   1775
after lying in wait. He laid waste to the land
and from that moment my mind was in dread
of his depredations. So I praise God
in His heavenly glory that I lived to behold
this head dripping blood and that after such harrowing   1780
I can look upon it in triumph at last.
Take your place, then, with pride and pleasure,
and move to the feast. Tomorrow morning
our treasure will be shared and showered upon you."

The Geat was elated and gladly obeyed   1785
the old man's bidding; he sat on the bench.
And soon all was restored, the same as before.
Happiness came back, the hall was thronged,
and a banquet set forth; black night fell
and covered them in darkness.
                Then the company rose   1790
for the old campaigner: the gray-haired prince
was ready for bed. And a need for rest
came over the brave shield-bearing Geat.
He was a weary seafarer, far from home,
so immediately a house-guard guided him out,   1795
one whose office entailed looking after
whatever a thane on the road in those days
might need or require. It was noble courtesy.

[Beowulf Returns Home]

That great heart rested. The hall towered,
gold-shingled and gabled, and the guest slept in it   1800
until the black raven with raucous glee
announced heaven's joy, and a hurry of brightness
overran the shadows. Warriors rose quickly,
impatient to be off: their own country
was beckoning the nobles; and the bold voyager   1805
longed to be aboard his distant boat.
Then that stalwart fighter ordered Hrunting
to be brought to Unferth, and bade Unferth
take the sword and thanked him for lending it.
He said he had found it a friend in battle   1810
and a powerful help; he put no blame
on the blade's cutting edge. He was a considerate man.
And there the warriors stood in their war-gear,
eager to go, while their honored lord
approached the platform where the other sat.   1815
The undaunted hero addressed Hrothgar.
Beowulf, son of Ecgtheow, spoke:
"Now we who crossed the wide sea
have to inform you that we feel a desire
to return to Hygelac. Here we have been welcomed   1820
and thoroughly entertained. You have treated us well.
If there is any favor on earth I can perform
beyond deeds of arms I have done already,
anything that would merit your affections more,
I shall act, my lord, with alacrity.   1825
If ever I hear from across the ocean
that people on your borders are threatening battle
as attackers have done from time to time,
I shall land with a thousand thanes at my back
to help your cause. Hygelac may be young   1830

to rule a nation, but this much I know
about the king of the Geats: he will come to my aid
and want to support me by word and action
in your hour of need, when honor dictates
that I raise a hedge of spears around you. 1835
Then if Hrethric should think about traveling
as a king's son to the court of the Geats,
he will find many friends. Foreign places
yield more to one who is himself worth meeting."
　　Hrothgar spoke and answered him: 1840
"The Lord in his wisdom sent you those words
and they came from the heart. I have never heard
so young a man make truer observations.
You are strong in body and mature in mind,
impressive in speech. If it should come to pass 1845
that Hrethel's descendant dies beneath a spear,
if deadly battle or the sword blade or disease
fells the prince who guards your people
and you are still alive, then I firmly believe
the seafaring Geats won't find a man 1850
worthier of acclaim as their king and defender
than you, if only you would undertake
the lordship of your homeland. My liking for you
deepens with time, dear Beowulf.
What you have done is to draw two peoples, 1855
the Geat nation and us neighboring Danes,
into shared peace and a pact of friendship
in spite of hatreds we have harbored in the past.
For as long as I rule this far-flung land
treasures will change hands and each side will treat 1860
the other with gifts; across the gannet's bath,
over the broad sea, whorled prows will bring
presents and tokens. I know your people
are beyond reproach in every respect,
steadfast in the old way with friend or foe." 1865
　　Then the earls' defender furnished the hero
with twelve treasures and told him to set out,
sail with those gifts safely home
to the people he loved, but to return promptly.
And so the good and gray-haired Dane, 1870
that highborn king, kissed Beowulf
and embraced his neck, then broke down
in sudden tears. Two forebodings
disturbed him in his wisdom, but one was stronger:[3]
nevermore would they meet each other 1875
face to face. And such was his affection
that he could not help being overcome:
his fondness for the man was so deep-founded,

---

3. We are not told what the other foreboding is, but it is probably the old man's awareness of the
imminence of his own death.

it warmed his heart and wound the heartstrings
tight in his breast.

The embrace ended   1880
and Beowulf, glorious in his gold regalia,
stepped the green earth. Straining at anchor
and ready for boarding, his boat awaited him.
So they went on their journey, and Hrothgar's generosity
was praised repeatedly. He was a peerless king   1885
until old age sapped his strength and did him
mortal harm, as it has done so many.

Down to the waves then, dressed in the web
of their chain-mail and war-shirts the young men marched
in high spirits. The coast-guard spied them,   1890
thanes setting forth, the same as before.
His salute this time from the top of the cliff
was far from unmannerly; he galloped to meet them
and as they took ship in their shining gear,
he said how welcome they would be in Geatland.   1895
Then the broad hull was beached on the sand
to be cargoed with treasure, horses and war-gear.
The curved prow motioned; the mast stood high
above Hrothgar's riches in the loaded hold.

The guard who had watched the boat was given   1900
a sword with gold fittings, and in future days
that present would make him a respected man
at his place on the mead-bench.

Then the keel plunged
and shook in the sea; and they sailed from Denmark.
Right away the mast was rigged with its sea-shawl;   1905
sail-ropes were tightened, timbers drummed
and stiff winds kept the wave-crosser
skimming ahead; as she heaved forward,
her foamy neck was fleet and buoyant,
a lapped prow loping over currents,   1910
until finally the Geats caught sight of coastline
and familiar cliffs. The keel reared up,
wind lifted it home, it hit on the land.

The harbor guard came hurrying out
to the rolling water: he had watched the offing   1915
long and hard, on the lookout for those friends.
With the anchor cables, he moored their craft
right where it had beached, in case a backwash
might catch the hull and carry it away.
Then he ordered the prince's treasure-trove   1920
to be carried ashore. It was a short step
from there to where Hrethel's son and heir,
Hygelac the gold-giver, makes his home
on a secure cliff, in the company of retainers.

The building was magnificent, the king majestic,   1925
ensconced in his hall; and although Hygd, his queen,
was young, a few short years at court,

her mind was thoughtful and her manners sure.
Haereth's daughter[4] behaved generously
and stinted nothing when she distributed   1930
bounty to the Geats.

             Great Queen Modthryth
perpetrated terrible wrongs.[5]
If any retainer ever made bold
to look her in the face, if an eye not her lord's[6]
stared at her directly during daylight,   1935
the outcome was sealed: he was kept bound,
in hand-tightened shackles, racked, tortured
until doom was pronounced—death by the sword,
slash of blade, blood-gush, and death-qualms
in an evil display. Even a queen   1940
outstanding in beauty must not overstep like that.
A queen should weave peace, not punish the innocent
with loss of life for imagined insults.
But Hemming's kinsman put a halt to her ways
and drinkers round the table had another tale: 1945
she was less of a bane to people's lives,
less cruel-minded, after she was married
to the brave Offa,[7] a bride arrayed
in her gold finery, given away
by a caring father, ferried to her young prince   1950
over dim seas. In days to come
she would grace the throne and grow famous
for her good deeds and conduct of life,
her high devotion to the hero king
who was the best king, it has been said,   1955
between the two seas or anywhere else
on the face of the earth. Offa was honored
far and wide for his generous ways,
his fighting spirit and his farseeing
defense of his homeland; from him there sprang Eomer,   1960
Garmund's grandson, kinsman of Hemming,[8]
his warriors' mainstay and master of the field.

   Heroic Beowulf and his band of men
crossed the wide strand, striding along
the sandy foreshore; the sun shone,   1965
the world's candle warmed them from the south
as they hastened to where, as they had heard,
the young king, Ongentheow's killer[9]

---

4. That is, Hygd.
5. A Danish queen whose wickedness is being used as a foil to Hygd.
6. Probably her father, although the Anglo-Saxon word can also refer to a husband.
7. A legendary king of the Angles, one of the Germanic peoples who invaded England and established a kingdom named Mercia in the north of the country prior to the composition

of *Beowulf*. Hemming is evidently a forebear of the Angles.
8. Garmund is Offa's father, Eomer his son.
9. Hygelac, king of the Geats; he led the attack against the Swedes, although a Geat named Eofor actually killed Ongentheow. This is the first reference to the feud between the Geats and the Swedes (or Shylfings); see below, lines 2379–96, 2468–89, 2922–98.

and his people's protector, was dispensing rings
inside his bawn. Beowulf's return   1970
was reported to Hygelac as soon as possible,
news that the captain was now in the enclosure,
his battle-brother back from the fray
alive and well, walking to the hall.
Room was quickly made, on the king's orders,   1975
and the troops filed across the cleared floor.
    After Hygelac had offered greetings
to his loyal thane in a lofty speech,
he and his kinsman, that hale survivor,
sat face to face. Hacreth's daughter[1]   1980
moved about with the mead-jug in her hand,
taking care of the company, filling the cups
that warriors held out. Then Hygelac began
to put courteous questions to his old comrade
in the high hall. He hankered to know   1985
every tale the Sea-Geats had to tell:
"How did you fare on your foreign voyage,
dear Beowulf, when you abruptly decided
to sail away across the salt water
and fight at Heorot? Did you help Hrothgar   1990
much in the end? Could you ease the prince
of his well-known troubles? Your undertaking
cast my spirits down, I dreaded the outcome
of your expedition and pleaded with you
long and hard to leave the killer be,   1995
let the South-Danes settle their own
blood-feud with Grendel. So God be thanked
I am granted this sight of you, safe and sound."
    Beowulf, son of Ecgtheow, spoke:
"What happened, Lord Hygelac, is hardly a secret   2000
any more among men in this world—
myself and Grendel coming to grips
on the very spot where he visited destruction
on the Victory-Shieldings and violated
life and limb, losses I avenged   2005
so no earthly offspring of Grendel's
need ever boast of that bout before dawn,
no matter how long the last of his evil
family survives.
              When I first landed
I hastened to the ring-hall and saluted Hrothgar.   2010
Once he discovered why I had come,
the son of Halfdane sent me immediately
to sit with his own sons on the bench.
It was a happy gathering. In my whole life
I have never seen mead enjoyed more   2015
in any hall on earth. Sometimes the queen

1. That is, Hygd.

herself appeared, peace-pledge between nations,[2]
to hearten the young ones and hand out
a torque to a warrior, then take her place.
Sometimes Hrothgar's daughter distributed   2020
ale to older ranks, in order on the benches:
I heard the company call her Freawaru
as she made her rounds, presenting men
with the gem-studded bowl, young bride-to-be
to the gracious Ingeld,[3] in her gold-trimmed attire.   2025
The friend of the Shieldings favors her betrothal:
the guardian of the kingdom sees good in it
and hopes this woman will heal old wounds
and grievous feuds.
                But generally the spear
is prompt to retaliate when a prince is killed,   2030
no matter how admirable the bride may be.
   "Think how the Heatho-Bards are bound to feel,
their lord, Ingeld, and his loyal thanes,
when he walks in with that woman to the feast:
Danes are at the table, being entertained,   2035
honored guests in glittering regalia,
burnished ring-mail that was their hosts' birthright,
looted when the Heatho-Bards could no longer wield
their weapons in the shield-clash, when they went down
with their beloved comrades and forfeited their lives.   2040
Then an old spearman will speak while they are drinking,
having glimpsed some heirloom that brings alive
memories of the massacre; his mood will darken
and heart-stricken, in the stress of his emotion,
he will begin to test a young man's temper   2045
and stir up trouble, starting like this:
'Now, my friend, don't you recognize
your father's sword, his favorite weapon,
the one he wore when he went out in his war-mask
to face the Danes on that final day?   2050
After Withergeld[4] died and his men were doomed,
the Shieldings quickly claimed the field;
and now here's a son of one or other
of those same killers coming through our hall
overbearing us, mouthing boasts,   2055
and rigged in armor that by right is yours.'
And so he keeps on, recalling and accusing,
working things up with bitter words
until one of the lady's retainers lies

---

2. Wealhtheow, Hrothgar's queen, is called a "peace-pledge between nations" because kings attempted to end feuds by marrying their daughters to the sons of the kings of enemy nations. But as we have already seen in the case of the marriage of the Dane Hildeburh to the Jute Finn, and as we shall shortly learn again, such a strategy seems rarely to have worked.

3. King of the Heatho-Bards, whose father, Froda, was killed by the Danes.

4. A Heatho-Bard warrior.

spattered in blood, split open   2060
on his father's account.[5] The killer knows
the lie of the land and escapes with his life.
Then on both sides the oath-bound lords
will break the peace, a passionate hate
will build up in Ingeld, and love for his bride   2065
will falter in him as the feud rankles.
I therefore suspect the good faith of the Heatho-Bards,
the truth of their friendship and the trustworthiness
of their alliance with the Danes.
                            But now, my lord,
I shall carry on with my account of Grendel,   2070
the whole story of everything that happened
in the hand-to-hand fight.
                            After heaven's gem
had gone mildly to earth, that maddened spirit,
the terror of those twilights, came to attack us
where we stood guard, still safe inside the hall.   2075
There deadly violence came down on Hondscio[6]
and he fell as fate ordained, the first to perish,
rigged out for the combat. A comrade from our ranks
had come to grief in Grendel's maw:
he ate up the entire body.   2080
There was blood on his teeth, he was bloated and dangerous,
all roused up, yet still unready
to leave the hall empty-handed;
renowned for his might, he matched himself against me,
wildly reaching. He had this roomy pouch,[7]   2085
a strange accoutrement, intricately strung
and hung at the ready, a rare patchwork
of devilishly fitted dragon-skins.
I had done him no wrong, yet the raging demon
wanted to cram me and many another   2090
into this bag—but it was not to be
once I got to my feet in a blind fury.
It would take too long to tell how I repaid
the terror of the land for every life he took
and so won credit for you, my king,   2095
and for all your people. And although he got away
to enjoy life's sweetness for a while longer,
his right hand stayed behind him in Heorot,
evidence of his miserable overthrow
as he dived into murk on the mere bottom.   2100
    "I got lavish rewards from the lord of the Danes
for my part in the battle, beaten gold
and much else, once morning came

---

5. A Danish attendant to Freawaru, whose
father killed a Heatho-Bard in the original
battle; this action is envisioned as taking place
at Ingeld's court after the marriage.

6. A Geat who was accompanying Beowulf;
his name means "glove."

7. The Anglo-Saxon word translated as
"pouch" literally means "glove."

and we took our places at the banquet table.
There was singing and excitement: an old reciter,   2105
a carrier of stories, recalled the early days.
At times some hero made the timbered harp
tremble with sweetness, or related true
and tragic happenings; at times the king
gave the proper turn to some fantastic tale,   2110
or a battle-scarred veteran, bowed with age,
would begin to remember the martial deeds
of his youth and prime and be overcome
as the past welled up in his wintry heart.
   "We were happy there the whole day long   2115
and enjoyed our time until another night
descended upon us. Then suddenly
the vehement mother avenged her son
and wreaked destruction. Death had robbed her,
Geats had slain Grendel, so his ghastly dam   2120
struck back and with bare-faced defiance
laid a man low. Thus life departed
from the sage Aeschere, an elder wise in counsel.
But afterward, on the morning following,
the Danes could not burn the dead body   2125
nor lay the remains of the man they loved
on his funeral pyre. She had fled with the corpse
and taken refuge beneath torrents on the mountain.
It was a hard blow for Hrothgar to bear,
harder than any he had undergone before.   2130
And so the heartsore king beseeched me
in your royal name to take my chances
underwater, to win glory
and prove my worth. He promised me rewards.
Hence, as is well known, I went to my encounter   2135
with the terror-monger at the bottom of the tarn.
For a while it was hand-to-hand between us,
then blood went curling along the currents
and I beheaded Grendel's mother in the hall
with a mighty sword. I barely managed   2140
to escape with my life; my time had not yet come.
But Halfdane's heir, the shelter of those earls,
again endowed me with gifts in abundance.
   "Thus the king acted with due custom.
I was paid and recompensed completely,   2145
given full measure and the freedom to choose
from Hrothgar's treasures by Hrothgar himself.
These, King Hygelac, I am happy to present
to you as gifts. It is still upon your grace
that all favor depends. I have few kinsmen   2150
who are close, my king, except for your kind self."
Then he ordered the boar-framed standard to be brought,
the battle-topping helmet, the mail-shirt gray as hoar-frost,
and the precious war-sword; and proceeded with his speech:

"When Hrothgar presented this war-gear to me   2155
he instructed me, my lord, to give you some account
of why it signifies his special favor.
He said it had belonged to his older brother,
King Heorogar, who had long kept it,
but that Heorogar had never bequeathed it   2160
to his son Heoroward, that worthy scion,
loyal as he was.
                    Enjoy it well."
   I heard four horses were handed over next.
Beowulf bestowed four bay steeds
to go with the armor, swift gallopers,   2165
all alike. So ought a kinsman act,
instead of plotting and planning in secret
to bring people to grief, or conspiring to arrange
the death of comrades. The warrior king
was uncle to Beowulf and honored by his nephew: 2170
each was concerned for the other's good.
   I heard he presented Hygd with a gorget,
the priceless torque that the prince's daughter,
Wealhtheow, had given him; and three horses,
supple creatures brilliantly saddled.   2175
The bright necklace would be luminous on Hygd's breast.
   Thus Beowulf bore himself with valor;
he was formidable in battle yet behaved with honor
and took no advantage; never cut down
a comrade who was drunk, kept his temper   2180
and, warrior that he was, watched and controlled
his God-sent strength and his outstanding
natural powers. He had been poorly regarded
for a long time, was taken by the Geats
for less than he was worth: and their lord too   2185
had never much esteemed him in the mead-hall.
They firmly believed that he lacked force,
that the prince was a weakling; but presently
every affront to his deserving was reversed.
   The battle-famed king, bulwark of his earls,   2190
ordered a gold-chased heirloom of Hrethel's[8]
to be brought in; it was the best example
of a gem-studded sword in the Geat treasury.
This he laid on Beowulf's lap
and then rewarded him with land as well,   2195
seven thousand hides;[9] and a hall and a throne.
Both owned land by birth in that country,
ancestral grounds; but the greater right
and sway were inherited by the higher born.

---

8. Hygelac's father and, through his daughter, Beowulf's grandfather.
9. A "hide" varied in size, but was considered

to be sufficient land to support a peasant and
his family.

[*The Dragon Wakes*]

A lot was to happen in later days   2200
in the fury of battle. Hygelac fell
and the shelter of Heardred's shield proved useless
against the fierce aggression of the Shylfings:[1]
ruthless swordsmen, seasoned campaigners,
they came against him and his conquering nation,   2205
and with cruel force cut him down
so that afterwards
           the wide kingdom
reverted to Beowulf. He ruled it well
for fifty winters, grew old and wise
as warden of the land
           until one began   2210
to dominate the dark, a dragon on the prowl
from the steep vaults of a stone-roofed barrow[2]
where he guarded a hoard; there was a hidden passage,
unknown to men, but someone managed[3]
to enter by it and interfere   2215
with the heathen trove. He had handled and removed
a gem-studded goblet; it gained him nothing,
though with a thief's wiles he had outwitted
the sleeping dragon. That drove him into rage,
as the people of that country would soon discover.   2220
   The intruder who broached the dragon's treasure
and moved him to wrath had never meant to.
It was desperation on the part of a slave
fleeing the heavy hand of some master,
guilt-ridden and on the run,   2225
going to ground. But he soon began
to shake with terror; . . . . . . in shock
the wretch . . . .
          . . . . panicked and ran
away with the precious   2230
metalwork. There were many other
heirlooms heaped inside the earth-house,
because long ago, with deliberate care,
somebody now forgotten
had buried the riches of a highborn race   2235
in this ancient cache. Death had come
and taken them all in times gone by
and the only one left to tell their tale,
the last of their line, could look forward to nothing
but the same fate for himself: he foresaw that his joy   2240
in the treasure would be brief.

1. Hygelac died in the raid against the Franks (see p. 140, n. 4); Heardred died in the long feud against the Swedes or Shylfings (see p. 156, n. 9).
2. A burial mound.
3. In the single manuscript of *Beowulf*, the page containing lines 2215–31 is badly damaged, and the translation is therefore conjectural. The ellipses of lines 2227–30 indicate lines that cannot be reconstructed at all.

           A newly constructed
barrow stood waiting, on a wide headland
close to the waves, its entryway secured.
Into it the keeper of the hoard had carried
all the goods and golden ware   2245
worth preserving. His words were few:
"Now, earth, hold what earls once held
and heroes can no more; it was mined from you first
by honorable men. My own people
have been ruined in war; one by one   2250
they went down to death, looked their last
on sweet life in the hall. I am left with nobody
to bear a sword or to burnish plated goblets,
put a sheen on the cup. The companies have departed.
The hard helmet, hasped with gold,   2255
will be stripped of its hoops; and the helmet-shiner
who should polish the metal of the war-mask sleeps;
the coat of mail that came through all fights,
through shield-collapse and cut of sword,
decays with the warrior. Nor may webbed mail   2260
range far and wide on the warlord's back
beside his mustered troops. No trembling harp,
no tuned timber, no tumbling hawk
swerving through the hall, no swift horse
pawing the courtyard. Pillage and slaughter   2265
have emptied the earth of entire peoples."
And so he mourned as he moved about the world,
deserted and alone, lamenting his unhappiness
day and night, until death's flood
brimmed up in his heart.   2270
              Then an old harrower of the dark
happened to find the hoard open,
the burning one who hunts out barrows,
the slick-skinned dragon, threatening the night sky
with streamers of fire. People on the farms
are in dread of him. He is driven to hunt out   2275
hoards under ground, to guard heathen gold
through age-long vigils, though to little avail.
For three centuries, this scourge of the people
had stood guard on that stoutly protected
underground treasury, until the intruder   2280
unleashed its fury; he hurried to his lord
with the gold-plated cup and made his plea
to be reinstated. Then the vault was rifled,
the ring-hoard robbed, and the wretched man
had his request granted. His master gazed   2285
on that find from the past for the first time.
   When the dragon awoke, trouble flared again.
He rippled down the rock, writhing with anger
when he saw the footprints of the prowler who had stolen
too close to his dreaming head.   2290

So may a man not marked by fate
easily escape exile and woe
by the grace of God.
                    The hoard-guardian
scorched the ground as he scoured and hunted
for the trespasser who had troubled his sleep.   2295
Hot and savage, he kept circling and circling
the outside of the mound. No man appeared
in that desert waste, but he worked himself up
by imagining battle; then back in he'd go
in search of the cup, only to discover   2300
signs that someone had stumbled upon
the golden treasures. So the guardian of the mound,
the hoard-watcher, waited for the gloaming
with fierce impatience; his pent-up fury
at the loss of the vessel made him long to hit back   2305
and lash out in flames. Then, to his delight,
the day waned and he could wait no longer
behind the wall, but hurtled forth
in a fiery blaze. The first to suffer
were the people on the land, but before long   2310
it was their treasure-giver who would come to grief.
    The dragon began to belch out flames
and burn bright homesteads; there was a hot glow
that scared everyone, for the vile sky-winger
would leave nothing alive in his wake.   2315
Everywhere the havoc he wrought was in evidence.
Far and near, the Geat nation
bore the brunt of his brutal assaults
and virulent hate. Then back to the hoard
he would dart before daybreak, to hide in his den.   2320
He had swinged[4] the land, swathed it in flame,
in fire and burning, and now he felt secure
in the vaults of his barrow; but his trust was unavailing.
    Then Beowulf was given bad news,
the hard truth: his own home,   2325
the best of buildings, had been burned to a cinder,
the throne-room of the Geats. It threw the hero
into deep anguish and darkened his mood:
the wise man thought he must have thwarted
ancient ordinance of the eternal Lord,   2330
broken His commandment. His mind was in turmoil,
unaccustomed anxiety and gloom
confused his brain; the fire-dragon
had razed the coastal region and reduced
forts and earthworks to dust and ashes,   2335
so the war-king planned and plotted his revenge.
The warriors' protector, prince of the hall-troop,

---

4. That is, singed, scorched.

ordered a marvelous all-iron shield
from his smithy works. He well knew
that linden boards would let him down   2340
and timber burn. After many trials,
he was destined to face the end of his days,
in this mortal world, as was the dragon,
for all his long leasehold on the treasure.

    Yet the prince of the rings was too proud   2345
to line up with a large army
against the sky-plague. He had scant regard
for the dragon as a threat, no dread at all
of its courage or strength, for he had kept going
often in the past, through perils and ordeals   2350
of every sort, after he had purged
Hrothgar's hall, triumphed in Heorot
and beaten Grendel. He outgrappled the monster
and his evil kin.

        One of his cruelest
hand-to-hand encounters had happened   2355
when Hygelac, king of the Geats, was killed
in Friesland: the people's friend and lord,
Hrethel's son, slaked a sword blade's
thirst for blood. But Beowulf's prodigious
gifts as a swimmer guaranteed his safety: 2360
he arrived at the shore, shouldering thirty
battle-dresses, the booty he had won.
There was little for the Hetware[5] to be happy about
as they shielded their faces and fighting on the ground
began in earnest. With Beowulf against them,   2365
few could hope to return home.

    Across the wide sea, desolate and alone,
the son of Ecgtheow swam back to his people.
There Hygd offered him throne and authority
as lord of the ring-hoard: with Hygelac dead,   2370
she had no belief in her son's ability
to defend their homeland against foreign invaders.
Yet there was no way the weakened nation
could get Beowulf to give in and agree
to be elevated over Heardred as his lord   2375
or to undertake the office of kingship.
But he did provide support for the prince,
honored and minded him until he matured
as the ruler of Geatland.

        Then over sea-roads
exiles arrived, sons of Ohthere.[6]   2380

---

5. A Frankish tribe.
6. King of the Swedes or Shylfings; after his
death his sons, Eanmund and Eadgils, were
driven out by their uncle Onela. They were
taken in by Heardred, Hygelac's son, who was

then king of the Geats, who was then in turn
attacked and killed (along with Eanmund) by
Onela. At this point Beowulf became king of
the Geats and supported Eadgils in his successful attack on Onela.

They had rebelled against the best of all
the sea-kings in Sweden, the one who held sway
in the Shylfing nation, their renowned prince,
lord of the mead-hall. That marked the end
for Hygelac's son: his hospitality   2385
was mortally rewarded with wounds from a sword.
Heardred lay slaughtered and Onela returned
to the land of Sweden, leaving Beowulf
to ascend the throne, to sit in majesty
and rule over the Geats. He was a good king.   2390

    In days to come, he contrived to avenge
the fall of his prince; he befriended Eadgils
when Eadgils was friendless, aiding his cause
with weapons and warriors over the wide sea,
sending him men. The feud was settled   2395
on a comfortless campaign when he killed Onela.

    And so the son of Ecgtheow had survived
every extreme, excelling himself
in daring and in danger, until the day arrived
when he had to come face to face with the dragon.   2400
The lord of the Geats took eleven comrades
and went in a rage to reconnoiter.
By then he had discovered the cause of the affliction
being visited on the people. The precious cup
had come to him from the hand of the finder,   2405
the one who had started all this strife
and was now added as a thirteenth to their number.
They press-ganged and compelled this poor creature
to be their guide. Against his will
he led them to the earth-vault he alone knew,   2410
an underground barrow near the sea-billows
and heaving waves, heaped inside
with exquisite metalwork. The one who stood guard
was dangerous and watchful, warden of the trove
buried under earth: no easy bargain   2415
would be made in that place by any man.

    The veteran king sat down on the cliff-top.
He wished good luck to the Geats who had shared
his hearth and his gold. He was sad at heart,
unsettled yet ready, sensing his death.   2420
His fate hovered near, unknowable but certain:
it would soon claim his coffered soul,
part life from limb. Before long
the prince's spirit would spin free from his body.

    Beowulf, son of Ecgtheow, spoke: 2425
"Many a skirmish I survived when I was young
and many times of war: I remember them well.
At seven, I was fostered out by my father,
left in the charge of my people's lord.
King Hrethel kept me and took care of me,   2430
was openhanded, behaved like a kinsman.
While I was his ward, he treated me no worse

as a wean[7] about the place than one of his own boys,
Herebeald and Haethcyn, or my own Hygelac.
For the eldest, Herebeald, an unexpected
deathbed was laid out, through a brother's doing,
when Haethcyn bent his horn-tipped bow
and loosed the arrow that destroyed his life.
He shot wide and buried a shaft
in the flesh and blood of his own brother.
That offense was beyond redress, a wrongfooting
of the heart's affections; for who could avenge
the prince's life or pay his death-price?
It was like the misery felt by an old man
who has lived to see his son's body
swing on the gallows. He begins to keen
and weep for his boy, watching the raven
gloat where he hangs: he can be of no help.
The wisdom of age is worthless to him.
Morning after morning, he wakes to remember
that his child is gone; he has no interest
in living on until another heir
is born in the hall, now that his first-born
has entered death's dominion forever.
He gazes sorrowfully at his son's dwelling,
the banquet hall bereft of all delight,
the windswept hearthstone; the horsemen are sleeping,
the warriors under ground; what was is no more.
No tunes from the harp, no cheer raised in the yard.
Alone with his longing, he lies down on his bed
and sings a lament; everything seems too large,
the steadings and the fields.
                   Such was the feeling
of loss endured by the lord of the Geats
after Herebeald's death. He was helplessly placed
to set to rights the wrong committed,
could not punish the killer in accordance with the law
of the blood-feud, although he felt no love for him.
Heartsore, wearied, he turned away
from life's joys, chose God's light
and departed, leaving buildings and lands
to his sons, as a man of substance will.
   "Then over the wide sea Swedes and Geats
battled and feuded and fought without quarter.
Hostilities broke out when Hrethel died.
Ongentheow's sons[8] were unrelenting,
refusing to make peace, campaigning violently

2435
2440
2445
2450
2455
2460
2465
2470
2475

7. A young child [translator's note]; a Northern Irish word.
8. Ohthere and Onela, who attacked the
Geats and killed Haethcyn; Haethcyn was
then avenged by his brother Hygelac, whose
attack on the Swedes resulted in the death
of Ongentheow at the hands of the Geat
Eofor (described below in lines 2922–98).
These events took place before those of lines
2379–96, which describe the Geats' role in
the struggle between Onela and Ohthere's two
sons after Ongentheow's death.

from coast to coast, constantly setting up
terrible ambushes around Hreosnahill.[9]
My own kith and kin avenged
these evil events, as everybody knows,
but the price was high: one of them paid   2480
with his life. Haethcyn, lord of the Geats,
met his fate there and fell in the battle.
Then, as I have heard, Hygelac's sword
was raised in the morning against Ongentheow,
his brother's killer. When Eofor cleft   2485
the old Swede's helmet, halved it open,
he fell, death-pale: his feud-calloused hand
could not stave off the fatal stroke.
    "The treasures that Hygelac lavished on me   2490
I paid for when I fought, as fortune allowed me,
with my glittering sword. He gave me land
and the security land brings, so he had no call
to go looking for some lesser champion,
some mercenary from among the Gifthas[1]   2495
or the Spear-Danes or the men of Sweden.
I marched ahead of him, always there
at the front of the line; and I shall fight like that
for as long as I live, as long as this sword
shall last, which has stood me in good stead   2500
late and soon, ever since I killed
Dayraven the Frank in front of the two armies.
He brought back no looted breastplate
to the Frisian king but fell in battle,
their standard-bearer, highborn and brave.   2505
No sword blade sent him to his death:
my bare hands stilled his heartbeats
and wrecked the bone-house. Now blade and hand,
sword and sword-stroke, will assay the hoard."

[Beowulf Attacks the Dragon]

    Beowulf spoke, made a formal boast   2510
for the last time: "I risked my life
often when I was young. Now I am old,
but as king of the people I shall pursue this fight
for the glory of winning, if the evil one will only
abandon his earth-fort and face me in the open."   2515
    Then he addressed each dear companion
one final time, those fighters in their helmets,
resolute and highborn: "I would rather not
use a weapon if I knew another way
to grapple with the dragon and make good my boast   2520
as I did against Grendel in days gone by.

9. The place of the battle can be translated as   1. A tribe related to the Goths.
Sorrow Hill.

But I shall be meeting molten venom
in the fire he breathes, so I go forth
in mail-shirt and shield. I won't shift a foot
when I meet the cave-guard: what occurs on the wall   2525
between the two of us will turn out as fate,
overseer of men, decides. I am resolved.
I scorn further words against this sky-borne foe.

   "Men-at-arms, remain here on the barrow,
safe in your armor, to see which one of us   2530
is better in the end at bearing wounds
in a deadly fray. This fight is not yours,
nor is it up to any man except me
to measure his strength against the monster
or to prove his worth. I shall win the gold   2535
by my courage, or else mortal combat,
doom of battle, will bear your lord away."

   Then he drew himself up beside his shield.
The fabled warrior in his war-shirt and helmet
trusted in his own strength entirely   2540
and went under the crag. No coward path.

   Hard by the rock-face that hale veteran,
a good man who had gone repeatedly
into combat and danger and come through,
saw a stone arch and a gushing stream   2545
that burst from the barrow, blazing and wafting
a deadly heat. It would be hard to survive
unscathed near the hoard, to hold firm
against the dragon in those flaming depths.
Then he gave a shout. The lord of the Geats   2550
unburdened his breast and broke out
in a storm of anger. Under gray stone
his voice challenged and resounded clearly.
Hate was ignited. The hoard-guard recognized
a human voice, the time was over   2555
for peace and parleying. Pouring forth
in a hot battle-fume, the breath of the monster
burst from the rock. There was a rumble under ground.
Down there in the barrow, Beowulf the warrior
lifted his shield: the outlandish thing   2560
writhed and convulsed and viciously
turned on the king, whose keen-edged sword,
an heirloom inherited by ancient right,
was already in his hand. Roused to a fury,
each antagonist struck terror in the other.   2565
Unyielding, the lord of his people loomed
by his tall shield, sure of his ground,
while the serpent looped and unleashed itself.
Swaddled in flames, it came gliding and flexing
and racing toward its fate. Yet his shield defended   2570
the renowned leader's life and limb
for a shorter time than he meant it to:

that final day was the first time
when Beowulf fought and fate denied him
glory in battle. So the king of the Geats   2575
raised his hand and struck hard
at the enameled scales, but scarcely cut through:
the blade flashed and slashed yet the blow
was far less powerful than the hard-pressed king
had need of at that moment. The mound-keeper   2580
went into a spasm and spouted deadly flames:
when he felt the stroke, battle-fire
billowed and spewed. Beowulf was foiled
of a glorious victory. The glittering sword,
infallible before that day,   2585
failed when he unsheathed it, as it never should have.
For the son of Ecgtheow, it was no easy thing
to have to give ground like that and go
unwillingly to inhabit another home
in a place beyond; so every man must yield   2590
the leasehold of his days.
                              Before long
the fierce contenders clashed again.
The hoard-guard took heart, inhaled and swelled up
and got a new wind; he who had once ruled
was furled in fire and had to face the worst.   2595
No help or backing was to be had then
from his highborn comrades; that hand-picked troop
broke ranks and ran for their lives
to the safety of the wood. But within one heart
sorrow welled up: in a man of worth   2600
the claims of kinship cannot be denied.
    His name was Wiglaf, a son of Weohstan's,
a well-regarded Shylfing warrior
related to Aelfhere.[2] When he saw his lord
tormented by the heat of his scalding helmet,   2605
he remembered the bountiful gifts bestowed on him,
how well he lived among the Waegmundings,
the freehold he inherited from his father[3] before him.
He could not hold back: one hand brandished
the yellow-timbered shield, the other drew his sword—   2610
an ancient blade that was said to have belonged
to Eanmund, the son of Ohthere, the one
Weohstan had slain when he was an exile without friends.
He carried the arms to the victim's kinfolk,
the burnished helmet, the webbed chain-mail   2615

---

2. Wiglaf is, like Beowulf, a member of the clan of the Waegmundings (see lines 2813–14), although both consider themselves Geats as well. See p. 120, n. 2. Nothing is known of Aelfhere.

3. Wiglaf's father is Weohstan, who, as we learn shortly, was the man who killed Eanmund,

Ohthere's son, when he had taken refuge among the Geats (lines 2379–84). How Wiglaf then became a Geat is not clear, although it may have been when Beowulf helped Eanmund's brother Eadgils avenge himself on Onela, who had usurped the throne of the Swedes; Eadgils then became king.

and that relic of the giants. But Onela returned
the weapons to him, rewarded Weohstan
with Eanmund's war-gear. He ignored the blood-feud,
the fact that Eanmund was his brother's son.[4]
Weohstan kept that war-gear for a lifetime,   2620
the sword and the mail-shirt, until it was the son's turn
to follow his father and perform his part.
Then, in old age, at the end of his days
among the Weather-Geats, he bequeathed to Wiglaf
innumerable weapons.
                            And now the youth   2625
was to enter the line of battle with his lord,
his first time to be tested as a fighter.
His spirit did not break and the ancestral blade
would keep its edge, as the dragon discovered
as soon as they came together in the combat.   2630
    Sad at heart, addressing his companions,
Wiglaf spoke wise and fluent words:
"I remember that time when mead was flowing,
how we pledged loyalty to our lord in the hall,
promised our ring-giver we would be worth our price,   2635
make good the gift of the war-gear,
those swords and helmets, as and when
his need required it. He picked us out
from the army deliberately, honored us and judged us
fit for this action, made me these lavish gifts—   2640
and all because he considered us the best
of his arms-bearing thanes. And now, although
he wanted this challenge to be one he'd face
by himself alone—the shepherd of our land,
a man unequaled in the quest for glory   2645
and a name for daring—now the day has come
when this lord we serve needs sound men
to give him their support. Let us go to him,
help our leader through the hot flame
and dread of the fire. As God is my witness,   2650
I would rather my body were robed in the same
burning blaze as my gold-giver's body
than go back home bearing arms.
That is unthinkable, unless we have first
slain the foe and defended the life   2655
of the prince of the Weather-Geats. I well know
the things he has done for us deserve better.
Should he alone be left exposed
to fall in battle? We must bond together,
shield and helmet, mail-shirt and sword."   2660
Then he waded the dangerous reek and went
under arms to his lord, saying only:

4. That is, Onela ignored the fact that Weohstan had killed his nephew Eanmund since he in
fact wanted Eanmund dead.

"Go on, dear Beowulf, do everything
you said you would when you were still young
and vowed you would never let your name and fame   2665
be dimmed while you lived. Your deeds are famous,
so stay resolute, my lord, defend your life now
with the whole of your strength. I shall stand by you."
        After those words, a wildness rose
in the dragon again and drove it to attack,   2670
heaving up fire, hunting for enemies,
the humans it loathed. Flames lapped the shield,
charred it to the boss, and the body armor
on the young warrior was useless to him.
But Wiglaf did well under the wide rim   2675
Beowulf shared with him once his own had shattered
in sparks and ashes.
                    Inspired again
by the thought of glory, the war-king threw
his whole strength behind a sword stroke
and connected with the skull. And Naegling snapped.   2680
Beowulf's ancient iron-gray sword
let him down in the fight. It was never his fortune
to be helped in combat by the cutting edge
of weapons made of iron. When he wielded a sword,
no matter how blooded and hard-edged the blade,   2685
his hand was too strong, the stroke he dealt
(I have heard) would ruin it. He could reap no advantage.
        Then the bane of that people, the fire-breathing dragon,
was mad to attack for a third time.
When a chance came, he caught the hero   2690
in a rush of flame and clamped sharp fangs
into his neck. Beowulf's body
ran wet with his life-blood: it came welling out.
        Next thing, they say, the noble son of Weohstan
saw the king in danger at his side   2695
and displayed his inborn bravery and strength.
He left the head alone,[5] but his fighting hand
was burned when he came to his kinsman's aid.
He lunged at the enemy lower down
so that his decorated sword sank into its belly   2700
and the flames grew weaker.
                        Once again the king
gathered his strength and drew a stabbing knife
he carried on his belt, sharpened for battle.
He stuck it deep in the dragon's flank.
Beowulf dealt it a deadly wound.   2705
They had killed the enemy, courage quelled his life;
that pair of kinsmen, partners in nobility,
had destroyed the foe. So every man should act,
be at hand when needed; but now, for the king,

---

5. That is, the dragon's flame-breathing head.

this would be the last of his many labors 2710
and triumphs in the world.
 Then the wound
dealt by the ground-burner earlier began
to scald and swell; Beowulf discovered
deadly poison suppurating inside him,
surges of nausea, and so, in his wisdom, 2715
the prince realized his state and struggled
toward a seat on the rampart. He steadied his gaze
on those gigantic stones, saw how the earthwork
was braced with arches built over columns.
And now that thane unequaled for goodness 2720
with his own hands washed his lord's wounds,
swabbed the weary prince with water,
bathed him clean, unbuckled his helmet.
 Beowulf spoke: in spite of his wounds,
mortal wounds, he still spoke 2725
for he well knew his days in the world
had been lived out to the end—his allotted time
was drawing to a close, death was very near.
 "Now is the time when I would have wanted
to bestow this armor on my own son, 2730
had it been my fortune to have fathered an heir
and live on in his flesh. For fifty years
I ruled this nation. No king
of any neighboring clan would dare
face me with troops, none had the power 2735
to intimidate me. I took what came,
cared for and stood by things in my keeping,
never fomented quarrels, never
swore to a lie. All this consoles me,
doomed as I am and sickening for death; 2740
because of my right ways, the Ruler of mankind
need never blame me when the breath leaves my body
for murder of kinsmen. Go now quickly,
dearest Wiglaf, under the gray stone
where the dragon is laid out, lost to his treasure; 2745
hurry to feast your eyes on the hoard.
Away you go: I want to examine
that ancient gold, gaze my fill
on those garnered jewels; my going will be easier
for having seen the treasure, a less troubled letting-go 2750
of the life and lordship I have long maintained."
 And so, I have heard, the son of Weohstan
quickly obeyed the command of his languishing
war-weary lord; he went in his chain-mail
under the rock-piled roof of the barrow, 2755
exulting in his triumph, and saw beyond the seat
a treasure-trove of astonishing richness,
wall-hangings that were a wonder to behold,
glittering gold spread across the ground,
the old dawn-scorching serpent's den 2760

packed with goblets and vessels from the past,
tarnished and corroding. Rusty helmets
all eaten away. Armbands everywhere,
artfully wrought. How easily treasure
buried in the ground, gold hidden   2765
however skillfully, can escape from any man!
    And he saw too a standard, entirely of gold,
hanging high over the hoard,
a masterpiece of filigree; it glowed with light
so he could make out the ground at his feet   2770
and inspect the valuables. Of the dragon there was no
remaining sign: the sword had dispatched him.
Then, the story goes, a certain man[6]
plundered the hoard in that immemorial howe,[7]
filled his arms with flagons and plates,   2775
anything he wanted; and took the standard also,
most brilliant of banners.
                          Already the blade
of the old king's sharp killing-sword
had done its worst: the one who had for long
minded the hoard, hovering over gold,   2780
unleashing fire, surging forth
midnight after midnight, had been mown down.
    Wiglaf went quickly, keen to get back,
excited by the treasure. Anxiety weighed
on his brave heart—he was hoping he would find   2785
the leader of the Geats alive where he had left him
helpless, earlier, on the open ground.
    So he came to the place, carrying the treasure
and found his lord bleeding profusely,
his life at an end; again he began   2790
to swab his body. The beginnings of an utterance
broke out from the king's breast-cage.
The old lord gazed sadly at the gold.
    "To the everlasting Lord of all,
to the King of Glory, I give thanks   2795
that I behold this treasure here in front of me,
that I have been allowed to leave my people
so well endowed on the day I die.
Now that I have bartered my last breath
to own this fortune, it is up to you   2800
to look after their needs. I can hold out no longer.
Order my troop to construct a barrow
on a headland on the coast, after my pyre has cooled.
It will loom on the horizon at Hronesness[8]
and be a reminder among my people—   2805
so that in coming times crews under sail
will call it Beowulf's Barrow, as they steer
ships across the wide and shrouded waters."

6. That is, Wiglaf.   8. The name means "Whaleness."
7. An Irish word for dwelling.

Then the king in his great-heartedness unclasped
the collar of gold from his neck and gave it   2810
to the young thane, telling him to use
it and the war-shirt and gilded helmet well.
"You are the last of us, the only one left
of the Waegmundings. Fate swept us away,
sent my whole brave highborn clan   2815
to their final doom. Now I must follow them."
  That was the warrior's last word.
He had no more to confide. The furious heat
of the pyre would assail him. His soul fled from his breast
to its destined place among the steadfast ones.   2820

[Beowulf's Funeral]

  It was hard then on the young hero,
having to watch the one he held so dear
there on the ground, going through
his death agony. The dragon from undercarth,
his nightmarish destroyer, lay destroyed as well,   2825
utterly without life. No longer would his snakefolds
ply themselves to safeguard hidden gold.
Hard-edged blades, hammered out
and keenly filed, had finished him
so that the sky-roamer lay there rigid,   2830
brought low beside the treasure-lodge.
  Never again would he glitter and glide
and show himself off in midnight air,
exulting in his riches: he fell to earth
through the battle-strength in Beowulf's arm.   2835
There were few, indeed, as far as I have heard,
big and brave as they may have been,
few who would have held out if they had had to face
the outpourings of that poison-breather
or gone foraging on the ring-hall floor   2840
and found the deep barrow-dweller
on guard and awake.
      The treasure had been won,
bought and paid for by Beowulf's death.
Both had reached the end of the road
through the life they had been lent.
        Before long   2845
the battle-dodgers abandoned the wood,
the ones who had let down their lord earlier,
the tail-turners, ten of them together.
When he needed them most, they had made off.
Now they were ashamed and came behind shields,   2850
in their battle-outfits, to where the old man lay.
They watched Wiglaf, sitting worn out,
a comrade shoulder to shoulder with his lord,
trying in vain to bring him round with water.

Much as he wanted to, there was no way   2855
he could preserve his lord's life on earth
or alter in the least the Almighty's will.
What God judged right would rule what happened
to every man, as it does to this day.
    Then a stern rebuke was bound to come   2860
from the young warrior to the ones who had been cowards.
Wiglaf, son of Weohstan, spoke
disdainfully and in disappointment:
"Anyone ready to admit the truth
will surely realize that the lord of men   2865
who showered you with gifts and gave you the armor
you are standing in—when he would distribute
helmets and mail-shirts to men on the mead-benches,
a prince treating his thanes in hall
to the best he could find, far or near—   2870
was throwing weapons uselessly away.
It would be a sad waste when the war broke out.
Beowulf had little cause to brag
about his armed guard; yet God who ordains
who wins or loses allowed him to strike   2875
with his own blade when bravery was needed.
There was little I could do to protect his life
in the heat of the fray, but I found new strength
welling up when I went to help him.
Then my sword connected and the deadly assaults   2880
of our foe grew weaker, the fire coursed
less strongly from his head. But when the worst happened
too few rallied around the prince.
    "So it is good-bye now to all you know and love
on your home ground, the open-handedness,   2885
the giving of war-swords. Every one of you
with freeholds of land, our whole nation,
will be dispossessed, once princes from beyond
get tidings of how you turned and fled
and disgraced yourselves. A warrior will sooner   2890
die than live a life of shame."
    Then he ordered the outcome of the fight to be reported
to those camped on the ridge, that crowd of retainers
who had sat all morning, sad at heart,
shield-bearers wondering about   2895
the man they loved: would this day be his last
or would he return? He told the truth
and did not balk, the rider who bore
news to the cliff-top. He addressed them all:
"Now the people's pride and love,   2900
the lord of the Geats, is laid on his deathbed,
brought down by the dragon's attack.
Beside him lies the bane of his life,
dead from knife-wounds. There was no way
Beowulf could manage to get the better   2905
of the monster with his sword. Wiglaf sits

at Beowulf's side, the son of Weohstan,
the living warrior watching by the dead,
keeping weary vigil, holding a wake
for the loved and the loathed.
                          Now war is looming   2910
over our nation, soon it will be known
to Franks and Frisians, far and wide,
that the king is gone. Hostility has been great
among the Franks since Hygelac sailed forth
at the head of a war-fleet into Friesland: 2915
there the Hetware harried and attacked
and overwhelmed him with great odds.
The leader in his war-gear was laid low,
fell among followers: that lord did not favor
his company with spoils. The Merovingian king   2920
has been an enemy to us ever since.
    "Nor do I expect peace or pact-keeping
of any sort from the Swedes. Remember:
at Ravenswood, Ongentheow
slaughtered Haethcyn, Hrethel's son,   2925
when the Geat people in their arrogance
first attacked the fierce Shylfings.
The return blow was quickly struck
by Ohthere's father.[9] Old and terrible,
he felled the sea-king and saved his own   2930
aged wife, the mother of Onela
and of Ohthere, bereft of her gold rings.
Then he kept hard on the heels of the foe
and drove them, leaderless, lucky to get away
in a desperate rout into Ravenswood.   2935
His army surrounded the weary remnant
where they nursed their wounds; all through the night
he howled threats at those huddled survivors,
promised to axe their bodies open
when dawn broke, dangle them from gallows   2940
to feed the birds. But at first light
when their spirits were lowest, relief arrived.
They heard the sound of Hygelac's horn,
his trumpet calling as he came to find them,
the hero in pursuit, at hand with troops.   2945
    "The bloody swathe that Swedes and Geats
cut through each other was everywhere.
No one could miss their murderous feuding.
Then the old man made his move,
pulled back, barred his people in: 2950
Ongentheow withdrew to higher ground.
Hygelac's pride and prowess as a fighter
were known to the earl; he had no confidence
that he could hold out against that horde of seamen,
defend his wife and the ones he loved   2955

9. Ongentheow.

from the shock of the attack. He retreated for shelter
behind the earthwall. Then Hygelac swooped
on the Swedes at bay, his banners swarmed
into their refuge, his Geat forces
drove forward to destroy the camp.   2960
There in his gray hairs, Ongentheow
was cornered, ringed around with swords.
And it came to pass that the king's fate
was in Eofor's hands,[1] and in his alone.
Wulf, son of Wonred, went for him in anger,   2965
split him open so that blood came spurting
from under his hair. The old hero
still did not flinch, but parried fast,
hit back with a harder stroke:
the king turned and took him on.   2970
Then Wonred's son, the brave Wulf,
could land no blow against the aged lord.
Ongentheow divided his helmet
so that he buckled and bowed his bloodied head
and dropped to the ground. But his doom held off.   2975
Though he was cut deep, he recovered again.
   "With his brother down, the undaunted Eofor,
Hygelac's thane, hefted his sword
and smashed murderously at the massive helmet
past the lifted shield. And the king collapsed,   2980
the shepherd of people was sheared of life.
Many then hurried to help Wulf,
bandaged and lifted him, now that they were left
masters of the blood-soaked battle-ground.
One warrior stripped the other,   2985
looted Ongentheow's iron mail-coat,
his hard sword-hilt, his helmet too,
and carried the graith[2] to King Hygelac,
he accepted the prize, promised fairly
that reward would come, and kept his word.   2990
For their bravery in action, when they arrived home,
Eofor and Wulf were overloaded
by Hrethel's son, Hygelac the Geat,
with gifts of land and linked rings
that were worth a fortune. They had won glory,   2995
so there was no gainsaying his generosity.
And he gave Eofor his only daughter
to bide at home with him, an honor and a bond.
   "So this bad blood between us and the Swedes,
this vicious feud, I am convinced,   3000
is bound to revive; they will cross our borders
and attack in force when they find out
that Beowulf is dead. In days gone by
when our warriors fell and we were undefended,
he kept our coffers and our kingdom safe.   3005

1. The killing of Ongentheow by Eofor is   2. Armor.
described in lines 2486–89.

He worked for the people, but as well as that
he behaved like a hero.
                    We must hurry now
to take a last look at the king
and launch him, lord and lavisher of rings,
on the funeral road. His royal pyre   3010
will melt no small amount of gold:
heaped there in a hoard, it was bought at heavy cost,
and that pile of rings he paid for at the end
with his own life will go up with the flame,
be furled in fire: treasure no follower   3015
will wear in his memory, nor lovely woman
link and attach as a torque around her neck—
but often, repeatedly, in the path of exile
they shall walk bereft, bowed under woe,
now that their leader's laugh is silenced,   3020
high spirits quenched. Many a spear
dawn-cold to the touch will be taken down
and waved on high; the swept harp
won't waken warriors, but the raven winging
darkly over the doomed will have news,   3025
tidings for the eagle of how he hoked[3] and ate,
how the wolf and he made short work of the dead."
    Such was the drift of the dire report
that gallant man delivered. He got little wrong
in what he told and predicted.
                    The whole troop   3030
rose in tears, then took their way
to the uncanny scene under Earnaness.[4]
There, on the sand, where his soul had left him,
they found him at rest, their ring-giver
from days gone by. The great man   3035
had breathed his last. Beowulf the king
had indeed met with a marvelous death.
    But what they saw first was far stranger:
the serpent on the ground, gruesome and vile,
lying facing him. The fire-dragon   3040
was scaresomely burned, scorched all colors.
From head to tail, his entire length
was fifty feet. He had shimmered forth
on the night air once, then winged back
down to his den; but death owned him now,   3045
he would never enter his earth-gallery again.
Beside him stood pitchers and piled-up dishes,
silent flagons, precious swords
eaten through with rust, ranged as they had been
while they waited their thousand winters under ground.   3050
That huge cache, gold inherited
from an ancient race, was under a spell—
which meant no one was ever permitted

---

3. Rooted about, a Northern Irish word [adapted from translator's note].

4. The place where Beowulf fought the dragon; it means "Eagleness."

to enter the ring-hall unless God Himself,
mankind's Keeper, True King of Triumphs, 3055
allowed some person pleasing to Him—
and in His eyes worthy—to open the hoard.

What came about brought to nothing
the hopes of the one who had wrongly hidden
riches under the rock-face. First the dragon slew 3060
that man among men, who in turn made fierce amends
and settled the feud. Famous for his deeds
a warrior may be, but it remains a mystery
where his life will end, when he may no longer
dwell in the mead-hall among his own. 3065
So it was with Beowulf, when he faced the cruelty
and cunning of the mound-guard. He himself was ignorant
of how his departure from the world would happen.
The highborn chiefs who had buried the treasure
declared it until doomsday so accursed 3070
that whoever robbed it would be guilty of wrong
and grimly punished for their transgression,
hasped in hell-bonds in heathen shrines.
Yet Beowulf's gaze at the gold treasure
when he first saw it had not been selfish. 3075

Wiglaf, son of Weohstan, spoke:
"Often when one man follows his own will
many are hurt. This happened to us.
Nothing we advised could ever convince
the prince we loved, our land's guardian, 3080
not to vex the custodian of the gold,
let him lie where he was long accustomed,
lurk there under earth until the end of the world.
He held to his high destiny. The hoard is laid bare,
but at a grave cost; it was too cruel a fate 3085
that forced the king to that encounter.
I have been inside and seen everything
amassed in the vault. I managed to enter
although no great welcome awaited me
under the earthwall. I quickly gathered up 3090
a huge pile of the priceless treasures
handpicked from the hoard and carried them here
where the king could see them. He was still himself,
alive, aware, and in spite of his weakness
he had many requests. He wanted me to greet you 3095
and order the building of a barrow that would crown
the site of his pyre, serve as his memorial,
in a commanding position, since of all men
to have lived and thrived and lorded it on earth
his worth and due as a warrior were the greatest. 3100
Now let us again go quickly
and feast our eyes on that amazing fortune
heaped under the wall. I will show the way
and take you close to those coffers packed with rings
and bars of gold. Let a bier be made 3105

and got ready quickly when we come out
and then let us bring the body of our lord,
the man we loved, to where he will lodge
for a long time in the care of the Almighty."
    Then Weohstan's son, stalwart to the end,   3110
had orders given to owners of dwellings,
many people of importance in the land,
to fetch wood from far and wide
for the good man's pyre:
                        "Now shall flame consume
our leader in battle, the blaze darken   3115
round him who stood his ground in the steel-hail,
when the arrow-storm shot from bowstrings
pelted the shield-wall. The shaft hit home.
Feather-fledged, it finned the barb in flight."
    Next the wise son of Weohstan   3120
called from among the king's thanes
a group of seven: he selected the best
and entered with them, the eighth of their number,
under the God-cursed roof; one raised
a lighted torch and led the way.   3125
No lots were cast for who should loot the hoard
for it was obvious to them that every bit of it
lay unprotected within the vault,
there for the taking. It was no trouble
to hurry to work and haul out   3130
the priceless store. They pitched the dragon
over the cliff-top, let tide's flow
and backwash take the treasure-minder.
Then coiled gold was loaded on a cart
in great abundance, and the gray-haired leader,   3135
the prince on his bier, borne to Hronesness.
    The Geat people built a pyre for Beowulf,
stacked and decked it until it stood foursquare,
hung with helmets, heavy war-shields
and shining armor, just as he had ordered.   3140
Then his warriors laid him in the middle of it,
mourning a lord far-famed and beloved.
On a height they kindled the hugest of all
funeral fires; fumes of woodsmoke
billowed darkly up, the blaze roared   3145
and drowned out their weeping, wind died down
and flames wrought havoc in the hot bone-house,
burning it to the core. They were disconsolate
and wailed aloud for their lord's decease.
A Geat woman too sang out in grief;   3150
with hair bound up, she unburdened herself
of her worst fears, a wild litany
of nightmare and lament: her nation invaded,
enemies on the rampage, bodies in piles,
slavery and abasement. Heaven swallowed the smoke.   3155

Then the Geat people began to construct
a mound on a headland, high and imposing,
a marker that sailors could see from far away,
and in ten days they had done the work.
It was their hero's memorial; what remained from the fire   3160
they housed inside it, behind a wall
as worthy of him as their workmanship could make it.
And they buried torques in the barrow, and jewels
and a trove of such things as trespassing men
had once dared to drag from the hoard.   3165
They let the ground keep that ancestral treasure,
gold under gravel, gone to earth,
as useless to men now as it ever was.
Then twelve warriors rode around the tomb,
chieftains' sons, champions in battle,   3170
all of them distraught, chanting in dirges,
mourning his loss as a man and a king.
They extolled his heroic nature and exploits
and gave thanks for his greatness; which was the proper thing,
for a man should praise a prince whom he holds dear   3175
and cherish his memory when that moment comes
when he has to be convoyed from his bodily home.
So the Geat people, his hearth-companions,
sorrowed for the lord who had been laid low.
They said that of all the kings upon earth   3180
he was the man most gracious and fair-minded,
kindest to his people and keenest to win fame.

ABOLQASEM FERDOWSI
940–1020

The *Shahnameh*, literally "book of kings," is sometimes called Persia's national epic. It is what the *Iliad* is to the Greeks, the *Aeneid* to the Romans, *Beowulf* to the English, or the *Song of Roland* to the French. But the label "epic" only begins to capture the scope and ambitions of Ferdowsi's capacious text, which opens with the creation of the world and ends with the lineage of medieval Persian kings; along the way, it includes fairies and jinns, flying horses and giant birds. Standing on the threshold of the fall of his Persian patrons to invading Turkish armies, Ferdowsi was writing with one eye on the glories of the past and one eye on the turbulent court politics of his own day.

Abolqasem Ferdowsi was born in Khorasan, a region encompassing what is now northeastern Iran and the adjoining regions of Afghanistan, Turkmenistan, and Uzbekistan, in a village near the city of Tus. He wrote his major work, the *Shahnameh*, under the patronage of the Iranian Samanid rulers of Khorasan (819–1005), who were eager to revive Persian literature and culture after a long period of dormancy following the Arab Islamic invasions of Persia that began in 633. The Samanid ruler Nuh ibn Mansur ordered that a prose compendium be produced of all the Persian literature that had been suppressed over the past centuries, drawing on oral and written sources of Persian mythology and the native monotheistic religion of Zoroastrianism. Ferdowsi tells us that the first poet told to turn this (now lost) prose account into an epic poem, Daqiqi-e Balkhi, died suddenly before he could finish more than a thousand lines. Ferdowsi claims to have incorporated Daqiqi's verses into his own *Shahnameh*—but because he ascribes to Daqiqi the most un-Islamic part of the poem, centering on the life of the prophet Zoroaster and the religion he founded, it is possible that the attribution is not so much fact as a clever tactic aimed at self-preservation. While Ferdowsi was at work on the *Shahnameh*, his Samanid patron fell from power. Though the rulers of this new regime, the Ghaznavid Turks, were ethnically distinct from and more rigorously Islamic than the Persian Samanids, they valued Persian culture highly. Ferdowsi therefore continued his work on the poem, sending selections to Mahmoud, the new Ghaznavid ruler, along with short poems praising his generosity.

Although the *Shahnameh* is an epic, it encompasses other genres as well. It begins with the creation of the world, the creation of the first human beings, and an account of their lineage, and thus resembles texts like *Gilgamesh* or **Genesis**. It is national in its evocation of the great mythic heroes of the Persian past, juxtaposed with a historical account of Persian rulers up through the Middle Ages. Beyond myth and history,

the *Shahnameh* also contains elements of romance, star-crossed lovers and tragic scenes of misrecognition, fantastical creatures and supernatural events. Further complicating all these diverse elements is their presentation, as the stories are told in intricately rhymed verse. In addition, the *Shahnameh* functions as a "mirror for princes"—that is, a guidebook for rulers: the exemplary kings appear as models to be emulated, while the deeds of bad rulers to be avoided. This aspect of the *Shahnameh* is most evident in the story of Alexander (Sekandar) but is woven throughout the text, especially in the repeated stories of father–son relationships that have gone tragically wrong.

The *Shahnameh* can be divided into three parts: a relatively brief opening section focusing on origin myths, a long second section on the heroes of Persian antiquity, and a third section on the history of the kings. The material becomes steadily more grounded in historical fact as the text goes on; heroic kings who live for several hundred years dominate the middle section, which makes up the bulk of the work, but rulers of normal life spans appear in the later ages. The figure of Alexander the Great, whose life story is excerpted here, is placed at the crucial junction linking the age of heroes with the history of the kings. Alexander appears as a transitional figure, as more than a man yet an integral part of the history of Persian rule. The description of the end of his reign is followed by an extremely brief overview of the dissolution of his empire into a number of small principalities before the rise of the Sassanid dynasty, whose royal lineage makes up the rest of the *Shahnameh*. The poem ends not in Ferdowsi's own times but instead with the last Sassanid ruler, Yazdgerd III, who was forced off his throne by the invading Arab Islamic armies in 651. This poetic celebration of the Persian mythic and historical heritage thus draws a discreet curtain over the period when the advent of Islam threatened to overwhelm the native culture. Moreover, the *Shahnameh* provides a powerful counternarrative to the history of conquest, a counternarrative that depends a great deal on the figure of Alexander the Great. For Persians, it is an article of faith that their nation has never been conquered, even though at times it may have adopted new customs, new religions, and new rulers. In keeping with this perspective, the figure of Alexander is presented in the *Shahnameh* not as a Macedonian invader but as a Persian prince. Instead of being the alien enemy of the Persian ruler, he is Darius's brother and rival.

The legends of Alexander the Great, who emerged from Macedonia to build an empire that stretched from Spain to India, were widely disseminated all around the Mediterranean Sea, reaching throughout Europe and much of Asia. The basic outline of the Alexander story as presented in the *Shahnameh* will be familiar to anyone who has read any one of the many versions of his legend, including the war against Darius (Dara), ruler of Persia; the battles against Porus (Foor), king of India; and the letters describing the marvels of the East exchanged by Alexander with his old teacher, the Greek philosopher Aristotle (Arestalis). Yet Ferdowsi faced a particular challenge in describing Alexander's journeys of conquest into the remotest reaches of the Orient, where he ultimately met his doom. For European readers, Alexander's adventures in Babylon were set in the exotic Orient; for Ferdowsi's readers, Babylon was just down the road. Ferdowsi therefore constructs an even more oriental Orient for his hero, sending Alexander as far as China in search of marvels. At the same time, Ferdowsi's Alexander is also made familiar to Persian readers, drawn into the fold of the lineage of Persian kings. The rivalry between Alexander and his brother ends in the death of Darius, who gives his kingdom to Alexander on the condition that Alexander marry his daughter and uphold the local religion of Zoroastrianism. Here, conquest is transformed into cultural assimilation, and the heroic age moves smoothly into the lists of Persian kings. Implicitly, the transition ushered in by Alexander foreshadows the greater transition that informs the last lines of the *Shahnameh*, which recount the rule of the Sassanid Yazdgerd III. He would be the last native ruler of Persia until the rise of the Samanid rulers of Khorasan—Ferdowsi's patrons— in 819.

The celebration of Persian identity so poetically expressed in the *Shahnameh* continues to be enormously popular not only within modern Iran but also in communities of Iranians throughout the world. Along with the lyric poetry of **Hafez**, Ferdowsi's narrative poetry is widely quoted and used for inscriptions. Unlike the delicate ghazals of Hafez, however, the *Shahnameh* has also been rendered as a popular series of graphic novels. The endurance of the *Shahnameh* is partly due to how little the Persian language (Farsi) has changed over the thousand years since Ferdowsi completed his epic work. Modern speakers of Persian can read Ferdowsi without difficulty, much as we might read Shakespeare's English. For them, Ferdowsi's Persian is a living language, as resonant in the present moment as at any time in the past millennium.

A NOTE ON TRANSLATION

The *Shahnameh* has repeatedly been translated into European languages, usually in the form of an excerpt taken from the tragic story of the hero Rostam and his doomed son Sohrab; one of the best-known examples is Matthew Arnold's poem "Sohrab and Rustum" (1853). This narrative appealed to nineteenth-century

European readers not just because of its emotional power and beauty but also because the story line of a father destroying his son corresponded well with an Orientalist view of the decadent East. The translation by Dick Davis reproduced here, by contrast, makes a real effort to bring the Persian text to readers of English on its own terms. Davis's versions of Persian narrative and lyric poetry have been particularly popular among diasporic Iranians, who are eager to rediscover their national literature within new cultural environments. Davis, himself a poet, renders Ferdowsi's heroic couplets in a lyrical, rhythmic prose punctuated by short passages in verse that mark moments of great emotional tension.

From Shahnameh[1]

The Birth of Sekandar

One night this lovely moon,[2] arrayed in jewels and scents, lay sleeping beside the king. Suddenly she sighed deeply, and the king[3] turned his head away, offended by the smell of her breath. This bad odor sickened him, and he frowned, wondering what could be done about it. He sent knowledgeable doctors to her; one who was especially expert was able to find a remedy. There is an herb that burns the palate, which they call "Sekandar" in Greece, and he rubbed this against the roof of her mouth. She wept a few tears and her face turned as red as brocade, because it burned her mouth, but the ugly smell was gone. But although this beautiful woman's breath was now as sweet as musk, the king no longer felt any love for her. His heart had grown cold toward his bride, and he sent her back to Filqus. The princess grieved, because she was pregnant, but she told no one of this.

When nine months had gone by she gave birth to a boy as splendid as the sun. Because of his stature and splendor, and the sweet smell that his flesh exhaled, she named him Sekandar, after the herb that had cured her of her malady. Her father the king told everyone that the boy was his and made no mention of Darab, because he was ashamed to tell people that Darab had rejected his daughter. The same night that Sekandar was born, a cream-colored mare in the royal stables, a huge warlike horse, gave birth to a gray foal with a lion-like chest and short pasterns.[4] Filqus took this as a good omen, raising his hands to the heavens in gratitude. At dawn the next day he had both the newborn child and the mare and her foal brought to him and passed his hands over the foal's eyes and chest, because he was exactly the same age as Sekandar.

So the heavens turned and the years passed. Sekandar grew to have a princely heart, and his speech was that of a warrior. Filqus treated him even more attentively than a son and loved to dress him as a champion. In a little while the boy gained in wisdom; he became adroit, intelligent, grave in his manner, and knowledgeable. He was made the kingdom's crown prince, and Filqus delighted in his presence. Sekandar learned the arts of kingship from

1. Translated by Dick Davis.
2. Nahid, daughter of Filqus (Philip), King of Macedon, sent to marry Darab, King of Persia. In Persian poetry, the moon often symbolizes feminine beauty.
3. Darab (Darius), King of Persia.
4. Bucephalus, who is featured prominently in classical Greek biographies of Alexander the Great.

his teachers, and it seemed he was born to administer justice, to occupy a throne, and to found an empire.

In Persia, after Nahid had returned to her father, Darab took another wife. She gave birth to a fine, princely son who was a year younger than Sekandar. On the day he was born he was named Dara, and it was hoped that his good fortune would be greater than his father's. Then, after twelve years, Darab's star declined: he grew sick and wasted away and knew he would be called to another place. He summoned his nobles and counselors and spoke to them at length about the business of government and kingship. Then he added: "Dara, my son, will guide you well. Listen to him and obey him, and may your souls know peace in obedience to his commands. This royal throne is no one's for long, and in the midst of pleasure we are called away. Strive to be kind and just, and rejoice when you remember me." Having said this he heaved a sigh from the depths of his being, and the rosy pomegranate petal turned as pale as fenugreek.[5]

* * *

Dara's Dying Words to Sekandar

Dara's counselors made their way to Sekandar and said, "Wise and victorious lord, we have killed your enemy: his days as king are over." When Sekandar heard Janushyar's words, he said to him and to Mahyar,[6] "Where is this enemy of mine whom you've cast aside in this way? Take me to him." The two led Sekandar, whose heart was bursting with rage, to where Dara lay with his chest covered in gore, and his face as pale as fenugreek. Sekandar gave orders that no one else should approach, and that Dara's two counselors be detained. Quick as the wind he dismounted and laid the wounded man's head on his thigh. He rubbed both his hands against Dara's face until he began to revive and speak. Then Sekandar removed the royal diadem from Dara's head and loosened his armor. No doctor was nearby, and when he saw Dara's wounds, a few tears dropped from Sekandar's eyes. "May this pass easily from you," he said, "and may the hearts of those who wish you ill tremble in terror! Get up, and let me lay you in a golden litter, or if you have the strength, sit yourself in the saddle. I will bring doctors from India and Greece, and I shall weep tears of blood for your pain. I shall restore your kingdom to you, and when you have recovered, we shall swear friendship. This instant I shall hang from a gibbet those who have injured you. When I heard last night what had happened, my heart filled with sorrow, my soul with anger. We are from the same stock, the same root, the same people: why should we destroy one another for ambition's sake?"

When he heard Sekandar, Dara said, "May wisdom always be your companion! I think that you will find the reward for what you have said from God himself. You said that Iran is mine, and that the crown and the throne of the brave are mine; but death is closer to me than the throne. The throne is over for me, and my luck has run out. So the high heavens revolve; their turning is toward sorrow, and their profit is pain. Look at me before you say 'I am exalted above all this great company of heroes.' Know that evil and good both come from God, and see that you remain grateful to him for as long as you live. My

5. A light green herb.
6. Janushyar and Mahyar, Zoroastrians serving in the royal retinue, have fatally wounded

Dara, Sekandar's half-brother and rival for the crown of Persia.

own state shows you the truth of what I say. Look how I, who had such sovereignty and glory and wealth, am now despised by everyone. I who never injured anyone, who had such armor and such armies, such splendid horses, such crowns and thrones, who had such sons and relatives, and so many allies whose hearts bore my brand. Earth and time were my slaves, and remained so while my luck held. But now I am separated from good fortune, and have fallen into the hands of murderers. I despair of my sons and family; the earth has turned dark for me, and my eyes are white like the eyes of a blind man. Our own people cannot help us; my one hope is in God the Creator. I lie here wounded on the earth, fallen into the trap of death, but this is the way of the heavens whether we are kings or heroes. Greatness too must pass: it is the prey, and its hunter is death."

Sekandar's pity made his face turn pale, and he wept for the wounded king, lying there stretched out on the earth. Dara said to him, "Do not weep, there is no profit in it. My part in the fires of life is now merely smoke. This was my fate from him who apportions our fates. This is the goal toward which the splendor of my earthly days has led me. Listen to the advice I shall give you, accept it into your heart, and remember it." Sekandar said, "It is for you to order me: I give you my word." Then Dara spoke quickly, going over his wishes and omitting nothing. He began by saying, "You have achieved fame, but see that you fear the world's Creator, who has made the heavens and the earth and time, and the strong and the weak. Look after my children and my family, and my veiled wise women. Ask for my daughter's hand in marriage, and keep her gently and in comfort in the court. Her mother named her Roshanak and saw that the world was always a place of happiness and delight for her. Do not despise my daughter, or let malevolent men speak badly of her. She has been brought up as a princess, and at our feasts she has always been the loveliest person present. It may be that you shall have a son with her, and that the name of Esfandyar[7] will be renewed in him, that he will preserve the fires of Zoroastrianism and live by the Zend-Avesta,[8] keeping the Feasts of Sadeh and No-Ruz[9] and preserving our fire temples. Such a son will honor Hormozd[1] and the sun and moon, and wash his soul and face in the waters of wisdom; he will renew the ways of Lohrasp and Goshtasp,[2] treating men according to their station whether it be high or low; he will make our faith flourish and his days will be fortunate."

Sekandar answered him, "Your heart is pure and your words are wise, O king. I accept all that you have said, and I shall not stray from your words while I am within the borders of your kingdom. I shall accomplish the good deeds you recommend, and your wisdom will be my guide." The master of the world grasped Sekandar's hand and began to weep bitterly.

7. A legendary Iranian hero, son of King Goshtasp; his battle with the mighty Rostam is recounted earlier in the *Shahnameh*.
8. The sacred scripture of Zoroastrianism: a collection of hymns and liturgical texts, together with their theological interpretations. The religion was founded by the prophet Zoroaster in Iran in the 6th century B.C.E. and was the state religion at the time of Alexander's conquest and from the 3rd century C.E. until shortly before the adoption of Islam.

9. The Persian New Year, which takes place on the spring equinox (March 20 or 21); Sadeh is a midwinter festival held fifty days earlier. Both festivals involve the celebration of light, especially fire.
1. An early Iranian god (also called Ahura Mazda), who was proclaimed the single uncreated God by Zoroaster and is the highest deity in Zoroastrianism.
2. Legendary Iranian kings.

> He kissed Sekandar's palm and said, "I pray
> That God will keep and guide you on your way.
> I give my flesh to dust, to God my spirit,
> My sovereignty is yours now to inherit."

He spoke, and his soul rose up from his body. All those gathered nearby began to weep, and Sekandar rent his clothes and poured dust on the royal diadem. Sekandar made a splendid tomb for him according to local custom and, now that the time for Dara's eternal sleep had come, the blood was washed from his body with clear rosewater. His body was wrapped in brocade woven with gold and sewn with jewels; it was then covered with camphor, even his face, so that no one could see it. As Dara's corpse was placed within its golden coffin the bystanders wept, and then it was carried in procession, passed hand to hand by the mourners, with Sekandar leading the cortege on foot, and as he approached the tomb, it seemed as if his skin would split with sorrow. The king's coffin was placed within the tomb according to the ancient royal rites, and the huge doors of the building were sealed. Then Sekandar had two gibbets built, one bearing the name Janushyar and the other Mahyar, and the two regicides were strung up on them. The soldiers who were there took rocks in their fists and stoned them to death, as a warning to those who would kill a king. When the Persians saw how Sekandar honored Dara and mourned for him, they offered the young king their homage and loyalty.

* * *

Sekandar's Letter to Foor

Having hidden his treasure in this way,[3] Sekandar led his army out from Milad and bore down on Qanuj like the wind. He wrote a threatening, bellicose letter, "From Sekandar, the son of Filqus, who lights the flames of prosperity and adversity, to Foor, the lord of India, favored by the heavens, commander of the armies of Sind."[4] The letter opened with praise of God the Creator who is eternal, saying that those to whom he gives victory never want for countries, crowns, and thrones, while those from whom he turns away become wretched, and the sun never shines on them. "You will have heard how God has given me *farr*,[5] victory, good fortune, crowns, thrones, and sovereignty over this dark earth. But none of this will last, and my days draw on; another will come after me to enjoy my conquests. My only ambition is to leave a good name and no disgrace behind me on this sublunar earth. When they bring this letter to you, free your dark soul from sorrow; descend from your throne, do not consult with your priests or advisors, but mount your horse and come to me asking for my protection. Those who try to trick me only prolong matters, and if for one moment you disobey me by choosing arrogance and warfare, I shall descend on your country like a fire, bringing an army of picked warriors, and once you see my cavalry you will regret your delay in submitting to me." The letter was sealed with Sekandar's mark, and a soldier who was eager for fame was chosen to take it. The messenger arrived at the court, and when Foor was told of his arrival he was summoned into the royal presence.

---

3. A concealment just described in a passage not included here.
4. China. "Foor": the Persian form of the Greek Porus.
5. God-given glory.

When Foor read Sekandar's letter he started up in rage and immediately wrote a furious reply, planting a tree in the garden of vengeance. "We should fear God, and not use such presumptuous language, because a boastful man will find himself friendless and with no resources. Have you no shame that you summon me like this? Isn't your wisdom disturbed by this kind of talk? If it were Filqus writing thus to Foor, that would be something, but you? You dare to stir up trouble in this way? Your victory over Dara has gone to your head, but the heavens had had enough of him, and fate deals in this way with people who won't listen to good advice. And you found your quarrel with Kayd[6] was like a feast, so now you think all kings are your prey to hunt down. The ancient kings of Iran never addressed us in this way. I am Foor, descended from the family of Foor, and we have never paid any attention to Caesars[7] from the west. When Dara asked for my help, I sent him war elephants to buy time, although I saw that neither his heart nor his fortune were as they should be. When he was murdered by a slave, good fortune deserted the Persians. If evil came to him from an evil counselor, is that any reason for you to lose your good sense? Don't be so eager for battle and so disrespectful toward me; soon enough you'll see my war elephants and armies crowding the way before you. All you think of is your own glory, but inside you are the color of Ahriman.[8] Don't sow these seeds of strife throughout the world; fear misfortune and the harm that will come to you. I mean well by this letter, and may it gratify your heart."

Sekandar Leads His Army Against Foor

After reading this letter, Sekandar immediately selected chieftains from his army, men who were worthy of command: old in their understanding but young in years. Then he led his men against Foor, and they were so numerous that the earth was like a heaving sea. They traveled by every pathway, so that there seemed to be no track that they didn't take, over mountains, along the seashores, and through the most difficult terrain. The army grew weary of harsh traveling and fierce battles, and one evening when they pitched camp, a group of them came before the king. They said,

> "Sovereign of Greece and of all Asia too,
> Earth cannot hold the massive armies you
> Lead out against the world: Foor will not fight,
> And China's emperor quails before your might.
> Why should your army's valiant soldiers die
> For worthless lands beneath an alien sky?
> In all our ranks we cannot find one horse
> That's fit for war; if we reverse our course
> The infantry and cavalry will stray
> By unfamiliar paths and lose their way.
> Before, we fought and gained our victories
> Against the strength of human enemies,

---

6. An Indian king.
7. That is, emperors.

8. In Zoroastrian theology, the god of evil and darkness, fundamentally opposed to Hormozd.

> But none of us desires to die in wars
> With mountains and the sea's infertile shores;
> Men do not fight with rocks and ocean tides,
> With barren plains and rugged mountain sides.
> Do not convert the glory of our fame
> To ignominious and ignoble shame."

Sekandar was angered by their words, and he made short work of their complaints. He said, "In the war with the Persians, no Greek soldier was injured; Dara was killed by his own slaves, and none of you suffered. I shall continue on my way without you, and place my foot on the dragon's heart alone. You will see that the wretched Foor will have no desire for either battles or banquets when I have dealt with him. My help comes from God and the Persian army, and I have no need of Greek goodwill." Frightened by his anger, the army begged him to pardon them and said, "We are all our Caesar's slaves, and we tread the earth only as he wills us to. We shall go on, and when there are no horses left, we shall fight on foot. If the earth becomes a sea with our blood, and the low places become hills of corpses, even if the heavens rain down mountainous rocks, no enemy will ever see our backs in battle. We are your slaves, here for you to command, and how could you suffer any injury from us?"

Sekandar then formed a new battle plan. He chose thirty thousand Persian warriors headed by experienced, well-armored chieftains. Behind them he placed forty thousand Greek cavalry, and behind them his warlike Egyptian cavalry, who fought with swords. Forty thousand of Dara's troops and men from the Persian royal family accompanied them. Sekandar picked out twelve thousand Greek and Egyptian cavalry to bring up the rear and scour the plains and valleys. With his army Sekandar had sixty astrologers and sages to advise him on the most auspicious days for combat.

When Foor became aware of the enemy's approach, he chose a place suitable for battle, and his troops crowded the plain for four miles, with elephants in the van and his warriors behind them. Meanwhile Sekandar's spies told him of the war elephants in Foor's army, and how with their overpowering trunks (that were under the protection of Saturn) they could destroy two miles of cavalry, who would be unable either to defeat them or to get back to their own ranks. The spies drew a picture of an elephant on a piece of paper and showed it to the king, who had a model of the animal made from wax. Then he turned to his advisors and said, "Who can think of some way to defeat this?" The wise men of his court pondered the problem and then gathered together, from Greece, Egypt, and Persia, a group of more than forty times thirty blacksmiths, all of whom were expert at their trade. They made a horse of iron, with an iron saddle and an iron rider; its joints were held together with nails and solder, and then they polished both the rider and his steed. It was mounted on wheels and filled with black oil. They pushed it in front of Sekandar, who was pleased by the device and saw that it would be very useful. He ordered that more than a thousand of these iron horses and riders be made. What king had ever seen an army of dappled, gray, bay, and black horses, all of them made of iron? The devices went forward on wheels, and looked exactly like cavalry prepared for war.

Sekandar's Battle Against the Indian Troops; He Kills Foor

As Sekandar approached Foor's forces, the two armies caught sight of each other; amid clouds of dust a great cry went up from each side, and the warriors advanced on each other eager for battle. Then Sekandar's men set fire to oil in the iron horses and routed Foor's forces. Flames flared out from the iron steeds, and as soon as the elephants saw this they plunged precipitately this way and that. Foor's army was in turmoil, and when the elephants wrapped their trunks around the burning horses, they were maddened by their wounds, and their mahouts were bewildered as to what to do. The whole Indian army, including its mighty elephants, began to flee, and Sekandar pursued his malicious enemies like the wind. As the air darkened at nightfall there was nowhere left for the army to fight. Sekandar and the Greeks halted at a place between two mountains and sent out scouts to keep their camp safe from the enemy.

When the sun rose like a gold ingot, making the world as bright as clear crystal, the din of trumpets, bugles, and fifes rang out, and the two armies, thrusting their lances into the heavens, prepared to fight again. Clutching his Greek sword, Sekandar came between the hosts and sent a horseman to shout from a distance to Foor,

> "Sekandar stands before his troops and seeks
> To talk with Foor, and hear the words he speaks."

When Foor heard this he hurried to the head of his troops. Sekandar said,

> "Two armies have been shattered on these plains
> Where feral scavengers eat human brains,
> And horses tread on bones. We're brave and young,
> Each of us is a noble champion—
> Our warriors have been killed, or they have fled:
> Why should they flee, or be left here for dead?
> Why should two countries fight when combat can
> Decide who is the victor, man to man?
> Prepare to face me, one of us alone
> Will live to claim these armies and this throne."

Foor agreed to his proposal, thinking that his own body was like a lion's and that his horse was the equal of any fierce dragon, while Sekandar was as thin as a reed, wore light armor, and rode an exhausted mount. He said,

> "This is a noble custom: hand to hand
> We will decide who's ruler of this land."

Grasping their swords, they advanced on one another in the space between the two hosts. When Sekandar saw his massive opponent, his fearsome sword in hand and mounted on a huge horse, he was astonished and almost despaired of his life. Nevertheless he went forward, and as he did so Foor was distracted by a cry that went up from the rear of his army and turned toward it. Like the wind then Sekandar bore down on him, and struck the lion-like warrior with a mighty sword blow. The blade sliced through Foor's neck and trunk, and he fell from his horse to the earth.

The Greek commander was overjoyed and his warriors rushed forward; the earth and clouds re-echoed with the thunder of a lion-skin drum, and the blare of trumpets. The Indian warriors looked on Sekandar with fury and were ready to fight, but a voice rang out from the Greek ranks: "Foor's head lies here in the dust, his mammoth body is hacked and torn, who is it you wish to fight for, who will benefit from more sword blows and destruction? Sekandar has become to you as Foor was; it is he you must look to now for battles and banquets." With a roar the Indian warriors called out their agreement, and they came forward to gaze at Foor's hacked and bloody body. A wail of sorrow went up from their ranks, and they threw down their weapons. Fearfully they went before Sekandar, groaning and heaping dust on their heads, but Sekandar returned their weapons, and his words were welcoming: "One Indian has died here, but you should not grieve. I shall cherish you more than he did and try to drive sorrow from your lives. I will distribute his wealth among you, and make the Indians powerful with crowns and throne." Then he mounted Foor's throne; on the one side there was mourning and on the other feasting. But this is the way of the passing world, which brings sorrow to those who dwell in it.

For two months Sekandar sat on the Indian throne, distributing wealth to the army; then he placed there as his regent an Indian nobleman called Savorg, saying to him, "Don't hide your gold away. Distribute and consume whatever comes to you, and put no faith in this passing world, which sometimes favors Sekandar, sometimes Foor, and sometimes gives us pain and rage, sometimes joy and feasting." Savorg too distributed gold and silver to the Indian warriors.

*　*　*

Sekandar Leads His Army to Egypt

When he returned from his pilgrimage he bestowed gold on Nasr,[9] enriching those who had been poor and obliged to find food by their own labors. Then he led his army to Jeddah, where he didn't stay long. The soldiers were set to work making ships and a number of boats, in which the world conqueror and his army set off for Egypt. The Egyptian king at that time was named Qaytun, and he possessed an unimaginably large army; when he heard that a victorious world conqueror was coming with a following wind from the shrine at Mecca, he set out with a large company of soldiers to welcome him and took coins, slaves, and crowns as presents. Sekandar was pleased to see him and stayed in Egypt for a year, until he and his troops were well rested.

Andalusia[1] was ruled over by a woman; she was wise, had innumerable troops at her disposal, and ruled in prosperity and happiness. The name of this generous and ambitious woman was Qaydafeh.[2] She sought out a painter from the

9. An Arab descendant of Ishmael (the older son of Abraham and the legendary forefather of the Arab people); he welcomes Sekandar to the Hijaz (modern Arabia) and Yemen. While there, Sekandar makes a pilgrimage to the Ka'aba at Mecca (a site of worship even before the rise of Islam).
1. Andalusia (or, more accurately, al-Andalus) became the name of modern Spain during the period of Islamic rule, which began about a thousand years after Alexander died and extended well past Ferdowsi's own time.
2. Queen of Andalusia; she corresponds to Candace, queen of the White Ethiopians, in Greek, Latin, and European versions of the Alexander story (also compare Queen Makeda in the Ethiopian *Kebra Nagast*).

ranks of her soldiers, someone who could make an accurate likeness, and said to him, "Go to Sekandar, and see that you make no mention of my country or of me. Look carefully at him, see what his complexion is, examine his face and stature, and then paint me a full-length portrait of him." The painter heard her and immediately mounted his horse, ready to carry out his sovereign's orders. As quick as a royal courier he made his way from Andalusia to Egypt and into the presence of Sekandar. He observed him when he gave audience and when he was in the saddle; then he took paper and Chinese ink,[3] drew his portrait exactly as he was in real life, and returned to Andalusia. Qaydafeh was moved when she saw Sekandar's face and sighed to herself, then hid the portrait away.

Sekandar asked Qaytun, "Who is Qaydafeh's equal in the world?"

> And King Qaytun replied, "In all the earth
> There's no one of her glory and her worth;
> Unless he were to read the muster rolls
> No one could count the soldiers she controls.
> You won't find anyone in any land
> Who has the wealth she's able to command,
> Who has her dignity, her eloquence,
> Her wisdom, goodness, and magnificence.
> She's built from stone a wide and wondrous town
> So strong no leopard's claws could tear it down—
> Four parasangs in length, no man can measure
> Its endless width. And if you ask for treasure,
> Hers is uncountable; for years there's been
> Talk in the world of this exalted queen."

Sekandar's Letter to Qaydafeh

Sekandar summoned a scribe and had a letter written on silk, from Sekandar, the slayer of lions and conqueror of cities, to Qaydafeh the wise, whose name is unequalled in glory. The letter opened by invoking God, who is generous and just and who bestows prosperity on those who merit it, and continued: "I have not rushed into war with you; rather, I have been weighing the reports of the splendor of your court. When they bring you this letter, may it enlighten your dark soul. Send tribute to me, and understand that you do not have the strength to oppose me. You are wise, so act with foresight, as a powerful and religious sovereign should. If you attempt any kind of trick against me, you will see nothing but adverse fortune come your way. You don't have to look far to learn this lesson: consider what happened to Dara and Foor." As soon as the ink had dried the letter was sealed with musk.

A quick messenger took the letter at Sekandar's command, and when Qaydafeh read it she was astonished at its language. Her answer was as follows: "Praise be to him who created the earth, who has made you victorious over Foor of India, over Dara, and over the nobles of Sind. Your victory over these warriors has made you willful. You have crowned yourself in victory, but how can you put me on their level? I am far greater than they were, in *farr* and

---

3. Very high quality ink.

in glory, in my armies, and in my royal wealth. How can I submit to a Greek overlord, and how can you expect me to tremble with fear because of your threats? My armies number more than a thousand thousand men, and princes command every one of those armies. Who are you that you should boast in this way? Your defeat of Dara has made you the prince of braggarts!" She placed her gold seal on the letter and dispatched the messenger, who rode like the wind.

The Greeks Capture Qaydafeh's Son

Sekandar read her letter and then he had the trumpets sounded and his army led out. They marched for a month until they reached the borders of Qaydafeh's lands. A king called Faryan reigned there, a man possessed of an army and wealth, and successful in his life. His city was built to withstand war, and its walls were so high that cranes could not overfly them. He and his army occupied this fortress, and Sekandar ordered that balistas and catapults be brought up to batter the walls. After a week of fighting his army entered the town, and the victor gave orders that no blood was to be spilled.

One of Qaydafeh's sons, named Qaydrus, was married to Faryan's daughter, and was in the city, as his father-in-law delighted in his company. Qaydrus and his wife, however, had been captured by a man named Shahrgir; Sekandar knew of this and looked for some way to free them. He summoned his vizier, a wise and reasonable man named Bitqun, and showed him his crown and throne, saying, "Qaydrus and his bride will come before you, and I shall call you Sekandar, the son of Filqus. You will be seated on the throne here like a king, and I will stand ready to serve you. You will give orders that Qaydrus's head is to be severed from his shoulders by the executioner. I will humble myself before you and plead for them; you will clear the audience hall of courtiers, and when I redouble my pleas, you will grant my request." The vizier was very troubled by all this, as he was unsure what it meant. Sekandar continued, "This business must remain secret. Call me in as an envoy and talk a little about Qaydafeh; then cordially send me off to her with ten horsemen, saying, 'Hurry and take this letter and bring me the answer.'" Bitqun replied, "I will do it: I'll carry out this deception according to your orders."

Dawn came, the sun drew its glittering dagger, and night fled away in fear. Bitqun sat on the royal throne, but there was shame in his face and anxiety in his heart. Sekandar stood before him as a servant: he had closed the doors to the court and opened the doors to deception. When Shahrgir led in Qaydafeh's weeping son as a captive, together with his young and beautiful wife, who was wringing her hands in grief, Bitqun quickly said, "Who is this man, who has cause to weep so much?" The young man answered, "Come to your senses! I am Qaydrus, Qaydafeh's son, and this is Faryan's daughter, my sole wife. I wish to take her home and cherish her like my own soul, but I am a prisoner in Shahrgir's hands, my soul wounded by the stars, my body by arrows." When Bitqun heard him he was distressed and angry. He started up and said to the executioner, "These two must be buried beneath the dust! Cut off their heads with your Indian sword: now, just as they are, in chains here."

Sekandar came forward and kissed the ground, and said, "Great king of royal lineage, if you will free them for my sake, I shall be able to hold my head up in any company. Why should you vengefully cut off the heads of innocent people? The world's Creator will not look well on us for this." Wise Bitqun answered him, "You have freed these two from death," and to Qaydrus he added, "You've kept your head, which was already leaving your shoulders! Now I shall send you and this man who has interceded for you to your mother, and he can explain what has happened. It would be good if she would then send us tribute: this would mean that no one will lose his skin in this quarrel. Look after this vizier of mine, who will offer your mother war with me or prosperity; act well toward him as he has done toward you, since a noble man's heart is moved to repay kindness. When he has received the queen's answer, send him safely back to me." Qaydrus replied,

> "I will not take my heart or ears or eyes
> From him; how could I treat him otherwise
> Since he has here restored to me my wife,
> My soul, the living sweetness of my life?"

Sekandar Goes as an Envoy to Qaydafeh

Sekandar selected ten suitable companions from among the Greeks: they were all privy to his identity and willing to keep his secret. He said to them, "On this journey address me as Bitqun." Qaydrus led the group, and Sekandar watched him and listened to him attentively. Their splendid horses galloped forward like fire, until the travelers came to a mountain made all of crystal, yet with fruit trees and many plants growing on its slopes. They continued into the queen's realm, and when Qaydafeh heard that her son, about whom she had been anxiously seeking news, was approaching, she went out to welcome him with a large escort of nobles. As soon as Qaydrus saw his mother he dismounted and made his obeisance before her. She told him to remount, and as they rode on together, she grasped his hand in hers. Qaydrus told her all that he had seen and heard, and he turned pale as he described his sufferings in Faryan's city, and how he was now bereft of his crown, throne, army, and wealth. And he added, "This man who has come with us saved my and my bride's lives; if he hadn't intervened, Sekandar would have ordered that my head be cut off and my body burned. Treat him well, and don't hold back with excuses that would make me break my promise to him."

Hearing her son's words, Qaydafeh was distraught with grief. She had the messenger summoned from her palace where he had been installed and motioned him to a fine throne. She questioned him closely and made much of him and saw that a special residence was set aside for his stay. There she sent fine foods, clothes, and carpets.

At dawn the next morning Sekandar made his way to the court to talk with the queen. Servants drew the curtain aside and let his horse enter. He stared in wonder at Qaydafeh on her ivory throne, with her crown studded with rubies and turquoise, wearing a Chinese cloak woven with gold, her many serving girls with their necklaces and earrings standing around her, her face shining like the sun, her throne supported on crystal columns, her gold dress woven with jewels and clasped with a precious black and white Yemeni stone. Under his breath he called on God repeatedly. He saw that her throne alone surpassed anything that Greece or Persia could provide. He came forward and kissed the ground, like a man anxious to make a good impression. Qaydafeh encouraged him by asking a number of questions; then, like the sun passing from the dome of the sky she declared that the audience for strangers was over, and summoned a meal, wine, and musicians. Tables made of teak and inlaid with gold on an ivory ground were brought in; various kinds of food were served, and wine was set out for when they had finished eating. Gold and silver trays were put before them; first they drank to Qaydafeh herself, and then, as she drank more deeply, the queen began to look closely at Sekandar. She said to her steward, "Bring me that shining silk with the charming face painted on it; bring it quickly, just as it is. Don't stand there wringing your hands, go!"

The steward brought the cloth and laid it before her. She stared at it for a long time and then looked at Sekandar's face: she saw no difference between them. Qaydafeh knew that her guest was the Greek king and the commander of his armies, that he had made himself his own messenger and bravely come into her presence. She said to him, "You seem a man well favored by fortune. Tell me, what message did Sekandar give to you?" And he replied, "The world's king spoke to me in the presence of our nobles. He said to tell the pure-hearted Qaydafeh, 'Pursue only honesty, pay attention to what I say, and do not turn your head aside from my orders. If your heart harbors any rebellion, I shall bring an army against you that will break it in pieces. I have found evidence of your greatness, and I have not hurried to declare war on you. Wisdom and modesty are yours, and your subtle policies maintain the world in safety. If you willingly pay me tribute, you need have no fear of me; if you refuse to go the way of rebellion and disaster, you will see from me nothing but kindness and righteousness.'"

Qaydafeh was infuriated when she heard this, but she thought that silence was the best policy. She said, "Go to your quarters now, and rest with your companions. When you come to me tomorrow, I shall give you my answer and some good advice for your return journey." Sekandar went to the building that had been assigned to him and spent the night considering what he should do. When the world's lamp appeared above the mountaintops, and the plains and foothills took on the appearance of glittering brocade, Sekandar made his way back to Qaydafeh's court; his lips were full of smiles, his heart of grief and anxiety. The chancellor recognized him as the foreign envoy and, after questioning him, led him into the queen's presence. The audience hall was full of strangers. The queen's throne was crystal patterned with agates and emeralds surrounding gems of royal worth; its base was sandal and aloes wood and it rested on pillars studded with turquoise. Sekandar was astonished at the splendor and glory he saw, and he thought, "This is indeed a throne room, and no God-fearing man ever saw its like." He came forward to the queen and was directed to a subsidiary golden throne. Qaydafeh said to him, "Well, Bitqun, why are you staring in this way? Is it that Greece can't produce the like of what you see here, in my humble country?"

Sekandar replied, "Your majesty, you should not speak contemptuously of this palace. It is far more glorious than the palaces of other kings and seems like a mine of precious stones." Qaydafeh laughed at his reaction, and she felt delight in her heart that she was able to tease him in this way. Then she cleared the court and motioned the envoy to come closer to her. She said to him,

"Filqus's son, I see you're fashioned for
Battles and royal banquets, peace and war!"

Sekandar turned pale at her words, and then blushed violently; his soul was filled with distress. He said, "Wise queen, such words are not worthy of you. I am Bitqun, don't say that I am a son of Filqus. I give thanks to God that there is no one of noble lineage here, because if he reported what you have said to my king my soul would soon be separated from my body." Qaydafeh replied,

"Enough excuses! If with your own eyes
You see yourself, then you must recognize
The truth of what I say, and don't attempt
Either to lie or treat me with contempt."

Then she produced the silk with the charming face painted upon it and laid it before him; if the painted face had moved at all you would have said that it was Sekandar himself. Sekandar saw it and he nervously chewed his lower lip; the day had suddenly turned as dark as night for him. He said, "A man should never go out in the world without a hidden dagger!" Qaydafeh answered, "If you had your sword belt on and stood before me with a dagger, you'd have neither the strength nor an adequate sword nor a place to fight nor a means of escape." Sekandar said, "A noble and ambitious man should not flinch at danger; a low-minded person will never rise in the world. If I had my arms and armor here, all your palace would be a sea of blood; I'd have killed you, or ripped open my own belly in front of those who hate me!"

Qaydafeh Gives Sekandar Some Advice

Qaydafeh laughed at his blustering manliness and his angry words. She said, "O lion-like king, don't let yourself be led astray by your male pride! The Indian king Foor wasn't killed because of your glory, and neither were Dara and the heroes of Sind. Their good fortune was at an end, and yours was in the ascendant; and now you're so full of your manly valor because you've become the greatest man on earth at the moment. But you should know that all good things come from God, and while you live you should be grateful to him. You say the world is yours because of your knowledge, but what you say does not seem true to me. What will knowledge avail you when you go into the maw of the dragon death? Acting as your own envoy is sewing your shroud while you are still young. I am not in the habit of shedding blood, nor of attacking rulers. When a monarch has power and is merciful and just, that is when he becomes knowledgeable. Know that whoever spills a king's blood will see nothing but fire as his reward. Be assured of your safety, and leave here with joy. But when you have gone change your habits: don't go acting as your own messenger again, because even the dust knows that you are Sekandar. And I'm not aware of any great hero whose portrait I don't possess, stored away with a reliable courtier. While you remain here I will call you Bitqun and seat you at court accordingly, so that no one will guess your secret or hear your name. I will send you on your way in safety, but you, my lord, must be reasonable and swear that you will never plot against my son, my country, or any of my people or allies, and that you will refer to me only as your equal, as the ruler of my own country."

Freed from the threat of being killed, Sekandar rejoiced to hear her words. He swore by the just God, by the Christian faith, and by the dust of battle that he would act only kindly and righteously toward her land, her son, and her noble allies, and that he would never plot their destruction. When she had heard his oath, Qaydafeh said, "There is one other piece of advice that should not be kept from you: know then that my son Taynush has little sense and pays scant attention to my knowledge and advice. He is Foor's son-in-law and he must not in any way suspect that you and Sekandar occupy the same skin, or even that you are friends. He is eager to avenge Foor, and to confound the earth and sky in war. Now, go joyfully and safely to your own quarters, and have no fear of the world's sorrows."

* * *

Sekandar Sees a Corpse in the Palace of Topazes

The king and his army marched onward for a month and were sorely tried by their journey. They came to a mountain, where they saw no sign of either wild or domestic animals. The mountain's crest was of lapis lazuli, and a palace stood there, made of topazes. It was filled with crystal chandeliers, and in its midst was a fountain of salt water. Next to this fountain was a throne for two people, on which was stretched a wretched corpse. He had a man's body, but his head was like that of a boar; there was a pillow of camphor beneath his head, and a brocade covering had been drawn up over his body. Instead of a lamp a brilliant red jewel shone there, illuminating the whole area; its rays twinkled like stars in the water, and all the chamber glowed as if in sunlight. Whoever went there to take something, or even simply set foot within the palace, found himself rooted to the spot; his whole body began to tremble, and he started to waste away.

A cry came from the salt water, saying, "O king, still filled with longing and desire, don't play the fool much longer! You have seen many things that no man ever saw, but now it's time to draw rein. Your life has shortened now, and the royal throne is without its king." Sekandar was afraid and hurried back to his camp as fast as wind-blown smoke. Quickly he led his army away, weeping and calling on God's name. From that mountain he headed toward the desert, afflicted with sorrow and concerned for his soul. And so he went forward, at the head of his troops, weeping and in pain.

Sekandar Sees the Speaking Tree

The desert road led to a city, and Sekandar was relieved when he heard human voices there. The whole area was one of gardens and fine buildings and was a place to delight any man. The city's noblemen welcomed him, calling out greetings and showering him with gold and jewels. "It is wonderful that you have come to visit us," they said. "No army has ever entered this town, and no one in it has ever heard the name of 'king.' Now that you have come our souls are yours, and may you live with bodily health and spiritual serenity." Sekandar was pleased by their welcome and rested from the journey across the desert. He said to them, "What is there here that's astonishing, that should be inquired into?" A guide said to him, "Victorious king, there is a marvel here, a tree that has two separate trunks together, one of which is female and the other male, and these splendid tree limbs can speak. At night the female trunk becomes sweet smelling and speaks, and when the daylight comes, the male speaks." Sekandar and his Greek cavalry, with the nobles of the town gathered around, listened and said, "When is it you say that the tree speaks in a loud voice?" The translator replied, "A little after day has disappeared one of the trunks begins to speak, and a lucky man will hear its voice; in the dark night the female speaks, and its leaves then smell like musk."

Sekandar answered, "When we go beyond the tree, what wonders are there on the other side?" The reply was, "When you pass the tree there is little argument about which way to take, as there is no place beyond there; guides say it is the world's end. A dark desert lies ahead of you, but no man is so weary of his own soul as to go there. None of us have ever seen or heard that there are any animals there, or that birds fly there." Sekandar and his troops went forward, and when they came near the speaking tree the ground throbbed with heat and the soil there was covered with the pelts of wild beasts. He asked his guide what the pelts were, and who it was that had skinned so many animals in this way. The man answered, "The tree has many worshippers, and when they come here to worship, they feed on the flesh of wild animals."

When the sun reached its zenith Sekandar heard a voice above him, coming from the leaves of the tree; it was a voice to strike terror and foreboding in a man. He was afraid and said to the interpreter, "You are wise and mean well, tell me what the leaves are saying, which makes my heart dissolve within me." "O king, favored by fortune, the leaves say, 'However much Sekandar wanders in the world, he has already seen his share of blessings: when he has reigned for fourteen years, he must quit the royal throne.'" At the guide's words Sekandar's heart filled with pain, and he wept bitterly. He was sad and silent then, speaking to no one, until midnight. Then the leaves of the other trunk began to speak, and Sekandar again asked the interpreter what they said. He replied, "The female tree says, 'Do not puff yourself up with greed; why torment your soul in this way? Greed makes you wander the wide world, harass mankind, and kill kings. But you are not long for this earth now; do not darken and deaden your days like this.'" Then the king said to the interpreter, "Pure of heart and noble as you are, ask them one question: Will this fateful day come in Greece; will my mother see me alive again, before someone covers my face in death?"

> The speaking tree replied, "Few days remain;
> You must prepare your final baggage train.
> Neither your mother, nor your family,
> Nor the veiled women of your land will see
> Your face again. Death will come soon: you'll die
> In a strange land, with strangers standing by.
> The stars and crown and throne and worldly glory
> Are sated with Sekandar and his story."

Sekandar left the tree, his heart wounded as if by a sword. When he returned to his camp, his chieftains went into the town to collect the gifts from the town's nobility. Among these was a cuirass that shone like the waters of the Nile and was as huge as an elephant skin: it had two long tusks attached to it and was so heavy it was hard to lift. There was other armor, as well as fine brocade, a hundred golden eggs each weighing sixty *man*,[4] and a rhinoceros made of gold and jewels. Sekandar accepted the gifts and led off his army, weeping bitter tears as he went.

Sekandar Visits the Emperor of China

Now Sekandar led his army toward China. For forty days they traveled, until they reached the sea. There the army made camp and the king pitched his brocade pavilion. He summoned a scribe to write a letter to the Chinese emperor from Sekandar, the seizer of cities. The message was filled with promises and threats, and when it was completed Sekandar himself went as the envoy, taking with him an intelligent companion who was one with him in heart and speech and who could advise him as to what to do and what not to do. He entrusted his troops to the army's commander and chose five Greeks as his escort.

When news reached the Chinese emperor that an envoy was approaching his country, he sent troops out to meet him. Sekandar reached the court and the emperor came forward in welcome, but his heart was filled with suspicious thoughts. Sekandar ran forward and made his obeisance to him, and then was seated in the palace for a long while. The emperor questioned him and made much of him and assigned him noble sleeping quarters. As the sun rose over the mountains, dying their summits gold, the envoy was summoned to court. Sekandar spoke at length, saying what was appropriate, and then handed over the letter. It was addressed from the king of Greece, possessor of the world, lord of every country, on whom other kings call down God's blessings. It continued, "My orders for China are that she remain prosperous, and that she should not prepare for war against me; it was war against me that destroyed Foor, and Dara, who was the lord of the world, and Faryan the Arab, and other sovereigns. From the east to the west no one ignores my commands, the heavens themselves do not know the number of my troops, and Venus[5] and the sun could not count them. If you disobey any command of mine you will bring distress on yourself and your country. When you read my letter, bring me tribute; do not trouble yourself about this, or look for evil allies to make war on me. If you come you will see me in the midst of my troops, and when I see that you are honest and mean well I shall confirm you in the possession of your crown and throne, and no misfortune will come to you. If, however, you are reluctant to come before your king, send me things that are peculiar to China—your country's gold work, horses, swords, seal rings, clothes, cloth, ivory thrones, fine brocade, necklaces, crowns—that is, if you have no wish to be harmed by me. Send my soldiers back to me, and rest assured that your wealth, throne, and crown are safe."

When the emperor of China saw what was in the letter, he started up in fury, but then chose silence as a better course. He laughed and said to the envoy, "May your king be a partner to the heavens! Tell me what you know about him. Tell me about his conversation, his height and appearance, and what kind of a man he is." The envoy said, "Great lord of China, you should understand that

---

4. A Persian unit of weight, usually equivalent to about 9 lbs.

5. The morning and the evening star, as well as the Roman goddess of love.

there is no one else in the world like Sekandar. In his manliness, policy, good fortune, and wisdom he surpasses all that anyone could imagine. He is as tall as a cypress tree, has an elephant's strength, and is as generous as the waters of the Nile; his tongue can be as cutting as a sword, but he can charm an eagle down from the clouds." When he heard all this, the emperor changed his mind. He ordered that wine and a banquet be laid out in the palace gardens. He drank till evening brought darkness to the world, and the company became tipsy. Then he said to the envoy, "May your king be Jupiter's[6] partner. At first light I'll compose an answer to his letter, and what I write will make the day seem splendid to your eyes." Sekandar was half drunk, and he staggered from the garden to his quarters with an orange in his hand.

When the sun rose in Leo[7] and the heavens dispelled the darkness, Sekandar went to the emperor, and all suspicious thoughts were far from his heart. The emperor asked him, "How did you spend the night? When you left you were quite overcome with wine." Then he summoned a scribe, who brought paper, musk, and ambergris, and dictated a letter. He began with praise of God, the lord of chivalry, justice, and ability, of cultivated behavior, abstinence, and piety, and called down his blessings on the Greek king. Then he continued, "Your eloquent envoy has arrived, bringing the king's letter. I have read through the royal words and discussed its contents with my nobles. As for your claims concerning the wars against Dara, Faryan, and Foor, in which you were victorious, so that you became a shepherd whose flock consists of kings, you should not consider what comes about through the will of the Lord of the Sun and Moon as the result of your own valor and the might of your army. When a great man's days are numbered, what difference does it make whether he dies in battle or at a banquet? If they died in battle with you this is because their fate was fixed for that day, and fate is not to be hurried or delayed. You should not pride yourself so much on your victories over them, because even if you are made of iron there is no doubt that you too will die. Where now are Feraydun, Zahhak, and Jamshid,[8] who came like the wind and left like a breath? I am not afraid of you and I will not make war against you, neither shall I puff myself up with pride as you are doing. It is not my habit to shed blood, and besides it would be unworthy of my faith for me to do evil in this way. You summon me, but to no purpose; I serve God, not kings. I send with this more riches than you have dreamed of, so that there shall be no doubting my munificence."

These words were an arrow in Sekandar's vital organs, and he blushed with shame. In his heart he said, "Never again shall I go somewhere disguised as my own envoy." He returned to his quarters and prepared to leave the Chinese court.

The proud emperor opened his treasuries' doors, since he was not a man who found generosity difficult. First he ordered that fifty crowns and ten ivory thrones encrusted with jewels be brought; then a thousand camel loads of gold and silver goods, and a thousand more of Chinese brocades and silks, of camphor, musk, perfumes, and ambergris. He had little regard for wealth, and it eased his heart to be bountiful in this way. He had ten thousand each of the pelts of gray

6. In Roman mythology, the king of the gods.
7. Sekandar's birth sign (the sun rises in Leo in midsummer), viewed in astrology as fiery and masculine.
8. Legendary Persian heroic rulers whose stories appear earlier in the *Shahnameh*.

squirrel, ermine, and sable brought, and as many carpets and crystal goblets, and his wise treasurer saw to their being loaded on pack animals. Then he added three hundred silver saddles and fifty golden ones, together with three hundred red-haired camels loaded with Chinese rarities. He chose as envoy an eloquent and dignified Chinese sage and told him to take his message to the Greek king with all goodwill and splendor, and to say that Sekandar would be warmly welcomed at the Chinese court for as long as he wished to stay there.

The envoy traveled with Sekandar, unaware that he was the Greek king. But when Sekandar's regent came forward and the king told him of his adventures, and the army congratulated him on his safe return and bowed to the ground before him, the envoy realized that he was indeed the Greek king and dismounted in consternation. Sekandar said to him, "There is no need for apologies, but do not tell your emperor of this!" They rested for a night, and the next morning Sekandar sat on the royal throne. He gave gifts to the envoy and said to him, "Go to your emperor and tell him that I say 'You have found honor and respect with me. If you wish to stay where you are, all China is yours, and if you wish to go elsewhere, that too is open to you. I shall rest here for a while, because such a large army as mine cannot be mobilized quickly.'" The envoy returned like the wind, and gave Sekandar's message to the emperor.

Sekandar Leads His Army to Babylon

Sekandar camped there for a month, and then led his army toward Babylon, and the air was darkened with the dust of their march. They pressed on for a month, and no one had any rest during this time. They came to a mountain range so high that its summit was hidden by dark clouds, as if it reached to Saturn. The king and his army could see no way forward but over the mountains and so with difficulty they climbed up toward the crest. The climb exhausted them, but once there they saw a deep lake lying below them. Joyfully and praising God, they began their descent; there was game of all kinds on every side, and for a while the soldiers lived off what they hunted.

Then in the distance a wild man appeared. He was covered in hair, and his body beneath the hair was a dark blue color, and he had huge ears, as big as an elephant's. The soldiers captured him and dragged him to Sekandar, who called on God in his astonishment at being confronted by such a creature. He said, "What kind of a man are you? What is your name? What can you find to live off in this lake, and what do you want from life?" The man replied, "O king, my mother and father call me Pillow-Ears." Then the king asked what it was that he could see in the middle of the lake, over toward where the sun rises. The man answered, "O king, and may you always be renowned in the world, that's a town that is like heaven; you'd say that earth had no part in its making. You won't see a single building there that isn't covered with fish skins and fish bones. On the walls they've painted the face of Afrasyah,[9] and he looks more splendid than the sun itself; and warlike Khosrow's[1] face is there too, and you can see his greatness and generosity by looking at it. They're painted on bones; you won't see

---

9. King of Turan, the archenemy of Iran; a powerful warrior, he was the agent of the evil god Ahriman.

1. One of the greatest of the Persian kings (531–579), famous for military conquests, cultural achievements, and major building projects.

one bit of soil in the whole city! The people eat fish there; that's the only thing they have to nourish them. If the king orders me to, I'll go there, but without any of your soldiers." Sekandar said to the man with huge ears, "Go, and bring back someone from the town, so that we can see something new."

Pillow-Ears hurried off to the town and soon came back with some of its inhabitants. Seventy men crossed the water with him; some were young and some old, and they were dressed in various kinds of silks. The older, more dignified men each carried a golden goblet filled with pearls, and the young ones each carried a crown; they came before Sekandar with their heads reverently bowed. They made their obeisance to him, and he talked with them for a long time. The army stayed there that night, and at cockcrow next morning the din of drums rang out from the king's pavilion. Sekandar continued the march to Babylon, and the air was dark with the dust sent up by his soldiers.

Sekandar's Letter to Arestalis[2] and Arestalis's Reply

The king knew that death was close, and that his days were darkening, and he decided that no one of royal lineage should be left alive in the world: he wanted to ensure that no man would be able to lead an army against Greece. With his mind fixed on this arrogant scheme, he wrote a letter to Arestalis, saying he would invite everyone of royal lineage to his court, where they were to come unsuspecting of what was in store for them. When this letter was delivered to the Greek sage, his heart seemed to break in two. Immediately he wrote a reply, weeping as if his ink were tears. "The king of the world's missive arrived, and he should give up this evil design of his. As for the evil you have already done, think no more of it but distribute goods to the poor. For the future, abstain from evil and give your soul to God; sow nothing but seeds of goodness in the world. From birth we are all marked for death, and we have no choice but to submit. No one who dies takes his sovereignty with him; he leaves, and hands on his greatness to another. Live within limits and do not shed the blood of the great families, which will make you cursed until the resurrection. And if there is no army or king in Persia, armies will sweep in from Turkestan, India, Scythia, and China, and it would be no surprise if whoever took Persia then marched on the west. The descendants of the Persian kings should not be harmed so much as by a breath of wind. Summon them to your court, but be generous to them, feast them, and consult with them. Treat each according to his rank and see that their names are listed in your pension rolls, since it is from them that you took the world, paying nothing for it. Do not give any of them power over another, or refer to any of them as king of the world, but make these royal nobles a shield to protect the west against foreign invasion."

Sekandar changed his mind when he read this letter. He summoned the world's nobly born, all who were chivalrous by nature, to his court, and assigned them suitable places there. He wrote a charter, which designated the portion of each, with the stipulation that none was to encroach on another's power: these nobles he called "kings of the peoples."

2. The Greek philosopher Aristotle (384– 322 B.C.E.), who tutored Alexander the Great. A fictional exchange of letters between Alexander and Aristotle (sometimes called *Wonders of the East*) circulated widely in Europe and the Islamic world throughout the Middle Ages.

That night Sekandar reached Babylon, where he was joyfully greeted by the local nobility. During the same night a woman gave birth to an astonishing child that had a lion's head, a human chest and human shoulders, a cow's tail, and hooves. The baby was stillborn, and it would have been better if the woman had had no offspring at all rather than such a monster. Immediately they brought the child to Sekandar, who took it as an omen, and ordered that it be buried. He told his astrologers of the child, who grew pensive and silent. He demanded their opinion, saying, "If you keep anything back from me I'll cut your heads from your bodies this minute, and your shroud will be a lion's maw." When the king stormed in this way, they said:

> "First then, as scribes have written, at your birth
> The lion's emblem, Leo, ruled the earth.
> You saw the dead child had a lion's head,
> Which means your majesty will soon be dead.
> The world will be a place of strife until
> A new king bends its peoples to his will."
> The king grew pensive, then replied, "I see
> Death comes, for which there is no remedy.
> I'm not long for this world, I know, but I
> Refuse to brood on this until I die.
> Death comes to us on the appointed day—
> We cannot make fate hurry, or delay."

Sekandar's Letter to His Mother

That day, in Babylon, he fell sick, and he knew that his end was approaching. He summoned an experienced scribe and dictated what was in his heart, in a letter to his mother. He said, "The signs of death cannot be hidden; I have lived the life allotted to me in this world, and we cannot hurry or delay our fate. Do not grieve at my death, for this is not a new thing in the world: all who are born must die, be they kings or paupers. I shall tell our chieftains that when they return from this land to Greece they must obey you alone. I have established those Persians who fought against our armies as lords over their realm, so that they shall have no desire to attack Greece; our country will be secure and at peace. See that my body is buried in Egypt, and that you fulfill all that I say here. Every year distribute ten thousand gold coins of my wealth to the peasantry. If Roshanak[3] bears a son, then my name will surely survive; no one but he must become king of Greece, and he will renew the country's prosperity. But if, when her labor pains come to her, she bears a daughter, marry the child to one of Filqus's sons and call him my son, not my son-in-law, so that my name shall be remembered in the world. As for Kayd's innocent daughter, send her back to her father in India, together with the crowns and silver and gold and all the dowry she brought. Now I have completed my affairs and have no choice but to prepare my heart for death. First, see that my coffin is of gold and that my body's shroud is worthy of me; let it be of Chinese silk impregnated with sweet scents, and see that no one neglects the offices due to me. The

3. Sekandar's wife, the daughter of Darab.

joints of my coffin should be sealed with pitch, as well as camphor, musk, and ambergris. Honey should be poured into the coffin, then a layer of brocade placed there, on which my body is to be laid; when my face has been covered there is no more to be said. When I have gone, wise mother, remember my words. As for the things that I have sent from India, China, Turan, Iran, and Makran, keep what you need and distribute the surplus. Dear mother, my desire is that you be sensible and serene in your soul; do not torment yourself on my behalf, since no one who lives in the world lives forever. When your days too draw to a close, my soul shall surely see yours again; patience is a greater virtue than love, and a person blown hither and thither by emotion is contemptible. For months and years you lovingly cared for my body; now pray to God for my soul; with these prayers you will still care for me. And consider, who is there in all the world whose soul is not cast down by death?"

He sealed the letter and ordered that it be taken with all speed from Babylon to Greece, to give news there that the imperial glory had been eclipsed.

Sekandar Dies in Babylon

When the army learned of the king's illness, the world grew dark before them. Their eyes turned toward the throne, and the world was filled with rumors. Knowing that he had few days left to live and hearing of his army's concern, Sekandar gave orders that his sickbed be taken from the palace out to the open plain. His saddened troops saw his face devoid of color, and the plain rang from end to end with lamentations, as if the soldiers were burning in flames; they cried, "It is an evil day when the Greeks lose their king: misfortune triumphs, and now our country will be destroyed. Our enemies have reached their hearts' desire, while for us the world has turned bitter, and we shall mourn publicly and in secret."

> Then in a failing voice their king replied,
> "Live humbly, fearfully, when I have died,
> And if you'd grow and prosper see that you
> Keep my advice henceforth, in all you do.
> This is your duty to me when I'm gone
> Lest time undo the work that I have done."
> He spoke, and then his soul rose from his breast:
> The king who'd shattered armies was at rest.

An earsplitting wail went up from his troops as they heaped dust on their heads and wept bitter tears. They set fire to the royal pavilion, and the very earth seemed to cry out in sorrow. They cut the tails of a thousand horses and set their saddles on them back to front, as a sign of mourning. As they brought the golden coffin their cries resounded in the heavens; a bishop washed the corpse in clear rosewater and scattered pure camphor over it. They shrouded their king in golden brocade, lamenting as they did so, then placed him beneath a covering of Chinese silk, his body soaked from head to toe in honey. The coffin lid was fastened, and the noble tree whose shade had spread so widely was no more.

They passed the coffin from hand to hand across the plain, and as they went forward, two opinions began to be heard. The Persians said, "He should not be buried anywhere but here: this is the land of emperors, what are they doing carrying the coffin about the world like this?" But a Greek guide said, "It would not be right to bury him here; if you hear my view you'll see that I'm right. Sekandar should be buried in the soil that nourished him." A Persian interrupted, "No matter how much you continue this conversation it won't get to the root of the matter. I'll show you a meadow near here that's been preserved since the time of our ancient kings: old folk call it Jorm. There is a wooded area there, and a lake; if you ask it a question, an answer will come from the mountain nearby. Take an old man there, together with the coffin, and ask your question; if the mountain answers, it will give you the best advice." As quickly as mountain sheep they made their way to the thicket called Jorm. And when they asked their question, the answer came, "What are you doing with this royal coffin? The dust of Sekandar belongs in Alexandria, the town he founded while he was alive." As soon as they heard this, the soldiers hurried from the area.

The Mourning for Sekandar

When Sekandar's body reached Alexandria the world was beset with new disputes. The coffin was set down on the plain, and the land was filled with rumor and gossip. As many as a hundred thousand children, men, and women flocked there. The philosopher Arestalis was there, his eyes filled with bitter tears; the world watched as he stretched out his hand to the coffin and said, "Where are your intelligence, knowledge, and foresight, now that a narrow coffin is your resting place? Why in the days of your youth did you choose the earth as your couch?"

The Greek sages crowded round, each speaking in turn, lamenting Sekandar's death. And then his mother came running, and placed her face on his chest, and said,

> "O noble king, world-conqueror, whose state
> Was princely, and whose stars were fortunate,
> You're far away from me and seem so near,
> Far from your kin, far from your soldiers here.
> Would that my soul were your soul's slave, that I
> Might see the hearts of those who hate you die."
> Then Roshanak ran grieving to his side,
> Crying, "Where are those kings now, and their pride?
> Where's Dara, who once ruled the world? Where's Foor?
> Where's Ashk? Faryan? The sovereign of Sharzoor,
> And all those other lords who put their trust
> In battle and were dragged down to the dust?
> You seemed a storm cloud charged with hail: I said
> That you could never die, that you had shed
> So much blood, fought so many wars, that there
> Must be some secret you would not declare,
> Some talisman that fate had given you
> To keep you safe whatever you might do.
> You cleared the world of petty kings, brought down
> Into the dirt an empire's ancient crown,
> And when the tree you'd planted was to bear
> Its fruits you died, and left me in despair."

When the sky's golden shield descended, the nobles were exhausted by their grief, and they placed the coffin in the ground. There is nothing in the world so terrible and fearful as the fact that one comes like the wind and departs as a breath, and that neither justice nor oppression are apparent in this. Whether you are a king or a pauper you will discover no rhyme or reason to it. But one must act well, with valor and chivalry, and one must eat well and rejoice: I see no other fate for you, whether you are a subject or a prince. This is the way of the ancient world: Sekandar departed, and what remains of him now is the words we say about him. He killed thirty-six kings, but look how much of the world remained in his grasp when he died. He founded ten prosperous cities, and those cities are now reed beds. He sought things that no man has ever sought, and what remains of him within the circle of the horizon is words, nothing more. Words are the better portion since they do not decay as an old building decays in the snow and rain. I have finished with Sekandar now, and with the barrier that he built may our days be fortunate and prosperous.

AVICENNA (IBN SINA)
ca. 980–1037

As the world of Islam stretched out eastward toward India and westward toward Spain, its literature began to reflect the integration of Muslim theology with different poetic modes. No Islamic tradition was a more fertile source of inspiration than the stories of the *mi'raj*, or miraculous night journey experienced by the Prophet Muhammad. The mi'raj story as told by the philosopher Avicenna in his *Book of the Prophet's Ascent to Heaven* is a particularly vivid example of this new blend of religion and poetry: in his hands, it not only narrates a well-known event in Muhammad's life but also presents an allegory of the thinking soul in a state of rapture.

Unlike the **Qur'an** and the biography of Muhammad written by **Ibn Ishaq**, the *Book of the Prophet's Ascent* or *Mi'raj-nameh* is composed in Persian rather than Arabic. It partakes in

the rich literary tradition of Persian poetry that intersected in an extraordinarily fertile way with Islam during the decades preceding and following the *Mi'raj-nameh*. Although scholars currently agree that the work can be attributed to Avicenna, his authorship is not entirely certain. We can be sure, however, that the blend of poetry, philosophy, and theology seen in this work is entirely in keeping with the Persian court culture centered on Baghdad under the rule of the Abbasid dynasty. Commonly known by the European form of his name, "Avicenna," Abu Ali al-Husayn ibn Abdullah ibn Sina was the foremost physician and philosopher of his time, author of hundreds of treatises, and one of the two main sources for the transmission of Aristotle's philosophy into the medieval West (the other was the Spanish Muslim Averroës, or Ibn Rushd).

Avicenna also wrote several works of literature that show a particular interest in how figurative language can reveal hidden truths. In the *Mi'raj-nameh*, for example, the Prophet's ascent through the Seven Heavens represents the way in which the rational soul is raised to a higher level of knowledge through the act of contemplation. Such language, which can be compared to the allegorical mode found in **Dante** and other European writers, both illuminates knowledge and conceals it. By using purposely obscure language that only certain readers can understand, the writer of allegory is able to create a closed interpretive community: a hidden sense can be accessed solely by the chosen few, while the the ignorant masses remain, in Avicenna's words, blind to "the inner meanings." Figurative language can be seen functioning similarly in the **Gospel of Matthew**, where Jesus' use of parables permits those "who hear with their ears" to understand, while others remain deaf to the word of God. This similarity is due not so much to a religious orientation shared by Christianity and Islam as to their common tendency to integrate Platonic philosophy into their account of how knowledge of the divine could be transmitted.

The story of the mi'raj is mentioned only very briefly in the Qur'an itself. Muhammad is said to have taken a journey by night from the "Sacred Mosque," the Holy Sanctuary at Mecca, to "the Farthest Mosque" ("al-Masjid al-Aqsa"; Qur'an 17.1, sura Al-Isra). The Farthest Mosque was identified in several different prophetic traditions (or hadith) as being located in Jerusalem, and a narrative of the two-part journey was soon produced. In the first part, or *isra*, Muhammad traveled from Mecca to Jerusalem, summoned by the angel Gabriel (Jibreel) and lifted up on the marvelous animal al-Buraq. The second part of the journey was the ascent, or *mi'raj*, in which Muhammad rose from the stone located at the Dome of the Rock, through the Seven Heavens, into the presence of the veiled Throne of God. Avicenna's version of the mi'raj story is also divided into two parts: a theoretical introduction on the nature of the mind and the ways in which knowledge is acquired, followed by the story of Muhammad's journey. Avicenna's way of proceeding is exegetical; after every few lines of the story, he gives a brief philosophical and literary explication of the allegorical meaning of that step of the mi'raj experience. For Avicenna, the many veils that Muhammad sees hiding the presence of God are a visible manifestation of the nature of all knowledge, concealed behind the veil of language.

From Mi'raj-nameh[1]

The Beginning of the Story

The best of creatures,[2] upon him be (God's) blessing and salvation, said: *I was sleeping one night in the house. It was a night with thunder and lightning. No animal made a sound, no bird chirped, no person was awake. I was not asleep, but lying between sleep and wakefulness.* That is, I had been desirous of perceiving truths by means of insight for a long time. At night humans are freer, for bodily occupations and sensual impediments are suspended.

---

1. Translated by Peter Heath.　　　　2. The Prophet Muhammad, founder of Islam.

So it happened one night when I was between wakefulness and sleep means that I was between the senses and the intellect; I fell into the sea of knowledge. *It was a night with thunder and lightning* means that the succor of the celestial caller prevailed so that the irascible faculty died and the faculty of imagination [*khayâl*] ceased its operations. Tranquility overcame preoccupation.

Then he said: *Suddenly Gabriel[3] descended in his own form with such beauty, splendor, and majesty that the house was alit*. He means: the faculty of the Holy Spirit in the form of the (divine) Command united with me. It had so great an effect that all the faculties of the rational soul became renewed and alit.

Describing the beauty of Gabriel, he said: *I saw him whiter than snow, fair of face, curly of lock. On his forehead was written in light, "There is no God but God, and Muhammad is the Apostle of God";[4] fairly large of eye, delicate of brow, with seventy thousand locks of red ruby dangling down, and six hundred thousand feathers of lustrous pearl opened up*. That is, in my inner eye [*başîrat*], by means of intellectual abstraction, I perceived such beauty and fairness that if a trace of that beauty were to appear to the senses, that sensible would look like what he described.

The meaning of "There is no God but God" being written on his forehead is that anyone whose eye beheld his beauty would be cleansed from the darkness of skepticism and idolatry, and would attain such certitude and belief in the affirmation of the Creator that every created thing that he beheld would increase his belief in his Oneness. And (Gabriel) was so elegant that if a person had seventy thousand tresses of musk and camphor, he would not attain his beauty. And he was so quick-moving that you would say that he flew with six hundred thousand feathers and wings. (But) he did not move in time and space.

Then he said: *When he reached me, he embraced me and kissed me between my two eyes and said, "O Sleeper, arise! How long you slumber!"* That is, when this Holy Faculty reached me, it caressed me and admitted me into its unveiling [*kashf*] and did (me) honor. Such yearning arose in my heart that it cannot be described. Then he said: *"How long you slumber!"* That is, why are you satisfied with counterfeit imaginings? There are worlds beyond this one you are in. You can only reach them in the wakefulness of knowledge. Because of compassion, I shall be your guide. Arise!

Then he said: *I was afraid and leapt up from my place because of that fear*. That is, because of his majesty, I could not think.

Then he said: *He said to me, "Be still, for I am your brother[5] Gabriel."* That is, by the grace of the unveiling [*kashf*] of wisdom, fear was stilled in me. He introduced himself, so that he removed my distress.

Then he said: *I said, "O Brother, an enemy has taken control of me (before)." He said, "I will not hand you over to the enemy." I said, "What are you going to do?" He said, "Arise! Be observant and take heart."* That is, illuminate the faculty of memory and obey me so that I may remove difficulties from you.

---

3. In Islamic tradition, the angel (messenger) who delivers the Qur'an to Muhammad; in Christian tradition, he announces to Mary that she would give birth to Jesus (Luke 1.26; cf. 1.19).
4. The *shahada*, or declaration of the oneness of God and the prophethood of Muhammad,

repeated in all of the five daily prayers; it is the central Islamic declaration of faith.
5. Angels and human beings (along with the jinn) are understood in Islam as orders of being all created by God and all directed to be obedient to the Qur'an.

Then he said: *I was amazed and astonished, and I followed Gabriel.* That is, I turned away from the world of sensibles. With the help of the instinctual intellect [*'aql-i gharîzî*], I followed the Holy Emanation.[6]

Then he said: *Behind Gabriel,* Burâq[7] *caught my eye.* That is, the Active Intelligence, which is the most predominant of the Holy Faculties. Its help comes to the Intelligences before it reaches the world of generation and corruption. Among the celestial Intelligences, it is it who is a ruler for the body. It is the bestower of help to souls at any time with whatever is appropriate. (Muhammad) likened it to *Burâq* because he was traveling [*dar ravish*], and a mount is a help for one who is travelling. In that journey it would be (Muhammad's) helper, so inevitably he called it a mount.

Then he said: *It was larger than an ass and smaller than a horse.* That is, it is greater than the human intellect and lesser than the First Intelligence.

Then he said: *Its face was like a human face.* That is, it inclines towards instructing [*tarbiyat*] humans; it has the same compassion for humans that a genus has for its species. And its resemblance to humans is by way of compassion and instruction. Then he said: *It is long of arm and long of leg.* That is, its beneficence reaches everywhere and its emanation renews everything.

Then he said: *I wanted to sit on it, (but) it shied away. Gabriel helped me until it was tamed.* That is, because I was in the physical world, I wanted to sit on it, that is, to unite with it. But it would not accept, until the Holy Faculty [*quvvat-i qudsî*] cleansed me of the preoccupations of ignorance and impediments of the body, so that I became pure [*mujarrad*] and, through it, attained the emanation and beneficence of the Active Intelligence.

Then he said: *When I had started on the road and passed the mountains of Mekka,*[8] *a traveler came after me and called out, "Stop!" Gabriel said, "Do not speak, go on!" So I went on.* By this he means the faculty of estimation. That is, when I was finished considering my external limbs and extremities, and was not contemplating the senses, and had gone on, the faculty of estimation called out from behind me, "Don't go!" (This is) because the faculty of estimation governs [*mutaṣarrif*], has great authority, and is active [*kârkun*] in all states. It is a tool and instrument for all animals. It stands in the place of intellect [*khirad*], accepting what is agreeable and rejecting what is contrary. It is an influence on human beings, but they should not obey estimation, for then they remain on the level of animals. A defect in their nobility thus appears. Whomever is helped by divine beneficence does not blindly follow estimation wherever he or she is.

Then he said: *A woman, alluring in (her) beauty, called from behind me, "Stop! So I can reach you." Again Gabriel said, "Go on, don't stop!"* That is, the faculty of imagination [*khayâl*], which is alluring and ornamented. He likened it to a woman because most natures incline toward it, and most people are in its grasp. Furthermore, whatever it does is baseless and is tainted by deceit and fraud, and this is (like) the doings of women, for the wiles and stratagems of women are known. And the faculty of imagination is also deceitful, lying, and

6. The creative impulse of God, here understood in Neoplatonic terms as light, which continually streams out from the divine source.
7. Muhammad's horse, upon which he is said to have made his miraculous night journey.

8. Mecca, Muhammad's birthplace and the site of the Ka'aba, which Muslims face when they pray and which is the central point of the pilgrimage prescribed as a religious duty.

treacherous. In this way it allures, hunting human beings with its representations then not fulfilling its promises, for show quickly becomes false. When humans go after imagination, they never attain intelligibles; they always follow (false) adornments and fall into the grip of meaningless concrete images.

Then he said: *When I went on, Gabriel said, "If you had waited for her until she reached you, you would have become a lover of the world."* That is, the conditions of the world are baseless and quickly disappear, and the vanities and preoccupations of the world, in relation to truths [*ma'âni*], are like the states and representations of imagination in relation to the secrets of intellect. Whoever becomes occupied with (imagination) stays away from intelligibles and, through the folly of passion, becomes a prisoner in the abyss of ignorance.

Then he said: *When I went away from the mountains and left these two persons, I traveled to the Sanctified Abode* [bait al-muqaddas],[9] *and I entered it. Someone came forward and gave me three goblets, one wine, one water, and one milk. I wanted to take the wine. Gabriel did not allow this. He pointed to the milk, so I took (it) and drank.* That is, when I went away from the senses and understood the condition of imagination and estimation, I gazed within myself and entered the spiritual realm. I saw three souls, one animal, one natural, and one rational.[1] I wanted to follow the animal (soul). He likened it to wine since its faculties, such as lust and anger, deceive, cloak, and increase ignorance, and wine intensifies these two appetites. He likened the natural (soul) to water since it sustains the body. A person survives by managing (this soul's) servants who work in the body. (Similarly), water is the cause of animal life; it promotes growth and increase. He likened the rational (soul) to milk since it is a beneficial nutriment, full of favor and usefulness.

Then he said, *I wanted to take the wine but he only allowed me to take the milk*, because most humans obey these two souls and do not transcend the natural and animal (souls), because they are deficient. (Such) people are deficient and remain deficient; whatever they seek, they seek only the corporeal and sensual, and the pleasure and utility of these two souls is corporeal. Inevitably, that which is animal is lust-driven or power-seeking, loving worldliness, drink, wine, sexual intercourse, and such things (on the one hand), or is irascibleness [*khashm*], which consists of driving away contraries and similar activities (on the other hand). These are all corporeal preoccupations, and a deficient person always seeks out such activities.

Those obedient to the natural soul are the same. They are always involved in eating and sleeping. But when a person is perfectly tempered, his or her rational soul becomes strong. It dominates the appetites of the (other) two souls. It commands the activity of the natural (soul's) faculties so that they benefit the body and sustain and govern the person. It also has the faculties of the animal (soul) in its bonds and orders actions at necessary and beneficial times. It directs the concupiscent (appetite) only toward modesty and well-being, so that the soul [*nafs*] continues to exist through reproduction, and the name "dead soul" is lifted from it. It directs the irascible faculty toward the conditions of bravery and piety, so that the name "ardorless" not befall it. It has all the faculties under its rule according to time, opportunity, and benefit.

9. The sacred precincts at Jerusalem.

1. Compare Aristotle's categories of the soul (*Nicomachean Ethics* I.13).

Human beings are called "human" [*kas*] by virtue of this. The dominion of the natural faculty is bestial, the dominion of the animal faculty is devilish, and the dominion of the rational faculty is angelic. Humankind is (such) by virtue of being closer to the angelic and further from the devilish and bestial, so that they are not unaware of their (physical) states, nor without a share of spiritual connection.

Then he said: *I arrived there and entered the mosque.*[2] *The muezzin gave the call for prayer. I was in front, and I saw the group of angels and prophets standing to the right and left. One by one they greeted me and renewed the covenant.* He means by this: when I finished examining and contemplating the animal and natural (souls), I entered the mosque, that is, I reached the brain. By "muezzin" he means the faculty of recollection. By his being "in front" he means cogitation. By "prophets and angels" he means the faculties of the mental spirits [*quvvathâ-yi arvâh-i dimâghî*], such as discernment, memory, recollection, and cogitation, and that which is like it.

Their greeting him is his comprehension of all the rational faculties, because Absolute Truth [*Haqq*], may He be praised and exalted, when He created human beings, divided their nature [*nahâd*] into two domains: an external one and an internal one. The external domain is the body. He gave it five senses so that it deals with sensibles. He also gave the internal (domain) five senses, as servants of the intellect. The external senses are the underlings of the internal senses, and the internal senses are the servants of the intellect. The common sense stands between the two (groups) as an intermediary. The external senses receive information from various sides and deposit it with the common sense. (Common sense) then gives it to the faculty of cogitation so that it acts on it. That which does not fully meet (cogitation's) criteria, it discards; estimation and imagination then take it, plunge into it, and make use of it. That which is intelligible and perfect is given to the faculty of memory to preserve its abstract (ideas). When they become useful to the intellect, recollection takes (them) from memory by means of representation [*musavvirat*] and gives (them) to it. This foundation is always well-laid [*mumahhad*].

Just as two of the external senses are the most noble, hearing and sight, and are the leaders of the rest, similarly, two of the internal senses are the most noble; cogitation and memory are the leaders of the rest. Imagination is on the level of taste. Estimation is equivalent to touch. Estimation is always active, just as touch is never constricted to a specific bodily part at any one time. The other faculties, however, are constricted to specific bodily parts.

Humans are complete [*tamâm*] when these five senses are in place and are working without fault, far from trouble. For if disruption or disturbance appears in one, they become defective [*nuqsânî*]. Similarly, the perfection [*kamâl*] of humans lies in their internal senses also being luminous and in their comprehending everything. For if they are negligent and do not preserve these faculties, they become deprived of and unable to control truths [*ma'ânî*]. In time of need they become lost, and then humans are deprived of the nobility of discernment. When humans know all of this, and the internal faculties become their

2. The site in Jerusalem later identified by Muslims as the Dome of the Rock. The rock in the mosque's foundation has a mark on it that Muslims believe to be the footprint of the Prophet, made at the time of his heavenly ascent.

guide, they attain the ultimate goal. If this is not the case, they are deprived of it. Just as someone who wishes to go on a roof first needs a ladder and then ascends rung by rung until he or she reaches the roof, rational faculties are like ladder rungs. When someone ascends, rung by rung, he or she reaches his or her goal.

Then he said: *When I was finished, I faced aloft. I found a ladder, one rung of silver, one rung of gold.* He means: from the external senses toward the internal senses. The intention of "silver and gold" is the nobility in rank of the one over the other.

Then he said: *When I reached the first heaven, a door opened. I entered and saw Ismâ'îl*[3] *seated on a chair, and a group was placed, face to face, in front of his eye. I greeted (them) and went on.* He means by this the sphere of the moon and by Ismâ'îl the body [*jirm*] of the moon. By this group (he means) those whose states are guided by the moon.

Then he said: *When I reached the second heaven, I entered. I saw an angel nearer than the former, with perfect beauty. He had a wondrous form, half of his body was of snow, half of fire. Neither mixed with the other, nor were they antagonistic toward one another. He greeted me and said, "Good tidings to you to whom goodness and fortune belong!"*

He means the sphere of Mercury.[4] The intention in this is that every heavenly body has a specific rule, either auspicious or sinister. Mercury, however, has two kinds of influence: conjoined with auspiciousness, it is auspicious; conjoined with sinisterness, it is sinister. For it is half auspicious and half sinister. The tidings of goodness and good fortune allude to the faculty of thought [*khâṭir*] and the many sciences that it bestows.

Then he said: *When I reached the third heaven, I saw an angel whose like in beauty and goodness I had never seen, joyful and glad and seated on a chair of light with angels gathered around.* He means that it was the sphere of Venus. There is no need to explain its beauty; it rules over joy and mirth.

Then he said: *When I reached the fourth heaven, I saw an angel, complete in statesmanship, seated on a throne of light. I greeted (him), he responded properly but with complete arrogance. Due to pride and haughtiness, he (usually) spoke to no one. (But) he smiled when he answered (my) greeting and said, "O Muhammad, I see complete goodness and felicity in your royal splendor [farr]. Good tidings to you!"*

By this throne he means the fourth sphere, and by this angel he means the Sun, which rules over the conditions of kings and great men. His smile indicates its influence for good fortune as an (astrological) ascendent, and his good tidings are its bounty [*faiḍ*] for the good of everyone.

Then he said: *When I reached the fifth heaven, I entered. I learned of hell. I saw a dominion full of darkness and fear. I saw the proprietor seated at its edge busy torturing and tormenting sinful people.* By this he means the fifth sphere. By the proprietor he means Mars, which rules over the conditions of the

---

3. Ishmael, the older son of Abraham and the legendary forefather of the Arab people; he is identified as a prophet in the Qur'an (19.54).
4. According to the Ptolemaic model, which dominated medieval Islamic astronomy as well as medieval European astronomy, the earth was in the center of a set of spheres to which were attached the heavenly bodies (starting with the moon) in the order given here; the outermost sphere belonged to the "Prime Mover."

bloodthirsty and sinful. By hell he means its sinister influence on the characteristics and conditions of people who are under its rule.

Then he said: *When I reached the sixth heaven, I saw an angel seated on a chair of light, engaged in praising and sanctifying (God). He had wings and tresses set with pearls and rubies. I greeted him. He responded, greeted (me), and gave tidings of goodness and happiness. He said to me, "I continually sent blessings to you."*

He means the sixth sphere, and by this angel he means Jupiter, which rules over folk of rectitude, piety, and knowledge. By those wings and tresses he means the effect of its light. By his blessings he means its influence for good, for it is the most auspicious (of the planets). All good things come to humankind from it; every benefit joined to a person is the result of its gaze. Because Absolute Truth, may He be exalted, through the perfection of His knowledge, has thus ordained. "He is the Manifest, True King."[5]

Then he said, *When I reached the seventh heaven, I saw an angel sitting on a chair of red ruby. Not everyone finds a way to him, but when someone does reach him, he is cherished. I greeted him. He responded and blessed me.*

By this he means the seventh sphere, and by this angel he means Saturn, which is red and the most sinister (of the planets). Everything it does, it does perfectly. When it does something sinister, it is completely so. When it does something auspicious, it exceeds everything else. *Not everyone finds a way to him* means that it rarely happens that it is in a good and auspicious location. But when it is, its effect is so good that it excels all else.

Then he said: *When I went on, I reached the Lote Tree of the Far Boundary.*[6] *I saw a world full of light and brightness so brilliant that the eye was dazzled. When I looked to the right and left, I saw all the spiritual angels busy at worship. I said, "O Gabriel, who are these people?" He said, "These never do anything except worship and praise God. They have specified oratories from which they never depart. As it is said in the Qur'ân, Each of us has a known station.'"*[7]

By this he means the eighth sphere, the sphere of the fixed stars. The constellations are there. By oratories and stations he means the twelve signs (of the zodiac). Each group of them resides in a specific quarter; they do not crowd one another. Thus the southern ones have nothing to do with the northern ones; each one has a place. Some of the constellations are on the ecliptic, some are in the south, and some are in the north.

Then he said: *I saw the Lote Tree, larger than all things, roots above and branches below, for its shade falls on heaven and earth.* By this he means the greatest sphere, within which are the rest of the spheres. It is larger than all, so that it is said in the Qur'ân: "Each gliding in a sphere."[8]

Then he said: *When I passed by I saw four seas, each one a (different) color.* That is, he cognized [taṣavvur] through (intellectual) abstraction [tajarrud] the principles of substantiality, materiality, corporality, and form, which are the principles [ḥaqâ'iq] of all this [în jumlat]. He found each one (to be) a different rank, and he expresses this rank by (the word) color.

---

5. Qur'an 20.114.
6. According to the Qur'an (53.13–16), the farthest that can be traveled in heaven as one

approaches God, marked by this nettle tree.
7. Qur'an 37.164.
8. Qur'an 21.33.

Then he said: *I saw many angels busy praising God and affirming His unity, all immersed in grace.* That is, abstract souls, free of concupiscent and irascible desire. They are pure. For each human being whose soul becomes pure and abstract in learning and knowledge, after becoming separated from the body, is held by Absolute Truth, may He be exalted, in neither place nor locality. He makes them like angels, adorned with eternal bliss.

He makes the comparison with angels because angels are the dwelling-place [*maskin*] of sinlessness and the celebration of God's praise. That is, they become free of corruption, death, the activities of the concupiscent faculties, and the preoccupations and accidents of the irascible (faculties). They attain the level of angelicness, always engaged in perceiving and learning about the invisible (world). They never look toward the lower world. This is because the body in relation to the soul is base. Noble people who look toward the lower place do so either because of necessity or because of the best interests of that location. When they become separated from that (lower) habitation by (attaining) perfection and hindrances are removed, they attain their perfect nobility. They become happy.

That is, they withdraw from sensual preoccupation toward rational perception and become so immersed in its pleasure and ease that they never recall anything base or look toward the lower world, for corporeal need has fallen away from them. At that time, they gain rank and nobility according to the measure of (their) knowledge and perception. "Some of them bow, some prostrate themselves."[9] Some are spiritual, some praise God and attest to His unity, some sanctify (Him), and some are drawn-near. On this basis, they continue forever.

Then he said: *When I went by this group, I reached a boundless sea. However much I gazed, I could not even perceive its middle. At the lower part of that sea, I saw a large stream, and I saw an angel who was pouring water from the sea into the stream. From the stream, water reached everywhere.*

By this sea he means the First Intelligence. By the stream he means the First Soul. For the First Soul is subordinate to the First Intelligence. The first thing that Absolute Truth, may He be exalted, manifested through the creativity [*ibdâ'*] of His power [*qudrat*] and knowledge, on the level of uniqueness, keeping it pure from the annoyance of mediation and bestowing upon it the highest rank, was the First Intelligence. As the prophet, upon whom be peace, said, "The first thing God created was the intelligence."[1] By this he means "first in rank," not "first in creation"; for that substance does not admit a temporal beginning.

When the First Intelligence appeared, the First Soul became manifest. The former was on the level of Adam, the latter on the level of Eve. Then after this, two substances became separated from (the First Intelligence) as substances and bodies, like spheres and heavenly bodies and their Souls and Intelligences. After this, it continued until the elements appeared, became divided, and assumed inclinations, (each) according to its constitution, each one in its own domain, in accordance to its nature, fineness, and coarseness, such as water and earth inclining below and air and fire inclining above. After this, it worked

9. Not from the Qur'ân or ḥadith [saying from the body of traditions relating to Muhammad]; perhaps a paraphrase? [translator's note].

1. This is a common—if weak— ḥadith [translator's note].

on minerals, and then on plants and animals, and then it brought forth human beings. They were preferred above all. They were bestowed with the faculty of soul and intellect, so that just as the First Intelligence, who was of noble rank, came in the beginning of creation, complete and beautiful, human beings also attained that rank in nobility at the end of creation. (Humans became) a point at the end so that the circle would be complete. This priority and posteriority about which I speak concerning existents is in rank, not in creation. The intent of that which he said concerning the sea and the water and the stream is what has been said (above).

Then he said: *At the bottom of that sea I saw a great valley, larger than any I had ever seen. However much I gazed, I found neither its beginning or end; nor could I define it by anything.* By this he means pure existence [*wujûd-i mujarrad*]. Nothing is more general than it. Only the perfect intellect can perceive pure existence.

Then he said: *In the sea's valley I saw an angel, of complete augustness, majesty, and beauty, who was gazing tranquilly at each of the two halves (of creation). He called me to himself. When I reached him, I said, "What is your name?" He said, "Michael [Mîkâ'îl].[2] I am the greatest of the angels. Whatever is difficult for you (to understand), ask of me. Whatever you desire, seek of me so that I can show to you the intended aims of everything."*

That is, when I knew all of this, I contemplated (further). I discerned the First Command [*amr-i avval*]. By that angel he means that which is called the Holy Spirit, said to be the Angel Drawn-Near [*malak muqarrab*]. Whoever makes his or her way to it, and receives help, comes to know so much through its help that he or she becomes cognizant of all unknown things, spiritual pleasures, and eternal felicities, the like of which he or she has never before experienced.

Then he said: *When I was finished with greeting and questioning him, I said, "I have suffered much pain and trouble to reach this place where I am. My goal in coming here was that I attain knowledge and direct vision of Absolute Truth, may He be exalted. Guide me to Him so that I attain my desire and partake of the full benefit, and so return to my house."*

That is, as he had wished from the divine Command, which is the pure Word [*kalimat*], when he was finished observing existents by way of insight, the eye of his heart became opened so that whatever was, he knew. By this he meant perceiving Absolute Existence, the First Cause, and the Necessary Existent and knowing its unity [*vaḥdat*], such that plurality could not be contained in it.

Then he said: *That angel took my hand, transported me through several thousand veils, and bore (me) to a world in which I saw nothing like what I had seen in this world. When he brought me to the Presence of Glory [ḥaḍrat-i 'izzat], the command came to me: "Draw nearer!"*

That is, that divine, holy Presence is free of body, substance, and accident, which exist in these worlds. It is above these categories. By necessity, it neither needs nor is connected to place, time, locality, how much, how, where, when, activity and passiveness, and the like. The Necessary Existent is neither body

---

2. An archangel, named in the Hebrew Bible (Daniel 10.13, 21), the New Testament (Jude 9; Revelation 12.7), and the Qur'an (2.98) and associated with righteous battle.

nor substance. It is pure and transcendent, beyond admitting those accidents. It is unique in purity. The associationalism [shirkat] of creation [maqdûr] is not contained in its singleness [fardâniyyat]. In its singleness, it is one. The multiplicity of number does not exist in its unicity [yagânagî]. In this regard, it is also able, knowing, and beneficent. It is thus unadulterated being. That unadulterated being is the world of pure unity, unaffected by the multiplicity of change and multitude.

Then he said: *I did not see sensation or movement in that Presence. I only saw tranquility* [farâghat], *stillness* [sukûn], *and sufficiency* [ghanâ]. That is, I saw the abstract knowledge of its existence to an extent that no living creature can encompass by means of sensation. For bodies are perceived through sensation, (external) forms and the imagination are preserved, and substances are cognized through the vigilance of the intellect. But the Necessary Existent is beyond these stages. It cannot be apprehended through sensation and imagination. In that Presence, there is no movement [harakat]. Movement is change in an existent, either by being acted upon in corporeal quantity and quality, or (by moving) from place to place desiring a benefit or fleeing an opponent or through bodily movement while remaining stationary. The former is by necessity, the latter by choice. All things that are moved need a mover. But movement is not admissible for it. The Necessary Existent is that which is the mover of all things.

Then he said: *From being in awe of God* [khudâvand], *I forgot everything that I had seen and known. Such unveiling, grandeur, and pleasure from proximity was produced that you would say that I was intoxicated.*

That is, when my knowledge made its way to the gnosis of unity [vâhdâniyyat] I was no longer engaged in perceiving and preserving particulars. The rational soul achieved so much pleasure from this knowledge that all the faculties of the natural and animal (souls) stopped working. I was so immersed in unity that I was no longer engaged in the world of substances and bodies.

Then he said: *So affected was I by (divine) proximity that I began to tremble. The command was coming, "Draw nearer!" When I drew nearer, He said, "Fear not, be calm!"*

That is, when I apprehended unity, I knew that the Necessary Existent was beyond these categories. I became afraid of my boldness for a journey that had become very long in affirming unity. I thought that it would harm me. *It was said, "Draw nearer!"* That is, draw nearer, away from this thought of mine and this fear and terror. For the realm of unity entails continual immersion in spiritual pleasure [ladhdhat-i rûhânî]. One is never affected by the animal (soul), and fear and hope are conditions of the animal (soul).

Then he said: *When I drew nearer, God's greeting came to me through a voice the like of which I had never heard.* That is, the reality of the discourse of the Necessary Existent, may it be exalted and sanctified, was unveiled to me. For its speech is not like the speech of creatures, with pronunciation and sound. Its speech is the affirmation of knowledge through pure abstraction in the soul. (It conveys) what it wishes by way of universality, not particularity.

Then he said: *The command came, "Praise!" I said, "'I do not enumerate Your praises, for You have praised Yourself.'³ I am unable (to say) the like of what You*

3. A well-known hadith [translator's note].

Yourself have said." That is, when he perceived the beauty of unity and apprehended the reality of the discourse of the Necessary Existent, and understood that its speech does not consist of pronunciation and sound, he attained pleasure the like of which he had never experienced. He understood that the Necessary Existent was deserving of all praise, but he knew he could not praise it with language that consisted of sounds and therefore fell under (the category of) language. This type of praise is only connected with particulars and universals, but it is not appropriate for the Necessary Existent, which is neither a universal or a particular. He knew that praising it through language was not correct, for it is not for the senses to do work befitting the intellect. The intellect knows that anyone praising one who is perfectly praiseworthy must be in agreement with him. For his knowledge must be equal to the one being praised if speech is to be suitable for the intention. The Necessary Existent is Single, One, and Incomparable, so the praise of a human is not concordant with it. Therefore (Muḥammad) left it to (the Necessary Existent's) own knowledge. It utters all knowledge, and its knowledge is the exposition of praise for itself, not through pronunciation or sound, nor through speech. It is its own adornment and it is its own splendor.

Then he said: *The command came, "Desire something!" I said, "Give permission that whatever (problem) I encounter, I (can) ask until its difficulties are solved."* That is, when it said to me, "What do you want?" I said, "Give permission!" That is, knowledge. Because in this intellectual journey, only pure intellect had remained, for he had reached the Presence of the Necessary Existent and become knowing. In Unity [*vahdâniyyat*], the only thing he could have asked for that would have been suitable for him was Absolute Knowledge [*'ilm-i muṭlaq*]. So he was given perfect knowledge [*'ilm-i tamâm*] in accordance with his rank. Hence, when there was afterwards any problem, he would petition (God's help) and find a clear solution. He would thus lay out the principles of religious law, such as prayer, fasting, and the like, according to the judgments of that knowledge, in the best interests of creation and never fall into error. In the reality of the Necessary Existent, he established the goal of his knowledge within the limits of his intellect, in language [*lafẓ*] harmonious with the hearing of created beings, so that meaning be clear and the curtain of (distortion due to) self-interest not be drawn up. The help of that knowledge was that the explanation of such a journey be given set in a story of an external journey, so that only one knowledgeable in the truth would be on the path of knowing and understanding the content of his speech.

Then he said: *When I did all this, I returned to the house. Because of the swiftness of the journey, the bedclothes were still warm.* That is, the journey was intellectual [*fikrî*]. He went by thought [*khâṭir*]. (His) intellect perceived the order of existents until the Necessary Existent. Then, when cognition [*tafakkur*] was complete, he returned to himself. No time had passed. Returning in that state was quicker than (the glance of) an evil eye. Whoever knows, knows what transpired. Whoever does not know, is excused.

It is not permissible to show the inner meanings [*ramz-hâ*] of these words to one of the ignorant masses. Only a rationalist ['*âqil*] is permitted to enjoy the inner meaning of these words. May God, may He be exalted, grant the favor of true speech and true knowledge.

SONG OF ROLAND
eleventh century

"Pagans are wrong and Christians are right." This poetic refrain, dividing the world into right and wrong, good and bad, white and black, Christian and non-Christian, expresses the fundamental outlook of the *Song of Roland*, which tells the story of how the heroic rearguard of Charlemagne's army was wiped out in an ambush at the mountain pass of Roncesvalles following their military victories in northern Spain. Yet this dualism goes beyond the metaphorical white hats and black hats of the Christian warriors and their "Saracen" (Muslim) opponents: from the first words of the poem, which identify Charlemagne as being at once "king" of the French people and "emperor" of the entire Christian world, the poem continuously defines things and persons from two points of view. The poetic rhythms of the text reaffirm this dualism as well, both within individual lines and in the doubling of stanzas (or *laisses*), when a heroic encounter on the battlefield is recounted first in simple terms, and a second time more elaborately. Yet the work never feels slow or repetitive: instead, the sequence of double stanzas heightens the reader's sense of anticipation, as the epic battle moves inexorably toward its bloody climax.

LIFE AND TIMES

At the very end of the earliest surviving copy of the *Song of Roland*, the so-called Oxford manuscript, the writer names himself: "Ci falt la geste que Turoldus declinet" ("here ends the story that Turoldus tells"). His name, a Latinized version of the Norman name "Turold" (Old Norse "Thorvaldr"), along with the French dialect of the poem, suggests that the poet who wrote and the courtly audiences who read—or, more likely, listened to—the *Song of Roland* were members of the new Anglo-Norman elite who dominated England following the Norman Conquest of 1066. These were the descendants of those same knights who, according to the twelfth-century chronicles of William of Malmesbury and Wace, had marched on the Anglo-Saxon armies of Harold, the last English claimant to the throne, while listening to their minstrel Taillefer "sing a song of Roland." This advancing Norman army would not be the last to find inspiration in the narrative of Charlemagne's heroic knight: in modern times, the *Song of Roland* has come to be seen as the foundational national epic of the French nation and, during the early twentieth century, was even used as a form of political propaganda.

THE SONG OF ROLAND

Although the Oxford manuscript dates to the mid-twelfth century, we know from Latin sources that the *Song of Roland* must have circulated much earlier in a variety of different forms, all of which were likely sung or recited. There may have been earlier manuscripts, now lost, but the text presented here is undoubtedly among the first versions of the song to be written down and thus fixed in its permanent form. Its oral origins persist, however, in the enigmatic "AOI" refrain, which appears at the close of several of the long *laisses* and may reflect a sung musical phrase or a chord played on the harp to note moments of particular drama. In the *Song of Roland*, we see one of the first manifestations of the rise of the vernacular into the realm of literature; before that time, written texts were almost exclusively in Latin, and the language spoken in daily life was thought to be simply a convenient medium for conversation, or for the evening entertainments of songs and recited tales as performed by jongleurs or minstrels. But by the time of the Oxford *Roland*, such works were entering into the poetic mainstream, beginning to take their place alongside the epic tradition of **Virgil's** *Aeneid* and the histories of Alexander the Great. Known as the *chansons de geste*, or "songs of great deeds," these popular epics would gradually develop into the romances of the later Middle Ages, such as **Sir Gawain and the Green Knight**.

In keeping with the thematic dualism that underlies the *Song of Roland*—its division of the world into "pagan" wrong and "Christian" right—the setting of time and place as recounted in the Oxford manuscript is likewise double. The poem explicitly tells the story of the aftermath of the Frankish campaign in Spain, when in the late summer of 778 the victorious army of Charlemagne was ambushed by a band of local inhabitants at the pass of Roncesvalles. But by describing the attackers as an overwhelmingly large "Saracen" force instead of scattered Basque guerrillas, the poem reinvents eighth-century history in terms of the eleventh-century present. The result was a story of Christian battle against Muslim armies, inseparable—for the medieval reader—from the waves of crusades then being launched by European nations in an effort to conquer the Holy City of Jerusalem. The *Song of Roland* thus simultaneously looks backward to an idealized past, when the mighty king and emperor Charlemagne built his Holy Roman Empire, and forward to an anticipated period of unified European Christian rule over Jerusalem and, by extension, the whole world.

The poem opens with Charlemagne contemplating his seven long years of armed assault on Spain and deciding to return to his kingdom north of the Pyrenees, to "the sweet land of France." His army has conquered all the cities of Spain with the exception of Zaragoza, but Charlemagne, weary of battle, decides that rather than attacking the city he will accept a pledge of loyalty from its Saracen king, Marsilion. This decision precipitates the two parallel plots of the *Song of Roland*, one centering on the conflict between Christian and Saracen armies and the other centering on dissension within Charlemagne's own retinue of noble knights—his *douzepers*, or company of "twelve peers." These two plots are linked by the shared theme of treachery, in the form both of the deceitful behavior of the Saracen Marsilion, who lies to Charlemagne and attacks his men as soon as the French army begins its retreat from Spain, and of the betrayal carried out by Ganelon, the noble knight appointed by Charlemagne (at the suggestion of Roland, Ganelon's stepson and rival) to serve as messenger to Marsilion. While the first plot is acted out on the grand scale of armies, nations, and religions, the second plot is carried out on a more intimate stage, as something of a family feud. Because Ganelon is married to Charlemagne's sister, Roland is Charlemagne's nephew; and though that position brings him honor, it also obliges him to avoid the appearance of favoritism and to constantly prove his bravery and loyalty—even if doing so requires the rashest of deeds.

Roland is the exemplar of the ethical code of knighthood that is repeatedly praised in the poem, a code that entails not just exhibiting the conventional chivalric virtues of truthfulness, bravery, and loyalty but also balancing their competing claims—a more complex task. Roland's death results precisely from his extreme expression of the knightly virtues: when the rearguard is suddenly ambushed, he refuses to sound the alarm that would call back the main forces of Charlemagne's army, because he believes that asking for aid would cause him shame and prefers death to disgrace. That Roland is excessive, almost reckless, in his bravery is highlighted by the contrast with Oliver, his closest companion and the brother of his fiancée, Aude. As the poet puts it while praising the shared excellence of the two knights, who are among the brightest lights in Charlemagne's retinue, "Roland is good [proz—literally, 'brave'], and Oliver is wise." Oliver's wisdom casts a shadow on Roland's more impetuous behavior: bravery is admirable, but taken to an extreme it leads not only to Roland's death but to the extermination of the entire rearguard. At the same time, it is important to stress that these deaths were not in vain, for it is the tragic fate of the rearguard that ultimately spurs Charlemagne to gather his forces and strike decisively at the Saracen armies of Spain. In this light, Roland's death appears as a necessary sacrifice, the loss that sets the stage for the greater victory.

The conflict of Muslim Spain and Christian France that erupts fully after Roland's death is initially played out between the armies of Marsilion and Charlemagne; after Marsilion is mortally wounded, however, the leadership of the Saracens shifts to Baligant, their "emir" (ruler), who suddenly appears in the poem. This thousand-line section of the text, about a quarter of the whole, is almost certainly a twelfth-century addition to the basic narrative of the Song of Roland. It gives the sense of the perpetual, ongoing nature of the "pagan" threat to Christendom, as another leader springs up almost immediately to replace his fallen predecessor. Yet in spite of the fundamental

opposition of Christian and pagan, right and wrong, the code of knightly behavior informs the behavior of warriors on both sides. When Charlemagne's knights meet the Saracen Baligant on the field (as described in a passage not included below), they are struck not by his difference from them but by the ways in which he seems to belong to their own kind: "God, what a noble lord," they exclaim, "if only he were made a Christian." Indeed, religious conversion, held out as a possible means of bridging the gap separating pagan and Christian on the battlefield, is achieved after the final conquest of Zaragoza by the armies of Charlemagne. The French offer the choice of conversion or death to all the inhabitants, with one significant exception: the Saracen queen Bramimunde, widow of King Marsilion. Charlemagne insists that she be converted pur amur, that is, "through love." For the writer of the Oxford Song of Roland, this phrase appears to imply a sincere religious conversion, suggesting that Bramimunde—now renamed "Juliana"—embraces Christianity out of love for Jesus Christ. Other versions of this story feature a Saracen queen whose motivation is more personal: namely, erotic love for one of the Christian knights. Such fantasies encouraged medieval readers to believe that their victory in the ongoing series of Crusades was inevitable, not just because of European military might but because of the Christian West's innate desirability.

In keeping with the double plot of the Song of Roland, with its grand narrative of battling armies and its intimate story of interpersonal conflict within Charlemagne's company, the poem has two separate climactic scenes of narrative closure. After the mass conversion and slaughter in Zaragoza, resolving the first level of the plot, Charlemagne and his men turn to the second level of the plot: the trial of

Ganelon. The emperor finds that the peers are divided regarding the degree of Ganelon's culpability: on the one hand, his behavior can be understood as treachery; on the other hand, it is arguably an appropriate expression of independence on the part of a powerful noble within the conventional obligations of a feudal relationship. In the end, after a trial by combat in which his champion is slain, Ganelon is condemned, his efforts at autonomy denounced as treason, and his punishment decreed: he is to be torn to pieces by four horses. Ganelon's broken body symbolizes the bonds of community shattered by the act of treason. The kinsmen who had stood with Ganelon and bound themselves as hostages before the trial are also condemned to death, by hanging; as the poet blandly puts it, "A traitor brings death, on himself and on others."

Despite these repeated scenes of closure, from the conversion and slaughter at Zaragoza to the punishment carried out after Ganelon's trial, the last lines of the *Song of Roland* insist on the essentially open-ended nature of the Christian mission. The poem ends with Charlemagne, exhausted and sorrowful after his years in Spain and the loss of his beloved nephew Roland, in the grip of a visionary dream in which the angel Gabriel commands him to embark upon a new campaign, renewing the unending cycle of battle between Christian and pagan. The king weeps bitterly, crying out, "God! . . . the pains, the labors of my life!"; nonetheless, he obeys the call.

For medieval readers, the *Song of Roland* was not an isolated, singular text but rather one episode within a whole cluster of stories about Charlemagne and his men, a cluster that was itself one among several comparable "cycles" of epic poetry. In the twelfth century, these *chansons de geste* were heroic models of the distant past that helped both inspire and perpetuate the ongoing warfare carried out by Crusaders in their repeated attempts to seize Jerusalem. In the twenty-first century, they are vivid reminders of an age in which warfare was the highest expression of human virtue, when the will of God was the compass that determined the actions of mankind.

From Song of Roland[1]

1

Charles the King, our Emperor, the Great,
has been in Spain for seven full years,
has conquered the high land down to the sea.
There is no castle that stands against him now,
no wall, no citadel left to break down—   5
except Saragossa, high on a mountain.[2]
King Marsilion holds it, who does not love God,

---

1. Translated by Frederick Goldin. Many of Goldin's notes have been adapted for use here.
2. Saragossa, in northeastern Spain, is not actually on a mountaintop. The poet's geography is not always accurate.

who serves Mahumet and prays to Apollin.[3]
He cannot save himself: his ruin will find him there. AOI.[4]

2

King Marsilion was in Saragossa.   10
He has gone forth into a grove, beneath its shade,
and he lies down on a block of blue marble,
twenty thousand men, and more, all around him.
He calls aloud to his dukes and his counts:
"Listen, my lords, to the troubles we have.   15
The Emperor Charles of the sweet land of France
has come into this country to destroy us.
I have no army able to give him battle,
I do not have the force to break his force.
Now act like my wise men: give me counsel,   20
save me, save me from death, save me from shame!"
No pagan there has one word to say to him
except Blancandrin, of the castle of Valfunde.

3

One of the wisest pagans was Blancandrin,
brave and loyal, a great mounted warrior,   25
a useful man, the man to aid his lord;
said to the King: "Do not give way to panic.
Do this: send Charles, that wild, terrible man,
tokens of loyal service and great friendship:
you will give him bears and lions and dogs,   30
seven hundred camels, a thousand molted hawks,
four hundred mules weighed down with gold and silver,
and fifty carts, to cart it all away:
he'll have good wages for his men who fight for pay.
Say he's made war long enough in this land: 35
let him go home, to France, to Aix, at last—
come Michaelmas[5] you will follow him there,
say you will take their faith, become a Christian,
and be his man with honor, with all you have.
If he wants hostages, why, you'll send them,   40
ten, or twenty, to give him security.
Let us send him the sons our wives have borne.
I'll send my son with all the others named to die.
It is better that they should lose their heads[6]
than that we, Lord, should lose our dignity   45
and our honors—and be turned into beggars!" AOI.

---

3. The Greek god Apollo; but the poet is mistaken, for these people worship only one god,
Allah. "Mahumet": Muhammad (ca. 570–632),
founder of the Islamic religion.
4. These three mysterious letters appear at certain moments throughout the text, 180 times in
all. No one has ever adequately explained them,
though every reader feels their effect.

5. The feast of St. Michael, September 29. *Aix*:
Aix-la-Chapelle, or Aachen, was the capital of
Charlemagne's empire.
6. The speaker expects that the hostages will
be killed by the French when the deception
becomes clear. Sometime before, hostages sent
by the French had been similarly slain (see
lines 207–09).

4

Said Blancandrin: "By this right hand of mine
and by this beard that flutters on my chest,
you will soon see the French army disband,
the Franks will go to their own land, to France. 50
When each of them is in his dearest home,
King Charles will be in Aix, in his chapel.
At Michaelmas he will hold a great feast—
that day will come, and then our time runs out,
he'll hear no news, he'll get no word from us. 55
This King is wild, the heart in him is cruel:
he'll take the heads of the hostages we gave.
It is better, Lord, that they lose their heads
than that we lose our bright, our beautiful Spain—
and nothing more for us but misery and pain!" 60
The pagans say: "It may be as he says."

5

King Marsilion brought his counsel to end,
then he summoned Clarin of Balaguét,
Estramarin and Eudropin, his peer,
And Priamun, Guarlan, that bearded one, 65
and Machiner and his uncle Maheu,
and Joüner, Malbien from over-sea,
and Blancandrin, to tell what was proposed.
From the worst of criminals he called these ten.
"Barons, my lords, you're to go to Charlemagne; 70
he's at the siege of Cordres,[7] the citadel.
Olive branches are to be in your hands—
that signifies peace and humility.
If you've the skill to get me an agreement,
I will give you a mass of gold and silver 75
and lands and fiefs, as much as you could want."
Say the pagans: "We'll benefit from this!" AOI.

6

Marsilion brought his council to an end,
said to his men: "Lords, you will go on now,
and remember: olive branches in your hands; 80
and in my name tell Charlemagne the King
for his god's sake to have pity on me—
he will not see a month from this day pass
before I come with a thousand faithful;
say I will take that Christian religion 85
and be his man in love and loyalty.
If he wants hostages, why, he'll have them."
Said Blancandrin: "Now you will get good terms." AOI.

---

7. Córdoba, in southern Spain, at that time the seat of a Muslim dynasty.

7

King Marsilion had ten white mules led out,
sent to him once by the King of Suatilie,[8]
with golden bits and saddles wrought with silver.
The men are mounted, the men who brought the message,
and in their hands they carry olive branches.
They came to Charles, who has France in his keeping.
He cannot prevent it: they will fool him. AOI.

90

95

8

The Emperor is secure and jubilant:
he has taken Cordres, broken the walls,
knocked down the towers with his catapults.
And what tremendous spoils his knights have won—
gold and silver, precious arms, equipment.
In the city not one pagan remained
who is not killed or turned into a Christian.
The Emperor is in an ample grove,
Roland and Oliver are with him there,
Samson the Duke and Ansëis the fierce,
Geoffrey d'Anjou, the King's own standard-bearer;
and Gerin and Gerer, these two together always,
and the others, the simple knights, in force:
fifteen thousand from the sweet land of France.
The warriors sit on bright brocaded silk;
they are playing at tables to pass the time,
the old and the wisest men sitting at chess,
the young light-footed men fencing with swords.
Beneath a pine, beside a wild sweet-briar,
there was a throne, every inch of pure gold.
There sits the King, who rules over sweet France.
His beard is white, his hair flowering white.
That lordly body! the proud fierce look of him!—
If someone should come here asking for him,
there'd be no need to point out the King of France.
The messengers dismounted, and on their feet
they greeted him in all love and good faith.

100

105

110

115

120

9

Blancandrin spoke, he was the first to speak,
said to the King: "Greetings, and God save you,
that glorious God whom we all must adore.
Here is the word of the great king Marsilion:
he has looked into this law of salvation,
wants to give you a great part of his wealth,
bears and lions and hunting dogs on chains,
seven hundred camels, a thousand molted hawks,
four hundred mules packed tight with gold and silver,
and fifty carts, to cart it all away;

125

130

8. A subordinate king, owing allegiance to Marsilion.

and there will be so many fine gold bezants,[9]
you'll have good wages for the men in your pay.
You have stayed long—long enough!—in this land,
it is time to go home, to France, to Aix.   135
My master swears he will follow you there."
The Emperor holds out his hands toward God,
bows down his head, begins to meditate. AOI.

10

The Emperor held his head bowed down;
never was he too hasty with his words: 140
his custom is to speak in his good time.
When his head rises, how fierce the look of him;
he said to them: "You have spoken quite well.
King Marsilion is my great enemy.
Now all these words that you have spoken here—   145
how far can I trust them? How can I be sure?"
The Saracen: "He wants to give you hostages.
How many will you want? ten? fifteen? twenty?
I'll put my son with the others named to die.[1]
You will get some, I think, still better born.   150
When you are at home in your high royal palace,
at the great feast of Saint Michael-in-Peril,[2]
the lord who nurtures me will follow you,
and in those baths[3]—the baths God made for you—
my lord will come and want to be made Christian."   155
King Charles replies: "He may yet save his soul." AOI.

11

Late in the day it was fair, the sun was bright.
Charles has them put the ten mules into stables.
The King commands a tent pitched in the broad grove,
and there he has the ten messengers lodged;   160
twelve serving men took splendid care of them.
There they remained that night till the bright day.
The Emperor rose early in the morning,
the King of France, and heard the mass and matins.
And then the King went forth beneath a pine,   165
calls for his barons to complete his council:
he will proceed only with the men of France. AOI.

12

The Emperor goes forth beneath a pine,
calls for his barons to complete his council:
Ogier the Duke, and Archbishop Turpin,   170

---

9. Gold coins; the name is derived from
Byzantium.
1. That is, if the promise is broken. "Saracen": the usual term for the enemy.
2. The epithet "in peril of the sea" was applied
to the famous sanctuary Mont-St.-Michel off

the Normandy coast because it could be reached
on foot only at low tide, and pilgrims were
endangered by the incoming tide. Eventually,
the phrase was applied to the saint himself.
3. Famous healing springs at Aix-la-Chapelle.

Richard the Old, and his nephew Henri;
from Gascony, the brave Count Acelin,
Thibaut of Reims, and his cousin Milun;
and Gerer and Gerin, they were both there,
and there was Count Roland, he came with them,   175
and Oliver, the valiant and well-born;
a thousand Franks of France, and more, were there.
Ganelon came, who committed the treason.
Now here begins the council that went wrong.[4] AOI.

                            13
"Barons, my lords," said Charles the Emperor,   180
"King Marsilion has sent me messengers,
wants to give me a great mass of his wealth,
bears and lions and hunting dogs on chains,
seven hundred camels, a thousand molting hawks,
four hundred mules packed with gold of Araby,   185
and with all that, more than fifty great carts;
but also asks that I go back to France:
he'll follow me to Aix, my residence,
and take our faith, the one redeeming faith,
become a Christian, hold his march[5] lands from me.   190
But what lies in his heart? I do not know."
And the French say: "We must be on our guard!" AOI.

                            14
The Emperor has told them what was proposed.
Roland the Count will never assent to that,
gets to his feet, comes forth to speak against it;   195
says to the King: "Trust Marsilion—and suffer!
We came to Spain seven long years ago,
I won Noples for you, I won Commibles,
I took Valterne and all the land of Pine,
and Balaguer and Tudela and Seville.   200
And then this king, Marsilion, played the traitor:
he sent you men, fifteen of his pagans—
and sure enough, each held an olive branch;
and they recited just these same words to you.
You took counsel with all your men of France;   205
they counseled you to a bit of madness:
you sent two Counts across to the Pagans,
one was Basan, the other was Basile.
On the hills below Haltille, he took their heads.
They were your men. Fight the war you came to fight!   210
Lead the army you summoned on to Saragossa!
Lay siege to it all the rest of your life!
Avenge the men that this criminal murdered!" AOI.

4. The poet anticipates that the plan adopted   that Ganelon will commit treason.
at the council will prove to be a mistake and   5. A frontier province or territory.

15

The Emperor held his head bowed down with this,
and stroked his beard, and smoothed his mustache down,   215
and speaks no word, good or bad, to his nephew.
The French keep still, all except Ganelon:
he gets to his feet and, come before King Charles,
how fierce he is as he begins his speech;
said to the King: "Believe a fool—me or   220
another—and suffer! Protect your interest!
When Marsilion the King sends you his word
that he will join his hands[6] and be your man,
and hold all Spain as a gift from your hands
and then receive the faith that we uphold—   225
whoever urges that we refuse this peace,
that man does not care, Lord, what death we die.
That wild man's counsel must not win the day here—
let us leave fools, let us hold with wise men!" AOI.

16

And after that there came Naimon the Duke—   230
no greater vassal in that court than Naimon—
said to the King: "You've heard it clearly now,
Count Ganelon has given you your answer:
let it be heeded, there is wisdom in it.
King Marsilion is beaten in this war,   235
you have taken every one of his castles,
broken his walls with your catapults,
burnt his cities and defeated his men.
Now when he sends to ask you to have mercy,
it would be a sin to do still more to him.   240
Since he'll give you hostages as guarantee,
this great war must not go on, it is not right."
And the French say: "The Duke has spoken well." AOI.

17

"Barons, my lords, whom shall we send down there,
to Saragossa, to King Marsilion?"   245
Naimon replies, "I'll go, if you grant it!
At once, my lord! give me the glove and the staff."[7]
The King replies: "You're a man of great wisdom:
now by my beard, now by this mustache of mine,
you will not go so far from me this year; or ever.   250
Go take your seat when no one calls on you."

18

"Barons, my lords, whom can we send down there,
to this Saracen who holds Saragossa?"

---

6. Part of the gesture of homage; the lord enclosed the joined hands of his vassal with his own.

7. Symbols of his commission from the Emperor Charles.

Roland replies: "I can go there! No trouble!"
"No, no, not you!" said Oliver the Count,   255
"that heart in you is wild, spoils for a fight,
how I would worry—you'd fight with them, I know.
Now I myself could go, if the King wishes."
The King replies: "Be still, the two of you!
Not you, not he—neither will set foot there.   260
Now by this beard, as sure as you see white,
let no man here name one of the Twelve Peers!"[8]
The French keep still, see how he silenced them.

19

Turpin of Reims has come forth from the ranks,
said to the King: "Let your Franks have a rest.   265
You have been in this land for seven years,
the many pains, the struggles they've endured!
I'm the one, Lord, give me the glove and the staff,
and I'll go down to this Saracen of Spain
and then I'll see what kind of man we have."   270
The Emperor replies to him in anger:
"Now you go back and sit on that white silk
and say no more unless I command it!" AOI.

20

"My noble knights," said the Emperor Charles,
"choose me one man: a baron from my march,   275
to bring my message to King Marsilion."
And Roland said: "Ganelon, my stepfather."
The French respond: "Why, that's the very man!
pass this man by and you won't send a wiser."
And hearing this Count Ganelon began to choke,   280
pulls from his neck the great furs of marten
and stands there now, in his silken tunic,
eyes full of lights, the look on him of fury,
he has the body, the great chest of a lord;
stood there so fair, all his peers gazed on him;   285
said to Roland: "Madman, what makes you rave?
Every man knows I am your stepfather,
yet you named me to go to Marsilion.
Now if God grants that I come back from there,
you will have trouble: I'll start a feud with you,   290
it will go on till the end of your life."
Roland replies: "What wild words—all that blustering!
Every man knows that threats don't worry me.
But we need a wise man to bring the message:
if the King wills, I'll gladly go in your place."   295

8. The elite knights who make up Charlemagne's inner circle.

21

Ganelon answers: "You will not go for me. AOI.
You're not my man, and I am not your lord.
Charles commands me to perform this service:
I'll go to Marsilion in Saragossa.
And I tell you, I'll play a few wild tricks   300
before I cool the anger in me now."
When he heard that, Roland began to laugh. AOI.

22

Ganelon sees: *Roland laughing at him!*
and feels such pain he almost bursts with rage,
needs little more to go out of his mind;   305
says to the Count: "I have no love for you,
you *made* this choice fall on me, and that was wrong.
Just Emperor, here I am, before you.
I have one will: to fulfill your command."

23

"I know now I must go to Saragossa. AOI.   310
Any man who goes there cannot return.
And there is this: I am your sister's husband,
have a son by her, the finest boy there can be,
Baldewin," says he, "who will be a good man.
To him I leave my honors, fiefs, and lands.   315
Protect my son: these eyes will never see him."
Charles answers him: "That tender heart of yours!
You have to go, I have commanded it."

24

And the King said: "Ganelon, come forward, AOI.
come and receive the staff and the glove.   320
You have heard it: the Franks have chosen you."
Said Ganelon: "Lord, it's Roland who did this.
In all my days I'll have no love for him,
or Oliver, because he's his companion,
or the Twelve Peers, because they love him so.   325
I defy them, here in your presence, Lord."
And the King said: "What hate there is in you!
You will go there, for I command you to."
"I can go there, but I'll have no protector. AOI.
Basile had none, nor did Basan his brother."   330

25

The Emperor offers him his right glove.
But Ganelon would have liked not to be there.
When he had to take it, it fell to the ground.
"God!" say the French, "What's that going to mean?
What disaster will this message bring us!"   335
Said Ganelon: "Lords, you'll be hearing news."

26

Said Ganelon: "Lord, give me leave to go,
since go I must, there's no reason to linger."
And the King said: "In Jesus' name and mine,"
absolved him and blessed him with his right hand.   340
Then he gave him the letter and the staff.

27

Count Ganelon goes away to his camp.
He chooses, with great care, his battle-gear,
picks the most precious arms that he can find.
The spurs he fastened on were golden spurs;   345
he girds his sword, Murgleis, upon his side;
he has mounted Tachebrun, his battle horse,
his uncle, Guinemer, held the stirrup.
And there you would have seen brave men in tears,
his men, who say: "Baron, what bad luck for you!   350
All your long years in the court of the King,
always proclaimed a great and noble vassal!
Whoever it was doomed you to go down there
Charlemagne himself will not protect that man.
Roland the Count should not have thought of this—   355
and you the living issue of a mighty line!"
And then they say: "Lord, take us there with you!"
Ganelon answers: "May the Lord God forbid!
It is better that I alone should die
     than so many good men and noble knights.
You will be going back, Lords, to sweet France: 360
go to my wife and greet her in my name,
and Pinabel, my dear friend and peer,
and Baldewin, my son, whom you all know:
give him your aid, and hold him as your lord."
And he starts down the road; he is on his way. AOI.   365

28

Ganelon rides to a tall olive tree,
there he has joined the pagan messengers.
And here is Blancandrin, who slows down for him:
and what great art they speak to one another.
Said Blancandrin: "An amazing man, Charles!   370
conquered Apulia, conquered all of Calabria,
crossed the salt sea on his way into England,
won its tribute,[9] got Peter's pence[1] for Rome:
what does he want from us here in our march?"

---

9. Although begun perhaps as early as the 8th century, the tribute was not the result of any effort of Charlemagne, who did not in fact visit England.

1. A tribute of one penny per house "for the use of Saint Peter," that is, for the pope in Rome.

Ganelon answers: "That is the heart in him.   375
There'll never be a man the like of him." AOI.

29

Said Blancandrin: "The Franks are a great people.
Now what great harm all those dukes and counts do
to their own lord when they give him such counsel:
they torment him, they'll destroy him, and others."   380
Ganelon answers: "Well, now, I know no such man
except Roland, who'll suffer for it yet.
One day the Emperor was sitting in the shade:
his nephew came, still wearing his hauberk,
he had gone plundering near Carcassonne;   385
and in his hand he held a bright red apple:
'Dear Lord, here, take,' said Roland to his uncle;
'I offer you the crowns of all earth's kings.'
Yes, Lord, that pride of his will destroy him,
for every day he goes riding at death.   390
And *should* someone kill him, we would have peace." AOI.

30

Said Blancandrin: "A wild man, this Roland!
wants to make every nation beg for his mercy
and claims a right to every land on earth!
But what men support him, if that is his aim?"   395
Ganelon answers: "Why, Lord, the men of France.
They love him so, they will never fail him.
He gives them gifts, masses of gold and silver,
mules, battle horses, brocaded silks, supplies.
And it is all as the Emperor desires: 400
he'll win the lands from here to the Orient." AOI.

31

Ganelon and Blancandrin rode on until
each pledged his faith to the other and swore
they'd find a way to have Count Roland killed.
They rode along the paths and ways until,   405
in Saragossa, they dismount beneath a yew.
There was a throne in the shade of a pine,
covered with silk from Alexandria.
There sat the king who held the land of Spain,
and around him twenty thousand Saracens.   410
There is no man who speaks or breathes a word,
poised for the news that all would like to hear.
Now here they are: Ganelon and Blancandrin.

32

Blancandrin came before Marsilion,
his hand around the fist of Ganelon,   415
said to the King: "May Mahumet save you,
and Apollin, whose sacred laws we keep!
We delivered your message to Charlemagne:

when we finished, he raised up both his hands
and praised his god. He made no other answer.   420
Here he sends you one of his noble barons,
a man of France, and very powerful.
You'll learn from him whether or not you'll have peace."
"Let him speak, we shall hear him," Marsilion answers. AOI.

33

But Ganelon had it all well thought out.   425
With what great art he commences his speech,
a man who knows his way about these things;
said to the King: "May the Lord God save you,
that glorious God, whom we must all adore.
Here is the word of Charlemagne the King: 430
you are to take the holy Christian faith;
he will give you one half of Spain in fief.
If you refuse, if you reject this peace,
you will be taken by force, put into chains,
and then led forth to the King's seat at Aix;   435
you will be tried; you will be put to death:
you will die there, in shame, vilely, degraded."
King Marsilion, hearing this, was much shaken.
In his hand was a spear, with golden feathers.
He would have struck, had they not held him back. AOI.   440

34

Marsilion the King—his color changed!
He shook his spear, waved the shaft to and fro.
When he saw that, Ganelon laid hand to sword,
he drew it out two fingers from its sheath;
and spoke to it: "How beautiful and bright!   445
How long did I bear you in the King's court
before I died! The Emperor will not say
I died alone in that foreign country:
they'll buy you first, with the best men they have!"
The pagans say: "Let us break up this quarrel!"   450

35

The pagan chiefs pleaded with Marsilion
till he sat down once again on his throne.
The Caliph[2] spoke: "You did us harm just now,
served us badly, trying to strike this Frenchman.
You should have listened, you should have heard him out."   455
Said Ganelon: "Lord, I must endure it.
I shall not fail, for all the gold God made,
for all the wealth there may be in this land,
to tell him, as long as I have breath, all
that Charlemagne—that great and mighty King!—   460
has sent through me to his mortal enemy."
He is buckled in a great cloak of sable,

2. A high official of King Marsilion.

covered with silk from Alexandria:
he throws it down. Blancandrin picks it up.
But his great sword he will never throw down!   465
In his right fist he grasps its golden pommel.
Say the pagans: "That's a great man! A noble!" AOI.

36

Now Ganelon drew closer to the King
and said to him: "You are wrong to get angry,
for Charles, who rules all France, sends you this word: 470
you are to take the Christian people's faith;
he will give you one half of Spain in fief,
the other half goes to his nephew: Roland—
quite a partner you will be getting there!
If you refuse, if you reject this peace,   475
he will come and lay siege to Saragossa;
you will be taken by force, put into chains,
and brought straight on to Aix, the capital.
No saddle horse, no war horse for you then,
no he-mule, no she-mule for you to ride: 480
you will be thrown on some miserable dray;
you will be tried, and you will lose your head.
Our Emperor sends you this letter."
He put the letter in the pagan's right fist.

37

Marsilion turned white; he was enraged;   485
he breaks the seal, he's knocked away the wax,
runs through the letter, sees what is written there:
"Charles sends me word, this king who rules in France:
I'm to think of his anger and his grief—
he means Basan and his brother Basile,   490
I took their heads in the hills below Haltille;
if I want to redeem the life of my body,
I must send him my uncle: the Algalife.[3]
And otherwise he'll have no love for me."
Then his son came and spoke to Marsilion,   495
said to the King: "Ganelon has spoken madness.
He crossed the line, he has no right to live.
Give him to me, I will do justice on him."
When he heard that, Ganelon brandished his sword;
he runs to the pine, set his back against the trunk.   500

38

King Marsilion went forth into the orchard,
he takes with him the greatest of his men;
Blancandrin came, that gray-haired counselor,
and Jurfaleu, Marsilion's son and heir,
the Algalife, uncle and faithful friend.   505

3. The Caliph.

Said Blancandrin: "Lord, call the Frenchman back.
He swore to me to keep faith with our cause."
And the King said: "Go, bring him back here, then."
He took Ganelon's right hand by the fingers,
leads him into the orchard before the King.   510
And there they plotted that criminal treason. AOI.

39

Said Marsilion: "My dear Lord Ganelon,
that was foolish, what I just did to you,
I showed my anger, even tried to strike you.
Here's a pledge of good faith, these sable furs,   515
the gold alone worth over five hundred pounds:
I'll make it all up before tomorrow night."
Ganelon answers: "I will not refuse it.
May it please God to reward you for it." AOI.

40

Said Marsilion: "I tell you, Ganelon,   520
I have a great desire to love you dearly.
I want to hear you speak of Charlemagne.
He is so old, he's used up all his time—
from what I hear, he is past two hundred!
He has pushed his old body through so many lands,   525
taken so many blows on his buckled shield,
made beggars of so many mighty kings:
when will he lose the heart for making war?"
Ganelon answers: "Charles is not one to lose heart.
No man sees him, no man learns to know him   530
who does not say: the Emperor is great.
I do not know how to praise him so highly
that his great merit would not surpass my praise.
Who could recount his glory and his valor?
God put the light in him of such lordliness,   535
he would choose death before he failed his barons."

41

Said the pagan: "I have reason to marvel
at Charlemagne, a man so old and gray—
he's two hundred years old, I hear, and more;
he has tortured his body through so many lands,   540
and borne so many blows from lance and spear,
made beggars of so many mighty kings:
when will he lose the heart for making war?"
"Never," said Ganelon, "while his nephew lives,
he's a fighter, there's no vassal like him
under the vault of heaven. And he has friends.   545
There's Oliver, a good man, his companion.
And the Twelve Peers, whom Charles holds very dear,
form the vanguard, with twenty thousand knights.
Charles is secure, he fears no man on earth." AOI.

42

Said the pagan: "Truly, how I must marvel
at Charlemagne, who is so gray and white—
over two hundred years, from what I hear;
gone through so many lands a conqueror,
and borne so many blows from strong sharp spears,
killed and conquered so many mighty kings:
when will he lose the heart for making war?"
"Never," said Ganelon, "while one man lives: Roland!
no man like him from here to the Orient!
There's his companion, Oliver, a brave man.
And the Twelve Peers, whom Charles holds very dear,
form the vanguard, with twenty thousand Franks.
Charles is secure, he fears no man alive." AOI.

550

555

560

43

"Dear Lord Ganelon," said Marsilion the King,
"I have my army, you won't find one more handsome:
I can muster four hundred thousand knights!
With this host, now, can I fight Charles and the French?"
Ganelon answers: "No, no, don't try that now,
you'd take a loss: thousands of your pagans!
Forget such foolishness, listen to wisdom:
send the Emperor so many gifts
there'll be no Frenchman there who does not marvel.
For twenty hostages—those you'll be sending—
he will go home: home again to sweet France!
And he will leave his rear-guard behind him.
There will be Roland, I do believe, his nephew,
and Oliver, brave man, born to the court.
These Counts are dead, if anyone trusts me.
Then Charles will see that great pride of his go down,
he'll have no heart to make war on you again." AOI.

565

570

575

44

"Dear Lord Ganelon," said Marsilion the King,
"What must I do to kill Roland the Count?"
Ganelon answers: "Now I can tell you that.
The King will be at Cize,[4] in the great passes,
he will have placed his rear-guard at his back:
there'll be his nephew, Count Roland, that great man,
and Oliver, in whom he puts such faith,
and twenty thousand Franks in their company.
Now send one hundred thousand of your pagans
against the French—let them give the first battle.
The French army will be hit hard and shaken.
I must tell you: your men will be martyred.
Give them a second battle, then, like the first.
One will get him, Roland will not escape.

580

585

590

4. The pass through the Pyrenees.

Then you'll have done a deed, a noble deed,
and no more war for the rest of your life!" AOI.   595

45

"If someone can bring about the death of Roland,
then Charles would lose the right arm of his body,
that marvelous army would disappear—
never again could Charles gather such forces.
Then peace at last for the Land of Fathers!"5   600
When Marsilion heard that, he kissed his neck.
Then he begins to open up his treasures. AOI.

46

Marsilion said, "Why talk. . . .
No plan has any worth which one. . . .6
Now swear to me that you will betray Roland."   605
Ganelon answers: "Let it be as you wish."
On the relics in his great sword Murgleis
he swore treason and became a criminal. AOI.

47

There stood a throne made all of ivory.
Marsilion commands them bring forth a book: 610
it was the law of Mahum and Tervagant.7
This is the vow sworn by the Saracen of Spain:
if he shall find Roland in the rear-guard,
he shall fight him, all his men shall fight him,
and once he finds Roland, Roland will die.   615
Says Ganelon: "May it be as you will." AOI.

48

And now there came a pagan, Valdabrun,
he was the man who raised Marsilion.
And, all bright smiles, he said to Ganelon:
"You take my sword, there's no man has one better: 620
a thousand coins, and more, are in the hilt.
It is a gift, dear lord, made in friendship,
only help us to Roland, that great baron,
let us find him standing in the rear-guard."
"It shall be done," replies Count Ganelon.   625
And then they kissed, on the face, on the chin.

49

And there came then a pagan, Climborin,
and, all bright smiles, he said to Ganelon:

---

5. "Tere Majur," in the original; it can mean
either "the great land" or "the land of fathers,
ancestors." It always refers to France.
6. Parts of lines 603–04 are unintelligible in

the manuscript.
7. Or Termagent, a fictitious deity whom medieval Christians believed to be worshipped by
Muslims.

"You take my helmet, I never saw one better,
only help us to Roland, lord of the march,   630
show us the way to put Roland to shame."
"It shall be done," replied Count Ganelon.
And then they kissed, on the face, on the mouth. AOI.

50

And then there came the Queen, Bramimunde;
said to the Count: "Lord, I love you well,   635
for my lord and all his men esteem you so.
I wish to send your wife two necklaces,
they are all gold, jacinths, and amethysts,
they are worth more than all the wealth of Rome.
Your Emperor has never seen their like."   640
He has taken them, thrusts them into his boot. AOI.

51

The King calls for Malduit, his treasurer:
"The gifts for Charles—is everything prepared?"
And he replies: "Yes, Lord, and well prepared:
seven hundred camels, packed with gold and silver,   645
and twenty hostages, the noblest under heaven." AOI.

52

Marsilion took Ganelon by the shoulder
and said to him: "You're a brave man, a wise man.
Now by that faith you think will save your soul,
take care you do not turn your heart from us.   650
I will give you a great mass of my wealth,
ten mules weighed down with fine Arabian gold;
and come each year, I'll do the same again.
Now you take these, the keys to this vast city:
present King Charles with all of its great treasure;   655
then get me Roland picked for the rear-guard.
Let me find him in some defile or pass,
I will fight him, a battle to the death."
Ganelon answers: "It's high time that I go."
Now he is mounted, and he is on his way. AOI.   660

53

The Emperor moves homeward, he's drawing near.
Now he has reached the city of Valterne:
Roland had stormed it, destroyed it, and it stood
from that day forth a hundred years laid waste.
Charles is waiting for news of Ganelon   665
and the tribute from Spain, from that great land.
In the morning, at dawn, with the first light,
Count Ganelon came to the Christian camp. AOI.

54

The Emperor rose early in the morning,
the King of France, and has heard mass and matins.   670

On the green grass he stood before his tent.
Roland was there, and Oliver, brave man,
Naimon the Duke, and many other knights.
Ganelon came, the traitor, the foresworn.
With what great cunning he commences his speech;   675
said to the King: "May the Lord God save you!
Here I bring you the keys to Saragossa.
And I bring you great treasure from that city,
and twenty hostages, have them well guarded.
And good King Marsilion sends you this word: 680
Do not blame him concerning the Algalife:
I saw it all myself, with my own eyes:
      four hundred thousand men, and all in arms,
their hauberks on, some with their helms laced on,
swords on their belts, the hilts enameled gold,
who went with him to the edge of the sea.   685
They are in flight: it is the Christian faith—
they do not want it, they will not keep its law.
They had not sailed four full leagues out to sea
when a high wind, a tempest swept them up.
They were all drowned; you will never see them;   690
if he were still alive, I'd have brought him.
As for the pagan King, Lord, believe this:
before you see one month from this day pass,
he'll follow you to the Kingdom of France
and take the faith—he will take your faith, Lord,   695
and join his hands and become your vassal.
He will hold Spain as a fief from your hand."
Then the King said: "May God be thanked for this.
You have done well, you will be well rewarded."
Throughout the host they sound a thousand trumpets.   700
The French break camp, strap their gear on their pack-horses.
They take the road to the sweet land of France. AOI.

55

King Charlemagne laid waste the land of Spain,
stormed its castles, ravaged its citadels.
The King declares his war is at an end.   705
The Emperor rides toward the land of sweet France.
Roland the Count affixed the gonfanon,[8]
raised it toward heaven on the height of a hill;
the men of France make camp across that country.
Pagans are riding up through these great valleys,   710
their hauberks on, their tunics of double mail,
their helms laced on, their swords fixed on their belts,
shields on their necks, lances trimmed with their banners.
In a forest high in the hills they gathered:
four hundred thousand men waiting for dawn.   715
God, the pity of it! the French do not know! AOI.

8. Pennant.

56

The day goes by; now the darkness of night.
Charlemagne sleeps, the mighty Emperor.
He dreamt he was at Cize, in the great passes,
and in his fists held his great ashen lance.   720
Count Ganelon tore it away from him
and brandished it, shook it with such fury
the splinters of the shaft fly up toward heaven.
Charlemagne sleeps, his dream does not wake him.

57

And after that he dreamed another vision: 725
he was in France, in his chapel at Aix,
a cruel wild boar was biting his right arm;
saw coming at him—from the Ardennes—a leopard,
it attacked him, fell wildly on his body.
And a swift hound running down from the hall   730
came galloping, bounding over to Charles,
tore the right ear off that first beast, the boar,
turns, in fury, to fight against the leopard.
And the French say: It is a mighty battle,
but cannot tell which one of them will win.   735
Charlemagne sleeps, his dream does not wake him. AOI.

58

The day goes by, and the bright dawn arises.
Throughout that host. . . .[9]
The Emperor rides forth with such fierce pride.
"Barons, my lords," said the Emperor Charles,   740
"look at those passes, at those narrow defiles—
pick me a man to command the rear-guard."
Ganelon answers: "Roland, here, my stepson.
You have no baron as great and brave as Roland."
When he hears that, the King stares at him in fury;   745
and said to him: "You are the living devil,
a mad dog—the murderous rage in you!
And who will precede me, in the vanguard?"
Ganelon answers, "Why, Ogier of Denmark,
you have no baron who could lead it so well."   750

59

Roland the Count, when he heard himself named,
knew what to say, and spoke as a knight must speak:
"Lord Stepfather, I have to cherish you!
You have had the rear-guard assigned to me.
Charles will not lose, this great King who rules France, 755
I swear it now, one palfrey, one war horse—
while I'm alive and know what's happening—
one he-mule, one she-mule that he might ride,

9. The rest of the line is unintelligible in the manuscript.

Charles will not lose one sumpter, not one pack horse
that has not first been bought and paid for with swords."
Ganelon answers: "You speak the truth, I know." AOI.   760

60

When Roland hears he will lead the rear-guard,
he spoke in great fury to his stepfather:
"Hah! you nobody, you base-born little fellow,
and did you think the glove would fall from my hands
as the staff fell[1] from yours before King Charles?" AOI.   765

61

"Just Emperor," said Roland, that great man,
"give me the bow that you hold in your hand.
And no man here, I think, will say in reproach
I let it drop, as Ganelon let the staff drop[2]
from his right hand, when he should have taken it."   770
The Emperor bowed down his head with this,
he pulled his beard, he twisted his mustache,
cannot hold back, tears fill his eyes, he weeps.

62

And after that there came Naimon the Duke,
no greater vassal in the court than Naimon,   775
said to the King: "You've heard it clearly now:
it is Count Roland. How furious he is.
He is the one to whom the rear-guard falls,
no baron here can ever change that now.
Give him the bow that you have stretched and bent,   780
and then find him good men to stand with him."
The King gives him the bow; Roland has it now.

63

The Emperor calls forth Roland the Count:
"My lord, my dear nephew, of course you know
I will give you half my men, they are yours.   785
Let them serve you, it is your salvation."
"None of that!" said the Count. "May God strike me
if I discredit the history of my line.
I'll keep twenty thousand Franks—they are good men.
Go your way through the passes, you will be safe.   790
You must not fear any man while I live."

64

Roland the Count mounted his battle horse. AOI.
Oliver came to him, his companion.
And Gerin came, and the brave Count Gerer,

---

1. Ganelon had let fall a glove, not a staff (line
333). For this and other less objective reasons,
some editors have questioned the authenticity of
this *laisse* (stanza).

2. In this *laisse* a reviser tried to make the text
more consistent by adding the reference to the
staff.

and Aton came, and there came Berenger,   795
and Astor came, and Anseïs, fierce and proud,
and the old man Gerard of Roussillon,
and Gaifier, that great and mighty duke.
Said the Archbishop: "I'm going, by my head!"
"And I with you," said Gautier the Count,   800
"I am Count Roland's man and must not fail him."
And together they choose twenty thousand men. AOI.

65

Roland the Count summons Gautier de l'Hum:
"Now take a thousand Franks from our land, France,
and occupy those passes and the heights there.   805
The Emperor must not lose a single man." AOI.
Gautier replies: "Lord, I'll fight well for you."
And with a thousand French of France, their land,
Gautier rides out to the hills and defiles;
will not come down, for all the bad news, again,   810
till seven hundred swords have been drawn out.
King Almaris of the Kingdom of Belferne
gave them battle that day, and it was bitter.

66

High are the hills, the valleys tenebrous,
the cliffs are dark, the defiles mysterious.   815
That day, and with much pain, the French passed through.
For fifteen leagues around one heard their clamor.
When they reach Tere Majur, the Land of Fathers,
they beheld Gascony, their lord's domain.
Then they remembered: their fiefs, their realms, their honors,   820
remembered their young girls, their gentle wives:
not one who does not weep for what he feels.
Beyond these others King Charles is in bad straits:
his nephew left in the defiles of Spain!
feels the pity of it; tears break through. AOI.   825

67

And the Twelve Peers are left behind in Spain,
and twenty thousand Franks are left with them.
They have no fear, they have no dread of death.
The Emperor is going home to France.
Beneath his cloak, his face shows all he feels.   830
Naimon the Duke is riding beside him;
and he said to the King: "What is this grief?"
And Charles replies: "Whoever asks me, wrongs me.
I feel such pain, I cannot keep from wailing.
France will be destroyed by Ganelon.   835
Last night I saw a vision brought by angels:
the one who named my nephew for the rear-guard
shattered the lance between my fists to pieces.
I have left him in a march among strangers.
If I lose him, God! I won't find his like." AOI.   840

68

King Charles the Great cannot keep from weeping.
A hundred thousand Franks feel pity for him;
and for Roland, an amazing fear.
Ganelon the criminal has betrayed him;
got gifts for it from the pagan king,   845
gold and silver, cloths of silk, gold brocade,
mules and horses and camels and lions.
Marsilion sends for the barons of Spain,
counts and viscounts and dukes and almaçurs,
and the emirs,[3] and the sons of great lords: 850
four hundred thousand assembled in three days.
In Saragossa he has them beat the drums,
they raise Mahumet upon the highest tower:
no pagan now who does not worship him
and adore him. Then they ride, racing each other,   855
search through the land, the valleys, the mountains;
and then they saw the banners of the French.
The rear-guard of the Twelve Companions
will not fail now, they'll give the pagans battle.

69

Marsilion's nephew has come forward   860
riding a mule that he goads with a stick;
said—a warrior's laugh on him—to his uncle:
"Dear Lord and King, how long I have served you,
and all the troubles, the pains I have endured,
so many battles fought and won on the field   865
Give me a fief, the first blow at Roland.
I will kill him, here's the spear I'll do it with.
If Mahumet will only stand by me,
I will set free every strip of land in Spain,
from the passes of Aspre to Durestant.   870
Charles will be weary, his Franks will give it up:
and no more war for the rest of your life!"
King Marsilion gave him his glove, as sign. AOI.

70

The King's nephew holds the glove in his fist,
speaks these proud words to Marsilion his uncle: 875
"You've given me, dear Lord, King, a great gift!
Choose me twelve men, twelve of your noble barons,
and I will fight against the Twelve Companions."
And Falsaron was the first to respond—
he was the brother of King Marsilion: 880
"Dear Lord, Nephew, it's you and I together!
We'll fight, that's sure! We'll battle the rear-guard
of Charlemagne's grand army! We are the ones!
We have been chosen. We'll kill them all! It is fated." AOI.

3. All lords of high rank.

71

And now again: there comes King Corsablis,   885
a Berber, a bad man, a man of cunning;
and now he spoke as a brave vassal speaks:
for all God's gold he would not be a coward.
Now rushing up: Malprimis de Brigal,
faster on his two feet than any horse;   890
and cries great-voiced before Marsilion:
"I'm on my way to Rencesvals to fight!
Let me find Roland, I won't stop till I kill him!"

[Lines 894–993 continue the roll call of volunteers.]

79

They arm themselves in Saracen hauberks,
all but a few are lined with triple mail;   995
they lace on their good helms of Saragossa,
gird on their swords, the steel forged in Vienne;
they have rich shields, spears of Valencia,
and gonfanons of white and blue and red.
They leave the mules and riding horses now,   1000
mount their war horses and ride in close array.
The day was fair, the sun was shining bright,
all their armor was aflame with the light;
a thousand trumpets blow: that was to make it finer.
That made a great noise, and the men of France heard.   1005
Said Oliver: "Companion, I believe
we may yet have a battle with the pagans."
Roland replies: "Now may God grant us that.
We know our duty: to stand here for our King.
A man must bear some hardships for his lord,   1010
stand everything, the great heat, the great cold,
lose the hide and hair on him for his good lord.
Now let each man make sure to strike hard here:
let them not sing a bad song about us!
Pagans are wrong and Christians are right!   1015
They'll make no bad example of me this day!" AOI.

80

Oliver climbs to the top of a hill,
looks to his right, across a grassy vale,
sees the pagan army on its way there;
and called down to Roland, his companion: 1020
"That way, toward Spain: the uproar I see coming!
All their hauberks, all blazing, helmets like flames!
It will be a bitter thing for our French.
Ganelon knew, that criminal, that traitor,
when he marked us out before the Emperor."   1025
"Be still, Oliver," Roland the Count replies.
"He is my stepfather—my stepfather.
I won't have you speak one word against him."

81

Oliver has gone up upon a hill,
sees clearly now: the kingdom of Spain,
and the Saracens assembled in such numbers: 1030
helmets blazing, bedecked with gems in gold,
those shields of theirs, those hauberks sewn with brass,
and all their spears, the gonfanons affixed;
cannot begin to count their battle corps,
there are too many, he cannot take their number.   1035
And he is deeply troubled by what he sees.
He made his way quickly down from the hill,
came to the French, told them all he had seen.

82

Said Oliver: "I saw the Saracens,
no man on earth ever saw more of them—   1040
one hundred thousand, with their shields, up in front,
helmets laced on, hauberks blazing on them,
the shafts straight up, the iron heads like flames—
you'll get a battle, nothing like it before.
My lords, my French, may God give you the strength.   1045
Hold your ground now! Let them not defeat us!"
And the French say: "God hate the man who runs!
We may die here, but no man will fail you." AOI.

83

Said Oliver: "The pagan force is great;
from what I see, our French here are too few.   1050
Roland, my companion, sound your horn then,
Charles will hear it, the army will come back."
Roland replies: "I'd be a fool to do it.
I would lose my good name all through sweet France.
I will strike now, I'll strike with Durendal,   1055
the blade will be bloody to the gold from striking!
These pagan traitors came to these passes doomed!
I promise you, they are marked men, they'll die." AOI.

84

"Roland, Companion, now sound the olifant,[4]
Charles will hear it, he will bring the army,   1060
the King will come with all his barons to help us."
Roland replies: "May it never please God
that my kin should be shamed because of me,
or that sweet France should fall into disgrace.
Never! Never! I'll strike with Durendal,   1065
I'll strike with this good sword strapped to my side,
you'll see this blade running its whole length with blood.

---

4. A form of *elephant*, which means "ivory" or "a horn made of ivory." It is used specifically, almost as a proper name, to denote Roland's horn, made of an elephant's tusk and adorned with gold and jewels about the rim.

These pagan traitors have gathered here to die.
I promise you, they are all bound for death." AOI.

85

"Roland, Companion, sound your olifant now, 1070
Charles will hear it, marching through those passes.
I promise you, the Franks will come at once."
Roland replies: "May it never please God
that any man alive should come to say
that pagans—pagans!—once made me sound this horn: 1075
no kin of mine will ever bear that shame.
Once I enter this great battle coming
and strike my thousand seven hundred blows,
you'll see the bloody steel of Durendal.
These French are good—they will strike like brave men. 1080
Nothing can save the men of Spain from death."

86

Said Oliver: "I see no blame in it—
I watched the Saracens coming from Spain,
the valleys and mountains covered with them,
every hillside and every plain all covered, 1085
hosts and hosts everywhere of those strange men—
and here we have a little company."
Roland replies: "That whets my appetite.
May it not please God and his angels and saints
to let France lose its glory because of me— 1090
let me not end in shame, let me die first.
The Emperor loves us when we fight well."

87

Roland is good, and Oliver is wise,
both these vassals men of amazing courage:
once they are armed and mounted on their horses, 1095
they will not run, though they die for it, from battle.
Good men, these Counts, and their words full of spirit.
Traitor pagans are riding up in fury.
Said Oliver: "Roland, look—the first ones,
on top of us—and Charles is far away. 1100
You did not think it right to sound your olifant:
if the King were here, we'd come out without losses.
Now look up there, toward the passes of Aspre—
you can see the rear-guard: it will suffer.
No man in that detail will be in another." 1105
Roland replies: "Don't speak such foolishness—
shame on the heart gone coward in the chest.
We'll hold our ground, we'll stand firm—we're the ones!
We'll fight with spears, we'll fight them hand to hand!" AOI.

88

When Roland sees that there will be a battle, 1110
it makes him fiercer than a lion or leopard;

shouts to the French, calls out to Oliver:
"Lord, companion: friend, do not say such things.
The Emperor, who left us these good French,
had set apart these twenty thousand men: 1115
he knew there was no coward in their ranks.
A man must meet great troubles for his lord,
stand up to the great heat and the great cold,
give up some flesh and blood—it is his duty.
Strike with the lance, I'll strike with Durendal—   1120
it was the King who gave me this good sword!
If I die here, the man who gets it can say:
it was a noble's, a vassal's, a good man's sword."

89

And now there comes the Archbishop Turpin.
He spurs his horse, goes up into a mountain,   1125
summons the French; and he preached them a sermon:
"Barons, my lords, Charles left us in this place.
We know our duty: to die like good men for our King.
Fight to defend the holy Christian faith.
Now you will have a battle, you know it now,   1130
you see the Saracens with your own eyes.
Confess your sins, pray to the Lord for mercy.
I will absolve you all, to save your souls.
If you die here, you will stand up holy martyrs,
you will have seats in highest Paradise."   1135
The French dismount, cast themselves on the ground;
the Archbishop blesses them in God's name.
He commands them to do one penance: strike.

90

The French arise, stand on their feet again;
they are absolved, released from all their sins: 1140
the Archbishop has blessed them in God's name.
Now they are mounted on their swift battle horses,
bearing their arms like faithful warriors;
and every man stands ready for the battle.
Roland the Count calls out to Oliver: 1145
"Lord, Companion, you knew it, you were right,
Ganelon watched for his chance to betray us,
got gold for it, got goods for it, and money.
The Emperor will have to avenge us now.
King Marsilion made a bargain for our lives,   1150
but still must pay, and that must be with swords." AOI.

91

Roland went forth into the Spanish passes
on Veillantif, his good swift-running horse.
He bears his arms—how they become this man!—
grips his lance now, hefting it, working it,   1155
now swings the iron point up toward the sky,
the gonfanon all white laced on above—

the golden streamers beat down upon his hands:
a noble's body, the face aglow and smiling.
Close behind him his good companion follows;   1160
the men of France hail him: their protector!
He looks wildly toward the Saracens,
and humbly and gently to the men of France;
and spoke a word to them, in all courtesy:
"Barons, my lords, easy now, keep at a walk.   1165
These pagans are searching for martyrdom.
We'll get good spoils before this day is over,
no king of France ever got such treasure!"
And with these words, the hosts are at each other. AOI.

92

Said Oliver: "I will waste no more words.   1170
You did not think it right to sound your olifant,
there'll be no Charles coming to your aid now.
He knows nothing, brave man, he's done no wrong;
those men down there—they have no blame in this.
Well, then, ride now, and ride with all your might!   1175
Lords, you brave men, stand your ground, hold the field!
Make up your minds, I beg you in God's name,
to strike some blows, take them and give them back!
Here we must not forget Charlemagne's war cry."
And with that word the men of France cried out.   1180
A man who heard that shout: Munjoie! Munjoie![5]
would always remember what manhood is.
Then they ride, God! Look at their pride and spirit!
and they spur hard, to ride with all their speed,
come on to strike—what else would these men do?   1185
The Saracens kept coming, never fearing them.
Franks and pagans, here they are, at each other.

93

Marsilion's nephew is named Aëlroth.
He rides in front, at the head of the army,
comes on shouting insults against our French: 1190
"French criminals, today you fight our men.
One man should have saved you: he betrayed you.
A fool, your King, to leave you in these passes.
This is the day sweet France will lose its name,
and Charlemagne the right arm of his body."   1195
When he hears that—God!—Roland is outraged!
He spurs his horse, gives Veillantif its head.
The Count comes on to strike with all his might,
smashes his shield, breaks his hauberk apart,
and drives: rips through his chest, shatters the bones,   1200
knocks the whole backbone out of his back,
casts out the soul of Aëlroth with his lance;
which he thrusts deep, makes the whole body shake,

5. For the poet's derivation of this war cry, see *laisse* 183, below.

throws him down dead, lance straight out,[6] from his horse;
he has broken his neck; broken it in two.   1205
There is something, he says, he must tell him:
"Clown! Nobody! Now you know Charles is no fool,
he never was the man to love treason.
It took his valor to leave us in these passes!
France will not lose its name, sweet France! today.   1210
Brave men of France, strike hard! The first blow is ours!
We're in the right, and these swine in the wrong!" AOI.

94

A duke is there whose name is Falsaron,
he was the brother of King Marsilion,
held the wild land of Dathan and Abiram;[7]   1215
under heaven, no criminal more vile;
a tremendous forehead between his eyes—
a good half-foot long, if you had measured it.
His pain is bitter to see his nephew dead;
rides out alone, baits the foe with his body,   1220
and riding shouts the war cry of the pagans,
full of hate and insults against the French:
"This is the day sweet France will lose its honor!"
Oliver hears, and it fills him with fury,
digs with his golden spurs into his horse,   1225
comes on to strike the blow a baron strikes,
smashes his shield, breaks his hauberk apart,
thrusts into him the long streamers of his gonfalon,
knocks him down, dead, lance straight out, from the saddle;
looks to the ground and sees the swine stretched out,   1230
and spoke these words—proud words, terrible words:
"You nobody, what are your threats to me!
Men of France, strike! Strike and we will beat them!"
Munjoie! he shouts—the war cry of King Charles. AOI.

95

A king is there whose name is Corsablis,   1235
a Berber, come from that far country.
He spoke these words to all his Saracens:
"Now here's one battle we'll have no trouble with,
look at that little troop of Frenchmen there,
a few odd men—they're not worth noticing!   1240
King Charles won't save a single one of them.
Their day has come, they must all die today."
And Archbishop Turpin heard every word:
no man on earth he wants so much to hate!
digs with spurs of fine gold into his horse,   1245
comes on to strike with all his awful might;

---

6. The lance is held, not thrown, and used to knock the enemy from his horse. To throw one's weapons is savage and ignoble. See *laisses* 154 and 160 and the outlandish names of the things the pagans throw at Roland, Gautier, and Turpin.

7. See Numbers 16.1–35.

smashed through his shield, burst the rings of his hauberk,
sent his great lance into the body's center,
drove it in deep, he made the dead man shake,
knocked him down, dead, lance straight out, on the road;   1250
looks to the ground and sees the swine stretched out;
there is something, he says, he must tell him:
"You pagan! You nobody! You told lies there:
King Charles my lord is our safeguard forever!
Our men of France have no heart for running.   1255
As for your companions—we'll nail them to the ground;
and then you must all die the second death.[8]
At them, you French! No man forget what he is!
Thanks be to God, now the first blow is ours";
and shouts Munjoie! Munjoie! to hold the field.   1260

[Lines 1261–1319 narrate a series of single combats, many of them similar.]

104

The battle is fearful and wonderful   1320
and everywhere. Roland never spares himself,
strikes with his lance as long as the wood lasts:
the fifteenth blow he struck, it broke, was lost.
Then he draws Durendal, his good sword, bare,
and spurs his horse, comes on to strike Chernuble,   1325
smashes his helmet, carbuncles shed their light,
cuts through the coif, through the hair on his head,
cut through his eyes, through his face, through that look,
the bright, shining hauberk with its fine rings,
down through the trunk to the fork of his legs,   1330
through the saddle, adorned with beaten gold,
into the horse; and the sword came to rest:
cut through the spine, never felt for the joint;
knocks him down, dead, on the rich grass of the meadow;
then said to him: "You were doomed when you started,   1335
Clown! Nobody! Let Mahum help you now.
No pagan swine will win this field today."

105

Roland the Count comes riding through the field,
holds Durendal, that sword! it carves its way!
and brings terrible slaughter down on the pagans.   1340
To have seen him cast one man dead on another,
the bright red blood pouring out on the ground,
his hauberk, his two arms, running with blood,
his good horse—neck and shoulders running with blood!
And Oliver does not linger, he strikes!   1345
and the Twelve Peers, no man could reproach them;
and the brave French, they fight with lance and sword.
The pagans die, some simply faint away!

8. The death of the soul, eternal damnation (see Revelation 2.11, 20.14, 21.8).

Said the Archbishop: "Bless our band of brave men!"
Munjoie! he shouts—the war cry of King Charles. AOI.   1350

106

Oliver rides into that battle-storm,
his lance is broken, he holds only the stump;
comes on to strike a pagan, Malsarun;
and he smashes his shield, all flowers and gold,
sends his two eyes flying out of his head,   1355
and his brains come pouring down to his feet;
casts him down, dead, with seven hundred others.
Now he has killed Turgis and Esturguz,
and the shaft bursts, shivers down to his fists.
Count Roland said: "Companion, what are you doing?   1360
Why bother with a stick in such a battle?
Iron and steel will do much better work!
Where is your sword, your Halteclere—that name!
Where is that crystal hilt, that golden guard?"
"Haven't had any time to draw it out,   1365
been so busy fighting," said Oliver. AOI.

107

Lord Oliver has drawn out his good sword—
that sword his companion had longed to see—
and showed him how a good man uses it:
strikes a pagan, Justin of Val Ferrée,   1370
and comes down through his head, cuts through the center,
through his body, his hauberk sewn with brass,
the good saddle beset with gems in gold,
into the horse, the backbone cut in two;
knocks him down, dead, before him on the meadow.   1375
Count Roland said: "Now I know it's you, Brother.
The Emperor loves us for blows like that."
Munjoie! that cry! goes up on every side. AOI.

108

Gerin the Count sits on his bay Sorél
and Gerer his companion on Passe-Cerf;   1380
and they ride, spurring hard, let loose their reins,
come on to strike a pagan, Timozel,
one on his shield, the other on his hauberk.
They broke their two lances in his body;
turn him over, dead, in a fallow field.   1385
I do not know and have never heard tell
which of these two was swifter, though both were swift.
Esperveris: he was the son of Borel
and now struck dead by Engeler of Bordeaux.
Turpin the Archbishop killed Siglorel,   1390
the enchanter, who had been in Hell before:
Jupiter brought him there, with that strange magic.
Then Turpin said: "That swine owed us his life!

Roland replies: "And now the scoundrel's dead.
Oliver, Brother, those were blows! I approve!"   1395

109

In the meantime, the fighting grew bitter.
Franks and pagans, the fearful blows they strike—
those who attack, those who defend themselves;
so many lances broken, running with blood,
the gonfanons in shreds, the ensigns torn,   1400
so many good French fallen, their young lives lost:
they will not see their mothers or wives again,
or the men of France who wait for them at the passes. AOI.
Charlemagne waits and weeps and wails for them.
What does that matter? They'll get no help from him.   1405
Ganelon served him ill that day he sold,
in Saragossa, the barons of his house.
He lost his life and limbs for what he did:
was doomed to hang in the great trial at Aix,
and thirty of his kin were doomed with him,   1410
who never expected to die that death. AOI.

110

The battle is fearful and full of grief.
Oliver and Roland strike like good men,
the Archbishop, more than a thousand blows,
and the Twelve Peers do not hang back, they strike!   1415
the French fight side by side, all as one man.
The pagans die by hundreds, by thousands:
whoever does not flee finds no refuge from death,
like it or not, there he ends all his days.
And there the men of France lose their greatest arms;   1420
they will not see their fathers, their kin again,
or Charlemagne, who looks for them in the passes.
Tremendous torment now comes forth in France,
a mighty whirlwind, tempests of wind and thunder,
rains and hailstones, great and immeasurable,   1425
bolts of lightning hurtling and hurtling down:
it is, in truth, a trembling of the earth.
From Saint Michael-in-Peril to the Saints,
from Besançon to the port of Wissant,
there is no house whose veil of walls does not crumble.   1430
A great darkness at noon[9] falls on the land,
there is no light but when the heavens crack.
No man sees this who is not terrified,
and many say: "The Last Day! Judgment Day!
The end! The end of the world is upon us!"   1435
They do not know, they do not speak the truth:
it is the worldwide grief for the death of Roland.

---

9. As during the crucifixion of Jesus, according to the gospel accounts (Matthew 27.45, Mark 15.33, Luke 23.44).

111

The French have fought with all their hearts and strength,
pagans are dead by the thousands, in droves:
of one hundred thousand, not two are saved.   1440
Said the Archbishop: "Our men! What valiant fighters!
No king under heaven could have better.
It is written in the Gesta Francorum:[1]
our Emperor's vassals were all good men."
They walk over the field to seek their dead,   1445
they weep, tears fill their eyes, in grief and pity
for their kindred, with love, with all their hearts.
Marsilion the King, with all his men
in that great host, rises up before them. AOI.

112

King Marsilion comes along a valley
with all his men, the great host he assembled: 1450
twenty divisions, formed and numbered by the King,
helmets ablaze with gems beset in gold,
and those bright shields, those hauberks sewn with brass.
Seven thousand clarions sound the pursuit,
and the great noise resounds across that country.   1455
Said Roland then: "Oliver, Companion, Brother,
that traitor Ganelon has sworn our deaths:
it is treason, it cannot stay hidden,
the Emperor will take his terrible revenge.
We have this battle now, it will be bitter,   1460
no man has ever seen the like of it.
I will fight here with Durendal, this sword,
and you, my companion, with Halteclere—
we've fought with them before, in many lands!
how many battles have we won with these two!   1465
Let no one sing a bad song of our swords." AOI.

113

When the French see the pagans so numerous,
the fields swarming with them on every side,
they call the names of Oliver, and Roland,
and the Twelve Peers: protect them, be their warranter.   1470
The Archbishop told them how he saw things:
"Barons, my lords, do not think shameful thoughts,
do not, I beg you all in God's name, run.
Let no brave man sing shameful songs of us:
let us all die here fighting: that is far better.   1475
We are promised: we shall soon find our deaths,
after today we won't be living here.
But here's one thing, and I am your witness:
Holy Paradise lies open to you,

---

1. The Deeds of the French (Latin), title of an account of these events that has not survived.

you will take seats among the Innocents."[2]   1480
And with these words the Franks are filled with joy,
there is no man who does not shout Munjoie! AOI.

114

A Saracen was there of Saragossa,
half that city was in this pagan's keeping,
this Climborin, who fled before no man,   1485
who took the word of Ganelon the Count,
kissed in friendship the mouth that spoke that word,
gave him a gift: his helmet and its carbuncle.
Now he will shame, says he, the Land of Fathers,
he will tear off the crown of the Emperor;   1490
sits on the horse that he calls Barbamusche,
swifter than the sparrowhawk, than the swallow;
digs in his spurs, gives that war horse its head,
comes on to strike Engeler of Gascony,
whose shield and fine hauberk cannot save him;   1495
gets the head of his spear into his body,
drives it in deep, gets all the iron through,
throws him back, dead, lance straight out, on the field.
And then he cries: "It's good to kill these swine!
At them, Pagans! At them and break their ranks!"   1500
"God!" say the French, "the loss of that good man!" AOI.

115

Roland the Count calls out to Oliver:
"Lord, Companion, there is Engeler dead,
we never had a braver man on horse."
The Count replies: "God let me avenge him";   1505
and digs with golden spurs into his horse,
grips—the steel running with blood—Halteclere,
comes on to strike with all his mighty power:
the blow comes flashing down; the pagan falls.
Devils take away the soul of Climborin.   1510
And then he killed Alphaïen the duke,
cut off the head of Escababi,
struck from their horses seven great Arrabites;
they'll be no use for fighting any more!
And Roland said: "My companion is enraged!   1515
Why, he compares with me! he earns his praise!
Fighting like that makes us dearer to Charles";
lifts up his voice and shouts: "Strike! you are warriors!" AOI.

[Lines 1519–1627 narrate another series of single combats.]

125

Marsilion sees his people's martyrdom.
He commands them: sound his horns and trumpets;

2. The infants slain by King Herod (see Matthew 2.16).

and he rides now with the great host he has gathered.   1630
At their head rides the Saracen Abisme:
no worse criminal rides in that company,
stained with the marks of his crimes and great treasons,
lacking the faith in God, Saint Mary's son.
And he is black, as black as melted pitch,   1635
a man who loves murder and treason more
than all the gold of rich Galicia,
no living man ever saw him play or laugh;
a great fighter, a wild man, mad with pride,
and therefore dear to that criminal king;   1640
holds high his dragon,[3] where all his people gather.
The Archbishop will never love that man,
no sooner saw than wanted to strike him;
considered quietly, said to himself:
"That Saracen—a heretic, I'll wager.   1645
Now let me die if I do not kill him—
I never loved cowards or cowards' ways." AOI.

126

Turpin the Archbishop begins the battle.
He rides the horse that he took from Grossaille,
who was a king this priest once killed in Denmark.   1650
Now this war horse is quick and spirited,
his hooves high-arched, the quick legs long and flat,
short in the thigh, wide in the rump, long in the flanks,
and the backbone so high, a battle horse!
and that white tail, the yellow mane on him,   1655
the little ears on him, the tawny head!
No beast on earth could ever run with him.
The Archbishop—that valiant man!—spurs hard,
he will attack Abisme, he will not falter,
strikes on his shield, a miraculous blow: 1660
a shield of stones, of amethysts, topazes,
esterminals,[4] carbuncles all on fire—
a gift from a devil, in Val Metas,
sent on to him by the Amiral Galafre.
There Turpin strikes, he does not treat it gently—   1665
after that blow, I'd not give one cent for it;
cut through his body, from one side to the other,
and casts him down dead in a barren place.
And the French say: "A fighter, that Archbishop!
Look at him there, saving souls with that crozier!"   1670

127

Roland the Count calls out to Oliver:
"Lord, Companion, now you have to agree
the Archbishop is a good man on horse,

---

3. Banner.   4. Precious ornaments.

there's none better on earth or under heaven,
he knows his way with a lance and a spear." 1675
The Count replies: "Right! Let us help him then."
And with these words the Franks began anew,
the blows strike hard, and the fighting is bitter;
there is a painful loss of Christian men.
To have seen them, Roland and Oliver, 1680
these fighting men, striking down with their swords,
the Archbishop with them, striking with his lance!
One can recount the number these three killed:
it is written—in charters, in documents;
the Geste tells it: it was more than four thousand. 1685
Through four assaults all went well with our men;
then comes the fifth, and that one crushes them.
They are all killed, all these warriors of France,
all but sixty, whom the Lord God has spared:
they will die too, but first sell themselves dear. AOI. 1690

128

Count Roland sees the great loss of his men,
calls on his companion, on Oliver:
"Lord, Companion, in God's name, what would you do?
All these good men you see stretched on the ground.
We can mourn for sweet France, fair land of France! 1695
a desert now, stripped of such great vassals.
Oh King, and friend, if only you were here!
Oliver, Brother, how shall we manage it?
What shall we do to get word to the King?"
Said Oliver: "I don't see any way. 1700
I would rather die now than hear us shamed." AOI.

129

And Roland said: "I'll sound the olifant,
Charles will hear it, drawing through the passes,
I promise you, the Franks will return at once."
Said Oliver: "That would be a great disgrace, 1705
a dishonor and reproach to all your kin,
the shame of it would last them all their lives.
When I urged it, you would not hear of it;
you will not do it now with my consent.
It is not acting bravely to sound it now— 1710
look at your arms, they are covered with blood."
The Count replies: "I've fought here like a lord."[5] AOI.

130

And Roland says: "We are in a rough battle.
I'll sound the olifant, Charles will hear it."

---

5. Some have found lines 1710–12 difficult. Oliver means, "We have fought this far—look at the enemy's blood on your arms: It is too late, it would be a disgrace to summon help when there is no longer any chance of being saved." But Roland thinks that that is the one time when it is not a disgrace.

Said Oliver: "No good vassal would do it. 1715
When I urged it, friend, you did not think it right.
If Charles were here, we'd come out with no losses.
Those men down there—no blame can fall on them."
Oliver said: "Now by this beard of mine,
If I can see my noble sister, Aude, 1720
once more, you will never lie in her arms!"[6] AOI.

131

And Roland said: "Why are you angry at me?"
Oliver answers: "Companion, it is your doing.
I will tell you what makes a vassal good:
it is judgment, it is never madness;
restraint is worth more than the raw nerve of a fool. 1725
Frenchmen are dead because of your wildness.
And what service will Charles ever have from us?
If you had trusted me, my lord would be here,
we would have fought this battle through to the end,
Marsilion would be dead, or our prisoner. 1730
Roland, your prowess—had we never seen it!
And now, dear friend, we've seen the last of it.
No more aid from us now for Charlemagne,
a man without equal till Judgment Day,
you will die here, and your death will shame France.
We kept faith, you and I, we were companions;
and everything we were will end today.
We part before evening, and it will be hard." AOI. 1735

132

Turpin the Archbishop hears their bitter words,
digs hard into his horse with golden spurs
and rides to them; begins to set them right:
"You, Lord Roland, and you, Lord Oliver,
I beg you in God's name do not quarrel. 1740
To sound the horn could not help us now, true,
but still it is far better that you do it:
let the King come, he can avenge us then—
these men of Spain must not go home exulting!
Our French will come, they'll get down on their feet, 1745
and find us here—we'll be dead, cut to pieces.
They will lift us into coffins on the backs of mules,
and weep for us, in rage and pain and grief,
and bury us in the courts of churches;
and we will not be eaten by wolves or pigs or dogs." 1750
Roland replies, "Lord, you have spoken well." AOI.

133

Roland has put the olifant to his mouth,
he sets it well, sounds it with all his strength.

6. Aude had been betrothed to Roland.

The hills are high, and that voice ranges far, 1755
they heard it echo thirty great leagues away.
King Charles heard it, and all his faithful men.
And the King says: "Our men are in a battle."
And Ganelon disputed him and said:
"Had someone else said that, I'd call him liar!" AOI. 1760

134

And now the mighty effort of Roland the Count:
he sounds his olifant; his pain is great,
and from his mouth the bright blood comes leaping out,
and the temple bursts in his forehead.
That horn, in Roland's hands, has a mighty voice: 1765
King Charles hears it drawing through the passes.
Naimon heard it, the Franks listen to it.
And the King said: "I hear Count Roland's horn;
he'd never sound it unless he had a battle."
Says Ganelon: "Now no more talk of battles! 1770
You are old now, your hair is white as snow,
the things you say make you sound like a child.
You know Roland and that wild pride of his—
what a wonder God has suffered it so long!
Remember? he took Noples without your command: 1775
the Saracens rode out, to break the siege;
they fought with him, the great vassal Roland.
Afterwards he used the streams to wash the blood
from the meadows: so that nothing would show.
He blasts his horn all day to catch a rabbit, 1780
he's strutting now before his peers and bragging—
who under heaven would dare meet him on the field?
So now: ride on! Why do you keep on stopping?
The Land of Fathers lies far ahead of us." AOI.

135

The blood leaping from Count Roland's mouth, 1785
the temple broken with effort in his forehead,
he sounds his horn in great travail and pain.
King Charles heard it, and his French listen hard.
And the King said: "That horn has a long breath!"
Naimon answers: "It is a baron's breath. 1790
There is a battle there, I know there is.
He betrayed him! and now asks you to fail him!
Put on your armor! Lord, shout your battle cry,
and save the noble barons of your house!
You hear Roland's call. He is in trouble." 1795

136

The Emperor commanded the horns to sound,
the French dismount, and they put on their armor:
their hauberks, their helmets, their gold-dressed swords,
their handsome shields; and take up their great lances,
the gonfalons of white and red and blue. 1800

The barons of that host mount their war horses
and spur them hard the whole length of the pass;
and every man of them says to the other:
"If only we find Roland before he's killed,
we'll stand with him, and then we'll do some fighting!"   1805
What does it matter what they say? They are too late.

137

It is the end of day, and full of light,
arms and armor are ablaze in the sun,
and fire flashes from hauberks and helmets,
and from those shields, painted fair with flowers,   1810
and from those lances, those gold-dressed gonfanons.
The Emperor rides on in rage and sorrow,
the men of France indignant and full of grief.
There is no man of them who does not weep,
they are in fear for the life of Roland.   1815
The King commands: seize Ganelon the Count!
and gave him over to the cooks of his house,
summons the master cook, their chief, Besgun:
"Guard him for me like the traitor he is:
he has betrayed the barons of my house."   1820
Besgun takes him, sets his kitchen comrades,
a hundred men, the best, the worst, on him;
and they tear out his beard and his mustache,
each one strikes him four good blows with his fist;
and they lay into him with cudgels and sticks,   1825
put an iron collar around his neck
and chain him up, as they would chain a bear;
dumped him, in dishonor, on a packhorse,
and guard him well till they give him back to Charles.

138

High are the hills, and tenebrous, and vast, AOI.   1830
the valleys deep, the raging waters swift;
to the rear, to the front, the trumpets sound:
they answer the lone voice of the olifant.
The Emperor rides on, rides on in fury,
the men of France in grief and indignation.   1835
There is no man who does not weep and wail,
and they pray God: protect the life of Roland
till they come, one great host, into the field
and fight at Roland's side like true men all.
What does it matter what they pray? It does no good.   1840
They are too late, they cannot come in time. AOI.

139

King Charles the Great rides on, a man in wrath,
his great white beard spread out upon his hauberk.[7]
All the barons of France ride spurring hard,

---

7. A gesture of defiance toward the enemy.

there is no man who does not wail, furious   1845
not to be with Roland, the captain count,
who stands and fights the Saracens of Spain,
so set upon, I cannot think his soul abides.
God! those sixty men who stand with him, what men!
No king, no captain ever stood with better. AOI.   1850

140

Roland looks up on the mountains and slopes,
sees the French dead, so many good men fallen,
and weeps for them, as a great warrior weeps:
"Barons, my lords, may God give you his grace,
may he grant Paradise to all your souls,   1855
make them lie down among the holy flowers.
I never saw better vassals than you.
All the years you've served me, and all the times,
the mighty lands you conquered for Charles our King!
The Emperor raised you for this terrible hour!   1860
Land of France, how sweet you are, native land,
laid waste this day, ravaged, made a desert.
Barons of France, I see you die for me,
and I, your lord—I cannot protect you.
May *God* come to your aid, that God who never failed.   1865
Oliver, brother, now I will not fail *you*.
I will die here—of grief, if no man kills me.
Lord, Companion, let us return and fight."

141

Roland returned to his place on the field,
strikes—a brave man keeping faith—with Durendal,   1870
struck through Faldrun de Pui, cut him to pieces,
and twenty-four of the men they valued most;
no man will ever want his vengeance more!
As when the deer turns tail before the dogs,
so the pagans flee before Roland the Count.   1875
Said the Archbishop: "You! Roland! What a fighter!
Now that's what every knight must have in him
who carries arms and rides on a fine horse:
he must be strong, a savage, when he's in battle;
for otherwise, what's he worth? Not four cents!   1880
Let that four-cent man be a monk in some minster,
and he can pray all day long for our sins."
Roland replies: "Attack, do not spare them!"
And with that word the Franks began again.
There was a heavy loss of Christian men.   1885

142

When a man knows there'll be no prisoners,
what will that man not do to defend himself!
And so the Franks fight with the fury of lions.
Now Marsilion, the image of a baron,

mounted on that war horse he calls Gaignun, 1890
digs in his spurs, comes on to strike Bevon,
who was the lord of Beaune and of Dijon;
smashes his shield, rips apart his hauberk,
knocks him down, dead, no need to wound him more.
And then he killed Yvorie and Yvon, 1895
and more: he killed Gerard of Rousillon.
Roland the Count is not far away now,
said to the pagan: "The Lord God's curse on you!
You kill my companions, how you wrong me!
You'll feel the pain of it before we part, 1900
you will learn my sword's name by heart today";
comes on to strike—the image of a baron.
He has cut off Marsilion's right fist;
now takes the head of Jurfaleu the blond—
the head of Jurfaleu! Marsilion's son. 1905
The pagans cry: "Help, Mahumet! Help us!
Vengeance, our gods, on Charles! the man who set
these criminals on us in our own land,
they will not quit the field, they'll stand and die!"
And one said to the other: "Let us run then." 1910
And with that word, some hundred thousand flee.
Now try to call them back: they won't return. AOI.

143

What does it matter? If Marsilion has fled,
his uncle has remained: the Algalife,[8]
who holds Carthage, Alfrere, and Garmalie, 1915
and Ethiopia: a land accursed;
holds its immense black race under his power,
the huge noses, the enormous ears on them;
and they number more than fifty thousand.
These are the men who come riding in fury, 1920
and now they shout that pagan battle cry.
And Roland said: "Here comes our martyrdom;
I see it now: we have not long to live.
But let the world call any man a traitor
    who does not make them pay before he dies!
My lords, attack! Use those bright shining swords! 1925
Fight a good fight for your deaths and your lives,
let no shame touch sweet France because of us!
When Charles my lord comes to this battlefield
and sees how well we punished these Saracens,
finds fifteen of their dead for one of ours, 1930
I'll tell you what he will do: he will bless us." AOI.

144

When Roland sees that unbelieving race,
those hordes and hordes blacker than blackest ink—

---

8. The Caliph, Marsilion's uncle, whom Ganelon lied about to Charlemagne (see lines 680–91).

no shred of white on them except their teeth—
then said the Count: "I see it clearly now,   1935
we die today: it is there before us.
Men of France, strike! I will start it once more."
Said Oliver: "God curse the slowest man."
And with that word, the French strike into battle.

145

The Saracens, when they saw these few French,   1940
looked at each other, took courage, and presumed,
telling themselves: "The Emperor is wrong!"
The Algalife rides a great sorrel horse,
digs into it with his spurs of fine gold,
strikes Oliver, from behind, in the back,   1945
shattered the white hauberk upon his flesh,
drove his spear through the middle of his chest;
and speaks to him: "Now you feel you've been struck!
Your great Charles doomed you when he left you in this pass.
That man wronged us, he must not boast of it.   1950
I've avenged all our dead in you alone!"

146

Oliver feels: he has been struck to death;
grips Halteclere, that steel blade shining, strikes
on the gold-dressed pointed helm of the Algalife,
sends jewels and flowers crackling down to the earth,   1955
into the head, into the little teeth;
draws up his flashing sword, casts him down, dead,
and then he says: "Pagan, a curse on you!
If only I could say Charles has lost nothing—
but no woman, no lady you ever knew   1960
will hear you boast, in the land you came from,
that you could take one thing worth a cent from me,
or do me harm, or do any man harm";
then cries out to Roland to come to his aid. AOI.

147

Oliver feels he is wounded to death,   1965
will never have his fill of vengeance, strikes,
as a baron strikes, where they are thickest,
cuts through their lances, cuts through those buckled shields,
through feet, through fists, through saddles, and through flanks.
Had you seen him, cutting the pagans limb   1970
from limb, casting one corpse down on another,
you would remember a brave man keeping faith.
Never would he forget Charles' battle-cry,
Munjoie! he shouts, that mighty voice ringing;
calls to Roland, to his friend and his peer: 1975
"Lord, Companion, come stand beside me now.
We must part from each other in pain today." AOI.

148

Roland looks hard into Oliver's face,
it is ashen, all its color is gone,
the bright red blood streams down upon his body,   1980
Oliver's blood spattering on the earth.
"God!" said the Count, "I don't know what to do,
Lord, Companion, your fight is finished now.
There'll never be a man the like of you.
Sweet land of France, today you will be stripped   1985
of good vassals, laid low, a fallen land!
The Emperor will suffer the great loss";
faints with that word, mounted upon his horse. AOI.

149

Here is Roland, lords, fainted on his horse,
and Oliver the Count, wounded to death: 1990
he has lost so much blood, his eyes are darkened—
he cannot see, near or far, well enough
to recognize a friend or enemy:
struck when he came upon his companion,
strikes on his helm, adorned with gems in gold,   1995
cuts down straight through, from the point to the nasal,[9]
but never harmed him, he never touched his head.
Under this blow, Count Roland looked at him;
and gently, softly now, he asks of him:
"Lord, Companion, do you mean to do this?   2000
It is Roland, who always loved you greatly.
You never declared that we were enemies."
Said Oliver: "Now I hear it is you—
I don't see you, may the Lord God see you.
Was it you that I struck? Forgive me then."   2005
Roland replies: "I am not harmed, not harmed,
I forgive you, Friend, here and before God."
And with that word, each bowed to the other.
And this is the love, lords, in which they parted.

150

Oliver feels: death pressing hard on him;   2010
his two eyes turn, roll up into his head,
all hearing is lost now, all sight is gone;
gets down on foot, stretches out on the ground,
cries out now and again: mea culpa![1]
his two hands joined, raised aloft toward heaven,   2015
he prays to God: grant him His Paradise;
and blesses Charles, and the sweet land of France,
his companion, Roland, above all men.
The heart fails him, his helmet falls away,
the great body settles upon the earth.   2020

---

9. The nosepiece protruding down from the
cone-shaped helmet.

1. My guilt (Latin); a formula used in the
confession of one's sins.

The Count is dead, he stands with us no longer.
Roland, brave man, weeps for him, mourns for him,
you will not hear a man of greater sorrow.

151

Roland the Count, when he sees his friend dead,
lying stretched out, his face against the earth,
softly, gently, begins to speak the regret:[2]
"Lord, Companion, you were brave and died for it.
We have stood side by side through days and years,
you never caused me harm, I never wronged you;
when you are dead, to be alive pains me."
And with that word the lord of marches faints
upon his horse, which he calls Veillantif.
He is held firm by his spurs of fine gold,
whichever way he leans, he cannot fall.

2025

2030

152

Before Roland could recover his senses
and come out of his faint, and be aware,
a great disaster had come forth before him:
the French are dead, he has lost every man
except the Archbishop, and Gautier de l'Hum,
who has come back, down from that high mountain:
he has fought well, he fought those men of Spain.
His men are dead, the pagans finished them;
flees now down to these valleys, he has no choice,
and calls on Count Roland to come to his aid:
"My noble Count, my brave lord, where are you?
I never feared whenever you were there.
It is Walter: I conquered Maëlgut,
my uncle is Droün, old and gray: your Walter
and always dear to you for the way I fought;
and I have fought this time: my lance is shattered,
my good shield pierced, my hauberk's meshes broken;
and I am wounded, a lance struck through my body.
I will die soon, but I sold myself dear."
And with that word, Count Roland has heard him,
he spurs his horse, rides spurring to his man. AOI.

2035

2040

2045

2050

2055

153

Roland in pain, maddened with grief and rage:
rushes where they are thickest and strikes again,
strikes twenty men of Spain, strikes twenty dead,
and Walter six, and the Archbishop five.
The pagans say: "Look at those criminals!
Now take care, Lords, they don't get out alive,
only a traitor will not attack them now!
Only a coward will let them save their skins!"

2060

2. What follows is a formal and customary lament for the dead.

And then they raise their hue and cry once more,
rush in on them, once more, from every side. AOI.   2065

154

Count Roland was always a noble warrior,
Gautier de l'Hum is a fine mounted man,
the Archbishop, a good man tried and proved:
not one of them will ever leave the others;
strike, where they are thickest, at the pagans.   2070
A thousand Saracens get down on foot,
and forty thousand more are on their mounts:
and I tell you, not one will dare come close,
they throw, and from afar, lances and spears,
wigars and darts, mizraks, javelins, pikes.   2075
With the first blows they killed Gautier de l'Hum
and struck Turpin of Reims, pierced through his shield,
broke the helmet on him, wounded his head;
ripped his hauberk, shattered its rings of mail,
and pierced him with four spears in his body,   2080
the war horse killed under him; and now there comes
great pain and rage when the Archbishop falls. AOI.

155

Turpin of Reims, when he feels he is unhorsed,
struck to the earth with four spears in his body,
quickly, brave man, leaps to his feet again;   2085
his eyes find Roland now, he runs to him
and says one word: "See! I'm not finished yet!
What good vassal ever gives up alive!";
and draws Almace, his sword, that shining steel!
and strikes, where they are thickest, a thousand blows, and more.   2090
Later, Charles said: Turpin had spared no one;
he found four hundred men prostrate around him,
some of them wounded, some pierced from front to back,
some with their heads hacked off. So says the Geste,
and so says one who was there, on that field,   2095
the baron Saint Gilles,[3] for whom God performs miracles,
who made the charter setting forth these great things
in the Church of Laon. Now any man
who does not know this much understands nothing.

156

Roland the Count fights well and with great skill,
but he is hot, his body soaked with sweat;   2100
has a great wound in his head, and much pain,
his temple broken because he blew the horn.
But he must know whether King Charles will come;

---

3. St. Gilles of Provence. These lines explain how the story of Rencesvals could be told after all
who had fought there died.

draws out the olifant, sounds it, so feebly.
The Emperor drew to a halt, listened.   2105
"Seigneurs," he said, "it goes badly for us—
My nephew Roland falls from our ranks today.
I hear it in the horn's voice: he hasn't long.
Let every man who wants to be with Roland
ride fast! Sound trumpets! Every trumpet in this host!"   2110
Sixty thousand, on these words, sound, so high
the mountains sound, and the valleys resound.
The pagans hear: it is no joke to them;
cry to each other: "We're getting Charles on us!"

157

The pagans say: "The Emperor is coming, AOI.   2115
listen to their trumpets—it is the French!
If Charles comes back, it's all over for us,
if Roland lives, this war begins again
and we have lost our land, we have lost Spain."
Some four hundred, helmets laced on, assemble,   2120
some of the best, as they think, on that field.
They storm Roland, in one fierce, bitter attack.
And now Count Roland has some work on his hands. AOI.

158

Roland the Count, when he sees them coming,
how strong and fierce and alert he becomes!   2125
He will not yield to them, not while he lives.
He rides the horse they call Veillantif, spurs,
digs into it with his spurs of fine gold,
and rushes at them all where they are thickest,
the Archbishop—that Turpin!—at his side.   2130
Said one man to the other: "Go at it, friend.
The horns we heard were the horns of the French,
King Charles is coming back with all his strength."[4]

159

Roland the Count never loved a coward,
a blusterer, an evil-natured man,   2135
a man on horse who was not a good vassal.
And now he called to Archbishop Turpin:
"You are on foot, Lord, and here I am mounted,
and so, here I take my stand: for love of you.
We'll take whatever comes, the good and bad,   2140
together, Lord: no one can make me leave you.
They will learn our swords' names today in battle,
the name of Almace, the name of Durendal!"
Said the Archbishop: "Let us strike or be shamed!
Charles is returning, and he brings our revenge."   2145

4. The lines could be spoken either by Roland and the archbishop or by the pagans.

160

Say the pagans: "We were all born unlucky!
The evil day that dawned for us today!
We have lost our lords and peers, and now comes Charles—
that Charlemagne!—with his great host. Those trumpets!
that shrill sound on us—the trumpets of the French!   2150
And the loud roar of that Munjoie! This Roland
is a wild man, he is too great a fighter—
What man of flesh and blood can ever hope
to bring him down? Let us cast at him, and leave him there."
And so they did: arrows, wigars, darts,   2155
lances and spears, javelots[5] dressed with feathers;
struck Roland's shield, pierced it, broke it to pieces,
ripped his hauberk, shattered its rings of mail,
but never touched his body, never his flesh.
They wounded Veillantif in thirty places,   2160
struck him dead, from afar, under the Count.
The pagans flee, they leave the field to him.
Roland the Count stood alone, on his feet. AOI.

161

The pagans flee, in bitterness and rage,
strain every nerve running headlong toward Spain,   2165
and Count Roland has no way to chase them,
he has lost Veillantif, his battle horse;
he has no choice, left alone there on foot.
He went to the aid of Archbishop Turpin,
unlaced the gold-dressed helmet, raised it from his head,   2170
lifted away his bright, light coat of mail,
cut his under tunic into some lengths,
stilled his great wounds with thrusting on the strips;
then held him in his arms, against his chest,
and laid him down, gently, on the green grass;   2175
and softly now Roland entreated him:
"My noble lord, I beg you, give me leave:
our companions, whom we have loved so dearly,
are all dead now, we must not abandon them.
I want to look for them, know them once more,   2180
and set them in ranks, side by side, before you."
Said the Archbishop: "Go then, go and come back.
The field is ours, thanks be to God, yours and mine."

162

So Roland leaves him, walks the field all alone,
seeks in the valleys, and seeks in the mountains.   2185
He found Gerin, and Gerer his companion,
and then he found Berenger and Otun,
Anseïs and Sansun, and on that field

5. Small spears or javelins.

he found Gerard the old of Roussillon;
and carried them, brave man, all, one by one,   2190
came back to the Archbishop with these French dead,
and set them down in ranks before his knees.
The Archbishop cannot keep from weeping,
raises his hand and makes his benediction;
and said: "Lords, Lords, it was your terrible hour.   2195
May the Glorious God set all your souls
among the holy flowers of Paradise!
Here is my own death, Lords, pressing on me,
I shall not see our mighty Emperor."

163

And Roland leaves, seeks in the field again;   2200
he has found Oliver, his companion,
held him tight in his arms against his chest;
came back to the Archbishop, laid Oliver
down on a shield among the other dead.
The Archbishop absolved him, signed him with the Cross.   2205
And pity now and rage and grief increase;
and Roland says: "Oliver, dear companion,
you were the son of the great duke Renier,
who held the march of the vale of Runers.
Lord, for shattering lances, for breaking shields,   2210
for making men great with presumption weak with fright,
for giving life and counsel to good men,
for striking fear in that unbelieving race,
no warrior on earth surpasses you."

164

Roland the Count, when he sees his peers dead,   2215
and Oliver, whom he had good cause to love,
felt such grief and pity, he begins to weep;
and his face lost its color with what he felt:
a pain so great he cannot keep on standing,
he has no choice, falls fainting to the ground.   2220
Said the Archbishop: "Baron, what grief for you."

165

The Archbishop, when he saw Roland faint,
felt such pain then as he had never felt;
stretched out his hand and grasped the olifant.
At Rencesvals there is a running stream: 2225
he will go there and fetch some water for Roland;
and turns that way, with small steps, staggering;
he is too weak, he cannot go ahead,
he has no strength: all the blood he has lost.
In less time than a man takes to cross a little field   2230
that great heart fails, he falls forward, falls down;
and Turpin's death comes crushing down on him.

166

Roland the Count recovers from his faint,
gets to his feet, but stands with pain and grief;
looks down the valley, looks up the mountain, sees: 2235
on the green grass, beyond his companions,
that great and noble man down on the ground,
the Archbishop, whom God sent in His name;
who confesses his sins, lifts up his eyes,
holds up his hands joined together to heaven, 2240
and prays to God: grant him that Paradise.
Turpin is dead, King Charles' good warrior.
In great battles, in beautiful sermons
he was ever a champion against the pagans.
Now God grant Turpin's soul His holy blessing. AOI. 2245

167

Roland the Count sees the Archbishop down,
sees the bowels fallen out of his body,
and the brain boiling down from his forehead.
Turpin has crossed his hands upon his chest
beneath the collarbone, those fine white hands. 2250
Roland speaks the lament, after the custom
followed in his land: aloud, with all his heart:
"My noble lord, you great and well-born warrior,
I commend you today to the God of Glory,
whom none will ever serve with a sweeter will. 2255
Since the Apostles no prophet the like of you[6]
arose to keep the faith and draw men to it.
May your soul know no suffering or want,
and behold the gate open to Paradise."

168

Now Roland feels that death is very near. 2260
His brain comes spilling out through his two ears;
prays to God for his peers: let them be called;
and for himself, to the angel Gabriel;
took the olifant: there must be no reproach!
took Durendal his sword in his other hand, 2265
and farther than a crossbow's farthest shot
he walks toward Spain, into a fallow land,
and climbs a hill: there beneath two fine trees
stand four great blocks of stone, all are of marble;
and he fell back, to earth, on the green grass, 2270
has fainted there, for death is very near.

169

High are the hills, and high, high are the trees;
there stand four blocks of stone, gleaming of marble.

---

6. Cf. Deuteronomy 34.10, on the death of Moses: "And there arose not a prophet since in
Israel like unto Moses, whom the Lord knew face to face."

Count Roland falls fainting on the green grass,
and is watched, all this time, by a Saracen: 2275
who has feigned death and lies now with the others,
has smeared blood on his face and on his body;
and quickly now gets to his feet and runs—
a handsome man, strong, brave, and so crazed with pride
that he does something mad and dies for it: 2280
laid hands on Roland, and on the arms of Roland,
and cried: "Conquered! Charles's nephew conquered!
I'll carry this sword home to Arabia!"
As he draws it, the Count begins to come round.

170

Now Roland feels: *someone taking his sword!*   2285
opened his eyes, and had one word for him:
"I don't know you, you aren't one of ours";
grasps that olifant that he will never lose,
strikes on the helm beset with gems in gold,
shatters the steel, and the head, and the bones,   2290
sent his two eyes flying out of his head,
dumped him over stretched out at his feet dead;
and said: "You nobody! how could you dare
lay hands on me—rightly or wrongly: how?
Who'll hear of this and not call you a fool?   2295
Ah! the bell-mouth of the olifant is smashed,
the crystal and the gold fallen away."

171

Now Roland the Count feels: his sight is gone;
gets on his feet, draws on his final strength,
the color on his face lost now for good.   2300
Before him stands a rock; and on that dark rock
in rage and bitterness he strikes ten blows:
the steel blade grates, it will not break, it stands unmarked.
"Ah!" said the Count, "Blessed Mary, your help!
Ah Durendal, good sword, your unlucky day,   2305
for I am lost and cannot keep you in my care.
The battles I have won, fighting with you,
the mighty lands that holding you I conquered,
that Charles rules now, our King, whose beard is white!
Now you fall to another: it must not be
a man who'd run before another man!   2310
For a long while a good vassal held you:
there'll never be the like in France's holy land."

172

Roland strikes down on that rock of Cerritania:
the steel blade grates, will not break, stands unmarked.
Now when he sees he can never break that sword,   2315
Roland speaks the lament, in his own presence:
"Ah Durendal, how beautiful and bright!

so full of light, all on fire in the sun!
King Charles was in the vales of Moriane
when God sent his angel and commanded him,   2320
from heaven, to give you to a captain count.
That great and noble King girded it on me.
And with this sword I won Anjou and Brittany,
I won Poitou, I won Le Maine for Charles,
and Normandy, that land where men are free,   2325
I won Provence and Aquitaine with this,
and Lombardy, and every field of Romagna,
I won Bavaria, and all of Flanders,
all of Poland, and Bulgaria, for Charles,
Constantinople, which pledged him loyalty,   2330
and Saxony, where he does as he wills;
and with this sword I won Scotland and Ireland,
and England, his chamber, his own domain—
the lands, the nations I conquered with this sword,
for Charles, who rules them now, whose beard is white!   2335
Now, for this sword, I am pained with grief and rage:
Let it not fall to pagans! Let me die first!
Our Father God, save France from that dishonor."

173

Roland the Count strikes down on a dark rock,
and the rock breaks, breaks more than I can tell,   2340
and the blade grates, but Durendal will not break,
the sword leaped up, rebounded toward the sky.
The Count, when he sees that sword will not be broken,
softly, in his own presence, speaks the lament:
"Ah Durendal, beautiful, and most sacred,   2345
the holy relics in this golden pommel!
Saint Peter's tooth and blood of Saint Basile,
a lock of hair of my lord Saint Denis,
and a fragment of blessed Mary's robe:
your power must not fall to the pagans,   2350
you must be served by Christian warriors.
May no coward ever come to hold you!
It was with you I conquered those great lands
that Charles has in his keeping, whose beard is white,
the Emperor's lands, that make him rich and strong."   2355

174

Now Roland feels: death coming over him,
death descending from his temples to his heart.
He came running underneath a pine tree
and there stretched out, face down, on the green grass,
lays beneath him his sword and the olifant.   2360
He turned his head toward the Saracen hosts,
and this is why: with all his heart he wants
King Charles the Great and all his men to say,
he died, that noble Count, a conqueror;

makes confession, beats his breast often, so feebly,   2365
offers his glove, for all his sins, to God. AOI.

175

Now Roland feels that his time has run out;
he lies on a steep hill, his face toward Spain;
and with one of his hands he beat his breast:
"Almighty God, *mea culpa* in thy sight,[7]
forgive my sins, both the great and the small,   2370
sins I committed from the hour I was born
until this day, in which I lie struck down."
And then he held his right glove out to God.
Angels descend from heaven and stand by him. AOI.   2375

176

Count Roland lay stretched out beneath a pine;
he turned his face toward the land of Spain,
began to remember many things now:
how many lands, brave man, he had conquered;
and he remembered: sweet France, the men of his line,   2380
remembered Charles, his lord, who fostered him:
cannot keep, remembering, from weeping, sighing;
but would not be unmindful of himself:
he confesses his sins, prays God for mercy:
"Loyal Father, you who never failed us,   2385
who resurrected Saint Lazarus from the dead,
and saved your servant Daniel from the lions:[8]
now save the soul of me from every peril
for the sins I committed while I still lived."
Then he held out his right glove to his Lord: 2390
Saint Gabriel took the glove from his hand.
He held his head bowed down upon his arm,
he is gone, his two hands joined, to his end.
Then God sent him his angel Cherubin[9]
and Saint Michael, angel of the sea's Peril;   2395
and with these two there came Saint Gabriel:
they bear Count Roland's soul to Paradise.

177

Roland is dead, God has his soul in heaven.
The Emperor rides into Rencesvals;
there is no passage there, there is no track,   2400
no empty ground, not an elle,[1] not one foot,
that does not bear French dead or pagan dead.
King Charles cries out: "Dear Nephew, where are you?
Where is the Archbishop? Count Oliver?

7. See Psalm 51.4: "Against thee, thee only,   9. The poet seems to have regarded this as the
have I sinned, and done this evil in thy sight."   name of a single angel, though "cherubim" is the
8. See Daniel 6.12–23. For the raising of   plural of "cherub."
Lazarus, see John 11.1–44.   1. That is, an ell (45 inches).

Where is Gerin, his companion Gerer? 2405
Where is Otun, where is Count Berenger,
Yves and Yvoire, men I have loved so dearly?
What has become of Engeler the Gascon,
Sansun the Duke, and Anseïs, that fighter?
Where is Gerard the Old of Roussillon, 2410
and the Twelve Peers, whom I left in these passes?"
And so forth—what's the difference? No one answered.
"God!" said the King, "how much I must regret
I was not here when the battle began";
pulls his great beard, a man in grief and rage. 2415
His brave knights weep, their eyes are filled with tears,
twenty thousand fall fainting to the ground;
Duke Naimon feels the great pity of it.

178

There is no knight or baron on that field
who does not weep in bitterness and grief; 2420
for they all weep: for their sons, brothers, nephew,
weep for their friends, for their sworn men and lords;
the mass of them fall fainting to the ground.
Here Naimon proved a brave and useful man:
he was the first to urge the Emperor: 2425
"Look ahead there, two leagues in front of us,
you can see the dust rising on those wide roads:
the pagan host—and how many they are!
After them now! Ride! Avenge this outrage!"
"Oh! God!" said Charles, "look how far they have gotten! 2430
Lord, let me have my right, let me have honor,
they tore from me the flower of sweet France."
The King commands Gebuïn and Othon,
Thibaut of Reims and Count Milun his cousin:
"Now guard this field, the valleys, the mountains, 2435
let the dead lie, all of them, as they are,
let no lion, let no beast come near them,
let no servant, let no groom come near them,
I command you, let no man come near these dead
until God wills we come back to this field." 2440
And they reply, gently, and in great love:
"Just Emperor, dear Lord, we shall do that."
They keep with them a thousand of their knights. AOI.

179

The Emperor has his high-pitched trumpets sound,
and then he rides, brave man, with his great host. 2445
They made the men of Spain show them their heels,
and they keep after them, all as one man.
When the King sees the twilight faltering,
he gets down in a meadow on the green grass,
lies on the ground, prays to the Lord his God 2450
to make the sun stand still for him in heaven,

hold back the night, let the day linger on.
Now comes the angel[2] always sent to speak with Charles;
and the angel at once commanded him:
"Charles, ride: God knows. The light will not fail you.   2455
God knows that you have lost the flower of France.
You can take vengeance now on that criminal race."
The Emperor, on that word, mounts his horse. AOI.

180

God made great miracles for Charlemagne,
for on that day in heaven the sun stood still.   2460
The pagans flee, the Franks keep at their heels,
catch up with them in the Vale Tenebrous,
chase them on spurring hard to Saragossa,
and always killing them, striking with fury;
cut off their paths, the widest roads away: 2465
the waters of the Ebro lie before them,
very deep, an amazing sight, and swift;
and there is no boat, no barge, no dromond,[3] no galley.
They call on Tervagant, one of their gods.
Then they jump in, but no god is with them: 2470
those in full armor, the ones who weigh the most,
sank down, and they were many, to the bottom;
the others float downstream: the luckiest ones,
who fare best in those waters, have drunk so much,
they all drown there, struggling, it is amazing.   2475
The French cry out: "Curse the day you saw Roland!" AOI.

181

When Charlemagne sees all the pagans dead,
many struck down, the great mass of them drowned—
the immense spoils his knights win from that battle!—
the mighty King at once gets down on foot,   2480
lies on the ground, and gives thanks to the Lord.
When he stands up again, the sun has set.
Said the Emperor: "It is time to make camp.
It is late now to return to Rencesvals;
our horses are worn out, they have no strength—   2485
take off their saddles, the bridles on their heads,
let them cool down and rest in these meadows."
The Franks reply: "Yes, as you well say, Lord." AOI.

182

The Emperor commands them to make camp.
The French dismount into that wilderness;   2490
they have removed the saddles from their horses,
and the bridles, dressed in gold, from their heads,
free them to the meadows and the good grass;

2. Gabriel. Cf. *laisses* 185, 291, and others.
3. A very large ship, with oarsmen and a single sail.

and that is all the care they can give them.
Those who are weary sleep on the naked earth;   2495
and all sleep, they set no watch that night.

183

The Emperor lay down in a meadow,
puts his great spear, brave man, beside his head;
he does not wish, on this night, to disarm:
he has put on his bright, brass-sewn hauberk,   2500
laced on his helm, adorned with gems in gold,
and girded on Joiuse, there never was its like:
each day it shines with thirty different lights.
There are great things that we can say about the lance
with which Our Lord was wounded on the Cross:[4]   2505
thanks be to God, Charles has its iron point,
he had it mounted in that sword's golden pommel.
For this honor, and for this mighty grace,
the name Joiuse[5] was given to that sword.
Brave men of France must never forget this: 2510
from this sword's name they get their cry Munjoie![6]
This is why no nation can withstand them.

184

The night is clear, the moon is shining bright,
Charles lies down in grief and pain for Roland,
and for Oliver, it weighs down on him hard,   2515
for the Twelve Peers, for all the men of France
whom he left dead, covered with blood, at Rencesvals;
and cannot keep from weeping, wailing aloud,
and prays to God: lead their souls to safety.
His weariness is great, for his pain is great;   2520
he has fallen asleep, he cannot go on.
Through all the meadows now the Franks are sleeping.
There is no horse that has the strength to stand:
if one wants grass, he grazes lying down.
He has learned much who knows much suffering.   2525

185

Charlemagne sleeps, a man worn out with pain.
God sent Saint Gabriel to him that night
with this command: watch over the Emperor.
All through the night the angel stands at his head;
and in a vision he brought the King dread tidings   2530
of a great battle soon to come against him:
revealed to him its grave signification:
Charles raised his eyes and looked up to the sky,
he sees the thunder, the winds, the blasts of ice,
the hurricanes, the dreadful tempests,   2535

4. See John 19.34.   6. My joy!
5. Joyful.

the fires and flames made ready in the sky.
And suddenly all things fall on his men.
Their lances burn, the wood of ash and apple,
and their shields burn down to their golden bosses,
the shafts of their sharp spears burst into pieces,   2540
then the grating of hauberks, helmets of steel.
He sees his warriors in great distress—
leopards and bears furious to devour them,
serpents, vipers, dragons, demons of hell,
swarms of griffins, thirty thousand and more,   2545
and all come swooping down upon the French;
and the French cry: "Charlemagne, come help us!"
The King is filled with rage and pain and pity,
wants to go there, but something blocks his way:
out of a wood a great lion coming at him,   2550
it is tremendous, wild, and great with pride:
seeks the King's very body, attacks the King!
and they lock arms, King and lion, to fight,
and still he cannot tell who strikes, who falls.
The Emperor sleeps, his dream does not wake him.   2555

186

And after this he was shown another vision:
he was in France, at Aix, on a stone step,
and two chains in his hands holding a bear;
from the Ardennes he saw thirty bears coming,
and each of them was speaking like a man;   2560
they said to him: "Lord, give him back to us,
you must not keep him longer, it is not right;
he is our kin, we must deliver him."
From his palace a greyhound now, running,
leaps on the greatest bear among them all,   2565
on the green grass beyond his companions,
there the King sees an amazing struggle
but cannot tell who conquers, who goes down.
These are the things God's angel showed this baron.
Charles sleeps until the morning and the bright day.   2570

[Lines 2571–3675 describe the death of Marsilion and Charlemagne's defeat of the army of
Baligant, the emir of Cairo and Marsilion's overlord.]

267

Night passes on, and the bright day appears.
Charles fortified the towers of Saragossa,
left a thousand knights there, fighting men all;
they guard the city in the Emperor's name.
Now the King mounts his horse, all his men mount,   3680
and Bramimunde, whom he leads prisoner,
though he has but one will: to do her good.
They turn toward home, in joy, in jubilation,
and pass in force, a mighty host, through Nerbone;

and Charles came to Bordeaux, that . . . city, sets[7]   3685
on the altar of the baron saint Sevrin
the olifant, filled with gold and pagan coins—
pilgrims passing can see it there today;
crosses the Gironde in great ships that lie there;
he has escorted as far as Blaye his nephew   3690
and Oliver, his noble companion,
and the Archbishop, who was so wise and brave;
and bids these lords be laid in white stone coffins:
at Saint-Romain the brave men lie there still;
the Franks leave them to the Lord and His Names.[8]   3695
And Charles rides over the valleys and the mountains,
would take no rest all the long way to Aix,
and rode until he dismounts at the steps.
When he is in his sovereign high palace,
he summons all his judges, sends messengers: 3700
Saxons, Bavarians, Frisians, men of Lorraine,
the Alemans, the men of Burgundy,
the Poitevins, the Normans, the Bretons,
the wisest men among the men of France.
And now begins the trial of Ganelon.   3705

268

The Emperor is home again from Spain,
and comes to Aix, best residence of France,
ascends to the palace; entered the hall.
And now comes Aude, fair maid, before the King;
and said to him: "Where is Roland the captain,   3710
who swore to me to take me for his wife?"
And Charlemagne feels the weight and grief of this,
tears fill his eyes, he weeps, pulls his white beard:
"Sweet friend, dear sister, you ask for a dead man.
I will give you a good man in his place,   3715
it is Louis, I cannot name a better—
he is my son, he will possess my marches."
And Aude replies: "How strange these words sound to me.
May it never please God or his angels or saints
that I should go on living after Roland";   3720
loses color, falls at Charlemagne's feet,
already dead, God take pity on her soul.
Brave men of France weep and lament for Aude.

269

Aude the fair maid is gone now to her end;
the King believes that she has only fainted;   3725
and he is moved, the Emperor weeps for Aude,
takes her two hands; now he has raised her up,

7. The line is incomplete in the manuscript.
8. A reference to prayers containing some of the many names (Adonai, Emmanuel, Yehovah, and so on) by which God is called in sacred writings. These prayers were considered effective in times of danger.

her head sinks down, fallen upon her shoulders;
when Charlemagne sees she is dead in his arms,
he has four countesses sent for at once,   3730
and Aude is borne to a minster of nuns;
all through the night till dawn they wake beside her,
then nobly buried her by an altar.
The King gave Aude great honors, the church great gifts. AOI.

270

The Emperor has come home again to Aix.   3735
In iron chains, the traitor Ganelon
stands before the palace, within the city.
He has been bound, and by serfs, to a stake;
they tie his hands with deerhide straps and thongs,
and beat him hard, with butcher's hooks, with clubs—   3740
for what better reward has this man earned?
There he stands, in pain and rage, awaiting his trial.

271

It is written in the ancient Geste
that Charles summons his vassals from many lands;
they are gathered in the chapel at Aix,   3745
a high day this, a very solemn feast,
the feast, some say, of the baron saint Sylvester.[9]
Now here begin the trial and the pleadings
of Ganelon, who committed treason.
The Emperor has had this man brought forth. AOI.   3750

272

"Barons, my lords," said Charlemagne the King,
"judge what is right concerning Ganelon.
He was with me, came in my army to Spain,
and took from me twenty thousand of my French,
and my nephew, whom you'll not see again,   3755
and Oliver, brave man, born to the court,
and the Twelve Peers—betrayed them all for money."
Said Ganelon: "Let me be called a traitor
    if I hide what I did. It was Roland
who cheated me of gold and goods; and so I wanted
to make him suffer and die; and found the way.   3760
But treason, no—I'll grant no treason there!"
The Franks reply: "We shall take counsel now."

273

And there Ganelon stood, before the King,
breathing power—that lordly color on his face:
the image of a great man, had he been loyal.   3765
He sees his judges, he sees the men of France,
and his kinsmen, the thirty with him there;

9. The feast of Saint Sylvester, December 31.

then he cried out, with that great ringing voice:
"Barons, hear me, hear me for the love of God!
I was in that army with the Emperor   3770
and served him well, in love and loyalty.
Then his nephew Roland began to hate me,
and he doomed me to die an outrageous death:
I was sent as messenger to King Marsilion.
I used my wits, and I came back alive.   3775
Now I had challenged Roland, that great fighter,
and Oliver, and all of their companions:
King Charles heard it, and all his noble barons.
I took *revenge*, but there's no treason there."
The Franks reply: "We shall go into council."   3780

274

When Ganelon sees that his great trial commences,
he got his thirty kinsmen all around him.
There is one man the others listen to:
it is Pinabel of the castle of Sorence,
a man who counsels well and judges well,   3785
a valiant fighter—no man can win his arms. AOI.
Said Ganelon: "In you, friend . . .¹
free me from death and from this accusation!"
Said Pinabel: "You will soon be out of this.
Let one Frenchman dare sentence you to hang: 3790
once the Emperor sets us down man to man,
I will give him the lie with this steel sword."
And Ganelon, the Count, falls at his feet.

275

Bavarians, Saxons have gone into council,
Poitevins and Normans and men of France,   3795
the Alemans, the Germans from the North,
men of Auvergne, the courtliest of all.
They keep their voices low, because of Pinabel;
said to each other: "Best to let it stop here—
let's leave this trial and then entreat the King   3800
to let Count Ganelon go free this time
and serve henceforth in love and loyalty.
Roland is dead: you won't see him again,
he will not come for gold or goods again:
only a fool would fight over this now."   3805
All go along, no one there disagrees
except one man, Lord Gefrei's brother: Tierri. AOI.

276

The barons now come back to Charlemagne,
say to the King: "Lord, this we beg of you:

1. The line is incomplete in the manuscript.

let Ganelon go free, renounce your claim,   3810
then let him serve you in love and loyalty:
let this man live, for his family is great.
Roland is dead: we'll not see a hair of him,
though we die for it, not a shred of his garment,
or get him back for gold or goods again."
And the King said: "You are all my traitors." AOI.   3815

277

When Charles perceives all have abandoned him,
he bowed his head with that and hid his face,
and in such pain calls himself wretched man.
But now we see: a warrior before him,
Tierri, brother of Gefrei, a duke of Anjou—   3820
the meager body on him, such a slight man!
his hair all black, and his face rather dark;
hardly a giant, but at least not too small;
said to the Emperor, as one born to the court:
"Dear Lord and King, do not lament before us.   3825
You know I have served you well: I have the right,
my forebears' right! to give this judgment here:
Whatever wrong Count Roland may have done
to Ganelon, he was in your service,
      and serving you should have protected him,
Ganelon is a traitor: he betrayed Roland.   3830
It's you he wronged when he perjured himself,
and broke faith. Therefore, I sentence him
to die, to hang . . . his body cast . . .²
like a traitor, a man who committed treason.
If his kinsman wants to give me the lie,   3835
here is my sword, girded on: and with this sword
I am ready to make my judgment good."
The Franks reply: "Now you have spoken well."

278

Now Pinabel has come before the King:
a huge man of swift grace, a valiant man—   3840
time has run out for the poor wretch he strikes!—
said to the King: "Lord, is this not your court?
Give orders then, tell them to stop this noise.
Here I see Tierri, who has given his judgment:
I declare it is false; I shall fight with him";   3845
places his deerhide glove in Charles's fist.
Said the Emperor: "I must have good surety."
Thirty kinsmen go hostage for his loyalty.
Then the King said: "I shall release him then";
and has them guarded until justice is done. AOI.   3850

---

2. The line is incomplete in the manuscript.

279

When Tierri sees the battle will take place
he gave to Charles his own right glove as gage.
The Emperor sets him free, for hostages;
then has four benches set round that battle ground:
there they will sit: the two men pledged to fight.   3855
The others judge they have been duly summoned,
Oger of Denmark had settled every question.
And then they call for their horses and arms.

280

Now since both men have been brought forth for battle, AOI.
they make confession and are absolved and blessed;   3860
they hear their mass, receive the Sacrament,
lay down great offerings in these minsters.
Now the two men have come back before Charles.
They have fastened their spurs upon their feet,
and they put on white hauberks, strong and light,   3865
and laced their bright helmets glowing upon their heads,
gird on their swords, the hilts of purest gold;
hang their great quartered shields upon their necks,
take hold of their sharp spears in their right fists;
now they are mounted upon their swift war horses.   3870
And then a hundred thousand warriors wept,
moved for love of Roland to pity Tierri.
The Lord well knows how this battle will end.

281

Down below Aix there is a broad meadow;
there the battle is joined between these barons.   3875
They are brave men, great warriors keeping faith,
and their horses are swift and spirited.
They spur them hard, reins loosened all the way,
come on to strike, the great strength that is theirs!
their two shields burst in that attack to pieces,   3880
their hauberks tear, their saddle girths rip open,
the bosses turn, the saddles fall to earth.
A hundred thousand men, who watch them, weep.

282

Now the two warriors are on the ground, AOI.
now on their feet, and with what speed! again—   3885
the grace and lightness, the strength of Pinabel!—
fall on each other, they have no horses now,
strike with their swords, the hilts of purest gold,
and strike again on these helmets of steel
tremendous blows—blows that cut through helms of steel!   3890
The knights of France are wild with grief and worry.
"Oh, God," said Charles, "make the right between them clear!"

283

Said Pinabel: "Tierri, now give it up!
I'll be your man, in love and loyalty,
I'll give you all I own, take what you please,   3895
only make peace with the King for Ganelon."
Tierri replies: "I cannot hear of that,
call me traitor if I consent to that!
May God do right between us two today." AOI.

284

Now Tierri spoke: "Pinabel, you are good,   3900
the great body on you formed like a lord's;
your peers know you: all that a vassal should be;
let this battle go then, let it end here,
I will make peace for you with Charlemagne.
But justice will be done on Ganelon,
such justice will be done on his body,   3905
no day will pass that men do not speak of it."
Said Pinabel: "May the Lord God forbid!
I will stand up for all my kin, I'll fight,
no man alive will make me quit my kin
and cry defeat and beg for his mercy,
I'd sooner die than be reproached for that."   3910
And they begin to beat down with their swords
on these helmets beset with gems in gold,
and the bright fires fly from that fight toward heaven;
and no chance now that these two can be parted:
it cannot end without one of them dead. AOI.   3915

285

Pinabel of Sorence, that valiant man,
strikes Tierri now on that helm of Provence:
the fire shoots out and sets the grass aflame;
and shows Tierri the point of that steel sword:
he brought it down. Pinabel brought it down   3920
on his forehead, and down across his face,
the whole right cheek is bloody from that blow,
his hauberk runs with blood down to his waist.
God protects him, he is not struck down dead. AOI.

286

And Tierri sees: he is struck on the face—   3925
the bright blood falling on the grass in the meadow;
strikes Pinabel on his helm of bright steel,
and shattered it, split it to the nosepiece,
struck his brain out spattering from his head;
and raised his sword; he has cast him down, dead.   3930
That was the blow, and the battle is won.
The Franks cry out: "God has made a miracle!
Now Ganelon must hang, it is right now,
and all his kin who stood for him in court." AOI.

287

Now when Tierri had won his great battle,   3935
there came to him the Emperor Charlemagne,
and forty of his barons along with him,
Naimon the Duke, and Oger of Denmark,
William of Blaye, and Gefrei of Anjou.
The King has taken Tierri into his arms,   3940
he wipes his face with his great furs of marten,
throws them aside; they clasp new furs round him.
Very gently, they disarm the warrior,
then they mount him on a mule of Araby,
and he comes home in joy among brave men.   3945
They come to Aix, it is there they dismount.
It is the time now for the executions.

288

Now Charlemagne summons his counts and dukes:
"What is your counsel regarding those I have held?
They came to court to stand for Ganelon,   3950
bound themselves hostages for Pinabel."
The Franks reply: "Not one of them must live."
The King commands his officer, Basbrun:
"Go, hang them all on the accursed tree,
and by this beard, by the white hairs in this beard,   3955
if one escapes, you are lost, a dead man."
Basbrun replies: "What should I do but hang them?";
leads them, by force, with a hundred sergeants.
They are thirty men, and thirty men are hanged.
A traitor brings death, on himself and on others. AOI.   3960

289

Bavarians and Alemans returned,
and Poitevins, and Bretons, and Normans,
and all agreed, the Franks before the others,
Ganelon must die, and in amazing pain.
Four war horses are led out and brought forward;   3965
then they attach his two feet, his two hands.
These battle horses are swift and spirited,
four sergeants come and drive them on ahead
toward a river in the midst of a field.
Ganelon is brought to terrible perdition,   3970
all his mighty sinews are pulled to pieces,
and the limbs of his body burst apart;
on the green grass flows that bright and famous blood.
Ganelon died a traitor's and recreant's death.
Now when one man betrays another,
it is not right that he should live to boast of it.   3975

290

When the Emperor had taken his revenge,
he called to him his bishops of France,

Bavaria, Germany: "In my household
there is a noble captive, and she has heard,
for so long now, such sermons and examples,   3980
she longs for faith in God, the Christian faith.
Baptize this Queen, that God may have her soul."
And they reply: "Let her be baptized now
by godmothers, ladies of noble birth."
At the baths of Aix there is a great crowd gathered,   3985
there they baptized the noble Queen of Spain,
and they found her the name Juliana;
she is Christian, by knowledge of the Truth.

291

When the Emperor had brought his justice to pass
and peace comes now to that great wrath of his,   3990
he put the Christian faith in Bramimunde;
the day passes, the soft night has gathered,
the King lay down in his vaulted chamber.
Saint Gabriel! come in God's name to say:
"Charles, gather the great hosts of your Empire!   3995
Go to the land of Bire, with all your force,
you must relieve King Vivien at Imphe,
the citadel, pagans have besieged it:
Christians are calling you, they cry your name!"
The Emperor would have wished not to go.   4000
"God!" said the King, "the pains, the labors of my life!";
weeps from his eyes, pulls his white beard.

Here ends the song   that Turold composes, paraphrases, amplifies,[3]
     that Turold completes, relates,
Here ends the tale   that Turold declaims, recounts, narrates,
     that Turold copies, transcribes,
Here ends the geste   for Turold grows weak, grows weary, declines,
Here ends the written history,
Here ends the source   that Turold turns into poetry.

---

3. The last line of the poem reads "Ci falt la geste que Turoldus declinet." The meaning of the words *geste* and *declinet* and the syntax of *que* have never been finally settled, and no line in the poem contains so many possible meanings as the last one. Some of the interpretations that have been proposed are given here, and every one is plausible.

PETRUS ALFONSI
1062–after 1116

etrus Alfonsi was a man of three worlds. Born a Sephardic Jew named Moses, he was educated in both Hebrew and Arabic and may have been a physician attached to one of the Islamic courts in al-Andalus (modern Spain). After migrating to England, Petrus made a strong impact on the history of science as well as literary history: the data he provided from Arabic sources played a vital role in the early development of astronomy, while his frame-tale narrative, the *Disciplina Clericalis* (*The Scholar's Guide*), was a conduit for the transmission of Eastern wisdom literature into Europe.

In 1106, Petrus converted to Christianity while living at Huesca, the capital of Aragon; he took his new first name from St. Peter, on whose feast day he was baptized, and his new second name from his godfather, King Alfonso I. Sometime during the decade following his conversion, he moved to England, where he was likely attached to the court of Henry I, King of England and Duke of Normandy. Living in both England and France, Petrus was a member of a circle of scientists and philosophers who were laying the foundation for the twelfth-century rebirth of scientific learning and, within the next century, the revival of Aristotelianism. He produced a translation into Latin from Arabic of astronomical tables, which provided the information needed to calculate the movement of the planets, eclipses of the sun and moon, and other cosmological phenomena.

Petrus wrote two major works, the *Disciplina Clericalis* and the *Dialogi contra Iudaeos* (*Dialogues against the Jews*). The latter work is a dialogue between Peter and himself—or, more precisely, between Moses (his old self, before his conversion) and the newly Christian Peter. Though there are only two parties in the dialogue, they debate three religious options: whether it is best to be a Jew, a Christian, or a Muslim. In this work, which greatly influenced later anti-Jewish polemics, Petrus Alfonsi displays a detailed knowledge of all three monotheistic religions.

His *Disciplina Clericalis* (sometimes translated as *The Scholar's Guide*), the work selected here, also takes the form of a dialogue, but the exchange is not confrontational: instead, it is the familiar and affectionate back-and-forth of an Arab father and his son, who also share the relationship of teacher and student. Like Petrus Alfonsi's earlier work, the *Disciplina Clericalis* displays an eclectic range of knowledge, but with a tone of tolerance rather than of religious polemic. It is the first frame-tale narrative to make its way from its Indian, Persian, and Arabic origins into the literature of the Latin West, paving the way for such later European story collections as Boccaccio's **Decameron**, Chaucer's **Canterbury Tales**, and **Christine de Pizan's City of Ladies**. Drawing on story traditions found in the **Pañcatantra** and the **Thousand and One Nights**, the *Disciplina Clericalis* recounts fantastic narratives of magic and mundane animal tales, snippets of Oriental Wisdom literature and comic anecdotes. The settings of the stories include the far-off regions of Baghdad, Babylon, and Mecca, as well as the more commonplace settings of the local marketplace and household.

Many manuscripts of the *Disciplina Clericalis* survive, along with a tremendous range of adaptations into vernacular languages: we have medieval versions, both in verse and prose, in French, Spanish, Catalan, Gascon, Italian, German, English, and Icelandic. These stories appealed to readers on a number of levels: they could be adapted as exemplary illustrations of moral truths, to be used in preaching, or they could simply be enjoyed as delightful narratives. Many of them found their way into other collections of tales: for example, the collection of **Aesop's** *Fables* published by the early English printer William Caxton includes stories from the *Disciplina Clericalis*.

Perhaps the most striking quality of the text, for modern readers as for medieval readers, appears in the correspondences between East and West that are threaded throughout the *Disciplina Clericalis*. When Petrus describes Balaam, a figure of the **Hebrew Bible** who also is found in Christian apocryphal traditions, he quickly adds that "in the Arabic language, he is called Luqman." Similarly, when he mentions the prophet Enoch, important in both Hebrew and Christian scripture, he explains that Enoch's other name is "Idris," the Islamic prophet described in sura 31 of the **Qur'an.** As a premodern figure standing at the crossroads of three religions and many cultures, Petrus Alfonsi offers a remarkable look into the complex and heterogeneous world of medieval Spain.

From The Scholar's Guide[1]

Prologue

Petrus Alfunsus, a servant of Jesus Christ and the author of this book, said: I give thanks to God, who is the first without beginning, the source of all good, the end without end, the fulfillment of all good, the all-knowing, who gives man knowledge and reason, who has favored us with His wisdom, enlightened us with the admirable clarity of His reason, and enriched us with the manifold grace of His Holy Spirit. And, because God has deigned to endow me, although a sinner, with wide learning, and so that the light entrusted to me may not remain hidden under a bushel,[2] inspired by the same Spirit, I have been impelled to compose this book for the benefit of many, begging Him to give a good end to this beginning of my little book and to guard me, lest anything be said in it which may displease His will. Amen. May God, therefore, who inspired me to compose this book and translate it into Latin, assist me in this modest work.

As I strove to know thoroughly the causes of the creation of man, frequently pondering them in my mind, I discovered that the human wit was intended, by order of its creator, to occupy itself, while it is in the world, in the study of holy philosophy, by means of which it acquires better and greater knowledge of its creator; that man should strive to live virtuously, guided by continence; learn to guard himself against the ever-present adversities; and walk in the path, in this world, which leads him to the Kingdom of Heaven. For, if he lives according to

---

1. Translated from the Latin by Joseph Ramon Jones and John Esten Keller.

2. See Matthew 5.14–16; Mark 4.21–22.

the aforementioned rule of holy discipline, he has fulfilled the end for which he was created and ought therefore to be called perfect.

I have also observed that the temperament of man is delicate; it must be instructed by being led, as it were, little by little, so that it will not become bored. I am mindful also of its hardness, which must to some extent be softened and sweetened, so that it may retain what it learns with greater facility, remembering that, as it is forgetful, it needs many things to help it remember what it tends to forget. For this reason I have compiled this small volume, taking it in part from the parables and counsels of the philosophers, in part from the parables and counsels of the Arabs, from tales and poems, and finally, from animal- and bird-fables. Nevertheless, I have taken pains to see that my writing may offer the readers and listeners a stimulus and an occasion to learn, knowing that if I should write more than is necessary, it might be a burden rather than an aid. The knowledgeable will remember what they have forgotten by means of the things which are contained here.

The title given to the book, taken from the subject itself, is THE SCHOLAR'S GUIDE, because it makes the scholar disciplined. And I have decided to avoid, as far as I am able, that anything should creep into my treatise which is contrary to our belief or repugnant to our faith. May God omnipotent, in whom I trust, help me in this task. Amen. If anyone examines this work with human and exterior eyes and finds in it something which human nature insufficiently guarded against, I advise him to read it again with sharper eye. And finally, I submit it for correction to him and to all those perfect in the Catholic faith. The philosopher believes that, in human writings, nothing is perfect.

ON THE FEAR OF GOD

The philosopher Enoch (who in Arabic is called Edric[3]), said to his son, "Let your concern be the fear of God, and wealth will come to you without toil."

Another wise man said, "All things fear him who fears God; he who does not fear God fears all things. He who fears God loves Him; he who loves Him, obeys Him."

An Arabic poet said, "You disobey God; you pretend, nevertheless, to love Him, which is incredible; for if you truly loved Him, you would obey Him; for he who loves, obeys."

ON HYPOCRISY

Socrates[4] said to his pupils, "Try not to be obedient and disobedient to God in the same matter."

They replied, "Explain your words."

And he answered them: "Avoid hypocrisy, which is pretending obedience to God in the sight of men and yet being disobedient in secret."

One of his disciples asked him, "Is there some other kind of hypocrisy which one should avoid?"

3. Idris; he is sometimes but not always (and certainly not in the Qur'an) identified with the Jewish prophet Enoch.

4. Greak philosopher (469–399 B.C.E.); his method of teaching through inquiry is recorded in Plato's dialogues.

Socrates answered, "There is the man who makes a show of obeying God in public as well as in private, in order to be taken for a saint by others and to be more honored by them. There is another cleverer than this one, who abandons this kind of hypocrisy in order to cultivate another greater kind: when he fasts or gives alms and someone asks whether he has done so, he will answer, 'God knows!' or, 'No,' in order to be held in greater reverence and so that people will say that he is not a hypocrite, since he does not want his good works known among men. I believe that there are very few who are not affected by some kind of hypocrisy. See to it that you are not seduced by it and deprived of the reward of your good works. To avoid this, do everything with pure intention, without seeking to acquire glory from your actions."

Another wise man says, "If you lean firmly on God, all things will prosper for you wherever you go."

THE ANT, THE COCK AND THE DOG

Balaam,[5] who is called Lucaman[6] in Arabic, said to his son, "Son, do not let the ant, who gathers in the summertime in order to have something to live on in winter, be wiser than you; do not let the cock, who wakes early in the morning while you sleep, be more vigilant than you; do not let the cock, who satisfies his ten wives, whereas you cannot control one, be stronger than you; do not let the dog, who does not forget his benefactors, though you forget yours, have a nobler heart than you; do not think that to have one enemy is a small number or a thousand friends too many. I will tell you a story:"

I. The Parable of the Half Friend

An Arab, on his deathbed, called his son and asked him, "How many friends have you acquired in your lifetime?"

The son answered, "I believe that I have a hundred friends."

The father said, "The wise man says, 'Do not praise your friend until you have tested him.' I was born before you, and I have scarcely acquired half a friend. How have you got a hundred? Go now and test them all, so that you may know whether any of them will turn out to be a whole friend."

The son asked, "How do you advise me to do it?"

The father said, "Kill a calf, cut it in pieces, and put it in a sack in such a way that the outside of the sack is bloodstained; and when you go to your friend, say, 'My good friend, I have killed a man by accident; I beg you to bury him secretly; no one will suspect you, and thus you will be able to save me.'"

The son did as his father commanded. The first friend to whom he went said to him, "Carry the dead man away on your own back. Since you did wrong, take your punishment. You will not enter my house."

---

5. The diviner or soothsayer in Numbers 22–24; his opposition to the people of Israel is largely ineffectual. Balaam does not appear by name in the Qur'an, but some commentators identify him with the man who fails to recog-nize the divine message at Qur'an 7.175–76. Few identify him with Luqman.

6. Traditional figure of wisdom, sometimes believed to be a prophet; sura 31 takes its name from him.

And when he did this to all his other friends, one by one, all gave him that same answer. He went back to his father and told him what he had done, and his father said, "It has happened to you as the wise man said: 'There are many who are called friends, but in time of necessity they are few.' And now go to my half friend and see what he says to you."

The son went to him and told him what he had told the others. The half friend said, "Come inside! This secret should be kept from the neighbors."

And then he sent his wife, with all his household, away, and he dug a grave. When the boy saw everything made ready, he revealed the truth of the matter to the half friend and thanked him earnestly. Then he recounted to his father what he had done.

The father said to him, "Regarding such a friend, the philosopher says, 'He who helps you when the world fails you is a true friend.'"

The son asked his father, "Have you ever seen a man who had a whole friend?"

The father: "I have not seen such a thing, but I have heard of it."

The son: "Tell me about it, in case I should acquire such a friend."

From II. The Parable of the Whole Friend

The father: Once there were two merchants, one in Egypt and another in Baldach.[7] They knew each other only by reputation, and they sent to each other by messenger for the things that they needed. It happened that the merchant from Baldach had to go to Egypt on business, and when the Egyptian merchant heard of his arrival, he ran out to meet him and received him into his house with great joy and served him in all things, as friends do, for eight days and entertained him with all sorts of music, which he maintained in his house.

At the end of the eight days, the merchant from Baldach fell sick. The master of the house, gravely worried about his friend, admitted all the doctors of Egypt to examine his guest. The doctors took his pulse and examined his urine again and again, but they could recognize no illness in him. And since they could find no bodily sickness in him, they knew that his suffering was due to love. When the Egyptian merchant learned this, he went to his friend and asked him if he were in love with some woman in the household.

The sick man said, "Show me all the women in your house, and if by chance I see her among them, I will point her out to you." When the Egyptian heard this, he brought out all the singers and serving women, but none pleased the friend. Then the Egyptian showed him all his daughters, but the friend rejected and ignored them completely, as he had the other women. The master, however, had in his house a young noblewoman whom he had been educating for some time, because he was planning to marry her. And he showed her to his sick friend.

The sick man, seeing her, said, "My death or life depends on her."

When he heard this, the Egyptian gave the young noblewoman to his friend for a wife, together with all the property which he himself would have received with her and with all the things which he would have given to the young woman if he had married her.

7. Baghdad.

When all these things had been accomplished, when the friend had married the girl and received all the things which came with her, and when he had finished his business, he returned to his own country.

Later, it happened that the Egyptian lost all that he had, and in great poverty, he decided to go to Baldach, so that his friend might have pity on him. Therefore naked and hungry, he made the journey to Baldach and arrived very late at night. Shame prevented his going to his friend's house, because he was afraid that if he were not recognized, he might perchance be driven out of the house. He therefore entered an ancient temple in order to pass the night there. And while he was there, unhappy and thinking many things to himself, near the temple in the city two men met and one killed the other and stealthily fled.

Many citizens, hearing the noise, came running and found the dead man. Seeking the person who had committed the murder, they entered the temple, expecting to find the murderer. There they found the Egyptian, and when they asked him who had killed the man, they heard from his own lips, "I killed him." (For he longed desperately to end his poverty at once by death.) They seized him and took him to jail.

When morning came, he was taken before the judges, and after he was condemned to death, he was led away to the cross. Many, as usual, had come to see the execution, and among them was the Egyptian's friend, the merchant on whose account he had come to Baldach. The merchant, looking at the condemned man closely, discovered that he was the friend whom he had left in Egypt. Realizing that if the Egyptian were to die, he would not be able to repay him, the merchant of Baldach determined to die in his place. He therefore exclaimed in a loud voice:

"Why do you condemn this innocent man? Where are you taking him? He does not deserve to die. I killed that man!"

And they seized him and led him, bound, to the cross and absolved the other from death.

But the murderer was in the crowd, observing these things and thinking to himself, "I killed that man and a guiltless man is condemned to death. This innocent man is sentenced to be punished, and I, a wicked man, enjoy freedom. What is the cause of this injustice? I do not know, unless it is God's patience. For God, the just judge, leaves no crime without punishment. I shall reveal myself as the perpetrator of this crime so that God will not punish me more severely at some later time. And thus, by freeing them from death, I shall atone for the sin which I committed."

He therefore exposed himself to danger, saying, "I did it, I did it! Free this innocent man!"

The judges, not a little amazed, bound the one and released the other. In doubt concerning the sentence, they brought the murderer and the other two who had already been freed, before the king. When they had told him everything, as it had happened, they caused even him to hesitate in judgment. On the advice of all, the king pardoned all three the crimes which they had committed, on the condition that they tell him the reason for their confessions. And they told the king the truth.

When all three had been released by common consent, the citizen of Baldach who had determined to die for his friend brought the Egyptian home and with every honor, according to custom, said to him: "If you agree to stay here with me, I will share all of my property with you, as is just. But if you should want to return to your country, we will divide equally all that I have."

And the Egyptian, who longed for his native land, accepted part of all the substance which his friend had offered him and then went back to his native land.

When the story had thus been told, the son said to the father, "Such a friend must be hard indeed to find!"

Another wise man said, concerning friends who have not been tested, "Guard yourself well from your enemies but a thousand times more carefully from your friends. For perhaps some day the friend may become an enemy, and then he will more easily be able to do you harm."

* * *

XI. The Parable of the Sword

It is told that a certain man, leaving on a journey, left his mother-in-law to guard his wife. The wife, however, was secretly in love with a young man and at once told her mother about it. The mother approved of the love affair and invited the young man to dinner. While they were eating, the husband returned and knocked at the door. The wife got up and went to open the door for her husband. The mother-in-law, remaining with her daughter's lover, did not know what to do, since there was no place to hide him. But while her daughter was opening the door for her husband, the old lady took an unsheathed sword, gave it to the young man, and ordered him to stand before the door where the husband would enter and not to answer if the husband said anything to him. He did as the old woman had ordered.

When the door had been opened and the husband saw the young man standing there, he stopped and asked, "Who are you?"

The young man did not answer, and the husband, who at first was surprised, began to be afraid.

The old lady said in a low voice, "Hush, dear son-in-law, so no one can hear you!" "What is it, dear lady?" he asked, even more amazed. The old lady: "My son, three men came here after this man, and we opened the door and let him come in with his sword until the men who wanted to kill him had left. He is afraid that you might be one of them, and he does not answer you for fright."

The husband replied to her, "You did well to save this man from death in that way."

And entering the house, he invited his wife's lover to sit down with him, and, reassuring him with pleasant conversation, he sent him on his way at night.

The pupil said, "You have told me surprising things about women, but what amazes me most is their presumptuous audaciousness. Nevertheless, if it is not too much trouble, I want you to tell me about their tricks. The more you tell me, the greater the reward you deserve."

To whom the teacher said, "Are these not enough for you? I have already told you three parables, and you still insist?"

The pupil replied, "When you say three parables, you exaggerate the number, for they were short ones. Now tell me a long story which will fill my ears and will thus satisfy me."

The teacher answered, "Be careful, so that what happened between a king and his story teller does not happen between us."

"What happened, dear teacher?"

"The following:"

XII. The Parable of the King and His Story Teller

A king had a story teller who usually told him five tales each night. It happened finally that the king, troubled with cares, could not sleep, and he ordered the story teller to tell him more tales. The story teller told him three more, but they were short, and the king asked for more. The story teller demurred because, as it seemed to him, he had already told a good many.

The king replied, "You have already told many, but they were very short. I want you to tell me a long one, and then I will let you go to bed."

The story teller agreed and began thus:

A peasant who had a thousand silver coins went to market and bought two thousand sheep, at six denarii[8] each. And when he was returning, it happened that the river was swollen with floodwaters, and he was not able to cross by the bridge or the ford. Worried, he began looking for a place where he could cross with his sheep. He finally found a small boat which would only hold two sheep and the shepherd at the same time. But driven by necessity, he put two sheep in the boat and crossed . . .

When the story teller had told this, he fell asleep.

The king woke him up so that he could finish the story that he had begun, and he said, "The river is very wide, the boat is very small, and the sheep are very numerous. Let the peasant ferry his sheep across first, and then I will finish the story."

And thus the story teller silenced the king who was eager to hear long tales.

"If you force me to invent more than the ones already told, I shall try to free myself by means of the stratagem of the tale just told."

Then the pupil said, "It is told in the ancient proverbs that he who weeps for pay does not feel the same grief as the man in bodily pain. And the story teller did not love the king as you love me. He wanted only to amuse him for a while with his stories, whereas you do not wish merely to amuse me, your pupil. Therefore I beg you not to stop the story-telling already begun but, on the contrary, to reveal women's tricks in detail."

From XIII. The Parable of the Weeping Bitch[9]

It is related that a nobleman had a very chaste and beautiful wife. He wanted to go to Rome to pray in the holy places, and he did not want to leave any other guardian for his wife but herself, trusting in her chaste habits and the honor of her uprightness. When the retinue was ready, he departed and the wife remained, living chastely and acting prudently in all things.

---

8. Silver Roman coins, reintroduced in the 8th century as the standard coin of Charle-magne's empire.
9. Female dog.

It happened that she needed something, and she left her own house and went to a neighboring house. As she came home after transacting her business, a young man saw her and fell madly in love with her. He, desiring to be loved by her for whom he burned so ardently, sent many messages to her. But she refused his messages and rejected him completely.

The young man seeing himself utterly scorned, grief-stricken, fell gravely ill; but nevertheless he would often go where he had seen his lady leave, hoping to meet her; but he was not able to effect it at all. Weeping for sorrow, he met an old woman wearing the habit of a nun, and she asked the cause of his unhappiness; but the young man was not very anxious to reveal what was going on in his mind.

The old woman said to him, "The longer a sick man delays in revealing his illness to the doctor, the more he will suffer from the illness."

Hearing this, he told her what had happened to him and his secret.

The old lady said to him, "With God's help I'll find a remedy for what you have told me."

And she left him and returned to her own house. She forced a little dog which she had at home to go without food for two days. On the third day she gave the hungry dog bread made with mustard, and as the dog ate the bread, its eyes began to water with the sharpness of the mustard. The old woman brought the little dog to the house of the chaste woman whom the young man loved, and the woman received her respectfully because of her very religious appearance. The little bitch was following the old woman. When the woman saw it weeping, she asked what was wrong with it and why it was crying.

The old woman said to her, "Dear friend, do not ask what is wrong, because the sorrow is so great that I can hardly talk about it."

And the woman begged her even more earnestly to tell her.

The old woman: "This little dog which you see was my daughter, who was very chaste and modest and was loved by a young man; but she was so chaste that she spurned him and rejected his love. The young man, pining away, became very ill. For her sin, my wretched daughter was turned into a little bitch." And so saying, the old lady burst into tears.

The decent woman said at this, "O dear lady, what shall I do? I am guilty of a similar crime; for a young man loves me, but because of my love of chastity I have disdained him, and he has also fallen ill."

"Dear friend, I advise you to have pity on him as quickly as possible and do what he asks, so that you may not be turned into a dog just as my daughter was. If I had known of the love between my daughter and the young man, my daughter would never have been transformed."

The chaste woman said to her, "I beg you to give me good advice, so that I may not be turned into a little bitch, deprived of my own form."

"Willingly," said the old woman, "for the love of God and the health of my soul and because I feel sorry for you, I will seek the young man, and if he can be found, I will bring him back to you."

The woman thanked her, and the wily old woman kept her word and brought back the young man, as she had promised and thus brought them together.

The pupil said to the teacher, "I have never heard anything so astounding, and I think it was done with black magic."

The teacher: "Have no doubt!"

The pupil: "I think that if any man is wise enough always to fear being deceived by women's tricks, perhaps he will be able to guard himself against them."

The teacher: "I know of a certain man who took great precautions to guard his wife; but he did not gain anything by it."

The pupil: "Tell me what he did, teacher, so I will be better able to guard my wife, if I ever marry."

MARIE DE FRANCE

1150?–1200?

"**M**arie ai num, si sui de France" (Marie is my name, and I am from France). With these words, the author of the *Lais* tells us her name and her homeland. Yet Marie was an English writer, composing in the Anglo-Norman dialect that had become the mother tongue of the English ruling classes following the Norman Conquest a century before. Her short, intense stories of love and loss reflect the complex cultural encounter of Celtic folktale, Anglo-French court setting, and English landscape, and they set the stage for the flowering of the romance genre in the last decades of the twelfth century.

We know little about Marie beyond what she herself tells us in the Prologue to her *Lais*, which is reprinted here, and in the closing lines of her collection of animal fables. She is likely to have been a nun—possibly an abbess in a position of authority within her community; in offering her collection of twelve *Lais* as a gift to Henry II, King of England and Duke of Normandy, she uses terms that presume some degree of familiarity, perhaps even a family relationship. It was not uncommon in twelfth-century Europe for the illegitimate female offspring of noble or royal figures to enter convents, less because these women were pious than because it was expedient to prevent them from marrying political rivals and bearing children who might complicate the smooth order of future succession. Marie's place in the world, attached at once to the cloister and to the court, may reflect some such family history.

In addition to her *Fables*, which she claims to have translated from a now-lost text by the Anglo-Saxon king Alfred, Marie's other surviving works include the mysterious journey to the afterlife recounted in *Saint Patrick's Purgatory* (adapted from a Latin original) and an account of the life and works of English saint Audrey. Her poems stand at the intersection of oral and written forms of literature, as well as at the crossroads of cultures—not just English and French, but Welsh or Breton as well. Celtic cultures had survived the warfare of English and French barons, both in the mountains of Wales and in

Cornwall, to the north of the English Channel, and in the upper regions of Normandy and Brittany, to the south. In her Prologue, Marie describes her desire to preserve these Breton songs: having heard them sung, she writes, "I don't want to neglect or forget them." She expresses a similar sentiment in the epilogue to her *Fables*, in which she tells the reader her own name "pur remembrance," "for remembrance." Through the *Lais*, Marie has ensured that both she and the ancient songs she has written down will live on in memory.

The two lais included here, "Lanval" and "Laüstic," represent two very different types: the first, more elaborate, offers a very fully developed psychology of the main characters, and the second, shorter and jewel-like, crystallizes an essential truth about the nature of love in poetic form. In "Lanval," we encounter the now-familiar world of Arthurian romance, with its tales of Arthur and Guenevere, Yvain and Gawain, and the hidden realm of Avalon. Yet Marie was the first to bring this oral Breton material into the mainstream of European literature, a move that was amplified by her French successor, Chrétien de Troyes (in his various Arthurian romances), and, later, by the anonymous English poet who wrote **Sir Gawain and the Green Knight** and by Thomas Malory in his *Morte d'Arthur*. In "Lanval," the realistic, practical world of the Arthurian court is suddenly punctured by the intrusion of the mysterious Otherworld when the knight's enigmatic lady appears to rescue her lover from the accusations of a false and potentially adulterous queen, and takes him home with her to Avalon.

"Laüstic" similarly recounts love's triumph, although here in a darker and more sorrowful vein. The affair of a woman and her husband's friend comes to a brutal end when the beautiful nightingale, whose nighttime song fuels the dreams of lovers, is killed by the jealous husband. The body of the bird becomes a token of their forbidden passion, first wrapped in an embroidered shroud by the lady, and then preserved in a begemmed reliquary by her lover. The miniature lai, like the miniature sarcophagus, remains as a potent reminder of the power of love.

From Lais[1]

Prologue

Whoever has received knowledge
and eloquence in speech from God
should not be silent or secretive
but demonstrate it willingly.
When a great good is widely heard of,   5
then, and only then, does it bloom,
and when that good is praised by many,
it has spread its blossoms.
The custom among the ancients—
as Priscian[2] testifies—   10
was to speak quite obscurely

---

1. Translated from the French by Robert Hanning and Joan Ferrante.

2. Latin grammarian (early 6th century C.E.), widely read in the Middle Ages.

in the books they wrote,
so that those who were to come after
and study them
might gloss the letter   15
and supply its significance from their own wisdom.
Philosophers knew this,
they understood among themselves
that the more time they spent,
the more subtle their minds would become   20
and the better they would know how to keep themselves
from whatever was to be avoided.
He who would guard himself from vice
should study and understand
and begin a weighty work   25
by which he might keep vice at a distance,
and free himself from great sorrow.
That's why I began to think
about composing some good stories
and translating from Latin to Romance;   30
but that was not to bring me fame:
too many others have done it.
Then I thought of the *lais* I'd heard.
I did not doubt, indeed I knew well,
that those who first began them   35
and sent them forth
composed them in order to preserve
adventures they had heard.
I have heard many told;
and I don't want to neglect or forget them.   40
To put them into word and rhyme
I've often stayed awake.

In your honor, noble King,[3]
who are so brave and courteous,
repository of all joys   45
in whose heart all goodness takes root,
I undertook to assemble these *lais*
to compose and recount them in rhyme.
In my heart I thought and determined,
sire, that I would present them to you.   50
If it pleases you to receive them,
you will give me great joy;
I shall be happy forever.
Do not think me presumptuous
if I dare present them to you.   55
Now hear how they begin.

---

3. Henry II, King of England, who also held substantial properties in France.

Lanval

I shall tell you the adventure of another *lai*,
just as it happened:
it was composed about a very noble vassal;
in Breton,[4] they call him Lanval.

Arthur, the brave and the courtly king,   5
was staying at Cardoel,[5]
because the Scots and the Picts
were destroying the land.
They invaded Logres[6]
and laid it waste.   10
At Pentecost,[7] in summer,
the king stayed there.
He gave out many rich gifts:
to counts and barons,
members of the Round Table[8]—   15
such a company had no equal in all the world—
he distributed wives and lands,
to all but one who had served him.
That was Lanval; Arthur forgot him,
and none of his men favored him either.   20
For his valor, for his generosity,
his beauty and his bravery,
most men envied him;
some feigned the appearance of love
who, if something unpleasant happened to him,   25
would not have been at all disturbed.
He was the son of a king of high degree
but he was far from his heritage.
He was of the king's household
but he had spent all his wealth,   30
for the king gave him nothing
nor did Lanval ask.
Now Lanval was in difficulty,
depressed and very worried.
My lords, don't be surprised: 35
a strange man, without friends,
is very sad in another land,
when he doesn't know where to look for help.
The knight of whom I speak,
who had served the king so long,   40
one day mounted his horse
and went off to amuse himself.

4. A Celtic language spoken in Brittany (a
region of modern northern France), closely
related to Welsh.
5. Carlisle, an English city on the border of
modern Scotland.
6. That is, England (a name often used in

tales of King Arthur).
7. A Christian feast day, observed seven Sundays after Easter.
8. King Arthur's legendary table, whose shape
symbolized the equality of every knight seated
at it.

He left the city
and came, all alone, to a field;
he dismounted by a running stream   45
but his horse trembled badly.
He removed the saddle and went off,
leaving the horse to roll around in the meadow.
He folded his cloak beneath his head
and lay down.   50
He worried about his difficulty,
he could see nothing that pleased him.
As he lay there
he looked down along the bank
and saw two girls approaching;   55
he had never seen any lovelier.
They were richly dressed,
tightly laced,
in tunics of dark purple;
their faces were very lovely.   60
The older one carried basins,
golden, well made, and fine;
I shall tell you the truth about it, without fail.
The other carried a towel.
They went straight   65
to where the knight was lying.
Lanval, who was very well bred,
got up to meet them.
They greeted him first
and gave him their message: 70
"Sir Lanval, my lady,
who is worthy and wise and beautiful,
sent us for you.
Come with us now.
We shall guide you there safely.   75
See, her pavilion is nearby!"
The knight went with them;
giving no thought to his horse
who was feeding before him in the meadow.
They led him up to the tent,   80
which was quite beautiful and well placed.
Queen Semiramis,[9]
however much more wealth,
power, or knowledge she had,
or the emperor Octavian[1]   85
could not have paid for one of the flaps.
There was a golden eagle on top of it,
whose value I could not tell,
nor could I judge the value of the cords or the poles
that held up the sides of the tent;   90

9. Legendary queen of Assyria (medieval Bab-   1. Augustus Caesar (63 B.C.E.–14 C.E.), the
ylon), renowned for her extravagance and her   first Roman emperor.
lust.

there is no king on earth who could buy it,
no matter what wealth he offered.
The girl was inside the tent:
the lily and the young rose
when they appear in the summer   95
are surpassed by her beauty.
She lay on a beautiful bed—
the bedclothes were worth a castle—
dressed only in her shift.
Her body was well shaped and elegant;   100
for the heat, she had thrown over herself,
a precious cloak of white ermine,
covered with purple alexandrine,[2]
but her whole side was uncovered,
her face, her neck and her bosom;   105
she was whiter than the hawthorn flower.
The knight went forward
and the girl addressed him.
He sat before the bed.
"Lanval," she said, "sweet love,   110
because of you I have come from my land;
I came to seek you from far away.
If you are brave and courtly,
no emperor or count or king
will ever have known such joy or good;   115
for I love you more than anything."
He looked at her and saw that she was beautiful;
Love stung him with a spark
that burned and set fire to his heart.
He answered her in a suitable way.   120
"Lovely one," he said, "if it pleased you,
if such joy might be mine
that you would love me,
there is nothing you might command,
within my power, that I would not do,   125
whether foolish or wise.
I shall obey your command;
for you, I shall abandon everyone.
I want never to leave you.
That is what I most desire."   130
When the girl heard the words
of the man who could love her so,
she granted him her love and her body.
Now Lanval was on the right road!
Afterward, she gave him a gift: 135
he would never again want anything,
he would receive as he desired;
however generously he might give and spend,

2. **Sumptuous silk fabric imported from Alexandria, Egypt; because of its expense, purple dye (like
ermine fur) was associated with royalty.**

she would provide what he needed.
Now Lanval is well cared for.
The more lavishly he spends,   140
the more gold and silver he will have.
"Love," she said, "I admonish you now,
I command and beg you,
do not let any man know about this.
I shall tell you why: 145
you would lose me for good
if this love were known;
you would never see me again
or possess my body."
He answered that he would do   150
exactly as she commanded.
He lay beside her on the bed;
now Lanval is well cared for.
He remained with her
that afternoon, until evening   155
and would have stayed longer, if he could,
and if his love had consented.
"Love," she said, "get up.
You cannot stay any longer.
Go away now; I shall remain   160
but I will tell you one thing:
when you want to talk to me
there is no place you can think of
where a man might have his mistress   165
without reproach or shame,
that I shall not be there with you
to satisfy all your desires.
No man but you will see me
or hear my words."   170
When he heard her, he was very happy,
he kissed her, and then got up.
The girls who had brought him to the tent
dressed him in rich clothes;
when he was dressed anew,   175
there wasn't a more handsome youth in all the world;
he was no fool, no boor.
They gave him water for his hands
and a towel to dry them,
and they brought him food.   180
He took supper with his love;
it was not to be refused.
He was served with great courtesy,
he received it with great joy.
There was an entremet³   185
that vastly pleased the knight
for he kissed his lady often

---

3. Dish served between courses at a banquet.

and held her close.
When they finished dinner,
his horse was brought to him.
The horse had been well saddled;
Lanval was very richly served.
The knight took his leave, mounted,
and rode toward the city,
often looking behind him.   195
Lanval was very disturbed;
he wondered about his adventure
and was doubtful in his heart;
he was amazed, not knowing what to believe;
he didn't expect ever to see her again.   200
He came to his lodging
and found his men well dressed.
That night, his accommodations were rich
but no one knew where it came from.
There was no knight in the city   205
who really needed a place to stay
whom he didn't invite to join him
to be well and richly served.
Lanval gave rich gifts,
Lanval released prisoners,   210
Lanval dressed jongleurs [performers],
Lanval offered great honors.
There was no stranger or friend
to whom Lanval didn't give.
Lanval's joy and pleasure were intense;   215
in the daytime or at night,
he could see his love often;
she was completely at his command.

In that same year, it seems to me,
after the feast of St. John,[4]   220
about thirty knights
were amusing themselves
in an orchard beneath the tower
where the queen was staying.
Gawain was with them   225
and his cousin, the handsome Yvain;
Gawain, the noble, the brave,
who was so loved by all, said:
"By God, my lords, we wronged
our companion Lanval,   230
who is so generous and courtly,
and whose father is a rich king,
when we didn't bring him with us."
They immediately turned back,
went to his lodging   235

4. John the Baptist; his feast day is June 24.

and prevailed on Lanval to come along with them.
At a sculpted window
the queen was looking out;
she had three ladies with her.
She saw the king's retinue,   240
recognized Lanval and looked at him.
Then she told one of her ladies
to send for her maidens,
the loveliest and the most refined;
together they went to amuse themselves   245
in the orchard where the others were.
She brought thirty or more with her;
they descended the steps.
The knights came to meet them,
because they were delighted to see them.   250
The knights took them by the hand;
their conversation was in no way vulgar.
Lanval went off to one side,
far from the others; he was impatient
to hold his love,   255
to kiss and embrace and touch her;
he thought little of others' joys
if he could not have his pleasure.
When the queen saw him alone,
she went straight to the knight.   260
She sat beside him and spoke,
revealing her whole heart:
"Lanval, I have shown you much honor,
I have cherished you, and loved you.
You may have all my love;   265
just tell me your desire.
I promise you my affection.
You should be very happy with me."
"My lady," he said, "let me be!
I have no desire to love you.   270
I've served the king a long time;
I don't want to betray my faith to him.
Never, for you or for your love,
will I do anything to harm my lord."
The queen got angry;   275
in her wrath, she insulted him:
"Lanval," she said, "I am sure
you don't care for such pleasure;
people have often told me
that you have no interest in women.   280
You have fine-looking boys
with whom you enjoy yourself.
Base coward, lousy cripple,
my lord made a bad mistake
when he let you stay with him.   285
For all I know, he'll lose God because of it."

When Lanval heard her, he was quite disturbed;
he was not slow to answer.
He said something out of spite
that he would later regret.
"Lady," he said, "of that activity
I know nothing,
but I love and I am loved
by one who should have the prize
over all the women I know.   295
And I shall tell you one thing;
you might as well know all:
any one of those who serve her,
the poorest girl of all,
is better than you, my lady queen,   300
in body, face, and beauty,
in breeding and in goodness."
The queen left him
and went, weeping, to her chamber.
She was upset and angry   305
because he had insulted her.
She went to bed sick;
never, she said, would she get up
unless the king gave her satisfaction
for the offense against her.   310
The king returned from the woods,
he'd had a very good day.
He entered the queen's chambers.
When she saw him, she began to complain.
She fell at his feet, asked his mercy,   315
saying that Lanval had dishonored her;
he had asked for her love,
and because she refused him
he insulted and offended her:
he boasted of a love   320
who was so refined and noble and proud
that her chambermaid,
the poorest one who served her,
was better than the queen.
The king got very angry;   325
he swore an oath:
if Lanval could not defend himself in court
he would have him burned or hanged.
The king left her chamber
and called for three of his barons;   330
he sent them for Lanval
who was feeling great sorrow and distress.
He had come back to his dwelling,
knowing very well
that he'd lost his love,   335
he had betrayed their affair.
He was all alone in a room,

disturbed and troubled;
he called on his love, again and again,
but it did him no good.   340
He complained and sighed,
from time to time he fainted;
then he cried a hundred times for her to have mercy
and speak to her love.
He cursed his heart and his mouth;   345
it's wonder he didn't kill himself.
No matter how much he cried and shouted,
ranted and raged,
she would not have mercy on him,
not even let him see her.   350
How will he ever contain himself?
The men the king sent
arrived and told him
to appear in court without delay:
the king had summoned him   355
because the queen had accused him.
Lanval went with his great sorrow;
they could have killed him, for all he cared.
He came before the king;
he was very sad, thoughtful, silent;   360
his face revealed great suffering.
In anger the king told him:
"Vassal, you have done me a great wrong!
This was a base undertaking,
to shame and disgrace me   365
and to insult the queen.
You have made a foolish boast:
your love is much too noble
if her maid is more beautiful,
more worthy, than the queen."   370
Lanval denied that he'd dishonored
or shamed his lord,
word for word, as the king spoke:
he had not made advances to the queen;
but of what he had said,   375
he acknowledged the truth,
about the love he had boasted of,
that now made him sad because he'd lost her.
About that he said he would do
whatever the court decided.   380
The king was very angry with him;
he sent for all his men
to determine exactly what he ought to do
so that no one could find fault with his decision.
They did as he commanded,   385
whether they liked it or not.
They assembled,
judged, and decided,

than Lanval should have his day;
but he must find pledges for his lord   390
to guarantee that he would await the judgment,
return, and be present at it.
Then the court would be increased,
for now there were none but the king's household.
The barons came back to the king   395
and announced their decision.
The king demanded pledges.
Lanval was alone and forlorn,
he had no relative, no friend.
Gawain went and pledged himself for him,   400
and all his companions followed.
The king addressed them: "I release him to you
on forfeit of whatever you hold from me,
lands and fiefs, each one for himself."
When Lanval was pledged, there was nothing else to do.   405
He returned to his lodging.
The knights accompanied him,
they reproached and admonished him
that he give up his great sorrow;
they cursed his foolish love.   410
Each day they went to see him,
because they wanted to know
whether he was drinking and eating;
they were afraid that he'd kill himself.
On the day that they had named,   415
the barons assembled.
The king and the queen were there
and the pledges brought Lanval back.
They were all very sad for him:
I think there were a hundred   420
who would have done all they could
to set him free without a trial
where he would be wrongly accused.
The king demanded a verdict
according to the charge and rebuttal.   425
Now it all fell to the barons.
They went to the judgment,
worried and distressed
for the noble man from another land
who'd gotten into such trouble in their midst.   430
Many wanted to condemn him
in order to satisfy their lord.
The Duke of Cornwall[5] said:
"No one can blame us;
whether it makes you weep or sing   435

---

5. Extreme southwestern part of England, a Celtic region that was the seat of Arthurian legend.

justice must be carried out.
The king spoke against his vassal
whom I have heard named Lanval;
he accused him of felony,
charged him with a misdeed—   440
a love that he had boasted of,
which made the queen angry.
No one but the king accused him:
by the faith I owe you,
if one were to speak the truth,   445
there should have been no need for defense,
except that a man owes his lord honor
in every circumstance.
He will be bound by his oath,
and the king will forgive us our pledges   450
if he can produce proof;
if his love would come forward,
if what he said,
what upset the queen, is true,
then he will be acquitted,   455
because he did not say it out of malice.
But if he cannot get his proof,
we must make it clear to him
that he will forfeit his service to the king;
he must take his leave."   460
They sent to the knight,
told and announced to him
that he should have his love come
to defend and stand surety for him.
He told them that he could not do it: 465
he would never receive help from her.
They went back to the judges,
not expecting any help from Lanval.
The king pressed them hard
because of the queen who was waiting.   470
When they were ready to give their verdict
they saw two girls approaching,
riding handsome palfreys.[6]
They were very attractive,
dressed in purple taffeta,   475
over their bare skin.
The men looked at them with pleasure.
Gawain, taking three knights with him,
went to Lanval and told him;
he pointed out the two girls.   480
Gawain was extremely happy, and begged him
to tell if his love were one of them.
Lanval said he didn't know who they were,
where they came from or where they were going.

6. Saddle horses, especially those used by ladies (as opposed to warhorses).

The girls proceeded   485
still on horseback;
they dismounted before the high table
at which Arthur, the king, sat.
They were of great beauty,
and spoke in a courtly manner: 490
"King, clear your chambers,
have them hung with silk
where my lady may dismount;
she wishes to take shelter with you."
He promised it willingly   495
and called two knights
to guide them up to the chambers.
On that subject no more was said.
The king asked his barons
for their judgment and decision;   500
he said they had angered him very much
with their long delay.
"Sire," they said, "we have decided.
Because of the ladies we have just seen
we have made no judgment.   505
Let us reconvene the trial."
Then they assembled, everyone was worried;
there was much noise and strife.
While they were in that confusion,
two girls in noble array,   510
dressed in Phrygian[7] silks
and riding Spanish mules,
were seen coming down the street.
This gave the vassals great joy;
to each other they said that now   515
Lanval, the brave and bold, was saved.
Gawain went up to him,
bringing his companions along.
"Sire," he said, "take heart.
For the love of God, speak to us.   520
Here come two maidens,
well adorned and very beautiful;
one must certainly be your love."
Lanval answered quickly
that he did not recognize them,   525
he didn't know them or love them.
Meanwhile they'd arrived,
and dismounted before the king.
Most of those who saw them praised them
for their bodies, their faces, their coloring;   530
each was more impressive
than the queen had ever been.
The older one was courtly and wise,

7. That is, Eastern.

she spoke her message fittingly:
"King, have chambers prepared for us
to lodge my lady according to her need;   535
she is coming here to speak with you."
He ordered them to be taken
to the others who had preceded them.
There was no problem with the mules.   540
When he had seen to the girls,
he summoned all his barons
to render their judgment;
it had already dragged out too much.
The queen was getting angry   545
because she had fasted so long.
They were about to give their judgment
when through the city came riding
a girl on horseback:
there was none more beautiful in the world.   550
She rode a white palfrey,
who carried her handsomely and smoothly:
he was well apportioned in the neck and head,
no finer beast in the world.
The palfrey's trappings were rich;   555
under heaven there was no count or king
who could have afforded them all
without selling or mortgaging lands.
She was dressed in this fashion:
in a white linen shift   560
that revealed both her sides
since the lacing was along the side.
Her body was elegant, her hips slim,
her neck whiter than snow on a branch,
her eyes bright, her face white,   565
a beautiful mouth, a well-set nose,
dark eyebrows and an elegant forehead,
her hair curly and rather blond;
golden wire does not shine
like her hair in the light.   570
Her cloak, which she had wrapped around her,
was dark purple.
On her wrist she held a sparrow hawk,
a greyhound followed her.[8]
In the town, no one, small or big,   575
old man or child,
failed to come look.
As they watched her pass,
there was no joking about her beauty.
She proceeded at a slow pace.   580
The judges who saw her
marveled at the sight;

8. Both animals were used in hunting.

no one who looked at her
was not warmed with joy.
Those who loved the knight   585
came to him and told him
of the girl who was approaching,
if God pleased, to rescue him.
"Sir companion, here comes one
neither tawny nor dark;   590
this is, of all who exist,
the most beautiful woman in the world."
Lanval heard them and lifted his head;
he recognized her and sighed.
The blood rose to his face;   595
he was quick to speak.
"By my faith," he said, "that is my love.
Now I don't care if I am killed,
if only she forgives me.
For I am restored, now that I see her."   600
The lady entered the palace;
no one so beautiful had ever been there.
She dismounted before the king
so that she was well seen by all.
And she let her cloak fall   605
so they could see her better.
The king, who was well bred,
rose and went to meet her;
all the others honored her
and offered to serve her.   610
When they had looked at her well,
when they had greatly praised her beauty,
she spoke in this way,
she didn't want to wait:
"I have loved one of your vassals: 615
you see him before you—Lanval.
He has been accused in your court—
I don't want him to suffer
for what he said; you should know
that the queen was in the wrong.   620
He never made advances to her.
And for the boast that he made,
if he can be acquitted through me,
let him be set free by your barons."
Whatever the barons judged by law   625
the king promised would prevail.
To the last man they agreed
that Lanval had successfully answered the charge.
He was set free by their decision
and the girl departed.   630
The king could not detain her,
though there were enough people to serve her.
Outside the hall stood

a great stone of dark marble
where heavy men mounted
when they left the king's court; 635
Lanval climbed on it.
When the girl came through the gate
Lanval leapt, in one bound,
onto the palfrey, behind her.
With her he went to Avalun,[9] 640
so the Bretons tell us,
to a very beautiful island;
there the youth was carried off.
No man heard of him again, 645
and I have no more to tell.

Laüstic (*The Nightingale*)

I shall tell you an adventure
about which the Bretons made a *lai*.
Laüstic was the name, I think,
they gave it in their land.
In French it is *rossignol*, 5
and *nightingale* in proper English.
At Saint-Malo,[1] in that country,
there was a famous city.
Two knights lived there,
they both had strong houses. 10
From the goodness of the two barons
the city acquired a good name.
One had married a woman
wise, courtly, and handsome;
she set a wonderfully high value on herself, 15
within the bounds of custom and usage.
The other was a bachelor,
well known among his peers
for bravery and great valor;
he delighted in living well. 20
He jousted often, spent widely
and gave out what he had.
He also loved his neighbor's wife;
he asked her, begged her so persistently,
and there was such good in him, 25
that she loved him more than anything,
as much for the good that she heard of him
as because he was close by.
They loved each other discreetly and well,
concealed themselves and took care 30
that they weren't seen

9. Avalon, in Celtic mythology the abode of
the blessed dead; in Arthurian legend, the
island where Arthur goes after he is mortally
wounded.

1. A seaport in northwest France, in Brittany.

or disturbed or suspected.
And they could do this well enough
since their dwellings were close,
their houses were next door,
and so were their rooms and their towers;   35
there was no barrier or boundary
except a high wall of dark stone.
From the rooms where the lady slept,
if she went to the window   40
she could talk to her love
on the other side, and he to her,
and they could exchange their possessions,
by tossing and throwing them.
There was scarcely anything to disturb them,   45
they were both quite at ease;
except that they couldn't come together
completely for their pleasure,
for the lady was closely guarded
when her husband was in the country.   50
Yet they always managed,
whether at night or in the day,
to be able to talk together;
no one could prevent
their coming to the window   55
and seeing each other there.
For a long time they loved each other,
until one summer
when the woods and meadows were green
and the orchards blooming.   60
The little birds, with great sweetness,
were voicing their joy above the flowers.
It is no wonder if he understands them,
he who has love to his desire.
I'll tell you the truth about the knight: 65
he listened to them intently
and to the lady on the other side,
both with words and looks.
At night, when the moon shone
when her lord was in bed,   70
she often rose from his side
and wrapped herself in a cloak.
She went to the window
because of her lover, who, she knew,
was leading the same life,   75
awake most of the night.
Each took pleasure in the other's sight
since they could have nothing more;
but she got up and stood there so often
that her lord grew angry   80
and began to question her, to ask
why she got up and where she went.

"My lord," the lady answered him,
"there is no joy in this world
like hearing the nightingale sing.   85
That's why I stand there.
It sounds so sweet at night
that it gives me great pleasure;
it delights me so and I so desire it
that I cannot close my eyes."   90
When her lord heard what she said
he laughed in anger and ill will.
He set his mind on one thing:
to trap the nightingale.
There was no valet in his house   95
that he didn't set to making traps, nets, or snares,
which he then had placed in the orchard;
there was no hazel tree or chestnut
where they did not place a snare or lime
until they trapped and captured him.   100
When they had caught the nightingale,
they brought it, still alive, to the lord.
He was very happy when he had it;
he came to the lady's chambers.
"Lady," he said, "where are you?   105
Come here! Speak to us!
I have trapped the nightingale
that kept you awake so much.
From now on you can lie in peace:
he will never again awaken you."   110
When the lady heard him,
she was sad and angry.
She asked her lord for the bird
but he killed it out of spite,
he broke its neck in his hands—   115
too vicious an act—
and threw the body on the lady;
her shift was stained with blood,
a little, on her breast.
Then he left the room.   120
The lady took the little body;
she wept hard and cursed
those who betrayed the nightingale,
who made the traps and snares,
for they took great joy from her.   125
"Alas," she said, "now I must suffer.
I won't be able to get up at night
or go and stand in the window
where I used to see my love.
I know one thing for certain: 130
he'd think I was pretending.
I must decide what to do about this.
I shall send him the nightingale

and relate the adventure."
In a piece of samite,   135
embroidered in gold and writing,
she wrapped the little bird.
She called one of her servants,
charged him with her message,
and sent him to her love.   140
He came to the knight,
greeted him in the name of the lady,
related the whole message to him,
and presented the nightingale.

When everything had been told and revealed to the knight,   145
after he had listened well,
he was very sad about the adventure,
but he wasn't mean or hesitant.
He had a small vessel fashioned,
with no iron or steel in it;   150
it was all pure gold and good stones,
very precious and very dear;
the cover was very carefully attached.
He placed the nightingale inside
and then he had the casket sealed—   155
he carried it with him always.

This adventure was told,
it could not be concealed for long.
The Bretons made a *lai* about it
which men call *The Nightingale*.   160

MEDIEVAL LYRICS

Lyric poetry gets its name from the lyre, a harplike musical instrument used to accompany the singing of verse in the ancient world; it was associated in Greek and Roman culture with the god Apollo, and connected in Jewish and Islamic culture with King David, supposed poet of the **Psalms**. Unlike narrative poetry, which features an extended story line and the development of complex characters, lyric poetry paints a brief, highly focused picture of a specific place, a particular moment, or an intense emotion. In some periods this poetry, like modern song lyrics, was conventionally set to music; at other times it was circulated in written form. But even on the page, it retains in its vividness and immediacy something of the spontaneous, performative quality of song.

The lyrics collected here span a wide range, in terms both of their thousand-year time period and of their geographical origin. Some are composed in elevated, learned languages spoken across national borders, such as Arabic, Hebrew, and Latin; others are written in the vernacular languages of Europe and the Islamic world, from the Old English of the extreme northwest to the Persian of the southeast. Yet certain themes appear repeatedly, like fragments of set melodies that are played over many times, in different keys and at different tempos. The preminent focus is love, whether amorous love for an individual person or spiritual love for the divine. Other recurrent themes include the sense of familiar place or homeland, often associated with the poetry of exile or with the elegiac mode, as the poet mourns a time and a place that seems to be lost forever; warfare, whose brutal violence and pain are coupled with extraordinary displays of heroism and the firm friendship of comrades; and poetry itself, the topic of a number of lyrics that meditate self-reflectively on the very task of literary composition, weighing the competing claims of supernatural inspiration against the simple, devoted labor of the artisan whose medium is the word and whose tool is the pen.

From the first poem onward, the lyrics collected here betray a fundamental ambivalence about the passion of love. On the surface level, there would seem to be a clear distinction between the love of one person for another, which is expressed physically, and the love directed toward God, which is expressed spiritually. In Boethius's lyric on Orpheus, the mythological musician unrivaled among mortals, this ambiguity takes the form of a stark opposition, leading to Orpheus's tragic mistake as he looks backward at his beloved wife Eurydice—he should, according to Boethius, have kept his gaze fixed on the proper, higher object, the love of the good. Orpheus's failure reveals the inescapable weakness of the lover, as his irrational passion brings about not only his own downfall but that of his beloved.

In Persian poetry and in the Arabic lyrics of medieval Spain, however, erotic love increasingly came to be represented as capable of refining or even perfecting the individual. Instead of opposing human love, expressed through the body, and divine love, expressed through the soul, the tradition that came to be known in Europe as "courtly love" posited that the human beloved was actually a medium through which one might glimpse the divine. The poems of **Ibn Arabi, Rumi**, and **Hafez** evoke this mediating quality possessed by the "beloved" or the "friend," an object of love that can equally be read as a human being adored by the poet or as the transcendent presence of God becoming fully immanent in this world. Something similar appears in the poetry of medieval Provence, in which the sensation of love brings the individual to the point of self-effacement—a moment memorably captured in **Bernart de Ventadorn**'s image of the lark that stretches its wings out to the sun, fully absorbed within the brilliant ray. In the writing of **Dante**, the divine reemerges as the focus of amorous love somewhat as the figure of the "friend" functioned in the Persian and Arabic traditions that lay behind Romance vernacular expressions of courtly love. But for Dante, the specifically Christian theology of redemption adds an additional layer to the process of mediation. In serving as a pathway to God, his Beatrice directs the poet's amorous gaze toward yet another intermediary, Christ.

Perhaps the most striking feature of the lyrics collected here is their simultaneous variety and unity; drawn from very different times and places, they display a remarkable harmony or resonance on the levels of both form and content. This connection can be illustrated with special poignancy in the lyrics of two women represented here, **Jahan Khatun** of Persia (modern Iran) and **Christine de Pizan**, a native of Italy who spent her life in France. Both born in the fourteenth century, living in regions of the world that were geographically and culturally very distinct, they share an ability to put into words the bittersweet experience of love. Jahan Khatun describes the painful experience of being a "stranger" in the court of the once-attentive beloved, while Christine de Pizan embraces the solitude of the *seulete*, the widow who holds close the memory of her absent beloved. Here, the power of lyric appears as an almost invisible but profoundly strong cord that enables the poetic imagination to create links across culture, across language—perhaps even across time.

A NOTE ON TRANSLATION

With the exception of one poem reproduced in its original Middle English, a language still comprehensible to the modern reader, all of the lyrics collected here are in translation. Unlike fiction or even narrative poetry, lyric poetry poses a special challenge to the translator because of the concentrated, highly focused quality of its language. Assonance and alliteration, rhythm and rhyme all demand to be reflected in the English version, despite the great challenge of retaining these poetic devices while still reproducing the meaning of the original verses.

The following translations reflect two different approaches: some translators have rendered the original text very literally, while others have sought equivalences, believing that the best way to capture the essential meaning of the source text is to rely on poetic modes that are natural to modern English even when those differ from literary devices in the author's language. One particularly remarkable example of the latter approach is Yusef Komunyakaa's translation of the Old English poem "**The Ruin**": Komunyakaa accurately renders the elements of the Anglo-Saxon world so hauntingly evoked in the lyric, while not hesitating to rely on analogies to convey the tenth-century experience of loss and exile to his twenty-first-century audience. Another can be found in Barbara Newman's rendering of the devout lyrics of the abbess **Hildegard of Bingen**, as the translator captures the passionate, even ecstatic quality of the medieval poet within a distinctively modern idiom.

BOETHIUS

A ncius Manlius Severinus Boethius (480–524) was a philosopher and poet who rose to political eminence, fell into disfavor, and spent his last days in prison under sentence of death. While awaiting execution he wrote his *Consolation of Philosophy*, a mixture of philosophical prose alternating with lyrical interludes. His work was widely read for more than a thousand years and was translated into English by not one but two monarchs, the Anglo-Saxon King Alfred and the Tudor Queen Elizabeth. The verse reproduced here marks a turning point in the *Consolation*, when the narrator learns that he must turn his intellectual gaze toward higher things, yet it also stands on its own as an elegiac tribute to the archetypal poet of classical myth, Orpheus.

From The Consolation of Philosophy[1]

III.12

Happy was he who could look upon
The clear fount of the good;
Happy who could loose the bonds
Of heavy earth.
Of old the Thracian poet[2] mourned   5

---

1. Translated from the Latin by Stephen J. Tester.

2. Orpheus; Thrace is northeast of Greece.

His wife's sad death,
He who before had made the woods so nimbly run
And rivers stand
With his weeping measures,
And the hind's fearless flank   10
Lay beside savage lions,
Nor was the hare afraid to look upon
The hound, made peaceful by his song;
When grief burned yet more fierce and hot
His inmost heart,   15
And measures that subdued all else
Soothed not their master,
Complaining of inexorable gods above
He approached the halls below.
There modulating gentle songs   20
On the sounding lyre
All that he drew from the foremost springs
Of his goddess mother,[3]
All that his unquelled grief bestowed
And love, that doubles grief,   25
Make his laments; he moves Taenarian hearts,
And with sweet prayer
Asks pardon of the lords of Hades' shades.
Taken by his strange song the doorkeeper
Three-headed Cerberus[4] stands benumbed;   30
Goddess-avengers of men's crimes[5] who make
The guilty quake with fear
Now full of sadness melt in tears;
Ixion's swift wheel
No longer spins his head,   35
And Tantalus tormented by long thirst
Scorns stooping to the water;
The vulture, while he is filled with Orpheus' measures,
Stops tearing at Tityus' liver.[6]
At last 'We are overborne' in pity says   40
The ruler of the shades;[7]
'We grant the man his wife to go with him,
Bought by his song;
Yet let our law restrict the gift,
That, while he Tartarus[8] quits,   45
He shall not turn his gaze.'
Who can give lovers laws?
Love is a greater law unto itself.

---

3. Calliope, the muse of epic poetry.
4. The monstrous dog that guards the entrance
of the underworld.
5. The Furies.
6. Three of the most famous examples of

those condemned to eternal punishment by
Zeus, king of the gods.
7. Hades.
8. That is, the underworld.

Woe! By the very boundaries of Night
Orpheus his Eurydice   50
Saw, lost, and killed.
To you this tale refers,
Who seek to lead your mind
Into the upper day;
For he who overcome should turn back his gaze   55
Towards the Tartarean cave,
Whatever excellence he takes with him
He loses when he looks on those below.

NOTKER BALBULUS

otker (ca. 840–912) was a monk at the powerful and influential monastery of St. Gall (in modern Switzerland), a paradise of devout learning in a region that was just entering into a period of cultural and intellectual revival. Although his surname means "the Stammerer," Notker more than compensated for his lack of oral eloquence with his extraordinary writing ability; he produced a great number of hymns and other compositions, many of which he himself set to music. His "Hymn to Holy Women" centers on the powerful symbol of the ladder, connecting heaven and earth, and stresses the role of woman in mediating the ascent of the soul. Eve, who introduced sin to humankind in Eden, is counterbalanced by Mary, whose willingness to become the vessel of the Incarnation brings about the salvation of the world.

A Hymn to Holy Women[1]

1. A ladder stretching up to heaven,
       circled by torments—

2. At whose foot an attentive
       dragon
   stands on guard, forever
       awake,

3. So that no one can climb even
       to the first rung and not be
       torn—

---

1. Translated from the Latin by Peter Dronke.

4. The ascent of the ladder barred
    by an Ethiop,[2] brandishing
  a drawn sword, threatening
    death,

5. While over the topmost rung
    leans a young man, radiant,
  a golden bough in his hand—

6. This is the ladder the love of
    Christ
  made so free for women
that, treading down the
    dragon
and striding past the Ethiop's
    sword,

7. By way of torments of every kind
    they can reach heaven's
    summit
and take the golden laurel
  from the hand of the strength-
    giving king.

8. What good did it do you,
    impious serpent,
  once to have deceived a
    woman,

9. Since a virgin brought forth
    God incarnate,
only-begotten of the Father:

10. He who took your spoils away
  and pierces your jaw with a hook[3]

11. To make of it an open gate
  for Eve's race, whom you long to
    hold.

12. So now you can see girls
    defeating you, envious one,

13. And married women now
    bearing sons who please
    God.

14. Now you groan at the loyalty
    of widows to their dead
    husbands,

15. You who once seduced a girl
    to disloyalty towards her
    creator.

16. Now you can see women made
    captains
in the war that is waged against
    you,

17. Women who spur on their sons
  bravely to conquer all your
    tortures.

18. Even courtesans, your vessels,
    are purified by God,

19. Transmuted into a burnished
    temple for him alone.

20. For these graces let us now
    glorify him together,
both the sinners and those who
    are just,

21. Him who strengthens those who
    stand
  and gives his right hand to
    the fallen,
that at least after crimes we may
    rise.

2. I.e., the devil.

3. See Job 40.20.

ANONYMOUS

This anonymous ninth-century lyric survives only in partial form in a single manuscript, a collection of miscellaneous poems and riddles known as the Exeter Book. Damaged by fire, the vellum page containing the poem has one significant gap near the beginning and is badly marred near the end. This frag- mentary nature is, however, appropriate to the poem's focus: the Roman ruins that dotted the medieval Anglo-Saxon countryside. "The Ruin" testifies to the ravages of time, which breaks down stone walls into rubble and causes the human beings who erected those walls to dwindle into nothing but a faint memory.

The Ruin[1]

Look at the elaborate crests chiseled into this stone wall
shattered by fate, the crumbled city squares,
and the hue and cry of giants rotted away.
There are caved-in roofs, towers in shambles,
rime on the limy mortar,   5
a storm-wall tilted and scarred,
half-fallen, slumped by time.
An earthly embrace holds the royal architects
rotting in their graves and lost to the cruel grip
of the ground, while a hundred generations   10
passed away. This wall, mapped and veined by lichen,
stained with red, outlasted one kingdom
after another, long stood upright after storms:
lofty and broad, it has fallen. The rampart
hewn and wedged together, sharpened roughly   15
and polished, an ancient structure well-worked by men . . .
ringed with encrustations of soil
still prods the brain and draws up a fiery clue.
Clever in the forging of chains,
some bold-minded man bound together the ribs   20
of the wall with amazing cables.

There were bright city plots linked by bathhouses,
a wealth of high, towering gables,
much clamor of the multitude,
many mead halls filled with revelry,   25
until a mighty Lot changed that.
Far and wide people fell dead:
days of pestilence ran rampant
and death clobbered ranks of the infamous swordsmen.
Their fortress became a tomb; the city rotted away: 30

1. Translated from the Old English by Yusef Komunyakaa.

those who should have braced it up, the multitudes,
were bones on the ground. Then, the courts knelt in dust
and the wide red roof of vaulted beams was left shedding tiles.
This ritual-place fell into ruin and piled-up heaps,
where once stood those lighthearted with gold,   35
clothed in splendor, proud and lifted by wine,
shorn in war-gear, and gazed upon a treasure
of silver and inlaid-plated gems,
on wealth and property, on precious stones
and this glorious citadel of a stout kingdom;   40
and the stone courts stood upright,
and the warming stream spouted its whole surge,
and a wall hugged everything to its bosom,
where the baths were steamy in its heart.
Streams poured across hot gray stones   45
until the round pool heated. . . .
It is still a fitting thing for this city.

ANONYMOUS

This anonymous Latin verse from the eleventh century features a conventional description of the natural landscape understood in terms of the "book of nature"—a complex unity of symbols that, when properly read, reveals the hidden message of the Creator. Here, each species of bird gives voice to its own song, together contributing to the complex harmony that is the song of summer. The duration of the song is both limited, confined to the summer months, and perpetual, as it is endlessly renewed with the cycle of the seasons.

Song of Summer[1]

The woodlands clothe the slender shoots
of boughs, laden with fruits;
from high perches wood pigeons sing
    songs to one and all.
Here the turtledove moans, here the thrush resounds,   5
here the age-old song of blackbirds rings out,
and the sparrow, not silent, with its chatter
    takes possession of the heights beneath the elms.

---

1. Translated from the Latin by Jan Ziolkowski.

Here the nightingale sings, delighting in leafy boughs,
pours out a long warbling through the breeze,   10
solemnly, and with tremulous voice the kite
    causes the sky to echo.
The eagle as it soars starward sings, upon the breezes
the lark sings and produces sounds in melodies.
From above it swoops, with a different melody   15
    as it touches ground.
The swift swallow ever makes its call,
the quail sings, the jackdaw resounds:
thus birds everywhere celebrate for everyone
    the song of summer.   20
None among the birds is like the bee,
who represents the ideal of chastity,
if not she who bore Christ in her womb
    inviolate.

IBN ZAYDUN

Ibn Zaydun (1003–1071) was a native of Córdoba, the seat of Muslim rule in medieval al-Andalus (modern Spain), at a time when the Umayyad dynasty was divided by internal conflict and, increasingly, besieged by enemies on its borders. Ibn Zaydun quickly became famous for his mastery of the sophisticated poetic form of the *qasida* (an Arabic counterpart to the Latin ode), almost single-handedly raising the reputation of the regional literature of al-Andalus to the level of that produced in the eastern cultural centers of Baghdad and Cairo. Several of his lyrics commemorate his tumultuous love for Wallada, the daughter of the Umayyad ruler of Córdoba who was herself a poet. After falling into political disfavor, Ibn Zaydun fled to Seville, where he wrote some of his most poignant verses on the experience of exile from his homeland, on those he had loved there, and on the beautiful "city of light" (*al-Zahra*), now only a shining memory.

From Al-Zahra[1]

With passion from this place
    I remember you.
        Horizon clear, limpid
The face of earth, and wind,

1. Translated from the Arabic by Christopher Middleton and Leticia Garza-Falcon.

Come twilight, desists,   5
    A tenderness sweeps me
When I see the silver
    Coiling waterways
        Like necklaces detached
From throats. Delicious those   10
    Days we spent while fate
        Slept. There was peace, I mean,
And us, thieves of pleasure.
    Now only flowers
        With frost-bent stems I see;   15
At my eyes their vivid
    Centers pull, they gaze
        Back at me, seeing me
Without sleep, and a light
    Flickers through their cups,   20
        In sympathy, I think.
The sun-baked rose-buds in
    Bushes, remember
        How their color had lit
Our morning air; and still   25
    Breaths of wind dispense
        At break of day, as then,
Perfume they gather up
    From waterlilies'
        Half-open drowsy eyes.   30
Such fresh memories
    Of you these few things
        Waken in my mind. For
Faraway as you are
    In this passion's grip   35
        I persist with a sigh
And pine to be at one
    With you. Please God no
        Calm or oblivion
Will occupy my heart,   40
    Or close it. Listen
        To the shiver of wings
At your side—it is my
    Desire, and still, still
        I am shaking with it [. . .]   45
Pure love we once exchanged,
    It was an unfenced
        Field and we ran there, free
Like horses. But alone
    I now can lay claim   50
        To have kept faith. You left,
Left this place. In sorrow
    To be here again,
        I am loving you.

WILLIAM IX

The earliest troubadour poet and the ninth Duke of Aquitaine, William (1071–1127) displayed the same aggressive spirit in his lyrics that he did on the field of battle. He passed his love of poetry on to his descendants, including his granddaughter Eleanor of Aquitaine, Queen of England and patron to several court poets, and her son Richard the Lion-Hearted, King of England and a poet in his own right. William appreciated the cultural treasures of poetry, song, and dance to be found in Muslim al-Andalus (Spain) and played a major role in their transmission into Occitan and French culture. In his audacious claim to write a verse "de dreit nien"—meaning both "about nothing at all" and "out of nothing at all"—William playfully puts himself in the position of the divine Creator, who made the world *ex nihilo*.

I'll make a verse of nothing at all[1]

I'll make a verse of nothing at all:
It won't be about me or about anyone else,
It won't be about love or about youthful joys,
　　Or about anything else;
In fact, I wrote it while I was dozing　　　　　　5
　　On the back of my horse.

I don't know exactly when I was born,
I'm not happy-go-lucky or quick to anger,
I'm not a stranger and not a close friend,
　　And I can't be any other way;　　　　　　　10
Because I was bewitched one dark night,
　　On a lonely hilltop.

I don't know when I go to sleep,
Or when I wake up, unless someone tells me about it.
My heart's not broken, not a bit,　　　　　　　15
　　By some sharp sad sorrow.
And I don't give a damn for that,
　　By Saint Martial![2]

I'm sick, and I'm afraid to die,
And I only know what I've heard said about it;　　20
I've got to find a doctor, one who understands me,
　　But I don't know such a one.

1. Translated from the Occitan-Provençal by Suzanne Akbari.
2. Bishop of Limoges and Toulouse in southern France; his shrine at Limoges was a key pilgrimage site in the 12th century.

He'll be a good doctor, if he can cure me of this,[3]
    But if I get any worse, there's no hope.

I have a lovely girl, but I don't know who she is,   25
Because I've never seen her, I swear it's true!
She never does what pleases me, she never gives me peace,
    And I don't care,
Because I never have a Norman or a Frenchman[4]
    In my house.   30

I've never seen her, and I love her with all my heart,
And she never treats me right, and she never treats me wrong;
I'm just as happy if I never see her again,
    I don't give a damn.
Because I know a girl even more lovely and pretty,   35
    She's worth ten of the other one.

I've made the verse, I don't know what it's about,
But I'll send it on to that one
Who will in turn send it to someone else
    Over there, out by Anjou,[5]   40
And maybe he'll send back to me, out of his private pocket,
    The secret clue.[6]

---

3. Of lovesickness, a state of body as well as mind.
4. Northerners, often the political enemies of the lords of Provence (modern southern France).
5. Dukedom in the west of France; in William IX's time, the Duke of Anjou was Geoffrey V Plantagenet, whose son Henry (later Henry II of England) married William's granddaughter, Eleanor of Aquitaine.
6. The *contraclau* that will unlock the riddling poem is a common feature of troubadour verse, especially in the poetic mode of *trobar clus*, or "enigmatic verse" (literally, "closed verse").

ARNAUT DANIEL

Born in Périgord (in modern France) of a noble family in the twelfth century, Arnaut had the reputation of being something of a ne'er-do-well: the short prose biographies or *vidas* attached to his lyrics refer to him as a jokester, gambler, and perpetual student. He excelled, however, in the remarkable craftsmanship of his poems; most notably, Arnaut's invention of the intricate and difficult verse form of the sestina earned him the praise of poets through the ages from **Dante** and **Petrarch** to Ezra Pound and T. S. Eliot. Dante offers his fellow poet the highest praise imaginable in his **Purgatorio**, calling Arnaut "il miglior fabbro" (the better craftsman) and granting him the singular privilege of speaking his native Occitan tongue within the Italian epic.

The Art of Love[1]

To this sweet and pretty air
I set words that I plane and finish;
and every word will fit well,
once I have passed the file there,
for at once Love polishes and aureates   5
my song, which proceeds from her,
ruler and guardian of merit.

Each day I am a better man and purer,
for I serve the noblest lady in the world,
and I worship her, I tell you this in the open.   10
I belong to her from my foot to the top of my head;
and let the cold wind blow,
love raining in my heart
keeps me warm when it winters most.

I hear a thousand masses and pay to have them said,   15
I burn lights of wax and oil,
so may God give me good luck with her,
for no defense against her does me any good.
When I look at her golden hair,
her soft young spirited body,   20
if someone gave me Luserna,[2] I'd still love her more.

I love her and seek her out with a heart so full,
I think I am stealing her out of my own hands by too much wanting,
if a man can lose a thing by loving it well.
For the heart of her submerges   25
mine and does not abate.
So usurious is her demand,
she gets craftsman and workshop together.

I do not want the empire of Rome,
do not make me pope of it   30
so that I could not turn back to her
for whom the heart in me burns and breaks apart.
If she does not cure me of this torment
with a kiss before new year's,
she murders me and sends herself to hell.   35

But this torment I endure
could not make me turn away from loving well,
though it holds me fast in loneliness,
for in this desert I cast my words in rhyme.
I labor in loving more than a man who works the earth,   40

1. Translated from the Occitan-Provençal by   2. A city, probably in Spain.
Frederick Goldin.

for the Lord of Moncli did not love
N'Audierna an egg's worth more.[3]

I am Arnaut, who hoards the wind,
and chases the hare on an ox,
and swims against the tide.   45

3. Neither the Lord of Moncli nor his love, N'Audierna, have been identified.

YEHUDA HALEVI

Yehuda HaLevi (ca. 1075–1141) was born under Muslim rule, in a region of northern Spain that was conquered by Christian armies while he was still a child. He spent his mature years in the thriving Jewish community located in the Muslim stronghold of Grenada, where he was famed both for his skills as a physician and as the finest writer of Hebrew verse since biblical times. A leader in the revival of Hebrew as a literary language in a period when Arabic was the standard written language for Muslims, Christians, and Jews alike, HaLevi adapted Arabic literary forms into a distinctly Hebrew idiom. While the first of the selections reproduced here addresses a real person and the second a divine being, they share a common language of passion and desire that grows out of the Islamic devotional poetics of al-Andalus.

To Ibn al-Mu'allim[1]

Gently, my hard-hearted, slender one,
be gentle with me and I'll bow before you.
I've ravished you only in looking—
my heart is pure, but not my eyes:
They'd gather from your features   5
the roses and lilies mingled there.
I'd lift the fire from your cheeks
to put out fire with fire,
and then when I was thirsty,
it's there I'd look for water.   10
I'd savor the lip that glows like ruby—
like coals in the tongs of my jaws.
My life hangs by scarlet threads;

1. Both poems are translated from the Hebrew by Peter Cole.

my death is now concealed in dusk. . . .
I find that nights have no end,   15
where once no dark divided my days:
For Time then was clay in my hands
and Fortune—the potter's wheel.[2]

Lord,

all my desire is here before you,
    whether or not I speak of it:
I'd seek your favor, for an instant, then die—
    if only you would grant my wish.
I'd place my spirit in your hand,   5
    then sleep—and in that sleep find sweetness.

I wander from you—and die alive;
    the closer I cling—I live to die.
How to approach I still don't know,
    nor on what words I might rely.   10
Instruct me, Lord; advise and guide me.
    Free me from my prison of lies.

Teach me while I can bear the affliction—
    do not, Lord, despise my plea;
before I've become my own burden   15
    and the little I am weighs on me,
and against my will, I give in
    as worms eat bones that weary of me.

I'll come to the place my forefathers reached,
    and by their place of rest find rest.   20
Earth's back to me is foreign;
    my one true home is in its dust.
Till now my youth has done what it would:
    When will I provide for myself?

The world He placed in my heart has kept me   25
    from tending to my end and after.
How could I come to serve my Lord,
    when I am still desire's prisoner?
How could I ask for a place on high,
    when I know the worm will be my sister?   30

How at that end could my heart be glad,
    when I do not know what death will bring?
Day after day and night after night
    reduce the flesh upon me to nothing.

2. The potter's wheel turns as does the wheel of Fortune, a common motif in medieval art.

Into the winds they'll scatter my spirit.   35
    To dust they'll return the little remaining.

What can I say—with desire my enemy,
    from boyhood till now pursuing me:
What is Time to me but your Will?
    If you're not with me, what will I be?   40
I stand bereft of any virtue:
    only your justice and mercy shield me.

But why should I speak, or even aspire?
    Lord, before you is all my desire.

HILDEGARD OF BINGEN

Although she lived within the walls of a cloister from early childhood, Hildegard of Bingen (1098–1179) was both powerful and prolific: elected head of the religious community at Bingen (in modern Germany), she founded two new monasteries at Rupertsberg and Eibingen, corresponded with two popes, and wrote a large number of works, including medical treatises, musical works, plays, and religious poems. Among her two most intriguing creations are *Scivias*, a vividly illustrated book recounting the divinely inspired visions she had experienced since the age of three, and the *lingua ignota*, or "unknown language," she invented for the private use of her fellow nuns at Bingen. The selections included here are songs of praise for the most special patron of the women enclosed at Bingen, playing on the double meaning of Mary's role as both verdant branch (*virga*) of the Lord and perpetual virgin (*virgo*).

Responsory for the Virgin[1]

Slender branch
from the stump of Jesse,[2]
God gazed at you like an eagle
staring into the sun.
Daughter of Zion![3] such daring!   5
the supernal father
saw a maiden's splendor
and her mortal flesh spoke his word.[4]

---

1. Both poems are translated from the Latin by Barbara J. Newman.
2. The father of David, who was the ancestor of Mary (see Matthew 1.1–16). The tree of Jesse was a common motif in medieval art, showing names of the patriarchs extending upward to its top, crowned with Jesus as a flower or fruit.
3. The promised land (literally, a section of Jerusalem).
4. For Jesus as the word of God made flesh, see John 1.1, 14.

In the depth of mystery her
mind was illumined   10
and bright was the rose[5] that
sprang from that maiden
when the supernal father
saw her virgin splendor
and her mortal flesh spoke his word.   15

Glorify the Father,
the Spirit and the Son.
As it was in the beginning
so it is now
and so be it ever.   20

The supernal father
saw a maiden's splendor
and her mortal flesh spoke his word.

Responsory for the Virgin

Priceless integrity!
Her virgin gate[1]
opened to none. But the Holy One
flooded her with warmth
until a flower sprang in her womb   5
and the Son of God came forth
from her secret chamber like the dawn.

Sweet as the buds of spring, her
son opened paradise
from the cloister of her womb.   10
And the Son of God came forth
from her secret chamber like the dawn.

---

5. A symbol of Mary.   1. That is, her unbroken hymen.

THE ARCHPOET

This author (d. 1165?) is known only by the nickname "Archipoeta" (literally, "chief of poets"), in the margin of the manuscripts containing his ten surviving poems. He was likely of German origin, attached to the traveling household of the archbishop of Cologne. Although the Archpoet's lyrics are commonly associated with the so-called Goliardic school of poetry, which was characterized by lewd drinking songs, political satire, and celebrations of the dissolute life of university students, they are likely not so much a pure expression of anarchy as the outpourings of a wanton persona invented in order to amuse his noble patron. "His Confession" includes the playful refrain "May God be gracious to this drinker," a pun on a standard Christian prayer for salvation that substitutes *potatori* (drinker) for *peccatori* (sinner); the refrain lives on as a popular student drinking song.

His Confession[1]

Seething over inwardly
   With fierce indignation,
In my bitterness of soul,
   Hear my declaration.
I am of one element,   5
   Levity my matter,
Like enough a withered leaf
   For the winds to scatter.

Since it is the property
   Of the sapient   10
To sit firm upon a rock,
   It is evident
That I am a fool, since I
   Am a flowing river,
Never under the same sky,   15
   Transient for ever.

Hither, thither, masterless
   Ship upon the sea,
Wandering through the ways of air,
   Go the birds like me.   20
Bound am I by ne'er a bond,
   Prisoner to no key,
Questing go I for my kind,
   Find depravity.

Never yet could I endure   25
   Soberness and sadness,
Jests I love and sweeter than
   Honey find I gladness.
Whatsoever Venus[2] bids
   Is a joy excelling,   30
Never in an evil heart
   Did she make her dwelling.

Down the broad way do I go,
   Young and unregretting,

1. Translated from the Latin by Helen Waddell.
2. Roman goddess of love.

Wrap me in my vices up,   35
   Virtue all forgetting,
Greedier for all delight
   Than heaven to enter in:
Since the soul in me is dead,
   Better save the skin.   40

Pardon, pray you, good my lord,
   Master of discretion,
But this death I die is sweet,
   Most delicious poison.
Wounded to the quick am I   45
   By a young girl's beauty:
She's beyond my touching? Well,
   Can't the mind do duty?

Hard beyond all hardness, this
   Mastering of Nature: 50
Who shall say his heart is clean,
   Near so fair a creature?
Young are we, so hard a law,
   How should we obey it?
And our bodies, they are young,   55
   Shall they have no say in't?

Sit you down amid the fire,
   Will the fire not burn you?
To Pavia[3] come, will you
   Just as chaste return you?   60
Pavia, where Beauty draws
   Youth with finger-tips,
Youth entangled in her eyes,
   Ravished with her lips.

Let you bring Hippolytus,[4]   65
   In Pavia dine him,
Never more Hippolytus
   Will the morning find him.
In Pavia not a road
   But leads to venery,   70
Nor among its crowding towers
   One to chastity.

Yet a second charge they bring:
   I'm for ever gaming.
Yea, the dice hath many a time   75
   Stripped me to my shaming.
What an if the body's cold,
   If the mind is burning,

3. Italian city then known for its wild life.
4. In Greek mythology, the chaste son of Theseus, famously devoted to the virgin huntress goddess Artemis.

On the anvil hammering,
    Rhymes and verses turning?   80

Look again upon your list.
    Is the tavern on it?
Yea, and never have I scorned,
    Never shall I scorn it,
Till the holy angels come,   85
    And my eyes discern them,
Singing for the dying soul,
    Requiem aeternam.[5]

For on this my heart is set:
    When the hour is nigh me,   90
Let me in the tavern die,
    With a tankard by me,
While the angels looking down
    Joyously sing o'er me,
Deus sit propitius   95
    Huic potatori.[6]

'Tis the fire that's in the cup
    Kindles the soul's torches,
'Tis the heart that drenched in wine
    Flies to heaven's porches.   100
Sweeter tastes the wine to me
    In a tavern tankard
Than the watered stuff my Lord
    Bishop hath decanted.

Let them fast and water drink,   105
    All the poets' chorus,
Fly the market and the crowd
    Racketing uproarious:
Sit in quiet spots and think,
    Shun the tavern's portal,   110
Write, and never having lived,
    Die to be immortal.

Never hath the spirit of
    Poetry descended,
Till with food and drink my lean   115
    Belly was distended,
But when Bacchus[7] lords it in
    My cerebral story,
Comes Apollo[8] with a rush,
    Fills me with his glory.   120

---

5. Eternal rest (Latin), the opening words of the Catholic Mass for the dead.
6. May God be gracious to this drinker (Latin).
7. Roman god of the vine.
8. God of musical and artistic inspiration, of light and the sun; Artemis/Diana is his sister.

Unto every man his gift.
  Mine was not for fasting.
Never could I find a rhyme
  With my stomach wasting.
As the wine is, so the verse: 125
  'Tis a better chorus
When the landlord hath a good
  Vintage set before us.

Good my lord, the case is heard,
  I myself betray me,
And affirm myself to be   130
  All my fellows say me.
See, they in thy presence are:
  Let whoe'er hath known
His own heart and found it clean,
  Cast at me the stone.   135

AVRAHAM IBN EZRA

Born in Tudela, on the border of Christian Spain and Muslim al-Andalus, Avraham Ibn Ezra (ca. 1093–ca. 1167) spent much of his life in transit. After he was driven south by increasing violence and anti-Judaism, Avraham lived in Toledo and in Córdoba, where he was the friend of another eminent Hebrew poet, **Yehuda HaLevi** (see above): his son later married HaLevi's daughter. Avraham Ibn Ezra produced a large number of translations of scientific and philosophical works in addition to his poetry. His verse maintains many of the traditional Andalusian metrical patterns even while moving in new thematic directions and embracing a new, biblically influenced style that avoids rhyme. Continued political discord caused Avraham to leave Spain: by 1140, he was in Rome, and later documentary evidence places him in France and England, together with many other Jews who had been displaced from Sefarad, their home within Muslim al-Andalus.

Elegy for a Son[1]

Come, father, approach and mourn,
  for the Lord our God has distanced from you
your son, your one and only child—
  Isaac whom you always loved.

1. Translated from the Hebrew by Peter Cole.

"I am a man who has witnessed affliction   5
    and watched as joy was driven away.
The fruit of my loins has been taken from me—
    words I never imagined I'd say.

I'd always envisioned him offering comfort,
    and being near me as I aged,   10
but all my labor has been in vain,
    for I've given birth to my own dismay—
    and how can I rejoice again
when Isaac has breathed his last and died?

Moment by bitter moment I weep   15
    and send up a mournful cry and lament,
thinking of how, three years ago,
    he died alone, in a foreign land,
after he'd wandered from place to place.
    And so my soul for his spirit moaned   20
until I'd be able to bring him home;
    all night and day, alone, I grieved.
        What pain and suffering I knew then!
And this is the story of Isaac, my son.

Be kind to me now—bear with me, friends!   25
    The comfort you offer adds to my grief.
So do not speak of my heart's desire,
    or even utter his name to me.
Time has quenched my final ember:
    How could it do any worse to me,   30
having decreed my ruin forever,
    and taken from me the light of my life?
        Now my flesh and heart are failing,
as Isaac's heart gave way when he died."

Lord, in whose hands all is held,   35
    whose will extends through all creatures,
speak to the heart of this grieving father
    who held your name in awe as a child.
Waken the spirit of consolation
    and let it pass through a heart now broken.   40
He taught, with his wife, his son to fear you,
    so he would follow on the path they do:
        While he was a boy, you set it before him,
for the sake of your servant, Isaac, their son.

BERNART DE VENTADORN

The early biographies or *vidas* tell us that Bernart (ca. 1135–ca. 1195) was the son of a baker; blessed with the gift of poetry, he made the mistake of falling in love with the wife of his noble patron and was forced to flee for his life. Whether or not this is a romantic fantasy, it is certainly true that Bernart made his way from southern France to the English court of Eleanor of Aquitaine, whose grandfather **William IX** had been the first known troubadour poet. Many of the musical settings of Bernart's lyrics survive, providing rare evidence of the intricate way the troubadours united what Bernart calls "the words and the sounds." This poem, widely imitated not just by Occitan poets but by French and Italian writers as well, illustrates Bernart's ability to couple vivid descriptions of the natural world with sophisticated allusions to myth, raising the lyric mode to its highest pitch.

When I see the lark stretch out[1]

When I see the lark stretch out, for joy,
Its wings against the sun's ray,
So that it forgets, and lets itself fall
Because of the sweetness that spreads through its heart,
I feel such great envy well up in me   5
Toward the one I see filled with gladness;
I can't believe that this doesn't cause
My heart to melt with desire.

Oh, I thought I knew all about
Love—I didn't know anything at all!   10
Because I can't keep myself from loving
The one who's never offered me any reward.
She took all my heart, and she took all of me,
And took herself too, and the whole entire world,
And when she took herself away, there was nothing left for me: 15
Just the blind desire, and the willing heart.

I never was the master of myself
Nor was I my own man ever since the moment
She let me look into her eyes,
In that mirror that pleases me so much.   20
Mirror, ever since I mirrored myself in you,
The sighs from down deep have led me to death,

---

1. Translated from the Occitan-Provençal by Suzanne Akbari.

And I've lost myself, just as he was lost:
The lovely Narcissus,[2] in the depths of the fountain.

I've lost all faith in the ladies;   25
I'll never trust them again,
Because just as I used to adore them,
Now I don't care for them at all.
Since I see that not one of them lends a hand
With that one who destroys me, who strikes me down,   30
I hate them all and don't believe a word they say,
Because I know very well that every one of them's the same.

In this, it's clear that my lady is
A woman like the rest of them, and I'll tell her so,
She doesn't want the things she ought to want   35
And whatever she ought not to do, she does.
I've fallen into bad grace,
And I'm totally like the fool perched on the bridge;
And I don't know why this has happened to me—
I guess I tried to climb up too high.   40

I've lost all grace, for sure,
And so I've lost the thing I've never been able to grasp,
For she who should have it most of all
Doesn't have a bit of it, and where will I ever find it?
Oh, how little they see, when they look at her: 45
They don't see this wretch, filled with longing,
The one who, without her, will never have anything at all;
She lets him die—she won't help him at all.

Since for my lady nothing is enough,
Neither prayer nor mercy, nor the rights that I should have,   50
Nor will it ever come to please her
That I love her, I won't say the words to her again.
Instead I'll leave her, I'll give up;
She's put me to death, and with death I'll answer her,
And I'll go, since she won't have me,   55
A wretch, in exile, I don't know where.

Tristan,[3] you'll get nothing from me,
Because I'm going away, a wretch, I don't know where.
I give up singing, it's all finished now,
To joy and love, I say goodbye.   60

---

2. In classical mythology, a beautiful youth who fell in love with his own reflection, wasted away, and died (see Ovid, *Metamorphoses* 3.405–501).

3. Legendary lover, loosely connected with the Arthurian tradition, whose passion for the married Iseult led to his banishment and death.

BEATRICE OF DIA

The troubadours of southern France included in their number female poets, called *trobairitz*, who were enthusiastic and skilled participants in the group's poetic contests of words. One of these was Beatrice, Countess of Dia (ca. 1150–1200), who was married to Guilhem de Poitiers, Count of Viennois, but (according to the short *vidas* attached to her poems) was the lover of the troubadour Raimbaut of Orange.

The striking similarity of some of Beatrice's lyrics to those of Raimbaut is not evidence of copying on the part of one or the other; rather, it reveals the poetic games of mimicry and emulation practiced within the troubadour community, whose members might treat each other's phrases like common melodic refrains. One of Beatrice's lyrics, set to the notes of a flute, is the only trobairitz poem to survive with its original musical setting.

A Lover's Prize[1]

I have been in great distress
for a knight for whom I longed;
I want all future times to know
how I loved him to excess
    Now I see I am betrayed—   5
he claims I did not give him love—
such was the mistake I made,
    naked in bed, and dressed.

How I'd long to hold him pressed
naked in my arms one night—   10
if I could be his pillow once,
would he not know the height of bliss?
    Floris was all to Blanchefleur,[2]
yet not so much as I am his:
I am giving my heart, my love,   15
    my mind, my life, my eyes.

Fair, gentle lover, gracious knight,
if once I held you as my prize
and lay with you a single night
and gave you a love-laden kiss—   20
    my greatest longing is for you
to lie there in my husband's place,
but only if you promise this:
    to do all I'd want to do.

1. Translated from the Occitan-Provençal by Peter Dronke.
2. Lovers in a popular medieval romance.

BERTRAN DE BORN

As Lord of Altaforte, a castle located on contested border territory in the south of France, Bertran (ca. 1140–ca. 1200) was inevitably drawn into regional disputes over Aquitaine waged by Henry II, King of England, and his sons. Bertran allied initially with Henry II's eldest son, Henry the Young King, in a rebellion against his father, and later with the Young King's brother, Richard the Lion-Hearted. His poetry reflects this life of warfare and political intrigue, centering on the clash of personal and regional loyalties, and exalting the values of masculine personal honor and fearlessness in battle. Although Bertran ended his days in the pious solitude of a Cistercian monastery, he continued to be remembered for his skillful political maneuvering: **Dante** places him in the depths of the *Inferno* as a sower of discord for his role in dividing father from son.

In Praise of War[1]

I love the joyful time of Easter,
that makes the leaves and flowers come forth,
and it pleases me to hear the mirth
of the birds, who make their song
resound through the woods,   5
and it pleases me to see upon the meadows
tents and pavilions planted,
and I feel a great joy
when I see ranged along the field
knights and horses armed for war.   10

And it pleases me when the skirmishers
make the people and their baggage run away,
and it pleases me when I see behind them coming
a great mass of armed men together,
and I have pleasure in my heart   15
when I see strong castles besieged,
the broken ramparts caving in,
and I see the host on the water's edge,
closed in all around by ditches,
with palisades, strong stakes close together   20

And I am as well pleased by a lord
when he is first in the attack,
armed, upon his horse, unafraid,
so he makes his men take heart
by his own brave lordliness.   25
And when the armies mix in battle,

---

1. Translated from the Occitan-Provençal by Frederick Goldin.

each man should be poised
to follow him, smiling,
for no man is worth a thing
till he has given and gotten blow on blow.   30

Maces and swords and painted helms,
the useless shields cut through,
we shall see as the fighting starts,
and many vassals together striking,
and wandering wildly,   35
the unreined horses of the wounded and dead.
And once entered into battle
let every man proud of his birth
think only of breaking arms and heads,
for a man is worth more dead than alive and beaten.   40

I tell you there is not so much savor
in eating or drinking or sleeping,
as when I hear them scream, "There they are! Let's get them!"
on both sides, and I hear riderless
horses in the shadows, neighing,   45
and I hear them scream, "Help! Help!"
and I see them fall among the ditches,
little men and great men on the grass,
and I see fixed in the flanks of the corpses
stumps of lances with silken streamers.   50

Barons, pawn your castles,
and your villages, and your cities
before you stop making war on one another.
Papiols,[2] gladly go
fast to my Lord Yes-and-No[3]   55
and tell him he has lived in peace too long.

2. Bertran's *joglar*, or minstrel, who will sing the lyric.   the time, Richard the Lion-Hearted, whom he
3. A mocking reference to Bertran's lord at   accuses of indecisiveness.

HEINRICH VON MORUNGEN

We know little about Heinrich (ca. 1150–1222), whose thirty-five surviving lyrics are among the earliest great examples of the German tradition of *Minnesang* (literally, "songs of love"), developed in response to the influence of the Occitan lyrics of the troubadours on the vernacular poetics of Europe. The figure of Minne, central to these poems, is rather different from the conventional depiction of the god of love found in Occitan, French, and Italian lyric: gendered female, Minne is in some ways similar to the mythical figure of Aphrodite or Venus from the Greco-Roman pantheon, but she has a dangerous, almost magical quality that emerges from Germanic folklore. In the lyric reproduced here, Heinrich vividly conjures up the torments of love, which consign the speaker not just to the pains of unrequited desire but even to a hellish—yet erotic—abyss.

The Wound of Love[1]

She has wounded me
    in my innermost soul,
within the mortal core,
when I told her
    that I was raving and anguished   5
in desire for her glorious lips.
Once I bade my own lips
    to commend me to her service,
    and to steal me
a tender kiss of hers,   10
    that I might for ever be well.

How I begin to hate
    her rose-red lips,
which I never yet forgot!
It troubles me still,   15
    that they once refused me
with such vehemence.
Thus I have grown so weak
    that I would far rather—alive—
    burn in the abyss   20
of hell than serve her still,
    not knowing to what end.

1. Translated from the German by Peter Dronke.

WALTHER VON DER VOGELWEIDE

Walther's surname simply means "of the bird field" or "forest," telling us only that he was not of a noble landowning family and that he was from a region remote from any city. Walther himself (ca. 1170–ca. 1230) tells us that he learned "to sing and to recite" ("singen unde sagen") while in Austria, likely referring to the cultural center of the court at Vienna. From an entry in the household accounts of the bishop of Passau recording the purchase of a fur coat for the young poet, we know that Walther must have been a member of the bishop's household during his travels across Europe; we can infer that Walther probably depended for his livelihood on numerous patrons, each willing for a while to support his poetic endeavors. Walther was a prolific writer whose lyrics address a wide range of strikingly naturalistic (rather than idealized) topics, composed in a style that emerges from Occitan and French models but takes on an idiosyncratic, deeply personal voice. His lyrics were widely admired but had few imitators, perhaps because of the unusual individuality of their tone.

Dancing Girl[1]

"Lady, accept this garland"—
these were the words I spoke to a pretty girl:
"then you will grace the dance
with the lovely flowers crowning you.
If I had priceless stones,   5
they would be for your hair—
indeed you must believe me,
by my faith, I mean it truly!"

She took my offering
as a gently nurtured child would take it.   10
Her cheeks became as red
as the rose that stands beside the lilies.
Her shining eyes were lowered then in shame,
yet she curtsied graciously.
That was my reward—   15
if any more becomes mine, I'll hold it secret.

"You are so fair,
that I want to give you my chaplet now,
the very best I have.
I know of many flowers, white and red,   20
so far away, on the heath over there,
where they spring up beautiful,
and where the birds are singing—
let us pluck them together there."

I thought that never yet   25
had I known such bliss as I knew then.
From the tree the flowers
rained on us endlessly as we lay in the grass.
Yes, I was filled with laughter in sheer joy.
Just then, when I was so gloriously   30
rich in my dreaming,
then day broke, and I was forced to wake.

1. Translated from the German by Peter Dronke.

She has stirred me so
that this summer, with every girl I meet,
I must gaze deep in her eyes: 35
perhaps one will be mine: then all my cares are gone.
What if she were dancing here?
Ladies, be so kind,
set your hats back a little.
Oh, if only, under a garland, I could see that face!   40

IBN 'ARABI

T he greatest poet of medieval al-
Andalus, Ibn 'Arabi (1165–1240)
was also one of its greatest philosophers—bested only by his countryman
Averroës (Ibn Rushd), whose commentary on Aristotle transformed the history of thought in the West. Born in
Murcia (in modern Spain), Ibn 'Arabi
received the standard education in
grammar and rhetoric appropriate to a
son of a minor court official, without
any specifically religious education.
After a conversion experience in his
early teens, however, Ibn 'Arabi devoted
himself fully to his lifelong task: the
integration of philosophy and theology
through the medium of mystical devotion. This goal is evident in his poetry's
language of passionate desire directed
toward the divine: the lover seeks at
once to possess the beloved completely
and to be annihilated by the beloved,
losing track of the self in the experience of the other.

Gentle Now, Doves[1]

Gentle now, doves of the thornberry
and moringa[2] thicket,
don't add to my heartache
your sighs.

Gentle now,   5
or your sad cooing
will reveal the love I hide,
the sorrow I hide away.

I echo back, in the evening,
in the morning, echo,   10
the longing of a love-sick lover,
the moaning of the lost.

1. Translated from the Arabic by Michael Sells.   2. Horseradish tree (of East India and Africa).

In a grove of Gháda,[3]
spirits wrestled,
bending the limbs down over me,
passing me away.

They brought yearning,
breaking of the heart,
and other new twists of pain,
putting me through it.

Who is there for me in Jám',
and the Stoning-Ground at Mína,
who for me at Tamarisk Grove,
or at the way-station of Na'mán?[4]

Hour by hour
they circle my heart
in rapture, in love-ache,
and touch my pillars with a kiss.

As the best of creation
circled the Ká'ba,[5]
which reason with its proofs
called unworthy.

He kissed the stones there—
and he was entrusted with the word!
What is the house of stone
compared to a man or woman?

They swore, how often!
they'd never change—piling up vows.
She who dyes herself red with henna
is faithless.

A white-blazed gazelle
is an amazing sight,
red-dye signaling,
eyelids hinting,

Pasture between breastbone
and innards.
Marvel,
a garden among the flames!

My heart can take on
any form:

15

20

25

30

35

40

45

50

3. A kind of tamarisk often featured in early Arabic love poetry.
4. All sites along the Muslim pilgrimage route leading to the shrine of the Ka'aba at Mecca.
5. The ritual circling of the Ka'aba is the climax of the pilgrimage.

for gazelles a meadow,
a cloister for monks,

For the idols, sacred ground,
Ka'ba for the circling pilgrim,
the tables of the Toráh,[6]   55
the scrolls of the Qur'án.

I profess the religion of love.
Wherever its caravan turns
along the way, that is the belief,
the faith I keep.   60

Like Bishr,
Hind and her sister,
love-mad Qays and the lost Láyla,
Máyya and her lover Ghaylán.[7]

---

6. The first five books of the Hebrew Bible
(traditionally written on a scroll).

7. Famous pairs of lover and beloved from the
Arabic and Persian tradition.

ALFONSO X

The King of Castile, León, and
Galicia, Alfonso X (1221–1284)
was both a political and an intellectual leader who transformed the status
of Castilian (an early version of Spanish) by making it the standard literary
and administrative language of his
realm and commissioning the translation of numerous scientific, historical,
and literary works from Arabic into
Castilian: consequently, he was commonly called Alfonso el Sabio ("the

Learned"). He was also a poet whose
own compositions were written in
Galician-Portuguese, a popular literary
vernacular of the period; they included
both devotional lyrics such as his *Can-
tigas de Santa Maria* (*Songs on the Virgin Mary*) and more secular works.
In "The Scorpions," we get a rare
insight into the complex position of
the monarch who must rule by force,
but who longs to escape into anonymous solitude.

The Scorpions[1]

I cannot find such great delight
in the song
of birds, or in their twittering,
in love or in ambition
or in arms—for I fear   5

---

1. Translated from the Galician-Portuguese by Peter Dronke.

that these indeed
are fraught with danger—
as in a good galleon
that can take me speedily
from this demonic landscape   10
where the scorpions dwell;
for within my heart
I have felt their sting!

And by the holy God I swear
I would wear   15
neither cloak nor beard,
nor would I involve myself in love
or arms, for injury
and lamentation
come from these at every season—   20
no, I'd pilot a merchant-ship
and sail across the ocean,
selling vinegar and flour,
and I would fly from the poison
of the scorpion, for I know   25
no other medicine against it.

I can take no pleasure here
in tilting,
nor, God save the mark,[2]
in mock-tournaments;   30
as for going armed by night
or patrolling,
I do it without any joy—
for I find more enchantment in the sea
than in being a knight: 35
long ago I was a mariner,
and henceforth I long to guard
myself against the scorpion, and return
to what I was in the beginning.

I must try to explain to you: 40
the demon
will never be able to trick me
now into speaking the language
of arms, for this is not my role—
(useless   45
for me to reason thus,
I have not even arms to try)—
rather, I long to go alone
and in a merchant's guise
to find some land   50
where they cannot strike at me:
the black scorpion, and the mottled.

2. An exclamation of scorn.

SHEM TOV ARDUTIEL

Shem Tov (late thirteenth century–after 1345) was a fluent writer in three languages, making him a valuable member of the court of Alfonso XI, King of Castile (modern Spain). He is known for his *Proverbios morales* (*Moral Proverbs*), a collection of edifying epigrams published under the Spanish form of his name, Santob de Carrión; for a number of translations from Arabic into Hebrew; and for his original compositions. His masterwork is "The Battles of the Pen and Scissors," an elaborate fantasy in which the poet sits down to work on a cold day only to find his inkpot frozen. A debate ensues between the pen, who argues that it is best to write with ink, and the scissors, who claims that one should cut words out of paper. Is the work a thinly veiled political satire, a playful entertainment, or an allegory of poetics itself? In the ambiguity is the pleasure of the text.

From The Battles of the Pen and the Scissors[1]

I. WRITER, YOU HOLD

Writer, you hold a flame in your hand,
    or is it the blade of a sword or a spear—
the tree of knowledge of good and evil,
    or a staff to make wondrous signs appear?

II. TO PRAISE THE PEN

Are there words enough in all of song
    to praise the pen? Who else could bear
the burden of bringing back the past
and preserving it then as though with myrrh?

It has no ear with which it might hear,
    or mouth with which to offer answers;
and yet the pen, in a single stroke,
at once does both—observes and remembers.

III. TOMORROW I'LL WRITE

At night he says: "Tomorrow I'll write,"
but there's nothing at all to back up his words;
the heaven's frost laughs in his face,
and the cackling of mocking ice is heard.

Don't pride yourself on tomorrow's prize,
when you have no notion of what it hides.

---

1. Translated from the Hebrew by Peter Cole.

IV. ENTER THE SCISSORS

A body fully drawn and rotted through,
like clothes eaten by moths—but this one's written:
a man with his hand in wisdom brought it forth,
    forming hole after hole in its skin.

V. WORK I WAS CUT OUT TO DO

I'm precious to every soul and man,
and lacking matter am only form.

I'm purest spirit—my body's nothing,
riding clouds and wings of the wind.

VI. THE PEN FIGHTS BACK

If only someone would shut you up,
    or that might be your wisdom's will;
for hope deferred you'll finish writing
    just makes the heart and soul feel ill.

Your languor casts us into a torpor—
then leaves us holding shreds of paper.

VII. THE SCISSORS LONGED

The scissors longed to be joined at last,
leaving nothing in the way of division—
so that its two might then be one,
to cut through what might come between them.

HADEWIJCH OF BRABANT

We know little about Hadewijch (thirteenth century) beyond the fact that she was an important member of a beguinage—a secular community of devout women who gathered voluntarily to serve the poor and worship Christ—located in the region of Brabant (now on the border of Belgium and the Netherlands). Already in Hadewijch's day, the beguines were regarded with suspicion by church authorities, and in the early fourteenth century they were condemned and some were executed on charges of heresy for their unconventional way of worshipping Christ through service to the poor. Hadewijch's surviving writings include letters, prose accounts of her divinely inspired visions, and devotional lyrics, which stand out for the way in which she expresses religious experience using figurative language derived from secular romance. Her god of love at first looks like the Cupid figure of French and Latin poetry but ultimately reveals himself to be the Son of God, embodied Love.

The Cult of Love[1]

1

The birds have long been silent
that were blithe here before:
their blitheness has departed,
they have lost their summer now;
they would swiftly sing again   5
if that summer came again,
which they have chosen above all
and for which they were born:
one hears it in their voices then.

2

I'll say no more of birds' laments: 10
their joy, their pain, is quickly gone;
I have more grievous cause to moan:
Love, to whom we should aspire,
weighs us down with her noble cares,
so we chase after false delights   15
and Love cannot enfold us then.
Ah, what has baseness done to us!
Who shall erase that faithlessness?

3

The mighty ones, whose hand is strong,
it is on them I still rely,   20
who work at all times in Love's bond,
heedless of pain, grief, tragedy;
they want to ride through all the land
that lovers loving by love have found,
so perfect is their noble heart;   25
they know what Love can teach by love,
how Love exalts lovers by love.

4

Why then should anyone refuse,
since by loving Love can be won?
Why not ride, longing, through the storm,   30
trusting in the power of Love,
aspiring to the cult of Love?
Love's peerlessness will then be seen—
there, in the brightness of Love's dawn,
where for Love's sake is shunned no pain   35
and no pain caused by Love weighs down.

1. Translated from the Flemish by Peter Dronke.

5

Often I call for help as a lost one,
but then, when you come close, my dear one,
with new solace you bear me up
and with high spirit I ride on,   40
sport with my dear so joyously
as if north and south and east
and west all lands belonged to me!
Then suddenly I am dashed down.—
Oh, what use to tell my pain?   45

ANONYMOUS

This poignant quatrain appears, in its original Middle English, in the middle of the highly formal Latin prose of the *Speculum Ecclesie*, or *Mirror of the Church* (1240), inserted at the point where the Apostle John is asked by the suffering Christ to take the Virgin Mary as his own mother. This pitiful scene elicits an affective response from the reader, heightened both by the intimate tone of the vernacular lines and by the poem's delicate wordplay, which aligns the setting sun in the sky with the dying Son on the cross, and echoes the Virgin's name in the sorrowful refrain "me rueth."

Calvary

Now goeth sonne[1] under wood,
Me rueth, Mary, thy fair rood;[2]
Now goeth sonne under tree,
Me rueth, Mary, thy son and thee.

1. Both "sun" and "son."

2. Both "face" and "cross."

JALÂLODDIN RUMI

Rumi (1207–1283) was born in the easternmost regions of Persia, in the town of Balkh (in modern Afghanistan), but spent almost all his life far to the west, in Konya (in modern Turkey): the name "Rumi" means "inhabitant of Rum," a term loosely used to designate the newly Islamicized regions formerly held by Christian Byzantium, the eastern capital of the Roman Empire. The son of a scholar and teacher, Rumi seemed about to follow in his father's footsteps, but he suddenly emerged as a prolific and extraordinarily powerful mystical poet, transformed by the first of three friendships that would help inspire him to give voice to his passionate spiritual impulses. His major achievement is the *Masnavi*, a collection of six books of rhymed couplets that lead the reader on a kind of spiritual ascent; it is beloved by Persian readers, who regard it as one of the greatest masterworks of their literary tradition. Rumi's shorter poems, however, have pierced national borders, making him the poet of the Middle East who is most widely read in the Western world, not so much for the undeniable literary merit of his verses as for their powerful spiritual call.

Dissolver of Sugar[1]

Dissolver of sugar, dissolve me,
if this is the time.
Do it gently with a touch of hand, or a look.
Every morning I wait at dawn. That's when it's happened before.
Or do it suddenly like an execution. How else   5
can I get ready for death?

You breathe without a body like a spark.
You grieve, and I begin to feel lighter.
You keep me away with your arm,
but the keeping away is pulling me in.   10

The Question

One dervish[1] to another, *What was your vision of God's presence?*
I haven't seen anything.
But for the sake of conversation, I'll tell you a story.

God's presence is there in front of me, a fire on the left,
a lovely stream on the right.   5
One group walks toward the fire, *into* the fire, another
toward the sweet flowing water.
No one knows which are blessed and which not.
Whoever walks into the fire appears suddenly in the stream.
A head goes under on the water surface, that head   10
pokes out of the fire.
Most people guard against going into the fire,
and so end up in it.
Those who love the water of pleasure and make it their devotion
are cheated with this reversal.   15
The trickery goes further.

---

1. All selections translated from the Persian by Coleman Barks.
1. An ascetic Sufi (a follower of a mystic form of Islam); Rumi founded an order of dervishes who, as he had often done, danced while reciting.

The voice of the fire tells the *truth*, saying *I am not fire*.
I am fountainhead. Come into me and don't mind the sparks.

If you are a friend of God, fire is your water.
You should wish to have a hundred thousand sets of mothwings,   20
so you could burn them away, one set a night.
The moth sees light and goes into fire. You should see fire
and go toward light. Fire is what of God is world-consuming.
Water, world-protecting.
Somehow each gives the appearance of the other. To these eyes you
    have now   25
what looks like water burns. What looks like
fire is a great relief to be inside.
You've seen a magician make a bowl of rice
seem a dish full of tiny, live worms.
Before an assembly with one breath he made the floor swarm   30
with scorpions that weren't there.
How much more amazing God's tricks.
Generation after generation lies down, defeated, they think,
but they're like a woman underneath a man, circling him.
One molecule-mote-second thinking of God's reversal of comfort and pain   35
is better than any attending ritual. That splinter
of intelligence is substance.
The fire and water themselves:
Accidental, done with mirrors.

An Empty Garlic

You miss the garden,
    because you want a small fig from a random tree.
You don't meet the beautiful woman.
You're joking with an old crone.
It makes me want to cry how she detains you,   5
stinking-mouthed, with a hundred talons,
putting her head over the roofedge to call down,
tasteless fig, fold over fold, empty
as dry-rotten garlic.

She has you tight by the belt,   10
even though there's no flower and no milk
inside her body.
Death will open your eyes
to what her face is: Leather spine
of a black lizard. No more advice.   15

Let yourself be silently drawn
by the stronger pull of what you really love.

Only Breath

Not Christian or Jew or Muslim, not Hindu
Buddhist, sufi, or zen. Not any religion

or cultural system. I am not from the East
or the West, not out of the ocean or up

from the ground, not natural or ethereal, not   5
composed of elements at all. I do not exist,

am not an entity in this world or in the next,
did not descend from Adam and Eve or any

origin story. My place is placeless, a trace
of the traceless. Neither body or soul.   10

I belong to the beloved, have seen the two
worlds as one and that one call to and know,

first, last, outer, inner, only that
breath breathing human being.

GUIDO GUINIZZELLI

Guido Guinizzelli (ca. 1240–1276) was the founder of a poetic lineage whose more famous members would be **Guido Cavalcanti** and **Dante Alighieri**. The *dolce stil nuovo*, or "sweet new style," influenced the development of medieval and Renaissance lyric more than any other movement since that of the Occitan troubadours. Guido served as a lawyer and judge in Bologna, where his political maneuvering ended with his exile in 1274, shortly before his death. Some twenty lyrics survive from Guido's pen; about ten more works exist in fragmentary form or are of doubtful authorship. Guido's masterpiece, "Love always repairs to the noble heart," became a kind of manifesto for the masters of the sweet new style, paraphrased by Dante in his **Purgatorio** and widely imitated by generations of poets. Perhaps the most striking feature of Guido's poetry is its philosophical quality—its ability to address profound intellectual truths within the ornate, sweet language of metaphor and allusion.

Love always repairs to the noble heart[1]

Love always repairs to the noble heart
   Like a bird winging back into its grove:
Nor was love made before the noble heart,
   Nor did nature, before the heart, make love.
For they were there as long as was the Sun,   5
   Whose splendor's ever bright;

---

1. Translated from the Italian by James J. Wilhelm.

Never did love before that shining come.
Love nestles deep inside nobility
    Exactly the way
One sees the heart within the fiery blaze.   10

Fire of love in noble heart is caught
    Like power gleaming inside a precious stone.
The value does not come down from the stars
    Until the Sun has blenched the stone all pure.
Only after the might of the Sun   15
    Has drawn out all that's vile
Does the star bestow its noble power.
Just so a heart transformed by nature pure,
    Noble and elect,
A woman starlike with her love injects.   20

Love for this reason stays in noble heart
    Like a waving flame atop a burning brand,
Shining, its own delight, subtle and bright;
    It is so proud, it knows no other way.
Yet a nature which is still debased   25
    Greets love as water greets the fire,
With the cold hissing against the heat.
Love in noble heart will find a haven
    Like the shine
Of a diamond glinting in ore within the mine.   30

Sun beats against the mud the livelong day;
    Mud it remains; Sun does not lose its ray;
The haughty one says: "I am noble by my tribe."
    He is the mud; Sun is the noble power.
Man must never believe   35
    That nobility exists outside the heart
In the grandness of his ancestry,
For without virtue, heart has no noble worth,
    It's a ray through a wave;
The heavens retain the sparkle and splendor they gave.   40

Shines among the powers of heaven
    God the creator, more than Sun in our eye;
Each angel knows the Maker beyond its sphere,
    And turning its circle, obeys God's noble power.
And thus it follows at once: 45
    The blesséd tasks of the Master transpire.
In the same way, in all truth, the beautiful lady
Should behave, for in her eyes reflects the desire
    Of a noble man
Who will turn his every thought to her command.   50

Lady, God will ask me: "Why did you presume?"
    When my soul stands before his mighty throne.

"You passed the heavens, came all the way to me,
    And cheapened me in the light of profane love.
To me is due all the praise   55
    And to the Queen of the Royal Realm[2]
Who makes all fraudulence cease."
I'll tell him then: "She had an angel look—
    A heavenly face.
What harm occurred if my love in her was placed?"   60

2. The Virgin Mary.

GUIDO CAVALCANTI

Drawing on the "sweet new style" developed by Tuscan poets such as **Guido Guinizzelli** but adding his own unique perspective on the ability of lyric to capture profound truths about the nature of the human soul, Guido Cavalcanti (ca. 1255–1300) paved the way for the flowering of Italian verse in **Dante** and **Petrarch**. An eager participant in the bitter Florentine political scene of the late thirteenth century, Guido was exiled from the city of his birth and died on the road while trying to return. His complex, intricate poems carry out a philosophical argument, progressing through logically connected stages whose startlingly vivid juxtaposed images convey the passions of the soul. In "Donna me prega" ("A lady asks me"), Guido uses the conventional figure of the beloved lady to instigate a philosophical discourse in eight parts on the nature of love; he ultimately concludes that the body's physical desires can be balanced with the demands of the intellect only through the rational effort to comprehend the power of love over the sense perceptions that knit together body and soul.

A lady asks me[1]

A lady asks me—and so I want to talk
About an accidental quality[2] that is all too often uncontrollable
And is so high and mighty that we call it "love."[3]
    If only he who denies that fact could feel its bitter truth!
And, for this case right here, I'd like to find someone who knows
        all about it,   5
Since I don't think that a man of lowly heart
    Could ever make sense of such an argument.
Because without a physical demonstration
I would never even try to claim to know
Where it can be found, and who first made it go,   10
    And what might be its power and its potency,

1. Translated from the Italian by Suzanne Akbari.
2. A quality that is not essential to a thing (a philosophical term).
3. The only use of the noun "love" (*amore*) in the poem; every other reference is simply to "it."

And, then, its inner nature, and every last one of its movements,
And the blissful biting pleasure that makes us call it "love,"[4]
And whether you can ever really make it open to the eye.

    In that region where memory is found   15
It finds its private place, formed with the same contours
Of airy lightness itself, by a circling darkness
    That comes from fiery Mars,[5] and stays right there.
It is a created thing, and has its own special name,
It's a habit of the soul, and the heart's willful flame.   20
    It rises up from a form that one has seen,
Which is taken up in the mind by the possible intellect[6]
As if it were a substance, and then it settles in that place.
There, it never has any power,
    Since that intellect does not descend any lower;   25
It just shines in itself, glowing in the eternal effect;
The mind doesn't take delight in this, but is rapt in contemplation,
And so does not create some empty idle image.

    It's not a power of the mind, but it comes from the faculty
That is perfection itself (so the wise men say);   30
It's not the power of reason but of the senses I'm speaking of.
    It keeps its role as judge, regardless of its strength,
Because strong intention always rules over reason:
It doesn't work so well in the one who tends toward vice.
    Its potency often brings death at its heels,   35
Because when the mind's power is impaired,
This pushes the mind down the wrong road;
But not because it is against Nature!
    When a man is—by chance—turned away from the highest good,
He can't say that he is truly alive,   40
Because he is not the master of himself.
The same thing happens when a man forgets about this.

    Its mode of being is such that, when desire is so very strong
That it goes beyond every limit imposed by Nature,
It doesn't pause to take a refreshing rest.   45
    It shifts about, changing color, drawing laughter out of tears,
And the form you see, out of fear, flies away from sight.
It doesn't stay long; beyond that, you will see
    That it's mostly found in those whose spirit is truly noble.
This new quality causes you to sigh   50
And makes you gaze intently at a place—a place you cannot see—
Fanning such an anger that it feels like flames
    (If you haven't felt it, you don't know what I mean),
And it doesn't let you reach out and touch what you want,

---

4. Cavalcanti uses *amare*, a form of the verb
"to love," and thus plays on the adjective *amaro*
(bitter); this pun is also frequent in other
romance vernacular poetry (French, Occitan).
5. Roman god of war; the dusky redness of his

planet reflects the darkness of the lover's
mind.
6. The storehouse of all possible ideas or concepts, according to medieval theories of the
mind.

And it doesn't let you look around for another source of joy: 55
For sure, your mind doesn't know anything at all.

It draws forth a quick glance from one who feels the same
And so it seems like pleasure's sure to follow:
It can't stay hidden anymore, once the eye-beams meet.[7]
The beautiful forms—not those lesser ones—are like arrows,   60
For the desire is lessened by the fear;
But the soul who is pierced gets just what he longs for.
And it can never be truly known through the eye:
To be able to see the faintest color white won't help you see this sight,
And—now listen to me!—you can't see form at all: 65
Ever so much less, then, can you see what comes from this.
Having no color, having no being in itself,
Placed in darkest shadows, it devours light itself.
Without any lying, I tell you, and you must believe me in this,
Only from this thing is true mercy born.   70

You can safely go, my song,
Wherever you want to go, because I've made you so pretty
That your clever argument will always be praised
By all those who have real understanding:
You don't want to hang around with anyone else.   75

---

7. The classical idea that love travels along the glance, sometimes identified with a dart, appears occasionally in medieval poetry and became a commonplace in the Renaissance.

DANTE ALIGHIERI

Dante's lyric poetry responds directly to his fellow poets of the "sweet new style," building on the concepts of nobility and gentility developed by **Guido Guinizzelli** and countering **Guido Cavalcanti's** philosophical condemnation of love as a dangerous passion that must be controlled by reason. Before turning to the epic genre in his *Divine Comedy*, Dante (1265–1321) wrote a large body of short lyrics, many of which he embedded within a longer prose commentary in his early masterpiece, the *Vita Nuova* (*New Life*), in which he forcefully contradicts Cavalcanti's view of love as irra-tional and destructive, insisting that the love of woman is the only path to spiritual transcendence. In the first poem presented here, Dante imagines a community in which those who truly comprehend the power of love, both the male writers of lyric and the women they adore, inhabit an enchanted space outside of time; in the second, he elaborates Guinizzelli's conception of the "gentle heart" into an allegory of desire in which love of a woman can redeem the soul of a man, and—a shockingly innovative claim—the love of a man can do the same for a woman.

Guido, I wish[1]

Guido, I wish that you and Lapo[2] and I,
Spirited on the wings of a magic spell,
Could drift in a ship where every rising swell
Would sweep us at our will across the skies;
Then tempest never, or any weather dire   5
Could ever make our blissful living cease;
No, but abiding in a steady, blesséd peace
Together we'd share the increase of desire.

And Lady Vanna and Lady Lagia[3] then
And she[4] who looms above the thirty best[5]   10
Would join us at the good enchanter's[6] behest;
And there we'd talk of Love without an end
To make those ladies happy in the sky—
With Lapo enchanted too, and you and I.

Love and the gentle heart[1]

Love and the gentle heart are one thing,
even as the sage[2] affirms in his poem,
and so one can be without the other
as much as rational soul without reason.
Nature creates them when she is amorous: 5
Love as lord and the heart as his mansion,
in which, sleeping, he rests
sometimes a brief and sometimes a long season.
Beauty appears in a wise lady, then,
which so pleases the eyes that in the heart   10
is born a desire for that which pleases;
and so long it lasts sometimes therein
that it wakens the spirit of Love.
And the same to a lady does a worthy man.

1. Translated from the Italian by James J.
Wilhelm.
2. Guido Cavalcanti; see pp. 356–58. Guido
and Lapo Gianni were poets in Dante's literary
circle.
3. Giovanna and Lagia were Guido's and
Lapo's ladies.

4. Beatrice, Dante's beloved.
5. Dante wrote a poem naming the most
beautiful women of Florence.
6. Merlin.
1. Translated from the Italian by Dino Cer-
vigni and Edward Vasta.
2. Guido Guinizzelli; see above, p. 354.

ALEXANDER THE WILD

A vivid full-page illustration of a man mounted on a rearing horse labeled "der wilde Alexander" (the wild Alexander), juxtaposed with a few lyrics, gives this late thirteenth-century poet his name. Like **Walther von der Vogelweide**, Alexander was a wandering poet who made his living by attaching himself to various courtly patrons; his vocabulary suggests that he was of South German or Swiss origin. In their vocabulary and poetic motifs, Alexander's lyrics grow out of the tradition of *Minnesang*, or "songs of love," but in their strong emphasis on social and moral issues they depart from that earlier mode. In "Strawberry Picking," Alexander conceals a stern moral lesson about the dangers of sin behind the veil of a colorful, naturalistic evocation of the summer landscape of a remembered childhood whose innocence proves to have been more apparent than real.

Strawberry Picking[1]

Long ago, when we were children,
in the time that spanned the years
when we ran across the meadows,
over from those, now back to these,
there, where we at times   5
found violets,
you now see cattle leap for flies.

I remember how we sat
deep in flowers, and decided
which girl was the prettiest.   10
Our young looks were radiant then
with the new garland
for the dance.
And so the time goes by.

Look, there we ran to find strawberries,   15
ran to the beech from the fir-tree,
over sticks and stones,
as long as the sun shone.
Then a forester called out
through the branches   20
"Come along, children, go home!"

All our hands were stained,
picking strawberries yesterday;
to us it was nothing but play.
Then, again and again, we heard   25

1. Translated from the German by Peter Dronke.

our shepherd calling
and moaning:
"Children, the forest is full of snakes!"

One child walked in the tall grass,
started, and cried aloud: 30
"Children, right here there was a snake!
He has bitten our pony—
it will never heal;
it must always
remain poisoned and unwell."   35

"Come along then, out of the forest!
If you do not now make haste
it will happen as I say:
if you are not sure to be gone
from the forest while there is day,   40
you will lose your way
and your joy will become a moan."

Do you know that five young women
loitered in the meadow-lands
till the king locked up his hall?   45
Great were their moans and their distress—
for the bailiffs tore
their clothes away,
so that they stood naked, without a dress.[2]

2. Probably an allusion to the parable of the Five Foolish Virgins in the New Testament: see Matthew 25.1–13.

DAFYDD AP GWILYM

Universally recognized as the outstanding Welsh poet of the Middle Ages, Dafydd (ca. 1310–1370) left a large corpus of almost two hundred lyrics on a variety of themes, ranging from the pains of love and the beauty of the natural world to dynamic scenes of village life and comic erotica: one of his popular (but rarely anthologized) lyrics is a encomium in praise of the penis ("Cywydd y gal"). Renowned for his popularization of the *cywydd* meter, a musical verse form that soon became standard among Welsh poets, Dafydd wrote during a time of political turmoil following the loss of Welsh independence in 1282—years that were also, paradoxically, a dynamic period of cultural revival. In "The Fox," Dafydd displays his two greatest strengths in portrayal: a natural landscape, conjured in vivid detail, and a sophisticated, highly individual subjectivity. For Dafydd, the subject is always the self, whose engagement with the world reveals both his own essential character and that of the world around him.

The Fox[1]

Yesterday was I, sure of purpose,
Under the trees (alas that the girl doesn't see it)
Standing under Ovid's[2] stems
And waiting for a pretty girl beneath the trees;
She made me weep on her way.   5
I saw when I looked there
(An ape's shape where I did not love)
A red fox (he doesn't love our hounds' place)
Sitting like a tame animal,
On his haunches near his den.   10

    I drew between my hands
A bow of yew there, it was brave,[3]
About, like an armed man,
On the brow of the hill, a stirring of high spirits,
Weapon for coursing along a district,   15
To hit him with a long, stout bolt.
I drew for a try a shaft
Clear past the jaw.
My grief, my bow went
In three pieces, luckless disaster.   20

    I got mad (I did not dread him,
Unhappy bear) at the fox.
He's a lad who'd love a hen,
A silly bird, and bird flesh;
He doesn't follow the cry of horns,   25
Rough his voice and his carol.

Ruddy is he in front of a talus[4] slope,
Like an ape among green trees.
At both ends of a field there turns up
A dog-shape looking for a goose.   30
Crows' beacon near the brink of a hill,
Acre-strider, color of an ember,
Likeness of a lure for crows and magpies at a fair,
Portent looking like a dragon.
Lord of excitement, chewer of a fat hen,   35
Of acclaimed fleece, glowing flesh.
An awl of hollowed-out fine earth,
Fire-dish at the edge of a shuttered window.
Copper bow of light feet,
Tongs like a beak of blood.   40

    Not easy for me to follow him,
And his dwelling toward Annwn.[5]

---

1. Translated from the Welsh by Richard Morgan Loomis.
2. Roman love poet (43 B.C.E.–17 C.E.).
3. Splendid; excellent.
4. A pile of rock fragments at the base of a cliff.
5. The otherworld of Welsh myth.

Red roamer, he was found to be too fierce,
He'd run ahead of a course of hounds.
Sharp his rushing, gorse-strider,   45
Leopard with a dart in his rump.

HAFEZ

S hams al-Din Muhammad (1350–
1390), whose pen name, "Hafez,"
simply means "accomplished reciter of
the Qur'an," was a native of Shiraz (a
city in modern Iran). His poems continue to be extraordinarily popular
among Persian speakers, who recite
their lines much as English speakers
spontaneously quote phrases from
Shakespeare. Hafez's verses are notoriously difficult to translate, due largely
to the nature of Persian poetry. It relies
on modes of metaphor very different
from those in the Western tradition,
and the verse forms favored by Hafez
have no English equivalent—in particular, the poem tends to have individual, free-standing lines rather than a
complex interwoven sequence of lines.
Hafez is sometimes viewed as a Sufi
writer in the tradition of **Rumi**, but his
poems are not as theologically oriented,
though they can be read as allegories
of devotion: Hafez celebrates the virtues of actual wine drinking and real,
embodied friends just as much as the
spiritual pleasures of the hereafter and
union with the divine beloved.

Plant friendship's tree[1]

Plant friendship's tree—the heart's desire
    Is the fruit it bears:

And uproot enmity—which brings
    Sorrows and cares.

Be friendly, easy, with drunkards—   5
    Good fellowship's theirs;

It's pride brings the hangover, not
    The wine-seller's wares.

Talk with your friends, deep in the night,
    And see how life fares   10

Since when we are gone the heavens
    Will bring others our cares;

---

1. Both poems are translated from the Persian by Dick Davis.

And welcome the spring in your heart
    Since the world never spares

To provide for us roses and song birds,   15
    Whoever despairs.

And love your belovèd—the heavens require you
    To be one who bears

The grief of Majnun[2] all your life:
    God grant me my prayers!   20

Your heart is so tired! You feel caught
    In the weary world's snares

But sip at your wine, and hear in your heart
    The hope it declares:

That Hafez will sit in his orchard   25
    By the stream that he shares

With his cypress-slim love, God willing,
    In the place that is theirs.

Thanks be to God

Thanks be to God now that the wine-shop door
Is open, since it's there I'm heading for;

The jars are groaning with fermented wine,
With wine that's real, and not a metaphor,

That brings us drunkenness, and pride, and pleasure,   5
While we bring weakness, need, and not much more!

The secret I've not told, and won't, to others
I'll tell my friend—of him I can be sure.

It's not a short tale, it describes the twists
In my belovèd's hair, and lovers' lore,   10

Majnun's grief, Layli's curls, Ayaz's foot
That royal Mahmud's face bowed down before;[1]

And like a hawk I've seeled[2] my eyes to all
The world, to glimpse the face that I adore.

---

2. The protagonist (sometimes called "Qays") of a classical Arabic love story; he was driven mad by his love for Layli.
1. Pairs of famous lovers: Layli and Majnun, and the sultan Mahmud and his beloved slave Ayaz.
2. Closed (literally, "sewn shut," as was done in the process of taming hunting birds).

Whoever strays within your street, it is
Your eyebrows' curve that he will pray before;[3]

O friends, to know the fire in Hafez' heart
Ask candles what they're burning, melting, for.

3. The eyebrows' curve repeats the curve of the *mihrab*, the prayer niche used by a Muslim to orient his or her prayer toward Mecca.

JAHAN KHATUN

Jahan Khatun ("Lady Jahan") was the daughter of the ruler of Fars, the central province of Persia (modern Iran); she lived most of her life in its capital, Shiraz, the home of several other poets of the fourteenth century, including Hafez. More than just scattered lyrics survive from the pen of Jahan Khatun: she is the author of a *divan*, or cycle of collected poems, with an introduction written by herself—a particularly unusual accomplishment in a period when female authors are rare. Although contemporary accounts of Jahan say that her love poems refer to a fellow poet with whom she exchanged verses, several of them apparently mourn a beloved stepmother who died at an early age. The lyric reprinted here includes several of the Eastern poetic tropes that entered Western literature by way of the Arabic literature of al-Andalus (Spain) and the troubadours of Provence, such as the midnight garden, with its roses and nightingales, and the lovesickness that no physician can cure.

Heart, in his beauty's garden[1]

Heart, in his beauty's garden, I—
  Like nightingales—complain,
And of his roses now for me
  Only the thorns remain;

My friends have gathered flowers, but I,   5
  Because of all his harshness,
Can find no flowers to gather here
  And search for them in vain.

My heart is filled with suffering;
  And all my doctor says is,   10
"Sugar from him, and nothing else,
  Will lessen your heart's pain."

1. Translated from the Persian by Dick Davis.

I've filled the world with love for him,
    So why do I receive
Such cruelty from my dearest love,   15
    Again, and yet again?

My free-will's gone from me, so how
    Can my poor ears accept
All the advice my clever tutor's
    Homilies contain?   20

No, in the pre-dawn darkness, I
    Am like the nightingale
That in the orchards sings the rose
    Its old love-sick refrain.

I hear it's strangers whom you welcome,   25
    Whom you make much of now;
Let me then be a stranger in
    The kingdom where you reign.

CHRISTINE DE PIZAN

Born in Italy but raised in France, Christine de Pizan (ca. 1364–ca. 1431) has the distinction of being the first professional European writer. Her father was physician and adviser to Charles V of France, and her husband had a promising career in the government administration; when first one and then the other died, Christine found herself a widow at the age of twenty-four, solely responsible for three children, a niece, and an aged mother. She supported them all with her pen, writing histories, books of myth, advice to princes, and allegorical visions for a series of royal and noble patrons. Christine's last poem is an exuberant song of praise of the young national heroine, Joan of Arc, who was then at the very height of her triumphs; Christine's early poems, one of which is reproduced here, comment on the tragic loss of her husband and consequent withdrawal from the world of erotic exchange. By embracing the role of the *seulete* (a term difficult to translate: literally, "the little solitary one"), Christine acknowledges her loss of the protection and rule of a husband, with all the difficulties that her new status entails—and all the freedom.

All alone am I, and alone I wish to stay[1]

All alone am I, and alone I wish to stay;
All alone, my sweet friend[2] has gone away.
All alone, no companion and no master,
All alone, with sorrow everlasting.
All alone, in weeping unconsoled,   5
All alone, more than any desperate soul.
All alone, left behind without a friend.

All alone am I, at the window, at the door,
All alone, hidden away in the corner.
All alone, fed only by my tears,   10
All alone, weighed down by doubt and fear.
All alone—and nothing suits me quite so well.
All alone, shut up in my quiet cell,
All alone, left behind without a friend.

All alone am I, every time, in every place,   15
All alone, wherever I go, wherever I stay.
All alone, more than any soul under the sun,
All alone, abandoned by each one.
All alone, pushed down by painful years,
All alone, wept empty of my tears,   20
All alone, left behind without a friend.

Prince, now my sorrow truly has arrived:
All alone am I, devoured on each side;
All alone, darkness looming without an end,
All alone, left behind without a friend.   25

1. Translated from the French by Suzanne   2. Her husband, now dead.
Akbari.

ANONYMOUS

This fifteenth-century lyric is an especially moving example of the lament, a genre of religious poem widely popular at the close of the Middle Ages, reflecting the strong devotion to the Virgin that pervaded English poetry on the eve of the Reformation. Written from the perspective of the Virgin Mary herself instead of (as would be more usual) from the perspective of one of her devotees, the poem offers a firm yet loving lesson to the reader: Mary asks the female reader to look at her own child while remembering the suffering of Mary's son, and to weep the tears of compassion that will cleanse the soul.

Lament of the Virgin

Of all women that ever were born,
That bear children, abide and see,
How my son lies me before,
Upon my knee, taken from the tree.
Your children ye dance upon your knee.   5
With laughing, kissing and merry cheer;
Behold my child, behold now me,
For now lies dead my dear son dear.

O woman, woman, well is thee,
Thy child's cap thee dotes upon;   10
Thou picks his hair, beholds his ble,[1]
Thou wost[2] not well when thou hast done.
But ever, alas, I make my moan
To see my son's head as it is here;
I pick out thorns by one and one,   15
For now lies dead my dear son dear.

O woman, a chaplet chosen thou has
Thy child to wear, it does thee great liking;
Thou pins it on with great solace,
And I sit with my son sore weeping.   20
His chaplet is thorns' sore pricking,
His mouth I kiss with a careful[3] cheer;
I sit weeping and thou singing,
For now lies dead my dear son dear.

O woman, look to me again,   25
That plays and kisses your children's pappis.[4]
To see my son I have great pain,
In his breast so great a gap is.
And on his body so many swappis.[5]
With bloody lips I kiss him here,   30
Alas! full hard methink me happis,[6]
For now lies dead my dear son dear.

O woman, thou takes thy child by the hand
And says, "My son, give me a strake!"[7]
My son's hands are sorely bleeding;   35
To look on him me list not lake.[8]
His hands he suffered for thy sake
Thus to be bored with nail and spear;
When thou make mirth great sorrow I make,
For now lies dead my dear son dear.   40
Behold, women, when that ye play

---

1. Complexion.
2. Know, be aware of.
3. Woeful.
4. Breasts.

5. Wounds.
6. I suffer.
7. Stroke—i.e., caress.
8. Is no pleasure to me.

And have your children on knees dansand;[9]
You feel their feet, so feat[1] are they,
And to your sight well likand,[2]
But the most[3] finger of any hand,   45
Through my son's feet I may put here,
And pull it out sorely bledand,[4]
For now lies dead my dear son dear.

Therefore, women, by town and street,
Your children's hands when ye behold   50
Their breasts, their body, and their feet,
Then good it were on my son think you wolde,[5]
How care has made my heart full cold
To see my son, with nail and spear,
With scourge and thorns many-fold,   55
Wounded and dead, my dear son dear.

Thou hast thy son full whole and sound,
And mine is dead upon my knee;
Thy child is loose and mine is bound,
Thy child is alive and mine dead is he.   60
Why was this ought[6] but for thee?
For my child trespassed never here.
Me thinks ye be holden[7] to weep with me,
For now lies dead my dear son dear.

Weep with me, both man and wife,   65
My child is yours and loves you well.
If your child had lost his life
You would weep at every mele.[8]
But for my son weep ye never a del.[9]
If you love yours, mine has no peer;   70
He sends yours both hap and hele[1]
And for you died my dear son dear.

Now all women that have your wit,[2]
And see my child on my knees dead,
Weep not for yours but weep for it,   75
And ye shall have full muchel mede.[3]
He would again for your love bleed
Rather than that ye damnéd were.
I pray you all to him take heed,
For now lies dead my dear son dear.   80
Farewell, woman, I may no more

9. Dancing.   7. Obliged.
1. Pretty.   8. Occasion.
2. Liking.   9. Not at all.
3. Largest.   1. Both fortune and health.
4. Bleeding.   2. I.e., wits.
5. Would.   3. A great reward.
6. At all.

For dread of death rehearse his pain.
Ye may laugh when ye list[4] and I weep sore,
That may ye see and ye look to me again.
To love my son and ye be fain,[5]   85
I will love yours with heart entere,[6]
And he shall bring your children and you, certain,
To bliss where is my dear son dear.

4. Wish.   6. Entire.
5. If you be willing.

CHARLES D'ORLEANS

Captured by the English during the Hundred Years' War, the young Duke of Orleans (1394–1465), close relative of the French king, was far too valuable a prisoner to be returned to his home: consequently, he spent the next twenty-four years in comfortable imprisonment in a series of English castles, becoming the valued friend and companion of English nobles and poets.

A skilled writer, Charles was the author of hundreds of lyrics composed in a variety of forms, including the very popular *balade*, a genre designed for musical performance in a court setting. "If you wish to sell your kisses" features a lover who offers to mortgage his heart in order to purchase his lady's embraces—an ironic exchange, in view of Charles's own status as royal hostage.

If you wish to sell your kisses[1]

If you wish to sell your kisses,
I will gladly buy some,
And in return you will have my heart as deposit.
To use them as inheritance,
By the dozens, hundreds, or thousands.   5
Don't sell them to me at as high a price
As you would to a total stranger
For you are receiving me as your liegeman.
    If you wish to sell your kisses,
    I will gladly buy some.   10
    And in return you will have my heart as deposit.
My complete wish and desire
Are yours in spite of all suspicion;
Allow, as a faithful and wise woman,
That for my reward and share   15
I may be among the first served,
    If you wish to sell your kisses.

1. Translated from the French by Sarah Spence.

FARID UD-DIN ATTAR

1145–1221

From the time of Goethe, *The Conference of the Birds* has been admired by Western readers captivated by Attar's ability to describe in poetic language the experience of divinity. Attar tells the story of a group of thirty birds who embark on a pilgrimage to find the mystical great bird, or "Simorgh," whose presence and leadership they long for. The Simorgh is a mythic creature taken from Persian heroic epic and folktale; it is described in such canonical texts as **Ferdowsi's Shahnameh**, where it is able to lift up the hero into the heavens. Attar turns this Simorgh into something quite different: a source of spiritual ascent. Although the Simorgh proves to be a manifestation of divinity, the birds finally discover it not in a remote location but within themselves. The Simorgh turns out to be *si morgh*— literally, "thirty birds." The spiritual journey of the *Conference*, like that told by **Augustine** in his *Confessions*, reaches its end in the depths of the individual's own soul.

LIFE AND TIMES

According to contemporary accounts, the poet's given name was Abu Hamid Muhammad ibn Abu Bakr Ibrahim, but he always was known by the name of his profession, pharmacist (*attar*). He was born in Nishapur, one of the two main cities in the region of Khorasan, which was also the homeland of the poets Ferdowsi, Omar Khayyam, and **Rumi**. Although Attar's life was long, it probably ended violently. The date of his death coincides with the demolition of Nishapur by the invading Mongol army and the massacre of every man, woman, and child within its walls. Despite Attar's subsequent great fame, in his own lifetime he seems to have been little known outside of his own city. A number of works have been attributed to him, but the only two whose authorship is certain are *The Conference of the Birds*, which internal evidence dates to 1177, and a prose account of holy men in the tradition of mystical Islam, the *Biographies of the Saints (Tazkirat al-Awliya)*.

The prose *Biographies* quickly became widely read, but Attar's poetry did not achieve general popularity until more than two centuries after his death. The increasing interest in Attar's poetry paralleled the rising popularity of the brand of mystical Islam espoused throughout his works, Sufism. This form of religious practice sought to build up Muslims' experience of divine presence through devout meditation (*dhikr*), such as the repeated invocation of the names of God or other acts of pious remembrance. There are many strands in Sufism, but they have in common a strong emphasis on the need to learn Sufi practice from others who have embarked on the same spiritual path, whether within an active community of Sufis, under the mentorship of an individual Sufi master, or from the writings of earlier Sufis. The bonds of affection that unite Sufis are described as loving friendships, and the ultimate "Friend" is God. The various strands of Sufism also agree on the goal of the practice: the total annihilation of the self in the experience of God. Paradoxically, this experience of self-annihilation re-creates the individual soul as a manifestation of God. Thus the famous Sufi Mansour al-Hallaj, according to Attar's account in the *Biographies of the Saints*, was once so enrapt in devout contemplation that he cried out ecstatically, "I am the Truth," perceiving himself as God. That Al-Hallaj was condemned for this apparently excessive claim and publicly crucified as a heretic demonstrates another aspect of Sufism. From one standpoint, Sufis could be seen as especially devout Muslims; but they could equally be seen as deviants from the straight path of Islam, dangerous innovators who were closer to the pious practices of Christian ascetics than to the exemplary life of moderation conducted by the Prophet Muhammad.

WORK

On its face, *The Conference of Birds* is a wondrous animal fable like the Greek tales of **Aesop** or the Indian **Pañcatantra**. Read within the framework of Sufi practice, however, the work immediately opens up as a figurative account of the soul's search for God, the Divine Friend. In some ways, this figurative language resembles the parables told by Jesus in the Gospels, here put to use in an extended literary form: the *Conference* uses the parable as a frame for a sequence of about one hundred shorter tales on saintly figures of Sufi tradition. The frame tale centers on a group of birds who set out on a pilgrimage in search of the Simorgh, the great bird who they hope will be their leader and Friend. Their search for the Simorgh is ultimately successful, but only for the thirty birds who persist until the very end. The others fall by the wayside, worn down by the difficulty of the struggle to purify the soul.

The story of Sheikh Sam'an is by far the longest of the exemplary tales embedded in the story of the birds' pilgrimage. Sheikh Sam'an is a holy man even before the story begins, spending his life at Mecca in the shadow of the holiest site in Islam, the Ka'aba. His life is turned upside down by a dream in which he finds himself not at the eastern heart of Islam but the western heart of Christendom—"Rome," the Islamic name for Constantinople. Instead of being at the threshold of the Ka'aba, he is in the sanctuary of a church, and instead of worshipping God, he is prostrated before a stone image. The sheikh wakes up terrified but is nonetheless impelled to go to the lands of the Christians, where he becomes enslaved by his devotion to a living idol, a beautiful woman whom he discovers as soon as he arrives at Rome (Constantinople). She returns his love, but demands that he make sacrifices for her. He must drink wine, burn his Qur'an, and bow down to images. Sheikh Sam'an's all-consuming love for this woman seems to be the most horrible deviance imaginable. Yet we know a happy ending must be coming, because in Sufism all-consuming love is always the only path to the Friend, even if the way must pass through the filth of sacrilege.

A series of oppositions structure the story of Sheikh Sam'an: Mecca and Rome (Constantinople), the Ka'aba and the church, the prayer niche (*mihrab*) and the idol. Through the power of love and the intervention of the Friend, who appears to Sheikh Sam'an's distressed followers in the form of a wise counselor, these seeming contradictions are resolved in unity. Complete submission to love ends in the soul becoming, in Attar's words, "a drop returned to Truth's great sea." Thrilled by the story, the birds are set aflame with a similar desire to carry out their pilgrimage in search of the Simorgh, who is also the Friend. The opposition of Islam and Christianity in the story, which is often viewed simply as a contrast between the right path to God and a falling away from the path, has a deeper significance when read in the light of Sufism, which enables Attar to present Sheikh Sam'an's all-consuming love for the Christian woman as not a path away from God but a path toward him. Throughout his writings, Attar makes it clear that all paths that are paved by love are equally paths to the Friend.

The geography of the story of Sheikh Sam'an is a microcosm of the geography of *The Conference of Birds* as a whole. Just as the sheikh travels away from the sacred center of Mecca in a journey that paradoxically leads to God, so too the birds seem to journey in the wrong direction; they traverse a sequence of seven valleys in their quest for the Simorgh, who proves to have been within themselves all along. Sensitive readers of Attar's poem quickly recognized this geography as a spiritual map of the soul's journey to God. The lyric poet Rumi recalls the *Conference*'s seven valleys when he praises Attar, saying that he has "roamed through the seven cities of love while we have barely turned down the first street." Rumi, along with **Hafez** and **Jahan Khatun**, would be among the next generations of Persian poets who would take up Attar's journey of the soul.

From The Conference of the Birds[1]

Love thrives on inextinguishable pain,
Which tears the soul, then knits the threads again.
A mote of love exceeds all bounds; it gives
The vital essence to whatever lives.
But where love thrives, there pain is always found; 5
Angels alone escape this weary round—
They love without that savage agony
Which is reserved for vexed humanity.
Islam and blasphemy have both been passed
By those who set out on love's path at last; 10
Love will direct you to Dame Poverty,
And she will show the way to Blasphemy.
When neither Blasphemy nor Faith remain,
The body and the Self have both been slain;
Then the fierce fortitude the Way will ask 15
Is yours, and you are worthy of our task.
Begin the journey without fear; be calm;
Forget what is and what is not Islam;
Put childish dread aside—like heroes meet
The hundred problems which you must defeat. 20

1. Translated from the Persian by Afkham Darbandi and Dick Davis.

The Story of Sheikh Sam'an

Sam'an was once the first man of his time.
Whatever praise can be expressed in rhyme
Belonged to him: for fifty years this sheikh[2]
Kept Mecca's holy place, and for his sake
Four hundred pupils entered learning's way.   5
He mortified his body night and day,
Knew theory, practice, mysteries of great age,
And fifty times had made the Pilgrimage.[3]
He fasted, prayed, observed all sacred laws—
Astonished saints and clerics thronged his doors.   10
He split religious hairs in argument;
His breath revived the sick and impotent.
He knew the people's hearts in joy and grief
And was their living symbol of Belief.
Though conscious of his credit in their sight,   15
A strange dream troubled him, night after night;
Mecca was left behind; he lived in Rome,[4]
The temple where he worshipped was his home,
And to an idol he bowed down his head.
"Alas!" he cried, when he awoke in dread,   20
"Like Joseph[5] I am in a well of need
And have no notion when I shall be freed.
But every man meets problems on the Way,
And I shall conquer if I watch and pray.
If I can shift this rock my path is clear;   25
If not, then I must wait and suffer here."
Then suddenly he burst out: "It would seem
That Rome could show the meaning of this dream;
There I must go!" And off the old man strode;
Four hundred followed him along the road.   30
They left the Ka'ba[6] for Rome's boundaries,
A gentle landscape of low hills and trees,
Where, infinitely lovelier than the view,
There sat a girl, a Christian girl who knew
The secrets of her faith's theology.   35
A fairer child no man could hope to see—
In beauty's mansion she was like a sun
That never set—indeed the spoils she won
Were headed by the sun himself, whose face
Was pale with jealousy and sour disgrace.   40
The man about whose heart her ringlets curled
Became a Christian and renounced the world;
The man who saw her lips and knew defeat

---

2. An honorific title meaning "wise" or "learned."

3. To Mecca. The hajj is one of the five fundamental obligations of Islam, and making it even once shows great commitment.

4. Constantinople, the capital of the Eastern Roman empire.

5. The son of Jacob, cast into a pit and then sold into slavery by his brothers (Genesis 37.19–28).

6. The Ka'aba (lit., the cube), the gray stone building that is the central point of the pilgrimage to Mecca; according to the Qur'an it was originally established by Abraham as a place to worship the one true God, and Muslims always face it when they pray.

Embraced the earth before her bonny feet;
And as the breeze passed through her musky hair   45
The men of Rome watched wondering in despair.
Her eyes spoke promises to those in love,
Their fine brows arched coquettishly above—
Those brows sent glancing messages that seemed
To offer everything her lovers dreamed.   50
The pupils of her eyes grew wide and smiled,
And countless souls were glad to be beguiled;
The face beneath her curls glowed like soft fire;
Her honeyed lips provoked the world's desire;
But those who thought to feast there found her eyes   55
Held pointed daggers to protect the prize,
And since she kept her counsel no one knew—
Despite the claims of some—what she would do.
Her mouth was tiny as a needle's eye,
Her breath as quickening as Jesus' sigh;   60
Her chin was dimpled with a silver well
In which a thousand drowning Josephs fell;
A glistering jewel secured her hair in place,
Which like a veil obscured her lovely face.
The Christian turned, the dark veil was removed,   65
A fire flashed through the old man's joints—he loved!
One hair converted hundreds; how could he
Resist that idol's face shown openly?
He did not know himself; in sudden fire
He knelt abjectly as the flames beat higher;   70
In that sad instant all he had been fled
And passion's smoke obscured his heart and head.
Love sacked his heart; the girl's bewitching hair
Twined round his faith impiety's smooth snare.
The sheikh exchanged religion's wealth for shame,   75
A hopeless heart submitted to love's fame.
"I have no faith," he cried. "The heart I gave
Is useless now; I am the Christian's slave."
When his disciples saw him weeping there,
And understood the truth of the affair,   80
They stared, confounded by his frantic grief,
And strove to call him back to his belief.
Their remonstrations fell on deafened ears;
Advice has no effect when no one hears.
In turn the sheikh's disciples had their say;   85
Love has no cure, and he could not obey.
(When did a lover listen to advice?
When did a nostrum cool love's flames to ice?)
Till evening came he could not move but gazed
With stupefaction in his face, amazed.   90

When gloomy twilight spread its darkening shrouds—
Like blasphemy concealed by guilty clouds—
His ardent heart gave out the only light,
And love increased a hundredfold that night.

He put aside the Self and selfish lust;   95
In grief he smeared his locks with filth and dust
And kept his haunted vigil, watched and wept,
Lay trembling in love's grip and never slept.
"O Lord, when will this darkness end?" he cried,
"Or is it that the heavenly sun has died?   100
Those nights I passed in faith's austerities
Cannot compare with this night's agonies;
But like a candle now my flame burns high
To weep all night and in the daylight die.
Ambush and blood have been my lot this night;   105
Who knows what torments day will bring to light?
This fevered darkness and my wretched state
Were made when I was made, and are my fate;
The night continues and the hours delay—
Perhaps the world has reached its Judgement Day;   110
Perhaps the sun's extinguished with my sighs,
Or hides in shame from my belovèd's eyes.
This long, dark night is like her flowing hair—
The thought in absence comforts my despair,
But love consumes me through this endless night—   115
I yield to love, unequal to the fight.
Where is there time enough to tell my grief?
Where is the patience to regain belief?
Where is the luck to waken me, or move
Love's idol to reciprocate my love?   120
Where is the reason that could rescue me,
Or by some trick prove my auxiliary?
Where is the hand to pour dust on my head,
Or lift me from the dust where I lie dead?
Where is the foot that seeks the longed-for place?   125
Where is the eye to show me her fair face?
Where is the loved one to relieve my pain?
Where is the guide to help me turn again?
Where is the strength to utter my complaint?
Where is the mind to counsel calm restraint?   130
The loved one, reason, patience—all are gone
And I remain to suffer love alone."

At this the fond disciples gathered round,
Bewildered by his groans' pathetic sound.
"My sheikh," urged one, "forget this evil sight;   135
Rise, cleanse yourself according to our rite."
"In blood I cleanse myself," the sheikh replied;
"In blood, a hundred times, my life is dyed."
Another asked: "Where is your rosary?"
He said: "I fling the beads away from me;   140
The Christian's belt[7] is my sole sanctuary!"

---

7. The *zonnar*, a belt or cord worn by Eastern Christians and Jews; thus a symbol of heresy [translators' note].

One urged him to repent; he said: "I do,
Of all I was, all that belonged thereto."
One counselled prayer; he said, "Where is her face
That I may pray toward that blessèd place?"   145
Another cried: "Enough of this; you must
Seek solitude and in repentant dust
Bow down to God." "I will," replied the sheikh,
"Bow down in dust, but for my idol's sake."
And one reproached him: "Have you no regret   150
For Islam and those rites you would forget?"
He said: "No man repents past folly more;
Why is it I was not in love before?"
Another said: "A demon's poisoned dart—
Unknown to you—has pierced your trusting heart."   155
The sheikh said: "If a demon straight from hell
Deceives me, I rejoice and wish her well."
One said: "Our noble sheikh has lost his way;
Passion has led his wandering wits astray."
"True, I have lost the fame I once held dear,"   160
Replied their sheikh, "and fraud as well, and fear."
One said: "You break our hearts with this disgrace."
He laughed: "The Christian's heart will take their place."
One said: "Stay with old friends awhile, and come—
We'll seek the Ka'ba's shade and journey home."   165
The sheikh replied: "A Christian monastery
And not the Ka'ba's shade suffices me."
One said: "Return to Mecca and repent!"
He answered: "Leave me here, I am content."
One said: "You travel on hell's road." "This sigh   170
Would shrivel seven hells" was his reply.
One said: "In hope of heaven turn again,"
He said: "Her face is heaven; I remain."
One said: "Before our God confess your shame."
He answered: "God Himself has lit this flame."   175
One said: "Stop vacillating now and fight;
Defend the ways our faith proclaims as right."
He said: "Prepare your ears for blasphemy;
An infidel does not prate piety."
Their words could not recall him to belief,   180
And slowly they grew silent, sunk in grief.
They watched; each felt the heart within him fail,
Fearful of deeds Fate hid beneath her veil.

At last white day displayed her golden shield;
Black night declined his head, compelled to yield—   185
The world lay drowned in sparkling light, and dawn
Disclosed the sheikh, still wretched and forlorn,
Disputing with stray dogs the place before
His unattainable belovèd's door.
There in the dust he knelt, till constant prayers   190
Made him resemble one of her dark hairs;

A patient month he waited day and night
To glimpse the radiance of her beauty's light.
At last fatigue and sorrow made him ill—
Her street became his bed and he lay still.   195
When she perceived he would—and could—not move,
She understood the fury of his love,
But she pretended ignorance and said:
"What is it, sheikh? Why is our street your bed?
How can a Muslim sleep where Christians tread?"   200
He answered her: "I have no need to speak;
You know why I am wasted, pale and weak.
Restore the heart you stole, or let me see
Some glimmer in your heart of sympathy;
In all your pride find some affection for   205
The grey-haired, lovesick stranger at your door.
Accept my love or kill me now—your breath
Revives me or consigns me here to death.
Your face and curls command my life; beware
Of how the breeze displays your vagrant hair;   210
The sight breeds fever in me, and your deep
Hypnotic eyes induce love's restless sleep.
Love mists my eyes, love burns my heart—alone,
Impatient and unloved, I weep and groan;
See what a sack of sorrow I have sewn!   215
I give my soul and all the world to burn,
And endless tears are all I hope to earn.
My eyes beheld your face, my heart despaired;
What I have seen and suffered none have shared.
My heart has turned to blood; how long must I   220
Subsist on misery? You need not try
To humble wretchedness, or kick the foe
Who in the dust submissively bows low.
It is my fortune to lament and wait—
When, if, love answers me depends on Fate.   225
My soul is ambushed here, and in your street
Relives each night the anguish of defeat;
Your threshold's dust receives my prayers—I give
As cheap as dust the soul by which I live.
How long outside your door must I complain?   230
Relent a moment and relieve my pain.
You are the sun and I a shadow thrown
By you—how then can I survive alone?
Though pain has worn me to a shadow's edge,
Like sunlight I shall leap your window's ledge;   235
Let me come in and I shall secretly
Bring seven heavens' happiness with me.
My soul is burnt to ash; my passion's fire
Destroys the world with unappeased desire.
Love binds my feet and I cannot depart;   240
Love holds the hand pressed hard against my heart.

My fainting soul dissolves in deathly sighs—
How long must you stay hidden from my eyes?"

She laughed: "You shameless fool, take my advice—
Prepare yourself for death and paradise! 245
Forget flirtatious games, your breath is cold;
Stop chasing love, remember you are old.
It is a shroud you need, not me! How could
You hope for wealth when you must beg for food?"
He answered her: "Say what you will, but I 250
In love's unhappy torments live and die;
To Love, both young and old are one—his dart
Strikes with unequalled strength in every heart."
The girl replied: "There are four things you must
Perform to show that you deserve my trust: 255
Burn the Koran, drink wine, seel up Faith's eye,
Bow down to images."[8] And in reply
The sheikh declared: "Wine I will drink with you;
The rest are things that I could never do."
She said: "If you agree to my commands, 260
To start with, you must wholly wash your hands
Of Islam's faith—the love which does not care
To bend to love's requests is empty air."
He yielded then: "I must and will obey;
I'll do whatever you are pleased to say. 265
Your slave submits—lead me with ringlets twined
As chains about my neck; I am resigned!"
She smiled: "Come then and drink," and he allowed
Her to escort him to a hall (the crowd
Of scholars followed, weeping and afraid) 270
Where Christians banqueted, and there a maid
Of matchless beauty passed the cup around.
Love humbled our poor sheikh—without a sound
He gave his heart into the Christians' hands;
His mind had fled, he bowed to her commands, 275
And from those hands he took the proffered bowl;
He drank, oblivion overwhelmed his soul.
Wine mingled with his love—her laughter seemed
To challenge him to take the bliss he dreamed.
Passion flared up in him; again he drank 280
And slave-like at her feet contented sank—
This sheikh who had the whole Koran by heart
Felt wine spread through him and his faith depart;
Whatever he had known deserted him,
Wine conquered and his intellect grew dim; 285
Wine sluiced away his conscience; she alone
Lived in his heart, all other thoughts had flown.
Now love grew violent as an angry sea,

8. Idolatry, like the drinking of wine, is forbidden to Muslims.

He watched her drink and moved instinctively—
Half-fuddled with the wine—to touch her neck.   290
But she drew back and held his hand in check,
Deriding him: "What do you want, old man?
Old hypocrite of love, who talks but can
Do nothing else? To prove your love, declare
That your religion is my rippling hair.   295
Love's more than childish games, if you agree—
For love—to imitate my blasphemy
You can embrace me here; if not, you may
Take up your stick and hobble on your way."
The abject sheikh had sunk to such a state   300
That he could not resist his wretched fate;
Now ignorant of shame and unafraid,
He heard the Christian's wishes and obeyed—
The old wine sidled through the old man's veins
And like a twisting compass turned his brains;   305
Old wine, young love, a lover far too old,
Her soft arms welcoming—could he be cold?
Beside himself with love and drink he cried:
"Command me now; whatever you decide
I will perform. I spurned idolatry   310
When sober, but your beauty is to me
An idol for whose sake I'll gladly burn
My faith's Koran." "Now you begin to learn,
Now you are mine, dear sheikh," she said. "Sleep well,
Sweet dreams; our ripening fruit begins to swell."   315

News spread among the Christians that this sheikh
Had chosen their religion for love's sake.
They took him to a nearby monastery,
Where he accepted their theology;
He burnt his dervish cloak and set his face   320
Against the faith and Mecca's holy place—
After so many years of true belief,
A young girl brought this learnèd sheikh to grief.
He said: "This dervish has been well betrayed;
The agent was mere passion for a maid.   325
I must obey her now—what I have done
Is worse than any crime beneath the sun."
(How many leave the faith through wine! It is
The mother of such evil vagaries.)
"Whatever you required is done," he said.   330
"What more remains? I have bowed down my head
In love's idolatry, I have drunk wine;
May no one pass through wretchedness like mine!
Love ruins one like me, and black disgrace
Now stares a once-loved dervish in the face.   335
For fifty years I walked an open road
While in my heart high seas of worship flowed;
Love ambushed me and at its sudden stroke

For Christian garments I gave up my cloak;
The Ka'ba has become love's secret sign,   340
And homeless love interprets the Divine.
Consider what, for your sake, I have done—
Then tell me, when shall we two be as one?
Hope for that moment justifies my pain;
Have all my troubles been endured in vain?"   345
The girl replied: "But you are poor, and I
Cannot be cheaply won—the price is high;
Bring gold, and silver too, you innocent—
Then I might pity your predicament;
But you have neither, therefore go—and take   350
A beggar's alms from me; be off, old sheikh!
Be on your travels like the sun—alone;
Be manly now and patient, do not groan!"
"A fine interpretation of your vow,"
The sheikh replied; "my love, look at me now—   355
I have no one but you; your cypress gait,
Your silver form, decide my wretched fate.
Take back your cruel commands; each moment you
Confuse me by demanding something new.
I have endured your absence, promptly done   360
All you have asked—what profit have I won?
I've passed beyond loss, profit, Islam, crime,
For how much longer must I bide my time?
Is this what we agreed? My friends have gone,
Despising me, and I am here alone.   365
They follow one way, you another—I
Stand witless here uncertain where to fly;
I know without you heaven would be hell,
Hell heaven with you; more I cannot tell."
At last his protestations moved her heart.   370
"You are too poor to play the bridegroom's part,"
She said, "but be my swineherd[9] for a year
And then we'll stay together, never fear."
The sheikh did not refuse—a fractious way
Estranges love; he hurried to obey.   375
This reverend sheikh kept swine—but who does not
Keep something swinish in his nature's plot?
Do not imagine only he could fall;
This hidden danger lurks within us all,
Rearing its bestial head when we begin   380
To tread salvation's path—if you think sin
Has no place in your nature, you can stay
Content at home; you are excused the Way.
But if you start our journey you will find
That countless swine and idols tease the mind—   385
Destroy these hindrances to love or you
Must suffer that disgrace the sad sheikh knew.

9. Pork is forbidden to Muslims.

Despair unmanned his friends; they saw his plight
And turned in helpless horror from the sight—
The dust of grief anointed each bowed head;   390
But one approached the hapless man and said:
"We leave for Mecca now, O weak-willed sheikh;
Is there some message you would have us take?
Or should we all turn Christians and embrace
This faith men call a blasphemous disgrace?   395
We get no pleasure from the thought of you
Left here alone—shall we be Christians too?
Or since we cannot bear your state should we,
Deserting you, incontinently flee;
Forget that you exist and live in prayer   400
Beside the Ka'ba's stone without a care?"
The sheikh replied: "What grief has filled my heart!
Go where you please—but quickly, now, depart;
Only the Christian keeps my soul alive,
And I shall stay with her while I survive   405
Though you are wise your wisdom cannot know
The wild frustrations through which lovers go.
If for one moment you could share my pain,
We could be old companions once again.
But now go back, dear friends; if anyone   410
Asks after me explain what I have done—
Say that my eyes swim blood, that parched I wait
Trapped in the gullet of a monstrous fate.
Say Islam's elder has outsinned the whole
Of heathen blasphemy, that self-control   415
Slipped from him when he saw the Christian's hair,
That faith was conquered by insane despair.
Should anyone reproach my actions, say
That countless others have pursued this Way,
This endless Way where no one is secure,   420
Where danger waits and issues are unsure."
He turned from them; a swineherd sought his swine.
His friends wept vehemently—their sheikh's decline
Seemed death to them. Sadly they journeyed home,
Resigning their apostate sheikh to Rome.   425

They skulked in corners, shameful and afraid.
A close companion of the sheikh had stayed
In Mecca while the group had journeyed west—
A man of wisdom, fit for any test,
Who, seeing now the vacant oratory   430
Where once his friend had worshipped faithfully,
Asked after their lost sheikh. In tears then they
Described what had occurred along the way;
How he had bound his fortunes to her hair,
And blocked the path of faith with love's despair;   435
How curls usurped belief and how his cloak
Had been consumed in passion's blackening smoke;

How he'd become a swineherd, how the four
Acts contrary to all Islamic law
Had been performed by him, how this great sheikh   440
Lived like a pagan for his lover's sake.
Amazement seized the friend—his face grew pale,
He wept and felt the heart within him fail.
"O criminals!" he cried. "O frailer than
Weak women in your faith—when does a man   445
Need faithful friends but in adversity?
You should be there, not prattling here to me.
Is this devoted love? Shame on you all,
Fair-weather friends who run when great men fall.
He put on Christian garments—so should you;   450
He took their faith—what else had you to do?
This was no friendship, to forsake your friend,
To promise your support and at the end
Abandon him—this was sheer treachery.
Friend follows friend to hell and blasphemy—   455
When sorrows come a man's true friends are found;
In times of joy ten thousand gather round.
Our sheikh is savaged by some shark—you race
To separate yourselves from his disgrace.
Love's built on readiness to share love's shame;   460
Such self-regarding love usurps love's name."
"Repeatedly we told him all you say,"
They cried. "We were companions of the Way,
Sworn to a common happiness or grief;
We should exchange the honours of belief   465
For odium and scorn; we should accept
The Christian cult our sheikh could not reject.
But he insisted that we leave—our love
Seemed pointless then; he ordered us to move.
At his express command we journeyed here   470
To tell his story plainly, without fear."

He answered them: "However hard the fight,
You should have fought for what was clearly right.
Truth struggled there with error; when you went
You only worsened his predicament.   475
You have abandoned him; how could you dare
To enter Mecca's uncorrupted air?"
They heard his speech; not one would raise his head.
And then, "There is no point in shame," he said.
"What's done is done; we must act justly now,   480
Bury this sin, seek out the sheikh and bow
Before him once again." They left their home
And made their way a second time to Rome;
They prayed a hundred thousand prayers—at times
With hope, at times disheartened by their crimes.   485
They neither ate nor slept but kept their gaze
Unswerving throughout forty nights and days.

Their wailing lamentations filled the sky,
Moving the green-robed angels[1] ranked on high
To clothe themselves with black, and in the end   490
The leader of the group, the sheikh's true friend,
His heart consumed by sympathetic grief,
Let loose the well-aimed arrows of belief.
For forty nights he had prayed privately,
Rapt in devotion's holy ecstasy—   495
At dawn there came a musk-diffusing breeze,
And in his heart he knew all mysteries.
He saw the Prophet, lovely as the moon,
Whose face, Truth's shadow, was the sun at noon,
Whose hair in two black heavy braids was curled—   500
Each hair, a hundred times, outpriced the world.
As he approached with his unruffled pace,
A smile of haunting beauty lit his face.
The sheikh's friend rose and said: "God's Messenger,
Vouchsafe your help. Our sheikh has wandered far;   505
You are our Guide; guide him to Truth again."
The Prophet answered: "I have loosed the chain
Which bound your sheikh—your prayer is answered, go.
Thick clouds of dust have been allowed to blow
Between his sight and Truth—those clouds have gone;   510
I did not leave him to endure alone.
I sprinkled on the fortunes of your sheikh
A cleansing dew for intercession's sake—
The dust is laid; sin disappeared before   ⎫
His new-made vow. A world of sin, be sure,   ⎬   515
Shall with contrition's spittle be made pure. ⎭
The sea of righteousness drowns in its waves
The sins of those sincere repentance saves."

With grateful happiness the friend cried out;
The heavens echoed his triumphant shout.   520
He told the good news to the group; again
They set out eagerly across the plain.
Weeping they ran to where the swineherd-sheikh,
Now cured of his unnatural mistake,
Had cast aside his Christian clothes, the bell,   525
The belt, the cap, freed from the strange faith's spell.
Seeing his friends approach his hiding-place,
He saw how he had forfeited God's grace;
He ripped his clothes in frenzies of distress;
He grovelled in the dust with wretchedness.   530
Tears flowed like rain; he longed for death; his sighs'
Great heat consumed the curtain of the skies;
Grief dried the blood within him when he saw
How he had lost all knowledge of God's law;
All he had once abandoned now returned   535

---

1. Green is the traditional color of Islam.

And he escaped the hell in which he'd burned.
He came hack to himself, and on his knees
Wept bitterly for past iniquities.
When his disciples saw him weeping there,
Bathed in shame's sweat, they reeled between despair   540
And joy—bewildered they drew near and sighed;
From gratitude they gladly would have died.
They said: "The mist has fled that hid your sun;
Faith has returned and blasphemy is gone;
Truth has defeated Rome's idolatry;   545
Grace has surged onward like a mighty sea.
The Prophet interceded for your soul;
The world sends up its thanks from pole to pole.
Why should you mourn? You should thank God instead
That out of darkness you've been safely led;   550
God who can turn the day to darkest night
Can turn black sin to pure repentant light—
He kindles a repentant spark, the flame
Burns all our sins and all sin's burning shame."

I will be brief: the sheikh was purified   555
According to the faith; his old self died—
He put the dervish cloak on as before.
The group set out for Mecca's gates once more.

And then the Christian girl whom he had loved
Dreamed in her sleep; a shaft of sunlight moved   560
Before her eyes, and from the dazzling ray
A voice said: "Rise, follow your lost sheikh's way;
Accept his faith, beneath his feet be dust;
You tricked him once, be pure to him and just,
And, as he took your path without pretence,   565
Take his path now in truth and innocence.
Follow his lead; you once led him astray—
Be his companion as he points the Way;
You were a robber preying on the road
Where you should seek to share the traveller's load.   570
Wake now, emerge from superstition's night."
She woke, and in her heart a steady light
Beat like the sun, and an unwonted pain
Throbbed there, a longing she could not restrain;
Desire flared up in her; she felt her soul   575
Slip gently from the intellect's control.
As yet she did not know what seed was sown—
She had no friend and found herself alone
In an uncharted world; no tongue can tell
What then she saw—her pride and triumph fell   580
Like rain from her; with an unearthly shout
She tore the garments from her back, ran out
And heaped the dust of mourning on her head.
Her frame was weak, the heart within her bled,

But she began the journey to her sheikh,   585
And like a cloud that seems about to break
And shed its downpour of torrential rain
(The heart's rich blood) she ran across the plain.
But soon the desert's endless vacancy
Bewildered her; wild with uncertainty,   590
She wept and pressed her face against the sand.
"O God," she cried, "extend your saving hand
To one who is an outcast of the earth,
To one who tricked a saint of unmatched worth—
Do not abandon me; my evil crime   595
Was perpetrated in a thoughtless time;
I did not know what I know now—accept
The prayers of one who ignorantly slept."

The sheikh's heart spoke: "The Christian is no more;
The girl you loved knocks at religion's door—   600
It is our way she follows now; go back
And be the comforter her sorrows lack."
Like wind he ran, and his disciples cried:
"Has your repentant vow so quickly died?
Will you slip back, a shameless reprobate?"   605
But when the sheikh explained the girl's sad state,
Compassion moved their hearts and they agreed
To search for her and serve her every need.
They found her with hair draggled in the dirt,
Prone on the earth as if a corpse, her skirt   610
Torn from her limbs, barefoot, her face death-pale.
She saw the sheikh and felt her last strength fail;
She fainted at his feet, and and as she slept
The sheikh hung over her dear face and wept.

She woke, and seeing tears like rain in spring   615
Knew he'd kept faith with her through everything.
She knelt before him, took his hands and said
"The shame I brought on your respected head
Burns me with shame; how long must I remain
Behind this veil of ignorance? Make plain   620
The mysteries of Islam to me here,
And I shall tread its highway without fear."
The sheikh spelt out the faith to her; the crowd
Of gratified disciples cried aloud,
Weeping to see the lovely child embrace   625
The search for Truth. Then, as her comely face
Bent to his words, her heart began to feel
An inexpressible and troubling zeal;
Slowly she felt the pall of grief descend,
Knowing herself still absent from the Friend.   630
"Dear sheikh," she said, "I cannot bear such pain;
Absence undoes me and my spirits wane.
I go from this unhappy world; farewell

World's sheikh and mine—further I cannot tell,
Exhaustion weakens me; O sheikh, forgive . . . "   635
And saying this the dear child ceased to live.
The sun was hidden by a mist—her flesh
Yielded the sweet soul from its weakening mesh.
She was a drop returned to Truth's great sea;
She left this world, and so, like wind, must we.   640

Whoever knows love's path is soon aware
That stories such as this are far from rare.
All things are possible, and you may meet
Despair, forgiveness, certainty, deceit.
The Self ignores the secrets of the Way,   645
The mysteries no mortal speech can say;
Assurance whispers in the heart's dark core,
Not in the muddied Self—a bitter war
Must rage between these two. Turn now and mourn
That your existence is so deeply torn!   650

The birds set off on their journey, pause, then choose a leader

They heard the tale; the birds were all on fire
To quit the hindrance of the Self; desire
To gain the Simorgh had convulsed each heart.

DANTE ALIGHIERI
1265–1321

"Midway along the journey of our life / I woke to find myself in a dark wood, / for I had wandered off from the straight path." With these opening words, Dante compels his reader to inhabit the point of view of a narrator who, halfway through not "my" but "our" lifetime, suddenly realizes that he is lost. His life is thus our life, and the ethical or righteous "straight path" that the narrator hopes to rediscover also comes to be the reader's own goal. Yet this identification of reader and narrator is countered, again and again in *The Divine Comedy*, by an insistence on the specific circumstances of Dante's own life: traveling into the underworld and into the other realms of the afterlife, we meet his old teacher, Brunetto Latini; the father of his close friend **Guido Cavalcanti**; his great-great-grandfather, Cacciaguida; and, most importantly, the beautiful Beatrice Portinari, whom Dante has loved (he tells us) since they were both children. In spite of the particularity of the details of this afterlife—or, perhaps, because of them—the reader constantly identifies with the narrator, experiencing the painful turns of the journey as well as the joyful expectation of heavenly bliss at the road's end.

LIFE AND TIMES

Dante Alighieri was born and raised in Florence, a northern Italian city that was at once central to his sense of identity and—as depicted in *The Divine Comedy*—a place that he loathed and despised, a degenerate community rife with corruption and discord. During the years around 1300, Florence, like other cities in northern Italy, was caught up in a large-scale confrontation between forces favoring the power of the church and those favoring the independence of city-states. Dante quickly became deeply involved with these issues, both as a member of the political governing body within the city of Florence and in his role as envoy from the city to the seat of the papal government in Rome. Dante's own view—expressed most explicitly in his *Monarchia* (1318), a political treatise that in some ways anticipates **Machiavelli's** *The Prince*—was that secular rule and ecclesiastical rule should be clearly divided. Dante argued that a strong ruler in the person of an idealized emperor was necessary for the church to appropriately exercise its moral and religious authority. Because it sought to place limitations on the exercise of political power by the church, *The Monarchia* was immediately condemned; it remained on the list (or "Index") of books that Catholics are forbidden to read until 1881.

Florence had taken a leading role in the disputes concerning secular and ecclesiastical power, split first into the factions of the Guelphs (who supported the pope) and the Ghibellines (who supported the Holy Roman Emperor). By the time Dante became involved in Florentine politics, the Guelphs had become dominant within the city, but an internal fracture soon developed between the Black Guelphs, who continued to support Boniface VIII, and the White Guelphs, who had come to oppose his despotism. Dante was allied with the latter, and when he was in Rome on a diplomatic mission, the Black Guelphs seized control of the city. Dante was consequently forbidden from ever reentering the city of his birth, under penalty of death by burning at the stake. Even worse, the split into the White and Black parties divided his family, as the Black Guelphs were led by the Donatis—relatives of his wife, Gemma Donati—and his wife and their four children remained in Florence.

Deeply embittered by the experience of exile, Dante spent the next twenty years wandering from city to city, all the while continuing with his political writing as well as his poetic efforts. The scandal arising from the *Monarchia* undoubtedly hampered Dante's efforts to return to Florence. In his *Divine Comedy*, he movingly recalls "the bitter taste of others' bread, how salty it is," and laments "how hard a path it is to go ascending and descending others' stairs." Dante never saw his sentence of exile lifted; indeed, Florence's city council finally revoked it only in 2008. That the vote was not unanimous—the motion passed 19 to 5—suggests that the city's political divisions may have lingered for seven hundred years.

WORK

Dante himself called his monumental poem simply the *Commedia*, or "comedy"; the adjective "divine" was added later by **Giovanni Boccaccio**, author of *The Decameron*, the other great work of medieval Italian literature. Boccaccio thereby signaled not just the subject matter of the work—that is, the realm of the afterlife, including the domains of hell, purgatory, and heaven—but also the elevated style in which it was written. The claim of direct inspiration by God, which Dante makes explicitly throughout the work, was taken at face value by the first generations of commentators, who accepted the work as the faithful poetic record of a real visionary experience. The theological content of the *Comedy* is both dense and elaborate: perhaps the most ambitious aspect of the poem's theology centers on purgatory, a place where souls are able to do penance for their sins even after death, to which Dante devotes the second of the three parts of his work. Purgatory would not become official Christian doctrine until well after the *Comedy* was completed, but Dante was responding to contemporary popular beliefs in the ability of the prayers of the living to affect the condition of the souls of the dead. He also reflects contemporary theological views of the persistence of the union of body and soul even after death, especially in the way that the shades that populate the afterworld of *The Divine Comedy* retain their individual bodily features though their flesh has been replaced by empty form. For modern readers, the term "comedy" might seem peculiar, conditioned as we are to associate comedy with laughter, just as we associate tragedy with tears. For medieval readers, however, following classical notions of genre, a comedy was simply a story that ended on a high note, with joy and—in the case of *The Divine Comedy*—with the narrator literally being lifted up into the heavens.

The Divine Comedy is divided into three books; each charts a different realm of the afterlife, from the depths of Hell in the *Inferno*, up the mountain of Purgatory in the *Purgatorio*, and finally through the ever-higher spheres of Heaven in the *Paradiso*. The three parts form a single path, as the narrator traverses a rugged landscape marked by hills, ravines, treacherous pathways, and difficult stairways, relying throughout on the help of a guide. For the journey through Hell and Purgatory, he follows in the footsteps of **Virgil**. The Roman poet is more than the literal guide of the wanderer within the fiction of the poem, for his *Aeneid*, the epic account of the fall of Troy and the foundation of Rome by Aeneas, is the constant poetic underpinning of Dante's own epic enterprise. But Virgil, as a pagan, cannot accompany him in Paradise: there Dante is led by Beatrice Portinari, his idealized love since childhood, who died in 1290. Both of these guides, as well as others who aid Dante along his way (such as Saint Lucy, who appears in the form of a golden eagle), are sent by a benefactor whom Dante only gradually comes to know: the *donna gentil* or "gracious lady" of Heaven, the Virgin Mary.

However important the theological message of *The Divine Comedy*, it never overshadows the essential realism and tangibility of the world Dante describes. From the horrible landscape of the ruined City of Dis seen in Hell to the brilliant light of the planets in Paradise, the reader's senses are continually stimulated. This stimulation is especially acute in the *Inferno*, where the vividness of the landscape is mirrored in the emotional affect of the narrator: he is moved to tears of pity by the sight of Paolo and Francesca, whose crime was to have given themselves over to the experience of love, but shows contempt for the traitor Bocca degli Abati, kicking him and pulling out tufts of his hair. In keeping with Christian doctrine, the souls in this underworld have no material bodies, yet their shades retain the appearance of the bodies they had in life, and the punishments they suffer in Hell leave marks on their flesh. In the circle of schismatics, whose sin is that they have divided the community of the faithful, Dante finds Muhammad, the Prophet of Islam, his body "split from the chin" down through his entrails. In this wound, as in the quartered body of Ganelon in the *Song of Roland*, the wrongful division of society, whether the body politic or the religious community, is made manifest on the canvas of the human body.

The structure of Hell, like that of Purgatory and Heaven, is highly symmetrical and full of numerical significance. *The Divine Comedy* is made up of one hundred chapters that Dante calls *cantos* (literally, "songs"), divided into three groups of thirty-three; the extra is added to the *Inferno*, which opens with an introductory canto. The numerological structure of the poem is also revealed in the landscape of each part. Hell is divided into nine circles, each containing a different category of sinners receiving their own proper form of punishment. The mountain of Purgatory is divided into nine parts as well, its seven main terraces (corresponding to the Seven Deadly Sins) surrounded by the entranceway of Ante-Purgatory and capped, at its summit, by the Earthly Paradise of Eden. Finally, the seven spheres of Heaven that lie above the mountain are brought to nine by the addition of those of the Fixed Stars and of the Primum Mobile—the first mover that imparts motion to all the other heavenly spheres. Beyond these nine are found only God and his angels. The constant play on the number three and its cube, three times three, highlights the Trinitarian theology that underlies the spiritual world of *The Divine Comedy*. Christian revelation places the earth at the center of the universe, surrounded by the spheres of the planets and of the stars and itself wounded by the cavernous pit of hell. At the base of the infernal pit, at the very center of the earth, Satan appears not wrapped in flames but rather frozen in a lake of ice. In Dante's memorable phrase, Satan is "the hairy worm . . . that pierces the earth's core" as if it were a rotten apple.

Climbing over the hairy body of Satan and twisting through a narrow passageway, Dante and his guide emerge from the bowels of the earth to the base of the mountain of Purgatory. A new mood infuses the work from this point on, as the hopefulness of the narrator reflects the very different circumstances of those who suffer pain in Purgatory. Here, unlike in Hell, suffering has a purpose, gradually redeeming the inhabitants from their former state of sin and enabling their souls to rise upward. At the summit of the mountain, Dante enters the Earthly Paradise of Eden, now hidden away in Purgatory to keep it from fallen humans. Here his wonder at a magnificent procession climaxes in a moment of staggering recognition: as he puts it, "I recognize signs of the ancient flame." Here Dante is met by Beatrice, his first love and the soul who will lead him the rest of the way on his upward journey.

Moving through the spheres of Paradise entails progressive dematerialization: instead of the rugged landscape of Hell, we find instead a sequence of spheres—each of which eclipses the last, each adorned with a symbolic form. In the sphere of the Crusaders, we see a mighty eagle; in the exalted spheres of the Empyrean, a celestial rose, studded with saintly souls. One of the very last of these symbolic forms is the great book "bound . . . by love," whose "scattered leaves" make up the universe. In this vivid image, the unity of divine revelation and of the written text of *The Divine Comedy* is complete. The love that binds the book reappears in the poem's last lines, as the narrator describes the endless motion of the heavens, turned by "the Love that moves the sun and the other stars." This earth-centered image of the cosmos would soon give way to a new worldview, with the sun at its center and with humanity placed in a very different relationship to its Creator.

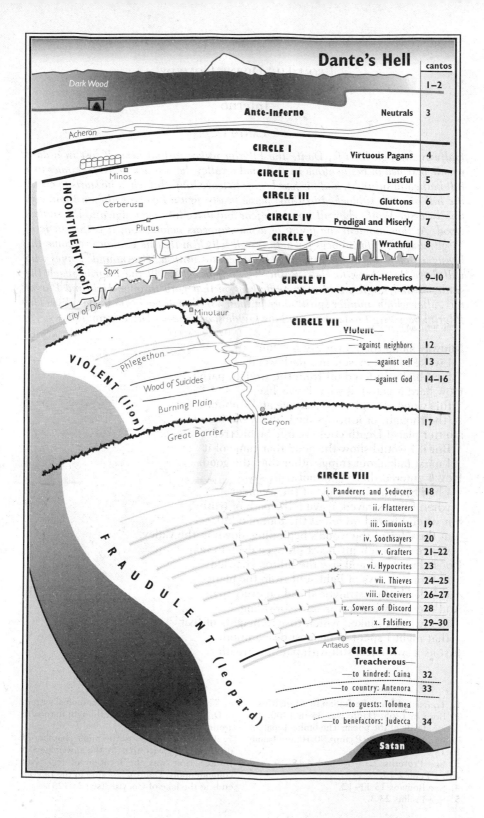

Dante's Hell

	cantos
Dark Wood	1–2
Ante-Inferno — Neutrals	3
Acheron	
CIRCLE I — Virtuous Pagans	4
Minos	
CIRCLE II — Lustful	5
Cerberus — **CIRCLE III** — Gluttons	6
Plutus — **CIRCLE IV** — Prodigal and Miserly	7
CIRCLE V — Wrathful	8
Styx	
CIRCLE VI — Arch-Heretics	9–10
City of Dis	
Minotaur	
CIRCLE VII Violent—	
—against neighbors	12
Phlegethon —against self	13
Wood of Suicides —against God	14–16
Burning Plain	
Great Barrier — Geryon	17
CIRCLE VIII	
i. Panderers and Seducers	18
ii. Flatterers	
iii. Simonists	19
iv. Soothsayers	20
v. Grafters	21–22
vi. Hypocrites	23
vii. Thieves	24–25
viii. Deceivers	26–27
ix. Sowers of Discord	28
x. Falsifiers	29–30
Antaeus	
CIRCLE IX Treacherous—	
—to kindred: Caina	32
—to country: Antenora	33
—to guests: Tolomea	
—to benefactors: Judecca	34
Satan	

INCONTINENT (wolf)

VIOLENT (lion)

FRAUDULENT (leopard)

From The Divine Comedy[1]

Inferno

CANTO I

*Halfway through his life, Dante the Pilgrim wakes to find himself lost in a dark
wood. Terrified at being alone in so dismal a valley, he wanders until he comes to a
hill bathed in sunlight, and his fear begins to leave him. But when he starts to climb
the hill his path is blocked by three fierce beasts: first a Leopard, then a Lion, and
finally a She-Wolf. They fill him with fear and drive him back down to the sunless
wood. At that moment the figure of a man appears before him; it is the shade of
Virgil, and the Pilgrim begs for help. Virgil tells him that he cannot overcome the
beasts which obstruct his path; they must remain until a "Greyhound" comes who
will drive them back to Hell. Rather by another path will the Pilgrim reach the
sunlight, and Virgil promises to guide him on that path through Hell and Purgatory, after which another spirit, more fit than Virgil, will lead him to Paradise. The
Pilgrim begs Virgil to lead on, and the Guide starts ahead. The Pilgrim follows.*

Midway along the journey of our life[2]
  I woke to find myself in a dark wood,
  for I had wandered off from the straight path.[3]   3
How hard it is to tell what it was like,
  this wood of wilderness, savage and stubborn
  (the thought of it brings back all my old fears),   6
a bitter place! Death could scarce be bitterer.
  But if I would show the good that came of it
  I must talk about things other than the good.   9
How I entered there I cannot truly say,
  I had become so sleepy[4] at the moment
  when I first strayed, leaving the path of truth;[5]   12
but when I found myself at the foot of a hill,
  at the edge of the wood's beginning, down in the valley,
  where I first felt my heart plunged deep in fear,   15
I raised my head and saw the hilltop shawled
  in morning rays of light sent from the planet
  that leads men straight ahead on every road.[6]   18
And then only did terror start subsiding,
  in my heart's lake,[7] which rose to heights of fear
  that night I spent in deepest desperation.   21
Just as a swimmer, still with panting breath,

---

1. Translated from the Italian by Mark Musa.
2. Born in 1265, Dante was 35 in 1300, the
fictional date of the poem. The biblical span of
human life is 70 (see Psalms 90.10 and Isaiah
23.15).
3. See Proverbs 2.13–14 and 4.18–19, and
also 2 Peter 2.15.
4. See Romans 13.11–12.
5. See Psalms 23.3.

6. The sun, which in the astronomical system
of Dante's time was a planet thought to revolve
around the earth.
7. This phrase refers to the inner chamber of
the heart, a cavity that in the physiology of
Dante's time was the location of fear. Not
coincidentally, Dante's last stop in the *Inferno*
ends at the lake of Cocytus (see 31.123).

now safe upon the shore, out of the deep,
   might turn for one last look at the dangerous waters,   24
so I, although my mind was turned to flee,
   turned round to gaze once more upon the pass
   that never let a living soul escape.[8]   27
I rested my tired body there awhile
   and then began to climb the barren slope
   (I dragged my stronger foot and limped along).[9]   30
Beyond the point the slope begins to rise
   sprang up a leopard, trim and very swift!
   It was covered by a pelt of many spots.   33
And, everywhere I looked, the beast was there
   blocking my way, so time and time again
   I was about to turn and go back down.   36
The hour was early in the morning then,
   the sun was climbing up with those same stars
   that had accompanied it on the world's first day,   39
the day Divine Love set their beauty turning;[1]
   so the hour and sweet season of creation
   encouraged me to think I could get past   42
that gaudy beast, wild in its spotted pelt,
   but then good hope gave way and fear returned
   when the figure of a lion loomed up before me,   45
and he was coming straight toward me, it seemed,
   with head raised high, and furious with hunger—
   the air around him seemed to fear his presence.   48
And now a she-wolf came, that in her leanness
   seemed racked with every kind of greediness
   (how many people she has brought to grief!).   51
This last beast brought my spirit down so low
   with fear that seized me at the sight of her,
   I lost all hope of going up the hill.[2]   54
As a man who, rejoicing in his gains,
   suddenly seeing his gain turn into loss,
   will grieve as he compares his then and now,   57
so she made me do, that relentless beast;
   coming toward me, slowly, step by step,
   she forced me back to where the sun is mute.   60
While I was rushing down to that low place,

8. This simile of Dante as the survivor of a passage through the sea invokes the story of the escape of the Israelites from Egypt through the Red Sea, a central metaphor throughout the *Comedy*: see Exodus 14. There is also probably an allusion to the opening of the *Aeneid*, where Aeneas and his men survive a storm.
9. The pilgrim is limping because he suffers from the injury of original sin.
1. In the Middle Ages it was thought that the world was created in spring, when the sun is in the constellation Aries.

2. The meaning of the leopard, lion, and she-wolf is open to a number of interpretations, the most plausible being that they represent the three major forms of sin found in Hell, respectively fraud, violence, and incontinence or immoderation (see 11.79 ff.). The structure of Hell indicates that the last is the least serious morally, but its role in this canto shows that it is the most difficult to overcome psychologically. Dante probably took the identities of these three beasts from a passage in Jeremiah 5.6.

my eyes made out a figure coming toward me
  of one grown faint, perhaps from too much silence.[3]   63
And when I saw him standing in this wasteland,
  "Have pity on my soul," I cried to him,
  "whichever you are, shade or living man!"   66
"No longer living man, though once I was,"
  he said, "and my parents were from Lombardy,
  both of them were Mantuans by birth.[4]   69
I was born, though somewhat late, *sub Julio*,[5]
  and lived in Rome when good Augustus reigned,
  when still the false and lying gods were worshipped.   72
I was a poet and sang of that just man,
  son of Anchises, who sailed off from Troy
  after the burning of proud Ilium.[6]   75
But why retreat to so much misery?
  Why not climb up this blissful mountain here,
  the beginning and the source of all man's joy?"   78
"Are you then Virgil, are you then that fount
  from which pours forth so rich a stream of words?"
  I said to him, bowing my head modestly.   81
"O light and honor of the other poets,
  may my long years of study, and that deep love
  that made me search your verses, help me now!   84
You are my teacher, the first of all my authors,
  and you alone the one from whom I took
  the noble style that was to bring me honor.   87
You see the beast that forced me to retreat;
  save me from her, I beg you, famous sage,
  she makes me tremble, the blood throbs in my veins."   90
"But you must journey down another road,"
  he answered, when he saw me lost in tears,
  "if ever you hope to leave this wilderness;   93
this beast, the one you cry about in fear,
  allows no soul to succeed along her path,
  she blocks his way and puts an end to him.   96
She is by nature so perverse and vicious,
  her craving belly is never satisfied,
  still hungering for food the more she eats.   99
She mates with many creatures, and will go on
  mating with more until the greyhound comes
  and tracks her down to make her die in anguish.[7]   102
He will not feed on either land or money:

---

3. The Roman poet Virgil's voice has not been
heard since he died in 19 B.C.E.
4. Lombardy is the most northern area of Italy;
Mantua is located to the east of Milan.
5. Virgil (70–19 B.C.E.) was born *sub Julio*,
during the reign of Julius Caesar (assassinated
in 44 B.C.E.), who was regarded by Dante as
the founder of the Roman Empire.

6. Aeneas, the hero of Virgil's *Aeneid*.
7. Dante's prediction of a modern political
redeemer is so enigmatic that there can be no
certainty of his identity. Most commentators
think it is Cangrande (i.e., the great dog) della
Scala of Verona, Dante's benefactor after his
exile from Florence.

his wisdom, love, and virtue shall sustain him;
  he will be born between Feltro and Feltro.[8]   105
He comes to save that fallen Italy
  for which the maid Camilla gave her life
  and Turnus, Nisus, Euryalus died of wounds.[9]   108
And he will hunt for her through every city
  until he drives her back to Hell once more,
  whence Envy first unleashed her on mankind.   111
And so, I think it best you follow me
  for your own good, and I shall be your guide
  and lead you out through an eternal place   114
where you will hear desperate cries, and see
  tormented shades, some old as Hell itself,
  and know what second death is, from their screams.[1]   117
And later you will see those who rejoice
  while they are burning, for they have hope of coming,
  whenever it may be, to join the blessèd[2]—   120
to whom, if you too wish to make the climb,
  a spirit, worthier than I, must take you;[3]
  I shall go back, leaving you in her care,   123
because that Emperor dwelling on high
  will not let me lead any to His city,
  since I in life rebelled against His law.[4]   126
Everywhere He reigns, and there He rules;
  there is His city, there is His high throne.
  Oh, happy the one He makes His citizen!"   129
And I to him: "Poet, I beg of you,
  in the name of God, that God you never knew,
  save me from this evil place and worse.   132
lead me there to the place you spoke about
  that I may see the gate Saint Peter guards
  and those whose anguish you have told me of."   135
Then he moved on, and I moved close behind him.

CANTO II

But the Pilgrim begins to waver, he expresses to Virgil his misgivings about his abil-ity to undertake the journey proposed by Virgil. His predecessors have been Aeneas and Saint Paul, and he feels unworthy to take his place in their company. But Vir-gil rebukes his cowardice, and relates the chain of events that led him to come to Dante. The Virgin Mary took pity on the Pilgrim in his despair and instructed Saint Lucia to aid him. The Saint turned to Beatrice because of Dante's great love for her, and Beatrice in turn went down to Hell, into Limbo, and asked Virgil to guide her friend until that time when she herself would become his guide. The Pilgrim takes heart at Virgil's explanation and agrees to follow him.

8. Feltre and Montefeltro are towns that roughly mark the limits of Cangrande's domains. But other interpretations are possible.
9. Characters in the *Aeneid* who die during Aeneas's conquest of Italy.
1. The second death is damnation; see Reve-

lation 21.8.
2. The souls in Purgatory; the blessed are the saved in Paradise.
3. Beatrice.
4. Virgil "rebelled" against God because he was not a Christian.

The day was fading and the darkening air
 was releasing all the creatures on our earth
 from their daily tasks, and I, one man alone, 3
was making ready to endure the battle
 of the journey, and of the pity it involved,
 which my memory, unerring, shall now retrace. 6
O Muses! O high genius! Help me now!
 O memory that wrote down what I saw,
 here your true excellence shall be revealed! 9
Then I began: "O poet come to guide me,
 tell me if you think my worth sufficient
 before you trust me to this arduous road. 12
You wrote about young Sylvius's father,[5]
 who went beyond, with flesh corruptible,
 with all his senses, to the immortal realm; 15
but if the Adversary of all evil
 was kind to him, considering who he was,
 and the consequence that was to come from him, 18
this cannot seem, to thoughtful men, unfitting,
 for in the highest heaven he was chosen
 father of glorious Rome and of her empire, 21
and both the city and her lands, in truth,
 were established as the place of holiness
 where the successors of great Peter sit.[6] 24
And from this journey you celebrate in verse,
 Aeneas learned those things that were to bring
 victory for him, and for Rome, the Papal seat; 27
then later the Chosen Vessel, Paul, ascended
 to bring back confirmation of that faith
 which is the first step on salvation's road.[7] 30
But why am I to go? Who allows me to?
 I am not Aeneas, I am not Paul,
 neither I nor any man would think me worthy; 33
and so, if I should undertake the journey,
 I fear it might turn out an act of folly—
 you are wise, you see more than my words express." 36
As one who unwills what he willed, will change
 his purpose with some new second thought,
 completely quitting what he first had started, 39
so I did, standing there on that dark slope,
 thinking, ending the beginning of that venture
 I was so quick to take up at the start. 42
"If I have truly understood your words,"
 that shade of magnanimity replied,
 "your soul is burdened with that cowardice 45
which often weighs so heavily on man,

---

5. Aeneas, who visited the underworld in *Aeneid* 6.
6. The Apostle Peter is considered by the Catholic Church to be the first pope.
7. St. Paul; see 2 Corinthians 12.2–4.

it turns him from a noble enterprise
   like a frightened beast that shies at its own shadow.   48
To free you from this fear, let me explain
   the reason I came here, the words I heard
   that first time I felt pity for your soul: 51
I was among those dead who are suspended,[8]
   when a lady summoned me. She was so blessed
   and beautiful, I implored her to command me.[9]   54
With eyes of light more bright than any star,
   in low, soft tones she started to address me
   in her own language, with an angel's voice: 57
'O noble soul, courteous Mantuan,
   whose fame the world continues to preserve
   and will preserve as long as world there is,   60
my friend, who is no friend of Fortune's, strays
   on a desert slope; so many obstacles
   have crossed his path, his fright has turned him back   63
I fear he may have gone so far astray,
   from what report has come to me in Heaven,
   that I may have started to his aid too late.   66
Now go, and with your elegance of speech,
   with whatever may be needed for his freedom,
   give him your help, and thereby bring me solace.   69
I am Beatrice, who urges you to go;
   I come from the place I am longing to return to;[1]
   love moved me, as it moves me now to speak.   72
When I return to stand before my Lord,
   often I shall sing your praises to Him.'
   And then she spoke no more. And I began,   75
'O Lady of Grace, through whom alone mankind
   may go beyond all worldy things contained
   within the sphere that makes the smallest round,[2]   78
your plea fills me with happy eagerness—
   to have obeyed already would still seem late!
   You needed only to express your wish.   81
But tell me how you dared to make this journey
   all the way down to this point of spacelessness,
   away from your spacious home that calls you back.'   84
'Because your question searches for deep meaning,
   I shall explain in simple words,' she said,
   'just why I have no fear of coming here.   87
A man must stand in fear of just those things
   that truly have the power to do us harm,
   of nothing else, for nothing else is fearsome.   90
God gave me such a nature through His Grace,
   the torments you must bear cannot affect me,
   nor are the fires of Hell a threat to me.   93

8. In Limbo, where the souls experience "neither joy nor sorrow" (4.84).
9. As we soon learn, the lady is Beatrice.

1. Paradise.
2. The sphere of the moon.

A gracious lady[3] sits in Heaven grieving
    for what happened to the one I send you to,
    and her compassion breaks Heaven's stern decree.   96
She called Lucia[4] and making her request,
    she said, "Your faithful one is now in need
    of you, and to you I now commend his soul."   99
Lucia, the enemy of cruelty,
    hastened to make her way to where I was,
    sitting by the side of ancient Rachel,[5]   102
and said to me: "Beatrice, God's true praise,
    will you not help the one whose love was such
    it made him leave the vulgar crowd for you?   105
Do you not hear the pity of his weeping,
    do you not see what death it is that threatens him
    along that river the sea shall never conquer?"[6]   108
There never was a worldly person living
    more anxious to promote his selfish gains
    than I was at the sound of words like these—   111
to leave my holy seat and come down here
    and place my trust in you, in your noble speech
    that honors you and all those who have heard it!'   114
When she had finished reasoning, she turned
    her shining eyes away, and there were tears
    How eager then I was to come to you!   117
And I have come to you just as she wished,
    and I have freed you from the beast that stood
    blocking the quick way up the mount of bliss.   120
So what is wrong? Why, why do you delay?
    Why are you such a coward in your heart,
    why aren't you bold and free of all your fear,   123
when three such gracious ladies, who are blessed,
    watch out for you up there in Heaven's court,
    and my words, too, bring promise of such good?"   126
As little flowers from the frosty night
    are closed and limp, and when the sun shines down
    on them, they rise to open on their stem,   129
my wilted strength began to bloom within me,
    and such warm courage flowed into my heart
    that I spoke like a man set free of fear.   132
"O she, compassionate, who moved to help me!
    And you, all kindness, in obeying quick
    those words of truth she brought with her for you—   135
you and the words you spoke have moved my heart
    with such desire to continue onward
    that now I have returned to my first purpose.   138
Let us start, for both our wills, joined now, are one.

---

3. The Virgin Mary.
4. St. Lucy, a 3rd-century martyr and the patron saint of those afflicted with poor or damaged sight.

5. Rachel signifies the contemplative life: see Genesis 29.16–17.
6. These are the metaphoric waters of 1.22–24.

You are my guide, you are my lord and teacher."
These were my words to him and, when he moved,   141
I entered on that deep and rugged road.

CANTO III

As the two poets enter the vestibule that leads to Hell itself, Dante sees the inscription above the gate, and he hears the screams of anguish from the damned souls. Rejected by God and not accepted by the powers of Hell, the first group of souls are "nowhere," because of their cowardly refusal to make a choice in life. Their punishment is to follow a banner at a furious pace forever, and to be tormented by flies and hornets. The Pilgrim recognizes several of these shades but mentions none by name. Next they come to the River Acheron, where they are greeted by the infernal boatman, Charon. Among those doomed souls who are to be ferried across the river, Charon sees the living man and challenges him, but Virgil lets it be known that his companion must pass. Then across the landscape rushes a howling wind, which blasts the Pilgrim out of his senses, and he falls to the ground.

I AM THE WAY INTO THE DOLEFUL CITY,
  I AM THE WAY INTO ETERNAL GRIEF,
  I AM THE WAY TO A FORSAKEN RACE.   3
JUSTICE IT WAS THAT MOVED MY GREAT CREATOR;
  DIVINE OMNIPOTENCE CREATED ME,
  AND HIGHEST WISDOM JOINED WITH PRIMAL LOVE.[7]   6
BEFORE ME NOTHING BUT ETERNAL THINGS
  WERE MADE, AND I SHALL LAST ETERNALLY.
  ABANDON EVERY HOPE, ALL YOU WHO ENTER.   9
I saw these words spelled out in somber colors
  inscribed along the ledge above a gate;
  "Master," I said, "these words I see are cruel."   12
He answered me, speaking with experience:
  "Now here you must leave all distrust behind;
  let all your cowardice die on this spot.   15
We are at the place where earlier I said
  you could expect to see the suffering race
  of souls who lost the good of intellect."[8]   18
Placing his hand on mine, smiling at me
  in such a way that I was reassured,
  he led me in, into those mysteries.   21
Here sighs and cries and shrieks of lamentation
  echoed throughout the starless air of Hell;
  at first these sounds resounding made me weep: 24
tongues confused, a language strained in anguish
  with cadences of anger, shrill outcries
  and raucous groans that joined with sounds of hands,   27
raising a whirling storm that turns itself
  forever through that air of endless black,
  like grains of sand swirling when a whirlwind blows.   30

7. God as Father, Son, and Holy Ghost.   8. "The good of intellect": i.e., God.

And I, in the midst of all this circling horror,
  began, "Teacher, what are these sounds I hear?
  What souls are these so overwhelmed by grief?"   33
And he to me: "This wretched state of being
  is the fate of those sad souls who lived a life
  but lived it with no blame and with no praise.   36
They are mixed with that repulsive choir of angels
  neither faithful nor unfaithful to their God,
  who undecided stood but for themselves.[9]   39
Heaven, to keep its beauty, cast them out,
  but even Hell itself would not receive them,
  to fear the damned might glory over them."   42
And I: "Master, what torments do they suffer
  that force them to lament so bitterly?"
  He answered: "I will tell you in few words: 45
these wretches have no hope of truly dying,
  and this blind life they lead is so abject
  it makes them envy every other fate.   48
The world will not record their having been there;
  Heaven's mercy and its justice turn from them.
  Let's not discuss them; look and pass them by."   51
And so I looked and saw a kind of banner
  rushing ahead, whirling with aimless speed
  as though it would not ever take a stand;   54
behind it an interminable train
  of souls pressed on, so many that I wondered
  how death could have undone so great a number.   57
When I had recognized a few of them,
  I saw the shade of the one who must have been
  the coward who had made the great refusal.[1]   60
At once I understood, and I was sure
  this was that sect of evil souls who were
  hateful to God and to His enemies.   63
These wretches, who had never truly lived,
  went naked, and were stung and stung again
  by the hornets and the wasps that circled them   66
and made their faces run with blood in streaks;
  their blood, mixed with their tears, dripped to their feet,
  and disgusting maggots collected in the pus.   69
And when I looked beyond this crowd I saw
  a throng upon the shore of a wide river,
  which made me ask, "Master, I would like to know: 72
who are these people, and what law is this
  that makes those souls so eager for the crossing—
  as I can see, even in this dim light?"   75
And he: "All this will be made plain to you

9. The "neutral angels," not mentioned in the Bible but discussed by theologians throughout the Middle Ages, were those who declined to choose either side when Satan rebelled against God.
1. This is Pope Celestine V, who was elected in July 1294 but resigned five months later.

as soon as we shall come to stop awhile
  upon the sorrowful shore of Acheron."[2]   78
And I, with eyes cast down in shame, for fear
  that I perhaps had spoken out of turn,
  said nothing more until we reached the river.   81
And suddenly, coming toward us in a boat,
  a man of years[3] whose ancient hair was white
  shouted at us, "Woe to you, perverted souls!   84
Give up all hope of ever seeing Heaven:
  I come to lead you to the other shore,
  into eternal darkness, ice, and fire.   87
And you, the living soul, you over there,
  get away from all these people who are dead."
  But when he saw I did not move aside,   90
he said, "Another way, by other ports,
  not here, shall you pass to reach the other shore;
  a lighter skiff than this must carry you."[4]   93
And my guide, "Charon, this is no time for anger!
  It is so willed, there where the power is
  for what is willed; that's all you need to know."   96
These words brought silence to the woolly cheeks
  of the ancient steersman of the livid marsh,
  whose eyes were set in glowing wheels of fire.   99
But all those souls there, naked, in despair,
  changed color and their teeth began to chatter
  at the sound of his announcement of their doom. 102
They were cursing God, cursing their own parents,
  the human race, the time, the place, the seed
  of their beginning, and their day of birth.   105
Then all together, weeping bitterly,
  they packed themselves along the wicked shore
  that waits for every man who fears not God.   108
The devil, Charon, with eyes of glowing coals,
  summons them all together with a signal,
  and with an oar he strikes the laggard sinner. 111
As in autumn when the leaves begin to fall,
  one after the other (until the branch
  is witness to the spoils spread on the ground), 114
so did the evil seed of Adam's Fall
  drop from that shore to the boat, one at a time,
  at the signal, like the falcon to its lure.[5]   117
Away they go across the darkened waters,
  and before they reach the other side to land,
  a new throng starts collecting on this side.   120

2. The first of the four rivers of Hell.
3. Charon; see *Aeneid* 6.
4. Charon knows that after death Dante will be taken not to Hell but to Purgatory in a "swift and light" vessel piloted by an angel; the arrival of the souls in Purgatory is described in

Purgatorio 2.22–48. This is the first of several places in the *Commedia* where Dante predicts his own salvation.
5. These similes are drawn from *Aeneid* 6.56–60 (all line references are to the edition in this anthology).

"My son," the gentle master said to me,
    "all those who perish in the wrath of God
    assemble here from all parts of the earth;   123
they want to cross the river, they are eager;
    it is Divine Justice that spurs them on,
    turning the fear they have into desire.   126
A good soul never comes to make this crossing,
    so, if Charon grumbles at the sight of you,
    you see now what his words are really saying."   129
He finished speaking, and the grim terrain
    shook violently; and the fright it gave me
    even now in recollection makes me sweat.   132
Out of the tear-drenched land a wind arose
    which blasted forth into a reddish light,
    knocking my senses out of me completely,   135
and I fell as one falls tired into sleep.[6]

CANTO IV

Waking from his swoon, the Pilgrim is led by Virgil to the First Circle of Hell,
known as Limbo, where the sad shades of the virtuous non-Christians dwell. The
souls here, including Virgil, suffer no physical torment, but they must live, in desire,
without hope of seeing God. Virgil tells about Christ's descent into Hell and His
salvation of several Old Testament figures. The poets see a light glowing in the dark-
ness, and as they proceed toward it, they are met by the four greatest (other than
Virgil) pagan poets: Homer, Horace, Ovid, and Lucan, who take the Pilgrim into
their group. As they come closer to the light, the Pilgrim perceives a splendid castle,
where the greatest non-Christian thinkers dwell together with other famous histori-
cal figures. Once within the castle, the Pilgrim sees, among others, Electra, Aeneas,
Caesar, Saladin, Aristotle, Plato, Orpheus, Cicero, Avicenna, and Averroës. But
soon they must leave; and the poets move from the radiance of the castle toward the
fearful encompassing darkness.

A heavy clap of thunder! I awoke
    from the deep sleep that drugged my mind—startled,
    the way one is when shaken out of sleep.   3
I turned my rested eyes from side to side,
    already on my feet and, staring hard,
    I tried my best to find out where I was,   6
and this is what I saw: I found myself
    upon the brink of grief's abysmal valley
    that collects the thunderings of endless cries.   9
So dark and deep and nebulous it was,
    try as I might to force my sight below,
    I could not see the shape of anything.   12
"Let us descend into the sightless world,"

6. Dante is describing an earthquake, which   unconscious that he crosses Acheron into Hell
medieval science understood as the escape of   proper.
vapors from within the earth; it is while he is

began the poet (his face was deathly pale):
"I will go first, and you will follow me."   15
And I, aware of his changed color, said:
"But how can I go on if you are frightened?
You are my constant strength when I lose heart."   18
And he to me: "The anguish of the souls
  that are down here paints my face with pity—
  which you have wrongly taken to be fear.   21
Let us go, the long road urges us."
  He entered then, leading the way for me
  down to the first circle of the abyss.   24
Down there, to judge only by what I heard,
  there were no wails but just the sounds of sighs
  rising and trembling through the timeless air,   27
the sounds of sighs of untormented grief
  burdening these groups, diverse and teeming,
  made up of men and women and of infants.   30
Then the good master said, "You do not ask
  what sort of souls are these you see around you.
  Now you should know before we go on farther,   33
they have not sinned. But their great worth alone
  was not enough, for they did not know Baptism,
  which is the gateway to the faith you follow,   36
and if they came before the birth of Christ,
  they did not worship God the way one should;
  I myself am a member of this group.   39
For this defect, and for no other guilt,
  we here are lost. In this alone we suffer:
  cut off from hope, we live on in desire."   42
The words I heard weighed heavy on my heart;
  to think that souls as virtuous as these
  were suspended in that limbo, and forever!   45
"Tell me, my teacher, tell me, O my master,"
  I began (wishing to have confirmed by him
  the teachings of unerring Christian doctrine),   48
"did any ever leave here, through his merit
  or with another's help, and go to bliss?"
  And he, who understood my hidden question,[7]   51
answered: "I was a novice in this place
  when I saw a mighty lord descend to us
  who wore the sign of victory as his crown.   54
He took from us the shade of our first parent,[8]
  of Abel, his good son, of Noah, too,
  and of obedient Moses, who made the laws;   57
Abram, the Patriarch, David the King,
  Israel with his father and his children,
  with Rachel, whom he worked so hard to win;   60

7. Dante's question is about the Harrowing of
Hell, when according to Christian doctrine,
Christ descended into Hell after the crucifix-
ion and rescued the souls of the righteous of
Israel; see also 12.44.
8. Adam.

and many more he chose for blessedness;
   and you should know, before these souls were taken,
   no human soul had ever reached salvation."   63
We did not stop our journey while he spoke,
   but continued on our way along the woods—
   I say the woods, for souls were thick as trees.   66
We had not gone too far from where I woke
   when I made out a fire up ahead,
   a hemisphere of light that lit the dark.   69
We were still at some distance from that place,
   but close enough for me vaguely to see
   that honorable souls possessed that spot.   72
"O glory of the sciences and arts,
   who are these souls enjoying special honor,
   dwelling apart from all the others here?"   75
And he to me: "The honored name they bear
   that still resounds above in your own world
   wins Heaven's favor for them in this place."[9]   78
And as he spoke I heard a voice announce:
   "Now let us honor our illustrious poet,
   his shade that left is now returned to us."   81
And when the voice was silent and all was quiet
   I saw four mighty shades approaching us,
   their faces showing neither joy nor sorrow.   84
Then my good master started to explain:
   "Observe the one who comes with sword in hand,
   leading the three as if he were their master.   87
It is the shade of Homer, sovereign poet,
   and coming second, Horace, the satirist;
   Ovid is the third, and last comes Lucan.[1]   90
Since they all share one name with me, the name
   you heard resounding in that single voice,
   they honor me and do well doing so."   93
So I saw gathered there the noble school
   of the master singer of sublimest verse,
   who soars above all others like the eagle.   96
And after they had talked awhile together,
   they turned and with a gesture welcomed me,
   and at that sign I saw my master smile.   99
Greater honor still they deigned to grant me:
   they welcomed me as one of their own group,
   so that I numbered sixth among such minds.   102
We walked together toward the shining light,
   discussing things that here are best kept silent,
   as there they were most fitting for discussion.   105
We reached the boundaries of a splendid castle

9. The "honored name" is "poet."   1. Horace, Ovid, and Lucan are famous
Roman poets.

that seven times was circled by high walls
  defended by a sweetly flowing stream.[2]   108
We walked right over it as on hard ground;
  through seven gates I passed with those wise spirits,
  and then we reached a meadow fresh in bloom.[3]   111
There people were whose eyes were calm and grave,
  whose bearing told of great authority;
  seldom they spoke and always quietly.   114
Then moving to one side we reached a place
  spread out and luminous, higher than before,
  allowing us to view all who were there.   117
And right before us on the lustrous green
  the mighty shades were pointed out to me
  (my heart felt glory when I looked at them).   120
There was Electra standing with a group,
  among whom I saw Hector and Aeneas,
  and Caesar, falcon-eyed and fully armed.[4]   123
I saw Camilla and Penthesilea;
  across the way I saw the Latian King,
  with Lavinia, his daughter, by his side.[5]   126
I saw the Brutus who drove out the Tarquin;
  Lucretia, Julia, Marcia, and Cornelia;
  off, by himself, I noticed Saladin,[6]   129
and when I raised my eyes a little higher
  I saw the master sage of those who know,[7]
  sitting with his philosophic family.   132
All gaze at him, all pay their homage to him;
  and there I saw both Socrates and Plato,
  each closer to his side than any other;   135
Democritus, who said the world was chance,
  Diogenes, Thales, Anaxagoras,
  Empedocles, Zeno, and Heraclitus;   138
I saw the one who classified our herbs:
  Dioscorides I mean. And I saw Orpheus,
  Tully, Linus, Seneca the moralist,[8]   141
Euclid the geometer, and Ptolemy,
  Hippocrates, Galen, Avicenna,

2. Commentators have suggested that this is a Castle of Fame, its seven walls symbolizing the seven liberal arts, a system of knowledge developed in the classical period.
3. A locale reminiscent of the classical Elysian fields as described in *Aeneid* 6.468–73.
4. Julius Caesar. "Electra": the mother of Dardanus, the founder of Troy. "Hector": the leading warrior of the Trojans in the *Iliad*. "Aeneas": the hero of the *Aeneid*.
5. Heiress to King Latinus who ruled the area of Italy where Rome was later located and who married Aeneas. "Camilla": a female warrior in the *Aeneid*, where she is compared to Penthesilea, who fought for the Trojans against the Greeks.

6. Admired for his chivalry in fighting against the Crusaders, he was sultan of Egypt and Syria and died in 1193. "Brutus": not the Brutus who killed Julius Caesar, but an earlier Roman who drove out the tyrant Tarquin. All four of the women mentioned were virtuous Roman matrons.
7. Aristotle (384–322 B.C.E.), Greek philosopher. The men mentioned in lines 132–38 are Greek philosophers of the 7th through the 4th centuries B.C.E.
8. Roman philosopher and dramatist, killed by Nero in 65 C.E. "Dioscorides": Greek physician (1st century C.E.). "Orpheus": mythical Greek poet. "Tully": Cicero (d. 43 B.C.E.), Roman orator.

and Averroës, who made the Commentary.[9]   144
I cannot tell about them all in full;
  my theme is long and urges me ahead,
  often I must omit things I have seen.   147
The company of six becomes just two;
  my wise guide leads me by another way
  out of the quiet into tempestuous air.   150
I come into a place where no light is.

CANTO V

From Limbo Virgil leads his ward down to the threshold of the Second Circle of Hell, where for the first time he will see the damned in Hell being punished for their sins. There, barring their way, is the hideous figure of Minòs, the bestial judge of Dante's underworld; but after strong words from Virgil, the poets are allowed to pass into the dark space of this circle, where can be heard the wailing voices of the Lustful, whose punishment consists in being forever whirled about in a dark, stormy wind. After seeing a thousand or more famous lovers—including Semiramis, Dido, Helen, Achilles, and Paris—the Pilgrim asks to speak to two figures he sees together. They are Francesca da Rimini and her lover, Paolo, and the scene in which they appear is probably the most famous episode of the Inferno. At the end of the scene, the Pilgrim, who has been overcome by pity for the lovers, faints to the ground.

This way I went, descending from the first
  into the second round, that holds less space
  but much more pain—stinging the soul to wailing.   3
There stands Minòs grotesquely, and he snarls,
  examining the guilty at the entrance;
  he judges and dispatches, tail in coils.[1]   6
By this I mean that when the evil soul
  appears before him, it confesses all,
  and he, who is the expert judge of sins,   9
knows to what place in Hell the soul belongs;
  the times he wraps his tail around himself
  tell just how far the sinner must go down.   12
The damned keep crowding up in front of him:
  they pass along to judgment one by one;
  they speak, they hear, and then are hurled below.   15
"O you who come to the place where pain is host,"
  Minòs spoke out when he caught sight of me,
  putting aside the duties of his office,   18
"be careful how you enter and whom you trust

---

9. Avicenna (d. 1037) and Averroës (d. 1198) were Islamic philosophers who wrote commentaries on Aristotle's works that were highly influential in Christian Europe. "Euclid": Greek mathematician (4th century B.C.E.). "Ptolemy": Greek astronomer and geographer (1st century C.E.) credited with devising the cosmological system that was accepted until the time of Copernicus in the 16th century (hence the term *Ptolemaic universe*). "Hippocrates and Galen": Greek physicians (4th and 2nd centuries B.C.E., respectively).
1. In *Aeneid* 6.207–11 Minos is described as judge of the underworld.

it's easy to get in, but don't be fooled!"
And my guide said to him: "Why keep on shouting?   21
Do not attempt to stop his fated journey;
   it is so willed there where the power is
   for what is willed,[2] that's all you need to know."   24
And now the notes of anguish start to play
   upon my ears; and now I find myself
   where sounds on sounds of weeping pound at me.   27
I came to a place where no light shone at all,
   bellowing like the sea racked by a tempest,
   when warring winds attack it from both sides.   30
The infernal storm, eternal in its rage,
   sweeps and drives the spirits with its blast:
   it whirls them, lashing them with punishment.   33
When they are swept back past their place of judgment,
   then come the shrieks, laments, and anguished cries;
   there they blaspheme God's almighty power.   36
I learned that to this place of punishment
   all those who sin in lust have been condemned,
   those who make reason slave to appetite;   39
and as the wings of starlings in the winter
   bear them along in wide-spread, crowded flocks,
   so does that wind propel the evil spirits: 42
now here, then there, and up and down, it drives them
   with never any hope to comfort them—
   hope not of rest but even of suffering less.   45
And just like cranes in flight, chanting their lays,
   stretching an endless line in their formation,
   I saw approaching, crying their laments,   48
spirits carried along by the battling winds,
   And so I asked, "Teacher, tell me, what souls
   are these punished in the sweep of the black wind?"   51
"The first of those whose story you should know,"
   my master wasted no time answering,
   "was empress over lands of many tongues;   54
her vicious tastes had so corrupted her
   she licensed every form of lust with laws
   to cleanse the stain of scandal she had spread;   57
she is Semiramis,[3] who, legend says,
   was Ninus' wife as well as his successor;
   she governed all the land the Sultan rules.   60
The next is she who killed herself for love
   and broke faith with the ashes of Sichaeus;[4]
   and there is Cleopatra, who loved men's lusting.   63

2. It is willed in Heaven by God, who has the power to accomplish whatever he wills.
3. Renowned for licentiousness, a mythical queen of Assyria and wife of Ninus, the legendary founder of Ninevah. Because both the capital of Assyria and Old Cairo were known as Babylon, her land is here confused with that ruled by the sultan of Egypt.
4. Dido, whose suicide for love of Aeneas is described in *Aeneid* 4.542–942, was the widow of Sichaeus. Cleopatra killed herself after the death of her lover, Mark Antony, in 30 B.C.E.

See Helen there, the root of evil woe
   lasting long years, and see the great Achilles,
   who lost his life to love, in final combat;[5]   66
see Paris, Tristan"[6]—then, more than a thousand
   he pointed out to me, and named them all,
   those shades whom love cut off from life on earth.   69
After I heard my teacher call the names
   of all these knights and ladies of ancient times,
   pity confused my senses, and I was dazed.   72
I began: "Poet, I would like, with all my heart,
   to speak to those two there who move together
   and seem to be so light upon the winds."[7]   75
And he: "You'll see when they are closer to us;
   if you entreat them by that love of theirs
   that carries them along, they'll come to you."   78
When the winds bent their course in our direction
   I raised my voice to them, "O wearied souls,
   come speak with us if it be not forbidden."   81
As doves, called by desire to return
   to their sweet nest, with wings raised high and poised,
   float downward through the air, guided by will,   84
so these two left the flock where Dido is
   and came toward us through the malignant air,
   such was the tender power of my call.   87
"O living creature, gracious and so kind,
   who makes your way here through this dingy air
   to visit us who stained the world with blood,   90
if we could claim as friend the King of Kings,
   we would beseech him that he grant you peace,
   you who show pity for our atrocious plight.   93
Whatever pleases you to hear or speak
   we will hear and we will speak about with you
   as long as the wind, here where we are, is silent.   96
The place where I was born lies on the shore
   where the river Po with its attendant streams
   descends to seek its final resting place.[8]   99
Love, quick to kindle in the gentle heart,
   seized this one for the beauty of my body,
   torn from me, (How it happened still offends me!)   102
Love, that excuses no one loved from loving,
   seized me so strongly with delight in him
   that, as you see, he never leaves my side.   105
Love led us straight to sudden death together.[9]

5. The medieval version of the Troy story described Achilles as enamored of a Trojan princess, Polyxena, and killed in an ambush set by Paris when he went to meet her. Helen's seduction by Paris (see line 67) was the cause of the Trojan War.
6. The lover of Iseult, wife of his lord King Mark.

7. Francesca da Rimini and her brother-in-law Paolo Malatesta.
8. The Po is a river in northern Italy that empties into the Adriatic sea at Ravenna.
9. These seven lines (100–106) should be compared to the love sonnets by Guido Guinizzelli and Dante included in *Medieval Lyrics* (pp. 354 and 358).

Caïna awaits the one who quenched our lives."[1]
These were the words that came from them to us.   108
When those offended souls had told their story,
    I bowed my head and kept it bowed until
    the poet said, "What are you thinking of?"   111
When finally I spoke, I sighed, "Alas,
    all those sweet thoughts, and oh, how much desiring
    brought these two down into this agony."   114
And then I turned to them and tried to speak;
    I said, "Francesca, the torment that you suffer
    brings painful tears of pity to my eyes.   117
But tell me, in that time of your sweet sighing
    how, and by what signs, did love allow you
    to recognize your dubious desires?"   120
And she to me: "There is no greater pain
    than to remember, in our present grief,
    past happiness (as well your teacher knows)!   123
But if your great desire is to learn
    the very root of such a love as ours,
    I shall tell you, but in words of flowing tears.   126
One day we read, to pass the time away,
    of Lancelot,[2] of how he fell in love;
    we were alone, innocent of suspicion.   129
Time and again our eyes were brought together
    by the book we read; our faces flushed and paled.
    To the moment of one line alone we yielded: 132
it was when we read about those longed-for lips
    now being kissed by such a famous lover,
    that this one (who shall never leave my side)   135
then kissed my mouth, and trembled as he did.
    Our Galehot[3] was that book and he who wrote it.
    That day we read no further."[4] And all the while   138
the one of the two spirits spoke these words,
    the other wept, in such a way that pity
    blurred my senses; I swooned as though to die,   141
and fell to Hell's floor as a body, dead, falls.

CANTO VI

On recovering consciousness the Pilgrim finds himself with Virgil in the Third Circle, where the Gluttons are punished. These shades are mired in filthy muck and are eternally battered by cold and dirty hail, rain, and snow. Soon the travelers come upon Cerberus, the three-headed, doglike beast who guards the Gluttons, but Virgil

1. Caïna is the circle of Cain (described in canto 32), where those who killed their kin are punished; the lovers were killed by Gianciotto Malatesta, Francesca's husband and Paolo's brother.
2. In Arthurian legend, the lover of Arthur's wife, Guinevere.

3. The knight who, in the French romance being read by the lovers, acted as a go-between for Lancelot and Guinevere.
4. Compare this line to Augustine's account in *Confessions* of his conversion by reading a passage in Paul's Epistle to the Romans.

*pacifies him with fistfuls of slime and the two poets pass on. One of the shades
recognizes Dante the Pilgrim and hails him. It is Ciacco, a Florentine who, before
they leave, makes a prophecy concerning the political future of Florence. As the
poets move away, the Pilgrim questions Virgil about the Last Judgment and other
matters until the two arrive at the next circle.*

Regaining now my senses, which had fainted
   at the sight of these two who were kinsmen lovers,
   a piteous sight confusing me to tears,   3
new suffering and new sinners suffering
   appeared to me, no matter where I moved
   or turned my eyes, no matter where I gazed.   6
I am in the third circle, in the round of rain
   eternal, cursed, cold, and falling heavy,
   unchanging beat, unchanging quality.   9
Thick hail and dirty water mixed with snow
   come down in torrents through the murky air,
   and the earth is stinking from this soaking rain.   12
Cerberus,[5] a ruthless and fantastic beast,
   with all three throats howls out his doglike sounds
   above the drowning sinners of this place.   15
His eyes are red, his beard is slobbered black,
   his belly swollen, and he has claws for hands;
   he rips the spirits, flays and mangles them.   18
Under the rain they howl like dogs, lying
   now on one side with the other as a screen,
   now on the other turning, these wretched sinners.   21
When the slimy Cerberus caught sight of us,
   he opened up his mouths and showed his fangs;
   his body was one mass of twitching muscles.   24
My master stooped and, spreading wide his fingers,
   he grabbed up heaping fistfuls of the mud
   and flung it down into those greedy gullets.   27
As a howling cur, hungering to get fed,
   quiets down with the first mouthful of his food,
   busy with eating, wrestling with that alone,   30
so it was with all three filthy heads
   of the demon Cerberus, used to barking thunder
   on these dead souls, who wished that they were deaf.   33
We walked across this marsh of shades beaten
   down by the heavy rain, our feet pressing
   on their emptiness that looked like human form.   36
Each sinner there was stretched out on the ground
   except for one[6] who quickly sat up straight,
   the moment that he saw us pass him by.   39
"O you there being led through this inferno,"
   he said, "try to remember who I am,

---

5. For this creature as one of the guardians of
Hell, see *Aeneid* 6.190–97.

6. A Florentine named Ciacco, known only
through his appearance here.

for you had life before I gave up mine."[7]   42
I said: "The pain you suffer here perhaps
   disfigures you beyond all recognition:
   I can't remember seeing you before.   45
But tell me who you are, assigned to grieve
   in this sad place, afflicted by such torture
   that—worse there well may be, but none more foul."   48
"Your own city," he said, "so filled with envy
   its cup already overflows the brim,
   once held me in the brighter life above.   51
You citizens gave me the name of Ciacco;
   and for my sin of gluttony I am damned,
   as you can see, to rain that beats me weak.   54
And my sad sunken soul is not alone,
   for all these sinners here share in my pain
   and in my sin." And that was his last word.   57
"Ciacco," I said to him, "your grievous state
   weighs down on me, it makes me want to weep;
   but tell me what will happen, if you know,   60
to the citizens of that divided state?
   And are there any honest men among them?
   And tell me, why is it so plagued with strife?"   63
And he replied:[8] "After much contention
   they will come to bloodshed; the rustic party
   will drive the other out by brutal means.   66
Then it will come to pass, this side will fall
   within three suns, and the other rise to power
   with the help of one now listing toward both sides.   69
For a long time they will keep their heads raised high,
   holding the others down with crushing weight,
   no matter how these weep or squirm for shame.   72
Two just men there are,[9] but no one listens,
   for pride, envy, avarice are the three sparks
   that kindle in men's hearts and set them burning."   75
With this his mournful words came to an end.
   But I spoke back: "There's more I want to know;
   I beg you to provide me with more facts: 78
Farinata and Tegghiaio, who were so worthy,
   Jacopo Rusticucci, Arrigo, Mosca,
   and all the rest so bent on doing good,[1]   81
where are they? Tell me what's become of them;
   one great desire tortures me: to know
   whether they taste Heaven's sweetness or Hell's gall."   84

---

7. "You were born before I died."
8. The enigmatic "prophecy" that follows
refers first to the triumph of the Whites, or
"the rustic party" (to which Dante was allied),
in 1300 and then their defeat by the Blacks,
aided by Pope Boniface ("one now listing
toward both sides"), in 1302, at which time

Dante was exiled.
9. The identity of these two is unknown.
1. Dante asks about famous Florentines; he
will find Farinata in canto 10, Tegghiaio and
Rusticucci in canto 16, and Mosca in canto
28. Arrigo does not appear.

"They lie below with blacker souls," he said,
  "by different sins pushed down to different depths;
  if you keep going you may see them all.   87
But when you are once more in the sweet world
  I beg you to remind our friends of me.
  I speak no more; no more I answer you."   90
He twisted his straight gaze into a squint
  and stared awhile at me, then bent his head,
  falling to join his other sightless peers.   93
My guide then said to me: "He'll wake no more
  until the day the angel's trumpet blows,
  when the unfriendly Judge shall come down here;   96
each soul shall find again his wretched tomb,
  assume his flesh and take his human shape,
  and hear his fate resound eternally."[2]   99
And so we made our way through the filthy mess
  of muddy shades and slush, moving slowly,
  talking a little about the afterlife.   102
I said, "Master, will these torments be increased,
  or lessened, on the final Judgment Day,
  or will the pain be just the same as now?"   105
And he: "Remember your philosophy:
  the closer a thing comes to its perfection,
  more keen will be its pleasure or its pain.   108
Although this cursèd race of punished souls
  shall never know the joy of true perfection,
  more perfect will their pain be then than now."[3]   111
We circled round that curving road while talking
  of more than I shall mention at this time,
  and came to where the ledge begins descending;   114
there we found Plutus, mankind's arch-enemy.[4]

CANTO VII

At the boundary of the Fourth Circle the two travelers confront clucking Plutus, the god of wealth, who collapses into emptiness at a word from Virgil. Descending farther, the Pilgrim sees two groups of angry, shouting souls who clash huge rolling weights against each other with their chests. They are the Prodigal and the Miserly. Their earthly concern with material goods prompts the Pilgrim to question Virgil about Fortune and her distribution of the worldly goods of men. After Virgil's explanation, they descend to the banks of the swamplike river Styx, which serves as the Fifth Circle. Mired in the bog are the Wrathful, who constantly tear and mangle each other. Beneath the slime of the Styx, Virgil explains, are the Slothful; the bubbles on the muddy surface indicate their presence beneath. The poets walk around the swampy area and soon come to the foot of a high tower.

2. Virgil refers to the Last Judgment, when the dead will regain their bodies.
3. They will be more perfect because body and soul will be reunited (a principle derived from Aristotelian science), which will only increase their pain.
4. Dante combines Pluto, the classical god of the underworld, with Plutus, the classical god of wealth.

"Pape Satàn, pape Satàn aleppe!"[5]
   the voice of Plutus clucked these words at us,
   and that kind sage, to whom all things were known,   3
said reassuringly: "Do not let fear
   defeat you, for whatever be his power,
   he cannot stop our journey down this rock."   6
Then he turned toward that swollen face of rage,
   crying, "Be quiet, cursèd wolf of Hell:
   feed on the burning bile that rots your guts.   9
This journey to the depths does have a reason,
   for it is willed on high, where Michael wrought
   a just revenge for the bold assault on God."[6]   12
As sails swollen by wind, when the ship's mast breaks,
   collapse, deflated, tangled in a heap,
   just so the savage beast fell to the ground.   15
And then we started down a fourth abyss,
   making our way along the dismal slope
   where all the evil of the world is dumped.   18
Ah, God's avenging justice! Who could heap up
   suffering and pain as strange as I saw here?
   How can we let our guilt bring us to this?   21
As every wave Charybdis[7] whirls to sea
   comes crashing against its counter-current wave,
   so these folks here must dance their roundelay.   24
More shades were here than anywhere above,
   and from both sides, to the sound of their own screams,
   straining their chests, they rolled enormous weights.   27
And when they met and clashed against each other
   they turned to push the other way, one side
   screaming, "Why hoard?," the other side, "Why waste?"   30
And so they moved back round the gloomy circle,
   returning on both sides to opposite poles
   to scream their shameful tune another time;   33
again they came to clash and turn and roll
   forever in their semicircle joust.
   And I, my heart pierced through by such a sight,   36
spoke out, "My Master, please explain to me
   who are these people here? Were they all priests,
   these tonsured[8] souls I see there to our left?"   39
He said, "In their first life all you see here
   had such myopic minds they could not judge
   with moderation when it came to spending;   42
their barking voices make this clear enough,

---

5. Virgil apparently understands this mysterious outburst regarding Satan, but commentators have remained baffled.
6. A reference to the battle in heaven between the Archangel Michael and Satan in the form of a dragon: see Revelation 12.7–9.

7. A famous whirlpool in the Straits of Messina, between Sicily and Italy, described in *Aeneid* 3.
8. The tonsure—a shaving of part of the head—was a mark of clerical status.

when they arrive at the two points on the circle
    where opposing guilts divide them into two.   45
The ones who have the bald spot on their heads
    were priests and popes and cardinals, in whom
    avarice is most likely to prevail."   48
And I: "Master, in such a group as this
    I should be able to recognize a few
    who dirtied themselves by such crimes as these."   51
And he replied, "Yours is an empty hope:
    their undistinguished life that made them foul
    now makes it harder to distinguish them.   54
Eternally the two will come to blows;
    then from the tomb they will be resurrected:
    these with tight fists, those without any hair.   57
It was squandering and hoarding that have robbed them
    of the lovely world, and got them in this brawl:
    I will not waste choice words describing it!   60
You see, my son, the short-lived mockery
    of all the wealth that is in Fortune's keep,
    over which the human race is bickering;   63
for all the gold that is or ever was
    beneath the moon won't buy a moment's rest
    for even one among these weary souls."   66
"Master, now tell me what this Fortune is
    you touched upon before. What is she like
    who holds all worldly wealth within her fists?"   69
And he to me, "O foolish race of man,
    how overwhelming is your ignorance!
    Now listen while I tell you what she means:[9]   72
that One, whose wisdom knows infinity,
    made all the heavens and gave each one a guide,
    and each sphere shining shines on all the others,   75
so light is spread with equal distribution:
    for worldly splendors He decreed the same
    and ordained a guide and general ministress   78
who would at her discretion shift the world's
    vain wealth from nation to nation, house to house,
    with no chance of interference from mankind;   81
so while one nation rules, another falls,
    according to whatever she decrees
    (her sentence hidden like a snake in grass).   84
Your knowledge has no influence on her;
    for she foresees, she judges, and she rules
    her kingdom as the other gods do theirs.   87
Her changing changes never take a rest;
    necessity keeps her in constant motion,
    as men come and go to take their turn with her.   90

9. Virgil now explains that each area of life is presided over by a "guide," a kind of angel, under the ultimate authority of God. The classical goddess Fortune—the "ministress" of line 78—who was thought to distribute the world's goods capriciously is here described as acting according to God's supervision.

And this is she so crucified and cursed;
 even those in luck, who should be praising her,
 instead revile her and condemn her acts.   93
But she is blest and in her bliss hears nothing;
 with all God's joyful first-created creatures
 she turns her sphere and, blest, turns it with joy. 96
Now let's move down to greater wretchedness;
 the stars that rose when I set out for you
 are going down—we cannot stay too long."[1]   99
We crossed the circle to its other bank,
 passing a spring that boils and overflows
 into a ditch the spring itself cut out.   102
The water was a deeper dark than perse,
 and we, with its gray waves for company,
 made our way down along a rough, strange path. 105
This dingy little stream, when it has reached
 the bottom of the gray malignant slopes,
 becomes a swamp that has the name of Styx.[2] 108
And I, intent on looking as we passed,
 saw muddy people moving in that marsh,
 all naked, with their faces scarred by rage.   111
They fought each other, not with hands alone,
 but struck with head and chest and feet as well,
 with teeth they tore each other limb from limb. 114
And the good teacher said: "My son, now see
 the souls of those that anger overcame;
 and I ask you to believe me when I say,   117
beneath the slimy top are sighing souls
 who make these waters bubble at the surface;
 your eyes will tell you this—just look around. 120
Bogged in this slime they say, 'Sluggish we were
 in the sweet air made happy by the sun,
 and the smoke of sloth was smoldering in our hearts; 123
now we lie sluggish here in this black muck!'
 This is the hymn they gurgle in their throats
 but cannot sing in words that truly sound."   126
Then making a wide arc, we walked around
 the pond between the dry bank and the slime,
 our eyes still fixed on those who gobbled mud. 129
We came, in time, to the foot of a high tower.[3]

CANTO VIII

But before they had reached the foot of the tower, the Pilgrim had noticed two signal flames at the tower's top, and another flame answering from a distance; soon he realizes that the flames are signals to and from Phlegyas, the boatman of the Styx, who

1. The stars that were rising at the start of the journey (1.37–40) are now setting: Good Friday has passed, and the time is now the early hours of Holy Saturday.
2. The second river of Hell.

3. This watchtower guards the entrance to lower Hell or the city of Dis—another name for Pluto, the classical god of the underworld, that is throughout the *Inferno* applied to Satan (see 11.65 and 34.20).

suddenly appears in a small boat speeding across the river. Wrathful and irritated though he is, the steersman must grant the poets passage, but during the crossing an angry shade rises from the slime to question the Pilgrim. After a brief exchange of words, scornful on the part of the Pilgrim, who has recognized this sinner, the spirit grabs hold of the boat. Virgil pushes him away, praising his ward for his just scorn, while a group of the wrathful attack the wretched soul, whose name is Filippo Argenti. At the far shore the poets debark and find themselves before the gates of the infernal City of Dis, where howling figures threaten them from the walls. Virgil speaks with them privately, but they slam the gate shut in his face. His ward is terrified, and Virgil too is shaken, but he insists that help from Heaven is already on the way.

I must explain, however, that before
  we finally reached the foot of that high tower,
  our eyes had been attracted to its summit   3
by two small flames we saw flare up just there;
  and, so far off the eye could hardly see,
  another burning torch flashed back a sign.   6
I turned to that vast sea of human knowledge:
  "What signal is this? And the other flame,
  what does it answer? And who's doing this?"   9
And he replied: "You should already see
  across the filthy waves what has been summoned,
  unless the marsh's vapors hide it from you."   12
A bowstring never shot an arrow off
  that cut the thin air any faster than
  a little boat I saw that very second   15
skimming along the water in our direction,
  with a solitary steersman, who was shouting,
  "Aha, I've got you now, you wretched soul!"   18
"Phlegyas, Phlegyas,[4] this time you shout in vain,"
  my lord responded, "you will have us with you
  no longer than it takes to cross the muck."   21
As one who learns of some incredible trick
  just played on him flares up resentfully—
  so, Phlegyas there was seething in his anger.   24
My leader calmly stepped into the skiff
  and when he was inside, he had me enter,
  and only then it seemed to carry weight.   27
Soon as my guide and I were in the boat
  the ancient prow began to plough the water,
  more deeply, now, than any time before.[5]   30
And as we sailed the course of this dead channel,
  before me there rose up a slimy shape
  that said: "Who are you, who come before your time?"   33
And I spoke back, "Though I come, I do not stay;
  but who are you, in all your ugliness?"
  "You see that I am one who weeps," he answered.   36

4. A mythological figure condemned to Hell for setting fire to the temple of Apollo in revenge for the god's seduction of his daughter: Dante found him in *Aeneid* 6.444–47.
5. Because of the weight of the living Dante.

And then I said to him: "May you weep and wail,
  stuck here in this place forever, you damned soul,
  for, filthy as you are, I recognize you."   39
With that he stretched both hands out toward the boat
  but, on his guard, my teacher pushed him back:
  "Away, get down there with the other curs!"   42
And then he put his arms around my neck
  and kissed my face and said, "Indignant soul,
  blessèd is she in whose womb you were conceived.[6]   45
In the world this man was filled with arrogance,
  and nothing good about him decks his memory;
  for this, his shade is filled with fury here.   48
Many in life esteem themselves great men
  who then will wallow here like pigs in mud,
  leaving behind them their repulsive fame."   51
"Master, it certainly would make me happy
  to see him dunked deep in this slop just once
  before we leave this lake—it truly would."   54
And he to me, "Before the other shore
  comes into sight, you will be satisfied:
  a wish like that is worthy of fulfillment."   57
Soon afterward, I saw the wretch so mangled
  by a gang of muddy souls that, to this day,
  I thank my Lord and praise Him for that sight: 60
"Get Filippo Argenti!"[7] they all cried.
  And at those shouts the Florentine, gone mad,
  turned on himself and bit his body fiercely.   63
We left him there, I'll say no more about him.
  A wailing noise began to pound my ears
  and made me strain my eyes to see ahead.   66
"And now, my son," the gentle teacher said,
  "coming closer is the city we call Dis,
  with its great walls and its fierce citizens."   69
And I, "Master, already I can see
  the clear glow of its mosques above the valley,
  burning bright red, as though just forged, and left   72
to smolder." And he to me: "Eternal fire
  burns within, giving off the reddish glow
  you see diffused throughout this lower Hell."   75
And then at last we entered those deep moats
  that circled all of this unhappy city
  whose walls, it seemed to me, were made of iron.   78
For quite a while we sailed around, until
  we reached a place and heard our boatsman shout
  with all his might, "Get out! Here is the entrance."   81
I saw more than a thousand fiendish angels[8]

6. See Luke 11.27, where these words are applied to Jesus.
7. A Florentine contemporary of Dante.
8. The rebel angels, cast out of Heaven; see Luke 10.18 and Revelation 12.9.

perching above the gates enraged, screaming:
  "Who is the one approaching? Who, without death,   84
dares walk into the kingdom of the dead?"
  And my wise teacher made some kind of signal
  announcing he would speak to them in secret.   87
They managed to suppress their great resentment
  enough to say: "You come, but he must go
  who thought to walk so boldly through this realm.   90
Let him retrace his foolish way alone,
  just let him try. And you who led him here
  through this dark land, you'll stay right where you are."   93
And now, my reader, consider how I felt
  when those foreboding words came to my ears!
  I thought I'd never see our world again!   96
"O my dear guide, who more than seven times
  restored my confidence, and rescued me
  from the many dangers that blocked my going on,   99
don't leave me, please," I cried in my distress,
  "and if the journey onward is denied us
  let's turn our footsteps back together quickly."   102
Then that lord who had brought me all this way
  said, "Do not fear, the journey we are making
  none can prevent: such power did decree it.   105
Wait here for me and feed your weary spirit
  with comfort and good hope; you can be sure
  I will not leave you in this underworld."   108
With this he walks away. He leaves me here,
  that gentle father, and I stay, doubting,
  and battling with my thoughts of "yes"—but "no."   111
I could not hear what he proposed to them,
  but they did not remain with him for long;
  I saw them race each other back for home.   114
Our adversaries slammed the heavy gates
  in my lord's face, and he stood there outside,
  then turned toward me and walked back very slowly   117
with eyes downcast, all self-assurance now
  erased from his forehead—sighing, "Who are these
  to forbid my entrance to the halls of grief!"   120
He spoke to me: "You need not be disturbed
  by my vexation, for I shall win the contest,
  no matter how they plot to keep us out!   123
This insolence of theirs is nothing new;
  they used it once at a less secret gate,[9]
  which is, and will forever be, unlocked;   126
you saw the deadly words inscribed above it;
  and now, already past it, and descending,
  across the circles, down the slope, alone,   129
comes one by whom the city will be opened."

---

9. A reference to Christ's descent into Hell after the crucifixion for the "harrowing": see above,
canto 4.53.

CANTO IX

The help from Heaven has not yet arrived; the Pilgrim is afraid and Virgil is obvi-ously worried. He reassures his ward by telling him that, soon after his own death, he was forced by the Sorceress Erichtho to resume mortal shape and go to the very bottom of Hell in order to bring up the soul of a traitor; thus Virgil knows the way well. But no sooner is the Pilgrim comforted than the Three Furies appear before him, on top of the tower, shrieking and tearing their breasts with their nails. They call for Medusa, whose horrible face has the power of turning anyone who looks on her to stone. Virgil turns his ward around and covers his eyes. After an "address to the reader" calling attention to the coming allegory, a strident blast splits the air, and the poets perceive an Angel coming through the murky darkness to open the gates of the City for them. Then the angel returns on the path whence he had come, and the two travelers enter the gate. Within are great open burning sarcophagi, from which groans of torment issue. Virgil explains that these are Arch-Heretics and their lesser counterparts.

The color of the coward on my face,
   when I realized my guide was turning back,
   made him quickly change the color of his own.   3
He stood alert, like one who strains to hear;
   his eyes could not see far enough ahead
   to cut the heavy fog of that black air.   6
"But surely we were meant to win this fight,"
   he said, "or else . . . but no, such help was promised!
   Oh, how much time it's taking him to come!"   9
I saw too well how quickly he amended
   his opening words with what he added on!
   They were different from the ones he first pronounced;   12
but nonetheless his words made me afraid,
   perhaps because the phrase he left unfinished
   I finished with worse meaning than he meant.   15
"Has anyone before ever descended
   to this sad hollow's depths from that first circle
   whose pain is all in having hope cut off?"[1]   18
I put this question to him. He replied,
   "It is not usual for one of us
   to make the journey I am making now.   21
But it happens I was down here once before,
   conjured by that heartless witch, Erichtho[2]
   (who could recall the spirit to its body).   24
Soon after I had left my flesh in death
   she sent me through these walls, and down as far
   as the pit of Judas to bring a spirit out;   27
and that place is the lowest and the darkest

---

1. "Has anyone from Limbo ever descended into lower Hell before?"
2. A legendary sorceress. The story of Virgil's prior descent into Hell is apparently Dante's own invention, although in the Middle Ages Virgil had the reputation of being a magician.

and the farthest from the sphere that circles all;[3]
   I know the road, and well, you can be sure.   30
This swamp that breathes with a prodigious stink
   lies in a circle round the doleful city
   that now we cannot enter without strife."   33
And he said other things, but I forget them,
   for suddenly my eyes were drawn above,
   up to the fiery top of that high tower   36
where in no time at all and all at once
   sprang up three hellish Furies[4] stained with blood,
   their bodies and their gestures those of females;   39
their waists were bound in cords of wild green hydras,
   horned snakes and little serpents grew as hair,
   and twined themselves around the savage temples.   42
And he who had occasion to know well
   the handmaids of the queen of timeless woe[5]
   cried out to me "Look there! The fierce Erinyes!   45
That is Megaera, the one there to the left,
   and that one raving on the right, Alecto,
   Tisiphone, in the middle." He said no more.   48
With flailing palms the three would beat their breasts,
   then tear them with their nails, shrieking so loud,
   I drew close to the poet, confused with fear.   51
"Medusa,[6] come, we'll turn him into stone,"
   they shouted all together glaring down,
   "how wrong we were to let off Theseus[7] lightly!"   54
"Now turn your back and cover up your eyes,
   for if the Gorgon comes and you should see her,
   there would be no returning to the world!"   57
These were my master's words. He turned me round
   and did not trust my hands to hide my eyes
   but placed his own on mine and kept them covered.   60
O all of you whose intellects are sound,
   look now and see the meaning that is hidden
   beneath the veil that covers my strange verses:[8]   63
and then, above the filthy swell, approaching,
   a blast of sound, shot through with fear, exploded,
   making both shores of Hell begin to tremble;   66
it sounded like one of those violent winds,
   born from the clash of counter-temperatures,
   that tear through forests; raging on unchecked,   69

---

3. Judecca, the last subdivision of the last circle of Hell, where Judas is punished.
4. Three mythological monsters who represent the spirit of vengeance, known in Greek as the Erinyes (see below, line 45, and line 46–48 for their individual names); they figure prominently in the *Aeneid* and other Latin poetry.
5. In classical mythology the queen of Hell is Hecate, or Proserpina, the wife of Pluto.

6. A mythological figure known as a Gorgon (line 56), so frightful in appearance that she turned those who gazed on her into stone.
7. Theseus, a legendary Athenian hero, descended into the underworld in order to try to rescue Proserpina, whom Pluto had abducted, and was rescued by Hercules.
8. Dante here reminds us of the need to interpret his poetry, although the lesson of this particular episode is far from self-evident.

it splits and rips and carries off the branches
    and proudly whips the dust up in its path
    and makes the beasts and shepherds flee its course!   72
He freed my eyes and said, "Now turn around
    and set your sight along the ancient scum,
    there where the marsh's mist is hovering thickest."   75
As frogs before their enemy, the snake,
    all scatter through the pond and then dive down
    until each one is squatting on the bottom,   78
so I saw more than a thousand fear-shocked souls
    in flight, clearing the path of one who came
    walking the Styx, his feet dry on the water.[9]   81
From time to time with his left hand he fanned
    his face to push the putrid air away,
    and this was all that seemed to weary him.   84
I was certain now that he was sent from Heaven.
    I turned to my guide, but he made me a sign
    to keep my silence and bow low to this one.   87
Ah, the scorn that filled his holy presence!
    He reached the gate and touched it with a wand;
    it opened without resistance from inside.   90
"O Heaven's outcasts, despicable souls,"
    he started, standing on the dreadful threshold,
    "what insolence is this that breeds in you?   93
Why do you stubbornly resist that will
    whose end can never be denied and which,
    more than one time, increased your suffering?   96
What do you gain by locking horns with fate?
    If you remember well, your Cerberus
    still bears his chin and throat peeled clean for that!"[1]   99
He turned then and retraced the squalid path,
    without one word to us, and on his face
    the look of one concerned and spurred by things   102
that were not those he found surrounding him.
    And then we started moving toward the city
    in the safety of the holy words pronounced.   105
We entered there, and with no opposition.
    And I, so anxious to investigate
    the state of souls locked up in such a fortress,   108
once in the place, allowed my eyes to wander,
    and saw, in all directions spreading out,
    a countryside of pain and ugly anguish.   111
As at Arles where the Rhône turns to stagnant waters
    or as at Pola near Quarnero's Gulf
    that closes Italy and bathes her confines,   114
the sepulchers make all the land uneven,

9. This is an angel, although described in a
way reminiscent of Mercury, the classical
messenger of the gods.

1. According to classical mythology, Hercules
dragged Cerberus into the daylight.

so they did here, strewn in all directions,
   except the graves here served a crueler purpose:[2]   117
for scattered everywhere among the tombs
   were flames that kept them glowing far more hot
   than any iron an artisan might use.   120
Each tomb had its lid loose, pushed to one side,
   and from within came forth such fierce laments
   that I was sure inside were tortured souls.   123
I asked, "Master, what kind of shades are these
   lying down here, buried in the graves of stone,
   speaking their presence in such dolorous sighs?"   126
And he replied: "There lie arch-heretics
   of every sect, with all of their disciples;
   more than you think are packed within these tombs.   129
Like heretics lie buried with their like
   and the graves burn more, or less, accordingly."
   Then turning to the right, we moved ahead   132
between the torments there and those high walls.

CANTO X

*They come to the tombs containing the Epicurean heretics, and as they are walking
by them, a shade suddenly rises to full height in one tomb, having recognized the
Pilgrim's Tuscan dialect. It is the proud Farinata, who, in life, opposed Dante's
party; while he and the Pilgrim are conversing, another figure suddenly rises out of
the same tomb. It is the shade of Cavalcante de Cavalcanti, who interrupts the conversation with questions about his son Guido. Misinterpreting the Pilgrim's confused silence as evidence of his son's death, Cavalcante falls back into his sepulcher
and Farinata resumes the conversation exactly where it had been broken off. He
defends his political actions in regard to Florence and prophesies that Dante, like
himself, will soon know the pain of exile. But the Pilgrim is also interested to know
how it is that the damned can see the future but not the present. When his curiosity
is satisfied, he asks Farinata to tell Cavalcante that his son is still alive, and that his
silence was caused only by his confusion about the shade's inability to know the
present.*

Now onward down a narrow path, between
   the city's ramparts and the suffering,
   my master walks, I following close behind.   3
"O lofty power who through these impious gyres[3]
   lead me around as you see fit," I said,
   "I want to know, I want to understand: 6
the people buried there in sepulchers,
   can they be seen? I mean, since all the lids
   are off the tombs and no one stands on guard."   9
And he: "They will forever he locked up,

---

2. Arles, located on the Rhone River in southern France, and Pola, located on the bay of
Quarnero in what is now Yugoslavia, were
sites of Roman cemeteries.
3. Circular turns.

when they return here from Jehoshaphat
  with the bodies that they left up in the world.[4]   12
The private cemetery on this side
  serves Epicurus[5] and his followers,
  who make the soul die when the body dies.   15
As for the question you just put to me,
  it will be answered soon, while we are here;
  and the wish you are keeping from me will be granted."[6]   18
And I: "O my good guide, I do not hide
  my heart; I'm trying not to talk too much,
  as you have told me more than once to do."   21
"O Tuscan walking through our flaming city,
  alive, and speaking with such elegance,
  be kind enough to stop here for a while.   24
Your mode of speech identifies you clearly
  as one whose birthplace is that noble city
  with which in my time, perhaps, I was too harsh."   27
One of the vaults resounded suddenly
  with these clear words, and I, intimidated,
  drew up a little closer to my guide,   30
who said, "What are you doing? Turn around
  and look at Farinata,[7] who has risen,
  you will see him from the waist up standing straight."   33
I already had my eyes fixed on his face,
  and there he stood out tall, with his chest and brow
  proclaiming his disdain for all this Hell.   36
My guide, with a gentle push, encouraged me
  to move among the sepulchers toward him:
  "Be sure you choose your words with care," he said.   39
And when I reached the margin of his tomb
  he looked at me, and half-contemptuously
  he asked, "And *who* would *your* ancestors be?"   42
And I who wanted only to oblige him
  held nothing back but told him everything.
  At this he lifted up his brows a little,   45
then said, "Bitter enemies of mine they were
  and of my ancestors and of my party;
  I had to scatter them not once but twice."[8]   48
"They were expelled, but only to return
  from everywhere," I said, "not once but twice—
  an art your men, however, never mastered!"[9]   51
Just then along that same tomb's open ledge

---

4. According to the Bible, the Last Judgment
when the dead will again receive their bodies
will take place in the Valley of Jehosaphat: see
Joel 3.2 and 3.12, and Matthew 25.31–32.
5. Greek philosopher (d. 270 B.C.E.) who
rejected the idea of the immortality of the soul.
6. Presumably Dante's desire to see the
Florentines who inhabit this circle.

7. Farinata degli Uberti (d. 1264), a leader of
the Ghibelline faction in Florence.
8. Dante's family were Guelphs, who were
driven out of Florence twice, in 1248 and
1260.
9. The Ghibellines were exiled in 1280, never
to return.

a shade appeared, but just down to his chin,
  beside this other; I think he got up kneeling.[1]   54
He looked around as though he hoped to see
  if someone else, perhaps, had come with me
  and, when his expectation was deceived,   57
he started weeping: "If it be great genius
  that carries you along through this blind jail,
  where is my son? Why is he not with you?"   60
"I do not come alone," I said to him,
  "that one waiting over there guides me through here,
  the one, perhaps, your Guido held in scorn."[2]   63
(The place of pain assigned him, and what he asked,
  already had revealed his name to me
  and made my pointed answer possible.)   66
Instantly, he sprang to his full height and cried,
  "What did you say? He *held*? Is he not living?
  The day's sweet light no longer strikes his eyes?"[3]   69
And when he heard the silence of my delay
  responding to his question, he collapsed
  into his tomb, not to be seen again.   72
That other stately shade, at whose request
  I had first stopped to talk, showed no concern
  nor moved his head nor turned to see what happened;   75
he merely picked up where we had left off:
  "If that art they did not master," he went on,
  "that gives me greater pain than does this bed.   78
But the face of the queen who reigns down here[4] will glow
  not more than fifty times before you learn
  how hard it is to master such an art;[5]   81
and as I hope that you may once more know
  the sweet world, tell me, why should your party be
  so harsh to my clan in every law they make?"   84
I answered: "The massacre and butchery
  that stained the waters of the Arbia red[6]
  now cause such laws to issue from our councils."   87
He sighed, shaking his head. "It was not I
  alone took part," he said, "not certainly
  would I have joined the rest without good cause.   90
But I alone stood up when all of them

---

1. This is Cavalcante de Cavalcanti, father of Dante's friend and fellow poet Guido (pp. 356–58); a Guelph, Guido married the daughter of Farinata in an unsuccessful attempt to heal the feud. In June 1300—after the fictional date of this conversation—Guido was exiled to a part of Italy where he caught the malaria from which he died in August. Dante was at that time a member of the governing body that made the decision to exile Guido.
2. The passage is ambiguous in the original Italian: as translated here, the "one" refers to Virgil; but the Italian word can also be translated to refer to Beatrice, so that these two lines would then read: "that one waiting over there guides me through here, / to her whom your Guido perhaps held in scorn."
3. In line 61 Dante used a verbal form known in Italian as the remote past, which leads Cavalcante to believe, wrongly, that now, in April 1300, Guido is dead—although, ironically, in about four months he will indeed die, as Dante knew when he was writing this canto.
4. Proserpina, who is also the goddess of the moon.
5. Farinata here predicts Dante's own exile.
6. A stream near the hill of Montaperti, where the Ghibellines defeated the Guelphs in 1260.

were ready to have Florence razed. It was *I*
who openly stood up in her defense."   93
"And now, as I would have your seed find peace,"
    I said, "I beg you to resolve a problem
    that has kept my reason tangled in a knot: 96
if I have heard correctly, all of you
    can see ahead to what the future holds
    but your knowledge of the present is not clear."   99
"Down here we see like those with faulty vision
    who only see," he said, "what's at a distance;
    this much the sovereign lord grants us here.   102
When events are close to us, or when they happen,
    our mind is blank, and were it not for others
    we would know nothing of your living state.   105
Thus you can understand how all our knowledge
    will be completely dead at that time when
    the door to future things is closed forever."[7]   108
Then I, moved by regret for what I'd done[8]
    said, "Now, will you please tell the fallen one
    his son is still on earth among the living;   111
and if, when he asked, silence was my answer,
    tell him: while he was speaking, all my thoughts
    were struggling with that point you solved for me."   114
My teacher had begun to call me back,
    so I quickly asked that spirit to reveal
    the names of those who shared the tomb with him.   117
He said, "More than a thousand lie with me,
    the Second Frederick[9] is here and the Cardinal[1]
    is with us. And the rest I shall not mention."   120
His figure disappeared. I made my way
    to the ancient poet, reflecting on
    those words which were prophetic enemies.[2]   123
He moved, and as we went along he said,
    "What troubles you? Why are you so distraught?"
    And I told him all the thoughts that filled my mind.   126
"Be sure your mind retains," the sage commanded,
    "those words you heard pronounced against yourself,
    and listen carefully now." He raised a finger: 129
"When at last you stand in the glow of her sweet ray,[3]
    the one whose splendid eyes see everything,
    from her you'll learn your life's itinerary."   132
Then to the left he turned. Leaving the walls,
    he headed toward the center by a path
    that strikes into a vale, whose stench arose,   135
disgusting us as high up as we were.

7. The damned can see the future but not the
present; after the Last Judgment, when human
time is abolished, they will know nothing.
8. See n. 3 to line 69 above.
9. Frederick II, Holy Roman Emperor from
1215 until his death in 1250; he reputedly

denied that there was life after death.
1. Ottaviano degli Ubaldini (d. 1273), who is
reputed to have said, "If I have a soul, I have
lost it for the Ghibellines."
2. That is, Farinata's prediction of his exile.
3. Beatrice's.

CANTO XI

Continuing their way within the Sixth Circle, where the heretics are punished, the poets are assailed by a stench rising from the abyss ahead of them which is so strong that they must stop in order to accustom themselves to the odor. They pause beside a tomb whose inscription declares that within is Pope Anastasius. When the Pilgrim expresses his desire to pass the time of waiting profitably, Virgil proceeds to instruct him about the plan of punishments in Hell. Then, seeing that dawn is only two hours away, he urges the Pilgrim on.

We reached the curving brink of a steep bank
   constructed of enormous broken rocks;
   below us was a crueler den of pain.   3
And the disgusting overflow of stench
   the deep abyss was vomiting forced us
   back from the edge. Crouched underneath the lid   6
of some great tomb, I saw it was inscribed:
   "Within lies Anastasius, the pope
   Photinus lured away from the straight path."[4]   9
"Our descent will have to be delayed somewhat
   so that our sense of smell may grow accustomed
   to these vile fumes; then we will not mind them,"   12
my master said. And I: "You will have to find
   some way to keep our time from being wasted."
   "That is precisely what I had in mind,"   15
he said, and then began the lesson:[5] "My son,
   within these boulders' bounds are three more circles,
   concentrically arranged like those above,   18
all tightly packed with souls; and so that, later,
   the sight of them alone will be enough,
   I'll tell you how and why they are imprisoned.   21
All malice has injustice as its end,
   an end achieved by violence or by fraud;
   while both are sins that earn the hate of Heaven,   24
since fraud belongs exclusively to man,
   God hates it more and, therefore, far below,
   the fraudulent are placed and suffer most.   27
In the first of the circles below are all the violent;
   since violence can be used against three persons,
   into three concentric rounds it is divided: 30
violence can be done to God, to self,
   or to one's neighbor—to him or to his goods,
   as my reasoned explanation will make clear.   33
By violent means a man can kill his neighbor

4. Pope Anastasius (d. 498) was thought, wrongly, to have accepted a heresy promoted by the 5th-century theologian Photinus that Christ was not divine but only human.
5. Virgil now describes the three remaining circles of Hell, the seventh, eighth, and ninth. The seventh is for the violent and is divided into three parts; the eighth and ninth are for the fraudulent, the eighth for those who deceive generally, the ninth for those who betray those who love them. For the scheme of Hell as a whole, see the diagram on p. 391.

or wound him grievously; his goods may suffer
   violence by arson, theft, and devastation;   36
so, homicides and those who strike with malice,
   those who destroy and plunder, are all punished
   in the first round, but all in different groups.   39
Man can raise violent hands against himself
   and his own goods; so in the second round,
   paying the debt that never can be paid,   42
are suicides, self-robbers of your world,
   or those who gamble all their wealth away
   and weep up there when they should have rejoiced.   45
One can use violence against the deity
   by heartfelt disbelief and cursing Him,
   or by despising Nature and God's bounty;   48
therefore, the smallest round stamps with its seal
   both Sodom and Cahors[6] and all those souls
   who hate God in their hearts and curse His name.   51
Fraud, that gnaws the conscience of its servants,
   can be used on one who puts his trust in you
   or else on one who has no trust invested.   54
This latter sort seems only to destroy
   the bond of love that Nature gives to man;
   so in the second circle there are nests   57
of hypocrites, flatterers, dabblers in sorcery,
   falsifiers, thieves, and simonists,[7]
   panders, seducers, grafters, and like filth.   60
The former kind of fraud both disregards
   the love Nature enjoys and that extra bond
   between men which creates a special trust;   63
thus, it is in the smallest of the circles,
   at the earth's center, around the throne of Dis,[8]
   that traitors suffer their eternal pain."   66
And I, "Master, your reasoning runs smooth,
   and your explanation certainly makes clear
   the nature of this pit and of its inmates,   69
but what about those in the slimy swamp,
   those driven by the wind, those beat by rain,
   and those who come to blows with harsh refrains?   72
Why are they, too, not punished here inside
   the city of flame, if they have earned God's wrath?
   If they have not, why are they suffering?"   75

6. In the Middle Ages the names of Sodom (see Genesis 18.20–19.29) and Cahors, a city in southern France, became synonymous with sodomites and userers, respectively. Usury, forbidden by the medieval church, is charging interest on loans; the logic of this prohibition—based on the argument that usury, like sodomy, is unnatural—is explained in lines 97–111 below.

7. Simony is the sin of selling a spiritual good, such as a church office or a sacrament like confession, for material gain. It is named after Simon Magus, a magician who sought to buy from the Apostles the power of baptism in Acts 8.9–24.

8. Dis is Satan, who is found at the bottom of Hell (see canto 34).

And he to me, "Why do you let your thoughts
   stray from the path they are accustomed to?
   Or have I missed the point you have in mind? 78
Have you forgotten how your *Ethics*[9] reads,
   those terms it explicates in such detail:
   the three conditions that the heavens hate, 81
incontinence, malice, and bestiality?
   Do you not remember how incontinence
   offends God least, and merits the least blame? 84
If you will reconsider well this doctrine
   and then recall to mind who those souls were
   suffering pain above, outside the walls, 87
you will clearly see why they are separated
   from these malicious ones, and why God's vengeance
   beats down upon their souls less heavily." 90
"O sun that shines to clear a misty vision,
   such joy is mine when you resolve my doubts
   that doubting pleases me no less than knowing! 93
Go back a little bit once more," I said,
   "to where you say that usury offends
   God's goodness, and untie that knot for me." 96
"Philosophy," he said, "and more than once,
   points out to one who reads with understanding
   how Nature takes her course from the Divine 99
Intellect, from its artistic workmanship,[1]
   and if you have your *Physics*[2] well in mind
   you will find, not many pages from the start, 102
how your art too, as best it can, imitates
   Nature, the way an apprentice does his master;
   so your art may be said to be God's grandchild. 105
From Art and Nature man was meant to take
   his daily bread to live—if you recall
   the book of Genesis near the beginning,[3] 108
but the usurer, adopting other means,
   scorns Nature in herself and in her pupil,
   Art—he invests his hope in something else.[4] 111
Now follow me, we should be getting on;
   the Fish are shimmering over the horizon,
   the Wain is now exactly over Caurus,[5] 114
and the passage down the bank is farther on."

---

9. Aristotle's *Nicomachean Ethics*.
1. The laws of nature are determined by God.
2. Aristotle's *Physics*, which argues that human art should follow natural laws.
3. In Genesis 3.17–19, God decrees that because of the Fall people must toil, supporting themselves by the sweat of their brows.
4. The usurer makes money not from labor but from money itself, which is an unnatural and therefore illicit art.
5. The position of stars shows that it is now about 4 A.M. on Holy Saturday.

CANTO XII

They descend the steep slope into the Seventh Circle by means of a great landslide, which was caused when Christ descended into Hell. At the edge of the abyss is the Minotaur, who presides over the circle of the Violent and whose own bestial rage sends him into such a paroxysm of violence that the two travelers are able to run past him without his interference. At the base of the precipice, they see a river of boiling blood, which contains those who have inflicted violence upon others. But before they can reach the river they are intercepted by three fierce Centaurs, whose task it is to keep those who are in the river at their proper depth by shooting arrows at them if they attempt to rise. Virgil explains to one of the centaurs (Chiron) that this journey of the Pilgrim and himself is ordained by God; and he requests him to assign someone to guide the two of them to the ford in the river and carry the Pilgrim across it to the other bank. Chiron gives the task to Nessus, one of the centaurs, who, as he leads them to the river's ford, points out many of the sinners there in the boiling blood.

Not only was that place, where we had come
   to descend, craggy, but there was something there
   that made the scene appalling to the eye. 3
Like the ruins this side of Trent left by the landslide
   (an earthquake or erosion must have caused it)
   that hit the Adige on its left bank,[6] 6
when, from the mountain's top where the slide began
   to the plain below, the shattered rocks slipped down,
   shaping a path for a difficult descent— 9
so was the slope of our ravine's formation.
   And at the edge, along the shattered chasm,
   there lay stretched out the infamy of Crete:[7] 12
the son conceived in the pretended cow.
   When he saw us he bit into his flesh,
   gone crazy with the fever of his rage. 15
My wise guide cried to him: "Perhaps you think
   you see the Duke of Athens come again,
   who came once in the world to bring your death?[8] 18
Begone, you beast, for this one is not led
   down here by means of clues your sister[9] gave him;
   he comes here only to observe your torments." 21
The way a bull breaks loose the very moment
   he knows he has been dealt the mortal blow,
   and cannot run but jumps and twists and turns, 24
just so I saw the Minotaur perform,

6. A famous landslide on a mountain on the Adige River near Trent, a city in northern Italy.
7. The Minotaur, half man and half bull, was conceived when Pasiphaë, the wife of King Minos of Crete, had a wooden cow built within which she placed herself so as to have intercourse with a bull. The story of the Minotaur

is told by Ovid, *Metamorphoses* 8.
8. Virgil is referring to Theseus, who killed the Minotaur in the labyrinth in which it was imprisoned.
9. Ariadne, daughter of Minos and Pasiphaë, who taught Theseus how to escape from the labyrinth within which the Minotaur was imprisoned.

and my guide, alert, cried out: "Run to the pass!
  While he still writhes with rage, get started down."   27
And so we made our way down through the ruins
  of rocks, which often I felt shift and tilt
  beneath my feet from weight they were not used to.   30
I was deep in thought when he began: "Are you,
  perhaps, thinking about these ruins protected
  by the furious beast I quenched in its own rage?   33
Now let me tell you that the other time
  I came down to the lower part of Hell,
  this rock had not then fallen into ruins;   36
but certainly, if I remember well,
  it was just before the coming of that One
  who took from Hell's first circle the great spoil,   39
that this abyss of stench, from top to bottom
  began to shake,[1] so I thought the universe
  felt love—whereby, some have maintained, the world   42
has more than once renewed itself in chaos.[2]
  That was the moment when this ancient rock
  was split this way—here, and in other places.   45
But now look down the valley. Coming closer
  you will see the river of blood that boils the souls
  of those who through their violence injured others."   48
(Oh, blind cupidity[3] and insane wrath,
  spurring us on through our short life on earth
  to steep us then forever in such misery!)   51
I saw a river—wide, curved like a bow—
  that stretched embracing all the flatland there,
  just as my guide had told me to expect.   54
Between the river and the steep came centaurs,[4]
  galloping in single file, equipped with arrows,
  off hunting as they used to in the world;   57
then, seeing us descend, they all stopped short
  and three of them departed from the ranks
  with bows and arrows ready from their quivers.   60
One of them cried from his distant post: "You there,
  on your way down here, what torture are you seeking?
  Speak where you stand, if not, I draw my bow."   63
And then my master shouted back: "Our answer
  we will give to Chiron[5] when we're at his side;
  as for you, I see you are as rash as ever!"   66

1. Because of the earthquake that accompanied Christ's death, which occurred just before his descent to Hell and the "harrowing," Christ's rescue from the First Circle of the virtuous Israelites (see above, canto 4.52–63).
2. A reference to a theory of the Greek philosopher Empedocles that the universe is held together by alternating forces of love and hate, and that if either one predominates the result is chaos. This classical theory is not consistent with the Christian belief that the universe is created and organized by God's love.
3. Desire for wealth.
4. Mythological creatures that are half man and half horse.
5. A centaur renowned for wisdom who educated many legendary Greek heroes, including Achilles.

He nudged me, saying: "That one there is Nessus,[6]
  who died from loving lovely Dejanira,
  and made of himself, of his blood, his own revenge.   69
The middle one, who contemplates his chest,
  is great Chiron, who reared and taught Achilles;
  the last is Pholus,[7] known for his drunken wrath.   72
They gallop by the thousands round the ditch,
  shooting at any daring soul emerging
  above the bloody level of his guilt."
    75
When we came closer to those agile beasts,
  Chiron drew an arrow, and with its notch
  he parted his beard to both sides of his jaws,   78
and when he had uncovered his great mouth
  he spoke to his companions: "Have you noticed,
  how the one behind moves everything he touches?   81
This is not what a dead man's feet would do!"
  And my good guide, now standing by the torso
  at the point the beast's two natures joined,[8] replied: 84
"He is indeed alive, and so alone
  that I must show him through this dismal valley;
  he travels by necessity, not pleasure.   87
A spirit[9] came, from singing Alleluia,
  to give me this extraordinary mission;
  he is no rogue nor I a criminal spirit.[1]   90
Now, in the name of that power by which I move
  my steps along so difficult a road,
  give us one of your troop to be our guide: 93
to lead us to the ford and, once we are there,
  to carry this one over on his back,
  for he is not a spirit who can fly."   96
Chiron looked over his right breast and said
  to Nessus, "You go, guide them as they ask,
  and if another troop protests, disperse them!"   99
So with this trusted escort we moved on
  along the boiling crimson river's bank,[2]
  where piercing shrieks rose from the boiling souls.   102
There I saw people sunken to their eyelids,
  and the huge centaur explained, "These are the tyrants
  who dealt in bloodshed and plundered wealth.   105
Their tears are paying for their heartless crimes:
  here stand Alexander and fierce Dionysius,
  who weighed down Sicily with years of pain;[3]   108

6. Nessus fell in love with Deianira, wife of Hercules, who killed him; while dying, Nessus poisoned with his own blood a robe that killed Hercules when he put it on.
7. Another centaur, killed by Hercules, whose rage is typical of the race.
8. When standing, Virgil reaches to the centaur's chest where his human and animal natures join.

9. Beatrice.
1. Virgil is answering the question of lines 61–62, which assumes that they are condemned spirits.
2. A river of blood, which we later learn is named Phlegethon (see 14.116).
3. Alexander the Great (d. 323 B.C.E.) and Dionysius of Syracuse in Sicily (d. 367 B.C.E.).

and there, that forehead smeared with coal-black hair,
   is Azzolino;[4] the other one, the blond,
   Opizzo d'Esti, who, and this is true,   111
was killed by his own stepson in your world."[5]
   With that I looked to Virgil, but he said
   "Let him instruct you now, don't look to me."   114
A little farther on, the centaur stopped
   above some people peering from the blood
   that came up to their throats. He pointed out   117
a shade off to one side, alone, and said:
   "There stands the one who, in God's keep, murdered
   the heart still dripping blood above the Thames."[6]   120
Then I saw other souls stuck in the river
   who had their heads and chests above the blood,
   and I knew the names of many who were there.   123
The river's blood began decreasing slowly
   until it cooked the feet and nothing more,
   and here we found the ford where we could cross.   126
"Just as you see the boiling river here
   on this side getting shallow gradually,"
   the centaur said, "I would also have you know   129
that on the other side the riverbed
   sinks deeper more and more until it reaches
   the deepest meeting place where tyrants moan: 132
it is there that Heaven's justice strikes its blow
   against Attila,[7] known as the scourge of earth,
   against Pyrrhus and Sextus,[8] and forever   135
extracts the tears the scalding blood produces.
   from Rinier da Corneto and Rinier Pazzo,[9]
   whose battlefields were highways where they robbed."   138
Then he turned round and crossed the ford again.

CANTO XIII

No sooner are the poets across the Phlegethon than they encounter a dense forest, from which come wails and moans, and which is presided over by the hideous harpies—half-woman, half-beast, bird-like creatures. Virgil tells his ward to break off a branch of one of the trees; when he does, the tree weeps blood and speaks. In life he was Pier della Vigna, chief counselor of Frederick II of Sicily; but he fell out of

4. Azzolino III (d. 1259), a brutal ruler in northern Italy.
5. Opizzo II d'Este (d. 1293), another cruel northern Italian tyrant, reputedly murdered by his son; he is called "stepson" either because of the unnaturalness of the crime or because Opizzo suspected his wife of adultery.
6. Guy de Montfort (d. 1298), who killed his cousin Prince Henry of Cornwall during a church service ("in God's keep") in the Italian city of Viterbo. Nessus's image of the blood

dripping from the victim's heart indicates his focus on the fact that the murder is still unavenged.
7. Attila the Hun (d. 453).
8. Sextus, the son of the Roman consul Pompey, became a pirate (1st century B.C.E.); Pyrrhus, Achilles' son, killed the aged Priam at the fall of Troy, as described in *Aeneid* 2.595–704.
9. Both Riniers were bandits of Dante's day; they are now weeping from pain, whereas in life they never wept for their sins.

favor, was accused unjustly of treachery, and was imprisoned, whereupon he killed himself. The Pilgrim is overwhelmed by pity. The sinner also explains how the souls of the suicides come to this punishment and what will happen to them after the Last Judgment. Suddenly they are interrupted by the wild sounds of the hunt, and two naked figures, Lano of Siena and Giacomo da Sant' Andrea, dash across the land- scape, shouting at each other, until one of them hides himself in a thorny bush; immediately a pack of fierce, black dogs rush in, pounce on the hidden sinner, and rip his body, carrying away mouthfuls of flesh. The bush, which has been torn in the process, begins to lament. The two learn that the cries are those of a Florentine who had hanged himself in his own home.

Not yet had Nessus reached the other side
   when we were on our way into a forest
   that was not marked by any path at all.   3
No green leaves, but rather black in color,
   no smooth branches, but twisted and entangled,
   no fruit, but thorns of poison bloomed instead.   6
No thick, rough, scrubby home like this exists—
   not even between Cecina and Corneto[1] —
   for those wild beasts that hate the run of farmlands.   9
Here the repulsive Harpies[2] twine their nests,
   who drove the Trojans from the Strophades
   with filthy forecasts of their close disaster.   12
Wide-winged they are, with human necks and faces,
   their feet are clawed, their bellies fat and feathered;
   perched in the trees they shriek their strange laments.   15
"Before we go on farther," my guide began,
   "remember, you are in the second round
   and shall be till we reach the dreadful sand,[3]   18
now look around you carefully and see
   with your own eyes what I will not describe,
   for if I did, you wouldn't believe my words."   21
Around me wails of grief were echoing,
   and I saw no one there to make those sounds;
   bewildered by all this, I had to stop.   24
I think perhaps he thought I might be thinking
   that all the voices coming from those stumps
   belonged to people hiding there from us,   27
and so my teacher said, "If you break off
   a little branch of any of these plants,
   what you are thinking now will break off too."[4]   30
Then slowly raising up my hand a bit

1. Two towns that mark the limits of the Maremma, a desolate area in Tuscany.
2. Birds with the faces of women and clawed hands; in *Aeneid* 3 they drive the wandering Trojans from their refuge in the Strophades Islands and predict their future suffering.

3. The "dreadful sand" is in the third ring or "round" of the seventh circle, described in the next canto.
4. Your thoughts that the moans come from people concealed among the trees will cease or "break off."

I snapped the tiny branch of a great thornbush,
and its trunk cried: "Why are you tearing me?"[5]   33
And when its blood turned dark around the wound,
it started saying more: "Why do you rip me?
Have you no sense of pity whatsoever?   36
Men were we once, now we are changed to scrub;
but even if we had been souls of serpents,
your hand should have shown more pity than it did."   39
Like a green log burning at one end only,
sputtering at the other, oozing sap,
and hissing with the air it forces out,   42
so from that splintered trunk a mixture poured
of words and blood. I let the branch I held
fall from my hand and stood there stiff with fear.   45
"O wounded soul," my sage replied to him,
"if he had only let himself believe
what he had read in verses I once wrote,[6]   48
he never would have raised his hand against you,
but the truth itself was so incredible,
I urged him on to do the thing that grieves me.   51
But tell him who you were; he can make amends,
and will, by making bloom again your fame
in the world above, where his return is sure."   54
And the trunk: "So appealing are your lovely words,
I must reply. Be not displeased if I
am lured into a little conversation.[7]   57
I am that one who held both of the keys
that fitted Frederick's heart; I turned them both,
locking and unlocking, with such finesse   60
that I let few into his confidence.
I was so faithful to my glorious office,
I lost not only sleep but life itself.   63
That courtesan who constantly surveyed
Caesar's household with her adulterous eyes,
mankind's undoing, the special vice of courts,[8]   66
inflamed the hearts of everyone against me,
and these, inflamed, inflamed in turn Augustus,
and my happy honors turned to sad laments.   69
My mind, moved by scornful satisfaction,

5. This episode derives from *Aeneid* 3, where Aeneas and his Trojan companions, stopping in their search for a new home, discover Polydorus transformed into a bush. Sent out by Priam during the war to solicit aid from the Thracians, Polydorus had been murdered by his hosts, and the javelins with which his body had been pierced had grown into the bush from which Aeneas breaks off a branch that bleeds. See also Ovid, *Metamorphoses* 2.
6. Had Dante been able to believe the story of Polydorus recounted in the *Aeneid*.

7. This is the soul of Pier della Vigna (ca. 1190–1249), who had risen to become minister to the Emperor Frederick II (on whom see n. 9 on 10.119); Frederick is referred to here as "Caesar" and "Augustus" because he sought to imitate the imperial court of Rome. Pier's name means Peter of the Vine, probably because his father had been a simple worker in a vineyard.
8. Pier means Envy, on whom he blames his fall from favor.

believing death would free me from all scorn,
  made me unjust to me, who was all just.[9]   72
By these strange roots of my own tree I swear
  to you that never once did I break faith
  with my lord, who was so worthy of all honor.   75
If one of you should go back to the world,
  restore the memory of me, who here
  remain cut down by the blow that Envy gave."   78
My poet paused awhile, then said to me,
  "Since he is silent now, don't lose your chance,
  ask him, if there is more you wish to know."   81
"Why don't you keep on questioning," I said,
  "and ask him, for my part, what I would ask,
  for I cannot, such pity chokes my heart."   84
He began again: "That this man may fulfill
  generously what your words cry out for,
  imprisoned soul, may it please you to continue   87
by telling us just how a soul gets bound
  into these knots, and tell us, if you know,
  whether any soul might someday leave his branches."   90
At that the trunk breathed heavily, and then
  the breath changed to a voice that spoke these words:
  "Your question will be answered very briefly.   93
The moment that the violent soul departs
  the body it has torn itself away from,
  Minòs sends it down to the seventh hole;   96
it drops to the wood, not in a place allotted,
  but anywhere that fortune tosses it.
  There, like a grain of spelt,[1] it germinates,   99
soon springs into a sapling, then a wild tree;
  at last the Harpies, feasting on its leaves,
  create its pain, and for the pain an outlet.   102
Like the rest, we shall return to claim our bodies,[2]
  but never again to wear them—wrong it is
  for a man to have again what he once cast off.   105
We shall drag them here and, all along the mournful
  forest, our bodies shall hang forever more,
  each one on a thorn of its own alien shade."   108
We were standing still attentive to the trunk,
  thinking perhaps it might have more to say,
  when we were startled by a rushing sound,   111
such as the hunter hears from where he stands:
  first the boar, then all the chase approaching,
  the crash of hunting dogs and branches smashing,   114
then, to the left of us appeared two shapes[3]

9. I unjustly committed suicide even though
I was innocent of the accusations brought
against me.
1. Wheat.
2. At the Last Judgment.

3. Lano of Siena and Giacomo da Sant' Andrea
of Padua, two Italians of a generation earlier
than Dante's; both were reputed to be spendthrifts.

naked and gashed, fleeing with such rough speed
 they tore away with them the bushes' branches.   117
The one ahead: "Come on, come quickly, Death!"
 The other, who could not keep up the pace,
 screamed, "Lano, your legs were not so nimble   120
when you jousted in the tournament of Toppo!"[4]
 And then, from lack of breath perhaps, he slipped
 into a bush and wrapped himself in thorns.   123
Behind these two the wood was overrun
 by packs of black bitches ravenous and ready,
 like hunting dogs just broken from their chains;   126
they sank their fangs in that poor wretch who hid,
 they ripped him open piece by piece, and then
 ran off with mouthfuls of his wretched limbs.   129
Quickly my escort took me by the hand
 and led me over to the bush that wept
 its vain laments from every bleeding sore.[5]   132
"O Giacomo da Sant' Andrea," it said,
 "what good was it for you to hide in me?
 What fault have I if you led an evil life?"   135
My master, standing over it, inquired:
 "Who were you once that now through many wounds
 breathes a grieving sermon with your blood?"   138
He answered us: "O souls who have just come
 in time to see this unjust mutilation
 that has separated me from all my leaves,   141
gather them round the foot of this sad bush.
 I was from the city that took the Baptist
 in exchange for her first patron,[6] who, for this,   144
swears by his art she will have endless sorrow;
 and were it not that on the Arno's[7] bridge
 some vestige of his image still remains,   147
those citizens who built anew the city
 on the ashes that Attila left behind
 would have accomplished such a task in vain;[8]   150
I turned my home into my hanging place."

CANTO XIV

They come to the edge of the Wood of the Suicides, where they see before them a
stretch of burning sand upon which flames rain eternally and through which a
stream of boiling blood is carried in a raised channel formed of rock. There, many
groups of tortured souls are on the burning sand; Virgil explains that those lying
supine on the ground are the Blasphemers, those crouching are the Usurers, and

4. Lano was killed at a battle on the river
Toppo in 1287.
5. Nothing is known about this suicide, who
hanged himself from his own house.
6. Florence; when the Florentines converted
to Christianity, John the Baptist replaced Mars

as patron of the city, and therefore Mars will
forever persecute the city with civil war.
7. The river that runs through Florence.
8. According to legend, Attila the Hun
destroyed Florence when he invaded Italy in
the 5th century.

those wandering aimlessly, never stopping, are the Sodomites. Representative of the
blasphemers is Capaneus, who died cursing his god. The Pilgrim questions his guide
about the source of the river of boiling blood; Virgil's reply contains the most elabo-
rate symbol in the Inferno, that of the Old Man of Crete, whose tears are the source
of all the rivers in Hell.

The love we both shared for our native city
   moved me to gather up the scattered leaves
   and give them back to the voice that now had faded.   3
We reached the confines of the woods that separate
   the second from the third round.[9] There I saw
   God's justice in its dreadful operation.   6
Now to picture clearly these unheard-of things:
   we arrived to face an open stretch of flatland
   whose soil refused the roots of any plant;   9
the grieving forest made a wreath around it,
   as the sad river of blood enclosed the woods.
   We stopped right here, right at the border line.   12
This wasteland was a dry expanse of sand,
   thick, burning sand, no different from the kind
   that Cato's[1] feet packed down in other times.   15
O just revenge of God! how awesomely
   you should be feared by everyone who reads
   these truths that were revealed to my own eyes!   18
Many separate herds of naked souls I saw,
   all weeping desperately; it seemed each group
   had been assigned a different penalty: 21
some souls were stretched out flat upon their backs,
   others were crouching there all tightly hunched,
   some wandered, never stopping, round and round.   24
Far more there were of those who roamed the sand
   and fewer were the souls stretched out to suffer,
   but their tongues were looser, for the pain was greater.   27
And over all that sandland, a fall of slowly
   raining broad flakes of fire showered steadily
   (a mountain snowstorm on a windless day),   30
like those that Alexander saw descending
   on his troops while crossing India's torrid lands:
   flames falling, floating solid to the ground,   33
and he with all his men began to tread
   the sand so that the burning flames might be
   extinguished one by one before they joined.[2]   36
Here too a never-ending blaze descended,
   kindling the sand like tinder under flint-sparks,
   and in this way the torment there was doubled.   39

9. The third ring of the seventh circle is surrounded by the second ring of the woods through
which Dante has just passed and the first ring of
the river of blood described in canto 12.
1. Roman general (1st century B.C.E.) who
campaigned in Libya.
2. Dante is here following an account by the
philosopher Albertus Magnus (d. 1280) of a
legendary adventure that befell Alexander the
Great in his conquest of India.

Without a moment's rest the rhythmic dance
   of wretched hands went on, this side, that side,
   brushing away the freshly fallen flames.   42
And I: "My master, you who overcome
   all opposition (except for those tough demons
   who came to meet us at the gate of Dis),   45
who is that mighty one that seems unbothered
   by burning, stretched sullen and disdainful there,
   looking as if the rainfall could not tame him?"[3]   48
And that very one, who was quick to notice me
   inquiring of my guide about him, answered:
   "What I was once, alive, I still am, dead!   51
Let Jupiter wear out his smith,[4] from whom
   he seized in anger that sharp thunderbolt
   he hurled, to strike me down, my final day;   54
let him wear out those others, one by one,
   who work the soot-black forge of Mongibello[5]
   (as he shouts, 'Help me, good Vulcan, I need your help,'   57
the way he cried that time at Phlegra's battle),[6]
   and with all his force let him hurl his bolts at me,
   no joy of satisfaction would I give him!"   60
My guide spoke back at him with cutting force,
   (I never heard his voice so strong before):
   "O Capaneus, since your blustering pride   63
will not be stilled, you are made to suffer more:
   no torment other than your rage itself
   could punish your gnawing pride more perfectly."   66
And then he turned a calmer face to me,
   saying, "That was a king, one of the seven
   besieging Thebes; he scorned, and would seem still   69
to go on scorning God and treat him lightly,
   but, as I said to him, he decks his chest
   with ornaments of lavish words that prick him.   72
Now follow me and also pay attention
   not to put your feet upon the burning sand,
   but to keep them well within the wooded line."   75
Without exchanging words we reached a place
   where a narrow stream came gushing from the woods
   (its reddish water still runs fear through me!);   78
like the one that issues from the Bulicame,[7]
   whose waters are shared by prostitutes downstream,
   it wore its way across the desert sand.   81
This river's bed and banks were made of stone,

---

3. Capaneus, one of the seven legendary kings who beseiged Thebes as described in the *Thebaid* by Statius (d. 95 C.E.). He was struck with a thunderbolt when he boasted that not even Jupiter could stop him.
4. Vulcan.
5. The Sicilian name for Mt. Etna, thought to be Vulcan's furnace. "Those others" are the Cyclopes, Vulcan's helpers.
6. Jove defeated the rebellious Titans at the battle of Phlegra (see 31.44).
7. A hot sulphurous spring that supplied water to brothels in an area of northern Italy.

so were the tops on both its sides; and then
   I understood this was our way across.   84
"Among the other marvels I have shown you,
   from the time we made our entrance through the gate
   whose threshold welcomes every evil soul,   87
your eyes have not discovered anything
   as remarkable as this stream you see here
   extinguishing the flames above its path."   90
These were my master's words, and I at once
   implored him to provide me with the food
   for which he had given me the appetite.   93
"In the middle of the sea there lies a wasteland,"
   he immediately began, "that is known as Crete,
   under whose king the world knew innocence.[8]   96
There is a mountain there that was called Ida;
   then happy in its verdure and its streams,
   now deserted like an old, discarded thing;   99
Rhea chose it once as a safe cradle
   for her son, and, to conceal his presence better,
   she had her servants scream loud when he cried.[9]   102
In the mountain's core an ancient man stands tall;
   he has his shoulders turned toward Damietta[1]
   and faces Rome as though it were his mirror.   105
His head is fashioned of the finest gold;
   pure silver are his arms and hands and chest;
   from there to where his legs spread, he is brass;   108
the rest of him is all of chosen iron,
   except his right foot which is terra cotta;
   he puts more weight on this foot than the other.[2]   111
Every part of him, except the gold, is broken
   by a fissure dripping tears down to his feet,
   where they collect to erode the cavern's rock;   114
from stone to stone they drain down here, becoming
   rivers: the Acheron, Styx, and Phlegethon,
   then overflow down through this tight canal   117
until they fall to where all falling ends:
   they form Cocytus.[3] What that pool is like
   I need not tell you. You will see, yourself."   120
And I to him: "If this small stream beside us
   has its source, as you have told me, in our world,
   why have we seen it only on this ledge?"   123
And he to me: "You know this place is round,

8. Saturn, mythical king of Crete during the golden age.
9. Jupiter was hidden by his mother, Rhea, from his father, Saturn, who tried to devour all his children to thwart a prophecy that he would be dethroned by one of them. So that Saturn would not hear the infant's cries, Rhea had her servants cry out and beat their shields with their swords.

1. A city in Egypt. The Old Man has been interpreted as an emblem of the decline of human history.
2. The four metals and the clay represent the degeneration of history; Dante took them from Daniel 2.31–35.
3. The frozen lake at the bottom of Hell: see 32.22–30 and 34.52.

and though your journey has been long, circling
    toward the bottom, turning only to the left,   126
you still have not completed a full circle;
    so you should never look surprised, as now,
    if you see something you have not seen before."   129
And I again: "Where, Master, shall we find
    Lethe and Phlegethon? You omit the first
    and say the other forms from the rain of tears."   132
"I am very happy when you question me,"
    he said, "but that the blood-red water boiled
    should answer certainly one of your questions.[4]   135
And Lethe you shall see, but beyond this valley,
    at a place where souls collect to wash themselves
    when penitence has freed them of their guilt.[5]   138
Now it is time to leave this edge of woods,"
    he added. "Be sure you follow close behind me:
    the margins are our road, they do not burn,   141
and all the flames above them are extinguished."

CANTO XV

*They move out across the plain of burning sand, walking along the ditchlike edge of
the conduit through which the Phlegethon flows, and after they have come some
distance from the wood they see a group of souls running toward them. One, Bru-
nette Latini, a famous Florentine intellectual and Dante's former teacher, recognizes the Pilgrim and leaves his band to walk and talk with him. Brunetto learns the
reason for the Pilgrim's journey and offers him a prophecy of the troubles lying in
wait for him—an echo of Ciacco's words in Canto VI. Brunetto names some of the
others being punished with him (Priscian, Francesco d'Accorso, Andrea de' Mozzi);
but soon, in the distance, he sees a cloud of smoke approaching, which presages a
new group, and because he must not associate with them, like a foot-racer Brunetto
speeds away to catch up with his own band.*

Now one of those stone margins bears us on
    and the river's vapors hover like a shade,
    sheltering the banks and the water from the flames.   3
As the Flemings, living with the constant threat
    of flood tides rushing in between Wissant
    and Bruges,[6] build their dikes to force the sea back;   6
as the Paduans build theirs on the shores of Brenta[7]
    to protect their town and homes before warm weather
    turns Chiarentana's snow to rushing water—   9
so were these walls we walked upon constructed,
    though the engineer, whoever he may have been,
    did not make them as high or thick as those.   12

4. See n. 2 to 12.101.
5. Lethe is crossed when Dante passes into
the Earthly Paradise on the top of Mount Purgatory.
6. Cities that, for Dante, mark the two ends of

the dike that protects Flanders from the sea.
7. A river that flows through Padua, fed by
the melting snows in the mountains of the
province of Chiarentana (modern Carinthia in
Austria).

We had left the wood behind (so far behind,
  by now, that if I had stopped to turn around,
  I am sure it could no longer have been seen)   15
when we saw a troop of souls come hurrying
  toward us beside the bank, and each of them
  looked us up and down, as some men look   18
at other men, at night, when the moon is new.
  They strained their eyebrows, squinting hard at us,
  as an old tailor might at his needle's eye.   21
Eyed in such a way by this strange crew,
  I was recognized by one of them, who grabbed
  my garment's hem and shouted: "How marvelous!"   24
And I, when he reached out his arm toward me,
  straining my eyes, saw through his face's crust,
  through his burned features that could not prevent   27
my memory from bringing back his name;
  and bending my face down to meet with his,
  I said: "Is this really you, here, Ser Brunetto?"[8]   30
And he: "O my son, may it not displease you
  if Brunetto Latini lets his troop file on
  while he walks at your side for a little while."   33
And I· "With all my heart I beg you to,
  and if you wish me to sit here with you,
  I will, if my companion does not mind."   36
"My son," he said, "a member of this herd
  who stops one moment lies one hundred years
  unable to brush off the wounding flames,   39
so, move on; I shall follow at your hem
  and then rejoin my family that moves
  along, lamenting their eternal pain."   42
I did not dare step off the margin-path
  to walk at his own level but, with head
  bent low in reverence, I moved along.   45
He began: "What fortune or what destiny
  leads you down here before your final hour?
  And who is this one showing you the way?"   48
"Up there above in the bright living life
  before I reached the end of all my years,
  I lost myself in a valley," I replied;   51
"just yesterday at dawn I turned from it.
  This spirit here appeared as I turned back,
  and by this road he guides me home again."   54
He said to me: "Follow your constellation
  and you cannot fail to reach your port of glory,
  not if I saw clearly in the happy life;   57
and if I had not died just when I did,

8. Brunetto Latini (ca. 1220–1294), active in Florentine politics and the author of—among other works—two books: a prose encyclopedia in French called the *Trésor*, which emphasizes the qualities needed for civic duty, and a shorter allegorical poem in Italian called the *Tesoretto*, which combines autobiography with philosophy.

I would have cheered you on in all your work,
   seeing how favorable Heaven was to you. 60
But that ungrateful and malignant race
   which descended from the Fiesole[9] of old,
   and still have rock and mountain in their blood, 63
will become, for your good deeds, your enemy—
   and right they are: among the bitter berries
   there's no fit place for the sweet fig to bloom.[1] 66
They have always had the fame of being blind,
   an envious race, proud and avaricious;
   you must not let their ways contaminate you. 69
Your destiny reserves such honors for you:
   both parties shall be hungry to devour you,
   but the grass will not be growing where the goat is.[2] 72
Let the wild beasts of Fiesole make fodder
   of each other, and let them leave the plant untouched
   (so rare it is that one grows in their dung-heap) 75
in which there lives again the holy seed
   of those remaining Romans who survived there
   when this new nest of malice was constructed." 78
"Oh, if all I wished for had been granted,"
   I answered him, "you certainly would not,
   not yet, be banished from our life on earth; 81
my mind is etched (and now my heart is pierced)
   with your kind image, loving and paternal,
   when, living in the world, hour after hour 84
you taught me how man makes himself eternal.[3]
   And while I live my tongue shall always speak
   of my debt to you, and of my gratitude. 87
I will write down what you tell me of my future
   and save it, with another text, to show
   a lady who can interpret, if I can reach her.[4] 90
This much, at least, let me make clear to you:
   if my conscience continues not to blame me,
   I am ready for whatever Fortune wants. 93
This prophecy is not new to my ears,
   and so let Fortune turn her wheel, spinning it
   as she pleases, and the peasant turn his spade."[5] 96
My master, hearing this, looked to the right,
   then, turning round and facing me, he said:
   "He listens well who notes well what he hears." 99
But I did not answer him; I went on talking,

9. A hill town north of Florence whose rustic
inhabitants were supposed to have joined with
noble Romans in the founding of Florence,
creating an unstable mixture.
1. The "bitter berries" are the Florentines
descended from Fiesole; the "sweet fig" is Brunetto's term for the aristocratic Dante.
2. Either both parties will ask you to join
them or both parties will want to devour you—

but keep yourself apart.
3. In the *Trésor* Brunetto says that earthly
glory gives man a second life through an
enduring reputation.
4. Beatrice.
5. The traditional image of Fortune and her
wheel is here compared to the rustic image of
the peasant turning the soil with his hoe.

walking with Ser Brunetto, asking him
who of his company were most distinguished. 102
And he: "It might be good to know who some are,
 about the rest I feel I should be silent,
 for the time would be too short, there are so many. 105
In brief, let me tell you, all here were clerics
 and respected men of letters of great fame,
 all befouled in the world by one same sin:[6] 108
Priscian is traveling with that wretched crowd
 and Francesco d'Accorso too,[7] and also there,
 if you could have stomached such repugnancy, 111
you might have seen the one the Servant of Servants
 transferred to the Bacchiglione from the Arno
 where his sinfully erected nerves were buried.[8] 114
I would say more, but my walk and conversation
 with you cannot go on, for over there
 I see a new smoke rising from the sand: 117
people approach with whom I must not mingle.
 Remember my *Trésor*, where I live on,
 this is the only thing I ask of you." 120
Then he turned back, and he seemed like one of those
 who run Verona's race across its fields
 to win the green cloth prize;[9] and he was like 123
the winner of the group, not the last one in.

CANTO XVI

Continuing through the third round of the Circle of Violence, the Pilgrim hears the distant roar of a waterfall, which grows louder as he and his guide proceed. Suddenly three shades, having recognized him as a Florentine, break from their company and converse with him, all the while circling like a turning wheel. Their spokesman, Jacopo Rusticucci, identifies himself and his companions (Guido Guerra and Tegghiaio Aldobrandi) as well-known and honored citizens of Florence, and begs for news of their native city. The three ask to be remembered in the world and then rush off. By this time the sound of the waterfall is so deafening that it almost drowns out speech, and when the poets reach the edge of the precipice, Virgil takes a cord which had been bound around his pupil's waist and tosses it into the abyss. It is a signal, and in response a monstrous form looms up from below, swimming through the air. On this note of suspense, the canto ends.

6. Sodomy, condemned in the Middle Ages as unnatural.
7. Priscian was a Greek grammarian (6th century C.E.), Francesco d'Accorso a Florentine law professor (d. 1293).
8. Andrea de' Mozzi, bishop of Florence (1287–95), transferred by Pope Boniface (designated here by an official title for the pope,

"the Servant of [Christ's] Servants") from Florence to Vicenza; the Arno runs through Florence, the Bacchiglione through Vicenza.
9. A footrace run at Verona on the first Sunday in Lent, the prize being a piece of green cloth. For the race to be run by the Christian, see 1 Corinthians 9.24–25.

Already we were where I could hear the rumbling
    of the water plunging down to the next circle,
    something like the sound of beehives humming,   3
when three shades with one impulse broke away,
    running, from a group of spirits passing us
    beneath the rain of bitter suffering.   6
They were coming toward us shouting with one voice:
    "O you there, stop! From the clothes you wear, you seem
    to be a man from our perverted city."[1]   9
Ah, the wounds I saw covering their limbs,
    some old, some freshly branded by the flames!
    Even now, when I think hack to them, I grieve.   12
Their shouts caught the attention of my guide,
    and then he turned to face me, saying, "Wait,
    for these are shades that merit your respect.   15
And were it not the nature of this place
    to rain with piercing flames, I would suggest
    you run toward *them*, for it would be more fitting."[2]   18
When we stopped, they resumed their normal pace
    and when they reached us, then they started circling;
    the three together formed a turning wheel,   21
just like professional wrestlers stripped and oiled,
    eyeing one another for the first, best grip
    before the actual blows and thrusts begin.[3]   24
And circling in this way each kept his face
    pointed up at me, so that their necks and feet
    moved constantly in opposite directions.   27
"And if the misery along these sterile sands,"
    one of them said, "and our charred and peeling flesh
    make us, and what we ask, repulsive to you,   30
let our great wordly fame persuade your heart
    to tell us who you are, how you can walk
    safely with living feet through Hell itself.   33
This one in front, whose footsteps I am treading,
    even though he runs his round naked and skinned,
    was of noble station, more than you may think: 36
he was the grandson of the good Gualdrada;
    his name was Guido Guerra,[4] and in his life
    he accomplished much with counsel and with sword.   39
This other one, who pounds the sand behind me,
    is Tegghiaio Aldobrandi,[5] whose wise voice
    the world would have done well to listen to.   42
And I, who share this post of pain with them,

1. Florence.
2. To hurry was considered undignified.
3. The three naked Florentines form a circle and are compared to oiled wrestlers (a sport practiced in Dante's time).
4. A leading participant in the civil strife in Florence (d. 1272).
5. An ally of Guido (see 6.79).

was Jacopo Rusticucci[6] and for sure
  my reluctant wife first drove me to my sin."   45
If I could have been sheltered from the fire,
  I would have thrown myself below with them,
  and I think my guide would have allowed me to;   48
but, as I knew I would be burned and seared,
  my fear won over my first good intention
  that made me want to put my arms around them.   51
And then I spoke: "Repulsion, no, but grief
  for your condition spread throughout my heart
  (and years will pass before it fades away),   54
as soon as my lord here began to speak
  in terms that led me to believe a group
  of such men as yourselves might be approaching.   57
I am from your city, and your honored names
  and your accomplishments I have always heard
  rehearsed, and have rehearsed, myself, with fondness.   60
I leave the bitter gall, and journey toward
  those sweet fruits promised me by my true guide,[7]
  but first I must go down to the very center."   63
"So may your soul remain to guide your body
  for years to come," that same one spoke again,
  "and your fame's light shine after you are gone,   66
tell us if courtesy and valor dwell
  within our city as they used to do,
  or have they both been banished from the place?   69
Guglielmo Borsiere,[8] who joined our painful ranks
  of late, and travels there with our companions,
  has given us reports that make us grieve."[9]   72
"A new breed of people with their sudden wealth
  have stimulated pride and unrestraint
  in you, O Florence, made to weep so soon."   75
These words I shouted with my head strained high,
  and the three below took this to be my answer
  and looked, as if on truth, at one another.   78
"If you always answer questions with such ease,"
  they all spoke up at once, "O happy you,
  to have this gift of ready, open speech;   81
therefore, if you survive these unlit regions
  and return to gaze upon the lovely stars,
  when it pleases you to say 'I was down there,'   84
do not fail to speak of us to living men."
  They broke their man-made wheel and ran away,
  their nimble legs were more like wings in flight.   87

---

6. An ally of Tegghiaio who blames his wife
for his sodomy (see 6.80).
7. Leave Hell and head for Paradise.
8. An elegant member of Florentine society.

9. An account of the recent dissension within
the city, to which Dante himself was soon to
fall victim.

"Amen" could not have been pronounced as quick
   as they were off, and vanished from our sight;
   and then my teacher thought it time to leave.   90
I followed him, and we had not gone far
   before the sound of water was so close
   that if we spoke we hardly heard each other.   93
As that river on the Apennines' left slope,[1]
   first springing from its source at Monte Veso,
   then flowing eastward holding its own course   96
(called Acquacheta at its start above
   before descending to its lower bed
   where, at Forli, it has another name),   99
reverberates there near San Benedetto
   dell'Alpe (plunging in a single bound),
   where at least a thousand vassals could be housed,   102
so down a single rocky precipice
   we found the tainted waters falling, roaring
   sound loud enough to deafen us in seconds.   105
I wore a cord that fastened round my waist,[2]
   with which I once had thought I might be able
   to catch the leopard with the gaudy skin.[3]   108
As soon as I removed it from my body
   just as my guide commanded me to do,
   I gave it to him looped into a coil.   111
Then taking it and turning to the right,
   he flung it quite a distance past the bank
   and down into the deepness of the pit.   114
"Now surely something strange is going to happen,"
   I thought to myself, "to answer the strange signal
   whose course my master follows with his eyes."   117
How cautious a man must be in company
   with one who can not only see his actions
   but read his mind and understand his thoughts![4]   120
He spoke: "Soon will rise up what I expect;
   and what you are trying to imagine now
   soon must reveal itself before your eyes."   123
It is always better to hold one's tongue than speak
   a truth that seems a bold-faced lie when uttered,
   since to tell this truth could be embarrassing;   126
but I shall not keep quiet; and by the verses
   of my *Comedy*—so may they be received
   with lasting favor, Reader—I swear to you   129
I saw a figure coming, it was swimming

---

1. Dante compares the roar of Phlegethon to
the Montone River in northern Italy, whose
course he traces in the next nine lines.
2. While commentators disagree, it seems
likely that this cord is a reference both to Job
41.1, where God says he can draw Leviathan
up with a hook and bind his tongue with a
cord, and to Francis of Assisi, who wore a cord

as a sign of humility and obedience. As a layman, Dante may have had a connection with
the Franciscan friars, a common circumstance
at the time.
3. The leopard of canto I, representing fraud.
4. Dante now realizes that Virgil can read his
thoughts.

through the thick and murky air, up to the top
 (a thing to startle even stalwart hearts),   132
like one returning who has swum below
 to free the anchor that has caught its hooks
 on a reef or something else the sea conceals,   135
spreading out his arms, and doubling up his legs.

CANTO XVII

The beast that had been seen approaching at the end of the last canto is the horrible
monster Geryon; his face is appealing like that of an honest man, but his body ends
in a scorpionlike stinger. He perches on the edge of the abyss and Virgil advises his
ward, who has noticed new groups of sinners squatting on the fiery sand, to learn
who they are, while he makes arrangements with Geryon for the descent. The sin-
ners are the Usurers, unrecognizable except by the crests on the moneybags hanging
about their necks, which identify them as members of the Gianfigliazzi, Ubriachi,
and Scrovegni families. The Pilgrim listens to one of them briefly but soon returns
to find his master sitting on Geryon's back. After he conquers his fear and mounts,
too, the monster begins the slow, spiraling descent into the Eighth Circle.

"And now, behold the beast with pointed tail
 that passes mountains, annulling walls and weapons,
 behold the one that makes the whole world stink!"[5]   3
These were the words I heard my master say
 as he signaled for the beast to come ashore,
 up close to where the rocky levee ends.   6
And that repulsive spectacle of fraud
 floated close, maneuvering head and chest
 on to the shore, but his tail he let hang free.   9
His face was the face of any honest man,
 it shone with such a look of benediction;
 and all the rest of him was serpentine;   12
his two clawed paws were hairy to the armpits,
 his back and all his belly and both flanks
 were painted arabesques and curlicues: 15
the Turks and Tartars never made a fabric
 with richer colors intricately woven,
 nor were such complex webs spun by Arachne.[6]   18
As sometimes fishing boats are seen ashore,
 part fixed in sand, and part still in the water;
 and as the beaver,[7] living in the land   21
of drunken Germans,[8] squats to catch his prey,
 just so that beast, the worst of beasts, hung waiting
 on the bank that bounds the stretch of sand in stone.   24

---

5. Geryon, the embodiment of fraud. For this
figure Dante drew upon classical literature,
where he had not three natures—human, rep-
tilian, and bestial—combined into one, as
here, but three bodies and three heads.
6. A woman in classical literature famous for

weaving, turned into a spider: see Ovid, *Meta-*
morphoses 6.
7. Which was thought to catch fish by putting
its tail into the water.
8. Accusing Germans of drunkenness was a
tradition going back to the Romans.

In the void beyond he exercised his tail,
  twitching and twisting-up the venomed fork
  that armed its tip just like a scorpion's stinger.   27
My leader said: "Now we must turn aside
  a little from our path, in the direction
  of that malignant beast that lies in wait."   30
Then we stepped off our path down to the right
  and moved ten paces straight across the brink
  to keep the sand and flames at a safe distance.   33
And when we stood by Geryon's side, I noticed,
  a little farther on, some people crouched
  in the sand quite close to the edge of emptiness.   36
Just then my master spoke: "So you may have
  a knowledge of this round that is complete,"
  he said, "go and see their torment for yourself.   39
But let your conversation there be brief;
  while you are gone I shall speak to this one
  and ask him for the loan of his strong back."   42
So I continued walking, all alone,
  along the seventh circle's outer edge
  to where the group of sufferers were sitting.   45
The pain was bursting from their eyes; their hands
  went scurrying up and down to give protection
  here from the flames, there from the burning sands.   48
They were, in fact, like a dog in summertime
  busy, now with his paw, now with his snout,
  tormented by the fleas and flies that bite him.   51
I carefully examined several faces
  among this group caught in the raining flames
  and did not know a soul, but I observed   54
that around each sinner's neck a pouch was hung,
  each of a different color, with a coat of arms,
  and fixed on these they seemed to feast their eyes.[9]   57
And while I looked about among the crowd,
  I saw something in blue on a yellow purse
  that had the face and bearing of a lion;   60
and while my eyes continued their inspection
  I saw another purse as red as blood
  exhibiting a goose more white than butter.   63
And one who had a blue sow, pregnant-looking,
  stamped on the whiteness of his moneybag
  asked me: "What are you doing in this pit?   66
Get out of here! And since you're still alive,
  I'll tell you that my neighbor Vitaliano
  will come to take his seat on my left side.[1]   69
Among these Florentines I sit, one Paduan:

9. These are usurers, men who lent money for interest, which was forbidden by the church in the Middle Ages (although often practiced). Each has a coat of arms on his purse by which he can be identified; all are Italians.
1. The speaker is from Padua and here maliciously identifies another Paduan who will soon be joining him.

time after time they fill my ears with blasts
of shouting: 'Send us down the sovereign knight[2]   72
who will come bearing three goats on his pouch.'"
   As final comment he stuck out his tongue—
   as far out as an ox licking its nose.   75
And I, afraid my staying there much longer
   might anger the one who warned me to be brief,
   turned my back on these frustrated sinners.   78
I found my guide already sitting high
   upon the back of that fierce animal;
   he said: "And now, take courage and be strong.   81
From now on we descend by stairs like these.
   Get on up front. I want to ride behind,
   to be between you and the dangerous tail."[3]   84
A man who feels the shivers of a fever
   coming on, his nails already dead of color,
   will tremble at the mere sight of cool shade;   87
I was that man when I had heard his words.
   But then I felt those stabs of shame that make
   a servant brave before his valorous master.   90
As I squirmed around on those enormous shoulders,
   I wanted to cry out, "Hold on to me,"
   but I had no voice to second my desire.   93
Then he who once before had helped me out
   when I was threatened put his arms around me
   as soon as I was settled, and held me tight;   96
and then he cried: "Now Geryon, start moving,
   descend with gentle motion, circling wide:
   remember you are carrying living weight."   99
Just as a boat slips back away from shore,
   back slowly, more and more, he left that pier;
   and when he felt himself all clear in space,   102
to where his breast had been he swung his tail
   and stretched it undulating like an eel,
   as with his paws he gathered in the air.   105
I doubt if Phaëthon[4] feared more—that time
   he dropped the sun-reins of his father's chariot
   and burned the streak of sky we see today—   108
or if poor Icarus[5] did—feeling his sides
   unfeathering as the wax began to melt,
   his father shouting: "Wrong, your course is wrong"—   111
than I had when I felt myself in air
   and saw on every side nothing but air;
   only the beast I sat upon was there.   114
He moves along slowly, and swimming slowly,

---

2. A prominent Florentine banker.
3. Virgil protects Dante from Geryon's scorpion's tail.
4. Son of Apollo, Phaëthon tried to drive the chariot of the sun, but when it got out of control

it scorched both Earth and the heavens, creating the Milky Way (Ovid, *Metamorphoses* 2).
5. Flying with wings made of wax and feathers, Icarus went too near the sun and fell (Ovid, *Metamorphoses* 8).

descends a spiral path—but I know this
  only from a breeze ahead and one below; 117
I hear now on my right the whirlpool roar
  with hideous sound beneath us on the ground;
  at this I stretch my neck to look below, 120
but leaning out soon made me more afraid,
  for I heard moaning there and saw the flames;
  trembling, I cowered back, tightening my legs, 123
and I saw then what I had not before:
  the spiral path of our descent to torment
  closing in on us, it seemed, from every side. 126
As the falcon on the wing for many hours,
  having found no prey, and having seen no signal
  (so that his falconer sighs: "Oh, he falls already"), 129
descends, worn out, circling a hundred times
  (instead of swooping down), settling at some distance
  from his master, perched in anger and disdain,[6] 132
so Geryon brought us down to the bottom
  at the foot of the jagged cliff, almost against it,
  and once he got our bodies off his back, 135
he shot off like a shaft shot from a bowstring.

CANTO XVIII

The Pilgrim describes the view he had of the Eighth Circle of Hell while descending
through the air on Geryon's back. It consists of ten stone ravines called Malebolge
(Evil Pockets), and across each bolgia *is an arching bridge. When the poets find*
themselves on the edge of the first ravine they see two lines of naked sinners, walking
in opposite directions. In one are the Pimps or Panderers, and among them the Pil-
grim recognizes Venedico Caccianemico; in the other are the Seducers, among
whom Virgil points out Jason. As the two move toward the next bolgia, *they are*
assailed by a terrible stench; for here the Flatterers are immersed in excrement.
Among them are Alessio Interminei and Thaïs the whore.

There is a place in Hell called Malebolge,
  cut out of stone the color of iron ore,
  just like the circling cliff that walls it in. 3
Right at the center of this evil plain
  there yawns a very wide, deep well, whose structure
  I will talk of when the place itself is reached.[7] 6
That belt of land remaining, then, runs round
  between the well and cliff, and all this space
  is divided into ten descending valleys, 9
just like a ground-plan for successive moats
  that in concentric circles bind their center
  and serve to protect the ramparts of the castle. 12
This was the surface image they presented;

6. Unless it sights prey or is called back with a
lure by its master, a trained falcon will continue
flying until exhaustion compels it to descend.

7. The last, or ninth, circle of Hell, described
in cantos 31–34.

and as bridges from a castle's portal stretch
　　from moat to moat to reach the farthest bank,　　　　　　15
so, from the great cliff's base, just spokes of rock,
　　crossing from bank to bank, intersecting ditches
　　until the pit's hub cuts them off from meeting.　　　　　18
This is the place in which we found ourselves,
　　once shaken from the back of Geryon.
　　The poet turned to the left, I walked behind him.　　　21
There, on our right, I saw new suffering souls,
　　new means of torture, and new torturers,
　　crammed into the depths of the first ditch.　　　　　24
Two files of naked souls walked on the bottom,
　　the ones on our side faced us as they passed,
　　the others moved as we did but more quickly.　　　　27
The Romans, too, in the year of the Jubilee[8]
　　took measures to accommodate the throngs
　　that had to come and go across their bridge:　　　　30
they fixed it so on one side all were looking
　　at the castle, and were walking to St. Peter's;
　　on the other, they were moving toward the mount.　　33
On both sides, up along the deadly rock,
　　I saw horned devils with enormous whips
　　lashing the backs of shades with cruel delight.　　　36
Ah, how they made them skip and lift their heels
　　at the very first crack of the whip! Not one of them
　　dared pause to take a second or a third!　　　　　39
As I walked on my eyes met with the glance
　　of one down there; I murmured to myself:
　　"I know this face from somewhere, I am sure."[9]　　42
And so I stopped to study him more closely;
　　my leader also stopped, and was so kind
　　as to allow me to retrace my steps;　　　　　45
and that whipped soul thought he would hide from me
　　by lowering his face— which did no good.
　　I said, "O you, there, with your head bent low,　　48
if the features of your shade do not deceive me,
　　you are Venedico Caccianemico, I'm sure.
　　How did you get yourself in such a pickle?"　　　51
"I'm not so keen on answering," he said,
　　"but I feel I must; your plain talk is compelling,
　　it makes me think of old times in the world.　　　54
I was the one who coaxed Ghisolabella
　　to serve the lusty wishes of the Marquis,
　　no matter how the sordid tale is told;　　　　57
I'm not the only Bolognese who weeps here—

8. The year 1300 was a Jubilee Year, and Dante here describes the crowd control on the bridge that ran between the Castle of St. Angelo and St. Peter's.

9. This is Venedico Caccianemico, a man from Bologna who was reputed to have turned his sister Ghisolabella over to the Marquis of Este.

hardly! This place is packed with us; in fact,
    there are more of us here than there are living tongues,   60
between Savena and Reno, saying 'Sipa';[1]
    I call on your own memory as witness:
    remember we have avaricious hearts."   63
Just at that point a devil let him have
    the feel of his tailed whip and cried: "Move on,
    you pimp, you can't cash in on women here!"   66
I turned and hurried to rejoin my guide;
    we walked a few more steps and then we reached
    the rocky bridge that juts out from the bank.   69
We had no difficulty climbing up,
    and turning right, along the jagged ridge,
    we left those shades to their eternal circlings.   72
When we were where the ditch yawned wide below
    the ridge, to make a passage for the scourged,
    my guide said: "Stop and stand where you can see   75
these other misbegotten souls, whose faces
    you could not see before, for they were moving
    in the same direction we were, over there."   78
So from the ancient bridge we viewed the train
    that hurried toward us along the other tract—
    kept moving, like the first, by stinging whips.   81
And the good master, without my asking him,
    said, "Look at that imposing one approaching,
    who does not shed a single tear of pain: 84
what majesty he still maintains down there!
    He is Jason,[2] who by courage and sharp wits,
    fleeced the Colchians of their golden ram.   87
He later journeyed through the isle of Lemnos,
    whose bold and heartless females, earlier,
    had slaughtered every male upon the island;   90
there with his words of love, and loving looks,
    he succeeded in deceiving young Hypsipyle,
    who had in turn deceived the other women.   93
He left her there, with child, and all alone:
    such sin condemns him to such punishment,
    and Medea, too, gets her revenge on him.   96
With him go all deceivers of this type,
    and let this be enough to know concerning
    the first valley and the souls locked in its jaws."   99
We were already where the narrow ridge
    begins to cross the second bank, to make it
    an abutment for another ditch's arch.   102

1. *Sipa* is a word for "yes" in the dialect spoken in the territory between the rivers Savena and Reno, which comprise the boundaries of Bologna.
2. Jason led the Argonauts on the voyage to the island of Colchis, where they stole the golden fleece. He seduced and abandoned Hypsipyle, who had hidden her father when the other women of Lemnos were killing all the males. He also abandoned Medea, the daughter of the King of Colchis. For his story, see Ovid, *Metamorphoses* 7.

Now we could hear the shades in the next pouch
  whimpering, making snorting grunting sounds
  and sounds of blows, slapping with open palms.   105
From a steaming stench below, the banks were coated
  with a slimy mold that stuck to them like glue,
  disgusting to behold and worse to smell.   108
The bottom was so hollowed out of sight,
  we saw it only when we climbed the arch
  and looked down from the bridge's highest point: 111
there we were, and from where I stood I saw
  souls in the ditch plunged into excrement
  that might well have been flushed from our latrines;   114
my eyes were searching hard along the bottom,
  and I saw somebody's head so smirched with shit,
  you could not tell if he were priest or layman.   117
He shouted up: "Why do you feast your eyes
  on me more than these other dirty beasts?"
  And I replied: "Because, remembering well,   120
I've seen you with your hair dry once or twice.
  You are Alessio Interminei from Lucca,[3]
  that's why I stare at you more than the rest."   123
He beat his slimy forehead as he answered:
  "I am stuck down here by all those flatteries
  that rolled unceasing off my tongue up there."   126
He finished speaking, and my guide began:
  "Lean out a little more, look hard down there
  so you can get a good look at the face   129
of that repulsive and disheveled tramp
  scratching herself with shitty fingernails,
  spreading her legs while squatting up and down: 132
it is Thaïs the whore,[4] who gave this answer
  to her lover when he asked: 'Am I very worthy
  of your thanks?': 'Very? Nay, incredibly so!'   135
I think our eyes have had their fill of this."

CANTO XIX

*From the bridge above the Third Bolgia can be seen a rocky landscape below filled
with holes, from each of which protrude a sinner's legs and feet; flames dance across
their soles. When the Pilgrim expresses curiosity about a particular pair of twitching
legs, Virgil carries him down into the bolgia so that the Pilgrim himself may question the sinner. The legs belong to Pope Nicholas III, who astounds the Pilgrim by
mistaking him for Boniface VIII, the next pope, who, as soon as he dies, will fall to
the same hole, thereby pushing Nicholas farther down. He predicts that soon after
Boniface, Pope Clement V will come, stuffing both himself and Boniface still
deeper. To Nicholas's rather rhetoric-filled speech the Pilgrim responds with equally
high language, inveighing against the Simonists, the evil churchmen who are*

---

3. A prominent citizen of Lucca, in northern
Italy.

4. A character in a play by the Roman writer
Terence (186 or 185–159? B.C.E.).

punished here. Virgil is much pleased with his pupil and, lifting him in an affectionate embrace, he carries him to the top of the arch above the next bolgia.

O Simon Magus![5] O scum that followed him!
  Those things of God that rightly should be wed
  to holiness, you, rapacious creatures,   3
for the price of gold and silver, prostitute.
  Now, in your honor, I must sound my trumpet
  for here in the third pouch is where you dwell.   6
We had already climbed to see this tomb,
  and were standing high above it on the bridge,
  exactly at the mid-point of the ditch.   9
O Highest Wisdom, how you demonstrate
  your art in Heaven, on earth, and here in Hell!
  How justly does your power make awards![6]   12
I saw along the sides and on the bottom
  the livid-colored rock all full of holes;
  all were the same in size, and each was round.   15
To me they seemed no wider and no deeper
  than those inside my lovely San Giovanni,[7]
  in which the priest would stand or baptize from;   18
and one of these, not many years ago,
  I smashed for someone who was drowning in it:
  let this be mankind's picture of the truth!   21
From the mouth of every hole were sticking out
  a single sinner's feet, and then the legs
  up to the calf—the rest was stuffed inside.   24
The soles of every sinner's feet were flaming;
  their naked legs were twitching frenziedly—
  they would have broken any chain or rope.   27
Just as a flame will only move along
  an object's oily outer peel, so here
  the fire slid from heel to toe and back.   30
"Who is that one, Master, that angry wretch,
  who is writhing more than any of his comrades,"
  I asked, "the one licked by a redder flame?"[8]   33
And he to me, "If you want to be carried down
  along that lower bank to where he is,
  you can ask him who he is and why he's here."   36
And I, "My pleasure is what pleases you:

---

5. Because in the Bible Simon Magus tried to buy spiritual power from the apostles (Acts 8.9–24), the selling of any spiritual good for material gain was known in the Middle Ages as simony. The most common form of simony was the selling of church offices.
6. Dante is here applauding the artfulness of divine justice because the simoniacs, who cared most for their purses, are here stuffed into fiery purses hewn into the rock; see line 72 below.

7. The baptistery in Florence where Dante was baptized. The subsequent personal reference has never been satisfactorily explained.
8. Pope Nicholas III (pope 1277–80). He mistakenly believes that one of his successors, Boniface VIII, has come to be squeezed into the hole (line 53). Like all damned souls, Nicholas has foreknowledge, and because Boniface did not die until 1303 Nicholas is surprised at what he thinks is his appearance in 1300.

you are my lord, you know that from your will
  I would not swerve. You even know my thoughts."   39
When we reached the fourth bank, we began to turn
  and, keeping to the left, made our way down
  to the bottom of the holed and narrow ditch.   42
The good guide did not drop me from his side
  until he brought me to the broken rock
  of that one who was fretting with his shanks.   45
"Whatever you are, holding your upside down,
  O wretched soul, stuck like a stake in ground,
  make a sound or something," I said, "if you can."   48
I stood there like a priest who is confessing
  some vile assassin who, fixed in his ditch,
  has called him back again to put off dying.[9]   51
He cried: "Is that *you*, here, already, upright?
  Is that you here already upright, Boniface?
  By many years the book has lied to me!   54
Are you fed up so soon with all that wealth
  for which you did not fear to take by guile
  the Lovely Lady,[1] then tear her asunder?"   57
I stood there like a person just made fun of,
  dumbfounded by a question for an answer,
  not knowing how to answer the reply.   60
Then Virgil said: "Quick, hurry up and tell him:
  'I'm not the one, I'm not the one you think!'"
  And I answered just the way he told me to.   63
The spirit heard, and twisted both his feet,
  then, sighing with a grieving, tearful voice,
  he said: "Well then, what do you want of me?   66
If it concerns you so to learn my name
  that for this reason you came down the bank,
  know that I once was dressed in the great mantle.   69
But actually I was the she-bear's son,[2]
  so greedy to advance my cubs, that wealth
  I pocketed in life, and here, myself.   72
Beneath my head are pushed down all the others
  who came, sinning in simony, before me,
  squeezed tightly in the fissures of the rock.   75
I, in my turn, shall join the rest below
  as soon as *he* comes, the one I thought you were
  when, all too quick, I put my question to you.   78
But already my feet have baked a longer time
  (and I have been stuck upside-down like this)
  than he will stay here planted with feet aflame: 81
soon after him shall come one from the West,[3]

9. Hired murderers were occasionally executed by being placed head-down in a ditch
and then buried alive.
1. The church.
2. The arms of Nicholas's family (the Orsini)

included a "she-bear."
3. Clement V, who became pope in 1305 after
agreeing with the French king to remove the
papacy to Avignon in France. He is "from the
West" because he was born in western France.

a lawless shepherd, one whose fouler deeds
   make him a fitting cover for us both.   84
He shall be another Jason,[4] like the one
   in Maccabees: just as his king was pliant,
   so France's king shall soften to this priest."   87
I do not know, perhaps I was too bold here,
   but I answered him in tune with his own words:
   "Well, tell me now: what was the sum of money   90
that holy Peter had to pay our Lord
   before He gave the keys into his keeping?
   Certainly He asked no more than 'Follow me.'[5]   93
Nor did Peter or the rest extort gold coins
   or silver from Matthias when he was picked
   to fill the place the evil one had lost.[6]   96
So stay stuck there, for you are rightly punished,
   and guard with care the money wrongly gained
   that made you stand courageous against Charles.[7]   99
And were it not for the reverence I have
   for those highest of all keys that you once held
   in the happy life—if this did not restrain me,   102
I would use even harsher words than these,
   for your avarice brings grief upon the world,
   crushing the good, exalting the depraved.   105
You shepherds it was the Evangelist[8] had in mind
   when the vision came to him of her who sits
   upon the waters playing whore with kings: 108
that one who with the seven heads was born
   and from her ten horns managed to draw strength
   so long as virtue was her bridegroom's joy.   111
You have built yourselves a God of gold and silver!
   How do you differ from the idolator,
   except he worships one, you worship hundreds?   114
O Constantine,[9] what evil did you sire,
   not by your conversion, but by the dower
   that the first wealthy Father got from you!"   117
And while I sang these very notes to him,

4. Jason became high priest of the Jews by bribing the king: see 2 Maccabees 4.7–9.
5. See Matthew 16.18–19: the keys are the church's power to bind (condemn) and to loose (absolve). For "follow me," see Matthew 4.18–19.
6. Matthias was chosen by lot to fill the place of Judas (Acts 1.23–26).
7. Nicholas was supposed to be involved in a plot against Charles of Anjou (1226–1285), ruler of Naples and Sicily.
8. John, author of Revelation, who in the Middle Ages was identified with the author of the Gospel according to John: for this passage,

which was originally interpreted as referring to pagan Rome but which Dante applies to the corrupt church, see Revelation 17.1–18. The "seven heads" are the seven Sacraments; the "ten horns," the Ten Commandments; the "bridegroom," God.
9. Roman emperor (d. 337) who was the supposed author of a document—known as the Donation of Constantine—in which he granted temporal power and the right to acquire wealth to Pope Sylvester I, "the first wealthy Father" of this passage. The document was proved to be a forgery in the 15th century.

his big flat feet kicked fiercely out of anger,
—or perhaps it was his conscience gnawing him.   120
I think my master liked what I was saying,
for all the while he smiled and was intent
on hearing the ring of truly spoken words.   123
Then he took hold of me with both his arms,
and when he had me firm against his breast,
he climbed back up the path he had come down.   126
He did not tire of the weight clasped tight to him,
but brought me to the top of the bridge's arch,
the one that joins the fourth bank to the fifth.   129
And here he gently set his burden down—
gently, for the ridge, so steep and rugged,
would have been hard even for goats to cross.   132
From there another valley opened to me.

CANTO XX

*In the Fourth Bolgia they see a group of shades weeping as they walk slowly along
the valley; they are the Soothsayers and their heads are twisted completely around so
that their hair flows down their fronts and their tears flow down to their buttocks.
Virgil points out many of them, including Amphiaraus, Tiresias, Aruns, and Manto.
It was Manto who first inhabited the site of Virgil's home city of Mantua, and the
poet gives a long description of the city's founding, after which he names more of the
condemned soothsayers: Eurypylus, Michael Scot, Guido Bonatti, and Asdente.*

Now I must turn strange torments into verse
to form the matter of the twentieth canto
of the first chant, the one about the damned.   3
Already I was where I could look down
into the depths of the ditch: I saw its floor
was wet with anguished tears shed by the sinners,   6
and I saw people in the valley's circle,
silent, weeping, walking at a litany pace
the way processions push along in our world.[1]   9
And when my gaze moved down below their faces,
I saw all were incredibly distorted,
the chin was not above the chest, the neck   12
was twisted—their faces looked down on their backs;
they had to move ahead by moving backward,
for they never saw what was ahead of them.   15
Perhaps there was a case of someone once
in a palsy fit becoming so distorted,
but none that *I* know of! I doubt there could be!   18
So may God grant you, Reader, benefit
from reading of my poem, just ask yourself
how I could keep my eyes dry when, close by,   21
I saw the image of our human form

1. A "litany" is a form of public prayer, often recited during stately "processions" in the church.

so twisted—the tears their eyes were shedding
    streamed down to wet their buttocks at the cleft.   24
Indeed I did weep, as I leaned my body
    against a jut of rugged rock. My guide:
    "So you are still like all the other fools?   27
In this place piety lives when pity is dead,
    for who could be more wicked than that man
    who tries to bend divine will to his own![2]   30
Lift your head up, lift it, see him for whom
    the earth split wide before the Thebans's eyes,
    while they all shouted, 'Where are you rushing off to,   33
Amphiaraus?[3] Why do you quit the war?'
    He kept on rushing downward through the gap
    until Minòs, who gets them all, got him.   36
You see how he has made his back his chest:
    because he wished to see too far ahead,
    he sees behind and walks a backward track.   39
Behold Tiresias,[4] who changed his looks:
    from a man he turned himself into a woman,
    transforming all his body, part for part;   42
then later on he had to take the wand
    and strike once more those two snakes making love
    before he could get back his virile parts.   45
Backing up to this one's chest comes Aruns,[5]
    who, in the hills of Luni, worked by peasants
    of Carrara dwelling in the valley's plain,   48
lived in white marble cut into a cave,
    and from this site, where nothing blocked his view,
    he could observe the sea and stars with ease.   51
And that one, with her hair loose, flowing back
    to cover both her breasts you cannot see,
    and with her hairy parts in front behind her,   54
was Manto,[6] who had searched through many lands
    before she came to dwell where I was born;
    now let me tell you something of her story.   57
When her father had departed from the living,
    and Bacchus' sacred city[7] fell enslaved,
    she wandered through the world for many years.   60
High in fair Italy there spreads a lake,
    beneath the mountains bounding Germany
    beyond the Tyrol, known as Lake Benaco;[8]   63

2. This is a rebuke to Dante, who errs by showing sympathy for the damned.
3. A priest swallowed up by the Earth in a battle against the Thebans as described in Statius's *Thebaid* (see n. 3 to 14.48). For Minos, see 5.4.
4. A soothsayer of Thebes, he struck two coupling serpents with his rod and was transformed into a woman. Seven years later he repeated the action and was changed back into a man. See Ovid, *Metamorphoses* 3.

5. An Etruscan soothsayer from the city of Luni, in the area of Carrera where marble is quarried, is described by the Roman poet Lucan (d. 65 C.E.) in his *Pharsalia*.
6. Another Theban soothsayer described by Roman poets.
7. Thebes.
8. The present-day Lake Garda in northern Italy, located in terms of an island where the boundaries of the three dioceses of Trent, Brescia, and Verona meet.

by a thousand streams and more, I think, the Alps
  are bathed from Garda to the Val Camonica[9]
  with the waters flowing down into that lake;   66
at its center is a place where all three bishops
  of Trent and Brescia and Verona could,
  if they would ever visit there, say Mass;   69
Peschiera[1] sits, a handsome well-built fortress,
  to ward off Brescians and the Bergamese,
  along the lowest point of that lake's shore,   72
where all the water that Benaco's basin
  cannot hold must overflow to make a stream
  that winds its way through countrysides of green;   75
but when the water starts to flow, its name
  is not Benaco, but Mencio, all the way
  to Governol,[2] where it falls into the Po;   78
but before its course is run it strikes a lowland,
  on which it spreads and turns into a marsh
  that can become unbearable in summer.   81
Passing this place one day the savage virgin
  saw land that lay in the center of the mire,
  untilled and empty of inhabitants.   84
There, to escape all human intercourse,
  she stopped to practice magic with her servants;
  there she lived, and there she left her corpse.   87
Later on, the men who lived around there gathered
  on that very spot, for it was well protected
  by the bog that girded it on every side.   90
They built a city over her dead bones,
  and for her, the first to choose that place, they named it
  Mantua,[3] without recourse to sorcery.   93
Once, there were far more people living there,
  before the foolish Casalodi listened
  to the fraudulent advice of Pinamonte.[4]   96
And so, I warn you, should you ever hear
  my city's origin told otherwise,
  let no false tales adulterate the truth."[5]   99
And I replied: "Master, your explanations
  are truth for me, winning my faith entirely;
  any others would be just like burned-out coals.   102
But speak to me of these shades passing by,
  if you see anyone that is worth noting;
  for now my mind is set on only that."   105

9. Garda is a town by the lake and Val Camonica a valley below it.
1. Peschiera is a town on the south shore of
the lake; the Brescians and the Bergamese are
inhabitants of two towns to the northwest of
Peschiera.
2. A town some 30 miles south of Peschiera.
Presumably Virgil provides this detailed geography to illustrate that he is a native of this region.

3. Virgil's native city.
4. A reference to the internal intrigues of the
rulers of Mantua in the 13th century.
5. Dante's Virgil contradicts the account of
Mantua's founding in *Aeneid* 10.198–200. It
is not clear why Dante has Virgil contradict
his own poem unless he is trying to clear Virgil
of any taint of himself being a magician (see
n. 2 to 9.23).

He said: "That one, whose beard flows from his cheeks
  and settles on his back and makes it dark,
  was (when the war stripped Greece of all its males, 108
so that the few there were still rocked in cradles)
  an augur who, with Calchas,[6] called the moment
  to cut the first ship's cable free at Aulis: 111
he is Eurypylus. I sang his story
  this way, somewhere in my high tragedy:
  you should know where—you know it, every line. 114
That other one, whose thighs are scarcely fleshed,
  was Michael Scot,[7] who most assuredly
  knew every trick of magic fraudulence. 117
See there Guido Bonatti; see Asdente,[8]
  who wishes now he had been more devoted
  to making shoes—too late now for repentance. 120
And see those wretched hags[9] who traded in
  needle, spindle, shuttle, for fortune-telling,
  and cast their spells with image-dolls and potions. 123
Now come along. Cain[1] with his thorn-bush straddles
  the confines of both hemispheres already
  and dips into the waves below Seville; 126
and the moon last night already was at full;
  and you should well remember that at times
  when you were lost in the dark wood she helped you." 129
And we were moving all the time he spoke.

CANTO XXI

*When the two reach the summit of the arch over the Fifth Bolgia, they see in the
ditch below the bubbling of boiling pitch. Virgil's sudden warning of danger fright-
ens the Pilgrim even before he sees a black devil rushing toward them, with a sinner
slung over his shoulder. From the bridge the devil flings the sinner into the pitch,
where he is poked at and tormented by the family of Malebranche devils. Virgil,
advising his ward to hide behind a rock, crosses the bridge to face the devils alone.
They threaten him with their pitchforks, but when he announces to their leader,
Malacoda, that Heaven has willed that he lead another through Hell, the devil's arrogance collapses. Virgil calls the Pilgrim back to him. Scarmiglione, who tries to take
a poke at him, is rebuked by his leader, who tells the travelers that the sixth arch is
broken here but farther on they will find another bridge to cross. He chooses a squad
of his devils to escort them there: Alichino, Calcabrina, Cagnazzo, Barbariccia,*

---

6. Calchas and Eurypylus were prophets (or
augurs) involved in the Trojan War; here Virgil
says that they determined when the Greeks
were to set out for the war from the island of
Aulis, although *Aeneid 2* gives a different
account.
7. A famous scientist, philosopher, and astrologer from Scotland, Scot spent many years at
the court of Frederick II (10.119) in Palermo
and died in 1235.
8. A shoemaker famous as a soothsayer in

13th-century Italy. Guido Bonatti: an astrologer at the court of Guido da Montefeltro (see
canto 27).
9. Common soothsayers and potion makers.
1. Popular belief held that God placed Cain
in the moon after the murder of Abel; "Cain
with his thorn-bush" means the moon with its
spots, which is now setting at the western edge
of the Northern Hemisphere. Overhead, in
Jerusalem, it is the dawn of Holy Saturday.

Libicocco, Draghignazzo, Ciriatto, Graffiacane, Farfarello, and Rubicante. The Pilgrim's suspicion about their unsavory escorts is brushed aside by his guide, and the squad starts off, giving an obscene salute to their captain, who returns their salute with a fart.

From this bridge to the next we walked and talked
   of things my Comedy does not care to tell;
   and when we reached the summit of the arch,   3
we stopped to see the next fosse[2] of Malebolge
   and to hear more lamentation voiced in vain:
   I saw that it was very strangely dark!   6
In the vast and busy shipyard of the Venetians[3]
   there boils all winter long a tough, thick pitch
   that is used to caulk the ribs of unsound ships.   9
Since winter will not let them sail, they toil:
   some build new ships, others repair the old ones,
   plugging the planks come loose from many sailings,   12
some hammer at the bow, some at the stern,
   one carves the oars while others twine the ropes,
   one mends the jib, one patches up the mainsail;   15
here, too, but heated by God's art, not fire,
   a sticky tar was boiling in the ditch
   that smeared the banks with viscous residue.   18
I saw it there, but I saw nothing in it,
   except the rising of the boiling bubbles
   breathing in air to burst and sink again.   21
I stood intently gazing there below,
   my guide, shouting to me: "Watch out, watch out!"
   took hold of me and drew me to his side.   24
I turned my head like one who can't resist
   looking to see what makes him run away
   (his body's strength draining with sudden fear),   27
but, looking back, does not delay his flight;
   and I saw coming right behind our backs,
   rushing along the ridge, a devil, black!   30
His face, his look, how frightening it was!
   With outstretched wings he skimmed along the rock,
   and every single move he made was cruel;   33
on one of his high-hunched and pointed shoulders
   he had a sinner slung by both his thighs,
   held tightly clawed at the tendons of his heels.   36
He shouted from our bridge: "Hey, Malebranche,[4]
   here's one of Santa Zita's elders for you!
   You stick him under—I'll go back for more;   39
I've got that city stocked with the likes of him,

---

2. Ditch or pouch.
3. The huge shipyard at Venice was called the Arsenal.
4. "Malebranche" (Evil-Claws) is the generic name for the devils in this ditch, and each has a proper name as well (lines 76, 105, 118–23). The elders of Saint Zita in Lucca (a town near Florence) were ten citizens who ran the government.

they're all a bunch of grafters, save Bonturo![5]
You can change a 'no' to 'yes' for cash in Lucca."   42
He flung him in, then from the flinty cliff
    sprang off. No hound unleashed to chase a thief
    could have taken off with greater speed than he.   45
That sinner plunged, then floated up stretched out,
    and the devils underneath the bridge all shouted:
    "You shouldn't imitate the Holy Face!   48
The swimming's different here from in the Serchio![6]
    We have our grappling-hooks along with us—
    don't show yourself above the pitch, or else!"   51
With a hundred prongs or more they pricked him, shrieking:
    "You've got to do your squirming under cover,
    try learning how to cheat beneath the surface."   54
They were like cooks who make their scullery boys
    poke down into the caldron with their forks
    to keep the meat from floating to the top.   57
My master said: "We'd best not let them know
    that you are here with me; crouch down behind
    some jutting rock so that they cannot see you;   60
whatever insults they may hurl at me,
    you must not fear, I know how things are run here;
    I have been caught in as bad a fix before."[7]   63
He crossed the bridge and walked on past the end;
    as soon as he set foot on the sixth bank
    he forced himself to look as bold as possible.   66
With all the sound and fury that breaks loose
    when dogs rush out at some poor begging tramp,
    making him stop and beg from where he stands,   69
the ones who hid beneath the bridge sprang out
    and blocked him with a flourish of their pitchforks,
    but he shouted: "All of you behave yourselves!   72
Before you start to jab me with your forks,
    let one of you step forth to hear me out,
    and then decide if you still care to grapple."   75
They all cried out: "Let Malacoda[8] go!"
    One stepped forward—the others stood their ground—
    and moving, said, "What good will this do him?"   78
"Do you think, Malacoda," said my master,
    "that you would see me here, come all this way,
    against all opposition, and still safe,   81
without propitious fate and God's permission?
    Now let us pass, for it is willed in Heaven
    that I lead another by this savage path."   84
With this the devil's arrogance collapsed,

---

5. A current official in Lucca, Bonturo Datí
was in fact known as the most corrupt of all;
the devil is being ironic.
6. The Serchio is a river near Lucca. The
Holy Face of Lucca was a venerated icon.

7. Virgil may be referring to his difficulties
with the devils in 8.82–130, when he and
Dante tried to enter the city of Dis.
8. Evil-Tail.

his pitchfork, too, dropped right down to his feet,
    as he announced to all: "Don't touch this man!"   87
"You, hiding over there," my guide called me,
    "behind the bridge's rocks, curled up and quiet,
    come back to me, you may return in safety."   90
At his words I rose and then I ran to him
    and all the devils made a movement forward;
    I feared they would not really keep their pact.   93
(I remember seeing soldiers under truce,
    as they left the castle of Caprona, frightened
    to be passing in the midst of such an enemy.)[9]   96
I drew up close to him, as close as possible,
    and did not take my eyes from all those faces
    that certainly had nothing good about them.   99
Their prongs were aimed at me, and one was saying:
    "Now do I let him have it in the rump?"
They answered all for one: "Sure, stick him good!"   102
But the devil who had spoken with my guide
    was quick to spin around and scream an order:
    "At ease there, take it easy, Scarmiglione!"   105
Then he said to us: "You cannot travel straight
    across this string of bridges, for the sixth arch
    lies broken at the bottom of its ditch;[1]   108
if you have made your mind up to proceed,
    you must continue on along this ridge;
    not far, you'll find a bridge that crosses it.[2]   111
Five hours more and it will be one thousand,
    two hundred sixty-six years and a day
    since the bridge-way here fell crumbling to the ground.[3]   114
I plan to send a squad of mine that way
    to see that no one airs himself down there;
    go along with them, they will not misbehave.   117
Front and center, Alichino, Calcabrina,"
    he shouted his commands, "you too, Cagnazzo;
    Barbariccia, you be captain of the squad.   120
Take Libicocco with you and Draghignazzo,
    toothy Ciriatto and Graffiacane,
    Farfarello and our crazy Rubicante.[4]   123
Now tour the ditch, inspect the boiling tar;
    these two shall have safe passage to the bridge
    connecting den to den without a break."   126

9. A battle outside Florence in 1289, in which Dante may have taken part.
1. The bridge across the fifth ditch was smashed, as Malacoda explains, by the earthquake that occurred at the time of the crucifixion.
2. As the travelers discover, this is a lie.
3. According to medieval tradition, Christ's death on the cross occurred on Good Friday at noon, in his thirty-third year, which would be 34 C.E.; the time at which Dante and Virgil are in this fifth ditch of Malebolge is 7 A.M. of Holy Saturday, 1300, which is 1266 years plus one day, less five hours later.
4. These names—like Scarmiglione in line 105—imply raffish irreverence in general, although some do have specific if ignoble meanings: Cagnazzo = "Big Dog," Barbariccia = "Curly Beard," Graffiacane = "Dog-Scratcher."

"O master, I don't like the looks of this,"
  I said, "let's go, just you and me, no escort,
  you know the way. I want no part of them!   129
If you're observant, as you usually are,
  why is it you don't see them grind their teeth
  and wink at one another?—we're in danger!"   132
And he to me: "I will not have you frightened;
  let them do all the grinding that they want,
  they do it for the boiling souls, not us."   135
Before they turned left-face along the bank
  each one gave their good captain a salute
  with farting tongue pressed tightly to his teeth,   138
and he blew back with his bugle of an ass-hole.

CANTO XXII

The note of grotesque comedy in the bolgia *of the* Malebranche *continues, with a comparison between Malacoda's salute to his soldiers and different kinds of military signals the Pilgrim has witnessed in his lifetime. He sees many Grafters squatting in the pitch, but as soon as the* Malebranche *draw near, they dive below the surface. One unidentified Navarrese, however, fails to escape and is hoisted up on Graffiacane's hooks;* Rubicante *and the other* Malebranche *start to tear into him, but Virgil, at his ward's request, manages to question him between torments. The sinner briefly tells his story, and then relates that he has left below in the pitch an Italian, Fra Gomita, a particularly adept grafter, who spends his time talking to Michel Zanche.*

The Navarrese sinner promises to lure some of his colleagues to the surface for the devils' amusement, if the tormentors will hide themselves for a moment. Cagnazzo is skeptical but Alichino agrees, and no sooner do the Malebranche *turn away than the crafty grafter dives below the pitch. Alichino flies after him, but too late; now Calcabrina rushes after Alichino and both struggle above the boiling pitch, and then fall in. Barbariccia directs the rescue operation as the two poets steal away.*

I have seen troops of horsemen breaking camp,
  opening the attack, or passing in review,
  I have even seen them fleeing for their lives;   3
I have seen scouts ride, exploring your terrain,
  O Aretines,[5] and I have seen raiding-parties
  and the clash of tournaments, the run of jousts—   6
to the tune of trumpets, to the ring of clanging bells,
  to the roll of drums, to the flash of flares on ramparts,
  to the accompaniment of every known device;   9
but I never saw cavalry or infantry
  or ships that sail by landmarks or by stars
  signaled to set off by such strange bugling!   12
So, on our way we went with those ten fiends.
  What savage company! But—in church, with saints—
  with rowdy good-for-nothings, in the tavern![6]   15

5. The people of Arezzo, a city south of   6. A popular proverb.
Florence.

My attention now was fixed upon the pitch
  to see the operations of this *bolgia*,
  and how the cooking souls got on down there. 18
Much like the dolphins that are said to surface
  with their backs arched to warn all men at sea
  to rig their ships for stormy seas ahead,[7] 21
so now and then a sinner's back would surface
  in order to alleviate his pain,
  then dive to hide as quick as lightning strikes. 24
Like squatting frogs along the ditch's edge,
  with just their muzzles sticking out of water,
  their legs and all the rest concealed below, 27
these sinners squatted all around their pond;
  but as soon as Barbariccia would approach
  they quickly ducked beneath the boiling pitch. 30
I saw (my heart still shudders at the thought)
  one lingering behind[8]—as it sometimes happens
  one frog remains while all the rest dive down – 33
and Graffiacane, standing in front of him,
  hooked and twirled him by his pitchy hair
  and hoisted him. He looked just like an otter! 36
By then I knew the names of all the fiends:
  I had listened carefully when they were chosen,
  each of them stepping forth to match his name. 39
"Hey, Rubicante, dig your claws down deep
  into his back and peel the skin off him,"
  this fiendish chorus egged him on with screams. 42
I said: "Master, will you, if you can, find out
  the name of that poor wretch who has just fallen
  into the cruel hands of his adversaries?" 45
My guide walked right up to the sinner's side
  and asked where he was from, and he replied:
  "I was born and bred in the kingdom of Navarre; 48
my mother gave me to a lord to serve,
  for she had me by some dishonest spendthrift
  who ran through all he owned and killed himself. 51
Then I became a servant in the household
  of good King Thibault. There I learned my graft,
  and now I pay my bill by boiling here." 54
Ciriatto, who had two tusks sticking out
  on both sides of his mouth, just like a boar's,
  let him feel how just one tusk could rip him open. 57
The mouse had fallen prey to evil cats,
  but Barbariccia locked him with his arms,
  shouting: "Get back while I've got hold of him!" 60
Then toward my guide he turned his face and said:

---

7. A common medieval belief.
8. The identity of this sinner is not known,
but he was employed in the household of
Thibaut II of Champagne, a man renowned
for his honesty who was also king of Navarre,
the area of Spain that is now Basque country.

"If you want more from him, keep questioning
  before he's torn to pieces by the others." 63
My guide went on: "Then tell me, do you know
  of some Italian stuck among these sinners
  beneath the pitch?" And he, "A second ago 66
I was with one who lived around those parts.
  Oh, I wish I were undercover with him now!
  I wouldn't have these hooks or claws to fear." 69
Libicocco cried: "We've waited long enough,"
  then with his fork he hooked the sinner's arm
  and, tearing at it, he pulled out a piece. 72
Draghignazzo, too, was anxious for some fun;
  he tried the wretch's leg, but their captain quickly
  spun around and gave them all a dirty look. 75
As soon as they calmed down a bit, my master
  began again to interrogate the wretch,
  who still was contemplating his new wound: 78
"Who was it, you were saying, that unluckily
  you left behind you when you came ashore?"
  "Gomita," he said, "the friar from Gallura,9 81
receptacle for every kind of fraud:
  when his lord's enemies were in his hands,
  the treatment they received delighted them: 84
he took their cash, and as he says, hushed up
  the case and let them off; none of his acts
  was petty grafting, all were of sovereign order. 87
He spends his time with don Michele Zanche
  of Logodoro, talking on and on
  about Sardinia—their tongues no worse for wear!1 90
Oh, but look how that one grins and grinds his teeth;
  I could tell you so much more, but I am afraid
  he is going to grate my scabby hide for me." 93
But their master-sergeant turned to Farfarello,
  whose wild eyes warned he was about to strike,
  shouting, "Get away, you filthy bird of prey." 96
"If you would like to see Tuscans or Lombards,"
  the frightened shade took up where he left off,
  "and have a talk with them, I'll bring some here; 99
but the Malebranche must back up a bit,
  or else those shades won't risk a surfacing;
  I, by myself, will bring you up a catch 102
of seven, without moving from this spot,
  just by whistling—that's our signal to the rest
  when one peers out and sees the coast is clear." 105
Cagnazzo raised his snout at such a story,
  then shook his head and said: "Listen to the trick
  he's cooked up to get off the hook by jumping!" 108

9. A friar who was chancellor of the Gallura district on the island of Sardinia. He was hanged by his master, a lord of Pisa, when it was discov-ered that he had sold prisoners their freedom.
1. Little is known of this sinner, except that he too was a Sardinian.

And he, full of the tricks his trade had taught him,
  said: "Tricky, I surely am, especially
  when it comes to getting friends into worse trouble."   111
But Alichin could not resist the challenge,
  and in spite of what the others thought, cried out:
  "If you jump, I won't come galloping for you,   114
I've got my wings to beat you to the pitch.
  We'll clear this ledge and wait behind that slope.
  Let's see if one of you can outmatch us!"   117
Now listen, Reader, here's a game that's strange:
  they all turned toward the slope, and first to turn
  was the fiend who from the start opposed the game.   120
The Navarrese had perfect sense of timing:
  feet planted on the ground, in a flash he jumped,
  the devil's plan was foiled, and he was free.   123
The squad was stung with shame but most of all
  the one who brought this blunder to perfection;[2]
  he swooped down, howling, "Now I've got you caught!"   126
Little good it did, for wings could not outstrip
  the flight of terror: down the sinner dived
  and up the fiend was forced to strain his chest   129
like a falcon swooping down on a wild duck:
  the duck dives quickly out of sight, the falcon
  must fly back up dejected and defeated.   132
In the meantime, Calcabrina, furious,
  also took off, hoping the shade would make it,
  so he could pick a fight with his companion.   135
And when he saw the grafter hit the pitch,
  he turned his claws to grapple with his brother,
  and they tangled in mid-air above the ditch;   138
but the other was a full-fledged hawk as well
  and used his claws on him, and both of them
  went plunging straight into the boiling pond.   141
The heat was quick to make them separate,
  but there seemed no way of getting out of there;
  their wings were clogged and could not lift them up.   144
Barbariccia, no less peeved than all his men,
  sent four fiends flying to the other shore
  with their equipment at top speed; instantly,   147
some here, some there, they took the posts assigned them.
  They stretched their hooks to reach the pitch-dipped pair,
  who were by now deep-fried within their crusts.   150
And there we left them, all messed up that way.

CANTO XXIII

The antics of Ciampolo, the Navarrese, and the Malebranche *bring to the Pilgrim's mind the fable of the frog, the mouse, and the hawk—and that in turn reminds him of the immediate danger he and Virgil are in from the angry* Malebranche. *Virgil senses the danger too, and grabbing his ward as a mother would her child, he dashes*

2. Alichin.

to the edge of the bank and slides down the rocky slope into the Sixth Bolgia—not a
moment too soon, for at the top of the slope they see the angry Malebranche. When
the Pilgrim looks around him he sees weeping shades slowly marching in single file,
each one covered from head to foot with a golden cloak lined with lead, which
weights them down. These are the Hypocrites. Two in this group identify themselves
as Catalano de' Malavolti and Loderingo degli Andalò, two Jovial Friars. The Pil-
grim is about to address them when he sees the shade of Caiaphas (the evil coun-
selor who advised Pontius Pilate to crucify Christ), crucified and transfixed by three
stakes to the ground. Virgil discovers from the two friars that in order to leave this
bolgia they must climb up a rockslide; he also learns that this is the only bolgia over
which the bridge is broken. Virgil is angry with himself for having believed Mala-
coda's lie about the bridge over the Sixth Bolgia (Canto XXI, iii).

In silence, all alone, without an escort,
  we moved along, one behind the other,
  like minor friars[3] bent upon a journey.   3
I was thinking over one of Aesop's fables[4]
  that this recent skirmish had brought back to mind,
  where he tells the story of the frog and mouse;   6
for "yon" and "there" could not be more alike
  than the fable and the fact, if one compares
  the start and finish of both incidents.   9
As from one thought another often rises,
  so this thought gave quick birth to still another,
  and then the fear I first had felt was doubled.   12
I was thinking: "Since these fiends, on our account,
  were tricked and mortified by mockery,
  they certainly will be more than resentful;   15
with rage now added to their evil instincts,
  they will hunt us down with all the savagery
  of dogs about to pounce upon the hare."   18
I felt my body's skin begin to tighten—
  I was so frightened!—and I kept looking back:
  "O master," I said, "if you do not hide   21
both of us, and very quick, I am afraid
  of the Malebranche—right now they're on our trail—
  I feel they're there, I think I hear them now."   24
And he replied: "Even if I were a mirror
  I could not reflect your outward image faster
  than your inner thoughts transmit themselves to me.   27
In fact, just now they joined themselves with mine,
  and since they were alike in birth and form,
  I decided to unite them toward one goal: 30
if the right-hand bank should slope in such a way
  as to allow us to descend to the next *bolgia,*
  we could escape that chase we have imagined."   33

3. Franciscan friars, who were known as "minor" or "lesser" friars because Francis of Assisi, the founder of the order, insisted upon humility.
4. The fable that Dante seems to be referring to tells how a frog offers to ferry a mouse across a river, then halfway over tries to drown him, only to be seized by a kite (a hawklike bird) while the mouse escapes.

He had hardly finished telling me his plan
   when I saw them coming with their wings wide open
   not too far off, and now they meant to get us!   36
My guide instinctively caught hold of me,
   like a mother waking to some warning sound,
   who sees the rising flames are getting close   39
and grabs her son and runs—she does not wait
   the short time it would take to put on something;
   she cares not for herself, only for him.   42
And over the edge, then down the stony bank
   he slid, on his back, along the sloping rock
   that walls the higher side of the next *bolgia*.   45
Water that turns a mill wheel never ran
   the narrow sluice at greater speed, not even
   at the point before it hits the paddle-blades,[5]   48
than down that sloping border my guide slid,
   bearing me with him, clasping me to his chest
   as though I were his child, not his companion.   51
His feet had hardly touched rock bottom, when
   there they were, the ten of them, above us
   on the height; but now there was no need to fear: 54
High Providence that willed for them to be
   the ministers in charge of the fifth ditch
   also willed them powerless to leave their realm.   57
And now, down there, we found a painted people,
   slow-motioned; step by step, they walked their round
   in tears, and seeming wasted by fatigue.   60
All were wearing cloaks with hoods pulled low
   covering the eyes (the style was much the same
   as those the Benedictines wear at Cluny),[6]   63
dazzling, gilded cloaks outside, but inside
   they were lined with lead, so heavy that the capes
   King Frederick used, compared to these, were straw.[7]   66
O cloak of everlasting weariness!
   We turned again, as usual, to the left
   and moved with them, those souls lost in their mourning;   69
but with their weight that tired-out race of shades
   paced on so slowly that we found ourselves
   in new company with every step we took;   72
and so I asked my guide: "Please look around
   and see, as we keep walking, if you find
   someone whose name or deeds are known to me."   75
And one who overheard me speaking Tuscan
   cried out somewhere behind us: "Not so fast,
   you there, rushing ahead through this heavy air,   78

5. A mill built on the land while the water of the river turns its wheel.
6. One of the largest monasteries in Europe, located in Burgundy in France; the Benedictines are monks who follow the Rule of St. Benedict (d. 587), one of the founders of monasticism.
7. Frederick II (see n. 9 to 10.119) was reported to have punished traitors by encasing them in lead and throwing them into heated cauldrons.

perhaps from me you can obtain an answer."
  At this my guide turned toward me saying, "Stop,
  and wait for him, then match your pace with his."   81
I paused and saw two shades with straining faces
  revealing their mind's haste to join my side,
  but the weight they bore and the crowded road delayed them.   84
When they arrived, they looked at me sideways
  and for some time, without exchanging words;
  then they turned to one another and were saying: 87
"He seems alive, the way his throat is moving,
  and if both are dead, what privilege allows them
  to walk uncovered by the heavy cloak?"   90
Then they spoke to me: "O Tuscan who has come
  to visit the college of the sullen hypocrites,
  do not disdain to tell us who you are."   93
I answered them: "I was born and I grew up
  in the great city on the lovely Arno's shore,
  and I have the body I have always had.   96
But who are you, distilling tears of grief,
  so many I see running down your cheeks?
  And what kind of pain is this that it can glitter?"   99
One of them answered: "The orange-gilded cloaks
  are thick with lead so heavy that it makes us,
  who are the scales it hangs on, creak as we walk.   102
Jovial Friars we were, both from Bologna.
  My name was Catalano, his, Loderingo,
  and both of us were chosen by your city,   105
that usually would choose one man alone,
  to keep the peace. Evidence of what we were
  may still be seen around Gardingo's parts."[8]   108
I began: "O Friars, all your wretchedness . . ."
  but said no more; I couldn't, for I saw
  one crucified with three stakes on the ground.[9]   111
And when he saw me all his body writhed,
  and through his beard he heaved out sighs of pain;
  then Friar Catalano, who watched the scene,   114
remarked: "That impaled figure you see there
  advised the Pharisees it was expedient
  to sacrifice one man for all the people.   117
Naked he lies stretched out across the road,
  as you can see, and he must feel the load
  of every weight that steps on him to cross.   120
His father-in-law[1] and the other council members,

8. Gardingo: a district in Florence, was destroyed by a civil war incited by their meddling in Florentine affairs. Jovial Friars: a military and religious order in Bologna called the Knights of the Blessed Virgin Mary, or popularly the Jovial Friars because of the laxity of its rules. The members were meant to fight only in order to protect the weak and enforce peace. Catalano and Loderingo were two citizens of Bologna who were involved in founding the Jovial Friars in 1261.
9. This is Caiaphas, the high priest under Pontius Pilate who advised that Christ be crucified (John 11.45–52).
1. Annas: see John 18.13.

who were the seed of evil for all Jews,
   are racked the same way all along this ditch."
                      123
And I saw Virgil staring down amazed
   at this body stretching out in crucifixion,
   so vilely punished in the eternal exile.   126
Then he looked up and asked one of the friars:
   "Could you please tell us, if your rule permits:
   is there a passage-way on the right, somewhere,   129
by which the two of us may leave this place
   without summoning one of those black angels
   to come down here and raise us from this pit?"   132
He answered: "Closer than you might expect,
   a ridge jutting out from the base of the great circle
   extends, and bridges every hideous ditch   135
except this one, whose arch is totally smashed
   and crosses nowhere; but you can climb up
   its massive ruins that slope against this bank."   138
My guide stood there awhile, his head bent low,
   then said: "He told a lie about this business,
   that one who hooks the sinners over there."[2]   141
And the friar: "Once, in Bologna, I heard discussed
   the devil's many vices; one of them is
   that he tells lies and is father of all lies."[3]   144
In haste, taking great strides, my guide walked off,
   his face revealing traces of his anger.
   I turned and left the heavy-weighted souls   147
to make my way behind those cherished footprints.

CANTO XXIV

*After an elaborate simile describing Virgil's anger and the return of his composure,
the two begin the difficult, steep ascent up the rocks of the fallen bridge. The Pilgrim can barely make it to the top even with Virgil's help, and after the climb he sits
down to catch his breath; but his guide urges him on, and they make their way back
to the bridge over the Seventh Bolgia. From the bridge confused sounds can be
heard rising from the darkness below. Virgil agrees to take his pupil down to the
edge of the eighth encircling bank, and once they are there, the scene reveals a terrible confusion of serpents, and Thieves madly running.*

   *Suddenly a snake darts out and strikes a sinner's neck, whereupon he flares up,
turning into a heap of crumbling ashes; then the ashes gather together into the
shape of a man. The metamorphosed sinner reveals himself to be Vanni Fucci, a
Pistoiese condemned for stealing the treasure of the sacristy of the church of San
Zeno at Pistoia. He makes a prophecy about the coming strife in Florence.*

In the season of the newborn year, when the sun
   renews its rays beneath Aquarius[4]
   and nights begin to last as long as days,   3

2. See 21.111.
3. For this description of the devil, see John
8.44.

4. January 21–February 21.

at the time the hoarfrost paints upon the ground
   the outward semblance of his snow-white sister[5]
   (but the color from his brush soon fades away),
the peasant wakes, gets up, goes out and sees
   the fields all white. No fodder for his sheep!
   He smites his thighs in anger and goes back   9
into his shack and, pacing up and down,
   complains, poor wretch, not knowing what to do;
   once more he goes outdoors, and hope fills him   12
again when he sees the world has changed its face
   in so little time, and he picks up his crook
   and out to pasture drives his sheep to graze—   15
just so I felt myself lose heart to see
   my master's face wearing a troubled look,
   and as quickly came the salve to heal my sore: 18
for when we reached the shattered heap of bridge,
   my leader turned to me with that sweet look
   of warmth I first saw at the mountain's foot.   21
He opened up his arms (but not before
   he had carefully studied how the ruins lay
   and found some sort of plan) to pick me up.   24
Like one who works and thinks things out ahead,
   always ready for the next move he will make,
   so, while he raised me up toward one great rock,   27
he had already singled out another,
   saying, "Now get a grip on that rock there,
   but test it first to see it holds your weight."   30
It was no road for one who wore a cloak!
   Even though I had his help and he weighed nothing,
   we could hardly lift ourselves from crag to crag.   33
And had it not been that the bank we climbed
   was lower than the one we had slid down[6]—
   I cannot speak for him—but I for one   36
surely would have quit. But since the Evil Pits
   slope toward the yawning well that is the lowest,
   each valley is laid out in such a way   39
that one bank rises higher than the next.
   We somehow finally reached the point above
   where the last of all that rock was shaken loose.   42
My lungs were so pumped out of breath by the time
   I reached the top, I could not go on farther,
   and instantly I sat down where I was.   45
"Come on, shake off the covers of this sloth,"
   the master said, "for sitting softly cushioned,
   or tucked in bed, is no way to win fame;   48
and without it man must waste his life away,
   leaving such traces of what he was on earth
   as smoke in wind and foam upon the water.   51

5. I.e., snow.
6. Because the whole of the eighth circle is tilted downward, the downside wall of each ditch is lower than that on the upside.

Stand up! Dominate this weariness of yours
  with the strength of soul that wins in every battle
  if it does not sink beneath the body's weight.   54
Much steeper stairs than these we'll have to climb;[7]
  we have not seen enough of sinners yet!
  If you understand me, act, learn from my words."   57
At this I stood up straight and made it seem
  I had more breath than I began to breathe,
  and said: "Move on, for I am strong and ready."   60
We climbed and made our way along the bridge,
  which was jagged, tight and difficult to cross,
  and steep—far more than any we had climbed.   63
Not to seem faint, I spoke while I was climbing;
  then came a voice from the depths of the next chasm,
  a voice unable to articulate.   66
I don't know what it said, even though I stood
  at the very top of the arch that crosses there;
  to me it seemed whoever spoke, spoke running.   69
I was bending over, but no living eyes
  could penetrate the bottom of that darkness;
  therefore I said: "Master, why not go down   72
this bridge onto the next encircling bank,[8]
  for I hear sounds I cannot understand,
  and I look down but cannot see a thing."   75
"No other answer," he replied, "I give you
  than doing what you ask, for a fit request
  is answered best in silence and in deed."   78
From the bridge's height we came down to the point
  where it ends and joins the edge of the eighth bank,
  and then the *bolgia* opened up to me:[9]   81
down there I saw a terrible confusion
  of serpents, all of such a monstrous kind
  the thought of them still makes my blood run cold.[1]   84
Let all the sands of Libya boast no longer,
  for though she breeds chelydri and jaculi,
  phareans, cenchres, and head-tailed amphisbenes,   87
she never bred so great a plague of venom,
  not even if combined with Ethiopia
  or all the sands that lie by the Red Sea.   90
Within this cruel and bitterest abundance
  people ran terrified and naked, hopeless
  of finding hiding-holes or heliotrope.[2]   93
Their hands were tied behind their backs with serpents,
  which pushed their tails and heads around the loins
  and coiled themselves in knots around the front.   96

7. Both the climb from the pit of Hell back to
Earth and the climb up Mount Purgatory.
8. Of the seventh ditch.
9. They cross the bridge over the seventh
ditch and then climb down the wall between
the seventh and eighth ditches.

1. The following list of exotic serpents derives
from a description by the Roman poet Lucan
(39–65 C.E.) of the plagues of Libya.
2. A fictitious stone that was supposed to
make the bearer invisible.

And then—at a sinner running by our bank
　　a snake shot out and, striking, hit his mark:
　　right where the neck attaches to the shoulder. 99
No *o* or *i* was ever quicker put
　　by pen to paper than he flared up and burned,
　　and turned into a heap of crumbled ash; 102
and then, these ashes scattered on the ground
　　began to come together on their own
　　and quickly take the form they had before: 105
precisely so, philosophers declare,
　　the phoenix dies to be reborn again
　　as she approaches her five-hundredth year;[3] 108
alive, she does not feed on herbs or grain,
　　but on teardrops of frankincense and balm,
　　and wraps herself to die in nard and myrrh. 111
As a man in a fit will fall, not knowing why
　　(perhaps some hidden demon pulls him down,
　　or some oppilation chokes his vital spirits), 114
then, struggling to his feet, will look around,
　　confused and overwhelmed by the great anguish
　　he has suffered, moaning as he stares about— 117
so did this sinner when he finally rose.
　　Oh, how harsh the power of the Lord can be,
　　raining in its vengeance blows like these! 120
My guide asked him to tell us who he was,
　　and he replied: "It's not too long ago
　　I rained from Tuscany to this fierce gullet. 123
I loved the bestial life more than the human,
　　like the bastard that I was; I'm Vanni Fucci,
　　the beast! Pistoia was my fitting den."[4] 126
I told my guide: "Tell him not to run away;
　　ask him what sin has driven him down here,
　　for I knew him as a man of bloody rage." 129
The sinner heard and did not try to feign;
　　directing straight at me his mind and face,
　　he reddened with a look of ugly shame, 132
and said: "That you have caught me by surprise
　　here in this wretched *bolgia*, makes me grieve
　　more than the day I lost my other life. 135
Now I am forced to answer what you ask:
　　I am stuck so far down here because of theft:
　　I stole the treasure of the sacristy— 138
a crime falsely attributed to another.

3. The "phoenix" is a mythical bird that is supposed to burn to death in its own nest every five hundred years, after which either itself or its son is reborn from the ashes; for these details, including its diet of exotic herbs and its funeral preparations (lines 110–11), see Ovid, *Metamorphoses* 15. In medieval mythography the phoenix was often taken as a symbol of Christ. 4. The illegitimate son of a noble father of Pistoia, a town just north of Florence: known as "the beast" because of the extravagance of his misbehavior. He reputedly robbed a church in Pistoia, a crime for which a similarly named man was wrongly hanged.

I don't want you to rejoice at having seen me,
 if ever you escape from these dark pits,   141
so open your ears and hear my prophecy:[5]
 Pistoia first shall be stripped of all its Blacks,
 and Florence then shall change its men and laws;   144
from Valdimagra Mars shall thrust a bolt
 of lightning wrapped in thick, foreboding clouds,
 then bolt and clouds will battle bitterly   147
in a violent storm above Piceno's fields,
 where rapidly the bolt will burst the cloud,
 and no White will escape without his wounds.   150
And I have told you this so you will suffer!"

CANTO XXV

*The wrathful Vanni Fucci directs an obscene gesture to God, whereupon he is
attacked by several snakes, which coil about him, tying him so tight that he cannot
move a muscle. As soon as he flees, the centaur Cacus gallops by with a fire-breathing
dragon on his back, and following close behind are three shades, concerned because
they cannot find Cianfa—who soon appears as a snake and attacks Agnèl; the two
merge into one hideous monster, which then steals off. Next, Guercio, in the form of
a snake, strikes Buoso, and the two exchange shapes. Only Puccio Sciancato is left
unchanged.*

When he had finished saying this, the thief
 shaped his fists into figs[6] and raised them high
 and cried: "Here, God, I've shaped them just for you!"   3
From then on all those snakes became my friends,
 for one of them at once coiled round his neck
 as if to say, "That's all you're going to say,"   6
while another twisted round his arms in front;
 it tied itself into so tight a knot,
 between the two he could not move a muscle.   9
Pistoia, ah, Pistoia! why not resolve
 to burn yourself to ashes, ending all,
 since you have done more evil than your founders?[7]   12
Throughout the circles of this dark inferno
 I saw no shade so haughty toward his God,
 not even he who fell from Thebes' high walls.[8]   15
Without another word he fled, and then
 I saw a raging centaur gallop up
 roaring: "Where is he, where is that untamed beast?"   18
I think that all Maremma[9] does not have

5. Vanni Fucci now prophesies, in the enigmatic terms appropriate to the genre, that the party of the Blacks (of which he was a member) will first be expelled from Pistoia by the Whites, but that then the Whites of Florence (Dante's party) will be defeated. The prophecy refers to events that occurred in either 1302 or 1306.
6. An obscene gesture made by thrusting a protruding thumb between the first and second fingers of a closed fist.
7. The most important founder of Pistoia was Catiline, who was a traitor against the Roman Republic in the 1st century B.C.E.
8. Capaneus (see 14.46–75).
9. A region infested with snakes; see 13.8.

as many snakes as he had on his back,
   right up to where his human form begins.   21
Upon his shoulders, just behind the nape,
   a dragon with its wings spread wide was crouching
   and spitting fire at whoever came its way.   24
My master said to me: "That one is Cacus,[1]
   who more than once in the grotto far beneath
   Mount Aventine spilled blood to fill a lake.   27
He does not go the same road as his brothers
   because of the cunning way he committed theft
   when he stole his neighbor's famous cattle-herd;   30
and then his evil deeds came to an end
   beneath the club of Hercules, who struck
   a hundred blows, and he, perhaps, felt ten."   33
While he was speaking Cacus galloped off;
   at the same time three shades appeared below us;
   my guide and I would not have seen them there   36
if they had not cried out: "Who are you two?"
   At this we cut our conversation short
   to give our full attention to these three.   39
I didn't know who they were, but then it happened,
   as often it will happen just by chance,
   that one of them was forced to name another: 42
"Where did Cianfa[2] go off to?" he asked. And then,
   to keep my guide from saying anything,
   I put my finger tight against my lips.   45
Now if, my reader, you should hesitate
   to believe what I shall say, there's little wonder,
   for I, the witness, scarcely can believe it.   48
While I was watching them, all of a sudden
   a serpent—and it had six feet—shot up
   and hooked one of these wretches with all six.   51
With the middle feet it hugged the sinner's stomach
   and, with the front ones, grabbed him by the arms,
   and bit him first through one cheek, then the other;   54
the serpent spread its hind feet round both thighs,
   then stuck its tail between the sinner's legs,
   and up against his back the tail slid stiff.   57
No ivy ever grew to any tree
   so tight entwined, as the way that hideous beast
   had woven in and out its limbs with his;   60
and then both started melting like hot wax
   and, fusing, they began to mix their colors
   (so neither one seemed what he was before),   63
just as a brownish tint, ahead of flame,
   creeps up a burning page that is not black
   completely, even though the white is dying.   66
The other two who watched began to shout:

---

1. A monster who lived in a cave on Mount
Aventine in Rome and was killed by Hercules,   from whom he stole cattle; see *Aeneid* 8.
   2. A noble Florentine, reputedly a thief.

"O Agnèl![3] If you could see how you are changing!
   You're not yourself, and you're not both of you!"   69
The two heads had already fused to one
   and features from each flowed and blended into
   one face where two were lost in one another;   72
two arms of each were four blurred strips of flesh;
   and thighs with legs, then stomach and the chest
   sprouted limbs that human eyes have never seen.   75
Each former likeness now was blotted out:
   both, and neither one it seemed—this picture
   of deformity. And then it sneaked off slowly.   78
Just as a lizard darting from hedge to hedge,
   under the stinging lash of the dog-days' heat,
   zips across the road, like a flash of lightning,   81
so, rushing toward the two remaining thieves,
   aiming at their guts, a little serpent,
   fiery with rage and black as pepper-corn,   84
shot up and sank its teeth in one of them,
   right where the embryo receives its food,
   then back it fell and lay stretched out before him.   87
The wounded thief stared speechless at the beast,
   and standing motionless began to yawn
   as though he needed sleep, or had a fever.   90
The snake and he were staring at each other;
   one from his wound, the other from its mouth
   fumed violently, and smoke with smoke was mingling.   93
Let Lucan from this moment on be silent,
   who tells of poor Nasidius and Sabellus,[4]
   and wait to hear what I still have in store;   96
and Ovid, too, with his Cadmus and Arethusa[5]—
   though he metamorphosed one into a snake,
   the other to a fountain, I feel no envy,   99
for never did he interchange two beings
   face to face so that both forms were ready
   to exchange their substance, each one for the other's,   102
an interchange of perfect symmetry:
   the serpent split its tail into a fork,
   and the wounded sinner drew his feet together;   105
the legs, with both the thighs, closed in to join
   and in a short time fused, so that the juncture
   didn't show signs of ever having been there,   108
the while the cloven tail assumed the features
   that the other one was losing, and its skin
   was growing soft, the other's getting scaly;   111
I saw his arms retreating to the armpits,
   and the reptile's two front feet, that had been short,
   began to stretch the length the man's had shortened;   114
the beast's hind feet then twisted round each other

3. Another noble Florentine thief.
4. Two soldiers bitten by serpents in Lucan's
Pharsalia.

5. See *Metamorphoses* 4.

and turned into the member man conceals,
while from the wretch's member grew two legs. 117
The smoke from each was swirling round the other,
exchanging colors, bringing out the hair
where there was none, and stripping off the other's. 120
The one rose up, the other sank, but neither
dissolved the bond between their evil stares,
fixed eye to eye, exchanging face for face; 123
the standing creature's face began receding
toward the temples; from the excess stuff pulled back,
the ears were growing out of flattened cheeks, 126
while from the excess flesh that did not flee
the front, a nose was fashioned for the face,
and lips puffed out to just the normal size. 129
The prostrate creature strains his face out long
and makes his ears withdraw into his head,
the way a snail pulls in its horns. The tongue, 132
that once had been one piece and capable
of forming words, divides into a fork,
while the other's fork heals up. The smoke subsides. 135
The soul that had been changed into a beast
went hissing off along the valley's floor,
the other close behind him, spitting words. 138
Then he turned his new-formed back on him and said
to the shade left standing there: "Let Buoso run
the valley on all fours, the way I did."[6] 141
Thus I saw the cargo of the seventh hold
exchange and interchange; and let the strangeness
of it all excuse me, if my pen has failed. 144
And though this spectacle confused my eyes
and stunned my mind, the two thieves could not flee
so secretly I did not recognize 147
that one was certainly Puccio Sciancato[7]
(and he alone, of that company of three
that first appeared, did not change to something else), 150
the other, he who made you mourn, Gaville.[8]

CANTO XXVI

From the ridge high above the Eighth Bolgia can be perceived a myriad of flames
flickering far below, and Virgil explains that within each flame is the suffering soul
of a Deceiver. One flame, divided at the top, catches the Pilgrim's eye and he is told
that within it are jointly punished Ulysses and Diomed. Virgil questions the pair for
the benefit of the Pilgrim. Ulysses responds with the famous narrative of his last voy-
age, during which he passed the Pillars of Hercules and sailed the forbidden sea
until he saw a mountain shape, from which came suddenly a whirlwind that spun
his ship around three times and sank it.

6. The identity of this Buoso is uncertain.
7. This third thief is also a noble Florentine.
8. The "little serpent" of line 83 above is now
identified as Francesco de Cavalcanti, a

Florentine nobleman who lived in Gaville: a
town south of Florence. When he was murdered by his townsmen, his kinsmen took brutal revenge.

Be joyful, Florence, since you are so great
   that your outstretched wings beat over land and sea,
   and your name is spread throughout the realm of Hell!   3
I was ashamed to find among the thieves
   five of your most eminent citizens,[9]
   a fact which does you very little honor.   6
But if early morning dreams have any truth,
   you will have the fate, in not too long a time,
   that Prato and the others crave for you.[1]   9
And were this the day, it would not be too soon!
   Would it had come to pass, since pass it must!
   The longer the delay, the more my grief.   12
We started climbing up the stairs of boulders
   that had brought us to the place from where we watched;
   my guide went first and pulled me up behind him.   15
We went along our solitary way
   among the rocks, among the ridge's crags,
   where the foot could not advance without the hand.   18
I know that I grieved then, and now again
   I grieve when I remember what I saw,
   and more than ever I restrain my talent   21
lest it run a course that virtue has not set;
   for if a lucky star or something better
   has given me this good, I must not misuse it.   24
As many fireflies (in the season when
   the one who lights the world hides his face least,
   in the hour when the flies yield to mosquitoes)   27
as the peasant on the hillside at his ease
   sees, flickering in the valley down below,
   where perhaps he gathers grapes or tills the soil—   30
with just so many flames all the eighth *bolgia*
   shone brilliantly, as I became aware
   when at last I stood where the depths were visible.   33
As he[2] who was avenged by bears beheld
   Elijah's chariot at its departure,
   when the rearing horses took to flight toward Heaven,   36
and though he tried to follow with his eyes,
   he could not see more than the flame alone
   like a small cloud once it had risen high—   39
so each flame moves itself along the throat
   of the abyss, none showing what it steals
   but each one stealing nonetheless a sinner.   42
I was on the bridge, leaning far over—so far
   that if I had not grabbed some jut of rock
   I could easily have fallen to the bottom.   45

9. Cianfa (25.43), Agnello (25.68), Francesco (25.82, 149), Buoso (25.140), and Puccio (25.148) are all Florentines.
1. A town just north of Florence, on the way to Pistoia. The reason for this threat is unclear.

2. Elisha, an Old Testament prophet, was mocked by children, who were then attacked by bears. He saw the ascent to heaven of the prophet Elijah in his chariot and continued Elijah's mission: 2 Kings 2.1–25.

And my guide, who saw me so absorbed, explained:
"There are souls concealed within these moving fires,
each one swathed in his burning punishment." 48
"O master," I replied, "from what you say
I know now I was right; I had guessed already
it might be so, and I was about to ask you: 51
Who's in that flame with its tip split in two,
like that one which once sprang up from the pyre
where Eteocles was placed beside his brother?"[3] 54
He said: "Within, Ulysses and Diomed[4]
are suffering in anger with each other,
just vengeance makes them march together now. 57
And they lament inside one flame the ambush
of the horse become the gateway that allowed
the Romans' noble seed[5] to issue forth. 60
Therein they mourn the trick that caused the grief
of Deïdamia,[6] who still weeps for Achilles;
and there they pay for the Palladium." 63
"If it is possible for them to speak
from within those flames," I said, "master, I pray
and repray you—let my prayer be like a thousand— 66
that you do not forbid me to remain
until the two-horned flame comes close to us;
you see how I bend toward it with desire!" 69
"Your prayer indeed is worthy of highest praise,"
he said to me, "and therefore I shall grant it;
but see to it your tongue refrains from speaking. 72
Leave it to me to speak, for I know well
what you would ask; perhaps, since they were Greeks,
they might not pay attention to your words."[7] 75
So when the flame had reached us, and my guide
decided that the time and place were right,
he addressed them and I listened to him speaking: 78
"O you who are two souls within one fire,
if I have deserved from you when I was living,
if I have deserved from you much praise or little, 81
when in the world I wrote my lofty verses,
do not move on; let one of you tell where
he lost himself through his own fault, and died." 84
The greater of the ancient flame's two horns

3. Eteocles and his brother, Polynices, were the sons of Oedipus; cursed by their father for their imprisonment of him, they engaged in a civil war over Thebes, killed each other, and were cremated on the same pyre, the flame of which divided into two as a sign of their enmity.
4. Two of the Greek leaders in the Trojan War. They devised the trick of the Trojan horse and stole the Palladium, a statue of Pallas Athena that protected the city. Their vil-lainy is described by Aeneas in *Aeneid* 2.
5. The Trojan survivors, who founded Rome.
6. Achilles' lover, who tried to prevent him from going to the Trojan War but was thwarted by Ulysses.
7. Virgil may assume that Greeks would disdain anyone who, like Dante, did not know Greek (and was therefore a "barbarian"); or that because he derives from the classical world he is the more appropriate interlocutor.

began to sway and quiver, murmuring
  just like a flame that strains against the wind;   87
then, while its tip was moving back and forth,
  as if it were the tongue itself that spoke,
  the flame took on a voice and said: "When I   90
set sail from Circe,[8] who, more than a year,
  had kept me occupied close to Gaëta
  (before Aeneas called it by that name),[9]   93
not sweetness of a son, not reverence
  for an aging father, not the debt of love
  I owed Penelope[1] to make her happy,   96
could quench deep in myself the burning wish
  to know the world and have experience
  of all man's vices, of all human worth.   99
So I set out on the deep and open sea
  with just one ship and with that group of men,
  not many, who had not deserted me   102
I saw as far as Spain, far as Morocco,
  both shores; I had left behind Sardinia,
  and the other islands which that sea encloses.   105
I and my mates were old and tired men.
  Then finally we reached the narrow neck
  where Hercules put up his signal-pillars   108
to warn men not to go beyond that point.[2]
  On my right I saw Seville, and passed beyond;
  on my left, Ceüta had already sunk behind me.   111
'Brothers,' I said, 'who through a hundred thousand
  perils have made your way to reach the West,
  during this so brief vigil of our senses   114
that is still reserved for us, do not deny
  yourself experience of what there is beyond,
  behind the sun, in the world they call unpeopled.[3]   117
Consider what you came from: you are Greeks!
  You were not born to live like mindless brutes
  but to follow paths of excellence and knowledge.'   120
With this brief exhortation I made my crew
  so anxious for the way that lay ahead,
  that then I hardly could have held them back;   123
and with our stern turned toward the morning light,
  we made our oars our wings for that mad flight,
  gaining distance, always sailing to the left.   126
The night already had surveyed the stars

8. Dante places Circe's home near Gaëta, on the coast of Italy north of Naples; she was a sorceress who transformed men into beasts.
9. Aeneas named it after his nurse Caieta, who died there: *Aeneid* 7.
1. Ulysses' faithful wife.
2. The straits of Gibraltar, with Seville on the European side and Ceüta on the African.

According to myth, Hercules separated a single mountain into two to mark the point beyond which human beings should not venture.
3. According to the geography of Dante's day, the Southern Hemisphere was made up entirely of water, with the only land being Mount Purgatory. To go "behind the sun" means to follow a westward course.

the other pole contains; it saw ours so low
   it did not show above the ocean floor.[4]   129
Five times we saw the splendor of the moon
   grow full and five times wane away again
   since we had entered through the narrow pass—   132
when there appeared a mountain shape, darkened
   by distance, that arose to endless heights.
   I had never seen another mountain like it.[5]   135
Our celebrations soon turned into grief:
   from the new land there rose a whirling wind
   that beat against the forepart of the ship   138
and whirled us round three times in churning waters;
   the fourth blast raised the stern up high, and sent
   the bow down deep, as pleased Another's will.   141
And then the sea was closed again, above us."

CANTO XXVII

As soon as Ulysses has finished his narrative, another flame—its soul within having recognized Virgil's Lombard accent—comes forward asking the travelers to pause and answer questions about the state of affairs in the region of Italy from which he came. The Pilgrim responds by outlining the strife in Romagna and ends by asking the flame who he is. The flame, although he insists he does not want his story to be known among the living, answers because he is supposedly convinced that the Pilgrim will never return to earth. He is another famous deceiver, Guido da Montefeltro, a soldier who became a friar in his old age; but he was untrue to his vows when, at the urging of Pope Boniface VIII, he counseled the use of fraud in the pope's campaign against the Colonna family. He was damned to Hell because he failed to repent his sins, trusting instead in the pope's fraudulent absolution.

By now the flame was standing straight and still,
   it said no more and had already turned
   from us, with sanction of the gentle poet,   3
when another, coming right behind it,
   attracted our attention to its tip,
   where a roaring of confusing sounds had started.   6
As the Sicilian bull—that bellowed first
   with cries of that one (and it served him right)
   who with his file had fashioned such a beast[6]—   9
would bellow with the victim's voice inside,
   so that, although the bull was only brass,
   the effigy itself seemed pierced with pain: 12
so, lacking any outlet to escape
   from the burning soul that was inside the flame,
   the suffering words became the fire's language.   15

4. They had crossed the equator and could see only the stars of the Southern Hemisphere.
5. This is Mount Purgatory.
6. According to classical legend, Phalaris, the tyrant of Agrigentum in Sicily, had an artisan build a brazen bull in which he roasted his victims alive, their shrieks emerging as the sounds of a bull's bellowing. His first victim was the artisan himself, Perillus.

But after they had made their journey upward
  to reach the tip, giving it that same quiver
  the sinner's tongue inside had given them,   18
we heard the words:[7] "O you to whom I point
  my voice, who spoke just now in Lombard,[8] saying:
  'you may move on, I won't ask more of you.'   21
although I have been slow in coming to you,
  be willing, please, to pause and speak with me.
  You see how willing I am—and I burn!   24
If you have just now fallen to this world
  of blindness, from that sweet Italian land
  where I took on the burden of my guilt,   27
tell me, are the Romagnols[9] at war or peace?
  For I come from the hills between Urbino
  and the mountain chain that lets the Tiber loose."   30
I was still bending forward listening
  when my master touched my side and said to me:
  "You speak to him; this one is Italian."   33
And I, who was prepared to answer him,
  began without delaying my response:
  "O soul who stands concealed from me down there,   36
your Romagna is not now and never was
  without war in her tyrants' hearts, although
  there was no open warfare when I came here.   39
Ravenna's[1] situation has not changed:
  the eagle of Polenta broods up there,
  covering all of Cervia with its pinions;   42
the land[2] that stood the test of long endurance
  and left the French piled in a bloody heap
  is once again beneath the verdant claws.   45
Verrucchio's Old Mastiff and its New One,[3]
  who both were bad custodians of Montagna,
  still sink their fangs into their people's flesh;   48
the cities by Lamone and Santerno[4]
  are governed by the Lion of the White Lair,
  who changes parties every change of season.   51

---

7. The speaker is Guido da Montefeltro (d. 1298), a nobleman deeply involved in the constant warfare of 13th-century Italy but who became a friar two years before his death (see line 67).

8. The dialect of northern Italy. Dante believed that since Virgil came from Mantua, his spoken language would be not Latin but this dialect.

9. The people of Romagna, an area northeast of Florence and bordering the Adriatic Sea; the city of Urbino marks its southern limit, the Apennine mountains its northern. The subsequent passage describes the political conditions in the cities of Romagna.

1. The major city of Romagna, ruled at the time by the Polenta family, who also controlled the small city of Cervia.

2. Forlì, which defeated French invaders but then fell under the control of the tyrannical Ordelaffi family, which had green paws on its coat of arms.

3. Malatesta de Verrucchio and his son Malatestino were tyrants of Rimini who killed their enemy Montagna.

4. The cities of Faenza and Imola, on the Lamone and Santerno Rivers respectively, governed by an unreliable ruler who had a lion on a white ground on his coat of arms.

As for the town[5] whose side the Savio bathes:
  just as it lies between the hills and plains,
  it lives between freedom and tyranny.   54
And now I beg you tell us who you are—
  grant me my wish as yours was granted you—
  so that your fame may hold its own on earth."   57
And when the fire, in its own way, had roared
  awhile, the flame's sharp tip began to sway
  to and fro, then released a blow of words: 60
"If I thought that I were speaking to a soul
  who someday might return to see the world,
  most certainly this flame would cease to flicker;   63
but since no one, if I have heard the truth,
  ever returns alive from this deep pit,
  with no fear of dishonor I answer you: 66
I was a man of arms and then a friar,
  believing with the cord to make amends;
  and surely my belief would have come true   69
were it not for that High Priest[6] (his soul be damned!)
  who put me back among my early sins;
  I want to tell you why and how it happened.   72
While I still had the form of the bones and flesh
  my mother gave me, all my actions were
  not those of a lion, but those of a fox;   75
the wiles and covert paths, I knew them all,
  and so employed my art that rumor of me
  spread to the farthest limits of the earth.   78
When I saw that the time of life had come
  for me, as it must come for every man,
  to lower the sails and gather in the lines,   81
things I once found pleasure in then grieved me;
  repentant and confessed, I took the vows
  a monk takes. And, oh, to think it could have worked!   84
And then the Prince of the New Pharisees
  chose to wage war upon the Lateran
  instead of fighting Saracens or Jews,[7]   87
for all his enemies were Christian souls
  (none among the ones who conquered Acri,[8]
  none a trader in the Sultan's kingdom).   90
His lofty papal seat, his sacred vows
  were no concern to him, nor was the cord
  I wore (that once made those it girded leaner).[9]   93
As Constantine once had Silvestro brought

---

5. Cesena, located on the Savio River, was a free municipality although its politics were dominated by a single family.
6. Pope Boniface VIII.
7. Boniface was struggling to retain the papacy against the challenge of another Roman family, the Colonnas.

8. City in the Holy Land, captured by the Crusaders and then recaptured by the Saracens.
9. Guido refers to the rough cord worn as a belt by Franciscan friars, a symbol of both obedience and poverty (hence it would make the wearer "leaner"); for another reference to this cord, see 16.106.

from Mount Soracte to cure his leprosy,[1]
  so this one sought me out as his physician   96
to cure his burning fever caused by pride.
  He asked me to advise him. I was silent,
  for his words were drunken. Then he spoke again: 99
'Fear not, I tell you: the sin you will commit,
  it is forgiven. Now you will teach me how
  I can level Palestrina[2] to the ground.   102
Mine is the power, as you cannot deny,
  to lock and unlock Heaven. Two keys I have,
  those keys my predecessor did not cherish."[3]   105
And when his weighty arguments had forced me
  to the point that silence seemed the poorer choice,
  I said: 'Father, since you grant me absolution   108
for the sin I find I must fall into now:
  ample promise with a scant fulfillment
  will bring you triumph on your lofty throne.'   111
Saint Francis[4] came to get me when I died,
  but one of the black Cherubim cried out:
  'Don't touch him, don't cheat me of what is mine!   114
He must come down to join my other servants
  for the false counsel he gave. From then to now
  I have been ready at his hair, because   117
one cannot be absolved unless repentant,
  nor can one both repent and will a thing
  at once—the one is canceled by the other!"[5]   120
O wretched me! How I shook when he took me,
  saying: 'Perhaps you never stopped to think
  that I might be somewhat of a logician!'[6]   123
He took me down to Minòs,[7] who eight times
  twisted his tail around his hardened back,
  then in his rage he bit it, and announced: 126
'He goes with those the thievish fire burns.'
  And here you see me now, lost, wrapped this way,
  moving, as I do, with my resentment."   129
When he had brought his story to a close,
  the flame, in grievous pain, departed from us
  gnarling and flickering its pointed horn.   132
My guide and I moved farther on; we climbed
  the ridge until we stood on the next arch
  that spans the fosse where penalties are paid   135
by those who, sowing discord, earned Hell's wages.

1. According to legend, the Emperor Constantine (d. 337) was cured of his leprosy by Pope Sylvester, who was hiding on Mount Soracte, some 20 miles north of Rome; see 19.115.
2. The fortress of the Colonnas.
3. The keys are those of damnation and absolution, given by Christ to Peter; see 19.92. Boniface's "predecessor" was Celestine V, who resigned after five months; see 3.59–60.

4. Francis of Assisi (1181/82–1226), founder of the order of friars joined by Guido.
5. Guido wanted forgiveness for his sin of guile at the same time as he was committing it; in willing the sin he showed that he was not truly repentant, the precondition for forgiveness.
6. The devil is referring to the logical law of noncontradiction.
7. For Minos, see 5.4.

CANTO XXVIII

In the Ninth Bolgia *the Pilgrim is overwhelmed by the sight of mutilated, bloody shades, many of whom are ripped open, with entrails spilling out. They are the Sowers of Scandal and Schism, and among them are Mahomet, Ali, Pier da Medicina, Gaius Scribonius Curio, Mosca de' Lamberti, and Bertran de Born. All bemoan their painful lot, and Mahomet and Pier da Medicina relay warnings through the Pilgrim to certain living Italians who are soon to meet terrible ends. Bertran de Born, who comes carrying his head in his hand like a lantern, is a particularly arresting example of a Dantean* contrapasso.

Who could, even in the simplest kind of prose
   describe in full the scene of blood and wounds
   that I saw now—no matter how he tried!   3
Certainly any tongue would have to fail:
   man's memory and man's vocabulary
   are not enough to comprehend such pain.   6
If one could bring together all the wounded
   who once upon the fateful soil of Puglia
   grieved for their life's blood spilled by the Romans,[8]   9
and spilled again in the long years of the war
   that ended in great spoils of golden rings
   (as Livy's history tells, that does not err),[9]   12
and pile them with the ones who felt the blows
   when they stood up against great Robert Guiscard,[1]
   and with those others whose bones are still in heaps   15
at Ceprano[2] (there where every Puglian
   turned traitor), and add those from Tagliacozzo,[3]
   where old Alardo conquered, weaponless—   18
if all these maimed with limbs lopped off or pierced
   were brought together, the scene would be nothing
   to compare with the foul ninth *bolgia's* bloody sight.   21
No wine cask with its stave or cant-bar sprung
   was ever split the way I saw someone
   ripped open from his chin to where we fart.   24
Between his legs his guts spilled out, with the heart
   and other vital parts, and the dirty sack
   that turns to shit whatever the mouth gulps down.   27
While I stood staring into his misery,
   he looked at me and with both hands he opened
   his chest and said: "See how I tear myself!   30

---

8. Puglia is in southern Italy, and Dante refers here to those killed when the Trojans conquered it in the *Aeneid* 7–12.
9. Livy is a Roman historian (d. 17 C.E.) and the "war" he chronicled is the Second Punic War (218–201 B.C.E.) between Rome and Carthage under Hannibal. After the Battle of Cannae (216) the victorious Carthaginians displayed rings taken from fallen Romans.
1. A Norman conqueror (1015–1085) who fought the Greeks and Saracens for control of Sicily and southern Italy in the 11th century.
2. A town that the barons of Puglia were pledged to defend for Manfred, the natural son of Frederick II (10.119), but whom they betrayed; he was then killed at the battle of Benevento in 1266.
3. A town where in 1268 Manfred's nephew Conradin was defeated by the strategy rather than the brute force of Alardo de Valery.

See how Mahomet[4] is deformed and torn!
    In front of me, and weeping, Ali walks,
    his face cleft from his chin up to the crown.   33
The souls that you see passing in this ditch
    were all sowers of scandal and schism in life,
    and so in death you see them torn asunder.   36
A devil stands back there who trims us all
    in this cruel way, and each one of this mob
    receives anew the blade of the devil's sword   39
each time we make one round of this sad road,
    because the wounds have all healed up again
    by the time each one presents himself once more.   42
But who are you there, gawking from the bridge
    and trying to put off, perhaps, fulfillment
    of the sentence passed on you when you confessed?"   45
"Death does not have him yet, he is not here
    to suffer for his guilt," my master answered;
    "but that he may have full experience,   48
I, who am dead, must lead him through this Hell
    from round to round, down to the very bottom,
    and this is as true as my presence speaking here."   51
More than a hundred in that ditch stopped short
    to look at me when they had heard his words,
    forgetting in their stupor what they suffered.   54
"And you, who will behold the sun, perhaps
    quite soon, tell Fra Dolcino[5] that unless
    he wants to follow me here quick, he'd better   57
stock up on food, or else the binding snows
    will give the Novarese their victory,
    a conquest not won easily otherwise."   60
With the heel of one foot raised to take a step,
    Mahomet said these words to me, and then
    stretched out and down his foot and moved away.   63
Another, with his throat slit, and his nose
    cut off as far as where the eyebrows start
    (and he only had a single ear to show),   66
who had stopped like all the rest to stare in wonder,
    stepped out from the group and opened up his throat,
    which ran with red from all sides of his wound,   69
and spoke: "O you whom guilt does not condemn,
    whom I have seen in Italy up there,
    unless I am deceived by similarity,   72
recall to mind Pier da Medicina,[6]

4. Muhammad, founder of Islam (570–632), regarded by some medieval Christians as a renegade Christian and a creator of religious disunity. Ali was his nephew and son-in-law, and his disputed claim to the rulership (or caliphate) divided Islam into Sunni and Shi'a sects.
5. In 1300 Fra Dolcino was head of a reformist order known as the Apostolic Brothers that was condemned as heretical by the pope. He and his followers escaped to the hills near the town of Novara, but starvation forced them out and many were executed.
6. The town of Medicina lies in the Po Valley between Vercelli and Marcabò. Nothing certain is known of Pier de Medicina.

should you return to see the gentle plain
   declining from Vercelli to Marcabò,   75
and inform the two best citizens of Fano[7]—
   tell Messer Guido and tell Angiolello—
   that, if our foresight here is no deception,   78
from their ship they shall be hurled bound in a sack
   to drown in the water near Cattolica,
   the victims of a tyrant's treachery;   81
between the isles of Cyprus and Mallorca
   so great a crime Neptune never witnessed
   among the deeds of pirates or the Argives.[8]   84
That traitor, who sees only with one eye
   and rules the land that someone with me here
   wishes he'd never fed his eyes upon,[9]   87
will have them come to join him in a parley,
   then see to it they do not waste their breath
   on vows or prayers to escape Focara's wind."   90
And I to him: "If you want me to bring back
   to those on earth your message—who is the one
   sated with the bitter sight? Show him to me."   93
At once he grabbed the jaws of a companion[1]
   standing near by, and squeezed his mouth half open,
   announcing, "Here he is, and he is mute.   96
This man, in exile, drowned all Caesar's doubts
   and helped him cast the die, when he insisted:
   'A man prepared, who hesitates, is lost.'"   99
How helpless and bewildered he appeared,
   his tongue hacked off as far down as the throat,
   this Curio, once so bold and quick to speak!   102
And one[2] who had both arms but had no hands,
   raising the gory stumps in the filthy air
   so that the blood dripped down and smeared his face,   105
cried: "You, no doubt, also remember Mosca,
   who said, alas, 'What's done is over with,'
   and sowed the seed of discord for the Tuscans."   108
"And of death for all your clan," I quickly said,
   and he, this fresh wound added to his wound,
   turned and went off like one gone mad from pain.   111
But I remained to watch the multitude,

---

7. A town on the Adriatic coast of Italy; its two leaders—named in the next line—were drowned in 1312 by the one-eyed tyrant Malatestino of Rimini (27.46) near the promontory of Focara (see line 90) after he had invited them to the town of La Cattolica for a parley.
8. Cyprus and Majorca are islands at the western and eastern ends of the Mediterranean. Neptune is the classical god of the sea and Argives is another name for Greeks.
9. This "someone" is Caius Curio, whose story is told in lines 94–102.

1. Caius Curio, a Roman of the 1st century B.C.E., was bribed by Julius Caesar to betray his friends; he urged Caesar to cross the Rubicon and invade the Roman Republic, starting a civil war.
2. A Florentine noble, who in 1215 started the civil strife that tore the city apart by advising a father to avenge the slight to his daughter by killing the man who had broken his engagement to her. Mosca's own family was a victim of the strife some 60 years later.

and saw a thing that I would be afraid
  to tell about without more evidence,   114
were I not reassured by my own conscience—
  that good companion enheartening a man
  beneath the breastplate of its purity.   117
I saw it, I'm sure, and I seem to see it still:
  a body with no head that moved along,
  moving no differently from all the rest;   120
he held his severed head up by its hair,
  swinging it in one hand just like a lantern,
  and as it looked at us it said: "Alas!"   123
Of his own self he made himself a light
  and they were two in one and one in two.
  How could this be? He who ordained it knows.   126
And when he had arrived below our bridge,
  he raised the arm that held the head up high
  to let it speak to us at closer range.   129
It spoke:[3] "Now see the monstrous punishment,
  you there still breathing, looking at the dead,
  see if you find suffering to equal mine!   132
And that you may report on me up there,
  know that I am Bertran de Born, the one
  who evilly encouraged the young king.   135
Father and son I set against each other:
  Achitophel with his wicked instigations
  did not do more with Absalom and David.   138
Because I cut the bonds of those so joined,
  I bear my head cut off from its life-source,
  which is back there, alas, within its trunk.   141
In me you see the perfect *contrapasso*!"[4]

CANTO XXIX

When the Pilgrim is rebuked by his mentor for his inappropriate interest in these wretched shades, he replies that he was looking for someone. Virgil tells the Pilgrim that he saw the person he was looking for, Geri del Bello, pointing a finger at him. They discuss Geri until they reach the edge of the next bolgía, *where all types of Falsifiers are punished. There miserable, shrieking shades are afflicted with diseases of various kinds and are arranged in various positions. Sitting back to back, madly scratching their leprous sores, are the shades of Griffolino da Arezzo and one Capoc-chio, who talk to the Pilgrim, the latter shade making wisecracks about the Sienese.*

The crowds, the countless, different mutilations,
  had stunned my eyes and left them so confused
  they wanted to keep looking and to weep,   3
but Virgil said: "What are you staring at?

3. This is Bertran de Born, a Provençal noble-man and poet, who reputedly advised the son of Henry II of England to rebel against his father. For Achitophel's similar scheming between David and his son Absalom, see 2 Sam- uel 15–17. A poem by Bertran is included in *Medieval Lyrics* (pp. 340–41).

4. Literally, "counter penalty": in Dante's hell, the sinner is punished by having to commit his sin for all of eternity.

Why do your eyes insist on drowning there
   below, among those wretched, broken shades?   6
You did not act this way in other *bolge*.
   If you hope to count them one by one, remember
   the valley winds some twenty-two miles around;[5]   9
and already the moon is underneath our feet;
   the time remaining to us now is short[6]—
   and there is more to see than you see here."   12
"If you had taken time to find out what
   I was looking for," I started telling him,
   "perhaps you would have let me stay there longer."   15
My guide was moving on, with me behind him,
   answering as I did while we went on,
   and adding: "Somewhere down along this ditch   18
that I was staring at a while ago,
   I think there is a spirit of my family
   mourning the guilt that's paid so dear down there."   21
And then my master said: "From this time on
   you should not waste another thought on him;
   think on ahead, and let him stay behind,   24
for I saw him standing underneath the bridge
   pointing at you, and threatening with his gesture,
   and I heard his name called out: Geri del Bello.[7]   27
That was the moment you were so absorbed
   with him who was the lord of Altaforte[8]
   that you did not look his way before he left."   30
"Alas, my guide," I answered him, "his death
   by violence, which has not yet been avenged
   by anyone who shares in his disgrace,   33
made him resentful, and I suppose for this
   he went away without a word to me,
   and because he did I feel great piety."   36
We spoke of this until we reached the start
   of the bridge across the next *bolgia*, from which
   the bottom, with more light, might have been seen.   39
Having come to stand above the final cloister
   of Malebolge, we saw it spreading out,
   revealing to our eyes its congregation.   42
Weird shrieks of lamentation pierced through me
   like arrow-shafts whose tips are barbed with pity,
   so that my hands were covering my ears.   45
Imagine all the sick in the hospitals
   of Maremma, Valdichiana, and Sardinia
   between the months of July and September,[9]   48

---

5. The reason for this exact measurement is not known. At 30.86 we are told that the circumference of the ninth circle is 11 miles, showing that Hell is shaped like a funnel.
6. This means that the sun (which they cannot see) is over their heads, and the time is about 2 P.M. The journey to the center of Hell lasts 24 hours, so only 4 hours are left.

7. First cousin to Dante's father; his death at the hands of a member of another Florentine family initiated a feud between the two families that lasted some 50 years.
8. Bertran de Born (see 28.134).
9. The region of Maremma, the river valley of Val di Chiana, and the island of Sardinia were all plagued by malaria.

crammed all together rotting in one ditch—
   such was the misery here; and such a stench
   was pouring out as comes from flesh decaying.   51
Still keeping to our left, we made our way
   down the long bridge onto the final bank,
   and now my sight was clear enough to find   54
the bottom where the High Lord's ministress,
   Justice infallible, metes out her punishment
   to falsifiers she registers on earth.   57
I doubt if all those dying in Aegina[1]
   when the air was blowing sick with pestilence
   and the animals, down to the smallest worm,   60
all perished (later on this ancient race,
   according to what the poets tell as true,
   was born again from families of ants)   63
offered a scene of greater agony
   than was the sight spread out in that dark valley
   of heaped-up spirits languishing in clumps.   66
Some sprawled out on others' bellies, some
   on others' backs, and some, on hands and knees,
   dragged themselves along that squalid alley.   69
Slowly, in silence, slowly we moved along,
   looking, listening to the words of all those sick,
   who had no strength to raise their bodies up.   72
I saw two sitting, leaning against each other
   like pans propped back to back against a fire,[2]
   and they were blotched from head to foot with scabs.   75
I never saw a curry-comb[3] applied
   by a stable-boy who is harried by his master,
   or simply wants to finish and go to bed,   78
the way those two applied their nails and dug
   and dug into their flesh, crazy to ease
   the itching that can never find relief.   81
They worked their nails down, scraping off the scabs
   the way one works a knife to scale a bream[4]
   or some other fish with larger, tougher scales.   84
"O you there scraping off your scabs of mail
   and even making pincers of your fingers,"
   my guide began to speak to one of them,   87
"so may your fingernails eternally
   suffice their task, tell us: among the many
   packed in this place is anyone Italian?"   90
"Both of us whom you see disfigured here,"
   one answered through his tears, "we are Italians.
   But you, who ask about us, who are you?"   93
"I am one accompanying this living man

1. A mythical island that was infected by Juno
with a pestilence that killed all its inhabitants
and was then repopulated when Jupiter turned
ants into men: see Ovid, *Metamorphoses* 7.
2. The image is of pans leaned against one
another before a kitchen fireplace.
3. A "curry-comb" is a bristled brush used to
groom horses.
4. A "bream" is a large fish like a carp.

descending bank from bank," my leader said,
  "and I intend to show him all of Hell."   96
With that each lost the other back's support
  and each one, shaky, turned to look at me,
  as others did who overheard these words.   99
My gentle master came up close to me
  and said: "Now ask them what you want to know,"
  and since he wanted me to speak, I started: 102
"So may the memory of you not fade
  from the minds of men up there in the first world,
  but rather live on under many suns,   105
tell me your names and where it was you lived;
  do not let your dreadful, loathsome punishment
  discourage you from speaking openly."   108
"I'm from Arezzo," one of them replied,
  "and Albert of Siena had me burned,
  but I'm not here for what I died for there;[5]   111
it's true I told him, jokingly, of course:
  'I know the trick of flying through the air,'
  and he, eager to learn and not too bright,   114
asked me to demonstrate my art; and only
  just because I didn't make him Daedalus,
  he had me burned by one whose child he was.   117
But here, to the last *bolgia* of the ten,
  for the alchemy[6] I practiced in the world
  I was condemned by Minòs, who cannot err."   120
I said to my poet: "Have you ever known
  people as silly as the Sienese?
  Even the French cannot compare with them!"   123
With that the other leper[7] who was listening
  feigned exception to my quip: "Excluding,
  of course, Stricca, who lived so frugally,   126
and Niccolo, the first to introduce
  the luxury of the clove for condiment
  into that choice garden where the seed took root,   129
and surely not that fashionable club
  where Caccia squandered all his woods and vineyards
  and Abbagliato flaunted his great wit!   132
That you may know who this is backing you
  against the Sienese, look sharply at me
  so that my face will give you its own answer,   135

---

5. Griffolino of Arezzo cheated Albero of
Siena by promising to teach him the art of
Daedalus—flying. The bishop of Siena, father
of the illegitimate Albero, had Griffolino
burned as a heretic.
6. A practice that sought to turn base metals
like lead into gold.
7. The speaker is Capocchio, a Florentine

burned in 1293 for alchemy, which he here
admits was mere counterfeiting. The people
he lists were rich young noblemen of Siena
who joined a "Spendthrifts' Club"—the "fashionable club" of line 130—and sought to outdo
each other in profligacy. For another member
of this club, Lano of Siena, see 13.115.

and you will recognize Capocchio's shade,
  betrayer of metals with his alchemy;
  you'll surely recall—if you're the one I think—   138
how fine an ape of nature[8] I once was."

CANTO XXX

Capocchio's remarks are interrupted by two mad, naked shades who dash up, and one of them sinks his teeth into Capocchio's neck and drags him off; he is Gianni Schicchi and the other is Myrrha of Cyprus. When they have gone, the Pilgrim sees the ill-proportioned and immobile shade of Master Adamo, a counterfeiter, who explains how members of the Guidi family had persuaded him to practice his evil art in Romena. He points out the fever-stricken shades of two infamous liars, Potiphar's Wife and Sinon the Greek, whereupon the latter engages Master Adamo in a verbal battle. Virgil rebukes the Pilgrim for his absorption in such futile wrangling, but his immediate shame wins Virgil's immediate forgiveness.

In ancient times when Juno was enraged
  against the Thebans because of Semele[9]
  (she showed her wrath on more than one occasion),   3
she made King Athamas go raving mad:
  so mad that one day when he saw his wife
  coming with his two sons in either arm,   6
he cried: "Let's spread the nets, so I can catch
  the lioness with her lion cubs at the pass!"
  Then he spread out his insane hands, like talons,   9
and, seizing one of his two sons, Learchus,
  he whirled him round and smashed him on a rock.
  She drowned herself with the other in her arms.   12
And when the wheel of Fortune brought down low
  the immeasurable haughtiness of Trojans,[1]
  destroying in their downfall king and kingdom,   15
Hecuba sad, in misery, a slave
  (after she saw Polyxena lie slain,
  after this grieving mother found her son   18
Polydorus left unburied on the shore),
  now gone quite mad, went barking like a dog—
  it was the weight of grief that snapped her mind.   21
But never in Thebes or Troy were madmen seen
  driven to acts of such ferocity
  against their victims, animal or human,   24
as two shades I saw, white with rage and naked,

8. By "ape of nature" Capocchio means that he merely imitated change in his alchemical displays rather than actually accomplishing it.
9. Daughter of the king of Thebes, Semele was loved by Jupiter and therefore incited the wrath of Juno, who drove her brother-in-law Athamas insane. While mad, Athamas thought his wife, Ino, and his two sons, Learchus and Melicertes, were a lioness and two cubs: he killed Learchus, and Ino drowned herself and Melicertes. See Ovid, *Metamorphoses* 4.
1. Parallel to the fate of Thebes is that of Troy, which is here represented by the madness into which Queen Hecuba fell when she saw her daughter Polyxena sacrificed on Achilles' tomb and the unburied body of her betrayed son Polydorus. See Ovid, *Metamorphoses* 13.

running, snapping crazily at things in sight,
 like pigs, directionless, broken from their pen. 27
One, landing on Capocchio, sank his teeth
 into his neck, and started dragging him
 along, scraping his belly on the rocky ground. 30
The Aretine[2] spoke, shaking where he sat:
 "You see that batty shade? He's Gianni Schicchi![3]
 He's rabid and he treats us all that way." 33
"Oh," I answered, "so may that other shade
 never sink its teeth in you—if you don't mind,
 please tell me who it is before it's gone." 36
And he to me: "That is the ancient shade
 of Myrrha,[4] the depraved one, who became,
 against love's laws, too much her father's friend. 39
She went to him, and there she sinned in love,
 pretending that her body was another's—
 just as the other there fleeing in the distance, 42
contrived to make his own the 'queen of studs,'
 pretending that he was Buoso Donati,
 making his will and giving it due form." 45
Now that the rabid pair had come and gone
 (from whom I never took my eyes away),
 I turned to watch the other evil shades. 48
And there I saw a soul shaped like a lute,
 if only he'd been cut off from his legs
 below the belly, where they divide in two. 51
The bloating dropsy,[5] disproportioning
 the body's parts with unconverted humors,
 so that the face, matched with the paunch, was puny, 54
forced him to keep his parched lips wide apart,
 as a man who suffers thirst from raging fever
 has one lip curling up, the other sagging. 57
"O you who bear no punishment at all
 (I can't think why) within this world of sorrow,"
 he said to us, "pause here and look upon 60
the misery of one Master Adamo:[6]
 in life I had all that I could desire,
 and now, alas, I crave a drop of water. 63
The little streams that flow from the green hills
 of Casentino, descending to the Arno,
 keeping their banks so cool and soft with moisture, 66

2. Griffolino (see 29.111).
3. A Florentine who impersonated Buoso Donati (line 44), who had just died, and dictated a new will that gave him Buoso's best beast ("the queen of studs" of line 43).
4. Myrrha impersonated another woman in order to sleep with her father: see Ovid, *Metamorphoses* 10.
5. A disease in which fluid ("humors" of line

53) gathers in the cells and the affected part becomes grotesquely swollen.
6. A counterfeiter, burned in 1281, who made coins stamped with the image of John the Baptist, the patron saint of Florence, that contained 21 rather than 24 carats of gold (see line 90); he worked for a noble family of Romena (individual members are mentioned in line 77), a town in the Florentine district of Casentino.

forever flow before me, haunting me;
  and the image of them leaves me far more parched
    than the sickness that has dried my shriveled face.   69
Relentless Justice, tantalizing me,
  exploits the countryside that knew my sin,
    to draw from me ever new sighs of pain: 72
I still can see Romena, where I learned
  to falsify the coin stamped with the Baptist,
    for which I paid with my burned body there;   75
but if I could see down here the wretched souls
  of Guido or Alexander or their brother,
    I would not exchange the sight for Branda's fountain.[7]   78
One is here already, if those maniacs
  running around this place have told the truth,
    but what good is it, with my useless legs?   81
If only I were lighter, just enough
  to move one inch in every hundred years,
    I would have started on my way by now   84
to find him somewhere in this gruesome lot,
  although this ditch winds round eleven miles
    and is at least a half a mile across.   87
It's their fault I am here with this choice family:
  they encouraged me to turn out florins
    whose gold contained three carats' worth of alloy."   90
And I to him: "Who are those two poor souls
  lying to the right, close to your body's boundary,
    steaming like wet hands in wintertime?"   93
"When I poured into this ditch, I found them here,"
  he answered, "and they haven't budged since then,
    and I doubt they'll move through all eternity.   96
One is the false accuser of young Joseph;
  the other is false Sinon, the Greek in Troy:[8]
    it's their burning fever makes them smell so bad."   99
And one of them, perhaps somewhat offended
  at the kind of introduction he received,
    with his fist struck out at the distended belly,   102
which responded like a drum reverberating;
  and Master Adam struck him in the face
    with an arm as strong as the fist he had received,   105
and he said to him: "Although I am not free
  to move around, with swollen legs like these,
    I have a ready arm for such occasions."   108
"*But* it was *not* as free and ready, was it,"
  the other answered, "when you went to the stake?
    Of course, when you were coining, it was readier!"   111
And he with the dropsy: "*Now* you tell the truth,

7. A fountain near Romena.
8. The "false accuser" is Potiphar's wife, who falsely accused Joseph of trying to lie with her (Genesis 39.6–20); Sinon is the Greek priest who persuaded the Trojans to accept the wooden horse (*Aeneid* 2).

but you were not as full of truth that time
    when you were asked to tell the truth at Troy!"   114
"My words were false—so were the coins you made,"
    said Sinon, "and *I* am here for one false act
    but *you* for more than any fiend in hell!"   117
"The horse, recall the horse, you falsifier,"
    the bloated paunch was quick to answer back,
    "may it burn your guts that all the world remembers!"   120
"May your guts burn with thirst that cracks your tongue,"
    the Greek said, "may they burn with rotting humors
    that swell your hedge of a paunch to block your eyes!"   123
And then the money-man: "So there you go,
    your evil mouth pours out its filth as usual;
    for if *I* thirst, and humors swell me up,   126
you burn more, and your head is fit to split,
    and it wouldn't take much coaxing to convince you
    to lap the mirror of Narcissus dry!"[9]   129
I was listening, all absorbed in this debate,
    when the master said to me: "Keep right on looking,
    a little more, and I shall lose my patience."   132
I heard the note of anger in his voice
    and turned to him; I was so full of shame
    that it still haunts my memory today.   135
Like one asleep who dreams himself in trouble
    and in his dream he wishes he were dreaming,
    longing for that which is, as if it were not,   138
just so I found myself: unable to speak,
    longing to beg for pardon and already
    begging for pardon, not knowing that I did.   141
"Less shame than yours would wash away a fault
    greater than yours has been," my master said,
    "and so forget about it, do not be sad.   144
If ever again you should meet up with men
    engaging in this kind of futile wrangling,
    remember I am always at your side;   147
to have a taste for talk like this is vulgar!"

CANTO XXXI

Through the murky air they move, up across the bank that separates the Malebolge *from the pit of Hell, the Ninth (and last) Circle of the* Inferno. *From a distance is heard the blast of a mighty horn, which turns out to have been that of the giant Nimrod. He and other giants, including Ephialtes, are fixed eternally in the pit of Hell; all are chained except Antaeus, who, at Virgil's request, lifts the two poets in his monstrous hand and deposits them below him, on the lake of ice known as Cocytus.*

The very tongue that first spoke—stinging me,
    making the blood rush up to both my cheeks—
    then gave the remedy to ease the pain,   3

9. Narcissus saw his reflection in a pool of water, referred to here as a "mirror" (Ovid, *Metamorphoses* 3).

just as, so I have heard, Achilles' lance,
   belonging to his father, was the source
   of pain, and then of balm, to him it struck.[1]   6
Turning our backs on that trench of misery
   gaining the bank again that walls it in,
   we cut across, walking in dead silence.   9
Here it was less than night and less than day,
   so that my eyes could not see far ahead;
   but then I heard the blast of some high horn   12
which would have made a thunder-clap sound dim;
   it drew my eyes directly to one place,
   as they retraced the sound's path to its source.   15
After the tragic rout when Charlemagne[2]
   lost all his faithful, holy paladins,
   the sound of Roland's horn was not as ominous.   18
Keeping my eyes still turned that way, I soon
   made out what seemed to be high, clustered towers.
   "Master," I said, "what city lies ahead?"   21
"Because you try to penetrate the shadows,"
   he said to me, "from much too far away,
   you confuse the truth with your imagination.   24
You will see clearly when you reach that place
   how much the eyes may be deceived by distance,
   and so, just push ahead a little more."   27
Then lovingly he took me by the hand
   and said: "But now, before we go on farther,
   to prepare you for the truth that could seem strange,   30
I'll tell you these aren't towers, they are giants;
   they're standing in the well around the bank—
   all of them hidden from their navels down."   33
As, when the fog begins to thin and clear,
   the sight can slowly make out more and more
   what is hidden in the mist that clogs the air,   36
so, as I pierced the thick and murky air,
   approaching slowly, closer to the well,
   confusion cleared and my fear took on more shape.   39
For just as Montereggion[3] is crowned with towers
   soaring high above its curving ramparts,
   so, on the bank that runs around the well,   42
towering with only half their bodies out,
   stood the terrible giants,[4] forever threatened
   by Jupiter in the heavens when he thunders.   45
And now I could make out one of the faces,

---

1. Achilles' father, Peleus, gave him a lance that would heal any wound it inflicted.
2. In *The Song of Roland*. Roland blows his horn to alert Charlemagne to the fact that the rear guard Roland commands has been slaughtered. Paladins are the twelve peers or great warriors of Charlemagne's court.

3. A castle surrounded by towers, built to protect Siena from attack by Florence.
4. These "giants" are the mythological Titans, monsters born of the Earth who assaulted Olympus and were defeated and imprisoned by Jupiter.

the shoulders, the chest and a good part of the belly
and, down along the sides, the two great arms.[5]   48
Nature, when she cast away the mold
    for shaping beasts like these, without a doubt
    did well, depriving Mars of more such agents.   51
And if she never did repent of whales
    and elephants, we must consider her,
    on sober thought, all the more just and wary: 54
for when the faculty of intellect
    is joined with brute force and with evil will,
    no man can win against such an alliance.   57
His face, it seemed to me, was about as long
    and just as wide as St. Peter's cone in Rome,[6]
    and all his body's bones were in proportion,   60
so that the bank which served to cover him
    from his waist down showed so much height above
    that three tall Frisians[7] on each other's shoulders   63
could never boast of stretching to his hair,
    for downward from the place men clasp their cloaks
    I saw a generous thirty hand-spans of him.[8]   66
"Raphel may a mech zabi almi!"[9]
    He played these sputtering notes with prideful lips
    for which no sweeter psalm was suitable.   69
My guide called up to him: "Blathering idiot,
    stick to your horn[1] and take it out on that
    when you feel a fit of anger coming on;   72
search round your neck and you will find the strap
    it's tied to, you poor muddle-headed soul,
    and there's the horn so pretty on your chest."   75
And then he turned to me: "His words accuse him.
    He is Nimrod, through whose infamous device
    the world no longer speaks a common language.   78
But let's leave him alone and not waste breath,
    for he can no more understand our words
    than anyone can understand his language."   81
We had to walk still farther than before,
    continuing to the left, a full bow's-shot,
    to find another giant,[2] huger and more fierce.   84
What engineer it took to bind this brute
    I cannot say, but there he was, one arm
    pinned to his back, the other locked in front,   87

5. This is Nimrod, described in Genesis as "a
mighty hunter before the Lord" (10.9) and
understood by medieval commentators to be a
giant. He ruled over Babylon, where the tower
of Babel was built (11.1–9).
6. This bronze pine cone, over 12 feet high,
stood outside St. Peter's Cathedral in Dante's
time; today it can be seen in the papal gardens
in the Vatican.
7. Inhabitants of the northernmost province
of what is now the Netherlands, considered

the tallest men of the time.
8. About 15 feet.
9. Appropriately for the builder of Babel, he
speaks an incomprehensible language.
1. Nimrod has a "horn" because in the Bible
he is described as a hunter (Genesis 10.9).
2. This is Ephialtes, a Titan who with his twin
brother Otus tried to attack Olympus by piling
Mount Ossa on Mount Pelion; see Virgil,
Aeneid 6.

with a giant chain winding around him tight,
    which, starting from his neck, made five great coils—
    and that was counting only to his waist.   90
"This beast of pride decided he would try
    to pit his strength against almighty Jove,"
    my leader said, "and he has won this prize.   93
He's Ephialtes, who made his great attempt
    when the giants arose to fill the Gods with panic;
    the arms he lifted then, he moves no more."   96
And I to him: "If it were possible,
    I would really like to have the chance to see
    the fantastic figure of Briareus."[3]   99
His answer was: "Not far from here you'll see
    Antaeus,[4] who can speak and is not chained;
    he will set us down in the very pit of sin.   102
The one you want to see is farther off;
    he too is bound and looks just like this one,
    except for his expression, which is fiercer."   105
No earthquake of the most outrageous force
    ever shook a tower with such violence
    as, suddenly, Ephialtes shook himself.   108
I never feared to die as much as then,
    and my fear might have been enough to kill me,
    if I had not already seen those chains.   111
We left him and continued moving on
    and came to where Antaeus stood, extending
    from the well a good five ells up to his head.[5]   114
"O you who in the celebrated valley[6]
    (that saw Scipio become the heir of glory,
    when Hannibal with all his men retreated)   117
once captured a thousand lions as your quarry
    (and with whose aid, had you chosen to take part
    in the great war with your brothers, the sons of earth   120
would, as many still think, have been the victors),
    do not disdain this modest wish: take us,
    and put us down where ice locks in Cocytus.[7]   123
Don't make us go to Tityus or Typhon;[8]
    this man can give you what all long for here,
    and so bend down, and do not scowl at us.   126
He still can spread your legend in the world,
    for he yet lives, and long life lies before him,
    unless Grace summons him before his time."   129
Thus spoke my master, and the giant in haste

---

3. Another Titan.
4. A Titan born too late to participate in the rebellion against Jupiter and therefore not chained; he was known for eating lions (line 118) and was defeated by Hercules in a wrestling match (line 132).
5. About 15 feet.

6. The "valley" of the Bagradas River in Tunisia, where the Roman Scipio defeated the Carthaginian Hannibal in 202 B.C.E.
7. The frozen lake of Cocytus is in the ninth and last circle of Hell.
8. Two more Titans.

stretched out the hands whose formidable grip
   great Hercules once felt, and took my guide.   132
And Virgil, when he felt the grasping hands,
   called out: "Now come and I'll take hold of you."
   Clasped together, we made a single burden.   135
As the Garisenda⁹ looks from underneath
   its leaning side, at the moment when a cloud
   comes drifting over against the tower's slant,   138
just so the bending giant Antaeus seemed
   as I looked up, expecting him to topple.
   I wished then I had gone another way.   141
But he, most carefully, handed us down
   to the pit that swallows Lucifer with Judas.¹
   And then, the leaning giant immediately   144
drew himself up as tall as a ship's mast.

CANTO XXXII

They descend farther down into the darkness of the immense plain of ice in which shades of Traitors are frozen. In the outer region of the ice-lake, Caïna, are those who betrayed their kin in murder; among them, locked in a frozen embrace, are Napoleone and Alessandro of Mangona, and others are Mordred, Focaccia, Sassol Mascheroni, and Camicion de' Pazzi. Then the two travelers enter the area of ice called Antenora, and suddenly the Pilgrim kicks one of the faces sticking out of the ice. He tries to force the sinner to reveal his name by pulling out his hair, and when another shade identifies him as Bocca degli Abati, the Pilgrim's fury mounts still higher. Bocca, himself furious, names several other sinners in Antenora, including Buoso da Duera, Tesauro dei Beccheria, Gianni de' Soldanier, Ganelou, and Tibbald. Going farther on, the Pilgrim sees two heads frozen in one hole, the mouth of one gnawing at the brain of the other.

If I had words grating and crude enough
   that really could describe this horrid hole
   supporting the converging weight of Hell,   3
I could squeeze out the juice of my memories
   to the last drop. But I don't have these words,
   and so I am reluctant to begin.   6
To talk about the bottom of the universe
   the way it truly is, is no child's play,
   no task for tongues that gurgle baby-talk.   9
But may those heavenly ladies² aid my verse
   who aided Amphion to wall-in Thebes,
   that my words may tell exactly what I saw.   12
O misbegotten rabble of all rabble,
   who crowd this realm, hard even to describe,
   it were better you had lived as sheep or goats!   15
When we reached a point of darkness in the well
   below the giant's feet, farther down the slope,

---

9. A leaning tower of Bologna: when a cloud passes over it, moving opposite to the tower's slant, it appears to be falling away from the sky.

1. Two of the inhabitants of Cocytus.
2. The Muses who helped the legendary musician Amphion raise the walls of Thebes with the music of his lyre.

and I was gazing still at the high wall,   18
I heard somebody say: "Watch where you step!
  Be careful that you do not kick the heads
  of this brotherhood of miserable souls."   21
At that I turned around and saw before me
  a lake of ice stretching beneath my feet,
  more like a sheet of glass than frozen water.[3]   24
In the depths of Austria's wintertime, the Danube
  never in all its course showed ice so thick,
  nor did the Don beneath its frigid sky,   27
as this crust here; for if Mount Tambernic[4]
  or Pietrapana would crash down upon it,
  not even at its edges would a crack creak.   30
The way the frogs (in the season when the harvest
  will often haunt the dreams of the peasant girl)
  sit croaking with their muzzles out of water,   33
so these frigid, livid shades were stuck in ice
  up to where a person's shame appears;
  their teeth clicked notes like storks' beaks snapping shut.[5] 36
And each one kept his face bowed toward the ice:
  the mouth bore testimony to the cold,
  the eyes, to sadness welling in the heart.   39
I gazed around awhile and then looked down,
  and by my feet I saw two figures clasped
  so tight that one's hair could have been the other's.   42
"Tell me, you two, pressing your chests together,"
  I asked them, "who are you?"[6] Both stretched their necks
  and when they had their faces raised toward me,   45
their eyes, which had before been only glazed,
  dripped tears down to their lips, and the cold froze
  the tears between them, locking the pair more tightly.   48
Wood to wood with iron was never clamped
  so firm! And the two of them like billy-goats
  were butting at each other, mad with anger.   51
Another one with both ears frozen off,
  and head still bowed over his icy mirror,
  cried out: "What makes you look at us so hard?   54
If you're interested to know who these two are:
  the valley where Bisenzio's waters[7] flow
  belonged to them and to their father, Albert;   57
the same womb bore them both, and if you scour
  all of Caïna,[8] you will not turn up one
  who's more deserving of this frozen aspic—   60

---

3. The water for this lake derives from the crack in the Old Man of Crete (14.103).
4. Probably Mount Tambura, close to Mount Pietrapana in the Italian Alps.
5. A harsh, clacking sound. "Where a person's shame appears" is the face because of blushing.
6. These are the two sons of Count Alberto degli Alberti of Florence; when he died (ca. 1280), they killed each other over politics and their inheritance.
7. Bisenzio is a river north of Florence.
8. Named after Cain: this first of the four subdivisions of Cocytus is where those who betrayed their kin are imprisoned.

not him who had his breast and shadow pierced
   with one thrust of the lance from Arthur's hand;[9]
   not Focaccia, not even this one here,   63
whose head gets in my way and blocks my view,
   known in the world as Sassol Mascheroni,[1]
   and if you're Tuscan you must know who he was.   66
To save me from your asking for more news:
   I was Camicion de' Pazzi,[2] and I await
   Carlin,[3] whose guilt will make my own seem less."   69
Farther on I saw a thousand doglike faces,
   purple from the cold. That's why I shudder,
   and always will, when I see a frozen pond.   72
While we were getting closer to the center
   of the universe,[4] where all weights must converge,
   and I was shivering in the eternal chill—   75
by fate or chance or willfully perhaps,
   I do not know—but stepping among the heads,
   my foot kicked hard against one of those faces.   78
Weeping, he screamed: "Why are you kicking me?[5]
   You have not come to take revenge on me
   for Montaperti, have you? Why bother me?"   81
And I: "My master, please wait here for me,
   let me clear up a doubt concerning this one,
   then I shall be as rapid as you wish."   84
My leader stopped, and to that wretch, who still
   had not let up in his barrage of curses,
   I said: "Who are you, insulting other people?"   87
"And you, who are *you* who march through Antenora[6]
   kicking other people in their faces?
   No living man could kick as hard!" he answered.   90
"I am a living man," was my reply,
   "and it might serve you well, if you seek fame,
   for me to put your name down in my notes."   93
And he said: "That's the last thing I would want!
   That's not the way to flatter in these lowlands!
   Stop pestering me like this—get out of here!"   96
At that I grabbed him by his hair in back[7]

---

9. "Not him . . . hand": This is Mordred, Arthur's nephew and son; when Arthur pierced him with a sword, he created a wound so large that the sun shone through, thus creating a hole in Mordred's shadow. Focaccia in the next line is a nobleman of Pistoia who killed his cousin.

1. A Florentine nobleman who murdered a relative.

2. A Florentine who killed his kinsman.

3. A Florentine who betrayed a castle belonging to his party. When he dies he will therefore be sent to the next subdivision, Antenora, for those who committed treachery against their country, city, or party—a harsher pun-

ishment, which Camicion says "will make my own [guilt] seem less."

4. The "center of the universe" is where gravity is most strong and to which all material things are drawn.

5. Bocca degli Abati (his name is betrayed by one of the fellow damned in line 106); Bocca betrayed his party at the battle of Montaperti in 1260.

6. Dante and Virgil have moved into the second subdivision of Caïna, which is named after Antenor, a Trojan who betrayed the city to the Greeks; it is the location of those who betrayed their country.

7. The hair at the nape of the neck.

and said: "You'd better tell me who you are
   or else I'll not leave one hair on your head."   99
And he to me: "Go on and strip me bald
   and pound and stamp my head a thousand times,
   you'll never hear my name or see my face."   102
I had my fingers twisted in his hair
   and already I'd pulled out more than one fistful,
   while he yelped like a cur with eyes shut tight,   105
when someone else[8] yelled: "What's the matter, Bocca?
   It's bad enough to hear your shivering teeth;
   now you bark! What the devil's wrong with you?"   108
"There's no need now for you to speak," I said,
   "you vicious traitor! Now I know your name
   and I'll bring back the shameful truth about you."   111
"Go away!" he answered. "Tell them what you want;
   but if you do get out of here, be sure
   you also tell about that blabbermouth,   114
who's paying here what the French silver cost him:
   'I saw,' you can tell the world, 'the one from Duera
   stuck in with all the sinners keeping cool.'   117
And if you should be asked: 'Who else was there?'
   Right by your side is the one from Beccheria[9]
   whose head was chopped off by the Florentines.   120
As for Gianni Soldanier,[1] I think you'll find him
   farther along with Ganelon and Tibbald,
   who opened up Faenza while it slept."   123
Soon after leaving him I saw two souls
   frozen together in a single hole,
   so that one head used the other for a cap.   126
As a man with hungry teeth tears into bread,
   the soul with capping head had sunk his teeth
   into the other's neck, just beneath the skull.   129
Tydeus[2] in his fury did not gnaw
   the head of Menalippus with more relish
   than this one chewed that head of meat and bones.   132
"O you who show with every bestial bite
   your hatred for the head you are devouring,"
   I said, "tell me your reason, and I promise,   135
if you are justified in your revenge,
   once I know who you are and this one's sin,
   I'll repay your confidence in the world above   138
unless my tongue dry up before I die."

---

8. This is Buoso da Duera, who betrayed
Manfred, the ruler of Naples, to his enemy
Charles of Anjou in 1265.
9. Tesauro de' Beccheria, a churchman executed for treason in Florence in 1258.
1. Gianni Soldanier was a Florentine nobleman who switched political parties; Ganelon
(line 122) is the betrayer of Roland in the
Song of Roland; Tibbald (line 122) was the
citizen of Faenza (a town east of Florence)
who betrayed it to its enemies.
2. In the war against Thebes, Tydeus was
mortally wounded by Menalippus, whom he
killed and whose skull he gnawed in fury while
dying.

CANTO XXXIII

Count Ugolino is the shade gnawing at the brain of his onetime associate Archbishop Ruggieri, and Ugolino interrupts his gruesome meal long enough to tell the story of his imprisonment and cruel death, which his innocent offspring shared with him. Moving farther into the area of Cocytus known as Tolomea, where those who betrayed their guests and associates are condemned, the Pilgrim sees sinners with their faces raised high above the ice, whose tears freeze and lock their eyes. One of the shades agrees to identify himself on condition that the ice be removed from his eyes. The Pilgrim agrees, and learns that this sinner is Friar Alberigo and that his soul is dead and damned even though his body is still alive on earth, inhabited by a devil. Alberigo also names a fellow sinner with him in the ice, Branca d'Oria, whose body is still functioning up on earth. But the Pilgrim does not honor his promise to break the ice from Alberigo's eyes.

Lifting his mouth from his horrendous meal,
   this sinner[3] first wiped off his messy lips
   in the hair remaining on the chewed-up skull,   3
then spoke: "You want me to renew a grief
   so desperate that just the thought of it,
   much less the telling, grips my heart with pain;   6
but if my words can be the seed to bear
   the fruit of infamy for this betrayer,
   who feeds my hunger, then I shall speak—in tears.   9
I do not know your name, nor do I know
   how you have come down here, but Florentine
   you surely seem to be, to hear you speak.   12
First you should know I was Count Ugolino
   and my neighbor here, Ruggieri the Archbishop;
   now I'll tell you why I'm so unneighborly.   15
That I, trusting in him, was put in prison
   through his evil machinations, where I died,
   this much I surely do not have to tell you.   18
What you could not have known, however, is
   the inhuman circumstances of my death.
   Now listen, then decide if he has wronged me!   21
Through a narrow slit of window high in that mew[4]
   (which is called the tower of hunger, after me,
   and I'll not be the last to know that place)   24
I had watched moon after moon after moon go by,
   when finally I dreamed the evil dream
   which ripped away the veil that hid my future.   27
I dreamed of this one here as lord and huntsman,
   pursuing the wolf and the wolf cubs up the mountain[5]
   (which blocks the sight of Lucca from the Pisans)   30

3. Ugolino, a governor of Pisa who was betrayed by his enemy Archbishop Ruggieri in 1288. His own crime is obliquely explained by his narrative.
4. A cage for birds; the prison in Pisa where Ugolino and his relatives were confined became known as the Torre de Fame or Tower of Hunger.

5. Mount San Giuliano lies between Pisa and Lucca. "The wolf and the wolf cubs": Ugolino and his four sons, each of whom are named in subsequent lines (50, 68, 89). In fact, Ugolino was imprisoned with two sons (who were grown men) and two adolescent grandsons.

with skinny bitches, well trained and obedient;
   he had out front as leaders of the pack
   Gualandi with Sismondi and Lanfranchi.[6]   33
A short run, and the father with his sons
   seemed to grow tired, and then I thought I saw
   long fangs sunk deep into their sides, ripped open.   36
When I awoke before the light of dawn,
   I heard my children sobbing in their sleep
   (you see they, too, were there), asking for bread.   39
If the thought of what my heart was telling me
   does not fill you with grief, how cruel you are!
   If you are not weeping now—do you ever weep?   42
And then they awoke. It was around the time
   they usually brought our food to us. But now
   each one of us was full of dread from dreaming;   45
then from below I heard them driving nails
   into the dreadful tower's door; with that,
   I stared in silence at my flesh and blood.   48
I did not weep, I turned to stone inside;
   they wept, and my little Anselmuccio spoke:
   'What is it, father? Why do you look that way?'   51
For them I held my tears back, saying nothing,
   all of that day, and then all of that night,
   until another sun shone on the world.   54
A meager ray of sunlight found its way
   to the misery of our cell, and I could see
   myself reflected four times in their faces;   57
I bit my hands in anguish. And my children,
   who thought that hunger made me bite my hands,
   were quick to draw up closer to me, saying: 60
'O father, you would make us suffer less,
   if you would feed on us: you were the one
   who gave us this sad flesh; you take it from us!'[7]   63
I calmed myself to make them less unhappy.
   That day we sat in silence, and the next day.
   O pitiless earth! You should have swallowed us!   66
The fourth day came, and it was on that day
   my Gaddo fell prostrate before my feet,
   crying: 'Why don't you help me? Why, my father?'[8]   69
There he died. Just as you see me here,
   I saw the other three fall one by one,
   as the fifth day and the sixth day passed. And I,   72
by then gone blind, groped over their dead bodies.
   Though they were dead, two days I called their names.
   Then hunger proved more powerful than grief."   75
He spoke these words; then, glaring down in rage,
   attacked again the wretched skull with his teeth
   sharp as a dog's, and as fit for grinding bones.   78

6. Pisan families of the political party opposed
to that of Ugolino.

7. See Job 1.21.

8. See Matthew 27.46.

O Pisa, blot of shame upon the people
   of that fair land where the sound of "sì" is heard![9]
   Since your neighbors hesitate to punish you,   81
let Capraia and Gorgona[1] move and join,
   damming up the River Arno at its mouth,
   and let every Pisan perish in its flood!   84
For if Count Ugolino was accused
   of turning traitor, trading-in your castles,[2]
   you had no right to make his children suffer.   87
Their newborn years (O newborn Thebes!)[3] made them
   all innocents: Brigata, Uguiccione,
   and the other two soft names my canto sings.   90
We moved ahead to where the frozen water
   wraps in harsh wrinkles another sinful race,
   with faces not turned down but looking up.[4]   93
Here, the weeping puts an end to weeping,
   and the grief that finds no outlet from the eyes
   turns inward to intensify the anguish: 96
for the tears they first wept knotted in a cluster
   and like a visor made for them in crystal,
   filled all the hollow part around their eyes.   99
Although the bitter coldness of the dark
   had driven all sensation from my face,
   as though it were not tender skin but callous,   102
I thought I felt the air begin to blow,
   and I: "What causes such a wind, my master?
   I thought no heat could reach into these depths."[5]   105
And he to me: "Before long you will be
   where your own eyes can answer for themselves,
   when they will see what keeps this wind in motion."   108
And one of the wretches with the frozen crust
   screamed out at us: "O wicked souls, so wicked
   that you have been assigned the ultimate post,   111
break off these hard veils covering my eyes
   and give relief from the pain that swells my heart—
   at least until the new tears freeze again."   114
I answered him: "If this is what you want,
   tell me your name; and if I do not help you,
   may I be forced to drop beneath this ice!"   117

9. I.e., Italy, where si means "yes."
1. Islands belonging to Pisa that lie close to the mouth of the Arno, which flows through Pisa.
2. In 1285 Ugolino conveyed three Pisan castles to Lucca and Florence.
3. In classical mythology, Thebes was notorious for its internecine violence, such as the story of Oedipus, his father, Laius, and his sons, Eteocles and Polynices (see 26.54).
4. Virgil and Dante pass into the third subdi-

vision of Cocytus, called Tolomea (line 124) after Ptolemy, governor of Jericho, who killed his father-in-law, Simon, and two of his sons while they were dining with him (I Maccabees 16.11–17). In Tolomea those who have betrayed their guests are punished.
5. Since the sun's heat was thought to cause wind, Dante wonders why he feels wind in this cold place. The answer will be given in 34.46–52.

He answered then: "I am Friar Alberigo,[6]
   I am he who offered fruit from the evil orchard:
   here dates are served me for the figs I gave."   120
"Oh, then!" I said. "Are you already dead?"
   And he to me: "Just how my body is
   in the world above, I have no way of knowing.   123
This zone of Tolomea is very special,
   for it often happens that a soul falls here
   before the time that Atropos[7] should send it.   126
And that you may more willingly scrape off
   my cluster of glass tears, let me tell you:
   whenever a soul betrays the way I did,   129
a demon takes possession of the body,
   controlling its maneuvers from then on,
   for all the years it has to live up there,   132
while the soul falls straight into this cistern here;
   and the shade in winter quarters just behind me
   may well have left his body up on earth.   135
But you should know, if you've just come from there:
   he is Ser Branca d'Oria;[8] and many years
   have passed since he first joined us here, icebound."   138
"I think you're telling me a lie," I said,
   "for Branca d'Oria is not dead at all;
   he eats and drinks, he sleeps and wears out clothes."   141
"The ditch the Malebranche watch above,"
   he said, "the ditch of clinging, boiling pitch,
   had not yet caught the soul of Michel Zanche,   144
when Branca left a devil in his body
   to take his place, and so did his close kinsman,
   his accomplice in this act of treachery.   147
But now, at last, give me the hand you promised.
   Open my eyes." I did not open them.
   To be mean to him was a generous reward.   150
O all you Genovese, you men estranged
   from every good, at home with every vice,
   why can't the world be wiped clean of your race?   153
For in company with Romagna's rankest soul[9]
   I found one of your men, whose deeds were such
   that his soul bathes already in Cocytus   156
but his body seems alive and walks among you.

---

6. A member of the Jovial Friars (see 23.103), he killed two of his relatives during a banquet at his house, signaling the assassins with an order to bring the fruit. In saying that he is now being served dates instead of figs, he is ironically complimenting God for his generosity, since a date would be more valuable than a fig.
7. One of the mythological figures known as the Fates; she is the one who cuts the thread of life.
8. A nobleman of Genoa (a "Genovese" in line 151), who with a "close kinsman" (line 146) killed his father-in-law, Michel Zanche (line 144), at a banquet in 1275 or 1290.
9. That is, Friar Alberigo (line 118); Romagna is the part of Italy from which he and Branca come.

CANTO XXXIV

Far across the frozen ice can be seen the gigantic figure of Lucifer, who appears
from this distance like a windmill seen through fog; and as the two travelers walk on
toward that terrifying sight, they see the shades of sinners totally buried in the frozen
water. At the center of the earth Lucifer stands frozen from the chest downward,
and his horrible ugliness (he has three faces) is made more fearful by the fact that in
each of his three mouths he chews on one of the three worst sinners of all mankind,
the worst of those who betrayed their benefactors: Judas Iscariot, Brutus, and Cas-
sius. Virgil, with the Pilgrim on his back, begins the descent down the shaggy body
of Lucifer. They climb down through a crack in the ice, and when they reach the
Evil One's thighs, Virgil turns and begins to struggle upward (because they have
passed the center of the earth), still holding on to the hairy body of Lucifer, until
they reach a cavern, where they stop for a short rest. Then a winding path brings
them eventually to the earth's surface, where they see the stars.

"Vexilla regis prodeunt Inferni,"[1]
   my master said, "closer to us, so now
   look ahead and see if you can make him out."   3
A far-off windmill turning its huge sails
   when a thick fog begins to settle in,
   or when the light of day begins to fade,   6
that is what I thought I saw appearing.
   And the gusts of wind it stirred made me shrink back
   behind my guide, my only means of cover.   9
Down here,[2] I stood on souls fixed under ice
   (I tremble as I put this into verse);
   to me they looked like straws worked into glass.   12
Some lying flat, some perpendicular,
   either with their heads up or their feet,
   and some bent head to foot, shaped like a bow.   15
When we had moved far enough along the way
   that my master thought the time had come to show me
   the creature who was once so beautiful,[3]   18
he stepped aside, and stopping me, announced:
   "This is he, this is Dis;[4] this is the place
   that calls for all the courage you have in you."   21
How chilled and nerveless, Reader, I felt then;
   do not ask me—I cannot write about it—
   there are no words to tell you how I felt.   24
I did not die—I was not living either!
   Try to imagine, if you can imagine,
   me there, deprived of life and death at once.   27

1. The first three words—"the banners of the
king advance"—are the opening lines of a 6th-
century Latin hymn traditionally sung during
Holy Week to celebrate Christ's Passion.
Dante has added the last word, *Inferni*—"the
banners of the king of Hell advance"—in order
to apply the words to Satan.
2. This is the last and lowest subdivision of
Caïna, known as Judecca after Judas; the sinners here are those who betrayed their benefactors.
3. Lucifer, the "light-bearer," was the most
beautiful of angels before he rebelled and was
renamed Satan.
4. A classical name for Pluto, here applied to
Satan (see also 11.65).

The king of the vast kingdom of all grief
  stuck out with half his chest above the ice;
  my height is closer to the height of giants   30
than theirs is to the length of his great arms;
  consider now how large all of him was:
  this body in proportion to his arms.   33
If once he was as fair as now he's foul
  and dared to raise his brows against his Maker,
  it is fitting that all grief should spring from him.   36
Oh, how amazed I was when I looked up
  and saw a head—one head wearing three faces![5]
  One was in front (and that was a bright red),   39
the other two attached themselves to this one
  just above the middle of each shoulder,
  and at the crown all three were joined in one: 42
The right face was a blend of white and yellow,
  the left the color of those people's skin
  who live along the river Nile's descent.[6]   45
Beneath each face two mighty wings stretched out,
  the size you might expect of this huge bird
  (I never saw a ship with larger sails):   48
not feathered wings but rather like the ones
  a bat would have. He flapped them constantly,
  keeping three winds continuously in motion   51
to lock Cocytus eternally in ice.
  He wept from his six eyes, and down three chins
  were dripping tears all mixed with bloody slaver.   54
In each of his three mouths he crunched a sinner,
  with teeth like those that rake the hemp and flax,
  keeping three sinners constantly in pain;   57
the one in front—the biting he endured
  was nothing like the clawing that he took:
  sometimes his back was raked clean of its skin.   60
"That soul up there who suffers most of all,"
  my guide explained, "is Judas Iscariot:
  the one with head inside and legs out kicking.   63
As for the other two whose heads stick out,
  the one who hangs from that black face is Brutus[7]—
  see how he squirms in silent desperation;   66
the other one is Cassius,[8] he still looks sturdy.
  But soon it will be night. Now is the time
  to leave this place, for we have seen it all."   69
I held on to his neck, as he told me to.
  while he watched and waited for the time and place,
  and when the wings were stretched out just enough,   72

---

5. Satan's three faces (and much else) make
him an infernal parody of the Trinity.
6. I.e., Ethiopians. The significance of these
three colors is not certain; it has been suggested that they represent hatred, impotence,
and ignorance as the opposites of the divine

attributes of love, omnipotence, and wisdom
(see 3.5–6).
7. The murderer of Julius Caesar in 44 B.C.E.
and thus for Dante a betrayer of the empire.
8. The other murderer of Caesar.

he grabbed on to the shaggy sides of Satan;
   then downward, tuft by tuft, he made his way
   between the tangled hair and frozen crust.   75
When we had reached the point exactly where
   the thigh begins, right at the haunch's curve,
   my guide, with strain and force of every muscle,   78
turned his head toward the shaggy shanks of Dis
   and grabbed the hair as if about to climb—
   I thought that we were heading back to Hell.[9]   81
"Hold tight, there is no other way," he said,
   panting, exhausted, "only by these stairs
   can we leave behind the evil we have seen."   84
When he had got me through the rocky crevice,
   he raised me to its edge and set me down,
   then carefully he climbed and joined me there.   87
I raised my eyes, expecting I would see
   the half of Lucifer I saw before.
   Instead I saw his two legs stretching upward.   90
If at that sight I found myself confused,
   so will those simple-minded folk who still
   don't see what point it was I must have passed.   93
"Get up," my master said, "get to your feet,
   the way is long, the road a rough climb up,
   already the sun approaches middle tierce!"[1]   96
It was no palace promenade we came to,
   but rather like some dungeon Nature built:
   it was paved with broken stone and poorly lit.   99
"Before we start to struggle out of here,
   O master," I said when I was on my feet,
   "I wish you would explain some things to me.   102
Where is the ice? And how can he be lodged
   upside-down? And how, in so little time,
   could the sun go all the way from night to day?"   105
"You think you're still on the center's other side,"
   he said, "where I first grabbed the hairy worm
   of rottenness that pierces the earth's core;   108
and you *were* there as long as I moved downward
   but, when I turned myself, you passed the point
   to which all weight from every part is drawn.[2]   111

---

9. Virgil's reversal marks the point at which the two travelers pass from the Northern to the Southern Hemisphere. They began by climbing down Satan's body, but now reverse directions and climb up from the Earth's center (hence when they have passed through the center Dante sees Satan's legs sticking up [line 90]). Note that the travelers pass through the glassy ice, a passage that probably echoes I Corinthians 13.12: "For now we see through a glass, darkly; but then face to face."

1. About 7:30 A.M. on Holy Saturday. Dante has added 12 hours to his scheme so that the travelers will emerge from the Earth and arrive at the shore of Mount Purgatory just before sunrise on the next day, Easter Sunday. 2. The center of the earth, which is for Dante the center of the universe, and therefore the place where gravity is the strongest. Being furthest from Heaven, it is also the place which is most material and least spiritual.

Now you are standing beneath the hemisphere[3]
    which is opposite the side covered by land,
    where at the central point was sacrificed   114
the Man whose birth and life were free of sin.
    You have both feet upon a little sphere
    whose other side Judecca occupies;   117
when it is morning here, there it is evening.[4]
    And he whose hairs were stairs for our descent
    has not changed his position since his fall.   120
When he fell from the heavens on this side,[5]
    all of the land that once was spread out here,
    alarmed by his plunge, took cover beneath the sea   123
and moved to our hemisphere; with equal fear
    the mountain-land, piled up on this side, fled
    and made this cavern here when it rushed upward.   126
Below somewhere there is a space, as far
    from Beelzebub[6] as the limit of his tomb,
    known not by sight but only by the sound   129
of a little stream[7] that makes its way down here
    through the hollow of a rock that it has worn,
    gently winding in gradual descent."   132
My guide and I entered that hidden road
    to make our way back up to the bright world.
    We never thought of resting while we climbed.   135
We climbed, he first and I behind, until,
    through a small round opening ahead of us
    I saw the lovely things the heavens hold,   138
and we came out to see once more the stars.[8]

3. I.e., under the Southern Hemisphere, exactly opposite Jerusalem where Christ ("the Man whose birth and life were free of sin") was crucified. Jerusalem is the center of the Northern Hemisphere (see Ezekiel 5.5) and is located directly over the cavity of Hell.
4. The "little sphere" upon which they stand is the other side of Judecca, which is a hollow. The sun is now over the Southern Hemisphere, and therefore it is night in the Northern, where Hell is located.
5. The land that was in the Southern Hemisphere before Satan fell fled to the Northern to avoid him; hence the Southern Hemisphere is composed of water. The exception is that when Satan plunged into the center of the world, the earth close to his body in the Northern Hemisphere moved "with equal fear" (line 124) to the Southern Hemisphere and became "mountain-land" (line 125), which is Mount Purgatory. "This cavern" (line 126) refers to

Hell: Mount Purgatory is thus comprised of the land displaced by Satan in his fall. This elaborate explanation for medieval geography is Dante's own poetic scheme.
6. Satan.
7. This stream must flow down from Purgatory, perhaps from Lethe. It finds its source in "a space" (line 127) on Mount Purgatory; thus it is "as far from Beelzebub as the limit of his tomb"—that is, it is located on the surface of the Southern Hemisphere, which since Satan is at the center of the earth is the same distance from him as Hell (his "tomb") is deep. When Dante has Virgil say that it is "below" (line 127) he must be writing from the perspective of the Northern Hemisphere, since Mount Purgatory is at this moment above the travelers.
8. Each of the three parts of the Divine Comedy end with the word "stars" as an affirmation of God's benevolent order.

From Purgatorio

CANTO I

Having left the Inferno behind, Dante announces his intention to sing of the second kingdom, Purgatory, and calls upon the Muses, in particular Calliope, to accompany his song. As the dawn approaches, he feels a sense of renewal, and, looking up into the heavens, he sees four stars. Turning his gaze earthward again, he discovers standing near him a dignified old man: Cato of Utica. Cato thinks Dante and Virgil are refugees from Hell, and he questions them as to how they managed to escape. Virgil explains that Dante is still a living man, and that, at the command of a lady from Heaven, he, Virgil, has been sent to guide this man on a journey for the purpose of his salvation. Already this journey has taken them through Hell, and now it is their intention to see the souls of Purgatory. Cato assents to their passage. He then instructs Virgil to bind a reed around the Pilgrim's waist and to be sure to cleanse him of every trace of stain from the infernal regions. The two poets descend to the shore, where they proceed to carry out Cato's instructions. The purgation is marked by a miracle: when Virgil pulls a reed from the ground, another springs up immediately to take its place.

For better waters, now, the little bark
   of my poetic powers hoists its sails,
   and leaves behind that cruelest of the seas.[9]   3
And I shall sing about that second realm
   where man's soul goes to purify itself
   and become worthy to ascend to Heaven.   6
Here let death's poetry arise to life,
   O Muses sacrosanct whose liege I am!
   And let Calliope[1] rise up and play   9
her sweet accompaniment in the same strain
   that pierced the wretched magpies with the truth
   of unforgivable presumptuousness.[2]   12
The tender tint of orient sapphire,
   suffusing the still reaches of the sky,
   as far as the horizon deeply clear,[3]   15
renewed my eyes' delight, now that I found
   myself free of the deathly atmosphere
   that had weighed heavy on my eyes and heart.   18
The lovely planet kindling love in man[4]
   made all the eastern sky smile with her light,
   veiling the Fish[5] that shimmered in her train.   21

9. The metaphor of the poem as a ship ("bark") is traditional; the "better waters" refer to Purgatory, while "that cruelest of the seas" is Hell.
1. The Muse of epic poetry.
2. The nine daughters of Pierus—the Pierides—challenged the Muses to a singing contest and, having lost, were turned into magpies: see Ovid, *Metamorphoses* 5.

3. The time is just before sunrise on Easter Sunday, 1300.
4. Venus, the morning star, although in fact on this date Venus would have been visible only after sunrise.
5. The constellation Pisces, in which Venus would have been located if it had risen before the sun on this date.

Then to my right I turned to contemplate
   the other pole and there saw those four stars
   the first man saw, and no man after him.[6]   24
The heavens seemed to revel in their flames.
   O widowed Northern Hemisphere, deprived
   forever of the vision of their light![7]   27
And when I looked away from those four stars,
   turning a little toward the other pole,
   where no sign of the Wain[8] was visible,   30
I saw near me an ancient man,[9] alone,
   whose face commanded all the reverence
   that any son could offer to his sire.   33
Long-flowing was his beard and streaked with white,
   as was his hair, which in two tresses fell
   to rest upon his chest on either side.   36
The rays of light from those four sacred stars
   struck with such radiance upon his face,
   it was as if the sun were shining there.   39
"Who are you two who challenged the blind stream[1]
   and have escaped from the eternal prison?"
   he said, moving his venerable locks.   42
"Who guided you? What served you as a lamp
   to light your way out of the heavy night
   that keeps the pit of Hell forever black?   45
Are all the laws of God's Abyss destroyed?
   Have new decisions now been made in Heaven
   so that, though damned, you come up to my cliff?"   48
My leader quickly seized me by the arm;
   his words, his touch, the way he looked at me,
   compelled my knees and brow to reverence.   51
Then he addressed him: "Not on my behalf
   have I come here; a lady sent from Heaven[2]
   asked me to guide this man along his way.   54
But since it is your will that we reveal
   the circumstances of our presence here,
   how can my will deny yours what it asks?   57
This man has not yet seen his final hour,
   although so close to it his folly brought him
   that little time was left to change his ways.   60

6. Prior to their expulsion from Eden, which is located on the summit of Mount Purgatory, Adam and Eve saw four stars above the South Pole. These stars symbolize the four cardinal virtues: prudence, temperance, justice, and fortitude.
7. Dante is lamenting the corruption of his present time compared to the perfection of life before the Fall.
8. The constellation Ursa Major, which never disappears from northern skies but is not visible to an observer in the Southern Hemi-sphere. "The other pole": the North Pole.
9. Cato (95–46 B.C.E.), a Roman known for his uncompromising morality and love of liberty; rather than submit to what he saw as Julius Caesar's tyranny, he committed suicide in Utica, a city in North Africa. Dante is here influenced by Virgil's treatment of Cato in the underworld, where he is presented not as a suicide but as the lawgiver to the righteous (*Aeneid* 6).
1. Lethe (see *Inferno* 34.130–32).
2. Beatrice.

So I was sent to help him, as I said;
　　there was no other way to save his soul
　　than by my guiding him along this road.　　63
Already I have shown him all the Damned:
　　I want to show him now the souls of those
　　who purge themselves of guilt in your domain.　　66
How we came here would take too long to tell;
　　from Heaven comes the power that has served
　　to lead him here to see and hear you now.　　69
May it please you to welcome him—he goes
　　in search of freedom, and how dear that is,
　　the man who gives up life for it well knows.　　72
You know, you found death sweet in Utica
　　for freedom's sake; there you put off that robe
　　which will be radiant on the Great Day.[3]　　75
We have not broken Heaven's timeless laws.
　　This man still lives; Minòs does not bind *me*;[4]
　　I come from that same Round where the chaste eyes　　78
of your dear Marcia[5] still plead with your soul,
　　O blessed heart, to hold her as your own;
　　for love of her, then, bend your will to ours,　　81
allow us to go through your seven realms,
　　and I shall tell her how you have been kind—
　　if you will let me speak your name below."　　84
"Marcia was so enchanting to my eyes,"
　　he answered then, "that while I was alive,
　　there was no wish of hers I would not grant.　　87
She dwells beyond the evil river now,
　　and can no longer move me by that law
　　decreed upon the day I issued forth.[6]　　90
But if a heavenly lady, as you say,
　　moves and directs you, why your flattery?
　　Ask in her name, there is no need for more.　　93
Go with this man, see that you gird his waist
　　with a smooth reed;[7] take care to bathe his face
　　till every trace of filth has disappeared,　　96
for it would not be fitting that he go
　　with vision clouded by the mists of Hell,
　　to face the first of Heaven's ministers.　　99
Around this little island at its base,
　　down there, just where the waves break on the shore,
　　you will find rushes growing in soft sand.　　102
No other plant producing leaves or stalk

---

3. "That robe" is the body, which will be glorified in its resurrection on Judgment Day.
4. See *Inferno* 5.4.
5. Cato's wife, now in Limbo (see *Inferno*
4.128); according to a story told by the Roman
poet Lucan (39–65 C.E.), Cato ceded Marcia
to his friend Hortensius, but on Hortensius's

death Marcia's entreaty to Cato that he remarry
her was granted.
6. Cato was freed during the Harrowing of
Hell (see *Inferno* 4.53) and is now unmoved
by the sufferings of those left behind. "The
evil river": Acheron.
7. The "reed" is a symbol of humility.

that hardens could survive in such a place—
   only the reeds that yield to buffeting.   105
When you are ready to begin to scale
   the mountainside, do not come back this way;
   the rising sun will show you where to climb."   108
With that he vanished. From my knees I rose,
   and silent, drawing closer to my guide,
   I looked into his eyes. He said to me: 111
"Follow my footsteps; now we must turn back,
   for over there the plain begins to slope,
   descending gently to the shore below."   114
The dawn was gaining ground, putting to flight
   the last hour of the night; I recognized,
   far off, the rippling waters of the sea.   117
We made our way along that lonely plain
   like men who seek the right path they have lost,
   counting each step a loss till it is found.   120
When we had reached a place where the cool shade
   allowed the dew to linger on the slope,
   resisting a while longer the sun's rays,   123
my master placed both of his widespread hands
   gently upon the tender grass, and I,
   who understood what his intention was,   126
offered my tear-stained face to him, and he
   made my face clean, restoring its true color,
   once buried underneath the dirt of Hell.   129
At last we touched upon the lonely shore
   that never yet has seen its waters sailed
   by one who then returned to tell the tale.   132
There, as another willed, he girded me.
   Oh, miracle! When he pulled out the reed,
   immediately a second humble plant   135
sprang up from where the first one had been picked.

CANTO II

As the sun rises, Dante and Virgil are still standing at the water's edge and wondering which road to take in order to ascend the mountain of Purgatory, when the Pilgrim sees a reddish glow moving across the water. The light approaches at an incredible speed, and eventually they are able to discern the wings of an angel. The angel is the miraculous pilot of a ship containing souls of the Redeemed, who are singing the psalm In exitu Israël de Aegypto. At a sign from the angel boatsman, these souls disembark, only to roam about on the shore. Apparently, they are strangers, and, mistaking Virgil and Dante for familiars of the place, they ask them which road leads up the mountainside. Virgil answers that they, too, are pilgrims, only recently arrived. At this point some of the souls realize that the Pilgrim is still alive, and they stare at him in fascination. Recognizing a face that he knows in this crowd of souls, Dante tries three times in vain to embrace the shade of his old friend Casella, a musician; then he asks Casella for a song and, as he sings, all the souls are held spellbound. Suddenly the Just Old Man, Cato, appears to disperse the rapt crowd, sternly rebuking them for their negligence and exhorting them to run to the mountain to begin their ascent.

The sun was touching the horizon now,[8]
  the highest point of whose meridian arc
  was just above Jerusalem; and Night,   3
revolving always opposite to him,
  rose from the Ganges with the Scales that fall
  out of her hand when she outweighs the day.   6
Thus, where we were, Aurora's lovely face
  with a vermilion flush on her white cheeks
  was aging in a glow of golden light.   9
We were still standing at the water's edge,
  wondering about the road ahead, like men
  whose thoughts go forward while their bodies stay,   12
when, suddenly, I saw, low in the west
  (like the red glow of Mars that burns at dawn
  through the thick haze that hovers on the sea),   15
a light—I hope to see it come again!—
  moving across the waters at a speed
  faster than any earthly flight could be.   18
I turned in wonder to my guide, and then,
  when I looked back at it again, the light
  was larger and more brilliant than before,   21
and there appeared, on both sides of this light,
  a whiteness indefinable, and then,
  another whiteness grew beneath the shape.   24
My guide was silent all the while, but when
  the first two whitenesses turned into wings,
  and he saw who the steersman was, he cried: 27
"Fall to your knees, fall to your knees! Behold
  the angel of the Lord! And fold your hands.
  Expect to see more ministers like him.   30
See how he scorns to use man's instruments;
  he needs no oars, no sails, only his wings
  to navigate between such distant shores.   33
See how he has them pointing up to Heaven:
  he fans the air with these immortal plumes
  that do not moult as mortal feathers do."   36
Closer and closer to our shore he came,
  brighter and brighter shone the bird of God,
  until I could no longer bear the light,   39
and bowed my head. He steered straight to the shore,
  his boat so swift and light upon the wave,
  it left no sign of truly sailing there;   42
and the celestial pilot stood astern
  with blessedness inscribed upon his face.
  More than a hundred souls were in his ship: 45

8. The opening nine lines designate the time by reference to Jerusalem (where the sun is setting), the Ganges (where it is midnight, and where the constellation Libra—the Scales—is in the sky), and Mount Purgatory (where the dawn—Aurora—is gradually reddening).

In exitu Israël de Aegypto,[9]
    they all were singing with a single voice,
    chanting it verse by verse until the end.   48
The angel signed them with the holy cross,
    and they rushed from the ship onto the shore;
    he disappeared, swiftly, as he had come.   51
The souls left there seemed strangers to this place:
    they roamed about, while looking all around,
    endeavoring to understand new things.   54
The sun, which with its shafts of light had chased
    the Goat out of the heavens' highest field,[1]
    was shooting rays of day throughout the sky,   57
when those new souls looked up to where we were,
    and called to us: "If you should know the road
    that leads up to the mountainside, show us."   60
And Virgil answered them: "You seem to think
    that we are souls familiar with this place,
    but we, like all of you, are pilgrims here;   63
we just arrived, not much ahead of you,
    but by a road which was so rough and hard—
    to climb this mountain now will be like play."   66
Those souls who noticed that my body breathed,
    and realized that I was still alive,
    in their amazement turned a deathly pale.   69
Just as a crowd, greedy for news, surrounds
    the messenger who bears the olive branch,
    and none too shy to elbow-in his way,   72
so all the happy souls of these Redeemed
    stared at my face, forgetting, as it were,
    the way to go to make their beauty whole.   75
One of these souls pushed forward, arms outstretched,
    and he appeared so eager to embrace me
    that his affection moved me to show mine.   78
O empty shades, whose human forms seem real!
    Three times I clasped my hands around his form,
    as many times they came back to my breast.[2]   81
I must have been the picture of surprise,
    for he was smiling as he drew away,
    and I plunged forward still in search of him.   84
Then, gently, he suggested I not try,
    and by his voice I knew who this shade was;
    I begged him stay and speak to me awhile.   87

---

9. "When Israel went out of Egypt" (Latin). This is the first verse of Psalm 113 (114 in Protestant Bibles), which is a song of thanksgiving for the liberation of the Israelites from Egypt. Christians understood this liberation as prefiguring the salvation of sinners through Christ. That the day is Easter Sunday gives the psalm special relevance.
1. The constellation Capricorn can now not be seen because of the growing light.
2. In his visit to the underworld in book 6 of the *Aeneid*, Aeneas also tries three times to embrace his father Anchisës.

"As once I loved you in my mortal flesh,
   without it now I love you still," he said.
   "Of course I'll stay. But tell me why you're here."   90
"I make this journey now, O my Casella,
   hoping one day to come back here again,"[3]
   I said. "But how did you lose so much time?"   93
He answered: "I cannot complain if he
   who, as he pleases, picks his passengers,
   often refused to take me in his boat,   96
for that Just Will is always guiding his.[4]
   But for the last three months, indulgently,
   he has been taking all who wish to cross;[5]   99
so, when I went to seek the shore again,
   where Tiber's waters turn to salty sea,[6]
   benignly, he accepted me aboard.   102
Now, back again he flies to Tiber's mouth,
   which is the meeting place of all the dead,
   except for those who sink to Acheron's shore."[7]   105
"If no new law prevents remembering
   or practicing those love songs that once brought
   peace to my restless longings in the world,"   108
I said, "pray sing, and give a little rest
   to my poor soul which, burdened by my flesh,
   has climbed this far and is exhausted now."   111
Amor che ne la mente mi ragiona,[8]
   began the words of his sweet melody—
   their sweetness still is sounding in my soul.   114
My master and myself and all those souls
   that came with him were deeply lost in joy,
   as if that sound were all that did exist.   117
And while we stood enraptured by the sound
   of those sweet notes—a sudden cry: "What's this,
   you lazy souls?" It was the Just Old Man.[9]   120
"What negligence to stand around like this!
   Run to the mountain, shed that slough which still
   does not let God be manifest to you!"   123
Just as a flock of pigeons in a field
   peacefully feeding on the grain and tares,
   no longer strutting proud of how they look,   126

3. He journeys now so that after death he may return to Purgatory. Casella, a Florentine musician, was said to have set some of Dante's lyrics to music. The question that follows assumes that Casella died well before the present moment.
4. The angel who chooses the souls to cross in his boat is directed by God.
5. Pope Boniface proclaimed 1300—the year of the poem's action—a Jubilee or Holy Year, when those making pilgrimage to Rome were granted release from punishments for their sins (see *Inferno* 18.28). Dante follows popular belief in assuming that this grant applies to the souls awaiting transport to Purgatory as well as to the living.
6. At Ostia, where the Tiber enters the sea.
7. Hell.
8. "Love that speaks to me in my mind" is the first line of a lyric that Dante included in his prose philosophical work, the *Convivio*, which he left incomplete.
9. Cato.

immediately abandon all their food,
    flying away, seized by a greater need—
    if something should occur that startles them—   129
so did that new-formed flock of souls give up
    their feast of song, and seek the mountainside,
    rushing to find a place they hoped was there.   132
And we were just as quick to take to flight.

*   *   *

CANTO XXI

*As the Pilgrim and Virgil walk along the Terrace of the Avaricious, a shade appears
and speaks to them. Virgil explains that the Pilgrim is still alive, and he relates the
nature and purpose of their journey, finally asking the shade why the mountain has
just trembled. The shade explains that the mountain of Purgatory is not subject to
the vicissitudes of Nature such as rain, wind, and lightning, but that when a soul
feels that the time of its purification has come to an end and it is ready to ascend to
Heaven, then the mountain shakes and voices shout praises to God. The shade
speaking is the one who has just experienced this release after more than five hundred years of purgation. He identifies himself as Statius, the author of the* Thebaid
and the unfinished Achilleid. *Statius claims that he has derived his poetic inspiration from the* Aeneid, *and he expresses his ardent wish to have lived when Virgil was
alive, and to have met the great poet. At these words the Pilgrim smiles knowingly,
and with his guide's permission, reveals to Statius that he is standing in the presence
of his mentor. Forgetting himself, Statius bends down to embrace Virgil's knees, but
is gently reminded by that prince of poets that they are only empty shades.*

The natural thirst which nothing satisfies
    except that water begged for long ago
    by the poor woman of Samaria   3
tormented me,[1] and haste was urging me
    along the crowded path, and I was still
    grieving at the just pain those souls must pay,   6
when suddenly—just as we read in Luke
    that Christ, new-risen from the tomb, appeared
    to the two men on the Emmaus road[2]—   9
a shade appeared! He had come from behind
    while we were trying not to step on shades,[3]
    quite unaware of him until he spoke: 12
"May God, my brothers, give you peace." At that,
    we quickly turned around, and Virgil then
    responded to his words appropriately,   15
and said: "May God's True Court which sentenced me
    to eternal banishment, lead you in peace
    into the Congregation of the Blest."   18

1. The thirst for knowledge can be quenched
only by divine revelation. In the previous canto
Dante has heard a cry of exultation and felt
Mount Purgatory shake; it is the meaning of
these events that he wishes to know. For the

woman of Samaria, see John 4.5–15.
2. Luke 24.13–17.
3. The avaricious are punished by being
bound prone to the Earth since they worshipped earthly things in life.

"What's that?" he said as we kept forging on.
   "If you are souls whom God will not receive,
   who let you climb His stairway this far up?"   21
And then my teacher said: "If you observe
   those marks the angel has traced on his brow,
   you'll see that he must dwell among the Just.[4]   24
But she who labors spinning day and night,
   had not spun out for him the flax which Clotho
   packs on her distaff for each one of us;[5]   27
therefore, his soul, sister to yours and mine,
   in coming up, could not come by itself,
   because it does not see as our eyes do.   30
And so I was brought up from Hell's wide throat
   to serve him as a guide, and guide I shall
   as far as my own knowledge will permit.   33
But can you tell me why the mountain shook
   so hard just now, and why all of the souls
   down to its marshy base, cried out as one?"   36
My leader's question pierced the needle's eye
   of my desire, and with the eager hope
   that this aroused, I felt my thirst relieved.   39
The shade said: "Sacred laws that rule this mount
   will not let anything take place that is
   uncustomary or irregular.   42
This place is not subject to any change:
   what Heaven takes from itself into itself,
   and nothing else, can serve as cause up here;[6]   45
therefore no rain, no hail, no snow can fall,
   nor dew nor hoarfrost form at any point
   beyond the three-step stairway down below.[7]   48
There are no clouds, misty or dense, no sign
   of lightning or of Thaumas' daughter,[8] she
   who often moves from place to place below;   51
nor can dry vapors rise beyond the height
   of those three steps of which I just now spoke,
   whereon Saint Peter's vicar[9] rests his feet.   54
Quakes may occur below, slight or severe,
   but tremors caused by winds hid in the earth
   (I know not why) have never reached this high.   57
Up here the mountain trembles when some soul

---

4. Before Dante entered Purgatory proper, an angel traced seven *P*s upon his forehead, one for each deadly sin (*peccatum* in Latin): see *Purgatorio* 9.112–14. The marks disappear one by one as he climbs the mountain and passes through each of the seven terraces appointed for the purgation of a sin.
5. According to classical mythology, the three Fates determine the span of a person's life: Clotho holds the spool, Lachesis spins the thread, and Atropos cuts it at the predestined time.

6. Purgatory is free from any earthly influence, and therefore any change must be caused by motion from above.
7. To reach the gate of Purgatory proper one must climb three steps, which represent the three stages of penance: contrition of heart, confession of mouth, and satisfaction by deeds.
8. Iris, goddess of the rainbow.
9. The angel who guards the entrance to Purgatory and who marked Dante's forehead.

feels itself pure enough to stand erect
    or start at once to climb—then, comes the shout. 60
The will to rise, alone, proves purity:
    once freed, it takes possession of the soul
    and wills the soul to change its company. 63
It willed to climb before, but the desire
    High Justice set against it, inspired it
    to wish to suffer—as once it wished to sin. 66
And I, who for five hundred years and more,
    have lain here in my pain, felt only now
    will free to raise me to a higher sill. 69
That's why you felt the quake and why you heard
    the pious dwellers on the mount praise God.
    May He soon call them up to be with Him." 72
This was his explanation. And my joy
    was inexpressible: the more the thirst,
    the more enjoyable becomes the drink. 75
And my wise leader: "Now I see what net
    holds you bound here, and how the mesh is torn,
    why the mount shakes, why you rejoice as one. 78
Now, if it please you, I would like to know
    who you once were, and learn from your own words
    why you have lain so many centuries here."[1] 81
"During the rule of the good Titus, who,
    assisted by the King of Kings, avenged
    the wounds that poured forth blood which Judas sold,[2] 84
I bore the title that endures the most
    and which is honored most," that soul replied;
    "renown I had, not yet the Christian faith.[3] 87
The spirit of my verses was so sweet
    that from Toulouse,[4] Rome called me to herself,
    and judged me worthy of the myrtle crown. 90
My name is Statius, still well known on earth.
    I sang of Thebes, then of Achilles' might,
    but found that second weight too great to bear. 93
The spark that kindled my poetic ardor
    came from the sacred flame that set on fire
    more than a thousand poets: I mean the *Aeneid*. 96
That was the mother of my poetry,
    the nurse that gave it suck. Without that poem,
    my verses would have not been worth a thing. 99
And if only I could have been alive
    when Virgil lived, I would consent to spend
    an extra year of exile on the mount." 102

1. The spirit reveals himself to be Statius (d. 96 C.E.), a Roman poet who composed an epic on the story of Thebes called the *Thebaid* and an unfinished epic on Achilles, the *Achilleid*.
2. The destruction of Jerusalem in 70 C.E. by the Roman emperor Titus in response to a rebellion was understood by Christians to be a divine punishment for the crucifixion of Christ.
3. He was a poet but not yet a Christian.
4. A city in southern France; Statius actually came from Naples, but Dante is following a medieval tradition.

At these words Virgil turned to me. His look
  told me in silence: "Silence!" But the power
  of a man's will is often powerless: 105
laughter and tears follow so close upon
  the passions that provoke them that the more
  sincere the man, the less they obey his will.   108
I smiled and unsmiled quicker than a blink,
  but he stopped speaking; staring straight at me,
  into the eyes, where secrets are betrayed: 111
"So may your toiling win you grace," he said,
  "tell me the reason for your smile just now—
  that smile that quickly came and quickly went."   114
Here I am caught between opposing sides:
  the one tells me be quiet, the other bids
  me to speak up. And so, I sigh. My guide   117
perfectly understood: "Don't be afraid
  to speak," he said: "speak to him, answer now
  the question he has asked so earnestly."   120
"You seem to find my smiling very strange,"
  I said to him, "O ancient spirit, but
  I have to tell you something stranger still: 123
This shade here who directs my eyes to Heaven
  is the poet Virgil, who bequeathed to you
  the power to sing the deeds of men and gods.   126
In truth, the only reason for my smile,
  is that you chose to mention Virgil here:
  your very words are guilty of my smile."   129
Already he was bending to embrace
  my teacher's feet, but Virgil: "Brother, no!
  You are a shade; it is a shade you see."   132
And Statius, rising: "Now you understand
  how much my love for you burns deep in me,
  when I forget about our emptiness   135
and deal with shadows as with solid things."

FROM CANTO XXII

Leaving the Fifth Terrace, the Pilgrim and Virgil, now accompanied by Statius, are directed to the next ledge by an angel who removes another P from the Pilgrim's forehead and pronounces those blessed who thirst for righteousness. Virgil tells Statius that he has felt a great deal of good will toward him ever since Juvenal had come down to Limbo with the report of Statius's love and admiration for Virgil. But he is puzzled as to how such a magnanimous spirit could find room in its heart for avarice. Statius explains that his sin was not Avarice, but Prodigality, and that whenever two sins are the immediate opposite of one another, they are purged together on the same terrace of the mountain of Purgatory. Virgil then asks Statius how he came to be a Christian, and Statius replies that it was Virgil's Fourth Eclogue that eventually led him to give ear to the Christian preachers. Once converted, however, he kept his faith a secret, and for this lack of zeal was consigned to spend four hundred years on the Terrace of the Slothful.

By now we had already left behind
   the angel who directs to the Sixth Round
   and from my brow erased another scar,[5]   3
saying that all who looked for righteousness
   are blest—omitting the *esuriunt,*
   and predicating only *sitiunt.*[6]   6
And I, lighter than I had felt before
   at any other stairs,[7] moved easily
   upward, behind those swiftly climbing shades.   9
Now, Virgil was already speaking: "Love,
   kindled by virtue, always kindles love,
   if the first flame is clearly visible;[8]   12
thus, ever since the day that Juvenal[9]
   came down to Hell's Limbo to be with us,
   and told me of the love you felt for me,   15
I have felt more good will toward you, more than
   was felt toward any person not yet seen;
   and so, these stairs will seem much shorter now.   18
But tell me   speak to me as to a friend,
   and as a friend, forgive me if I seem
   too bold in slackening decorum's reins—   21
how could your heart find room for avarice,
   with that abundant store of sound, good sense
   which you acquired with such diligence?"   24
These words of Virgil brought to Statius' lips
   a briefly lingering smile; then he replied:
   "All you have said reveals your love for me.   27
Appearances will often, it is true,
   give rise to false assumptions, when the truth
   to be revealed is hidden from our eyes.   30
Your question makes it clear to me that you
   believe my sin on earth was Avarice—
   perhaps because you found me where you did.   33
In truth, I had no part of Avarice;
   in fact, too little! The sin I purged below,
   thousands of months, was Prodigality.[1]   36
And if I had not come to change my ways
   while meditating on those lines you wrote,
   where you, enraged by human nature, cry: 39

5. The "scar" is a *P* for avarice, the sin cleansed on the previous terrace.
6. The angel quotes the beginning of the Fourth Beatitude from the Sermon on the Mount. "Blessed are they which do hunger and thirst after righteousness: for they shall be filled" (Matthew 5.6). He mentions only "thirst" (*sitiunt* in Latin), omitting hunger, which will appear at the end of the journey through the sixth terrace, where gluttony is purged.
7. Dante grows lighter as he is gradually relieved of the sins, symbolized by the *P*s on his forehead, that weigh him down.
8. Virtuous love, such as Statius displayed at the end of canto 21, will elicit a similar response.
9. A Roman poet, contemporary with Statius but who outlived him (dying about 140 C.E.), located with Virgil in Limbo, as described in *Inferno* 4.
1. Prodigality is a vice opposite to Avarice but its counterpart: both involve an excess in the use of money; in *Inferno* 7 the avaricious and the prodigal are punished together.

'To what extremes, O cursèd lust for gold
    will you not drive man's appetite?'[2] I would
    be rolling weights now in the dismal jousts.[3]   42
But when I understood how hands could spread
    their wings too wide in spending, then that sin,
    and all my others, I repented of.   45
How many shall rise bald the Final Day
    through ignorance of this vice, forbidding them
    repentance during life or on death's bed?[4]   48
And know that when the vice of any sin
    is the rebuttal of its opposite,
    the two of them wither together here.   51
So, though to purge myself I spent my time
    among those souls who weep for Avarice,
    my sin was just the opposite of theirs."
"Now, when you sang about the bitter strife   54
    of the twin sources of Jocasta's grief,"[5]
    the bard of the Bucolics[6] said to him,   57
"from what you wrote in Clio's[7] company,
    it does not seem that you were faithful then
    to that faith without which virtue is vain.[8]   60
If this be so, tell me—what heavenly sun
    or earthly beam lit up your course so that
    you could set sail behind the Fisherman."[9]   63
Statius said: "It was you directed me
    to drink Parnassus' waters[1]—it was you
    whose radiance revealed the way to God.   66
You were the lonely traveller in the dark
    who holds his lamp behind him, shedding light
    not for himself but to make others wise;   69
for you once wrote: 'The world is born again;
    Justice returns, and the first age of man,
    and a new progeny descends from heaven.'[2]   72
Through you I was a poet, through you, a Christian.
    And now, to show you better what I mean,
    I shall fill in my outline with more color.   75

2. Statius is quoting from *Aeneid* 3.
3. Be punished in the fourth circle of Hell, described in *Inferno* 7.
4. The close-cropped heads of the prodigal are described in *Inferno* 7.57.
5. Statius's *Thebaid* deals with the history of Thebes: Jocasta's husband, Laius, was unwittingly killed by their son, Oedipus, who then—again in ignorance—married Laius's widow, Oedipus's own mother. Their sons, Polynices and Eteocles, imprisoned their father in a dungeon and then fought over the throne of Thebes in a war in which they killed each other. It is this fratricidal war, in which Jocasta lost both her sons at once, to which Virgil refers.

6. Virgil's *Bucolics* contain his *Georgics* and *Eclogues*, which is quoted in lines 70–72.
7. The Muse of history, whom Statius invokes in the *Thebaid*.
8. I.e., Christianity.
9. I.e., followed Peter, a fisherman who became a fisher of men (see Mark 1.17).
1. Dante follows a tradition that takes *Parnassus*, a mountain in Greece, as the home of the Muses.
2. A slightly altered citation from Virgil's Fourth *Eclogue*. A pastoral poem written about 40 B.C.E., it celebrated the birth of the son of an important Roman politician but was taken by medieval Christians as a prophecy of the birth of Christ.

By then, the world was laboring in the birth
  of the true faith, sown by the messengers
  of the Eternal Kingdom;[3] and your words,   78
which I just quoted now, so harmonized
  with what the new preachers were saying then,
  that I would often go to hear them speak.   81
These men became so holy in my eyes
  that when Domitian[4] persecuted them,
  I wept, as they wept in their suffering,   84
and, for as long as I remained alive,
  I helped them, and their righteous way of life
  taught me to scorn all other faiths but theirs.   87
Before I brought the Greeks to Theban streams
  with my poetic art,[5] I was baptized,
  but was a secret Christian out of fear,   90
pretending to be pagan many years;
  and for this lack of zeal, I had to run
  four hundred years on the Fourth Circle.[6] Now,   93
please tell me, you who did remove the veil
  that once concealed from me the good I praise,
  tell me, while there is still some time to climb,   96
where is our ancient Terence, do you know?
  And Plautus, and Caecilius and Varius?[7]
  Have they been damned? If so, where are they lodged?"   99
"They all, along with Persius and me
  and others," said my guide, "are with that Greek
  the Muses suckled more than all the rest,   102
in the First Round of Hell's unlighted jail.
  We often talk about the mountain slope
  where our nine nurses[8] dwell eternally.   105
Euripides walks with us; Antiphon,
  Simonides, and Agathon are there,
  and other Greeks who wear the laurel crown.[9]   108
With us are many of your people too:
  Antigone, Deïphyle, Argia,
  Ismene, sad as she has ever been,   111
and she who showed Langia to the Greeks,
  and Thetis, and the daughter of Tiresias,
  Deïdamia with her sisters, too."[1]   114
The poets now were free of walls and stairs,
  both of them standing silent on the ledge,
  eager again to gaze at everything.   117

3. The apostles.
4. Roman emperor, 81–91 c.e., thought by early Christian historians to have persecuted Christians although there is little evidence for this.
5. The *Thebaid* describes how six Greek rulers joined with Polynices to invade Thebes and topple Eteocles from the throne.
6. Where Sloth, which is the cause of the

failure to perform religious duties, is purged.
7. These men and Persius (line 100) are Roman poets now in Limbo with Homer (lines 101–2).
8. The Muses walk on Mount Parnassus.
9. Greek dramatists and poets.
1. Characters from Statius's *Thebaid* and *Achilleid*, which Dante considered historical epics.

Already the four handmaids of the day[2]
  were left behind, and at the chariot-pole,
  the fifth was tilting up the blazing tip,   120
when my guide said: "I think we ought to move
  with our right shoulders to the outer edge,
  the way we always have gone round this mount."[3]   123
So, habit was our guide there, and we went
  our way with much less hesitation now,
  since worthy Statius gave us his assent.   126
They walked ahead and I, behind, alone,
  was paying close attention to their words,
  which taught me things about the art of verse.[4]   129

*   *   *

FROM CANTO XXIV

*The Pilgrim and Virgil are now on the sixth terrace, where Gluttony is punished.
Among other sinners, they meet Bonagiunta Orbicciana, a Florentine poet who was
acquainted with Dante. This selection from this canto begins with Bonagiunta citing one of Dante's most famous sonnets.*

"But, tell me, do I not see standing here
  him who brought forth the new poems that begin:
  'Ladies who have intelligence of Love.'"[5]   51
I said to him, "I am one who, when Love
  inspires me, takes careful note and then,
  gives form to what he dictates in my heart."   54
"My brother, now I see," he said, "the knot
  that held Guittone and the Notary
  and me back from the sweet new style[6] I hear!   57
Now, I see very clearly how your wings
  fly straight behind the dictates of that Love—
  this, certainly, could not be said of ours;   60
and no one who examines the two styles
  can clarify the difference more than I."
  Then, pleased with what he said, he said no more.   63

*   *   *

FROM CANTO XXVI

*Dante and Virgil are now on the seventh terrace, where Lechery is punished. Here
they meet another of Dante's literary contemporaries and continue the discussion of
literary issues.*

2. The hours, the fifth of which is guiding the
chariot of the sun: it is between 10 and 11 A.M.
3. Mount Purgatory is climbed by turning to
the right; the travelers descended into Hell by
turning to the left.
4. The canto continues with a new episode,
not relevant to the literary issues that have so
far occupied it.
5. The first line of the first lyric in Dante's
New Life, which tells the story in poetry and

prose of his transformation by his love for
Beatrice.
6. The *dolce stil novo* that Dante saw as char-
acterizing his own poetry and that was first
defined for him by Guido Guinizzelli, whom
he will meet in canto 26. The Notary (Giacomo
da Lentini) and Guittone d'Arezzo, like Bonagiunta, were Italian poets of the generation
before Dante's.

As for my name, I can fulfill your wish:
  I am Guido Guinizzelli[7]—here so soon,
  for I repented long before I died."   93
As King Lycurgus raged with grief, two sons
  discovered their lost mother and rejoiced[8]—
  I felt the same (though more restrained) to hear   96
that spirit name himself—father of me
  and father of my betters, all who wrote
  a sweet and graceful poetry of love.   99
I heard no more, I did not speak, I walked
  deep in my thoughts, my eyes fixed on his shade;
  the flames kept me from coming close to him.   102
At last my eyes were satisfied. And then
  I spoke, convincing him of my deep wish
  to serve him in whatever way I could.[9]   105
He answered me: "What I just heard you say
  has made a deep impression on my mind,
  which even Lethe[1] cannot wash away.   108
But if what you have told me is the truth,
  now tell me what it is that makes you show
  in words and looks this love you have for me?"   111
And I to him: "Those graceful poems of yours,
  which, for as long as our tongue serves for verse,
  will render precious even the ink you used."   114
"My brother, I can show you now," he said
  (he pointed to a spirit up ahead)[2]
  "a better craftsman of his mother tongue.   117
Poets of love, writers of tales in prose—
  better than all of them he was! They're fools
  who think him of Limoges a greater poet![3]   120
They judge by reputation, not by truth,
  their minds made up before they know the rules
  of reason and the principles of art.   123
Guittone[4] was judged this way in the past;
  many praised him and him alone—though, now,
  most men have been won over to the truth.   126
But now, if that high privilege be yours
  of climbing to the cloister, there where Christ
  is Abbot of the holy college, then,   129
please say a *Paternoster*[5] for me there—
  at least the part appropriate for us,
  who are by now delivered from all evil."   132

7. Bolognese poet (d. ca. 1276), considered
the greatest Italian poet prior to Dante. A
poem by him is included in *Medieval Lyrics:*
(pp. 354–56).
8. In an episode in Statius's *Thebaid*, a woman
condemned to death by the warrior Lycurgus
is saved at the last moment by the arrival of
her twin sons.
9. Dante here swears an oath to Guinizzelli to
which the reader is not given access.

1. The river of forgetfulness that the fully
purged souls will pass through in order to
renounce their earthly lives.
2. Guinizzelli is indicating Arnaut Daniel
(d. ca. 1210), a Provençal poet. A poem by him
is included in *Medieval Lyrics* (pp. 326–28)
3. The reference is to Giraut de Borneil
(d. ca. 1220), another Provençal poet.
4. See *Purgatorio* 24.56.
5. The Lord's Prayer.

Then, to make room for someone else, perhaps,
   he disappeared into the depths of fire
   the way fish seeking deeper waters fade.   135
I moved up toward the shade just pointed out,
   and told him my desire had prepared
   a gracious place of welcome for his name.   138
He readily and graciously replied:[6]
   "Tan m'abellis vostre cortes deman,
   Qu'ieu no me puesc no voill a vos cobrire.   141
Ieu sui Arnaut, que plor e vau cantan;
   consiros vei la passada folor,
   e vei jausen lo joi qu'esper, denan.   144
Ara vos prec, per aquella valor
   que vos guida al som de l'escalina,
   sovenha vos a temps de ma dolor!"   147
Then in the purifying flames he hid.

FROM CANTO XXVII

*The sun is near setting when the poets leave the souls of the Lustful and encounter
the angel of Chastity, singing the beatitude "Blessed are the Pure of Heart." The
angel tells them that they can go no farther without passing through the flames, but,
numbed with fear, the Pilgrim hesitates for a long time. Finally Virgil prevails upon
him and they make the crossing through the excruciating heat. As they emerge on
the other side, they hear the invitation "Come O ye blessed of my Father," and an
angel exhorts them to climb as long as there is still daylight. But soon the sun sets
and the poets are overcome by sleep. Toward morning the Pilgrim dreams of Leah
and Rachel, who represent the active and contemplative lives, respectively. When
he awakes, he is refreshed and eager and races up the remaining steps. In the last
few lines, included here, Virgil describes the moral development achieved by the
Pilgrim—such that he no longer needs his guidance. These are the last words that
Virgil will speak in the poem.*

* * *

And now, before the splendor of the dawn
   (more welcomed by the homebound pilgrim now,
   the closer he awakes to home each day),   111
night's shadows disappeared on every side;
   my sleep fled with them: I rose to my feet,
   for my great teachers were already up.   114
"That precious fruit which all men eagerly
   go searching for on many different boughs
   will give, today, peace to your hungry soul."[7]   117
These were the words that Virgil spoke to me,

---

6. Arnaut speaks not in Italian but in Provençal. His speech can be translated: "Your elegant request so pleases me, / I could not possibly conceal my name. / I am Arnaut, singing now through my tears, / regretfully recalling my past follies / and joyfully anticipating joy, / I beg you, in the name of the great power / guiding you to the summit of the stairs, / remember in good times my suffering here."

7. On this day Dante will enter the Earthly Paradise and find Beatrice, who will conduct him through Paradise.

and never was a more auspicious gift
   received, or given, with more joyfulness.   120
Growing desire, desire to be up there,
   was rising in me: with every step I took
   I felt my wings were growing for the flight.   123
Once the stairs, swiftly climbed, were all behind
   and we were standing on the topmost step,
   Virgil addressed me, fixing his eyes on mine: 126
"You now have seen, my son, the temporal
   and the eternal fire,[8] you've reached the place
   where my discernment now has reached its end.   129
I led you here with skill and intellect;
   from here on, let your pleasure be your guide:
   the narrow ways, the steep, are far below.   132
Behold the sun shining upon your brow,
   behold the tender grass, the flowers, the trees,
   which, here, the earth produces of itself.   135
Until those lovely eyes rejoicing come,
   which, tearful, once urged me to come to you,[9]
   you may sit here, or wander, as you please.   138
Expect no longer words or signs from me.
   Now is your will upright, wholesome and free,
   and not to heed its pleasure would be wrong: 141
I crown and miter you lord of yourself!"

FROM CANTO XXX

Dante has arrived at the Earthly Paradise on the top of Mount Purgatory. There Beatrice appears. The Pilgrim turns to Virgil to confess his overpowering emotions, only to find that Virgil has disappeared! Beatrice speaks sternly to Dante, calling him by name and reprimanding him for having wasted his God-given talents, wandering from the path that leads to Truth. So hopeless, in fact, was his case, to such depths did he sink, that the journey to see the souls of the Damned in Hell was the only way left of setting him back on the road to salvation.

* * *

Sometimes, as day approaches, I have seen
   all of the eastern sky a glow of rose,
   the rest of heaven beautifully clear,   24
the sun's face rising in a misty veil
   of tempering vapors that allow the eye
   to look straight at it for a longer time: 27
even so, within a nebula of flowers
   that flowed upward from angels' hands and then
   poured down, covering all the chariot,[1]   30
appeared a lady—over her white veil
   an olive crown and, under her green cloak,
   her gown, the color of eternal flame.[2]   33

8. Purgatory and Hell.
9. See *Inferno* 2.55–74.
1. Beatrice appears in a chariot accompanied by messengers of eternal life.
2. The colors are symbolic: white signifies hope; green, faith: and red, charity.

And instantly—though many years had passed
  since last I stood trembling before her eyes,
  captured by adoration, stunned by awe[3]—   36
my soul, that could not see her perfectly,
  still felt, succumbing to her mystery
  and power, the strength of its enduring love.   39
No sooner were my eyes struck by the force
  of the high, piercing virtue I had known
  before I quit my boyhood years,[4] than I   42
turned to the left—with all the confidence
  that makes a child run to its mother's arms,
  when he is frightened or needs comforting—   45
to say to Virgil: "Not one drop of blood
  is left inside my veins that does not throb:
  I recognize signs of the ancient flame."[5]   48
But Virgil was not there. We found ourselves
  without Virgil, sweet father, Virgil to whom
  for my salvation I gave up my soul.[6]   51
All the delights around me, which were lost
  by our first mother,[7] could not keep my cheeks,
  once washed with dew, from being stained with tears.   54
"Dante,[8] though Virgil leaves you, do not weep,
  not yet, that is, for you shall have to weep
  from yet another wound.[9] Do not weep yet."   57
Just as an admiral, from bow or stern,
  watches his men at work on other ships,
  encouraging their earnest labors—so,   60
rising above the chariot's left rail
  (when I turned round, hearing my name called out,
  which of necessity I here record),   63
I saw the lady who had first appeared
  beneath the angelic festival of flowers
  gazing upon me from beyond the stream.   66
Although the veil that flowed down from her head,
  fixed by the crown made of Minerva's leaves,[1]
  still kept me from a perfect view of her,   69
I sensed the regal sternness of her face,
  as she continued in the tone of one
  who saves the sharpest words until the end: 72
"Yes, look at me! Yes, I am Beatrice!
  So, you at last have deigned to climb the mount?
  You learned at last that here lies human bliss?"   75
I lowered my head and looked down at the stream,

---

3. Beatrice died in 1290, so it has been 10 years since Dante saw her.
4. Dante was 9 when he fell in love with Beatrice.
5. A quotation from Virgil's *Aeneid* 4; it is Dido's response upon first seeing Aeneas.
6. This tercet echoes Virgil's *Georgics* 4.525–27, in which Orpheus looks back and laments

the loss of Eurydice.
7. Eve, who caused the loss of the Eden in which Dante is now located.
8. This is the only time Dante's name appears in the *Commedia*.
9. The sharp words Beatrice will now speak.
1. These are olive leaves, sacred to Minerva, the Roman goddess of wisdom.

but, filled with shame at my reflection there,
   I quickly fixed my eyes upon the grass.   78
I was the guilty child facing his mother,
   abject before her harshness: harsh, indeed,
   is unripe pity not yet merciful.[2]   81

*   *   *

From Paradiso

CANTO XXXIII

Dante has been led by Beatrice and other guides to the highest point of the universe, the Empyrean. The final canto of the poem begins with a prayer by Bernard of Clairvaux (1091–1153), abbot of the monastery of Clairvaux in France and one of the great spiritual leaders and mystical writers of the Middle Ages. Bernard is present here both as a mystic and because of the role his writings played in developing the cult of the Virgin Mary. St. Bernard lovingly praises the Virgin Mary and then recounts the Pilgrim's journey through Hell, Purgatory, and the celestial spheres, entreating the Virgin to clear away the obstacles from the Pilgrim's eyes so that he may behold God's glory. Bernard then signals the Pilgrim to look upward, but he has already done so, spurred on by his clearer sight. He sees the multiform world bound in a single unity with love. Then, as he gazes into the Divine Light, he sees three rings of three different colors all of which share and are bound by one and the same circumference. The first ring of color reflects the second; both reflect the third: the miracle of the Trinity. Again the poet's words begin to fail him. He fixes his eyes on the second ring of reflected light and perceives God in the image of man, but he is unable to grasp how the forms coincide. Then with a sudden flash the Pilgrim's mind is illuminated by the Truth and he feels, now that the ultimate vision has been granted him, his desire and will turning in harmony with Divine Love, "the Love that moves the sun and the other stars."

"Oh Virgin Mother, daughter of your son,
   most humble, most exalted of all creatures
   chosen of God in His eternal plan,   3
you are the one who ennobled human nature
   to the extent that He did not disdain,
   Who was its Maker, to make Himself man.   6
Within your womb rekindled was the love
   that gave the warmth that did allow this flower[3]
   to come to bloom within this timeless peace.   9
For all up here you are the noonday torch
   of charity, and down on earth, for men,
   the living spring of their eternal hope.   12
Lady, you are so great, so powerful,
   that who seeks grace without recourse to you
   would have his wish fly upward without wings.   15

2. Beatrice's "pity" is "unripe" because it is not yet time for her to show it to Dante, the erring child.

3. In *Paradiso* 30 Dante saw the blessed souls arranged in a vast rose, to which Bernard now refers.

Not only does your loving kindness rush
  to those who ask for it, but often times
  it flows spontaneously before the plea.   18
In you is tenderness, in you is pity,
  in you munificence—in you unites
  all that is good in God's created beings.   21
This is a man who from the deepest pit
  of all the universe up to this height
  has witnessed, one by one, the lives of souls,   24
who begs you that you grant him through your grace
  the power to raise his vision higher still
  to penetrate the final blessedness.   27
And I who never burned for my own vision
  more than I burn for his, with all my prayers
  I pray you—and I pray they are enough—   30
that you through your own prayers dispel the mist
  of his mortality, that he may have
  the Sum of Joy revealed before his eyes.   33
I pray you also, Queen who can achieve
  your every wish, keep his affections sound
  once he has had the vision and returns.   36
Protect him from the stirrings of the flesh:
  you see, with Beatrice, all the Blest,
  hands clasped in prayer, are praying for my prayer."   39
Those eyes so loved and reverenced by God,
  now fixed on him who prayed, made clear to us
  how precious true devotion is to her;   42
then she looked into the Eternal Light,
  into whose being, we must believe, no eyes
  of other creatures pierce with such insight.   45
And I who was approaching now the end
  of all man's yearning, strained with all the force
  in me to raise my burning longing high.   48
Bernard then gestured to me with a smile
  that I look up, but I already was
  instinctively what he would have me be: 51
for now my vision as it grew more clear
  was penetrating more and more the Ray
  of that exalted Light of Truth Itself.   54
And from then on my vision rose to heights
   higher than words, which fail before such sight,
  and memory fails, too, at such extremes.   57
As he who sees things in a dream and wakes
  to feel the passion of the dream still there
  although no part of it remains in mind,   60
just such am I: my vision fades and all
  but ceases, yet the sweetness born of it
  I still can feel distilling in my heart: 63
so imprints on the snow fade in the sun,

and thus the Sibyl's oracle of leaves
was swept away and lost into the wind.[4]   66
O Light Supreme, so far beyond the reach
of mortal understanding, to my mind
relend now some small part of Your own Self,   69
and give to my tongue eloquence enough
to capture just one spark of all Your glory
that I may leave for future generations;   72
for, by returning briefly to my mind
and sounding, even faintly, in my verse,
more of Your might will be revealed to men.   75
If I had turned my eyes away, I think,
from the sharp brilliance of the living Ray
which they endured, I would have lost my senses.   78
And this, as I recall, gave me more strength
to keep on gazing till I could unite
my vision with the Infinite Worth I saw.   81
O grace abounding and allowing me to dare
to fix my gaze on the Eternal Light,
so deep my vision was consumed in It!   84
I saw how it contains within its depths
all things bound in a single book by love
of which creation is the scattered leaves: 87
how substance, accident, and their relation[5]
were fused in such a way that what I now
describe is but a glimmer of that Light.   90
I know I saw the universal form,
the fusion of all things, for I can feel,
while speaking now, my heart leap up in joy.   93
One instant brings me more forgetfulness
than five and twenty centuries brought the quest
that stunned Neptune when he saw Argo's keel.[6]   96
And so my mind was totally entranced
in gazing deeply, motionless, intent;
the more it saw the more it burned to see.   99
And one is so transformed within that Light
that it would be impossible to think
of ever turning one's eyes from that sight,   102
because the good which is the goal of will
is all collected there, and outside it
all is defective that is perfect there.   105

---

4. In *Aeneid* 3 Virgil describes how the Sibyl of Cumae writes down the future on leaves that the wind then scatters.
5. In the philosophical tradition followed by Dante, a "substance" is that which subsists in and of itself, an "accident" exists only as a quality or an attribute of a substance, and their "relation" is the way substances and accidents are bound together.
6. The voyage of Jason and the Argonauts after the golden fleece was thought to have occurred about 1300 B.C.E.; see *Inferno* 18.86–87.

Now, even in the things I do recall
  my words have no more strength than does a babe
    wetting its tongue, still at its mother's breast.   108
Not that within the Living Light there was
  more than a sole aspect of the Divine
    which always is what It has always been,   111
yet as I learned to see more, and the power
  of vision grew in me, that single aspect
    as I changed, seemed to me to change Itself.   114
Within Its depthless clarity of substance
  I saw the Great Light shine into three circles
    in three clear colors bound in one same space;[7]   117
the first seemed to reflect the next like rainbow
  on rainbow, and the third was like a flame
    equally breathed forth by the other two.   120
How my weak words fall short of my conception,
  which is itself so far from what I saw
    that "weak" is much too weak a word to use!   123
O Light Eternal fixed in Self alone,
  known only to Yourself, and knowing Self,
    You love and glow, knowing and being known!   126
That circling which, as I conceived it, shone
  in You as Your own first reflected light
    when I had looked deep into It a while,   129
seemed in Itself and in Its own Self-color
  to be depicted with man's very image.[8]
    My eyes were totally absorbed in It.   132
As the geometer who tries so hard
  to square the circle, but cannot discover,
    think as he may, the principle involved,[9]   135
so did I strive with this new mystery:
  I yearned to know how could our image fit
    into that circle, how could it conform;   138
but my own wings could not take me so high—
  then a great flash of understanding struck
    my mind, and suddenly its wish was granted.   141
At this point power failed high fantasy[1]
  but, like a wheel in perfect balance turning,
    I felt my will and my desire impelled   144
by the Love that moves the sun and the other stars.[2]

---

7. Signifying the Trinity.
8. Dante seems to see a human image in the center of the Godhead.
9. The problem of constructing a square equal in area to a circle is a proverbially insoluble mathematical problem.
1. By "fantasy" Dante means the capacity of the mind to form images; it is "high" because it is capable of representing in visible form invisible truths.
2. As in the *Inferno* and the *Purgatorio*, the last word of the *Paradiso* is "stars," returning us to the perspective of the human gazing up at that which is beyond the human.

KEBRA NAGAST
fourteenth century

The *Kebra Nagast* or *Book of the Glory of Kings* is, like the **Hebrew Bible**, the **New Testament Gospels**, and the **Qur'an**, both literature and sacred scripture. It is revered by Ethiopian Christians as a true account of the union of King Solomon and the Queen of Sheba, the birth of their son Menelik, and the movement of the ark of the covenant from Jerusalem to the Ethiopian capital of Axum, and continues to be read as a divinely inspired work by Rastafari communities in Jamaica and throughout the world. Yet the aims of the *Kebra Nagast* concern nation building as much as religious unity, as the Christian religious appropriation of the identity of the "true Israel" and the Ethiopian national appropriation of "real" Jewish identity go hand in hand. The movement of the ark from Jerusalem to the heart of Ethiopia, like the movement of the sacred images of the gods from Troy to Rome in **Virgil's** *Aeneid*, provides a tangible focal point for the advance of empire and stakes a nation's claim to supremacy.

THE TEXT IN CONTEXT:
MEDIEVAL CHRISTIAN ETHIOPIA

The Christian communities of Ethiopia date their origins to the first decades following the crucifixion of Jesus Christ, relying on verses in the Acts of the Apostles that recount the baptism of a visiting official from the court of the Queen of Sheba, his subsequent return, and the conversion of the nation. By the fifth century, however, the Ethiopian Church had come to claim a far older relationship with

Christianity, pointing to its ties with the forefathers of Jesus—especially Solomon, son of King David and himself ruler of Jerusalem. The connection of Jerusalem and the Ethiopian Christian capital at Axum was expressed both through holy texts such as the *Kebra Nagast* and through the art and architecture of the region. Ethiopian Christians believe that one of their most sacred sites, the church of Our Lady Mary of Zion, houses the very same ark of the covenant that the Jews carried with them through the desert on their way to the promised land, as recounted in Exodus. Reflecting its importance, the daughter churches of Ethiopia continue to provide to each individual congregation a reproduction of the tablets of the law whose originals are kept in the ark. Although the common vernacular language of the region is Amharic, the language used in the religious services of the Ethiopian Church is Ge'ez, which is also the language of the *Kebra Nagast* and other sacred scripture.

WORK

The *Kebra Nagast* is a compilation produced by a community of religious scholars, united by the divine inspiration that lies behind the written text. It establishes the origins of the national religion of Ethiopia in part by emphasizing the antiquity of the ruling house. The text includes a postscript that claims it was originally written in Coptic (a language used by the Christian communities of Egypt and North Africa), then translated into Arabic in 1225, and finally rendered in the local

Ethiopian language of Ge'ez. Only the Ge'ez version of the work survives, and scholars agree that it dates from the fourteenth century; they conjecture, from the presence of Arabic vocabulary in the Ge'ez text, that there must have been a lost Arabic version, but have found no trace of a previous version in Coptic.

The Kebra Nagast begins with a broad overview of the book's own purpose and origins, followed by a brief account of world geography. But the main thread of the narrative is a love story—that of Solomon, king of the Jews and ruler of Jerusalem, and Makeda, the lovely and accomplished Queen of Sheba. After learning from a traveling merchant about the profound wisdom of Solomon, the queen decides to travel to Jerusalem. There, she is as enraptured by Solomon's wisdom as he is by her beauty, and converts from her people's traditional worship of the sun, moon, and stars to instead revering the "God of Israel." The blissful union of Solomon and Makeda results in the birth of a child, Menelik (Bayna-Leḥkem), who will be heir to the Ethiopian throne. Although Solomon adores the queen as well as the firstborn son she has given him, it is impossible for him to install Menelik as his heir in Jerusalem. But as a sign of his special favor, Solomon determines to ensure that his son would carry with him back to Ethiopia a very special treasure: the luxurious cloth used to cover the ark of the covenant holding the tablets of the law, which had been carefully preserved in the great temple. When Menelik is on the journey homeward, however, he makes an extraordinary discovery. The young men of Jerusalem that Solomon has sent along to accompany his son to Ethiopia have brought with them not only the ceremonial cloth but the ark itself.

The Kebra Nagast is remarkable for the extraordinary variety of literary and theological sources on which it draws, ranging from the Hebrew Scriptures and the Gospels to rabbinic commentaries, Christian apocrypha, Islamic texts, and fanciful Syriac legends. This synthesis, which reflects the extent to which the ancient Ethiopian capital of Axum was a cultural crossroads, illustrates the cultural interchange that permeated the Red Sea region. The uniquely Ethiopian Christian identity crystalized in the Kebra Nagast has been mirrored in the work's reception in later periods, especially its central role in the black diaspora. Rastafari communities hold the Kebra Nagast in special reverence, envisioning the migration of the ark from Jerusalem to the Ethiopian capital of Axum as a model for their own migration into the New World, and their anticipated return—whether in body or in spirit—to the Ethiopian homeland of Zion. Western knowledge of the text was very limited until the late eighteenth century, when the Scottish explorer James Bruce carried home from Ethiopia a collection of valuable manuscripts that included a copy of the Kebra Nagast. The first English translation, by E. A. Wallis Budge, was published in 1922, and an updated version of Budge's work is reproduced here. The ornate style chosen by Budge, with its elevated, ceremonial diction, accurately reflects the liturgical language of the Ge'ez original. The formal, bejeweled style of the Kebra Nagast is suitable tribute to the "glory of kings" memorialized in the work.

From Kebra Nagast[1]

17. The Glory of Zion

And as concerning Zion, the Tabernacle of the Law of God:[2] at the very beginning, as soon as God had stablished the heavens, He ordained that it should become the habitation of His glory upon the earth. And willing this He brought it down to the earth, and permitted Moses to make a likeness of it. And He said unto him, "Make an ark (or, tabernacle) of wood that cannot be eaten by worms, and overlay it with pure gold. And thou shalt place therein the Word of the Law, which is the Covenant that I have written with Mine own fingers, that they may keep My law, the Two Tables of the Covenant."[3] Now the heavenly and spiritual [original] within it is of divers colours, and the work thereof is marvellous, and it resembleth jasper, and the sparkling stone, and the topaz, and the hyacinthine stone (?), and the crystal, and the light, and it catcheth the eye by force, and it astonisheth the mind and stupefieth it with wonder; it was made by the mind of God and not by the hand of the artificer, man, but He Himself created it for the habitation of His glory. And it is a spiritual thing and is full of compassion; it is a heavenly thing and is full of light; it is a thing of freedom and a habitation of the Godhead, Whose habitation is in heaven, and Whose place of movement is on the earth, and it dwelleth with men and with the angels, a city of salvation for men, and for the Holy Spirit a habitation. And within it are a Gomor[4] of gold [containing] a measure of the manna which came down from heaven; and the rod of Aaron which sprouted after it had become withered though no one watered it with water,[5] and one had broken it in two places, and it became three rods being [originally only] one rod.

And Moses covered [the Ark] with pure gold, and he made for it poles wherewith to carry it and rings [in which to place them], and they carried it before the people until they brought it into the land of [their] inheritance, which is Jerusalem, the City of Zion. And when they were crossing the Jordan and the priests were carrying it, the waters stood upright like a wall until all the people had passed over, and after all the people had passed over the priests passed over bearing the Ark, and they set it down in the city of Judah, the land of [their] inheritance. And prophets were appointed over the children of Israel in the Tabernacle of Testimony, and the priests wore the ephod, so that they might minister to the Tabernacle of Testimony, and the high priests offered up offerings, so that they might obtain remission of their own sins and of the sins of the people likewise.

And God commanded Moses and Aaron to make holy vessels for the Tabernacle of Testimony for the furnishing of the Holy of Holies, namely, vessels of gold, bowls and pots, pitchers and sacred tables, netted cloths and tops for pillars, lamps and vessels for filling them, torch-holders and snuffers, tongs, candlesticks, and rings and rods for carrying them, large bowls and lavers, embroidered curtains and hangings, crowns and worked vestments, purple cloths and leather work, carpets and draperies, unguents for anointing priests

1. Translated from the Ge'ez by E. A. Wallis Budge, who sometimes adds words in square brackets.
2. The ark of the covenant, containing the Ten Commandments (the tablets of the law) given to Moses at Sinai.
3. See Exodus 25.10–16.
4. Gomer or omer, a Hebrew dry measure equivalent to about 4 quarts.
5. See Numbers 17.8.

and kings, hyacinthine and purple hangings, rugs of double thickness and hangings of silk (?), skins of kids and red hides of rams, and sardius stones,[6] and rubies, and sapphires, and emeralds [and to place them] in the Tabernacle of Witness, where dwelleth Zion, the habitation of His glory. [And God told them] to make for it the "belly of a ship" with the Two Tables, which were written by the fingers of God—Zion shall rest upon them—And thou shalt make for it a tabernacle of wood that the worms cannot eat, whereon Zion shall rest, two cubits and half a cubit shall be the length thereof, and a cubit and half a cubit the breadth thereof, and thou shalt cover it with pure gold, both the outside thereof and the inside thereof. And thou shalt make the fittings and the cover thereof of fine gold, and there shall be rings round about it; and thou shalt make in the four sides four holes for the carrying-poles. And thou shalt make it of wood that the worms cannot eat, and thou shalt cover it with pure gold, and in this ye shall carry the Tabernacle of the Law.

In this wise did God command Moses on Mount Sinai, and He showed him the work thereof, and the construction and the pattern of the Tent, according to which he was to make it. And it (i.e., Zion) was revered and had exceedingly great majesty in Israel, and it was acknowledged by God to be the habitation of His glory. And He Himself came down on the mountain of His holiness, and He held converse with His chosen ones, and He opened to them [a way of] salvation, and He delivered them from the hand of their enemies. And he spake with them from the pillar of cloud, and commanded them to keep His Law and His commandments, and to walk in the precepts of God.

* * *

19. How this Book came to be found

And Dĕmâtĕyôs (Domitius), the Archbishop of Rôm (i.e., Constantinople, Byzantium), said, "I have found in the Church of [Saint] Sophia among the books and the royal treasures a manuscript [which stated] that the whole kingdom of the world [belonged] to the Emperor of Rôm and the Emperor of Ethiopia."

20. The Division of the Earth

From the middle of Jerusalem, and from the north thereof to the south-east is the portion of the Emperor of Rôm; and from the middle of Jerusalem from the north thereof to the south and to Western India is the portion of the Emperor of Ethiopia. For both of them are of the seed of Shem, the son of Noah, the seed of Abraham, the seed of David, the children of Solomon. For God gave the seed of Shem glory because of the blessing of their father Noah. The Emperor of Rôm is the son of Solomon, and the Emperor of Ethiopia is the firstborn and eldest son of Solomon.

21. The Queen of the South

And how this Queen was born I have discovered written in that manuscript, and in this manner also doth the Evangelist mention that woman. And our Lord Jesus Christ, in condemning the Jewish people, the crucifiers, who lived at that

---

6. Precious stones (sard is a reddish-orange variety of carnelian).

time, spake, saying: "The Queen of the South shall rise up on the Day of Judgment and shall dispute with, and condemn, and overcome this generation who would not hearken unto the preaching of My word, for she came from the ends of the earth to hear the wisdom of Solomon."[7] And the Queen of the South of whom He spake was the Queen of Ethiopia. And in the words "ends of the earth" [He maketh allusion] to the delicacy of the constitution of women, and the long distance of the journey, and the burning heat of the sun, and the hunger on the way, and the thirst for water. And this Queen of the South was very beautiful in face, and her stature was superb, and her understanding and intelligence, which God had given her, were of such high character that she went to Jerusalem to hear the wisdom of Solomon; now this was done by the command of God and it was His good pleasure. And moreover, she was exceedingly rich, for God had given her glory, and riches, and gold, and silver, and splendid apparel, and camels, and slaves, and trading men (or, merchants). And they carried on her business and trafficked for her by sea and by land, and in India, and in 'Aswân (Syene).

22. Tâmrîn, the Merchant

And there was a certain wise man, the leader of a merchant's caravan, whose name was Tâmrîn, and he used to load five hundred and twenty camels, and he possessed about three and seventy ships.

Now at that time King Solomon wished to build the House of God,[8] and he sent out messages among all the merchants in the east and in the west, and in the north and in the south, bidding the merchants come and take gold and silver from him, so that he might take from them whatsoever was necessary for the work. And certain men reported to him concerning this rich Ethiopian merchant, and Solomon sent to him a message and told him to bring whatsoever he wished from the country of Arabia, red gold, and black wood that could not be eaten by worms, and sapphires. And that merchant, whose name was Tâmrîn, the merchant of the Queen of Ethiopia, went to Solomon the King; and Solomon took whatsoever he desired from him, and he gave to the merchant whatsoever he wished for in great abundance. Now that merchant was a man of great understanding, and he saw and comprehended the wisdom of Solomon, and he marvelled [thereat], and he watched carefully so that he might learn how the King made answer by his word, and understand his judgment, and the readiness of his mouth, and the discreetness of his speech, and the manner of his life, and his sitting down and his rising up, and his occupations, and his love, and his administration, and his table, and his law. To those to whom Solomon had to give orders he spake with humility and graciousness, and when they had committed a fault he admonished them [gently]. For he ordered his house in the wisdom and fear of God, and he smiled graciously on the fools and set them on the right road, and he dealt gently with the maidservants. He opened his mouth in parables, and his words were sweeter than the purest honey; his whole behaviour was admirable, and his whole aspect pleasant. For wisdom is beloved by men of understanding, and is rejected by fools.

7. See Matthew 12.42, Luke 11.31.
8. That is, the temple of Solomon in Jerusa- lem (see I Kings 4–7), identified in the Middle Ages with the al-Aqsa mosque.

And when that merchant had seen all these things he was astonished, and he marvelled exceedingly. For those who were wont to see Solomon held him in complete affection, and he [became] their teacher; and because of his wisdom and excellence those who had once come to him did not wish to leave him and go away from him. And the sweetness of his words was like water to the man who is athirst, and like bread to the hungry man, and like healing to the sick man, and like apparel to the naked man. And he was like a father to the orphans. And he judged with righteousness and accepted the person of no man (*i.e.*, he was impartial). He had glory, and riches, which God had given unto him, in great abundance, namely, gold, and silver, and precious stones, and rich apparel, and cattle, and sheep, and goats innumerable. Now in the days of Solomon the King gold was as common as bronze, and silver as lead, and bronze and lead and iron were as abundant as the grass of the fields and the reeds of the desert; and cedarwood was also abundant. And God had given unto him glory, and riches, and wisdom, and grace in such abundance that there was none like unto him among his predecessors, and among those who came after him there was none like unto him.

23. How the Merchant returned to Ethiopia

And it came to pass that the merchant Tâmrîn wished to return to his own country, and he went to Solomon and bowed low before him, and embraced him, and said unto him, "Peace be to thy majesty! Send me away and let me depart to my country to my Lady, for I have tarried long in beholding thy glory, and thy wisdom, and the abundance of dainty meats wherewith thou hast regaled me. And now I would depart to my Lady. Would that I could abide with thee, even as one of the very least of thy servants, for blessed are they who hear thy voice and perform thy commands! Would that I could abide here and never leave thee! but thou must send me away to my Lady because of what hath been committed to my charge, so that I may give unto her her property. And as for myself, I am her servant." And Solomon went into his house and gave unto him whatever valuable thing he desired for the country of Ethiopia, and he sent him away in peace. And Tâmrîn bade him farewell, and went forth, and journeyed along his road, and came to his Lady, and delivered over to her all the possessions which he had brought. And he related unto her how he had arrived in the country of Judah [and] Jerusalem, and how he had gone into the presence of Solomon the King, and all that he had heard and seen. And he told her how Solomon administered just judgment, and how he spake with authority, and how he decided rightly in all the matters which he enquired into, and how he returned soft and gracious answers, and how there was nothing false about him, and how he appointed inspectors over the seven hundred woodmen who hauled the timber and the eight hundred masons who hewed the stone, and how he sought to learn from all the merchants and dealers concerning the cunning craft and the working thereof, and how he received information and imparted it two-fold, and how all his handicraft and his works were performed with wisdom.

And each morning Tâmrîn related to the Queen [about] all the wisdom of Solomon, how he administered judgment and did what was just, and how he ordered his table, and how he made feasts, and how he taught wisdom, and how he directed his servants and all his affairs on a wise system, and how they went on their errands at his command, and how no man defrauded another, and how no man purloined the property of his neighbour, and how there was neither a thief nor a robber in his days. For in his wisdom he knew those who had done wrong, and he chastised them, and made them afraid, and they did not repeat their evil deeds, but they lived in a state of peace which had mingled therein the fear of the King.

All these things did Tâmrîn relate unto the Queen, and each morning he recalled the things that he had seen with the King and described them unto her. And the Queen was struck dumb with wonder at the things that she heard from the merchant her servant, and she thought in her heart that she would go to him; and she wept by reason of the greatness of her pleasure in those things that Tâmrîn had told her. And she was exceedingly anxious to go to him, but when she pondered upon the long journey she thought that it was too far and too difficult to undertake. And time after time she asked Tâmrîn questions about Solomon, and time after time Tâmrîn told her about him, and she became very wishful and most desirous to go that she might hear his wisdom, and see his face, and embrace him, and petition his royalty. And her heart inclined to go to him, for God had made her heart incline to go and had made her to desire it.

* * *

25. How the Queen came to Solomon the King

And she arrived in Jerusalem, and brought to the King very many precious gifts which he desired to possess greatly. And he paid her great honour and rejoiced, and he gave her a habitation in the royal palace near him. And he sent her food both for the morning and evening meal, each time fifteen measures by the kôrî[9] of finely ground white meal, cooked with oil and gravy and sauce in abundance, and thirty measures by the kôrî of crushed white meal wherefrom bread for three hundred and fifty people was made, with the necessary platters and trays, and ten stalled oxen, and five bulls, and fifty sheep, without (counting) the kids, and deer, and gazelles and fatted fowls, and a vessel of wine containing sixty gerrât measures, and thirty measures of old wine, and twenty-five singing men and twenty-five singing women, and the finest honey and rich sweets, and some of the food which he himself ate, and some of the wine whereof he drank. And every day he arrayed her in eleven garments which bewitched the eyes. And he visited her and was gratified, and she visited him and was gratified, and she saw his wisdom, and his just judgments and his splendour, and his grace, and heard the eloquence of his speech. And she marvelled in her heart, and was utterly astonished in her mind, and she recognized in her understanding, and perceived very clearly with her eyes how admirable he was; and she wondered exceedingly because of what she saw and heard with him—how perfect he was in composure, and wise in understanding, and pleasant in graciousness, and commanding in stature. And she observed the subtlety of his voice, and the discreet utterances of his lips, and that he gave his commands with dignity, and that his replies were made quietly and with the fear of God. All these things she saw, and she was astonished at the abundance of his wisdom, and there was nothing whatsoever wanting in his word and speech, but everything that he spake was perfect.

9. An Ethiopian unit of measure (as is gerrât, below).

And Solomon was working at the building of the House of God, and he rose up and went to the right and to the left, and forward and backward. And he showed the workmen the measurement and weight and the space covered [by the materials], and he told the workers in metal how to use the hammer, and the drill, and the chisel (?), and he showed the stone-masons the angle [measure] and the circle and the surface [measure]. And everything was wrought by his order, and there was none who set himself in opposition to his word; for the light of his heart was like a lamp in the darkness, and his wisdom was as abundant as the sand. And of the speech of the beasts and the birds there was nothing hidden from him, and he forced the devils to obey him by his wisdom. And he did everything by means of the skill which God gave him when he made supplication to Him; for he did not ask for victory over his enemy, and he did not ask for riches and fame, but he asked God to give him wisdom and understanding whereby he might rule his people, and build His House, and beautify the work of God and all that He had given him [in] wisdom and understanding.

* * *

28. How Solomon gave Commandments to the Queen

And the King answered[1] and said unto her, "Verily, it is right that they (*i.e.*, men) should worship God, Who created the universe, the heavens and the earth, the sea and the dry land, the sun and the moon, the stars and the brilliant bodies of the heavens, the trees and the stones, the beasts and the feathered fowl, the wild beasts and the crocodiles, the fish and the whales, the hippopotamuses and the water lizards, the lightnings and the crashes of thunder, the clouds and the thunders, and the good and the evil. It is meet that Him alone we should worship, in fear and trembling, with joy and with gladness. For He is the Lord of the Universe, the Creator of angels and men. And it is He Who killeth and maketh to live, it is He Who inflicteth punishment and showeth compassion, Who raiseth up from the ground him that is in misery, Who exalteth the poor from the dust, Who maketh to be sorrowful and Who maketh to rejoice, Who raiseth up and Who bringeth down. No one can chide Him, for He is the Lord of the Universe, and there is no one who can say unto Him, 'What hast Thou done?' And unto Him it is meet that there should be praise and thanksgiving from angels and men. And as concerning what thou sayest, that 'He hath given unto you the Tabernacle of the Law,' verily there hath been given unto us the Tabernacle of the God of Israel, which was created before all creation by His glorious counsel. And He hath made to come down to us His commandments, done into writing, so that we may know His decree and the judgment that He hath ordained in the mountain of His holiness."

And the Queen said, "From this moment I will not worship the sun, but will worship the Creator of the sun, the God of Israel. And that Tabernacle of the God of Israel shall be unto me my Lady, and unto my seed after me, and unto all my kingdoms that are under my dominion. And because of this I have found favour before thee, and before the God of Israel my Creator, Who hath brought me unto thee, and hath made me to hear thy voice, and hath shown me thy face, and hath made me to understand thy commandment." Then she returned to [her] house.

1. She had asked, "Whom is it right for me to worship?"

And the Queen used to go [to Solomon] and return continually, and hearken unto his wisdom, and keep it in her heart. And Solomon used to go and visit her, and answer all the questions which she put to him, and the Queen used to visit him and ask him questions, and he informed her concerning every matter that she wished to enquire about. And after she had dwelt [there] six months the Queen wished to return to her own country, and she sent a message to Solomon, saying, "I desire greatly to dwell with thee, but now, for the sake of all my people, I wish to return to my own country. And as for that which I have heard, may God make it to bear fruit in my heart, and in the hearts of all those who have heard it with me. For the ear could never be filled with the hearing of thy wisdom, and the eye could never be filled with the sight of the same."

Now it was not only the Queen who came [to hear the wisdom of Solomon], but very many used to come from cities and countries, both from near and from far; for in those days there was no man found to be like unto him for wisdom (and it was not only human beings who came to him, but the wild animals and the birds used to come to him and hearken unto his voice, and hold converse with him), and then they returned to their own countries, and every one of them was astonished at his wisdom, and marvelled at what he had seen and heard.

And when the Queen sent her message to Solomon, saying that she was about to depart to her own country, he pondered in his heart and said, "A woman of such splendid beauty hath come to me from the ends of the earth! What do I know? Will God give me seed in her?" Now, as it is said in the Book of Kings, Solomon the King was a lover of women.[2] And he married wives of the Hebrews, and the Egyptians, and the Canaanites, and the Edomites, and the Îyôbâwîyân (Moabites?), and from Rîf and Kuĕrguĕ, and Damascus, and Sûrest (Syria), and women who were reported to be beautiful. And he had four hundred queens and six hundred concubines. Now this which he did was not for [the sake of] fornication, but as a result of the wise intent that God had given unto him, and his remembering what God had said unto Abraham, "I will make thy seed like the stars of heaven for number, and like the sand of the sea."[3] And Solomon said in his heart, "What do I know? Peradventure God will give me men children from each one of these women." Therefore when he did thus he acted wisely, saying, "My children shall inherit the cities of the enemy, and shall destroy those who worship idols."

Now those early peoples lived under the law of the flesh, for the grace of the Holy Spirit had not been given unto them. And to those [who lived] after Christ, it was given to live with one woman under the law of marriage. And the Apostles laid down for them an ordinance, saying, "All those who have received His flesh and His blood are brethren. Their mother is the Church and their father is God, and they cry out with Christ Whom they have received, saying, 'Our Father, Who art in heaven.'" And as concerning Solomon no law had been laid down for him in respect of women, and no blame can be imputed to him in respect of marrying [many] wives. But for those who believe, the law and the command have been given that they shall not marry many wives, even as Paul saith, "Those who marry many wives seek their own punishment. He

2. 1 Kings 11.1.   3. Genesis 22.17.

who marrieth one wife hath no sin."[4] And the law restraineth us from the sister [-in-law],[5] in respect of the bearing of children. The Apostles speak [concerning it] in the [Book of] Councils.

29. Concerning the Three Hundred and Eighteen [Patriarchs]

Now we ordain even as did they. We know well what the Apostles who were before us spake. We the Three Hundred and Eighteen have maintained and laid down the orthodox faith, our Lord Jesus Christ being with us. And He hath directed us what we should teach, and how we should fashion the faith.

[The narrative of Solomon and the Queen of Sheba continued]

And King Solomon sent a message unto the Queen, saying, "Now that thou hast come here why wilt thou go away without seeing the administration of the kingdom, and how the meal[s] for the chosen ones of the kingdom are eaten after the manner of the righteous, and how the people are driven away after the manner of sinners? From [the sight of] it thou wouldst acquire wisdom. Follow me now and seat thyself in my splendour in the tent, and I will complete thy instruction, and thou shalt learn the administration of my kingdom; for thou hast loved wisdom, and she shall dwell with thee until thine end and for ever." Now a prophecy maketh itself apparent in [this] speech.

And the Queen sent a second message, saying, "From being a fool, I have become wise by following thy wisdom, and from being a thing rejected by the God of Israel, I have become a chosen woman because of this faith which is in my heart; and henceforth I will worship no other god except Him. And as concerning that which thou sayest, that thou wishest to increase in me wisdom and honour, I will come according to thy desire." And Solomon rejoiced because of this [message], and he arrayed his chosen ones [in splendid apparel], and he added a double supply to his table, and he had all the arrangements concerning the management of his house carefully ordered, and the house of King Solomon was made ready [for guests] daily. And he made it ready with very great pomp, in joy, and in peace, in wisdom, and in tenderness, with all humility and lowliness; and then he ordered the royal table according to the law of the kingdom.

And the Queen came and passed into a place set apart in splendour and glory, and she sat down immediately behind him where she could see and learn and know everything. And she marvelled exceedingly at what she saw, and at what she heard, and she praised the God of Israel in her heart; and she was struck with wonder at the splendour of the royal palace which she saw. For she could see, though no one could see her, even as Solomon had arranged in wisdom for her. He had beautified the place where she was seated, and had spread over it purple hangings, and laid down carpets, and decorated it with *miskât* (moschus),[6] and marbles, and precious stones, and he burned aromatic powders, and sprinkled oil of myrrh and cassia round about, and scattered frankincense and costly incense in all directions. And when they brought her into this

---

4. Compare 1 Corinthians 7.1–40.

5. Leviticus 18.18.

6. Nutmeg.

abode, the odour thereof was very pleasing to her, and even before she ate the dainty meats therein she was satisfied with the smell of them. And with wise intent Solomon sent to her meats which would make her thirsty, and drinks that were mingled with vinegar, and fish and dishes made with pepper. And this he did and he gave them to the Queen to eat. And the royal meal had come to an end three times and seven times, and the administrators, and the counsellors, and the young men and the servants had departed, and the King rose up and he went to the Queen, and he said unto her—now they were alone together—"Take thou thine ease here for love's sake until daybreak." And she said unto him, "Swear to me by thy God, the God of Israel, that thou wilt not take me by force. For if I, who according to the law of men am a maiden, be seduced, I should travel on my journey [back] in sorrow, and affliction, and tribulation."

* * *

31. Concerning the sign which Solomon gave the Queen

And the Queen rejoiced, and she went forth in order to depart, and the King set her on her way with great pomp and ceremony. And Solomon took her aside so that they might be alone together, and he took off the ring that was upon his little finger, and he gave it to the Queen, and said unto her, "Take [this] so that thou mayest not forget me. And if it happen that I obtain seed from thee, this ring shall be unto it a sign; and if it be a man child he shall come to me; and the peace of God be with thee! Whilst I was sleeping with thee I saw many visions in a dream, [and it seemed] as if a sun had risen upon Israel, but it snatched itself away and flew off and lighted up the country of Ethiopia; peradventure that country shall be blessed through thee; God knoweth. And as for thee, observe what I have told thee, so that thou mayest worship God with all thy heart and perform His Will. For He punisheth those who are arrogant, and He showeth compassion upon those who are humble, and He removeth the thrones of the mighty, and He maketh to be honoured those who are needy. For death and life are from Him, and riches and poverty are bestowed by His Will. For everything is His, and none can oppose His command and His judgment in the heavens, or in the earth, or in the sea, or in the abysses. And may God be with thee! Go in peace." And they separated from each other.

32. How the Queen brought forth and came to her own Country

And the Queen departed and came into the country of Bálá Zadîsârĕyâ nine months and five days after she had separated from King Solomon. And the pains of childbirth laid hold upon her, and she brought forth a man child, and she gave it to the nurse with great pride and delight. And she tarried until the days of her purification were ended, and then she came to her own country with great pomp and ceremony. And her officers who had remained there brought gifts to their mistress, and made obeisance to her, and did homage to her, and all the borders of the country rejoiced at her coming. Those who were nobles among them she arrayed in splendid apparel, and to some she gave gold and silver, and hyacinthine and purple robes; and she gave them all manner of things that could be desired. And she ordered her kingdom aright, and none disobeyed her command; for she loved wisdom and God strengthened her kingdom.

And the child grew and she called his name Bayna-Leḥkem. And the child reached the age of twelve years, and he asked his friends among the boys who were being educated with him, and said unto them, "Who is my father?" And they said unto him, "Solomon the King." And he went to the Queen his mother, and said unto her, "O Queen, make me to know who is my father." And the Queen spake unto him angrily, wishing to frighten him so that he might not desire to go [to his father] saying, "Why dost thou ask me about thy father? I am thy father and thy mother; seek not to know any more." And the boy went forth from her presence, and sat down. And a second time, and a third time he asked her, and he importuned her to tell him. One day, however, she told him, saying, "His country is far away, and the road thither is very difficult; wouldst thou not rather be here?" And the youth Bayna-Leḥkem was handsome, and his whole body and his members, and the bearing of his shoulders resembled those of King Solomon his father, and his eyes, and his legs, and his whole gait resembled those of Solomon the King. And when he was two and twenty years old he was skilled in the whole art of war and of horsemanship, and in the hunting and trapping of wild beasts, and in everything that young men are wont to learn. And he said unto the Queen, "I will go and look upon the face of my father, and I will come back here by the Will of God, the Lord of Israel."

33. How the King of Ethiopia travelled

And the Queen called Tâmrîn, the chief of her caravan men and merchants, and she said unto him, "Get ready for thy journey and take this young man with thee, for he importuneth me by night and by day. And thou shalt take him to the King and shalt bring him back hither in safety, if God, the Lord of Israel, pleaseth." And she prepared a retinue suitable to their wealth and honourable condition, and made ready all the goods that were necessary for the journey, and for presenting as gifts to the King, and all that would be necessary for ease and comfort by the way. And she made ready everything for sending him away, and she gave to the officers who were to accompany him such moneys as they would need for him and for themselves on the journey. And she commanded them that they were not to leave him there, but only to take him to the King, and then to bring him back again to her, when he should assume the sovereignty over her land.

Now there was a law in the country of Ethiopia that [only] a woman should reign, and that she must be a virgin who had never known man, but the Queen said [unto Solomon], "Henceforward a man who is of thy seed shall reign, and a woman shall nevermore reign; only seed of thine shall reign and his seed after him from generation to generation. And this thou shalt inscribe in the letters of the rolls in the Book of their Prophets in brass, and thou shalt lay it in the House of God, which shall be built as a memorial and as a prophecy for the last days. And the people shall not worship the sun and the magnificence of the heavens, or the mountains and the forests, or the stones and the trees of the wilderness, or the abysses and that which is in the waters, or graven images and figures of gold, or the feathered fowl which fly; and they shall not make use of them in divining, and they shall not pay adoration unto them. And this law shall abide for ever. And if there be anyone who shall transgress this law, thy seed shall judge him for ever. Only give us the fringes of the covering of the holy heavenly Zion, the Tabernacle of the Law of God, which we would embrace (or, greet). Peace be to the strength of thy kingdom and to thy brilliant wisdom, which God, the Lord of Israel our Creator, hath given unto thee."

And the Queen took the young man aside and when he was alone with her she gave him that symbol which Solomon had given her, that is to say, the ring on his finger, so that he might know his son, and might remember her word and her covenant which she had made [with him], that she would worship God all the days of her life, she and those who were under her dominion, with all [the power] which God had given her. And then the Queen sent him away in peace.

And the young man [and his retinue] made straight their way and they journeyed on and came into the country of the neighbourhood of Gâzâ.[7] Now this is the Gâzâ which Solomon the King gave to the Queen of Ethiopia. And in the Acts of the Apostles Luke the Evangelist wrote, saying, "He was the governor of the whole country of Gâzâ, an eunuch of Queen Hendakê, who had believed on the word of Luke the Apostle."[8]

34. How the young man arrived in his mother's country

And when the young man arrived in his mother's country he rejoiced there in the honour [which he received], and in the gifts [that were made] to him. And when the people saw him they thought him to be the perfect likeness of Solomon the King. And they made obeisance to him, and they said unto him, "Hail, the royal father liveth!" And they brought unto him gifts and offerings, fatted cattle and food, as to their king. And [the people of] the whole country of Gâzâ, as far as the border of Judah, were stirred up and they said, "This is King Solomon." And there were some who said, "The King is in Jerusalem building his house" now he had finished building the House of God—and others said, "This is Solomon the King, the son of David."[9] And they were perplexed, and they disputed with one another, and they sent off spies mounted on horses, who were to seek out King Solomon and to find out if he were actually in Jerusalem, or if he were with them [in Gâzâ]. And the spies came to the watchmen of the city of Jerusalem, and they found King Solomon there, and they made obeisance to him, and they said unto him, "Hail, may the royal father live! [Our] country is disturbed because there hath come into it a merchant who resembleth thee in form and appearance, without the smallest alteration or variation. He resembleth thee in noble carriage and in splendid form, and in stature and in goodly appearance; he lacketh nothing in respect of these and is in no way different from thyself. His eyes are gladsome, like unto those of a man who hath drunk wine, his legs are graceful and slender, and the tower of his neck is like unto the tower of David thy father. He is like unto thee exactly in every respect, and every member of his whole body is like unto thine."

7. The seaport and surrounding region, located in modern Israel (Palestine).
8. See Acts 8.27.

9. The second king of Israel, according to the Hebrew Bible, traditionally credited with authorship of the Psalms.

And King Solomon answered and said unto them, "Where is it then that he wisheth to go?" And they answered and said unto him, "We have not enquired of him, for he is awesome like thyself. But his own people, when we asked them, 'Whence have ye come and whither do ye go?' said, 'We have come from the dominions of Hendakê (Candace) and Ethiopia, and we are going to the country of Judah to King Solomon.'" And when King Solomon heard this his heart was perturbed and he was glad in his soul, for in those days he had no children, except a boy who was seven years old and whose name was Îyôrbe'âm (Rehoboam). It happened to Solomon even as Paul stateth, saying, "God hath made foolishness the wisdom of this world,"[1] for Solomon had made a plan in his wisdom and said, "By one thousand women I shall beget one thousand men children, and I shall inherit the countries of the enemy, and I will overthrow [their] idols." But [God] only gave him three children. His eldest son was the King of Ethiopia, the son of the Queen of Ethiopia, and was the firstborn of whom [God] spake prophetically, "God sware unto David in righteousness, and repented not, 'Of the fruit of thy body will I make to sit upon thy throne.'"[2] And God gave unto David His servant grace before Him, and granted unto him that there should sit upon the throne of Godhead One of his seed in the flesh, from the Virgin, and should judge the living and the dead, and reward every man according to his work, One to whom praise is meet, our Lord Jesus Christ, for ever and ever, Amen. And He gave him one on the earth who should become king over the Tabernacle of the Law of the holy, heavenly Zion, that is to say, the King of Ethiopia. And as for those who reigned, who were not [of] Israel, that was due to the transgression of the law and the commandment, whereat God was not pleased.

* * *

36. How King Solomon conversed with his son

And Joas (Benaiah), the son of Yôdâhê, went out and brought Bayna-Leḥkem inside. And when King Solomon saw him he rose up, and moved forward to welcome him, and he loosed the band of his apparel from his shoulder, and he embraced him, with his hands [resting] on his breast, and he kissed his mouth, and forehead, and eyes, and he said unto him, "Behold, my father David hath renewed his youth and hath risen from the dead." And Solomon the King turned round to those who had announced the arrival of the young man, and he said unto them, "Ye said unto me, 'He resembleth thee,' but this is not my stature, but the stature of David my father in the days of his early manhood, and he is handsomer than I am." And Solomon the King rose up straightway, and he went into his chamber, and he arrayed the young man in apparel made of cloth embroidered with gold, and a belt of gold, and he set a crown upon his head, and a ring upon his finger. And having arrayed him in glorious apparel which bewitched the eyes, he seated him upon his throne, that he might be equal in rank to himself. And he said unto the nobles and officers of Israel, "O ye who treat me with contumely among yourselves and say that I have no son, look ye, this is my son, the fruit that hath gone forth from my body, whom God, the Lord of Israel, hath given me, when I expected it not."

1. 1 Corinthians 1.20.   2. See 2 Samuel 7.12–16, Psalm 132.11–12.

And his nobles answered and said unto him, "Blessed be the mother who hath brought forth this young man, and blessed be the day wherein thou hadst union with the mother of this young man. For there hath risen upon us from the root of Jesse[3] a shining man who shall be king of the posterity of our posterity of his seed. Concerning his father none shall ask questions, and none shall say, 'Whence is his coming?' Verily he is an Israelite of the seed of David, fashioned perfectly in the likeness of his father's form and appearance; we are his servants, and he shall be our king." And they brought unto him gifts, each according to his greatness. And the young man took that ring which his mother had given him when they were alone together, and he said unto his father, "Take this ring, and remember the word which thou didst speak unto the Queen, and give unto us a portion of the fringe of the covering of the Tabernacle of the Law of God, so that we may worship it all our days, and all those who are subject unto us, and those who are in the kingdom of the Queen." And the King answered and said unto him, "Why givest thou me the ring as a sign? Without thy giving me a sign I discovered the likeness of thy form to myself, for thou art indeed my son."

And the merchant Tâmrîn spake again unto King Solomon, saying, "Hearken, O King, unto the message which thy handmaiden, the Queen my mistress, sent by me: 'Take this young man, anoint him, consecrate him, and bless him, and make him king over our country, and give him the command that a woman shall never again reign [in this country], and send him back in peace. And peace be with the might of thy kingdom, and with thy brilliant wisdom. As for me, I never wished that he should come where thou art, but he urged me exceedingly that he should be allowed to come to thee. And besides, I was afraid for him lest he should fall sick on the journey, either through thirst for water, or the heat of the sun, and I should bring my grey hairs down to the grave with sorrow. Then I put my trust in the holy, heavenly Zion, the Tabernacle of the Law of God, that thou wilt not withhold it in thy wisdom. For thy nobles cannot return to their houses and look upon their children, by reason of the abundance of wisdom and food which thou givest them, according to their desire, and they say, The table of Solomon is better for us than enjoying and gratifying ourselves in our own houses. And because of this I, through my fear, sought protection so that thou mightest not stablish him with thee, but mightest send him [back] to me in peace, without sickness and suffering, in love and in peace, that my heart might rejoice at having encountered thee.' "

And the King answered and said unto him, "Besides travailing with him and suckling him, what else hath a woman to do with a son? A daughter belongeth to the mother, and a boy to the father. God cursed Eve, saying, 'Bring forth children in anguish and with sorrow of heart, and [after] thy bringing forth shall take place thy return to thy husband';[4] with an oath He said, 'Bring forth,' and having sworn, thy return to thy husband [shall follow]. As for this my son, I will not give him to the Queen, but I will make him king over Israel. For this is my firstborn, the first of my race whom God hath given me."

3. Father of David, forefather of Jesus (see Matthew 1.6–16). In the Middle Ages, representations of the genealogy of Jesus often took the form of a tree, rooted in the body (usually, the genitals) of Jesse and rising upward through the generations to culminate in Jesus, borne like a fruit at its top.

4. Genesis 3.16.

And then Solomon sent unto the young man evening and morning dainty meats, and apparel of honour, and gold and silver. And he said unto him, "It is better for thee to dwell here in our country with us, where the House of God is, and where the Tabernacle of the Law of God is, and where God dwelleth." And the young man his son sent a message unto him, saying, "Gold, and silver, and [rich] apparel are not wanting in our country. But I came hither in order to hear thy wisdom, and to see thy face, and to salute thee, and to pay homage to thy kingdom, and to make obeisance to thee, and then [I intended thee] to send me away to my mother and to my own country. For no man hateth the place where he was born, and everyone loveth the things of his native country. And though thou givest me dainty meats I do not love them, and they are not suitable for my body, but the meats whereby I grow and become strong are those that are gratifying to me. And although [thy] country pleaseth me even as doth a garden, yet is not my heart gratified therewith; the mountains of the land of my mother where I was born are far better in my sight. And as for the Tabernacle of the God of Israel, if I adore it where I am, it will give me glory, and I shall look upon the House of God which thou hast builded, and I will make offering and make supplication to it there. And as for Zion, the Tabernacle of the Law of God, give me [a portion of] the fringe of the covering thereof, and I will worship it with my mother and with all those who are subject to my sovereignty. For my Lady the Queen hath already rooted out all those who served idols, and those who worshipped strange objects, and stones and trees, and she hath rooted them out and hath brought them to Zion, the Tabernacle of the Law of God. For she had heard from thee and had learned, and she did according to thy word, and we worship God." And the King was not able to make his son consent to remain [in Jerusalem] with all [his persuadings].

* * *

45. How those who were sent away wept and made a plan

And the children of the nobles of Israel, who were commanded to depart with the son of the king, took counsel together, saying, "What shall we do? For we have left our country and our birth-place, and our kinsfolk and the people of our city. Now, come ye, let us establish a covenant between us only, whereof our kinsfolk shall know nothing, that we will love each other in that country : none shall hasten or tarry here, and we will neither fear nor have any doubt. For God is here, and God is there, and may God's Will be done! And to Him be praise for ever and ever! Amen." And 'Azâryâs and 'Êlmîyâs, sons of the priests, answered, "Let not the other matter—that our kinsfolk hate us—cause us sorrow, but let us sorrow on account of our Lady Zion, because they are making us to leave her. For in her they have committed us to God, and we have served her to this day; and let us be sorrowful because they have made us to leave her. It is because of her and because of this that they have specially made us to weep." And the others answered and said unto them, "Verily she is our Lady and our hope, and our object of boasting, and we have grown up under her blessedness. And how is it possible for us to forsake Zion our mistress? For we have been given to her. And what shall we do? If we resist his command the king will kill us, and we are unable to transgress the word of our fathers or the king's command. And what shall we do concerning Zion our Lady?"

And 'Azâryâs, the son of Zadok the priest, answered and said, "I will counsel you what we shall do. But make a covenant with me to the end of your lives; and swear to me that ye will not repeat it whether we live or whether we die, or whether we be taken captive or whether we go forth [unhindered]." And they swore an oath to him in the Name of the Lord God of Israel, and by the heavenly Zion, the Tabernacle of the Law of God, and by what God had promised unto Abraham, and by the purity and excellence of Isaac, and by His making Jacob to arrive in and inherit a land whereto he was a stranger, and his seed after him.

And when they had sworn thus to him, he answered and said unto them, "Come now, let us take [with us] our Lady Zion; but how are we to take her? I will show you. And carry ye out my plan and if God willeth we shall be able to take our Lady with us. And if they should gain knowledge of our doings and slay us, that shall not trouble us, because we shall die for our Lady Zion." And they all rose up, and kissed his head, and his face, and his eyes, and they said unto him, "We will do everything that thou hast counselled us to do; whether we die or whether we live, we are with thee for the sake of our Lady Zion. If we die it will not cause us sorrow, and if we live—the Will of God be done!" And one of them, the son of Yôas (Benaiah), whose name was Zechariah, said, "I cannot sit down because of the great gladness that is in my heart. Tell me, moreover, canst thou indeed carry her off, and is it not a lie? Thou canst go into the House of God in the place of thy father Zadok, and the keys are continually in thy hand. But ponder well what we counsel thee before they take the keys out of thy hand. Thou knowest the hidden openings (or, windows) which King Solomon made; but none of the priests may enter therein except thy father once each year in order to offer up sacrifice in the Holy of Holies on behalf of himself and on behalf of the people.[5] Ponder, consider, and sleep not in the matter of thy wish to carry away Zion. And we will depart with her as soon as she hath been committed to our care, and we shall have joy and our fathers sorrow when she arriveth with us in the country of Ethiopia."

And Azâryâs said unto them, "Do ye what I tell you, and we shall succeed. Give ye to me each of you ten *dîdrachmas*,[6] and I will give them to a carpenter so that he will make haste to prepare for me good planks of wood—now because of his love of money he will fasten them together very quickly—of the height, and breadth, and length and size of our Lady [Zion]. And I will give him the dimensions of myself, and I will say unto him, 'Prepare for me pieces of wood for a framework (?) so that I may make a raft therefrom; for we are going to travel over the sea, and in the event of the ship sinking I shall be able to get up on the raft, and we shall be saved from the sea.' And I will take the framework without the pieces of wood thereof being fixed together, and I will have them put together in Ethiopia. And I will set them down in the habitation of Zion, and will drape them with the draperies of Zion, and I will take Zion, and will dig a hole in the ground, and will set Zion there, until we journey and take it away with us thither. And I will not tell the matter to the king until we have travelled far."

---

5. See Leviticus 16.
6. Greek coins worth two drachmas (the literal meaning of their name), each about a third of an ounce of silver.

And they each gave him ten *dîdrachmas*, and this money amounted to one hundred and forty *dîdrachmas*, and he took them and gave them to a carpenter, who straightway fashioned a good piece of work from the remains of the wood of the house of the sanctuary, and Azâryâs rejoiced and showed it to his brethren.

* * *

48. How they carried away Zion

And behold, the Angel of the Lord appeared again to Azâryâs and he stood up above him like a pillar of fire, and he filled the house with his light. And he raised up Azâryâs and said unto him, "Stand up, be strong, and rouse up thy brother Êlmĕyâs, and 'Abĕsâ, and Mâkarî, and take the pieces of wood and I will open for thee the doors of the sanctuary. And take thou the Tabernacle of the Law of God, and thou shalt carry it without trouble and discomfort. And I, inasmuch as I have been commanded by God to be with it for ever, will be thy guide when thou shalt carry it away."

And Azâryâs rose up straightway, and woke up the three men his brethren, and they took the pieces of wood, and went into the house of God—now they found all the doors open, both those that were outside and those that were inside—to the actual place where Azâryâs found Zion, the Tabernacle of the Law of God; and it was taken away by them forthwith, in the twinkling of an eye, the Angel of the Lord being present and directing. And had it not been that God willed it Zion could not have been taken away forthwith. And the four of them carried Zion away, and they brought it into the house of Azâryâs, and they went back into the house of God, and they set the pieces of wood on the place where Zion had been, and they covered them over with the covering of Zion, and they shut the doors, and went back to their houses. And they took lamps and set them in the place where [Zion] was hidden, and they sacrificed the sheep thereto, and burned offerings of incense thereto, and they spread purple cloths over it and set it in a secret place for seven days and seven nights.

THE THOUSAND AND ONE NIGHTS (ALF LAYLA WA-LAYLA)
fourteenth century

A text built from many texts, *The Thousand and One Nights* is an extraordinarily flexible and capacious storytelling machine, one that has absorbed stories from a range of cultures across Asia and North Africa and then cast them back out again into the world in many new forms, including theater, opera, film, cartoons, video games, fashion, children's toys, and, of course, other texts. Considered in the work's many manifestations, the "nights" are not "one thousand and one"—they are innumerable.

THE TEXT IN CONTEXT

The Thousand and One Nights was written by many unknown authors, scattered over many centuries and countries of the Middle East. The first document bearing any physical evidence of *The Thousand and One Nights* was a single piece of very rare old Syrian paper that dates from 879 C.E. Discovered in 1948 by a scholar studying in a Cairo archive, the page contained, among various other scrawls and jottings, a signature, a date, and a few words from the opening lines of the *Nights*. The next trace of the *Nights* appears in the tenth century, when Ibn al-Nadim, a book dealer in Baghdad, mentions in his catalogue a number of story collections; among them is a book of tales concerning "Shahrazad," which, he notes, is adapted from a Persian original called *Hazar Afsan*, or *Thousand Tales*. Another tenth century writer, al-Mas'udi, also mentions Shahrazad and the now-lost Persian *Hazar Afsan*, and adds the title of the Arabic version of the work: *Alf Layla*, or *Thousand Nights*. The title that comes down to us in the earliest complete manuscript, a Syrian text dating from the fourteenth century, is the familiar *Alf Layla wa-Layla*, or *Thousand and One Nights*. The number—one thousand and one—seems precise, and in fact the first generation of Western readers took it literally, assuming that the manuscript, which contained far fewer than one thousand stories, must be incomplete. But its sense is instead symbolic: adding one more to a thousand implies an unending abundance. There is always one more tale to be told.

The Thousand and One Nights is an Arabic text, but one derived from a Persian source (reflected in the Persian names of the characters of the frame story—Shahrazad and her sister Dunyazad, King Shahrayar and his brother Shahzaman). Behind both the Arabic and the Persian texts may lie a Sanskrit original, just as the Indian *Pañcatantra* lies behind the other widely disseminated Arabic story collection, *Kalila and Dimna*; but this original, if it exists, has never been discovered. Whatever its early sources, the *Nights* quickly swelled with new stories from Arab traditions as its influence spread. One cluster of stories centers on Baghdad and its early ninth-century ruler, Harun al-Rashid, and his vizier Ja'far al-Barmaki. Other groups of stories, which entered the collection at a later date, reflect the culture of medieval Cairo; still others allude to the itinerant heritage of the Bedouin of the Arabian Peninsula. The text of the *Nights*—if we can call such a flexible and changeable organism a "text"—was above all an inspiration for sharing stories, and was thus subject to change with each new telling.

Though the content of the *Nights* is unique, its literary form—the frame tale—is common in Eastern and Western traditions. The frame tale is an open-ended genre, in which an outer story or "frame" provides a structure within which other, shorter stories can be told. Frame tales are among the most popular of literary forms, surviving in the major works of **Boccaccio** and **Chaucer** as well as in the writings of **Apuleius, Petrus Alfonsi, Marie de France**, and many others. The genre most likely has its origins in India. The *Pañcatantra*, a Sanskrit collection of animal stories, is among the world's best-known and oldest frame tales, and it was the inspiration for the Arabic *Kalila and Dimna*, which was quickly disseminated throughout medieval Europe. While *Kalila and Dimna* was popular in the West because of the didactic and edifying quality of the tales (they each conclude, as do **Aesop's Fables,** with a moral), *The Thousand and One Nights* were avidly read by Europeans for less noble reasons: they believed the *Nights* could offer insights into the duplicitous and irrational character of "the Oriental," and they found pleasure in the tales' sensuous details and often unrestrained sexuality. The long history of "Orientalist" approaches to *The Thousand and One Nights* in the West takes nothing away from our own enjoyment of the tales, but it is certainly a reminder of the dangers of interpreting any text as somehow embodying the culture in which it originated.

WORK

The overall frame of *The Thousand and One Nights* centers on a good king who has become a tyrant. After discovering the secret promiscuity of his wife, King Shahrayar decides that he will avoid the deception of women forever by taking a new bride every night and putting her to death in the morning. The deaths rapidly mount, the kingdom is filled with mourning parents—and to the horror and despair of the king's loyal vizier, his daughter, Shahrazad, volunteers to marry the king. He tries to dissuade her, but Shahrazad has a plan. By telling a story to the king every night, each one more marvelous and entrancing than the last, Shahrazad will continually defer the doom that awaits his bride. Yet she also has another goal, beyond self-preservation or even the salvation of her countrywomen. By telling stories that repeatedly address the problems of rule—both the rule of oneself and the rule of others—she will teach the king how to restore order in his own realm, as well as in his own soul.

Even among frame tales, *The Thousand and One Nights* is unique for its enchantingly intricate nested structure. Very often, a character in a tale will pause to tell yet another tale, with one story inside the next inside the next, like Russian nested dolls. In "The Story of the Merchant and the Demon," for example, three old men tell stories, each more fantastic than the last, to the dangerous jinn in their sucessful effort to purchase the merchant's freedom. "The Story of the Fisherman and the Demon" even more elaborately nests smaller stories within the larger one, always with a strong focus on the irresistibility of storytelling, as characters within the larger tale express their eagerness to hear every new story. When the fisherman comments offhandedly on finding himself in a situation "like that of King Yunan and the sage Duban," the jinn cannot resist asking, "What is their story?" Once his curiosity is piqued, the delightful power of the tale quickly defuses his potential for evil. And within that story, King Yunan himself tells "The Tale of the Husband and the Parrot." This structure makes *The Thousand and One Nights* an unusually playful text, seemingly spontaneous and improvisational even on the page, and wonderfully suited to public entertainment and oral performance.

Perhaps the *Nights* is most extraordinary for the persistence of its fertile, regenerative quality even after being taken up by Western readers and rendered in a host of European and, later, American translations and adaptations. This process began in 1704, with the publication in French (by Antoine Galland) of a selection of tales from the earliest surviving complete manuscript. Readers were immediately captivated by the work: an unauthorized English translation of the French version appeared in 1706, and Galland himself quickly produced additional volumes for publication. When he ran out of tales to translate from the Syrian manuscript (which, like all the early collections, contains only about 280), Galland turned to other sets of Arabic tales, including the famous stories of Aladdin and Ali Baba. As he sought to reach the target number of one thousand and one, Galland even added some tales for which there were no written Arabic sources but only oral versions picked up from Arab visitors to Paris. The tremendous European appetite for *The Thousand and One Nights* led to the production of composite Arabic story collections in Cairo during the eighteenth and nineteenth centuries, and subsequently these versions were published in Arabic editions and translated. We can thus think of two separate lineages for the modern reception of the *Nights*: one can be traced back to the earliest complete text, the fourteenth-century Syrian manuscript translated by Galland, and the other to the later composite texts assembled in eighteenth- and nineteenth-century Cairo. The selections reproduced here come from the Syrian manuscript, but it would be wrong to think of these as the "authentic" tales and to dismiss those in the Cairo versions as unimportant innovations. Instead, the Syrian manuscript can best be thought of as a snapshot, an image captured of the *Nights* at a certain moment in time, in a certain cultural location. The Cairo manuscripts also represent a specific time and place in the life of the *Nights*—one intimately connected with the history of French and, later, British rule in Egypt.

Western reception of *The Thousand and One Nights* has been uniformly enthusiastic, and yet wildly heterogeneous—a good example of the changing fortunes in the relations between Europe and the Middle East. This heterogeneity can be seen, for example, in the nineteenth-century English translations of the *Nights*, all of which were based on the enlarged Cairo compilations. The earliest of these was by Edward Lane, an Englishman living in Cairo; it tries to conjure up an entire way of life through the medium of the *Nights*. For Lane, the stories are not so much an end in themselves as a way for him to re-create the daily experiences of a nineteenth-century Egyptian who might have listened to such stories as they were performed in the coffeehouse. The translation of the philologist John Payne, published for a very limited audience of specialists, sought to use the *Nights* to construct an ethnographic portrait of Egyptian society, while the sexually explicit, extensively footnoted, and deliberately archaic translation by the extraordinary explorer Sir Richard Burton is in a category by itself. The variety of these encounters with the *Nights*, all so different yet all produced in the same language over the span of a few decades, was wittily summed up by a nineteenth-century commentator in the *Edinburgh Review* who states that each version has "its proper destination: Galland for the nursery, Lane for the library, Payne for the study, and Burton for the sewers."

The influence of *The Thousand and One Nights* continued to spread out across the globe. Thus late nineteenth-century portrait photography in Japan shows a fascination with the "Arabian Nights" theme, which had become fashionable in stage costume and dress styles, theater and opera, music and ballet. Today, reflections of the *Nights* are visible in children's cartoons, adult film, graphic novels, and coloring books. In the modern Middle East, however, attitudes toward *The Thousand and One Nights* are more ambivalent; they have even at times led to censorship, whether because of the text's graphic language or, more likely, because of the complicated history of the *Nights* in shaping European fantasies about the Orient.

While Eastern studies of the *Nights* have tended to consider the work in the context of folklore and oral storytelling,

Western scholars are often preoccupied with the effort to nail down the work's point of origin. They want to know: Which is the original version? When was it composed? Is *The Thousand and One Nights* an Arab text? a Persian text? Indian? These questions ultimately slip away, because what the text *is* turns out to be much less interesting than what it *does*. *The Thousand and One Nights* has its life in transit—always becoming something new, leaving its reader in a perpetual state of anticipation. It is less a collection of stories than a machine that makes stories possible.

From The Thousand and One Nights[1]

Prologue

[*The Story of King Shahrayar and Shahrazad, His Vizier's[2] Daughter*]

It is related—but God knows and sees best what lies hidden in the old accounts of bygone peoples and times—that long ago, during the time of the Sasanid dynasty,[3] in the peninsulas of India and Indochina, there lived two kings who were brothers. The older brother was named Shahrayar, the younger Shahzaman. The older, Shahrayar, was a towering knight and a daring champion, invincible, energetic, and implacable. His power reached the remotest corners of the land and its people, so that the country was loyal to him, and his subjects obeyed him. Shahrayar himself lived and ruled in India and Indochina, while to his brother he gave the land of Samarkand[4] to rule as king.

Ten years went by, when one day Shahrayar felt a longing for his brother the king, summoned his vizier (who had two daughters, one called Shahrazad, the other Dinarzad) and bade him go to his brother. Having made preparations, the vizier journeyed day and night until he reached Samarkand. When Shahzaman heard of the vizier's arrival, he went out with his retainers to meet him. He dismounted, embraced him, and asked him for news from his older brother, Shahrayar. The vizier replied that he was well, and that he had sent him to request his brother to visit him. Shahzaman complied with his brother's request and proceeded to make preparations for the journey. In the meantime, he had the vizier camp on the outskirts of the city, and took care of his needs. He sent him what he required of food and fodder, slaughtered many sheep in his honor, and provided him with money and supplies, as well as many horses and camels.

For ten full days he prepared himself for the journey; then he appointed a chamberlain in his place, and left the city to spend the night in his tent, near the vizier. At midnight he returned to his palace in the city, to bid his wife good-bye. But when he entered the palace, he found his wife lying in the arms of one of the kitchen boys. When he saw them, the world turned dark before his eyes and, shaking his head, he said to himself, "I am still here, and this is what she has

---

1. All selections translated from the Arabic by Husain Haddawy except for "The Third Old Man's Tale," translated from the Arabic by Jerome W. Clinton.
2. Literally, "one who bears burdens": the

highest state official or administrator under a caliph or shah.
3. The last pre-Islamic dynasty (226–652).
4. A city and province in central Asia, now in Uzbekistan.

done when I was barely outside the city. How will it be and what will happen behind my back when I go to visit my brother in India? No. Women are not to be trusted." He got exceedingly angry, adding, "By God, I am king and sovereign in Samarkand, yet my wife has betrayed me and has inflicted this on me." As his anger boiled, he drew his sword and struck both his wife and the cook. Then he dragged them by the heels and threw them from the top of the palace to the trench below. He then left the city and going to the vizier ordered that they depart that very hour. The drum was struck, and they set out on their journey, while Shahzaman's heart was on fire because of what his wife had done to him and how she had betrayed him with some cook, some kitchen boy. They journeyed hurriedly, day and night, through deserts and wilds, until they reached the land of King Shahrayar, who had gone out to receive them.

When Shahrayar met them, he embraced his brother, showed him favors, and treated him generously. He offered him quarters in a palace adjoining his own, for King Shahrayar had built two beautiful towering palaces in his garden, one for the guests, the other for the women and members of his household. He gave the guest house to his brother, Shahzaman, after the attendants had gone to scrub it, dry it, furnish it, and open its windows, which overlooked the garden. Thereafter, Shahzaman would spend the whole day at his brother's, return at night to sleep at the palace, then go back to his brother the next morning. But whenever he found himself alone and thought of his ordeal with his wife, he would sigh deeply, then stifle his grief, and say, "Alas, that this great misfortune should have happened to one in my position!" Then he would fret with anxiety, his spirit would sag, and he would say, "None has seen what I have seen." In his depression, he ate less and less, grew pale, and his health deteriorated. He neglected everything, wasted away, and looked ill.

When King Shahrayar looked at his brother and saw how day after day he lost weight and grew thin, pale, ashen, and sickly, he thought that this was because of his expatriation and homesickness for his country and his family, and he said to himself, "My brother is not happy here. I should prepare a goodly gift for him and send him home." For a month he gathered gifts for his brother; then he invited him to see him and said, "Brother, I would like you to know that I intend to go hunting and pursue the roaming deer, for ten days. Then I shall return to prepare you for your journey home. Would you like to go hunting with me?" Shahzaman replied, "Brother, I feel distracted and depressed. Leave me here and go with God's blessing and help." When Shahrayar heard his brother, he thought that his dejection was because of his homesickness for his country. Not wishing to coerce him, he left him behind, and set out with his retainers and men. When they entered the wilderness, he deployed his men in a circle to begin trapping and hunting.

After his brother's departure, Shahzaman stayed in the palace and, from the window overlooking the garden, watched the birds and trees as he thought of his wife and what she had done to him, and sighed in sorrow. While he agonized over his misfortune, gazing at the heavens and turning a distracted eye on the garden, the private gate of his brother's palace opened, and there emerged, strutting like a dark-eyed deer, the lady, his brother's wife, with twenty slave-girls, ten white and ten black. While Shahzaman looked at them, without being seen, they continued to walk until they stopped below his window, without looking in his direction, thinking that he had gone to the hunt with his brother. Then they sat down, took off their clothes, and suddenly there were ten slave-girls and ten black slaves dressed in the same clothes as the girls. Then the ten black slaves mounted the ten girls, while the lady called, "Mas'ud, Mas'ud!" and a black slave jumped from the tree to the ground, rushed to her, and, raising her legs, went between her thighs and made love to her. Mas'ud topped the lady, while the ten slaves topped the ten girls, and they carried on till noon. When they were done with their business, they got up and washed themselves. Then the ten slaves put on the same clothes again, mingled with the girls, and once more there appeared to be twenty slave-girls. Mas'ud himself jumped over the garden wall and disappeared, while the slave-girls and the lady sauntered to the private gate, went in and, locking the gate behind them, went their way.

All of this happened under King Shahzaman's eyes. When he saw this spectacle of the wife and the women of his brother the great king—how ten slaves put on women's clothes and slept with his brother's paramours and concubines and what Mas'ud did with his brother's wife, in his very palace—and pondered over this calamity and great misfortune, his care and sorrow left him and he said to himself, "This is our common lot. Even though my brother is king and master of the whole world, he cannot protect what is his, his wife and his concubines, and suffers misfortune in his very home. What happened to me is little by comparison. I used to think that I was the only one who has suffered, but from what I have seen, everyone suffers. By God, my misfortune is lighter than that of my brother." He kept marveling and blaming life, whose trials none can escape, and he began to find consolation in his own affliction and forget his grief. When supper came, he ate and drank with relish and zest and, feeling better, kept eating and drinking, enjoying himself and feeling happy. He thought to himself, "I am no longer alone in my misery; I am well."

For ten days, he continued to enjoy his food and drink, and when his brother, King Shahrayar, came back from the hunt, he met him happily, treated him attentively, and greeted him cheerfully. His brother, King Shahrayar, who had missed him, said, "By God, brother, I missed you on this trip and wished you were with me." Shahzaman thanked him and sat down to carouse with him, and when night fell, and food was brought before them, the two ate and drank, and again Shahzaman ate and drank with zest. As time went by, he continued to eat and drink with appetite, and became lighthearted and carefree. His face regained color and became ruddy, and his body gained weight, as his blood circulated and he regained his energy; he was himself again, or even better. King Shahrayar noticed his brother's condition, how he used to be and how he had improved, but kept it to himself until he took him aside one day and said, "My brother Shahzaman, I would like you to do something for me, to satisfy a wish, to answer a question truthfully." Shahzaman asked, "What is it, brother?" He replied, "When you first came to stay with me, I noticed that you kept losing weight, day after day, until your looks changed, your health deteriorated, and your energy sagged. As you continued like this, I thought that what ailed you was your homesickness for your family and your country, but even though I kept noticing that you were wasting away and looking ill, I refrained from questioning you and hid my feelings from you. Then I went hunting, and when I came back, I found that you had recovered and had regained your health. Now I want you to tell me everything and to explain the cause of your deterioration and the cause of your subsequent recovery, without hiding anything from me." When Shahzaman heard what King Shahrayar said, he bowed his head, then said, "As for the cause of my recovery, that I cannot tell you, and I wish that you would excuse me from telling you." The king was greatly astonished at his brother's reply and, burning with curiosity, said, "You must tell me. For now, at least, explain the first cause."

Then Shahzaman related to his brother what happened to him with his own wife, on the night of his departure, from beginning to end, and concluded, "Thus all the while I was with you, great King, whenever I thought of the event and the misfortune that had befallen me, I felt troubled, careworn, and unhappy, and my health deteriorated. This then is the cause." Then he grew silent. When King Shahrayar heard his brother's explanation, he shook his head, greatly amazed at the deceit of women, and prayed to God to protect him from their wickedness, saying, "Brother, you were fortunate in killing your wife and her lover, who gave you good reason to feel troubled, careworn, and ill. In my opinion, what happened to you has never happened to anyone else. By God, had I been in your place, I would have killed at least a hundred or even a thousand women. I would have been furious; I would have gone mad. Now praise be to God who has delivered you from sorrow and distress. But tell me what has caused you to forget your sorrow and regain your health?" Shahzaman replied, "King, I wish that for God's sake you would excuse me from telling you." Shahrayar said, "You must." Shahzaman replied, "I fear that you will feel even more troubled and careworn than I." Shahrayar asked, "How could that be, brother? I insist on hearing your explanation."

Shahzaman then told him about what he had seen from the palace window and the calamity in his very home—how ten slaves, dressed like women, were sleeping with his women and concubines, day and night. He told him everything from beginning to end (but there is no point in repeating that). Then he concluded, "When I saw your own misfortune, I felt better—and said to myself, 'My brother is king of the world, yet such a misfortune has happened to him, and in his very home.' As a result I forgot my care and sorrow, relaxed, and began to eat and drink. This is the cause of my cheer and good spirits."

When King Shahrayar heard what his brother said and found out what had happened to him, he was furious and his blood boiled. He said, "Brother, I can't believe what you say unless I see it with my own eyes." When Shahzaman saw that his brother was in a rage, he said to him, "If you do not believe me, unless you see your misfortune with your own eyes, announce that you plan to go hunting. Then you and I shall set out with your troops, and when we get outside the city, we shall leave our tents and camp with the men behind, enter the city secretly, and go together to your palace. Then the next morning you can see with your own eyes."

King Shahrayar realized that his brother had a good plan and ordered his army to prepare for the trip. He spent the night with his brother, and when God's morning broke, the two rode out of the city with their army, preceded by the camp attendants, who had gone to drive the poles and pitch the tents where the king and his army were to camp. At nightfall King Shahrayar summoned his chief chamberlain and bade him take his place. He entrusted him with the army and ordered that for three days no one was to enter the city. Then he and his brother disguised themselves and entered the city in the dark.

They went directly to the palace where Shahzaman resided and slept there till the morning. When they awoke, they sat at the palace window, watching the garden and chatting, until the light broke, the day dawned, and the sun rose. As they watched, the private gate opened, and there emerged as usual the wife of King Shahrayar, walking among twenty slave-girls. They made their way under the trees until they stood below the palace window where the two kings sat. Then they took off their women's clothes, and suddenly there were ten slaves, who mounted the ten girls and made love to them. As for the lady, she called, "Mas'ud, Mas'ud," and a black slave jumped from the tree to the ground, came to her, and said, "What do you want, you slut? Here is Sa'ad al-Din Mas'ud." She laughed and fell on her back, while the slave mounted her and like the others did his business with her. Then the black slaves got up, washed themselves, and, putting on the same clothes, mingled with the girls. Then they walked away, entered the palace, and locked the gate behind them. As for Mas'ud, he jumped over the fence to the road and went on his way.

When King Shahrayar saw the spectacle of his wife and the slave-girls, he went out of his mind, and when he and his brother came down from upstairs, he said, "No one is safe in this world. Such doings are going on in my kingdom, and in my very palace. Perish the world and perish life! This is a great calamity, indeed." Then he turned to his brother and asked, "Would you like to follow me in what I shall do?" Shahzaman answered, "Yes. I will." Shahrayar said, "Let us leave our royal state and roam the world for the love of the Supreme Lord. If we should find one whose misfortune is greater than ours, we shall return. Otherwise, we shall continue to journey through the land, without need for the trappings of royalty." Shahzaman replied, "This is an excellent idea. I shall follow you."

Then they left by the private gate, took a side road, and departed, journeying till nightfall. They slept over their sorrows, and in the morning resumed their day journey until they came to a meadow by the seashore. While they sat in the meadow amid the thick plants and trees, discussing their misfortunes and the recent events, they suddenly heard a shout and a great cry coming from the middle of the sea. They trembled with fear, thinking that the sky had fallen on the earth. Then the sea parted, and there emerged a black pillar that, as it swayed forward, got taller and taller, until it touched the clouds. Shahrayar and Shahzaman were petrified; then they ran in terror and, climbing a very tall tree, sat hiding in its foliage. When they looked again, they saw that the black pillar was cleaving the sea, wading in the water toward the green meadow, until it touched the shore. When they looked again, they saw that it was a black demon, carrying on his head a large glass chest with four steel locks. He came out, walked into the meadow, and where should he stop but under the very tree where the two kings were hiding. The demon sat down and placed the glass chest on the ground. He took out four keys and, opening the locks of the chest, pulled out a full-grown woman. She had a beautiful figure, and a face like the full moon, and a lovely smile. He took her out, laid her under the tree, and looked at her, saying, "Mistress of all noble women, you whom I carried away on your wedding night, I would like to sleep a little." Then he placed his head on the young woman's lap, stretched his legs to the sea, sank into sleep, and began to snore.

Meanwhile, the woman looked up at the tree and, turning her head by chance, saw King Shahrayar and King Shahzaman. She lifted the demon's head from her lap and placed it on the ground. Then she came and stood under the tree and motioned to them with her hand, as if to say, "Come down slowly to me." When they realized that she had seen them, they were frightened, and they begged her and implored her, in the name of the Creator of the heavens, to excuse them from climbing down. She replied, "You must come down to me." They motioned to her, saying, "This sleeping demon is the enemy of mankind. For God's sake, leave us alone." She replied, "You must come down, and if you don't, I shall wake the demon and have him kill you." She kept gesturing and pressing, until they climbed down very slowly and stood before her. Then she lay on her back, raised her legs, and said, "Make love to me and satisfy my need, or else I shall wake the demon, and he will kill you." They replied, "For God's sake, mistress, don't do this to us, for at this moment we feel nothing but dismay and fear of this demon. Please, excuse us." She replied, "You must," and insisted, swearing, "By God who created the heavens, if you don't do it, I shall wake my husband the demon and ask him to kill you and throw you into the sea." As she persisted, they could no longer resist and they made love to her, first the older brother, then the younger. When they were done and withdrew from her, she said to them, "Give me your rings," and, pulling out from the folds of her dress a small purse, opened it, and shook out ninety-eight rings of different fashions and colors. Then she asked them, "Do you know what these rings are?" They answered, "No." She said, "All the owners of these rings slept with me, for whenever one of them made love to me, I took a ring from him. Since you two have slept with me, give me your rings, so that I may add them to the rest, and make a full hundred. A hundred men have known me under the very horns of this filthy, monstrous cuckold, who has imprisoned me in this chest, locked it with four locks, and kept me in the middle of this raging, roaring sea. He has guarded me and tried to keep me pure and chaste, not realizing that nothing can prevent or alter what is predestined and that when a woman desires something, no one can stop her." When Shahrayar and Shahzaman heard what the young woman said, they were greatly amazed, danced with joy, and said, "O God, O God! There is no power and no strength, save in God the Almighty, the Magnificent. Great is women's cunning." Then each of them took off his ring and handed it to her. She took them and put them with the rest in the purse. Then sitting again by the demon, she lifted his head, placed it back on her lap, and motioned to them, "Go on your way, or else I shall wake him."

They turned their backs and took to the road. Then Shahrayar turned to his brother and said, "My brother Shahzaman, look at this sorry plight. By God, it is worse than ours. This is no less than a demon who has carried a young woman away on her wedding night, imprisoned her in a glass chest, locked her up with four locks, and kept her in the middle of the sea, thinking that he could guard her from what God had foreordained, and you saw how she has managed to sleep with ninety-eight men, and added the two of us to make a hundred. Brother, let us go back to our kingdoms and our cities, never to marry a woman again. As for myself, I shall show you what I will do."

Then the two brothers headed home and journeyed till nightfall. On the morning of the third day, they reached their camp and men, entered their tent, and sat on their thrones. The chamberlains, deputies, princes, and viziers came to attend King Shahrayar, while he gave orders and bestowed robes of honor, as well as other gifts. Then at his command everyone returned to the city, and he went to his own palace and ordered his chief vizier, the father of the two girls Shahrazad and Dinarzad, who will be mentioned below, and said to him, "Take that wife of mine and put her to death." Then Shahrayar went to her himself, bound her, and handed her over to the vizier, who took her out and put her to death. Then King Shahrayar grabbed his sword, brandished it, and, entering the palace chambers, killed every one of his slave-girls and replaced them with others. He then swore to marry for one night only and kill the woman the next morning, in order to save himself from the wickedness and cunning of women, saying, "There is not a single chaste woman anywhere on the entire face of the earth." Shortly thereafter he provided his brother Shahzaman with supplies for his journey and sent him back to his own country with gifts, rarities, and money. The brother bade him good-bye and set out for home.

Shahrayar sat on his throne and ordered his vizier, the father of the two girls, to find him a wife from among the princes' daughters. The vizier found him one, and he slept with her and was done with her, and the next morning he ordered the vizier to put her to death. That very night he took one of his army officers' daughters, slept with her, and the next morning ordered the vizier to put her to death. The vizier, who could not disobey him, put her to death. The third night he took one of the merchants' daughters, slept with her till the morning, then ordered his vizier to put her to death, and the vizier did so. It became King Shahrayar's custom to take every night the daughter of a merchant or a commoner, spend the night with her, then have her put to death the next morning. He continued to do this until all the girls perished, their mothers mourned, and there arose a clamor among the fathers and mothers, who called the plague upon his head, complained to the Creator of the heavens, and called for help on Him who hears and answers prayers.

Now, as mentioned earlier, the vizier, who put the girls to death, had an older daughter called Shahrazad and a younger one called Dinarzad. The older daughter, Shahrazad, had read the books of literature, philosophy, and medicine. She knew poetry by heart, had studied historical reports, and was acquainted with the sayings of men and the maxims of sages and kings. She was intelligent, knowledgeable, wise, and refined. She had read and learned. One day she said to her father, "Father, I will tell you what is in my mind." He asked, "What is it?" She answered, "I would like you to marry me to King Shahrayar, so that I may either succeed in saving the people or perish and die like the rest." When the vizier heard what his daughter Shahrazad said, he got angry and said to her, "Foolish one, don't you know that King Shahrayar has sworn to spend but one night with a girl and have her put to death the next morning? If I give you to him, he will sleep with you for one night and will ask me to put you to death the next morning, and I shall have to do it, since I cannot disobey him." She said, "Father, you must give me to him, even if he kills me." He asked, "What has possessed you that you wish to imperil yourself?" She replied, "Father, you must give me to him. This is absolute and final." Her father the vizier became furious and said to her, "Daughter, 'He who misbehaves, ends up in trouble,' and 'He who considers not the end, the world is not his friend.' As the popular saying goes, 'I would be sitting pretty, but for my curiosity.' I am afraid that what happened to the donkey and the ox with the merchant will happen to you." She asked, "Father, what happened to the donkey, the ox, and the merchant?" He said:

[The Tale of the Ox and the Donkey]

There was a prosperous and wealthy merchant who lived in the countryside and labored on a farm. He owned many camels and herds of cattle and employed many men, and he had a wife and many grown-up as well as little children. This merchant was taught the language of the beasts, on condition that if he revealed his secret to anyone, he would die; therefore, even though he knew the language of every kind of animal, he did not let anyone know, for fear of death. One day, as he sat, with his wife beside him and his children playing before him, he glanced at an ox and a donkey he kept at the farmhouse, tied to adjacent troughs, and heard the ox say to the donkey, "Watchful one, I hope that you are enjoying the comfort and the service you are getting. Your ground is swept and watered, and they serve you, feed you sifted barley, and offer you clear, cool water to drink. I, on the contrary, am taken out to plow in the middle of the night. They clamp on my neck something they call yoke and plow, push me all day under the whip to plow the field, and drive me beyond my endurance until my sides are lacerated, and my neck is flayed. They work me from nighttime to nighttime, take me back in the dark, offer me beans soiled with mud and hay mixed with chaff, and let me spend the night lying in urine and dung. Meanwhile you rest on well-swept, watered, and smoothed ground, with a clean trough full of hay. You stand in comfort, save for the rare occasion when our master the merchant rides you to do a brief errand and returns. You are comfortable, while I am weary; you sleep, while I keep awake."

When the ox finished, the donkey turned to him and said, "Greenhorn, they were right in calling you ox, for you ox harbor no deceit, malice, or meanness. Being sincere, you exert and exhaust yourself to comfort others. Have you not heard the saying 'Out of bad luck, they hastened on the road'? You go into the field from early morning to endure your torture at the plow to the point of exhaustion. When the plowman takes you back and ties you to the trough, you go on butting and beating with your horns, kicking with your hoofs, and bellowing for the beans, until they toss them to you; then you begin to eat. Next time, when they bring them to you, don't eat or even touch them, but smell them, then draw back and lie down on the hay and straw. If you do this, life will be better and kinder to you, and you will find relief."

As the ox listened, he was sure that the donkey had given him good advice. He thanked him, commended him to God, and invoked His blessing on him, and said, "May you stay safe from harm, watchful one." All of this conversation took place, daughter, while the merchant listened and understood. On the following day, the plowman came to the merchant's house and, taking the ox, placed the yoke upon his neck and worked him at the plow, but the ox lagged behind. The plowman hit him, but following the donkey's advice, the ox, dissembling, fell on his belly, and the plowman hit him again. Thus the ox kept getting up and falling until nightfall, when the plowman took him home and tied him to the trough. But this time the ox did not bellow or kick the ground with his hoofs. Instead, he withdrew, away from the trough. Astonished, the plowman brought him his beans and fodder, but the ox only smelled the fodder and pulled back and lay down at a distance with the hay and straw, complaining till the morning. When the plowman arrived, he found the trough as he had left it, full of beans and fodder, and saw the ox lying on his back, hardly breathing, his belly puffed, and his legs raised in the air. The plowman felt sorry for him and said to himself, "By God, he did seem weak and unable to work." Then he went to the merchant and said, "Master, last night, the ox refused to eat or touch his fodder."

The merchant, who knew what was going on, said to the plowman, "Go to the wily donkey, put him to the plow, and work him hard until he finishes the ox's task." The plowman left, took the donkey, and placed the yoke upon his neck. Then he took him out to the field and drove him with blows until he finished the ox's work, all the while driving him with blows and beating him until his sides were lacerated and his neck was flayed. At nightfall he took him home, barely able to drag his legs under his tired body and his drooping ears. Meanwhile the ox spent his day resting. He ate all his food, drank his water, and lay quietly, chewing his cud in comfort. All day long he kept praising the donkey's advice and invoking God's blessing on him. When the donkey came back at night, the ox stood up to greet him saying, "Good evening, watchful one! You have done me a favor beyond description, for I have been sitting in comfort. God bless you for my sake." Seething with anger, the donkey did not reply, but said to himself, "All this happened to me because of my miscalculation. 'I would be sitting pretty, but for my curiosity.' If I don't find a way to return this ox to his former situation, I will perish." Then he went to his trough and lay down, while the ox continued to chew his cud and invoke God's blessing on him.

"You, my daughter, will likewise perish because of your miscalculation. Desist, sit quietly, and don't expose yourself to peril. I advise you out of compassion for you." She replied, "Father, I must go to the king, and you must give me to him." He said, "Don't do it." She insisted, "I must." He replied, "If you don't desist, I will do to you what the merchant did to his wife." She asked, "Father, what did the merchant do to his wife?" He said:

[The Tale of the Merchant and His Wife]

After what had happened to the donkey and the ox, the merchant and his wife went out in the moonlight to the stable, and he heard the donkey ask the ox in his own language, "Listen, ox, what are you going to do tomorrow morning, and what will you do when the plowman brings you your fodder?" The ox replied, "What shall I do but follow your advice and stick to it? If he brings me my fodder, I will pretend to be ill, lie down, and puff my belly." The donkey shook his head, and said, "Don't do it. Do you know what I heard our master the merchant say to the plowman?" The ox asked, "What?" The donkey replied, "He said that if the ox failed to get up and eat his fodder, he would call the butcher to slaughter him and skin him and would distribute the meat for alms and use the skin for a mat. I am afraid for you, but good advice is a matter of faith; therefore, if he brings you your fodder, eat it and look alert lest they cut your throat and skin you." The ox farted and bellowed.

The merchant got up and laughed loudly at the conversation between the donkey and the ox, and his wife asked him, "What are you laughing at? Are you making fun of me?" He said, "No." She said, "Tell me what made you laugh." He replied, "I cannot tell you. I am afraid to disclose the secret conversation of the animals." She asked, "And what prevents you from telling me?" He answered, "The fear of death." His wife said, "By God, you are lying. This is nothing but an excuse. I swear by God, the Lord of heaven, that if you don't tell me and explain the cause of your laughter, I will leave you. You must tell me." Then she went back to the house crying, and she continued to cry till the morning. The merchant said, "Damn it! Tell me why you are crying. Ask for God's forgiveness, and stop questioning and leave me in peace." She said, "I insist and will not desist." Amazed at her, he replied, "You insist! If I tell you what the donkey said to the ox, which made me laugh, I shall die." She said, "Yes, I insist, even if you have to die." He replied, "Then call your family," and she called their two daughters, her parents and relatives, and some neighbors. The merchant told them that he was about to die, and everyone, young and old, his children, the farmhands, and the servants began to cry until the house became a place of mourning. Then he summoned legal witnesses, wrote a will, leaving his wife and children their due portions, freed his slave-girls, and bid his family good-bye, while everybody, even the witnesses, wept. Then the wife's parents approached her and said, "Desist, for if your husband had not known for certain that he would die if he revealed his secret, he wouldn't have gone through all this." She replied, "I will not change my mind," and everybody cried and prepared to mourn his death.

Well, my daughter Shahrazad, it happened that the farmer kept fifty hens and a rooster at home, and while he felt sad to depart this world and leave his children and relatives behind, pondering and about to reveal and utter his secret, he overheard a dog of his say something in dog language to the rooster, who, beating and clapping his wings, had jumped on a hen and, finishing with her, jumped down and jumped on another. The merchant heard and understood what the dog said in his own language to the rooster, "Shameless, no-good rooster. Aren't you ashamed to do such a thing on a day like this?" The rooster asked, "What is special about this day?" The dog replied, "Don't you know that our master and friend is in mourning today? His wife is demanding that he disclose his secret, and when he discloses it, he will surely die. He is in this predicament, about to interpret to her the language of the animals, and all of us are mourning for him, while you clap your wings and get off one hen and jump on another. Aren't you ashamed?" The merchant heard the rooster reply, "You fool, you lunatic! Our master and friend claims to be wise, but he is foolish, for he has only one wife, yet he does not know how to manage her." The dog asked, "What should he do with her?"

The rooster replied, "He should take an oak branch, push her into a room, lock the door, and fall on her with the stick, beating her mercilessly until he breaks her arms and legs and she cries out, 'I no longer want you to tell me or explain anything.' He should go on beating her until he cures her for life, and she will never oppose him in anything. If he does this, he will live, and live in peace, and there will be no more grief, but he does not know how to manage." Well, my daughter Shahrazad, when the merchant heard the conversation between the dog and the rooster, he jumped up and, taking an oak branch, pushed his wife into a room, got in with her, and locked the door. Then he began to beat her mercilessly on her chest and shoulders and kept beating her until she cried for mercy, screaming, "No, no, I don't want to know anything. Leave me alone, leave me alone. I don't want to know anything," until he got tired of hitting her and opened the door. The wife emerged penitent, the husband learned good management, and everybody was happy, and the mourning turned into a celebration.

"If you don't relent, I shall do to you what the merchant did to his wife." She said, "Such tales don't deter me from my request. If you wish, I can tell you many such tales. In the end, if you don't take me to King Shahrayar, I shall go to him by myself behind your back and tell him that you have refused to give me to one like him and that you have begrudged your master one like me." The vizier asked, "Must you really do this?" She replied, "Yes, I must."

Tired and exhausted, the vizier went to King Shahrayar and, kissing the ground before him, told him about his daughter, adding that he would give her to him that very night. The king was astonished and said to him, "Vizier, how is it that you have found it possible to give me your daughter, knowing that I will, by God, the Creator of heaven, ask you to put her to death the next morning and that if you refuse, I will have you put to death too?" He replied, "My King and Lord, I have told her everything and explained all this to her, but she refuses and insists on being with you tonight." The king was delighted and said, "Go to her, prepare her, and bring her to me early in the evening."

The vizier went down, repeated the king's message to his daughter, and said, "May God not deprive me of you." She was very happy and, after preparing herself and packing what she needed, went to her younger sister, Dinarzad, and said, "Sister, listen well to what I am telling you. When I go to the king, I will send for you, and when you come and see that the king has finished with me, say, 'Sister, if you are not sleepy, tell us a story.' Then I will begin to tell a story, and it will cause the king to stop his practice, save myself, and deliver the people." Dinarzad replied, "Very well."

At nightfall the vizier took Shahrazad and went with her to the great King Shahrayar. But when Shahrayar took her to bed and began to fondle her, she wept, and when he asked her, "Why are you crying?" she replied, "I have a sister, and I wish to bid her good-bye before daybreak." Then the king sent for the sister, who came and went to sleep under the bed. When the night wore on, she woke up and waited until the king had satisfied himself with her sister Shahrazad and they were by now all fully awake. Then Dinarzad cleared her throat and said, "Sister, if you are not sleepy, tell us one of your lovely little tales to while away the night, before I bid you good-bye at daybreak, for I don't know what will happen to you tomorrow." Shahrazad turned to King Shahrayar and said, "May I have your permission to tell a story?" He replied, "Yes," and Shahrazad was very happy and said, "Listen":

[The Story of the Merchant and the Demon]

THE FIRST NIGHT

It is said, O wise and happy King, that once there was a prosperous merchant who had abundant wealth and investments and commitments in every country. He had many women and children and kept many servants and slaves. One day, having resolved to visit another country, he took provisions, filling his saddlebag with loaves of bread and with dates, mounted his horse, and set out on his journey. For many days and nights, he journeyed under God's care until he reached his destination. When he finished his business, he turned back to his home and family. He journeyed for three days, and on the fourth day, chancing to come to an orchard, went in to avoid the heat and shade himself from the sun of the open country. He came to a spring under a walnut tree and, tying his horse, sat by the spring, pulled out from the saddlebag some loaves of bread and a handful of dates, and began to eat, throwing the date pits right and left until he had had enough. Then he got up, performed his ablutions, and performed his prayers.

But hardly had he finished when he saw an old demon, with sword in hand, standing with his feet on the ground and his head in the clouds. The demon approached until he stood before him and screamed, saying, "Get up, so that I may kill you with this sword, just as you have killed my son." When the merchant saw and heard the demon, he was terrified and awestricken. He asked, "Master, for what crime do you wish to kill me?" The demon replied, "I wish to kill you because you have killed my son." The merchant asked, "Who has killed your son?" The demon replied, "You have killed my son." The merchant said, "By God, I did not kill your son. When and how could that have been?" The demon said, "Didn't you sit down, take out some dates from your saddlebag, and eat, throwing the pits right and left?" The merchant replied, "Yes, I did." The demon said, "You killed my son, for as you were throwing the stones right and left, my son happened to be walking by and was struck and killed by one of them, and I must now kill you." The merchant said, "O my lord, please don't kill me." The demon replied, "I must kill you as you killed him—blood for blood." The merchant said, "To God we belong and to God we turn. There is no power or strength, save in God the Almighty, the Magnificent. If I killed him, I did it by mistake. Please forgive me." The demon replied, "By God, I must kill you, as you killed my son." Then he seized him, and throwing him to the ground, raised the sword to strike him. The merchant began to weep and mourn his family and his wife and children. Again, the demon raised his sword to strike, while the merchant cried until he was drenched with tears, saying, "There is no power or strength, save in God the Almighty, the Magnificent." Then he began to recite the following verses:

Life has two days: one peace, one wariness,
And has two sides: worry and happiness.
Ask him who taunts us with adversity,
"Does fate, save those worthy of note, oppress?
Don't you see that the blowing, raging storms   5
Only the tallest of the trees beset,
And of earth's many green and barren lots,
Only the ones with fruits with stones are hit,
And of the countless stars in heaven's vault
None is eclipsed except the moon and sun?   10
You thought well of the days, when they were good,
Oblivious to the ills destined for one.
You were deluded by the peaceful nights,
Yet in the peace of night does sorrow stun."

When the merchant finished and stopped weeping, the demon said, "By God, I must kill you, as you killed my son, even if you weep blood." The merchant asked, "Must you?" The demon replied, "I must," and raised his sword to strike.

But morning overtook Shahrazad, and she lapsed into silence, leaving King Shahrayar burning with curiosity to hear the rest of the story. Then Dinarzad said to her sister Shahrazad, "What a strange and lovely story!" Shahrazad replied, "What is this compared with what I shall tell you tomorrow night if the king spares me and lets me live? It will be even better and more entertaining." The king thought to himself, "I will spare her until I hear the rest of the story; then I will have her put to death the next day." When morning broke, the day dawned, and the sun rose; the king left to attend to the affairs of the kingdom, and the vizier, Shahrazad's father, was amazed and delighted. King Shahrayar governed all day and returned home at night to his quarters and got into bed with Shahrazad. Then Dinarzad said to her sister Shahrazad, "Please, sister, if you are not sleepy, tell us one of your lovely little tales to while away the night." The king added, "Let it be the conclusion of the story of the demon and the merchant, for I would like to hear it." Shahrazad replied, "With the greatest pleasure, dear, happy King":

THE SECOND NIGHT

It is related, O wise and happy King, that when the demon raised his sword, the merchant asked the demon again, "Must you kill me?" and the demon replied, "Yes." Then the merchant said, "Please give me time to say good-bye to my family and my wife and children, divide my property among them, and appoint guardians. Then I shall come back, so that you may kill me." The demon replied, "I am afraid that if I release you and grant you time, you will go and do what you wish, but will not come back." The merchant said, "I swear to keep my pledge to come back, as the God of Heaven and earth is my witness." The demon asked, "How much time do you need?" The merchant replied, "One year, so that I may see enough of my children, bid my wife good-bye, discharge my obligations to people, and come back on New Year's Day." The demon asked, "Do you swear to God that if I let you go, you will come back on New Year's Day?" The merchant replied, "Yes, I swear to God."

After the merchant swore, the demon released him, and he mounted his horse sadly and went on his way. He journeyed until he reached his home and came to his wife and children. When he saw them, he wept bitterly, and when his family saw his sorrow and grief, they began to reproach him for his behavior, and his wife said, "Husband, what is the matter with you? Why do you mourn, when we are happy, celebrating your return?" He replied, "Why not mourn when I have only one year to live?" Then he told her of his encounter with the demon and informed her that he had sworn to return on New Year's Day, so that the demon might kill him.

When they heard what he said, everyone began to cry. His wife struck her face in lamentation and cut her hair, his daughters wailed, and his little children cried. It was a day of mourning, as all the children gathered around their father to weep and exchange good-byes. The next day he wrote his will, dividing his property, discharged his obligations to people, left bequests and gifts, distributed alms, and engaged reciters to read portions of the Quran in his house. Then he summoned legal witnesses and in their presence freed his slaves and slave-girls, divided among his elder children their shares of the property, appointed guardians for his little ones, and gave his wife her share, according to her marriage contract. He spent the rest of the time with his family, and when the year came to an end, save for the time needed for the journey, he performed his ablutions, performed his prayers, and, carrying his burial shroud, began to bid his family good-bye. His sons hung around his neck, his daughters wept, and his wife wailed. Their mourning scared him, and he began to weep, as he embraced and kissed his children good-bye. He said to them, "Children, this is God's will and decree, for man was created to die." Then he turned away and, mounting his horse, journeyed day and night until he reached the orchard on New Year's Day.

He sat at the place where he had eaten the dates, waiting for the demon, with a heavy heart and tearful eyes. As he waited, an old man, leading a deer on a leash, approached and greeted him, and he returned the greeting. The old man inquired, "Friend, why do you sit here in this place of demons and devils? For in this haunted orchard none come to good." The merchant replied by telling him what had happened to him and the demon, from beginning to end. The old man was amazed at the merchant's fidelity and said, "Yours is a magnificent pledge," adding, "By God, I shall not leave until I see what will happen to you with the demon." Then he sat down beside him and chatted with him. As they talked . . .

But morning overtook Shahrazad, and she lapsed into silence. As the day dawned, and it was light, her sister Dinarzad said, "What a strange and wonderful story!" Shahrazad replied, "Tomorrow night I shall tell something even stranger and more wonderful than this."

THE THIRD NIGHT

When it was night and Shahrazad was in bed with the king, Dinarzad said to her sister Shahrazad, "Please, if you are not sleepy, tell us one of your lovely little tales to while away the night." The king added, "Let it be the conclusion of the merchant's story." Shahrazad replied, "As you wish":

I heard, O happy King, that as the merchant and the man with the deer sat talking, another old man approached, with two black hounds, and when he reached them, he greeted them, and they returned his greeting. Then he asked them about themselves, and the man with the deer told him the story of the merchant and the demon, how the merchant had sworn to return on New Year's Day, and how the demon was waiting to kill him. He added that when he himself heard the story, he swore never to leave until he saw what would happen between the merchant and the demon. When the man with the two dogs heard the story, he was amazed, and he too swore never to leave them until he saw what would happen between them. Then he questioned the merchant, and the merchant repeated to him what had happened to him with the demon.

While they were engaged in conversation, a third old man approached and greeted them, and they returned his greeting. He asked, "Why do I see the two of you sitting here, with this merchant between you, looking abject, sad, and dejected?" They told him the merchant's story and explained that they were sitting and waiting to see what would happen to him with the demon. When he heard the story, he sat down with them, saying, "By God, I too like you will not leave, until I see what happens to this man with the demon." As they sat, conversing with one another, they suddenly saw the dust rising from the open country, and when it cleared, they saw the demon approaching, with a drawn steel sword in his hand. He stood before them without greeting them, yanked the merchant with his left hand, and, holding him fast before him, said, "Get ready to die." The merchant and the three old men began to weep and wail.

But dawn broke and morning overtook Shahrazad, and she lapsed into silence. Then Dinarzad said, "Sister, what a lovely story!" Shahrazad replied, "What is this compared with what I shall tell you tomorrow night? It will be even better; it will be more wonderful, delightful, entertaining, and delectable if the king spares me and lets me live." The king was all curiosity to hear the rest of the story and said to himself, "By God, I will not have her put to death until I hear the rest of the story and find out what happened to the merchant with the demon. Then I will have her put to death the next morning, as I did with the others." Then he went out to attend to the affairs of his kingdom, and when he saw Shahrazad's father, he treated him kindly and showed him favors, and the vizier was amazed. When night came, the king went home, and when he was in bed with Shahrazad, Dinarzad said, "Sister, if you are not sleepy, tell us one of your lovely little tales to while away the night." Shahrazad replied, "With the greatest pleasure":

THE FOURTH NIGHT

It is related, O happy King, that the first old man with the deer approached the demon and, kissing his hands and feet, said, "Fiend and King of the demon kings, if I tell you what happened to me and that deer, and you find it strange and amazing, indeed stranger and more amazing than what happened to you and the merchant, will you grant me a third of your claim on him for his crime and guilt?" The demon replied, "I will." The old man said:

[The First Old Man's Tale]

Demon, this deer is my cousin, my flesh and blood. I married her when I was very young, and she a girl of twelve, who reached womanhood only afterward. For thirty years we lived together, but I was not blessed with children, for she bore neither boy nor girl. Yet I continued to be kind to her, to care for her, and to treat her generously. Then I took a mistress, and she bore me a son, who grew up to look like a slice of the moon.[5] Meanwhile, my wife grew jealous of my mistress and my son. One day, when he was ten, I had to go on a journey. I entrusted my wife, this one here, with my mistress and son, bade her take good

---

5. The moon is a symbol of beauty for men and women.

care of them, and was gone for a whole year. In my absence my wife, this cousin of mine, learned soothsaying and magic and cast a spell on my son and turned him into a young bull. Then she summoned my shepherd, gave my son to him, and said, "Tend this bull with the rest of the cattle." The shepherd took him and tended him for a while. Then she cast a spell on the mother, turning her into a cow, and gave her also to the shepherd.

When I came back, after all this was done, and inquired about my mistress and my son, she answered, "Your mistress died, and your son ran away two months ago, and I have had no news from him ever since." When I heard her, I grieved for my mistress, and with an anguished heart I mourned for my son for nearly a year. When the Great Feast of the Immolation[6] drew near, I summoned the shepherd and ordered him to bring me a fat cow for the sacrifice. The cow he brought me was in reality my enchanted mistress. When I bound her and pressed against her to cut her throat, she wept and cried, as if saying, "My son, my son," and her tears coursed down her cheeks. Astonished and seized with pity, I turned away and asked the shepherd to bring me a different cow. But my wife shouted, "Go on. Butcher her, for he has none better or fatter. Let us enjoy her meat at feast time." I approached the cow to cut her throat, and again she cried, as if saying, "My son, my son." Then I turned away from her and said to the shepherd, "Butcher her for me." The shepherd butchered her, and when he skinned her, he found neither meat nor fat but only skin and bone. I regretted having her butchered and said to the shepherd, "Take her all for yourself, or give her as alms to whomever you wish, and find me a fat young bull from among the flock." The shepherd took her away and disappeared, and I never knew what he did with her.

Then he brought me my son, my heartblood, in the guise of a fat young bull. Then my son saw me, he shook his head loose from the rope, ran toward me, and, throwing himself at my feet, kept rubbing his head against me. I was astonished and touched with sympathy, pity, and mercy, for the blood hearkened to the blood and the divine bond, and my heart throbbed within me when I saw the tears coursing over the cheeks of my son the young bull, as he dug the earth with his hoofs. I turned away and said to the shepherd, "Let him go with the rest of the flock, and be kind to him, for I have decided to spare him. Bring me another one instead of him." My wife, this very deer, shouted, "You shall sacrifice none but this bull." I got angry and replied, "I listened to you and butchered the cow uselessly. I will not listen to you and kill this bull, for I have decided to spare him." But she pressed me, saying, "You must butcher this bull," and I bound him and took the knife . . .

But dawn broke, and morning overtook Shahrazad, and she lapsed into silence, leaving the king all curiosity for the rest of the story. Then her sister Dinarzad said, "What an entertaining story!" Shahrazad replied. "Tomorrow night I shall tell you something even stranger, more wonderful, and more entertaining if the king spares me and lets me live."

6. The Feast of Sacrifice, celebrated throughout the Muslim world at the end of the pilgrimage to Mecca; to commemorate Abraham, who was willing to sacrifice his son Isaac when commanded by God but was allowed to offer a ram instead, Muslims sacrifice animals to God.

THE FIFTH NIGHT

The following night, Dinarzad said to her sister Shahrazad, "Please, sister, if you are not sleepy, tell us one of your little tales." Shahrazad replied, "With the greatest pleasure":

I heard, dear King, that the old man with the deer said to the demon and to his companions:

I took the knife and as I turned to slaughter my son, he wept, bellowed, rolled at my feet, and motioned toward me with his tongue. I suspected something, began to waver with trepidation and pity, and finally released him, saying to my wife, "I have decided to spare him, and I commit him to your care." Then I tried to appease and please my wife, this very deer, by slaughtering another bull, promising her to slaughter this one next season. We slept that night, and when God's dawn broke, the shepherd came to me without letting my wife know, and said, "Give me credit for bringing you good news." I replied, "Tell me, and the credit is yours." He said, "Master, I have a daughter who is fond of soothsaying and magic and who is adept at the art of oaths and spells. Yesterday I took home with me the bull you had spared, to let him graze with the cattle, and when my daughter saw him, she laughed and cried at the same time. When I asked her why she laughed and cried, she answered that she laughed because the bull was in reality the son of our master the cattle owner, put under a spell by his stepmother, and that she cried because his father had slaughtered the son's mother. I could hardly wait till daybreak to bring you the good news about your son."

Demon, when I heard that, I uttered a cry and fainted, and when I came to myself, I accompanied the shepherd to his home, went to my son, and threw myself at him, kissing him and crying. He turned his head toward me, his tears coursing over his cheeks, and dangled his tongue, as if to say, "Look at my plight." Then I turned to the shepherd's daughter and asked, "Can you release him from the spell? If you do, I will give you all my cattle and all my possessions." She smiled and replied, "Master, I have no desire for your wealth, cattle, or possessions. I will deliver him, but on two conditions: first, that you let me marry him; second, that you let me cast a spell on her who had cast a spell on him, in order to control her and guard against her evil power." I replied, "Do whatever you wish and more. My possessions are for you and my son. As for my wife, who has done this to my son and made me slaughter his mother, her life is forfeit to you." She said, "No, but I will let her taste what she has inflicted on others." Then the shepherd's daughter filled a bowl of water, uttered an incantation and an oath, and said to my son, "Bull, if you have been created in this image by the All-Conquering, Almighty Lord, stay as you are, but if you have been treacherously put under a spell, change back to your human form, by the will of God, Creator of the wide world." Then she sprinkled him with the water, and he shook himself and changed from a bull back to his human form.

As I rushed to him, I fainted, and when I came to myself, he told me what my wife, this very deer, had done to him and to his mother. I said to him, "Son, God has sent us someone who will pay her back for what you and your mother and I have suffered at her hands." Then, O demon, I gave my son in marriage to the shepherd's daughter, who turned my wife into this very deer, saying to me, "To me this is a pretty form, for she will be with us day and night, and it is better to turn her into a pretty deer than to suffer her sinister looks." Thus she stayed with us, while the days and nights followed one another, and the months and years went by. Then one day the shepherd's daughter died, and my son went to the country of this very man with whom you have had your encounter. Some time later I took my wife, this very deer, with me, set out to find out what had happened to my son, and chanced to stop here. This is my story, my strange and amazing story.

The demon assented, saying, "I grant you one-third of this man's life."

Then, O King Shahrayar, the second old man with the two black dogs approached the demon and said, "I too shall tell you what happened to me and to these two dogs, and if I tell it to you and you find it stranger and more amazing than this man's story will you grant me one-third of this man's life?" The demon replied, "I will." Then the old man began to tell his story, saying . . .

But dawn broke, and morning overtook Shahrazad, and she lapsed into silence. Then Dinarzad said, "This is an amazing story," and Shahrazad replied, "What is this compared with what I shall tell you tomorrow night if the king spares me and lets me live!" The king said to himself, "By God, I will not have her put to death until I find out what happened to the man with the two black dogs. Then I will have her put to death, God the Almighty willing."

THE SIXTH NIGHT

When the following night arrived and Shahrazad was in bed with King Shahrayar, her sister Dinarzad said, "Sister, if you are not sleepy, tell us a little tale. Finish the one you started." Shahrazad replied, "With the greatest pleasure":

I heard, O happy King, that the second old man with the two dogs said:

[The Second Old Man's Tale]

Demon, as for my story, these are the details. These two dogs are my brothers. When our father died, he left behind three sons, and left us three thousand dinars,[7] with which each of us opened a shop and became a shopkeeper. Soon my older brother, one of these very dogs, went and sold the contents of his shop for a thousand dinars, bought trading goods, and, having prepared himself for his trading trip, left us. A full year went by, when one day, as I sat in my shop, a beggar stopped by to beg. When I refused him, he tearfully asked, "Don't you recognize me?" and when I looked at him closely, I recognized my brother. I embraced him and took him into the shop, and when I asked him about his plight, he replied, "The money is gone, and the situation is bad." Then I took him to the public bath, clothed him in one of my robes, and took him home with me. Then I examined my books and checked my balance, and found out that I had made a thousand dinars and that my net worth was two thousand dinars. I divided the amount between my brother and myself, and said to him, "Think as if you have never been away." He gladly took the money and opened another shop.

7. Gold coins; the basic Muslim money units [translator's note].

Soon afterward my second brother, this other dog, went and sold his merchandise and collected his money, intending to go on a trading trip. We tried to dissuade him, but he did not listen. Instead, he bought merchandise and trading goods, joined a group of travelers, and was gone for a full year. Then he came back, just like his older brother. I said to him, "Brother, didn't I advise you not to go?" He replied tearfully, "Brother, it was foreordained. Now I am poor and penniless, without even a shirt on my back." Demon, I took him to the public bath, clothed him in one of my new robes, and took him back to the shop. After we had something to eat, I said to him, "Brother, I shall do my business accounts, calculate my net worth for the year, and after subtracting the capital, whatever the profit happens to be, I shall divide it equally between you and myself. When I examined my books and subtracted the capital, I found out that my profit was two thousand dinars, and I thanked God and felt very happy. Then I divided the money, giving him a thousand dinars and keeping a thousand for myself. With that money he opened another shop, and the three of us stayed together for a while. Then my two brothers asked me to go on a trading journey with them, but I refused, saying, "What did you gain from your ventures that I can gain?"

They dropped the matter, and for six years we worked in our stores, buying and selling. Yet every year they asked me to go on a trading journey with them, but I refused, until I finally gave in. I said, "Brothers, I am ready to go with you. How much money do you have?" I found out that they had eaten and drunk and squandered everything they had, but I said nothing to them and did not reproach them. Then I took inventory, gathered all I had together, and sold everything. I was pleased to discover that the sale netted six thousand dinars. Then I divided the money into two parts, and said to my brothers, "The sum of three thousand dinars is for you and myself to use on our trading journey. The other three thousand I shall bury in the ground, in case what happened to you happens to me, so that when we return, we will find three thousand dinars to reopen our shops." They replied, "This is an excellent idea." Then, demon, I divided my money and buried three thousand dinars. Of the remaining three I gave each of my brothers a thousand and kept a thousand for myself. After I closed my shop, we bought merchandise and trading goods, rented a large seafaring boat, and after loading it with our goods and provisions, sailed day and night, for a month.

But morning overtook Shahrazad, and she lapsed into silence. Then her sister Dinarzad said, "Sister, what a lovely story!" Shahrazad replied, "Tomorrow night I shall tell you something even lovelier, stranger, and more wonderful if I live, the Almighty God willing."

THE SEVENTH NIGHT

The following night Dinarzad said to her sister Shahrazad, "For God's sake, sister, if you are not sleepy, tell us a little tale." The king added, "Let it be the completion of the story of the merchant and the demon." Shahrazad replied, "With the greatest pleasure":

I heard, O happy King, that the second old man said to the demon:

For a month my brothers, these very dogs, and I sailed the salty sea, until we came to a port city. We entered the city and sold our goods, earning ten dinars for every dinar. Then we bought other goods, and when we got to the seashore to embark, I met a girl who was dressed in tatters. She kissed my hands and said, "O my lord, be charitable and do me a favor, and I believe that I shall be able to reward you for it." I replied, "I am willing to do you a favor regardless of any reward." She said, "O my lord, marry me, clothe me, and take me home with you on this boat, as your wife, for I wish to give myself to you. I, in turn, will reward you for your kindness and charity, the Almighty God willing. Don't be misled by my poverty and present condition." When I heard her words, I felt pity for her, and guided by what God the Most High had intended for me, I consented. I clothed her with an expensive dress and married her. Then I took her to the boat, spread the bed for her, and consummated our marriage. We sailed many days and nights, and I, feeling love for her, stayed with her day and night, neglecting my brothers. In the meantime they, these very dogs, grew jealous of me, envied me for my increasing merchandise and wealth, and coveted all our possessions. At last they decided to betray me and, tempted by the Devil, plotted to kill me. One night they waited until I was asleep beside my wife; then they carried the two of us and threw us into the sea.

When we awoke, my wife turned into a she-demon and carried me out of the sea to an island. When it was morning, she said, "Husband, I have rewarded you by saving you from drowning, for I am one of the demons who believe in God.[8] When I saw you by the seashore, I felt love for you and came to you in the guise in which you saw me, and when I expressed my love for you, you accepted me. Now I must kill your brothers." When I heard what she said, I was amazed and I thanked her and said, "As for destroying my brothers, this I do not wish, for I will not behave like them." Then I related to her what had happened to me and them, from beginning to end. When she heard my story, she got very angry at them, and said, "I shall fly to them now, drown their boat, and let them all perish." I entreated her, saying, "For God's sake, don't. The proverb advises 'Be kind to those who hurt you.' No matter what, they are my brothers after all." In this manner, I entreated her and pacified her. Afterward, she took me and flew away with me until she brought me home and put me down on the roof of my house. I climbed down, threw the doors open, and dug up the money I had buried. Then I went out and, greeting the people in the market, reopened my shop. When I came home in the evening, I found these two dogs tied up, and when they saw me, they came to me, wept, and rubbed themselves against me. I started, when I suddenly heard my wife say, "O my lord, these are your brothers." I asked, "Who has done this to them?" She replied, "I sent to my sister and asked her to do it. They will stay in this condition for ten years, after which they may be delivered." Then she told me where to find her and departed. The ten years have passed, and I was with my brothers on my way to her to have the spell lifted, when I met this man, together with this old man with the deer. When I asked him about himself, he told me about his encounter with you, and I resolved not to leave until I found out what would happen between you and him. This is my story. Isn't it amazing?

---

8. According to the Qur'an, God created both humans and demons (jinns), some of whom accepted Islam.

The demon replied, "By God, it is strange and amazing. I grant you one-third of my claim on him for his crime."

Then the third old man said, "Demon, don't disappoint me. If I told you a story that is stranger and more amazing than the first two would you grant me one-third of your claim on him for his crime?" The demon replied, "I will." Then the old man said, "Demon, listen":

But morning overlook Shahrazad, and she lapsed into silence. Then her sister said, "What an amazing story!" Shahrazad replied, "The rest is even more amazing." The king said to himself, "I will not have her put to death until I hear what happened to the old man and the demon; then I will have her put to death, as is my custom with the others."

THE EIGHTH NIGHT

The following night Dinarzad said to her sister Shahrazad, "For God's sake, sister, if you are not sleepy, tell us one of your lovely little tales to while away the night." Shahrazad replied, "With the greatest pleasure":

[The Third Old Man's Tale][9]

The demon said, "This is a wonderful story, and I grant you a third of my claim on the merchant's life."

The third sheikh approached and said to the demon, "I will tell you a story more wonderful than these two if you will grant me a third of your claim on his life, O demon!"

To which the demon agreed.

So the sheikh began:

O sultan and chief of the demons, this mule was my wife. I had gone off on a journey and was absent from her for a whole year. At last I came to the end of my journey and returned home late one night. When I entered the house I saw a black slave lying in bed with her. They were chatting and dallying and laughing and kissing and quarreling together. When she saw me my wife leaped out of bed, ran to the water jug, recited a spell over it, then splashed me with some of the water and said, "Leave this form for the form of a dog."

Immediately I became a dog and she chased me out of the house. I ran out of the gate and didn't stop running until I reached a butcher's shop. I entered it and fell to eating the bones lying about. When the owner of the shop saw me, he grabbed me and carried me into his house. When his daughter saw me, she hid her face and said, "Why are you bringing this strange man in with you?"

"What man?" her father asked.

"This dog is a man whose wife has put a spell on him," she said, "but I can set him free again." She took a jug of water, recited a spell over it, then splashed a little water from it on me, and said, "Leave this shape for your original one."

---

9. Translated by Jerome W. Clinton. Because the earliest manuscript does not include a story for the third sheikh, later narrators sup- plied one. This brief anecdote comes from a manuscript found in the library of the Royal Academy in Madrid.

And I became myself again. I kissed her hand and said, "I want to cast a spell on my wife as she did on me. Please give me a little of that water."

"Gladly," she said, "if you find her asleep, sprinkle a few drops on her and she will become whatever you wish."

Well, I did find her asleep, and I sprinkled some water on her and said, "Leave this shape for the shape of a she mule." She at once became the very mule you see here, oh sultan and chief of the demons."

The demon then turned to him and asked, "Is this really true?"

"Yes," he answered, nodding his head vigorously, "it's all true."

When the sheikh had finished his story, the demon shook with laughter and granted him a third of his claim on the merchant's blood.

Then the demon released the merchant and departed. The merchant turned to the three old men and thanked them, and they congratulated him on his deliverance and bade him good-bye. Then they separated, and each of them went on his way. The merchant himself went back home to his family, his wife, and his children, and he lived with them until the day he died. But this story is not as strange or as amazing as the story of the fisherman.

Dinarzad asked, "Please, sister, what is the story of the fisherman?" Shahrazad said: . . .

[The Story of the Fisherman and the Demon]

It is related that there was a very old fisherman who had a wife and three daughters and who was so poor that they did not have even enough food for the day. It was this fisherman's custom to cast his net four times a day. One day, while the moon was still up, he went out with his net at the call for the early morning prayer. He reached the outskirts of the city and came to the seashore. Then he set down his basket, rolled up his shirt, and waded to his waist in the water. He cast his net and waited for it to sink; then he gathered the rope and started to pull. As he pulled little by little, he felt that the net was getting heavier until he was unable to pull any further. He climbed ashore, drove a stake into the ground, and tied the end of the rope to the stake. Then he took off his clothes, dove into the water, and went around the net, shaking it and tugging at it until he managed to pull it ashore. Feeling extremely happy, he put on his clothes and went back to the net. But when he opened it, he found inside a dead donkey, which had torn it apart. The fisherman felt sad and depressed and said to himself, "There is no power and no strength save in God, the Almighty, the Magnificent," adding, "Indeed, this is a strange catch!" Then he began to recite the following verses:

> O you who brave the danger in the dark,
> Reduce your toil, for gain is not in work.
> Look at the fisherman who labors at his trade,
> As the stars in the night their orbits make,
> And deeply wades into the raging sea,
> Steadily gazing at the swelling net,
> Till he returns, pleased with his nightly catch,
> A fish whose mouth the hook of death has cut,

5

> And sells it to a man who sleeps the night,
> Safe from the cold and blessed with every wish.　　　　10
> Praised be the Lord who blesses and withholds:
> This casts the net, but that one eats the fish.

*But morning overtook Shahrazad, and she lapsed into silence. Then her sister
Dinarzad said, "Sister, what a lovely story!" Shahrazad replied, "Tomorrow night
I shall tell you the rest, which is stranger and more wonderful, if the king spares
me and lets me live!"*

THE NINTH NIGHT

*The following night Dinarzad said to her sister Shahrazad, "Sister, if you are
not sleepy, finish the fisherman's story." Shahrazad replied, "With the greatest
pleasure":*

I heard, O happy King, that when the fisherman finished reciting his verses, he
pushed the donkey out of the net and sat down to mend it. When he was done, he
wrung it out and spread it to dry. Then he waded into the water and, invoking the
Almighty God, cast the net and waited for it to sink. Then he pulled the rope little
by little, but this time the net was even more firmly snagged. Thinking that it was
heavy with fish, he was extremely happy. He took off his clothes and, diving into
the water, freed the net and struggled with it until he reached the shore, but
inside the net he found a large jar full of nothing but mud and sand. When he saw
this, he felt sad and, with tears in his eyes, said to himself, "This is a strange day!
God's we are and to God we turn," and he began to recite the following verses:

> O my tormenting fate, forbear,
> Or if you can't, at least be fair.
> I went to seek my daily bread,
> But they said to me it was dead.
> And neither luck nor industry　　　　5
> Brought back my daily bread to me.
> The Pleiads[1] many fools attain,
> While sages sit in dark disdain.

Then the fisherman threw the jar away, washed his net, and, wringing it out,
spread it to dry. Then he begged the Almighty God for forgiveness and went
back to the water. For the third time, he cast the net and waited for it to sink.
But when he pulled it up, he found nothing inside but broken pots and bottles,
stones, bones, refuse, and the like. He wept at this great injustice and ill luck
and began to recite the following verses:

> Your livelihood is not in your own hands;
> Neither by writing nor by the pen you thrive.
> Your luck and your wages are by lot;
> Some lands are waste, and some are fertile lands.
> The wheel of fortune lowers the man of worth,　　　　5

---

1. Cluster of stars in the constellation of Taurus.

Raising the base man who deserves to fall.
Come then, O death, and end this worthless life,
Where the ducks soar, while the falcons are bound to earth.
No wonder that you see the good man poor,
While the vicious exalts in his estate.   10
Our wages are alloted; 'tis our fate
To search like birds for gleanings everywhere.
One bird searches the earth from east to west,
Another gets the tidbits while at rest.

Then the fisherman raised his eyes to the heavens and, seeing that the sun had risen and that it was morning and full daylight, said, "O Lord, you know that I cast my net four times only. I have already cast it three times, and there is only one more try left. Lord, let the sea serve me, even as you let it serve Moses."[2] Having mended the net, he cast it into the sea, and waited for it to sink. When he pulled, he found that it was so heavy that he was unable to haul it. He shook it and found that it was caught at the bottom. Saying "There is no power or strength save in God, the Almighty, the Magnificent," he took off his clothes and dove for the net. He worked at it until he managed to free it, and as he hauled it to the shore, he felt that there was something heavy inside. He struggled with the net, until he opened it and found a large long-necked brass jar, with a lead stopper bearing the mark of a seal ring.[3] When the fisherman saw the jar, he was happy and said to himself, "I will sell it in the copper market, for it must be worth at least two measures of wheat." He tried to move the jar, but it was so full and so heavy that he was unable to budge it. Looking at the lead stopper, he said to himself, "I will open the jar, shake out the contents, then roll it before me until I reach the copper market." Then he took out a knife from his belt and began to scrape and struggle with the lead stopper until he pried it loose. He held the stopper in his mouth, tilted the jar to the ground, and shook it, trying to pour out its contents, but when nothing came out, he was extremely surprised.

After a while, there began to emerge from the jar a great column of smoke, which rose and spread over the face of the earth, increasing so much that it covered the sea and rising so high that it reached the clouds and hid the daylight. For a long time, the smoke kept rising from the jar; then it gathered and took shape, and suddenly it shook and there stood a demon, with his feet on the ground and his head in the clouds. He had a head like a tomb, fangs like pincers, a mouth like a cave, teeth like stones, nostrils like trumpets, ears like shields, a throat like an alley, and eyes like lanterns. In short, all one can say is that he was a hideous monster. When the fisherman saw him, he shook with terror, his jaws locked together, and his mouth went dry. The demon cried, "O Solomon,[4] prophet of God, forgive me, forgive me. Never again will I disobey you or defy your command."

2. That is, by parting and returning at his command (Exodus 14.21–29); like Jews and Christians, Muslims view Moses as a prophet.
3. A ring set with an engraved stone, commonly used to imprint an authenticating mark; or it might be engraved with talismanic words and used as a charm.
4. Solomon (Suleiman), king of Israel (see 1 Kings 1–11), is mentioned as a prophet in the Qur'an.

But morning overtook Shahrazad, and she lapsed into silence. Then Dinarzad said, "Sister, what a strange and amazing story!" Shahrazad replied, "Tomorrow night I shall tell you something stranger and more amazing if I stay alive."

THE TENTH NIGHT

The following night, when Shahrazad was in bed with King Shahrayar, her sister Dinarzad said, "Please, sister, finish the story of the fisherman." Shahrazad replied, "With the greatest pleasure":

I heard, O happy King, that when the fisherman heard what the demon said, he asked, "Demon, what are you saying? It has been more than one thousand and eight hundred years since the prophet Solomon died, and we are now ages later. What is your story, and why were you in this jar?" When the demon heard the fisherman, he said, "Be glad!" The fisherman cried, "O happy day!" The demon added, "Be glad that you will soon be put to death." The fisherman said, "You deserve to be put to shame for such tidings. Why do you wish to kill me, I who have released you and delivered you from the bottom of the sea and brought you back to this world?" The demon replied, "Make a wish!" The fisherman was happy and asked, "What shall I wish of you?" The demon replied, "Tell me how you wish to die, and what manner of death you wish me to choose." The fisherman asked, "What is my crime? Is this my reward from you for having delivered you?" The demon replied, "Fisherman, listen to my story." The fisherman said, "Make it short, for I am at my rope's end."

The demon said, "You should know that I am one of the renegade, rebellious demons. I, together with the giant Sakhr, rebelled against the prophet Solomon, the son of David, who sent against me Asif ibn-Barkhiya, who took me by force and bade me be led in defeat and humiliation before the prophet Solomon. When the prophet Solomon saw me, he invoked God to protect him from me and my looks and asked me to submit to him, but I refused. So he called for this brass jar, confined me inside, and sealed it with a lead seal on which he imprinted God's Almighty name. Then he commanded his demons to carry me and throw me into the middle of the sea. I stayed there for two hundred years, saying to myself, 'Whoever sets me free during these two hundred years, I will make him rich.' But the two hundred years went by and were followed by another two hundred, and no one set me free. Then I vowed to myself, 'Whoever sets me free, I will open for him all the treasures of the earth,' but four hundred years went by, and no one set me free. When I entered the next hundred years, I vowed to myself, 'Whoever delivers me, during these hundred years, I will make him king, make myself his servant, and fulfill every day three of his wishes,' but that hundred years too, plus all the intervening years, went by, and no one set me free. Then I raged and raved and growled and snorted and said to myself, 'Whoever delivers me from now on, I will either put him to the worst of deaths or let him choose for himself the manner of death.' Soon you came by and set me free. Tell me how you wish to die."

When the fisherman heard what the demon said, he replied, "To God we belong and to Him we return. After all these years, with my bad luck, I had to set you free now. Forgive me, and God will grant you forgiveness. Destroy me, and God will inflict on you one who will destroy you." The demon replied, "It must be. Tell me how you wish to die." When the fisherman was certain that he was going to die, he mourned and wept, saying, "O my children, may God not deprive us of each other." Again he turned to the demon and said, "For God's sake, release me as a reward for releasing you and delivering you from this jar." The demon replied, "Your death is your reward for releasing me and letting me escape." The fisherman said, "I did you a good turn, and you are about to repay me with a bad one. How true is the sentiment of the following lines:

> Our kindness they repaid with ugly deeds,
> Upon my life, the deeds of men depraved.
> He who the undeserving aids will meet
> The fate of him who the hyena saved."

The demon said, "Be brief, for as I have said, I must kill you." Then the fisherman thought to himself, "He is only a demon, while I am a human being, whom God has endowed with reason and thereby made superior to him. He may use his demonic wiles on me, but I will use my reason to deal with him." Then he asked the demon, "Must you kill me?" When the demon replied, "I must," the fisherman said, "By the Almighty name that was engraved on the ring of Solomon the son of David, will you answer me truthfully if I ask you about something?" The demon was upset and said with a shudder, "Ask, and be brief!"

But morning overtook Shahrazad, and she lapsed into silence. Then Dinarzad said, "Sister, what an amazing and lovely story!" Shahrazad replied, "What is this compared with what I shall tell you tomorrow night if the king spares me and lets me live! It will be even more amazing."

THE ELEVENTH NIGHT

The following night Dinarzad said to her sister Shahrazad, "Sister, if you are not sleepy, finish the story of the fisherman and the demon." "Shahrazad replied, "With the greatest pleasure":

I heard, O King, that the fisherman said, "By the Almighty name, tell me whether you really were inside this jar." The demon replied, "By the Almighty name, I was imprisoned in this jar." The fisherman said, "You are lying, for this jar is not large enough, not even for your hands and feet. How can it be large enough for your whole body?" The demon replied, "By God, I was inside. Don't you believe that I was inside it?" The fisherman said, "No, I don't." Whereupon the demon shook himself and turned into smoke, which rose, stretched over the sea, spread over the land, then gathered, and, little by little, began to enter the jar. When the smoke disappeared completely, the demon shouted from within, "Fisherman, here I am in the jar. Do you believe me now?"

The fisherman at once took out the sealed lead stopper and hurriedly clamped it on the mouth of the jar. Then he cried out, "Demon, now tell me how you wish to die. For I will throw you into this sea, build a house right here, and sit here and stop any fisherman who comes to fish and warn him that there is a demon here, who will kill whoever pulls him out and who will let him choose how he wishes to die." When the demon heard what the fisherman said and found himself imprisoned, he tried to get out but could not, for he was prevented by the seal of Solomon the son of David. Realizing that the fisherman had tricked him, the demon said, "Fisherman, don't do this to me. I was only joking with you." The fisherman replied, "You are lying, you the dirtiest and meanest of demons," and began to roll the jar toward the sea. The demon shouted, "Don't, don't!" But the fisherman replied, "Yes, yes." Then in a soft and submissive voice the demon asked, "Fisherman, what do you intend to do?" The fisherman replied, "I intend to throw you into the sea. The first time you stayed there for eight hundred years. This time I will let you stay until Doomsday. Haven't I said to you, 'Spare me, and God will spare you. Destroy me, and God will destroy you'? But you refused, and persisted in your resolve to do me in and kill me. Now it is my turn to do you in." The demon said, "Fisherman, if you open the jar, I will reward you and make you rich." The fisherman replied. "You are lying, you are lying. Your situation and mine is like that of King Yunan and the sage Duban." The demon asked, "What is their story?" The fisherman said:

[The Tale of King Yunan and the Sage Duban]

Demon, there was once a king called Yunan, who reigned in one of the cities of Persia, in the province of Zuman.[5] This king was afflicted with leprosy, which had defied the physicians and the sages, who, for all the medicines they gave him to drink and all the ointments they applied, were unable to cure him. One day there came to the city of King Yunan a sage called Duban. This sage had read all sorts of books, Greek, Persian, Turkish, Arabic, Byzantine, Syriac, and Hebrew, had studied the sciences, and had learned their groundwork, as well as their principles and basic benefits. Thus he was versed in all the sciences, from philosophy to the lore of plants and herbs, the harmful as well as the beneficial. A few days after he arrived in the city of King Yunan, the sage heard about the king and his leprosy and the fact that the physicians and the sages were unable to cure him. On the following day, when God's morning dawned and His sun rose, the sage Duban put on his best clothes, went to King Yunan and, introducing himself, said, "Your Majesty, I have heard of that which has afflicted your body and heard that many physicians have treated you without finding a way to cure you. Your Majesty, I can treat you without giving you any medicine to drink or ointment to apply." When the king heard this, he said, "If you succeed, I will bestow on you riches that would be enough for you and your grandchildren. I will bestow favors on you, and I will make you my companion and friend." The king bestowed robes of honor on the sage, treated him kindly, and then asked him, "Can you really cure me from my leprosy without any medicine to drink or ointment to apply?" The sage replied, "Yes, I will cure you externally." The king was astonished, and he began to feel respect as well as great affection for the sage. He said, "Now, sage, do what you have promised." The sage replied, "I hear and obey. I will do it tomorrow morning, the

5. Modern Armenia.

Almighty God willing." Then the sage went to the city, rented a house, and there he distilled and extracted medicines and drugs. Then with his great knowledge and skill, he fashioned a mallet with a curved end, hollowed the mallet, as well as the handle, and filled the handle with his medicines and drugs. He likewise made a ball. When he had perfected and prepared everything, he went on the following day to King Yunan and kissed the ground before him.

But morning overtook Shahrazad, and she lapsed into silence. Then her sister Dinarzad said, "What a lovely story!" Shahrazad replied, "You have heard nothing yet. Tomorrow night I shall tell you something stranger and more amazing if the king spares me and lets me live!"

THE TWELFTH TIGHT

The following night Dinarzad said to her sister Shahrazad, "Please, sister, finish the rest of the story of the fisherman and the demon." Shahrazad replied, "With the greatest pleasure":

I heard, O King, that the fisherman said to the demon:

The sage Duban came to King Yunan and asked him to ride to the playground to play with the ball and mallet. The king rode out, attended by his chamberlains, princes, viziers, and lords and eminent men of the realm. When the king was seated, the sage Duban entered, offered him the mallet, and said, "O happy King, take this mallet, hold it in your hand, and as you race on the playground, hold the grip tightly in your fist, and hit the ball. Race until you perspire, and the medicine will ooze from the grip into your perspiring hand, spread to your wrist, and circulate through your entire body. After you perspire and the medicine spreads in your body, return to your royal palace, take a bath, and go to sleep. You will wake up cured, and that is all there is to it." King Yunan took the mallet from the sage Duban and mounted his horse. The attendants threw the ball before the king, who, holding the grip tightly in his fist, followed it and struggled excitedly to catch up with it and hit it. He kept galloping after the ball and hitting it until his palm and the rest of his body began to perspire, and the medicine began to ooze from the handle and flow through his entire body. When the sage Duban was certain that the medicine had oozed and spread through the king's body, he advised him to return to his palace and go immediately to the bath. The king went to the bath and washed himself thoroughly. Then he put on his clothes, left the bath, and returned to his palace.

As for the sage Duban, he spent the night at home, and early in the morning, he went to the palace and asked for permission to see the king. When he was allowed in, he entered and kissed the ground before the king; then, pointing toward him with his hand, he began to recite the following verses:

> The virtues you fostered are great;
> For who but you could sire them?
> Yours is the face whose radiant light
> Effaces the night dark and grim.
> Forever beams your radiant face;

5

> That of the world is still in gloom.
> You rained on us with ample grace,
> As the clouds rain on thirsty hills,
> Expending your munificence,
> Attaining your magnificence. 10

When the sage Duban finished reciting these verses, the king stood up and embraced him. Then he seated the sage beside him, and with attentiveness and smiles, engaged him in conversation. Then the king bestowed on the sage robes of honor, gave him gifts and endowments, and granted his wishes. For when the king had looked at himself the morning after the bath, he found that his body was clear of leprosy, as clear and pure as silver. He therefore felt exceedingly happy and in a very generous mood. Thus when he went in the morning to the reception hall and sat on his throne, attended by the mamluks[6] and chamberlains, in the company of the viziers and the lords of the realm, and the sage Duban presented himself, as we have mentioned, the king stood up, embraced him, and seated him beside him. He treated him attentively and drank and ate with him.

But morning overtook Shahrazad, and she lapsed into silence. Then her sister Dinarzad said, "Sister, what a lovely story!" Shahrazad replied, "The rest of the story is stranger and more amazing. If the king spares me and I am alive tomorrow night, I shall tell you something even more entertaining."

THE THIRTEENTH NIGHT

The following night Dinarzad said to her sister Shahrazad, "Sister, if you are not sleepy, tell us one of your lovely little tales to while away the night." Shahrazad replied, "With the greatest pleasure":

I heard, O happy King who is praiseworthy by the Grace of God, that King Yunan bestowed favors on the sage, gave him robes of honor, and granted his wishes. At the end of the day he gave the sage a thousand dinars and sent him home. The king, who was amazed at the skill of the sage Duban, said to himself, "This man has treated me externally, without giving me any draught to drink or ointment to apply. His is indeed a great wisdom for which he deserves to be honored and rewarded. He shall become my companion, confidant, and close friend." Then the king spent the night, happy at his recovery from his illness, at his good health, and at the soundness of his body. When morning came and it was light, the king went to the royal reception hall and sat on the throne, attended by his chief officers, while the princes, viziers, and lords of the realm sat to his right and left. Then the king called for the sage, and when the sage entered and kissed the ground before him, the king stood up to salute him, seated him beside him, and invited him to eat with him. The king treated him intimately, showed him favors, and bestowed on him robes of honor and many other gifts. Then he spent the whole day conversing with him, and at the end of

---

6. Literally, "slaves"; here, members of a military class who were originally slaves from the Caucasus region.

the day he ordered that he be given a thousand dinars. The sage went home and spent the night with his wife, feeling happy and thankful to God the Arbiter.

In the morning, the king went to the royal reception hall, and the princes and viziers came to stand in attendance. It happened that King Yunan had a vizier who was sinister, greedy, envious, and fretful, and when he saw that the sage had found favor with the king, who bestowed on him much money and many robes of honor, he feared that the king would dismiss him and appoint the sage in his place; therefore, he envied the sage and harbored ill will against him, for "nobody is free from envy." The envious vizier approached the king and, kissing the ground before him, said, "O excellent King and glorious Lord, it was by your kindness and with your blessing that I rose to prominence; therefore, if I fail to advise you on a grave matter, I am not my father's son. If the great King and noble Lord commands, I shall disclose the matter to him." The king was upset and asked, "Damn you, what advice have you got?" The vizier replied, "Your Majesty, 'He who considers not the end, fortune is not his friend.' I have seen your Majesty make a mistake, for you have bestowed favors on your enemy who has come to destroy your power and steal your wealth. Indeed, you have pampered him and shown him many favors, but I fear that he will do you harm." The king asked, "Whom do you accuse, whom do you have in mind, and at whom do you point the finger?" The vizier replied, "If you are asleep, wake up, for I point the finger at the sage Duban, who has come from Byzantium." The king replied, "Damn you, is he my enemy? To me he is the most faithful, the dearest, and the most favored of people, for this sage has treated me simply by making me hold something in my hand and has cured me from the disease that had defied the physicians and the sages and rendered them helpless. In all the world, east and west, near and far, there is no one like him, yet you accuse him of such a thing. From this day onward, I will give him every month a thousand dinars, in addition to his rations and regular salary. Even if I were to share my wealth and my kingdom with him, it would be less than he deserves. I think that you have said what you said because you envy him. This is very much like the situation in the story told by the vizier of King Sindbad[7] when the king wanted to kill his own son.

But morning overtook Shahrazad, and she lapsed into silence. Then her sister Dinarzad said, "Sister, what a lovely story!" Shahrazad replied, "What is this compared with what I shall tell you tomorrow night! It will be stranger and more amazing."

THE FOURTEENTH NIGHT

The following night, when the king got into bed and Shahrazad got in with him, her sister Dinarzad said, "Please, sister, if you are not sleepy, tell us one of your lovely little tales to while away the night." Shahrazad replied, "Very well":

I heard, O happy King, that King Yunan's vizier asked, "King of the age, I beg your pardon, but what did King Sindbad's vizier tell the king when he wished to kill his own son?" King Yunan said to the vizier, "When King Sindbad, provoked by an envious man, wanted to kill his own son, his vizier said to him, 'Don't do what you will regret afterward.'"

---

7. Not to be confused with Sindbad the Sailor.

[The Tale of the Husband and the Parrot]

I have heard it told that there was once a very jealous man who had a wife so splendidly beautiful that she was perfection itself. The wife always refused to let her husband travel and leave her behind, until one day when he found it absolutely necessary to go on a journey. He went to the bird market, bought a parrot, and brought it home. The parrot was intelligent, knowledgeable, smart, and retentive. Then he went away on his journey, and when he finished his business and came back, he brought the parrot and inquired about his wife during his absence. The parrot gave him a day-by-day account of what his wife had done with her lover and how the two carried on in his absence. When the husband heard the account, he felt very angry, went to his wife, and gave her a sound beating. Thinking that one of her maids had informed her husband about what she did with her lover in her husband's absence, the wife interrogated her maids one by one, and they all swore that they had heard the parrot inform the husband.

When the wife heard that it was the parrot who had informed the husband, she ordered one of her maids to take the grinding stone and grind under the cage, ordered a second maid to sprinkle water over the cage, and ordered a third to carry a steel mirror and walk back and forth all night long. That night her husband stayed out, and when he came home in the morning, he brought the parrot, spoke with it, and asked about what had transpired in his absence that night. The parrot replied, "Master, forgive me, for last night, all night long, I was unable to hear or see very well because of the intense darkness, the rain, and the thunder and lightning." Seeing that it was summertime, during the month of July, the husband replied, "Woe unto you, this is no season for rain." The parrot said, "Yes, by God, all night long, I saw what I told you." The husband, concluding that the parrot had lied about his wife and had accused her falsely, got angry, and he grabbed the parrot and, taking it out of the cage, smote it on the ground and killed it. But after the parrot's death, the husband heard from his neighbors that the parrot had told the truth about his wife, and he was full of regret that he had been tricked by his wife to kill the parrot.

King Yunan concluded, "Vizier, the same will happen to me."

But morning overtook Shahrazad, and she lapsed into silence. Then her sister Dinarzad said, "What a strange and lovely story!" Shahrazad replied, "What is this compared with what I shall tell you tomorrow night! If the king spares me and lets me live, I shall tell you something more amazing." The king thought to himself, "By God, this is indeed an amazing story."

THE FIFTEENTH NIGHT

The following night Dinarzad said to her sister Shahrazad, "Please, sister, if you are not sleepy, tell us one of your lovely little tales, for they entertain and help everyone to forget his cares and banish sorrow from the heart." Shahrazad replied, "With the greatest pleasure." King Shahrayar added, "Let it be the remainder of the story of King Yunan, his vizier, and the sage Duban, and of the fisherman, the demon, and the jar." Shahrazad replied, "With the greatest pleasure":

I heard, O happy King, that King Yunan said to his envious vizier, "After the husband killed the parrot and heard from his neighbors that the parrot had told him the truth, he was filled with remorse. You too, my vizier, being envious of this wise man, would like me to kill him and regret it afterward, as did the husband after he killed the parrot." When the vizier heard what King Yunan said, he replied, "O great king, what harm has this sage done to me? Why, he has not harmed me in any way. I am telling you all this out of love and fear for you. If you don't discover my veracity, let me perish like the vizier who deceived the son of the king." King Yunan asked his vizier, "How so?" The vizier replied:

[The Tale of the King's Son and the She-Ghoul]

It is said, O happy King, that there was once a king who had a son who was fond of hunting and trapping. The prince had with him a vizier appointed by his father the king to follow him wherever he went. One day the prince went with his men into the wilderness, and when he chanced to see a wild beast, the vizier urged him to go after it. The prince pursued the beast and continued to press in pursuit until he lost its track and found himself alone in the wilderness, not knowing which way to turn or where to go, when he came upon a girl, standing on the road, in tears. When the young prince asked her, "Where do you come from?" she replied, "I am the daughter of an Indian king. I was riding in the wilderness when I dozed off and in my sleep fell off my horse and found myself alone and helpless." When the young prince heard what she said, he felt sorry for her, and he placed her behind him on his horse and rode on. As they passed by some ruins, she said, "O my lord, I wish to relieve myself here." He let her down and she went into the ruins. Then he went in after her, ignorant of what she was, and discovered that she was a she-ghoul, who was saying to her children, "I brought you a good, fat boy." They replied, "Mother, bring him to us, so that we may feed on his innards." When the young prince heard what they said, he shook with terror, and fearing for his life, ran outside. The she-ghoul followed him and asked, "Why are you afraid?" and he told her about his situation and his predicament, concluding, "I have been unfairly treated." She replied, "If you have been unfairly treated, ask the Almighty God for help, and He will protect you from harm." The young prince raised his eyes to Heaven . . .

But morning overtook Shahrazad, and she lapsed into silence. Then her sister Dinarzad said, "What a strange and lovely story!" Shahrazad replied, "What is this compared with what I shall tell you tomorrow night! It will be even stranger and more amazing."

THE SIXTEENTH NIGHT

The following night Dinarzad said, "Please, sister, if you are not sleepy, tell us one of your lovely little tales." Shahrazad replied, "I shall with pleasure":

I heard, O King, that the vizier said to King Yunan:

When the young prince said to the she-ghoul, "I have been unfairly treated," she replied, "Ask God for help, and He will protect you from harm." The young prince raised his eyes to Heaven and said, "O Lord, help me to prevail upon my enemy, for 'everything is within your power.'" When the she-ghoul heard his invocation, she gave up and departed, and he returned safely to his father and told him about the vizier and how it was he who had urged him to pursue the beast and drove him to his encounter with the she-ghoul. The king summoned the vizier and had him put to death.

The vizier added, "You too, your Majesty, if you trust, befriend, and bestow favors on this sage, he will plot to destroy you and cause your death. Your Majesty should realize that I know for certain that he is a foreign agent who has come to destroy you. Haven't you seen that he cured you externally, simply with something you held in your hand?" King Yunan, who was beginning to feel angry, replied, "You are right, vizier. The sage may well be what you say and may have come to destroy me. He who has cured me with something to hold can kill me with something to smell." Then the king asked the vizier, "My vizier and good counselor, how should I deal with him?" The vizier replied, "Send for him now and have him brought before you, and when he arrives, strike off his head. In this way, you will attain your aim and fulfill your wish." The king said, "This is good and sound advice." Then he sent for the sage Duban, who came immediately, still feeling happy at the favors, the money, and the robes the king had bestowed on him. When he entered, he pointed with his hand toward the king and began to recite the following verses:

> If I have been remiss in thanking you,
> For whom then have I made my verse and prose?
> You granted me your gifts before I asked,
> Without deferment and without excuse.
> How can I fail to praise your noble deeds,   5
> Inspired in private and in public by my muse?
> I thank you for your deeds and for your gifts,
> Which, though they bend my back, my care reduce.

The king asked, "Sage, do you know why I have had you brought before me?" The sage replied, "No, your Majesty." The king said, "I brought you here to have you killed and to destroy the breath of life within you." In astonishment Duban asked, "Why does your Majesty wish to have me put to death, and for what crime?" The king replied, "I have been told that you are a spy and that you have come to kill me. Today I will have you killed before you kill me. 'I will have you for lunch before you have me for dinner.'" Then the king called for the executioner and ordered him, saying, "Strike off the head of this sage and rid me of him! Strike!"

When the sage heard what the king said, he knew that because he had been favored by the king, someone had envied him, plotted against him, and lied to the king, in order to have him killed and get rid of him. The sage realized then that the king had little wisdom, judgment, or good sense, and he was filled with regret, when it was useless to regret. He said to himself, "There is no power and no strength, save in God the Almighty, the Magnificent. I did a good deed but was rewarded with an evil one." In the meantime, the king was shouting at the executioner, "Strike off his head." The sage implored, "Spare me, your Majesty, and God will spare you; destroy me, and God will destroy you." He repeated the statement, just as I did, O demon, but you too refused, insisting on killing me. King Yunan said to the sage, "Sage, you must die, for you have cured me with a mere handle, and I fear that you can kill me with anything." The sage replied, "This is my reward from your Majesty. You reward good with evil." The king said, "Don't stall; you must die today without delay." When the sage Duban became convinced that he was going to die, he was filled with grief and sorrow, and his eyes overflowed with tears. He blamed himself for doing a favor for one who does not deserve it and for sowing seeds in a barren soil and recited the following verses:

> Maimuna was a foolish girl,
> Though from a sage descended,
> And many with pretense to skill
> Are e'en on dry land upended.

The executioner approached the sage, bandaged his eyes, bound his hands, and raised the sword, while the sage cried, expressed regret, and implored, "For God's sake, your Majesty, spare me, and God will spare you; destroy me, and God will destroy you." Then he tearfully began to recite the following verses:

> They who deceive enjoy success,
> While I with my true counsel fail
> And am rewarded with disgrace.
> If I live, I'll nothing unveil;
> If I die, then curse all the men,
> The men who counsel and prevail.

Then the sage added, "Is this my reward from your Majesty? It is like the reward of the crocodile." The king asked, "What is the story of the crocodile?" The sage replied, "I am in no condition to tell you a story. For God's sake, spare me, and God will spare you. Destroy me, and God will destroy you," and he wept bitterly.

Then several noblemen approached the king and said, "We beg your Majesty to forgive him for our sake, for in our view, he has done nothing to deserve this." The king replied, "You do not know the reason why I wish to have him killed. I tell you that if I spare him, I will surely perish, for I fear that he who has cured me externally from my affliction, which had defied the Greek sages, simply by having me hold a handle, can kill me with anything I touch. I must kill him, in order to protect myself from him." The sage Duban implored again, "For God's sake, your Majesty, spare me, and God will spare you. Destroy me, and God will destroy you." The king insisted, "I must kill you."

Demon, when the sage realized that he was surely going to die, he said, "I beg your Majesty to postpone my execution until I return home, leave instructions for my burial, discharge my obligations, distribute alms, and donate my scientific and medical books to one who deserves them. I have in particular a book entitled *The Secret of Secrets*, which I should like to give you for safekeeping in your library." The king asked, "What is the secret of this book?" The sage replied, "It contains countless secrets, but the chief one is that if your Majesty has my head struck off, opens the book on the sixth leaf, reads three lines from the left page, and speaks to me, my head will speak and answer whatever you ask."

The king was greatly amazed and said, "Is it possible that if I cut off your head and, as you say, open the book, read the third line, and speak to your head, it will speak to me? This is the wonder of wonders." Then the king allowed the sage to go and sent him home under guard. The sage settled his affairs and on the following day returned to the royal palace and found assembled there the princes, viziers, chamberlains, lords of the realm, and military officers, as well as the king's retine, servants, and many of his citizens. The sage Duban entered, carrying an old book and a kohl[8] jar containing powder. He sat down, ordered a platter, and poured out the powder and smoothed it on the platter. Then he said to the king, "Take this book, your Majesty, and don't open it until after my execution. When my head is cut off, let it be placed on the platter and order that it be pressed on the powder. Then open the book and begin to ask my head a question, for it will then answer you. There is no power and no strength save in God, the Almighty, the Magnificent. For God's sake, spare me, and God will spare you; destroy me, and God will destroy you." The king replied, "I must kill you, especially to see how your head will speak to me." Then the king took the book and ordered the executioner to strike off the sage's head. The executioner drew his sword and, with one stroke, dropped the head in the middle of the platter, and when he pressed the head on the powder, the bleeding stopped. Then the sage Duban opened his eyes and said, "Now, your Majesty, open the book." When the king opened the book, he found the pages stuck. So he put his finger in his mouth, wetted it with his saliva, and opened the first page, and he kept opening the pages with difficulty until he turned seven leaves. But when he looked in the book, he found nothing written inside, and he exclaimed, "Sage, I see nothing written in this book." The sage replied, "Open more pages." The king opened some more pages but still found nothing, and while he was doing this, the drug spread through his body—for the book had been poisoned—and he began to heave, sway, and twitch.

But morning overtook Shahrazad, and she lapsed into silence. Then her sister Dinarzad said, "Sister, what an amazing and entertaining story!" Shahrazad replied, "What is this compared with what I shall tell you tomorrow night if the king spares me and lets me live!"

THE SEVENTEENTH NIGHT

The following night Dinarzad said to her sister Shahrazad, "Please, sister, if you are not sleepy, tell us one of your lovely little tales to while away the night." The king added, "Let it be the rest of the story of the sage and the king and of the fisherman and the demon." Shahrazad replied, "Very well, with the greatest pleasure":

---

8. An ancient cosmetic used to darken the eyelids and as mascara, long commonly employed by women in the Middle East.

I heard, O King, that when the sage Duban saw that the drug had spread through the king's body and that the king was heaving and swaying, he began to recite the following verses:

> For long they ruled us arbitrarily,
> But suddenly vanished their powerful rule.
> Had they been just, they would have happily
> Lived, but they oppressed, and punishing fate
> Afflicted them with ruin deservedly,
> And on the morrow the world taunted them,
> "'Tis tit for tat; blame not just destiny."

As the sage's head finished reciting the verses, the king fell dead, and at that very moment the head too succumbed to death. Demon, consider this story.

But morning overtook Shahrazad, and she lapsed into silence. Then her sister Dinarzad said, "Sister, what an entertaining story!" Shahrazad replied, "What is this compared with what I shall tell you tomorrow night if I live!"

THE EIGHTEENTH NIGHT

The following night, Dinarzad said to her sister Shahrazad, "Please, sister, if you are not sleepy, tell us one of your lovely little tales to while away the night." The king added, "Let it be the rest of the story of the fisherman and the demon." Shahrazad replied, "With the greatest pleasure":

I heard, O King, that the fisherman said to the demon, "Had the king spared the sage, God would have spared him and he would have lived, but he refused and insisted on destroying the sage, and the Almighty God destroyed him. You too, demon, had you from the beginning agreed to spare me, I would have spared you, but you refused and insisted on killing me; therefore, I shall punish you by keeping you in this jar and throwing you into the bottom of the sea." The demon cried out, "Fisherman, don't do it. Spare me and save me and don't blame me for my action and my offense against you. If I did ill, you should do good. As the saying goes, 'Be kind to him who wrongs you.' Don't do what Imama did to 'Atika." The fisherman asked, "What did Imama do to 'Atika?" The demon replied, "This is no time and this narrow prison is no place to tell a story, but I shall tell it to you after you release me." The fisherman said, "I must throw you into the sea. There is no way I would let you out and set you free, for I kept imploring you and calling on you, but you refused and insisted on killing me, without any offense or injury that merits punishment, except that I had set you free. When you treated me in this way, I realized that you were unclean from birth, that you were ill-natured, and that you were one who rewards good with ill. After I throw you into the sea, I shall build me a hut here and live in it for your sake, so that if anyone pulls you out, I shall acquaint him with what I suffered at your hands and shall advise him to throw you back into the sea and let you perish or languish there to the end of time, you the dirtiest of demons." The demon replied, "Set me free this time, and I pledge never to bother you or harm you, but to make you rich." When he heard this, the fisherman made the demon pledge and covenant that if the fisherman released him and let him out, he would not harm him but would serve him and be good to him.

After the fisherman secured the demon's pledge, by making him swear by the Almighty Name, he opened the seal of the jar, and the smoke began to rise. When the smoke was completely out of the jar, it gathered and turned again into a full-fledged demon, who kicked the jar away and sent it flying to the middle of the sea. When the fisherman saw what the demon had done, sure that he was going to meet with disaster and death, he wet himself and said, "This is a bad omen." Then he summoned his courage and cried out, "Demon, you have sworn and given me your pledge. Don't betray me. Come back, lest the Almighty God punish you for your betrayal. Demon, I repeat to you what the sage Duban said to King Yunan, 'Spare me, and God will spare you; destroy me, and God will destroy you.'" When the demon heard what the fisherman said, he laughed, and when the fisherman cried out again, "Demon, spare me," he replied, "Fisherman, follow me," and the fisherman followed him, hardly believing in his escape, until they came to a mountain outside the city. They climbed over to the other side and came to a vast wilderness, in the middle of which stood a lake surrounded by four hills.

The demon halted by the lake and ordered the fisherman to cast his net and fish. The fisherman looked at the lake and marveled as he saw fish in many colors, white, red, blue, and yellow. He cast his net, and when he pulled, he found four fish inside, one red, one white, one blue, and one yellow. When he saw them, he was full of admiration and delight. The demon said to him, "Take them to the king of your city and offer them to him, and he will give you enough to make you rich. Please excuse me, for I know no other way to make you rich. But don't fish here more than once a day." Then, saying, "I shall miss you," the demon kicked the ground with his foot, and it opened and swallowed him. The fisherman, O King, returned to the city, still marveling at his encounter with the demon and at the colored fish. He entered the royal palace, and when he offered the fish to the king, the king looked at them . . .

But morning overtook Shahrazad, and she lapsed into silence. Then Dinarzad said, "Sister, what an amazing and entertaining story!" Shahrazad replied, "What is this compared with what I shall tell you tomorrow night if the king spares me and lets me live!"

THE NINETEENTH NIGHT

The following night Dinarzad said to her sister Shahrazad, "Sister tell us the rest of the story and what happened to the fisherman." Shahrazad replied, "With the greatest pleasure":

I heard, O King, that when the fisherman presented the fish to the king, and the king looked at them and saw that they were colored, he took one of them in his hand and looked at it with great amazement. Then he said to his vizier, "Take them to the cook whom the emperor of Byzantium has given us as a present." The vizier took the fish and brought them to the girl and said to her, "Girl, as the saying goes, 'I save my tears for the time of trial.' The king has been presented these four fish, and he bids you fry them well." Then the vizier went back to report to the king, and the king ordered him to give the fisherman four hundred dirhams.[9] The vizier gave the money to the fisherman, who, receiving it, gathered it in the folds of his robe and went away, running, and as he ran, he stumbled and kept falling and getting up, thinking that he was in a dream. Then he stopped and bought some provisions for his family.

So far for the fisherman, O King. In the meantime the girl scaled the fish, cleaned them, and cut them into pieces. Then she placed the frying pan on the fire and poured in the sesame oil, and when it began to boil, she placed the fish in the frying pan. When the pieces were done on one side, she turned them over, but no sooner had she done this than the kitchen wall split open and there emerged a maiden with a beautiful figure, smooth cheeks, perfect features, and dark eyes. She wore a short-sleeved silk shirt in the Egyptian style, embroidered all around with lace and gold spangles. In her ears she wore dangling earrings; on her wrists she wore bracelets; and in her hand she held a bamboo wand. She thrust the wand into the frying pan and said in clear Arabic, "O fish, O fish, have you kept the pledge?" When the cook saw what had happened, she fainted. Then the maiden repeated what she had said, and the fish raised their heads from the frying pan and replied in clear Arabic, "Yes, yes. If you return, we shall return; if you keep your vow, we shall keep ours; and if you forsake us, we shall be even." At that moment the maiden overturned the frying pan and disappeared as she had come, and the kitchen wall closed behind her.

When the cook came to herself, she found the four fish charred, and she felt sorry for herself and afraid of the king, saying to herself, "'He broke his lance on his very first raid.'" While she remonstrated with herself, the vizier suddenly stood before her, saying, "Give me the fish, for we have set the table before the king, and he is waiting for them." The girl wept and told the vizier what she had seen and witnessed and what had happened to the fish. The vizier was astonished and said, "This is very strange." Then he sent an officer after the fisherman, and he returned a while later with the fisherman. The vizier shouted at him, saying, "Bring us at once four more fish like the ones you brought us before, for we have had an accident with them." When he followed with threats, the fisherman went home and, taking his fishing gear, went outside the city, climbed the mountain, and descended to the wilderness on the other side. When he came to the lake, he cast his net, and when he pulled up, he found inside four fish, as he had done the first time. Then he brought them back to the vizier, who took them to the girl and said, "Fry them in front of me, so that I can see for myself." The girl prepared the fish at once, placed the frying pan over the fire, and threw them in. When the fish were done, the wall split open, and the maiden appeared in her elegant clothes, wearing necklaces and other jewelry and holding in her hand the bamboo wand. Again she thrust the wand into the frying pan and said in clear Arabic, "O fish, have you kept the pledge?" and again the fish raised their heads and replied, "Yes, yes. If you return, we shall return; if you keep your vow, we shall keep ours; and if you forsake us, we shall be even."

9. Small silver coins.

But morning overtook Shahrazad, and she lapsed into silence. Then Dinarzad said, "What an entertaining story!" Shahrazad replied, "What is this compared with what I shall tell you tomorrow night if I live, the Almighty God willing!"

THE TWENTIETH NIGHT

The following night Dinarzad said to her sister Shahrazad, "Please, sister, if you are not sleepy, tell us one of your lovely little tales to while away the night." Shahrazad replied, "With the greatest pleasure":

I heard, O happy King, that after the fish spoke, the maiden overturned the frying pan with the wand and disappeared into the opening from which she had emerged, and the wall closed behind her. The vizier said to himself, "I can no longer hide this affair from the king," and he went to him and told him what had happened to the fish before his very eyes.

The king was exceedingly amazed and said, "I wish to see this with my own eyes." Then he sent for the fisherman, who came after a little while, and the king said to him, "I want you to bring me at once four more fish like the ones you brought before. Hurry!" Then he assigned three officers to guard the fisherman and sent him away. The fisherman disappeared for a while and returned with four fish, one red, one white, one blue, and one yellow. The king commanded, "Give him four hundred dirhams," and the fisherman, receiving the money, gathered it in the folds of his robe and went away. Then the king said to the vizier, "Fry the fish here in my presence." The vizier replied, "I hear and obey," and he called for a stove and a frying pan and sat to clean the fish. Then he lit the fire and, pouring the sesame oil, placed the fish in the frying pan.

When they were almost done, the palace wall split open, and the king and vizier began to tremble, and when they looked up, they saw a black slave who stood like a towering mountain or a giant descendant of the tribe of 'Ad.[1] He was as tall as a reed, as wide as a stone bench, and he held a green palm leaf in his hand. Then in clear but unpleasant language, he said, "O fish, O fish, have you kept the pledge?" and the fish raised their heads from the frying pan and said, "Yes, yes. If you return, we shall return; if you keep your vow, we shall keep ours; and if you forsake us, we shall be even." At that moment, the black slave overturned the frying pan, in the middle of the hall, and the fish turned into charcoal. Then the black slave departed as he had come, and the wall closed behind him. When the black slave disappeared, the king said, "I cannot sleep over this affair, for there is no doubt a mystery behind these fish." Then he bade the fisherman be brought before him again.

When the fisherman arrived, the king said to him, "Damn you, where do you catch these fish?" The fisherman replied, "My lord, I catch them in a lake that lies among four hills, on the other side of the mountain." The king turned to the vizier and asked, "Do you know this lake?" The vizier replied, "No, by God, your Majesty. For sixty years, I have hunted, traveled, and roamed far and wide, sometimes for a day or two, sometimes for a month or two, but I have

---

1. Tribe supposedly destroyed by God's wrath (Qur'an 41.15).

never seen or known that such a lake existed on the other side of the mountain." Then the king turned to the fisherman and asked him, "How far is this lake from here?" The fisherman replied, "King of the age, it is one hour from here." The king was astonished, and he ordered his soldiers to be ready. Then he rode out with his troops, behind the fisherman, who led the way under guard, muttering curses on the demon as he went.

They rode until they were outside the city. Then they climbed the mountain, and when they descended to the other side, they saw a vast wilderness that they had never seen in all their lives, as well as the four hills and the lake in whose clear water they saw the fish in four colors, red, white, blue, and yellow. The king stood marveling; then he turned to the vizier, princes, chamberlains, and deputies and asked, "Have any of you ever seen this lake before?" They replied, "Never." He asked, "And none of you knew where it was?" They kissed the ground before him and replied, "By God, your Majesty, till now we have never in our lives seen this lake or known about it, even though it is close to our city." The king said, "There is a mystery behind this. By God, I shall not return to the city until I find the answer to the mystery behind this lake and these fish in four colors." Then he ordered his men to halt and pitch the tents, and he dismounted and waited.

When it was dark, he summoned the vizier, who was an experienced and wise man of the world. The vizier came to the king, without being seen by the soldiers, and when he arrived, the king said, "I wish to reveal to you what I intend to do. At this very hour, I shall go all by myself to look for an answer to the mystery of this lake and these fish. Early tomorrow morning you shall sit at the entrance of my tent and tell the princes that the king is indisposed and that he has given you orders not to let anyone be admitted to his presence. You must not let anyone know about my departure and absence, and you must wait for me for three days." The vizier, unable to disobey him, abided by the order, saying, "I hear and obey."

Then the king packed, prepared himself, and girded himself with the royal sword. Then he climbed one of the four hills, and when he reached the top, he journeyed on for the rest of the night. In the morning, when the sun rose and steeped the mountaintop with light, the king looked and sighted a dark mass in the distance. When he saw it, he was glad, and he headed in its direction, saying to himself, "There may be someone there to give me information." He journeyed on, and when he arrived, he found a palace, built under a lucky star, with black stones and completely overlaid with iron plates. It had double doors, one open, one shut. Pleased, the king knocked gently at the door and waited patiently for a while without hearing any reply. He knocked again, this time more loudly than before, but again waited without hearing any reply or seeing anyone. He knocked for the third time and kept knocking repeatedly but once more waited without hearing any reply or seeing anyone. Then he said to himself, "There is no doubt that there is no one inside, or perhaps the palace is deserted." Summoning his courage, he entered and shouted from the hallway, "O inhabitants of the palace, I am a stranger and a hungry traveler. Have you any food? Our Lord will requite you and reward you for it." He shouted a second and a third time but heard no reply. Feeling bold and determined, he advanced from the hallway into the center of the palace and looked around, but saw no one.

But morning overtook Shahrazad, and she lapsed into silence. Then Dinarzad said, "Sister, what an amazing and entertaining story!" Shahrazad replied, "What is this compared with what I shall tell you tomorrow night if I live, the Almighty God willing!"

THE TWENTY-FIRST NIGHT

The following night Dinarzad said to her sister Shahrazad, "For God's sake, sister, if you are not sleepy, tell us one of your lovely little tales to while away the night." Shahrazad replied, "With the greatest pleasure":

I heard, O King, that the king walked to the center of the palace and looked around, but saw no one. The palace was furnished with silk carpets and leather mats and hung with drapes. There were also settees, benches, and seats with cushions, as well as cupboards. In the middle there stood a spacious courtyard, surrounded by four adjoining recessed courts facing each other. In the center stood a fountain, on top of which crouched four lions in red gold, spouting water from their mouths in droplets that looked like gems and pearls, and about the fountain singing birds fluttered under a high net to prevent them from flying away. When the king saw all this, without seeing anyone, he was astonished and regretted that he found none to give him any information. He sat pensively by one of the recessed courts, when he heard sad moans and lamentations and the following plaintive verses:

> My soul is torn between peril and toil;
> O life, dispatch me with one mighty blow.
> Lover, neither a bankrupt nor a noble man
> Humbled by love's law do you pity show.
> Ev'n from the breeze I jealously used to guard you,
> But at the blow of fate the eyes blind go.
> When, as he pulls to shoot, the bowstring breaks
> What can the bowman facing his foes do?
> And when the foes begin to congregate
> How can he then escape his cruel fate?

When the king heard the lamentation and the verses, he rose and moved toward the source of the voice until he came to a doorway behind a curtain, and when he lifted the curtain, he saw at the upper end of the room a young man sitting on a chair that rose about twenty inches above the floor. He was a handsome young man, with a full figure, clear voice, radiant brow, bright face, downy beard, and ruddy cheeks, graced with a mole like a speck of amber, just as the poet describes it:

> Here is a slender youth whose hair and face
> All mortals envelope with light or gloom.
> Mark on his cheek the mark of charm and grace,
> A dark spot on a red anemone.

The king greeted the seated young man, pleased to see him. The young man wore a long-sleeved robe of Egyptian silk with gold embroidery, and on his head he wore an Egyptian conical head covering, but his face showed signs of grief and sorrow. When the king greeted him, the young man greeted him back courteously and said, "Pardon me, sir, for not rising, for you deserve even a greater honor." The king replied, "Young man, you are pardoned. I myself am your guest, having come to you on a serious mission. Pray tell me the story behind the lake and the colored fish, as well as this palace and the fact that you sit alone and mourn with no one to console you." When the young man heard this, his tears began to flow over his cheeks until they drenched his breast. Then he sang the following *Mawwaliya* verses:[2]

> Say to the man whom life with arrows shot,
> "How many men have felt the blows of fate!"
> If you did sleep, the eyes of God have not;
> Who can say time is fair and life in constant state?

Then he wept bitterly. The king was astonished and asked, "Young man, why do you cry?" The young man replied, "Sir, how can I refrain from crying in my present condition?" Then he lifted the skirt of his robe, and the king saw that while one half of the young man, from the navel to the head, was human flesh, the other half, from the navel to the feet, was black stone.

But morning overcame Shahrazad, and she lapsed into silence. Then King Shah-rayar thought to himself, "This is an amazing story. I am willing to postpone her execution even for a month, before having her put to death." While the king was thinking to himself, Dinarzad said to her sister Shahrazad, "Sister, what an enter-taining story!" Shahrazad replied, "What is this compared with what I shall tell you tomorrow night if I live, the Almighty God willing!"

THE TWENTY-SECOND NIGHT

The following night Shahrazad said:

I heard, O King, that when the king saw the young man in this condition, he felt very sad and sorry for him, and said with a sigh, "Young man, you have added one more worry to my worries. I came to look for an answer to the mystery of the fish, in order to save them, but ended up looking for an answer to your case, as well as the fish. There is no power and no strength save in God, the Almighty, the Magnificent. Hurry up, young man, and tell me your story." The young man replied, "Lend me your ears, your eyes, and your mind." The king replied, "My ears, my eyes, and my mind are ready." The young man said:

[*The Tale of the Enchanted King*]

My story, and the story of the fish, is a strange and amazing one, which, if it could be engraved with needles at the corner of the eye,[3] would be a lesson to

2. Poem in colloquial language, often sung to the accompaniment of a reed pipe.
3. I.e., if a master calligrapher could by a miracle of his art write the entire story at the cor-

ner of an eye, it would then be read as a double miracle: one for the extraordinary events, one for the extraordinary art.

those who would consider. My lord, my father was the king of this city, and his name was King Mahmud of the Black Islands. For these four hills were islands. He ruled for seventy years, and when he died, I succeeded him and married my cousin. She loved me very much, so much so that if I was away from her even for a single day, she would refuse to eat and drink until I returned to her. In this way, we lived together for five years until one day she went to the bath and I ordered the cook to grill meat and prepare a sumptuous supper for her. Then I entered this palace, lay down in this very spot where you are sitting now, and ordered two maids to sit down, one at my head and one at my feet, to fan me. But I felt uneasy and could not go to sleep. While I lay with my eyes closed, breathing heavily, I heard the girl at my head say to the one at my feet, "O Mas'uda, what a pity for our poor master with our damned mistress, and him so young!" The other one replied, "What can one say? May God damn all treacherous, adulterous women. Alas, it is not right that such a young man like our master lives with this bitch who spends every night out." Mas'uda added, "Is our master stupid? When he wakes up at night, doesn't he find that she is not by his side?" The other replied, "Alas, may God trip the bitch our mistress. Does she leave our master with his wits about him? No. She places a sleeping potion in the last drink he takes, offers him the cup, and when he drinks it, he sleeps like a dead man. Then she leaves him and stays out till dawn. When she returns, she burns incense under his nose, and when he inhales it, he wakes up. What a pity!"

My lord, when I heard the conversation between the two maids, I was extremely angry and I could hardly wait for the night to come. When my wife returned from the bath, we had the meal served but ate very little. Then we retired to my bed and I pretended to drink the contents of the cup, which I poured out, and went to sleep. No sooner had I fallen on my side than my wife said, "Go to sleep, and may you never rise again. By God, your sight disgusts me and your company bores me." Then she put on her clothes, perfumed herself with burning incense and, taking my sword, girded herself with it. Then she opened the door and walked out. My lord, I got up . . .

But morning overtook Shahrazad, and she lapsed into silence. Then Dinarzad said, "O my lady, what an amazing and entertaining story!" Shahrazad replied, "What is this compared with what I shall tell you tomorrow night!"

THE TWENTY-THIRD NIGHT

The following night Dinarzad said to her sister Shahrazad, "Please, sister, if you are not sleepy, tell us one of your lovely little tales." Shahrazad replied, "With the greatest pleasure":

It is related, O King, that the enchanted young man said to the king:

Then I followed her, as she left the palace and traversed my city until she stood at the city gate. There she uttered words I could not understand, and the locks fell off and the gate opened by itself. She went out, and I followed her until she slipped through the trash mounds and came to a hut built with palm leaves, leading to a domed structure built with sun-dried bricks. After she entered, I climbed to the top of the dome, and when I looked inside, I saw my wife standing before a decrepit black man sitting on reed shavings and dressed in tatters. She kissed the ground before him and he raised his head and said, "Damn you, why are you late? My black cousins were here. They played with the bat and ball, sang, and drank brewed liquor. They had a good time, each with his own girlfriend, except for myself, for I refused even to drink with them because you were absent."

My wife replied, "O my lord and lover, don't you know that I am married to my cousin, who finds me most loathsome and detests me more than anyone else? Were it not for your sake, I would not have let the sun rise before reducing his city to rubble, a dwelling place for the bears and the foxes, where the owl hoots and the crow crows, and would have hurled its stones beyond Mount Qaf."[4] He replied, "Damn you, you are lying. I swear in the name of black chivalry that as of tonight, if our cousins visit me and you fail to be present, I will never befriend you, lie down with you, or let my body touch yours. You cursed woman, you have been playing with me like a piece of marble, and I am subject to your whims, you cursed, rotten woman." My lord, when I heard their conversation, the world started to turn black before my eyes, and I lost my senses. Then I heard my wife crying and imploring, "O my lover and my heart's desire, if you remain angry at me, whom else have I got, and if you turn me out, who will take me in, O my lord, my lover, and light of my eye?" She kept crying and begging until he was appeased. Then, feeling happy, she took off her outer garments, and asked, "My lord, have you anything for your little girl to eat?" The black man replied, "Open the copper basin," and when she lifted the lid, she found some leftover fried rat bones. After she ate them, he said to her, "There is some brewed liquor left in that jug. You may drink it." She drank the liquor and washed her hands and lay beside the black man on the reed shavings. Then she undressed and slipped under his tatters. I climbed down from the top of the dome and, entering through the door, grabbed the sword that my wife had brought with her, and drew it, intending to kill both of them. I first struck the black man on the neck and thought that I had killed him.

But morning overtook Shahrazad, and she lapsed into silence. Then Dinarzad said, "Sister, what an entertaining story!" Shahrazad replied, "Tomorrow night I shall tell you something more entertaining if I live!"

THE TWENTY-FOURTH NIGHT

The following night Dinarzad said to her sister Shahrazad, "For God's sake, sister, if you are not sleepy, tell us one of your lovely little tales." Shahrazad replied, "With the greatest pleasure":

I heard, O King, that the enchanted young man said to the king:

My lord, I struck the black man on the neck, but failed to cut the two arteries. Instead I only cut into the skin and flesh of the throat and thought that I had killed him. He began to snort violently, and my wife pulled away from him. I

4. Legendary mountain cited for its remoteness.

retreated, put the sword back in its place, and went back to the city. I entered the palace and went to sleep in my bed till morning. When my wife arrived and I looked at her, I saw that she had cut her hair and put on a mourning dress. She said, "Husband, don't reproach me for what I am doing, for I have received news that my mother has died, that my father was killed in the holy war, and that my two brothers have also lost their lives, one in battle, the other bitten by a snake. I have every reason to weep and mourn." When I heard what she said, I did not reply, except to say, "I don't reproach you. Do as you wish."

She mourned for an entire year, weeping and wailing. When the year ended, she said to me, "I want you to let me build inside the palace a mausoleum for me to use as a special place of mourning and to call it the house of sorrows." I replied, "Go ahead." Then she gave the order, and a house of mourning was erected for her, with a domed mausoleum and a tomb inside. Then, my lord, she moved the wounded black man to the mausoleum and placed him in the tomb. But, although he was still alive, from the day I cut his throat, he never spoke a word or was able to do her any good, except to drink liquids. She visited him in the mausoleum every day, morning and evening, bringing with her beverages and broth, and she kept at it for an entire year, while I held my patience and left her to her own devices. One day, while she was unaware, I entered the mausoleum and found her crying and lamenting:

> When I see your distress,
> It pains me, as you see.
> And when I see you not,
> It pains me, as you see.
> O speak to me, my life,
> My master, talk to me.

Then she sang:

> The day I have you is the day I crave;
> The day you leave me is the day I die.
> Were I to live in fear of promised death,
> I'd rather be with you than my life save.

Then she recited the following verses:

> If I had every blessing in the world
> And all the kingdom of the Persian king,
> If I see not your person with my eyes,
> All this will not be worth an insect's wing.

When she stopped crying, I said to her, "Wife, you have mourned and wept enough and further tears are useless." She replied, "Husband, do not interfere with my mourning. If you interfere again, I will kill myself." I kept quiet and left her alone, while she mourned, wept, and lamented for another year. One day, after the third year, feeling the strain of this drawn-out, heavy burden, something happened to trigger my anger, and when I returned, I found my wife in the mausoleum, beside the tomb, saying, "My lord, I have not had any word from you. For three years I have had no reply." Then she recited the following verses:

> O tomb, O tomb, has he his beauties lost,
> Or have you lost yourself that radiant look?
> O tomb, neither a garden nor a star,
> The sun and moon at once how can you host?

These verses added anger to my anger, and I said to myself, "Oh, how much longer shall I endure?" Then I burst out with the following verses:

> O tomb, O tomb, has he his blackness lost,
> Or have you lost yourself that filthy look?
> O tomb, neither a toilet nor a heap of dirt,
> Charcoal and mud at once how can you host?

When my wife heard me, she sprang up and said, "Damn you, dirty dog. It was you who did this to me, wounded my beloved, and tormented me by depriving me of his youth, while he has been lying here for three years, neither alive nor dead." I said to her, "You, dirtiest of whores and filthiest of all venal women who ever desired and copulated with black slaves, yes it was I who did this to him." Then I grabbed my sword and drew it to strike her. But when she heard me and realized that I was determined to kill her, she laughed and said, "Get away, you dog. Alas, alas, what is done cannot be undone; nor will the dead come back to life, but God has delivered into my hand the one who did this to me and set my heart ablaze with the fire of revenge." Then she stood up, uttered words I could not understand, and cried, "With my magic and cunning, be half man, half stone." Sir, from that instant, I have been as you now see me, dejected and sad, helpless and sleepless, neither living with the living nor dead among the dead.

But morning overtook Shahrazad, and she lapsed into silence. Then Dinarzad said, "Sister, what an amazing and entertaining story!" Shahrazad replied, "Tomorrow night I shall tell you something more entertaining if the king spares me and lets me live!"

THE TWENTY-FIFTH NIGHT

The following night Dinarzad said to her sister Shahrazad, "Sister, if you are not sleepy, tell us one of your lovely little tales to while away the night." Shahrazad replied, "With the greatest pleasure":

It is related, O King, that the enchanted young man said to the king:

"After my wife turned me into this condition, she cast a spell on the city, with all its gardens, fields, and markets, the very place where your troops are camping now. My wife turned the inhabitants of my city, who belonged to four sects, Muslims, Magians,[5] Christians, and Jews, into fish, the Muslims white, the Magians red, the Christians blue, and the Jews yellow. Likewise, she turned the islands into four hills surrounding the lake. As if what she has done to me and the city is not enough, she strips me naked every day and gives me a hundred lashes with

---

5. Priests of Zoroastrianism, a dualistic religion (emphasizing the cosmic struggle between good and evil) that was dominant in Persia before Islam.

the whip until my back is lacerated and begins to bleed. Then she clothes my upper half with a hairshirt like a coarse rug and covers it with these luxurious garments." Then the young man burst into tears and recited the following verses:

> O Lord, I bear with patience your decree,
> And so that I may please you, I endure,
> That for their tyranny and unfair use
> Our recompense your Paradise may be.
> You never let the tyrant go, my Lord;   5
> Pluck me out of the fire, Almighty God.

The king said to the young man, "Young man, you have lifted one anxiety but added another worry to my worries. But where is your wife, and where is the mausoleum with the wounded black man?" The young man replied, "O King, the black slave is lying in the tomb inside the mausoleum, which is in the adjoining room. My wife comes to visit him at dawn every day, and when she comes, she strips me naked and gives me a hundred lashes with the whip, while I cry and scream without being able to stand up and defend myself, since I am half stone, half flesh and blood. After she punishes me, she goes to the black slave to give him beverages and broth to drink. Tomorrow at dawn she will come as usual." The king replied, "By God, young man, I shall do something for you that will go down in history and commemorate my name." Then the king sat to converse with the young man until night fell and they went to sleep.

The king got up before dawn, took off his clothes, and, drawing his sword, entered the room with the domed mausoleum and found it lit with candles and lamps and scented with incense, perfume, saffron, and ointments. He went straight to the black man and killed him. Then he carried him out and threw him in a well inside the palace. When he came back, he put on the clothes of the black man, covered himself, and lay hiding at the bottom of the tomb, with the drawn sword hidden under his clothes.

A while later, the cursed witch arrived, and the first thing she did was to strip her husband naked, take a whip, and whip him again and again, while he cried, "Ah wife, have pity on me; help me; I have had enough punishment and pain; have pity on me." She replied, "You should have had pity on me and spared my lover."

But morning overtook Shahrazad, and she lapsed into silence. Then Dinarzad said, "Sister, what an amazing and entertaining story!" Shahrazad replied, "What is this compared with what I shall tell you tomorrow night if I live!" King Shahrayar, with a mixture of amazement, pain, and sorrow for the enchanted youth, said to himself, "By God, I shall postpone her execution for tonight and many more nights, even for two months, until I hear the rest of the story and find out what happened to the enchanted young man. Then I shall have her put to death, as I did the others." So he said to himself.

THE TWENTY-SIXTH NIGHT

The following night Dinarzad said to Shahrazad, "Sister, if you are not sleepy, tell us one of your lovely little tales to while away the night." Shahrazad replied, "With the greatest pleasure":

I heard, O King, that after the witch punished her husband by whipping him until his sides and shoulders were bleeding and she satisfied her thirst for revenge, she dressed him with the coarse hairshirt and covered it with the outer garments. Then she headed to the black man, with the usual cup of drink and the broth. She entered the mausoleum, reached the tomb, and began to cry, wail, and lament, saying, "Lover, denying me yourself is not your custom. Do not be stingy, for my foes gloat over our separation. Be generous with your love, for forsaking is not your custom. Visit me, for my life is in your visit. O my lord, speak to me; O my lord, entertain me." Then she sang the following verses of the *Mufrad*[6] variety:

> For how long is this cruel disdain,
> Have I not paid with enough tears?
> O lover, talk to me,
> O lover, speak to me,
> O lover, answer me.

The king lowered his voice, stammered, and simulating the accent of black people, said, "Ah, ah, ah! There is no power and no strength save in God the Almighty, the Magnificent." When she heard him speak, she screamed with joy and fainted, and when she came to herself, she cried, "Is it true that you spoke to me?" The king replied, "Damn you, you don't deserve that anyone should speak to you or answer you." She asked, "What is the cause?" He replied, "All day long you punish your husband, while he screams for help. From sunset till dawn he cries, implores, and invokes God against you and me, with his deafening and enervating cries that deprive me of sleep. If it had not been for this, I would have recovered a long time ago, and this is why I have not spoken to you or answered you." She said, "My lord, if you allow me, I shall deliver him from his present condition." He replied, "Deliver him and rid us of his noise."

She went out of the mausoleum, took a bowl, and, filling it with water, uttered a spell over it, and the water began to boil and bubble as in a caldron over fire. Then she sprinkled the young man with the water and said, "By the power of my spell, if the Creator has created you in this form, or if he has turned you into this form out of anger at you, stay as you are, but if you have been transformed by my magic and cunning, turn back to your normal form, by the will of God, Creator of the world." The young man shook himself at once and stood up, erect and sound, and he rejoiced and thanked God for his deliverance. Then his wife said to him, "Get out of my sight and don't ever come back, for if you do and I see you here, I shall kill you." She yelled at him, and he went away.

Then she returned to the mausoleum and, descending to the tomb, called out, "My sweet lord, come out and let me see your handsome face." The king replied in a muffled voice, "You have rid me of the limb, but failed to rid us of the body." She asked, "My sweet lord, what do you mean by the body?" He replied, "Damn you, cursed woman, it is the inhabitants of this city and its four islands, for every night at midnight, the fish raise their heads from the lake to implore and invoke God against me, and this is why I do not recover. Go to

6. Literally "single," a verse form.

them and deliver them at once; then come back to hold my hand and help me rise, for I am beginning to feel better already." When she heard him, she rejoiced and replied joyfully, "Yes, my lord, yes, with God's help, my sweetheart." Then she rose, went to the lake, and took a little of its water.

But morning overtook Shahrazad, and she lapsed into silence. Then Dinarzad said, "What an amazing and entertaining story!" Shahrazad replied, "What is this compared with what I shall tell you tomorrow night if the king spares me and I live!"

THE TWENTY-SEVENTH NIGHT

The following night Dinarzad said to her sister Shahrazad, "If you are not sleepy, tell us one of your lovely little tales to while away the night." Shahrazad replied, "With the greatest pleasure":

It is related, O King, that the wife uttered some words over the lake, and the fish began to dance, and at that instant the spell was lifted, and the townspeople resumed their usual activities and returned to their buying and selling. Then she went back to the palace, entered the mausoleum, and said, "My lord, give me your gracious hand and rise." The king replied in a muffled voice, "Come closer to me." She moved closer, while he urged her "Come closer still," and she moved until her body touched his. Then he pushed her back and with one stroke of the sword sliced her in half, and she fell in two to the ground.

Then the king went out and, finding the enchanted young man waiting for him, congratulated him on his deliverance, and the young man kissed his hand, thanked him, and invoked God's blessing on him. Then the king asked him, "Do you wish to stay here or come with me to my city?" The young man replied, "King of the age, and Lord of the world, do you know the distance between your city and mine?" The king replied, "It is a half-day journey." The young man said, "O King, you are dreaming, for between your city and mine it is a full year's journey. You reached us in half a day because the city was enchanted." The king asked, "Still, do you wish to stay here in your city or come with me?" The young man replied, "O King, I shall not part from you, even for one moment." The king was happy and said, "Thank God who has given you to me. You shall be a son to me, for I have never had one." They embraced, holding each other closely, and felt happy. Then they walked together back to the palace, and when they entered the palace, the enchanted young king announced to the eminent men of his kingdom and to his retinue that he was going on a journey.

He spent ten days in preparation, packing what he needed, together with the gifts that the princes and merchants of the city had given him for his journey. Then he set out with the king, with his heart on fire to be leaving his city for a whole year. He left, with fifty Mamluks and many guides and servants, bearing one hundred loads of gifts, rarities, and treasures, as well as money. They journeyed on, evening and morning, night and day, for a whole year until God granted them safe passage and they reached their destination. Then the king sent someone to inform the vizier of his safe return, and the vizier came out with all the troops and most of the townspeople to meet him. Having given him up for lost, they were exceedingly happy, and the city was decorated and its streets were spread with silk carpets. The vizier and the soldiers dismounted and, kissing the ground before the king, congratulated him on his safety and invoked God's blessing on him.

Then they entered the city, and the king sat on his throne and, meeting with the vizier, explained to him why he had been absent for an entire year. He told him the story of the young man and how he, the king, had dealt with the young man's wife and saved him and the city, and the vizier turned to the young man and congratulated him on his deliverance. Then the princes, viziers, chamberlains, and deputies took their places, and the king bestowed on them robes of honor, gifts, and other favors. Then he sent for the fisherman, who was the cause of saving the young man and the city, and when the fisherman stood before the king, the king bestowed on him robes of honor, and then asked him, "Do you have any children?" The fisherman replied that he had one boy and two girls. The king had them brought before him, and he himself married one of the girls, while he married the other to the enchanted young man. Moreover, the king took the fisherman's son into his service and made him one of his attendants. Then he conferred authority on the vizier, appointing him king of the city of the Black Islands, supplied him with provisions and fodder for the journey, and ordered the fifty Mamluks, who had come with them, as well as a host of other people, to go with him. He also sent with him many robes of honor and many fine gifts for all the princes and prominent men there. The vizier took his leave, kissed the king's hand, and departed. The king, the enchanted young man, and the fisherman lived peacefully thereafter, and the fisherman became one of the richest men of his time, with daughters married to kings.

But morning overtook Shahrazad, and she lapsed into silence. Then Dinarzad said, "What an amazing and entertaining story!" Shahrazad replied, "What is this compared with what I shall tell you tomorrow night if the king spares me and lets me live!"

GIOVANNI BOCCACCIO
1313–1375

In 1362, Boccaccio had a midlife crisis: told by a monk that his death was approaching and that he must renounce his frivolous devotion to poetry, he decided to sell or throw away all his books. His intimate friend, **Petrarch**, urged him to reconsider; but if Boccaccio insisted on getting rid of his books, Petrarch added eagerly, "I am indeed grateful that you have offered them to me." Just two years later, Boccaccio again fell into a dark mood, this time almost led by his admiration of Petrarch's Latin masterworks to burn all of his own writings composed in the "low" language of Italian in order to clear the ground for the revival of a pure, classical Latin. Thankfully,

Boccaccio did not give in to his urge, for today's readers have all but forgotten the learned encyclopedic compendia that he was certain would endure the test of time. Instead, modern audiences respond with a delighted sense of familiarity to the "medieval" Boccaccio of the *Decameron*, whose unruly and uncouth tales much more accurately represent the chaos of everyday life than would be allowed by the strictures of Renaissance art and religion. In this work overflowing with multiple narratives of priests and sailors, merchants and princesses, Boccaccio disregarded all conceivable rules of decorum in order to celebrate the variety and fecundity of Mediterranean culture.

LIFE AND TIMES

Boccaccio was born in 1313, the illegitimate son of a merchant associated with the powerful Bardi banking family. Boccaccio's father arranged for his son's education, which included the study of accounting, doubtless hoping that the boy would enter his own line of work. When the young Boccaccio became restless during his apprenticeship in the countinghouses of the Bardi family, his father obligingly arranged for him to study law instead, but all Boccaccio wanted to do was to become a poet. He found a temporary outlet for his literary ambitions in the household of Robert of Anjou, a stimulating environment rich in art and culture. In his letters, Boccaccio describes these as the happiest days of his life, and it was with regret that he left Naples in 1340 to seek more permanent employment in Florence, where he spent most of the rest of his life.

At this time, an extraordinary movement was just beginning in mid-fourteenth-century Italy that would spread across both northern and southern Europe. Humanism would affect language, literature, philosophy, and theology, but in its foundational moment, it centered on the role of language: in response to the late medieval flowering of vernacular literature found in the French of the *Song of Roland*, in the Provençal of troubadour lyric, and, above all, in the "illustrious vernacular" of Dante's *Divine Comedy*, a new generation of writers became determined to restore Latin to its ancient glory and to create a neoclassical literature that would follow in the footsteps of **Virgil, Ovid,** and—most particularly—the orator Cicero. The self-proclaimed leader of this movement was Petrarch, who, only a few years older than Boccaccio, was nonetheless recognized by the younger poet as his mentor and superior. Under Petrarch's guidance, Boccaccio turned away from his early narrative poems in the Italian language, such as the *Teseida* (the source of **Chaucer**'s Knight's Tale), *Diana's Hunt* (*Caccia di Diana*), and *Amorous Vision* (*Amorosa visione*), which nevertheless inspired a wide range of Renaissance poetry in France and England as well as in Italy. His embrace of Latin entailed not only a change of language but also a change of literary form, leading Boccaccio to produce learned Latin encyclopedias, such as an account of the rise and fall of famous men on the wheel of Fortune (*De casibus virorum illustrium*) and a genealogy of the Greek and Roman gods (*De genealogia deorum gentilium*). Boccaccio enthusiastically signed on to Petrarch's project, both by producing his own Latin literary works and by participating in the humanist effort to revive ancient Greek poetry—most directly in his effort to produce a Latin translation of Homer's *Iliad* and *Odyssey*. Finding his own command of Greek too limited for such an important undertaking, Boccaccio had to content himself with hiring a native Greek speaker to carry out the work.

At exactly this moment of linguistic and cultural transition, an event took place that transformed the landscape of medieval Europe: from 1348 to 1351, the Black Death swept through the region, killing a third of the population. Mortality rates were particularly high in cities; indeed, in some locations half or even three-quarters of the population died. This event is the setting of Boccaccio's *Decameron*, which opens with a harrowing account of the effects of plague—not just the direct effects of the disease on individuals' bodies but its indirect effects on the body politic of Florence, torn apart and almost destroyed by the ravages of illness so horrific that, in Boccaccio's words, "brother abandoned brother" and, "almost unbelievable, fathers and mothers neglected to tend and care for their children, as if they were not their own." The two main forces of social order in the time of plague were the city governments, which sought to control the spread of disease and limit its impact on public health, and the church, which tried to reassure vulnerable citizens that at least their immortal souls would come through the pestilence unscathed. The role of the church as a source of social order and civic harmony is parodied in the *Decameron*'s playful account of rogues who deceive their confessors, nuns who allow the convent gardener to "cultivate their gardens," and priests who care more for their earnings than for the welfare of their flock. But despite its sometimes satirical tone, the *Decameron* does not depict a world in which the authority of the church is rejected: on the contrary, the church is seen as a regulating force in society like any other, and therefore similarly vulnerable to corruption and abuse.

WORK

Written before Boccaccio's first meeting with Petrarch in 1350 but after plague first struck Florence in 1348, the *Decam-eron* marks a pivotal point both in literary history and in Boccaccio's own life. Because its vernacular prose captures the rhythms of everyday speech and renders the voice of the carpenter or merchant as vividly as that of the priest or great lord, the *Decameron* brings to life the bustling life of medieval Florence, a city where trade and banking flourished. Not only the hubbub of the city but also the broader panorama of Mediterranean interconnections emerge in the tales that recount travel to North Africa, to Muslim-held regions of Spain, to Sicily, to Greece. In some tales, such as that of the Muslim princess Alatiel, action takes place aboard ship, representing powerfully the dynamic cultural and economic exchanges occurring in the Mediterranean.

The cross-cultural interactions prominently depicted in the tales also inform the genre of the *Decameron*, which follows the frame-tale model of Indo-Persian works such as the **Pañcatantra** and *The Thousand and One Nights*. Its framing story of seven young women and three young men who have fled Florence in the time of the Black Death contains within it a series of short tales written in a wide range of genres, styles, and moods. The young people deliver their tales in a light and playful tone that belies the desperation engendered by their flight from the plague-ridden city, much as the storyteller Shahrazad, in *The Thousand and One Nights*, tells of marvels and wonders even as the threat of execution hangs over her head. Although written models for the frame-tale structure did make their way from Asia to Europe, influencing such works as **Petrus Alfonsi**'s *Disciplina Clericalis*, oral sources are more likely to have been the principal inspiration behind Boccaccio's collection. These include not only the stories of traders and sailors that circulated throughout the Mediterranean region but also the folktales that had long been part of

European tradition, as evidenced in such collections as the scatological and highly sexualized comic fabliaux surviving in French manuscripts.

The community of ten young men and women who recount the stories of the *Decameron* flee the city in the time of plague out of a concern for more than their own personal health. The stories that they tell are a kind of medicine concocted to heal both the individual spirit and the collective social fabric, focused on everyday themes such as how happiness follows misfortune, how women deceive their husbands, the power of the witty retort, and the value of generosity. The urgency and panic caused by pestilence is reflected but contained in the frame narrative, which begins with the group selecting as their leader Pampinea, the eldest of the young women, so that the community will be united under a single will. The leadership then rotates among them over a ten-day period, allowing each of the men and women to serve as "king" or "queen" of the day. Dioneo, the young man who tells the most unsavory and sexualized of the tales, claims for himself the privilege of telling the last tale of each day. Thus, through a series of comic inversions, the usual order of things is turned upside down: instead of a single male ruler, the group is governed first by a woman and then by a rotation of leaders, and a special status is awarded to the man who poses the loudest challenge to proper norms of behavior. Yet this chaotic quality does not escape the orderly structure: when the ten days come to an end, the community chooses to return to Florence, restored by the medicine of laughter and fellowship and determined to do all they can to rebuild a society in peril.

The *Decameron* includes many tales of the European fabliau type, but others have origins that are more broadly Mediterranean. The Mediterranean scope of the *Decameron* appears, for example, in the story of Alatiel, a Muslim princess who has a string of erotic adventures on her way to marry the Sultan of Algarve—that is, the ruler of *al-Gharb*, which literally means "the West." The distinctions between East and West that are almost second nature to modern readers are foreign to the world of the *Decameron*, where the West can be home to Islam just as easily as the East can be the natural turf of Italian merchants, as comfortable in the cities of Asia as they are in the cities of their native land. This interpenetration of worlds also appears in the two stories devoted to the Sultan Saladin, who displays an impartial wisdom in the story of the Three Rings, in which the comparative merits of Judaism, Christianity, and Islam are assessed, and in the story of Messer Torello, in which Saladin visits Italy disguised as a merchant and reveals himself to be an exotic paragon of munificence.

The informality of the prose in many of the tales is countered by what might be called the "high style" of the frame narrative, as well as by the care with which the work is structured. For example, the "Valley of Ladies" is a luscious verdant landscape that marks the transition between the Sixth and Seventh Days of the *Decameron*, but its concentric circles also provide a resonant symbolic echo of Dante's underworld, suggesting that the delightful feminine "valley" might prove to be less an erotic paradise than a torturous hell. Similarly, the numerical skeleton of the *Decameron*—ten tales told on each of the ten days of the expedition— reinforces an underlying sense of order and symmetry that flies in the face of the spontaneity and dynamism of the tales' content and tone. Chaos, in the *Decameron*, is consistently subordinated to order, reaffirming the ability of humanity to surmount any disruption, even the upheaval wrought by pestilence. By insisting that the triumph of order can be achieved through human effort, the *Decameron* contradicts its most important predecessor and model: Dante's *Divine Comedy*, in which God is repeatedly identified as the only source of form and harmony in the universe. The hundred cantos of the *Divine Comedy* represent the perfect order of divine creation; the hundred tales of the *Decameron*, in contrast, represent the fertile creativity of the human mind.

In a letter to his friend Boccaccio, Petrarch gently criticizes the low vernacular of the *Decameron* but praises the quality of the collection's last tale, the story of patient Griselda. In order that the story might survive the passage of time, Petrarch writes, "I attacked this story of yours," rendering it into immortal Latin. Ironically, Petrarch's effort to preserve Boccaccio's story by translating it into Latin reveals more about the limited shelf life of Latin humanism than it does about the defects of the vernacular: it is Boccaccio's own version, along with Chaucer's translation of the Griselda story into English in his *Clerk's Tale*, that continues to enchant readers today.

From Decameron[1]

Day 1, Story 1

Ser Cepparello deceives a holy friar with a false confession and dies, and although he was one of the worst of men during his life, he is reputed after his death to be a saint and is called Saint Ciappelletto.

Dearest ladies, it is fitting that everything man does should take as its origin the wonderful and holy name of Him who was the maker of all things. Thus, since I am the first and must begin our storytelling, I intend to begin with one of His marvelous works so that, once you have heard it, our hope in Him, as in that which is immutable, will be strengthened, and we will forever praise His name. Now, it is clear that the things of this world are all transitory and fading, so that both in themselves and in what they give rise to, they are filled with suffering, anguish, and toil, as well as being subject to countless dangers. We, who live in the midst of these things and are a part of them, would certainly not be able to resist and defend ourselves against them, if the special grace of God did not lend us strength and discernment. It is wrong to believe that this grace descends to us and enters us because of any merit of our own. Rather, it is sent by His loving kindness and is obtained through the prayers of those who, though mortal like us, truly followed His will while they were alive and now enjoy eternal bliss with Him. To them, as to advocates informed by experience of our frailty, we offer up prayers about our concerns, perhaps because we do not dare to present them personally before the sight of so great a judge. And yet in Him, who is generous and filled with pity for us, we perceive something more. Although human sight is not sharp enough to penetrate the secrets of the divine mind in any way, it sometimes happens that we are deceived by popular opinion into making some-

1. Translated from the Italian by Wayne Rebhorn.

one our advocate before Him in all His majesty whom He has cast into eternal exile. And yet He, from whom nothing is hidden, pays more attention to the purity of the supplicant than to his ignorance or to the damned state of his intercessor, listening to those who pray as if their advocate were actually blessed in His sight. All of this will appear clearly in the tale I intend to tell—clearly, I say, not in keeping with the judgment of God, but with that of men.

The story is told that Musciatto Franzesi,[2] an extremely rich and celebrated merchant in France, who had been made a knight, was once supposed to move to Tuscany with Lord Charles Lackland, the King of France's brother, whom Pope Boniface[3] had sent for and was encouraging to come. Musciatto recognized that his affairs, as those of merchants often are, were tangled up here and there and could not be put right quickly and easily, but he thought of a number of different people to whom he could entrust them and thus found a way to take care of everything. There was, however, one exception. He was unsure whom he could leave behind to recover the loans he had made to a number of people in Burgundy.[4] The reason for his uncertainty was that he had heard the Burgundians were a quarrelsome lot, evil by nature and untrustworthy, and he could think of no one he could rely on who would be sufficiently wicked that his wickedness would match theirs. After he had given the matter a great deal of thought, there came to mind a certain Ser Cepparello da Prato, who was often a guest in his house in Paris. Because the man was small of stature and dressed like a dandy, the French, not knowing what "Cepparello" signified and thinking it meant "hat," that is, "garland," in their language, called him, because he was small as we have said, not Ciappello, but Ciappelletto. And so, he was called Ciappelletto everywhere, while only a select few knew he was really Ser Cepparello.[5]

Let me tell you about the kind of life this Ciappelletto led. A notary, he would feel the greatest shame if even one of the very few legal documents he drew up was found to be other than false. He had composed as many of these phony ones as people requested, and he did so for free more willingly than someone else would have done for a sizeable payment. Furthermore, he supplied false testimony with the greatest delight, whether it was asked for or not, and since people in France in those days placed the greatest trust in oaths, and since he did not care if his were false, he won a great many law cases through his wickedness whenever he was asked to swear upon his oath to tell the truth. Because it gave him real pleasure, he went to great lengths to stir up bad feelings, hatred, and scandals among friends and relatives and everyone else, and the greater the evils he saw arise as a result, the greater his happiness. Invited

2. Musciatto di Messer Guido Franzesi (d. 1310), a merchant from Tuscany who became rich while serving as counselor to King Philip of France; he advised the king to falsify his coinage and to confiscate funds from the Italian merchants living in France. Many of The Decameron's tales refer to historical persons.

3. Boniface VIII (ca. 1235 or 1240–1303; pope, 1294–1303). "Tuscany": the region in northern Italy surrounding Florence.

4. Large, wealthy region in central France.

5. Cepparello da Prato's name appears in documents of the period as a tax collector for King Philip. The "Ser" before his name (short for "Messer") is an honorific (like "Sir"), and his first name is the diminutive (-ello) of Ciapo, short for Jacopo (James), although Boccaccio plays with the fact that ceppo meant "log" or "stump." "Cepparello" could thus be translated "Little Log." The French-speaking Burgundians transform his name into "Ciappelletto," a double diminutive, which in their language would be the rather precious nickname "Little Garland of Flowers."

to be an accomplice in a murder or some other criminal act, he would never refuse to go. Indeed, he would do so with a ready will and often found himself happily wounding or killing men with his own hands. He was the greatest blasphemer of God and the saints, and since he would do so at the slightest provocation, he came off as the most irascible man alive. He never went to church and used abominable words to mock all its sacraments as being beneath contempt. On the other hand, he happily spent time in taverns and frequented other places of ill repute. Of women, he was as fond as dogs are of being beaten with a stick, and he took more delight in their opposite than any degenerate ever did. He would rob and steal with a conscience like that of a holy man giving alms. He was a total glutton and a great drinker, so much so that sometimes it would make him disgustingly ill. Plus, he was a devout cardsharp and gambled with loaded dice. But why do I lavish so many words on him? He was perhaps the worst man who had ever been born. For a long time his wickedness had preserved the wealth and rank of Messer Musciatto who often protected him from both private persons, who were frequently the victims of his abuse, and from the courts, which always were.

Thus, when this Ser Cepparello crossed the mind of Messer Musciatto, who was well acquainted with his life, he thought to himself that this would be just the man he needed to deal with the wickedness of the Burgundians. He therefore had Ciappelletto sent for and spoke to him as follows:

"Ser Ciappelletto, as you know, I am about to leave here for good, and since, among others, I have to deal with the Burgundians, who are full of tricks, I know of no one more qualified than you to recover my money from them. Since you're not doing anything at present, if you take care of this business for me, I intend to obtain the favor of the court for you here and to award you a fair portion of what you recover."

Ser Ciappelletto, who was indeed unemployed and in short supply of worldly goods, saw the man who had long been his refuge and defense about to depart, and so, without a moment's hesitation, constrained, as it were, by necessity, he made up his mind and said he would be more than willing to do what Musciatto wanted. The two of them then worked out the details of their agreement, and Ser Ciappelletto received Musciatto's power of attorney as well as letters of introduction from the king. Soon after Messer Musciatto's departure, Ciappelletto went off to Burgundy, where almost no one knew him. There, in a kind and gentle manner quite beyond his nature, as though he were holding back his wrath till the end, he began recovering Musciatto's money and taking care of what he had been sent to do.

Before long, while he was lodging in the house of two Florentine brothers who lent money at interest and who treated him with great respect out of love for Messer Musciatto, he happened to fall ill. The two brothers immediately sent for doctors and servants to take care of him and to provide him with everything he might need to recover his health. All their help was in vain, however, for, in the opinion of the doctors, the good man, who was already old and had lived a disorderly life, was going from bad to worse every day, as people did who had a fatal illness. The two brothers were very upset about this, and one day, right next to the bedroom in which Ser Ciappelletto lay sick, they began talking together.

"What are we going to do about this guy?" said the one of them to the other. "We've got a terrible mess on our hands on account of him, because if we kick him out of our house, as sick as he is, people would condemn us for doing it. Plus, they'd really think we're stupid since we did not just take him in at first, but also went to great lengths to find servants and doctors for him, and now, although he couldn't have done anything to offend us, they see him suddenly kicked out of our house when he's deathly ill. On the other hand, he's been such a bad man that he won't want to make his confession or receive any of the sacraments of the Church, and if he dies without confession, no church will want to receive his body, and they'll wind up tossing him into some garbage pit like a dog. But if he goes ahead and makes his confession, the same thing will happen. Since his sins are so many and so horrible, no friar or priest will be willing or able to absolve him, and so, without absolution, he'll be tossed into a garbage pit just the same. And when that happens, the people of this town—both because of our profession, which they think is truly wicked and which they badmouth all day long, and because of their desire to rob us—well, they'll rise up and riot when they see it. And as they come running to our house, they'll be screaming, 'These Lombard dogs[6] that the Church refuses to accept, we won't put up with them any longer!' And maybe they won't just steal our stuff, but on top of that, they'll take our lives. So, no matter how things work out, it'll be bad for us if this guy dies."

Ser Ciappelletto, who, as we said, was lying close to where they were talking, and whose hearing was sharp, as it often is in those who are sick, caught every word they were saying about him and reacted by sending for them to come to him.

"I don't want you to fear anything on my account," he told them, "or be afraid you'll be harmed because of me. I heard what you were saying about me, and I'm very sure that the outcome will be exactly what you've predicted if things happen the way you've been imagining them. However, it's all going to turn out differently. I've done the Lord God so many injuries during my life-time that doing Him one more at the hour of my death won't make a difference to Him one way or the other. So go and arrange for the holiest and worthiest friar you can find to come to me—if such a one exists—and leave everything to me, for I'm sure I can set both your affairs and my own in order so that all will be well and you'll be satisfied with the result."

Although the two brothers didn't derive much hope from this, they neverthe-less went off to a monastery and asked for a wise and holy man to hear the confession of a Lombard who was sick in their house. They were assigned an elderly friar, a grand master of the Scriptures, who had lived a good and holy life and was a very venerable figure towards whom all the townspeople felt an immense special devotion, and they took this man back home with them.

When the friar reached the bedroom where Ser Ciappelletto was lying, he seated himself beside the sick man, and after speaking some words of comfort, asked him how much time had passed since he had made his last confession. Ser Ciappelletto, who had never been to confession, replied to him:

"Father, it used to be my custom to go to confession at least once a week, without counting the many weeks in which I went more often. Since I've been

6. I.e., Italian bankers (Lombardy is a region in northern Italy).

sick for about a week now, the truth is that the suffering I've endured from my illness has been so great that it has prevented me from going to confession."

"My son," said the friar, "you've done well, and you should continue that practice in the future. Considering how often you've made your confession, I don't think it will be a lot of trouble for me to hear it and to examine you."

"Master friar," said Ser Ciappelletto, "don't speak like that. Although I've gone to confession many, many times, I've always had a longing to make a general confession of all the sins I could remember, starting from the day of my birth and coming right down to the present. Therefore, my good father, I beg you to examine me point by point about everything just as if I'd never been to confession. And don't be concerned about me because I'm sick, for I would much rather mortify this flesh of mine than indulge it by doing something that might lead to the perdition of my soul, which my Savior redeemed with His precious blood."

These words pleased the holy man immensely and seemed to him to argue a well-disposed mind. Consequently, after commending Ser Ciappelletto warmly for making frequent confessions, he began by asking him if he had ever committed the sin of lust with a woman.

"Father," Ser Ciappelletto replied with a sigh, "I'm ashamed to tell you the truth on this subject for fear I might be committing the sin of pride."

"Don't be afraid to speak," said the holy friar. "Telling the truth was never a sin either in confession or anywhere else."

"Since you give me such reassurance," said Ser Ciappelletto, "I'll go ahead and tell you: I'm as much a virgin today as when I came forth from my mama's body."

"Oh, God's blessings on you!" said the friar. "What a good man you've been! In fact, by acting as you have, you are all the more meritorious, because, if you had wanted to, you had more freedom to do the opposite than we and others like us do, since we are bound by the vows of religion."

Next, he asked Ciappelletto if he had displeased God through the sin of gluttony. Breathing a heavy sigh, Ser Ciappelletto replied that he had done so many times. For although it was his habit to fast on bread and water at least three days a week, in addition to doing so during the periods of fasting that devout people observed on holy days throughout the year, he had nevertheless drunk that water with as much delight and gusto as any great wine-drinker ever drank his wine, and especially if he was exhausted from performing acts of devotion or making a pilgrimage. Moreover, he was often filled with a longing to have those little salads of baby field greens that women fix when they go to the country, and sometimes, as he ate them, doing so seemed better to him than it should have seemed to someone, like himself, who fasted out of piety, which was the precise reason why he was fasting.

"My son," replied the friar, "these sins are natural and quite trivial, so I don't want you to burden your conscience with them any more than necessary. No matter how truly holy a man may be, eating after a long fast and drinking after hard work will always seem good to him."

"Oh, father," said Ser Ciappelletto, "don't say that just to console me. Surely you must realize that I know how every act we perform in the service of God has to be done wholeheartedly and with an unspotted soul, and how anybody who does otherwise is committing a sin."

Feeling quite content, the friar said: "I am overjoyed that you think like this. It pleases me greatly that on this topic your conscience is pure and good. But tell me: have you committed the sin of avarice by desiring more than what was proper or by keeping what you should not have kept?"

"Father," said Ser Ciappelletto, "I don't want you to suspect me of this because I'm living in the house of these usurers. I'm not here to do business. On the contrary, I've come with the intention of admonishing and chastising them and of leading them away from their abominable moneymaking. What is more, I think I would have succeeded if God had not visited this tribulation upon me. Now, you should know that although my father left me a rich man, I gave away the greater part of what he had to charity after his death. Then, however, in order to sustain my life and to be able to aid Christ's poor, I have done a little bit of trading, and in doing so, I did indeed desire to make money. But I've always divided what I earned down the middle with God's poor, devoting my half to my needs, and giving the other half to them, and my Creator has aided me so well in this that my business has continually gotten better and better."

"Well done," said the friar. "But say, how often have you gotten angry?"

"Oh," said Ser Ciappelletto, "that's something, just let me tell you, that's happened to me a lot. For who could restrain himself, seeing the disgusting things men do all day long, neither observing God's commandments, nor fearing His chastisement? There've been many days when I would have preferred to die rather than live to listen to young people swearing and forswearing themselves, and to watch them pursuing vanities, frequenting taverns rather than going to church, and following the ways of the world rather than those of God."

"My son," said the friar, "this is righteous anger, and for my part, I cannot impose any penance on account of it. But was there ever a case in which your anger led you to commit murder or to hurl abuse at anyone or to do them any other sort of injury?"

Ser Ciappelletto answered him: "Alas, sir, how can you, who appear to be a man of God, speak such words? If I'd had even the teeniest little thought about doing any one of the things you've mentioned, do you think I'd believe that God would have shown me so much favor? Those are things that thugs and criminals would do, and whenever I've come upon a person of that sort, I've always said, 'Be gone! And may God convert you!'"

"God bless you, my son!" said the friar. "Now tell me: have you ever borne false witness against anyone or spoken ill of others or taken things from them without their permission?"

"Yes, sir," replied Ser Ciappelletto, "I really have spoken ill of others. Because once I had a neighbor who, without the least justification, was forever beating his wife, and so one time, I criticized him to his wife's relatives because of the great pity I felt for the wretched creature. Whenever he'd had too much to drink, God alone could tell you how he used to smack her around."

"Well, then," said the friar, "you tell me you've been a merchant. Have you ever deceived anyone, as merchants do?"

"Yes, sir, by gosh," replied Ser Ciappelletto, "but I don't know who he was, except that he was a man who brought me money he owed me for some cloth I'd sold him, and I put it in a box without counting it. Then, a good month later, I discovered that there were four more pennies in it than there should have been. Well, I kept them for an entire year with the intention of returning them to him, but when I never saw him again, I gave them away to charity."

"That was a trifle," said the friar, "and you did well to have acted as you did."

On top of this, the holy friar went on to ask him about many other things and got the same kind of reply in each case. But then, just as he was about to proceed to absolution, Ser Ciappelletto said: "I still have a sin or two more, sir, that I haven't told you about."

The friar asked him what they were, and Ciappelletto replied: "I remember how one Saturday I didn't show proper reverence for the Holy Sabbath because after nones[7] I had my servant sweep the house."

"Oh, my son," said the friar, "that's a trifle."

"No," said Ser Ciappelletto, "don't call it a trifle, for the Sabbath cannot be honored too much, seeing that it was on just such a day our Savior came back to life from the dead."

Then the friar asked: "Have you done anything else?"

"Yes, sir," replied Ser Ciappelletto. "Once, not thinking about what I was doing, I spat in the house of God."

The friar smiled and said: "My son, that's nothing to worry about. We, who are in holy orders, spit there all day long."

"And what you're doing is vile," said Ser Ciappelletto, "for nothing should be kept as clean as the Holy Temple in which we offer sacrifice to God."

In brief, he told the holy friar many things of this sort, until he finally began sighing and then burst into tears—for he was someone who knew only too well how to do this when he wanted to.

"My son," said the holy friar, "what's wrong?"

"Alas, sir," Ser Ciappelletto replied, "there's still one sin of mine remaining that I've never confessed because I feel so much shame in speaking about it. As you can see, every time I remember it, it makes me weep, and I think there can be no doubt that God will never have mercy on me because of it."

"Come on now, son," said the holy friar, "what are you talking about? If all the sins that have ever been committed by all of humanity, or that will be committed by them as long as the world lasts, were united in one single man, and yet he were as penitent and contrite as I see you are, then truly the benignity and mercy of God are so great that if that man were to confess them, he would be forgiven willingly. Therefore, don't be afraid to speak."

Ser Ciappelletto continued to weep violently as he replied: "Alas, father, my sin is so great that I can hardly believe God will ever pardon it unless you use your prayers on my behalf."

"Speak freely," said the friar, "for I promise I'll pray to God for you."

Ser Ciappelletto just kept on crying and refusing to talk about it, and the friar went on encouraging him to speak. Then, after Ser Ciappelletto had kept the friar in suspense with his weeping for a very long time, he heaved a great sigh and said: "Father, since you've promised to pray to God for me, I will tell

---

7. One of the canonical hours, at which prescribed prayers were offered daily and which thus served to divide the day: nones was the service at about 3 p.m.

you about it. You should know that when I was a little boy, I once cursed my mama." And having said this, he started weeping violently all over again.

"Oh, my son," said the friar, "does this seem such a great sin to you? Why, men curse God all day long, and yet He freely pardons anyone who repents of having cursed Him. And you don't think that He will pardon you for this? Don't weep and don't worry, for surely, even if you had been one of those who placed Him on the cross, He would pardon you because of the contrition I see in you."

"Alas, father," replied Ser Ciappelletto, "what are you saying? My sweet mama, who carried me in her body, day and night, for nine months, and who held me in her arms more than a hundred times—I was too wicked when I cursed her! My sin is too great! And if you don't pray to God for me, it will not be forgiven."

When the friar saw that there was nothing left to say to Ser Ciappelletto, he absolved him and gave him his blessing, taking him to be a very holy man, for he fully believed that what Ser Ciappelletto had said was true—and who would not have believed it, seeing a man at the point of death speak like that?

Then, after all this, the friar said to him: "Ser Ciappelletto, with the help of God you'll soon be well, but if it should happen that God calls that blessed, well-disposed soul of yours to Him, would you like to have your body buried at our monastery?"

"Yes, sir," replied Ser Ciappelletto. "In fact, I wouldn't want to be anywhere else, since you've promised to pray to God for me, not to mention the fact that I have always been especially devoted to your Order. Therefore, when you return to your monastery, I beg you to have them send me that most true body of Christ which you consecrate upon the altar every morning,[8] for, although I'm unworthy of it, I would like, with your permission, to partake of it, and afterward, to receive Holy Extreme Unction[9] so that if I have lived a sinner, at least I may die a Christian."

The holy man said he was greatly pleased that Ser Ciappelletto had spoken so well, and told him that he would arrange for the Host to be brought to him right away. And so it was.

The two brothers, who were afraid that Ser Ciappelletto was going to deceive them, had placed themselves near a partition that divided the room where he was lying from the one they were in, and as they eavesdropped, they were able to understand everything he said to the friar. Upon hearing him confess the things he had done, they sometimes had such a desire to laugh that they almost burst, and from time to time they would say to one another: "What kind of man is this, whom neither old age, nor sickness, nor the fear of death, which is imminent, nor the fear of God, before whose judgment he must stand in just a short while, could induce him to give up his wickedness and want to die any differently than he lived?" But, seeing as how he had spoken in such a way that he would be received for burial in a church, everything else was of no consequence to them.

8. I.e., the consecrated bread that Catholics consume in the Eucharist, as the body of Christ.

9. The Catholic sacrament administered to the sick who are in danger of dying.

A little later Ser Ciappelletto took communion, and as his condition was rapidly deteriorating, he received Extreme Unction and then died just a little after vespers[1] of the day on which he had made his good confession. Using Ser Ciappelletto's own money, the two brothers took care of all the arrangements necessary for him to be given an honorable burial, and sent word to the friars' house that they should come in the evening to perform the customary wake and take away the body in the morning.

The holy friar who had confessed Ser Ciappelletto, having heard that he had passed away, came to an understanding with the prior of the monastery, and after the chapter-house bell had been rung and the friars were gathered together, he explained to them how Ser Ciappelletto had been a holy man, according to what he had deduced from the confession he had heard. And in the hope that the Lord God was going to perform many miracles through Ser Ciappelletto, he persuaded the others to receive the body with the greatest reverence and devotion. The credulous prior and the other friars agreed to this plan, and in the evening they all went to the room where Ser Ciappelletto's body was laid and held a great and solemn vigil over it. Then, in the morning, they got dressed in their surplices and copes, and with their books in their hands and the cross before them, they went for the body, chanting along the way, after which they carried it to their church with the greatest ceremony and solemnity, followed by almost all the people of the city, men and women alike. Once the body had been placed in the church, the holy friar who had confessed Ser Ciappelletto mounted the pulpit and began to preach marvelous things about him, about his life, his fasts, his virginity, his simplicity and innocence and sanctity, recounting, among other things, what he had confessed to him in tears as his greatest sin, and how he had scarcely been able to get it into his head that God would forgive him for it. After this, the holy friar took the opportunity to reprimand the people who were listening.

"And you, wretched sinners," he said, "for every blade of straw your feet trip over, you blaspheme against God and His Mother and all the Saints in Paradise."

Besides this, the holy friar said many other things about Ser Ciappelletto's faith and purity, so that in short, by means of his words, which the people of the countryside believed absolutely, he managed to plant the image of Ser Ciappelletto so deeply inside the minds and hearts of everyone present that when the service was over, there was a huge stampede as the people rushed forward to kiss Ser Ciappelletto's hands and feet. They tore off all the clothing he had on, each one thinking himself blessed if he just got a little piece of it. Furthermore, the body had to be kept there all day long so that everyone could come to see him. Finally, when night fell, he was given an honorable burial in a marble tomb located in one of the chapels. The next day people immediately began going there to light candles and pray to him, and later they made vows to him and hung up *ex voto*[2] of wax in fulfillment of the promises they had made. So great did the fame of Ciappelletto's holiness and the people's devotion to him grow that there was almost no one in some sort of difficulty who did not

1. A canonical hour, about 6 P.M.

2. Votive offerings (*ex voto* means "out of a vow"; Lat.).

make a vow to him rather than to some other saint. In the end, they called him Saint Ciappelletto, as they still do, and claim that God has performed many miracles through him and will perform them every day for those who devoutly entrust themselves to him.

Thus lived and died Ser Cepparello da Prato who, as you have heard, became a saint. Nor do I wish to deny the possibility that he sits among the Blessed in the presence of God. For although his life was wicked and depraved, it is possible that at the very point of death he became so contrite that God took pity on him and accepted him into His kingdom. However, since this is hidden from us, what I will say in this case, on the basis of appearances, is that he is more likely in the hands of the devil down in Hell than up there in Paradise. And if that is so, then we may recognize how very great God's loving kindness is toward us, in that He does not consider our sinfulness, but the purity of our faith, and even though we make our intercessor one of His enemies, thinking him His friend, God still grants our prayers as if we were asking a true saint to obtain His grace for us. And therefore, so that all of us in this merry company may, by His grace, be kept safe and sound during our present troubles, let us praise His name, which is what we began with, and venerate Him, commending ourselves to Him in our need, in the certain knowledge that we will be heard.

And at this point he[3] fell silent.

Day 2, Story 7

The Sultan of Babylon sends one of his daughters to be married to the King of Algarve,[4] and in a series of misadventures spanning a period of four years, she passes through the hands of nine men in various places, until she is finally restored to her father as a virgin and goes off, as she was doing at the start, to marry the King of Algarve.

If Emilia's tale had gone on perhaps just a little bit longer, the pity the young ladies were feeling for Madam Beritola because of her misfortunes would have made them weep. But since the tale had come to an end, it was the Queen's[5] pleasure to have Panfilo continue the storytelling. Most obedient, he began as follows:

It is difficult, charming ladies, for us to know what is truly in our best interest. For, as we have frequently observed, there are many who have thought that if only they were rich, they would be able to lead secure, trouble-free lives, and they have not just prayed to God for wealth, but have made every effort to acquire it, sparing themselves neither effort nor danger in the process. However, no sooner did they succeed than the prospect of a substantial legacy led

3. Panfilo, one of the young men of the *brigata* or "group" of storytellers; he recounts the first story.
4. Medieval Islamic kingdom in present-day southern Portugal (conquered in 1253 by the Christian Alfonso III) and, across the Mediterranean, in the northern part of modern Morocco; *al-Gharb* in Arabic means "the West." "Babylon": the name commonly applied to Cairo in the Middle Ages.
5. The ruler of the day; each day of the *Decameron* has an appointed king or queen from among the *brigata*.

to their being murdered by people who would never have considered harming them before then. Others have risen from low estate to the heights of power, passing through the dangers of a thousand battles and shedding the blood of their brothers and friends to get there, all because of their belief that to rule was felicity itself. And yet, as they could have seen and heard for themselves, it was a felicity fraught with endless cares and fears, and when it cost them their lives, they finally realized that at the tables of royalty chalices may contain poison, even though made of gold. Again, there have been many who have ardently yearned for physical strength and beauty, while others have sought bodily ornaments with equal passion, only to discover that the things they unwisely desired were the cause of misery or even death.

But to avoid reviewing every conceivable human desire, let me simply affirm that no person alive can choose any one of them in complete confidence that it will remain immune from the vicissitudes of Fortune.[6] Thus, if we wish to live upright lives, we should resign ourselves to acquiring and preserving whatever is bestowed on us by the One who alone knows what we need and has the ability to provide it for us. However, just as there are myriad ways in which men are driven to sin because of their desires, so you, gracious ladies, sin above all in one particular way, namely, in your desire to be beautiful, for finding that the attractions bestowed on you by nature are insufficient, you make use of the most extraordinary art trying to improve on them. And therefore, I would like to tell you a tale about a Saracen[7] girl's unfortunate beauty, which in the space of about four years turned her into a newly-wed nine separate times.

A long time ago Babylon was ruled by a Sultan named Beminedab,[8] in whose reign very little happened that went contrary to his wishes. Among his many children of both sexes, he had a daughter named Alatiel[9] who was at that time, according to what everyone said who saw her, the most beautiful woman in the world. The Sultan had been recently attacked by a huge army of Arabs, but thanks to the timely assistance of the King of Algarve, he had been able to defeat them decisively. Consequently, when, as a special favor, the King asked to be given Alatiel as his wife, the Sultan agreed, and after having seen her aboard a well-armed, well-equipped ship and having provided her with an honorable escort of men and women as well as with many elegant and expensive trappings, he commended her to God's protection and sent her on her way.

When the sailors saw that the weather was favorable, they unfurled their sails into the wind, and for some while after leaving the port of Alexandria,[1] their voyage prospered. One day, however, after they had already passed Sardinia and seemed close to their journey's end, cross winds suddenly arose that were so violent and buffeted the ship so badly that time and again not only the lady, but the crew thought they were done for. Nevertheless, they held out valiantly, and by marshaling all their skill and all their strength, they resisted the onslaught of the heavy seas for two days. As night approached for the third

6. The goddess whose wheel—ready to turn an individual from high to low at a moment—was often invoked in the Middle Ages.
7. Muslim (the term usually refers to an Arab, but sometimes to a European convert).
8. A fictitious name, though "Amminadab" is

mentioned in passing in Numbers (1.7, 7.12) and in the genealogy of Jesus (Matthew 1.4).
9. A fictitious name, which may be a punning anagram of "La Lieta" (The Happy One).
1. In northern Egypt, not far from Cairo.

time since the start of the storm, however, not only did it not abate, but rather, it kept growing stronger, until they felt the ship beginning to break apart. Although they were not far to the north of Majorca, the sailors had no idea of their location, and because it was a dark night and the sky was covered with pitch-black clouds, they were unable to determine their position either by using nautical instruments or by making visual observations.

It now became a case of every man for himself, and the officers, seeing no other means of escape, lowered a dinghy into the water and jumped into it, choosing to put their faith in it rather than in the foundering ship. Right behind them, however, came all the other men on board, leaping down into the boat one after the other, despite the fact that those who had gotten there first were trying, knife in hand, to fend them off. Although they all thought this was the way to escape death, they actually ran right into it, for the dinghy, not built to hold so many people in such weather, went down, taking everyone with it.

Meanwhile, the ship, though torn open and almost completely filled with water, was being blown swiftly along by a fierce wind that finally drove it aground on a beach on the island of Majorca. By now the only people remaining on board were the lady and her female attendants, all of whom lay prostrate, looking as if they were dead, overcome by both the tempest and their fear. The ship's impetus had been so great that it had thrust itself deep into the sand almost a stone's throw from the shore, where, now that the wind could no longer make it budge, it remained all night long, relentlessly pounded by the sea.

By daybreak the tempest had calmed down considerably, and the lady, who was feeling half-dead, raised her head and, weak though she was, began calling to her servants one after the other. She did so in vain, however, because they were too far away to hear her. Puzzled when she got no reply and could see no one about, she began to feel quite panic-stricken, and then, staggering to her feet, she finally found her ladies-in-waiting and all the other women who were lying about everywhere. As she ran from one to the other, she called and shook them repeatedly. Few, however, showed any sign of life, most having died from a combination of terror and horrible stomach convulsions, a discovery that only served to intensify the lady's fears. Since she was all alone there and had no idea of her whereabouts, she felt a desperate need of assistance and prodded those who were still alive until she got them to their feet. But when they realized that no one knew where the men had gone and saw that the boat was stuck in the sand and full of water, they all began weeping and wailing.

The hour of nones was already upon them before they saw anyone on the shore or elsewhere in the vicinity who might be moved to pity them and come to their assistance, for by chance, at that very hour, a nobleman named Pericone da Vislago,[2] who was returning from one of his estates, happened to come riding by on horseback, accompanied by several of his servants. The instant he saw the ship, he figured out what had happened and ordered one of his men to climb aboard as quickly as possible and to report what he discovered there.

2. A fictitious character; his first name is a diminutive of the Catalan name "Pere" (Peter), and his last name refers to a castle in Majorca, a large island south of Catalonia (the northeast corner of modern Spain).

Although the servant had to struggle, he managed to get onto the ship, where he found the young noblewoman, frightened out of her wits, hiding with her few remaining companions under the end of the bowsprit. On seeing him, they started weeping and repeatedly begged him for mercy, although when they realized he could not understand them, nor they him, they tried to explain their misfortune by means of gestures.

Once he had sized up the situation to the best of his ability, the servant reported what he had discovered to Pericone, who promptly had his men bring the women down along with the most valuable objects they could salvage from the ship. Then he escorted the women to one of his castles where he arranged for them to be fed and allowed to rest in order to restore their spirits. From their rich attire he deduced that he had stumbled across some great lady, and he quickly recognized which one she was by the deference which the other women paid to her alone. Although she was pallid and extremely disheveled because of her exhausting experiences at sea, her features still struck Pericone as extremely beautiful, and for this reason he resolved on the spot to take her to wife if she had no husband, and if marriage were out of the question, to make her his mistress.

Quite a robust man with a commanding presence, Pericone had her waited on hand and foot, and when, after a few days, she had recovered completely, he found her to be more beautiful than he could have imagined. Although it pained him that they could not understand one another and he could not determine who she was, nevertheless, her beauty had set him all ablaze, and he tried, by means of pleasant, loving gestures, to coax her to give into his desires without a struggle. But it was all in vain: she kept refusing to let him get on familiar terms with her, and as she did so, Pericone's passion just got hotter and hotter.

The lady had no idea where she was, but she guessed, after having observed the local customs for a few days, that she was among Christians and in a place where she saw that there was little to be gained by revealing her identity, even if she had known how to do so. She recognized what was going on with Pericone, and although she concluded that sooner or later she was going to have to satisfy his desires whether she liked it or not, nevertheless, she proudly resolved to rise above her wretched predicament. To her three remaining women, she gave orders never to reveal their identities to anyone unless they found themselves in a place where doing so would clearly help them gain their freedom. Beyond that, she implored them to preserve their chastity, declaring that she herself was determined to let no one except her husband ever enjoy her favors. Her women commended her resolve and said they would do their utmost to follow her instructions.

Pericone's passion was burning more fiercely from day to day, growing ever hotter as he got closer to the object of his desire and it was ever more firmly denied him. When he saw that his coaxing her was getting him nowhere, he sharpened his wits and decided to make use of deception, keeping force in reserve as a last resort. On several occasions he had noticed that the lady liked wine, which she was unaccustomed to drinking because the laws of her religion forbade it, and by using it as Venus's[3] assistant, he thought he would be

3. The Roman goddess of love.

able to have his way with her. Thus, one evening, pretending not to care about the very thing for which she had shown such distaste, he held a sumptuous banquet with all the trappings of a holiday celebration, at which the lady was present. Since the meal was graced with a wide array of dishes, he ordered the man who was serving her to give her a variety of different wines to drink with them. The man did his job only too well, and the lady, caught off guard and carried away by the pleasures of drinking, consumed more wine than was consistent with her honor. Forgetting all the adversities she had been through, she became positively merry, and when she saw other women doing Majorcan dances, she herself did one in the Alexandrian manner.

On seeing this, Pericone thought he was getting close to what he wanted, and he called for more food and drink in order to prolong the banquet into the wee hours of the night. Finally, after the guests were gone, he accompanied her, alone, to her bedroom. There, unhindered by any feeling of shame, and more heated by the wine than restrained by her sense of honor, she undressed in front of him as if he were one of her women, and got into bed. Pericone was not slow to follow her, and after extinguishing the lights, he quickly got in from the other side. Lying down beside her, he took her in his arms, and without even token resistance on her part, began playing the game of love with her. Up until that moment, she had no conception of the kind of horn men do their butting with, but once she did, she almost regretted not having given in to Pericone's solicitations. And from then on, she would no longer wait for an invitation to enjoy such sweet nights, but often issued the invitation herself, not by means of words, since she did not know how to make herself understood, but by means of actions.

Fortune, however, was not content to have made the wife of a king into the mistress of a lord, but was preparing a more terrible alliance for the lady in place of the very pleasurable one she had with Pericone. For Pericone had a twenty-five-year-old brother named Marato, fair and fresh as a rose, who had seen the lady and felt powerfully attracted to her. As far as he could judge from her reactions, it seemed very likely to him that he stood in her good graces, and since he thought the only thing between him and what he desired was the strict watch that Pericone kept over her, he devised a cruel plan which he quickly turned into a terrible reality.

There happened to be a ship down in the port just then that was loaded up with merchandise and bound for Chiarenza in Romania.[4] Although it had already hoisted sail, ready to depart with the first favorable wind, Marato made a deal with its two young Genoese masters for them to take himself and the lady on board the following night. With this out of the way, Marato made up his mind about how he would proceed, and as soon as night fell, he wandered unobserved over to Pericone's house, taking along with him several of his most trusted companions whom he had enlisted specifically to help him carry out his plan. Since Pericone had no reason to be on his guard, Marato was able to hide himself inside the house just as he had told his men he was going to do.

---

4. Another named used by the medieval Italians for Morea, or the Peloponnese (southern Greece); Chiarenza (also "Klarenza") was a main seaport in Achaea, a region of the northwest Peloponnese.

Then, in the dead of night, he opened the door and led them to the room in which Pericone and the lady were sleeping. They slew Pericone in his bed and seized the lady, now wide awake and in tears, threatening to kill her if she made any noise. Then, after taking many of Pericone's most precious possessions, they left the house without being heard and hurried down to the harbor where Marato and the lady immediately boarded the ship while his companions returned to the city. The crew set sail, and with a good, fresh wind behind them, began their voyage.

The lady grieved bitterly over this second misfortune, just as she had over the first one, but Marato made good use of Saint Sprouts-in-the-Hand, God's gift to all of us, and began consoling her in such a way that she was soon on intimate terms with him and forgot all about Pericone. Things thus seemed to be going pretty well for her, but Fortune, not content it seems with the lady's previous tribulations, was already preparing her a new one. For what with her beauty, which was, as we have said many times before, quite stunning, and her extremely refined manners, the two masters of the ship contracted such a violent love for her that they forgot about everything else and sought only to serve her and provide for her pleasures, at the same time, however, making sure that Marato never caught on to what they were doing.

When they discovered they were both in love with her, they talked things over in secret and agreed to make the acquisition of her love a joint venture—as if love could be shared like merchandise or money. The fact that Marato kept a close watch on her hindered their plan, but one day, when the ship was sailing ahead at full speed and he stood at the stern gazing out to sea, never suspecting that there was a plot against him, they both crept up on him, grabbed him quickly from behind, and threw him into the water. By the time anyone noticed that he had fallen overboard, they were already more than a mile away. When the lady heard what had happened and realized that there was no way of going to his rescue, she began filling the ship once more with the sound of her grief.

Her two lovers came straightway to console her, and with the aid of sweet words and the most extravagant promises, of which she understood very little, they worked at getting her to calm down. She was really lamenting her own misfortune more than the loss of Marato, and when, after their lengthy speeches, which they repeated twice over, she seemed much less distressed to them, the pair had a private discussion to decide who would be the first one to take her to bed with him. Each man wanted that honor, and failing to reach an agreement, they started a violent argument about it. Their words kept fanning the flames of their anger until they reached for their knives and in a fury hurled themselves at one another, and before any of the ship's crew could separate them, they had both been stabbed repeatedly. One of them died instantly from his wounds, and although the other survived, he was left with serious injuries to many parts of his body.

The lady was very upset over what had happened, for she could see that she was all alone there now, with no one to turn to for aid or advice, and she was terrified that the relatives and friends of the two masters would take their anger out on her. However, partly because of the injured man's pleas on her behalf and partly because the ship quickly reached Chiarenza, she escaped the danger of being killed. Upon arriving, she disembarked with the injured man and went to stay with him at an inn, from which rumors of her stunning beauty spread throughout the city, eventually reaching the ears of the Prince of Morea[5] who was living in Chiarenza at the time. He insisted on seeing her, and once he had, not only did he find that her beauty surpassed anything he had heard about it, but he immediately fell in love with her so passionately that he could think of nothing else.

Having learned about the circumstances of her arrival in the city, he saw no reason why he should not be able to have her, and in fact, while he was still trying to figure out a way to do so, the relatives of the injured man found out what he was up to and sent the lady to him without a moment's hesitation. The Prince was absolutely delighted by this turn of events, as was the lady, who felt she had escaped a very dangerous situation, indeed. Observing that she was endowed with refined manners as well as beauty, the Prince concluded, not having any other way to determine her identity, that she had to be a noblewoman, which had the effect of redoubling his love for her and led not only to his keeping her in high style, but to his treating her more like a wife than a mistress.

When the lady compared her present situation with the awful experiences she had been through, she considered herself pretty well off, and now that she had recovered fully and felt happy again, her beauty flowered to such an extent that all of Romania seemed to be talking about nothing else. And that is why the Duke of Athens,[6] a handsome, well-built youth, who was a friend and relative of the Prince, was moved by a desire to see her. And so, under the pretext that he was just paying a visit to the Prince, as he used to do on occasion, he arrived in Chiarenza at the head of a splendid, noble retinue, and was received there with honor amid great rejoicing.

A few days later, the two men fell to talking about the lady's beauty, and the Duke asked if she was really so marvelous an object as people said. "Far more so!" replied the Prince. "But rather than take my word for it, I'd prefer it if you judged with your own eyes."

The Prince invited the Duke to follow him, and together they went to the lady's room. Having already been informed of their approach, she welcomed them with the greatest civility, her face glowing with happiness. They had her sit down between them, but took no pleasure in conversing with her since she understood little or nothing of their language. Instead, as if she were some marvel, they wound up simply gazing at her, and especially the Duke, who could hardly bring himself to believe she was a mere mortal. He did not realize he was drinking down the poison of Love through his eyes as he stared at her, and although he may have believed he could satisfy his desire simply by looking, the wretch was actually being caught up in the snare of her beauty and was falling passionately in love with her. After he and the Prince had taken their leave and he had had some time for reflection, he concluded that the Prince was the happiest of men in having such a beautiful creature at his beck and call. Many and varied were his thoughts on the subject until finally, his burning passion overcame his sense of honor, and he decided that, whatever

5. A fictional character.
6. Also a fictional character; but Boccaccio was acquainted with a real Duke of Athens,

Walter of Brienne, who became ruler of Florence in 1342–43.

the consequences, he would do everything in his power to deprive the Prince of that happiness and make it his own.

Determined to move with dispatch, he set aside all considerations of reason and justice, concentrating entirely on his treachery, and one day, in further-ance of his wicked plan, made arrangements with one of the Prince's most trusted servants, a man named Ciuriaci, to have his horses and baggage secretly readied for a sudden departure. When night fell, the aforementioned Ciuriaci silently let him and an accomplice, both fully armed, into the Prince's cham-ber. It was a very hot night, and although the lady lay sleeping, the Duke saw the Prince standing completely naked next to a window that faced the sea, enjoying a light breeze coming from that direction. The Duke, who had told his accomplice what to do ahead of time, stole quietly across the room to the win-dow and thrust a dagger into the Prince's back, using such force that it went straight through him, after which he quickly picked him up and hurled him out of the window. The palace stood high above the sea, and the window by which the Prince had been standing overlooked a cluster of houses that had been reduced to ruins by the pounding of the waves. People went there seldom, if ever, and consequently, as the Duke had foreseen, no one noticed the Prince's body as it fell, for there was no one there to see it.

When the Duke's accomplice saw that the deed was done, he quickly took out a noose he had brought with him for the purpose, and while pretending to embrace Ciuriaci, threw it around his neck, and drew it so tight that the man could not make a sound. The Duke then came over, and together they stran-gled Ciuriaci before throwing him down where they had just thrown the Prince. Once this was done, they made sure that neither the lady nor anyone else had heard them, after which the Duke took up a lantern, carried it over to the bed, and quietly took all the covers off of her as she lay there sound asleep. Looking her over from head to toe, he was enraptured, and if he had found her attractive when dressed, now that she was naked, his admiration knew no bounds. The flames of the Duke's desire were burning even more fiercely than before, and unperturbed by the crime he had just committed, he lay down beside her, his hands still bloody, and made love to her, while she, half-asleep, thought he was the Prince.

After a while, having enjoyed himself to the limit with her, the Duke got up and summoned a few of his men whom he ordered to hold the lady in such a way that she could not make a sound and to carry her out through the secret door by which he had entered. Then, without making a sound, they put her on a horse, and the Duke led them all in the direction of Athens. Since he already had a wife, however, he did not take this unhappiest of ladies to Athens itself, but to an extremely attractive villa he had, not far from the city, that over-looked the sea. There he kept her in seclusion, but ordered that she be treated with respect and given everything she needed.

The next day the Prince's courtiers waited until nones for him to get up, but when they still heard no sound coming from his room, they pushed open the doors, which were unlocked, only to discover that no one was there. Working on the assumption that he had gone off somewhere in secret to spend a few days in the happy company of his beautiful mistress, they did not give the mat-ter a second thought.

Things stood thus until the next day, when an idiot who had wandered into the ruins where the bodies of the Prince and Ciuriaci were lying, dragged Ciuriaci out by the rope around his neck, and walked about, pulling the body behind him. When people recognized who it was, they were dumbfounded and managed to coax the idiot into taking them to the place from which he had brought the body. There, to the immense sorrow of the entire city, they found the dead Prince. After burying him with full honors, they opened an investigation to discover who was responsible for the heinous crime, and when they learned that the Duke of Athens, who had departed in secret, was nowhere to be found, they concluded correctly that he was the culprit and that he must have taken the lady away with him. After hastily choosing a brother of their dead prince as their new ruler, they urged him with all the eloquence at their command to seek revenge. And when yet more evidence appeared, confirming that their suspicions were true, the new Prince summoned his friends, relatives, and servants from various places to support his cause, quickly assembled a huge, formidable army, and set out to make war on the Duke of Athens.

The moment the Duke heard what was happening, he, too, mobilized his entire army for his defense. Many noblemen came to his aid, including two who were sent by the Emperor of Constantinople, namely his son Constantine and his nephew Manuel,[7] who arrived at the head of a large, well-trained force. They were warmly welcomed by the Duke, and even more so by the Duchess, who was Constantine's sister.

As war came closer day by day, the Duchess found a convenient moment to invite the two young men to her room, where she told them the entire story in great detail. Weeping copiously as she explained the causes of the war, she complained bitterly about the disrespect the Duke was showing her by keeping some woman as his mistress, whose existence he thought was a secret from her, and she begged them, for the sake of the Duke's honor and her own happiness, to take whatever measures were necessary to set things right. Since the young men already knew the whole story, they did not ask her very many questions, but did their best to comfort her and give her every reason to be hopeful. Then, after being informed as to where the lady was staying, they took their leave of her.

Since they had often heard the lady praised for her marvelous beauty, they were actually quite eager to see her and begged the Duke to present her to them. He promised he would, forgetting what had happened to the Prince for having done something similar. And the next morning, after arranging to have a magnificent banquet served in a lovely garden that was on the estate where the lady was staying, he took the two young men, along with a few other companions, to dine with her there. Sitting down next to her, Constantine stared at her in wonder, vowing to himself that he had never seen anything so lovely and that no one would blame the Duke, or anybody else, for resorting to treachery and other dishonest means in order to gain possession of so beautiful an object. And as he looked her over again and again, each time he admired her more than the time before, until finally the same thing happened to him that

<hr>

7. Names that appear repeatedly among the Christian rulers of the Byzantine Empire, whose capital was Constantinople (renamed Istanbul after it fell to the Ottoman Turks in 1453), the former seat of the Eastern Roman Empire.

had happened to the Duke. As a result, by the time he left, he was so much in love with her that he abandoned any thought of going to war and concentrated on how he might take her away from the Duke, all the while doing a very good job of concealing his passion from everyone.

As Constantine was burning in that fire, the moment arrived to march against the Prince who had by now almost reached the Duke's territories. In accordance with their strategic plan, the Duke, Constantine, and all the others left Athens and went to take up positions along certain stretches of the frontier where they intended to block the Prince's advance. While they waited there for several days, Constantine, whose thoughts and feelings were entirely focused on the lady, fancied that since the Duke was no longer anywhere near her, he now had an excellent opportunity to get what he wanted. Pretending to be seriously ill in order to have a pretext for returning to Athens, with the permission of the Duke he handed over his command to Manuel and went back to stay with his sister in the city. Several days later, after he got her talking about the disrespect she thought the Duke was showing her with his kept woman, he told her that if she wanted, he could certainly be of considerable assistance to her in this business, for he could have the woman removed from where she was staying and taken elsewhere. Thinking that Constantine was prompted by his love for her rather than for the lady, the Duchess said that it would please her very much, provided it was done in such a way that the Duke never found out she had given her consent to the scheme. Constantine reassured her completely on this point, and accordingly, the Duchess gave him permission to proceed in whatever way he thought best.

Constantine had a swift boat fitted out in secret, and one evening, after giving those of his men who were on board their instructions, he sent it to a spot near the garden on the estate where the lady was staying. Then, with another group of men, he went to her villa, where he was warmly received by her servants and by the lady herself, who at his request, went with him and his men to take a walk in the garden, accompanied by her servants.

Pretending he wanted to speak to her on behalf of the Duke, he led her down toward a gate overlooking the sea which had been unlocked earlier by one of his crew. There, at a given signal, the boat pulled up, and Constantine had his men seize her and quickly put her on board. Then he turned to her servants and said: "Don't anyone move or make a sound unless you want to be killed. My intention here is not to steal the Duke's mistress, but to take away the shame he's inflicted on my sister."

Seeing that no one dared to respond to him, he boarded the boat with his men, and sitting down beside the weeping lady, he ordered them to put their oars into the water and get under way. They did not row so much as fly along, arriving at Aegina[8] just before dawn the next day.

Disembarking there in order to rest, Constantine had his fun with the lady, who did nothing but lament her unlucky beauty. Then they boarded the boat once again and in just a few days reached Chios,[9] where Constantine decided to put up, thinking he would be safe there both from his father's reprimands

---

8. An island less than 25 miles southwest of Athens.

9. An island almost directly east of Athens, just off the coast of Turkey; Alatiel is steadily moving eastward.

and from the possibility that someone might take away from him the lady he himself had stolen. For several days the beauty bewailed her misfortune, but eventually, thanks to Constantine's unremitting efforts to console her, she began to enjoy, as she had every other time, the lot that Fortune had assigned her.

This was the state of affairs when Osbech,[1] at that time the King of the Turks, who was constantly at war with the Emperor, chanced to come to Smyrna,[2] where he learned that Constantine was leading a dissolute life on Chios with some woman of his whom he had abducted and had consequently not bothered to set up any defenses there. Arriving one night with a squadron of light warships, Osbech quietly entered the town with his men, capturing many people in their beds before they were even aware that the enemy was upon them, and killing those who awoke in time to run and get their weapons. They then set fire to the town, loaded their booty and their prisoners onto the ships, and went back to Smyrna. Upon reviewing their spoils after their return, the young Osbech was delighted to discover the beautiful lady, whom he recognized as being the one he had captured in bed together with Constantine as they lay sleeping. He married her on the spot, and after the wedding spent the next several months very happily in bed with her.

In the period before these events occurred, the Emperor had been negotiating a pact with Basano, the King of Cappadocia,[3] to have his forces attack Osbech from one direction while the Emperor assaulted him from the other. He had not yet brought their negotiations to a conclusion, however, because he would not agree to some of Basano's demands which he found quite unreasonable. But on hearing what had happened to his son, the Emperor was so distraught that he accepted the King of Cappadocia's terms at once and urged him to attack Osbech as soon as he possibly could, while he himself made preparations to come down on Osbech from the other direction.

When Osbech heard about all this, rather than let himself get caught in the middle between two powerful rulers, he assembled his army and marched against the King of Cappadocia, leaving the lovely lady at Smyrna under the protection of a loyal retainer and friend. Some time later, he confronted the King of Cappadocia and attacked him, but in the battle his army was defeated and put to flight, and he himself was killed. Unopposed, the victorious Basano then marched on Smyrna, and as he went, all the peoples along the way submitted to him as their conqueror.

The retainer in whose care Osbech had left the lovely lady, a man named Antioco, was so taken with her beauty that he betrayed the trust of his friend and master, and despite his advanced years, fell in love with her. It pleased her immensely that he knew her language, because for a number of years she had been forced to live as if she were a deaf-mute, incapable of understanding others or getting them to understand her. Spurred on by love, in the first few

1. Uzbek was in fact the Mongol khan of the Golden Horde (ruled ca. 1312–ca. 1342) in what is now southern Russia. Boccaccio turns him into the King of the Turks, a separate ethnic group, and invents his war with Constantinople.
2. A city on the western coast of Turkey (modern Izmir), opposite Chios; by the early 14th century it was no longer under Christian control.
3. A region in central modern Turkey; though Christians lost control of the area during the 12th century, the Italian-sounding name of the fictional character "Basano" implies Christian rule.

days Antioco began taking so many liberties with her that before long they had cast aside any concern for their master, who was away fighting in the war, and they became not merely friends, but lovers who gave one another the greatest pleasure imaginable over and over again as they lay together between the sheets.

When they heard that Osbech had been defeated and killed, however, and that Basano was on his way, carrying everything before him, they were of one mind in deciding to leave rather than wait for his arrival. Taking with them a substantial quantity of Osbech's most valuable possessions, they fled together in secret to Rhodes,[4] where they had not been very long before Antioco contracted a fatal illness. At the time he happened to have a Cypriot[5] merchant staying in his house, a very close friend whom he loved dearly, and as Antioco felt the end approaching, he decided to leave his friend both his possessions and his beloved lady. And so, when he felt his death was imminent, he summoned the two of them and said:

"I have no doubt that my strength is failing, which saddens me because my life has never been as happy as it's been of late. Truthfully, though, there's one thing that reconciles me to my death, and it's that I will die, if die I must, in the arms of the two people I love more than anyone else in the world, that is, in your arms, my dear dear friend, and in those of this lady, whom I've loved more than I love myself for as long as I've known her. But still, what really does trouble me is that when I die, she'll be left all alone here in a strange land, with no one to turn to for help or counsel. And this worry would weigh on me even more than it does if I didn't have you here, because I believe that, out of love for me, you will take good care of her just as you would of me. Consequently, in the event of my death, I commit her, together with all my worldly goods, to your charge, and I entreat you as earnestly as I can to make use of them in whatever way you think will offer my soul some measure of consolation. And as for you, my dearest lady, I beg you not to forget me after my death, for then I can boast up there that I have been loved down here by the most beautiful woman ever fashioned by nature. And now, if you two will just reassure me on these two points, you may have no doubt but that I will die content."

Both Antioco's merchant friend and the lady wept as they listened to his words, and when he was finished, they comforted him and swore on their honor to do what he requested if he should happen to die. And not long after this, he did, in fact, pass away, and they saw to it that he was given an honorable burial.

A few days later, when the Cypriot merchant had taken care of all his business in Rhodes, he decided to take ship on a Catalan merchant vessel then in port that was about to sail to Cyprus. He asked the lady what she wanted to do, in light of the fact that he was compelled to return to Cyprus, and she replied that if he had no objection, she would gladly go with him, because she hoped that, out of love for Antioco, he would think of her like a sister and would treat her accordingly. The merchant said he would be happy to do whatever she wished, and with an eye to protecting her from any harm that might befall her before they reached Cyprus, he told everyone she was his wife. When they got

4. An island off the southwest coast of Turkey (southeast of Chios and Smyrna), and a much-disputed military stronghold.

5. Native of Cyprus, a large island in the northeastern Mediterranean (south of Turkey).

on board, they were, consequently, assigned a small cabin in the stern, and to ensure that their actions were consistent with their words, he slept in the same narrow little bunk with her. What happened next was something that neither one of them had intended when they left Rhodes. Stimulated by the darkness as well as by the warmth and comfort of the bed, which are forces not to be underestimated, they were both seized by the same desires, and forgetting all about the loyalty and love they owed Antioco, before long they were fondling one another, with the inevitable result that even before they reached Paphos,[6] the Cypriot's hometown, they were sleeping together like a regular married couple. And for quite some time after they reached their destination, she stayed on with the merchant in his house.

By chance, a gentleman named Antigono happened to come to Paphos on some business or other at a time when the Cypriot merchant was away on a trading mission in Armenia. An elderly man, Antigono had acquired even more wisdom than years, albeit very little wealth in the process, because every time he had undertaken a commission in the service of the King of Cyprus, Fortune had always been his enemy. One day, as he was passing by the house where the lovely lady was staying, he happened to catch sight of her at one of the windows. He just could not stop staring at her, not only because she was so beautiful, but also because he had a vague recollection that he had seen her at some other time, although where exactly it had been, he simply could not remember.

For a long time, the lovely lady had been Fortune's plaything, but the moment was approaching when her sufferings would be over. Observing Antigono, she recalled having seen him in Alexandria where he had served her father in a position of some importance, and all of a sudden she was filled with hope that there might be some possibility of her returning once more to her royal station with the help of this man's advice. Since her merchant was out of the way, she sent for the old counselor at the first opportunity, and when he arrived, she asked him shyly if he was, as she thought, Antigono di Famagosto. Antigono replied that he was, adding: "My lady, I think I've seen you before, but I can't, for the life of me, remember where. Please be good enough, therefore, unless you have some objection, to remind me who you are."

When the lady heard that he was indeed Antigono, to his complete astonishment she burst into tears and threw her arms about his neck. Then, after a moment, she asked him if he had ever seen her in Alexandria. The instant Antigono heard her question, he recognized that she was Alatiel, the Sultan's daughter, who everybody thought had died at sea. He tried to bow to her as court etiquette required, but she would not permit it, asking him, instead, to come and sit with her a while. When he was seated, he asked her with due reverence how and when and from where she had come to Cyprus, for all of Egypt was convinced that she had drowned at sea many years before.

"I really wish that had happened," replied the lady, "instead of my having led the sort of life I've led. Furthermore, I think my father would agree with me if he ever found out about it." Then, having said this, she began weeping copiously once again.

6. In classical times, a major center of the worship of Aphrodite, Greek goddess of love.

"My lady, don't distress yourself unnecessarily," said Antigono. "Tell me about your misfortunes, if you like, and about the life you've led. Perhaps things can be handled in such a way that, with God's help, we'll be able to find a solution for your problem."

"Antigono," said the lovely lady, "when I first saw you here, I felt I was looking at my own father, and although I could have concealed my identity from you, I was moved to reveal it by the same love and tender affection I am bound to feel for him. Actually, there are few people I would have been as happy to have seen here as I am to have seen you, and therefore, I'm going to reveal to you, as to a father, the story of my misfortunes, which I've always kept hidden from everyone else. If, after you've heard it, you can see any means of restoring me to my original condition, I implore you to make use of it. If not, I beg you never to tell anyone that you've either seen me or heard anything about me."

This said, she gave him an account, without ever ceasing to weep, of every thing that had happened to her from the day she was shipwrecked off Majorca up to the present moment. Her story made Antigono start weeping himself out of pity for her, and after pondering the matter a while, he said: "My lady, since no one ever knew who you were during all your misadventures, have no doubt but that I can restore you, more precious than ever, first to your father and then, as his bride, to the King of Algarve."

Questioned by her as to how he would manage this, he explained in detail just what she had to do. Then, to prevent anything from happening that might cause a delay, Antigono returned at once to Famagosto where he presented himself before the King.

"My lord," he said, "if it please you, you can do something at very little cost that will greatly redound to your honor, while simultaneously being of inestimable service to me, who have grown poor while acting on your behalf."

When the King asked how this might be done, Antigono answered:

"The beautiful young daughter of the Sultan, who was long thought to have drowned at sea, has turned up in Paphos. For many years she has suffered through extreme hardships in order to preserve her honor, and now she is living here in poverty and wants to return to her father. If it should be your pleasure to send her back to him under my escort, it would greatly enhance your honor and would mean a rich reward for me. It is, moreover, inconceivable that the Sultan would ever forget such a service."

Moved by regal feelings of magnanimity, the King said that it was indeed his pleasure to send the lady home, and he dispatched an honor guard to escort her to Famagosto where he and the Queen received her with the most incredible pomp and circumstance. When they asked her about her adventures, she replied by recounting the whole story just as Antigono had taught her to tell it.

A few days later, at her request, the King sent her back to the Sultan under Antigono's protection and with a splendid retinue of distinguished gentlemen and ladies. No one need ask how warm a welcome she got there or how Antigono and her entire entourage were received. After letting her rest a while, the Sultan wanted to know how it had come about that she was still alive, where she had been living for all this time, and why she had never sent him word about her situation.

The lady, who had memorized Antigono's instructions to the letter, answered the Sultan as follows: "Father, some twenty days after I left you, our ship foundered in a fierce storm and ran aground one night on some beach or other in the West near a place called Aigues Mortes.[7] I never found out what happened to the men who were on board. All I do remember is that when dawn arrived, I felt as though I was rising from the dead and returning to life. Some peasants, who had spotted the wrecked ship, came running from all over to plunder it. When I was put ashore with two of my women, they were instantly snatched up by some young men who then fled, carrying them off in different directions, and I have no idea what became of them. As for me, although I tried to fight them off, two young men grabbed me and started to drag me away by my hair. I was weeping violently the whole time, but then, just as they started heading down a road in the direction of a dense forest, four horsemen happened to come riding by, and the instant my abductors caught sight of them, they let go of me and immediately fled away.

"When they saw what was happening, the four horsemen, who seemed like persons of some authority, galloped over to me. They asked me a lot of questions, and I gave them a lot of answers, but it was impossible for us to understand one another. Then, after a long consultation among themselves, they put me on one of their horses and led me to a convent of women who practiced these men's religion. I have no idea what they said there, but the women gave me a very kind welcome and always treated me with respect. While I was in the convent, I joined them in reverently worshipping Saint Grows-Big-in-Deep-Valley,[8] to whom the women of that country are passionately devoted. After I'd lived there a while and had learned something of their language, they asked me who I was and what country I'd come from. Knowing where I was, I feared that if I told them the truth, they might expel me as an enemy to their religion, and so I replied that I was the daughter of an important nobleman of Cyprus, who had been sending me to be married in Crete when, unfortunately, we were driven onto their shores by a storm and shipwrecked.

"Fearful of a worse fate, I made a regular habit of observing their customs of every sort until, eventually, I was asked by the women's superior, whom they call their abbess, whether I wanted to return to Cyprus, and I replied that there was nothing I desired more. Out of concern for my honor, however, she was unwilling to entrust me to just anyone coming to Cyprus, at least up until about two months ago, when certain French gentlemen, some of whom were related to the abbess, arrived there with their wives. When she heard that they were going to Jerusalem to visit the Sepulcher, where the man they consider their God was buried after the Jews had killed him, she placed me in their care and asked them to hand me over to my father in Cyprus.

"It would make too long a story if I were to describe how much I was honored and how warm a welcome I was given by these noblemen and their wives.

---

7. Literally, "dead [i.e., stagnant] waters" (Lat. *Aquae Mortuae*), named from the marshes on which this fortified city was built. On the southern coast of modern France, it was linked by trade routes with the Italian cities of Florence and Genoa.

8. Although the saint's name here appears to be a clever invention, there actually was a shrine of San Cresci in Valcava ("Saint Grows in Deep Valley") located about 15 miles north of Florence.

Suffice it to say that we all took ship and in just a few days reached Paphos, where it suddenly hit me that I'd come to a place where I didn't know a soul and thus had no idea what to tell the noblemen who wanted to follow the venerable lady's instructions and hand me over to my father. Perhaps God took pity on me, however, for he arranged to have Antigono there on the shore at Paphos at the precise moment we were getting off the ship. I called out to him at once, using our own language so as not to be understood by the noblemen and their wives, and told him to welcome me as his daughter. He grasped my meaning instantly and made a tremendous fuss over me. After entertaining those noblemen and their wives as well as his limited means allowed, he took me to the King of Cyprus, and I cannot begin to describe how much he honored me, not only with the welcome he gave me there, but by sending me back here to you. If anything else remains to be said, I leave it to Antigono, for he has heard me recount my adventures time and time again."

"My lord," said Antigono, turning to the Sultan, "she has now told you exactly the same story she's recounted to me many times and what the noblemen who were accompanying her told me as well. There's only one part that she's left out, which I think she omitted because it would not be appropriate for her to talk about it, and that is how much praise the gentlemen and ladies with whom she was traveling lavished on her not just because of the honest life she'd led with the pious women, but also because of her virtue and her laudable character. She also failed to mention how all of them, the men as well as the women, grieved and wept bitter tears when the time came to say farewell to her and place her in my charge. Were I to recount in detail everything they told me on this subject, I'd be talking not just all day, but all night, too. Let it suffice for me to say just this much, that from what their words have shown me, and from what I myself have been able to see, you may boast of having a daughter who is far lovelier, chaster, and more courageous than that of any monarch wearing a crown today."

The Sultan was absolutely overjoyed to hear these things, and he repeatedly asked God to grant him the grace to bestow proper rewards on all those who had treated his daughter so honorably, and in particular on the King of Cyprus who had sent her home with such pomp and ceremony. A few days later, having ordered the most lavish gifts for Antigono, he gave him leave to return to Cyprus, sending letters and special envoys along with him to convey his heartfelt gratitude to the King for what he had done for his daughter. Then, since he wanted to bring what he had started long before to its conclusion, namely to make her the wife of the King of Algarve, he wrote to the King, explaining everything that had happened, and adding that if he still wished to have her, he should send his envoys to fetch her. The King of Algarve was quite delighted by this proposition, sent an honorable escort for her, and gave her a joyous welcome. Thus, although she had slept with eight men perhaps ten thousand times, she not only came to the king's bed as a virgin, but made him believe she really was one, and for a good many years after that, lived a perfectly happy life with him as his queen. And that is the reason why we say:

> A mouth that's been kissed never loses its charm,
> But just like the moon, it's forever renewed.

Day 4, Story 9

Messer Guglielmo Rossiglione slays his wife's lover, Messer Guglielmo Guardastagno,[9] and gives her his heart to eat, but when she finds out about it later, she throws herself down to the ground from a high window, and after her death, is buried with her beloved.

Neifile's story had inspired great feelings of pity in the entire company, and when it was finished, the King, who had no intention of infringing on Dioneo's privilege, saw that there was no one else left to speak. Consequently, he began as follows:

Considering how much you are saddened, my most compassionate ladies, by lovers' misfortunes, the tale that presents itself to me will make you feel at least as much pity as the last one did, since the people involved in the events I am about to relate were of loftier rank and met with a crueler fate than those of whom we have already spoken.

You must know, then, that according to the people of Provence, there were once two noble knights living in that region, each of whom had a castle and a large number of vassals under him. One was named Messer Guglielmo Rossiglione and the other Messer Guglielmo Guardastagno, and since both excelled in feats of arms, they used to arm themselves from head to toe, and not only would they go together to tournaments and jousts and other contests involving martial prowess, but they would do so wearing exactly the same device.[1]

Although the castles in which the two of them resided were a good ten miles apart, Messer Guglielmo Guardastagno chanced to fall madly in love with Messer Guglielmo Rossiglione's very beautiful and charming wife, and despite all the affection and camaraderie the men shared, he made use of one means and then another to make her aware of his feelings. The lady, knowing him to be a most gallant knight, was flattered and soon became so infatuated with him that there was nothing she burned and yearned for more, until the only thing she was still waiting for was to have him proposition her. Nor was it very long before he did, after which they met with some frequency and made passionate love together.

Since they were not very discreet in their encounters, one day her husband chanced to discover them and became so deeply incensed that the great love he felt for Guardastagno was transformed into mortal hatred. Better at keeping it hidden, however, than the two lovers had been with their affair, he made up his mind, no matter what, to kill the man.

With Rossiglione in this frame of mind, a grand tournament happened to be announced in France. He immediately sent word of it to Guardastagno, asking him if he would like to come to his castle where the two of them could decide together whether they wanted to go and how they would get there. Quite delighted, Guardastagno replied that he would come without fail the next day and have supper with him.

---

9. The love triangle appears to be fictitious, but the names refer to the Provençal troubadour poet Guilhem de Cabestaing (1162–1212) and his lord Raimon de Castel-Rossillon (d. 1209).

1. The individual emblem, worn on armor or carried as a banner, that enabled a knight to be recognized on the field of battle.

When he received Guardastagno's message, Rossiglione thought the time had come to kill him. The next day, after arming himself, he got on his horse, and with a few of his men he went about a mile away from his castle, where he set up an ambush in a woods through which Guardastagno was bound to pass. After a long wait, he caught sight of him approaching, unarmed, followed by two servants, who were likewise unarmed, because he never thought for a moment that he might need to protect himself against his friend. When Rossiglione saw Guardastagno reach the spot he had chosen, he rushed out at him, with murder and vengeance in his heart, holding his lance above his head and shouting, "Traitor, you're a dead man!" And before the words were even out of his mouth, he thrust his lance right through Guardastagno's chest.

Unable to defend himself, let alone even utter a word, Guardastagno fell, impaled by the lance, and died almost instantly, at which point his servants, without waiting to see who had killed him, turned their horses' heads around and fled back to their master's castle as fast as they could.

After dismounting from his horse, Rossiglione cut open Guardastagno's chest with a knife, tore out the heart with his own hands, and wrapping it up in a banderole, told one of his men to take it with him. Having given them all strict instructions not to dare to say so much as a word about what had happened, he got back on his horse and returned to his castle, by which time it was nightfall.

The lady, who had heard that Guardastagno was supposed to come to supper and was waiting for him with the greatest impatience, was mystified when he did not show up with her husband and asked him: "How is it, my lord, that Guardastagno hasn't arrived?"

"My lady," replied her husband, "I've received word from him that he can't be here until tomorrow"—a statement that left her feeling somewhat perturbed.

Having dismounted, Rossiglione had his cook summoned and said to him: "Take this boar's heart and make sure that you prepare the finest, most delectable dish you can with it. Then, when I'm seated at table, send it to me on a silver serving plate."

The cook took the heart, and calling upon all his knowledge and all his skill, he minced it, seasoned it with a number of savory spices, and made a very tasty dish out of it indeed.

When it was time to eat, Messer Guglielmo sat down at the table with his wife. The meal was served, but he was preoccupied with the crime he had committed and ate very little. When the cook sent him the special dish, he had it placed before the lady, saying he had no appetite that evening. He heartily commended the dish, however, and the lady, who did have an appetite, started to eat it, and finding it quite tasty, consumed every last scrap.

When the knight saw that his wife had finished the whole thing, he asked her: "My lady, what did you think of the dish?"

"In good faith, my lord," she replied, "I liked it very much."

"So help me God," said the knight, "I do believe you did. But I'm really not surprised that you liked it dead, because you liked it more than anything else in the world when it was alive."

Upon hearing these words, the lady hesitated a moment. Then she asked: "How's that? What is this thing you've given me to eat?"

"What you ate," said the knight, "was actually the heart of Messer Guglielmo Guardastagno, whom you, like the faithless woman you are, were so infatuated with. And you may rest assured that it really was his, because I ripped it out of his chest myself, with these hands, just a little while before I came back here."

When she heard what had happened to the man she loved more than anything else in the world, there's no need to ask if she was grief-stricken. After a brief pause, she said:

"In doing what you did, you've behaved like a wicked, faithless knight, for if I was not forced into it by him, but freely chose to abuse you by making him the master of my love, then you should have punished me for it, not him. But now that I've eaten such a noble dish, made from the heart of so gallant and courteous a knight as Messer Guglielmo Guardastagno, God forbid that any food should ever pass my lips again."

Then she stood up, and going to a window right behind her, without the slightest hesitation she let herself fall backwards out of it. Because it was so high above the ground, the lady did not merely die, but was completely dashed to pieces.

Messer Guglielmo was profoundly shaken by what he had witnessed and conscience-stricken over having done wrong. Moreover, he feared what his fellow-countrymen and the Count of Provence might do. Consequently, he had his horses saddled and rode away.

By the next morning, news of what had happened had spread throughout the entire region, and people came from both Messer Guglielmo Guardastagno's castle and that of the lady's family to gather up the two bodies, which were taken, amid a great outpouring of grief and lamentation, to the chapel inside the lady's castle and buried there in a single tomb together. Upon it there was an inscription in verse, indicating who was buried inside and the manner as well as the cause of their deaths.

Day 10, Story 9

Disguised as a merchant, Saladin[2] *is honorably entertained by Messer Torello, who, when a Crusade is launched, establishes a time period for his wife to wait to remarry. He is taken prisoner, but because of his skill in training falcons, he comes to the attention of the Sultan, who recognizes him, reveals himself in turn, and entertains him lavishly. Having fallen ill, Messer Torello is transported by magic in a single night to Pavia, where his wife's second marriage is about to be celebrated. She recognizes him, and he then returns with her to his house.*

Filomena had brought her story to a close, and when one and all had finished heaping praise on Titus for his magnificent act of gratitude, the King, who was reserving the last place for Dioneo,[3] began speaking as follows:

2. Salah ah-Din Yusuf ibn Ayyub (1138–1193), Sultan of Egypt and Syria, who led Muslim campaigns against the Christians in Palestine and recaptured Jerusalem in 1187. Although he was the Crusaders' greatest opponent, in European literature he was represented as a paragon of chivalry and generosity.
3. Dioneo requests and is granted the privilege of speaking last on each day of the *Decameron*; his tales are usually among the most bawdy.

Pretty ladies, not only is what Filomena says about friendship undoubtedly true, but she was right to complain in her final comments about how little regard people have for it nowadays. If we had come here to correct the errors of the world, or even to criticize them, I would follow up on what she said with a substantial discourse of my own. But since our purpose is different, it occurs to me to tell you a story, long perhaps but enjoyable from start to finish, that concerns one of the generous deeds performed by Saladin. Thus, even though our defects may prevent us from winning the deepest sort of friendship with another person, by imitating the things you will hear about in my tale, we may at least derive a certain delight from being courteous to others and hope that sooner or later we will receive our reward for doing so.

Let me begin by saying, then, that during the reign of Emperor Frederick I,[4] according to a number of accounts, the Christians launched a great Crusade to recover the Holy Land. Saladin, a most worthy lord who was then the Sultan of Babylon, having heard about what was happening sometime in advance, decided to go in person and see what preparations the Christian leaders were making so that he would be better prepared to protect himself from them. Consequently, having settled all his affairs in Egypt, he pretended to be going on a pilgrimage[5] and set out disguised as a merchant, taking with him only three servants and two of his wisest senior counselors. After they had inspected many Christian kingdoms, one evening close to vespers, as they were riding through Lombardy on their way to cross the mountains, they happened to come upon a gentleman on the road between Milan and Pavia. He was named Messer Torello di Stra da Pavia,[6] and he was going, together with his servants, his dogs, and his falcons, to stay at a lovely estate he owned on the banks of the Ticino.

As soon as Messer Torello caught sight of them, he concluded that they were foreigners of gentle birth, and he was eager to offer them some sort of honorable entertainment. So, when Saladin asked one of Messer Torello's servants how much father it was to Pavia and whether they could still reach it in time to enter the city, Messer Torello prevented his man from saying a word by replying himself: "Gentlemen, by the time you reach Pavia, it'll be too late for you to get in."

"Then," said Saladin, "since we're strangers here, would you be so kind as to tell us where we can find the best lodgings."

"I'll do so gladly," said Messer Torello. "I was thinking just now that I would send one of these servants of mine on an errand to a spot not too far from Pavia. I'll have him go with you, and he'll take you to a place where you'll find quite suitable accommodations."

Messer Torello then went up to the most discreet of his servants, told him what to do, and sent him off with Saladin's party. Meanwhile, he himself quickly rode on to his estate where he arranged for the best possible supper to be prepared and for tables to be set up in one of his gardens, after which he went to wait for his guests at the entrance. Meanwhile, the servant, conversing

4. Also called Frederick Barbarossa (1122–1190); Holy Roman Emperor, 1152–90; he joined two kings, Richard the Lion-Hearted of England and Philip of France, in leading the Third Crusade in 1189–92. The Crusades were military campaigns against the Muslims to gain possession of the Holy Land.
5. Because pilgrimage is central to both Muslim and medieval Christian worship, Saladin's alibi would work well for both Muslim and Christian audiences.
6. That is, Torello whose hometown was Stra in the province of Pavia, a town south of Milan, on the east bank of the Ticino River.

with the gentlemen about various subjects, took them on a roundabout route, leading them along various by-roads, until he had brought them, without their suspecting it, to his master's estate.

As soon as Messer Torello saw them, he went out on foot to meet them and said with a laugh: "Gentlemen, you are very welcome here, indeed."

An extremely astute man, Saladin realized that the knight had not invited them there when they first met for fear they would have turned him down, and that he had cleverly arranged to have them brought to his house so that they could not refuse to spend the evening with him. Thus, after returning Messer Torello's greeting, he said:

"Sir, were it possible to lodge a complaint against courteous people, we would lodge one against you, for even leaving aside the fact that you have taken us somewhat out of our way, you have more or less constrained us to accept this noble courtesy of yours when the only thing we did to deserve your good will was to exchange a single greeting with you."

"Gentlemen," replied knight, who was both wise and eloquent, "if I may judge from your appearance, the courtesy you are going to receive from me is a poor thing in comparison with what you deserve. Truth to tell, however, you could not have found decent lodgings outside of Pavia, and that's why I hope you won't be upset to have gone somewhat out of your way in exchange for a little less discomfort here."

While he was speaking, his servants gathered around Saladin's party, and as soon as they had dismounted, took charge of the horses. Messer Torello then led the three gentlemen to the rooms that had been prepared for them. There, after they had been helped off with their boots, he offered them some deliciously cool wine as a refreshment and detained them with pleasant conversation until such time as they might go to supper.

Since Saladin and his companions and servants all knew Italian, they had no difficulty understanding Messer Torello or making themselves understood, and they were all of the opinion that this knight was the most agreeable and well-mannered gentleman and a better conversationalist than anyone they had ever encountered. For his part, Messer Torello concluded that they were all quite eminent men, much more distinguished than he had originally thought, and he regretted deeply that he could not entertain them in company that evening or offer them a more elaborate banquet. He therefore resolved to make amends the next morning, and having told one of his servants what he wanted him to do, he sent the man off to Pavia, which never locked its gates and was not that far away, bearing a message for Messer Torello's wife, a woman of great intelligence and exceptional spirit. This done, he led his guests into the garden and politely asked them who they were, where they had come from, and what their destination was.

"We are Cypriot merchants," replied Saladin. "We've just arrived from Cyprus, and now we're heading to Paris on business."

"Would to God," said Messer Torello, "that this country of ours bred gentlemen comparable to the merchants I see coming from Cyprus."

On these and other matters they chatted for a while until it was time for supper. Messer Torello then asked them if they would do him the honor of being seated at his table, and although it was an impromptu meal, the food was quite good and the service, excellent. Nor had the tables long been cleared before

Messer Torello, seeing how tired his guests were, showed them to the very comfortable beds that had been prepared for them to sleep in, following which, a little while later, he too retired for the night.

Meanwhile, the servant sent to Pavia delivered his message to Messer Torello's wife, who, in a spirit more like a queen's than an ordinary woman's, promptly summoned a large number of his friends and servants, and had all the preparations for a magnificent banquet set in motion. She had invitations delivered by torchlight to many of the most important nobles in the city, saw to it that a supply of fine clothes and silks and furs was at the ready, and took care of everything else, down to the very last detail, that her husband had asked her to do.

The next day, after the gentlemen had risen, Messer Torello set out on horseback with them, and having called for his falcons, he led the group to a nearby stretch of shallow water where he showed off how his birds could fly. Then, when Saladin asked if there was someone who could escort them to Pavia and direct them to the best inn in the city, Messer Torello replied, "I'll do it myself, because I'm obliged to go there any way." They took him at his word and happily set off down the road together, reaching the city just after tierce.[7] Thinking they were being escorted to the finest inn available, they arrived, instead, at Messer Torello's mansion where they found a good fifty of the most important nobles in Pavia who had assembled there to receive them and who immediately gathered around them in order to hold their reins and stirrups for them.

When Saladin and his companions saw this, they realized only too well what it all meant.

"Messer Torello," they said, "this isn't what we asked you to do for us. You treated us so very well last night, much better than we deserve, which is why you could have just let us go on our way."

"Gentlemen," replied Messer Torello, "with regard to the service that was done for you last night, I am more indebted to Fortune than to you, for it was she who overtook you on the road at a hour when you had no choice but to come to my humble abode. However, with regard to the service that will be done for you this morning, I will be beholden only to you, as will all these gentlemen you see here about you, although if you think it polite to decline an invitation to dine with them, then you are certainly at liberty to do so."

Acknowledging defeat, Saladin and his companions dismounted and were welcomed by the gentlemen who happily led them to a richly furnished set of rooms that had been prepared for them. After they had removed their traveling clothes and taken a little refreshment, they made their way to the hall, where everything was magnificently arranged. Having washed their hands, they were seated at table with great pomp and circumstance and were served so many courses in such splendid style that if the Emperor himself had been present, it would have been impossible to honor him more highly. In fact, even though Saladin and his companions were great lords and were accustomed to the grandest displays of opulence, they were nevertheless overcome with wonder at their treatment here, which, considering the position of the knight, who they knew was just a private citizen, not a ruler, seemed to them about as fine as anything they had ever experienced.

7. A canonical hour, about 9 A.M.

Once the meal was over and the tables cleared away, they discussed serious affairs for a while until, at Messer Torello's suggestion, the weather being quite hot, the gentlemen from Pavia all went off to take a nap, leaving him alone with his three guests. To make sure they got to see all of his most precious possessions, he escorted them into another room and sent for his good lady. A tall, strikingly beautiful woman, she presented herself before them, decked out in her rich garments and flanked by her two little children, who looked like a pair of angels, and welcomed them cordially to her home. The moment the three men saw her, they rose to their feet, gave her a most respectful greeting in return, and invited her to sit down with them, all the while making a great fuss over her beautiful little children. After starting a pleasant conversation with them, during which Messer Torello left the room for a while, she graciously asked them where they were from and where they were going, to which they gave her the same answer they had given her husband.

"Then I see that my woman's intuition may well be useful," said the lady, with a smile, "for I want to ask you a special favor, namely that you will neither refuse nor look down on the trifling gift I'm going to have them bring for you. Instead, you should bear in mind that women, with their tiny hearts, give tiny presents, and consequently, you should judge what you are going to get more by the good intentions of the giver than the size of the gift."

She then sent for two pairs of robes for each of the guests, one lined with silk and the other with fur—all of them more suitable for lords than for private citizens or merchants—as well as three doublets of taffeta and a number of undergarments.

"Take these robes," she said. "They're just like the ones I've always dressed my husband in. As far as the other things are concerned, although they're of no great value, you may find they'll come in handy, considering how far away you are from your wives, not to mention the fact that you've come a long way and still have a long way to go, and I know how you merchants always like to be neat and trim."

The gentlemen were astonished, for it had become abundantly clear that Messer Torello was intent upon showing them every conceivable courtesy. Considering how magnificent the robes were and how unlike the ones any merchant would wear, they were afraid that he had recognized who they really were, but one of them nevertheless replied to his wife:

"My lady, these things are exquisite and should not be accepted lightly, but we feel compelled to do so because of your prayers, to which we cannot say no."

Thus they took her gifts, and since Messer Torello had now returned, the lady, having bid them farewell, left the room and went away to see that their servants were supplied with similar gifts according to their rank. In response to Messer Torello's repeated entreaties, the gentlemen agreed to spend the entire day with him, and after they had slept for a while, they got dressed in their robes and rode through the city with him until it was time for supper, at which point they sat down to a magnificent feast in the company of many noble guests.

In due course they went to bed, and when they arose at daybreak, they discovered that they now had three fine, sturdy palfreys in place of their tired old nags and that their servants likewise had been provided with fresh, strong horses. Upon seeing all this, Saladin turned to his companions and said:

"I swear to God there's never been a more perfect gentleman than this, or one who is more courteous and considerate. If the kings of Christendom are as good at being kings as this man is at being a knight, the Sultan of Babylon will be unable to resist even one of them, let alone all those we've seen preparing to descend on him."

But since they knew there was no way for them to refuse Messer Torello's gifts, they thanked him most politely and mounted their horses.

Messer Torello, together with many of his companions, escorted them quite some distance down the road leading out of the city. Finally, even though it weighed heavily on Saladin that he had to part company from his host, to whom he had formed a deep attachment, he felt he could not delay his departure any longer and begged him to turn back. Messer Torello, who found it just as hard to bid his guests farewell, said:

"Since you want me to go, gentlemen, that's what I'll do. But there's one thing I must tell you: I don't know who you are, nor do I wish to know more than you care to reveal, but whoever you may be, you cannot make me believe you are merchants. Now, that said, I wish you Godspeed."

Saladin, who had already taken leave of Messer Torello's companions, turned to face him.

"Sir," he said, "we may yet have the chance to show you some of our merchandise and make a believer out of you. In the meantime, may God be with you."

Saladin then rode off with his companions, utterly determined that, if he managed to survive the war he was facing and avoid defeat, he would show Messer Torello no less hospitality than Messer Torello had shown him. As they went on, he talked to his companions about the gentleman and his wife and about all his gifts and favors and acts of kindness, praising them ever more highly each time he returned to the subject. But finally, when he had with no little labor surveyed all of the West, he put to sea and returned with his companions to Alexandria, where, now that he had all the information he needed, he prepared his defenses. As for Messer Torello, he went back to Pavia, and although he pondered at length who the three men might be, he never arrived at the truth or even came anywhere near it.

When the time arrived for the Crusade to begin and great preparations for it were underway everywhere, Messer Torello, despite the tears and entreaties of his wife, was wholly committed to going with them. He therefore got all of his equipment ready, and just as he was about to ride off on his horse, he said to his wife, whom he loved deeply:

"As you can see, my lady, I'm joining this Crusade, both for the sake of my personal honor and for the salvation of my soul. I'm placing our good name and our possessions in your care. And since I feel less assurance about my return than about my departure, considering the thousand accidents that can occur, I would ask this favor of you: no matter what happens to me, if you don't have any trustworthy news that I'm still alive, I nevertheless want you to wait for a year and a month and a day before you get married again, starting from this, the day of my departure."

"Messer Torello," replied the lady, who was weeping bitterly, "I don't know how I'm going to bear the sorrow you'll be leaving me in after you're gone, but if I'm strong enough to survive it, and if anything should happen to you, you may live and die in the certain knowledge that for the rest of my days, I shall remain wedded to Messer Torello and his memory."

"My lady," said Messer Torello, "I feel confident that you'll do everything in your power to keep your promise, but you're a beautiful young woman who comes from an important family, and everyone knows what a wonderful person you are. Consequently, I haven't the slightest doubt that if there's the least suspicion of my death, many fine gentlemen will come asking your brothers and kinsmen for your hand, and that no matter how much you may try to resist, they'll subject you to so much pressure that you'll eventually be forced to comply with their wishes. And that's the reason why I'm not asking you to wait any longer than the time limit I've set for you."

"I'll do whatever I can to keep my promise to you," said the lady, "but even if I'm forced to act otherwise, I'll certainly follow those instructions you've given me. However, I pray to God that neither you nor I ever have to deal with such extremities."

When she finished speaking, the lady wept and embraced Messer Torello. She then removed a ring from her finger and gave it to him, saying: "If I should happen to die before I see you again, remember me whenever you look at it."

Messer Torello took the ring, mounted his horse, and after saying farewell to everyone, went on his way. Upon reaching Genoa with his company, he boarded a galley and set sail, arriving at Acre in short order, where he met up with the rest of the Christian forces.[8] Almost immediately, however, a deadly epidemic broke out that overwhelmed the army, in the course of which, whether because of his skill or his good fortune, Saladin had no difficulty in capturing almost all the Christians who survived, and whom he then divided up and sent away to be incarcerated in various cities. Among those taken was Messer Torello, who was led off to prison in Alexandria. No one recognized him there, and being afraid to reveal his true identity, he had no choice but to apply himself to the training of hawks. Since he was a past master of this art, his abilities soon brought him to the notice of Saladin, who had him released from prison and appointed him his falconer.

Neither man recognized the other, and Messer Torello, whom Saladin referred to simply as "the Christian," thought of nothing except Pavia and tried many times to escape, but always without success. Consequently, when a group of emissaries from Genoa, who had come to Saladin to ransom certain fellow citizens of theirs, were about to depart, Messer Torello decided he would write to his wife, both to let her know that he was alive and would return to her as soon as possible, and to ask her to wait for him. When he finished the letter, he earnestly begged one of the emissaries, whom he knew, to see that it got into the hands of his uncle, who was the Abbot of San Pietro in Ciel d'Oro.[9]

8. Acre, also called Saint John of Acre, was the main European stronghold in the region of Jerusalem. The city was captured by Christian Crusaders in 1104, retaken by Saladin in 1187, and then attacked by Christian armies in 1189 (the "Siege of Acre") and captured in 1191. Its reconquest by Muslims in 1291 marks the fall of the "Latin Kingdom of Jerusalem."
9. The church of San Pietro (St. Peter) stands in the center of Pavia.

This, then, is how things stood with Messer Torello until one morning, as Saladin was speaking with him about his birds, he just so happened to smile, moving his mouth in a way that the Sultan had noted in particular when he was staying at Messer Torello's house in Pavia. It put Saladin in mind of his former host, and after staring intently at him for a while, he felt pretty sure he knew who it was. He thus dropped the subject they had been discussing, and said: "Tell me, Christian, what country do you come from in the West?"

"My lord," answered Messer Torello, "I'm a poor man of humble condition, and I come from a city in Lombardy called Pavia."

When Saladin heard this, he was now almost completely certain that what he suspected was correct, and he happily said to himself, "God has given me a chance to show this man how much I appreciated his hospitality." He did not say another word on the subject, however, but had them put all of his robes on display in another room, and took Messer Torello there to see them.

"Have a look at these clothes, Christian," he said, "and tell me whether you've ever come across any of them before?"

Messer Torello began inspecting them, and albeit he spotted the garments his wife had given to Saladin, it was inconceivable to him that they could possibly be the same ones. Consequently, he replied: "My lord, I don't recognize any of them, although it's certainly true that these two look like robes I once wore myself, as did three merchants who happened to come to my house."

Saladin could no longer restrain himself and embraced Messer Torello tenderly.

"You are Messer Torello di Stra," he said, "and I am one of the three merchants to whom your wife gave these robes. And the time has now come for me to show you exactly what kind of merchandise I have, as I told you, when I left you, might well happen one day."

Upon hearing this, Messer Torello felt both overjoyed and ashamed, overjoyed to have had such a distinguished guest, and ashamed because he thought he had entertained him poorly. But then Saladin went on:

"Messer Torello, since God has sent you to me, from now on you should consider yourself, and not me, the master here."

After much mutual rejoicing at their reunion, Saladin had him dressed in regal robes, and having presented him to a gathering of his greatest lords, and spoken at length in praise of him as a most worthy gentleman, he ordered all those who valued his favor to honor Messer Torello's person as they did his own. And from then on, that is what everyone did, and especially the two lords who had accompanied Saladin when he stayed at Messer Torello's house.

For a while Messer Torello's sudden elevation to the heights of glory took his mind off his affairs in Lombardy, all the more so because he had no doubt that his letters had reached his uncle.

On the day that the Crusaders had been captured by Saladin, however, there was a Provençal knight of little account named Messer Torello di Dignes[1] who had died and been buried on the battlefield, or rather in the Christian camp itself, and since Messer Torello di Stra was well known for his nobility throughout the army, whenever anyone heard people saying "Messer Torello is dead," it was assumed they were referring to Messer Torello di Stra and not the man

---

1. Also "Digne," a town in the French Alps at one time controlled by the rulers of Naples.

from Dignes. Before those who had been deceived had a chance to be unde-ceived, however, Messer Torello was taken prisoner, and as a result, many Ital-ians returned home bearing the news of his death with them, including some who were so presumptuous that they did not hesitate to say they had seen his corpse and been present at the burial. Finally, this came to the knowledge of Messer Torello's wife and family, and was the cause of the most intense, inex-pressible sorrow not just for them, but for everyone who had known him.

It would take a long time, indeed, to describe the nature and the depth of the lady's grief, the sadness and the woe she experienced. After she had mourned for several months straight in utter misery, however, her sorrow showed signs of abating, and since many of the most influential men in Lom-bardy were seeking her hand, her brothers and the rest of her relatives began urging her to get married. Although she repeatedly refused to do so, always amid floods of tears, her resistance was overcome in the end, and she agreed to give them what they wanted, but only on the condition that she could refrain from taking a husband until the period of time she had promised to wait for Messer Torello was up.

This, then, was how things stood with the lady in Pavia when, about a week or so before the date when she was supposed to be married, Messer Torello happened to catch sight one day in Alexandria of a man he had seen embarking with the Genoese emissaries on the galley that was taking them home. He therefore sent for him and asked him how their trip had been and when it was that they had reached Genoa.

"My lord," the man replied, "I was left behind in Crete, where I later learned that the galley had had a disastrous voyage. As it was approaching Sicily, a furi-ous northerly gale arose, driving it onto the Barbary reefs, so that no one man-aged to escape, and that included two of my brothers who perished along with the rest."

Messer Torello had no reason to doubt the man's account, which was only too true, and when he realized that there were just a few days left until the end of the time period he had asked his wife to wait and that nothing was known in Pavia about his present situation, he was absolutely convinced that she was going to be getting married again. So deep was the despair into which he fell that he lost his appetite, lay down on his bed, and resolved to die.

As soon as Saladin, who loved Messer Torello with great tenderness, heard what had happened, he came to see him. Having discovered, after earnest and repeated entreaties, the reason for his grief and his sickness, he scolded him severely for not having told him about it before. Then, however, the Sultan begged him to take heart, assuring Messer Torello that if he did so, he would arrange for him to be in Pavia on the date prescribed. Saladin then went on to explain how this would be done.

Messer Torello took him at his word, and since he had often heard that such things were possible and had actually happened on numerous occasions, he began to feel more optimistic and urged Saladin to take care of it at once. The Sultan therefore ordered one of his necromancers, a man whose skill he had already tested, to find a way to transport Messer Torello on a bed to Pavia in a single night. The magician replied that it would be done, but that for Messer Torello's own good, he would first put him to sleep.

When all this was arranged, Saladin returned to Messer Torello, whom he still found fully determined either to be back in Pavia by the date prescribed, if it were possible, or to die, if it were not.

"Messer Torello," he said, "God knows I can't blame you in the least for loving your wife so passionately and being so fearful of losing her to another. For I believe that of all the women I've ever seen, she's the one whose way of life, whose manners, and whose demeanor—to say nothing of her beauty, which fades like a flower—seem to me most precious and commendable. Since Fortune has brought you here to me, I should have liked nothing better than for the two of us to have spent the rest of our lives together, ruling as equals over this realm of mine. God has not granted me this wish, however, and now that you've made up your mind to die unless you can return to Pavia by the appointed date, I really would have preferred to have known about all this in time for me to have sent you home with all the honor and pomp, as well as the splendid escort, your virtues deserve. But since even this has not been granted to me, and you, moreover, are set upon going there at once, I will do what I can to get you to Pavia in the manner I've described to you."

"My lord," replied Messer Torello, "apart from your words, your actions have given me sufficient proof of your good will toward me, which is far, far above anything I've merited, so that even if you'd said nothing, I should have lived and died utterly convinced that what you say is true. But seeing as how my mind's made up, I beg you to act quickly and do what you promised me, because tomorrow is the last day she'll still be waiting for me."

Saladin assured him that everything had been taken care of, and on the next day, it being his intention to send Messer Torello away that night, he had a very lovely, luxurious bed set up in one of his great halls. Its mattresses were all covered in the Eastern fashion with velvet and cloth of gold, and on top of them there lay a quilt embroidered with enormous pearls and the rarest of precious stones arranged in oval patterns—the quilt was later considered a priceless treasure in these parts—as well as two pillows selected to match the bedding. When this was ready, he ordered them to dress Messer Torello, who had by now recovered his strength, in a robe of the Saracen fashion, the richest and most beautiful thing anyone had ever seen, while they took one of Saladin's longest turbans and wrapped it around his head in their usual style.

It was already late in the day when Saladin, with many of his lords in attendance, went to Messer Torello's room and sat down beside him.

"Messer Torello," he began, practically in tears, "the hour is approaching for you to be separated from me, and since I cannot accompany you myself or send anyone with you, because the nature of the journey you have to make won't permit it, I must take my leave of you here in this room to which I've come for that purpose. But before I bid you Godspeed, I beg you, in the name of the love and friendship that exists between us, not to forget me, and if it's possible, before our days have ended, to come and see me at least one more time after you've taken care of your affairs in Lombardy. For not only will I rejoice to see you again, but I'll be able to compensate then for the delight I must now forgo because of your hasty departure. Until such time as that should occur, I hope it won't be a burden for you to visit me by means of your letters and to ask me for whatever you please, for there is certainly no man alive whom I'd be happier to serve than you."

Unable to hold back his own tears, Messer Torello only managed to utter a few words, declaring that it would be impossible for him ever to forget Saladin's kind deeds and noble spirit and that he would, without fail, do what Saladin requested if he were given the opportunity. Saladin embraced him and kissed him tenderly. Then, weeping copiously, he said "Godspeed" and left the room, after which the other lords all took their leave of him and accompanied Saladin to the hall where the bed had been set up.

It was getting late, and since the magician was anxious to send him quickly on his way, a doctor arrived with a potion which he got Messer Torello to drink, persuading him that it would enable him to keep up his strength. Soon afterward he fell asleep, and as he slept, he was carried at Saladin's command and laid upon the beautiful bed where the Sultan placed a large, exquisite, and extremely valuable crown, which he marked in such a way that later on everyone saw clearly that it was a present from him to Messer Torello's wife. Then, onto Messer Torello's finger he slipped a ring containing a ruby that gleamed like a lighted torch and whose value could scarcely be assessed. Next, he had him girded with a sword so richly ornamented that its value, too, would be difficult to determine, and in addition, he had them fasten a brooch on his chest that was studded both with pearls, the like of which had never been seen, and with many other precious stones. Finally, Saladin had them fill two enormous golden bowls with doubloons and set them on either side of him, while all around him were strewn numerous strings of pearls, plus rings and belts and other things that would take too long to describe. When they were done, he kissed Messer Torello one more time, and he had hardly finished telling the magician to hurry up when the bed and Messer Torello were suddenly whisked away right before his eyes, leaving Saladin behind still talking with his lords about his departed friend.

As he requested, Messer Torello was set down in the church of San Pietro in Ciel d'Oro in Pavia, with all the jewels and finery that have been mentioned, and he was still fast asleep when the hour of matins was rung and the sacristan entered the church with a light in his hand. He immediately caught sight of the opulent bed, and after his initial amazement, he was so terrified that he turned on his heels and fled back the way he had come. The abbot and the other monks were equally amazed to see him running away, and they asked him for an explanation, which he immediately produced for them.

"Come on," said the abbot, "you're not a child any more, and you're hardly a newcomer to this church, either, so you shouldn't get frightened so easily. Let's all go now and see what gave you such a scare."

After lighting a number of lanterns, the abbot entered the church with his monks, where they saw this marvelous, luxurious bed on which the knight lay sleeping. Then, as they were casting a wary and timorous eye over all the princely jewels, the effect of the potion just happened to wear off, Messer Torello woke up, and a great sigh escaped his lips. When the monks saw this, they were terrified, as was the abbot, and they all ran away screaming "Lord, help us!"

Opening his eyes, Messer Torello looked about him and discovered, to his immense satisfaction, that he was in the very place where he had asked to be taken. Although he had been aware of Saladin's generosity in the past, when he sat up now and observed, one by one, the treasures around him, he was all the more conscious of it and judged it to be even greater than he had thought it was before. He could hear the monks running away, however, and divining the reason why, he did not make another move, but began calling the abbot by name, telling him not to be afraid, as it was only his nephew Torello.

Hearing these words, the abbot became even more frightened, because for many months he had thought that Messer Torello was dead. But after a while, as he continued to hear his name being called, he reassured himself with rational arguments, made the sign of the holy cross, and went up to him.

"O my father," said Messer Torello, "what are you afraid of? I'm alive, by the grace of God, and I've come back here from across the sea."

Although Messer Torello had a full beard and was dressed in Arab clothing, after a little while the abbot managed to recognize him. Now, he was feeling thoroughly reassured, and taking him by the hand, he said, "Welcome home, my son."

"Our fear shouldn't surprise you," he continued, "because there's no one in this city who isn't firmly convinced that you're dead. What's more, I can tell you that your wife, Madonna Adalieta, has been overcome by the threats and the pleading of her relatives, and has been forced to remarry against her will. In fact, this is the very morning when she's to go to her new husband, and they've made all the necessary preparations there for the nuptials and the wedding feast."

Messer Torello got up off the luxurious bed, and after warmly embracing the abbot and the monks, he begged them, each and every one, to say nothing about his return to anybody until he had taken care of some business of his. Next, having put all of the rich jewels in a safe place, he gave the abbot an account of everything that had happened to him up to then. Delighted by his good fortune, the abbot joined him in giving thanks to God. When they were done, Messer Torello asked him for the name of his wife's new husband, and the abbot told him what it was.

"Before anyone learns of my return," said Messer Torello, "I intend to see how my wife conducts herself at these nuptials. And so, even though it's not customary for the religious to attend such festivities, I'd ask you, for my sake, to make arrangements for the two of us to go there."

The abbot said he would be happy to oblige him, and right after daybreak, he sent a message to the new bridegroom, saying that he wished to attend the nuptials with a companion of his. In reply, the gentleman declared he would be quite delighted to see them.

When the hour for the banquet arrived, Messer Torello, still wearing the clothes he had arrived in, went with the abbot to the bridegroom's house, where everyone who saw him stared at him in amazement, although none of them managed to recognize who he was. The abbot told them all that Messer Torello was a Saracen who was being sent by the Sultan as his ambassador to the King of France. Accordingly, Messer Torello was seated at a table directly across from his wife, whom he gazed at with the utmost pleasure, thinking all the while that, from the look on her face, she was not too happy about this marriage. She likewise glanced at him from time to time, not because she recognized him in any way—his thick beard, his foreign dress, and her own firm belief that he was dead made that impossible—but because of the unusual clothes he had on.

Finally, when Messer Torello felt the time was right to put his wife to the test and see if she remembered him, he took the ring she had given to him at his departure, and holding it in his hand, called over a young man who was waiting on her.

"Tell the new bride on my behalf," he said, "that in my country, whenever a stranger, like me, is attending the wedding feast of a newly married woman, like her, it's customary for the bride to take a cup from which she herself has been drinking, fill it with wine, and send it to him as a token of her appreciation for his coming there to dine with her. Then, when the stranger has drunk his fill, he puts the cover back on, and the bride drinks up what remains."

The young man delivered this message to the lady, who, being both wise and well-mannered, and believing that she was dealing with an important dignitary, hastened to show him how pleased she was that he had come. Accordingly, she ordered that a large gold cup, which stood on the table before her, should be washed, filled with wine, and taken over to the gentleman.

They carried it to Messer Torello, who had placed his wife's ring in his mouth, and he drank in such a way as to let it fall into the cup without anyone noticing. Then, when there was only a tiny bit of wine left in it, he replaced the cover and sent it back to the lady. In deference to the custom of his country, she took it, removed the lid, and put it to her lips. At that moment, she caught sight of the ring. After gazing at for some time without saying a word, she identified it as the one she had given Messer Torello when he left her. She then picked it up and stared intently at the man she had assumed was a stranger. Now that she could see who it really was, she seized the table in front of her and hurled it to the ground, shouting as if she had gone mad:

"This is my lord, this is really Messer Torello."

Then she dashed over to where he was sitting, and without giving a thought to her clothing or any of the things on the table, she flung herself across it as far as she could and hugged him to her in a tight embrace. Nor could she be induced to let go of his neck for anything the people there could say or do, until Messer Torello himself told her to exercise a little self-control, for she would have plenty of time to embrace him later on.

The lady accordingly stood back up, and although by now the wedding feast was in total disarray, the return of so distinguished a knight actually made it happier than ever. Then, at Messer Torello's request, everyone grew silent, and he told them the story of what had happened to him from the day of his departure up to that very hour. He concluded by saying that the gentleman who, in the belief that he was dead, had married his wife could hardly take offense if he now reclaimed her as his own, since he was alive after all.

Though somewhat embarrassed, the bridegroom freely replied in a friendly manner that Messer Torello was at liberty to dispose of that which belonged to him in whatever way he pleased. The lady accordingly returned the ring and the crown her new bridegroom had given her and put on the ring she had taken from the cup as well as the crown that the Sultan had sent her. They then left the house they were in, and with all the pomp of a wedding procession, they made their way to Messer Torello's estate, where the merry-making went on for hours, lifting the spirits of his unhappy friends and relatives and all the townspeople, who considered his return only a little less than a miracle.

After giving away some of his precious jewels to the gentleman who had paid for the wedding-feast as well as to the abbot and to numerous others, Messer Torello sent more than one messenger to Saladin with word of his happy home-coming, declaring himself to be the Sultan's friend and servant. And for many years after that, he lived with his worthy wife, behaving in a more courteous manner than ever.

This, then, was how the tribulations of Messer Torello and his beloved wife came to an end, and how they were rewarded for their prompt and cheerful acts of courtesy. There are many people who strive to do the like, but although they have the wherewithal, they perform such deeds so ineptly that before they are finished, those who receive them wind up paying more for them than they are worth. And so, if such people get no credit for what they do, neither they nor anyone else should be surprised.

Day 10, Story 10

Induced by the entreaties of his vassals to take a wife, the Marquis of Saluzzo,[2] wanting to choose one his own way, takes the daughter of a peasant. After he has had two children with her, he makes it look to her as though they have been put to death. Later on, pretending to have grown weary of her, he claims he has married another woman and arranges to have his own daughter brought home as though she were his bride, meanwhile having turned his wife out of doors wearing nothing but her shift. On finding that she has borne everything with patience, however, he takes her back home again, dearer to him than ever, shows her their grown-up children, and honors her as Marchioness and causes everyone else do so as well.

When the King had finished his long story, which everyone seemed to have really enjoyed, Dioneo laughed and said: "The good man who was looking forward the next night to making the bogeyman's erect tail droop[3] would have given less than two cents for all the praise you are bestowing on Messer Torello." Then, knowing that he was the only one left to speak, he began as follows:

My gentle ladies, the way I see it, we have given this entire day over to kings and sultans and people of that ilk, and therefore, lest I stray too far away from the path you are on, I want to tell you about a marquis whose behavior was not an example of magnanimity, but of senseless brutality. And even though things turned out well for him in the end, I would not recommend that you follow his lead, because it is a real shame that he derived any benefit from it at all.

A long time ago, there was a young man named Gualtieri who, as the head of the family, had succeeded to the Marquisate of Saluzzo, and being unmarried and childless, spent all of his time out hawking and hunting. He never gave a thought to finding a wife and starting a family, for which he should have been considered very wise, but his vassals were not content with this and repeatedly begged him to get married so that he would not be left without an heir and they without a lord. Moreover, they offered to find him a woman whose character and family were

---

2. An Italian town south of Turin, in the foothills of the Alps; a marquis (lord) of Saluzzo named Gualtieri is named in a document dated 1174–75.
3. An allusion to the bawdy first tale told on day seven.

such that there would be every reason to feel hopeful about the match and he could expect to be quite happy with her. In response Gualtieri said:

"My friends, you are forcing me to do something I had absolutely resolved never to do, considering how hard it is to find a person whose character will be a match for your own, how very many of the other sort there are out there, and how miserable life will be for a man if he stumbles upon a wife who is not well suited to him. Furthermore, it's foolish of you to believe that you can figure out what daughters will be like by considering how their fathers and mothers behave and on that basis to argue that you are going to find one who will please me. For I don't know how you can get any information about the fathers, let alone find out the secrets of the mothers, and even if you could, daughters are often very different from either one of their parents. But look, since you want to bind me in these chains, I'm willing to do it. Nevertheless, so that I won't have anybody to blame except myself if it turns out badly, I want to be the one who's responsible for finding her. And let me assure you that no matter what woman I choose, if you fail to honor her as your lady, you will learn to your great misfortune just how serious a matter it was for you to have begged me to take a wife against my will."

The gentlemen replied that they were satisfied, as long as he was amenable to taking a wife.

For quite some time Gualtieri had been taken with the behavior of a poor girl who lived in a village not far from his home, and since she was also very beautiful, he thought that life with her might be rather agreeable. Thus, without searching any farther, he resolved to marry her, and having summoned her father, who was very poor indeed, he made arrangements with him to take her as his wife.

This done, Gualtieri called all his friends in the area together and said to them:

"My friends, since it is still your pleasure that I agree to take a wife, I am prepared to do so, though more to gratify you than from any interest I have in getting married. You know what you promised me, namely, that you would be content with whatever woman I chose and would honor her as your lady. Now the time has arrived for me to keep my promise to you and for you to keep yours to me. I've located a young woman after my own heart who lives quite nearby, and just a few days from now I intend to marry her and lead her home as my bride. So, see to it that the wedding feast is splendid and that you give her an honorable reception. That way I'll be able to pronounce myself satisfied that you've kept your word to me just as you'll be able to say I've kept mine to you."

The gentlemen all replied joyfully that they were very pleased with this decision and that no matter whom he chose, they would accept her as their lady and would honor her as such in every way they could. After that, they got everything ready so that the feast would be as grand and lavish and happy as possible, and Gualtieri did likewise, arranging for the most magnificent and beautiful wedding, to which he invited a host of his friends and relatives as well as many great noblemen and others who lived in the area. In addition, he had them make a fair number of beautiful dresses out of expensive material, all tailored to fit a girl who seemed to him the same size as the one he intended to marry. Finally, he ordered belts and rings, a lovely, costly crown, and everything else a new bride would require.

On the day set for the wedding, halfway between prime and tierce,[4] Gualtieri mounted his horse, as did all those who had come to honor him, and after everything necessary had been seen to, he announced, "Gentlemen, it's time to go and fetch the new bride." Then off he rode with the entire company. Before long they reached the little village, and when they got to the house belonging to the girl's father, they spotted her carrying water back from the spring, hurrying so that she could go with the other women to watch Gualtieri's spouse as she arrived. The moment Gualtieri saw her, he called her by her name, which was Griselda,[5] and asked her where her father was, to which she bashfully replied, "He's in the house, my lord."

Gualtieri dismounted and told everyone to wait for him while he went into the hovel by himself. There he found her father, whose name was Giannucole, and said to him: "I've come to marry Griselda, but first, here in your presence, there are certain things I need to find out from her." Then he asked her whether, if he were to wed her, she would do her best to please him and never get upset at anything he ever said or did, and whether she would be obedient, and about many other things of this sort, to all of which she replied that she would.

At this point Gualtieri, taking her by the hand, led her outside and in the presence of his entire company as well as all the other living people there, he had her stripped naked. Then he called for the clothing and shoes he had ordered for her and quickly had them dress her, after which he had them place a crown on her hair, disheveled though it was. And as everyone looked on in wonder, he proclaimed: "My lords, this is the woman I want to marry, provided that she wants to marry me." Then, turning to her as she stood there, feeling stunned and quite embarrassed, he asked her: "Griselda, will you have me as your husband?"

"Yes, my lord," she replied.

"And I," he said, "will take you as my wife." And thus, right there, in the presence of the entire assembly, he married her. He then had her seated on a palfrey[6] and led her, honorably attended, to his house where the wedding was celebrated in as beautiful, festive, and magnificent a style as if he had married the daughter of the King of France.

The young bride appeared to change her mind and her manners along with her clothes. As we have already said, she had a fine figure and lovely features, and in keeping with her beauty, she now became so charming, so disarming, and so well-mannered that she did not seem like a shepherdess and the daughter of Giannucole, but like the child of some noble lord, leading everyone who had known her earlier to marvel at her transformation. Moreover, she was so obedient and attentive to her husband that he thought himself the happiest, most contented man in the world. At the same time she was so gracious and kind to her husband's subjects that they all loved her with utter devotion, honored her of their own free will, and prayed for her well-being, her prosperity, and her advancement. And whereas they used to say that Gualtieri had shown some lack of discretion in marrying her, now they declared him to be the wisest, most discerning man on earth because no one else could have ever perceived her lofty virtues, which were hidden under the poor rags of her peasant's clothing. In short, she comported herself so well that

---

4. Two canonical hours: about 7:30 A.M.
5. This name seems to have been invented by Boccaccio, perhaps as an ironic variation of Criseida, the aristocratic romance heroine of his courtly poem *Il Filostrato*.
6. A horse for riding (as opposed to a warhorse), especially one used by ladies.

before long she had everyone talking, not only in her husband's domain, but far and wide, about how fine her character was and how virtuous her behavior, and she got people to change their minds if they had ever criticized her husband on her account at the time of his marriage.

She had not lived with Gualtieri very long before she became pregnant and in time, to his great happiness, gave birth to a little girl. But a little while later the strange idea popped into his head to test her patience by subjecting her to constant tribulations and generally making life intolerable for her. Consequently, he started by goading her with words, pretending to be angry and telling her that his vassals were thoroughly disgruntled with her because of her base origin, especially now that they saw her bearing children, and that, furthermore, they were upset about the little girl who had just been born and were doing nothing but grumbling about it.

The lady did not change her expression or show the least resentment when she heard these words. "My lord," she said, "do with me whatever you think best for your honor and your peace of mind, and I will be entirely content with it, for I know that I'm less important than your vassals are and that I am unworthy of the honor which you have so graciously bestowed on me." This reply was very gratifying to Gualtieri, for he realized that she had not gotten puffed up with pride because of the honors that he or the others had paid her.

Some time later, having already given her to understand in general terms that his subjects could not endure the little girl she had given birth to, he gave certain instructions to one of his servants and sent him to her.

"My lady," said the servant, with the most sorrowful expression on his face, "if I don't want to be put to death, I have to do what my lord has commanded, and he has commanded me to take this daughter of yours and to . . ." And at this point he could say no more.

When the lady heard the servant's words and saw his face, and when she recalled what her husband had said to her, she concluded that the man had been ordered to put her child to death. In response, although she was so sad that her heart was breaking, she immediately took her daughter from the cradle, and without ever changing her expression, she kissed her and blessed her and placed her in the servant's arms. "There," she said to him, "do exactly what your lord, who is my lord as well, has ordered, but don't leave her to be devoured by beasts and the birds unless he has told you to do so."

The servant took the child and reported what the lady had said to Gualtieri, who, marveling at her constancy, sent him away with the baby to one of his relatives in Bologna, asking her to raise and educate the child with some care, but never to reveal whose daughter she was.

Shortly afterwards, the lady became pregnant once again, and when she came to term, she gave birth to a baby boy, which made Gualtieri very happy. Nevertheless, not content with what he had already done, he wounded his wife even more deeply. One day, glowering at her with feigned fury, he said:

"Woman, ever since you gave birth to this boy, I've found it completely impossible to live with my vassals, so bitterly do they complain that one of Giannucole's grandsons is to succeed me as their lord. So, if I don't want to be deposed by them, I'm afraid that I'll have to do in this case what I did in the other one, and that I'll also eventually have to leave you and find another wife."

The lady listened patiently, and her only reply was: "My lord, you should think about your own happiness and about how to satisfy your desires. Don't waste another thought on me, for nothing is of any value to me unless I see that it gives you pleasure."

Not many days after that, Gualtieri sent for his son the same way he had for his daughter, and having likewise pretended to have him put to death, he sent him to be brought up in Bologna just as he had done with the girl. In response, his wife said nothing more and did not change the expression on her face any more than she had in her daughter's case, all to Gualtieri's great astonishment, who told himself that no other woman could do what she did. And if it were not for the fact that he saw her treat the children with the utmost tenderness as long as he permitted her to do so, he would have concluded that she acted as she did because she had stopped caring for them. He knew, however, that her behavior was the product of her discretion.

Since Gualtieri's subjects believed he had arranged to have his two children murdered, they condemned him, blaming it all on his cruelty, whereas they felt nothing but the most profound pity for his wife. But to the women who mourned with her for her children because they had suffered such a death, she never said anything except that if such was the pleasure of the man who had conceived them, then it was her pleasure as well.

Finally, many years after the birth of his daughter, Gualtieri decided the time had come to put his wife's patience to the ultimate test. Accordingly, he spoke with a large company of his vassals and told them that under no circumstances could he put up with Griselda as his wife any longer. He said that he had come to realize just how bad and immature a decision he had made when he chose her, and that he would therefore do everything he could to procure a dispensation from the Pope so that he could put Griselda aside and take another wife. A large number of the worthy men took him to task over this plan, but his only reply was that it had to be done that way.

Upon learning of her husband's intentions, the lady grieved bitterly inside, for it seemed to her that what she had to look forward to was returning to her father's house and perhaps tending his sheep as she had done before, while being forced to see the man she loved with all her heart in another woman's embrace. But still, just as she had borne all of Fortune's other afflictions, she was determined to keep her countenance unchanged and endure this one as well.

A little later Gualtieri arranged to have counterfeit letters sent to him from Rome and led his subjects to believe that they contained the Pope's dispensation, which allowed him to put Griselda aside and take another wife. Hence, he summoned her to appear, and in the presence of a large number of people, he said to her: "Woman, through the concession granted me by the Pope I am now free to put you aside and choose another wife. Since my ancestors have always been great noblemen and rulers in these parts, whereas yours have always been peasants, I no longer want you as my wife. You should return to Giannucole's house with the dowry you brought me, and I will bring home another woman I've found who is a more appropriate match for me."

When she heard these words, the lady managed to hold back her tears only by making an enormous effort that went well beyond the normal capacity of women.

"My lord," she said, "I have always known that my lowly condition and your nobility were in no way suited to one another, just as I have acknowledged that the position I have held with you was a gift from you and from God, nor have I taken what was given to me and treated it as if it were my own rather than as something lent to me. So, if it pleases you to have it back, then it must also please me—and it does—to return it to you. Here's the ring with which you married me: take it. As for your ordering me to carry away the dowry I brought here, to do that will not require a paymaster on your part, nor a purse, let alone a packhorse, on mine, for I haven't forgotten that I was completely naked when you took me.[7] And if you think it proper to let everybody see this body which bore the children you sired, I will depart naked as well, but I beg you, in return for the virginity I brought here and cannot take away again, that it may please you to let me take away at least one single shift in addition to my dowry."

Although Gualtieri had a greater desire to weep than anything else, he maintained his stony expression and said: "Very well, take a shift with you."

The people standing about there begged him to give her a dress so that the woman who had been his wife for thirteen years or longer should not suffer the shame of leaving his house wearing only a shift like a pauper. All their pleading was in vain, however, and thus she left the house in her shift, barefoot, and with nothing to cover her head.[8] After having said good-bye to them all, she returned to her father's home, accompanied by the weeping and wailing of everyone who saw her.

Since Giannucole never really believed it possible for his daughter to last very long as Gualtieri's wife, he had been expecting just such a development every day and had kept the clothes that she had taken off the morning Gualtieri married her. He brought them to her, and after she had put them on, she devoted herself to all the menial chores in her father's house just as she had been accustomed to do, bravely enduring the fierce assault of a hostile Fortune.

As soon as he had sent Griselda away, Gualtieri led his vassals to believe that he had chosen as his wife a daughter of one of the Counts of Panago.[9] And having ordered great preparations to be made for the wedding, he sent for Griselda to come to him. When she appeared, he said to her:

"I'm going to bring home the lady whom I have recently chosen to marry, and I want her to be given an honorable reception the moment she arrives. Since you know that I don't have any women in my house who can prepare the rooms properly and do many of the things that a festive occasion of this sort requires, and since you understand such household matters better than anyone else, I want you to see to it that all the arrangements are taken care of and that you invite as many ladies as you think necessary and receive them as though you were the mistress of the house. Then, when the wedding celebration is over, you can return home."

Gualtieri's words pierced Griselda's heart like a dagger, for she had not been able to renounce the love she bore him in the same way that she had relinquished the good fortune she once had. Nevertheless, she replied: "My lord, I am ready and willing."[1] And so, clad in homespun garments of coarse wool, she entered the house, which only a little while before she had left in a shift. Then

7. Compare Job 1.21: "Naked came I out of my mother's womb, and naked I shall return thither: the Lord gave, and the Lord hath taken away; blessed be the name of the Lord." Readers of Boccaccio's tale of Griselda (notably, his friend Petrarch) strongly associated her experiences with the biblical character of Job.
8. Only very poor (or very immodest) women would go out without a shawl or veil to cover their head.
9. Also "Panico," a city near Bologna ruled by counts of the Alberti family.
1. Compare Luke 1.38, "Behold the handmaid of the Lord." The Latin of the Vulgate, "Ecce ancilla Dei," was commonly written out in medieval pictures of the Annunciation.

she began sweeping and tidying up the rooms, had wall hangings and drapes to cover the benches put in place, got the kitchen ready to go, and turned her hand to everything just as if she were some little household serving wench, never stopping until it was all as neat and trim as the occasion called for. Finally, after having invitations sent to all the women in those parts on Gualtieri's behalf, she stopped and waited for the celebration to begin. When the wedding day arrived, though the clothes she wore were poor, she displayed the spirit and bearing of a lady, receiving, with a happy smile on her face, all the women who came to the feast.

Gualtieri had seen to it that his children were brought up with care in Bologna by his kinswoman, who had been married into the house of the counts of Panago. His daughter, who had now reached the age of twelve, was the most beautiful creature ever seen, and his son was six. Gualtieri sent word to his kinswoman's husband, asking him if he would be so kind as to accompany his daughter and her brother to Saluzzo, to arrange a noble, honorable escort for her, and not to reveal to anyone who she was in reality, but simply to tell them that he was bringing her to Gualtieri as his bride.

The nobleman did everything the Marquis requested, and a few days after he set out on his journey with the girl and her brother and their noble retinue, he reached Saluzzo, arriving around the dinner hour, where he found that all the people there, as well as many others from neighboring communities, were waiting for Gualtieri's new bride. She was welcomed by the ladies, and as soon as she entered the hall where the tables were set up, Griselda, dressed just as she was, happily went to meet her, and said: "You are welcome here, my lady."

The ladies had begged Gualtieri, earnestly but in vain, either to have Griselda remain in another room or to lend her one of the dresses that had once been hers, so that she would not appear in front of the guests looking as she did. But she was nevertheless seated at the tables along with all the rest of them, after which dinner was served. As everyone stared at the girl, they said that Gualtieri had done well by the exchange, and Griselda joined in, praising her warmly, and her little brother as well.

It seemed to Gualtieri that he had now seen as much as he could have ever desired of his wife's patience, for he had observed that no event, however outrageous, had produced any sort of change in her at all. Moreover, he felt sure that her reaction was not the result of obtuseness, since he knew just how wise she was. He therefore decided that it was time to deliver her from the bitter sorrow he guessed she was keeping hidden beneath her impassive exterior, and having summoned her, he smiled and asked her in the presence of all the assembled people: "What do you think of our bride?"

"My lord," replied Griselda, "she seems quite fine to me, and if, as I believe, her wisdom matches her beauty, I have no doubt whatsoever that living with her will make you the happiest gentleman in the world. However, I beg you with all my heart not to inflict on her the same wounds you once gave the other spouse you used to have, because I find it hard to believe she'll be able to endure them, considering how much younger she is and also how refined an upbringing she has had, whereas the other one experienced continual hardships from the time she was a little girl."

Seeing that she firmly believed the girl was going to be his wife, and yet had nothing but good things to say, Gualtieri had her sit down beside him.

"Griselda," he said, "the time has finally come both for you to taste the fruit of your long patience, and for those who have thought me cruel, unjust, and brutish to realize that what I've done I've done with a purpose. For I wanted to teach you how to be a wife, to teach them how to manage one, and at the same time to beget for myself perpetual peace and quiet for the rest of my life with you. When I was at the point of taking a wife, peace was something I really feared I wouldn't have, and that's why I decided to choose one by means of a test and have, as you know, inflicted so many wounds and so much suffering on you.

"And since I've never seen you deviate from my wishes in either word or deed, and since it seems to me that you will provide me with all the happiness I desired, I intend to restore to you in a single hour that which I took from you little by little, and with the sweetest of cures to heal the wounds I gave you. Receive this girl, then, with a glad heart, the one you believed to be my wife, as well as her brother, for they are, in fact, our children, yours as well as mine, the very ones whom you and many others believed for a long time I had cruelly ordered to be put to death. And I am your husband, who loves you more than anything else, and I believe I may boast that there is no one else who could be as content with his wife as I am with you."

When he finished speaking, he embraced her and kissed her, and while she wept for joy, they both got up and went over to where their daughter sat, listening in amazement to what they were saying. Both of them embraced her and her brother tenderly, thus dispelling any confusion that they, like many others present, were feeling. The ladies were overjoyed, and getting up from the tables, they went with Griselda into a chamber where, with a more auspicious view of her future, they divested her of her old clothes and dressed her in one of her own stately gowns. Then, like the lady of the castle, which she always appeared to be even when clad in rags, they led her back into the hall, where her rejoicing with her children was simply wonderful to see. Indeed, everyone was so happy about what had happened that the feasting and the celebrating were redoubled and continued unabated for several more days. They all declared that Gualtieri was very wise, although they thought that the tests to which he had subjected his wife were harsh and intolerable, but they considered Griselda to be the wisest of them all.

A few days later the Count of Panago returned to Bologna, and Gualtieri, having taken Giannucole away from his drudgery, set him up in a position befitting the man who was his father-in-law, so that he was treated with honor and lived in great comfort during his last remaining years. As for Gualtieri himself, he arranged a noble match for his daughter and lived a long, contented life with Griselda, always honoring her in every way he could.

What more is there left to say except that divine spirits may rain down from the heavens even into the houses of the poor, just as there are others in royal palaces who might be better suited to tending pigs than ruling men. Who, aside from Griselda, would have been able to endure so cheerfully the cruel, unheard-of trials to which Gualtieri subjected her and not have her face streaked with tears? Perhaps it would have served him right if, instead, he had stumbled across the kind of woman who, upon being thrown out of the house in her shift, would have found some guy to give her fur a good shaking and gotten a nice new dress in the bargain.

GEOFFREY CHAUCER
1340?–1400

While there was plenty of literature in English before Chaucer, later generations of writers would identify his *Canterbury Tales* as the foundation of the English poetic tradition. Chaucer was the first to conceive of poetry in English not as the product of an isolated, provincial nation located in an obscure corner of Europe but as a vital agent in the fourteenth-century emergence of the vernacular as a literary language. For this reason, Chaucer's models and rivals were not so much the English authors of **Beowulf** and **Sir Gawain and the Green Knight** as the Europeans **Dante, Petrarch,** and **Boccaccio.** Queen Elizabeth's tutor, Roger Ascham, recognized Chaucer's foundational role by calling him "our English **Homer.**" The sentiment was reiterated by Dryden, who translated several of the tales alongside selections from **Ovid's** *Metamorphoses,* declaring "I hold him in the same degree of veneration as the Grecians held Homer or the Romans **Virgil.**" In his *Faerie Queene,* Spenser calls Chaucer the "well of English undefiled," a stream of poetic influence still visible in the opening lines of T. S. Eliot's *The Waste Land.* For these writers, Chaucer's vivid, naturalistic English was the firm ground on which they could anchor a national literature.

LIFE

Chaucer's family origins were solidly middle class. His father and grandfather had been wine merchants, and by placing the youthful Chaucer as a servant at the royal court they set in motion a social transition that would ultimately lead to the family's participation in the upper classes of English society. Chaucer's granddaughter, Alice de la Pole, married a duke, and her grandson was named as the heir to his uncle, Richard III (though he never reached the throne). Chaucer's own family history is an example of the increasing social fluidity of late medieval English culture, in which status could change dramatically over just a few generations. Unlike many premodern poets who were supported by wealthy patrons, Chaucer was obliged to hold a mundane day job for most of his career. He had the time-consuming and tedious position of record keeper at the customs authority in London, and later supervised a number of building projects in his role as clerk of public works. In his *House of Fame,* Chaucer describes poring over his financial ledgers all day, and his books of poetry and fiction all night.

Chaucer's entry into the bureaucracy of English government followed from his early placement in a series of households within the royal family, beginning as a page in the retinue of the Countess of Ulster, daughter-in-law of King Edward III. In fact, the very first documentation of the poet's existence appears in a record of clothes purchased for the then-teenage Chaucer when he was attached to the countess's household. Later in his career, Chaucer was directly rewarded for his work for the court by Edward's grandson, King Richard II, and had the support of Edward's son John of Gaunt, the Duke of Lancaster (who, through a late third marriage, also became Chaucer's brother-in-law). Chaucer had a genius for keeping on the right side of power in a difficult and competitive era, a time characterized by civil unrest, international war, and, ultimately, seizure of the throne in 1399 by John of Gaunt's son and Richard II's cousin, Henry IV. Chaucer appears to have seamlessly transferred his loyalty from Richard to the new king, addressing one of his final lyrics, "A Complaint to His Purse," to the "conqueror of Brutus's Albion, who by lineage and free election is the true king." His subtle and politically astute poetry is as much the product of social and economic turmoil as is Dante's *Divine Comedy*: unlike Dante, however, who ended his days in exile, Chaucer knew how to play all sides against each other in order to protect himself.

As a soldier in the Hundred Years' War and, later, a diplomatic envoy for the English government, Chaucer traveled repeatedly to France, Spain, and—most importantly—Italy; there he encountered the work of Dante, Petrarch, and Boccaccio, which became central to his own writing. French literature had already had a strong impact on English writers of the period, but Italian literature was something new and exciting: through Chaucer, the humanist tradition championed by Petrarch began to be felt in England, along with the high allegorical mode of Dante and the story collections of Boccaccio. While the exact chronology of Chaucer's works is uncertain, they are often divided roughly into three periods: the so-called French phase, which includes the *Book of the Duchess*, an elegiac dream vision that owes much to the *Romance of the Rose* and the poetry of Machaut and Froissart; the Italian phase, which features the *Parliament of Fowls* and the *House of Fame*, both of which refer explicitly to Dante's *Divine Comedy*; and the English phase, during which Chaucer composed his *Canterbury Tales*. This sequence has many faults—most seriously, it tends to privilege the final, culminating period of the poet's career as specifically "English." Yet despite simplifying, it provides a useful way to contextualize a series of major works, each of which represents a significant innovation beyond what had come before.

In addition to the literature of his French and Italian contemporaries, Chaucer was deeply indebted to the major classical authors, especially Ovid and Virgil. A more particular influence, however, was the late antique philosophical poem of **Boethius**, the *Consolation of Philosophy*. Chaucer was a penetrating reader of the *Consolation*, which he translated into English, and he repeatedly turned to Boethian themes such as the competing roles of Fortune and Providence, the place of free will in the human soul, and the role of love as source of both chaos and order. In his dream visions and *Troilus and Criseyde*, Chaucer ostentatiously displays his classical learning and makes continual reference to the poems of his French and Italian contemporaries. But in the *Canterbury Tales*, Chaucer suddenly begins to wear his learning much more lightly: allusions become indirect and often parodic, and the focus of the poetry shifts instead to the landscape of society and, especially, to the relationship between the nature of a storyteller and the story he or she tells.

TIMES

Chaucer's England was the crucible of Reformation: the last years of the fourteenth century witnessed the emergence of religiously unorthodox communities loosely grouped under the term "Lollardy," an originally derogatory term used to identify such would-be reformers as dangerous heretics who sowed discord in the church. Lollard preachers argued that the Bible should be available in the vernacular language so that each person could know scripture at first hand, that images were really idols leading away from rather than toward God, and that pilgrimages were nothing more than social gatherings thinly disguised as devotional practice. In Chaucer's day, such unorthodox views were regarded with suspicion but were not yet as energetically suppressed as they would be just a few years after his death, when those suspected of Lollardy might be burned in the public square along with their unauthorized translations. Chaucer's Parson, who recounts a penitential treatise as the concluding story of the Canterbury Tales, is mocked by the Host, who exclaims, "I smell a Lollard in the wind." This kind of mockery, still just barely playful in the last decade of the fourteenth century, would soon evolve into denunciation and persecution. After this violent suppression, the aims of the Lollards would reemerge more successfully in the sixteenth century.

The same impulse that led medieval English men and women to want to read the Bible in English also led to other expressions of religious piety, including the tremendously popular stories of the lives of saints (two of which appear in the Canterbury Tales, in the Prioress's Tale and the Second Nun's Tale) and autobiographies of devout women such as Julian of Norwich and Margery Kempe. Chaucer's Wife of Bath is far less focused on heavenly goals than were these women: for her, pilgrimage is less about retracing the pathway to God than about "wandering by the way." Like Margery Kempe, however, the Wife of Bath is a strong female representative of the emerging bourgeois class whose wealth was built on local industries such as brewing (Margery Kempe) and weaving (the Wife of Bath), and whose independence was expressed physically through the act of travel both within England and abroad. Chaucer's pilgrims exemplify the late

medieval English eagerness to find the right path to God, whether through the unmediated experience of scripture, as advocated by the Lollards, or through the highly overdetermined mediation of pardons (certificates from Rome that guaranteed the devout buyer a shorter stay in purgatory).

The same instability that had come to threaten the church's control of the Christian flock in England, through the rise of Lollardy, also affected the smooth working of government. The reign of Richard II, who had ascended the throne as a child in 1377 following the death of his grandfather Edward III, was marked by capricious rule, discord between the king's advisers and the major lords of the realm, and repeated heavy taxation necessitated by the ongoing war between England and France. Discord within the capital city of London itself was particularly intense, as the burghers of the city became increasingly involved in the disputes between Parliament and the king. The greatest disruption took place in 1381, as a popular uprising broke out in the countryside in response to the imposition of yet another heavy tax. The Peasants' Revolt, as it was later called, moved rapidly through the towns and fields outside London, entering the city with violence. When the archbishop of Canterbury confronted the mob, urging the peasants to return to their homes, he was decapitated and his head impaled on a pike on London Bridge. The peasants rampaged through the streets, sacking and burning the palace of the king's uncle and chief adviser, John of Gaunt. Gaunt was connected to Chaucer both as his main patron and through family ties, but the revolt struck still closer to home for Chaucer: the mob slaughtered a group of Flemish immigrant workers in a London street where Chaucer had lived as a boy, and it entered the city through a major gate—Aldgate—above which Chaucer had his lodgings.

Although Chaucer must have witnessed this violence at first hand, his allusions to social unrest are always oblique and, above all, cautious.

WORK

The Canterbury Tales is a frame-tale poem; like *The Thousand and One Nights* and Boccaccio's *Decameron*, it has a beginning and ending within which a series of tales are related. Unlike *The Thousand and One Nights*, which has (for the most part) a single storyteller, and the *Decameron*, which has a relatively homogenous company of noble young narrators, *The Canterbury Tales* revels in the extraordinary range of possible tales and possible tale-tellers. From the humble Miller to the chivalric Knight, from the bossy Wife of Bath to the effete Pardoner, Chaucer's diverse pilgrims span the range of medieval English life. The pilgrims are, in a way, types or ideals of each manner of life available to the individual: the company includes a nun, a lawyer, a squire, a sailor, and so on. But each teller is also an individual, characterized as such not only in the prefatory prologues that introduce each tale but also in the manner in which the tale itself is told. Petty rivalries, as between the Miller and the Reeve or between the Friar and the Summoner, are played out during the interludes between tales; tale-tellers pay back or "quite" one another by telling stories that indirectly comment on their fellows, causing sometimes argument and discord, sometimes laughter, or sometimes—as at the end of the Pardoner's Tale—both.

Chaucer's Wife of Bath is endowed with a vivid personality and a complex inner life that she herself tells us all about. In her Prologue, she sets her female experience against the misogynist stereotypes of women as lawless, sexually voracious, and manipulative creatures, a view promoted by certain traditions of medieval religious thought. Yet the reader is forced to ask if the Wife's frank celebration of her own sexuality, and her account of the torment she has inflicted on her three old husbands, does not in fact confirm those stereotypes. An answer is suggested by the Wife's claim that she is only playing: indeed, at one point she speaks as if she were showing her almost exclusively male audience how she would conduct a kind of school for wives. She seems, in other words, to be putting on a performance, pretending to reveal to her fascinated audience the secrets that women share among themselves and thereby letting men witness the intimate life of a woman. Yet as the Prologue proceeds we feel that her playful dramatics give way to a more serious, more authentic self-revelation. We learn that not only have her husbands suffered in marriage but that she has too, that she is unavoidably (if cheerfully) aware of her advancing years, and that what she seems to value most is neither money nor the sex she so aggressively celebrates but the companionship and love she comes finally to share with her fifth husband. In the same way, her tale gradually reveals itself to be more than simply a nostalgic wish fulfillment for the return of youth and beauty. When the criminal knight tries to learn what women most desire, he is offered a series of misogynist answers; but when forced to marry he discovers, through the moral lecture his old wife delivers, that she possesses a wisdom that he himself lacks. This is why he leaves the final decision about what form she will assume up to her, and in granting her mastery he is rewarded not merely with youth and beauty but with a marriage of mutual affection. It is through this experience, then, rather than by relying on the authority of time-honored opinions, that the knight comes to learn about the true nature of women.

The Pardoner offers a performance that is very similar to the Wife of Bath's, but his subject is not marriage but religion. His function is to raise money for a charitable institution—in this case, a hospital—by selling papal indulgences. Sinners bought these documents—in effect, made a charitable gift to the church—so that they might be spared some of the punishment that awaited them or their loved ones in purgatory. On no account, despite what this Pardoner says, did indulgences remit the guilt of sin: only Christ could do that. In his Prologue, the Pardoner openly admits that he is a bad man—in fact, he proclaims both his vicious nature and his impenitent lack of concern for his own spiritual future so loudly and so brazenly that we may think he protests too much. Even in his Prologue we get hints that the Pardoner harbors somewhere in his tortured soul the thought that he is, in spite of himself, doing God's work. And in fact the story he tells is one of the most brilliantly effective religious stories in all of medieval literature. It belongs to the genre of the exemplum, a short tale of the sort that preachers would use to enliven their sermons. It demonstrates with an almost mathematical efficiency that the wages of sin are death, and it also provides us with a startling insight into the Pardoner himself. For he too is seeking the spiritual death of damnation, and in the figure of the eerie old man he expresses with a painful vivid-ness the common medieval understanding of damnation as a condition of perpetual dying, a dying that never finds death. Just as the Wife of Bath is more than a stereotype, so too the Pardoner is more than an impenitent sinner. On the contrary, Chaucer allows us to see the deep suffering endured by a man who mocks religious truths while simultaneously yearning for them.

CHAUCER'S LANGUAGE

Chaucer's Middle English strikes the present-day reader as both familiar and strange, separated from Modern English by peculiarities of pronunciation and word order, but recognizable as its ancestor through names and terms that have remained essentially unchanged. Unlike the Old English of *Beowulf*, which must be learned as though it were a foreign language, Middle English is usually approached as if it were a dialect or an idiom—close to home, but still uncannily strange. We reproduce below the first eighteen lines of the General Prologue to the *Tales*, not only to illustrate the gap between English of the fourteenth century and the twenty-first, and to provide a frame of reference for the modern English translation that follows, but also to give a taste of the unfamiliar familiar tongue of the father of English poetry.

Whan that Aprill with his shoures soote
The droghte of March hath perced to the roote,
And bathed every veyne in swich licour
Of which vertu engendred is the flour;
Whan Zephirus eek with his sweete breeth
Inspired hath in every holt and heeth
The tender croppes, and the yonge sonne
Hath in the Ram his halve cours yronne,
And smale foweles maken melodye,
That slepen al the nyght with open ye
(So priketh hem nature in hir corages);
Thanne longen folk to goon on pilgrimages,
And palmeres for to seken straunge strondes,

To ferne halwes, kowthe in sondry londes;
And specially from every shires ende
Of Engelond to Caunterbury they wende,
The hooly blissful martir for to seke,
That hem hath holpen whan that they were seeke.

FROM THE CANTERBURY TALES[1]

The General Prologue

Here begins the Book of the Tales of Canterbury.

When April comes and with its showers sweet
Has, to the root, pierced March's drought complete,
And then bathed every vein in such elixir
That, by its strength, engendered is the flower;
When Zephirus[2] with his sweet breath   5
Inspires life anew, through grove and heath,
In tender shoots, and when the spring's young sun
Has, in the Ram,[3] full half its course now run,
And when small birds begin to harmonize
That sleep throughout the night with open eyes   10
(So nature, stirring them, pricks up their courage),
Then folks, too, long to go on pilgrimage,
And palmers hope to seek there, on strange strands,[4]
Those far-off shrines well known in many lands;
And especially, from every shire's end   15
Of England, to Canterbury they wend;
The holy, blessed martir[5] they all seek,
Who has helped them when they were sick and weak.
     It happened, in that season, on a day
In Southwark,[6] at the Tabard as I lay   20
Ready to start out on my pilgrimage
To Canterbury, with true, devoted courage,
At night, there came into that hostelry,[7]
Fully nine-and-twenty in a company
Of sundry folks, as chance would have them fall   25
In fellowship, and pilgrims were they all,

1. Translated from Middle English by Sheila Fisher.
2. Zephyr, the west wind.
3. Aries, the first sign of the zodiac in the solar year (March 21–April 20).
4. Shores, beaches. "Palmers": pilgrims who had returned from the Holy Land (they carried palm fronds in imitation of Jesus and his apostles during their entry into Jerusalem).
5. St. Thomas Becket (ca. 1118–1170), killed by assailants loyal to King Henry II of England as he stood before the altar of his church at Canterbury; until the Reformation, the site was something of a national center of religious devotion.
6. A suburb of London, south of the Thames, where theaters, brothels, and other businesses of dubious repute set up shop beyond the reach of the city's laws.
7. I.e., the Tabard.

Who, toward Canterbury, wished to ride.
The chambers and the stables were all wide,
And we were put at ease with all the best.
And, shortly, when the sun went to its rest, 30
I had so spoken with them, every one,
That I was in their fellowship anon,
And to rise early I gave them my vow,
To make our way, as I will tell you now.

But, nonetheless, while I have time and space, 35
Before much further in this tale I pace,
It seems quite right and proper to relate
To you the full condition and the state
Of each of them, just as they seemed to me,
And what they were, and of what degree, 40
And also of the clothes they were dressed in,
And with a knight, then, I will first begin.

A KNIGHT there was, and that, a worthy man,
Who, from the time when he first began
To ride to war, he loved most chivalry, 45
Truth and honor, largesse and courtesy.
Full worthy he, to fight in his lord's war,
No other man had ridden half so far,
As much in Christian as in heathen lands,
And all honor his worthiness commands; 50
At Alexandria[8] he was, when it was won.
At banquets, he was many times the one
Seated with honor above all knights in Prussia;
In Lithuania, he'd raided, and in Russia,
Unrivalled among knightly Christian men. 55
In Granada, at the siege, he'd also been
Of Algeciras; he rode at Belmarin.
At Ayas and at Adalia had he been
When they fell; and then in the Great Sea[9]
At fine armed conquests, he fought worthily. 60
In fifteen mortal battles had he been,
And thrice he fought for God at Tlemcen
Alone in lists, and always slew his foe.
And this same worthy knight had been also
At one time fighting alongside Balat's lord 65
Against another Turkish heathen horde;
And always was his fame a sovereign prize.
Not only was he was worthy, he was wise;
And in his bearing, meek as is a maid.
In all his life, no rude word had he said 70
To any man, however much his might.
He was a true and perfect gentle knight.

8. A city in northern Egypt, sacked by Peter I of Cyprus in 1365. The following places named, ranging from eastern Europe to the Muslim-held regions in southern Spain and North Africa, demonstrate both the large number and the wide variety of the Knight's campaigns.
9. The Mediterranean.

But now to tell you about his array,
His horse was good, but his dress was not gay.
His tunic was of fustian, coarse and plain, 75
Which by his rusty mailcoat was all stained,
For just lately he'd come from his voyage,
And now he went to make his pilgrimage.
    With him there was his son, a young SQUIRE,
A lover and in arms, a bachelor, 80
His locks waved like they'd seen a curling press.
About twenty years of age he was, I guess.
In his stature, he was of average length,
And wonderfully deft, and of great strength.
He'd ridden sometimes with the cavalry 85
In Flanders, in Artois, and Picardy,[1]
And fared quite well, within small time and space,
In hope of standing in his lady's grace.
Embroidered was he, as if he were a bed
All full of fresh spring flowers, white and red. 90
Singing he was, or fluting, all the day;
He was as fresh as is the month of May.
Short was his gown, its sleeves hung long and wide.
Well could he sit his horse, and nicely ride.
And also he wrote songs, both verse and note, 95
He jousted and he danced, he drew and wrote.
So hotly loved he that when nighttime came,
The nightingale and he slept both the same.[2]
Courteous and meek, to serve, quite able,
He carved before his father at the table.[3] 100
    A YEOMAN[4] had he—no servants beside,
For at this time, that's how he chose to ride,
And he was clad in coat and hood of green.
A sheaf of peacock arrows, bright and keen,
Under his belt, he bore quite properly 105
(For he could tend his gear quite yeomanly;
His arrows did not droop with feathers low),
And in his hand he bore a mighty bow.
A close-cropped head had he, a face well browned.
No man more skilled in woodcraft might be found. 110
Upon his arm he wore a gay wrist guard,
And by his side a small shield and a sword,
By his other side, a bright, gay dagger fell,
As sharp as a spear's point, and sheathed up well;
On his breast, a silver Christopher[5] was seen. 115

1. Regions in modern Belgium and northern France.
2. That is, not at all. In Persian, Arabic, Occitan, and French poetry, the nightingale was a symbol of erotic love.
3. One of the duties of a squire, and also a sign of obedience and loyalty.
4. A superior grade of servant in a noble household.
5. A medal bearing the image of the patron saint of travelers.

He bore a horn, its baldric was of green;
A forester, he was, truly, as I guess.
    There was also a Nun, a PRIORESS,
Who in her smiling was simple and gracious;
Her greatest oath was "by Saint Eligius";[6]   120
And she was known as Madame Eglentine.[7]
Quite well she sang the liturgy divine,
Intoning it in her nose quite properly;
And French she spoke quite well and elegantly,
After the school of Stratford-at-the-Bow,[8]   125
Because Parisian French she did not know.
In dining, she was well taught overall;
She let no morsel down from her lips fall,
Nor wet her fingers in her sauce so deep;
Deftly she could lift up a bite, and keep   130
A single drop from falling on her breast.
In courtesy, she found what pleased her best.
Her upper lip she wiped so nice and clean
That in her cup no single speck was seen
Of grease, because she drank her drink so neat.   135
Quite daintily, she reached out for her meat.
And truthfully, she was so very pleasant,
And amiable, her manners excellent;
She pained herself to imitate the ways
Of court, and to be stately all her days,   140
And to be held worthy of reverence.
But, now, to speak about her conscience,
She was so full of pity and charity,
That she'd cry for a mouse that she might see
Caught in a trap, if it bled or was dead.   145
With her, she had her small hounds, which she fed
With roasted flesh, or milk and pure white bread.[9]
Sorely she wept if one of them were dead,
Or if men smote it so hard it would smart;
With her, all was conscience and tender heart.   150
Quite properly, her pleated wimple draped,
Her eyes blue gray as glass, her nose well-shaped,
Her mouth quite small, and also soft and red.
But, certainly, she had a fair forehead;
It was almost a span[1] in breadth, I own;   155
For, truth to tell, she was not undergrown.
Quite elegant, her cloak, I was aware.
Made of small corals on her arm she'd bear,
A rosary, set off with beads of green,
And thereon hung a broach of golden sheen,   160

---

6. The patron saint of goldsmiths, said to have been a remarkably attractive man.
7. The name of a kind of wild rose (more appropriate to a romance heroine than a nun).
8. A village 2 miles from London.

9. A diet enjoyed only by the wealthy; in this period, most ate black or brown bread, with little meat.
1. A handspan (a wide forehead was a sign of beauty).

On which the letter "A," inscribed and crowned
With "Amor vincit omnia"[2] was found.
    Another NUN riding with her had she,
Who was her secretary, and priests three.
    A MONK there was, the handsomest to see,   165
An outrider, who most loved venery,[3]
A manly man, to be an abbot able.
Many a striking horse had he in stable,
And when he rode, men might his bridle hear
Jingling in a whistling wind as clear   170
And just as loud as tolls the chapel bell
Of the house where he was keeper of the cell.
The rule of Saints Maurus and Benedict,[4]
Because it was so old and somewhat strict—
This same Monk let the old things pass away   175
And chose the new ways of the present day.
For that text he'd not give you one plucked hen
That said that hunters are not holy men,
Or that a monk who disobeys his order
Is likened to a fish out of the water—   180
That is to say, a monk out of the cloister.
But that text, he held not worth an oyster.
And I said his opinion was good.
What! Should he study, and make himself mad should
He, always poring over books in cloister,   185
Or should he work with his hands and labor
As Augustine bids?[5] How shall the world be served?
For Augustine, let this work be reserved!
A fine hard-pricking spursman he, all right;
He had greyhounds as swift as birds in flight;   190
In pricking and in hunting for the hare,
Lay all his lust; for no cost would he spare.
I saw his sleeves were fur lined at the hand
With rich, gray squirrel, the finest in the land;
And to fasten his hood beneath his chin,   195
He had, all wrought from gold, a fancy pin;
A love knot on the larger end was cast.
His head was bald, and it shone just like glass,
His face shone, too, as though he'd been anointed.
He was a lord full fat and well appointed;   200
His eyes rolled in his head and shone as bright
As fires under furnace pots, cast light;
His boots were supple, his horses strong and fit;
Now, certainly, he was a fair prelate;

2. "Love conquers all" (Latin).
3. Hunting; also, sexual pleasure (Latin, *veneria*). "Outrider": here, the monk whose duty was to look after the lands belonging to the monastery.
4. The founder (d. 547) of the Benedictine

order; Maurus was his (d. 584), his disciple, founded an abbey in France.
5. The rule of St. Augustine of Hippo (354–430), author of the *Confessions*, requires that monks engage in manual labor.

He was not pale like a tormented ghost.   205
A fat swan[6] loved he best of any roast.
His palfrey was as brown as is a berry.
    A FRIAR there was, a wanton one, and merry,
A limitor,[7] quite an important man.
In all four orders[8] is no one who can   210
Talk quite so smoothly, with such winning speech.
Many marriages made he in the breach
For young women and at his own expense.
In him, his order found a fine defense.
Quite well beloved and on close terms was he   215
With the franklins[9] all throughout his country,
And with all the town's most worthy women,
For he had the right to hear confession,
As he said, more than a curate surely,
For, by his order, he was licensed fully.   220
So, quite sweetly, would he hear confession,
And quite pleasant was his absolution:
He was an easy man in giving penance,
Where he knew he'd get more than a pittance.
If to a poor order one has given,   225
It's a sure sign that one's been well shriven;
If a man gave, he knew well what it meant:
He dared boast that this person would repent.
For many a man is just so hard of heart,
He may not weep, though he may sorely smart.   230
Therefore, instead of giving tears and prayers,
Men must yield up their silver to poor friars.
His hood's tip always was stuffed full of knives
And pins, for him to give out to fair wives.
Certainly his merry voice was pleasing: 235
And he could play the fiddle well and sing;
For ballads, he took first prize utterly.
His neck was white as is the fleur-de-lis.[1]
A strong champion was he in a brawl.
The taverns in each town, he knew them all;   240
Each innkeeper and every barmaid, too,
More than lepers[2] or beggar girls, he knew,
Because, for such a worthy man as he,
It would not do, with his ability,
With sick lepers to have an acquaintance.   245
It is not right; it hardly can advance
Him if he has to waste time with the poor,

---

6. An expensive and rare delicacy; ordinarily, monks abstained from eating meat.
7. A friar licensed to beg in a specific territory.
8. In the 14th century, Franciscans, Augustinians, Carmelites, and Dominicans. Friars, unlike monks, circulated among the people.
9. Upper-middle-class landowners, ranked below the gentry.
1. A lily (in heraldry, the royal arms of France).
2. Shunned through antiquity and the Middle Ages, but healed by Jesus (see Mark 1.40–45; Luke 17.11–19).

Just with the rich and victualers, for sure.
And over all, where profit should arise,
Polite was he, and served in humble guise.　250
No man was so effective anywhere:
He was, in his house, the best beggar there.
For private begging turf, he laid out rent;
None of his brothers came there where he went;
And although one were a shoeless widow,　255
So charming was his "In principio,"[3]
A farthing he would get before he went.
His income was much higher than his rent.
And he could rage just like a little whelp.
On love-days,[4] like a judge, well could he help,　260
For there, he was not like a cloisterer
In a threadbare cloak, like a poor scholar,
But like a master or the pope as well.
Of double worsted, rounded as a bell
Fresh from the casting, was his short, rich cloak.　265
With affection, he lisped when he spoke,
To make his English sweet upon his tongue;
In his harping, whenever he had sung,
His eyes would twinkle in his head as bright
As do the stars upon a frosty night.　270
This worthy limitor was named Huberd.

　　A MERCHANT was there, too, with a forked beard,
In mixed-hued clothes; high on his horse he sat;
Upon his head, a Flemish beaver hat,
And his fair boots were fastened stylishly.　275
He uttered his ideas quite solemnly,
Sounding always increase in his winning.
He wished the sea safe, more than anything,
Between the ports of Middleburgh and Orwell.[5]
Well could he in exchange his florins sell.[6]　280
This worthy man quite deftly used his wit:
Were he in debt, no one would know of it,
So stately was he in his management
Of borrowing, buying, selling where he went.
Surely, he was a worthy man, in all,　285
But, truth to say, I don't know what he's called.

　　A CLERK from Oxford[7] was with us also,
Whose work in logic started long ago.
As skinny was his horse as is a rake,
And he was not so fat, I undertake;　290
He looked hollow, and thus, grave and remote.

---

3. "In the beginning" (Latin), the opening words of the Vulgate translation of the Gospel of John, whose first fourteen verses were used by friars in devotions and in greetings.
4. Days when disputes were judged out of court.

5. Cities in the Netherlands and England, respectively.
6. I.e., he also profited in currency exchange. Florins were gold coins minted in Florence, Italy.
7. A student.

Quite threadbare was his outermost short coat;
He had as yet no clerical appointment,
And wasn't made for secular employment.
For he would rather have, at his bed's head,   295
Twenty books, all well bound in black or red,
Of Aristotle[8] and his philosophy
Than rich robes, or fiddle, or gay psaltery.
But, for all that he was a philosopher,
He had but little gold piled in his coffer;[9]   300
For, anything that his friends to him lent,
On books and on his learning, it got spent.
Busily, for the souls of them he prayed
Who, so that he could go to school, had paid.
Of his studies, he took most care and heed.   305
Not one word spoke he more than he had need,
And that was said with dignity and respect,
And short, and quick, and full of intellect;
Resounding in moral virtue was his speech,
And gladly would he learn, and gladly teach.   310
    A SERGEANT OF THE LAW,[1] wary and wise,
Who often in Saint Paul's court[2] did advise,
There was also, quite rich in excellence.
Dignified and judicious in each sense—
Or he seemed such, his words were all so wise.   315
He was often a judge at the assize,[3]
With full commission—and through royal consent.
For all his learning and his fame's extent,
Fees and robes, he did have, many a one.
So great a land buyer elsewhere was none: 320
He would directly buy up the estate;
His purchase, no one could invalidate.
Nowhere was such a busy man as he;
He seemed than he was, actually.
Busier he knew the precedents for everything   325
The law had done since William was the king.[4]
Fine legal texts, thus could he draft and draw
In which no one could find a single flaw;
Every statute, he could recite by rote.
He rode there in a simple mixed-hued coat.   330
A striped silk belt around his waist he wore;
About his dress, I won't tell any more.
    A FRANKLIN rode there in his company,
And his beard was as white as is the daisy;

8. The rediscovered works of Aristotle (384–
322 B.C.E.) were widely read and commented
on in medieval universities, especially his
works on logic and science.
9. A joke that relies on understanding "philosopher" as also meaning "alchemist" (one
who sought to create gold out of base metals).
1. A judge.

2. By St. Paul's Cathedral, a meeting place
for lawyers and their clients.
3. Circuit court, presided over by itinerant
judges.
4. I.e., since modern law was established by
William I, the Norman who conquered England in 1066.

His mood was sanguine,[5] his face rosy red.   335
Well loved he, in the morning, wine-soaked bread;
To live in sheer delight was his one care,
For he was Epicurus's[6] own heir,
Who thought to lead life in all its pleasure
Was true perfect bliss beyond all measure.   340
A householder, and a full great one, was he;
A Saint Julian[7] he was, in his country.
His bread, his ale, were always very fine;
No other man had better stocks of wine.
His house was never lacking in baked meat,   345
Or fish or flesh, in plenty so complete
That it snowed, in his house, with food and drink,
With any dainties of which men could think.
According to the seasons of the year,
New dishes on his table would appear.   350
Fat partridges in coops, when he did like;
He kept his fish pond stocked with bream and pike.
And woe unto his cook if he'd not got
His gear set and the sauce, spicy and hot.
Covered and ready did his table stay   355
Set up for meals within the hall all day.
At county courts, he was the lord and sire;
And went to Parliament to serve his shire.
A two-edged dagger and a purse of silk
Hung from his girdle, white as morning's milk.   360
A sheriff had he been, an auditor,[8]
And nowhere such a worthy landholder.
    A HABERDASHER and a CARPENTER,
A WEAVER, DYER, and a TAPESTRY MAKER—
They were all clothed in the same livery   365
Of one great parish guild fraternity.[9]
All fresh and newly furbished was their gear;
On their knives no brass mountings were found here,
But only silver; fashioned just as fit,
Their girdles and their purses, every bit.   370
Each of them seemed such a worthy burgess[1]
He might sit in the guildhall on the dais.
And each, with all the wisdom that he can,
Was suited to be made an alderman.
Income had they enough, and property,   375
To this their wives would certainly agree;
Or else, quite surely, they would all be blamed.
It is quite nice "My Lady" to be named,

---

5. In medieval physiology, the dominance of blood (one of the four bodily humors), indicated by his red face, was believed to explain a cheerful disposition.
6. Greek philosopher (340–270 B.C.E.), viewed in the Middle Ages as a proponent of hedonism.

7. The legendary patron saint of innkeepers.
8. An official responsible for verifying accounts.
9. A trade group whose purposes were social, religious, and economic.
1. Propertied citizen.

At feasts and vigils, to march first in line,
And have, borne royally, a mantel[2] fine.   380
     For this trip, a COOK rode with them then
To boil the marrowbones up with the hens,
Along with spices tart and galingale.[3]
Well did he know a draught of London ale.
He could both roast and simmer, boil and fry,   385
Make stews and hash and also bake a pie.
But it was a real shame, it seemed to me,
That on his shin, a pus-filled sore had he.
A milky pudding made he with the best.
     A SHIPMAN was there, who lived in the west;   390
He came from Dartmouth,[4] for all that I guessed.
To ride a packhorse he did try his best,
In a gown of coarse wool cloth cut to the knee.
A dagger hanging on a strap had he
Around his neck, under his arm coming down.   395
The hot summer had turned his skin all brown.
And certainly, he was a good fellow.
So many draughts of fine wine from Bordeaux[5]
Had he drawn, while the merchants were asleep.
In a good conscience, small stock did he keep.   400
If, when he fought, he had the upper hand,
He sent them all, by water, back to land.
But in the art of reckoning the tides,
The currents and all perils near, besides,
The moon and piloting and anchorage,   405
No one was so skilled from Hull to Carthage.[6]
Hardy and wise in what was undertaken,
With many tempests had his beard been shaken.
He knew well all the harbors that there were,
Stretching from Gotland to Cape Finisterre,[7]   410
And each inlet from Brittany to Spain;
His sailing ship was called the "Magdalene."[8]
     With us was a DOCTOR OF MEDICINE;
No one was like him, all the world within,
To speak of medicine and surgery,   415
For he was schooled well in astrology.
Through natural magic,[9] he gave patients hope
By keeping close watch on their horoscope.
He could divine when planets were ascendant

---

2. I.e., a mantle (Chaucer's spelling, now obsolete).
3. Aromatic root, also used as a powder.
4. Port on the southwest coast of England.
5. A center of the wine trade, in southwest France.
6. I.e., from northern England to North Africa (Carthage) or Spain (Cartagena; Chaucer has "Cartage"); the Shipman is widely traveled.
7. From an island off the coast of Sweden to the west coast of Spain.
8. Named after Mary Magdalen, Jesus' disciple; according to a French tradition, she, her brother Lazarus, and some companions came to the port city of Marseille in the south of France and converted all of Provence.
9. As opposed to black magic.

To aid the star signs governing his patient.   420
Of every malady, he knew the source
In humors hot, cold, moist, or dry, of course,
And where they were engendered, from which humor.[1]
He was a perfect, true practitioner.
The cause and root known of the malady,   425
At once he gave the sick their remedy.
Quite ready had he his apothecaries
To send him their drugs and electuaries,[2]
For each made profit for the other one—
Their friendship had not recently begun.   430
Well knew he his old Aesculapius,[3]
Dioscorides, and also Rufus,
Old Hippocrates, Hali, and Galen,
Rhazes, Avicenna, Serapion,
Averroës, Damascien, Constantinus,   435
Bernard, Gaddesden, Gilbertus Anglicus.
Of his own diet, moderate was he,
For it contained no superfluity,
But was nourishing and digestible.
His study was but little on the Bible.   440
In blood red and in blue he was all clad,
A lining of two kinds of silk he had.
Yet he was quite cautious with expenses;
He saved what he earned in pestilences.
In medicine, gold[4] works well for the heart,   445
Therefore, he'd loved gold from the very start.

 A good WIFE was there from nearby to BATH;
It was a pity she was deaf by half.
In cloth-making she had such a talent
She far passed those from Ypres and from Ghent.[5]   450
And throughout all her parish, there was no
Wife who might first to the offering go
Before her; if one did, so mad was she
That she lost any sense of charity.
Her coverchiefs of fine linen were found;   455
I dare swear that they weighed a full ten pounds,
The ones that, Sundays, sat upon her head.
Her stockings were all fine and scarlet red,
Quite tightly laced, her shoes quite soft and new.[6]
Bold was her face, and fair, and red of hue.   460
Worthy she was as any woman alive,
Husbands at the church door, she had had five,

---

1. According to humoral physiology, illness was caused by imbalance in the four humors— the different combinations of the four qualities (hot, cold, moist, dry).
2. Medicinal pastes.
3. Greek god of healing. The list that follows names medical authors from ancient Greece, the Arabic world (including Avicenna), and medieval England (John of Gaddesden [d. 1348/49] and Gilbert the Englishman [d. ca. 1250]).
4. Used as a medicine in the Middle Ages.
5. Two cities in Flanders (modern Belgium) renowned for cloth production.
6. I.e., of good quality, supple leather.

Not counting other company in youth—
No need to speak of that now, to tell the truth.
And thrice she had been to Jerusalem;[7]   465
Many a foreign sea, she'd covered them;
At Rome she'd been, and also at Boulogne,
At Saint James in Galicia and Cologne.
She knew much of wandering by the way.
Gap toothed[8] she was, it is the truth to say.   470
On her ambling horse, quite easily she sat,
Wearing a wimpled headdress and a hat
Like a buckler or a shield as broad and round;
A foot-mantle about her large hips wound,
And on her feet a pair of sharp spurs poked.   475
In fellowship, quite well she laughed and joked.
The remedies of love she knew by heart,
For of that old dance, she knew all the art.

    A good man was there of religion,
Of a town, he served as the poor PARSON.   480
But he was rich in holy thought and work.
He was also a learned man, a clerk,
And Christ's gospel truthfully he would preach;
His parishioners devoutly he would teach.
Gracious he was, a wonder of diligence,   485
And in adversity, he had such patience,
And in this, he had often tested been.
For tithes, he found it loathsome to curse men,
But he would rather give, there is no doubt,
To his poor parishioners, round about,   490
From Mass offerings and his own pay, too.
With little, he could easily make do.
Wide was his parish, the houses far asunder,
But he would not leave them, for rain or thunder,
If sickness or if trouble should befall   495
The farthest in his parish, great or small,
He'd go on foot; his staff in hand he'd keep.
This noble example he gave to his sheep:
That first he wrought, and afterward, he taught.
Out of the Gospels, those words he had caught,   500
And his own metaphor he added, too:
If gold should rust, then what will iron do?
For if a priest is foul, in whom we trust,
No wonder that a foolish man should rust;
And it's a shame, if care he does not keep—   505
A shepherd to be shitty with clean sheep.
Well should a priest a good example give,
By his own cleanness, how his sheep should live.

7. The major pilgrimage site for medieval Christians; lesser popular pilgrimage sites—in Italy, France, Spain, and Germany, respectively—follow.

8. According to medieval lore, a sign of a tendency to wander, associated especially with sexual excess.

His parish, he would not put out for hire
And leave his sheep encumbered in the mire   510
To run to London to Saint Paul's[9] to switch
And be a chantry priest[1] just for the rich,
Nor by guild brothers would he be detained;[2]
But he stayed home and with his flock remained,
So that the wolf would not make it miscarry;   515
He was a shepherd, not a mercenary.
And though he holy was, and virtuous,
To sinners, he was not contemptuous,
Nor haughty nor aloof was he in speech,
With courtesy and kindness would he teach.   520
To draw folks up to heaven with his fairness,
By good example: this was all his business.
But if there were a person who was stubborn,
Whoever he was, high or low rank born,
Then he would scold him sharply, at the least.   525
There is nowhere, I know, a better priest.
He expected no pomp or reverence;
For him, no finicky, affected conscience,
But the words of Christ and his apostles twelve
He taught: but first, he followed them himself.   530
        With him, his brother who was a PLOWMAN rode;
Of dung, this man had hauled out many a load;
A true laborer, and a good one was he,
Living in peace and perfect charity.
God loved he best with all of his whole heart   535
At all times, though it caused him joy or smart,
And next, his neighbor, just as he loved himself.
He would thresh, dig ditches, and also delve,
For Christ's sake and the sake of each poor man,
And without pay, he'd do all that he can.   540
His tithes, with all due fairness, he'd not shirk,
But paid from what he owned and with his work.
In a workman's smock, he rode on a mare.
        A REEVE and a MILLER were also there,
A SUMMONER and then a PARDONER,   545
A MAN and myself—that's all there were.
        The MILLER was a stout churl, it is true;
Quite big he was in brawn, and in bones, too.
That stood him in good stead; for where he came,
He'd win the ram[3] in every wrestling game.   550
He was short necked and broad, a thick-thewed thug;
There was no door around he couldn't lug
Right off its hinges, or break with his head.

---

9. The largest cathedral in medieval England.
1. A priest supported by an endowment to say daily mass for the souls of particular individuals (usually wealthy men or their family members).

2. I.e., he would not take the lucrative position of priest for a guild.
3. I.e., the prize for the winner of a village wrestling contest.

His beard, just like a sow or fox, was red,[4]
And also broad, as though it was a spade.   555
Right up atop his nose's ridge was laid
A wart; on it, a tuft of hairs grew now,
Red as the bristles in ears of a sow;
His nostrils were quite black, and also wide.
A sword and buckler bore he by his side.   560
His mouth was as great as a great cauldron.
A jangling goliard, he was quite the one—
Of sin and harlotries, he most would tell.
He made three times his pay and stole corn well;
And yet, he had a thumb of gold, all right.[5]   565
A blue hood wore he, and a coat of white.
A bagpipe he knew how to blow and play.
And sounding it, he led us on our way.

    A good MANCIPLE[6] did business for a law school;
All food buyers could follow well his rule   570
For prudent buying; it would earn them merit;
For, whether he paid straight or took on credit,
In buying, he watched carefully and waited,
So he was in good shape and well ahead.
Now, is it not from God a sign of grace   575
That this unlearned man's wit can outpace
The wisdom of a heap of learned men?
Of his masters, he had more than thrice ten,
Who were quite skilled and expert in the law,
And in that house, a full dozen one saw   580
Worthy to be stewards of rents and land
For any lord who dwells now in England,
To make him live within the means he had
In debtless honor (unless he were mad),
Or as frugally as he could desire,   585
And able thus to help out all the shire
In any circumstance that may befall:
And yet this Manciple hoodwinked them all.

    The REEVE was a slender, choleric[7] man.
He shaved his beard as closely as one can;   590
His hair, short and up by his ears, he'd crop,
And, like a priest's, he'd dock it on the top.
Quite long his legs were; they were also lean,
And just like sticks; no calf was to be seen.
He could well guard the granary and bin;   595

---

4. His coloration, together with the description of his nostrils and mouth, would suggest to medieval readers a temperament given to strong displays of temper or rage.

5. "An honest miller has a golden thumb" was a proverb expressing the general belief that all millers were dishonest (either because no such miller existed or because millers cheated their customers with a heavy thumb on the scale).

6. Agent responsible for buying supplies and paying bills, especially for a college or monastery.

7. Dominated by choler, the humor associated with irascibility. "Reeve": farm or estate manager.

No auditor around could with him win.
He knew well, by the drought and by the rain,
The yieldings of his seed and of his grain.
His lord's sheep, his cattle, and his dairy,
His swine and horses, his livestock and poultry   600
Were wholly under this Reeve's governing,
And by his contract, he gave reckoning,
Because his lord, in age, was twenty years.
No man alive could bring him in arrears.[8]
No bailiff, herdsman, worker there might be   605
But he knew all their tricks and treachery;
As they feared death, of him they were all scared.
His dwelling place upon a heath was fair;
All shaded with green trees on every hand.
He could, much better than his lord, buy land.   610
Quite richly had he stocked up, privately.
And he could please his lord so cleverly
That he'd lend to him from his lord's own goods,
And have his thanks, then, plus a coat and hood.
When he was young, he had learned a fine trade,   615
A good wright, a skilled carpenter he made.
The Reeve on his stout farm horse sat that day,
Which was called Scot and was a dapple gray.
His overcoat was long, of darkish blue,
And by his side, a rusty blade hung, too.   620
From Norfolk[9] was this Reeve, of whom I tell,
From near a town that men call Baldeswell.
Like a friar's, he tucked his coat up fast.
In our company, he always rode the last.
    A SUMMONER[1] was with us in that place,   625
Who had a fiery-red cherubic face,
Pimply was he, with eyes swollen and narrow.
Hot he was and lecherous as a sparrow,[2]
With scabbed black brows; his beard had lost some hair.
And of his visage, children were quite scared.   630
Not lead monoxide, mercury, or sulphur,
Not borax, white lead, or cream of tartar—
No single ointment that would cleanse or bite—
Could help him to remove those pustules white,
Nor cure the pimples sitting on his cheeks.   635
Well loved he garlic, onions, also leeks,[3]
And drinking blood red wine, strongly fermented;
Then he would speak and cry as though demented.
And when of this good wine he'd drunk his fill,

---

8. I.e., convict him of having unpaid debts.
9. County northeast of London.
1. An officer of the ecclesiastical courts who served summonses to individuals charged with offenses against canon law.
2. A proverbially lecherous bird; this behavior is a manifestation of the Summoner's "hot" temperament.
3. These foods, according to medieval medicine, would increase the heat of the body and thus also cause lust, outbursts of fury, and outbreaks of the skin.

No words but Latin from his mouth would spill.   640
A few such terms he knew, like two or three,
That he had learned by hearing some decree—
It's no wonder, for he heard it all day;
And thus you know full well how any jay[4]
Can call out "Walter" as well as the pope.   645
But whoever might on other matters grope,
Then his philosophy was spent thereby;
Always, "Questio quid iuris,"[5] cry would he.
He was a noble rascal in his kind;
A better fellow men would never find.   650
And he would suffer, for a quart of wine,
A good fellow to have his concubine
A full year, and excuse him thus completely;
For he himself could pluck a finch[6] discreetly.
If he found a good fellow anywhere,   655
Then he would quickly teach to him that there
Was no need to fear archdeacons' curses,[7]
Unless men's souls were found in their purses;
For in their purses, they will punished be.
"The purse is the archdeacon's hell," said he.   660
He downright lied, I know, in what he said;
Excommunication guilty men should dread.
Absolving saves, but cursing slays indeed;
Of *Significavit*,[8] men should well take heed.
Under his thumb, he had, as it did please   665
Him, the young girls there of the diocese;
He counseled all who told him things in secret.
A garland he had fashioned and then set,
Big as an ale-house sign, upon his head.
He'd made a buckler from a loaf of bread.   670
     With him, there rode a gentle PARDONER
Of Roncevalles,[9] and good, close friends they were.
He'd come straight from the papal court at Rome,
And loudly sang, "Come hither, love, to me!"
With a stiff bass, the Summoner sang along;   675
No trumpet's sound was ever half so strong.
This Pardoner had hair yellow as wax,
But smooth it hung as does a hank of flax;
In skinny strands, the locks hung from his head,
And with them, he his shoulders overspread;   680
But thin it lay; its strands hung one by one.
For stylishness, a hood he would wear none,

---

4. A popinjay, or parrot.
5. "The question [is], what [point] of law [applies]" (Latin); a phrase familiar to the Summoner from the ecclesiastical courts.
6. To trick or blackmail; to have sexual relations.
7. I.e., excommunication.

8. Literally, "he has signified" (Latin): the writ issued for the arrest of an excommunicated person.
9. A church-affiliated hospital in London, supported in part by the sale of pardons—papal indulgences purchased to shorten the time spent by souls in purgatory.

Since it was trussed up within his wallet.
He thought he wore the latest fashions yet;
With loose hair, his head save for his cap, was bare.   685
Such staring eyes he had, just like a hare.
A veronica[1] he'd sewn on his cap.
His wallet lay before him in his lap,
With pardons hot from Rome stuffed to the brim.
A voice high as a goat's came out of him.   690
No beard had he, nor should he wait for one;
His face smooth like his shaving'd just been done.
I think he was a gelding or a mare.
But, in his craft, from Berwick down to Ware,[2]
No pardoner like him in all the land.   695
In his bag was a pillowcase on hand,
And he declared it was Our Lady's[3] veil;
He said he had a big piece of the sail
Saint Peter used upon his boat when he,
Before Christ took him, had gone out to sea.   700
He had a fake gold cross bedecked with stones,
A glass he had that carried some pig bones.[4]
But with these relics, whenever he spied
A poor parson out in the countryside,
On that day, much more money would he make   705
Than, in two months, the poor parson might take;
And thus, with his feigned flattery and japes,
He made the parson and people his apes.
But to tell the whole truth, now, finally,
In church, a noble ecclesiastic, he.   710
Well could he read a lesson or a story,
But best of all, he sang the offertory;
For well he knew, when that song had been sung,
Then he must preach and smoothly file his tongue
To win his silver, as quite well could he;   715
Therefore, he sang quite loud and merrily.
     Now, I have told you truly, in a clause,
The rank, the dress, the number, and the cause
That brought together all this company
In Southwark, at this noble hostelry   720
That's called the Tabard, next door to the Bell.
But now it's time that to you I should tell
How that we all behaved on that same night
When we should in that hostelry alight;
Afterward, I will tell of our voyage   725

---

1. A reproduction of Jesus' features, as were said to have been miraculously impressed on the cloth offered to him by St. Veronica on his way to his crucifixion. The veronica was also a key point of reference for medieval artists who wished to claim a divine origin for their craft.

2. I.e., from northernmost England to the south.
3. The Virgin Mary.
4. The Pardoner has a variety of false saints' relics; such relics were believed to possess the saints' spiritual power and thus found eager buyers.

And all the rest about our pilgrimage.
But first I pray you, by your courtesy,
That you not blame my own vulgarity,
Although I might speak plainly in this matter,
When I tell you their words and their demeanor,   730
Or if I speak their words, exact and true.
For this you all know just as well as I do:
Whoever tells a tale after a man,
He must repeat, as closely as he can,
Every last word, if that is his duty,   735
Even if he has to speak quite rudely,
Or otherwise, he makes his tale untrue,
Or makes things up, or finds words that are new.
He may not spare, though that man were his brother;
He might as well say one word as another.   740
Christ himself plainly spoke in Holy Writ,
You know no vulgarity is in it.
And Plato says, whoever can him read,
That words must be the cousin to the deed.[5]
Also, I pray you that you will forgive me   745
Although I've not ranked folks by their degree
Here in this tale, the way that they should stand.
My wit is short, you may well understand.
         Our Host put us at ease with his great cheer;
At once, he set up supper for us here.   750
He served us all with victuals that were fine;
It pleased us well to drink his good, strong wine.
An impressive man our HOST was, all in all;
He could have been a marshal in a hall.
A large man he, with eyes both bright and wide—   755
No fairer burgess anywhere in Cheapside[6]—
Bold in his speech, and wise, and quite well taught.
And in his manhood, he did lack for naught.
Moreover, he was quite a merry man;
After supper, to amuse us, he began,   760
And spoke of pleasure, among other things,
When we had settled up our reckonings.
He then said thus: "Now, my good lords, truly,
To me, you are quite welcome, heartily;
For, by my word, if that I shall not lie,   765
So merry a company, this whole year, I
Have not seen in this inn, as I see now.
I'd gladly make you happy, knew I how.
I've just thought what would be entertaining;
It'd please you, and it wouldn't cost a thing.   770
         You go to Canterbury—bless the Lord,

5. Apparently an allusion to Plato's *Timaeus* 29B, borrowed by Chaucer from Boethius's *Consolation of Philosophy* (ca. 525 C.E.) or from the *Roman de la Rose* (ca. 1275).
6. A major business district in London.

May the blissful martyr pay you your reward!
I know well, as you travel by the way,
You all intend to tell tales and to play;
For truly, comfort and mirth both have flown   775
If you ride on the way dumb as a stone;
Now, I know a way I can divert you,
As I have said, and give you comfort, too.
And if it pleases you to give assent
So you all agree to trust my judgment,   780
And to do according to what I say,
Tomorrow, when you all ride by the way,
Now, by the soul of my father who is dead,
Unless you're merry, I'll give you my head!
Hold up your hands, now, without further speech."   785
    All our assent took not long to beseech.
It did not seem worthwhile to make a fuss,
For we did not need more time to discuss,
And we told him to give his verdict then.
"My lords," said he, "this plan is best. Now, listen.   790
But take it not, I pray you, with disdain.
This is the point, to speak now, short and plain:
Each one of you, to help shorten our way,
Along this journey, two tales you will say,
Toward Canterbury, as I mean you to,   795
And homeward, you'll tell us another two,
Of adventures that in old times did befall.
The one who bears himself the best of all—
That is to say, the one of you who might
Tell tales that have most meaning and delight—   800
Shall have a supper paid for by us all,
Sitting right near this post here in this hall,
When we all come again from Canterbury.
And to make you all even more merry,
I will myself quite gladly with you ride,   805
Right at my own expense, and be your guide.
Whoever will my judgment now gainsay
Shall pay for all we spend along the way.
If it be so, and all of you agree,
Without more words, at once, now you tell me,   810
And I'll make myself ready long before."
    This thing was granted, and our oaths we swore
With quite glad hearts, and we prayed him also
That he fully would agree to do so,
And that he would become our governor,   815
And of our tales, the judge and record keeper,
And set the supper at a certain price,
And we would all be ruled by his advice
In all respects; and thus, with one assent
We were all accorded with his judgment.   820

And thereupon, the wine was fetched in fast;
We drank, and to our rest we went at last,
Without us any longer tarrying.
    In the morning, as day began to spring,
Up rose our Host, and was, for us, the cock,   825
And gathered us together in a flock;
With slow gait, we started on our riding,
Till we came to Saint Thomas's Watering;[7]
And there, our Host began to stop his horse
And said, "My lords, listen—if you please, of course.   830
Let me remind you that you gave your word.
If evening-song and morning-song accord,[8]
Let see now who shall tell us the first tale.
As ever may I drink of wine or ale,
Whoso now rebels against my judgment   835
Shall pay for all that by the way is spent.
Now let's draw straws, and then we shall depart;
Whoever has the shortest straw will start.
Sir Knight, my master and my lord," he said,
"Now you draw first, for thus I have decided.   840
Come near," said he, "my lady Prioress.
And you, sir Clerk, leave off your bashfulness.
Don't study now. Lay hands to, every man!"
At once, to draw straws, everyone began;
To quickly tell the way it did advance,   845
Were it by fortune or by luck or chance,
The truth is this: the draw fell to the Knight,
For which we were quite glad, as it was right;
By agreement and arrangement, now he must
Tell us his tale, as it was only just,   850
As you have heard; what more words need be spent?
And when this good man saw the way it went,
Because he wise was, and obedient
To keep the word he gave by free assent,
He said, "Now, since I shall begin the game,   855
What, welcome is this straw, in the Lord's name!
Now, let us ride, and hearken what I say."
And with that word, we rode forth on our way,
And he began with then a merry cheer
His tale at once, and said as you may hear.   860

---

7. A spring dedicated to St. Thomas (not far from the inn).

8. I.e., if your intention at night matches what you promised in the morning.

The Wife of Bath's Prologue and Tale

The Wife of Bath's Prologue

"Experience, though no authority
Were in this world, is right enough for me
To speak of the woe that is in marriage;
For, my lords, since I was twelve years of age,[1]
Thanks be to God, eternally alive,   5
Husbands at the church door, I have had five—
If quite so often I might wedded be—
And all were worthy men in their degree.
But it was told me not so long ago,[2]
That since just once our Christ did ever go   10
To a wedding, in Cana in Galilea,[3]
That by that same example, he taught me
That only one time I should wedded be.
Lo, listen, what a sharp word then spoke he,
Beside a well when Jesus, God and man,   15
Spoke in reproof of the Samaritan:[4]
"Thou hast had five husbands,' then said he,
'And that same man here who now hath thee
Is not thy husband,' said he by the well.
But what he meant thereby, I cannot tell;   20
Except I ask, why is it the fifth man
Was not husband to the Samaritan?
How many might she have in marriage?
Yet I've never heard tell, in all my age,
About this, any number definite.   25
Up and down, men gloss[5] and guess about it,
But well I know, expressly, it's no lie,
That God bade us to wax and multiply;[6]
This gentle text, I can well understand.
Also, well I know, he said my husband   30
Should leave mother and father and cleave to me.[7]
But of no number a mention made he,
Of bigamy, or of octogamy;[8]
Why then should men speak of it villainy?
    Lo, here is the wise king, Don[9] Solomon;   35
I think he had some wives, well more than one.
Now would to God it lawful were for me

---

1. The minimum age of marriage, in canon law.
2. Many of the biblical sources cited by the Wife of Bath in the argument that follows can be found in St. Jerome's *Adversus Jovinianum* (392 C.E.), a polemical diatribe that is highly critical of both women and marriage.
3. See John 2.2.
4. A woman from Samaria (see John 4.7–18).
5. Interpret.

6. Genesis 1.28.
7. Genesis 2.24.
8. Marriage to two or to eight. Usually, *bigamy* involves concurrent marriages (as below, in references to biblical figures), but the Wife of Bath often instead means consecutive marriages.
9. Master. The biblical king Solomon was proverbially renowned for his great wisdom and for his hundreds of wives and concubines (see 1 Kings 11.3).

To be refreshed here half so much as he!
A gift from God had he with all his wives!
No man has such a gift who's now alive.   40
This noble king, God knows, as I would judge it,
That first night had many a merry fit
With each of them, so well was he alive.
Blessèd be God that I have wedded five!
Of whom I have picked out the very best,   45
For both their nether purse[1] and money chest.
Different schools can turn out perfect clerks,
And different practices in sundry works
Make the workman perfect, it's no lie;
From my five husbands, studying am I.   50
Welcome the sixth, when he shall come along.
In truth, I won't keep chaste for very long.
And when my husband from this world has passed,
Another Christian man will wed me fast;
Then the apostle[2] says that I am free   55
To wed, by God, where it most pleases me.
He says to be wedded is not sinning;
Better to be wedded than be burning.
What do I care if folks speak villainy
About accursed Lamech's bigamy?[3]   60
Abraham was a holy man, I know;
And as I understand it, Jacob also;
And each of them had wives now, more than one,
As many other holy men have done.
Where, can you say, in any kind of age,   65
That our high God has forbidden marriage
Expressly, in a word? I pray, tell me.
Or where did he command virginity?
I know as well as you, or else you should,
The apostle, when he speaks of maidenhood,   70
Said that a precept for it he had none.[4]
Men may counsel a woman to be one,
But counseling does not make a commandment.
All of it left to our own judgment;
For if our God commanded maidenhood,   75
Then wedding with the deed, he'd damn for good.
And surely, if no seed were ever sown,
From what, then, would virginity be grown?
And at the least, Paul never dared demand
Something his own Master won't command.   80
The prize is set up for virginity;
Catch it who may; who runs the best, let's see.
　　　To everyone, this word does not apply,

---

1. I.e., scrotum.
2. St. Paul; see 1 Corinthians 7.39, 9.
3. See Genesis 4.19. Lamech (cursed as a murderer) is the first man in the Bible said to

have had more than one wife (or a wife and a concubine) at the same time, but he was hardly the last, as the Wife of Bath points out.
4. 1 Corinthians 7.25.

But only where God's might wants it to lie.
I know the apostle was a virgin;   85
Nonetheless, although he wrote and said then
He wished that everyone was such as he,
This is but counsel to virginity.[5]
He gave me leave to be a wife, all the same,
With his permission, so it is no shame,   90
If my mate dies, to go then and wed me,
Without objections about bigamy.
Though it may be good not to touch women[6]—
In his bed or on his couch, he meant then—
Fire and flax together make peril so—   95
What this example resembles, you all know.
The sum is this: he held virginity
More perfect than to wed from frailty.
Frailty I call it, unless he and she
Wished to lead all their lives in chastity.   100
      I grant it well that I have no envy,
Though maidenhood's preferred to bigamy.
To be clean pleases them, body and spirit;
Of my state, I make no boast about it,
For you well know, a lord in his household,   105
He has not every vessel made of gold;[7]
Some come from wood, and serve their lord withal.
In sundry ways, folks to him God does call,
Each has God's special gift while he must live,
Some this, some that, it pleases God to give.[8]   110
      Virginity thus is great perfection,
And also continence spurred by devotion,
But Christ, who of perfection is the well,
Bade not that every person should go sell
All that he has and give it to the poor,   115
And follow in his footsteps thus, for sure.
He spoke to those who would live perfectly,[9]
And my lords, by your leave, that is not me.
I will bestow the flower of my life
In married acts and fruits, and be a wife.   120
      Tell me, for what purpose and conclusion
Were the members[1] made for generation,
And by so perfectly wise a maker wrought?
Trust it well now: they were not made for nought.
Say what you will, or hedge it by glossing,   125
That they were made simply for the purging
Of urine; and both our small things also
Were made so male from female we could know,
And for no other cause—do you say no?
Experience well knows it is not so.   130

5. 1 Corinthians 7.8.   8. See 1 Corinthians 7.7.
6. 1 Corinthians 7.1.   9. See Matthew 19.21.
7. See 2 Timothy 2.20.   1. I.e., sexual organs.

So the clerks will not be angry at me,
They were made for both: I say this truly.
That is, to do our business and for ease
In engendering, where God we don't displease.
Why should men otherwise in their books set   135
It down that man should yield his wife her debt?[2]
Now how to her should he make his payment,
Unless he'd used his silly[3] instrument?
Thus, they were bestowed upon a creature
To purge urine, and so we could engender.   140
     But I don't say that each one's obligated,
Who has the harness that I've just related,
To go and use it for engendering.
Then for chastity, men wouldn't care a thing.
Christ was a maiden and shaped like a man,   145
And many saints, since first the world began;
They lived forever in perfect chastity.
I won't envy any virginity.
Let them be bread of wheat that's been refined,
As barley bread, let us wives be defined;   150
And yet, with barley bread, as Mark can tell,
Our Lord has refreshed many men quite well.[4]
In whatever rank God's called to us,
I'll persevere; I'm not fastidious.
In wifehood, I will use my instrument   155
As freely as my Maker has it sent.
If I'm aloof, then God send me dismay!
My husband can well have it, night and day,
When it pleases him to come and pay his debt.
A husband I will have—I won't stop yet—   160
Who shall be both my debtor and my slave,
With tribulation, unless he behaves,
Upon his flesh while I may be his wife.
I have the power, during all my life
Over his own body, and not he.   165
Thus the Apostle has told this to me,
And bade our husbands they should love us well.[5]
This meaning, I like more than I can tell"—
     Up the Pardoner starts, immediately;
"Now, Madame, by God and Saint John," said he,   170
"You are a noble preacher on this strife.
Alas! I was about to wed a wife.
Why on my flesh now pay a price so dear?
I'd rather not wed any wife this year!"
     "Just wait! My tale is not begun," said she.   175
"No, you'll drink from another cask, you'll see,
Before I go, that will taste worse than ale.

---

2. The marital debt, mutually owed; see 1 Corinthians 7.3–4.
3. Innocent.

4. See not Mark but John 6.9–13.
5. Ephesians 5.25.

And when I will have told you all my tale
Of the tribulation that's in marriage—
About which I'm an expert in my age—   180
That is to say that I have been the whip—
Then you can choose if you might want to sip
Out of the cask that I will open here.
Beware of it, before you come too near;
For I shall give examples, more than ten.   185
'Whoever won't be warned by other men,
By him will other men corrected be.'
Those same words were written by Ptolemy;[6]
Read his *Almageste,* and there you'll find it still."
    "Madame, I pray you, if it be your will,"   190
Said this Pardoner, "now as you began,
Tell forth your tale, and don't spare any man;
Teach us young men all about your practice."
    "Gladly," said she, "since you might well like this;
But yet I pray to all this company,   195
If I speak after my own fantasy,
Do not be aggrieved by what I say,
For my intent is only now to play.
    And now, sir, now I'll tell on with my tale.
As ever I might drink of wine or ale,   200
I'll tell the truth; those husbands that I had,
Some three of them were good, and two were bad.
The three who were good men were rich and old;
And so they barely could the statute hold
Through which they all had bound themselves to me.   205
By God, you know what I mean, certainly!
So help me God, I laugh to remember
How pitifully at night I made them labor!
In faith, I set no store by their pleasure.
To me, they had given land and treasure;   210
No longer need I use my diligence
To win their love or do them reverence.
They loved me so well that, by God above,
I set no value then upon their love!
A wise woman will be the busy one   215
To get herself love, yes, where she has none.
But since I had them wholly in my hand,
And since to me they'd given all their land,
Why should I take care that I should them please
Unless it were for my profit and my ease?   220
I set them so to hard work, by my lights,
That they sung "Wey-la-way!" on many nights.
I don't think the bacon was meant for them now

---

6. Greek astronomer and mathematician (2nd century C.E.); his textbook, the *Almagest*, dominated astronomy for more than a thousand years; a preface containing proverbial wisdom attributed to Ptolemy was later added to the text.

That some men win in Essex at Dunmow.[7]
I governed them so well, after my law,   225
That each of them was eager, as I saw,
To bring me home some gay things from the fair.
They were glad when my speech to them was fair;
I scolded them, as God knows, spitefully.
    Now, listen how I acted properly,   230
You wise wives, who can so well understand.
Thus should you accuse falsely, out of hand.
For half so boldly knows no living man
How to swear and lie just as a woman can.
This statement about wise wives, I don't make—   235
Unless it be when they've made some mistake.
A wise wife, who knows what's good for her,
Will swear the tattling crow is mad for sure,[8]
And make sure that her maid has assented
As her witness. But hear now what I said: 240
    'Sir old dotard, is this your array?
Why is it that my neighbor's wife's so gay?
She is honored everywhere she goes;
I sit at home; I have no decent clothes.
What do you do at my neighbor's house there?   245
Are you so amorous? Is she so fair?
What do you whisper to our maid? Bless me!
Sir old lecher, now let your jokes be!
If, without guilt, I have a chum or friend,
Just like a fiend, you scold me without end   250
If I should play or walk down to his house!
But you come home as drunken as a mouse,
And then preach from your bench, no proof from you!
And it's great mischief, as you tell me too,
A poor woman to wed, for the expense;   255
If she's rich and born to lofty parents,
Then you say that a torment it will be
To bear her pride and sullen melancholy.
And if she should be fair, you horrid cur,
You say every lecher soon will have her;   260
For she can't long in chastity abide,
Who is always assailed on every side.
    You say some folk want us for our richness,
Some for our figure, and some for our fairness,
Some because she can either dance or sing,   265
Some for gentility and socializing;
And some because their hands and arms are small;
By your lights, to the devil thus goes all.
You say men cannot defend a castle wall
When it's so long assailed by large and small.   270

---

7. A village ca. 35 miles northeast of London. In the 13th century, the custom began of awarding a side of bacon to the couple who swore not to have quarreled or regretted their marriage during the first year after their wedding.
8. The talking bird who reveals a wife's infidelity by repeating words it has heard is a common motif in folktales.

And if she should be ugly, you say she
Will covet every man that she may see,
For like a spaniel, she will on him leap
Until she finds a man to buy her cheap.
No goose goes out there on the lake so gray   275
That she will be without a mate, you say.
You say it's hard for men to have controlled
A thing that no man willingly would hold.
Thus you say, scoundrel, when you go to bed,
That no wise man has any need to wed,   280
Nor one who toward heaven would aspire.
With wild thunder claps and lightning's fire
May your old withered neck break right in two!

    You say that leaky houses, and smoke too,
And scolding wives all cause a man to flee   285
Out of his own house; ah now, God bless me!
What can ail such an old man, who must chide?
You say that we wives will our vices hide
Till we're hitched, and then we show them to you—
Well may that be the proverb of a shrew!   290

    You say horses, hounds, asses, and oxen
At different times can be tried out by men;
Wash bowls and basins, spoons and stools, you say,
All household things men try before they pay;
The same thing goes for clothes and gear and pots;   295
But to try out a wife, a man may not
Till they are wedded—you old dotard shrew!—
And then we show our vices, so say you.

    You say also that it displeases me
Unless you will always praise my beauty,   300
Or else always pour over my face,
And call me "Fair Madame" in every place.
Unless you make a feast upon the day
That I was born, and dress me fresh and gay;
Unless to my nurse, you do all honor,   305
And to the chambermaid within my bower,[9]
And to my father's folk and kin all day—
Old barrelful of lies, all this you say!

    Yet of Jenkin, who is our apprentice,
Whose curly hair shines just like gold—for this,   310
And because he will squire me around,
A cause for false suspicions, you have found.
I don't want him, though you should die tomorrow!

    Tell me: why do you hide, to my sorrow,
The keys now of your chest[1] away from me?   315
They are my goods as well as yours, bless me!
Will you make an idiot of your dame?
Now, by that good lord who is called Saint James,
You will not, though it might make you crazy,
Be master of both my goods and body;   320

9. Bedroom.   1. Strongbox.

One of them you'll forgo, to spite your eyes.
What good is it to ask around and spy?
I think you want to lock me in your chest!
You should say, 'Wife, go where you think is best;
Enjoy yourself; I'll believe no tales of this.   325
I know you for my own true wife, Dame Alice.'
We love no man who will take heed or charge
Of where we go; we want to be at large.
      And of all men, quite blessèd must he be,
That wise astrologer, Don Ptolemy,   330
Who says this proverb in his *Almageste*,
'Of all men, his wisdom is the highest
Who never cares who holds the world in hand.'
By this proverb, you should well understand,
If you have enough, why then should you care   335
How merrily some other folks might fare?
For certainly, old dotard, by your leave,
You'll have some quaint things sure enough come eve.
He is too great a niggard who would spurn
A man to light a candle at his lantern;   340
By God, from that, he doesn't have less light.
If you've enough, complaining isn't right.
      You also say if we make ourselves gay
With our clothing and with precious array,
That it is peril to our chastity;   345
Woe to you—you then enforce it for me,
And say these words in the Apostle's name:
'In clothing made from chastity and shame
You women all should dress yourselves,' said he,
'Not with well-coifed hair and with gay jewelry,   350
Not with rich clothes, with pearls, or else with gold.'[2]
With your text and your rubric,[3] I don't hold,
Or follow them as much as would a gnat.
      You said this: that I was just like a cat;
Whoever wanted to singe a cat's skin   355
He could be sure the cat would then stay in;
And if the cat's skin were so sleek and gay,
She'd not stay in the house for half a day;
Forth she'd go, before the day was dawning,
To show her skin and to go caterwauling.   360
That is to say, if I am gay, sir shrew,
I'll run to put my poor old clothes on view.
      Sir old fool, what help is it if you spy?
Though you prayed Argus[4] with his hundred eyes
To be my bodyguard, as he'd know best,   365
He'd not guard me till I let him, I'll be blessed.
I'd hoodwink him, as I am prospering!

---

2. See I Timothy 2.9–10.
3. Direction written in red.
4. In classical myth, a monster used by

Hera/Juno, queen of the gods, to watch over
one of her husband's paramours.

Yet you also say that there are three things,
And that these same things trouble all this earth,
And that no man might yet endure the fourth.[5]   370
Oh, dear sir shrew, Jesus shorten your life!
Yet you will preach and say a hateful wife
Is one of these misfortunes that you reckon.
Aren't there other kinds of comparison
That, for all your parables, you could use,   375
Unless a poor wife were the one you'd choose?

    You liken, too, a woman's love to hell,
To barren land where water may not dwell.
You liken it also to a wild fire;
The more it burns, the more it has desire   380
To consume everything that burned will be.
You say that just as worms destroy a tree,
A wife destroys her husband, you have found;
This, they well know who to wives have been bound.'

    My lords, right thus, as you can understand,   385
I stiffly[6] kept my old husbands in hand
And swore they said thus in their drunkenness;
And all was false; except I took witness
On Jenkin there, and on my niece, also.
Oh Lord! The pain I did them and the woe.   390
And, by God's sweet pain, they were not guilty!
For, like a horse, I could bite and whinny.
I knew how to complain well even when
I had the guilt, or I'd been ruined then.
Whoever comes first to the mill, first grinds;   395
Complaining first, our war stopped, I did find.
They were glad to excuse themselves quite quickly
For things of which they never had been guilty.
Of wenches, I'd accuse them out of hand
When, in their sickness, they could hardly stand.   400

    Yet it tickled his heart, because then he
Thought that I had for him such great fancy!
I swore that all my walking out at night
Was to spy on wenches he was holding tight;
Using that cover, I enjoyed much mirth.   405
For all such wit is given us at birth;
Deceit, weeping, and spinning God did give
To women by nature, all the time they live.
And thus of one thing, I can surely boast:
In the end, I'm the one who won the most   410
By tricks or force or by some other thing
As much as constant grumbling and grousing.
Namely, then, they would have bad luck in bed:
I did them no pleasure, and I chided;
I would no longer in the bed abide,   415
If I felt his arm come over my side,

<hr>

5. See Proverbs 30.21–23.   6. Firmly.

Till he had paid his ransom down to me;
Then I'd suffer him to do his foolery.
Therefore, to every man this tale I tell:
Win whoso may, for all is there to sell;   420
With empty hands men may no hawks then lure.
For profit, I would all their lust endure,
And I would fake it with feigned appetite;
And yet in bacon,[7] I had no delight.
That was the reason I would always chide them,   425
For though the pope were sitting right beside them,
At their own table, I would never spare.
In truth, I repaid them word for word there.
So help me, oh true God omnipotent,
If now I made my will and testament,   430
There was not one unpaid word I did owe.
By my own wit, I brought it all about so
That they must give it up, and for the best,
Or otherwise, we never would have rest;
Though he looked as crazy as a lion,   435
He would fail at gaining his conclusion.
      Then I would say to him, 'sweetheart, take heed—
See how meek our sheep Willie looks, indeed!
Come near, my spouse, and let me kiss your cheek!
Truly you should be all patient and meek,   440
And have, too, a carefully spiced conscience,
Since you always preach about Job's patience.[8]
Suffer always, since you can so well preach;
Unless you do, for sure we shall you teach
That it's nice to have a wife in peace now.   445
Doubtless, one of the two of us must bow,
And so, since man is more reasonable
Than woman, to suffer you are able.
What ails you now that thus you grouse and groan?
Do you just want my quaint thing[9] for your own?   450
Why, take it all! Lo, have it through and through!
You love it well, by Peter,[1] curse on you;
For if I wanted to sell my *belle chose*,[2]
Then I could walk as fresh as is a rose;
But I will keep it just for your own tooth.   455
You are to blame, by God! I tell the truth.'
These are the kinds of words I had on hand.
And now I will speak of my fourth husband.
      My fourth husband was a reveler—
That is to say, he had a paramour—   460
And young and full of wantonness was I,
Stubborn, strong and jolly as a magpie.
How I'd danced when the small harp was playing;

---

7. I.e., preserved (old) meat; or perhaps a reference to the prize at Dunmow.
8. Proverbial; see the book of Job.

9. Genitals.
1. St. Peter.
2. Pretty thing (French).

Like a nightingale's was all my singing,
When I had drunk my draught of fine sweet wine!   465
Metellius, the foul churl, the swine,
Who, with a staff, bereft his wife of life,
Because she drank wine;[3] if I were his wife,
He wouldn't frighten me away from drink!
And after wine, on Venus[4] I must think,   470
For just as sure as cold engenders hail,
A lecherous mouth must have lecherous tail.
In wine-drunk women, there is no defence—
This, lechers know from their experience.

    But—Lord Christ!—when memories come back to me,   475
About my youth and all my jollity,
It tickles me right down to my heart's root.
To this day, it does my heart good, to boot,
That I have had my world right in my time.
But age, alas, that poisons what is prime,   480
Has bereft me of my beauty and my pith.[5]
Let it go. Farewell! The devil go therewith!
The flower's gone; there is no more to tell;
The bran, as I best can, now must I sell;
But yet to be right merry I have planned.   485
And now I will tell of my fourth husband.

    I say, I had in my heart a great spite
That he in any other took delight.
By God and Saint Judocus,[6] he's repaid!
Of the same wood, a cross for him I made;   490
Not in a foul manner with my body,
But I made folks such cheer that certainly
I made him fry enough in his own grease
Because his jealous anger would not cease.
By God, on earth I was his purgatory,   495
For which, I hope his soul will be in glory.
God knows, he often sat and sang "Alack"
When his shoe so bitterly pinched him back.
There was no man who knew, save God and he,
In what ways I twisted him so sorely.   500
When I came from Jerusalem, he died;
Buried beneath the cross's beam,[7] he lies.
His tomb is not fancy or curious
As was the sepulcher of Darius,
Which Appelles had formed so skillfully;[8]   505
A waste to bury him expensively.

---

3. One of the historical anecdotes compiled in the rhetorical handbook by Valerius Maximus (1st century C.E.), which presents Metellius's act as justified.
4. Roman goddess of love.
5. Energy.
6. St. Judoc or Josse, a 7th-century Breton saint (never canonized) whose emblem was

the pilgrim's staff.
7. I.e., in a place of honor within the church itself.
8. According to the (fictional) account in Walter of Châtillon's 12th-century Latin epic, *Alexandreis*, the famous painter Apelles (4th c. B.C.E.) decorated the tomb of the Persian king Darius (d. 486 B.C.E.).

Let him fare well. God rest his soul, I ask it!
He is now in his grave and in his casket.
  Now of my fifth husband I will tell.
May God let his soul never go to hell!   510
Yet to me he was the biggest scoundrel;
On my whole row of ribs, I feel it still,
And ever shall until my dying day.
But in our bed, he was so fresh and gay,
And he knew so well just how to gloss me   515
When he wanted my *belle chose,* as you'll see;
Although he'd beaten me on every bone,
Quickly he'd win back my love for his own.
I believe that I loved him best since he
Could be standoffish with his love for me.   520
We women have, and no lie this will be,
In this matter, our own quaint[9] fantasy:
Whatever thing won't lightly come our way,
Then after it we'll cry and crave all day.
Forbid us something, and that desire we;   525
Press on us fast, and then we're sure to flee.
With standoffishness, we spread out all our wares;
Great crowds at market make the goods dear there,
Too great a bargain isn't thought a prize;
And this knows every woman who is wise.   530
  My fifth husband—now God his soul should bless—
Whom I took for love and not for richness,
Formerly, he was a clerk at Oxford,
And had left school, and went back home to board
With my close friend who in our town did dwell.   535
God save her! Her name's Alison, as well.
She knew both my heart and my privacy
More than our parish priest did, so help me!
With her, I shared my secrets one and all.
For had my husband pissed upon a wall,   540
Or done a thing that should have cost his life,
To her and to another worthy wife,
And to my niece, whom I did love so well,
All of his secrets I'd be sure to tell.
God knows too that I did this quite often   545
So I made his face both red and hot then
From shame itself. He blamed himself that he
Had ever shared with me his privacy.
  And so it happened that one time in Lent—
For often times to my close friend I went,   550
Because I always did love being gay,
And to walk out in March, April, and May,
From house to house, and sundry tales to hear—

9. "Queynt," meaning "quaint" in the modern
English sense and also a pun on the slang
word for the female sex organ; the pun is especially likely coming a few lines after the last
reference to Wife's *"belle chose"* (510).

Jenkin the clerk, Alison, my friend dear,
And I myself, into the fields all went. 555
My husband was at London all that Lent;
More leisure for my playing, I then had,
To see and to be seen (and I was glad)
By lusty folks. Did I know where good grace
Was destined to find me, or in what place? 560
Therefore, I made all my visitations
To vigils and also to processions,
To preachings and to these pilgrimages,
To miracle plays[1] and to marriages,
And always wore my gowns of scarlet bright. 565
Neither the worms nor moths nor any mites,
On my soul's peril, had my gowns abused.
Do you know why? Because they were well used.
    Now I'll tell you what happened then to me.
I say that out into the fields walked we, 570
Till truly, we had such a flirtation,
This clerk and I, that I made due provision
And spoke to him, and said to him how he,
Were I a widow, should be wed to me.
For certainly—and I'm not boasting here— 575
I have not ever lacked provisions clear
For marriage, or for such things, so to speak.
I hold a mouse's heart not worth a leek
Who's only got one hole where it can run,
And if that fails, then everything is done. 580
    I made him think he had enchanted me—
My mother taught me all that subtlety—
And said I had dreamed this of him all night:
As I lay on my back he'd slain me quite,
And I dreamed full of blood then was my bed; 585
'But yet I hope you'll do me good,' I said,
'For blood betokens gold, as was taught me.'
And all was false; I had no dream, you see,
But I always followed my mother's lore,
In this as well as other things before. 590
    But now, sirs, let's see what I shall say then.
Aha! By God, I've got my tale again.
    When my fourth husband lay up on his bier,
I wept quite long and made a sorry cheer,
As wives must, for it is common usage. 595
With my coverchief, I hid my visage,
But since I was provided with my next mate,
I didn't weep much—this to you I'll state.
    To church was my husband borne next morning
With the neighbors, who for him were mourning; 600
And there Jenkin, our clerk, was one of those.

1. Medieval dramas focused on the lives and acts of the saints or on events from the Bible (also called "mystery plays"); performed in the vernacular, they were extremely popular.

So help me God, when I saw how he goes
Behind the bier, I thought he had a pair
Of legs and feet that were so clean and fair,
I gave him all my heart for him to hold.   605
He was, I think, just twenty winters old,
And I was forty, if I tell the truth;
But yet I always had a coltish tooth[2]
Gap toothed was I, and that became me well;
With Venus's seal[3] I'm printed, I can tell.   610
So help me God, I was a lusty one,
And fair and rich and young and well begun,
And truly, as my husbands all told me,
I had the best *quoniam*[4] there might be.
For certainly, I'm all Venerian   615
In feeling, and my heart is Martian.[5]
Venus gave me my love and lecherousness,
And Mars gave me my sturdy hardiness;
My ascendant's sign's Taurus,[6] with Mars therein.
Alas! Alas! That ever love was sin!   620
I always followed my inclination
By virtue of my stars' constellation;
Thus I could not withdraw—I was made so—
My chamber of Venus from a good fellow.
Yet I have Mars's mark[7] upon my face,   625
And also in another private place.
For as God so wise is my salvation,
I have never loved in moderation,
But I always followed my appetite,
Should he be long or short or black or white;   630
I took no heed, so long as he liked me,
Of how poor he was, or of what degree.
        What should I say, but at the month's end, he,
This pretty clerk, this Jenkin, so handy,[8]
Has wedded me with great solemnity,   635
And I gave him all land and property
That ever had been given me before.
But after, I was made to rue that sore;
My desires he would not suffer to hear.
By God, he hit me once upon the ear,   640
Because, out of his book, a leaf I rent,
And from that stroke, my ear all deaf then went.
But, like a lioness, I was stubborn,
And with my tongue, I was a jangler[9] born,
And I would walk around, as I once did,   645
From house to house, although he did forbid;

2. I.e., youthful appetites.
3. An alluring birthmark.
4. Literally, "whereas" (Latin): another slang form for female genitals.
5. Belonging to Mars, the Roman god of war.
6. Sign of the zodiac (April 21–May 20) in which Venus is dominant.
7. Probably a red birthmark.
8. Clever; courteous.
9. Chatterer.

Because of this, quite often he would preach,
And from old Roman stories, he would teach;
How one Simplicius Gallus[1] left his wife,
And her forsook for the rest of his life,   650
Because one day, and for no reason more,
Bareheaded she was looking out the door.

    Another Roman he told me by name,
Who, since his wife was at a summer's game
Without his knowledge, he then her forsook.   655
And then he would into his Bible look
For the proverb of Ecclesiasticus[2]
Where he commands, and he does forbid thus:
That man shall not suffer wife to roam about.
Then would he say right thus, without a doubt: 660
    'Whoever builds his house up all from willow
And pricks his blind horse over fields so fallow,
And lets his wife go seeking shrines so hallowed,
Is worthy to be hanging on the gallows!'
But all for nought: I didn't give a straw   665
For all his old proverbs or his saws,
Nor by him would I then corrected be.
I hate him who my vices tells to me,
And so do more of us, God knows, than me.
This drove him mad about me, utterly;   670
For I wouldn't bear with any of this.

    I'll tell you the truth now, by Saint Thomas,[3]
Why once out of his book a leaf I rent,
For which he hit me so that deaf I went.

    He had a book that, gladly, night and day,   675
For his pleasure, he would be reading always;[4]
It's called Valerius and Theophrastus;
He always laughed as he read it to us.
And also there was once a clerk at Rome,
A cardinal, who was called Saint Jerome,   680
Who made a book against Jovinian;
In which book was also Tertullian,
Crisippus, Trotula, and Heloise,
An abbess near to Paris, if you please,
And too the Parables of Solomon,   685

---

1. This story and the next (lines 647–49) are found in Valerius Maximus.
2. See Ecclesiasticus 25.25–26.
3. Thomas Becket, to whose shrine the pilgrims are traveling.
4. This single anthology contains a number of works, all hostile or cast as hostile to women: *Letter of Valerius Concerning Not Marrying*, by Walter Map (12th century); *Against Jovinian* (a 4th-century monk), by the Church Father Jerome (d. 420), which mentions a lost *Golden Book of Marriage* by the Greek philosopher Theophrastus (d. 285 B.C.E.) and writings by the Church Father Tertullian (d. ca. 220) and Crisippus (otherwise unknown); Trotula, a legendary 11th-century Italian female doctor; Heloise (d. 1164), a participant in a scandalous love affair who wrote that philosophers should never marry; the biblical book of Proverbs; and the *Art of Love* by Ovid (43 B.C.E.–17 C.E.), a how-to book on seduction.

Ovid's *Ars,* and more books, many a one,
And all of these in one volume were bound,
And every night and day, some time he found
When he had some leisure and vacation
From his other worldly occupation,   690
To read then in this book of wicked wives.
He knew of them more legends and more lives
Then there are of good wives in the Bible.
For trust it well, it is impossible
For any clerk to speak some good of wives,   695
Unless he speaks about holy saints' lives:
This for no other women will he do.
Now who painted the lion, tell me who?[5]
By God, if women had written stories,
Like clerks do within their oratories,   700
They would have written of men more wickedness
Than all the mark of Adam could redress.
The children of Venus and Mercury[6]
In their actions, are always contrary;
Mercury loves both wisdom and science;   705
Venus, revelry and extravagance.
Because of their different dispositions,
Each falls in the other sign's exaltation.
And thus, God knows, Mercury's despondent
In Pisces,[7] when Venus is ascendant,   710
And Venus falls where Mercury is raised.
Therefore, no woman by a clerk is praised.
The clerk, when he is old and may not do
Of Venus's work what's worth his old shoe,
Then he sits down and writes in his dotage   715
That women cannot keep up their marriage!
        But now to my purpose, why I told you
That I was beaten for a book, it's true!
One night Jenkin, who was our lord and sire,
Read in this book, as he sat by the fire,   720
Of Eve first: because of her wickedness,
All mankind was brought into wretchedness,
And thus Jesus Christ himself was slain then,
Who bought us with his own heart's blood again.
Lo, here, expressly, of woman you find   725
That woman was the loss of all mankind.
        He read to me how Samson lost his hair:
His lover cut it while he did sleep there;
And through this treason, he lost both his eyes.[8]
        And then he read to me, if I don't lie,   730

5. In one of Aesop's fables, a lion argues that the representation of a man killing a lion did not prove the man's superiority: if a lion could create an artwork, it would depict the opposite.
6. Winged messenger of the Roman gods, the god of commerce and trickery.
7. Sign of the zodiac (February 20–March 20).
8. See Judges 13–16 for the story of Delilah and Samson, whose superhuman strength lay in his hair.

About Dianyra and Hercules;[9]
She made him set himself on fire, if you please.
   Nor forgot he the woe throughout his life
That Socrates[1] endured from his two wives,
How Xantippa cast piss upon his head.   735
This foolish man sat still like he were dead;
He wiped his head and no more dared say plain,
But 'Before thunder stops, there comes the rain!'
   Of Pasiphaë, who was the queen of Crete,
From evilness, the tale seemed to him sweet;   740
Fie! Speak no more—it is a grisly thing—
Of her lust and horrible desiring.[2]
   Of Clytemnestra, who, from lechery,
Falsely made her husband die,[3] you see,
He read out that tale with great devotion.   745
   He told me also on what occasion
Amphiaraus at Thebes had lost his life.[4]
My husband had a legend of his wife,
Eriphyle, who, for a brooch of gold
Has privately unto the Greeks then told   750
Where her husband had kept his hiding place,
And thus at Thebes he suffered sorry grace.
   Of Livia and Lucia,[5] then heard I:
How both of them had made their husbands die,
The one for love, the other one for hate.   755
This Livia, for sure, one evening late,
Poisoned her husband for she was his foe;
Lecherous Lucia loved her husband so
That, to make sure he'd always on her think,
She gave to him such a kind of love-drink   760
He was dead before it was tomorrow;
And thus, always, husbands have had sorrow.
   Then he told me how one Latumius
Complained once to his fellow Arrius
That in his garden there grew such a tree   765
On which, he said, that all of his wives three
Hung themselves with spite, one then another.
Said this Arrius, 'Beloved brother,
Give me a shoot from off that blessèd tree,

---

9. The greatest hero of classical mythology, who died because his wife unwittingly gave him a poisoned cloak. (Many of the following exempla are drawn from myth.)
1. The Greek philosopher (469–399 B.C.E.) immortalized in the dialogues of his pupil Plato; Xantippa is protrayed as a shrew in ancient biographies.
2. The union of Pasiphaë with a bull produced the Minotaur.
3. Conspiring with her lover, the queen of Mycenae murdered her husband, Agamemnon,

when he returned from leading the Greeks in the Trojan War.
4. He was forced to join the war against Thebes, whose disastrous outcome he foresaw, by his wife, who had been bribed.
5. According to Jerome, Livia, who had a lover, deliberately poisoned her husband, Drusus (d. 23 C.E.), whose father later became the Roman emperor Tiberius, and Lucia (Lucilla) accidentally poisoned her husband, the poet Lucretius (d. 55 B.C.E.), with a love potion.

And in my garden, planted it will be.'[6]   770
      And later on, about wives he has read,
And some had slain their husbands in their bed,
And let their lechers hump them all the night,
While on the floor the corpses lay upright.
And some have driven nails into the brain,   775
While they did sleep, and thus they had them slain.
And some did give them poison in their drink.
He spoke more slander than the heart can think,
And on top of it, he knew more proverbs
Than in this world there can grow grass and herbs.   780
'Better,' he said, 'that your habitation
Be either with a lion or foul dragon,
Than with a woman who is used to chide.
Better,' said he, 'high on the roof abide,
Than down in the house with an angry wife;[7]   785
They're so wicked and contrary all their lives,
That they hate what their husbands love always.'
He said, 'A woman casts her shame away,
When she casts off her shift.' He spoke more so:
'A fair woman, unless she's chaste also,   790
Is just like a gold ring in a sow's nose.'[8]
Who would imagine, or who would suppose
The woe that in my heart was, and the pain?
      And when I saw he never would refrain
From reading on this cursed book all night,   795
Then suddenly, three leaves I have ripped right
Out of his book, as he read, and also
With my fist, I took him on the cheek so
That backward in our fire, right down fell he.
He starts up like a lion who's gone crazy,   800
And with his fist, he hit me on the head
So on the floor I lay like I were dead.
And when he saw how still it was I lay,
He was aghast, and would have fled away,
Till, at last, out of my swoon I awoke.   805
'Oh! Hast thou slain me, false thief?' then I spoke,
'And for my land, hast thou now murdered me?
Before I'm dead, yet will I still kiss thee.'
      And fairly he kneeled down when he came near,
And he said, 'Alison, my sister dear,   810
Never more will I hit you, in God's name!
If I've done so, you are yourself to blame.
I pray you, your forgiveness now I seek.'
And right away, I hit him on the cheek,
And said, 'thief, now this much avenged am I;   815
I may no longer speak, now I will die.'
But then, at last, after much woe and care,

6. A story told in the *Letter of Valerius*.   8. Proverbs 11.22.
7. Proverbs 21.9.

We two fell into an agreement there,
He gave me all the bridle in my hand
To have the governing of house and land,   820
And of his tongue, and of his hands, then, too;
I made him burn his book without ado.
And when I had then gotten back for me,
By mastery, all the sovereignty,
And when he said to me, 'My own true wife,   825
Do as you like the rest of all your life;
Keep your honor, and keep my rank and state'—
After that day, we never had debate.
God help me so, there's no wife you would find
From Denmark to India who was so kind,   830
And also true, and so was he to me.
I pray to God, who sits in majesty,
To bless his soul with all his mercy dear.
Now will I tell my tale, if you will hear."

Behold the words between the Summoner and the Friar.

The Friar laughed, when he had heard all this;   835
"Madame," said he, "so have I joy or bliss,
This is a long preamble to a tale!"
The Summoner had heard his windy gale,
"By God's two arms," the Summoner said, "lo!
Always will a friar interfere so.   840
Lo, good men, a fly and then a friar
Will both fall in every dish and matter.
Of preambulation, what's to say of it?
What! Amble, trot, keep still, or just go sit!
You're hindering our sport in this manner."   845
        "You say so, sir Summoner?" said the Friar;
"Now, by my faith, I shall, before I go,
Tell a tale of a summoner, you know,
That all the folks will laugh at in this place."
        "Now, elsewise, Friar, I do curse your face,"   850
Said this Summoner. "And I curse myself, too,
Unless I tell some tales, at least a few,
Of friars before I come to Sittingbourne[9]
So that, be sure, I will make your heart mourn.
I know full well that you're out of patience."   855
        Our Host cried out, "Peace now! And that at once!"
And he said, "Let the woman tell her tale.
You act like folks who are all drunk on ale.
Do, madame, tell your tale, and all the rest."
        "All ready, sir," said she, "as you think best,   860
If I have license of this worthy Friar."
        "Yes, madame," said he, "tell on. I will hear."

Here the Wife of Bath ends her Prologue.

9. A town on the road to Canterbury, 40 miles from London.

The Wife of Bath's Tale

Here begins the Tale of the Wife of Bath.

In the olden days of good King Arthur,
Of whom Britons still speak with great honor,
This whole land was all filled up with fairies.   865
The elf queen, with her pretty company,
Went dancing then through many a green mead.
I think this was the old belief, indeed;
I speak of many hundred years ago.
But now no one sees elves and fairies go,   870
For now all the charity and prayers
Of limitors[1] and other holy friars,
Who haunt through every land and every stream
As thick as motes floating in a sun beam,
Blessing halls and chambers, kitchens, bowers,   875
Cities, boroughs, castles, and high towers,
Barns and villages, cowsheds and dairies—
This is the reason why there are no fairies.
For there where once was wont to walk an elf,
Now there the begging friar walks himself   880
In the afternoons and in the mornings,
He says his matins[2] and his holy things
As he walks all throughout his begging grounds.
Now women may go safely all around.
In every bush and under every tree,   885
There is no other incubus[3] but he,
And he'll do them no harm but dishonor.
    So it happened that this good King Arthur
Once had a lusty knight, a bachelor,
Who, one day, came riding from the river,   890
And it chanced that, as he was born, alone,
He saw a maiden walking on her own,
From which maid, then, no matter what she said,
By very force, he took her maidenhead;
This oppressive violence caused such clamor,   895
And such a suit for justice to King Arthur
That soon this knight was sentenced to be dead,
By the course of law, and should have lost his head—
By chance that was the law back long ago—
Except the queen and other ladies also   900
So long had then prayed to the king for grace
Till he had granted his life in that place,
And gave him to the queen, to do her will,
To choose whether she would him save or kill.
    The queen then thanked the king with all her might, 905

---

1. Friars licensed to beg in a specific territory.
2. I.e., morning prayers.

3. An evil spirit believed to have sex with women as they sleep.

And after this, thus spoke she to the knight,
When, on a day, she saw that it was time.
"You stand," she said, "in this state for your crime:
That of your life, you've no security.
I grant you life, if you can tell to me   910
What thing it is that women most desire.
Keep your neck-bone from the ax now, sire!
And if, at once, the answer you don't know,
Still, I will give you leave so you can go
A twelvemonth and a day, to search and learn   915
Sufficient answer before you return;
Before you leave, I'll have security
That here you'll surrender up your body."

    Woe was this knight, and he sighs sorrowfully;
But what! He can't do all he likes completely.   920
And at last, he decided that he'd wend
His way and come back home at the year's end,
With such an answer as God would convey;
He takes his leave and goes forth on his way.

    He seeks in every house and every place   925
Where he has hopes that he'll find some good grace
To learn the thing that women love the most,
But he could not arrive on any coast
Where he might find out about this matter,
Two creatures who agreed on it together.   930
Some said that all women best loved richness,
Some said honor, and some said jolliness,
Some, rich array, and some said lust in bed,
And often times to be widowed and wed.

    Some said that our hearts were most often eased   935
When we could be both flattered and well pleased.
He got quite near the truth, it seems to me.
A man shall win us best with flattery,
Solicitude, and eager busyness.
Thus we are captured, both the more and less.   940

    And some said that the best of all love we
To do what pleases us, and to be free,
And that no man reproves us for our folly,
But says that we are wise and never silly.
For truly, there is not one of us all,   945
If any one will claw us where it galls,
That we won't kick when what he says is true.
Try, and he'll find it so who will so do;
For, be we ever so vicious within,
We want to be held wise and clean of sin.   950

    And some say that we find it very sweet
Dependable to be thought, and discreet,
And in one purpose steadfastly to dwell,
And not betray a thing that men us tell.
A rake handle isn't worth that story.   955
We women can't keep secrets, by God's glory;

See Midas—will you hear the tale withal?[4]
     Once Ovid, among some other things small,
Said Midas covered up with his long hair,
On his head two ass's ears that grew there,   960
And this flaw he did hide as best he might
Quite cleverly from every mortal's sight,
So that, save for his wife, no one did know.
He loved her most, and trusted her also;
He prayed her that to no other creature   965
She would tell how he was so disfigured.
     She swore to him, "No"; all this world to win,
She would not do that villainy or sin,
To make her husband have so foul a name.
She wouldn't tell because of her own shame.   970
But, nonetheless, it seemed to her she died
Because so long she must that secret hide;
She thought it swelled so sorely near her heart
That some word from her must, by needs, depart;
Since she dared not tell it to any man,   975
Down to the marsh that was nearby, she ran—
Until she got there, her heart was on fire—
And as a bittern[5] bellows in the mire,
Down by the water, she did her mouth lay:
"Thou water, with your sound do not betray: 980
To thee I tell, and no one else," she said;
"My husband has long ass ears on his head!
Now is my heart all whole; now is it out.
I could no longer keep it, without doubt."
Here you see, if a time we might abide,   985
Yet it must out; we can no secret hide.
If of this tale you want to hear the rest,
Read Ovid, and there you will learn it best.
     This knight, about whom my tale is concerned,
Seeing that the answer he'd not learned—   990
That is to say, what women love the best—
Sorrowful was the spirit in his breast.
But home he goes; no more might he sojourn;
The day had come when homeward he must turn.
And on his way, it happened he did ride,   995
With all his cares, near to a forest's side,
Where he saw come together for a dance,
Some four and twenty ladies there by chance;
Toward which dance he eagerly did turn,
In hopes some wisdom from them he might learn.   1000
But truly, before he had arrived there,
The dancing ladies vanished—who knew where.
No creature saw he left there who bore life,
Save on the green, he saw sitting a wife[6]—

4. See Ovid, *Metamorphoses* 11.172–93 (where
Midas's secret is discovered by a servant, not
by his wife).

5. A wading bird with a deep, booming call.
6. A woman.

A fouler creature, none imagine might.   1005
This old wife then arose to meet the knight.
"Sir knight, there's no road out of here," said she.
"What you are seeking, by your faith, tell me.
Perhaps, then, you'll be better prospering."
She said, "These old folks can know many things."   1010
      "Beloved mother," said this knight, "it's fate
That I am dead unless I can relate
What thing it is that women most desire.
Could you tell me, I'd well repay your hire."
      "Pledge me your troth," said she, "here in my hand,   1015
And swear to me the next thing I demand,
You shall do it if it lies in your might,
And I'll tell you the answer before night."
      "I grant," he said, "you have this pledge from me."
      "Then, Sire, I dare well boast to you," said she,   1020
"Your life is safe, and I will stand thereby;
Upon my life, the queen will say as I.
Let see who is the proudest of them yet
Who wears either a coverchief or hair-net
Who dares say 'Nay' to what I will you teach.   1025
Let us go forth without a longer speech."
Then she whispered a message in his ear,
And bade him to be glad, and have no fear.
      When they came to the court, this knight did say
That, as he'd pledged, he had held to his day,   1030
And he said his answer was ready then.
Many noble wives and many maidens
And many widows, because wise are they,
With the queen sitting as the judge that day,
Were all assembled, his answer to hear;   1035
And then this knight was told he should appear.
      It was commanded that there should be silence
And that the knight should tell in audience
The thing that worldly women love the best.
The knight did not stand like a beast at rest;   1040
At once to his question then he answered
With manly voice, so all the court it heard:
      "My liege lady, generally," said he,
"Women desire to have sovereignty
As well over their husbands as their loves,   1045
And to be in mastery them above.
This is your greatest desire, though me you kill.
Do as you like; I am here at your will."
In all the court, there was no wife or maiden
Nor widow who denied what he had said then,   1050
But they said he was worthy of his life.
And with that word, then, up jumps the old wife,
Whom the knight had seen sitting on the green:
"Mercy," said she, "my sovereign lady queen!
Before your court departs, by me do right.   1055

I taught this very answer to this knight;
For which he pledged to me his troth and hire,
So that the first thing I'd of him require,
This he would do, if it lay in his might.
Before the court, then I pray you, sir knight," 1060
Said she, "that you now take me for your wife,
For well you know that I have saved your life.
Upon my faith, if I say false, say 'nay.' "
    This knight answered, "Alas, and well away!
I know that was my promise, I'll be blessed. 1065
But for God's love now, choose a new request!
Take all my goods, and let my body go."
    "Oh no," said she, "I curse us both then so!
For though I may be foul and poor and old,
I'd not want all the metal, ore, or gold 1070
That's buried in the earth or lies above,
Unless I were your lady and your love."
    "My love?" said he, "oh, no, my damnation!
Alas, that one of my birth and station
Ever should so foully disparaged be!" 1075
But all for naught; the end is this, that he
Constrained was here; by needs, he must her wed,
And take his old wife, and go off to bed.
    Now here some men would want to say perhaps
That I take no care—so it is a lapse— 1080
To tell you all the joy and the array
That at the wedding feast was on that day:
To which, my answer here is short and small:
I say there was no joy or feast at all.
Only sorrow and heaviness, I say. 1085
For privately he wedded her next day,
And all day after, he hid like an owl,
For woe was he that his wife looked so foul.
    Great was the woe the knight had in his thoughts,
When he was with his wife to their bed brought; 1090
He wallows and he writhes there, to and fro.
His old wife just lay smiling, even so,
And said, "Oh husband dear, God save my life!
Like you, does every knight fare with his wife?
Is this the law here in the house of Arthur? 1095
Is each knight to his wife aloof with her?
I am your own love, and I am your wife;
And I am she who has just saved your life.
Surely, toward you I have done only right;
Why fare you thus with me on this first night? 1100
You're faring like a man who's lost his wits,
What's my guilt? For love of God, now tell it,
And it will be amended if I may."
    "Amended?" said this knight, "Alas! No way!
It will not be amended, this I know. 1105
You are so loathly, and so old also,

And come from such low lineage, no doubt,
Small wonder that I wallow and writhe about.
I would to God my heart burst in my breast!"
    "Is this," said she, "the cause of your unrest?" 1110
    "Yes," said he, "no wonder is, that's certain."
    "Sir," said she, "I could mend this again,
If I liked, before there'd passed days three,
If you might now behave well toward me.
    But since you speak now of such gentleness[7] 1115
As descends to you down from old richness,
So that, because of it, you're gentle men,
Such arrogance is just not worth a hen.
See who is most virtuous all their lives,
In private and in public, and most strives 1120
To always do what gentle deeds he can:
Now take him for the greatest gentle men.
Christ wills we claim from him our gentleness,
Not from our elders and from their old richness.
Though they leave us their worldly heritage, 1125
And we claim that we're from high lineage,
Yet they may not bequeath a single thing
To us here of their virtuous living,
Which is what made them be called gentle men;
This is the path they bade us follow then. 1130
    Well can he, the wise poet of Florence,
Who's named Dante,[8] speak forth with this sentence.
Lo, Dante's tale is in this kind of rhyme:
'Seldom up his family tree's branches climbs
A man's prowess, for God, in his goodness, 1135
Wills that from him we claim our gentleness';
For, from our elders, we may no thing claim
But temporal things that may hurt us and maim.
    And every man knows this as well as me,
If gentleness were planted naturally 1140
In a certain lineage down the line, yet
They'd not cease in public or in private,
From gentleness, to do their fair duty;
They might not then do vice or villainy.
    Take fire and bring it in the darkest house, 1145
From here to mountains of the Caucasus,[9]
And let men shut the doors and go return;
Yet still the fire will lie as fair and burn
Like twenty thousand men might it behold;
Its natural duty it will always hold, 1150
On my life, till extinguished it may be.

---

7. Gentility; nobility.
8. Dante Alighieri (1265–1321), Florentine poet whose *Divine Comedy* had a significant influence on Chaucer; the following lines echo

Purgatorio 7.121–23.
9. The mountain range on the southwest border of Russia, between the Black and Caspian Seas.

Here, may you well see how gentility
Is not connected to one's possessions,
Since folks don't follow its operation
Always, as does the fire, lo, in its kind.   1155
For, God knows it, men may well often find
That a lord's son does shame and villainy;
And he who wants praise for his gentility,
Since a gentle house he was born into,
And had elders full of noble virtue,   1160
And who will not himself do gentle deeds,
And dead gentle ancestors hardly heeds,
He is not gentle, be he duke or earl;
A villain's sinful deeds do make a churl.
For such gentleness is only fame   1165
From your elders' high goodness and their name,
Which is a thing your person does not own.
Your gentleness must come from God alone.
Thus our true gentleness must come from grace;
It's not a thing bequeathed us with our place.   1170
        Think how noble, as says Valerius,
Was this one Tullius Hostillius,[1]
Nobility did poverty succeed.
Read Seneca, and Boethius[2] read;
There you shall see expressly that, indeed,   1175
The man is gentle who does gentle deeds.
And therefore, my dear husband, I conclude:
Though my ancestors were humble and rude,
Yet may the high God, and for this I pray,
Grant me grace to live virtuously each day.   1180
I am gentle, whenever I begin,
To live virtuously and to waive sin.
        You reproach me for poverty, indeed,
High God above, on whom we base our creed,
In willing poverty did live his life.   1185
And certainly each man, maiden, or wife
May understand that Jesus, heaven's king,
Would not choose a vicious way of living.
Glad poverty's an honest thing, it's true;
Thus Seneca and other clerks say, too.   1190
He who sees he's well paid by poverty,
Though he had no shirt, he seems rich to me.
He is a poor man who can only covet,
For he wants what he lacks power to get;
He who has naught, and does not covet, too,   1195
Is rich, though he a peasant seems to you.
True poverty, it sings out properly;

1. Third king of Rome (7th century B.C.E.);
according to legend, he began life as a herdsman.
2. Christian Roman philosopher (d. 474),
whose *Consolation of Philosophy*, written in

prison before his execution, was translated
from Latin by Chaucer. Seneca the Younger
(d. 65 C.E.), Roman Stoic moralist and dramatist who committed suicide by order of the
emperor Nero.

Now Juvenal[3] says of it merrily:
'The poor man, when he should go by the way,
Before the thieves, this man can sing and play.'   1200
Poverty is a hateful good, I guess,
A great encouragement to busyness;
Great improver of wisdom and good sense
For him who can suffer it with patience.
Poverty, though miserable seems its name,   1205
Is a possession no one else will claim.
Poverty often, when a man is low,
Can make him both his God and himself know.
Poverty's an eyeglass, it seems to me,
Through which he might his good and true friends see.   1210
And sire, now, if I don't grieve you, therefore
For poverty don't blame me anymore.
    Now, sire, with old age you have reproached me;
And truly, sire, though no authority
Were in books, you gentlemen of honor   1215
Say folks to an old man should show favor
And call him father, in your gentleness;
And I shall find authorities, I guess.
    Now, since you say that I am foul and old,
You don't have to fear to be a cuckold;   1220
For filth and age, so far as I can see,
Are great wardens upon one's chastity.
But, nonetheless, since I know your delight,
I shall fulfill your worldly appetite.
    Choose now," said she, "of these things, one of two: 1225
Till I die, to have me foul and old, too,
And be to you a true and humble wife,
And never displease you in all my life,
Or else you can have now a fair, young thing,
And take your chances with the visiting   1230
That happens at your house because of me,
Or in some other place, as well may be.
Choose yourself whichever one will please you."
    This knight now ponders and sighs sorely, too,
But finally, he said in this way here: 1235
"My lady and my love and wife so dear,
I put myself in your wise governing;
Choose yourself which one may be most pleasing
And most honor to both you and me too.
I do not care now which one of the two;   1240
What pleases you suffices now for me."
    "Then have I got mastery from you," said she,
"Since I may choose and govern all the rest?"
    "Yes, truly, wife," said he, "I think it best."
    "Kiss me," said she, "we are no longer angry,   1245

---

3. Roman poet (d. ca. 120 C.E.); the quotation is from *Satire* 10.22.

For, by my troth,[4] to you I will both be—
Yes, now both fair and good, as will be plain.
I pray to God that I might die insane,
Unless to you I'm also good and true
As any wife's been, since the world was new.   1250
Unless tomorrow I'm as fair to see
As any queen or empress or lady,
Who is between the east and then the west,
Do with my life and death as you think best.
Cast up the curtain; how it is, now see."   1255
        And when the knight saw all this verily,
That she now was so fair and so young, too,
For joy he seized her within his arms two,
His heart was all bathed in a bath of bliss.
A thousand times in a row, he did her kiss,   1260
And she obeyed him then in everything
That was to his pleasure or his liking.
        And thus they both lived until their lives' end
In perfect joy; and Jesus Christ us send,
Husbands meek and young and fresh in bed,   1265
And the grace to outlive those whom we wed;
I pray that Jesus may shorten the lives
Of those who won't be governed by their wives;
And old and stingy niggards who won't spend,
To them may God a pestilence soon send!   1270

The Pardoner's Prologue and Tale

The Introduction to the Pardoner's Tale

The words of the Host to the Physician and the Pardoner.

        Our Host swore as though he had gone crazy;
"Harrow! Now, by Christ's nails and blood!" said he,
"This was a false churl and a false judge then.[1]
May death shameful as man can imagine
Come to such judges and attorneys too!   5
This innocent maid's slain, alas, it's true!
Alas, too dearly she has bought her beauty!
Therefore, I say always that men can see
That both Fortune's gifts and also Nature's
Bring about the deaths of many creatures.   10
Her beauty was her death, I think it's plain.
Alas, so piteously was she slain!
Of both the gifts that I do speak of now
Men often have more harm than good, I vow.

---

4. I.e., "I swear."
1. The Host is deeply upset by the preceding tale, told by the Physician, which recounts

the death of a beautiful and virtuous maiden as a result of the machinations of a lecherous Roman magistrate.

But it's the truth now, my own master dear,[2]   15
This is truly a piteous tale to hear.
But nonetheless, no matter; let it be.
I pray God to save your gentle body,
Your chamber pots and urinals[2] too, then,
And drinks named for Hippocrates and Galen,   20
And each box filled with electuary;[3]
God bless them, and our lady Saint Mary!
So may I prosper, you're a proper man,
And just like a prelate, by Saint Ronan![4]
That's not right? I can't speak jargon, I believe;   25
But I know well that you made my heart grieve,
And I almost had a cardiac unrest.
          God's bones! Unless some medicine I test,
Or else a draught of moist and malty ale,
Or unless I now hear a merry tale,   30
My heart's lost for pity of this maiden.
You, *bel ami*,[5] you Pardoner," he said then,
"Tell us some mirth or jokes now right away."
          "It shall be done, by Saint Ronan, I say!
But first, here at this alehouse sign," he said,   35
"I will both drink and eat a loaf of bread."
          But right away out cried the gentle folks,
"No, do not let him tell us dirty jokes!
Tell us some moral thing, so we may learn
Some wisdom; then we'll listen to his turn."   40
"I grant this, sure," said he, "but I must think
Upon some honest thing while here I drink."

The Pardoner's Prologue

Here follows the Prologue of the Pardoner's Tale.

*Radix malorum est Cupiditas. Ad
Thimotheum, 6.
[The root of all evil is cupidity.
1 Timothy 6:10]*

          "My lords," said he, "in churches when I preach,
I take great pains to form impressive speech,
And ring it out as loudly as a bell,   45
For I know all by heart that I do tell.
My one theme is the same and always was—

2. Tools of his trade for the Physician, who would diagnose illness largely by assessing the color and consistency of the patient's urine.
3. Medicinal paste. The Greeks Hippocrates (d. ca. 377 B.C.E.) and Galen (d. ca. 199 C.E.) were the greatest physicians of antiquity.
4. Irish saint (the best known of this name d. 535); also, perhaps, a pun on *runnions*, kidneys or testicles.
5. Literally, "fair friend" (French), with the mocking connotations of "pretty boy."

Radix malorum est Cupiditas.

    First, I tell them from whence I have come,
And I show my papal bulls,[6] and then some.
Our liege lord's seal on my letters patent,[7]
For protection, I show first as warrant,
So no man is so bold, not priest nor clerk,
To bother me amid Christ's holy work.
And afterward, then forth my tales I tell;
The bulls of popes and cardinals as well,
Of bishops and of patriarchs I show,
And I speak some words in Latin so
I can give to my sermons some flavor,
And to stir them to devoted ardor.
Then I show cases of long crystal stones,[8]
All crammed tight full of clotted rags and bones—
Relics they are, each one supposes then.
I have a shoulder bone mounted in latten[9]
Which came from the sheep of a holy Jew.
'My good men,' I say, 'heed my words, now do:
If this bone here is washed in any well,
If cow or calf or sheep or ox should swell
That's eaten any snake, or a snake's stung,
Take water from that well and wash its tongue,
And it's all quickly healed; and furthermore,
Of pox and pustules and of every sore
Shall every sheep be healed that of this well
Drinks a draught. Now take heed of what I tell:
If the good man who owns the beasts will seek,
Right before the cock crows, every week,
To drink from this well, fasting as he ought,
As this same holy Jew our elders taught,
His beasts and his stock sure will multiply.
    Sires, it heals jealousy, if you will try.
When a man in a jealous rage will stoop,
With this same water, then, have made his soup;
Mistrust of his wife he'll no longer heed,
Though he did know the truth of her misdeed—
Though she'd taken a priest, or two, or three.
    I have a mitten, too, as you can see.
He who puts his hand inside this mitten
Will have multiplying of his grain then,
Once he's sown it, whether it's wheat or oats,
So long as here he offers pence or groats.[1]
    Good men and women, I warn of one thing:

50

55

60

65

70

75

80

85

90

---

6. Official papal documents; here, indulgences purchased to shorten a sinner's time in purgatory.

7. An open letter authorizing his actions, authenticated with the pope's or bishop's seal.

8. Jars; relics of a saint's body and clothing were believed to possess extraordinary powers.

9. Yellow metal alloy.

1. Small coins, worth 4 pence (pennies).

If now, in this church, there is a being
Who's done a sin so horrible that he
Dares not, for shame, absolved of it to be,
Or any woman, whether young or old,   95
Who has made her husband be a cuckold,
Such folks will have no power and no grace
To offer for my relics in this place.
Whoever finds himself free from such blame,
He will come up and offer, in God's name.   100
I'll absolve him by the authority
That, through the bull, has been granted to me.'
        Year by year, a hundred marks[2] by this game,
I've won since I a pardoner became.
I stand like a clerk up in my pulpit,   105
And when the stupid people down do sit,
I preach just as you heard me say before
And tell a hundred false tricks or some more.
I take pains in stretching forth my neck then;
East and west, to them I nod and beckon,   110
As does a dove that in a barn is sitting.
My hands and tongue so eagerly are flitting
That it's a joy to see my busyness.
Of avarice and such accursedness
Is all my preaching, thus to make them free   115
To give their pence, and namely, straight to me.
For my intention is only to win,
And nothing for the correction of sin.
I don't care, once they've had their burying,
If their souls then go blackberrying![3]   120
Surely, many sermons one could mention
Often times come from evil intention;
Some for pleasing folks, some for flattery,
To be advanced then by hypocrisy,
And some for vainglory, and some for hate.   125
When in no other way I dare debate,
Then I will sting him with my tongue so smart
In preaching, so that he can't help but start
To be falsely defamed if perchance he
Has trespassed against my brethren and me.   130
For though I may not speak his proper name,
Men shall well know he is one and the same,
By signs and by certain other measures.
Thus I repay folks who cause us displeasure;
My venom I spit out under the hue   135
Of holiness, to seem holy and true.
        But shortly my intention I'll explain:
I preach of naught but avarice and gain.

2. A great sum (in Chaucer's day, about what   was worth about 160 pennies.
a craftsman might earn in ten years); a mark   3. I.e., go to hell.

Therefore my theme is still, and always was,
Radix malorum est Cupiditas.   140
Thus the very same vice that I practice,
I preach against, and that is avarice.
Though I myself am guilty of that sin,
Yet still I can make other folks begin
To leave avarice and sorely repent.   145
But that is not my principal intent;
I preach of nothing except avarice.
On that matter, suffice enough of this.
      Then I tell them exempla that I know
From the old stories of quite long ago.   150
For stupid people love tales that are old;
Such things they can repeat as their minds hold.
What, do you think that while I may thus preach,
And win gold and silver with what I teach,
That I'll live in poverty willfully?   155
No, no, I would never think that, truly!
For I will preach and beg in sundry lands;
And I will do no labor with my hands,
Nor make baskets, to sustain my living,
For I will not idly go out begging.   160
No apostles will I counterfeit yet;
Money and wool, cheese and wheat I will get,
Although by the poorest page they're given,
Or the village's poorest widow, then,
Even if her children died from hunger.   165
No, from the vine, I will drink the liquor
And have a jolly wench in every town.
But in conclusion, hark, lords of renown:
Your preference is that I should tell a tale.
Now have I drunk a draught of corny[4] ale,   170
And, by God, I hope I'll tell you something
That, by reason, shall be to your liking.
Though I myself am quite a vicious man,
A moral tale yet to you tell I can,
Which I am wont to preach so I can win.   175
Now hold your peace! My tale I will begin."

The Pardoner's Tale

Here begins the Pardoner's Tale.

      In Flanders[5] once there was a company
Of young folk who haunted after folly,
Such as gambling and brothels and taverns,
Where, carousing with harps, lutes, and citterns,
They'd dance and play at dice both day and night,   180

---

4. Beer tasting strongly of corn or malt.
5. The coast of the Low Countries (modern

provinces of Belgium and the Netherlands),
across the North Sea from southern England.

And eat also, and drink beyond their might;
To the devil they make sacrifices
In his temple with their cursed devices
By overindulgence abominable.   185
Their oaths are both so great and damnable
That it is grisly just to hear them swear.
Our blessed Lord's body into bits they tear[6]—
They thought the Jews then should have torn him more;
Each laughed hard at the sins the others bore.   190
Right away there came the women tumblers,
Slim and small, and then the young fruit peddlers,
Singers with harps, bawds, sellers of wafers,
Who are the very devil's officers
To kindle and blow fires of lechery,   195
Which are annexed quite close to gluttony.
Holy Writ I take here for my witness:
There's lechery in wine and drunkenness.
        Lo, how drunken Lot, unnaturally,
Lay by his daughters two, unwittingly;[7]   200
So drunk was he, he knew not what he wrought.
        Herod, whoever has his stories sought,
When at his feast all filled with wine was he,
At his own table, he gave the decree
To slay John the Baptist, who was guiltless.[8]   205
        Seneca[9] too says a good word doubtless;
He says that no difference can he find
Between a man who is out of his mind
And one who's always drunk—and that is true—
Except madness, when it befalls a shrew,   210
Will last much longer than does drunkenness.
O gluttony, so full of cursedness!
O, the first cause of all our confusion!
O, the origin of our damnation,
Till Christ had bought us with his blood again!   215
Lo, how dearly, to say it shortly then,
Was bought back this accursed villainy!
Corrupted was this world for gluttony.
Adam, our father, and his wife also,
From Paradise to labor and to woe   220
Were driven for that vice, it is no lie.
For while Adam was fasting, as read I,
He was in Paradise; and when, then, he
Ate of the fruit forbidden from that tree,
At once he was cast out to woe and pain.   225
O gluttony, of you we should complain!
O if man knew how many maladies
Follow him from excess and gluttonies,

6. I.e., in such oaths as "God's teeth!"
7. See Genesis 19.30–38.
8. Matthew 14.6–11; Mark 6.19–28.

9. Seneca the Younger (d. 65 C.E.), Roman tragedian and Stoic moralist; see *Epistle* 83.18.

He'd be as moderate as he was able
About his diet, sitting at his table.   230
Alas, the short throat and the tender mouth
Make it so east and west and north and south,
Men must toil hard in earth, water, and air
So dainty meat and drink gluttons have there!
About this matter, O Paul, you well treat: 235
"Meat to belly, and belly then to meat,"
As Paul has said, "God shall destroy them both."[1]
Alas, a foul thing, by my faith and oath,
To say this word, and fouler the deed to dread
When a man drinks so of wines white and red   240
That of his throat he then makes his privy
Through this accursed superfluity.
      The apostle, weeping, piteously says too,
"There walk many about whom I've told you—
I say now weeping, with voice piteous —   245
These ones are enemies of Christ's cross thus,
Of whom the end is death; their paunch is God!"[2]
O paunch! O belly! O you stinking cod,[3]
Bag all filled up with corruption and dung!
For your foul sound at either end is sung.   250
Great cost and labor food for you to find!
These cooks, look how they pound, stew, strain, and grind,
So they turn substance into accident,[4]
And fill your greedy need up with their talent!
Out from the hard bones' middle knocked have they   255
The marrow, for they throw nothing away
That goes through the gullet soft and sweetly.
Spicings from leaf, bark, and root completely
Shall make his sauces up for his delight,
To stir in him a keener appetite.   260
Sure, he who haunts such delicacies nice
Is dead while he is living in such vice.
      A lecherous thing is wine, and drunkenness
Is full of fighting and of wretchedness.
O drunken man, disfigured is your face,   265
Sour is your breath, foul are you to embrace,
And through your drunken nose the sound does play
As though "Samson, Samson," you always say,
And yet, God knows, Samson never drank wine.[5]
You fall just like you were a stuck-through swine;   270
Your tongue is lost, and all decent behavior,
For drunkenness is the true sepulcher
Both of man's wit and of his discretion.
One in whom drink has its domination—
He can no secret keep, it must be said.   275

1. 1 Corinthians 6.13.
2. Philippians 3.18–19.
3. I.e., belly, but also the scrotum ("bag").
4. I.e., turn what is real into inessential attributes (terms from logic).
5. See Judges 13.4, 7, 14. "Samson" is here
merely drunken slurring.

Now keep yourself from wine, both white and red,
Especially, from the white wine of Lepe[6]
That is for sale in Fish Street or in Cheap,[7]
Because this wine from Spain creeps stealthily
Through other wines that grow close by, you see,   280
From which there rises such fumosity[8]
That when a man has drunk draughts, two or three,
And then supposes he's back home in Cheap,
He is in Spain, right in the town of Lepe—
He's not in La Rochelle, nor in Bordeaux[9]—   285
And then always, "Samson, Samson!" he'll go.
    But hearken, now, my lords; one word, I pray,
That all the sovereign acts, I dare well say,
Of victories in the Old Testament,
Through the one, true God, who's omnipotent,   290
Were done in abstinence and done in prayer.
Look in the Bible; you will learn it there.
    Now, look, Attilla,[1] the great conqueror,
Died in his sleep, with shame and dishonor,
His nose bleeding from drunkenness, you see.   295
A captain should live in sobriety.
And beyond this, consider now quite well
What commanded was unto Lemuel[2]—
Not Samuel, but Lemuel, I say;
Read the Bible, and find it told this way   300
About wine-giving to those who mete justice.
Suffice what it says there; enough of this.
    Since of gluttony I've finished speaking,
Now I'll turn and I'll forbid you gambling.
Gambling is the true mother of lying,   305
And of deceit and accursed perjuring,
Blasphemy, manslaughter, and waste also
Of goods and time, and further still to go,
It is shameful and contrary to honor
To be thought of as a common gambler.   310
The higher in estate that he stands yet,
The more he is considered desolate.
If a prince himself resorts to gambling,
In all his policies and governing,
He is, by common consent and opinion,   315
Held to be less in his reputation.
    Stilbo, who was a wise ambassador,
Was sent into Corinth with great honor
Out of Sparta to make an alliance.[3]

---

6. A coastal town in southwest Spain.
7. Streets in London.
8. Strong fumes.
9. Two seaports in southwest France in a region known for producing fine wines.
1. King of the Huns (d. 453), a nomadic people of central Asia who, under his leadership,
gained control of large areas of central and eastern Europe.
2. That kings should not drink wine (see Proverbs 31.4–5).
3. In ancient Greece, Sparta was renowned for its citizens' moral rectitude; Corinth had a reputation for immorality.

And when he came, it happened then by chance 320
That the greatest men from that land around,
Playing at dice there, all of them he found.
And for this reason, soon as it might be,
He stole home again to his own country,
And he said, "There I will not lose my name, 325
Nor in this way will I myself defame;
Never will I ally you with gamblers.
Now send forth other wise ambassadors;
For, by my word here, I would rather die
Than with these gamblers thus you to ally. 330
You, who are so glorious in honors,
Shall not ally yourselves with these gamblers
Through any will of mine or any treaty."
Lo, this wise philosopher, thus said he.

  And moreover, to the king Demetrius, 335
The king of Parthia,[4] as the book tells us,
Had sent in scorn a pair of dice of gold,
For he'd used dice before, it had been told;
Thus he held his glory and renown, too,
To have little repute and no value. 340
Lords may well locate other kinds of play
Honest enough to drive the day away.

  Now will I speak of oaths both false and great
A word or two, as these old books relate.
Swearing is a thing abominable, 345
And false swearing is more condemnable.
God on high forbade swearing completely,
As witness Matthew;[5] but especially
Of swearing says Jeremiah the holy,
"You shall not lie, but swear all oaths truly, 350
And swear in judgment and in righteousness";[6]
But idle swearing is accursedness.
Behold and see that in the first table
Of high God's commandments honorable,
How the second commandment demands this: 355
"Take not my name in vain or else amiss."
Lo, he'd rather forbid us such swearing
Than homicide or other cursed thing;
I say that, in their order, thus it stands;
He knows who the commandments understands, 360
How God's second commandment is just that.
And furthermore, here I will tell you flat
That vengeance will not vacate one's house thus
If one with one's oaths is too outrageous.
Now "By God's precious heart," and "By his nails," 365
And "By the blood of Christ that is at Hales,[7]

---

4. Modern northeastern Iran; Demetrius was a Syrian king. "The book" (also the source of the story of Stilbo) is John of Salisbury's *Policraticus* (1159), 1.5.

5. See Matthew 5.34.
6. See Jeremiah 4.2.
7. An abbey in Gloucestershire, believed to possess some of Christ's blood.

Seven's my chance, and yours is five and three!"
"By God's arms, I swear, if you play falsely,
This dagger right through your heart will go!"—
This fruit comes from these two bitched bones[8] so: 370
Perjury, ire, falseness, and homicide.
Now, for the love of Christ who for us died,
Leave all your oaths, both the small and the great.
But, sires, here now my tale I will relate.

  Thus, these three debauchers of whom I tell, 375
Long before prime[9] had rung from any bell,
Had sat down in a tavern there to drink;
And as they sat, they all heard a bell clink
And toll, for a corpse was brought to his grave.
Thus, one of them then called out to his knave:[1] 380
"Go at once," he said, "and now ask quickly
What corpse is passing nearby that we see;
Make sure that his name you report clearly."
  "Sire," said this boy, "this isn't necessary;
It was told to me just two hours before 385
You came, he was an old fellow of yours,
And suddenly, he was slain here tonight,
Stone drunk as he sat on his bench upright.
There came a secret thief called Death, men say,
Who, in this country, all the people slay, 390
In two he smote his heart then with his spear,
And went away with no more words from here.
He's slain a thousand in this pestilence.[2]
Master, before you come in his presence,
It seems to me that it's necessary 395
To be wary of this adversary.
Be prepared to meet him forevermore;
Thus my dame taught me; I can say no more."
"By Saint Mary," the tavern-keep said, too,
"He's slain this year, and thus the child speaks true, 400
In a great village, a mile hence, I'd gauge,
Both man and woman, farmer, child, and page;
I believe that he has his dwelling there.
It'd be great wisdom for you to prepare,
Before he did someone a dishonor." 405
  "Yes, by God's arms," then said this debaucher,
"Is it such peril if one with him meets?
I shall seek him in all byways and streets,
So to God's worthy bones I make my vow!
Hark, good fellows, we three are all one now; 410
Let's each hold up his hand to the other,

---

8. I.e., cursed dice.
9. One of the canonical hours, at which prescribed prayers were offered daily and which
thus served to divide the day: prime was the
service at about 6 A.M.

1. Servant boy.
2. Bubonic plague, Black Death; a major outbreak in the mid-14th century killed at least
one-third of the population of Europe.

And each one become the other's brother;
We will slay this false traitor Death today.
He shall be slain who does so many slay,
By God's dignity, before it is night!" 415
    These three then pledged their word as best they might
To live and die each one for the other,
As though he were his natural-born brother.
And up they start, in their rage all drunken,
And forth they all go toward that village, then, 420
Of which the tavern-keep did speak before.
And many grisly oaths those three then swore,
And Christ's blessed body they did tear and shred—
If they can catch him, then Death shall be dead!
    When they had gone not fully half a mile, 425
Right where they would have climbed over a stile,
An old and poor man with those three did meet.
There this old man quite meekly did them greet,
And said thus, "Now, my lords, may God you see!"
    The proudest one of these debauchers three 430
Answered him back, "What, churl, with sorry grace!
Why are you all wrapped up, except your face?
Why do you live so long to such great age?"
    This old man did look into his visage,
And answered thus: "Since I cannot find a 435
Man, even if I walked to India,
Neither in a city or a village,
Who would exchange his youth for my age,
Therefore, I must have my old age still,
For as long a time as it is God's will. 440
Alas, Death does not want to have my life.
I walk here like a wretch in restless strife,
And on the ground, which is my mother's gate,
I knock with my staff, early and late,
And I say, 'Dear mother, let me in! 445
Lo, how I vanish, flesh and blood and skin!
Alas, now when shall my bones find their rest?
Mother, I would exchange my treasure chest
That such a long time in my chamber's been,
Yea, for a haircloth shroud to wrap me in!' 450
But yet, to me, she will not give that grace,
And thus, all pale and withered is my face.
    But, sires, to you it does no courtesy
To speak to an old man with villainy,
Unless he should trespass in word or deed. 455
In Holy Writ, you may yourselves well read:
'Before an old man, hoary on his head,
You should stand up.'[3] Thus I warn you instead:
Unto an old man, no harm must you do

3. Leviticus 19.32.

More than you would want men to do to you   460
In old age, if so long you might abide.
Let God be with you, where you walk or ride!
I must go now to where I have to go."
      "Nay, by God, old churl, you will not do so,"
This other gambler said to him quickly;   465
"By Saint John, you don't leave so easily!
You spoke now of this traitor Death today,
Who, in this country, all our friends does slay.
Have here my word, as you're his spy, I say,
Tell where he is, or for it you will pay,   470
By God and by the holy sacrament!
For surely, with him now, you do consent
To slay all us young folk, you false old thief!"
      "Sires," he said, "if you're eager, to be brief,
To find Death, go turn up this crooked way;   475
By my faith, I left him in that grove today,
Under a tree, and there his time he'll bide;
Nothing in your boast will make him hide.
You see that oak? Right there, him you will find.
May God save you, who bought again mankind,   480
And you amend!" Thus said here this old man;
      And then each one of these debauchers ran
Till he came to that tree, and there they found
Of florins fine of gold, coined new and round
Well nigh to eight full bushels' worth, they thought.   485
No longer, then, after Death have they sought,
Each of them so glad was of that sight,
Because the florins were so fair and bright,
That they all sat down by that precious hoard.
The worst of them spoke first of their reward.   490
      "Brethren," said he, "take heed of what I say;
My wit is great, although I jest and play.
This treasure to us Fortune now did give
In mirth and jolliness our life to live;
Easily as it comes, so will we spend.   495
God's precious dignity, what did portend
Today that we would have so much good grace?
If this gold might be carried from this place
Back home to my house, or else home to yours—
You know this gold is ours forevermore—   500
Then we would be in high felicity.
But truly, by day, this might never be.
Men would all say that we're thieves bold and strong;
For our own treasure, we'd hang before long.
This treasure must be carried out by night   505
As wisely and as slyly as we might.
Thus, I advise a cut[4] among us all

---

4. I.e., straws. "The cut" is the longer straw.

Be drawn, and then see where the cut will fall;
He who wins the cut, with heart blithely cast,
Shall run to town, and that with speed quite fast, 510
And bring us bread and wine quite privately.
And two of us shall guard all stealthily
This treasure well; if he does not tarry,
When it's night, we will this treasure carry,
Where we have all by one accord best thought." 515
Then one of them the cut in his fist brought,
And bade them draw and see where it would fall;
And it fell to the youngest of them all,
Who set out for town immediately.
And just as soon as on his way went he, 520
One of them spoke up thus to the other:
"You know well that you are my sworn brother;
At once about your profit let me tell.
Our fellow now is gone, as you know well.
Here is gold, and that in quite some plenty, 525
Which shall divided be among us three.
But nonetheless, if I can shape it so
It's divided between us two, you know,
Wouldn't I have done a good friend's turn to you?"
            The other said, "I don't know what you'll do, 530
He knows that with us both the gold did stay;
What shall we do? To him, what shall we say?"
        "Shall it be secret?" then said the first shrew.[5]
"And I shall tell you now in words a few
What we shall do, and bring it well about." 535
"I grant it," said the other, "without doubt,
By my word, that I will not betray you."
        "Now," said the first, "You know well we are two,
And we two shall be stronger than one yet.
See to it, right away, when he is set, 540
Rise up just as though with him you would play;
I'll stab him through his two sides right away
While you struggle with him as though it's a game,
And with your dagger, see you do the same;
And then shall all this gold divided be, 545
My dear friend, only between you and me.
Then may we both all of our lusts fulfill,
And play at dice just as much as we will."
Thus these two shrews have one accord that day
To slay the third, as you have heard me say. 550
        This youngest one, who went into the town,
Quite often in his heart rolls up and down
The beauty of these florins new and bright.
"O Lord!" said he, "if it were so I might
Have all this treasure for myself alone, 555
There is no man who lives beneath the throne

5. Villain.

Of God who would live quite so merrily!"
At last the fiend, who is our enemy,
Put in his thought that he should poison buy,
With which he might make his two fellows die;   560
The fiend found him to live in such a way
That him to sorrow he could bring that day.
For this was utterly his full intent,
To slay them both, and never to repent.
Forth he goes, no longer would he tarry,   565
Into town, to an apothecary,
And prayed the man that to him he would sell
Some poison that would help to kill rats well;
And in his yard there was a weasel, who,
As he then said, had slain his capons, too.   570
He'd happily take vengeance, if he might,
On vermin that destroyed him in the night.

    Said the apothecary, "I will give
You something here, as God lets my soul live,
Such that, in this world, there's no single creature   575
Who has drunk or eaten of this mixture
One little grain or just the smallest bit,
Who won't find at once that his life's forfeit;
Yes, he will die, and in a shorter while
Than it will take you to walk but a mile,   580
This poison is so violent and strong."

    This cursed man in his hand took along
This poison in a box, and then he ran
Into a nearby street right to a man,
And borrowed from him there large bottles three,   585
And this poison in two of them poured he;
The third one he kept clean for his own drink.
For all that night, to work hard he did think
In carrying the gold out of that place.
And when this debaucher, with sorry grace,   590
Had with the wine filled the great bottles three,
Back to his fellows once again goes he.

    What need is there to preach about this more?
For just as they had planned his death before,
Quickly they slew him, and when it was done,   595
Then right away spoke up the other one:
"Let us sit and drink and now make merry.
Afterward, we will his body bury."
And with that word, by chance, he did happen
To take up the bottle which held poison,   600
And drank, and gave drink to his fellow, too,
And thus at once they died, both of those two.

    Surely, I suppose that Avicenna[6]
Never wrote, in his treatise or fen, a

---

6. Ibn Sina (ca. 980–1037), Islamic philosopher whose work on medicine was widely disseminated, including in Europe. His *Canon of Medicine* is divided into shorter sections that in the Latin translation are called "fens."

More wondrous display of poisoning 605
Than these wretches showed before their ending.
Thus ended now are these two homicides,
And also the false poisoner besides.

   O cursed sin of all accursedness!
O homicidal traitors! O wickedness! 610
O gluttony! O gambling and lechery!
You blasphemer of Christ with villainy
And great oaths, through habit and through pride!
Alas, mankind, how may it be denied
That to your creator, who has you wrought 615
And with his precious heart's blood has you bought,
Against nature, you're false and unkind, alas?

   Now, good men, God forgive you your trespass.
Beware the sin of avarice so grave!
My holy pardon may you now all save, 620
If you offer coins of gold or sterling,
Or else a silver brooch or spoon or ring.
Bow your head now beneath this holy bull!
Come up, you wives, and offer me your wool!
Your names I enter in my roll right so; 625
Into the bliss of heaven shall you go.
I absolve you here through my high power,
To be clean and clear, you who will offer,
As when you were born.—Lo, sires, I thus preach then.
Now Jesus Christ, who is our soul's physician, 630
Grant to you his pardon to receive,
For that is best; I will you not deceive.

   But, sires, one word I forgot in my tale:
My bag holds pardons and relics for sale,
As fair as has any man in England, 635
Which were given me by the pope's own hand.
If anyone wants, out of devotion,
To offer and have my absolution,
Come forth now and kneel down here, everyone,
And meekly you can receive my pardon; 640
Or you can take my pardon as you wend,
All new and fresh, as every mile does end,
As long as you give, and always renew,
Nobles[7] or pence, which are both good and true.
To each one who's here, it is an honor 645
For you to have a sufficient pardoner
To absolve you in this land as you ride
For whatever happens by the wayside.
Perhaps there may fall one or two of you
Down from his horse and break his neck in two. 650
Look what security it's for you all
That I into your fellowship did fall,

---

7. Gold coins, each worth about 80 pence.

Who may absolve you, the more and the less,
When the soul may from your body pass.
I advise that our Host shall here begin   655
Because he is most enveloped in sin.
Come forth, sir Host; to give be the first one,
And you shall kiss the relics every one,
Yes, for a groat! Now unbuckle your purse."
        "No! No!" said he, "then may I have Christ's curse!   660
Leave it," said he, "it shall not be, I swear!
You would make me kiss your old underwear,
And swear it was the relic of a saint,
Though on it with your asshole you did paint!
Now, by Saint Helen's cross,[8] you understand,   665
I wish I had your balls right in my hand
Instead of relics in their reliquary.
Let them be cut off! Them, I'll help you carry!
They'll be enshrined for good in a hog's turd!"
        This Pardoner answered back not one word;   670
So angry he was, no word would he say.
        "Now," said our Host, "I will no longer play
With you, or with another angry man."
But right away the worthy Knight began,
When he saw all of the people laughing,   675
"No more of this, for enough of this thing!
Sir Pardoner, be glad and of good cheer;
And you, sir Host, who are to me so dear,
I pray you the Pardoner to kiss here.
And Pardoner, I pray you, draw you near.   680
As we have done, now let us laugh and play."
At once they kissed and rode forth on their way.

Here is ended the Pardoner's Tale.

---

8. St. Helen or St. Helena (d. ca. 328), mother of the Emperor Constantine, was credited with
having discovered the cross on which Jesus was crucified.

CODICIBVS SACRIS HOSTILI CLADE PERVSTIS
ESDRA DŌ FERVENS HOC REPARAVIT OPVS

This page from the Codex Amiatinus (ca. 8th century C.E.), the earliest surviving manuscript of the Latin Vulgate Bible, depicts the Jewish scribe Ezra. Ezra is traditionally credited with reestablishing the primacy of the Law in Jewish society.

Frontispiece from the world's earliest dated printed book: a Chinese translation of the Buddhist *Diamond Sūtra*. This translation, consisting of a series of woodblock prints on a sixteen-foot scroll, was printed in 868 C.E.

A fragment of the Qur'an (specifically, the beginning of sura 33) written in Kufic script, the oldest calligraphic form of Arabic script. This parchment manuscript, decorated with designs in black and red ink and gold leaf, dates from the ninth or tenth century C.E.

HWÆT WE GARDE

na ingear dagum· þeod cyninga
þrym ge frunon huða æþelingas elle
fremedon· oft scyld sceffing sceaþe
þreatum moneðu mægþum meodo setla
ofteah egsode eorl syððan ærest wer
fea sceaft funden he þæs frofre geba
weox under wolcnum weorð myndum þah
oð þ him æghpylc þara ymb sittendra
ofer hron rade hyran scolde gomban
gyldan þ wæs god cyning· ðæm eafera wæs
æfter cenned geong ingeardum þone god
sende folce tofrofre fyren ðearfe on
geat þ hie ær drugon aldor ase lange
hpile him þæs lif frea wuldres wealdend
worold are forgeaf beowulf wæs bren
blæd wide sprang scyldes eafera scede
landum in· Spa sceal
ge wyrcean fromum feoh giftum on fæder

A single leaf from a fan-shaped album of excerpts from the Buddhist *Lotus Sūtra* that was produced near the end of the Heian Period in Japan (i.e., sometime during the late twelfth century). In addition to the calligraphic excerpt on the right, this page features a genre painting of servants performing their duties. The illustrations in these fan-shaped albums were typically unrelated to the quoted sutra.

A page from what is perhaps the most famous printed book of all time: the Gutenberg Bible (ca. 1453–56). Printed in Mainz, Germany, this Bible was one of the first books (and certainly the most notable one) to be printed in Europe using a movable-type printing press. Only twenty-one copies survive.

ARte mea reliquas illuſtro Typographus artes,
  Imprimo dum varios ære micante libros.
Quæ prius auſta ſitu, quæ puluere plena iacebant,
Vidimus obſcura noſte ſepulta premi.

Hæc veterum renouo neglecta volumina Patrum
  Atq̢ ſcolis curo publica faſta legi.
Artem prima nouam reperiſſe Moguntia fertur,
  Vrbs grauis, et multis ingenioſa modis.
Qua nihil vtilius videt, aut precioſius orbis,
  Vix melius quicquam ſecla futura dabunt.

A woodcut print from Jost Amman's *The Book of Trades* (1568), a short
guide to the various ranks of European society, illustrates the operation of
a printer's workshop. Though this book was published over a century after
Johannes Gutenberg's revolutionary innovations in movable-type printing,
the technology pictured here is quite similar to that used by Gutenberg.

A page from an illuminated manuscript of the Persian epic *Shahnameh*. This version is attributed to Muzaffar Ali, a famous Persian miniaturist who thrived during the reign of Shah Tahmasp (1525–76).

dead girl who is the central figure in *Pearl*. In his closing words to Gawain, the Green Knight might be speaking of the Pearl-maiden herself when he tells the selfless knight, "I declare you purged, as polished and as pure / as the day you were born, without blemish or blame."

Sir Gawain and the Green Knight[1]

FITT I

Once the siege and assault of Troy had ceased,
with the city a smoke-heap of cinders and ash,
the traitor who contrived such betrayal there
was tried for his treachery,[2] the truest on earth,
Aeneas, it was, with his noble warriors   5
who went conquering abroad, laying claim to the crowns
of the wealthiest kingdoms in the western world.
Mighty Romulus[3] quickly careered towards Rome
and conceived a city in magnificent style
which from then until now has been known by his name.   10
Ticius constructed townships in Tuscany
and Langobard did likewise building homes in Lombardy.[4]
And further afield, over the Sea of France,
Felix Brutus[5] founds Britain on broad banks
        most grand.   15
    And wonder, dread and war
    have lingered in that land
    where loss and love in turn
    have held the upper hand.

After Britain was built by this founding father   20
a bold race bred there, battle-happy men
causing trouble and torment in turbulent times,
and through history more strangeness has happened here
than anywhere else I know of on Earth.
But most regal of rulers in the royal line   25
was Arthur, who I heard is honored above all,
and the inspiring story I intend to spin
has moved the hearts and minds of many—
an awesome episode in the legends of Arthur.

1. Translated from Middle English by Simon Armitage.
2. According to one medieval tradition, the unnamed Trojan traitor was Antenor—a neutral character in Virgil's *Aeneid*, which ties the founding of Rome to the noble warrior Aeneas, who escaped the fall of his city. Another tradition blames Aeneas himself. Medieval historians invented additional Trojan genealogies for other European nations.
3. The legendary founder of Rome, along with his brother Remus; traditionally he is Aeneas's descendant, not his contemporary.
4. Two regions in northern Italy; Ticius and Langobard are other "Trojan" founders.
5. Great-grandson of Aeneas. "Felix": literally, "happy" or "fortunate" (Latin).

So listen a little while to my tale if you will   30
and I'll tell it as it's told in the town where it trips from
   the tongue;
  and as it has been inked
  in stories bold and strong,
  through letters which, once linked,   35
  have lasted loud and long.

It was Christmas at Camelot[6]—King Arthur's court,
where the great and the good of the land had gathered,
the right noble lords of the ranks of the Round Table
all roundly carousing and reveling in pleasure.   40
Time after time, in tournaments of joust,
they had lunged at each other with leveled lances
then returned to the castle to carry on their caroling,
for the feasting lasted a full fortnight and one day,
with more food and drink than a fellow could dream of.   45
The hubbub of their humor was heavenly to hear:
pleasant dialogue by day and dancing after dusk,
so house and hall were lit with happiness
and lords and ladies were luminous with joy.
With all the wonder in the world they gathered there as one: 50
the most chivalrous and courteous knights known to Christendom;
the most wonderful women to have walked in this world;
the handsomest king to be crowned at court.
Fine folk with their futures before them, there in
   that hall.
  Their highly honored king   55
  was happiest of all:
  no nobler knights had come
  within a castle's wall.

With New Year so young it still yawned and stretched   60
helpings were doubled on the dais[7] that day.
And as king and company were coming to the hall
the choir in the chapel fell suddenly quiet,
then a chorus erupted from the courtiers and clerks:
"Noel," they cheered, then "Noel, Noel,"   65
"New Year Gifts!" the knights cried next
as they pressed forwards to offer their presents,
teasing with frivolous favors and forfeits,
till those ladies who lost couldn't help but laugh,
and the undefeated were far from forlorn.[8]   70
Their merrymaking rolled on in this manner until mealtime,

6. Located by tradition in various places, but usually in southern England (often Cornwall) or southern Wales.
7. A raised platform (the setting described here is not the famous Round Table but a conventional hall, in which those of highest rank sit at a table on the dais while the rest are at a long table or tables perpendicular to it).
8. Because the forfeit in this game is a kiss, both winners and losers are happy with the outcome.

when, worthily washed, they went to the table,
and were seated in order of honor, as was apt,
with Guinevere[9] in their gathering, gloriously framed
at her place on the platform, pricelessly curtained   75
by silk to each side, and canopied across
with tasteful tapestries of Toulouse and Turkestan,[1]
studded with stones and stunning gems
beyond pocket or purse, beyond what pennies
        could buy.   80
    But not one stone outshone
    the quartz of the queen's eyes;
    with hand on heart, no one
    could argue otherwise.

But Arthur would not eat until all were served.   85
He brimmed with ebullience, being almost boyish
in his love of life, and what he liked the least
was to sit still watching the seasons slip by.
His blood was busy and he buzzed with thoughts,
and the matter which played on his mind at that moment   90
was his pledge to take no portion from his plate
on such a special day until a story was told:
some far-fetched yarn or outrageous fable,
the tallest of tales, yet one ringing with truth,
like the action-packed epics of men-at-arms.   95
Or till some chancer had challenged his chosen knight,
dared him, with a lance, to lay life on the line,
to stare death face-to-face and accept defeat
should fortune or fate smile more favorably on his foe.
Within Camelot's castle this was the custom,   100
and at feasts and festivals when the fellowship
        would meet.
    With features proud and fine
    he stood there tall and straight,
    a king at Christmastime   105
    amid great merriment.

And still he stands there just being himself,
chatting away charmingly, exchanging views.
Good Sir Gawain is seated by Guinevere,
and at Arthur's other side sits Agravain the Hard Hand,   110
both nephews of the king and notable knights.
At the head of the board sat Bishop Baldwin,
with Ywain, son of Urien, to eat beside him.
First those sitting on the dais were splendidly served,
then those stalwarts seated on the benches to the sides.   115
The first course comes in to the fanfare and clamor
of blasting trumpets hung with trembling banners,

9. The wife of King Arthur.
1. A city in southern France and a region of Asia, respectively.

then pounding double-drums and dinning pipes,
weird sounds and wails of such warbled wildness
that to hear and feel them made the heart float free.   120
Flavorsome delicacies of flesh were fetched in
and the freshest of foods, so many in fact
there was scarcely space to present the stews
or to set the soups in the silver bowls on
      the cloth.   125
      Each guest received his share
      of bread or meat or broth;
      a dozen plates per pair—
      plus beer or wine, or both!

Now, on the subject of supper I'll say no more   130
as it's obvious to everyone that no one went without.
Because another sound, a new sound, suddenly drew near,
which might signal the king to sample his supper,
for barely had the horns finished blowing their breath
and with starters just spooned to the seated guests,   135
a fearful form appeared, framed in the door:
a mountain of a man, immeasurably high,
a hulk of a human from head to hips,
so long and thick in his loins and his limbs
I should genuinely judge him to be a half giant,   140
or a most massive man, the mightiest of mortals.
But handsome, too, like any horseman worth his horse,
for despite the bulk and brawn of his body
his stomach and waist were slender and sleek.
In fact in all features he was finely formed   145
      it seemed.
      Amazement seized their minds,
      no soul had ever seen
      a knight of such a kind—
      entirely emerald green.   150

And his gear and garments were green as well:
a tight fitting tunic, tailored to his torso,
and a cloak to cover him, the cloth fully lined
with smoothly shorn fur clearly showing, and faced
with all-white ermine, as was the hood,   155
worn shawled on his shoulders, shucked from his head.
On his lower limbs his leggings were also green,
wrapped closely round his calves, and his sparkling spurs
were green-gold, strapped with stripy silk,
and were set on his stockings, for this stranger was shoeless.   160
In all vestments he revealed himself veritably verdant!
From his belt hooks and buckle to the baubles and gems
arrayed so richly around his costume
and adorning the saddle, stitched onto silk.
All the details of his dress are difficult to describe,   165
embroidered as it was with butterflies and birds,

green beads emblazoned on a background of gold.
All the horse's tack—harness strap, hind strap,
the eye of the bit, each alloy and enamel
and the stirrups he stood in were similarly tinted,   170
and the same with the cantle and the skirts of the saddle,
all glimmering and glinting with the greenest jewels.
And the horse: every hair was green, from hoof
        to mane.
    A steed of pure green stock.   175
    Each snort and shudder strained
    the hand-stitched bridle, but
    his rider had him reined.

The fellow in green was in fine fettle.
The hair of his head was as green as his horse,   180
fine flowing locks which fanned across his back,
plus a bushy green beard growing down to his breast,
which hung with the splendid hair from his head
and was lopped in a line at elbow length
so half his arms were gowned in green growth,   185
crimped at the collar, like a king's cape.
The mane of his mount was groomed to match,
combed and knotted into curlicues
then tinseled with gold, tied and twisted
green over gold, green over gold. . . .   190
The fetlocks were finished in the same fashion
with bright green ribbon braided with beads,
as was the tail—to its tippety-tip!
And a long, tied thong lacing it tight
where bright and burnished gold bells chimed clearly.   195
No waking man had witnessed such a warrior
or weird warhorse—otherworldly, yet flesh
        and bone.
    His look was lightning bright
    said those who glimpsed its glow.   200
    It seemed no man there might
    survive his violent blow.

Yet he wore no helmet and no hauberk either,
no armored apparel or plate was apparent,
and he swung no sword nor sported any shield,   205
but held in one hand a sprig of holly—
of all the evergreens the greenest ever—
and in the other hand held the mother of all axes,
a cruel piece of kit I kid you not:
the head was an ell in length at least   210
and forged in green steel with a gilt finish;
its broad-edged blade brightly burnished,
it could shear a man's scalp and shave him to boot.
The handle which fitted that fiend's great fist
was inlaid with iron, end to end,   215

with green pigment picking out impressive designs.
From stock to neck, where it stopped with a knot,
a lace was looped the length of the haft,
trimmed with tassels and tails of string
fastened firmly in place by forest-green buttons.   220
And he kicks on, canters through that crowded hall
towards the top table, not the least bit timid,
cocksure of himself, sitting high in the saddle.
"And who," he bellows, without breaking breath,
"is governor of this gaggle? I'll be glad to know.   225
It's with him and no one else that I'll hold
            a pact."
        He held them with his eyes,
        and looked from right to left,
        not knowing, of those knights,   230
        which person to respect.

The guests looked on. They gaped and they gawked
and were mute with amazement: what did it mean
that human and horse could develop this hue,
should grow to be grass-green or greener still,   235
like green enamel emboldened by bright gold?
Some stood and stared then stepped a little closer,
drawn near to the knight to know his next move;
they'd seen some sights, but this was something special,
a miracle or magic, or so they imagined.   240
Yet several of the lords were like statues in their seats,
left speechless and rigid, not risking a response.
The hall fell hushed, as if all who were present
had slipped into sleep or some trancelike state.
            No doubt   245
        not all were stunned and stilled
        by dread, but duty bound
        to hold their tongues until
        their sovereign could respond.

Then the king acknowledged this curious occurrence,   250
cordially addressed him, keeping his cool.
"A warm welcome, sir, this winter's night.
My name is Arthur, I am head of this house.
Won't you slide from that saddle and stay awhile,
and the business which brings you we shall learn of later."   255
"No," said the knight, "by Him in highest heaven,
I'm not here to idle in your hall this evening.
But because your acclaim is so loudly chorused,
and your castle and brotherhood are called the best,
the strongest men to ever mount the saddle,   260
the worthiest knights ever known to the world,
both in competition and true combat,
and since courtesy, so it's said, is championed here,
I'm intrigued, and attracted to your door at this time.

Be assured by this holly stem here in my hand   265
that I mean no menace. So expect no malice,
for if I'd slogged here tonight to slay and slaughter
my helmet and hauberk wouldn't be at home
and my sword and spear would be here at my side,
and more weapons of war, as I'm sure you're aware;   270
I'm clothed for peace, not kitted out for conflict.
But if you're half as honorable as I've heard folk say
you'll gracefully grant me this game which I ask for
        by right."
      Then Arthur answered, "Knight   275
      most courteous, you claim
      a fair, unarmored fight.
      We'll see you have the same."

"I'm spoiling for no scrap, I swear. Besides,
the bodies on these benches are just bum-fluffed bairns.   280
If I'd ridden to your castle rigged out for a ruck
these lightweight men wouldn't last a minute.
But it's Yuletide—a time of youthfulness, yes?
So at Christmas in this court I lay down a challenge:
if a person here present, within these premises,   285
is big or bold or red-blooded enough
to strike me one stroke and be struck in return,
I shall give him as a gift this gigantic cleaver
and the axe shall be his to handle how he likes.
I'll kneel, bare my neck and take the first knock.   290
So who has the gall? The gumption? The guts?
Who'll spring from his seat and snatch this weapon?
I offer the axe—who'll have it as his own?
I'll afford one free hit from which I won't flinch,
and promise that twelve months will pass in peace,   295
        then claim
      the duty I deserve
      in one year and one day.
      Does no one have the nerve
      to wager in this way?"   300

Flustered at first, now totally foxed
were the household and the lords, both the highborn and the low.
Still stirruped, the knight swiveled round in his saddle
looking left and right, his red eyes rolling
beneath the bristles of his bushy green brows,   305
his beard swishing from side to side.
When the court kept its counsel he cleared his throat
and stiffened his spine. Then he spoke his mind:
"So here is the House of Arthur," he scoffed,
"whose virtues reverberate across vast realms.   310
Where's the fortitude and fearlessness you're so famous for?
And the breathtaking bravery and the big-mouth bragging?
The towering reputation of the Round Table,

skittled and scuppered by a stranger—what a scandal!
You flap and you flinch and I've not raised a finger!"   315
Then he laughed so loud that their leader saw red.
Blood flowed to his fine-featured face and he raged
      inside.
    His men were also hurt—
    those words had pricked their pride.   320
    But born so brave at heart
    the king stepped up one stride.

"Your request," he countered, "is quite insane,
and folly finds the man who flirts with the fool.
No warrior worth his salt would be worried by your words,   325
so in heaven's good name hand over the axe
and I'll happily fulfill the favor you ask."
He strides to him swiftly and seizes his arm;
the man dismounts in one mighty leap.
Then Arthur grips the axe, grabs it by its haft   330
and takes it above him, intending to attack.
Yet the stranger before him stands up straight,
highest in the house by at least a head.
Quite simply he stands there stroking his beard,
fiddling with his coat, his face without fear,   335
about to be bludgeoned, but no more bothered
than a guest at the table being given a goblet
      of wine.
    By Guinevere, Gawain
    now to his king inclines   340
    and says, "I stake my claim.
    This melee must be mine."

"Should you call me, courteous lord," said Gawain to his king,
"to rise from my seat and stand at your side,
politely take leave of my place at the table   345
and quit without causing offence to my queen,
then I shall come to your counsel before this great court.
For I find it unfitting, as my fellow knights would,
when a deed of such daring is dangled before us
that you take on this trial—tempted as you are—   350
when brave, bold men are seated on these benches,
men never matched in the mettle of their minds,
never beaten or bettered in the field of battle.
I am weakest of your warriors and feeblest of wit;
loss of my life would be least lamented.   355
Were I not your nephew my life would mean nothing;
to be born of your blood is my body's only claim.
Such a foolish affair is unfitting for a king,
so, being first to come forward, it should fall to me.
And if my proposal is improper, let no other person   360
      stand blame."

The knighthood then unites
and each knight says the same:
their king can stand aside
and give Gawain the game.   365

So the sovereign instructed his knight to stand.
Getting to his feet he moved graciously forward
and knelt before Arthur, taking hold of the axe.
Letting go of it, Arthur then held up his hand
to give young Gawain the blessing of God   370
and hope he finds firmness in heart and fist.
"Take care, young cousin, to catch him cleanly,
use full-blooded force then you needn't fear
the blow which he threatens to trade in return."
Gawain, with the weapon, walked towards the warrior,   375
and they stood face-to-face, not one man afraid.
Then the green knight spoke, growled at Gawain:
"Before we compete, repeat what we've promised.
And start by saying your name to me, sir,
and tell me the truth so I can take it on trust."   380
"In good faith," said the knight, "Gawain is my name.
I heave this axe, and whatever happens after,
in twelvemonth's time I'll be struck in return
with any weapon you wish, and by you and you
          alone."   385
     The green man speaks again:
     "I swear on all I know,
     I'm glad it's you, Gawain,
     who'll drive the axe-head home."

"Gawain," said the green knight, "by God, I'm glad   390
the favor I've called for will fall from your fist.
You've perfectly repeated the promise we made
and the terms of the contest are crystal clear.
Except for one thing: you must solemnly swear
that you'll seek me yourself; that you'll search me out   395
to the ends of the earth to earn the same blow
as you'll dole out today in this decorous hall."
"But where will you be? Where's your abode?
You're a man of mystery, as God is my maker.
Which court do you come from and what are you called?   400
There is knowledge I need, including your name,
then I shall use all my wit to work out the way,
and keep to our contract, so cross my heart."
"But enough at New Year. It needs nothing more,"
said the warrior in green to worthy Gawain.   405
"I could tell you the truth once you've taken the blow;
if you smite me smartly I could spell out the facts
of my house and home and my name, if it helps,
then you'll pay me a visit and vouch for our pact.

Or if I keep quiet you might cope all the better,   410
loafing and lounging here, looking no further. But
          we stall!
     Now grasp that gruesome axe
     and show your striking style."
     He answered, "Since you ask,"   415
     and touched the tempered steel.

In the standing position he prepared to be struck,
bent forward, revealing a flash of green flesh
as he heaped his hair to the crown of his head,
the nape of his neck now naked and ready.   420
Gawain grips the axe and heaves it heavenwards,
plants his left foot firmly on the floor in front,
then swings it swiftly towards the bare skin.
The cleanness of the strike cleaved the spinal cord
and parted the fat and the flesh so far   425
that the bright steel blade took a bite from the floor.
The handsome head tumbles onto the earth
and the king's men kick it as it clatters past.
Blood gutters brightly against his green gown,
yet the man doesn't shudder or stagger or sink   430
but trudges towards them on those tree-trunk legs
and rummages around, reaches at their feet
and cops hold of his head and hoists it high,
and strides to his steed, snatches the bridle,
steps into the stirrup and swings into the saddle   435
still gripping his head by a handful of hair.
Then he settles himself in his seat with the ease
of a man unmarked, never mind being minus
          his head!
     He wheeled his bulk about,   440
     that body which still bled.
     They cowered in the court
     before his speech was said.

For that scalp and skull now swung from his fist;
to the noblest at the table he turned the face   445
and it opened its eyelids, stared straight ahead
and spoke this speech, which you'll hear for yourselves:
"Sir Gawain, be wise enough to keep your word
and faithfully follow me until you find me,
as you vowed in this hall within hearing of these horsemen.   450
You're charged with getting to the Green Chapel,
to reap what you've sown. You'll rightfully receive
that what is due to be dealt to you as New Year dawns.
Men know my name as the Green Chapel knight,
and even a fool couldn't fail to find me.   455
So come, or be called a coward forever."
With a tug of the reins he twisted around
and, head still in hand, galloped out of the hall,

so the hooves brought fire from the flame in the flint.
Which kingdom he came from they hadn't a clue,   460
no more than they knew where he made for next.
        And then?
    Well, with the green man gone
    they laughed and grinned again.
    And yet such goings-on   465
    were magic to those men.

And although King Arthur was awestruck at heart
no sign of it showed. Instead he spoke
to his exquisite queen with courteous words:
"Dear lady, don't be daunted by this deed today,   470
it's in keeping that such strangeness should occur at Christmas
between sessions of banter and seasonal song,
amid the lively pastimes of ladies and lords.
And at least I'm allowed to eat at last,
having witnessed such wonder, wouldn't you say?"   475
Then he glanced at Gawain and spoke gracefully:
"Now hang up your axe²—one hack is enough."
So it dangled from the drape behind the dais
so that men who saw it would be mesmerized and amazed,
and give voice, on its evidence, to that stunning event.   480
Then the two of them turned and walked to the table,
the monarch and his knight, and men served the meal—
double dishes apiece, rare delicacies,
all manner of food—and the music of minstrels.
And they danced and sang till the sun went down   485
        that day.
    But mind your mood, Gawain,
    lest dread make you delay,
    or lose this lethal game
    you've promised you will play.   490

Fitt 2

This happening was a gift—just as Arthur had asked for
and had yearned to hear of while the year was young.
And if guests had no subject as they strolled to their seats,
now this serious concern sustained their chatter.
And Gawain had been glad to begin the game,   495
but don't be so shocked should the plot turn pear-shaped:
for men might be merry when addled with mead
but each year, short lived, is unlike the last
and rarely resolves in the style it arrived.
So the festival finishes and a new year follows   500
in eternal sequence, season by season.
After lavish Christmas come the lean days of Lent³

---

2. A punning phrase, as it applies both literally and figuratively—"stop what you're doing."

3. The forty days before Easter, a penitential period of prayer and restricted eating.

when the flesh is tested with fish and simple food.
Then the world's weather wages war on winter:
cold shrinks earthwards and the clouds climb;   505
sun-warmed, shimmering rain comes showering
onto meadows and fields where flowers unfurl;
woods and grounds wear a wardrobe of green;
birds burble with life and build busily
as summer spreads, settling on slopes as   510
        it should.
    Now every hedgerow brims
    with blossom and with bud,
    and lively songbirds sing
    from lovely, leafy woods.   515

So summer comes in season with its subtle airs,
when the west wind sighs among shoots and seeds,
and those plants which flower and flourish are a pleasure
as their leaves let drip their drink of dew
and they sparkle and glitter when glanced by sunlight.   520
Then autumn arrives to harden the harvest
and with it comes a warning to ripen before winter.
The drying airs arrive, driving up dust
from the face of the earth to the heights of heaven,
and wild sky wrestles the sun with its winds,   525
and the leaves of the lime lie littered on the ground,
and grass that was green turns withered and gray.
Then all which had risen over-ripens and rots
and yesterday on yesterday the year dies away,
and winter returns, as is the way of the world   530
        through time.
    At Michaelmas[4] the moon
    stands like that season's sign,
    a warning to Gawain
    to rouse himself and ride.   535

Yet by All Saints' Day[5] he was still at Arthur's side,
and they feasted in the name of their noble knight
with the revels and riches of the Round Table.
The lords of that hall and their loving ladies
were sad and concerned for the sake of their knight,   540
but nevertheless they made light of his load.
Those joyless at his plight made jokes and rejoiced.
Then sorrowfully, after supper, he spoke with his uncle,
and openly talked of the trip he must take:
"Now, lord of my life, I must ask for your leave.   545
You were witness to my wager. I have no wish
to retell you the terms—they're nothing but a trifle.
I must set out tomorrow to receive that stroke
from the knight in green, and let God be my guide."

4. The feast of St. Michael, September 29.   5. November 1.

Then the cream of Camelot crowded around: 550
Ywain and Eric and others of that ilk,
Sir Dodinal the Dreaded, the Duke of Clarence,
Lancelot, Lionel, Lucan the Good,
and Sir Bors and Sir Bedevere—both big names,
and powerful men such as Mador de la Port.[6]   555
This courtly committee approaches the king
to offer up heartfelt advice to our hero.
And sounds of sadness and sorrow were heard
that one as worthy and well liked as Gawain
should suffer that strike but offer no stroke in   560
       reply.
    Yet keeping calm the knight
    just quipped, "Why should I shy
    away? If fate is kind
    or cruel, man still must try."   565

He remained all that day and in the morning he dressed,
asked early for his arms and all were produced.
First a rug of rare cloth was unrolled on the floor,
heaped with gear which glimmered and gleamed,
and the stout knight steps onto it and handles the steel.   570
He tries on his tunic of extravagant silk,
then the neatly cut cloak, closed at the neck,
its lining finished with a layer of white fur.
Then they settled his feet into steel shoes
and clad his calves, clamped them with greaves,   575
then hinged and highly polished plates
were knotted with gold thread to the knight's knees.
Then leg guards were fitted, lagging the flesh,
attached with thongs to his thick-set thighs.
Then comes the suit of shimmering steel rings   580
encasing his body and his costly clothes:
well burnished braces to both of his arms,
good elbow guards and glinting metal gloves,
all the trimmings and trappings of a knight tricked out
       to ride: 585
    a metal suit that shone;
    gold spurs which gleam with pride;
    a keen sword swinging from
    the silk belt to his side.

Fastened in his armor he seemed fabulous, famous,   590
every link looking golden to the very last loop.
Yet for all that metal he still made it to mass,
honored the Almighty before the high altar.
After which he comes to the king and his consorts
and asks to take leave of the ladies and lords;   595
they escort and kiss him and commended him to Christ.

6. Literally, "of the Door" (French).

Now Gringolet is rigged out and ready to ride
with a saddle which flickered with fine gold fringes
and was set with new studs for the special occasion.
The bridle was bound with stripes of bright gold,   600
the apparel of the panels was matched in appearance
to the color of the saddlebows and cropper and cover,
and nails of red gold were arrayed all around,
shining splendidly like splintered sunlight.
Then he holds up his helmet and hastily kisses it;   605
it was strongly stapled and its lining was stuffed,
and sat high on his head, fastened behind
with a colorful cloth to cover his neck
embroidered and bejeweled with brilliant gems
on the broad silk border, and with birds on the seams   610
such as painted parrots perched among periwinkles
and turtle doves and true lover's knots, tightly entwined
as if women had worked at it seven winters
    at least.
  The diamond diadem   615
  was greater still. It gleamed
  with flawless, flashing gems
  both clear and smoked, it seemed.

Then they showed him the shining scarlet shield
with its pentangle[7] painted in pure gold.   620
He seized it by its strap and slung it round his neck;
he looked well in what he wore, and was worthy of it.
And why the pentangle was appropriate to that prince
I intend to say, though it will stall our story.
It is a symbol that Solomon once set in place[8]   625
and is taken to this day as a token of fidelity,
for the form of the figure is a five-pointed star
and each line overlaps and links with the last
so is ever eternal, and when spoken of in England
is known by the name of the endless knot.   630
So it suits this soldier in his spotless armor,
fully faithful in five ways five times over.
For Gawain was as good as the purest gold—
devoid of vices but virtuous, loyal
    and kind,   635
  so bore that badge on both
  his shawl and shield alike.
  A prince who talked the truth:
  known as the noblest knight.

First he was deemed flawless in his five senses;   640
and secondly his five fingers were never at fault;

---

7. I.e., a pentagram, a figure believed to have
mystical powers.
8. Folklore associated the proverbially wise
king of the ancient Hebrews with mystic
knowledge.

and thirdly his faith was founded in the five wounds
Christ received on the cross, as the creed recalls.
And fourthly, if that soldier struggled in skirmish
one thought pulled him through above all other things: 645
the fortitude he found in the five joys
which Mary had conceived in her son, our Savior.[9]
For precisely that reason the princely rider
had the shape of her image inside his shield,
so by catching her eye his courage would not crack.   650
The fifth set of five which I heard the knight followed
included friendship and fraternity with fellow men,
purity and politeness that impressed at all times,
and pity, which surpassed all pointedness. Five things
which meant more to Gawain than to most other men.   655
So these five sets of five were fixed in this knight,
each linked to the last through the endless line,
a five-pointed form which never failed,
never stronger to one side or slack at the other,
but unbroken in its being from beginning to end   660
however its trail is tracked and traced.
So the star on the spangling shield he sported
shone royally, in gold, on a ruby red background,
the pure pentangle as people have called it
      for years.   665
     Then, lance in hand, held high,
     and got up in his gear
     he bids them all good-bye
     one final time, he fears.

Spiked with the spurs the steed sped away   670
with such force that the fire-stones sparked underfoot.
All sighed at the sight, and with sinking hearts
they whispered their worries to one another,
concerned for their comrade. "A pity, by Christ,
if a lord so noble should lose his life.   675
To find his equal on earth would be far from easy.
Cleverer to have acted with caution and care,
deemed him a duke—a title he was due—
a leader of men, lord of many lands;
better that than being battered into oblivion,   680
beheaded by an ogre, through headstrong pride.
Whoever knew any king to take counsel of a knight
in the grip of an engrossing Christmas game?"
Warm tears welled up in their weepy eyes
as gallant Sir Gawain galloped from court   685
      that day.
     He sped from home and hearth

9. The events labeled by Catholics the Annunciation (the announcement that Christ would
be born), the Nativity (Christ's birth), the Resurrection, the Ascension (of Christ into
heaven), and the Assumption (the bodily taking up of Mary into heaven).

and went his winding way
on steep and snaking paths,
just as the story says.   690

Now through England's realm he rides and rides,
Sir Gawain, God's servant, on his grim quest,
passing long dark nights unloved and alone,
foraging to feed, finding little to call food,
with no friend but his horse through forests and hills   695
and only our Lord in heaven to hear him.
He wanders near to the north of Wales
with the Isles of Anglesey[1] off to the left.
He keeps to the coast, fording each course,
crossing at Holy Head and coming ashore   700
in the wilds of the Wirral,[2] whose wayward people
both God and good men have quite given up on.
And he constantly enquires of those he encounters
if they know, or not, in this neck of the woods,
of a great green man or a Green Chapel.   705
No, they say, never. Never in their lives.
They know of neither a chap nor a chapel
            so strange.
    He trails through bleak terrain.
    His mood and manner change   710
    at every twist and turn
    towards that chosen church.

In a strange region he scales steep slopes;
far from his friends he cuts a lonely figure.
Where he bridges a brook or wades through a waterway   715
it's no surprise to find that he faces a foe
so foul or fierce he is bound to use force.
So momentous are his travels among the mountains
to tell just a tenth would be a tall order.
Here he scraps with serpents and snarling wolves,   720
here he tangles with wodwos[3] causing trouble in the crags,
or with bulls and bears and the odd wild boar.
Hard on his heels through the highlands come giants.
Only diligence and faith in the face of death
will keep him from becoming a corpse or carrion.   725
And the wars were one thing, but winter was worse:
clouds shed their cargo of crystallized rain
which froze as it fell to the frost-glazed earth.
Nearly slain by sleet he slept in his armor,
bivouacked in the blackness amongst bare rocks   730
where meltwater streamed from the snow-capped summits
and high overhead hung chandeliers of ice.

1. Off the northwest corner of Wales.
2. A forest in the English county of Cheshire;
Gawain, after reaching the northern limits of
Wales, heads east.
3. Woodwoses, or wild men of the woods.

So in peril and pain Sir Gawain made progress,
crisscrossing the countryside until Christmas
   Eve. Then   735
  at that time of tiding,
  he prayed to highest heaven.
  Let Mother Mary guide him
  towards some house or haven.

Next morning he moves on, skirts the mountainside, 740
descends a deep forest, densely overgrown,
with vaulting hills to each half of the valley
and ancient oaks in huddles of hundreds.
Hazel and hawthorn are interwoven,
decked and draped in damp, shaggy moss,   745
and bedraggled birds on bare, black branches
pipe pitifully into the piercing cold.
Under cover of the canopy he girded Gringolet
through mud and marshland, a man all alone,
concerned and afraid in case he should fail   750
in the worship of our Deity, who, on that date
was born the Virgin's son to save our souls.
He prayed with heavy heart. "Father, hear me,
and Lady Mary, our mother most mild,
let me happen on some house where mass might be heard, 755
and matins in the morning; meekly I ask,
and here I utter my pater, ave
   and creed."[4]
  He rides the path and prays,
  dismayed by his misdeeds,   760
  and signs Christ's cross and says,
  "Be near me in my need."

No sooner had he signed himself three times
than he became aware, in those woods, of high walls
in a moat, on a mound, bordered by the boughs 765
of thick-trunked timber which trimmed the water.
The most commanding castle a knight ever kept,
positioned in a site of sweeping parkland
with a palisade of pikes pitched in the earth
in the midst of tall trees for two miles or more. 770
He stopped and stared at one side of that stronghold
as it sparkled and shone within shimmering oaks,
and with helmet in hand he offered up thanks
to Jesus and Saint Julian,[5] both gentle and good,
who had courteously heard him and heeded his cry. 775
"A lodging at last. So allow it, my Lord."
Then he girded Gringolet with his gilded spurs,

4. The Paternoster (Our Father), Ave Maria (Hail Mary), and Apostle's Creed—all foundational prayers said daily, as were mass and matins.

5. Julian the Hospitaller, legendary patron of travelers and innkeepers.

and purely by chance chose the principal approach
to the building, which brought him to the end of the bridge
      with haste.   780
    The drawbridge stood withdrawn,
    the front gates were shut fast.
    Such well-constructed walls
    would blunt the storm wind's blast.

In the saddle of his steed he halts on the slope   785
of the delving moat with its double ditch.
Out of water of wondrous depth, the walls
then loomed overhead to a huge height,
course after course of crafted stone,
then battlements embellished in the boldest style   790
and turrets arranged around the ramparts
with lockable loopholes set into the lookouts.
The knight had not seen a more stunning structure.
Further in, his eye was drawn to a hall
attended, architecturally, by many tall towers   795
with a series of spires spiking the air
all crowned by carvings exquisitely cut.
Uncountable chimneys the color of chalk
sprutted[6] from the roof and sparkled in the sun.
So perfect was that vision of painted pinnacles   800
clustered within the castle's enclosure
it appeared that the place was cut from paper.[7]
Then a notion occurred to that noble knight:
to seek a visit, get invited inside,
to be hosted and housed, and all the holy days   805
      remain.
    Responding to his call
    a pleasant porter came,
    a watchman on the wall,
    who welcomed Sir Gawain.   810

"Good morning," said Gawain, "will you go with a message
to the lord of this house to let me have lodging?"
"By Saint Peter,"[8] said the porter, "it'll be my pleasure,
and I'll warrant you'll be welcome for as long as you wish."
Then he went on his way, but came back at once   815
with a group who had gathered to greet the stranger;
the drawbridge came down and they crossed the ditch
and knelt in the frost in front of the knight
to welcome this man in a way deemed worthy.
Then they yielded to their guest, yanked open the gate,   820
and bidding them to rise he rode across the bridge.
He was assisted from the saddle by several men

6. I.e., sprouted.
7. Paper castles were sometimes used at elaborate feasts to decorate food.

8. An appropriate oath for a porter, since Jesus gave this apostle "the keys of the kingdom of heaven" (Matthew 16.19).

and the strongest amongst them stabled his steed.
Then knights, and the squires of knights, drew near,
to escort him, with courtesy, into the castle.   825
As he took off his helmet, many hasty hands
stretched to receive it and to serve this noble knight,
and his sword and his shield were taken aside.
Then he made himself known to nobles and knights
and proud fellows pressed forwards to confer their respects.   830
Still heavy with armor he was led to the hall
where a fire burned bright with the fiercest flames.
Then the master of the manor emerged from his chamber,
to greet him in the hall with all due honor,
saying, "Behave in my house as your heart pleases.   835
To whatever you want you are welcome, do what
            you will."
    "My thanks," Gawain exclaimed,
    "May Christ reward you well."
    Then firmly, like good friends,   840
    arm into arm they fell.

Gawain gazed at the lord who greeted him so gracefully,
the great one who governed that grand estate,
powerful and large, in the prime of his life,
with a bushy beard as red as a beaver's,   845
steady in his stance, solid of build,
with a fiery face and fine conversation:
and it suited him well, so it seemed to Gawain,
to keep such a castle and captain his knights.
Escorted to his quarters the lord quickly orders   850
that a servant be assigned to assist Gawain,
and many were willing to wait on his word.
They brought him to a bedroom, beautifully furnished
with fine silken fabrics finished in gold
and curious coverlets lavishly quilted   855
in bright ermine and embroidered to each border.
Curtains ran on cords through red-gold rings,
tapestries from Toulouse and Turkistan
were fixed against walls and fitted underfoot.
With humorous banter Gawain was helped out   860
of his chain-mail coat and costly clothes,
then they rushed to bring him an array of robes
of the choicest cloth. He chose, and changed,
and as soon as he stood in that stunning gown
with its flowing skirts which suited his shape   865
it almost appeared to the persons present
that spring, with its spectrum of colors, had sprung;
so alive and lean were that young man's limbs
a nobler creature Christ had never created, they declared.
        This knight,   870
    whose country was unclear,
    now seemed to them by sight

a prince without a peer
in fields where fierce men fight.

In front of a flaming fireside a chair   875
was pulled into place for Gawain, and padded
with covers and quilts all cleverly stitched,
then a cape was cast across the knight
of rich brown cloth with embroidered borders,
finished inside with the finest furs,   880
ermine, to be exact, and a hood which echoed it.
Resplendently dressed he settled in his seat;
as his limbs thawed, so his thoughts lightened.
Soon a table was set on sturdy trestles
covered entirely with a clean white cloth   885
and cruets of salt and silver spoons.
In a while he washed and went to his meal.
Staff came quickly and served him in style
with several soups all seasoned to taste,
double helpings as was fitting, and a feast of fish,   890
some baked in bread, some browned over flames,
some boiled or steamed, some stewed in spices
and subtle sauces which the knight savored.
Four or five times he called it a feast,
and the courteous company happily cheered him   895
            along:
    "On penance plates you dine⁹—
    there's better board to come."
    The warming, heady wine
    then freed his mind for fun.   900

Now through tactful talk and tentative enquiry
polite questions are put to this prince;
he responds respectfully, and speaks of his journey
from the Court of Arthur, King of Camelot,
the royal ruler of the Round Table,   905
and he says they now sit with Gawain himself,
who has come here at Christmastime quite by chance.
Once the lord has gathered that his guest is Gawain
he likes it so well that he laughs out loud.
All the men of that manor were of the same mind,   910
being happy to appear promptly in his presence,
this person famed for prowess and purity,
whose noble skills were sung to the skies,
whose life was the stuff of legend and lore.
Then knight spoke softly to knight, saying   915
"Watch now, we'll witness his graceful ways,
hear the faultless phrasing of flawless speech;
if we listen we will learn the merits of language
since we have in our hall a man of high honor.

9. Because Christmas Eve is a fast day, he is served only fish, not meat.

Ours is a graceful and giving God   920
to grant that we welcome Gawain as our guest
as we sing of His birth who was born to save us.
            We few
      shall learn a lesson here
      in tact and manners true,   925
      and hopefully we'll hear
      love's tender language, too."[1]

Once dinner was done Gawain drew to his feet
and darkness neared as day became dusk.
Chaplains went off to the castle's chapels   930
to sound the bells hard, to signal the hour
of evensong, summoning each and every soul.
The lord goes alone, then his lady arrives,
concealing herself in a private pew.
Gawain attends, too; tugged by his sleeve   935
he is steered to a seat, led by the lord
who greets Gawain by name as his guest.
No man in the world is more welcome, are his words.
For that he is thanked. And they hug there and then,
and sit as a pair through the service in prayer.   940
Then she who desired to see this stranger
came from her closet with her sisterly crew.
She was fairest amongst them—her face, her flesh,
her complexion, her quality, her bearing, her body,
more glorious than Guinevere, or so Gawain thought,   945
and in the chancel of the church they exchanged courtesies.
She was hand in hand with a lady to her left,
someone altered by age, an ancient dame,
well respected, it seemed, by the servants at her side.
Those ladies were not the least bit alike: 950
one woman was young, one withered by years.
The body of the beauty seemed to bloom with blood,
the cheeks of the crone were wattled and slack.
One was clothed in a kerchief clustered with pearls
which shone like snow—snow on the slopes   955
of her upper breast and bright bare throat.
The other was noosed and knotted at the neck,
her chin enveloped in chalk-white veils,
her forehead fully enfolded in silk
with detailed designs at the edges and hems;   960
nothing bare, except for the black of her brows
and the eyes and nose and naked lips
which were chapped and bleared and a sorrowful sight.
A grand old mother, a matriarch she might
            be hailed.   965
      Her trunk was square and squat,
      her buttocks bulged and swelled.

1. Though Gawain is usually presented as a chaste and mighty knight, another tradition casts
him as a lover.

Most men would sooner squint
at her whose hand she held.

Then Gawain glanced at the gracious-looking woman,   970
and by leave of the lord he approached those ladies
saluting the elder with a long, low bow,
holding the other for a moment in his arms,
kissing her respectfully and speaking with courtesy.
They request his acquaintance, and quickly he offers   975
to serve them unswervingly should they say the word.
They take him between them and talk as they walk
to a hearth full of heat, and hurriedly ask
for specially spiced cakes, which are speedily fetched,
and wine filled each goblet again and again.   980
Frequently the lord would leap to his feet
insisting that mirth and merriment be made:
hauling off his hood he hoisted it on a spear—
a prize, he promised, to the person providing
most comfort and cheer at Christmastime.   985
"And my fellows and friends shall help in my fight
to see that it hangs from no head but my own."
So the laughter of that lord lights up the room,
and Gawain and the gathering are gladdened by games
          till late.   990
     So late, his lordship said,
     that lamps should burn with light.
     Then, blissful, bound for bed,
     Sir Gawain waved good night.

So the morning dawns when man remembers   995
the day our Redeemer was born to die,
and every house on earth is joyful for Lord Jesus.
Their day was no different, being a diary of delights:
banquets and buffets were beautifully cooked
and dutifully served to diners at the dais.   1000
The ancient elder sat highest at the table
with the lord, I believe, in the chair to her left;
the sweeter one and Gawain took seats in the center
and were first at the feast to dine; then food
was carried around as custom decrees   1005
and served to each man as his status deserved.
There was feasting, there was fun, and such feelings of joy
as could not be conveyed by quick description,
yet to tell it in detail would take too much time.
But I'm aware that Gawain and the beautiful woman   1010
found such comfort and closeness in each other's company
through warm exchanges of whispered words
and refined conversation free from foulness
that their pleasure surpassed all princely sports
          by far.   1015
     Beneath the din of drums

men followed their affairs,
and trumpets thrilled and thrummed
as those two tended theirs.

They drank and danced all day and the next   1020
and danced and drank the day after that,
then Saint John's Day[2] passed with a gentler joy
as the Christmas feasting came to a close.
Guests were to go in the grayness of dawn,
so they laughed and dined as the dusk darkened,   1025
swaying and swirling to music and song.
Then at last, in the lateness, they upped and left
toward distant parts along different paths.
Gawain offered his good-byes, but was ushered by his host
to his host's own chamber and the heat of its chimney,   1030
waylaid by the lord so the lord might thank him
profoundly and profusely for the favor he had shown
in honoring his house at that hallowed season
and lighting every corner of the castle with his character.
"For as long as I live my life shall be better   1035
that Gawain was my guest at God's own feast."
"By God," said Gawain, "but the gratitude goes to you.
May the High King of Heaven repay your honor.
Your requests are now this knight's commands.
I am bound by your bidding, no boon is too high   1040
    to say."
        At length his lordship tried
        to get his guest to stay.
        But proud Gawain replied
        he must now make his way.   1045

Then the lord of the castle inquired courteously
of what desperate deed in the depth of winter
should coax him from Camelot, so quickly and alone,
before Christmas was over in his king's court.
"What you ask," said the knight, "you shall now know.   1050
A most pressing matter prized me from that place:
I myself am summoned to seek out a site
and I have not the faintest idea where to find it.
But find it I must by the first of the year, and not fail
for all the acres in England, so the Lord help me.   1055
Consequently this inquiry I come to ask of you:
that you tell me, in truth, if you have heard the tale
of a green chapel and the ground where it stands,
or the guardian of those grounds who is colored green.
For I am bound by a bond agreed by us both   1060
to link up with him there, should I live that long.
As dawn on New Year's Day draws near,
if God sees fit, I shall face that freak

2. December 27 (celebrating the Apostle John).

more happily than I would the most wondrous wealth!
With your blessing, therefore, I must follow my feet.   1065
In three short days my destiny is due,
and I would rather drop dead than default from duty."
Then laughing the lord of the house said, "Stay longer.
I'll direct you to your rendezvous when the time is right,
you'll get to the green chapel, so give up your grieving.   1070
You can bask in your bed, bide your time,
save your fond farewells till the first of the year
and still meet him by midmorning to do as you might.
    So stay.
    A guide will get you there   1075
    at dawn on New Year's Day.
    The place you need is near,
    two miles at most away."

Then Gawain was giddy with gladness, and declared,
"For this more than anything I thank you thoroughly,   1080
and shall work to do well at whatever you wish,
until that time, attending every task."
The lord squeezed Gawain's arm and seated him at his side,
and called for the ladies to keep them company.
There was pleasure aplenty in their private talk,   1085
the lord delighting in such lively language,
like man who might well be losing his mind.
Then speaking to Gawain, he suddenly shouted:
"You have sworn to serve me, whatever I instruct.
Will you hold to that oath right here and now?"   1090
"You may trust my tongue," said Gawain, in truth,
"for within these walls I am servant to your will."
The lord said warmly, "You were weary and worn,
hollow with hunger, harrowed by tiredness,
yet joined in my reveling right royally every night.   1095
You relax as you like, lie in your bed
until mass tomorrow, then go to your meal
where my wife will be waiting; she will sit at your side
to accompany and comfort you in my absence from court.
    So lounge: 1100
    at dawn I'll rise and ride
    to hunt with horse and hound."
    The gracious knight agreed
    and, bending low, he bowed.

"Furthermore," said the master, "let's make a pact.   1105
Here's a wager: what I win in the woods will be yours,
and what you gain while I'm gone you will give to me.
Young sir, let's swap, and strike a bond,
let a bargain be a bargain, for better or worse."
"By God," said Gawain, "I agree to the terms,   1110
and I find it pleasing that you favor such fun."
"Let drink be served and we'll seal the deal,"

the lord cried loudly, and everyone laughed.
So they reveled and caroused uproariously,
those lords and ladies, for as long as they liked;   1115
then with immaculate exchanges of manners and remarks
they slowed and they stood and they spoke softly.
And with parting kisses the party dispersed,
footmen going forward with flaring torches,
and everybody was brought to their bed at long last,   1120
       to dream.
    Before they part the pair
    repeat their pact again.
    That lord was well aware
    of how to host a game.   1125

Fitt 3

Well before sunrise the servants were stirring;
the guests who were going had called for their grooms,
and they scurried to the stables to strap on the saddles,
trussing and tying all the trammel and tack.
The high-ranking nobles got ready to ride,   1130
jumped stylishly to their saddles and seized the reins,
then cantered away on their chosen courses.
The lord of that land was by no means last
to be rigged out for riding with the rest of his men.
After mass he wolfed down a meal, then made   1135
for the hills in a hurry with his hunting horn.
So as morning was lifting its lamp to the land
his lordship and his huntsmen were high on horseback,
and the canny kennel men had coupled the hounds
and opened the cages and called them out.   1140
On the bugles they blew three long, bare notes
to a din of baying and barking, and any dogs
which wandered at will where whipped back into line
by a hundred hunters, or so I heard tell,
       at least.   1145
    The handlers hold their hounds,
    the huntsmen's hounds run free.
    Each bugle blast rebounds
    between the trunks of trees.

As the cry went up the wild creatures quaked.   1150
The deer in the dale, quivering with dread
hurtled to high ground, but were headed off
by the ring of beaters who bellowed boisterously.
The stags of the herd with their high-branched heads
and the broad-horned bucks were allowed to pass by,   1155
for the lord of the land had laid down a law
that man should not maim the male in close season.[3]

3. I.e., the season closed to hunting.

But the hinds were halted with hollers and whoops
and the din drove the does to sprint for the dells.
Then the eye can see that the air is all arrows: 1160
all across the forest they flashed and flickered,
biting through hides with their broad heads.
What! They bleat as they bleed and they die on the banks,
and always the hounds are hard on their heels,
and the hunters on horseback come hammering behind   1165
with stone-splitting cries, as if cliffs had collapsed.
And those animals which escaped the aim of the archers
were steered from the slopes down to rivers and streams
and set upon and seized at the stations below.
So perfect and practiced were the men at their posts   1170
and so great were the greyhounds which grappled with the deer
that prey was pounced on and dispatched with speed
       and force.
    The lord's heart leaps with life.
    Now on, now off his horse   1175
    all day he hacks and drives.
    And dusk comes in due course.

So through a lime-leaf border the lord led the hunt,
while good Gawain lay slumbering in his sheets,
dozing as the daylight dappled the walls,   1180
under a splendid cover, enclosed by curtains.
And while snoozing he heard a slyly made sound,
the sigh of a door swinging slowly aside.
From below the bedding he brings up his head
and lifts the corner of the curtain a little   1185
wondering warily what it might be.
It was she, the lady, looking her loveliest,
most quietly and craftily closing the door,
nearing the bed. The knight felt nervous;
lying back he assumed the shape of sleep   1190
as she stole towards him with silent steps,
then cast up the curtain and crept inside,
then sat down softly at the side of his bed.
And awaited his wakening for a good long while.
Gawain lay still, in his state of false sleep,   1195
turning over in his mind what this matter might mean,
and where the lady's unlikely visit might lead.
Yet he said to himself, "Instead of this stealth
I should openly ask what her actions imply."
So he stirred and stretched, turned on his side,   1200
lifted his eyelids and, looking alarmed,
crossed himself hurriedly with his hand, as if saving
       his life.
    Her chin is pale, her cheeks
    are ruddy red with health;   1205
    her smile is sweet, she speaks
    with lips that love to laugh:

"Good morning, Sir Gawain," said the graceful lady,
"You sleep so soundly one might sidle in here.
You're tricked and trapped! But let's make a truce,   1210
or I'll bind you in your bed, and you'd better believe me."
The lady laughed, making light of his quandary.
"Good morning, madam," Gawain said merrily.
"I'll contentedly attend whatever task you set,
and in serving your desires I shall seek your mercy,   1215
which seems my best plan, in the circumstances!"
And he loaded his light-hearted words with laughter.
"But my gracious lady, if you grant me leave,
will you pardon this prisoner and prompt him to rise,
then I'll quit these covers and pull on my clothes,   1220
and our words will flow more freely back and forth."
"Not so, beautiful sir," the sweet lady said.
"Bide in your bed—my own plan is better.
I'll tuck in your covers corner to corner,
then playfully parley with the man I have pinned.   1225
Because I know your name—the knight Sir Gawain,
famed through all realms whichever road he rides,
whose princely honor is highly praised
amongst lords and ladies and everyone alive.
And right here you lie. And we are left all alone,   1230
with my husband and his huntsmen away in the hills
and the servants snoring and my maids asleep
and the door to this bedroom barred with a bolt.
I have in my house an honored guest
so I'll make the most of my time and stay talking   1235
       a while.
    You're free to have my all,
    do with me what you will.
    I'll come just as you call
    and swear to serve you well."   1240

"In good faith," said Gawain, "such gracious flattery,
though in truth I'm not now such a noble knight.
I don't dare to receive the respect you describe
and in no way warrant such worthy words.
But by God, I'd be glad, if you give me the right,   1245
to serve your desires, and with action or speech
bring you perfect pleasure. It would be pure joy."
Said the gracious lady, "Sir Gawain, in good faith,
how improper on my part if I were to imply
any slur or slight on your status as a knight.   1250
But what lady in this land wouldn't latch the door,
wouldn't rather hold you as I do here—
in the company of your clever conversation,
forgetting all grief and engaging in joy—
than hang on to half the gold that she owns?   1255
I praise the Lord who upholds the high heavens,
for I have what I hoped for above all else by

His grace."
That lovely looking maid,
she charmed him and she chased.   1260
But every move she made
he countered, case by case.

"Madam," said our man, "may Mary reward you,
in good faith, I have found your fairness noble.
Some fellows are praised for the feats they perform;   1265
I hardly deserve to receive such respect.
It is you who is genuinely joyful and generous."
"By Mary," she declared, "it's quite the contrary.
Were I the wealthiest woman in the world
with priceless pearls in the palm of my hand   1270
to bargain with and buy the best of all men,
then for all the signs you have shown me, sir,
of kindness, courtesy and exquisite looks—
a picture of perfection now proved to be true—
no person on this planet would be picked before you."   1275
"In fairness," said Gawain, "you found far better.
But I'm proud of the price you would pay from your purse,
and will swear to serve you as my sovereign lady.
Let Gawain be your servant and Christ your Savior."
Then they muse on many things through morning and midday,   1280
and the lady stares with a loving look,
but Gawain acts graciously and remains on guard,
and although no woman could be warmer or more winning,
he is cool in his conduct, on account of the scene he
          foresees: 1285
the strike he must receive,
as cruel fate decrees.
The lady begs her leave—
at once Gawain agrees.

She glanced at him, laughed and gave her good-bye,   1290
then stood, and stunned him with astounding words:
"May the Lord repay you for your prize performance.
But I know that Gawain could never be your name."
"But why not?" the knight asked nervously,
afraid that some fault in his manners had failed him.   1295
The beautiful woman blessed him, then rebuked him:
"A good man like Gawain, so greatly regarded,
the embodiment of courtliness to the bones of his being,
could never have lingered so long with a lady
without craving a kiss, as politeness requires,   1300
or coaxing a kiss with his closing words."
"Very well," said Gawain, "Let it be as you wish.
I shall kiss at your command, as becomes a knight,
and further, should it please you, so press me no more."
The lady comes close, cradles him in her arms,   1305
leans nearer and nearer, then kisses the knight.

Then they courteously commend one another to Christ,
and without one more word the woman is away.
Rapidly he rises and makes himself ready,
calls for his chamberlain, chooses his clothes,   1310
makes himself ready then marches off to mass.
Then he went to a meal which was made and waiting,
and was merry and amused till the moon had silvered
       the view.
    No man felt more at home   1315
    tucked in between those two,
    the cute one and the crone.
    Their gladness grew and grew.

And the lord of the land still led the hunt,
driving hinds to their death through holts and heaths,   1320
and by the setting of the sun had slaughtered so many
of the does and other deer that it beggared belief.
Then finally the folk came flocking to one spot
and quickly they collected and counted the kill.
Then the leading lords and their loyal men   1325
chose the finest deer—those fullest with fat—
and ordered them cut open by those skilled in the art.
They assessed and sized every slain creature
and even on the feeblest found two fingers worth of fat.
Through the sliced-open throat they seized the stomach   1330
and the butchered innards were bound in a bundle.
Next they lopped off the legs and peeled back the pelt
and hooked out the bowels through the broken belly,
but carefully, being cautious not to cleave the knot.
Then they clasped the throat, and clinically they cut   1335
the gullet from the windpipe, then garbaged the guts.
Then the shoulder blades were severed with sharp knives
and slotted through a slit so the hide stayed whole.
Then the beasts were prized apart at the breast,
and they went to work on the gralloching⁴ again,   1340
riving open the front as far as the hind fork,
fetching out the offal, then with further purpose
filleting the ribs in the recognized fashion.
And the spine was subject to a similar process,
being pared to the haunch so it held as one piece   1345
then hoisting it high and hacking it off.
And its name is the numbles,⁵ as far as I know, and
       just that.
    Its hind legs pulled apart
    they slit the fleshy flaps,   1350
    then cleave and quickly start
    to break it down its back.

---

4. Disemboweling (from a Gaelic term).   5. Organs of a deer that can be eaten.

Then the heads and necks of hinds were hewn off,
and the choice meat of the flanks chopped away from the chine,
and a fee for the crows was cast into the copse.   1355
Then each side was skewered, stabbed through the ribs
and heaved up high, hung by its hocks,
and every person was paid with appropriate portions.
Using pelts for plates, the dogs pogged out
on liver and lights and stomach linings   1360
and a blended sop of blood and bread.
The kill horn was blown and the bloodhounds bayed.
Then hauling their meat they headed for home,
sounding howling wails on their hunting horns,
and as daylight died they had covered the distance   1365
and had come to the castle where the knight was ensconced,
   adjourned
  in peace, with fires aflame.
  The huntsman has returned,
  and when he greets Gawain   1370
  warm feelings are confirmed.

Then the whole of the household was ordered to the hall,
and the women as well with their maids in waiting.
And once assembled he instructs the servants
that the venison be revealed in full view,   1375
and in excellent humor he asked that Gawain
should see for himself the size of the kill,
and showed him the side slabs sliced from the ribs.
"Are you pleased with this pile? Have I won your praise?
Does my skill at this sport deserve your esteem?"   1380
"Yes indeed," said the other. "It's the hugest haul
I have seen, out of season, for several years."
"And I give it all to you, Gawain," said the master,
"for according to our contract it is yours to claim."
"Just so," said Gawain, "and I'll say the same,   1385
for whatever I've won within these walls
such gains will be graciously given to you."
So he held out his arms and hugged the lord
and kissed him in the comeliest way he could.
"You're welcome to my winnings—to my one profit,   1390
though I'd gladly have given you any greater prize."
"I'm grateful," said the lord, "and Gawain, this gift
would carry more worth if you cared to confess
by what wit you won it. And when. And where."
"That wasn't our pact," he replied. "So don't pry.   1395
You'll be given nothing greater, the agreement we have
   holds good!"
  They laugh aloud and trade
  wise words which match their mood.
  When supper's meal is made   1400
  they dine on dainty food.

Later, they lounged by the lord's fire,
and were served unstintingly with subtle wines
and agreed to the game again next morning
and to play by the rules already in place: 1405
any takings to be traded between the two men
at night when they met, no matter what the merchandise.
They concurred on this contract in front of the court,
and drank on the deal, and went on drinking
till late, when they took their leave at last,   1410
and every person persent departed to bed.
By the third cackle of the crowing cock
the lord and his liegemen are leaping from their beds,
so that mass and the morning meal are taken,
and riders are rigged out ready to run as   1415
        day dawns.
     They leave the levels, loud
     with howling hunting horns.
     The huntsmen loose the hounds
     through thickets and through thorns.   1420

Soon they picked up a scent at the side of a swamp,
and the hounds which first found it were urged ahead
by wild-words and shrill shouting.
The pack responded with vigor and pace,
alert to the trail, forty lurchers[6] at least.   1425
Then such a raucous din rose up all around them
it ricocheted and rang through the rocky slopes.
The hounds were mushed with hollers and the horn,
then suddenly they swerved and swarmed together
in a wood, between a pool and a precipice.   1430
On a mound, near a cliff, on the margins of a marsh
where toppled stones lay scattered and strewn,
they coursed towards their quarry with huntsmen at heel.
Then a crew of them ringed the hillock and the cliff,
until they were certain that inside their circle   1435
was the beast whose being three bloodhounds had sensed.
Then they riled the creature with their rowdy ruckus,
and suddenly he breaks the barrier of beaters,
—the biggest of wild boars has bolted from his cover—
ancient in years and estranged from the herd,   1440
savage and strong, a most massive swine,
truly grim when he grunted. And the group were aggrieved,
for three were thrown down by the first of his thrusts;
then he fled away fast without further damage.
The other huntsmen bawled "hi" and "hay, hay,"   1445
blasted on their bugles, blew to regroup,
so the dogs and the men made a merry din,
tracking him nosily, testing him time and time

6. Hunting dogs.

again.

The boar would stand at bay   1450
and aim to maul and maim
the thronging dogs, and they
would yelp and yowl in pain.

Then the arches advanced with their bows and took aim,
shooting arrows at him which were often on target,   1455
but their points could not pierce his impenetrable shoulders
and bounced away from his bristly brow.
The smooth, slender shafts splintered into pieces,
and the heads glanced away from wherever they hit.
Battered and baited by such bombardment,   1460
in frenzied fury he flies at the men,
hurts them horribly as he hurtles past
so that many grew timid and retreated a tad.
But the master of the manor gave chase on his mount,
the boldest of beast hunters, his bugle blaring,   1465
trumpeting the tally-ho and tearing through thickets
till the setting sun slipped from the western sky.
So the day was spent in pursuits of this style,
while our lovable young lord had not left his bed,
and, cosseted in costly quilted covers, there he   1470
        remained.
    The lady, at first light,
    did not neglect Gawain,
    but went to wake the knight
    and meant to change his mind.   1475

She approaches the curtains, parts them and peeps in,
at which Sir Gawain makes her welcome at once,
and with prompt speech she replies to the prince,
settling by his side and laughing sweetly,
looking at him lovingly before launching her words.   1480
"Sir, if you truly are Gawain it seems wondrous to me
that a man so dedicated to doing his duty
cannot heed the first rule of honorable behavior,
which has entered through one ear and exited the other;
you have already lost what yesterday you learned   1485
in the truest lesson my tongue could teach."
"What lesson?" asked the knight. "I know of none,
though if discourtesy has occurred then blame me, of course."
"I encouraged you to kiss," the lady said kindly,
"and to claim one quickly when one is required,   1490
an act which ennobles any knight worth the name."
"Dear lady," said the other, "don't think such a thing,
I dare not kiss in case I am turned down.
If refused, I'd be at fault for offering in the first place."
"In truth," she told him, "you cannot be turned down.   1495
If someone were so snooty as to snub your advance,
a man like you has the means of his muscles."

"Yes, by God," said Gawain, "what you say holds good.
But such heavy-handedness is frowned on in my homeland,
and so is any gift not given with grace.   1500
What kiss you command I will courteously supply,
have what you want or hold off, whichever
        the case."
     So bending from above
     the fair one kissed his face.   1505
     The two then talk of love:
     its grief; also its grace.

"I would like to learn," said the noble lady,
"and please find no offence, but how can it follow
that a lord so lively and young in years,   1510
a champion in chivalry across the country—
and in chivalry, the chiefmost aspect to choose,
as all knights acknowledge, is loyalty in love,
for when tales of truthful knights are told
in both title and text the topic they describe   1515
is how lords have laid down their lives for love,
endured for many days love's dreadful ordeal,
then vented their feelings with avenging valor
by bringing great bliss to a lady's bedroom—
and you the most notable knight who is known,   1520
whose fame goes before him . . . yes, how can it follow
that twice I have taken this seat at your side
yet you have not spoken the smallest syllable
which belongs to love or anything like it.
A knight so courteous and considerate in his service   1525
really ought to be eager to offer this pupil
some lessons in love, and to lead by example.
Why, are you, whom all men honor, actually ignorant,
or do you deem me too dull to hear of dalliances?
     I come   1530
    to learn of love and more,
    a lady all alone.
    Perform for me before
    my husband heads for home."

"In faith," said Gawain, "may God grant you fortune.   1535
It gives me great gladness and seems a good game
that a woman so worthy should want to come here
and take pains to play with your poor knight,
unfit for her favors—I am flattered indeed.
But to take on the task of explaining true love   1540
or touch on the topics those love tales tell of,
with yourself, who I sense has more insight and skill
in the art than I have, or even a hundred
of the likes of me, on earth where I live,
would be somewhat presumptuous, I have to say.   1545
But to the best of my ability I'll do your bidding,

bound as I am to honor you forever
and to serve you, so let our Savior preserve me!"
So the lady tempted and teased him, trying
to entice him to wherever her intentions might lie.   1550
But fairly and without fault he defended himself,
no sin on either side transpiring, only happiness
       that day.
    At length, when they had laughed,
    the woman kissed Gawain.   1555
    Politely then she left
    and went her own sweet way.

Roused and risen he was ready for mass,
and then men sumptuously served the morning meal.
Then he loitered with the ladies the length of the day   1560
while the lord of the land ranged left and right
in pursuit of that pig which stampeded through the uplands,
breaking his best hounds with its back-snapping bite
when it stood embattled . . . then bowmen would strike,
goading it to gallop into open ground   1565
where the air was alive with the huntsman's arrows.
That boar made the best men flinch and bolt,
till at last his legs were like lead beneath him,
and he hobbled away to hunker in a hole
by a stony rise at the side of a stream.   1570
With the bank at his back he scrapes and burrows,
frothing and foaming foully at the mouth,
whetting his white tusks. The hunters waited,
irked by the effort of aiming from afar
but daunted by the danger of daring to venture   1575
       too near.
    So many men before
    had fallen prey. They feared
    that fierce and frenzied boar
    whose tusks could slash and tear.   1580

Till his lordship hacks up, urging on his horse,
spots the swine at standstill encircled by men,
then handsomely dismounts and unhands his horse,
brandishes a bright sword and goes bounding onwards,
wades through the water to where the beast waits.   1585
Aware that the man was wafting a weapon
the hog's hairs stood on end, and its howling grunt
made the fellows there fear for their master's fate.
Then the boar burst forward, bounded at the lord,
so that beast and hunter both went bundling   1590
into white water, and the swine came off worst,
because the moment they clashed the man found his mark,
knifing the boar's neck, nailing his prey,
hammering it to the hilt, bursting the hog's heart.
Screaming, it was swept downstream, almost slipping   1595

         beneath.
   At least a hundred hounds
   latch on with tearing teeth.
   Then, dragged to drier ground,
   the dogs complete its death.   1600

The kill was blown on many blaring bugle
and the unhurt hunters hollered and whooped.
The chief amongst them, in charge of the chase,
commanded the bloodhounds to bay at the boar,
then one who was wise in woodland ways   1605
began carefully to cut and carve up the carcass.
First he hacks off its head and hoists it aloft,
then roughly rives it right along the spine;
he gouges out the guts and grills them over coals,
and blended with bread they are tidbits for the bloodhounds.   1610
Next he fetches out the fillets of glimmering flesh
and retrieves the intestines in time-honored style,
then the two sides are stitched together intact
and proudly displayed on a strong pole.
So with the swine swinging they swagger home,   1615
the head of the boar being borne before the lord
who had fought so fiercely in the ford till the beast
         was slain.
   The day then dragged, it seemed,
   before he found Gawain,   1620
   who comes when called, most keen
   to countenance the claim.

Now the lord is loud with words and laughter
and speaks excitedly when he sees Sir Gawain;
he calls for the ladies and the company of the court   1625
and he shows off the meat slabs and shares the story
of the boar's hulking hugeness, and the full horror
of the fight to the finish as it fled through the forest.
And Gawain is quick to compliment the conquest,
praising it as proof of the lord's prowess,   1630
for such prime pieces of perfect pork
and such sides of swine were a sight to be seen.
Then admiringly he handles the boar's huge head,
feigning fear to flatter the master's feelings.
"Now Gawain," said the lord, "I give you this game,   1635
as our wager warranted, as well you remember."
"Certainly," said Sir Gawain. "It shall be so.
And graciously I shall give you my gains in exchange."
He catches him by the neck and courteously kisses him,
then a second time kisses him in a similar style.   1640
"Now we're even," said Gawain, "at this eventide;
the clauses of our contract have been kept and you have what
         I owe."

"By Saint Giles,"[7] the just lord says,
"You're now the best I know.   1645
By wagering this way
your gains will grow and grow."

Then the trestle tables were swiftly assembled
and cast with fine cloths. A clear, living light
from the waxen torches awakened the walls.   1650
Places were set and supper was served,
and a din arose as they reveled in a ring
around the fire on the floor, and the feasting party
made much pleasant music at the meal and after,
singing seasonal songs and carol dancing   1655
with as much amusement as a mouth could mention.
The young woman and Gawain sat together all the while.
And so loving was that lady towards the young lord,
with stolen glances and secret smiles
that the man himself was maddened and amazed,   1660
but his breeding forbade him rebuking a lady,
and though tongues might wag he returned her attention
            all night.
      Before his friends retire
      his lordship leads the knight,   1665
      heads for his hearth and fire
      to linger by its light.

They supped and swapped stories, and spoke again
of the night to come next, which was New Year's Eve.
Gawain pleaded politely to depart by morning,   1670
so in two days' time he might honor his treaty.
But the lord was unswerving, insisting that he stayed:
"As an honest soul I swear on my heart,
you shall find the Green Chapel to finish your affairs
long before dawn on New Year's Day.   1675
So lie in your room and laze at your leisure
while I ride my estate, and, as our terms dictate,
we'll trade our trophies when the hunt returns.
I have tested you twice and found you truthful.
But think tomorrow *third time throw best*.   1680
Now, a lord can feel low whenever he likes,
so let's chase cheerfulness while we have the chance."
So those gentlemen agreed that Gawain would stay,
and they took more drink, then by torchlight retired to
            their beds.   1685
      Our man then sleeps, a most
      reposed and peaceful rest.

---

7. A frequent subject of medieval art, always depicted with a hind.

> As hunters must, his host
> is up at dawn and dressed.

After mass the master grabs a meal with his men   1690
and asks for his mount on that marvelous morning.
All those grooms engaged to go with their lord
were high on their horses before the hall gates.
The fields were dazzling, fixed with frost,
and the crown of sunrise rose scarlet and crimson,   1695
scalding and scattering cloud from the sky.
At the fringe of the forest the dogs were set free
and the rumpus of the horns went ringing through the rocks.
They fall on the scent of a fox, and follow,
turning and twisting as they sniff out the trail.   1700
A young harrier yowls and a huntsman yells,
then the pack come panting to pick up the scent,
running as a rabble along the right track.
The fox scurries ahead, they scamper behind,
and pursue him at speed when he comes within sight,   1705
haranguing him with horrific ranting howls.
Now and then he doubles back through thorny thickets,
or halts and harkens in the hem of a hedge,
until finally, by a hollow, he hurdles a fence,
and carefully he creeps by the edge of a copse,   1710
convinced that his cunning has conned those canines!
But unawares he wanders where they lie in wait,
where greyhounds are gathered together, a group
> > of three.
> He springs back with a start,   1715
> then twists and turns and flees.
> With heavy, heaving heart
> he tracks towards the trees.

It was one of life's delights to listen to those hounds
as they massed to meet him, marauding together.   1720
They bayed bloodily at the sight of his being,
as if clustering cliffs had crashed to the ground.
Here he was ambushed by bushwhacking huntsmen
waiting with a welcome of wounding words;
there he was threatened and branded a thief,   1725
and the team on his tail gave him no time to tarry.
Often, in the open, the pack tried to pounce,
then that crafty Reynard[8] would creep into cover.
So his lordship and his lords were merrily led
in this manner through the mountains until midafternoon,   1730
while our handsome hero snoozed contentedly at home,
kept from the cold of the morning by curtains.

---

8. Conventional name for a fox (from the 12th-century beast fable *Roman de Renart*, whose
hero was a fox).

But love would not let her ladyship sleep
and the fervor she felt in her heart would not fade.
She rose from her rest and rushed to his room   1735
in a flowing robe that reached to the floor
and was finished inside with fine-trimmed furs.
Her head went unhooded, but heavenly gems
were entwined in her tresses in clusters of twenty.
She wore nothing on her face; her neck was naked,   1740
and her shoulders were bare to both back and breast.
She comes into his quarters and closes the door,
throws the window wide open and wakes Gawain,
right away rouses him with ringing words for
        his ear.   1745
   "Oh, sir, how can you sleep
   when morning comes so clear?"
   And though his dreams are deep
   he cannot help but hear.

Yes he dozes in a daze, dreams and mutters   1750
like a mournful man with his mind on dark matters—
how destiny might deal him a death blow on the day
when he grapples with the guardian of the Green Chapel;
of how the strike of the axe must be suffered without struggle.
But sensing her presence there he surfaces from sleep,   1755
comes quickly from the depths of his dreams to address her.
Laughing warmly she walks towards him
and finds his face with the friendliest kiss.
In a worthy style he welcomes the woman
and seeing her so lovely and alluringly dressed,   1760
every feature so faultless, her complexion so fine,
a passionate heat takes hold in his heart.
They traded smiles and speech tripped from their tongues,
and a bond of friendship was forged there, all blissful
        and bright.   1765
   They talk with tenderness
   and pride, and yet their plight
   is perilous unless
   sweet Mary minds her knight.

For that noble princess pushed him and pressed him,   1770
nudged him ever nearer to a limit where he needed
to allow her love or impolitely reject it.
He was careful to be courteous and avoid uncouthness,
and more so for the sake of his soul should he sin
and be counted a betrayer by the keeper of the castle.   1775
"I shall not succumb," he swore to himself.
With affectionate laughter he fenced and deflected
all the loving phrases which leapt from her lips.
"You shall bear the blame," said the beautiful one,
"if you feel no love for the lady you lie with,   1780
and wound her, more than anyone on earth, to the heart.

Unless, of course, there is a lady in your life
to whom you are tied and so tightly attached
that the bond will not break, as I must now believe.
So in honesty and trust now tell me the truth;   1785
for all the love alive, do not lessen the truth
      with guile."
    "You judge wrong, by Saint John,"
    he said to her, and smiled.
    "There is no other one   1790
    nor will be for this while!"

"Those words," said the woman, "are the worst of all.
But I asked, and you answered, and now I ache.
Kiss me as I wish and I shall walk away
in mourning like a lady who loved too much."   1795
Stooping and sighing she kisses him sweetly,
then withdraws from his side, saying as she stands,
"But before we part will you find me some small favor?
Give me some gift—a glove at least,
that might leaven my loss when we meet in my memory."   1800
"Well it were," said Gawain. "I wish I had here
my most precious possession as a present for your love,
for over and over you deserve and are owed
the highest prize I could hope to offer.
But I would not wish on you a worthless token,   1805
and it strikes me as unseemly that you should receive
nothing greater than a glove as a keepsake from Gawain.
I am here on an errand in an unknown land
without men bearing bags of beautiful things,
which my regard for you, lady, makes me regret;   1810
but man must live by his means, and neither mope
      nor moan."
    The pretty one replies:
    "Nay, knight, since you decline
    to pass to me a prize.   1815
    you must have one of mine."

She offers him a ring of rich, red gold,
and the stunning stone set upon it stood proud,
beaming and burning with the brightness of the sun;
what wealth it was worth you can well imagine.   1820
But he would not accept it, and said straight away,
"By God, no tokens will I take at this time;
I have nothing to give, so nothing will I gain."
She insists he receive it but still he resists,
and swears, on his name as a knight, not to swerve.   1825
Snubbed by his decision, she said to him then,
"You refuse my ring because you find it too fine,
and don't care to be deeply indebted to me;
so I give you my girdle, a lesser thing to gain."
From around her body she unbuckled the belt   1830

which fastened the frock beneath her fair mantle,
a green silk girdle trimmed with gold,
exquisitely edged and hemmed by hand.
And she sweetly beseeched Sir Gawain to receive it,
in spite of its slightness, and hoped he would accept.   1835
But still he maintained he intended to take
neither gold nor girdle, until by God's grace
the challenge he had chosen was finally achieved.
"With apologies I pray you be not displeased,
but end all your offers, for always against them   1840
     I am.
    For all your grace I owe
    a thousand thank-you's, ma'am.
    I shall through sun and snow
    remain your loyal man."   1845

"And now he spurns my silk," the lady responded,
"so simple in itself, or so it appears,
so little and unlikely, worth nothing, or less.
But the knight who knew of the power knitted in it
would pay a high price to possess it, perhaps.   1850
For the body which is bound within this green belt,
as long as it is buckled robustly about him,
will be safe against anyone who seeks to strike him,
and all the slyness on earth wouldn't see him slain."
The man mulled it over, and it entered his mind   1855
it might just be the jewel for the jeopardy he faced
and save him from the strike in his challenge at the chapel.
With luck, it might let him escape with his life.
So relenting at last he let her speak,
and promptly she pressed him to take the present,   1860
and he granted her wish, and she gave with good grace,
though went on to beg him not to whisper a word
of this gift to her husband, and Gawain agreed;
those words of theirs within those walls
     should stay.   1865
    His thanks are heartfelt, then.
    No sooner can he say
    how much it matters, when
    the third kiss comes his way.

Then the lady departed, leaving him alone,   1870
for no more merriment could be had from that man.
And once she has quit he clothes himself quickly,
rises and dresses in the richest of robes,
stowing the love-lace safely aside,
hiding it away from all hands and eyes.   1875
Then he went at once to the chapel of worship,
privately approached the priest and implored him
to allow his confession, and to lead him in life
so his soul might be saved when he goes to his grave.

Then fully and frankly he spoke of his sins,   1880
no matter how small, always seeking mercy,
beseeching the counselor that he receive absolution.
The priest declares him so clean and so pure
that the Day of Doom[9] could dawn in the morning.
Then in merrier mood he mingled with the ladies,   1885
caroling and carousing and carrying on
as never before, until nightfall. Folk feel
   and hear
  and see his boundless bliss
  and say, "Such charm and cheer;   1890
  he's at his happiest
  since his arrival here."

And long let him loiter there, looked after by love.
Now the lord of the land was still leading his men,
finishing off the fox he had followed for so long.   1895
He vaults a fence to flush out the victim,
hearing that the hounds are harrying hard.
Then Reynard scoots from a section of scrub
and the rabble of the pack rush right at his heels.
Aware of its presence the wary lord waits,   1900
then bares his bright sword and swishes at the beast,
which shirks from its sharpness, and would have shot away
but a hound flew forward before it could flee
and under the hooves of the horses they have him,
worrying the wily one with wrathful baying.   1905
The lord hurtles from his horse and heaves the fox up,
wrestles it from the reach of those ravenous mouths,
holds it high over head and hurrahs manfully
while the bloodthirsty bloodhounds bay and howl.
And the other huntsmen hurried with their horns   1910
to catch sight of the slaughter and celebrate the kill.
And when the courtly company had come together
the buglers blew with one mighty blast,
and the others hallooed with open throats.
It was the merriest music ever heard by men,   1915
that rapturous roar which for Reynard's soul
   was raised.
  The dogs, due their reward,
  are patted, stroked and praised.
  Then red fur rips—Reynard   1920
  out of his pelt is prised.

Then with night drawing near they headed homewards,
blaring their bugles with the fullness of their breath.
And at last the lord lands at his lovely home,
to find, by the heat of the fireside, his friend   1925
the good Sir Gawain, in glad spirits

9. Judgment Day.

on account of the company he had kept with the ladies.
His blue robe flowed as far as the floor,
his soft-furred surcoat suited him well,
and the hood which echoed it hung from his shoulders,   1930
Both hood and coat were edged in ermine.
He meets the master in the middle of the room,
greets him graciously, with Gawain saying:
"I shall first fulfill our formal agreement
which we fixed in words when the drink flowed freely."   1935
He clasps him tight and kisses him three times
with as much emotion as a man could muster.
"By the Almighty," said the master, "you must have had luck
to profit such a prize—if the price was right."
"Oh fiddlesticks to the fee," said the other fellow.   1940
"As long as I have given the goods which I gained."
"By Mary," said the master, "mine's a miserable match.
I've hunted for hours with nothing to my name
but this foul-stinking fox—fling its fur to the devil—
so poor in comparison with such priceless things,   1945
these presents you impart, three kisses perfect
            and true."
    "Enough!" the knight entreats,
    "I thank you through and through."
    The standing lord then speaks   1950
    of how the fox fur flew!

And with meals and mirth and minstrelsy
they made as much amusement as any mortal could,
and among those merry men and laughing ladies
Gawain and his host got giddy together;   1955
only lunatics and drunkards could have looked more delirious.
Every person present performed party pieces
till the hour arrived when revelers must rest,
and the company in that court heard the call of their beds.
And lastly, in the hall, humbly to his host,   1960
our knight says good night and renews his gratitude.
"Your uncountable courtesies have kept me here
this Christmas—be honored by the High King's kindness.
If it suits, I submit myself as your servant.
But tomorrow morning I must make a move;   1965
if you will, as you promised, please appoint some person
to guide me, God willing, towards the Green Chapel,
where my destiny will dawn on New Year's Day."
"On my honor," he replied. "With hand on heart,
every promise I made shall be put into practice."   1970
He assigns him a servant to steer his course,
to lead him through the land without losing time,
to ride the fastest route between forest
            and fell.[1]

1. A high field.

Gawain will warmly thank   1975
his host in terms that tell;
towards the womenfolk
the knight then waves farewell.

It's with a heavy heart that guests in the hall
are kissed and thanked for their care and kindness,   1980
and they respond with speeches of the same sort,
commending him to our Savior with sorrowful sighs.
Then politely he leaves the lord and his household,
and to each person he passes he imparts his thanks
for taking such trouble in their service and assistance   1985
and such attention to detail in attendance of duty.
And every guest is grieved at the prospect of his going,
as if honorable Gawain were one of their own.
By tapering torchlight he was taken to his room
and brought to his bed to be at his rest.   1990
But if our knight sleeps soundly I couldn't say,
for the matter in the morning might be muddying
            his thoughts.
    So let him lie and think,
    in sight of what he sought.   1995
    In time I'll tell if tricks
    work out the way they ought.

                        Fitt 4

Now night passes and New Year draws near,
drawing off darkness as our Deity decrees.
But wild-looking weather was about in the world: 2000
clouds decanted their cold rain earthwards;
the nithering² north needled man's very nature;
creatures were scattered by the stinging sleet.
Then a whip-cracking wind comes whistling between hills
driving snow into deepening drifts in the dales.   2005
Alert and listening, Gawain lies in his bed;
his lids are lowered but he sleeps very little
as each crow of the cock brings his destiny closer.
Before day had dawned he was up and dressed
for the room was livened by the light of a lamp.   2010
To suit him in his metal and to saddle his mount
he called for a servant, who came quickly,
bounded from his bedsheets bringing his garments.
He swathes Sir Gawain in glorious style,
first fastening clothes to fend off the frost,   2015
then his armor, looked after all the while by the household:
the buffed and burnished stomach and breastplates,
and the rings of chain mail, raked free of rust,
all gleaming good as new, for which he is grateful

2. Oppressing.

        indeed.   2020
   With every polished piece
   no man shone more, it seemed
   from here to ancient Greece.
   He sent then for his steed.

He clothes himself in the costliest costume: 2025
his coat with the brightly emblazoned badge
mounted on velvet; magical minerals
inside and set about it; embroidered seams;
a lining finished with fabulous furs. . . .
And he did not leave off the lady's lace girdle;   2030
for his own good, Gawain won't forget that gift.
Then with his sword sheathed at his shapely hips
he bound himself twice about with the belt,
touchingly wrapped it around his waist.
That green silk girdle truly suited Sir Gawain   2035
and went well with the rich red weaves that he wore.
But our man bore the belt not merely for its beauty,
or the appeal of its pennants, polished though they were,
or the gleam of its edges which glimmered with gold,
but to save his skin when presenting himself,   2040
without shield or sword, to the axe. To its swing
         and thwack!
   Now he is geared and gowned
   he steps outside and thinks
   those nobles of renown   2045
   are due his thorough thanks.

Then his great horse Gringolet was got up ready.
The steed had been stabled in comfort and safety
and snorted and stamped in readiness for the ride.
Gawain comes closer to examine his coat,   2050
saying soberly to himself, swearing on his word:
"There are folk in this castle who keep courtesy to the forefront;
their master maintains them—happiness to them all.
And let his lordship's lady be loved all her life.
That they chose, out of charity, to cherish a guest,   2055
showing kindness and care, then may heaven's King
who reigns overall reward them handsomely.
For as long as I live in the lands of this world
I shall practice every means in my power to repay him."
Then he steps in the stirrup and vaults to the saddle   2060
and his servant lifts his shield which he slings on his shoulder,
then he girds on Gringolet with his golden spurs
who clatters from the courtyard, not stalling to snort
         or prance.
   His man was mounted, too,   2065
   who lugged the spear and lance.
   "Christ keep this castle true,"
   he chanted. "Grant good chance."

The drawbridge was dropped, and the double-fronted gates
were unbarred and each half was heaved wide open. 2070
As he clears the planking he crosses himself quickly,
and praises the porter, who kneels before the prince
and prays that God be good to Gawain.
Then he went on his way with the one whose task
was to point out the road to that perilous place 2075
where the knight would receive the sorry stroke.
They scrambled up bankings where branches were bare,
clambered up cliff faces where the cold clings.
The clouds which had climbed now cooled and dropped
so the moors and the mountains were muzzy with mist 2080
and every hill wore a hat of mizzle[3] on its head.
The streams on the slopes seemed to fume and foam,
whitening the wayside with spume and spray.
They wandered onwards through the wildest woods
till the sun, at that season, came skyward, showing 2085
   its hand.
  On hilly heights they ride,
  snow littering the land.
  The servant at his side
  then has them slow and stand. 2090

"I have accompanied you across this countryside, my lord,
and now you are near the site you have named
and have steered and searched for with such singleness of mind.
But there's something I should like to share with you, sir,
because upon my life, you're a lord that I love, 2095
so if you value your health you'll hear my advice:
the place you proceed to is held to be perilous.
In that wilderness lives a wildman, the worst in the world,
he is brooding and brutal and loves bludgeoning people.
He's more powerful than any person alive on this earth 2100
and four times the figure of any fighting knight
in Arthur's house, or Hector[4] or any other hero.
This grizzliness goes on at the green chapel,
and to pass through that place unscathed is impossible,
for he deals out death blows by dint of his hands, 2105
a man without measure who shows no mercy.
Be it chaplain or churl who rides by the chapel,
monk or priest, whatever man or person,
he loves murdering more than he loves his own life.
So I say, just as sure as you sit in your saddle, 2110
if you come there you'll be killed, of that there's no question.
Trust me, he could trample you twenty times over
   or more.
  He's lurked about too long
  engaged in grief and gore. 2115

3. Drizzle, light rain.
4. Son of King Priam, and the greatest Trojan warrior; he was especially admired in the Middle Ages.

His hits are swift and strong—
he'll fell you to the floor."

"Therefore, good Sir Gawain, let the man go,
and for God's sake travel an alternate track,
ride another road, and be rescued by Christ.   2120
I'll head off home, and with hand on heart
I shall swear by God and all his good saints,
and on all earthly holiness, and other such oaths,
that your secret is safe, and not a soul will know
that you fled in fear from the fellow I described."   2125
"Many thanks," said Gawain, in a terse tone of voice,
"and for having my interests at heart, be lucky.
I'm certain such a secret would be silent in your keep.
But as faithful as you are, if I failed to find him
and were to flee in fear in the fashion you urge,   2130
I'd be christened a coward, and could not be excused.
So I'll trek to the chapel and take my chances,
say my piece to that person, speak with him plainly,
whether fairness or foulness follows, however fate
       behaves.   2135
  He may be stout and stern
  and standing armed with stave,
  but those who strive to serve
  our Lord, our Lord will save."

"By Mary," said the servant, "you seem to be saying   2140
you're hell-bent on heaping harm on yourself
and losing your life, so I'll delay you no longer.
Set your helmet on your head and your lance in your hand
and ride a route through that rocky ravine
till you're brought to the bottom of that foreboding valley,   2145
then look towards a glade a little to the left
and you'll see in the clearing the site itself,
and the hulking person who inhabits the place.
Now God bless and good-bye, brave Sir Gawain;
for all the wealth in the world I wouldn't walk with you   2150
or go further in this forest by a single footstep."
With a wrench on the reins he reeled around
and heel-kicked the horse as hard as he could,
and was gone from Gawain, galloping hard
       for home.   2155
  "By Christ, I will not cry,"
  announced the knight, "or groan,
  but find my fortune by
  the grace of God alone."

Then he presses ahead, picks up a path,   2160
enters a steep-sided grove on his steed
then goes by and by to the bottom of a gorge
where he wonders and watches—it looks a wild place:

no sign of a settlement anywhere to be seen
but heady heights to both halves of the valley   2165
and set with saber-toothed stones of such sharpness
no cloud in the sky could escape unscratched.
He stalls and halts, holds the horse still,
glances side to side to glimpse the green chapel
but sees no such thing, which he thinks is strange,   2170
except at mid-distance what might be a mound,
a sort of bald knoll on the bank of a brook
where fell water surged with frenzied force,
bursting with bubbles as if it had boiled.
He heels the horse, heads for that mound,   2175
grounds himself gracefully and tethers Gringolet,
looping the reins to the limb of a lime.
Then he strides forwards and circles the feature,
baffled as to what that bizarre hill could be:
it had a hole at one end and at either side,   2180
and its walls, matted with weeds and moss,
enclosed a cavity, like a kind of old cave
or crevice in the crag—it was all too unclear to
      declare.
      "Green Church?" chunters the knight.   2185
      "More like the devil's lair
      where, at the nub of night,
      he makes his morning prayer."

"For certain," he says, "this is a soulless spot,
a ghostly cathedral overgrown with grass,   2190
the kind of kirk where that camouflaged man
might deal in devotions on the devil's behalf.
My five senses inform me that Satan himself
has tricked me in this tryst, intending to destroy me.
This is a haunted house—may it go to hell.   2195
I never came across a church so cursed."
With head helmeted and lance in hand
he scrambled towards skylight in that strange abyss.
Then he heard on the hillside, from behind a hard rock
and beyond the brook, a blood-chilling noise.   2200
What! It cannoned through the cliffs as if they might crack,
like the scream of a scythe being ground on a stone.
What! It whined and wailed, like a waterwheel.
What! It rasped and rang, raw on the ear.
"My God," cried Gawain, "that grinding is a greeting.   2205
My arrival is honored with the honing of an axe
      up there.
      Then let the Lord decide.
      'Oh well,' won't help me here.
      I might well lose my life   2210
      but freak sounds hold no fear."

Then Gawain called as loudly as his lungs would allow,
"Who has power in this place to honor his pact?

Because good Gawain now walks on this ground.
If anyone wants anything then hurry and appear   2215
to do what he needs—it's now or it's never."
"Abide," came a voice from above the bank.
"You'll cop for what's coming to you quickly enough."
Yet he went at his work, whetting the blade,
not showing until it was sharpened and stropped.   2220
Then out of the crags he comes, through the cave mouth,
whirling into view with a wondrous weapon,
a Danish-style axe[5] for dealing the dint,
with a brute of a blade curving back to the haft
filed on a stone, a four footer at least   2225
by the look of the length of its shining lace.
And again he was green, like a year ago,
with green flesh, hair and beard, and a fully green face,
and firmly on green feet he came stomping forwards,
the handle of that axe like a staff in his hand.   2230
At the edge of the water, he will not wade
but vaults the stream with the shaft, and strides
with an ominous face onto earth covered over
             with snow.
        Our brave knight bowed, his head   2235
        hung low—but not too low!
        "Sweet Sir," the green man said,
        "Your visit keeps your vow."

The green knight spoke again, "God guard you, Gawain.
Welcome to my world after all your wandering.   2240
You have timed your arrival like a true traveler
to begin this business which binds us together.
Twelve months ago at this time you took what was yours,
and with New Year come you are called to account.
We're very much alone, beyond view in this valley,   2245
no person to part us—we can do as we please.
Pull your helmet from your head and take what you're owed.
Show no more struggle than I showed myself
when you severed my head with a single smite."
"No," said good Gawain, "by my life-giving God,   2250
I won't gripe or begrudge the grimness to come,
so keep to one stroke and I'll stand stock-still,
won't whisper a word of unwillingness, or one
             complaint."
        He bowed to take the blade   2255
        and bared his neck and nape,
        but, loath to look afraid,
        he feigned a fearless state.

Suddenly the green knight summons up his strength,
hoists the axe high over Gawain's head,   2260

5. A long-bladed battle-axe, as favored by the Vikings.

lifts it aloft with every fiber of his life
and begins to bring home a bone-splitting blow.
Had he seen it through as thoroughly as threatened
the knight, being brave, would have died from the blow.
But glimpsing the axe at the edge of his eye   2265
bringing death earthwards as it arced through the air,
and sensing its sharpness, Gawain shrank at the shoulders.
The swinging axman swerved from his stroke,
and reproached the young prince with some proud words:
"Call yourself good Sir Gawain?" he goaded,   2270
"who faced down every foe in the field of battle
but now flinches with fear at the foretaste of harm.
Never have I know such cowardice in a knight.
Did I budge or even blink when you aimed the axe,
or carp or quibble in King Arthur's castle,   2275
or flap when my head went flying to my feet?
But entirely untouched, you are terror struck.
I'll be found the better fellow, since you were so feeble
      and frail."
    Gawain confessed, "I flinched   2280
    at first, but will not fail.
    Though once my head's unhitched
    it's off once and for all!"

"So be brisk with the blow, bring on the blade.
Deal me my destiny and do it out of hand,   2285
and I'll stand the stroke without shiver or shudder
and be wasted by your weapon. You have my word."
"Take this then," said the other, throwing up the axe,
with a menacing glare like the gaze of a maniac.
Then he launches his swing but leaves him unscathed,   2290
withholds his arm before harm could be done.
And Gawain was motionless, never moved a muscle,
but stood stone-still, or as still as a tree stump
anchored in the earth by a hundred roots.
Then the warrior in green mocked Gawain again: 2295
"Now you've plucked up your courage I'll dispatch you properly.
May the honorable knighthood heaped on you by Arthur—
if it proves to be powerful—protect your neck."
That insulting slur drew a spirited response:
"Thrash away then, thug, your threats are hollow.   2300
Such huffing and fussing—you'll frighten your own heart."
"By God," said the green man, "since you speak so grandly
there'll be no more shilly-shallying, I shall shatter you
      right now."
    He stands to strike, a sneer   2305
    from bottom lip to brow.
    Who'd fault Gawain if fear
    took hold. All hope is down.

Hoisted and aimed, the axe hurtled downwards,
the blade baring down on the knight's bare neck,   2310

a ferocious blow, but far from being fatal
it skewed to one side, just skimming the skin
and finely snicking the fat of the flesh
so that bright red blood shot from body to earth.
Seeing it shining on the snowy ground   2315
Gawain leapt forward a spear's length at least,
grabbed hold of his helmet and rammed it on his head,
brought his shield to his side with a shimmy of his shoulder,
then brandished his sword before blurting out brave words,
because never since birth, as his mother's babe,   2320
was he half as happy as here and now.
"Enough swiping, sir, you've swung your swing.
I've borne one blow without backing out,
go for me again and you'll get some by return,
with interest! Hit out, and be hit in an instant,   2325
          and hard.
      One axe attack—that's all.
      Now keep the covenant
      agreed in Arthur's hall
      and hold the axe in hand."   2330

The warrior steps away and leans on his weapon,
props the handle in the earth and slouches on the head
and studies how Gawain is standing his ground,
bold in his bearing, brave in his actions,
armed and ready. In his heart he admires him.   2335
Then remarking merrily, but in a mighty voice,
with reaching words he rounded on the knight:
"Be a mite less feisty, fearless young fellow,
you've suffered no insulting or heinous incident
beyond the game we agreed on in the court of your king.   2340
One strike was promised—consider yourself well paid!
From any lingering loyalties you are hereby released.
Had I mustered all my muscles into one mighty blow
I would have hit more harshly and done you great harm.
But my first strike fooled you—a feint, no less—   2345
not fracturing your flesh, which was only fair
in keeping with the contract we declared that first night,
for with truthful behavior you honored my trust
and gave up your gains as a good man should.
Then I missed you once more, and this for the morning   2350
when you kissed my pretty wife then kindly kissed me.
So twice you were truthful, therefore twice I left
          no scar.
      The person who repays
      will live to feel no fear.   2355
      The third time, though, you strayed,
      and felt my blade therefore."

"Because the belt you are bound with belongs to me;
it was woven by my wife so I know it very well.
And I know of your courtesies, and conduct, and kisses,   2360

and the wooing of my wife—for it was all my work!
I sent her to test you—and in truth it turns out
you're by the far the most faultless fellow on earth.
As a pearl is more prized than a pea which is white,
in good faith, so is Gawain, amongst gallant knights.   2365
But a little thing more—it was loyalty that you lacked:
not because you're wicked, or a womanizer, or worse,
but you loved your own life; so I blame you less."
Gawain stood speechless for what seemed a great while,
so shocked and ashamed that he shuddered inside.   2370
The fire of his blood brought flames to his face
and he shrank out of shame at what the other had said.
Then he tried to talk, and finding his tongue, said:
"A curse upon cowardice and covetousness.
They breed villainy and vice, and destroy all virtue."   2375
Then he grabbed the girdle and ungathered its knot
and flung it in fury at the man before him.
"My downfall and undoing; let the devil take it.
Dread of the death blow and cowardly doubts
meant I gave in to greed, and in doing so forgot   2380
the freedom and fidelity every knight knows to follow.
And now I am found to be flawed and false,
through treachery and untruth I have totally failed," said
            Gawain.
        "Such terrible mistakes,   2385
        and I shall bear the blame.
        But tell me what it takes
        to clear my clouded name."

The green lord laughed, and leniently replied:
"The harm which you caused me is wholly healed.   2390
By confessing your failings you are free from fault
and have openly paid penance at the point of my axe.
I declare you purged, as polished and as pure
as the day you were born, without blemish or blame.
And this gold-hemmed girdle I present as a gift,   2395
which is green like my gown. It's yours, Sir Gawain,
a reminder of our meeting when you mix and mingle
with princes and kings. And this keepsake will be proof
to all chivalrous knights of your challenge in this chapel.
But follow me home. New Year's far from finished—   2400
we'll resume our reveling with supper and song.
            What's more
        my wife is waiting there
        who flummoxed you before.
        This time you'll have in her   2405
        a friend and not a foe."

"Thank you," said the other, taking helmet from head,
holding it in hand as he offered his thanks.
"But I've loitered long enough. The Lord bless your life
and bestow on you such honor as you surely deserve.   2410

And mind you commend me to your fair wife,
both to her and the other, those honorable ladies
who kidded me so cleverly with their cunning tricks.
But no wonder if a fool finds his way into folly
and be wiped of his wits by womanly guile—   2415
it's the way of the world. Adam fell because of a woman,
and Solomon because of several, and as for Samson,
Delilah was his downfall, and afterwards David
was bamboozled by Bathsheba and bore the grief.[6]
All wrecked and ruined by their wrongs; if only   2420
we could love our ladies without believing their lies.
And those were foremost of all whom fortune favored,
excellent beyond all others existing under heaven,"
              he cried.
        "Yet all were charmed and changed   2425
        by wily womankind.
        I suffered just the same,
        but clear me of my crime."

"But the girdle," he went on, "God bless you for this gift.
And shall wear it with good will, but not for its gold,   2430
nor its silks and streamers, and not for the sake
of its wonderful workmanship or even its worth,
but as a sign of my sin—I'll see it as such
when I swagger in the saddle—a sad reminder
that the frailty of his flesh is man's biggest fault,   2435
how the touch of filth taints his tender frame.
So when praise for my prowess in arms swells my pride,
one look at this love-lace will lessen my ardor.
But I will ask one thing, if it won't offend:
since I stayed so long in your lordship's land   2440
and was hosted in your house—let Him reward you
who upholds the heavens and sits upon high—
will you make known your name? And I'll ask nothing else."
"Then I'll treat you to the truth," the other told him,
"Here in my homelands they call me Bertilak de Hautdesert.   2445
And in my manor lives the mighty Morgan le Fay,[7]
so adept and adroit in the dark arts,
who learned magic from Merlin—the master of mystery—
for in earlier times she was intimately entwined
with that knowledgeable man, as all you knights know   2450
              back home.
        Yes, 'Morgan the Goddess'—
        I will announce her name.

---

6. A series of figures from the Hebrew Bible: in Gawain's telling, Adam was persuaded to sin by Eve, Solomon was led into sin by his many wives and concubines, Samson was tricked and betrayed by Delilah, and David was tempted to adultery and, in effect, murder by the beautiful Bathsheba.

7. Literally, "Morgan the Fairy"; in Arthurian tradition, the half-sister of Arthur. Having fallen in love with her, the sorcerer Merlin taught her.

There is no nobleness
she cannot take and tame."   2455

"She guided me in this guise to your great hall
to put pride on trial, and to test with this trick
what distinction and trust the Round Table deserves.
She imagined this mischief would muddle your minds
and that grieving Guinevere would go to her grave   2460
at the sight of a specter making ghostly speeches
with his head in his hands before the high table.
So that ancient woman who inhabits my home
is also your aunt—Arthur's half sister,
the daughter of the duchess of Tintagel; the duchess   2465
who through Uther, was mother to Arthur, your king.
So I ask you again, come and greet your aunt
and make merry in my house; you're much loved there,
and, by my faith, I am as fond of you my friend
as any man under God, for your great truth."   2470
But Gawain would not. No way would he go.
So they clasped and kissed and made kind commendations
to the Prince of Paradise, and then parted in the cold,
            that pair.
        Our man, back on his mount   2475
        now hurtles home from there.
        The green knight leaves his ground
        to wander who-knows-where.

So he winds through the wilds of the world once more,
Gawain on Gringolet, by the grace of God,   2480
under a roof sometimes and sometimes roughing it,
and in valleys and vales had adventures and victories
but time is too tight to tell how they went.
The nick to his neck was healed by now;
thereabouts he had bound the belt like a baldric—   2485
slantwise, as a sash, from shoulder to side,
laced in a knot looped below his left arm,
as a sign that his honor was stained by sin.
So safe and sound he sets foot in court,
and great joy came to the king in his castle   2490
when tidings of Gawain's return had been told.
The king kissed his knight and so did the queen,
and Gawain was embraced by his band of brothers,
who made eager enquiries, and he answered them all
with the tale of his trial and tribulations,   2495
and the challenge at the chapel, and the great green chap,
and the love of the lady, which led to the belt.
And he showed them the scar at the side of his neck,
confirming his breach of faith, like a badge
            of blame.   2500
        He grimaced with disgrace,
        he writhed in rage and pain.

Blood flowed towards his face
and showed his smarting shame.

"Regard," said Gawain, as he held up the girdle,   2505
"the symbol of sin, for which my neck bears the scar;
a sign of my fault and offence and failure,
of the cowardice and covetousness I came to commit.
I was tainted by untruth. This, its token,
I will drape across my chest till the day I die.   2510
For man's crimes can be covered but never made clean;
once sin is entwined it is attached for all time."
The king gave comfort, then the whole of the court
allow, as they laugh in lovely accord,
that the lords and ladies who belong to the Table,   2515
every knight in the brotherhood, should bear such a belt,
a bright green belt worn obliquely to the body,
crosswise, like a sash, for the sake of this man.
So that slanting green stripe was adopted as their sign,
and each knight who held it was honored ever after,   2520
as all the best books on romance remind us:
an adventure which happened in Arthur's era,
as the chronicles of this country have stated clearly.
Since fearless Brutus first set foot
on these shores, once the siege and assault at Troy   2525
            had ceased,
      our coffers have been crammed
      with stories such as these.
      Now let our Lord, thorn-crowned,
      bring us to perfect peace. AMEN.   2530

HONY SOYT QUI MAL PENCE[8]

---

8. I.e., "Honi soit qui mal y pense" (Middle French): "Shame on him who thinks ill of it." This closing phrase, added by a later scribe or reader of the poem, links the poem to the Order of the Garter, which was established around 1350 and which uses this phrase as its motto.

CHRISTINE DE PIZAN

ca. 1364–ca. 1431

"My head bowed as if in shame and my eyes full of tears, I sat slumped against the arm of my chair with my cheek resting on my hand. All of a sudden, I saw a beam of light, like the rays of the sun, shine down into my lap." Christine de Pizan's best-known allegory, *The Book of the City of Ladies*, opens with the narrator lamenting her female nature: she has been reading book after book about the character of women, learning that she, like all of her kind, is unfit for pursuing study, unable to perform meaningful work, and particularly likely to sin. Comforted by three crowned women, shining "goddesses" who embody Reason, Rectitude, and Justice, the narrator relearns the history of mankind—this time, through the lens of the feminine. From the stories of women of ancient times such as Dido and Lucrece to the lives of medieval saints, the goddesses work with the narrator to build the City of Ladies, stone by shining stone.

LIFE AND TIMES

Although Christine de Pizan lived almost her whole life in and around Paris, and wrote all of her works in the French language, she always remained (as she puts it in her *Book of Deeds of Arms and Chivalry*) "an Italian woman." Christine was the daughter of Tommaso da Pizzano, a doctor of medicine and of astrology, who moved from Italy to France to serve at the royal court of Charles V, and thus her fortunes were from childhood dependent on the favor and financial support of the ruling family. (The name "de Pizan," sometimes also spelled "de Pisan," reflects the family's landholdings in the town of Pizzano, on the outskirts of Bologna.) Her relationship to the royal household was reinforced after she wed Etienne de Castel, who worked as an administrative secretary and aide at the court. The marriage seems to have been a success: in her autobiographical writings, Christine refers to those ten years as the happiest of her life, and describes their abrupt end as the shattering of a ship tossed by a storm upon the rocks. Her ship had lost its "captain," and Christine had lost her "dearest friend." At the age of twenty-five, Christine found herself obliged to support herself, her three young children, a niece, and her widowed mother, at a time when few opportunities for paid work were available to women. Her solution: to live by her pen, becoming the first known female professional writer in European history.

The years around 1400 were tumultuous ones, especially for those near the royal court of France: the popular and effective ruler Charles V had died two decades before, leaving a son, Charles VI, who was at best erratic and at times descended into mental instability. His queen, Isabeau of Bavaria, attempted to maintain stable rule, aided by one of the king's brothers, but her efforts were thwarted by her own foreign birth and by rivalry on the part of other family members (especially Charles VI's uncle, the Duke of Burgundy). At the same time, the nation was engaged in repeated conflicts with England, in the course of the Hundred Years' War (1337–1453), and repeated bouts of plague following the devastating outbreak of the mid-fourteenth century roiled the country. Christine represents this political and social instability throughout her works, nowhere more memorably than in *Christine's Vision*, in which the "Crowned Dame" who represents the French nation laments the wicked children who tear her clothing and wound her body. By writing books of counsel and advice for the royal court, as well as works praising the virtues of the past king Charles V and the present queen Isabeau of Bavaria, Christine hoped to do her part in healing the body politic.

THE BOOK OF THE CITY OF LADIES

Christine de Pizan produced an extraordinary volume of writings, even compared with the prodigious output of her contemporaries **Petrarch, Boccaccio,** and **Chaucer.** She wrote hundreds of poems, both short lyrics and narrative works; allegorical visions, often incorporating autobiographical accounts of her life and times; and encyclopedic surveys of history and of myth. *The Book of the City of Ladies* is her most mature work, combining a remarkable ability to compile large amounts of information into a memorable form with the poetic gifts of metaphor and allegory: the city of ladies is a monumental edifice, built up piece by piece with "stones" made up of tales of individual women. Instead of being lofty, abstract figures, the goddesses of Reason, Rectitude, and Justice give Christine practical advice, urging her to wield "the pick of understanding" to dig out the badly shaped stones—that is, texts that describe women as ignorant and sinful—and instead to lay the foundations with the straight stones that are stories of great women of the past.

The three books of the *City of Ladies*, each supervised by a different goddess, demarcate progressive levels of the city-building project, moving upward from the foundations of book 1 to the walls of book 2 and finally to the houses and roofs of book 3. The first book, which is excerpted here, features women who ruled cities and empires, including Dido of Carthage and Semiramis of Babylon: these women, who had been condemned as lascivious and unstable by writers such as **Virgil** and **Dante,** become for Christine exemplars of the female ability to rule. Figures of myth also appear throughout book 1 as models for women's behavior: **Ovid**'s Io, for example, is transformed from a foolish cow to a brilliant woman who gave the gift of learning and language to the Egyptians, while Minerva appears not as a goddess but as a woman who taught the Greeks their alphabet and ruled the city of Athens, where classical civilization flowered. The later books include historical examples of notable women of Christine's own time, both the lofty and the humble: not just duchesses and princesses but also Novella, the woman who sometimes lectured in the legal classroom of her father at the University of Bologna, and Anastasia, a brilliant painter of manuscript illustrations in medieval Paris.

Christine's works were quickly translated into other languages, and an English translation of the *City of Ladies* was read at the Tudor court. It is tempting to think of Christine's "city" as a hospitable home for the queens Mary I and Elizabeth, who would soon sit on the English throne. Although Christine's works were extremely popular during her lifetime and for more than a century after her death, they fell into neglect in subsequent generations. In the early 1970s, however, readers began to search out female authors of the premodern past. Along with **Marie de France,** Christine de Pizan is one of a long forgotten generation of medieval foremothers who laid the foundations for women writers of today.

From The Book of the City of Ladies[1]

FROM *PART ONE*

1. *Here begins* The Book of the City of Ladies

One day, I was sitting in my study surrounded by many books of different kinds, for it has long been my habit to engage in the pursuit of knowledge. My mind had grown weary as I had spent the day struggling with the weighty tomes of various authors whom I had been studying for some time. I looked up from my book and decided that, for once, I would put aside these difficult texts and find instead something amusing and easy to read from the works of the poets. As I searched around for some little book, I happened to chance upon a work which did not belong to me but was amongst a pile of others that had been placed in my safekeeping. I opened it up and saw from the title that it was by Matheolus.[2] With a smile, I made my choice. Although I had never read it, I knew that, unlike many other works, this one was said to be written in praise of women. Yet I had scarcely begun to read it when my dear mother called me down to supper, for it was time to eat. I put the book to one side, resolving to go back to it the following day.

The next morning, seated once more in my study as is my usual custom, I remembered my previous desire to have a look at this book by Matheolus. I picked it up again and read on a little. But, seeing the kind of immoral language and ideas it contained, the content seemed to me likely to appeal only to those who enjoy reading works of slander and to be of no use whatsoever to anyone who wished to pursue virtue or to improve their moral standards. I therefore leafed through it, read the ending, and decided to switch to some more worthy and profitable work. Yet, having looked at this book, which I considered to be of no authority, an extraordinary thought became planted in my mind which made me wonder why on earth it was that so many men, both clerks and others, have said and continue to say and write such awful, damning things about women and their ways. I was at a loss as to how to explain it. It is not just a handful of writers who do this, nor only this Matheolus whose book is neither regarded as authoritative nor intended to be taken seriously. It is all manner of philosophers, poets and orators too numerous to mention, who all seem to speak with one voice and are unanimous in their view that female nature is wholly given up to vice.

As I mulled these ideas over in my mind again and again, I began to examine myself and my own behaviour as an example of womankind. In order to judge in all fairness and without prejudice whether what so many famous men have said about us is true, I also thought about other women I know, the many princesses and countless ladies of all different social ranks who have shared their private and personal thoughts with me. No matter which way I looked at it and no matter how much I turned the question over in my mind, I could find no evidence from my own experience to bear out such a negative view of female nature and habits. Even so, given that I could scarcely find a moral

1. Translated from the French by Rosalind Brown-Grant.
2. The French poet's Latin poem, *Liber Lamentationum* (ca. 1295), which became enormously popular in its French translation by Jean le Fèvre as *The Lamentations of Matheolus* (ca. 1320), attacked women and marriage.

work by any author which didn't devote some chapter or paragraph to attacking the female sex, I had to accept their unfavourable opinion of women since it was unlikely that so many learned men, who seemed to be endowed with such great intelligence and insight into all things, could possibly have lied on so many different occasions. It was on the basis of this one simple argument that I was forced to conclude that, although my understanding was too crude and ill-informed to recognize the great flaws in myself and other women, these men had to be in the right. Thus I preferred to give more weight to what others said than to trust my own judgement and experience.

I dwelt on these thoughts at such length that it was as if I had sunk into a deep trance. My mind became flooded with an endless stream of names as I recalled all the authors who had written on this subject. I came to the conclusion that God had surely created a vile thing when He created woman. Indeed, I was astounded that such a fine craftsman could have wished to make such an appalling object which, as these writers would have it, is like a vessel in which all the sin and evil of the world has been collected and preserved. This thought inspired such a great sense of disgust and sadness in me that I began to despise myself and the whole of my sex as an aberration in nature.

With a deep sigh, I called out to God: 'Oh Lord, how can this be? Unless I commit an error of faith, I cannot doubt that you, in your infinite wisdom and perfect goodness, could make anything that wasn't good. Didn't you yourself create woman especially and then endow her with all the qualities that you wished her to have? How could you possibly have made a mistake in anything? Yet here stand women not simply accused, but already judged, sentenced and condemned! I just cannot understand this contradiction. If it is true, dear Lord God, that women are guilty of such horrors as so many men seem to say, and as you yourself have said that the testimony of two or more witnesses is conclusive, how can I doubt their word? Oh God, why wasn't I born a male so that my every desire would be to serve you, to do right in all things, and to be as perfect a creature as man claims to be? Since you chose not to show such grace to me, please pardon and forgive me, dear Lord, if I fail to serve you as well as I should, for the servant who receives fewer rewards from his lord is less obligated to him in his service.'

Sick at heart, in my lament to God I uttered these and many other foolish words since I thought myself very unfortunate that He had given me a female form.

2. The three ladies

Sunk in these unhappy thoughts, my head bowed as if in shame and my eyes full of tears, I sat slumped against the arm of my chair with my cheek resting on my hand. All of a sudden, I saw a beam of light, like the rays of the sun, shine down into my lap. Since it was too dark at that time of day for the sun to come into my study, I woke with a start as if from a deep sleep. I looked up to see where the light had come from and all at once saw before me three ladies, crowned and of majestic appearance, whose faces shone with a brightness that lit up me and everything else in the place. As you can imagine, I was full of amazement that they had managed to enter a room whose doors and windows were all closed. Terrified at the thought that it might be some kind of apparition come to tempt me, I quickly made the sign of the cross on my forehead.

With a smile on her face, the lady who stood at the front of the three addressed me first: 'My dear daughter, don't be afraid, for we have not come to do you any harm, but rather, out of pity on your distress, we are here to comfort you. Our aim is to help you get rid of those misconceptions which have clouded your mind and made you reject what you know and believe in fact to be the truth just because so many other people have come out with the opposite opinion. You're acting like that fool in the joke who falls asleep in the mill and whose friends play a trick on him by dressing him up in women's clothing. When he wakes up, they manage to convince him that he is a woman despite all evidence to the contrary! My dear girl, what has happened to your sense? Have you forgotten that it is in the furnace that gold is refined, increasing in value the more it is beaten and fashioned into different shapes? Don't you know that it's the very finest things which are the subject of the most intense discussion? Now, if you turn your mind to the very highest realm of all, the realm of abstract ideas, think for a moment whether or not those philosophers whose views against women you've been citing have ever been proven wrong. In fact, they are all constantly correcting each other's opinions, as you yourself should know from reading Aristotle's *Metaphysics* where he discusses and refutes both their views and those of Plato and other philosophers.[3] Don't forget the Doctors of the Church either, and Saint Augustine[4] in particular who all took issue with Aristotle himself on certain matters, even though he is considered to be the greatest of all authorities on both moral and natural philosophy. You seem to have accepted the philosophers' views as articles of faith and thus as irrefutable on every point.

'As for the poets you mention, you must realize that they sometimes wrote in the manner of fables which you have to take as saying the opposite of what they appear to say. You should therefore read such texts according to the grammatical rule of *antiphrasis*, which consists of interpreting something that is negative in a positive light, or vice versa. My advice to you is to read those passages where they criticize women in this way and to turn them to your advantage, no matter what the author's original intention was. It could be that Matheolus is also meant to be read like this because there are some passages in his book which, if taken literally, are just out-and-out heresy. As for what these authors—not just Matheolus but also the more authoritative writer of the *Romance of the Rose*[5]—say about the God-given, holy state of matrimony, experience should tell you that they are completely wrong when they say that marriage is insufferable thanks to women. What husband ever gave his wife the power over him to utter the kind of insults and obscenities which these authors claim that women do? Believe me, despite what you've read in books, you've never actually *seen* such a thing because it's all a pack of outrageous lies. My

3. The influential Greek philosophers Plato (429–347 B.C.E.) and his student Aristotle (384–322 B.C.E.) were widely read in Latin translation in the Middle Ages.
4. Augustine of Hippo (354–430). Doctors of the Church: title given in the Middle Ages to certain saints who were also outstanding theologians.
5. A very popular French allegorical romance, written in two parts—by Guillaume de Lorris (ca. 1237) and by Jean de Meun (ca. 1275); Christine's objections are mainly to the continuation, which includes a number of misogynistic passages.

dear friend, I have to say that it is your naivety which has led you to take what they come out with as the truth. Return to your senses and stop worrying your head about such foolishness. Let me tell you that those who speak ill of women do more harm to themselves than they do to the women they actually slander.'

3. Christine recounts how the lady who had spoken to her told her who she was, what her function and purpose was, and how she prophesied that Christine would build a city with the help of the three ladies

On receiving these words from the distinguished lady, I didn't know which of my senses was the more struck by what she said: whether it was my ears as I took in her stirring words, or my eyes as I admired her great beauty and dress, her noble bearing and face. It was the same for the other ladies too: my gaze darted back and forth from one to the other since they were all so alike that you could hardly tell them apart. All except for the third lady, who was no less imposing than the other two. This lady had such a stern face that whoever glanced into her eyes, no matter how brazen they were, would feel afraid of committing some misdeed since she seemed to threaten punishment to all wrongdoers. Out of respect for the ladies' noble appearance, I stood up before them but was far too dumbfounded to utter a single word. I was extremely curious to know who they were and would have dearly loved to dare ask them their names, where they were from, why they had come, and what the priceless symbols were that each of them held like a sceptre in her right hand. Yet I didn't think myself worthy to put these questions to such honourable ladies as these, so I held my tongue and carried on gazing at them. Though still frightened, I was also in part reassured, for the lady's words had already begun to assuage my fears.

Presently, the wise lady who had addressed me first seemed to read my mind and began to answer my unspoken questions with these words: 'My dear daughter, you should know that it is by the grace of God, who foresees and ordains all things, that we, celestial creatures though we may be, have been sent down to earth in order to restore order and justice to those institutions which we ourselves have set up at God's command. All three of us are His daughters, for it was He who created us. My task is to bring back men and women when they drift away from the straight and narrow. Should they go astray but yet have the sense to know me when they see me, I come to them in spirit and speak to their conscience, instructing them in the error of their ways and showing them how exactly it is that they have done wrong. Then I teach them to follow the correct road and to avoid doing what is undesirable. Because it is my role to light their way to the true path and to teach both men and women to acknowledge their flaws and weaknesses, you see me here holding up a shining mirror like a sceptre in my right hand. You can be sure that whoever looks into this mirror, no matter who they may be, will see themselves as they truly are, such is its great power. Not for nothing is it encrusted with precious stones, as you can see. With the help of this mirror, I can determine the nature, quantity and essence of all things and can take full measure of them. Without this mirror, nothing can come to good. Since you obviously want to know what function my two sisters perform, each of them will shortly speak to you in turn and will add her weight to my words by giving you a clear explanation of both her name and her powers.

'First, however, I will tell you exactly why we are here. I want you to know that, as we do nothing without good reason, our appearance here today has a definite purpose. Though we do not attempt to be known in all places, since not everyone strives to acquaint themselves with us, we have none the less come to visit you, our dear friend. Because you have long desired to acquire true knowledge by dedicating yourself to your studies, which have cut you off from the rest of the world, we are now here to comfort you in your sad and dejected state. It is your own efforts that have won you this reward. You will soon see clearly why it is that your heart and mind have been so troubled.

'Yet we also have a further, more important reason for coming to visit you, which we'll now go on to tell you about. Our wish is to prevent others from falling into the same error as you and to ensure that, in future, all worthy ladies and valiant women are protected from those who have attacked them. The female sex has been left defenceless for a long time now, like an orchard without a wall, and bereft of a champion to take up arms in order to protect it. Indeed, this is because those trusty knights who should by right defend women have been negligent in their duty and lacking in vigilance, leaving womankind open to attack from all sides. It's no wonder that women have been the losers in this war against them since the envious slanderers and vicious traitors who criticize them have been allowed to aim all manner of weapons at their defenceless targets. Even the strongest city will fall if there is no one to defend it, and even the most undeserving case will win if there is no one to testify against it. Out of the goodness and simplicity of their hearts, women have trusted in God and have patiently endured the countless verbal and written assaults that have been unjustly and shamelessly launched upon them. Now, however, it is time for them to be delivered out of the hands of Pharaoh.[6] For this reason, we three ladies whom you see before you have been moved by pity to tell you that you are to construct a building in the shape of a walled city, sturdy and impregnable. This has been decreed by God, who has chosen you to do this with our help and guidance. Only ladies who are of good reputation and worthy of praise will be admitted into this city. To those lacking in virtue, its gates will remain forever closed.'

4. How, before the lady revealed her name, she spoke at greater length about the city which Christine was destined to build, and explained that she was entrusted with the task of helping her to construct the enclosure and external walls

'So you see, my dear daughter, that you alone of all women have been granted the honour of building the City of Ladies. In order to lay the foundations, you shall draw fresh water from us three as from a clear spring. We will bring you building materials which will be stronger and more durable than solid, uncemented marble. Your city will be unparalleled in splendour and will last for all eternity.

6. Like the Israelites from Egypt; in this comparison, Christine is implicitly cast as Moses.

'Haven't you read that King Tros founded the city of Troy with the help of Apollo, Minerva and Neptune,[7] whom the people of that time believed to be gods? Haven't you also heard of Cadmus, who created the city of Thebes at the gods' command?[8] Yet, in the course of time, even these cities fell into ruin and decay. However, in the manner of a true sibyl, I prophesy to you that this city which you're going to build with our help will never fall or be taken. Rather, it will prosper always, in spite of its enemies who are racked by envy. Though it may be attacked on many sides, it will never be lost or defeated.

'In the past, as the history books tell you, certain courageous ladies who refused the yoke of servitude founded and established the realm of Amazonia.[9] For many years afterwards, this realm was maintained under the rule of various queens, all of whom were noble ladies chosen by the women themselves, and who governed well and wisely, making every effort to keep their country safe. These women were very strong and powerful, having extended their rule over many of the lands of the east and having subjugated to their will all the neighbouring countries. They were feared by everyone, even the Greeks, who were the bravest nation in the world at that time. None the less, even the Amazons' power began to crumble in due course, as is the way with all earthly rulers. Now, the only trace that is left of that proud realm is its name.

'By contrast, the city which you're going to build will be much more powerful than these. As has been decided amongst the three of us, it is my task to help you begin by giving you tough, indestructible cement which you will need to set the mighty foundations and to support the great walls that you must raise all around. These walls should have huge high towers, solid bastions surrounded by moats, and outer forts with both natural and manmade defences. This is what a powerful city must have in order to resist attack. On our advice, you will sink these foundations deep in order to make them as secure as possible, and you will construct such high walls that the city inside will be safe from assault. Dear Christine, I have now told you all about why we have come. However, in order to convince you to give greater weight to my words, I'm going to reveal my name to you. The very sound of it should reassure you that, if you follow my instructions, you will find me to be an infallible guide to you in all your endeavours. I am called Lady Reason, so rest assured that you are in good hands. For the moment, I will say no more.'

* * *

14. More discussion and debate between Christine and Reason

'My lady, you have truly spoken well, and your words are like music to my ears. Yet, despite what we've said about intelligence, it's undeniable that women are by nature fearful creatures, having weak, frail bodies and lacking in physical

7. According to classical myth, the city of Troy (in modern-day Turkey) was founded by the son of Tros, aided by Apollo (god of the sun, prophecy, and music), Athena (called by the Romans Minerva, goddess of wisdom and war), and Poseidon (Neptune, god of the sea).
8. According to myth, the earliest inhabitants of the new city were men who grew from the dragon's teeth that Cadmus had sown in the ground on the instructions of Athena. Christine would have been most familiar with the verson of the story told in Ovid, *Metamorphoses* 3.1–137.
9. The country believed to be inhabited only by Amazons, the warrior women featured in several Greek myths; its location, a matter of dispute, was usually held to be somewhere near the Black Sea.

strength. Men have therefore argued that it is these things that make the female sex inferior and of lesser value. To their minds, if a person's body is defective in some way, this undermines and diminishes that person's moral qualities and thus it follows that he or she is less worthy of praise.'

Reason's reply was, 'My dear daughter, this is a false conclusion which is completely untenable. It is definitely the case that when Nature fails to make a body which is as perfect as others she has created, be it in shape or beauty, or in some strength or power of limb, she very often compensates for it by giving that body some greater quality than the one she has taken away. Here's an example: it's often said that the great philosopher Aristotle was very ugly, with one eye lower than the other and a deformed face. Yet, if he was physically misshapen, Nature certainly made up for it by endowing him with extraordinary intellectual powers, as is attested by his own writings. Having this extra intelligence was worth far more to him than having a body as beautiful as that of Absalom.

'The same can be said of the emperor Alexander the Great,[1] who was extremely short, ugly and sickly, and yet, as is well known, he had tremendous courage in his soul. This is also true of many others. Believe me, my dear friend, it doesn't necessarily follow that a fine, strong body makes for a brave and courageous heart. Courage comes from a natural, vital force which is a gift from God that He allows Nature to implant in some rational beings more than in others. This force resides in the mind and the heart, not in the bodily strength of one's limbs. You very often see men who are well built and strong yet pathetic and cowardly, but others who are small and physically weak yet brave and tough. This applies equally to other moral qualities. As far as bravery and physical strength are concerned, neither God nor Nature has done the female sex a disservice by depriving it of these attributes. Rather, women are lucky to be deficient in this respect because they are at least spared from committing and being punished for the acts of appalling cruelty, the murders and terrible violent deeds which men who are equipped with the necessary strength have performed in the past and still do today. It probably would have been better for such men if their souls *had* spent their pilgrimage through this mortal life inside the weak body of a woman. To return to what I was saying, I am convinced that if Nature decided not to endow women with a powerful physique, she none the less made up for it by giving them a most virtuous disposition: that of loving God and being fearful of disobeying His commandments. Women who don't act like this are going against their own nature.

'However, dear Christine, you should note that God clearly wished to prove to men that, just because *all* women are not as physically strong and courageous as men generally are, this does not mean that the entire female sex is lacking in such qualities. There are in fact several women who have displayed the necessary courage, strength and bravery to undertake and accomplish extraordinary deeds which match those achieved by the great conquerors and knights mentioned in books. I'll shortly give you an example of such a woman.

'My dear daughter and beloved friend, I've now prepared a trench for you which is good and wide, and have emptied it of earth which I have carried away in great loads on my shoulders. It's now time for you to place inside the trench

1. The greatest Greek general of antiquity (356–323 B.C.E.), renowned in the Middle Ages as an ideal of knighthood and the power to rule.

some heavy, solid stones which will form the foundations of the walls for the City of Ladies. So take the trowel of your pen and get ready to set to with vigour on the building work. Here is a good, strong stone which I want you to lay as the first of your city's foundations. Don't you know that Nature herself used astrological signs to predict that it should be placed here in this work? Step back a little now and let me put it into position for you.'

15. About Queen Semiramis

'Semiramis[2] was a truly heroic woman who excelled in the practice and pursuit of arms. Because of her great military prowess, the people of the time—who were all pagans—said that she was so invincible both on land and sea that she must be the sister of the great god Jupiter and the daughter of the old god Saturn whom they regarded as the rulers of these two domains. This lady was married to King Ninus, who named the city of Nineveh after himself. With the help of his wife Semiramis, who rode into battle at his side, this fine lord conquered the mighty city of Babylon, the vast land of Assyria and many other countries.

'When Semiramis was still quite young, it so happened that her husband Ninus was killed by an arrow during an assault on a city. Once he had been buried with all due ceremony as befitted a king, his wife didn't lay down her arms but rather took them up with renewed vigour and seized the reins of power over the kingdoms and territories that she and her husband had conquered together in battle. She gained full control over these lands, thanks to her military skills, and likewise accomplished so many other marvellous deeds that no man could match her in strength and ability. This supremely courageous lady had no fear of pain and was undaunted by anything. Semiramis confronted any type of danger with such courage that she crushed all her enemies who thought that, once she was widowed, they could overthrow her in the lands which she had conquered. However, she had such a fearsome reputation as a warrior that she not only kept all the lands she had already taken but even added others to her empire. Accompanied by vast numbers of troops, she attacked Ethiopia with such force that she defeated it completely. From there she set off with a huge army to conquer India, a country on which no one had ever dared wage war. She attacked this nation so ruthlessly that it fell entirely into her hands. To keep the tale short, she then went on to attack still more countries so that, in the end, the whole of the East came under her control. Thanks to these magnificent and mighty conquests, Semiramis was able to rebuild and fortify the city of Babylon which had been founded by Nimrod and the giants on the plains of Shinar.[3] Though the city was already powerful and fiercely protected, she strengthened it still further with more defences and deep moats all around.

'One time, Semiramis was sitting in her room surrounded by her handmaidens, who were busy combing her hair, when news suddenly came that one of her territories had rebelled against her. She jumped up immediately and swore

2. Legendary Assyrian queen, credited with conquering many lands but later conventionally associated with despotism and sexual appetites (specifically, incest; e.g., see Dante, *Inferno* 5.52–60). Christine's positive representation of Semiramis, identified during the Middle Ages as the Queen of Babylon, is unusual in the Middle Ages.
3. See Genesis 10.10.

on her kingdom that the half of her hair which had not yet been plaited would remain loose until she could avenge this outrage and take the country back into her control. Without further delay, she ordered huge numbers of her troops to prepare for battle and attacked the rebels with such ferocity and might that they submitted once more to her rule. These rebels and all her other subjects were so intimidated by her that none ever dared to revolt against her again. In memory of this great and noble deed, an enormous bronze statue of her, richly decorated in gold, was erected on a massive pillar in the middle of Babylon. This statue, which stood for many years, depicted a princess holding a sword in her hand with only one side of her hair plaited. Queen Semiramis founded and built several new cities and fortresses, and performed so many other notable feats that no man has ever been commemorated in the history books for having as much courage and for doing as many marvellous things as she did.

'It's true that some authors have criticized Semiramis—and rightly so, if she had been a Christian—for having married her own son whom she had borne to her husband, the lord Ninus. Yet she had two main reasons for doing so: firstly, she wanted no other crowned lady to share her empire with her, as would have been the case if her son had married another woman; and secondly, in her opinion, no other man than her son was worthy of her. This terrible transgression of hers can partly be excused by the fact that, at that time, there was no written law: people observed only the law of nature whereby they were free to do as they pleased without fear of committing a sin. There's no doubt that, since she was so proud and honourable, if she *had* thought she was doing anything wrong or that she might be subject to criticism for her actions, she would have refrained from doing as she did.

'The first foundation stone of our city is now in place, but we must follow it up with many more stones in order to raise high the walls of the building.'

16. About the Amazons

There is a country near the land of Europe which lies on the Ocean,[4] that great sea that covers the whole world. This place is called Scythia, or the land of the Scythians. It once happened that, in the course of a war, all the noblest male inhabitants of this country were killed. When their womenfolk saw that they had lost all their husbands, brothers and male relatives, and that only very young boys and old men were left, they took courage and called together a great council of women, resolving that, henceforth, they would lead the country themselves, free from male control. They issued an edict which forbade any man from entering their territory, but decided that, in order to ensure the survival of their race, they would go into neighbouring countries at certain times of the year and return thereafter to their own land. If they gave birth to male children, they would send them away to be with their fathers, but the female children they would bring up themselves. In order to uphold this law, they chose two of the highest-born ladies to be queens, one of whom was called Lampheto and the other Marpasia. No sooner was this done than they expelled

---

4. On medieval maps, the name given to a sea that surrounded the entire landmass of the known world. The region known in classical times as Scythia includes areas of modern Ukraine, Russia, and Kazakhstan.

all the men who were left in the country. Next, they took up arms, women and girls together, and waged war on their enemies, laying waste to their lands with fire and sword and crushing all opposition until none remained. In short, they wreaked full revenge for their husbands' deaths.

'This is how the women of Scythia began to bear arms. They were later known as the Amazons, a name which means "they who have had a breast removed." It was their custom that, by a technique known only to this race of women, the most noble of them would have the left breast burnt off at a very early age in order to free them up to carry a shield. Those young girls who were of non-noble birth would lose the right breast so that they could more easily handle a bow. They took such pleasure in the pursuit of arms that they greatly expanded their territory by the use of force, thus spreading their fame far and wide. To get back to what I was saying, the two queens Lampheto and Marpasia each led a great army into various countries and were so successful that they conquered a large part of Europe and the region of Asia, subjugating many kingdoms to their rule. They founded many towns and cities including the Asian city of Ephesus,[5] which has long been justly renowned. Of these two queens, it was Marpasia who died first in battle and who was replaced by a young daughter of hers, a beautiful and noble maiden called Synoppe. This girl was so proud that she chose never to sleep with a man, preferring instead to remain a virgin until her death. Her only love and sole pleasure in life was the pursuit of arms: she never tired of going into battle and seizing new lands. She also avenged her mother's death fully by putting to the sword the entire enemy population and laying waste to their whole country, adding it to the others which she went on to conquer.'

17. About the Amazon queen, Thamiris

'As you will now go on to hear, the state founded by the Amazons flourished for a very long time, with a whole succession of valiant ladies becoming queen. Since it would be tedious to tell you all their names, I'll limit myself to the most famous individuals.

'One of the Amazon queens was the noble Thamiris, who was as brave as she was wise. Thanks to her intelligence, cunning and military prowess, she defeated and captured Cyrus,[6] a great and powerful king of Persia who had performed many marvellous feats, including the conquest of the mighty Babylon and a large part of the whole world. Having vanquished so many countries, Cyrus decided to attack the realm of the Amazons in an attempt to bring them too under his control. Once this wise queen had been informed by her spies that Cyrus was advancing towards her with an army big enough to defeat the entire world, she realized that there was no way to beat his troops by force and that she would have to use guile. So, like the battle-hardened leader she was, on learning that, as she had intended, Cyrus had now come well inside her territory having met no opposition, Thamiris ordered all her ladies to put on their armour and cleverly sent them off to set up strategic ambushes in the mountains and forests through which Cyrus would have to pass.

5. In Asia Minor, near the coast of the Aegean Sea (in modern Turkey).
6. The founder of the Persian Empire (d. 529 B.C.E), who conquered Babylon (but did not suffer the death described here).

'Hidden from view, Thamiris and her army waited for Cyrus and his men to move into the narrow passages and gullies between the trees and rocks where he had to pick his way. At the key moment, she had her horns sounded, taking Cyrus completely by surprise. To his dismay, he found his army attacked on all sides by ladies who were hurling down great piles of rocks to crush them. Because of the difficult terrain, his men could neither advance nor retreat: if they tried to go forwards or backwards, they were ambushed and killed as soon as they emerged at either end of the passages. All were crushed and slain, except Cyrus and his barons, who were taken prisoner by order of the queen. When the massacre was over, Thamiris had them brought before her pavilion, which she had ordered to be put up before the fighting began. She was so full of anger at Cyrus for having killed one of her beloved sons whom she had sent to his court that she decided to show no mercy. She had all his barons decapitated in front of him, saying: "Cyrus, you who were so cruel and bloodthirsty from killing other men, can now finally drink your fill." Thereupon she had his head cut off and thrown into a barrel in which all the blood of his barons had been collected.

'My sweet daughter and dear friend, I'm reminding you of these things because they are relevant to what we've been discussing, even though you are already familiar with them. Indeed, you yourself have recounted these stories elsewhere in your Book of the Mutation of Fortune and Letter of Othea to Hector. I'll now go on to tell you some more.'

18. How the mighty Hercules and his companion Theseus came from Greece to attack the Amazons with a great army and fleet of ships, and how the two maidens Menalippe and Hippolyta brought them down, horses and all, in a big heap

'What else shall I tell you about them? The ladies of Amazonia were so successful in warfare that they were feared and respected by all other nations. Their reputation for being invincible and their unquenchable thirst for conquering new lands which led them to lay waste any country which refused to surrender to them, spread even as far as the distant land of Greece. This made the Greeks very afraid that the Amazons would one day attempt to use force against them.

'Then living in Greece at the very height of his powers was the great and mighty Hercules.[7] In his day, he performed more feats of strength than any mortal man whose deeds are recorded in the history books, fighting with giants, lions, snakes and terrifying monsters, and beating them all. In short, the only man who ever matched him for strength was the magnificent Samson.[8] Hercules was of the opinion that the Greeks shouldn't wait for the Amazons to come to them but would be much better advised to invade them first instead. In order to execute this plan, he ordered ships to be made ready for war and gathered together a large group of young noblemen to go and attack the Amazons in numbers. When Theseus, the good and valiant king of Athens, heard what was happening, he declared that they wouldn't go without him. He joined forces with Hercules and they sailed off with a huge army towards the land of

7. The greatest hero of classical mythology; many of his feats were performed in connec- tion with his twelve famous labors.
8. See Judges 13–16.

the Amazons. When they were just off the coast, Hercules, despite his extraordinary strength and bravery and the fact that he had so many troops with him, did not dare to moor the ships and disembark during the daytime as he knew just how fierce and courageous the Amazons were. This would be an almost unbelievable thing to say were it not that so many history books have recounted how this man, who could not be beaten by any creature alive, was extremely wary of these women's strength. He and his army therefore waited until nightfall when, at that hour when all living things are fast asleep, they leapt out of their ships and ran ashore. They swept through towns, setting fire to everything and killing all those who were caught unawares and had no time to defend themselves. The news about what had happened spread like wildfire and, as soon as they could, the brave Amazons rushed over themselves to pick up their weapons and to head down in great waves to attack the enemy's ships.

'The queen of the Amazons at that time was called Orithyia, a very valiant lady who had conquered many lands. She was the mother of the good Queen Penthesilea, about whom I'll tell you more later. Orithyia had succeeded the courageous Queen Antiope who had ruled the Amazons and governed the country with superb military skill, achieving many great things in her time. Orithyia soon heard the news that the Greeks, entirely unprovoked, had landed like a pack of thieves in the night and were going around killing everyone. As you can imagine, she was livid with rage, and vowed that they would regret having made her so angry. Cursing her enemy, whom she didn't fear in the least, she immediately called her troops together for battle. You should have seen the ladies as they dashed about for their arms and lined up at their queen's side. By daybreak, all her battalions were ready.

'Two of the strongest and most courageous maidens, the finest and most valiant of all the Amazons, Menalippe and Hippolyta, who were closely related to the queen, decided not to wait for her order once they heard that her plan was to get all her ladies together and order them into battle formation. Instead, as quickly as they could, they threw on their arms and, with lances at the ready and shields of tough elephant hide slung round their necks, they headed off on their swift chargers directly towards the port. Boiling with the most terrible rage and fury, they lowered their lances and aimed straight for the leaders of the Greek army: Menalippe against Hercules and Hippolyta against Theseus. Despite the great strength, bravery and courage of their enemies, the women's anger soon bore fruit as each of them struck against her adversary with such power that the two knights were brought down, horses and all, in a big heap. The women too fell from their horses, but they immediately recovered themselves and attacked the knights with their swords.

'How can one praise these maidens highly enough for having brought down, completely unaided, two of the most valiant knights who ever lived? The story would be almost impossible to believe if so many reliable authors had not made mention of it in their works. Those writers who were themselves clearly amazed by the story attempted to find excuses for Hercules in particular, given his exceptional physical strength, claiming that he only fell because his horse stumbled on the impact of the blow, adding that he would never have been brought down if he had been on foot. These two knights were completely shamefaced to have been knocked off their horses by the two maidens. Although the women continued to fight long and hard with their swords in a drawn-out battle, they were eventually beaten by the two knights, which is hardly suprising given that there were no two other heroes like them in the whole world.

'Hercules and Theseus were so highly gratified at having taken the two maidens prisoner that they wouldn't have exchanged them for the wealth of an entire city. They returned to their ship to disarm and refresh themselves, for they were only too aware that the battle had been a hard one to win. The two knights treated their captives with the greatest of honour and, once the ladies had disarmed and revealed themselves in all their true splendour and beauty, they were even more delighted. As they feasted their eyes on the two ladies, it seemed to them that they had never won a prize which gave them greater pleasure.

'When Queen Orithyia heard that the two maidens had been captured, she advanced towards the Greeks with a huge army. She was deeply distressed by what had happened but, out of fear that more harm would come to the two prisoners if she attacked the Greeks, she called a halt and sent a couple of her baronesses to parley with the enemy and to tell them that whatever ransom they demanded for the return of the girls, she would pay it. Hercules and Theseus received the two messengers with great respect and courteously replied that if the queen chose to make peace with them and promise that she and her ladies would never wage war on the Greeks but would be their allies, they would make a reciprocal pact with her. As for the ransom, they were prepared to surrender the two women and keep only their arms as a token and reminder of the victory that they had won over them. Since Orithyia's only concern was to have the two maidens whom she loved dearly returned safely to her, she was obliged to agree to the Greeks' demands. Once all the negotiations were done and the terms accepted by both parties, the queen arrived unarmed to celebrate the peace treaty with a feast, accompanied by a whole host of ladies and girls who were more beautifully arrayed than any the Greeks had ever seen. This feast took place amidst much happiness and joy.

'Yet Theseus was extremely reluctant to let Hippolyta go as he had already fallen deeply in love with her. He therefore begged Hercules to ask Orithyia to allow him to marry Hippolyta and take her back to Greece with him, a request to which the queen gave her consent. After a magnificent wedding feast, the Greeks left for home with Hippolyta at Theseus's side. She later bore him a son called Hippolytus who became a famous knight of exemplary prowess and skill. When the people of Greece learnt that peace had been made with the Amazons, they were overjoyed because there was no other race in the world whom they feared more.'

19. About Queen Penthesilea and how she went to the rescue of the city of Troy

'This Queen Orithyia lived for a long time and died at a fine old age, having kept the realm of Amazonia in a flourishing state and expanded its dominion. The Amazons crowned as her successor her own daughter, the brave Penthesilea, who surpassed all others in intelligence, courage, prowess and virtue. She too was forever eager to take up arms and fight, increasing the Amazons' power further than ever before in her relentless pursuit of territory. She was so feared by her enemies that none dared approach her and so proud that she never slept with a man but preferred to remain a virgin all her life.

'It was during her reign that the terrible war between the Greeks and the Trojans broke out.[9] Because of the name that the great Hector had made for himself as the finest, bravest and most highly skilled knight in the world, Penthesilea, who was naturally drawn to him since they shared the same qualities, heard so much about him that she began to love him with a pure and noble heart and desired above all else to go and see him. In order to fulfil this wish, she left her country with a great host of noble ladies and maidens all expert in the arts of war and richly armed, setting off to the city of Troy which lay a great distance away. However, distances always seem shorter when one's heart is filled with a strong desire.

'Unfortunately, when Penthesilea arrived in Troy, it was already too late: she discovered that Hector had been killed by Achilles during a battle in which the flower of Trojan chivalry had been wiped out. Penthesilea was received with all honours by the Trojans—King Priam, Queen Hecuba and all the barons—yet she was inconsolable and heartbroken to find that Hector was dead. The king and queen, who never left off grieving for the death of their son, offered to show her his body since they had been unable to let her see him alive. They took her to the temple where his tomb had been prepared, truly the very noblest and finest sepulchre that has ever been recorded in the history books. There, in a beautiful, sumptuous chapel all decorated with gold and precious stones, sat the embalmed and robed body of Hector on a throne in front of the main altar dedicated to the gods. He appeared to be more alive than dead as he brandished a naked sword in his hand and his haughty face still seemed to be throwing out a challenge to the Greeks. He was draped in a long, full garment which was woven with fine gold and trimmed and embroidered with jewels. This garment came down to the floor, covering the lower half of his body, which lay completely immersed in a precious balm that gave off a most delicious scent. The Trojans worshipped this body, bathed in the dazzling light of hundreds of candles, as if it were one of their gods. A costlier tomb surely never was seen. Here they brought Queen Penthesilea, who no sooner glimpsed the body through the open chapel door than she fell on her knees in front of Hector and greeted him as if he were still alive. She then went up close towards him and gazed deeply on his face. Through her tears she cried out: "O flower of chivalry, the very epitome and pinnacle of bravery: who can dare to call themselves valiant or even strap on a sword now that the finest and most shining example of knighthood has gone? Alas, cursed be the day that he whose vile hand deprived the world of its greatest treasure was ever born! Most noble prince, why was Fortune so contrary as to prevent me from being by your side when this traitor was plotting your downfall? This never would have happened because I would not have allowed it. If your killer were still alive, I would surely avenge your death and thus extinguish the great sorrow and anger which are burning up my heart as I see you lifeless before me and unable to speak to me, as was my only desire. Yet, since Fortune decreed that it should be so and I can do nothing to gainsay her, I swear by the very highest gods of our faith and solemnly promise you, my dear lord, that as long as I have breath in my body I will make the Greeks pay for

---

9. The Trojan War, a central theme of classical literature; it was the subject of Homer's *Iliad* and the backdrop of Virgil's *Aeneid*. Hector was the greatest warrior among the Trojans; Achilles, the greatest among the Greeks.

your death." As she knelt before the corpse, Penthesilea's words reached the great crowd of barons, knights and ladies who were all gathered there and moved them to tears. She could barely drag herself away from the tomb but, finally, she kissed his hand that was holding the sword and took her leave, saying: "Most excellent knight, what must you have been like when you were alive, given that the mere image of you in death is so full of majesty!"

'Weeping tender tears, she left his side. As soon as she could, she put on her armour and, with her army of noble ladies, dashed out of the city to attack the Greeks who were holding Troy in a state of siege. To make a brief tale of it, she and her army set to with such vigour that, if she had lived longer, no Greek would ever again have set foot in Greece. She struck down and nearly killed Pyrrhus, Achilles's son, who was a very fine soldier. It was only with great difficulty that his men were able to rescue him and drag him, half-dead, back to safety. Thinking that he was unlikely to survive, the Greeks were distraught, for he had been their greatest hope. If Penthesilea felt hatred for the father, she certainly didn't spare the son.

'In short, though Penthesilea performed the most extraordinary feats, she finally succumbed after having spent several days with her army in the thick of battle. When the Greeks were at their lowest ebb, Pyrrhus, who had recovered from his wounds but was overcome with shame and sorrow that she had done him such grievous harm, ordered his valiant men to concentrate solely on surrounding Penthesilea and separating her from her companions. He wanted to kill her with his own hands and would pay a handsome reward to anyone who managed to trap her. Pyrrhus's men took a long time to do his bidding because Penthesilea dealt out such fearsome blows that they were extremely afraid of approaching her. However, in the end, after an enormous amount of effort on their part, they finally managed to encircle her one day and isolate her from her ladies. The Greeks attacked the other Amazons so fiercely that they were powerless to help their queen and Penthesilea herself was exhausted after having accomplished more in that time than even Hector himself could have done. Despite the astonishing strength with which she defended herself, the Greeks were able to smash all her weapons and tear off a good part of her helmet. When Pyrrhus saw her bare blonde head, he struck her such a blow that he split her whole skull in two. Thus died the great and good Penthesilea, a huge loss both to the Trojans and to her own countrywomen, who were immediately plunged into grief, which was understandable since from that day forth the Amazons never knew any other queen to rival her. With heavy hearts, they carried her dead body back home.

'So, you have now heard how the realm of Amazonia was founded and how it lasted for over eight hundred years. You can work this out by checking in the history books for the length of time it took from the beginning of their reign up to when Alexander the Great conquered the entire world, at which point they were still reckoned to be a powerful nation. The accounts of his exploits tell how he went to their country and was received by the queen and her ladies. Alexander lived a long time after the destruction of Troy and more than four hundred years after the founding of Rome,[1] which itself postdated the fall of Troy by a great deal. So, if you make the effort to compare these histories and calculate the timescale involved, you will see that the reign of the Amazons was

1. Generally given in legend as 753 B.C.E.

extremely long-lived. You'll also realize that, of all the kingdoms that lasted this long, there is none that could boast such a large number of illustrious rulers who accomplished such extraordinary deeds as this great nation could of its queens and ladies.'

* * *

33. Christine asks Reason if any woman has ever invented new forms of knowledge

I, Christine, on hearing Reason's words, took up this matter and said to her, 'My lady, I can clearly see that you are able to cite an endless number of women who were highly skilled in the arts and sciences. However, I'd like to ask you if you know of any woman who was ingenious, or creative, or clever enough to invent any new useful and important branches of knowledge which did not previously exist. It's surely less difficult to learn and follow a subject which has already been invented than it is to discover something new and unknown by oneself.'

Reason replied, 'Believe me, many crucial and worthy arts and sciences have been discovered thanks to the ingenuity and cleverness of women, both in the theoretical sciences which are expressed through the written word, and in the technical crafts which take the form of manual tasks and trades. I'll now give you a whole set of examples.

'First of all, I'll tell you about the noble Nicostrata, whom the Italians called Carmentis. This lady was the daughter of the king of Arcadia[2] whose name was Pallas. She was extraordinarily intelligent and endowed by God with special intellectual gifts, having such a vast knowledge of Greek literature and being able to write so wisely, elegantly and with such eloquence that the poets of the time claimed in their verse that she was loved by the god Mercury.[3] They similarly thought that her son, who was in his day equally renowned for his intelligence, was the offspring of this god, rather than of her husband. Because of various upheavals that occurred in her native land, Nicostrata, accompanied by her son and a whole host of other people who wanted to go with her, set off for Italy in a large fleet of ships and sailed up the River Tiber. It was here that she went ashore and climbed up a great hill which she named Mount Palatine after her father. On this hill, where the city of Rome was subsequently founded, she, her son and her followers built themselves a castle. As she found the indigenous population to be very primitive, she laid down a set of rules for them to observe and encouraged them to live a rational and just existence. Thus it was she who first established laws in this country that was to become so famous for developing a legal system from which all known laws would be derived.

'Amongst all the other attributes that this lady possessed, Nicostrata was particularly blessed with the gift of divine inspiration and prophecy. She was thus able to predict that her adopted country would one day rise above all others to become the most magnificent and glorious realm on earth. To her mind, therefore, it would not be fitting for this country which would outshine and conquer the rest of the world to use an inferior and crude set of alphabetical letters which

2. Region of central Greece, conventionally associated with pastoral poetry.
3. Messenger of the Roman gods; as a herald, he was a god of commerce and—especially important in the Middle Ages—skill in speaking and eloquence generally.

had originated in a foreign country. Moreover, Nicostrata wished to transmit her own wisdom and learning to future generations in a suitable form. She therefore set her mind to inventing a new set of letters which were completely different from those used in other nations. What she created was the ABC—the Latin alphabet—as well as the rules for constructing words, the distinction between vowels and consonants and the bases of the science of grammer. She gave this knowledge and this alphabet to the people, in the hope that they would become universally known. It was truly no small or insignificant branch of knowledge that this lady invented, nor should she receive only paltry thanks for it. This ingenious science proved so useful and brought so much good into the world that one can honestly say that no nobler discovery was ever made.

'The Italians were not lacking in gratitude for this great gift, and rightly so, since they heralded it as such a marvellous invention that they venerated her more highly than any man, worshipping Nicostrata/Carmentis like a goddess in her own lifetime. When she died, they built a temple dedicated to her memory, situated at the foot of the hill where she had made her home. In order to preserve her fame for posterity, they borrowed various terms from the science she had invented and even used her own name to designate certain objects. In honour of the science of Latin that she had invented, the people of the country called themselves Latins. Furthermore, because *ita* in Latin is the most important affirmative term in that language, being the equivalent of *oui* in French, they did not stop at calling their own realm the land of the Latins, but went so far as to use the name Italy to refer to the whole country beyond their immediate borders, which is a vast area comprising many different regions and kingdoms. From this lady's name, Carmentis, they also derived the Latin word *carmen*, meaning "song." Even the Romans, who came a long time after her, called one of the gates of the city the *Porta Carmentalis*. These names have not been changed since and are still the same today, no matter how the fortunes of the Romans have fared or which mighty emperor was in power.

'My dear Christine, what more could you ask for? Could any mortal man be said to have done anything so splendid? But don't think that she's the only example of a woman who invented many new branches of learning . . .'

34. About Minerva, who invented countless sciences, including the art of making arms from iron and steel

'Minerva, as you yourself have noted elsewhere, was a maiden from Greece who was also known as Pallas.[4] This girl was so supremely intelligent that her contemporaries foolishly declared her to be a goddess come down from the heavens, since they had no idea who her parents were and she performed deeds that had never been done before. As Boccaccio himself points out,[5] the fact that they knew so little about her origins meant that they were all the more astonished at her great wisdom, which surpassed that of every other woman of her time. She

4. An epithet of Athena.
5. In his *Genealogy of the Gentile Gods*, the Italian writer Giovanni Boccaccio (1313–1375) describes the descent of the gods, their evolution from actual human beings to divine figures, and the figurative significance of their names and deeds.

employed her skilfulness and her immense ingenuity not just in one domain but in many. First of all, she used her brilliance to invent various Greek letters called characters which can be used to write down a maximum number of ideas in a minimum number of words. This wonderfully clever invention is still used by the Greeks today. She also invented numbers and developed ways of using them to count and perform quick calculations. In short, she was so ingenious that she created many arts and techniques that had not previously been discovered, including the art of making wool and cloth. It was she who first had the idea of shearing sheep and developing the whole process of untangling, combing and carding the wool with various instruments, cleaning it, breaking down the fibres on metal spikes and spinning it on the distaff, whilst also inventing the tools needed for weaving it into cloth and making it into fine fabric.

'Likewise, she discovered how to make oil from pressing olives and how to extract the juice from other sorts of fruit.

'Likewise, she invented the art of building carts and chariots in order to carry things more easily from one place to another.

'Likewise, an invention of this lady's which was all the more marvellous for being such an unlikely thing for a woman to think of, was the art of forging armour for knights to protect themselves in battle and weapons of iron and steel for them to fight with. She taught this art first to the people of Athens, whom she also instructed in how to organize themselves into armies and battalions and to fight in serried ranks.

'Likewise, she invented flutes, pipes, trumpets and other wind instruments.

'This lady was not only extraordinarily intelligent but also supremely chaste, remaining a virgin all her life. It was because of her exemplary chastity that the poets claimed in their fables that she struggled long and hard with Vulcan, the god of fire,[6] but finally overcame and defeated him. This story can be interpreted to mean that she conquered the passions and desires of the flesh which so vigorously assail the body when one is young. The Athenians held this girl in the highest esteem, worshipping her as if she were a deity and calling her the goddess of arms and warfare because she was the first to invent these arts. She was also known as the goddess of wisdom, thanks to her great intelligence.

'After her death, the people of Athens built a temple dedicated to her, in which they placed a statue representing wisdom and warfare in the likeness of a girl. This statue had terrible fierce eyes to symbolize both the duty of a knight to enforce justice and the inscrutability of the thoughts of a wise man. The statue had a helmet on its head, to suggest the idea that a knight must be hardened in battle and have unfailing courage, and that the plans of a wise man should be shrouded in secrecy. It was also dressed in chainmail, to represent the power of the estate of knighthood as well as the foresight of a wise man who arms himself against the vicissitudes of Fortune. The statue held a great spear or lance as an emblem of the fact that a knight must be the rod of justice and that a wise man launches his attacks from a safe distance. Round the statue's neck hung a shield or buckler of crystal, meaning that a knight must always be vigilant and ready to defend the country and the people and that a wise man has a clear understand-

6. The Greek Hephaistos; according to one myth, he attempted to rape Athena/Minerva.

ing of all things. In the centre of this shield was the image of the head of a serpent known as a Gorgon,[7] to suggest the idea that a knight must be cunning and stalk his enemies like a snake whilst a wise man must be wary of all the harm that others might do to him. To guard the statue, they placed next to it a night bird—an owl—to signify that a knight must be prepared, if needs be, to protect the country both day and night, and that a wise man must be alert at all times to do what is right. This lady Minerva was greatly revered for a long time and her fame spread to many other countries, where they also dedicated temples to her. Even centuries later, when the Romans were at the height of their powers, they incorporated her image into their pantheon of gods.'

* * *

37. About all the great good that these ladies have brought into the world

'My lady, I'm delighted to hear from your lips that so much good has been brought into the world thanks to the intelligence of women. Yet there are still those men who go around claiming that women know nothing of any worth. It's also a common way to mock someone for saying something foolish by telling them that they're thinking like a woman. On the whole, men seem to hold the view that women have never done anything for humankind but bear children and spin wool.'

Reason's reply was: 'Now can you understand the terrible ingratitude of those men who say such things? It's as if they're enjoying all the benefits without having any idea of where they come from or whom they should thank for them. You can clearly see how God, who does nothing without good cause, wanted to show men that they should no more denigrate the female sex than they should their own sex. He chose to endow women's minds with the capacity not simply to learn and grasp all kinds of knowledge but also to invent new ones by themselves, discovering sciences which have done more good and have been more useful to humanity than any others. Just take the example of Carmentis, whom I told you about before. Her invention of the Latin alphabet pleased God so much that He wished it to replace the Hebrew and Greek alphabets which had been so prestigious. It was by His will that the alphabet spread throughout most of Europe, a vast expanse of land, where it is used in countless books and volumes in all disciplines which recall and preserve for ever the glorious deeds of men and the marvellous workings of God, in addition to all the arts and sciences. But don't let it be said that I'm telling you these things out of bias: these are the words of Boccaccio himself and thus the truth of them is indisputable.

'One could sum up by saying that the good things that this Carmentis has done are truly infinite, since it is thanks to her that men have been brought out of their ignorant state and become civilized, even if they themselves have not acknowledged this fact. Thanks to her, men possess the art of encoding their thoughts and wishes into secret messages which they can send all over the

7. In classical mythology, one of three snake-haired female monsters, the sight of which turned viewers to stone; one was Medusa, whose head was cut off by the hero Perseus and then set in Athena's shield (see Ovid, *Metamorphoses* 7.772–803).

world. They have the means to make their desires known and understood by others, and they have access to knowledge of past and present events as well as to some aspects of the future. Moreover, thanks to this lady's invention, men can draw up treaties and strike up friendships with people in faraway places; through their correspondence back and forth, they can get to know each other without ever meeting face to face. In short, it is impossible to count up all the advantages that the invention of the alphabet has brought: it is writing which allows us to describe and to know God's will, to understand celestial matters, the sea, the earth, all individuals and all objects. I ask you, then, was there ever a man who did more good than this?'

38. *More on the same topic*

'One might also ask if any man ever did as much for the benefit of humankind as this noble Queen Ceres,[8] whom I was telling you about before. Who could ever deserve more praise than she who led men, who were no better than savage primitives, out of the woods where they were roaming like wild beasts without any laws, and instead took them to dwell in towns and cities and taught them how to live a law-abiding existence? It was she who introduced men to far better nourishment than their previous diet of acorns and wild apples, giving them wheat and corn which makes their bodies more beautiful, their complexions clearer and their limbs stronger and more supple. This is much more suitable and substantial food for human beings to eat. It was she who showed men how to clear the land which was full of thistles, thorns, scrubby bushes and wild trees, and to plough the earth and sow seed by which means agriculture became a sophisticated rather than a crude process and could be used for the common good of all. It was she who enriched humankind by turning coarse primitives into civilized citizens and by transforming men's minds from being lazy, unformed and shrouded in ignorance to being capable of more suitable meditations and of the contemplation of higher matters. Finally, it was she who sent men out into the fields to work the land, men whose efforts sustain the towns and cities and provide for those inhabitants who are freed up to perform other tasks which are essential for human existence.

'Isis[9] is a similar example in terms of horticulture. Who could ever match the enormous benefits which she brought into the world when she discovered how to grow trees which bear fine fruit and to cultivate other excellent herbs which are so suitable for a human diet?

'Minerva too used her wisdom to endow human beings with many vital things such as woollen clothing, instead of the animal pelts which were all there was previously to wear. For the benefit of humankind, she invented carts and chariots to relieve men of the burden of carrying their possessions from place to place in their arms. Not to mention, my dear Christine, what she gave to noblemen and knights when she taught them the art and skill of making armour to give their bodies greater protection in battle, armour which was

8. The Roman goddess of agriculture—the equivalent of Demeter, one of the most important of the Greek deities (described in a chapter not included here).

9. One of the principal Egyptian deities, the goddess of earth; she was credited with teaching the Egyptians how to cultivate wheat and barley.

stronger, more practical and much finer than the leather hides which they had had to put on in the past.'

I answered Reason, saying, 'Indeed, my lady, from what you're telling me I've now realized the full extent to which those men who attack women have failed to express their gratitude and acknowledgement. They have absolutely no grounds for criticizing women: it's not just that every man who is born of woman receives so much from her, but also that there is truly no end to the great gifts which she has so generously showered on him. Those clerks who slander women, attacking them either verbally or in their writings, really should shut their mouths once and for all. They and all those who subscribe to their views should bow their heads in shame for having dared to come out with such things, considering that the reality is utterly different from what they've claimed. Indeed, they owe a huge debt of thanks to this noble lady Carmentis, for having used her fine mind to instruct them like a teacher with her pupils—a fact which they can't deny—and to endow them with the knowledge that they themselves hold in the highest regard, which is the noble Latin alphabet.

'But what about all the many noblemen and knights who go against their duty by launching their sweeping attacks on women? They too should hold their tongues, given that all their skills in bearing arms and fighting in orga-nized ranks, of which they're so inordinately proud, have come down to them from a woman. More generally, does any man who eats bread and lives in a civilized fashion in a well-ordered city or who cultivates the land have the right to slander and criticize women, as so many of them do, seeing all that has been done for them? Certainly not. It is women like Minerva, Ceres and Isis who have brought them so many advantages which they will always be able to live off and which will for ever enhance their daily existence. Are these things to be taken lightly? I think not, my lady, for it seems to me that the teachings of Aristotle, which have so greatly enriched human knowledge and are rightly held in such high esteem, put together with all those of every other philoso-pher who ever lived, are not worth anything like as much to humankind as the deeds performed by these ladies, thanks to their great ingenuity.'

Reason replied to me, 'These ladies were not the only ones to do so much good. There have been many others, some of whom I'll now go on to tell you about.'

* * *

46. About the good sense and cleverness of Queen Dido

'As you yourself pointed out earlier, good judgement consists of weighing up carefully what you wish to do and working out how to do it. To prove to you that women are perfectly able to think in this way, even about the most impor-tant matters, I'll give you a few examples of some high-born ladies, the first of whom is Dido.[1] As I'll go on to tell you, this Dido, whose name was originally Elissa, revealed her good sense through her actions. She founded and built a city in Africa called Carthage and was its queen and ruler. It was in the way that she established the city and acquired the land on which it was built that

1. The legendary founder of Carthage (a city that was located northeast of modern Tunis, in Tunisia); the dominant version of her story focuses on her love for the Trojan refugee Aeneas and her suicide after he leaves her to fulfill his destiny as forefather of the Roman people (see Virgil's *Aeneid*, esp. book 4).

she demonstrated her great courage, nobility and virtue, qualities which are indispensable to anyone who wishes to act prudently.

'This lady was descended from the Phoenicians, who came from the remotest regions of Egypt to settle in Syria where they founded and built several fine towns and cities. Amongst these people was a king named Agenor, who was a direct ancestor of Dido's father. This king, who was called Belus, ruled over Phoenicia and conquered the kingdom of Cyprus. He had only two children: a son, Pygmalion, and a daughter, Dido.

'On his deathbed, Belus ordered his barons to honour his children and be loyal to them, making them swear an oath that they would do so. Once the king was dead, they crowned his son Pygmalion and married the beautiful Elissa to a duke named Acerbas Sychaea, or Sychaeus, who was the most powerful lord in the country after the king. This Sychaeus was a high priest in the temple dedicated to Hercules, whom they worshipped, as well as being an extremely wealthy man. He and his wife loved each other very deeply and led a happy life together. But King Pygmalion was an evil man, the cruellest and most envious person you ever saw, whose greed knew no bounds. Elissa, his sister, was all too aware of what he was like. Seeing how rich her husband was and how well known for his fabulous wealth, she advised Sychaeus to be on his guard against the king and to put his treasure in a safe place where her brother couldn't lay his hands on it. Sychaeus followed his wife's advice but failed to watch his own back against possible attack from the king as she had told him to do. Thus it happened that, one day, the king had him killed in order to steal his great riches from him. Elissa was so distraught at his death that she nearly died of grief. For a long time, she gave herself over to weeping and wailing for the loss of her beloved lord, cursing her brute of a brother for having ordered his murder. However, the wicked king, whose wishes had been thwarted since he had only managed to recover a tiny part of Sychaeus's wealth, bore a deep grudge against his sister, whom he suspected of having hidden it all away.

'Realizing that her own life was in danger, Elissa's good sense told her to leave her native land and live elsewhere. Her mind made up, she carefully considered all that she needed to do and then steeled herself to put her plans into effect. This lady knew very well that the king did not enjoy the full support of his barons or his subjects because of his great cruelty and the excessive burdens he imposed on them. She therefore rallied to her cause some of the princes, townspeople and even the peasants. Having sworn them to secrecy, she outlined her plans to them in such persuasive terms that they declared their loyalty to her and agreed to go with her.

'As quickly and as quietly as she could, Elissa had her ship prepared. In the dead of night, she set sail with all her treasure and her many followers aboard, urging the sailors to make the ship go as fast as possible. Yet this lady's cleverness didn't end there. Knowing that her brother would send his men after her as soon as he learnt of her flight, she had great chests, trunks and boxes secretly filled up with heavy, worthless objects to make it look as if they contained treasure. The idea was that she would give these chests and boxes to her brother's men if they would only leave her alone and let her continue on her course. It all happened just as she planned, for they had not long been at sea when a whole host of the king's men came racing after her to stop her. In measured tones, she pointed out to them that as she was only setting out on a pilgrimage, they should allow her to sail on unhindered. However, seeing that they remained unconvinced by her explanation, she declared that if it was her treasure her brother was after, she would be prepared to give it to him, even though he had no right to interfere with her wishes. The king's men, who knew that this was his sole desire, forced her to part with it as that way they could do the king's bidding and she could appease her brother. With a sad face, as if it cost her dear, the lady made them load up all the chests and boxes on to their ships. Thinking that they had done well and that the king would be delighted with the news, his men immediately went on their way.

'Uttering not a single word of protest, the queen's only thoughts were of setting sail once more. They journeyed on, by day and night, until they came to the island of Cyprus, where they stopped for a short while to refresh themselves. As soon as she had made her sacrifices to the gods, the lady went back to the ship, taking with her the priest from the temple of Jupiter and his family. This priest had predicted that a lady would come from the land of the Phoenicians and that he would leave his country to join her. Casting off again, they left the island of Crete behind them and passed the island of Sicily on their right. They sailed along the whole length of the coast of Massylia until they finally arrived in Africa, where they landed. No sooner had they docked than the people living there rushed down to see the ship and to find out where those aboard were from.

'When they saw the lady and realized that she and her people had come in peace, they went and brought them food in abundance. Elissa talked to them in a very friendly way, explaining to them that she had heard such good things about their country that she wished to make her home there, if they had no objections. They replied that they were happy for her to do so. Insisting that she didn't want to establish a large colony on this foreign soil, the lady asked them to sell her a piece of land by the coast which was no bigger than what could be covered by the hide of a cow. Here she would build some dwellings for herself and her people. They granted her wishes and, as soon as the terms of the deal had been agreed upon, her cleverness and good sense came to the fore. Taking the cowhide, the lady had it cut into the tiniest strips possible, which were then tied together to form a rope. This rope was laid out on the ground by the seashore where it enclosed a huge plot of land. Those who had sold her the land were amazed and stunned by her cunning ruse, yet they had to abide by the deal they had struck with her.

'So it was that this lady took possession of all this territory in Africa. On her plot of land, a horse's head was discovered. This head, along with the movements and noises of the birds in the sky, they interpreted as prophetic signs that the city which they were about to found would be full of warriors who would excel themselves in the pursuit of arms. The lady immediately sent all over for workmen and spent her wealth freely to pay for their labour. The place which she had built was a magnificent and mighty city called Carthage, the citadel and main fortress of which were called Byrsa, which means "cowhide."[2]

'Just as she was beginning to build her city, she received news that her brother was coming after her and her followers for having made a fool of him

2. In Greek.

and tricked him out of his treasure. She told his messengers that she had most definitely given the treasure to the king's men for them to take back to him, but that perhaps it was they who had stolen it and replaced it with worthless objects instead. It was possibly even the gods who had decided to metamorphose the treasure and stop the king from having it because of the sin he had committed in ordering her husband's murder. As for her brother's threats, she had faith that, with the help of the gods, she could defend herself against him. Elissa therefore assembled all her fellow Phoenicians together and told them that she wanted no one to stay with her against their will nor suffer any harm for her sake. If any or all of them wanted to return home, she would reward them for their hard work and let them go. They all replied with one voice that they would live and die by her side, and would never leave her even for a single day.

'The messengers departed and the lady worked as fast as she could to finish the city. Once it was completed, she established laws and rules for her people to live an honest and just existence. She conducted herself with such wisdom and prudence that her fame spread all over the world and talk of her was on everyone's lips. Thanks to her bold and courageous actions and her judicious rule, she became so renowned for her heroic qualities that her name was changed to Dido, which means "virago"[3] in Latin: in other words, a woman who has the virtue and valour of a man. She lived a glorious life for many years, one which would have lasted even longer had Fortune not turned against her. As this goddess is wont to be envious of those she sees prosper, she concocted a bitter brew for Dido to drink, which I'll tell you about all in good time.'

* * *

48. About Lavinia, daughter of King Latinus

'Lavinia, queen of the Laurentines,[4] was similarly renowned for her good sense. Descended from the same Cretan king, Saturn, whom I've just mentioned, she was the daughter of King Latinus. She later wed Aeneas, although before her marriage she had been promised to Turnus, king of the Rutulians. Her father, who had been informed by an oracle that she should be given to a Trojan prince, kept putting off the wedding despite the fact that his wife, the queen, was very keen for it to take place. When Aeneas arrived in Italy, he requested King Latinus's permission to enter his territory. He was not only granted leave to do so but was immediately given Lavinia's hand in marriage. It was for this reason that Turnus declared war on Aeneas, a war which caused many deaths and in which Turnus himself was killed. Having secured the victory, Aeneas took Lavinia as his wife. She later bore him a son, even though he himself died whilst she was still pregnant. As her time grew near, she became very afraid that a man called Ascanius, Aeneas's elder son by another woman,[5] would attempt to murder her child and usurp the throne. She therefore went off to give birth in the woods and named the newborn baby Julius Silvius. Vowing never to marry again, Lavinia conducted herself with exemplary good judgement in her widow-

---

3. Literally, "manlike woman" (Latin), in a heroic sense; while the English word sometimes retains this meaning, it also (and more often) came to mean "a shrew."
4. Inhabitants of Laurentum, on the coast of

Latium just south of the mouth of the Tiber, where Aeneas and his men are said to have landed in Italy.
5. Aeneas's wife Creusa, who had died during the Greek sack of Troy.

hood and managed to keep the kingdom intact, thanks to her astuteness. She was able to win her stepson's affection and thus defuse any animosity on his part towards her or his stepbrother. Indeed, once he had finished building the city of Alba, Ascanius left to make his home there. Meanwhile, Lavinia ruled the country with supreme skill until her son came of age. This child's descendants were Romulus and Remus, who later founded the city of Rome. They in turn were the ancestors of all the noble princes who came after them.

'What more can I tell you, my dear Christine? It seems to me that I've cited sufficient evidence to make my point, having given enough examples and proofs to convince you that God has never criticized the female sex more than the male sex. My case is conclusive, as you have seen, and my two sisters here will go on to confirm this for you in their presentation of the facts. I think that I have fulfilled my task of constructing the enclosure walls of the City of Ladies, since they're all now ready and done. Let me give way to my two sisters: with their help and advice you'll soon complete the building work that remains.'

END OF THE FIRST PART OF *THE BOOK OF THE CITY OF LADIES*.

Travel and Encounter

Long before the early modern Age of Exploration, when Portuguese, Dutch, Spanish, and English sailors began to map out trade routes to East Asia and the Americas, medieval writers had begun to write travelers' accounts of eastward voyages. Some of these were largely fictional—entertainment for an audience eager to hear about exotic wonders. Others were based on real experience, offering practical knowledge concerning local languages and currencies and describing the safest and most lucrative routes a traveler might take. The three works collected here—the firsthand account of the merchant **Marco Polo**, the personal narrative of the learned and pious **Muhammad ibn Battuta**, and the half-fact, half-fantasy compilation that makes up the wildly popular *Book of John Mandeville*—represent both aspects of the travel genre.

Writing about travel in medieval Europe was at first centered on the practical experience of pilgrims, who made the difficult journey over land and sea to Jerusalem in order to retrace the footsteps of Jesus Christ. The fourth-century account of the nun Egeria, part of whose detailed letter recording her own visit to Jerusalem was copied and survived, illustrates the early popularity of this genre, which was both practical and inspirational—setting forth the spiritual journey behind the physical travel. People read such narratives not

just in order to plan their own itinerary but also to imagine voyages that they could never take in person, instead tracing the journey within their own souls. By the thirteenth century, the genre of the pilgrimage account had been taken up by traveling preachers (mainly Franciscan friars) who had voyaged to the distant East in order to bring new converts into the fold of Christianity. Figures such as the Italian Oderic of Pordenone and the Flemish William of Rubruck composed full descriptions of their journeys within India and China; intended to provide useful local information for subsequent waves of Christian missionaries, these works were also eagerly seized by other kinds of travelers who wished to undertake the difficult journey to East Asia.

Alongside the pious pilgrimage narratives and handbooks for missionaries a third genre developed, illustrated by Marco Polo's book: highly practical guides for merchants that provided the information on local customs, currencies, and commodities necessary to facilitate trade and exchange. And all three of these modes of travel writing stimulated the imaginations of armchair travelers who could enjoy vicarious journeys as they constructed a fantasy of the exotic East. The increasingly dynamic perspective on travel and exploration seen in these writings is also visible in medieval maps, especially in the shift away from the symbolic geography of the world map, or "mappamundi," oriented toward the east, with the Garden of Eden at the top and centered on Jerusalem. It was replaced by Ptolemaic

A page from an illustrated version of *The Book of John Mandeville*, produced in Bohemia ca. 1410, showing Mandeville on his way to Constantinople.

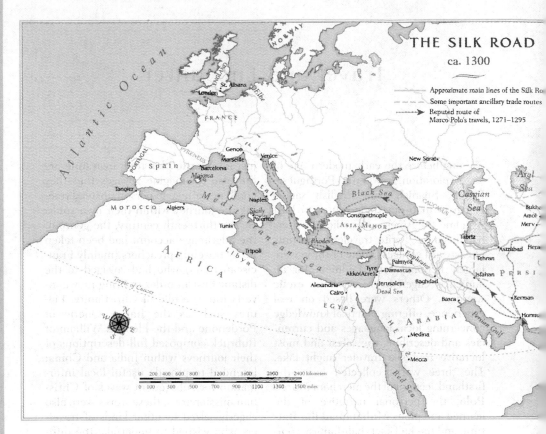

THE SILK ROAD
ca. 1300

———— Approximate main lines of the Silk Ro
- - - - Some important ancillary trade routes
·······➤ Reputed route of
Marco Polo's travels, 1271–1295

maps, based on the empirical observations and instructions of the second-century C.E. Greek astronomer Ptolemy from a text rediscovered around 1400, and by late medieval portolan charts (from Italian *portolano*, "having to do with ports or harbors"). These were oriented toward the north, to aid navigation by the Pole Star, and included highly detailed renderings of coastlines and harbors as well as a series of crisscrossing lines indicating the various

compass headings a navigator might use. This emphasis on navigation began to be reflected in monumental maps of the later Middle Ages, including the beautiful Catalan Atlas produced in 1375 by the Majorcan Jew Abraham Cresques. This extraordinarily detailed map, renowned for its accuracy and completeness, was almost immediately acquired by Charles V, King of France. Even earlier, however, Muslim cartographers had achieved a high degree of

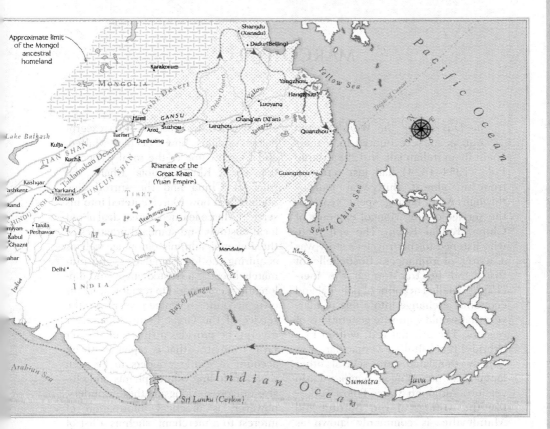

Map labels: Approximate limit of the Mongol ancestral homeland; Shangdu (Xanadu); Dadu (Beijing); Karakorum; MONGOLIA; Gobi Desert; Ordos Desert; Yellow Sea; Pacific Ocean; Yangzhou; Hangzhou; Yellow; Luoyang; Hami; GANSU; Chang'an (Xi'an); Lanzhou; Yangtze; Quanzhou; Lake Balkash; Turfan; Suzhou; Anxi; Dunhuang; Kulja; TIAN SHAN; Kucha; Taklamakan Desert; KUNLUN SHAN; Khanate of the Great Khan (Yuan Empire); Guangzhou; Kashgar; ashkent; Yarkand; Khotan; TIBET; South China Sea; kand; HINDU KUSH; Brahmaputra; HIMALAYAS; miyan; Taxila; Peshawar; Kabul; Ghazni; Ganges; Mekong; Mandalay; Irrawaddy; ahar; Delhi; INDIA; Bay of Bengal; Arabian Sea; Indian Ocean; Sumatra; Java; Sri Lanka (Ceylon); Tropic of Cancer

realism in their maps, as can be seen in the so-called *Tabula Rogeriana* (*Book of Roger*; Latin), finished in 1154 by Muhammad al-Idrisi, an Arab mapmaker and encyclopedist, at the request of Roger II, the Norman Christian ruler of Sicily. The volume contains seventy large maps, each highly detailed, that together constitute a single monumental world map. It was oriented toward the south (as is typical of medieval Islamic maps, and like the Catalan Atlas), and its division into seven latitudinal zones is in keeping with Ptolemaic conventions. The result was an exceptionally complete—and practical—vision of the world. In the *Book of Roger* we witness the mixing of cultures characteristic of the medieval Mediterranean. The Catalan Atlas of 250 years later, with its crisscrossed navigational lines, shows late medieval Europe poised on the threshold of a dynamic period of world exploration.

MARCO POLO

The *Diversity of the World* started out as story recounted by a merchant in an Italian jail. In 1298, Marco Polo (1254–1324) had just returned from an almost thirty-year journey through Asia, having spent years in the service of the Mongol emperor of China, Kublai Khan. The cell mate who listened to the traveler's story was a writer of romances, Rustichello of Pisa, and he transformed the merchant's detailed account of political and economic exchange into a tale of marvels that would captivate generations of readers. The original text, written in a hybrid French-Italian vernacular, was quickly translated into several other languages (including a popular Latin version). Although Marco Polo's work—like the writings of **Ibn Battuta** and **Mandeville**—is commonly known as his *Travels,* this is a modern name for a genre that was just beginning to emerge during the Middle Ages. The first generations to read Marco's story would have known it as *Le Devisement dou monde.* That title is translated here as *The Diversity of the World,* but the first word could also accurately be rendered as "division" or "description." This notion of diversity—exuberant, fertile heterogeneity—is key to Marco Polo's account, which highlights the tremendous range of cultures, peoples, and practices to be found along the trade routes winding from the Mediterranean Sea to the Indian Ocean and beyond.

The story opens by describing how Marco's father Niccolò and uncle Maffeo had traveled as far as China along the Asian trade route known as the Silk Road. After their return to Italy in 1269, they set forth again—this time joined by Marco. His extended journey throughout the Middle East and Asia would last almost three decades. The first excerpt below explains how Niccolò, Maffeo, and Marco came to the royal palace of the "Great Khan" (Kublai Khan), the ruler of China and the surrounding regions, and how Marco entered into his service. Marco learned a great deal about local customs and standard practices of the imperial administration as well as acquiring the local languages, and ultimately became a trusted envoy and diplomatic messenger. He remained, by his own account, seventeen years in the service of the Great Khan. In another excerpt, he provides a survey of "Lesser Java" (Sumatra) that is replete with an account of exotic wonders to be seen there, including wild elephants and elusive unicorns. Alongside these wonders, however, is practical information of interest to a merchant, such as a list of the spices and other trade-worthy goods that are plentiful in the region. Marco also supplies information useful to navigation, such as his note that the Pole Star—the main reference point in the Northern Hemisphere—"is not visible here." It is easy to see why Christopher Columbus carried a heavily annotated copy of Marco Polo's *Diversity of the World* with him on his voyages to the New World. In the final excerpted passage, Marco describes the virtuous and devout Brahmans of India, who eat and drink in extreme moderation and who so revere all living things that they refrain from killing even an insect. Some aspects of this account of the Brahmans are fanciful, in the tradition of "Wonders of the East" literature that began with ancient Greek writings on the eastern voyages of Alexander the Great. Yet other passages contain factual, detailed ethnographic description and offer a practical guide to exploration.

From The Diversity of the World[1]

FROM PROLOGUE

XIV. How the two brothers and Marc came to where the Great Khan was in the city of Clemeinfu

My lords Nicolau and Mafeu, and Marc, Nicolau's son, set out on the road and rode, winter and summer, until they came to the Great Khan, who was then in a large and very rich city called Clemeinfu.[2] What they found en route I won't mention now, for we will tell you about that later in the book, in due order. Know that it took them three and a half years' effort to get there; this was because of the snow, the rain, and the great rivers they had to cross, and because they couldn't ride as hard in winter as in summer. And he says in truth that when the Great Khan learned that my lords Nicolau and Mafeu were coming, he sent his messengers out forty days' journey to meet them, and they were well served and well honored in everything.

XV. How the two brothers and Marc went to the palace to meet the Great Khan

What should I tell you? When my lords Nicolau and Mafeu had arrived in this great city, they went to the chief palace, where they found the Great Khan with a great company of barons. They knelt before him and made every effort to humble themselves. The Great Khan had them stand and received them honorably, welcoming them with great joy and celebration. He kept asking them how they were and how they had done. And the two brothers told him that they had done very well, since they found him healthy and hale. Then they presented the warrants and letters the pope had sent him,[3] which made him very happy. Then they gave him the holy oil, which made him very happy and which he greatly prized. When the Great Khan saw Marc, who was a young man, he asked who he was. "Lord," said my lord Nicolau, he is my son and your man." "He is welcome," said the Great khan. Why should I make a long tale of it? Know, in truth, that the arrival of these messengers brought great joy and celebration to the Great Khan and his entire court; they were well served and well honored in everything. They remained at court and were honored above all other barons.

XVI. How the Great Khan sent Marc as his messenger

Now it so happened that Marc, my lord Nicolau's son, learned the Tartars' customs, languages, and writing so well that it was a marvel: for I tell you truthfully that not long after coming to the great lord's court, he learned to read and write four languages. He was wise and exceedingly perspicacious, and the Great Khan was very well disposed toward him for the goodness and great valor he saw in him. When the Great Khan saw how wise Marc was, he sent

---

1. Translated by Sharon Kinoshita.
2. The summer residence of Kublai Khan (1215–1294), northwest of modern Beijing; also spelled *Kaipingfu* (literally, "Kaiping governmental capital"). Kublai Khan, a Mongol

emperor, conquered China and founded the Yuan dynasty.
3. On their earlier visit to China, Kublai Khan had asked Niccolò and Maffeo to go to Rome and deliver a message to the pope on his behalf.

him as an envoy to a land a good six months' distant. The young man fulfilled the embassy wisely and well. And having often seen and heard the Great Khan say that the messengers he had sent to different parts of the world were fools and ignoramuses (when they returned and reported on the missions they had been sent on but were unable to say anything else about the countries they had visited) and that he would rather hear about the news and the customs and practices of the foreign country than about the affairs for which he had sent them, Marco, well aware of all this, when he went on this mission, put a good deal of effort into being able to tell the Great Khan about all the novelties and oddities he had seen.

XVII. How Marc returned from his embassy and recounts his embassy to the Great Khan

When Marc had returned from his embassy, he went before the Great Khan and gave a complete report on his mission; and having accomplished this very well, he then told him of all the novelties and things he had seen on the way— so well and intelligently that the Great Khan and everyone who heard him marveled, saying to each other: if this young man lives, he will surely become a man of great wisdom and valor. What should I tell you? From the time of that embassy on, the young man was referred to as my lord Marc Pol—and so will he henceforth be called in our book. And this with good reason, for he was wise and accomplished.

Why should I make a long story of it? Know in truth that my lord Marc remained with the Great Khan a good seventeen years; and in all this time he never stopped going on embassies. For the Great Khan—seeing that my lord Marc brought him such news from all over and acquitted his missions so well—gave all the good, long embassies to my lord Marc. And he fulfilled his tasks very well and was able to relate many novelties and oddities. My lord Marc's conduct pleased the Great Khan so well that he was very favorably disposed toward him; he honored him and kept him so close to him that the other lords were very envious. This was how my lord Marc came to know more about things in that country than any other man: he looked around those foreign parts more than any man ever born, besides putting all his effort into this knowledge.

LESSER JAVA AND THE POLE STAR

CLXVI. Here the island of Lesser Java is described

On leaving the island of Pentain and heading southeast about 100 miles, you find the island of Lesser Java:[4] but know that it is not so small as to be any less than two thousand miles around. We will tell you the whole truth about this island.

Now, know that on this island there are eight kingdoms and eight crowned kings. On this island they are all idolators and have their own languages, for know that each kingdom has a language of its own. This island has the very

---

4. Modern Sumatra (which takes its name from the city-state described in the following chapter).

greatest abundance of treasure, costly spices, aloewood, and spikenard, and many other spices that never make it to our countries. Now I want to tell you about the customs of all these people, one at a time. First I'll tell you something that everyone will take as a marvel. Know in truth that this island is so far south that the North Star does not appear in the slightest. Now we'll return to men's customs and will tell you about the kingdom of Ferlec.

Know that this kingdom of Ferlec converted to Muhammad's law as a result of Saracen[5] merchants who often came there by ship: only the city people; the mountain people are like animals, for I tell you in truth that they eat human flesh and all other flesh—good and bad. They worship many things; for, when they get up in the morning, they worship the first thing they see. Now I've told you about Ferlec; next I'll tell you about the kingdom of Basma.

On leaving the kingdom of Ferlec you enter the kingdom of Basma. This Basma is its own kingdom; the people have their own language but no laws—they are like beasts. They call themselves subjects of the Great Khan but send him no tribute, for they are so far away that the Great Khan's people would not be able to get there. But all those on the island call themselves his subjects and sometimes send him oddities. They have wild elephants and lots of unicorns that are no smaller than elephants: they have hair like buffalo and feet like elephants, with a very thick, black horn in the middle of the forehead. And I tell you it doesn't do harm with its horn but with its tongue. For its tongue has very long spines, such that whatever harm it inflicts, it inflicts with its tongue. Its head is like that of a wild boar; it always carries its head bent down towards the ground and likes to stay in the mud and the muck. It's a very ugly beast to see. They are not as we say and describe here when they say that it lets itself be captured by a virgin. But I tell you it's just the opposite of what we all say it is like. They have a great abundance of swans of many different kinds; they have goshawks, black as crows; they are very large and hawk very well.

And I would tell you and have you know that those who bring little men from India are involved in a great lie and deception; for I tell you that those they call men are made on this island—I'll tell you how. It is true that on this island there's a kind of very small monkey whose faces are like men's: men take such monkeys and remove their hair, leaving the hair of their beards and chests. Then they dry them and shape them and rub them with camphor and other things so that they seem to have been human. This is a great deception, for they are made as you've just heard. For never in India or other, more savage parts have such little men as these seem to be ever been seen.

Now we won't tell you anything more of this kingdom, for there's nothing else there worth mentioning. Therefore we'll leave this and tell you about another kingdom called Sumatra.

CLXVII. Here the kingdom of Sumatra is described

Now, know that, leaving Basma, you find the kingdom of Sumatra, which is on the same island. I, Marc Pol, stayed there for five months, on account of the weather, which didn't allow us to continue on our way. Moreover, I tell you

5. The term generally used in the medieval West to mean "Muslim." "Muhammad's law": Islam.

that the North Star does not appear there; what's more, I tell you the Master constellation[6] doesn't appear at all. They are savage idolaters; their king is rich and powerful, and they call themselves subjects of the Great Khan. And here's how we stayed there five months: we disembarked from our ships and built castles out of wood and logs, then stayed in those castles for fear of those bestial men who eat men. They have the best fish in the world. They don't have any wheat but live on rice. They have no wine, except as I'll describe to you. Know in truth that they have a kind of tree; they cut its branches and put a large pot under the remaining stump; and I tell you that in a day and a night it fills up with wine that is very good to drink. The trees look like small date trees and have four branches; lop it off, and get the wine I've described to you, which is very good. I'll tell you something else as well: when this branch no longer give wine, they water the foot of the trees; and it doesn't take long for the branches to give wine which, I tell you, is white and red. They have a great quantity of Indian nuts, big and good. They eat every sort of flesh, good and bad.

BRAHMANS AND THE BUDDHA

CLXXVII. *Concerning the island of Seilan*

These Brahmans[7] live longer than anyone in the world because of how little they eat and for their great abstinence. They have very good teeth on account of an herb they're in the habit of eating, which is a great aid to digestion and is healthy for the human body. And know that these Brahmans are not bled from their veins nor have blood drawn from anywhere.

Among them there are some, living under a rule,[8] called Ciugui. They live longer than the others, for they live between 150 and 200 years. They are very able physically: they come and go wherever they want and fulfill all the services necessary to their church and their idols, and serve them as well as if they were younger. This is possible because of their great abstinence in eating little and good food, for they are in the habit of eating more rice and milk than anything else. Moreover, I tell you that these Ciugui, who live as long as I've told you, eat something I'll tell you about that will seem like a great thing to you: I tell you that they take quicksilver[9] and sulfur and mix them together into a beverage which they then drink. They say this prolongs their life, and they live quite long. I tell you that they do this twice a month. And know that these people drink this from childhood to live longer. And without fail those that live as long as I've described are accustomed to this sulfur-and-quicksilver drink.

Also in this kingdom of Maabar is a religion, also called Ciugui, involving such great abstinence and such a strong, tough life as I will describe to you. Know, truthfully, that they go around completely naked, wearing no covering, not covering their privates or any members. They worship cattle; and all of them wear a small cow, made of copper or gilded bronze, on their foreheads.

---

6. Ursa Major, or the Big Dipper.
7. Natives of India renowned for their virtuous mode of life in the ancient and medieval West, as described in the fictional letters exchanged between Alexander the Great and

their ruler, Didymus. They are loosely connected with the Brahmin caste.
8. A prescribed guide of conduct, as for a monastic "rule."
9. Mercury.

Understand that they have it tied to them. Moreover, I tell you that they burn cow's dung and make a powder of it, then anoint their bodies with it in several places, as reverentially as Christians do with holy water. They don't eat from bowls or trenchers, but eat their food off apple of paradise[1] or other big leaves—not green but dried. For they say the green ones have souls, and it would be a sin [to use them]. For I tell you that they refrain from harming all the world's creatures, for they believe that would be a sin and they would rather die than commit what they believe to be a sin. And when other men ask them why they go around naked, unashamed at showing their members, they say: "We go naked because we want nothing in this world, for we came into this world naked, without any clothing. The reason we are not ashamed to show our member is this: we do not sin with it, so we are no more ashamed of it than you would be to show your hand or face or other part with which you commit no lustful sin. It's because you've used your member sinfully and lust-fully that you cover it and are ashamed of it; but we are no more ashamed of showing it than we would be to show a finger, for we do not sin with it." This is the explanation they give to men who ask them why they are unashamed to show their member. And I tell you that they kill no creatures or animals in the world—neither flies nor fleas nor lice nor worms—for they say they have souls and that they won't eat them for the sin they would incur. What's more, I tell you they eat nothing green—neither herbs nor roots—until they are dried, for they say anything green has a soul. And I tell you that they sleep on the ground completely naked, with nothing either under them or over them. And it's a great marvel that they don't die and that they live as long as I've described above. And they are very abstemious in their food, for they fast all year and drink nothing other than water.

And I'll tell you something else: they test those that live under a rule (those who live in their churches to serve their idols), as I shall tell you. They bring the maidens who have been offered to the idols and have them touch the men serving the idols. The maidens touch them here and there, all over their bod-ies. They fondle them and give them the world's greatest solace. And as for the man whom the maidens touch in the way I've told you: if his member doesn't move in any way more than before the maidens touched him, he is good and they keep him among them. As for the other whom the maidens touch, if his member moves and stands upright, they don't keep him: they expel him imme-diately and say they don't want a lustful man among them. And I'll tell you how cruel and perfidious their idols are. They say that this is why they burn their dead: they say that, if they didn't burn their dead, they would make worms.

CLXXVIII. The island of Seilan is described again

Seilan[2] is a big island, as I've described to you earlier in this book. Now it's true that on this island there's a very high mountain with cliffs so sheer that no one can climb it, except in this way: many iron chains hang from this mountain, arranged so that men can climb this chain to the top of the mountain. And I tell you that they say that on top of this mountain is the monument of Adam

1. The citron tree.   2. Ceylon (modern Sri Lanka).

our first father. The Saracens say that this tomb is Adam's and the idolators say that it's the monument of Sergamoni Borcam.[3]

This Sergamoni was the first man in whose name idols were first made, for according to their customs he was the best man who ever lived among them. He was the first man they held holy and in whose name they made idols. He was the son of a great, wealthy, and powerful king. And this son of his had such a good life that he didn't want to hear about any worldly things nor did he want to become king. His father, seeing that his son didn't want to become king or hear about anything worldly, got very angry. He offered him very great things: he said he wanted to crown him king of the kingdom and that he could rule as he liked; what's more, he wanted to give up the crown, and would not rule over anything: he [his son] alone would be master. His son said that he didn't want a thing; when his father saw that he wanted nothing to do with earthly power, he got so angry that he almost died of affliction. And no wonder: for this was his only son, and he had no one to whom to leave his kingdom. So this is how the king reacted: he said to himself that he would make it so that his son would willingly return to earthly things and take up the crown and the kingdom. He put him in a very beautiful palace and gave him 30,000 beautiful serving maids, so that there were no men around him but only these maids. Maids put him to bed and served him at table and kept him company all day. They sang and danced before him, and made things as pleasant as possible, just as the king had ordered. And I tell you that all these maids were powerless to move the king's son to the least bit of lust: he remained more steadfast and chaste than before. He led a very good life, according to their customs. And I tell you that he was such a delicate young man that he had never left the palace—had never seen a dead man or anyone not completely healthy. For his father never allowed any elderly or infirm man into his presence. Now it happened that one day this young man was riding out on the road; then he saw a dead man. As someone who had never seen such a thing, he was completely stunned; he asked those accompanying him what it was, and they told him it was a dead man. "What?" said the king's son, "Then do all men die?" "Yes, truly," they replied. The young man didn't say a thing and rode on, lost in thought. After that, he hadn't ridden very far when he came across a very old man who couldn't move and had no teeth in his mouth, having lost them all on account of his great age. When the king's son saw this old man, he asked what this thing was and why he couldn't move. And those accompanying him said that old age kept him from moving and old age had made him lose his teeth. When the king's son had heard of the dead man and the old man, he returned to the palace, saying to himself that he would not remain in this bad world but would go seeking the one who had made it and did not die. Then he left the palace and his father; he went to some great, faraway mountains. And there he remained his whole life, simply and chastely, practicing great abstinence. And certainly, had he been Christian, he would have been a great saint with our lord Jesus Christ.

And when this king's son died, he was carried to his father the king. When he saw that the one he loved more than himself was dead, you needn't ask if he was

---

3. "Sergamoni" is probably a mistranscription of "Sakyamuni," one of the honorific names applied to Siddhartha Gautama (d. ca. 483 B.C.E.?), founder of Buddhism; "Borcam" may be a mistranscription of "Buddha."

vexed and distressed: he mourned greatly, and had a likeness made of pure gold and precious stones, and had all his subjects honor and worship him as a god. And they said he had died 84 times. For they said that when he first died, he became a cow; then he died again and became a horse; and thus they said he had died 84 times, each time becoming an animal—a dog or something else. But the 84th time he died, he became a god. And they hold idols to be the best and most powerful gods they have. And know that this was the idolaters' first idol; all the idols are descended from him. This was on the island of Seilan in India.

Now you have heard how about the earliest idol. And I tell you truly that idolaters come on pilgrimage from very distant parts, just as Christians go on pilgrimage to Saint James.[4] And the idolaters say that this monument, on this mountain, belongs to the king's son you've heard about, and that the teeth, hair, and bowl there also belonged to the king's son, whose name was Sergamoni Borcam, meaning "Saint Sergamoni." And the Saracens, who also come on pilgrimage here in great numbers, say that this is the monument of Adam our first father and that the teeth, hair, and bowl were also Adam's. Now you've heard how the idolaters say that this is the king's son who was their first idol and their first god, and how the Saracens say that it's Adam, our first father. But God knows who he is and who he was, for we do not believe that Adam is here in this place, because the Scripture of the Holy Church says that he's in another part of the world.

Now it happened that the Great Khan heard that Adam's monument was atop this mountain, along with his teeth, his hair, and the bowl he had eaten from; and he said to himself it was fitting that he should have these teeth and bowl and hair. So he sent a great embassy there: this was in the year 1284 of the Incarnation of Christ. What should I say of it? Know truly that the Great Khan's messengers set out on the road with a great entourage and traveled so far by land and by sea that they came to the island of Seilan. They went to the king and importuned him so much that they got the two molars, which were fat and large; and they also got the hairs and the bowl. The bowl was of very beautiful green porphyry. And when the Great Khan's messengers got these things I've told you about, they got on the road and returned to their lord. As they approached the great city of Ganbalu,[5] where the Great Khan was staying, they sent word that they were coming and that they were bringing what he had sent them to get. The Great Khan then ordered that everyone—the monks and others—should go to meet these relics that were understood to be Adam's. Why should I prolong my account? Know that, in truth, all the people of Ganbalu went to meet these relics; and the monks received it and brought it to the Great Khan, who received them with great joy, celebration, and reverence. And I tell you that they found in their writings that this bowl had such properties that if you filled it with food enough for one man, there would be enough for five; and the Great Khan said that he had tested it, and that it was true.

In such a way as you have heard, the Great Khan got the relics that you've heard about. And it cost him quite a great amount of treasure to acquire them.

Now we've told the whole truth of this whole story in order. From here we'll leave it and will tell you about other things. We'll tell you right away about the city of Cail.

4. St. James of Compostella (in Spain), perhaps the most important pilgrimage site in medieval Europe.

5. Also spelled *Khanbaliq* (literally, "great residence of the Khan"); modern Beijing.

IBN BATTUTA

Muhammad ibn Abdullah ibn Battuta (1304–1368/69) was born in Tangier, in what is now Morocco, to a Muslim Berber family. Well-educated and upper-class, Ibn Battuta was a member of a transnational urban elite that was relatively free to move about the Islamic world. His travels began in 1325, when he undertook the prescribed religious pilgrimage (or *hajj*) to Mecca and Medina; later, he would voyage to Africa's eastern coast, central Asia, and India. After a stay in Delhi, Ibn Battuta was sent by his patron on a diplomatic mission to the emperor of China. Upon his return to Morocco, Ibn Battuta's royal patron was amazed by the traveler's engrossing account of his experiences and commanded the court secretary, Muhammad ibn Juzayy, to write it down. Like the romancer Rustichello, who embroidered the practical report of the merchant **Marco Polo**, Ibn Juzayy embellished the account he was given. Specifically, he used Ibn Battuta's personal experiences as a foundation or framework to which he attached fragments of other, earlier travel narratives (such as that of Ibn Jubayr). Ibn Battuta's tale bears witness to the momentous events of his age: the increasing political chaos in India and Persia following the end of Mongol rule in 1336, the succession disputes that plagued Egypt after 1341, and the terrifying advent of the Black Death in 1348.

The geographical range of the excerpts from Ibn Battuta's account presented here stretches from areas of the Middle East under Islamic rule to the distant reaches of East Asia. His descriptions of the regions surrounding Jerusalem, in-cluding the Cave of the Patriarchs at Hebron, the site of Jesus' birth at Bethlehem, and "Lot's Lake" (the Dead Sea), are remarkable for the picture they summon up of an environment in which sites holy to Jews, Christians, and Muslims sit side by side, and where worshippers coexist in harmony. Ibn Battuta's account of the combined Jewish, Christian, and Muslim procession to the local shrine dedicated to Moses that took place in Damascus at the time of the Black Death is particularly striking, illustrating how a catastrophic event can bring a community together to worship, even across faiths. Nonetheless, he views Jerusalem not primarily in connection with Jewish history or with the lifetime of Jesus, but rather as the place where the Prophet Muhammad ascended into the heavens in his heavenly night journey, or *mi'raj*, leaving his footprint in the stone at the Dome of the Rock. Ibn Battuta also describes the imperial city of Constantinople (modern Istanbul), then still under Christian rule. He gives an overview of the geography of the city, the distribution of its different populations, and its most awe-inspiring monument: the cathedral of Hagia Sophia, "one of the greatest churches of the Greeks." Ibn Battuta is obliged to explain to his Muslim readers what a "monastery" is, because the life of renunciation undertaken by Christian monks and nuns would seem bizarre and unnatural to them. For these readers, Ibn Battuta's firsthand account of Christian life in Constantinople would have offered some of the most exotic ethnography of the entire work. Finally, Ibn Battuta recounts the marvels of Ceylon (Sri Lanka): priceless rubies, the

Lake of Monkeys, the repulsive "flying leech," and the mountaintop shrine where one can see the rock containing the footprint of Adam, father of human-kind. Marco Polo describes the same site, in an excerpt also reproduced in this cluster: but where Ibn Battuta sees a location holy to Abrahamic tradition, Marco finds only sordid evidence of the pagan origins of idolatry.

From Travels[1]

* * *

From Gaza I travelled to the city of Abraham [Hebron], the mosque of which is of elegant, but substantial, construction, imposing and lofty, and built of squared stones. At one angle of it there is a stone, one of whose faces measures twenty-seven spans. It is said that Solomon commanded the *jinn*[2] to build it. Inside it is the sacred cave containing the graves of Abraham, Isaac, and Jacob,[3] opposite which are three graves, which are those of their wives. I questioned the imám, a man of great piety and learning, on the authenticity of these graves, and he replied: "All the scholars whom I have met hold these graves to be the very graves of Abraham, Isaac, Jacob and their wives. No one questions this except introducers of false doctrines; it is a tradition which has passed from father to son for generations and admits of no doubt." This mosque contains also the grave of Joseph, and somewhat to the east of it lies the tomb of Lot,[4] which is surmounted by an elegant building. In the neighbourhood is Lot's lake [the Dead Sea], which is brackish and is said to cover the site of the settlements of Lot's people. On the way from Hebron to Jerusalem, I visited Bethlehem, the birthplace of Jesus. The site is covered by a large building; the Christians regard it with intense veneration and hospitably entertain all who alight at it.

We then reached Jerusalem (may God ennoble her!), third in excellence after the two holy shrines of Mecca and Madína,[5] and the place whence the Prophet was caught up into heaven.[6] Its walls were destroyed by the illustrious King Saladin[7] and his successors, for fear lest the Christians should seize it and fortify themselves in it. The sacred mosque is a most beautiful building, and is said to be the largest mosque in the world. Its length from east to west is put at 752 "royal" cubits[8] and its breadth at 435. On three sides it has many entrances,

---

1. Translated from the Arabic by H. A. R. Gibb.
2. See Qur'an 21.81–82, 34.12–13. "Jinn": in Islam, supernatural beings that, like angels and humans, are created by Allah.
3. Three Hebrew patriarchs, also revered by Muslims and Christians; Jacob was the son of Isaac, who was the son of Abraham.
4. Abraham's nephew; he escaped God's complete destruction of Gomorrah and Sodom, where he lived (see Genesis 19.1–29).
5. Islam's holiest sites: Mecca contains the Ka'aba, the building that Muslims face when they pray and that is the central point of the pilgrimage prescribed as a religious duty; Med-

ina, about 210 miles northwest, is where Muhammad and his followers fled to escape enemies in Mecca.
6. The *mi'raj*; this miraculous ascent of the Prophet Muhammad through the seven heavens is recounted in a number of Arabic and Persian texts, including Avicenna's *Mi'raj-nameh*.
7. Salah al-Din Yusuf ibn Ayyub (ca. 1138–1193), Sultan of Egypt and Syria. He successfully led Muslim campaigns against the Christians in Palestine, and his capture of Jerusalem in 1187 led to the Third Crusade.
8. About 1,630 by 940 feet.

but on the south side I know of one only, which is that by which the imám enters. The entire mosque is an open court and unroofed, except the mosque al-Aqsá, which has a roof of most excellent workmanship, embellished with gold and brilliant colours. Some other parts of the mosque are roofed as well. The Dome of the Rock is a building of extraordinary beauty, solidity, elegance, and singularity of shape. It stands on an elevation in the centre of the mosque and is reached by a flight of marble steps. It has four doors. The space round it is also paved with marble, excellently done, and the interior likewise. Both outside and inside the decoration is so magnificent and the workmanship so surpassing as to defy description. The greater part is covered with gold so that the eyes of one who gazes on its beauties are dazzled by its brilliance, now glowing like a mass of light, now flashing like lightning. In the centre of the Dome is the blessed rock from which the Prophet ascended to heaven, a great rock projecting about a man's height, and underneath it there is a cave the size of a small room, also of a man's height, with steps leading down to it. Encircling the rock are two railings of excellent workmanship, the one nearer the rock being artistically constructed in iron, and the other of wood.

Among the grace-bestowing sanctuaries of Jerusalem is a building, situated on the farther side of the valley called the valley of Jahannam [Gehenna] to the east of the town, on a high hill. This building is said to mark the place whence Jesus ascended to heaven. In the bottom of the same valley is a church venerated by the Christians, who say that it contains the grave of Mary. In the same place there is another church which the Christians venerate and to which they come on pilgrimage. This is the church of which they are falsely persuaded to believe that it contains the grave of Jesus. All who come on pilgrimage to visit it pay a stipulated tax to the Muslims, and suffer very unwillingly various humiliations. Thereabouts also is the place of the cradle of Jesus,[9] which is visited in order to obtain blessing.

I journeyed thereafter from Jerusalem to the fortress of Askalon,[1] which is a total ruin. Of the great mosque, known as the mosque of 'Omar, nothing remains but its walls and some marble columns of matchless beauty, partly standing and partly fallen. Amongst them is a wonderful red column, of which the people tell that the Christians carried it off to their country but afterwards lost it, when it was found in its place at Askalon. Thence I went on to the city of ar-Ramlah, which is also called Filastín [Palestine], in the *qibla* of those mosque they say three hundred of the prophets are buried. From ar-Ramlah I went to the town of Nábulus [Shechem],[2] a city with an abundance of trees and perennial streams, and one of the richest in Syria for olives, the oil of which is exported thence to Cairo and Damascus. It is at Nábulus that the carob-sweet is manufactured and exported to Damascus and elsewhere. It is made in this way: the carobs are cooked and then pressed, the juice that runs out is gathered and the sweet is manufactured from it. The juice itself too is exported to Cairo and Damascus. Nábulus has also a species of melon which is called by its name, a good and delicious fruit. Thence I went to Ajalún mak-

9. In the Church of the Nativity, located in Bethlehem (about 5 miles southwest of Jerusalem).
1. Former Crusader stronghold, demolished by the Muslims in 1270 (modern Ashkelon is a port city in Israel, just north of the Gaza Strip).
2. Modern Ramallah and Nablus, in the Palestinian West Bank.

ing in the direction of Ládhiqíya, and passing through the Ghawr,[3] followed the coast to 'Akká [Acre], which is in ruins. Acre[4] was formerly the capital and port of the country of the Franks in Syria, and rivalled Constantinople itself.

* * *

One of the celebrated sanctuaries at Damascus is the Mosque of the Footprints (al-Aqdám), which lies two miles south of the city, alongside the main highway which leads to the Hijáz, Jerusalem, and Egypt. It is a large mosque, very blessed, richly endowed, and very highly venerated by the Damascenes. The footprints from which it derives its name are certain footprints impressed upon a rock there, which are said to be the mark of Moses' foot. In this mosque there is a small chamber containing a stone with the following inscription "A certain pious man saw in his sleep the Chosen One [Muhammad], who said to him 'Here is the grave of my brother Moses.' " I saw a remarkable instance of the veneration in which the Damascenes hold this mosque during the great pestilence,[5] on my return journey through Damascus in the latter part of July 1348. The viceroy Arghún Sháh ordered a crier to proclaim through Damascus that all the people should fast for three days[6] and that no one should cook anything eatable in the market during the daytime. For most of the people there eat no food but what has been prepared in the market. So the people fasted for three successive days, the last of which was a Thursday, then they assembled in the Great Mosque, amírs, sharífs, qádís,[7] theologians, and all the other classes of the people, until the place was filled to overflowing, and there they spent the Thursday night in prayers and litanies. After the dawn prayer next morning they all went out together on foot, holding Korans in their hands, and the amírs barefooted. The procession was joined by the entire population of the town, men and women, small and large; the Jews came with their Book of the Law[8] and the Christians with their Gospel, all of them with their women and children. The whole concourse, weeping and supplicating and seeking the favour of God through His Books and His Prophets, made their way to the Mosque of the Footprints, and there they remained in supplication and invocation until near midday. They then returned to the city and held the Friday service, and God lightened their affliction; for the number of deaths in a single day at Damascus did not attain two thousand, while in Cairo and Old Cairo it reached the figure of twenty-four thousand a day.

* * *

The city[9] is enormous in size, and in two parts separated by a great river [the Golden Horn], in which there is a rising and ebbing tide. In former times there was a stone bridge over it, but it fell into ruins and the crossing is now made in boats. The part of the city on the eastern bank of the river is called Istambúl,

---

3. The Jordan Valley.
4. Site of the last Crusader stronghold in the region, which fell in 1291.
5. The outbreak of bubonic plague that began in Asia and by 1350 had killed more than a third of the population of Europe.
6. I.e., take no food or drink during daylight.

7. I.e., emirs (rulers), nobles, and judges.
8. The Torah (the first five books of the Bible).
9. Constantinople, modern Istanbul; Ibn Battuta later refers to its imperial quarter as "Istambul" (lit., "to the city"). The capital of the Byzantine Empire, the city came under Ottoman Muslim rule in 1453.

and contains the residence of the Emperor, the nobles and the rest of the population. Its bazaars and streets are spacious and paved with flagstones; each bazaar has gates which are closed upon it at night, and the majority of the artisans and sellers in them are women. The city lies at the foot of a hill which projects about nine miles into the sea, its breadth being the same or greater. On the top of the hill there is a small citadel and the Emperor's palace. Round this hill runs the city-wall, which is very strong and cannot be taken by assault from the sea front. Within its circuit there are about thirteen inhabited villages. The principal church is in the midst of this part of the city. The second part, on the western bank of the river, is called Galata, and is reserved to the Frankish Christians who dwell there. They are of different kinds, including Genoese, Venetians, Romans and people of France; they are subject to the authority of the king of Constantinople, who sets over them one of their own number of whom they approve, and him they call the *Comes*.[1] They are bound to pay a tax every year to the king of Constantinople, but often they revolt against him and he makes war on them until the Pope makes peace between them. They are all men of commerce and their harbour is one of the largest in the world; I saw there about a hundred galleys and other large ships, and the small ships were too many to be counted. The bazaars in this part of the town are good but filthy, and a small and very dirty river runs through them. Their churches too are filthy and mean.

Of the great church I can only describe the exterior, for I did not see its interior. It is called by them Ayá Súfiyá [St. Sophia],[2] and the story goes that it was built by Asaph, the son of Berechiah, who was Solomon's cousin. It is one of the greatest churches of the Greeks, and is encircled by a wall so that it looks as if it were a town. It has thirteen gates and a sacred enclosure, which is about a mile long and closed by a great gate. No one is prevented from entering this enclosure, and indeed I went into it with the king's father; it resembles an audience-hall paved with marble, and is traversed by a stream which issues from the church. Outside the gate of this hall are platforms and shops, mostly of wood, where their judges and the recorders of their bureaux sit. At the gate of the church there are porticoes where the keepers sit who sweep its paths, light its lamps and close its gates. They allow none to enter it until he prostrates himself to the huge cross there, which they claim to be a relic of the wood upon which the pseudo-Jesus was crucified.[3] This is over the gate of the church, set in a golden case whose height is about ten cubits, across which a similar golden case is placed to form a cross. This gate is covered with plaques of silver and gold and its two rings are of pure gold. I was told that the number of monks and priests in this church runs into thousands, and that some of them are descendants of the apostles, and that inside it is another church exclusively for women, containing more than a thousand virgins and a still greater number of aged women who devote themselves to religious practices. It is the custom of the king, the nobles and the rest of the people to come every morning to visit

1. Companion (Latin); here, an attendant of the ruler.
2. Modern Hagia Sophia ("Holy Wisdom"; Greek); established as a Christian church in 360, it was converted to a mosque after the Ottoman conquest and is now a public museum.

3. A reference to the Muslim belief that Jesus, although miraculously born without a human father to the Virgin Mary and a prophet of God, was not crucified; instead, they believe, a substitute took his place before the execution.

this church. The Pope comes to visit it once a year. When he is four days' journey from the town the king goes out to meet him, and dismounts before him and when he enters the city walks on foot in front of him. During his stay in Constantinople the king comes to salute[4] him every morning and evening.

A monastery is the Christian equivalent of a religious house or convent among the Muslims, and there are a great many such monasteries at Constantinople. Among them is the monastery which King George built outside Istambúl and opposite Galata, and two monasteries outside the principal church, to the right as one enters it. These two monasteries are inside a garden traversed by a stream of water; one of them is for men and the other for women. In each there is a church and they are surrounded by the cells of men and women who have devoted themselves to religious exercises. Each monastery possesses pious endowments for the clothing and maintenance of the devotees. Inside every monastery there is a small convent designed for the ascetic retreat of the king who built it, for most of these kings, on reaching the age of sixty or seventy, build a monastery and put on garments of hair,[5] investing their sons with the sovereignty and occupying themselves with religious exercises for the rest of their lives. They display great magnificence in building these monasteries, and construct them of marble and mosaic-work. I entered a monastery with the Greek whom the king had given me as a guide. Inside it was a church containing about five hundred virgins wearing hair-garments; their heads were shaved and covered with felt bonnets. They were exceedingly beautiful and showed the traces of their austerities. A youth sitting on a pulpit was reading the gospel to them in the most beautiful voice I have ever heard; round him were eight other youths on pulpits with their priest, and when the first youth had finished reading another began. The Greek said to me "These girls are kings' daughters who have given themselves to the service of this church, and likewise the boys who are reading [are kings' sons]." I entered with him also into churches in which there were the daughters of ministers, governors, and the principal men of the city, and others where there were aged women and widows, and others where there were monks, each church containing a hundred men or so. Most of the population of the city are monks, ascetics, and priests, and its churches are not to be counted for multitude. The inhabitants of the city, soldiers and civilians, small and great, carry over their heads huge parasols, both in winter and summer, and the women wear large turbans.

I was out one day with my Greek guide, when we met the former king George who had become a monk. He was walking on foot, wearing haircloth garments and a bonnet of felt, and he had a long white beard and a fine face, which bore traces of his austerities. Behind and before him was a body of monks, and he had a staff in his hand and a rosary on his neck. When the Greek saw him he dismounted and said to me "Dismount, for this is the king's father." When my guide saluted him the king asked him about me, then stopped and sent for me. He took my hand and said to the Greek (who knew the Arabic tongue) "Say to this Saracen (meaning Muslim) 'I clasp the hand which has entered Jerusalem and the foot which has walked within the Dome of the Rock and the great church of the Holy Sepulchre and Bethlehem,' " and he laid his hand upon my

4. Greet.
5. I.e., rough animal hair worn against the skin as penance.

feet and passed it over his face. I was astonished at their good opinion of one who, though not of their religion, had entered these places. Then he took my hand and as I walked with him asked me about Jerusalem and the Christians who were there, and questioned me at length. I entered with him the sacred enclosure of the church which we have described above. When he approached the principal gate, a party of priests and monks came out to salute him, for he is one of their chief men in monasticism, and on seeing them he let go my hand. I said to him "I should like to enter the church with you." Then he said to the interpreter, "Say to him 'He who enters it must needs prostrate himself before the great cross, for this is a rule which the ancients laid down and which cannot be contravened.'" So I left him and he entered alone and I did not see him again. After leaving the king I entered the bazaar of the scribes, where I was noticed by the judge, who sent one of his assistants to ask the Greek about me. On learning that I was a Muslim scholar he sent for me and I went up to him. He was an old man with a fine face and hair, wearing the black garments of a monk, and had about ten scribes in front of him writing. He rose to meet me, his companions rising also, and said "You are the king's guest and we are bound to honour you." He then asked me about Jerusalem, Syria, and Egypt, and spoke with me for a long time. A great crowd gathered round him, and he said "You must come to my house that I may entertain you." After that I went away, but I did not see him again.

* * *

In the island of Ceylon[6] rubies are found in all parts. The land is private property, and a man buys a parcel of it and digs for rubies. Some of them are red, some yellow [topazes], and some blue [sapphires]. Their custom is that all rubies of the value of a hundred *fanams* belong to the sultan, who pays their price and takes them; those of less value belong to the finders. A hundred *fanams* equal in value six gold dinars.[7]

We went on from Kunakár and halted at a cave called after Ustá Mahmúd the Lúrí, a pious man who dug out this cave at the foot of a hill beside a small lake. Thence we travelled to the Lake of Monkeys. There are in these mountains vast numbers of monkeys. They are black and have long tails, and their males are bearded like men. Shaykh 'Othmán and his sons and others as well told me that these monkeys have a chief, whom they obey as if he were a king. He fastens on his head a fillet of leaves and leans upon a staff. On his right and his left are four monkeys carrying staves in their hands. When the chief monkey sits down the four monkeys stand behind him, and his female and young come and sit in front of him every day. The other monkeys come and sit at a distance from him, then one of the four monkeys addresses them and all the monkeys withdraw. After this each one brings a banana or a lemon or some such fruit, and the monkey chief with his young and the four monkeys eat. One of the Yogis told me that he had seen the four monkeys in the presence of their chief beating a monkey with sticks and after the beating pulling out its

---

6. Modern Sri Lanka.
7. The dinar, used in the Muslim world, was about 4 grams of gold.

hair. We continued our journey to a place called "The Old Woman's Hut," which is the end of the inhabited part, and marched thence by a number of grottoes. In this place we saw the flying leech, which sits on trees and in the vegetation near water. When a man approaches it jumps out at him, and wheresoever it alights on his body the blood flows freely. The inhabitants keep a lemon in readiness for it; they squeeze this over it and it falls off them, then they scrape the place on which it alighted with a wooden knife which they have for the purpose.

The mountain of Sarandíb [Adam's Peak] is one of the highest in the world.[8] We saw it from the sea when we were nine days' journey away, and when we climbed it we saw the clouds below us, shutting out our view of its base. On it there are many evergreen trees and flowers of various colours, including a red rose as big as the palm of a hand. There are two tracks on the mountain leading to the Foot, one called Bábá track and the other Mámá track, meaning Adam and Eve. The Mámá track is easy and is the route by which the pilgrims return, but anyone who goes by that way is not considered by them to have made the pilgrimage at all. The Bábá track is difficult and stiff climbing. Former generations cut a sort of stairway on the mountain, and fixed iron stanchions on it, to which they attached chains for climbers to hold on by. There are ten such chains, two at the foot of the hill by the "threshold," seven successive chains farther on, and the tenth is the "Chain of the Profession of Faith," so called because when one reaches it and looks down to the foot of the hill, he is seized by apprehensions and recites the profession of faith for fear of falling. When you climb past this chain you find a rough track. From the tenth chain to the grotto of Khidr[9] is seven miles; this grotto lies in a wide plateau, and near by it is a spring full of fish, but no one catches them. Close to this there are two tanks cut in the rock on either side of the path. At the grotto of Khidr the pilgrims leave their belongings and ascend thence for two miles to the summit of the mountain where the Foot is.

The blessed Footprint, the Foot of our father Adam, is on a lofty black rock in a wide plateau. The blessed Foot sank into the rock far enough to leave its impression hollowed out. It is eleven spans long. In ancient days the Chinese came here and cut out of the rock the mark of the great toe and the adjoining parts. They put this in a temple at Zaytún,[1] where it is visited by men from the farthest parts of the land. In the rock where the Foot is there are nine holes cut out, in which the infidel pilgrims place offerings of gold, precious stones, and jewels. You can see the darwíshes,[2] after they reach the grotto of Khidr, racing one another to take what there is in these holes. We, for our part, found nothing in them but a few stones and a little gold, which we gave to the guide. It is customary for the pilgrims to stay at the grotto of Khidr for three days, visiting the Foot every morning and evening, and we followed this practice. When the three days were over we returned by the Mámá track, halting at a number of villages on the mountain. At the foot of the mountain there is an ancient tree whose leaves never fall, situated in a place that cannot be got at. I have never

---

8. In fact, the mountain is about 7,300 feet high.

9. An enigmatic figure, attested in the Qur'an (18.65) and venerated as a prophet in Islam.

1. In southeast China (modern Quanzhou), a great port in the Middle Ages.

2. I.e., dervishes, or ascetic Sufis (followers of a mystic form of Islam).

met anyone who has seen its leaves. I saw there a number of Yogis who never quit the base of the mountain waiting for its leaves to fall. They tell lying tales about it, one being that whosoever eats of it regains his youth, even if he be an old man, but that is false. Beneath the mountain is the great lake from which the rubies are taken; its water is a bright blue to the sight.

THE BOOK OF JOHN MANDEVILLE

The Book of John Mandeville (ca. 1360), today sometimes titled *Mandeville's Travels*, is almost exactly contemporary with but also quite different from Ibn Battuta's account: one is written by a Christian native of northern Europe, the other by a Muslim native of the Mediterranean coast of Africa; one is largely compiled from earlier books about the Orient, the other based primarily on personal experience of travel and cultural encounter. Yet the two have much in common—especially their evocation of the multicultural, multifaith environment of the major cities of the East. The author emphasizes the first-person quality of his work, beginning it with what can only be described as a claim of witness: "I, John Mandeville, knight, born and brought up in England in the town of St. Albans, have seen and gone around many lands, of which I will speak more fully." Ironically, this claim is not true, or at least not entirely true. There is no corroborating evidence of a John Mandeville of St. Albans; the text was written not in English but in French; and the work was most likely composed not in England but on the Continent. It was, however, written in a dialect of French (Anglo-Norman) that was spoken in the British Isles, and so the claim of authorship by an Englishman—especially in view of the text's rampant nationalism—is entirely plausible. The

claim of actual experience of the regions described is at least partially false: though the author may have visited some of these lands, including Constantinople and the regions around Jerusalem, the account of territories lying farther eastward is clearly adapted from earlier written sources. But the importance of *The Book of John Mandeville* lies not in the veracity of its ethnographic description, as in **Marco Polo**'s and **Ibn Battuta**'s works, but rather in its extraordinary popularity: more widely read than any other travel narrative of the period, "Mandeville's" book was translated, adapted, reprinted, and retold innumerable times.

Despite questions about its own authenticity, *The Book of John Mandeville* displays a strong interest in the practice of exploration, as can be seen in the account of navigation by the stars excerpted here. This chapter epitomizes the work's striking juxtaposition of information useful to the explorer and bizarre details designed to titillate the armchair traveler: we hear about the spherical shape of the world and the geography of eastern regions, on the one hand, and the practice of cannibalism on the other, as children are fattened up expressly to produce "the best and sweetest meat in the world." *The Book of John Mandeville* concludes with an account of the Great Khan, ruler of China—the same ruler sought by Ibn

Battuta on his mission to Beijing, and a descendant of Kublai Khan, who was served so loyally by Marco Polo. The *Book*'s last lines return to the opening claim of eyewitness testimony, as "John Mandeville" reassures us, once again, of the utter reliability of his half-truthful story of wonders. The influence of *The Book of John Mandeville* would con-tinue to be felt for hundreds of years, across a wide range of genres, from the spiritual pilgrimage of Bunyan's *Pilgrim's Progress* (which alludes to Mandeville's "Valley Perilous") to the compilation of travels found in Hakluyt's *Principal Navigations*, and extending even as far as the fantastical "Xanadu" of Samuel Taylor Coleridge.

From The Book of John Mandeville[1]

XX. About the evil customs used in the Isle of Lamory, and how the Earth and the Sea are of round form by proof of the Antarctic Star

From this country one goes by the Ocean Sea and many diverse islands and many countries that would be too long to name and describe; and fifty-two days' journey from this land that I have spoken about, there is another land that is quite large and has the name Lamory.[2]

In this land there is a very great heat, and the custom is such that the men and the women all go naked. They jeer when they see any foreigner who is clothed, and they say that God who made Adam was naked—and [that] both Adam and Eve were made naked—and that people should not be ashamed to show themselves as God has made them, for nothing is ugly that comes from nature. And they say that those who are clothed are people of another era, or they are people who do not believe in God; and indeed they say that they believe in God who created the world and made Adam and Eve and all other things.

Since they have no married women, all the women of the country are thus common and refuse no man; and they say that they sin if they refuse men and that God commanded it of Adam and his descendents where he said: "*Crescite et multiplicamini et replete terram.*"[3] Therefore no man in all this country can say: "this is my wife." Nor can any woman say: "this is my husband." And when the women have children, they give them to those they like who have had sex-ual relations with them. The land is also common, for some hold it in one year and others in another, and each takes whatever part he wants; and also all the goods of the country are common, wheat and other things, for nothing is enclosed, nothing is locked up at all; each takes what he likes without restric-tion and one person is as rich as another. But they have an evil custom, for they more willingly eat human flesh than any other flesh. And the country abounds in wheat, meat, fish, gold, silver, and other goods. The merchants go there and take children with them for sale to the inhabitants, and the latter

1. Translated from the French by Iain Macleod Higgins.
2. Sumatra. The land just discussed is Coro-mandel, on the southeast coast of India.
3. "Increase and multiply and fill the Earth" (Genesis 1.28; Vulgate). Passages in Latin in Mandeville's text remained in that language in the many medieval vernacular translations, as here.

buy them; and if they are fat, they eat them right away, and if they are lean, they fatten them, and they say that this is the best and sweetest meat in the world.

In this land and in many others over there the Tramontane star[4] cannot be seen at all. It is the star of the sea that does not move which is towards the north. But one can see another star opposite it, towards the south, which is called Antarctic.[5] And just as sailors here take their bearings and steer themselves by that star to the north, so the sailors over there use this star to the south, which is never visible to us, and the one to the north is not visible to them.

Through this we can perceive that the earth and the sea are of round form, for the part of the firmament that appears in one country does not appear in another. And it can be easily discovered by experience and by clever research that, if a man found passage by ship and people who wanted to go explore the world, he could sail all around the world, both above and below. This thing I prove according to what I have seen, for I have been towards the regions of Brabant and seen with the astrolabe[6] that the Tramontane is 53 degrees high. And further forward in Germany and Bohemia it is 58 degrees, and further forward towards the northern regions it is 62 degrees and several minutes high, for I myself have measured it with the astrolabe.

Now you ought to know that opposite this Tramontane is the other star that is called Antarctic, as I have said above. And these two stars are not very mobile, and the whole firmament turns on them as a wheel turns on its axle, such that these stars divide the firmament into two equal parts so that there is as much below as above.

Afterwards, I went towards the meridional regions—that is, towards the south—and found that the Antarctic star is first seen in Libya, and the farther forward I went in those parts the higher I found this star, such that towards upper Libya it was 18 degrees and several minutes high (60 minutes make one degree). Then in going by sea and by land towards those regions that I have spoken about and to other islands and lands beyond this country, I found the Antarctic star 33 degrees and several minutes high.

If I had found company and ship to go further, I believe it to be certain that we would have seen the whole roundness of the firmament all around. For, as I told you above, half of the firmament is between these two stars. I have seen all of this half; and of the other half to the north under the Tramontane, I have seen 62 degrees and 10 minutes, and towards the meridional [southern] parts under the Antarctic I have seen 33 degrees and 16 minutes. Now half of the firmament in total has only 180 degrees, and of these 180 I have seen 62 of one part and 33 of the other, which is 95 degrees and almost half a degree. Thus I have not seen only 94 degrees and half a degree of the whole firmament; and that is not one quarter of the firmament, for a quarter of the roundness of the firmament is 90 degrees, and lacks 5 and a half degrees of the

4. The North Star.
5. Although no star in the Southern Hemisphere corresponds to the North Star in marking the celestial pole, navigators could steer by the Southern Cross.
6. An astronomical device, used for naviga-

tion, that was introduced to Europe from Islamic Spain; it quickly came into widespread use. "Brabant": a duchy in what is now the southern Netherlands and central and northern Belgium.

quarter. So I have seen three quarters of all the roundness of the firmament and 5 and a half degrees more. For this reason I say for certain that a man could travel around all the land in the world, both below and above, and return to his own country, if he had company and shipping and always found men, lands, and islands just as in this country.

For you know that those who are in the place of the Antarctic are exactly foot against foot[7] with those who live beneath the Tramontane, just as we and those who live under us are foot against foot: for all the parts of sea and land have their habitable and navigable opposites, and islands here as well as there. Know that according to what I can perceive and understand, the lands of Prester John,[8] Emperor of India, are under us. For in going from Scotland or England towards Jerusalem one is always climbing; for our land is in the low part of the earth to the west, and Prester John's land is the low part of the earth to the east, and they have day there when we have night, and just the opposite: they have night when we have day. For the earth and the sea are of round form, as I told you above, and as one climbs on one side one descends on the other.

Now you have heard said before that Jerusalem is in the middle of the world, and this can be shown over there by a spear fixed in the ground at the hour of noon at the equinox that casts no shadow on any side. That it is in the middle of the world David testifies in the Psalter, where he says "*Deus operatus est salutem in medio terre.*"[9] Thus those who leave from these parts of the west to go towards Jerusalem take as many days of climbing to go all the way there as they would take from Jerusalem to the other ends of the earth's surface over there. And when one takes more days towards India and the farther islands, one is going around all the roundness of the land and the sea under our countries over here.

For this reason I have often recalled a thing I heard told when I was young: how a brave man once left from our regions to go explore the world. He passed India and the islands beyond India, where there are more than 5000 islands, and he went so far by sea and by land, and he went round so much of the world through many seasons that he found an island where he heard his own language spoken and the oxen called with the same words as in his own country. This amazed him very much. For he did not know how it could be. But I say that he had gone so far by land and by sea that he had gone around the whole earth, that he came back having gone right round to his own borderlands— and if he had gone forward he would have found his own country and his own knowledge. But he went back by the way he had come and lost much effort, as he himself said a great while after he had returned. For it happened afterwards that he was in Norway, and a storm on the sea caught him and he came to an island, and when he was on that island he recognized it as the island where he had heard his own language spoken in guiding the oxen pulling the plough.

---

7. I.e., at the Antipodes (literally, "having opposite feet"; Greek).
8. According to a legend invented in the 12th century, an Oriental (usually Indian) Christian ruler eager to join with the Christian nations of Europe to drive the Muslim forces out of the Holy Land. Voyagers looked for the Land of Prester John in Asia and elsewhere— especially Ethiopia, which had long been recognized as a Christian kingdom.
9. "God worked salvation in the middle of the Earth" (Psalm 74.12, slightly misquoted).

That was indeed a possible thing, although it seems to simple people that no one could go beneath the earth and that one must fall into the sky below. But this cannot be, any more than we could fall into the sky from the land where we are. For in whatever part of the earth one dwells, either above or below, it always seems to those living there that they walk more upright than any other people; and just as it seems to us that they are under us, so it seems to them that we are under them. For if one could fall from the earth to the firmament, [there is] all the more reason [to believe that] the earth and the sea—that are so large and so heavy—ought to fall right to the firmament. But that could not be, and this is why Our Lord says "*Non timeas me qui suspendi terram ex nichilo.*"[1]

Although this is a possible thing that one could thus go around the whole world, nevertheless not one person in a thousand would travel the right way so as to return to his own country. For because of the large size of the earth and the sea, one could go by thousands of other ways, such that no one could return exactly to the regions from which he left, except by chance or God's true grace.

For the earth is very broad and very big, and is 20,425 miles in roundness and all around,[2] above and below, according to the opinion of the ancients. I do not reject their word, but according to my small intelligence, it seems to me that with all due respect it is larger. The better to understand what I mean, let there be imagined a figure of a large circle, and around the point of this large circle—the part called the centre—let there be another smaller circle. Then let the large circle be divided by lines into many parts, and let all the lines come together in the centre such that the small circle that is around the centre will be divided into as many parts as the large circle, although the spaces will be smaller. Now let the large circle stand for the firmament and the little circle for the earth. The firmament is divided by astronomers into twelve signs, and each sign is divided into thirty degrees; around the whole firmament there are 360 degrees. Now let the earth be divided into as many parts as the firmament, and each part will correspond to a degree of the firmament. Know that according to the authorities in astronomy, 600 stades[3] of the earth correspond to one degree of the firmament; there are 87,004 stades. Now let this be multiplied by 340 [360]; there will be 31,600 miles, each of eight stades, according to the miles of our country. Such is the earth in roundness and all around, according to my opinion and my understanding.

Know that, according to the opinion of the wise ancient philosophers and astronomers, our country, Ireland, Wales, Scotland, England, Norway, and the other islands bordering them are not on the earth's surface calculated above, as it appears in all the books of astronomy. For the surface of the earth is divided into seven parts by the seven planets, and these parts are called climates, and our parts are not in the seven climates.[4] For they descend to the

1. "Do not fear me, who suspended the Earth from nothing" (a somewhat garbled echo of Job 26.7).
2. The actual circumference of the earth is more than 24,000 miles.
3. The stade, or stadium, is one-eighth of a Roman mile (a little more than 600 feet).

4. Ancient and medieval astronomers (following the 2nd-century C.E. Greek astronomer Ptolemy) divided the Northern Hemisphere into seven zones of latitude or "climates"; the British Isles lie above the northernmost of the seven climates.

west owing to the roundness of the world, and the islands of India are there, and they are opposite us who are in the low part, and the seven climates extend all around the world.

From XXXIV. *About the customs of the kings and others dwelling on the islands near Prester John's Land, and about the honor that the son does to his dead father*

* * *

On this island they have a custom throughout the whole country that when someone's father dies and he wishes to greatly honor his father, he sends for all his friends and relatives and monks and priests and a great many minstrels. Then the body is carried onto a mountain with great ceremony and great joy, and when they have carried [it] all the way there, the greatest priest cuts off the head and sets it on a large platter made of gold or silver, if he is a rich man, and then delivers the head to the son, and the son and the other relatives chant many prayers to God. Then the priests and the monks cut all the flesh of the body into pieces, and then they say their prayers, and the birds of the country, which have long known this custom, come flying above—such as vultures, eagles, and all other birds that eat flesh—and the priests throw pieces of the flesh to them, and they carry it not far away and eat it. Then just as the chaplains over here chant "*Subvenite sancti Dei etc.*"[5] for the dead, so these priests there at this point chant aloud in their language, "See how worthy a man he was that God's angels seek him out and carry him to Paradise." At this point it seems to the son that he is very much honoured when the birds have eaten his father, and whoever has the greatest number of birds is the most honoured. Then the son takes his relatives and his friends back to his house and makes a great feast for them, and all the friends tell their story of how the birds came — five here, ten there, twenty here—and enjoy themselves most abundantly in the telling. When they are at the house the son has his father's head cooked and gives each of his most special friends a little of the flesh from it instead of a dish of something else, and from the skull he has a goblet made, and he drinks from it—and his relatives do too—with great devotion in memory of the holy man whom the birds have eaten. And the son will keep this goblet and drink from it all his life in his father's memory.

From this island after ten days on the return journey through the Great Khan's land, there is another very good island and large kingdom where there is a rich and strong king, and amongst the rich men of his country there is a very rich man who is neither prince, duke, commander, or count. But there are many who have their lands from him, and he is extremely rich, for each year he has in payment a good three thousand horses laden with wheat and rice, and he leads a very noble life according to the custom over there, for he has fifty maiden ladies-in-waiting who always serve him at meals and in going to bed and do whatever he likes. When he is eating a meal, they bring him his food five dishes at a time, and while carrying it in they sing a song. Then they cut his

5. Aid him, saints of God.

food up for him and put it in his mouth, for he touches nothing but just holds his hands in front of him on the table, for he has such long nails that he could not grasp or hold anything. It is a noble thing for men to have long nails and to let them always grow and be looked after as much as they can. There are many men in the country who let them grow so much that they encircle the whole hand, and it is a very noble thing; and the noble thing for women in this country is to have small feet. Therefore as soon as they are born, they have their feet bound so tightly that they grow only half as long as they should grow. These ladies-in-waiting always sing while he eats, and when he is no longer eating any of these five dishes, they bring him another five dishes and sing as before, and they do this right to the end of the meal. It is done this way every day, and this is how he spends his life, and so did his ancestors and so will those who come after him, without anyone doing a fair deed of arms, but he always lives like this in comfort like a pig that is being fattened. He has very fine and very rich palace where he lives whose walls are a good two leagues in circumference, and he has inside it many beautiful gardens, and all the floors of the halls and the rooms are paved with gold and silver. In the middle of one of the gardens there is a small mountain where there is a meadow and in this meadow there is a little church with towers and pinnacles all of gold, and he often likes to sit in this little church both to take the air and to enjoy himself, for this church was made for no other purpose than for his pleasure alone.

From this country one goes by land through the Great Khan's land, about which I told you before, so no further account is needed.

Know that in all these countries about which I have spoken, and on all these islands, and amongst all these diverse peoples that I have described to you, and the diverse laws and the diverse beliefs they have, there is no people—because they have reason and understanding—who do not have some articles of our faith and some good points of our belief, and who do not believe in God who made the world, whom they call god of nature, according to the prophet, who said: "*Et metuent eum omnes fines terre.*" And elsewhere: "*Omnes gentes servient ei.*"[6]

But they do not know how to speak perfectly, for they have no one to explain it to them, except insofar as they understand it with their natural understanding. They do not know how to speak about the Son, nor about the Holy Spirit. But they all know how to speak about the Bible, especially about Genesis, the sayings of the prophets, and the books of Moses.

Indeed, they say that the creatures that they worship are not gods at all, but they worship them for the virtue that is in them, which could not exist without God's grace. About simulacra and idols, they say that there are no people who do not have simulacra, and they say this because we Christians have images of Our Lady and other saints that we worship. But they do not know what we worship: not the images of wood or stone, but the saints in whose name they are made. For just as the letter instructs and teaches the clergy what and how they should believe, so the images and the depictions teach the laity to think about and worship the saints in whose name they are made.

---

6. Respectively, "And all the ends of the Earth shall fear Him" (Psalm 67.7, slightly misquoted); "All nations shall serve Him" (Psalm 72.11).

They say also that God's angels speak to them in those idols, and that they perform great miracles; and they speak the truth that there is an angel within. But there are two kinds of angel, good and bad: Cacho [kakos] and Calo [kallos], as the Greeks say, and Cacho is bad and Calo is good.[7] But it is not the good angel, but the bad that is in the idols, to deceive them and keep them in their error.

There are many other diverse countries and many other wonders over there that I have not seen at all, and do not know how to speak properly about. And even in countries where I have been there are many diversities of which I have made no mention, for it would be a long thing to describe everything. Therefore what I have described for you about some countries should do you for now. For if I described as many things as there are over there, someone else who took the trouble and labored bodily to go into those far places and find out about the country would be hindered by my words from reporting on anything foreign, for he would have nothing new to say in which the listeners could take pleasure, and it is always said that new things give pleasure. Thus I shall keep quiet now without recounting any more diversities that exist over there, so that whoever wishes to go into those parts might find there enough to say.

And I, the above-named John Mandeville—who left our countries and crossed the sea in the year of grace 1322, who has since sought out many lands and many journeys and many countries, and who has been in much good company and in many a fine undertaking (although I never did any fair deed nor fine adventure), and now have come to rest, despite myself, because of arthritic gout, which constrains me—while taking pleasure in my miserable rest, in recording the time past, have compiled these things and put them into writing, such as I could remember, in the year of grace 1356, in the thirty-fourth year since I left our countries.

7. A difficult passage: the contrast is between the evil (Greek *kakos*) and the beautiful (Greek *kallos*) image.

II

India's Classical Age

During the ancient period (ca. 1200 B.C.E.–400 C.E.), society on the Indian subcontinent evolved in several distinct stages. Beginning from agrarian villages, it developed a caste system and a religion centered on Vedic scripture and ritual; as the rural economy increasingly supported the growth of towns and cities, the first subcontinent-wide empires arose. The caste system grew more intricate, with five main categories that included so-called untouchables as well as numerous specific castes, even as the coexistence of monogamy, polygamy, and polyandry complicated the rules of social classification. The Vedic canon of scripture, commentaries, and code books came to articulate the concepts of *Brahman*, or undifferentiated godhead, and *ātman*, enduring individual self or soul; *mokṣa*, the soul's liberation from mundane existence, so that it can be reunited with godhead; and karma, or action and its consequences, as well as *dharma*, law and duty as defined by the gods. Vedic ritual, designed to please many deities and to increase its performer's chances of attaining *mokṣa*, was complemented by sophisticated debates about the nature of good and evil, morality and power, and ethics and justice, thereby laying the

This detail from a seventh-century Buddhist wall painting depicts the Hindu deity Indra kneeling in veneration before the Buddha.

foundation for Hinduism in the classical period. By the start of the Common Era, India was well-defined as a distinct cultural zone within Asia, characterized by its acceptance of pantheism and polytheism, its religious pluralism and tolerance, and its accommodation of social and cultural diversity.

THE TRANSITION TO THE CLASSICAL PERIOD

In the closing centuries of the ancient period, the subcontinent underwent several far-reaching changes that were part of a lengthy transition to the classical period (ca. 400–1100 C.E.). One major shift was a transformation of its political organization, which became evident under the Maurya dynasty (ca. 321–180 B.C.E.). Established immediately after Alexander the Great's invasion of India (327 B.C.E.), the Mauryan empire unified most of the country—then inhabited by about 50 million people—under a centralized administration and a single system of laws. The new empire interconnected its districts with highways, easing the movement of goods and people; and it established diplomatic and trade links with Greece, Rome, Egypt, Syria, and Central Asia. The visionary Mauryan emperor Aśoka (ruled 269–232 B.C.E.), in particular, influenced subsequent Indian and Asian history on a significant scale. He institutionalized the idea that a king "turns the wheel of *dharma*" on earth, and hence is fully responsible for his people's well-being under cosmic or universal law. His royal chancery standardized the Brahmi script system, which was used in his famous rock inscriptions, paving the way for the subcontinent's future literacy and the spread of writing throughout Southeast Asia. The standardization also emphasized multilingual pluralism, as Brahmi writing was simultaneously transcribed into the Greek and Kharoṣṭhī scripts (the latter a variant of the Aramaic), which were used widely along the ancient Silk Road linking Asia to Europe.

Equally important, Aśoka personally converted to Buddhism, patronized the Third Buddhist Council, and sent Buddhist embassies to various parts of Asia. Because of his adoption of *ahiṃsā* (nonviolence) as a state policy, as well as his unusual balance between Buddhist proselytizing and the official tolerance of many religions (Hinduism, Jainism, and Greek polytheism, among others), he became the first figure of transnational importance in the history of Buddhism; he is portrayed in the canon of Theravada Buddhism as second in importance only to Gautama Buddha. Aśoka's conception and practice of imperial rule became a multifaceted model for Indian empires and kingdoms in the classical period and later.

Another change during the transitional centuries was the consolidation of royal patronage for the arts, architecture and construction, and public works. Aśoka built many of the oldest, most venerated monuments of Buddhism, and he invested in hospitals, libraries, monasteries, and institutions of learning; his support initiated the growth and spread of Buddhist art and architecture across Asia over many centuries. A successor of the Mauryan state, the Kuṣāṇa empire (first–third century C.E.), particularly under Kaniṣka (ruled ca. 100 C.E.), sponsored the Indo-Greek sculpture and architecture of Gandhara and Mathura, which displayed the influence of the Greek colony Alexander established near Peshawar, Pakistan. After he, like Aśoka, converted to Buddhism, Kaniṣka hosted the Fourth Buddhist Council in Kashmir, which launched Mahāyāna Buddhism and its subsequent momentous spread to China and Japan. He patronized painters, musicians, and poets, including the poet-dramatist Aśvaghoṣa, whose *Buddhacarita* (*The Life of the Buddha,* second century C.E.) invented the style of Sanskrit *kāvya,* or poetry, that was to dominate the classical period.

SOCIAL AND POLITICAL CONTEXTS OF CLASSICAL LITERATURE

The "classical" phase—during which Indian literature achieved an exceptional degree of aesthetic balance, stylistic refinement, intellectual sophistication, and originality—began in the second century C.E.; it came to maturity during the Gupta empire (ca. 320–550), specifically under Candragupta Vikramāditya (ruled ca. 375–415). Despite turbulence in its latter half, the classical period lasted until the end of the eleventh century, after which Islam, having arrived from the Middle East, irreversibly transformed the subcontinent's politics, society, and economy.

Stretching across the whole of northern India, and building alliances with lesser powers to its south, the Gupta empire achieved a remarkable expansion and stabilization of the Indian economy. Agriculture and dairy farming yielded an array of grains, fresh produce, and milk products; at the same time, weaving and spinning guilds, salt and mineral mines, metalworks, jewelers' workshops, and specialized castes of artisans produced a wide range of luxury goods and items for everyday consumption. An efficient bureaucracy, regulated coinage, and banking led to an increase in travel and pilgrimage and the growth of shipping, ports, inland cities, and overland and maritime commerce. While trade with the Roman Empire declined, that with China and Southeast Asia—especially the Indonesian archipelago—flourished, creating prosperity across the countryside as well as in urban areas. The economic improvements of the Gupta empire continued, on a smaller scale, in the successor kingdoms of Harṣavardhana of Kannauj (seventh century, near Delhi) and of dynasties in central and eastern India (eighth–eleventh centuries).

The Gupta empire's prosperity and political stability had broad ramifications for the subcontinent's arts, religions, and literature. Like the Mauryas and Kuśānas before them, the Guptas had a pluralistic policy of supporting Hinduism, Jainism, and Buddhism, though more lavishly; but they themselves were Hindus, and their patronage powerfully aided the consolidation of what we now call classical Hinduism. Mainly because of their stimulus, Hinduism shifted from an elite focus on Vedic ritual and sacrifice to a more populist form of engagement, centered on pilgrimages to holy river sites and public worship in temples. It devalued many of the Vedic gods, who resembled the gods in the Greek and Roman pantheons, and elevated Viṣṇu (the god of preservation) and Śiva (the god of destruction) to the status of major deities. Moreover, it produced a vast new canon of theological and mythological works, called Purāṇas, focused on these gods; eventually, they significantly displaced the Vedas (ca. 1200–900 B.C.E.), the original revealed scripture, in the popular imagination. The Guptas aided this shift by financing temple architecture and construction on a grand scale; these edifices later served as models for temple complexes not only in India but also in Borobudur (Indonesia) and Angkor Wat (Cambodia). They also championed major advances in classical Indian stone and metal sculpture—examples are now widely represented in major museums around the world—which influenced the plastic arts throughout Asia.

INDIA
100–1000

0   200   400   600   800 kilometers
0   100   200   300   400   500 miles

BACTRIA
Balkh
Oxus
CHINA
AFGHANISTAN
HINDU KUSH
KARAKORAM RANGE
KASHMIR
TIBET
GANDHARA
Srinagara
Helmand (Etymander)
Taxila
Kandahar
Indus
Jhelum (Hydaspes)
Chenab
Ravi
Sutlej
Beas
Brahmaputra

approximate extent
of the Gupta empire
ca. 370

Hastinapura
Gupta kingdom
ca. 320
H I M A L A Y A S

Mathura
Jumna
Kanyakubja
Banaras
Pataliputra
Prayaga
Nalanda
Ganges
MAGADHA

Indus
Tropic of Cancer

Vidisa
Ujjayini
VINDHYA RANGE
Narmada

Dvaraka

area added to
Gupta empire
ca. 410

Deccan Plateau
Krishna
Godavari

Arabian Sea

Bay of Bengal

Uraiyur
Maturai

Korkai
LANKA

Indian Ocean

OVERVIEW OF SOUTH
& SOUTHEAST ASIA

CHINA
area of main map

MYANMAR
(BURMA)

INDIA

Sri Lanka

Malay
Peninsula
MALAYSIA
Borneo

Sumatra

INDONESIA
Java

The Dashavatar temple, dedicated to Viṣṇu, in Deogarh, India—characteristic of temple architecture during the height of the Gupta dynasty in the fifth century.

The Gupta dynasty extended patronage at their court to writers, scholars, and artists as well; they appointed a *rāja-kavi*, or poet laureate; and they maintained royal libraries. They initiated the tradition of underwriting the preparation and conservation of manuscripts by professional scribes, and the production of dramas and other entertainments. Kālidāsa's plays were written for and staged at the Gupta court; centuries later, the courtier-poet Rājaśekhara (one of the writers in our anthology) could draw on this tradition as he hosted play productions at his home. The Guptas also reinforced the older Mauryan and Kuṣāṇa practice of patronizing the writing and collection of manuscripts at monasteries and temples of various faiths. Among the classical authors represented here, **Kālidāsa** was probably the emperor Candragupta Vikramāditya's poet laureate, and **Bāṇa** was King Harṣavardhana's court poet and official biographer. **Somadeva** served the notable queen Sūryamati of Kashmir, whereas **Bhartṛhari**, **Bhavabhūti**, and **Murāri** worked for lesser royal patrons. The poet **Dharmakīrti** and the editor Vidyākara, from whose classical anthology many of our Sanskrit lyrics are

drawn, were monks at Buddhist monasteries under Gupta-style patronage.

Most important, the Guptas' paradigm of royal patronage spread literacy and literature beyond the networks of the *brāhmaṇa* (priestly) caste, which had largely monopolized writing and scholarship in earlier Hindu society. Now, the caste groups of *kṣatriyas* (warriors) and *vaiśyas* (traders) were able to develop their own literate cultures, and the Buddhists and Jains—who had broken away around the sixth century B.C.E.—were able to extend and refine theirs. By the end of the Gupta empire, the Jains in particular had defined a cultural role for themselves that has proved central to Indian history: drawing on royal patronage from across the subcontinent, they became its informal "librarians," collecting and preserving manuscripts in virtually every language and period. Classical Tamil lyric poetry (called *cuṅkam* poetry), for instance, whose canon was closed by the third century, was preserved for the next sixteen hundred years only in Jain monastic libraries. The Tamil people themselves rediscovered their classical heritage in the late nineteenth century, when, in a chance encounter, a Jain monk passed on a *caṅkam* manuscript to the leading Tamil scholar of the day.

CLASSICAL GENRES AND THE CLASSICAL POET

The classical period witnessed an expansion in how literature and the figure of the writer were understood. Sanskrit prose had appeared early in the ancient period, but during the first millennium B.C.E. its purposes were solely theological and practical. In the classical period, as prose became a medium with aesthetic qualities, it was used to compose fictional narratives in the genre of *kathā* (tale) or nonfictional narratives in the genre of *ākhyāyikā* (history, biography). Bāṇa (seventh century) is represented below by a few vignettes in verse, but his fame in Sanskrit *kāvya* is as the inventor of both *kathā* and *ākhyāyikā* in beautiful prose. His *Kādambarī* is the first novelistic fiction in Indian literature, an achievement that several modern languages of the subcontinent commemorate by using *kādambarī* as their term for "novel"; his *Harṣacarita* is the first biography, based on facts and legends about his patron, King Harṣavardhana.

In the ancient period, the **Rāmāyana** and the **Mahābhārata** described themselves as *kāvyas*—that is, as epics in verse. The classical period, in both theory and practice, expanded the term's application to the full range of literary composition in verse, prose, and mixtures of verse and prose, whether oral or written. The category thus came to include drama, epics, tales, and lyrics, as well as didactic and nonfictional composition—but it contained only those works that displayed aesthetic qualities appropriate to their form and genre. Within classical *kāvya*, major forms, such as long poems in interwoven cantos, had equal footing with minor forms, such as topical satires, prayers, bene-

dictions, and epigrams, which could be as short as a single verse. By the end of the first millennium C.E., Sanskrit literature had burgeoned, abandoning its original, narrow definition to refashion itself into a vast storehouse of texts in several dozen genres.

Whereas the *kavi* (poet) of the ancient period dealt primarily with oral transmission, the classical Indian author inhabited a more complex literary world permeated with orality, performance, and writing. His social life was also busy: as we know from the *Kāmasūtra* (fourth century) and other texts, the classical intellectual was a connoisseur of the arts and a man about town, with a taste for life's tangible pleasures. As a poet, he had to be trained in grammar, poetics, and philosophy; moreover, he had to command not just his mother tongue but also a regional lingua franca and Sanskrit. So that he could produce and interpret allusions, it was essential that *kāvya* as well as religious discourse and mythology (especially Hindu and Buddhist) be a part of his repertoire. A poet could not be original unless he knew what had been done in the past, and he could not be inventive unless he had mastered all the tools of his trade.

While classical society valued learning and versatility, these qualities were not sufficient to ensure greatness: an author had to display imagination and brilliance of conception (*pratibhā*) as well as urbane decorum (*aucitya*). And as the classical period progressed, he increasingly had to display his individuality. Among the writers we have selected, Kālidāsa and Bhartṛhari from the fifth century are shadowy figures; Murāri, **Rājaśekhara**, and Somadeva, several centuries later, have constructed more individuated literary personae. In the classical period, literature (*sāhitya*) by definition produced "mutual benefit" for the author and audience; a poet therefore had to employ his learning and skill to create something of moral or spiritual value for himself and for his readers and listeners. Most important, a classical *kavi* had to use all his resources to reach through and speak directly to his reader, a connoisseur who ideally was in sympathy with him—his true "companion at heart" (*sahṛdaya*). In a famous verse included in this anthology, the seventh-century poet-dramatist Bhavabhūtī memorably describes his search for the ideal reader:

The people in this world who
   scorn me
no doubt have a special wisdom,
so I don't write for them:

instead, I write with the thought
that since the world is wide and
   time is endless,
one day someone will be born

whose nature is the same as mine.

     (trans. Vinay Dharwadker)

As the classical era drew to a close, the corresponding ideal of the poet is conveyed by Kṣemendra, a minor Sanskrit writer of the twelfth century:

A poet should learn with his eyes
the forms of leaves
he should know how to make
people laugh when they are
   together
he should get to see
what they are really like
he should know about oceans
   and mountains
in themselves
and the sun and the moon and
   the stars
his mind should enter into the seasons
he should go
among many people
in many places
and learn their languages

     (trans. W. S. Merwin
    and J. Moussaieff Masson)

THE ROLE OF POETICS IN THE CLASSICAL PERIOD

One aspect of the new literary culture of the classical period was a fresh interest in theoretical reflection on the nature of beauty. Probably the result of imperial patronage of intellectual activity, poetics had a double relation to literature and the arts in classical India: it laid out both the ideals to which artistic practitioners should aspire, based on general considerations, and broad aesthetic rules, derived from the actual practice of past writers. Classical works of poetics and aesthetics therefore functioned simultaneously as philosophical expositions and as practical guides or manuals.

The earliest of these, and the broadest in its influence, was Bharata's *Nāṭyaśāstra* (*The Discipline of the Performing Arts*, second century B.C.E.–second century C.E.), which may have been composed during Kuṣāṇa imperial rule. A treatise on drama, stagecraft, dance, and music, it comprehensively charts their varieties, materials, techniques, and goals. It also provides guidelines for the training of performers, covering topics from acting, directing, set design, costume, and makeup to song and instrumental music. Within this framework, the *Nāṭyaśāstra* discusses ten main forms of drama, including the play in multiple acts; dramatic structure and language as well as types of character; and diction, versification, and meter.

According to Bharata, the overall goal of a literary work is to lead its audience to experience a *rasa*. *Rasa* is literally the taste, essence, or flavor of a human emotion, but it can be captured only via representation—that is, in works of art: the raw emotion of real life (called *bhāva*) is something quite different. A writer extracts the universal essence of an ordinary, specific *bhāva*; an actor or dancer on stage does the same, but instead of using

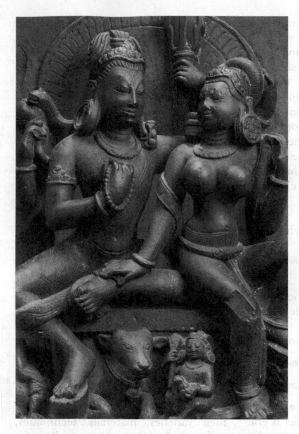

This tenth-century sculpture of Śiva and his consort, Pārvatī, depicts the gods in a particular gesture and attitude that has a long history in Indian art and a specific name: "Uma Maheshvara."

words alone he selects and combines all the elements of his craft, including song, gesture, movement, and melody. Through *rasa*, the audience experiences an emotion in its pure, sublime form, without the messiness that accompanies it in everyday life; such an experience refines the audience's aesthetic and moral sensibilities, thereby achieving the primary goal of "culture" or self-cultivation. A poet's aim therefore should be to take any one or more of the nine emotional states fundamental to human experience—love, joy, pity, anger, valor, terror, disgust, wonder, and peace—and transform them into the best words in the best order for a sublime effect on his readers or listeners. Bharata's analysis of the performing arts became the dominant poetic theory of the classical period, and its influ-

ence ultimately spread throughout Southeast Asia, from Java and Bali to Thailand and Cambodia. Its greatest adherent in India was Kālidāsa.

The second major aesthetic theory appeared in Daṇḍin's *Kāvayādarśa* (*The Ideal of Poetry*, or *The Mirror of Literature*, sixth–seventh century), which limited itself to imaginative writing. A poet and theorist from the Tamil region in southern India, Daṇḍin asked a simple question: what makes a poem poetic? His answer, in effect, was that the poetic quality of poetry or the literariness of literature lies in a distinctive handling of language—in deviation from everyday speech and practical communication by the use of *alaṃkāra*, "embellishment." To achieve this deflection from the "normal," authors rely on a large repertoire of devices, falling broadly into the categories of figures of speech (such as alliteration, onomatopoeia, and rhyme) and figures of thought (such as metonymy, or association, and metaphor). Among the poets in our anthology, Bhavabhūtī and Murāri especially are masters of *alaṃkāra* in the Daṇḍin tradition, inventing superb metaphors with effortless skill. The first Indian work of poetics devoted exclusively to literature, Daṇḍin's exposition was widely celebrated in its time; within a few decades, it found its way to China, where, in translation, it became a theoretical template for T'ang and later Chinese poetry.

The third major aesthetic system of the classical period was articulated in Ānandavardhana's *Dhvanyāloka* (*The Radiance of Suggestion*, ninth century), a work produced in Kashmir. According to followers of this school of thought, the aesthetic effects of an artwork can largely be explained by how it conveys its meanings to an audience: they view such a conclusion as logical, since meaningless discourse (babble) fails to create beauty. In the perspective that Ānandavardhana adopts, meaning is grounded in language, and each word signifies at three levels: denotation, which supplies the word's literal or conventional meaning; connotation, which includes one or more secondary associative meanings; and suggestion, which produces a broader range of meanings evoked by the word's placement in a particular larger structure, such as a sentence, verse, or prose passage. For example, the word "village" by itself denotes "a small group of houses in a rural area"; it connotes life on a farm, a world with barnyard animals, a close-knit community, and a lack of urban amenities. In a phrase like "the village on the banks of the Ganges," however, the word suggests other, unexpected meanings: an exotic landscape, the coolness and serenity of a river, timelessness and simplicity, peace and holiness. This last method of signification, called *dhvani*, is the principal device of poetry.

Persuaded by Ānandavardhana, many poets and readers of the late classical period and after came to believe that the beauty of poetry lies primarily in its power to create new meanings through the subtle use of suggestion. *Dhvanyāloka*, of course, also describes the technique of poetic suggestion as practiced by earlier writers; Bhartṛhari and Dharmakīrti are among the poets who exemplify the use of suggestion early in the classical period. But whichever theory or combination of theories they followed—*rasa, alaṃkāra,* or *dhvani*—classical authors and audiences alike found themselves engaged in unprecedented ways not only with the practice of literature but also with larger questions about its nature, function, and value.

Over a thousand years, between the transition from the ancient period and the arrival of Islam as a political power on the subcontinent, the varieties of literature in India gradually multiplied into an unprecedented diversity of texts and genres. Besides a voluminous body of *kāvya* in Sanskrit, the rich literary culture encompassed writing in regional Prakrits—languages such as Mahārāṣṭrī, Magadhī, and Śaurasenī —as well as the remarkable, completely different canon of *caṅkam* poetry in classical Tamil. A vital achievement of the period was the establishment of a reciprocal relation between literary theory and practice, which defined the materials, means, sources, and ends of poetry afresh and encouraged both authors and audiences to engage in sophisticated debates about the function and value of literature. Classical India thus radically altered the literary landscape it had inherited from the ancient period.

VIṢṆUŚARMAN

second or third century

Animal fables are among the earliest and most fundamental stories in world literature. A fable is usually a short tale with a moral, often involving supernatural events and nonhuman characters; its narrative is designed to teach a lesson, capture a general truth, or give practical advice, especially on conduct. Animal fables are particularly effective because they exploit the natural characteristics of various species to create parallels with humans, using wit and humor to make us laugh in recognition. We learn by identifying with the animals and taking pleasure in the identification.

According to its prologue, the *Pañcatantra*, the best-known ancient collection of Indian animal fables and folktales, was written with specific students in mind. Its author, a *brāhmaṇa* scholar named Viṣṇuśarman, was assigned the task of training three dull-headed and reluctant princes in the principles of statecraft. Viṣṇuśarman chose animal fables, practical in their wisdom and both entertaining and instructive, to teach the young men the arts of governance and diplomacy. The *Pañcatantra* is the collected record of this royal tutelage, and a delightful source on which storytellers throughout the world have drawn for millennia.

CONTEXT

Animal fables appeared in different parts of the ancient world between about 700 B.C.E. and 300 C.E.: among the Greeks, in **Aesop's Fables**; in India, among the Buddhists, in the *Jātaka* tales, and among the Hindus, in the *Pañcatantra* and the *Hitopdeśa*; and,

among the Jews, in the Talmud. These societies may have created such stories independently of each other; or fables invented in one or more places may have circulated widely through trade and conquest. The Indian and Arab traders who brought live peacocks to King Solomon in biblical times, or sold the subcontinent's muslin cloth to Egyptians (used to wrap the mummies interred in pyramids), may also have carried the Indian animal fables that are recorded in the Talmud. Likewise, the soldiers in Alexander's army who were left behind in a Greek colony in Gandhara (the Peshawar valley in modern Pakistan) around 327 B.C.E. may have retold Aesop's fables to their Indian contemporaries. In each of these places, animal fables caught the imagination of their audiences and quickly spread to other places, in oral and in written retellings.

WORK

Viṣṇuśarman probably composed his innovative work while serving a royal patron late in the transition from ancient to classical times. Its title, *Pañcatantra*, means "the five books, sciences, or rules of conduct," and it is divided into five large sections, each focusing on a single theme related to strategies for success in worldly affairs. Book 1, "The Loss of Friends," brings together tales about how two crafty jackals create conflict between a lion, the king of beasts, and a mighty bull, his competitor; book 2, "The Winning of Friends," tells stories of four animals in the forest who successfully pursue the ideals of friendship and harmony;

book 3, "Crows and Owls," concentrates on tales about the perpetual war between two species of birds, sworn enemies of each other; and books 4 and 5, "Loss of Gains" and "Ill-Considered Action," contain stories warning against foolishness in financial transactions and everyday conduct.

The animal fables of the *Pañcatantra* are told in many different voices, but the stories are interlinked—one leads to another. The work as a whole is organized as a frame narrative, an older Indian invention: one story is told inside another, which in turn may be set inside another story, and so on. Each of the *Pañcatantra*'s five books has its own frame story, which concentrates on its main theme and introduces a number of characters, many of whom then in turn tell each other smaller stories, which ultimately lead back to the outer frame. Such a nesting of narratives emerged as a basic structural principle in the earlier Sanskrit epics, the *Rāmāyaṇa* and the *Mahābhārata*, as well as in the Buddhist *Jātaka* tales composed in Pali.

The five fables presented here are drawn from three different books of the *Pañcatantra*; the first three are from "The Loss of Friends," the fourth from "Owls and Crows," and the last from "Ill-Considered Action." Each story has a particular animal narrator or set of narrators, and begins and ends with a short verse that summarizes the tale's lesson or moral; each animal narrator and character in the story has a name, which highlights his or her moral quality or character trait. Thus, Rusty is the lion in "The Loss of Friends" who is in conflict with Lively the bull; Victor the jackal is the narrator of "Leap and Creep" and "The Blue Jackal," whereas Constance the plover is the narrator of "Forethought, Readywit, and Fatalist"; Red-Eye the owl tells "Mouse-maid Made Mouse"; and a group of judges collectively narrate "The Loyal Mungoose."

Each of the five fables constructs an imaginative context for practical advice that is easy to grasp. In "Leap and Creep," for example, the main characters are a louse and a flea; the louse, who lives in the sheets of a king's bed, makes the mistake of accepting the flea as her guest. When he fails to heed her warning, the consequences for the louse are fatal. The moral of this tale is that one should never let a stranger share one's home. In contrast, "Mouse-maid Made Mouse" depicts a brāhmaṇa sage whose miraculous powers enable him to transform a mouse into a baby girl, as a gift for his childless wife. When the girl reaches puberty, the sage attempts to find her a bridegroom, but the girl finds flaws in and rejects each of the grand figures he suggests. When he presents a mouse, however, she is instinctively attracted to him, and the sage changes the mouse-maid back. The message, in this case, is that every type of creature has an inherent and unchangeable nature, which defines the creature's place in the world as well as his or her destiny.

Over the centuries, the *Pañcatantra*'s fables have found many audiences. For all classes and ages, including children, they have offered a guide to prudent behavior in daily life; at the same time, they were used by leaders and rulers as a handbook on how to manage affairs of state. The tales were an extraordinary cultural success story in their own time and subsequently traveled far and wide: they appeared in early Persian and Syriac versions (sixth century); in a classic Arabic rendering, *Kalilah wa Dimnah* (ca. 750); in Greek and Latin retellings; and then in early modern European versions, including the first renderings in German (1483) and English (1570), as well as the well-known fables of La Fontaine in French (late seventeenth century). By the end of the Renaissance, animal fables from ancient India, the Middle East, and Greece had become part of a transnational narrative culture that could no longer be traced back to any single point of origin, though the influence of the *Pañcatantra* remained preeminent.

From Pañcatantra[1]

From *Book I*

The Loss of Friends

* * *

> "With no stranger share your house;
> Leap, the flea, killed Creep, the louse."

"How was that?" asked Rusty. And Victor[2] told the story of

LEAP AND CREEP

In the palace of a certain king stood an incomparable bed, blessed with every cubiculary virtue. In a corner of its coverlet lived a female louse named Creep. Surrounded by a thriving family of sons and daughters, with the sons and daughters of sons and daughters, and with more remote descendants, she drank the king's blood as he slept. On this diet she grew plump and handsome.

While she was living there in this manner, a flea named Leap drifted in on the wind and dropped on the bed. This flea felt supreme satisfaction on examining the bed—the wonderful delicacy of its coverlet, its double pillow, its exceptional softness like that of a broad, Gangetic sand-bank, its delicious perfume.[3] Charmed by the sheer delight of touching it, he hopped this way and that until—fate willed it so—he chanced to meet Creep, who said to him: "Where do *you* come from? This is a dwelling fit for a king. Begone, and lose no time about it." "Madam," said he, "you should not say such things. For

> The Brahman reverences fire,[4]
> Himself the lower castes' desire;
> The wife reveres her husband dear;
> But all the world must guests revere.

Now I am your guest. I have of late sampled the various blood of Brahmans, warriors, businessmen, and serfs, but found it acid, slimy, quite unwholesome. On the contrary, he who reposes on this bed must have a delightful vital fluid, just like nectar. It must be free from morbidity, since wind, bile, and phlegm are kept in harmony by constant and heedful use of potions prepared by physicians. It must be enriched by viands unctuous, tender, melting in the mouth; viands prepared from the flesh of the choicest creatures of land, water, and air, seasoned

---

1. Translated by Arthur W. Ryder.
2. In the principal frame narrative of book 1, Victor the jackal tells this story to Rusty the lion.

3. This is a parody of the involved style of description found in the more ornate classical *kāvya* poems. "Gangetic": of the Ganges River.
4. A reference to the sacred fire of Hindu ritual.

furthermore with sugar, pomegranate, ginger, and pepper. To me it seems an elixir of life. Therefore, with your kind permission, I plan to taste this sweet and fragrant substance, thus combining pleasure and profit."

"No," said she. "For fiery-mouthed stingers like you, it is out of the question. Leave this bed. You know the proverb:

> The fool who does not know
> His own resource, his foe,
> His duty, time, and place,
> Who sets a reckless pace,
> Will by the wayside fall,
> Will reap no fruit at all."

Thereupon he fell at her feet, repeating his request. And she agreed, since courtesy was her hobby, and since, when the story of that prince of sharpers, Muladeva,[5] was being repeated to the king while she lay on a corner of the coverlet, she had heard how Muladeva quoted this verse in answer to the question of a certain damsel:

> Whoever, angry though he be,
> Has spurned a suppliant enemy,
> In Shiva, Vishnu, Brahma,[6] he
> Has scorned the Holy Trinity.

Recalling this, she agreed, but added: "However, you must not come to dinner at a wrong place or time." "What is the right place and what is the right time?" he asked. "Being a newcomer, I am not *an courant*." And she replied: "When the king's body is mastered by wine, fatigue, or sleep, then you may quietly bite him on the feet. This is the right place and the right time." To these conditions he gave his assent.

In spite of this arrangement, the famished bungler, when the king had just dozed off in the early evening, bit him on the back. And the poor king, as if burned by a firebrand, as if stung by a scorpion, as if touched by a torch, bounded to his feet, scratched his back, and cried to a servant: "Rascal! Somebody bit me. You must hunt through this bed until you find the insect."

Now Leap heard the king's command and in terrified haste crept into a crevice in the bed. Then the king's servants entered, and following their master's orders, brought a lamp and made a minute inspection. As fate would have it, they came upon Creep as she crouched in the nap of the fabric, and killed her with her family.

> "And that is why I say:
> With no stranger share your house, . . .

and the rest of it. And another thing. My lord and king does wrong in neglecting the servants who are his by inheritance. For

> Whoever leaves his friends,
> Strange folk to cherish,
> Like foolish Fierce-Howl, will
> Untimely perish."

"How was that?" asked Rusty. And Victor told the story of

5. A hero in the well-known Sanskrit romance *Bṛhatkathā* (*The Great Story*). See also Somadeva's *Kathāsaritsāgara* (p. 962).

6. Gods of the Hindu triad: Śiva is the destroyer, Viṣṇu is the preserver, and Brahmā is the creator.

THE BLUE JACKAL

There was once a jackal named Fierce-Howl, who lived in a cave near the suburbs of a city. One day he was hunting for food, his throat pinched with hunger, and wandered into the city after nightfall. There the city dogs snapped at his limbs with their sharp-pointed teeth, and terrified his heart with their dreadful barking, so that he stumbled this way and that in his efforts to escape and happened into the house of a dyer. There he tumbled into a tremendous indigo vat, and all the dogs went home.

Presently the jackal—further life being predestined—managed to crawl out of the indigo vat and escaped into the forest. There all the thronging animals in his vicinity caught a glimpse of his body dyed with the juice of indigo, and crying out: "What is this creature enriched with that unprecedented color?" they fled, their eyes dancing with terror, and spread the report: "Oh, oh! Here is an exotic creature that has dropped from somewhere. Nobody knows what his conduct might be, or his energy. We are going to vamoose. For the proverb says:

> Where you do not know
> Conduct, stock, and pluck,
> "'Tis not wise to trust,
> If you wish for luck."

Now Fierce-Howl perceived their dismay, and called to them: "Come, come, you wild things! Why do you flee in terror at sight of me? For Indra,[7] realizing that the forest creatures have no monarch, anointed me—my name is Fierce-Howl—as your king. Rest in safety within the cage formed by my resistless paws."

On hearing this, the lions, tigers, leopards, monkeys, rabbits, gazelles, jackals, and other species of wildlife bowed humbly, saying: "Master, prescribe to us our duties." Thereupon he appointed the lion prime minister and the tiger lord of the bedchamber, while the leopard was made custodian of the king's betel,[8] the elephant doorkeeper, and the monkey the bearer of the royal parasol. But to all the jackals, his own kindred, he administered a cuffing, and drove them away. Thus he enjoyed the kingly glory, while lions and others killed food-animals and laid them before him. These he divided and distributed to all after the manner of kings.

While time passed in this fashion, he was sitting one day in his court when he heard the sound made by a pack of jackals howling near by. At this his body thrilled, his eyes filled with tears of joy, he leaped to his feet, and began to howl in a piercing tone. When the lions and others heard this, they perceived that he was a jackal, and stood for a moment shamefaced and downcast, then they said: "Look! We have been deceived by this jackal. Let the fellow be killed." And when he heard this, he endeavored to flee, but was torn to bits by a tiger and died.

> "And that is why I say:
> Whoever leaves his friends, ...

and the rest of it."

* * *

---

7. The king of the gods.

8. A plant whose leaves are chewed as a digestive and stimulant in India.

FORETHOUGHT, READYWIT, AND FATALIST[9]

In a great lake lived three full-grown fishes, whose names were Forethought, Readywit, and Fatalist. Now one day the fish named Forethought overheard passersby on the bank and fishermen saying: "There are plenty of fish in this pond. Tomorrow we go fishing."

On hearing this, Forethought reflected: "This looks bad. Tomorrow or the day after they will be sure to come here. I will take Readywit and Fatalist and move to another lake whose waters are not troubled." So he called them and put the question.

Thereupon Readywit said: "I have lived long in this lake and cannot move in such a hurry. If fishermen come here, then I will protect myself by some means devised for the occasion."

But poor, doomed Fatalist said: "There are sizable lakes elsewhere. Who knows whether they will come here or not? One should not abandon the lake of his birth merely because of such small gossip. And the proverb says:

> Since scamp and sneak and snake
> So often undertake
> A plan that does not thrive,
> The world wags on, alive.

Therefore I am determined not to go." And when Forethought realized that their minds were made up, he went to another body of water.

On the next day, when he had gone, the fishermen with their boys beset the inner pool, cast a net, and caught all the fish without exception. Under these circumstances Readywit, while still in the water, played dead. And since they thought: "This big fellow died without help," they drew him from the net and laid him on the bank, from which he wriggled back to safety in the water. But Fatalist stuck his nose into the meshes of the net, struggling until they pounded him repeatedly with clubs and so killed him.

"And that is why I say:

> Forethought and Readywit thrive;
> Fatalist can't keep alive."

* * *

From *Book III*

Crows and Owls

* * *

> "Though mountain, sun, and cloud, and wind
>   Were suitors at her feet.
> The mouse-maid turned a mouse again—
>   Nature is hard to beat."

"How was that?" asked Live-Strong. And Red-Eye told the story of

---

9. In the frame story Constance the plover tells this story to her mate, Sprawl.

MOUSE-MAID MADE MOUSE[1]

The billows of the Ganges were dotted with pearly foam born of the leaping of fishes frightened at hearing the roar of the waters that broke on the rugged, rocky shore. On the bank was a hermitage crowded with holy men devoting their time to the performance of sacred rites—chanting, self-denial, self-torture, study, fasting, and sacrifice. They would take purified water only, and that in measured sips. Their bodies wasted under a diet of bulbs, roots, fruits, and moss. A loin-cloth made of bark formed their scanty raiment.

The father of the hermitage was named Yajnavalkya. After he had bathed in the sacred stream and had begun to rinse his mouth, a little female mouse dropped from a hawk's beak and fell into his hand. When he saw what she was, he laid her on a banyan leaf, repeated his bath and mouth-rinsing, and performed a ceremony of purification. Then through the magic power of his holiness, he changed her into a girl, and took her with him to his hermitage.

As his wife was childless, he said to her: "Take her, my dear wife. She has come into life as your daughter, and you must rear her carefully." So the wife reared her and spoiled her with petting. As soon as the girl reached the age of twelve, the mother saw that she was ready for marriage, and said to her husband: "My dear husband, how can you fail to see that the time is passing when your daughter should marry?"

And he replied: "You are quite right, my dear. The saying goes:

> Before a man is gratified,
> These gods must treat her as a bride—
> The fire, the moon, the choir of heaven;
> In this way, no offense is given.
>
> Holiness is the gift of fire;   5
> A sweet voice, of the heavenly choir;
> The moon gives purity within:
> So is a woman free from sin.
>
> Before nubility, 'tis said
> That she is white; but after, red;   10
> Before her womanhood is plain,
> She is, though naked, free from stain.
>
> The moon, in mystic fashion, weds
> A maiden when her beauty spreads;
> The heavenly choir, when bosoms grow;   15
> The fire, upon the monthly flow.
>
> To wed a maid is therefore good
> Before developed womanhood;
> Nor need the loving parents wait
> Beyond the early age of eight.[2]   20

---

1. In the frame story of Book III, Red-Eye, the counselor of the king of the owls, tells this story to Live-Strong, the counselor of the king of the crows.
2. Eight was considered a good age for marriage.

> The early signs one kinsman slay;
> The bosom takes the next away;
> Friends die for passion gratified;
> The father, if she ne'er be bride.

> For if she bides a maiden still,   25
> She gives herself to whom she will;
> Then marry her in tender age:
> So warns the heaven-begotten sage.

> If she, unwed, unpurified,
> Too long within the home abide,   30
> She may no longer married be:
> A miserable spinster, she.

> A father then, avoiding sin,
> Weds her,[3] the appointed time within
> (Where'er a husband may be had)   35
> To good, indifferent, or bad.

Now I will try to give her to one of her own station. You know the saying:

> Where wealth is very much the same,
> And similar the family fame,
> Marriage (or friendship) is secure;
> But not between the rich and poor.

And finally:

> Aim at seven things in marriage;
> All the rest you may disparage;

But

> Get money, good looks,
> And knowledge of books,
> Good family, youth,
> Position, and truth.

"So, if she is willing, I will summon the blessèd sun, and give her to him." "I see no harm in that," said his wife. "Let it be done."

The holy man therefore summoned the sun, who appeared without delay, and said: "Holy sir, why am I summoned?" The father said: "Here is a daughter of mine. Be kind enough to marry her." Then, turning to his daughter, he said: "Little girl, how do you like him, this blessèd lamp of the three worlds?"[4] "No, father," said the girl. "He is too burning hot. I could not like him. Please summon another one, more excellent than he is."

Upon hearing this, the holy man said to the sun: "Blessèd one, is there any superior to you?" And the sun replied: "Yes, the cloud is superior even to me. When he covers me, I disappear."

So the holy man summoned the cloud next, and said to the maiden: "Little girl, I will give you to him." "No," said she. "This one is black and frigid. Give me to someone finer than he."

3. Following the Indian tradition of arranged marriages, the father finds a suitable bride-groom for his daughter.
4. That is, heaven, earth, and the underworld.

Then the holy man asked: "O cloud, is there anyone superior to you?" And the cloud replied: "The wind is superior even to me."

So he summoned the wind, and said: "Little girl, I give you to him." "Father," said she, "this one is too fidgety. Please invite somebody superior even to him." So the holy man said: "O wind, is there anyone superior to you?" "Yes," said the wind. "The mountain is superior to me."

So he summoned the mountain and said to the maiden: "Little girl, I give you to him." "Oh, father," said she. "He is rough all over, and stiff. Please give me somebody else."

So the holy man asked: "O kingly mountain, is there anyone superior even to you?" "Yes," said the mountain. "Mice are superior to me."

Then the holy man summoned a mouse, and presented him to the girl, saying: "Little girl, do you like this mouse?"

The moment she saw him, she felt: "My own kind, my own kind," and her body thrilled and quivered, and she said: "Father dear, turn me into a mouse, and give me to him. Then I can keep house as my kind of people ought to do."

And her father, through the magic power of his holiness, turned her into a mouse, and gave her to him.

* * *

From *Book V*

Ill-Considered Action

* * *

> Let the well-advised be done;
> Ill-advised leave unbegun;
> Else, remorse will be let loose,
> As with lady and mungoose.

"How was that?" asked Jewel. And they told the story of

THE LOYAL MUNGOOSE[5]

There was once a Brahman named Godly in a certain town. His wife mothered a single son and a mungoose. And as she loved little ones, she cared for the mungoose also like a son, giving him milk from her breast, and salves, and baths, and so on. But she did not trust him, for she thought: "A mungoose is a nasty kind of creature. He might hurt my boy." Yes, there is sense in the proverb:

> A son will ever bring delight,
> Though bent on folly, passion, spite,
> Though shabby, naughty, and a fright.[6]

One day she tucked her son in bed, took a water-jar, and said to her husband: "Now, Professor,[7] I am going for water. You must protect the boy from the mun-

---

5. A band of judges tells this story to Jewel the merchant. A mungoose (mongoose) is a small mammal and a natural enemy of snakes, which it can kill and eat.

6. A great value is placed on sons in the Indian family.

7. Priestly *brāhmaṇas* study the Vedas and other ritual texts.

goose." But when she was gone, the Brahman went off somewhere himself to beg food,[8] leaving the house empty.

While he was gone, a black snake issued from his hole and, as fate would have it, crawled toward the baby's cradle. But the mungoose, feeling him to be a natural enemy, and fearing for the life of his baby brother, fell upon the vicious serpent halfway, joined battle with him, tore him to bits, and tossed the pieces far and wide. Then, delighted with his own heroism, he ran, blood trickling from his mouth, to meet the mother; for he wished to show what he had done.

But when the mother saw him coming, saw his bloody mouth and his excitement, she feared that the villain must have eaten her baby boy, and without thinking twice, she angrily dropped the water-jar upon him, which killed him the moment that it struck. There she left him without a second thought, and hurried home, where she found the baby safe and sound, and near the cradle a great black snake, torn to bits. Then, overwhelmed with sorrow because she had thoughtlessly killed her benefactor, her son, she beat her head and breast.

At this moment the Brahman came home with a dish of rice gruel which he had got from someone in his begging tour, and saw his wife bitterly lamenting her son, the mungoose. "Greedy! Greedy!" she cried. "Because you did not do as I told you, you must now taste the bitterness of a son's death, the fruit of the tree of your own wickedness. Yes, this is what happens to those blinded by greed. For the proverb says:

> Indulge in no excessive greed
> (A little helps in time of need)—
> A greedy fellow in the world
> Found on his head a wheel that whirled."[9]

---

8. *Brāhmaṇas* are entitled to live on alms: those priests without ritual commissions are obliged to live by begging.

9. This verse is the lead-in to the next story.

THE CLASSICAL TAMIL LYRIC

ca. third century

Little-known outside India even in the early twenty-first century, the literature of the ancient Tamil people raises questions that are among some of the most intriguing for modern readers of world literature. How could a predominantly rural community, with no connection to an empire, create a body of poetry that has such range and depth in its representation of human experience? What makes it possible for classical Tamil poetry, composed by the beginning of the Common Era, to largely match in its qualities the classical poetry in imperial and urban languages such as Greek and Latin, Sanskrit and Mandarin?

CONTEXT

Ancient Tamil culture flourished in the southernmost region of the Indian peninsula, which has been the Tamil homeland ever since. Based mainly on agriculture, trade, and handicrafts, as well as hunting and fishing, its economy supported a network of small villages, market towns, and ports, governed by local chieftains in the countryside and by kings (ruling minor kingdoms) in a few larger cities. Yet the poets of this apparently unsophisticated society invented an aesthetic and a style of poetry able to richly explore the complexities of nature and culture, of human subjectivity in interaction with its environment, and of the impersonal forces at work in the cosmos. Their medium of expression was their mother tongue, Tamil, one of the twenty-three languages in the Dravidian language family; it acquired its classical form before the Common Era, and the poetry they composed in it became canonical between about 100 B.C.E. and 250 C.E. Used continuously since the ancient period, Tamil is one of India's two classical literary languages (the other is Sanskrit).

The Tamil people, most of whom still live in southern India, appear to have been visited by travelers from Rome and Greece in this early period; later they may have traveled to eastern Africa and they undoubtedly established contact with people and places across Southeast Asia, from Indonesia and Thailand to Cambodia and Vietnam. The Tamil script, derived from the Brahmi script that appeared on the subcontinent after about 500 B.C.E., influenced the development of the scripts of the Burmese, Thai, Khmer, and Lao languages, among others; and, since the early modern period, Tamil emigrants have settled in significant numbers in what are now Sri Lanka, Malaysia, Singapore, and Fiji.

WORK

Classical Tamil poetry, a body of work that was complete by the third century C.E., has been preserved and transmitted in eight anthologies whose contents are mainly short and medium-length poems—most about love, war, and public and political life, but some also dealing with religion; in a set of ten long poems on love, war, cities, landscapes, and gods, some framed as guides, handbooks of advice, and vivid descriptions; and in a master work of grammar, linguistics, and rhetoric. The canon totals 2,381 poems, attributed to 473 poets known by their personal names or by poetic epithets (among them, twelve women) and to 102 poets who remain anonymous. Sixteen of the named poets are represented in the anthologies by substantial selections, others by only one poem each. The canon appears to have taken form through a centuries-long collective process of refinement rather than through the labor of any individual editor.

This entire body of poetry is known as *cankam* poetry—that is, poetry of the academy or fraternity (a community trained in grammar, rhetoric, poetics, and ethics). Its authors were called *puḷavārs*, scholars or wise men, and a seventh-century commentator claimed that they belonged to three distinct, successive *cankams*. According to the accompanying literary folklore, the works of the first have been lost; of the second, only the master work of grammar survives; and the eight anthologies and the ten long poems represent the third, most recent *cankam*. All three academies produced their work in a broadly secular framework, before the rise, spread, and consolidation of Hinduism in its classical form, and before the arrival of Buddhism and Jainism in southern India. As a result, classical Tamil poetry, as we have inherited it, differs fundamentally from classical

Sanskrit poetry in its orientation. While a great deal of classical Sanskrit lyric, narrative, and dramatic poetry, from about the fourth century onward, takes Hindu, Buddhist, and even Jain ideas, beliefs, and practices for granted, classical Tamil poetry does not. The ancient Tamil scholar-poets, composing their poems before the third century, make no references to karma or *dharma*, caste or pollution, Śiva or Viṣṇu, the *Rāmāyaṇa* or the *Mahābhārata*—or to *rasa* and Sanskrit poetics. *Caṅkam* poetry is thus "pre-Hindu" or even "pre-Sanskrit," and hence a truly alternative indigenous classical poetry of the Indian subcontinent.

The independence of *caṅkam* poetry is evident in its forms, genres, imagery, symbolism, figuration, and textual organization, as well as in its themes. Its canon is organized not by author but by genre: all the poems are classified and presented by theme, as either *akam* or *puṟam*. Akam means "interior," and this genre deals with the heart, love, self, the interiority of experience, home, family, the private and domestic spheres, and intimate emotions. In contrast, *puṟam* means "exterior," and poems within the genre convey an individual's experience of his or her public world—the shared world of war, social conflict, ethics, and community; of kings, heroes, poets, and ordinary citizens.

Within this broad distinction, the ancient Tamils conceived of an individual's inner or subjective world as consisting of five symbolic and figurative "interior landscapes," representing five principal phases of love. An individual in a specific phase of love is thought to inhabit a particular type of natural landscape, whose properties permeate all his or her experiences. The first phase is lovers' unions, which ideally take place at night on hillsides; the second phase is separation, anxious waiting, and secret meetings, which symbolically occur by the seashore at nightfall; the third phase is hardship, cast as the lovers' journey through a desert or wilderness in the heat of the sun; the fourth phase is happiness after marriage and patient waiting in domesticity, at home, on the edge of the forest in the evening; the fifth phase is unfaithfulness after marriage, imagined to occur in the agricultural lowland, where the loved one meets others working in the fields in the morning. By placing an individual as a character in the appropriate landscape, an *akam* lyric dramatizes his or her experience of, and emotions in, a particular situation. Since every character, emotion, and situation has many nuances, and the details of every interior landscape can vary, no two *akam* poems cover exactly the same terrain; and only when all the poems in the genre are taken together do they map out the full complexity of love and of human inner experience.

Having set up the facets and phases of love as a series of interior landscapes, the classical Tamil poets then turn to *puṟam* poetry as the "public" opposite of personal experience. These poems are often set in a town or city; they are about real people and real places, public issues and public events, common problems and common tragedies. They praise and attack kings, celebrate victories and criticize policies, reflect on ethical and economic principles, mourn the death of heroes and the destruction of cities, uphold virtues and values.

The thematic and rhetorical difference between *akam* and *puṟam* poems is quite sharp and deliberate. The love poems usually depict a young man, a young woman, and the young woman's girlfriend (who serves as a confidante and a go-between), often in the voice of one of the female characters (though the great majority of poets are male); that all are nameless enhances both the privacy and the universality of the inner world. In contrast, the public poems offer a wider range of social types and are articulated in a wider range of voices; those of supplicating poets, concerned citizens, grieving daughters, and bereaved mothers are especially common. At the same time, the two genres complement each other by bringing love and war, as well as nature and culture, within the ambit of the ancient Tamils' agricultural way of life centered on small villages, with bustling market towns, port cities, and political capitals in the distance, on the horizon.

The poems we have selected, taken from only the shorter lyric poems in the classical Tamil anthologies, fall into two main parts, representing the *akam* and the *puṟam* genre, respectively. The *akam* poems are further subdivided into the five interior landscapes. Thus, the poems grouped under "The Hills" are all about lovers' unions; they consistently use images, symbols, and associations drawn from that landscape to evoke or dramatize various aspects of the first phase of love. Kapilar's "In His Country," for instance, depicts a young girl's longing for a dashing hunter who is still out of her reach; the same poet's "Forest Animals Walk There," in contrast, represents a young woman in a much later stage, as she grants her beloved permission to marry her. Kapilar's third poem in the section, "He Is from Those Mountains," portrays yet another type: the young woman whose joy is mixed with a great deal of anguish, because her lover is careless, insensitive, and lackadaisical. His fourth poem, "The Colors on the Elephant's Body," is a heady celebration, again from a woman's perspective, of a perfect match of desire and temperament.

The poems included in each of the other *akam* sections below likewise follow the conventions associated with their respective landscapes. The poems grouped under "Seashore" all deal with the phase of love that involves anxious waiting and secret meetings; this association of the seaside with love's trying circumstances is quite different from modern Euro-American conventions, which often present a seashore as an ideally "romantic" setting for lovers. The poems in the "Wasteland" section focus on the sufferings of the young lovers apart; in Auvaiyār's "The Round Blazing Sun," for example, a girl lies awake and imagines her lover crossing the wilderness alone, and she longs to bring him (and herself) the comfort of love. The selections in the "Forest" and "Lowland" sections then depict lovers' experiences of domestic happiness (as in Cīttalai Cattaṉār's "Rains in Season") and of the anguish of marital infidelity (as in the anonymous "From the Long Fronds"), respectively.

Finally, under the *puṟam* poems are lyrics that explore many different facets of public and social life in ancient Tamil society. Iḷam Peruvaḻuti's "This World Lives Because" presents an ethical ideal of conduct as a citizen, whereas Auvaiyār's "Earth's Bounty" pays homage to the land as well as its young men. In contrast, Poṉmuṭiyār's "A Young Warrior" captures the devastating tragedy of war. Complementing the preceding *akam* poems in both theme and tone, these writings on public events complete the unique imaginative accomplishment of *caṅkam* poetry: the depiction of the inner and outer worlds of the classical Tamil people.

Akam Poems[1]

Five Interior Landscapes[2]

1. *The Hills: Lovers' Unions*

[IN HIS COUNTRY]

What she said to her girl friend[3]

In his country,[4]

summer west wind blows
flute music
through bright beetle-holes in the waving bamboos.
The sweet sound of waterfalls is continuous,   5
dense as drums.
The urgent lowing voices of a herd of stags
are oboes,
the bees on the flowering slopes
become lutes.   10

Excited by such teeming voices,
an audience of female monkeys
watches in wonder
the peacock in the bamboo hill
sway and strut   15
like a dancer
making an entrance
on a festival stage.

He had a garland on his chest,[5]
a strong bow in his grip,
arrow already chosen,   20
and he asked which way
the elephant went
with an arrow buried in its side.

He stood at the edge   25
of a ripe-eared millet field.

---

1. Translated by A. K. Ramanujan.
2. Imaginative landscapes that lovers supposedly inhabit, each evoking the emotions and
experiences of a different phase of love. In this
geography, hills are associated with lovers'
unions; seashores, with anxious waiting and
secret meetings; wastelands, with perilous
journeys, separation, and hardship; the edge
of forests, with patient waiting and happiness
in marriage; and lowlands, with unfaithfulness
after marriage.

3. An *akam* poem usually carries an initial
statement, such as this, which identifies its
speaker and characters and helps explain their
feelings and actions.
4. Here, hill country; all the flora and fauna
mentioned in this poem are characteristic of
the uplands in the Tamil country.
5. This young man not only belongs to the hill
country but is also a local hero, which is why
the young woman who is the speaker of the
poem finds him irresistible.

But, among all the people
who saw him standing there,
why is it
that I alone   30
lie in bed
in this harsh night,
eyes streaming,
arms growing lean?

Kapilar

[FOREST ANIMALS WALK THERE]

What she said

Forest animals walk there[6]
and elephants roam.
In the sky's high places
thunder rumbles.
But you come alone   5
in the night
along the narrow paths
of snakes and tigers,

O man of the mountain country,

    that country of fruitful hills,
    ancient conquests,   10
    and wide spaces,
    where the music of waterfalls
    mingles with bee sounds
    as drums with lute-strings.[7]   15

If you wish to marry me, you can.[8]
But one thing: do not come
along those narrow paths;

though, if you must, please,
when you leave here   20
and reach your village in the hills,
think of us
living in anxiety here,
and get that long horn you use
to signal your hounds   25

6. The lower slopes of the hills, which often
are forested.
7. Drums are associated with war and hunting;
lute strings, with music, emotion, and love.
8. In giving him permission to marry her, the

speaker is also proposing to the young man.
(Note the contrast with social conventions in
northern India, where marriages arranged by
couples' families became the norm in this
period.)

and hunters
straying in the bamboo jungle,

and blow on it
a little.

Kapilar

[HE IS FROM THOSE MOUNTAINS]

What she said

He is from those mountains

    where the little black-faced monkey,
    playing in the sun,
    rolls the wild peacock's eggs
    on the rocks   5

Yes, his love is always good
as you say, my friend,

but only for those strong enough
to bear it,

who will not cry their eyes out   10
or think anything of it

when he leaves.

Kapilar

[THE COLORS ON THE ELEPHANT'S BODY]

What she said to her friend

The colors on the elephant's body
shine, as he grazes
with his herd
on bamboo shoots,
breaking down branches;   5
then, in thirst,
he goes to a watering place,
kills a crouching tiger
poised for attack.
Pouring rains   10
clean the tusks, wash down the blood on their tips,
as he walks slowly along slopes
of jagged rock.
He's arrogant
after finishing off a vicious enemy,   15
and with six-legged bees making lute-music

over the juices of his lust
he mounts his female,
then goes to sleep
in our man's banana groves.   20

    Friend,
    comforting me once, you said lovingly,
    "The man is just right
    for your rank and nature."
    Sweet words those, bless you,   25
    they've come true:
    garlands smell on him
    like nectar to people who crave it,
    his chest's embrace so tight
    there's no place   30
    even for the waist of a bee,
    and love
    is tireless still
    as on the very first day.

                Kapilar

2. The Seashore: Anxious Waiting

[NEAR THE SALT PANS]

What her girl friend said to him

Near the salt pans
the clusters of *neytal* and blue lily[9]
are closing for the day.
The sea restlessly
brings in the lapping tide,   5
the side-pincered crab
surfaces from its wet nest
of black clay,
and the seaside falls silent
in the absence of users.   10

Don't ask the charioteer
to yoke the thick-legged donkey,
    used to the crooked plow,
to your chariot strung with bells.

And for our lovely girl's sake,   15
her eyes cool as rain,
stay tonight
and go on tomorrow,
    man from the great waters.

---

9. Flowers of the Tamil coast. "*Neytal*": dark lily.

In that shining big sea,   20
fishermen with big boats
    careless of the killer shark
dive for the right-spiralled oyster,

sound loud
the conch shells   25
that contain voices,

are met and welcomed
by bustling Korkai city[1]
as they disembark on the long sandy coasts.
There,   30
you'll see
our good little town.[2]

            Centan Kannanār

[ON THE NEW SAND]

What her girl friend said, the lover within earshot, behind a fence[3]

On the new sand
where fishermen,
    their big nets
      ripped apart by an angry sea,
dry their great hauls of fish   5

in a humming neighborhood
of meat smells,

a laurel tree blossoms
all at once in bright clusters
fragrant as a festival,   10

but this unfair town
is noisy with gossip.

And what with an unfair Mother too
keeping strict watch over us,

will our love just perish here   15
in sallow patches,

    this love for our man
    of the seashore

1. On the southeast tip of India.
2. By emphasizing her hometown's prosperity, the speaker seeks to impress the well-to-do young man, a visitor from a distant place.

3. This scenario—speech directed at one character but primarily meant to be overheard by another—is common in *akam* poems.

where petals
loosened by the traffic of birds
mix with the mud of the backwaters,   20

where the big-maned chariot horses galloping there
are washed clean
by the waves of the sea?

Ulōccaṉār

3. The Wasteland: Lovers' Hardships

[THE ROUND BLAZING SUN]

What she said, thinking of him crossing the wilderness alone

The round blazing sun
creeps in the sky,
raging as a fire
in the forest,

and the silk-cotton tree[4]   5
is leafless
yet in flower
without a bud,

    like a long array
    of red lamps
    in the month of Kārttikai[5]   10
    lit happily
    by bustling women,

in the fruitless forest
where the pools are dry, dusty.   15

If only
he'd spend the time with me,
it would go fast,

if only he'd walk swiftly with me
on the dunes   20
overhung with flowering boughs,
all fragrant,
where the forest stream flows now
and the sand
is laid out like a woman's bodice,   25

    he could have what arms desire,
    loving embraces,
    body entering body,

---

4. A tree that tolerates a desert environment. 5. Overlapping with November and December.

and then my guiltless eyes
that now fill
ceaselessly like barren pools
fed by secret springs
                                30

could put aside
their daily sorrow
and find some sleep.
                                35

                Auvaiyār

[A HEN-EAGLE BROODS, SICK]

What he said to his heart, arguing against further ambition and travel

A hen-eagle broods, sick
in the great branches
lifted to the sky,

in a neem tree[6]
with cracked trunk and dotted shade
                                5

       where unschooled children
       scratch their squares
       on a rock
       flat as a touchstone
       and play marbles with gooseberries
                         10

       in that wilderness
       with fierce little settlements
       of marauders,
            the bow their only plow,

and as evening comes creeping in,
                         15
sapping my strength, what can I do
but think of her,

who is sweet as a deed
long wished for and done,

standing there
                         20
in this hour of memories
in front of a house lamp

blazing?

             Iḷaṅkīraṉār

---

6. The margosa tree, common in India and Africa; because it thrives in arid environments, it is associated here with the wilderness or wasteland.

4. The Forest: Happiness after Marriage

[HER ARMS HAVE THE BEAUTY]

What he said

Her arms have the beauty
of a gently moving bamboo.
Her large eyes are full of peace.
She is faraway,
her place not easy to reach.   5

My heart is frantic
with haste,

      a plowman with a single plow
      on land all wet
      and ready for seed.   10

          Ōrēruḻavaṉār
          ("The Poet of the Plowman with the Single Plow")[7]

[RAINS IN SEASON]

What he said to his charioteer, on his way back

Rains in season,
forests grow beautiful.
Black pregnant clouds
bring the monsoons, and stay.
Between flower and blue-gem   5
flower on the bilberry tree
the red-backed moths multiply,
and fallen jasmines
cover the ground.[8]
   It looks like   10
a skilled man's work of art,
this jasmine country.

Friend, drive softly here.
Put aside the whip for now.
Slow down   15
these leaping pairs of legs,
these majestic horses
galloping in style
as if to music.

---

7. The literal meaning of the poet's name (probably a literary pseudonym).

8. In *akam* poetry, fecundity is strongly associated with marriage and the interior landscape of the forest.

Think of the stag, his twisted antlers   20

    like banana stems
    after the clustering bud
    and the one big blossom
    have dropped,

think of the lovely bamboo-legged doe   25
ready in desire:

if they hear the clatter
of horse and chariot.
how can they mate
at their usual dead of night?   30

Cīttalai Cattanār

FROM SEVEN SAID BY THE FOSTER-MOTHER[9]

The way
they lay together

    like deer, mother-doe,
    and fawn.

with their boy   5
between them, was very sweet:

neither in this world
hugged by the wide blue sea
nor in the one above

is such a thing easy to get.   10

5. The Lowland: Unfaithfulness

[IN HIS COUNTRY]

What she said

In his country,

spotted crabs
born in their mother's death
grow up with crocodiles
that devour their young.[1]   5

Why is he here now?

---

9. The young couple probably lives with the husband's adoptive parents.
1. Predatory creatures of the lowland land-scape, underscoring its association with sexual predators and infidelity.

And why does he
take those women,

    a jangle of gold bangles
    as they make love,   10

only to leave them?

                      Ōrampōkiyār

[FROM THE LONG FRONDS]

What her girl friend asked and what she replied regarding his return

"From the long fronds
of a deserted talipot tree
with clusters thick and hard
like an old date-palm's,

a male bird calls to its mate,   5
and the listening tiger
roars in echo

on those difficult roads
where hot winds blow—

    but then your lover who went there[2]   10
    has returned,
    has hugged you sweetly ever since
    and you've lain together
    inseparably
    in one place,   15

    and yet
    why do you look like a ruin,
    why do you grieve, my girl?"

So you ask, friend.
It could look like that to someone   20
who doesn't know.
          What's the use
of longing faithfully
for his strong chest

    that's now like the cold beaches   25
    of Tonti city[3]
    famous in the mouths of many?

2. The wasteland or wilderness, associated with absence (perhaps the husband is a trader).
3. A port on the eastern coast, linked by the young woman with scandal and gossip. While imaginatively inhabiting the lowland, she invokes the seashore because her husband's unfaithfulness has given her cause for anxious waiting, typically associated in *akam* poetry with "cold beaches."

When love is gone,
what's copulation worth?

Anonymous

Puṟam Poems[1]

The Exterior Landscape[2]

[THIS WORLD LIVES BECAUSE]

This world lives
because

some men
do not eat alone,
not even when they get   5
the sweet ambrosia of the gods;

they've no anger in them,
they fear evils other men fear
but never sleep over them;

give their lives for honor,   10
will not touch a gift of whole worlds
if tainted;

there's no faintness in their hearts
and they do not strive
for themselves.   15

Because such men are,
this world is.

Iḷam Peruvaḷuti

EARTH'S BOUNTY

Bless you, earth:

field,
forest,
valley,
or hill,   5

---

1. Translated by A. K. Ramanujan.
2. *Puṟam* poems are set in a single, shared "exterior landscape"; this public space contrasts with the five interior landscapes of *akam* poetry.

you are only
as good
as the good young men
in each place.

Auvaiyār

CHILDREN

Even when a man has earned much
of whatever can be earned,
shared it with many,
even when he is master of great estates,

if he does not have   5
children

     who patter on their little feet,
     stretch tiny hands,
     scatter, touch,
     grub with mouths   10
     and grab with fingers,
     smear rice and ghee
     all over their bodies,
     and overcome reason with love,

all his days   15
have come to nothing.

Pāṇṭiyaṉ Aṟivuṭai Nampi

A YOUNG WARRIOR

O heart
sorrowing
for this lad

once scared of a stick
lifted in mock anger   5
when he refused
a drink of milk,
     now
not content with killing
war elephants   10
with spotted trunks,

this son
of the strong man who fell yesterday

seems unaware of the arrow
in his wound.   15

his head of hair is plumed
like a horse's,

he has fallen
on his shield,

his beard still soft.[3]   20

Poṇmuṭiyār

A MOTHER'S LIST OF DUTIES

To bring forth and rear a son is my duty.
To make him noble is the father's.
To make spears for him is the blacksmith's.
To show him good ways is the king's.

And to bear   5
a bright sword and do battle,
to butcher enemy elephants,
and come back:

that is the young man's duty.

Poṇmuṭiyār

3. I.e., still a teenager.

KĀLIDĀSA
fifth century

Kālidāsa's classical Sanskrit play *Śakuntalā and the Ring of Recollection*, composed around the fifth century, is the first romantic comedy in world drama. It gives us a fine-tuned account of the process of falling in love, from the first encounter to an impromptu wedding, with only the gods as the passionate couple's witnesses; and it shows us how the lovers reunite, after a terrible breakup and after overcoming impossible obstacles, to live happily ever after. When Goethe read the play in its first English translation by Sir William Jones, he fell in love with it; indeed, he adapted some of Kālidāsa's stage conventions for the prologue of his own *Faust*, Part I, a very different kind of play. The dramatic structure created for *Śakuntalā*, with some of its surprisingly modern themes, remains the stock formula for romantic comedy. Since the classical period, the play has also been considered the most perfect expression of the theory of *rasa*, a centerpiece of India's classical aesthetics.

LIFE

Kālidāsa probably lived in north-central India sometime between 390 and 470, early in the classical period. Legend suggests that he was born and raised in the countryside (possibly near the modern city of Ujjain), with few resources or opportunities and little education to nurture his imagination and talent for words. Nevertheless, he turned to poetry in his youth, and some believe that he gained a regional reputation as a nature poet in Sanskrit. He may then have found a royal patron in Candragupta Vikramāditya, the most famous ruler of the Gupta dynasty, which established ancient India's largest and most prosperous empire (320–550). According to one popular literary account, Kālidāsa moved to the imperial capital of Pataliputra (now Patna, in the modern Indian state of Bihar) as the court poet, married a Gupta princess, and perhaps even had a political career as governor of the province of Kashmir. Seven works are attributed to him: four long poems in different genres and three full-length plays, including *Śakuntalā*.

CONTEXT

The classical period of Sanskrit literature stretched from about the fourth to the twelfth century; during this time, the language itself achieved its classical form, when it was at its most "refined" (the literal meaning of *saṃskṛta*). The Sanskrit term for its classical (and epic) poetry is *kāvya*, and *kavi* is its related word for poet. *Kāvya* designates both "poetry to be heard" (in oral recitation) and "poetry to be seen" (in performance on stage); it encompasses prose and verse, narrative and lyric, epic and drama; and it can be composed in major and minor as well as continuous and discontinuous forms. Whatever shape it takes, *kāvya* by definition must be well-crafted: it uses language that is embellished with figures of speech and thought, such as metaphors, and its goal is to induce in its audience a heightened state or an experience of the sublime. Besides *alaṃkāra* (verbal ornamentation), *kāvya* also uses the power of *dhvani* (suggestion in language) to create imaginative effects beyond the levels of denotation (literal meanings) and connotation (secondary meanings). Even a simple phrase like "the village on the Ganges" works by suggestion: the phrase as a whole, understood in context, evokes an image of serenity, rustic beauty, holiness, and harmony with nature that far exceeds the denotations and connotations of its individual words.

Verse and prose (and mixtures of the two), drama and narrative, and epic and lyric are all equally capable of producing a sublime experience in a listener, viewer, or reader. According to the theory of *rasa* in classical Sanskrit poetics, the heightened experience conveyed by genuine poetry is based on the nine fundamental emotional states (called *bhāva*) that we experience in the course of our lives: love, joy, pity, anger, valor, terror, disgust, wonder, and peace. They are accompanied by more transitory, secondary feelings, such as dejection, jealousy, anxiety, excitement, pride, sorrow, and impatience (Sanskrit theorists usually list thirty-three of these), in different combinations. Each *bhāva* also has a characteristic physical manifestation in the person who experiences it.

The goal of a poem is to create a beautiful representation of one or more of the fundamental emotional states, so that its audience can experience each in its pure "essence," or *rasa* (which literally means juice, extract, essence, or flavor). Only works of art can create and communicate such an essence: they extract the full flavor of a *bhāva* by blending its characteristics with various subsidiary states and the physical signs associated with it. Thus, a love poem can give us the *rasa* of love by combining longing or desire with lovesickness ("I can't eat or sleep if I'm not with her"), anxiety ("Why hasn't he called me today?"), jealousy ("Is she seeing someone else?"), or dejection ("He doesn't even notice me"), employing images such as a pallid face, sunken eyes, tears, a stunned look, and so on. The nine *rasas* created in art correspond exactly to the nine states found in real life. But for connoisseurs, the sublime experience of a *rasa* is superior to anything felt in the corresponding raw emotion and is essential to a refined sensibility. A high proportion of classical Sanskrit drama, poetry, and narrative (whether long or short, in prose or verse) was composed and understood in accordance with this aesthetic. Since his own times, Kālidāsa has been judged to be the best practitioner of the poetics of *rasa*, both in his long poems and in his plays, and the theory of *rasa* is thus closely linked with his work. *Śakuntalā* is universally viewed as his highest achievement in drama.

WORK

Abhijñānaśākuntalam, translated here as *Śakuntalā and the Ring of Recollection*, is classified in Indian poetics as a *nāṭaka*, the most important dramatic genre. A *nāṭaka* is a play in five to ten acts, with a prologue and interludes; its main characters are elevated figures, drawn from mythology or history— usually, a noble hero and a beautiful, extraordinary woman. Its secondary characters may come from different castes, social classes, and geographical regions. As a consequence, this type of play uses several regional languages while relying mainly on Sanskrit. It may employ verse as well as prose in its dialogue, and it contains music, song, and dance, which may be integral parts of the action or may provide entertainment in the prologue or interludes.

Śakuntalā follows this generic pattern quite closely. It is a multilingual play: the royal hero and his courtiers speak in Sanskrit, whereas women and lower-caste characters speak in various Prakrits (non-Sanskrit mother tongues, such as Magadhī and Śaurasenī, which were often regional and were considered relatively "unrefined"). It is divided into a prologue, interludes, and seven acts, which are arranged symmetrically around the fourth act, the longest and dramatically the most important. Its chief characters are a king and a woman of semidivine origin; they and their well-known story come from the *Mahābhārata*, the Sanskrit epic that defines itself as a "poetic history of mankind" (though begun much earlier, it was probably taking its final shape around Kālidāsa's time). Besides a large number of named secondary characters from various social backgrounds, the play also features brief appearances by "celestial" characters who mediate between the human world and the gods.

Kālidāsa takes the basic story of Śakuntalā from *The Book of the Beginning*, the first major book of the *Mahābhārata*, but adapts it substantially for his play; he reworks his epic material much as ancient Greek dramatists, such as **Aeschylus** and **Sophocles**, reshaped stories about Troy in plotting their tragedies. In the *Mahābhārata*, the story of Duṣyanta and Śakuntalā is important because the son born of their liaison is Bharata, the prince who goes on to establish the great empire ruled by his dynasty. Indeed, the *Mahābhārata* itself is literally "the great poem about the descendents of Bharata"; and today's Republic of India is officially called *Bhārata-varṣa*, "the land of Bharata's descendents." In the epic's Śakuntalā episode, Duṣyanta, a powerful king on a hunting expedition, encounters Śakuntalā in the ashram (hermitage) of her foster father, Kaṇva. Intensely attracted to Śakuntalā and taking advantage of Kaṇva's brief absence, Duṣyanta frankly propositions her. Somewhat surprisingly, given her sheltered upbringing, Śakuntalā responds like a woman familiar with sexual negotiations: she agrees to "marry" Duṣyanta, but only if he promises to make any son born of their union the heir to his throne. The king eagerly agrees, they make love, and he leaves for his capital, promising to send for her soon. Kaṇva returns, already aware of what has transpired while he was gathering food, and gives Śakuntalā his blessing.

But Duṣyanta does not keep his word. Left in the ashram, Śakuntalā raises a handsome son; when the boy is six years old, she goes to the king's palace where, in the presence of courtiers, she reminds Duṣyanta of his promise. The king, fearing that this relationship may discredit him, refuses to recognize her or their son. Śakuntalā is enraged and confronts him, and he slanders her and casts doubt on his son's paternity. Śakuntalā leaves, humiliated and furious; but a "celestial voice" declares to the king and his courtiers that she has been faithful and that he is the father of her son. Following this divine intervention, Duṣyanta sends for Śakuntalā and explains his actions and makes amends, installing her as his lawful queen and anointing the boy as his heir.

In drawing on the Mahābhārata, Kālidāsa views the story of Śakuntalā through the double lens of verisimilitude and of aucitya, (propriety, fitness, or decorum) a key concept in classical Indian morality and aesthetics. From his critical perspective, the epic offers a narrative unbecoming a great king: Duṣyanta's proposition to Śakuntalā is merely sexual, her response is much too calculated for an innocent country girl, and the swiftness of their "marriage" and Duṣyanta's departure is improbable. Moreover, the quarrel between Śakuntalā and the king at court is undignified and downright ugly, and Duṣyanta's subsequent reversal and explanation lack credibility.

So Kālidāsa imaginatively recasts most of the story in a new vein, in which Bharata must be conceived and born out of true love—rather than just a sexual transaction—between his parents, and the fundamental sequence of union–separation–reunion that binds them together must be tied to an emotional pattern that is true to human experience. Kālidāsa therefore invents much of his plot so that the audience could find Śakuntalā's story emotionally deeper, psychologically more plausible, and morally and aesthetically more appropriate in its outcome. At a pragmatic level, then, Kaṇva's absence from the ashram and his adoptive daughter must last for several days. Śakuntalā's entire character has to be reconceived in keeping with her upbringing apart from normal society: Kālidāsa presents her as an innocent teenager, untutored in the ways of men and seducers. Her encounter with the handsome king is a genuinely overwhelming experience of love at first sight (Act I), and she sees the impetuous "secret marriage" as a union of soul mates (Act III). Duṣyanta himself cannot be less than noble in his thoughts, intentions, and actions; hence, unlike the Mahābhārata, which gives him no psychological depth, the play details his emotional entanglement with Śakuntalā (Acts II–III). Kālidāsa also eliminates the callousness, self-regard, and cynical manipulation that he displays in the original narrative by introducing the famous devices of the royal ring and the curse: when Duṣyanta and Śakuntalā part (Act III), he gives her a ring as a token of their bond; when she arrives, pregnant, at his court (Act V), a curse placed on her makes him forget their relationship; and because she has lost the ring, she cannot prove who she is.

The first half of the play thus sets up what has become a universal framework for romantic comedy ever since: after a brief initial union, the lovers are forced apart by their circumstances, and have to overcome seemingly insurmountable obstacles (imposed by their families, by society at large, or even by the gods) before they can happily come together once again. How Duṣyanta can remember and recognize Śakuntalā after the loss of the ring, whether he suffers any remorse for his cruelty when she presents herself at his palace, how—and whether—she survives when her companions at the ashram also turn her away after the king's rejection, and where and how the two can be plausibly reunited become the dramatic problems that Kālidāsa has to solve in the play's second half (Acts V–VII).

But while plot and characterization function superbly in Western poetic terms to drive the play forward—initial situation, complications, crisis, discovery, and reversal—Kālidāsa's handling of *rasa* is what affects the audience at every turn. Each act emphasizes one fundamental emotional state and combination of subsidiary emotions, or moves sequentially from one state to another. Act I, which depicts Duṣyanta and Śakuntalā's first meeting, foregrounds love, colored by excitement and infatuation; Act II, about Duṣyanta's feelings, combines love with joy and laughter, building up anticipation; Act III, which focuses on the lovers' intimacy, heightens the desire that leads to union. Act IV then portrays love under conditions of separation, associating it with distraction, impatience, and anxiety, while Act V evokes pity, fear, and anger in succession. In the final movement, Act VI combines pity with love, linking those emotions to dejection and tears, whereas Act VII moves from valor

and wonder back to love, but now with sorrow as well as joy and peace. Kālidāsa thus takes us aesthetically through the entire range of our most basic emotions—from love and joy to pity, anger, terror, valor, and wonder, and then back to joy and on to peace—leaving out only the negative *rasa* of disgust. In the process, he also touches on all our important subsidiary or transitory emotions and their accompanying physical signs, from excitement and laughter to sorrow and tears, until we reach the powerful catharsis of the scene of reunion. *Śakuntalā* thus offers us a full experience of the drama of love with a happy ending—a romantic comedy, as generally understood.

Since about the sixth century, Kālidāsa and his plays and poems, especially *Śakuntalā*, have been constant points of reference in Indian literature: he is mentioned, quoted, or discussed by poets and dramatists as well as scholars and theorists across the subcontinent, in all its languages. Europeans discovered Kālidāsa and *Śakuntalā* in the late eighteenth century; since then, the play has been translated into many of the world's languages, with new renderings appearing in English regularly since the nineteenth century. We know that it was produced in the classical period in India using the theatrical conventions and techniques of Sanskrit-based performance arts; but as courtly and public theater sharply declined in India under Muslim rule between the twelfth and eighteenth centuries, *Śakuntalā*, like other Sanskrit plays, disappeared from the stage. Even with the emergence of modern theater in India and with its dissemination abroad in translation, *Śakuntalā* is now rarely performed. Despite its remarkable survival and continuous influence over some 1,500 years, and its wide appeal to readers around the world, Kālidāsa's play seems better equipped to reveal its beauty and complexity as "drama" than as "theater."

Śakuntalā and the Ring of Recollection[1]

CHARACTERS

Players in the prologue:
DIRECTOR: *Director of the players and manager of the theater.*
ACTRESS: *The lead actress.*

Principal roles:
KING: *Duṣyanta, the hero; ruler of Hastināpura; a royal sage of the lunar dynasty of Puru.*
ŚAKUNTALĀ: *The heroine; daughter of the royal sage Viśvāmitra and the celestial nymph Menakā; adoptive daughter of the ascetic Kaṇva.*
BUFFOON: *Māḍhavya, the king's comical brahman companion.*

Members of Kaṇva's hermitage:
ANASŪYĀ and PRIYAMVADĀ: *Two young female ascetics; friends of Śakuntalā.*
KAṆVA: *Foster father of Śakuntalā and master of the hermitage; a sage belonging to the lineage of the divine creator Marīci, and thus related to Mārīca.*
GAUTAMĪ: *The senior female ascetic.*
ŚĀRṄGARAVA and ŚĀRADVATA: *Kaṇva's disciples.*
Various inhabitants of the hermitage: a monk with his two pupils, two boy ascetics (named Gautama and Nārada), a young disciple of Kaṇva, a trio of female ascetics.

Members of the king's forest retinue:
CHARIOTEER: *Driver of the king's chariot.*
GUARD: *Raivataka, guardian of the entrance to the king's quarters.*
GENERAL: *Commander of the king's army.*
KARABHAKA: *Royal messenger.*
Various attendants, including Greco-Bactrian bow-bearers.

Members of the king's palace retinue:
CHAMBERLAIN: *Vātāyana, chief officer of the king's household.*
PRIEST: *Somarāta, the king's religious preceptor and household priest.*
DOORKEEPER: *Vetravatī, the female attendant who ushers in visitors and presents messages.*
PARABHṚTIKĀ and MADHUKARIKĀ: *Two maids assigned to the king's garden.*
CATURIKĀ: *A maidservant.*

City dwellers:
MAGISTRATE: *The king's low-caste brother-in-law; chief of the city's policemen.*
POLICEMEN: *Sūcaka and Jānuka.*
FISHERMAN: *An outcaste.*

Celestials:
MĀRĪCA: *A divine sage; master of the celestial hermitage in which Śakuntalā gives birth to her son; father of Indra, king of the gods, whose armies Duṣyanta leads.*
ADITI: *Wife of Mārīca.*
MĀTALI: *Indra's charioteer.*
SĀNUMATĪ: *A nymph; friend of Śakuntalā's mother Menakā.*

Various members of Mārīca's hermitage: two female ascetics, Mārīca's disciple Gālava.
BOY: *Sarvadamana, son of Śakuntalā and Duṣyanta; later known as Bharata.*

Offstage voices:
VOICES OFFSTAGE: *From the backstage area or dressing room; behind the curtain, out of view of the audience. The voice belongs to various players before they enter the stage, such as the monk,*

1. Translated by Barbara Stoler Miller.

Śakuntalā's friends, the buffoon,
Mātali; also to figures who never
enter the stage, such as the angry
sage Durvāsas, the two bards
who chant royal panegyrics
(vaitālikau).
VOICE IN THE AIR: *A voice chanting in
the air from somewhere offstage:*

the bodiless voice of Speech
quoted in Sanskrit by Priyaṁvadā;
the voice of a cuckoo who
represents the trees of the forest
blessing Śakuntalā in Sanskrit:
the voice of Haṁsapadikā singing
a Prakrit love song.

The setting of the play shifts from the forest hermitage (Acts I–IV) to the palace (Acts V–VI) to the celestial hermitage (Act VII). The season is early summer when the play begins and spring during the sixth act; the passage of time is otherwise indicated by the birth and boyhood of Śakuntalā's son.

Act I

The water that was first created,
the sacrifice-bearing fire, the priest,
the time-setting sun and moon,
audible space that fills the universe,
what men call nature,[2] the source of all seeds,   5
the air that living creatures breathe—
through his eight embodied forms,
may Lord Śiva come to bless you![3]

Prologue

DIRECTOR: [*Looking backstage.*] If you are in costume now, madam,
please come on stage!   10
ACTRESS: I'm here, sir.[4]
DIRECTOR: Our audience is learned. We shall play Kālidāsa's new
drama called *Śakuntalā and the Ring of Recollection.* Let the players
take their parts to heart!
ACTRESS: With you directing, sir, nothing will be lost.   15
DIRECTOR: Madam, the truth is:

I find no performance perfect
until the critics are pleased;
the better trained we are
the more we doubt ourselves.   20

2. Here, earth.
3. This verse is a *nāndī* (benedictory verse) recited at the beginning of a Sanskrit play, immediately after the preparatory rituals performed before a dramatic performance in ancient India. The benedictory verses of Sanskrit plays usually invoke the blessings of Śiva, dancer of the cosmic dance of creation and destruction as well as patron god of the drama. In this verse, Kālidāsa praises Śiva as the cosmic divinity pervading the universe in his eight manifest forms—the five elements (ether, air, fire, water, and earth), the sun and moon, and the sacrificing priest.
4. The prologues to many plays present the actress as the director's wife.

ACTRESS: So true . . . now tell me what to do first!
DIRECTOR: What captures an audience better than a song?
  Sing about the new summer season and its pleasures:

> To plunge in fresh waters
> swept by scented forest winds   25
> and dream in soft shadows
> of the day's ripened charms.

ACTRESS: [*Singing.*]

> Sensuous women
> in summer love
> weave   30
> flower earrings
> from fragile petals
> of mimosa
> while wild bees
> kiss them gently.[5]   35

DIRECTOR: Well sung, madam! Your melody enchants the audience.
  The silent theater is like a painting. What drama should we play to
  please it?
ACTRESS: But didn't you just direct us to perform a new play called
  Śakuntalā and the Ring of Recollection?   40
DIRECTOR: Madam, I'm conscious again! For a moment I forgot.

> The mood of your song's melody
> carried me off by force,
> just as the swift dark antelope
> enchanted King Duṣyanta.   45

[*They both exit; the prologue ends. Then the* KING *enters with his*
CHARIOTEER, *in a chariot, a bow and arrow in his hand, hunting an
antelope.*]

CHARIOTEER: [*Watching the* KING *and the antelope.*]

> I see this black buck move
> as you draw your bow
> and I see the wild bowman Śiva,
> hunting the dark antelope.[6]

---

5. Such verses are sung by women in Prakrit
and set to a melody, whereas the Sanskrit
kāvya verses of the play are recited or sung to a
simple tune that follows the rhythmic pattern
of the verse quarter. The women's songs
generally feature nature descriptions or the
nuances of love in natural settings.
6. The comparison is based on an ancient
myth of Śiva's pursuit of the creator god
Prajāpati, who had taken the form of an antelope. The verse flatters the king.

KING: Driver, this antelope has drawn us far into the forest. There he   50
is again:

> The graceful turn of his neck
> as he glances back at our speeding car,
> the haunches folded into his chest
> in fear of my speeding arrow,   55
> the open mouth dropping
> half-chewed grass on our path—
> watch how he leaps, bounding on air,
> barely touching the earth.

[He shows surprise.]
Why is it so hard to keep him in sight?   60
CHARIOTEER: Sir, the ground was rough. I tightened the reins to slow
the chariot and the buck raced ahead. Now that the path is smooth,
he won't be hard to catch.
KING: Slacken the reins!
CHARIOTEER: As you command, sir. [He mimes the speeding chariot.]   65
Look!

> Their legs extend as I slacken the reins,
> plumes and manes set in the wind, ears angle back;
> our horses outrun their own clouds of dust,
> straining to match the antelope's speed.   70

KING: These horses would outrace the steeds of the sun.[7]

> What is small suddenly looms large,
> split forms seem to reunite,
> bent shapes straighten before my eyes—
> from the chariot's speed   75
> nothing ever stays distant or near.

CHARIOTEER: The antelope is an easy target now. [He mimes the fixing
of an arrow.]
VOICE OFFSTAGE: Stop! Stop, king! This antelope belongs to our
hermitage! Don't kill him!
CHARIOTEER: [Listening and watching.] Sir, two ascetics are protecting   80
the black buck from your arrow's deadly aim.
KING: [Showing confusion.] Rein in the horses!
CHARIOTEER: It is done!
[He mimes the chariot's halt. Then a MONK enters with TWO PUPILS, his
hand raised.]
MONK: King, this antelope belongs to our hermitage.
Withdraw your well-aimed arrow! Your weapon should rescue victims,   85
not destroy the innocent!
KING: I withdraw it. [He does as he says.]

---

7. The seven horses that draw the sun god's chariot.

MONK: An act worthy of the Puru dynasty's shining light!

> Your birth honors
> the dynasty of the moon![8]   90
> May you beget a son
> to turn the wheel of your empire![9]

THE TWO PUPILS: [*Raising their arms.*] May you beget a son to turn the
wheel of your empire!
KING: [*Bowing.*] I welcome your blessing.   95
MONK: King, we were going to gather firewood.[1] From here you can see
the hermitage[2] of our master Kaṇva on the bank of the Mālinī river. If
your work permits, enter and accept our hospitality.

> When you see the peaceful rites of devoted ascetics,
> you will know how well your scarred arm protects us.[3]   100

KING: Is the master of the community there now?
MONK: He went to Somatīrtha,[4] the holy shrine of the moon, and
put his daughter Śakuntalā in charge of receiving guests. Some
evil threatens her, it seems.
KING: Then I shall see her. She will know my devotion and commend   105
me to the great sage.
MONK: We shall leave you now. [*He exits with his pupils.*]
KING: Driver, urge the horses on! The sight of this holy hermitage will
purify us.
CHARIOTEER: As you command, sir. [*He mimes the chariot's speed.*] 110
KING: [*Looking around.*] Without being told one can see that this is a
grove where ascetics live.
CHARIOTEER: How?
KING: Don't you see—

> Wild rice grains under trees   115
> where parrots nest in hollow trunks,
> stones stained by the dark oil
> of crushed iṅgudī nuts,[5]
> trusting deer who hear human voices
> yet don't break their gait,   120
> and paths from ponds streaked
> by water from wet bark cloth.[6]

8. Known as the "lunar dynasty," because it traces its descent to the moon god.
9. Any ancient Indian emperor is a *cakravartin*, a turner of the wheel of empire.
1. For the fire rituals and Vedic sacrifices performed at the hermitage.
2. It includes men and women and is organized like an extended family.

3. One of a king's chief duties is to protect hermits and ascetics.
4. A place of pilgrimage in western India.
5. These nuts are pressed by forest dwellers for oil.
6. Forest dwellers wear a cloth made of tree bark.

CHARIOTEER: It is perfect.

KING: [*Having gone a little inside.*] We should not disturb the grove!
Stop the chariot and let me get down! 125

CHARIOTEER: I'm holding the reins. You can dismount now, sir.

KING: [*Dismounting.*] One should not enter an ascetics' grove in
hunting gear. Take these! [*He gives up his ornaments and his
bow.*] Driver, rub down the horses while I pay my respects to
the residents of the hermitage! 130

CHARIOTEER: Yes, sir! [*He exits.*]

KING: This gateway marks the sacred ground. I will enter.
[*He enters, indicating he feels an omen.*]

> The hermitage is a tranquil place,
> yet my arm is quivering . . .
> do I feel a false omen of love 135
> or does fate have doors everywhere?

VOICE OFFSTAGE: This way, friends!

KING: [*Straining to listen.*] I think I hear voices to the right of the grove.
I'll find out.
[*Walking around and looking.*]
Young female ascetics with watering pots cradled on their hips are 140
coming to water the saplings. [*He mimes it in precise detail.*] This
view of them is sweet.

> These forest women have beauty
> rarely seen inside royal palaces—
> the wild forest vines far surpass 145
> creepers in my pleasure garden.

I'll hide in the shadows and wait.
[*ŚAKUNTALĀ and her two friends enter, acting as described.*]

ŚAKUNTALĀ: This way, friends!

ANASŪYĀ: I think Father Kaṇva cares more about the trees in the hermitage than he cares about you. You're as delicate as a jasmine, yet 150
he orders you to water the trees.

ŚAKUNTALĀ: Anasūyā, it's more than Father Kaṇva's order. I feel a
sister's love for them. [*She mimes the watering of trees.*]

KING: [*To himself.*] Is this Kaṇva's daughter? The sage does show poor
judgment in imposing the rules of the hermitage on her. 155

> The sage who hopes to subdue
> her sensuous body by penances
> is trying to cut firewood
> with a blade of blue-lotus leaf.

Let it be! I can watch her closely from here in the trees. 160
[*He does so.*]

ŚAKUNTALĀ: Anasūyā, I can't breathe! Our friend Priyaṁvadā tied my
bark dress too tightly! Loosen it a bit!

ANASŪYĀ: As you say. [*She loosens it.*]

PRIYAMVADĀ: [*Laughing.*] Blame your youth for swelling your breasts. Why blame me? 165

KING: This bark dress fits her body badly, but it ornaments her beauty . . .

> A tangle of duckweed adorns a lotus,
> a dark spot heightens the moon's glow,
> the bark dress increases her charm— 170
> beauty finds its ornaments anywhere.

ŚAKUNTALĀ: [*Looking in front of her.*] The new branches on this mimosa tree are like fingers moving in the wind, calling to me. I must go to it! [*Saying this, she walks around.*]

PRIYAMVADĀ: Wait, Śakuntalā! Stay there a minute! When you stand by this mimosa tree, it seems to be guarding a creeper. 175

ŚAKUNTALĀ: That's why your name means "Sweet-talk."[7]

KING: "Sweet-talk" yes, but Priyamvadā speaks the truth about Śakuntalā:

> Her lips are fresh red buds,
> her arms are tendrils,
> impatient youth is poised 180
> to blossom in her limbs.

ANASŪYĀ: Śakuntalā, this is the jasmine creeper who chose the mango tree in marriage,[8] the one you named "Forestlight." Have you forgotten her?

ŚAKUNTALĀ: I would be forgetting myself! [*She approaches the creeper* 185 *and examines it.*] The creeper and the tree are twined together in perfect harmony. Forestlight has just flowered and the new mango shoots are made for her pleasure.

PRIYAMVADĀ: [*Smiling.*] Anasūyā, don't you know why Śakuntalā looks so lovingly at Forestlight? 190

ANASŪYĀ: I can't guess.

PRIYAMVADĀ: The marriage of Forestlight to her tree makes her long to have a husband too.

ŚAKUNTALĀ: You're just speaking your own secret wish. [*Saying this, she pours water from the jar.*]

KING: Could her social class be different from her father's?[9] There's no 195 doubt!

---

7. The characters of the two friends correspond to their names: Anasūyā (Without Envy) is a serious, straightforward, decisive young woman, while Priyamvadā (Sweet Talker) loves to tease and laugh and has a way with words. As noted above, the women speak Prakrit, whereas the king and other upper-class male characters speak Sanskrit.

8. In calling the jasmine creeper *svayamvara-vadhū* (bride by her own choice), Anasūyā refers to the public ceremony called *svayamvara* (choosing one's own bridegroom) in which women of the warrior class chose their own husbands, thus foreshadowing Śakuntalā's action later in the play.

9. Marrying outside one's class in the fourfold Hindu scheme of classes (*varṇa*) is forbidden. As the sage Kaṇva's daughter, Śakuntalā would be a *brāhmaṇa*, and the king, being of the *kṣatriya* (warrior) class, would not be allowed to marry her.

> She was born to be a warrior's bride,
> for my noble heart desires her—
> when good men face doubt,
> inner feelings are truth's only measure. 200

Still, I must learn everything about her.

ŚAKUNTALĀ: [Flustered.] The splashing water has alarmed a bee. He is flying from the jasmine to my face. [She dances to show the bee's attack.]

KING: [Looking longingly.]

> Bee, you touch the quivering
> corners of her frightened eyes, 205
> you hover softly near
> to whisper secrets in her ear;
> a hand brushes you away,
> but you drink her lips' treasure—
> while the truth we seek defeats us, 210
> you are truly blessed.

ŚAKUNTALĀ: This dreadful bee won't stop. I must escape. [She steps to one side, glancing about.] Oh! He's pursuing me.... Save me! Please save me! This mad bee is chasing me!

BOTH FRIENDS: [Laughing.] How can we save you? Call King Duşyanta. 215 The grove is under his protection.

KING: Here's my chance. Have no fear ... [With this half-spoken, he stops and speaks to himself.] Then she will know that I am the king.... Still, I shall speak.

ŚAKUNTALĀ: [Stopping after a few steps.] Why is he still following me? 220

KING: [Approaching quickly.]

> While a Puru king rules the earth
> to punish evildoers,
> who dares to molest
> these innocent young ascetics?

[Seeing the KING, all act flustered.]

ANASŪYĀ: Sir, there's no real danger. Our friend was frightened when 225 a bee attacked her. [She points to ŚAKUNTALĀ.]

KING: [Approaching ŚAKUNTALĀ.] Does your ascetic practice go well? [ŚAKUNTALĀ stands speechless.]

ANASŪYĀ: It does now that we have a special guest. Śakuntalā, go to our hut and bring the ripe fruits. We'll use this water to bathe his feet.[1] 230

KING: Your kind speech is hospitality enough.

PRIYAMVADĀ: Please sit in the cool shadows of this shade tree and rest, sir.

1. A traditionally mandated rite of hospitality.

KING: You must also be tired from your work.

ANASŪYĀ: Śakuntalā, we should respect our guest. Let's sit down. [*All 235 sit.*]

ŚAKUNTALĀ: [*To herself.*] When I see him, why do I feel an emotion that the forest seems to forbid?

KING: [*Looking at each of the girls.*] Youth and beauty complement your friendship.

PRIYAṂVADĀ: [*In a stage whisper.*] Anasūyā, who is he? He's so polite, 240 fine looking, and pleasing to hear. He has the marks of royalty.

ANASŪYĀ: I'm curious too, friend. I'll just ask him. [*Aloud.*] Sir, your kind speech inspires trust. What family of royal sages do you adorn? What country mourns your absence? Why does a man of refinement subject himself to the discomfort of visiting an ascetics' grove?[2] 245

ŚAKUNTALĀ: [*To herself.*] Heart, don't faint! Anasūyā speaks your thoughts.

KING: [*To himself.*] Should I reveal myself now or conceal who I am? I'll say it this way: [*Aloud.*] Lady, I have been appointed by the Puru king as the officer in charge of religious matters. I have come to this 250 sacred forest to assure that your holy rites proceed unhindered.

ANASŪYĀ: Our religious life has a guardian now.

[ŚAKUNTALĀ *mimes the embarrassment of erotic emotion.*]

BOTH FRIENDS: [*Observing the behavior of* ŚAKUNTALĀ *and the* KING; *in a stage whisper.*] Śakuntalā, if only your father were here now!

ŚAKUNTALĀ: [*Angrily.*] What if he were?

BOTH FRIENDS: He would honor this distinguished guest with what he 255 values most in life.

ŚAKUNTALĀ: Quiet! Such words hint at your hearts' conspiracy. I won't listen.

KING: Ladies, I want to ask about your friend.

BOTH FRIENDS: Your request honors us, sir. 260

KING: Sage Kaṇva has always been celibate, but you call your friend his daughter. How can this be?

ANASŪYĀ: Please listen, sir. There was a powerful royal sage[3] of the Kauśika clan . . .

KING: I am listening. 265

ANASŪYĀ: He begot our friend, but Kaṇva is her father because he cared for her when she was abandoned.

KING: "Abandoned"? The word makes me curious. I want to hear her story from the beginning.

ANASŪYĀ: Please listen, sir. Once when this great sage was practicing 270 terrible austerities on the bank of the Gautamī river, he became so powerful that the jealous gods sent a nymph named Menakā to break his self-control.[4]

KING: The gods dread men who meditate.

---

2. Anasūyā uses the formal, florid style of courtly conversation.
3. Viśvāmitra, who was born in the warrior class but acquired the spiritual powers of a *brāhmaṇa* sage.

4. A standard theme in classical Indian mythology, appearing in the narratives of the life of the Buddha as well. The gods feel threatened by the supernatural powers that ascetics amass through self-denial.

ANASŪYĀ: When springtime came to the forest with all its charm, the   275
sage saw her intoxicating beauty . . .
KING: I understand what happened then. She is the nymph's daughter.
ANASŪYĀ: Yes.
KING: It had to be!

> No mortal woman could give birth to such beauty—   280
> lightning does not flash out of the earth.

[ŚAKUNTALĀ *stands with her face bowed. The* KING *continues speaking
to himself.*]
My desire is not hopeless. Yet, when I hear her friends teasing her
about a bridegroom, a new fear divides my heart.
PRIYAMVADĀ: [*Smiling, looking at* ŚAKUNTALĀ, *then turning to the* KING.]
Sir, you seem to want to say more.
[ŚAKUNTALĀ *makes a threatening gesture with her finger.*]
KING: You judge correctly. In my eagerness to learn more about your   285
pious lives, I have another question.
PRIYAMVADĀ: Don't hesitate! Ascetics can be questioned frankly.
KING: I want to know this about your friend:

> Will she keep the vow of hermit life
> only until she marries . . .   290
> or will she always exchange
> loving looks with deer in the forest?

PRIYAMVADĀ: Sir, even in her religious life, she is subject to her father,
but he does intend to give her to a suitable husband.
KING: [*To himself.*] His wish is not hard to fulfill.   295

> Heart, indulge your desire—
> now that doubt is dispelled,
> the fire you feared to touch
> is a jewel in your hands.

ŚAKUNTALĀ: [*Showing anger.*] Anasūyā, I'm leaving!   300
ANASŪYĀ: Why?
ŚAKUNTALĀ: I'm going to tell Mother Gautamī that Priyamvadā is talk-
ing nonsense.
ANASŪYĀ: Friend, it's wrong to neglect a distinguished guest and leave
as you like.[5]   305
[ŚAKUNTALĀ *starts to go without answering.*]
KING: [*Wanting to seize her, but holding back, he speaks to himself.*] A
lover dare not act on his impulsive thoughts!

> I wanted to follow the sage's daughter,
> but decorum abruptly pulled me back;

5. Śakuntalā's failure here foreshadows her neglect of this duty and its consequences later in the
play.

I set out and returned again   310
    without moving my feet from this spot.

PRIYAMVADĀ: [Stopping ŚAKUNTALĀ.] It's wrong of you to go!
ŚAKUNTALĀ: [Bending her brow into a frown.] Give me a reason why!
PRIYAMVADĀ: You promised to water two trees for me. Come here and
pay your debt before you go! [She stops her by force.]   315
KING: But she seems exhausted from watering the trees:

        Her shoulders droop, her palms
        are red from the watering pot—
        even now, breathless sighs
        make her breasts shake;   320
        beads of sweat on her face
        wilt the flower at her ear;
        her hand holds back
        disheveled locks of hair.

Here, I'll pay her debt!   325
[He offers his ring. Both friends recite the syllables of the name on
the seal and stare at each other.][6]
Don't mistake me for what I am not! This is a gift from the king to
identify me as his royal official.
PRIYAMVADĀ: Then the ring should never leave your finger. Your word
has already paid her debt. [She laughs a little.] Śakuntalā, you are
freed by this kind man . . . or perhaps by the king. Go now!   330
ŚAKUNTALĀ: [To herself.] If I am able to . . . [Aloud.] Who are you to
keep me or release me?
KING: [Watching ŚAKUNTALĀ.] Can she feel toward me what I feel
toward her? Or is my desire fulfilled?

        She won't respond directly to my words,   335
        but she listens when I speak;
        she won't turn to look at me,
        but her eyes can't rest anywhere else.

VOICE OFFSTAGE: Ascetics, be prepared to protect the creatures of our
forest grove! King Duṣyanta is hunting nearby!   340

        Dust raised by his horses' hooves
        falls like a cloud of locusts swarming
        at sunset over branches of trees
        where wet bark garments hang.

        In terror of the chariots, an elephant   345
        charged into the hermitage
        and scattered the herd of black antelope,
        like a demon foe of our penances—

6. A clear indication that women were part of the literate courtly culture of classical India.

his tusks garlanded with branches
from a tree crushed by his weight,   350
his feet tangled in vines
that tether him like chains.

[*Hearing this, all the girls are agitated.*]

KING: [*To himself.*] Oh! My palace men are searching for me and
wrecking the grove. I'll have to go back.

BOTH FRIENDS: Sir, we're all upset by this news. Please let us go to our   355
hut.

KING: [*Showing confusion.*] Go, please. We will try to protect the
hermitage.
[*They all stand to go.*]

BOTH FRIENDS: Sir, we're ashamed that our bad hospitality is our only
excuse to invite you back.   360

KING: Not at all. I am honored to have seen you.
[*ŚAKUNTALĀ exits with her two friends, looking back at the* KING,
lingering artfully.]
I have little desire to return to the city. I'll join my men and have
them camp near the grove. I can't control my feelings for Śakuntalā.

My body turns to go,
my heart pulls me back,   365
like a silk banner
buffeted by the wind.
[*All exit.*]

Act II

[*The* BUFFOON *enters, despondent.*]

BUFFOON: [*Sighing.*] My bad luck! I'm tired of playing sidekick to a
king who's hooked on hunting.[7] "There's a deer!" "There's a boar!"
"There's a tiger!" Even in the summer midday heat we chase from
jungle to jungle on paths where trees give barely any shade. We drink
stinking water from mountain streams foul with rusty leaves. At odd   5
hours we eat nasty meals of spit-roasted meat. Even at night I can't
sleep. My joints ache from galloping on that horse. Then at the
crack of dawn, I'm woken rudely by a noise piercing the forest.
Those sons of bitches hunt their birds then. The torture doesn't
end—now I have sores on top of my bruises. Yesterday, we lagged   10
behind. The king chased a buck into the hermitage. As luck would
have it, an ascetic's daughter called Śakuntalā caught his eye. Now
he isn't even thinking of going back to the city. This very dawn I
found him wide-eyed, mooning about her. What a fate! I must see
him after his bath. [*He walks around, looking.*] Here comes my   15

7. The *brāhmaṇa vidūṣaka* (buffoon), though
the king's constant companion, differs from him
in every respect, from his obsession with creature comforts and his cowardice to his coarse
language. A caricature of the learned *brāhmaṇa*
and Sanskrit scholar, the buffoon speaks only
Prakrit and is incapable of versifying.

friend now, wearing garlands of wild flowers. Greek women carry his
bow in their hands.[8] Good! I'll stand here pretending my arms and
legs are broken. Maybe then I'll get some rest.

> [*He stands leaning on his staff. The* KING *enters with his retinue, as
> described.*]

KING: [*To himself.*]

> My beloved will not be easy to win,
> but signs of emotion revealed her heart—   20
> even when love seems hopeless,
> mutual longing keeps passion alive.

[*He smiles.*] A suitor who measures his beloved's state of mind by his
own desire is a fool.

> She threw tender glances   25
> though her eyes were cast down,
> her heavy hips swayed
> in slow seductive movements.
> she answered in anger
> when her friend said, "Don't go!"   30
> and I felt it was all for my sake . . .
> but a lover sees in his own way.

BUFFOON: [*Still in the same position.*] Dear friend, since my hands
can't move to greet you, I have to salute you with my voice.

KING: How did you cripple your limbs?   35

BUFFOON: Why do you ask why I cry after throwing dust in my eyes
yourself?

KING: I don't understand.

BUFFOON: Dear friend, when a straight reed is twisted into a crooked
reed, is it by its own power, or is it the river current?[9]   40

KING: The river current is the cause.

BUFFOON: And so it is with me.

KING: How so?

BUFFOON: You neglect the business of being a king and live like a
woodsman in this awful camp. Chasing after wild beasts every day   45
jolts my joints and muscles till I can't control my own limbs anymore.
I beg you to let me rest for just one day!

KING: [*To himself.*] He says what I also feel. When I remember Kaṇva's daughter, the thought of hunting disgusts me.

> I can't draw my bowstring   50
> to shoot arrows at deer

8. In Kālidāsa's plays the king's bow bearers
are identified as *yavanī* (Greek women). North
Indian kings of the Gupta age and earlier
employed Bactrian Greek women as body-
guards and bow bearers.

9. Like Shakespeare's fools, the buffoon likes
to speak in riddles.

who live with my love
and teach her tender glances.[1]

BUFFOON: Sir, you have something on your mind. I'm crying in a
wilderness.[2]   55

KING: [Smiling.] Yes, it is wrong to ignore my friend's plea.

BUFFOON: Live long! [He starts to go.]

KING: Dear friend, stay! Hear what I have to say!

BUFFOON: At your command, sir!

KING: When you have rested, I need your help in some work that you   60
will enjoy.

BUFFOON: Is it eating sweets? I'm game!

KING: I shall tell you. Who stands guard?

GUARD: [Entering.] At your command, sir!

KING: Raivataka! Summon the general!   65

[The GUARD exits and reenters with the GENERAL.]

GUARD: The king is looking this way, waiting to give you his orders.
Approach him, sir!

GENERAL: [Looking at the KING.] Hunting is said to be a vice,[3] but our
king prospers.

> Drawing the bow only hardens his chest,   70
> he suffers the sun's scorching rays unburned,
> hard muscles mask his body's lean state
> like a wild elephant, his energy sustains him.

[He approaches the KING.] Victory, my lord! We've already tracked
some wild beasts. Why the delay?   75

KING: Māḍhavya's[4] censure of hunting has dampened my spirit.

GENERAL: [In a stage whisper, to the BUFFOON.] Friend, you stick to
your opposition! I'll try to restore our king's good sense. [Aloud.] This
fool is talking nonsense. Here is the king as proof:

> A hunter's belly is taut and lean,   80
> his slender body craves exertion;
> he penetrates the spirit of creatures
> overcome by fear and rage;
> his bowmanship is proved
> by arrows striking a moving target—   85
> hunting is falsely called a vice.
> What sport can rival it?

BUFFOON: [Angrily.] The king has come to his senses. If you keep
chasing from forest to forest, you'll fall into the jaws of an old bear
hungry for a human nose . . .   90

---

1. A comparison of women's eyes with the
eyes of deer, conventional in Sanskrit poetry.
2. A paraphrase of the Sanskrit proverbial
expression araṇyaruditām (a cry in the wilderness); this is an expression of his puzzlement
at the king's behavior.
3. The censure of hunting in Hindu law reflects
the influence of the theory of karma and rebirth
and the impact of nonviolent creeds.
4. The buffoon's.

KING: My noble general, we are near a hermitage; your words cannot please me now.

> Let horned buffaloes plunge into muddy pools!
> Let herds of deer huddle in the shade to eat grass!
> Let fearless wild boars crush fragrant swamp grass! 95
> Let my bowstring lie slack and my bow at rest!

GENERAL: Whatever gives the king pleasure.

KING: Withdraw the men who are in the forest now and forbid my soldiers to disturb the grove!

> Ascetics devoted to peace 100
> possess a fiery hidden power,
> like smooth crystal sunstones
> that reflect the sun's scorching rays.

GENERAL: Whatever you command, sir!

BUFFOON: Your arguments for keeping up the hunt fall on deaf ears! 105
[*The* GENERAL *exits.*]

KING: [*Looking at his* RETINUE.] You women, take away my hunting gear! Raivataka, don't neglect your duty!

RETINUE: As the king commands!
[*They exit.*]

BUFFOON: Sir, now that the flies are cleared out, sit on a stone bench under this shady canopy. Then I'll find a comfortable seat too. 110

KING: Go ahead!

BUFFOON: You first, sir!
[*Both walk about, then sit down.*]

KING: Mādhavya, you haven't really used your eyes because you haven't seen true beauty.

BUFFOON: But you're right in front of me, sir! 115

KING: Everyone is partial to what he knows well, but I'm speaking about Śakuntalā, the jewel of the hermitage.

BUFFOON: [*To himself.*] I won't give him a chance! [*Aloud.*] Dear friend, it seems that you're pursuing an ascetic's daughter.

KING: Friend, the heart of a Puru king wouldn't crave a forbidden 120 fruit . . .

> The sage's child is a nymph's daughter,
> rescued by him after she was abandoned,
> like a fragile jasmine blossom
> broken and caught on a sunflower pod. 125

BUFFOON: [*Laughing.*] You're like the man who loses his taste for dates and prefers sour tamarind!⁵ How can you abandon the gorgeous gems of your palace?

KING: You speak this way because you haven't seen her.

5. A fruit, the extract of which is used to flavor Indian sauces.

BUFFOON: She must be delectable if you're so enticed!   130
KING: Friend, what is the use of all this talk?

> The divine creator imagined perfection
> and shaped her ideal form in his mind—
> when I recall the beauty his power wrought,
> she shines like a gemstone among my jewels.   135

BUFFOON: So she's the reason you reject the other beauties!
KING: She stays in my mind:

> A flower no one has smelled,
> a bud no fingers have plucked,
> an uncut jewel, honey untasted,   140
> unbroken fruit of holy deeds—
> I don't know who is destined
> to enjoy her flawless beauty.

BUFFOON: Then you should rescue her quickly! Don't let her fall into
the arms of some ascetic who greases his head with iṅgudī oil!   145
KING: She is someone else's ward and her guardian is away.
BUFFOON: What kind of passion did her eyes betray?
KING: Ascetics are timid by nature:

> Her eyes were cast down in my presence,
> but she found an excuse to smile—   150
> modesty barely contained the love
> she could neither reveal nor conceal.

BUFFOON: Did you expect her to climb into your lap when she'd barely
seen you?
KING: When we parted her feelings for me showed despite her mod-   155
esty.

> "A blade of kuśa grass[6]
> pricked my foot,"
> the girl said for no reason
> after walking a few steps away;   160
> then she pretended to free
> her bark dress from branches
> where it was not caught
> and shyly glanced at me.

BUFFOON: Stock up on food for a long trip! I can see you've turned that   165
ascetics' grove into a pleasure garden.
KING: Friend, some of the ascetics recognize me. What excuse can we
find to return to the hermitage?

6. Used in Hindu sacred rites.

BUFFOON: What excuse? Aren't you the king? Collect a sixth of their
wild rice as tax! 170

KING: Fool! These ascetics pay tribute that pleases me more than
mounds of jewels.

> Tribute that kings collect
> from members of society decays,
> but the share of austerity 175
> that ascetics give lasts forever.[7]

VOICE OFFSTAGE: Good, we have succeeded!

KING: [Listening.] These are the steady, calm voices of ascetics.

GUARD: [Entering.] Victory, sir! Two boy ascetics are waiting near the
gate. 180

KING: Let them enter without delay!

GUARD: I'll show them in. [He exits; reenters with the boys.] Here you
are!

FIRST BOY: His majestic body inspires trust. It is natural when a king is
virtually a sage.[8] 185

> His palace is a hermitage
> with its infinite pleasures,
> the discipline of protecting men
> imposes austerities every day—
> pairs of celestial bards praise 190
> his perfect self-control,
> adding the royal word "king"
> to "sage," his sacred title.

SECOND BOY: Gautama, is this Duṣyanta, the friend of Indra?[9]

FIRST BOY: Of course! 195

SECOND BOY:

> It is no surprise that this arm of iron
> rules the whole earth bounded by dark seas—
> when demons harass the gods, victory's hope
> rests on his bow and Indra's thunderbolt.

BOTH BOYS: [Coming near.] Victory to you, king! 200

KING: [Rising from his seat.] I salute you both!

BOTH BOYS: To your success, sir! [They offer fruits.]

KING: [Accepting their offering.] I am ready to listen.

BOTH BOYS: The ascetics know that you are camped nearby and send
a petition to you. 205

7. The king values the sacred power that the
sages amass through self-denial.
8. While Duṣyanta may appear worldly to a
modern audience, his sacred royal office, his
respect for the sages, and his disciplined
adherence to the standards of dharma make
him, in the sages' eyes, a person of tremendous self-control.
9. His friendship with Indra underscores the
king's status as the earthly counterpart of the
king of the gods.

KING: What do they request?

BOTH BOYS: Demons are taking advantage of Sage Kaṇva's absence to harass us.[1] You must come with your charioteer to protect the hermitage for a few days!

KING: I am honored to oblige. 210

BUFFOON: [In a stage whisper.] Your wish is fulfilled!

KING: [Smiling.] Raivataka, call my charioteer! Tell him to bring the chariot and my bow!

GUARD: As the king commands! [He exits.]

BOTH BOYS: [Showing delight.]

> Following your ancestral duties 215
> suits your noble from—
> the Puru kings are ordained
> to dispel their subjects' fear.

KING: [Bowing.] You two return! I shall follow.

BOTH BOYS: Be victorious! [They exit.] 220

KING: Mādhavya, are you curious to see Śakuntalā?

BUFFOON: At first there was a flood, but now with this news of demons, not a drop is left.

KING: Don't be afraid! Won't you be with me?

BUFFOON: Then I'll be safe from any demon . . . 225

GUARD: [Entering.] The chariot is ready to take you to victory . . . but Karabhaka has just come from the city with a message from the queen.

KING: Did my mother send him?

GUARD: She did. 230

KING: Have him enter then.

GUARD: Yes. [He exits; reenters with KARABHAKA.] Here is the king. Approach!

KARABHAKA: Victory, sir! Victory! The queen has ordered a ceremony four days from now to mark the end of her fast. Your Majesty will 235 surely give us the honor of his presence.

KING: The ascetics' business keeps me here and my mother's command calls me there. I must find a way to avoid neglecting either!

BUFFOON: Hang yourself between them the way Triśaṅku[2] hung between heaven and earth. 240

KING: I'm really confused . . .

> My mind is split in two
> by these conflicting duties,
> like a river current split
> by boulders in its course. 245

---

1. The motif of a royal hero slaying demons who destroy the sacred rituals of forest sages is traditional.
2. A mythic king who was left suspended between heaven and earth in a contest of power between the sage Viśvāmitra and the gods.

[*Thinking.*] Friend, my mother has treated you like a son. You must go back and report that I've set my heart on fulfilling my duty to the ascetics. You fulfill my filial duty to the queen.

BUFFOON: You don't really think I'm afraid of demons?

KING: [*Smiling.*] My brave brahman, how could you be?   250

BUFFOON: Then I can travel like the king's younger brother.

KING: We really should not disturb the grove! Take my whole entourage with you!

BUFFOON: Now I've turned into the crown prince!

KING: [*To himself.*] This fellow is absent-minded. At any time he may   255
tell the palace women about my passion. I'll tell him this: [*Taking the* BUFFOON *by the hand, he speaks aloud.*] Dear friend, I'm going to the hermitage out of reverence for the sages. I really feel no desire for the young ascetic Śakuntalā.

> What do I share with a rustic girl   260
> reared among fawns, unskilled in love?
> Don't mistake what I muttered
> in jest for the real truth, friend!

[*All exit.*]

Act III

[*A disciple of* KAṆVA *enters, carrying kuśa grass for a sacrificial rite.*]

DISCIPLE: King Duṣyanta is certainly powerful. Since he entered the hermitage, our rites have not been hindered.

> Why talk of fixing arrows?
> The mere twang of his bowstring
> clears away menacing demons   5
> as if his bow roared with death.

I'll gather some more grass for the priests to spread on the sacrificial altar. [*Walking around and looking, he calls aloud.*] Priyaṁvadā, for whom are you bringing the ointment of fragrant lotus root fibers and leaves? [*Listening.*] What are you saying? Śakuntalā is suffering   10
from heat exhaustion? They're for rubbing on her body? Priyaṁvadā, take care of her! She is the breath of Father Kaṇva's life. I'll give Gautamī this water from the sacrifice to use for soothing her.

[*He exits; the interlude ends. Then the* KING *enters, suffering from love, deep in thought, sighing.*]

KING:

> I know the power ascetics have
> and the rules that bind her,
> but I cannot abandon my heart   15
> now that she has taken it.

[*Showing the pain of love.*] Love, why do you and the moon both contrive to deceive lovers by first gaining our trust?

Arrows of flowers and cool moon rays   20
are both deadly for men like me—
the moon shoots fire through icy rays
and you hurl thunderbolts of flowers.

[*Walking around.*] Now that the rites are concluded and the priests
have dismissed me, where can I rest from the weariness of this   25
work? [*Sighing.*] There is no refuge but the sight of my love. I must
find her. [*Looking up at the sun.*] Śakuntalā usually spends the heat
of the day with her friends in a bower of vines on the Mālinī riverbank. I shall go there. [*Walking around, miming the touch of breeze.*]
This place is enchanted by the wind.   30

A breeze fragrant with lotus pollen
and moist from the Mālinī waves
can be held in soothing embrace
by my love-scorched arms.

[*Walking around and looking.*]

I see fresh footprints   35
on white sand in the clearing,
deeply pressed at the heel
by the sway of full hips.

I'll just look through the branches. [*Walking around, looking, he
becomes joyous.*] My eyes have found bliss! The girl I desire is lying   40
on a stone couch strewn with flowers, attended by her two friends.
I'll eavesdrop as they confide in one another. [*He stands watching.
ŚAKUNTALĀ appears as described, with her two friends.*]
BOTH FRIENDS: [*Fanning her affectionately.*] Śakuntalā, does the breeze
from this lotus leaf please you?
ŚAKUNTALĀ: Are you fanning me?   45
[*The friends trade looks, miming dismay.*]
KING: [*Deliberating.*] Śakuntalā seems to be in great physical pain. Is
it the heat or is it what is in my own heart? [*Miming ardent desire.*]
My doubts are unfounded!

Her breasts are smeared with lotus balm,
her lotus-fiber bracelet hangs limp,   50
her beautiful body glows in pain—
love burns young women like summer heat
but its guilt makes them more charming.

PRIYAMVADĀ: [*In a stage whisper.*] Anasūyā, Śakuntalā has been pining
since she first saw the king. Could he be the cause of her sickness?   55
ANASŪYĀ: She must be suffering from lovesickness. I'll ask her . . .
[*Aloud.*] Friend, I have something to ask you. Your pain seems so
deep . . .

ŚAKUNTALĀ: [*Raising herself halfway.*] What do you want to say?

ANASŪYĀ: Śakuntalā, though we don't know what it is to be in love,   60
your condition reminds us of lovers we have heard about in stories.
Can you tell us the cause of your pain? Unless we understand your
illness, we can't begin to find a cure.

KING: Anasūyā expresses my own thoughts.

ŚAKUNTALĀ: Even though I want to, suddenly I can't make myself tell   65
you.

PRIYAMVADĀ: Śakuntalā, my friend Anasūyā means well. Don't you see
how sick you are? Your limbs are wasting away. Only the shadow of
your beauty remains . . .

KING: What Priyamvadā says is true: 70

> Her cheeks are deeply sunken,
> her breasts' full shape is gone,
> her waist is thin, her shoulders bent,
> and the color has left her skin—
> tormented by love,   75
> she is sad but beautiful to see,
> like a jasmine creeper
> when hot wind shrivels its leaves.

ŚAKUNTALĀ: Friends, who else can I tell? May I burden you?

BOTH FRIENDS: We insist! Sharing sorrow with loving friends makes it   80
bearable.

KING:

> Friends who share her joy and sorrow
> discover the love concealed in her heart—
> though she looked back longingly at me,
> now I am afraid to hear her response.   85

ŚAKUNTALĀ: Friend, since my eyes first saw the guardian of the hermits'
retreat, I've felt such strong desire for him!

KING: I have heard what I want to hear.

> My tormentor, the god of love,
> has soothed my fever himself,   90
> like the heat of late summer
> allayed by early rain clouds.

ŚAKUNTALĀ: If you two think it's right, then help me to win the
king's pity. Otherwise, you'll soon pour sesame oil and water[3] on my
corpse . . .   95

KING: Her words destroy my doubt.

---

3. Offerings to the dead in Hindu funeral rites. Śakuntalā and her friends have learned of the
king's real identity, because the hermits have asked him to guard their hermitage from demons.

PRIYAMVADĀ: [*In a stage whisper.*] She's so dangerously in love that there's no time to lose. Since her heart is set on the ornament of the Puru dynasty, we should rejoice that she desires him.

ANASŪYĀ: What you say is true. 100

PRIYAMVADĀ: [*Aloud.*] Friend, by good fortune your desire is in harmony with nature. A great river can only descend to the ocean. A jasmine creeper can only twine around a mango tree.

KING: Why is this surprising when the twin stars of spring serve the crescent moon?[4] 105

ANASŪYĀ: What means do we have to fulfill our friend's desire secretly and quickly?

PRIYAMVADĀ: "Secretly" demands some effort. "Quickly" is easy.

ANASŪYĀ: How so?

PRIYAMVADĀ: The king was charmed by her loving look; he seems thin 110 these days from sleepless nights.

KING: It's true . . .

> This golden armlet
> slips to my wrist
> without touching the scars 115
> my bowstring has made;
> its gemstones are faded
> by tears of secret pain
> that every night wets my arm
> where I bury my face. 120

PRIYAMVADĀ: [*Thinking.*] Compose a love letter and I'll hide it in a flower. I'll deliver it to his hand on the pretext of bringing an offering to the deity.

ANASŪYĀ: This subtle plan pleases me. What does Śakuntalā say?

ŚAKUNTALĀ: I'll try my friend's plan. 125

PRIYAMVADĀ: Then compose a poem to declare your love!

ŚAKUNTALĀ: I'm thinking, but my heart trembles with fear that he'll reject me.

KING: [*Delighted.*]

> The man you fear will reject you
> waits longing to love you, timid girl— 130
> a suitor may lose or be lucky,
> but the goddess always wins.

BOTH FRIENDS: Why do you belittle your own virtues? Who would cover his body with a piece of cloth to keep off cool autumn moonlight? 135

ŚAKUNTALĀ: [*Smiling.*] I'm trying to follow your advice. [*She sits thinking.*]

---

4. The king refers metaphorically to the two friends attending Śakuntalā as stars attending a young moon that is waning.

KING: As I gaze at her, my eyes forget to blink.

> She arches an eyebrow,
> struggling to compose the verse—
> the down rises on her cheek,   140
> showing the passion she feels.[5]

ŚAKUNTALĀ: I've thought of a verse, but I have nothing to write it on.

PRIYAMVADĀ: Engrave the letters with your nail on this lotus leaf! It's
as delicate as a parrot's breast.

ŚAKUNTALĀ: [*Miming what* PRIYAMVADĀ *described.*] Listen and tell me   145
this makes sense!

BOTH FRIENDS: We're both paying attention.

ŚAKUNTALĀ: [*Singing.*]

> I don't know
> your heart,
> but day and night   150
> for wanting you,
> love violently
> tortures
> my limbs,
> cruel man.   155

KING: [*Suddenly revealing himself.*]

> Love torments you, slender girl,
> but he completely consumes me—
> daylight spares the lotus pond
> while it destroys the moon.

BOTH FRIENDS: [*Looking, rising with delight.*] Welcome to the swift   160
success of love's desire!
[ŚAKUNTALĀ *tries to rise.*]

KING: Don't exert yourself!

> Limbs lying among crushed petals
> like fragile lotus stalks
> are too weakened by pain   165
> to perform ceremonious acts.

ANASŪYĀ: Then let the king sit on this stone bench!
[*The* KING *sits;* ŚAKUNTALĀ *rises in embarrassment.*]

PRIYAMVADĀ: The passion of two young lovers is clear. My affection for
our friend makes me speak out again now.[6]

---

5. Such quivering of the cheek is held to be a
sign of inner emotion, which the actress is
supposed to be able to represent.

6. Śakuntalā's modesty and good breeding
prevent her from making her own declaration
of love.

KING: Noble lady, don't hesitate! It is painful to keep silent when one   170
must speak.

PRIYAMVADĀ: We're told that it is the king's duty to ease the pain of his
suffering subjects.

KING: My duty, exactly!

PRIYAMVADĀ: Since she first saw you, our dear friend has been reduced   175
to this sad condition. You must protect her and save her life.

KING: Noble lady, our affection is shared and I am honored by all you
say.

ŚAKUNTALĀ: [*Looking at* PRIYAMVADĀ.] Why are you keeping the king
here? He must be anxious to return to his palace.   180

KING:

> If you think that my lost heart
> could love anyone but you,
> a fatal blow strikes a man
> already wounded by love's arrows!

ANASŪYĀ: We've heard that kings have many loves. Will our dear   185
friend become a sorrow to her family after you've spent time with
her?

KING: Noble lady, enough of this!

> Despite my many wives,
> on two the royal line rests—   190
> sea-bound earth
> and your friend.[7]

BOTH FRIENDS: You reassure us.

PRIYAMVADĀ: [*Casting a glance.*] Anasūyā, this fawn is looking for its
mother. Let's take it to her!   195
[*They both begin to leave.*]

ŚAKUNTALĀ: Come back! Don't leave me unprotected!

BOTH FRIENDS: The protector of the earth is at your side.

ŚAKUNTALĀ: Why have they gone?

KING: Don't be alarmed! I am your servant.

> Shall I set moist winds in motion   200
> with lotus-leaf fans to cool your pain,
> or rest your soft red lotus feet[8]
> on my lap to stroke them, my love?

ŚAKUNTALĀ: I cannot sin against those I respect!
[*Standing as if she wants to leave.*]

7. Royal polygamy was common in ancient India; it served to make and cement political alliances. Here the king speaks of the conventional ideal of a ruler's two "chief queens": the royal consort, whose son will inherit the king-dom, and the earth, personified as the king's spouse.

8. A common metaphor for feet in Indian verse.

KING: Beautiful Śakuntalā, the day is still hot.   205

> Why should your frail limbs
> leave this couch of flowers
> shielded by lotus leaves
> to wander in the heat?

[*Saying this, he forces her to turn around.*]

ŚAKUNTALĀ: Puru king, control yourself! Though I'm burning with   210
love, how can I give myself to you?

KING: Don't fear your elders! The father of your family knows the law.
When he finds out, he will not blame you.

> The daughters of royal sages often marry
> in secret[9] and then their fathers bless them.   215

ŚAKUNTALĀ: Release me! I must ask my friends' advice!

KING: Yes, I shall release you.

ŚAKUNTALĀ: When?

KING:

> Only let my thirsting mouth
> gently drink from your lips,   220
> the way a bee sips nectar
> from a fragile virgin blossom.

[*Saying this, he tries to raise her face.* ŚAKUNTALĀ *evades him with a dance.*]

VOICE OFFSTAGE: Red goose,[1] bid farewell to your gander! Night has
arrived!

ŚAKUNTALĀ: [*Flustered.*] Puru king, Mother Gautamī is surely coming   225
to ask about my health. Hide behind this tree!

KING: Yes.

> [*He conceals himself and waits. Then* GAUTAMĪ *enters with a vessel
> in her hand, accompanied by* ŚAKUNTALĀ's *two friends.*]

BOTH FRIENDS: This way, Mother Gautamī!

GAUTAMĪ: [*Approaching* ŚAKUNTALĀ.] Child, does the fever in your
limbs burn less?   230

ŚAKUNTALĀ: Madam, I do feel better.

GAUTAMĪ: Kuśa grass and water will soothe your body. [*She sprinkles*
ŚAKUNTALĀ's *head.*] Child, the day is ended. Come, let's go back to
our hut! [*She starts to go.*]

ŚAKUNTALĀ: [*To herself.*] My heart, even when your desire was within   235
reach, you were bound by fear. Now you'll suffer the torment of
separation and regret. [*Stopping after a few steps, she speaks aloud.*]

---

9. The *gāndharva* form of marriage, a secret
marriage of mutual consent, was permitted for
the warrior class. By the beginning of Act IV
this has taken place.

1. Also known as the sheldrake (*cakravāka*).
In Sanskrit poetry, separated lovers are symbolized by these birds, subject to a curse that
separates them from their mates every night.

Bower of creepers, refuge from my torment, I say goodbye until our
joy can be renewed . . . [*Sorrowfully,* ŚAKUNTALĀ *exits with the other
women.*]

KING: [*Coming out of hiding.*] Fulfillment of desire is fraught with   240
obstacles.

> Why didn't I kiss her face
> as it bent near my shoulder,
> her fingers shielding lips
> that stammered lovely warning?   245

Should I go now? Or shall I stay here in this bower of creepers that
my love enjoyed and then left?

> I see the flowers her body pressed
> on this bench of stone,
> the letter her nails inscribed   250
> on the faded lotus leaf,
> the lotus-fiber bracelet
> that slipped from her wrist—
> my eyes are prisoners
> in this empty house of reeds.   255

VOICE IN THE AIR: King!

> When the evening rituals begin,
> shadows of flesh-eating demons swarm
> like amber clouds of twilight,
> raising terror at the altar of fire.   260

KING: I am coming.
    [*He exits.*]

Act IV

[*The two friends enter, miming the gathering of flowers.*]

ANASŪYĀ: Priyamvadā, I'm delighted that Śakuntalā chose a suitable
husband for herself, but I still feel anxious.

PRIYAMVADĀ: Why?

ANASŪYĀ: When the king finished the sacrifice, the sages thanked him
and he left. Now that he has returned to his palace women in the   5
city, will he remember us here?

PRIYAMVADĀ: Have faith! He's so handsome, he can't be evil. But I
don't know what Father Kaṇva will think when he hears about what
happened.

ANASŪYĀ: I predict that he'll give his approval.   10

PRIYAMVADĀ: Why?

ANASŪYĀ: He's always planned to give his daughter to a worthy husband. If fate accomplished it so quickly, Father Kaṇva won't object.

PRIYAṀVADĀ: [*Looking at the basket of flowers.*] We've gathered enough
flowers for the offering ceremony.   15
ANASŪYĀ: Shouldn't we worship the goddess who guards Śakuntalā?
PRIYAṀVADĀ: I have just begun. [*She begins the rite.*]
VOICE OFFSTAGE: I am here!
ANASŪYĀ: [*Listening.*] Friend, a guest is announcing himself.
PRIYAṀVADĀ: Śakuntalā is in her hut nearby, but her heart is far away.   20
ANASŪYĀ: You're right! Enough of these flowers!
        [*They begin to leave.*]
VOICE OFFSTAGE: So . . . you slight a guest . . .

> Since you blindly ignore
> a great sage like me,
> the lover you worship   25
> with mindless devotion
> will not remember you,
> even when awakened—
> like a drunkard who forgets
> a story he just composed!   30

PRIYAṀVADĀ: Oh! What a terrible turn of events! Śakuntalā's distraction has offended someone she should have greeted. [*Looking
ahead.*] Not just an ordinary person, but the angry sage Durvāsas
himself cursed her and went away in a frenzy of quivering, mad
gestures. What else but fire has such power to burn?   35
ANASŪYĀ: Go! Bow at his feet and make him return while I prepare the
water for washing his feet!
PRIYAṀVADĀ: As you say. [*She exits.*]
ANASŪYĀ: [*After a few steps, she mimes stumbling.*] Oh! The basket of
flowers fell from my hand when I stumbled in my haste to go. [*She   40
mimes the gathering of flowers.*]
PRIYAṀVADĀ: [*Entering.*] He's so terribly cruel! No one could pacify
him! But I was able to soften him a little.
ANASŪYĀ: Even that is a great feat with him! Tell me more!
PRIYAṀVADĀ: When he refused to return, I begged him to forgive a
daughter's first offense, since she didn't understand the power of   45
his austerity.
ANASŪYĀ: Then? Then?
PRIYAṀVADĀ: He refused to change his word, but he promised that
when the king sees the ring of recollection, the curse will end. Then
he vanished.   50
ANASŪYĀ: Now we can breathe again. When he left, the king himself
gave her the ring engraved with his name. Śakuntalā will have her
own means of ending the curse.
PRIYAṀVADĀ: Come friend! We should finish the holy rite we're performing for her.   55
        [*The two walk around, looking.*]
Anasūyā, look! With her face resting on her hand, our dear friend
looks like a picture. She is thinking about her husband's leaving,
with no thought for herself, much less for a guest.

ANASŪYĀ: Priyaṁvadā, we two must keep all this a secret between us.
Our friend is fragile by nature; she needs our protection.   60
PRIYAṀVADĀ: Who would sprinkle a jasmine with scalding water?
    [*They both exit: the interlude ends. Then a* DISCIPLE *of* KAṆVA *enters,
just awakened from sleep.*]
DISCIPLE: Father Kaṇva has just returned from his pilgrimage and
wants to know the exact time. I'll go into a clearing to see what
remains of the night. [*Walking around and looking.*] It is dawn.

> The moon sets over the western mountain   65
> as the sun rises in dawn's red trail—
> rising and setting, these two bright powers
> portend the rise and fall of men.
>
> When the moon disappears, night lotuses
> are but dull souvenirs of its beauty—   70
> when her lover disappears, the sorrow
> is too painful for a frail girl to bear.

ANASŪYĀ: [*Throwing aside the curtain and entering.*][2] Even a person
withdrawn from worldly life knows that the king has treated Śakuntalā badly.   75
DISCIPLE: I'll inform Father Kaṇva that it's time for the fire oblation.
[*He exits.*]
ANASŪYĀ: Even when I'm awake, I'm useless. My hands and feet don't
do their work. Love must be pleased to have made our innocent
friend put her trust in a liar . . . but perhaps it was the curse of
Durvāsas that changed him . . . otherwise, how could the king have   80
made such promises and not sent even a message by now? Maybe
we should send the ring to remind him. Which of these ascetics who
practice austerities can we ask? Father Kaṇva has just returned from
his pilgrimage. Since we feel that our friend was also at fault, we
haven't told him that Śakuntalā is married to Duṣyanta and is   85
pregnant. The problem is serious. What should we do?
PRIYAṀVADĀ: [*Entering, with delight.*] Friend, hurry! We're to celebrate
the festival of Śakuntalā's departure for her husband's house.
ANASŪYĀ: What's happened, friend?
PRIYAṀVADĀ: Listen! I went to ask Śakuntalā how she had slept. Father   90
Kaṇva embraced her and though her face was bowed in shame, he
blessed her: "Though his eyes were filled with smoke, the priest's
oblation luckily fell on the fire. My child, I shall not mourn for you
. . . like knowledge given to a good student I shall send you to your
husband today with an escort of sages."   95
ANASŪYĀ: Who told Father Kaṇva what happened?
PRIYAṀVADĀ: A bodiless voice was chanting when he entered the fire
sanctuary. [*Quoting in Sanskrit.*]

2. The *javanikā* (impeller), a curtain hung
over two doors separating the backstage area
from the stage of the ancient Indian play-
house. An agitated entrance was indicated
when, as here, a character entered the stage
by throwing aside the curtain.

Priest, know that your daughter
carries Duṣyanta's potent seed
for the good of the earth—   100
like fire in mimosa[3] wood.

ANASŪYĀ: I'm joyful, friend. But I know that Śakuntalā must leave us
today and sorrow shadows my happiness.

PRIYAMVADĀ: Friend, we must chase away sorrow and make this hermit   105
girl happy!

ANASŪYĀ: Friend, I've made a garland of mimosa flowers. It's in the
coconut-shell box hanging on a branch of the mango tree. Get it for
me! Meanwhile I'll prepare the special ointments of deer musk,
sacred earth, and blades of dūrvā grass.[4]   110

PRIYAMVADĀ: Here it is!

[ANASŪYĀ exits; PRIYAMVADĀ gracefully mimes taking down the box.]

VOICE OFFSTAGE: Gautamī! Śārṅgarava and some others have been
appointed to escort Śakuntalā.

PRIYAMVADĀ: [Listening.] Hurry! Hurry! The sages are being called to
go to Hastināpura.   115

ANASŪYĀ: [Reentering with pots of ointments in her hands.] Come,
friend! Let's go!

PRIYAMVADĀ: [Looking around.] Śakuntalā stands at sunrise with
freshly washed hair while the female ascetics bless her with handfuls
of wild rice and auspicious words of farewell. Let's go to her together. 120

[The two approach as ŚAKUNTALĀ enters with GAUTAMĪ and other
female ascetics, and strikes a posture as described. One after another,
the female ascetics address her.]

FIRST FEMALE ASCETIC: Child, win the title "Chief Queen" as a sign of
your husband's high esteem!

SECOND FEMALE ASCETIC: Child, be a mother to heroes!

THIRD FEMALE ASCETIC: Child, be honored by your husband!

BOTH FRIENDS: This happy moment is no time for tears, friend.   125

[Wiping away her tears, they calm her with dance gestures.]

PRIYAMVADĀ: Your beauty deserves jewels, not these humble things
we've gathered in the hermitage.

[Two boy ascetics enter with offerings in their hands.]

BOTH BOYS: Here is an ornament for you!

[Everyone looks amazed.]

GAUTAMĪ: Nārada, my child, where did this come from?

FIRST BOY: From Father Kaṇva's power.   130

GAUTAMĪ: Was it his mind's magic?

SECOND BOY: Not at all! Listen! You ordered us to bring flowers from
the forest trees for Śakuntalā.

One tree produced this white silk cloth,
another poured resinous lac to redden her feet—   135

3. Here, the samī tree, which Indians con-   of farewell to a young woman moving from her
sider the repository of fire.   father's to her husband's home.
4. Materials prepared by women for the ritual

the tree nymphs produced jewels in hands
that stretched from branches like young shoots.[5]

PRIYAMVADĀ: [*Watching* ŚAKUNTALĀ.] This is a sign that royal fortune
will come to you in your husband's house.
[ŚAKUNTALĀ *mimes modesty.*]

FIRST BOY: Gautama, come quickly! Father Kaṇva is back from bath-   140
ing. We'll tell him how the trees honor her.

SECOND BOY: As you say.
[*The two exit.*]

BOTH FRIENDS: We've never worn them ourselves, but we'll put these
jewels on your limbs the way they look in pictures.

ŚAKUNTALĀ: I trust your skill.   145
[*Both friends mime ornamenting her. Then* KAṆVA *enters, fresh from
his bath.*]

KAṆVA:

> My heart is touched with sadness
> since Śakuntalā must go today,
> my throat is choked with sobs,
> my eyes are dulled by worry—
> if a disciplined ascetic   150
> suffers so deeply from love,
> how do fathers bear the pain
> of each daughter's parting?[6]

[*He walks around.*]

BOTH FRIENDS: Śakuntalā, your jewels are in place; now put on the
pair of silken cloths.   155
[*Standing,* ŚAKUNTALĀ *wraps them.*]

GAUTAMĪ: Child, your father has come. His eyes filled with tears of joy
embrace you. Greet him reverently!

ŚAKUNTALĀ: [*Modestly.*] Father, I welcome you.

KAṆVA: Child,

> May your husband honor you   160
> the way Yayāti honored Śarmiṣṭhā.
> As she bore her son Puru,[7]
> may you bear an imperial prince.

GAUTAMĪ: Sir, this is a blessing, not just a prayer.

KAṆVA: Child, walk around the sacrificial fires![8]   165

---

5. The verse suggests that Śakuntalā is a kinswoman of the tree goddesses (*yakṣīs*), worshipped in popular cults. *Lac*: a substance
secreted by a species of beetle, used by Indian
women as a cosmetic dye for fingernails and
toenails.

6. A celebrated passage, prized for its convincing portrait of an Indian father's sorrow at
losing his daughter to another household.
7. Yayāti and Puru are ancestors of Duṣyanta.
8. Holy objects, persons, and places are honored by ritually walking around them.

[*All walk around*: KAṆVA *intoning a prayer in Vedic meter.*[9]]

> Perfectly placed around the main altar,
> fed with fuel, strewn with holy grass,
> destroying sin by incense from oblations,
> may these sacred fires purify you!

You must leave now! [*Looking around.*] Where are Śārṅgarava and   170
the others?

DISCIPLE: [*Entering.*] Here we are, sir!

KAṆVA: You show your sister the way!

ŚĀRṄGARAVA: Come this way!
        [*They walk around.*]

KAṆVA: Listen, you trees that grow in our grove!   175

> Until you were well watered
> she could not bear to drink;
> she loved you too much
> to pluck your flowers for her hair;
> the first time your buds bloomed,   180
> she blossomed with joy—
> may you all bless Śakuntalā
> as she leaves for her husband's house.

[*Miming that he hears a cuckoo's cry.*]

> The trees of her forest family
> have blessed Śakuntalā—   185
> the cuckoo's melodious song
> announces their response.

VOICE IN THE AIR:

> May lakes colored by lotuses mark her path!
> May trees shade her from the sun's burning rays!
> May the dust be as soft as lotus pollen!   190
> May fragrant breezes cool her way!

[*All listen astonished.*]

GAUTAMĪ: Child, the divinities of our grove love you like your family
and bless you. We bow to you all!

ŚAKUNTALĀ: [*Bowing and walking around; speaking in a stage whisper.*]
Priyaṁvadā, though I long to see my husband, my feet move with
sorrow as I start to leave the hermitage.   195

PRIYAṀVADĀ: You are not the only one who grieves. The whole hermitage feels this way as your departure from our grove draws near.

---

9. The version of the *triṣṭubh* meter used in the Vedic hymns, the oldest scriptures of the Hindu
tradition.

> Grazing deer
> drop grass,
> peacocks 200
> stop dancing,
> vines loose
> pale leaves
> falling
> like tears. 205

ŚAKUNTALĀ: [Remembering.] Father, before I leave, I must see my sister, the vine Forestlight.

KAṆVA: I know that you feel a sister's love for her. She is right here.

ŚAKUNTALĀ: Forestlight, though you love your mango tree, turn to embrace me with your tendril arms! After today, I'll be so far away . . . 210

KAṆVA:

> Your merits won you the husband
> I always hoped you would have
> and your jasmine has her mango tree—
> my worries for you both are over.

Start your journey here! 215

ŚAKUNTALĀ: [Facing her two friends.] I entrust her care to you.

BOTH FRIENDS: But who will care for us? [They wipe away their tears.]

KAṆVA: Anasūyā, enough crying! You should be giving Śakuntalā courage!
[All walk around.]

ŚAKUNTALĀ: Father, when the pregnant doe who grazes near my hut 220 gives birth, please send someone to give me the good news.

KAṆVA: I shall not forget.

ŚAKUNTALĀ: [Miming the interrupting of her gait.] Who is clinging to my skirt?
[She turns around.]

KAṆVA: Child. 225

> The buck whose mouth you healed with oil
> when it was pierced by a blade of kuśa grass
> and whom you fed with grains of rice—
> your adopted son will not leave the path.

ŚAKUNTALĀ: Child, don't follow when I'm abandoning those I love! I 230 raised you when you were orphaned soon after your birth, but now I'm deserting you too. Father will look after you. Go back! [Weeping, she starts to go.]

KAṆVA: Be strong!

> Hold back the tears that blind
> your long-lashed eyes— 235
> you will stumble if you cannot see
> the uneven ground on the path.

ŚĀRṄGARAVA: Sir, the scriptures prescribe that loved ones be escorted
only to the water's edge. We are at the shore of the lake. Give us
your message and return!   240

ŚAKUNTALĀ: We shall rest in the shade of this fig tree.
[*All walk around and stop;* KAṆVA *speaks to himself.*]

KAṆVA: What would be the right message to send to King Duṣyanta?
[*He ponders.*]

ŚAKUNTALĀ: [*In a stage whisper.*] Look! The wild goose cries in anguish
when her mate is hidden by lotus leaves. What I'm suffering
is much worse.   245

ANASŪYĀ: Friend, don't speak this way!

> This goose spends
> every long night
> in sorrow
> without her mate,   250
> but hope lets her
> survive
> the deep pain
> of loneliness.

KAṆVA: Śārṅgarava, speak my words to the king after you present   255
Śakuntalā!

ŚĀRṄGARAVA: As you command, sir!

KAṆVA:

> Considering our discipline,
> the nobility of your birth
> and that she fell in love with you   260
> before her kinsmen could act,
> acknowledge her with equal rank
> among your wives—
> what more is destined for her,
> the bride's family will not ask.   265

ŚĀRṄGARAVA: I grasp your message.

KAṆVA: Child, now I must instruct you. We forest hermits know something about worldly matters.

ŚĀRṄGARAVA: Nothing is beyond the scope of wise men.

KAṆVA: When you enter your husband's family: 270

> Obey your elders, be a friend to the other wives!
> If your husband seems harsh, don't be impatient!
> Be fair to your servants, humble in your happiness!
> Women who act this way become noble wives;
> sullen girls only bring their families disgrace.   275

But what does Gautamī think?

GAUTAMĪ: This is good advice for wives, child. Take it all to heart!

KAṆVA: Child, embrace me and your friends!

ŚAKUNTALĀ: Father, why must Priyaṁvadā and my other friends turn back here? 280

KAṆVA: They will also be given in marriage. It is not proper for them to go there now. Gautamī will go with you.

ŚAKUNTALĀ: [*Embracing her father.*] How can I go on living in a strange place, torn from my father's side, like a vine torn from the side of a sandalwood tree growing on a mountain slope?[1] 285

KAṆVA: Child, why are you so frightened?

> When you are your husband's honored wife,
> absorbed in royal duties and in your son,[2]
> born like the sun to the eastern dawn,
> the sorrow of separation will fade. 290

[ŚAKUNTALĀ *falls at her father's foot.*]

Let my hopes for you be fulfilled!

ŚAKUNTALĀ: [*Approaching her two friends.*] You two must embrace me together!

BOTH FRIENDS: [*Embracing her.*] Friend, if the king seems slow to recognize you, show him the ring engraved with his name! 295

ŚAKUNTALĀ: Your suspicions make me tremble!

BOTH FRIENDS: Don't be afraid! It's our love that fears evil.

ŚĀRṄGARAVA: The sun is high in the afternoon sky. Hurry, please!

ŚAKUNTALĀ: [*Facing the sanctuary.*] Father, will I ever see the grove again? 300

KAṆVA:

> When you have lived for many years
> as a queen equal to the earth
> and raised Duṣyanta's son
> to be a matchless warrior,
> your husband will entrust him 305
> with the burdens of the kingdom
> and will return with you
> to the calm of this hermitage.[3]

GAUTAMĪ: Child, the time for our departure has passed. Let your father turn back! It would be better, sir, if you turn back yourself. She'll 310 keep talking this way forever.

KAṆVA: Child, my ascetic practice has been interrupted.

ŚAKUNTALĀ: My father's body is already tortured by ascetic practices. He must not grieve too much for me!

1. Śakuntalā's sorrow reflects the experience of every Indian bride as she permanently leaves the home of her birth to join the extended family into which she has married.
2. The son, heir to the throne, will ensure an honored place for Śakuntalā among the hith-erto childless wives of King Duṣyanta.
3. It was a custom of Hindu kings and commoners of the three higher castes to retire to the forest with their wives to concentrate on the spiritual life.

KAṆVA: [*Sighing.*]

> When I see the grains of rice   315
> sprout from offerings you made
> at the door of your hut,
> how shall I calm my sorrow!

[ŚAKUNTALĀ *exits with her escort.*]

BOTH FRIENDS: [*Watching* ŚAKUNTALĀ.] Śakuntalā is hidden by forest trees now.   320

KAṆVA: Anasūyā, your companion is following her duty. Restrain yourself and return with me!

BOTH FRIENDS: Father, the ascetics' grove seems empty without Śakuntalā. How can we enter?

KAṆVA: The strength of your love makes it seem so. [*Walking around*   325 *in meditation.*] Good! Now that Śakuntalā is on her way to her husband's family, I feel calm.

> A daughter belongs to another man—
> by sending her to her husband today,
> I feel the satisfaction   330
> one has on repaying a loan.

[*All exit.*]

Act V

[*The* KING *and the* BUFFOON *enter; both sit down.*]

BUFFOON: Pay attention to the music room, friend, and you'll hear the notes of a song strung into a delicious melody . . . the lady Haṁsapadikā is practicing her singing.

KING: Be quiet so I can hear her!

VOICE IN THE AIR: [*Singing.*]

> Craving sweet   5
> new nectar,
> you kissed
> a mango bud once—
> how could you
> forget her, bee,   10
> to bury your joy
> in a lotus?

KING: The melody of the song is passionate.

BUFFOON: But did you get the meaning of the words?

KING: I once made love to her. Now she reproaches me for loving   15 Queen Vasumatī. Friend Mādhavya, tell Haṁsapadikā that her words rebuke me soundly.

BUFFOON: As you command! [*He rises.*] But if that woman grabs my
hair tuft, it will be like a heavenly nymph grabbing some ascetic . . .
there go my hopes of liberation![4]   20

KING: Go! Use your courtly charm to console her.

BUFFOON: What a fate!
[*He exits.*]

KING: [*To himself.*] Why did hearing the song's words fill me with such
strong desire? I'm not parted from anyone I love . . .

> Seeing rare beauty,   25
> hearing lovely sounds,
> even a happy man
> becomes strangely uneasy . . .
> perhaps he remembers,
> without knowing why,   30
> loves of another life
> buried deep in his being.[5]

[*He stands bewildered. Then the* KING'S CHAMBERLAIN *enters.*]

CHAMBERLAIN: At my age, look at me!

> Since I took this ceremonial bamboo staff
> as my badge of office in the king's chambers   35
> many years have passed; now I use it
> as a crutch to support my faltering steps.

A king cannot neglect his duty. He has just risen from his seat of
justice and though I am loath to keep him longer, Sage Kaṇva's
pupils have just arrived. Authority to rule the world leaves no time   40
for rest.

> The sun's steeds were yoked before time began,
> the fragrant wind blows night and day,
> the cosmic serpent always bears earth's weight,[6]
> and a king who levies taxes has his duty.   45

Therefore, I must perform my office. [*Walking around and looking.*]

> Weary from ruling them like children,
> he seeks solitude far from his subjects,

<hr>

4. The buffoon is referring, in his own inimi-
table way, to the seduction of the ascetic by
the courtesan and the thwarting of the former's quest for liberation from karma and
rebirth. The buffoon's joke turns on the word
mokṣa, which means "release," in the physical
sense as well as in the spiritual one of libera-

tion from karma.
5. An allusion to the power of art to revive
buried memories of experiences from former
lives.
6. According to Hindu mythology the earth
rests on Śeṣa, the cosmic serpent. "Sun's
steeds": horses for the sun god's chariot.

like an elephant bull who seeks cool shade
after gathering his herd at midday.   50

[*Approaching.*] Victory to you, king! Some ascetics who dwell in the
forest at the foothills of the Himālayas have come. They have women
with them and bring a message from Sage Kaṇva. Listen, king, and
judge!

KING: [*Respectfully.*] Are they Sage Kaṇva's messengers?   55

CHAMBERLAIN: They are.

KING: Inform the teacher Somarāta that he should welcome the ascetics with the prescribed rites and then bring them to me himself. I'll
wait in a place suitable for greeting them.

CHAMBERLAIN: As the king commands. [*He exits.*]   60

KING: [*Rising.*] Vetravatī, lead the way to the fire sanctuary.

DOORKEEPER: Come this way, king!

KING: [*Walking around, showing fatigue.*] Every other creature is happy
when the object of his desire is won, but for kings success contains
a core of suffering.   65

> High office only leads to greater greed;
> just perfecting its rewards is wearisome—
> a kingdom is more trouble than it's worth,
> like a royal umbrella one holds alone.

TWO BARDS OFFSTAGE: Victory to you, king!   70

FIRST BARD:

> You sacrifice your pleasures every day
> to labor for your subjects—
> as a tree endures burning heat
> to give shade from the summer sun.

SECOND BARD:

> You punish villains with your rod of justice,   75
> you reconcile disputes, you grant protection—
> most relatives are loyal only in hope of gain,
> but you treat all your subjects like kinsmen.

KING: My weary mind is revived. [*He walks around.*]

DOORKEEPER: The terrace of the fire sanctuary is freshly washed and 80
the cow is waiting to give milk for the oblation. Let the king ascend!

KING: Vetravatī, why has Father Kaṇva sent these sages to me?

> Does something hinder their ascetic life?
> Or threaten creatures in the sacred forest?
> Or do my sins stunt the flowering vines?   85
> My mind is filled with conflicting doubts.

DOORKEEPER: I would guess that these sages rejoice in your virtuous conduct and come to honor you.

[*The ascetics enter;* ŚAKUNTALĀ *is in front with* GAUTAMĪ: *the* CHAMBERLAIN *and the* KING'S PRIEST *are in front of her.*]

CHAMBERLAIN: Come this way, sirs!

ŚĀRṄGARAVA: Śāradvata, my friend:

> I know that this renowned king is righteous
> and none of the social classes follows evil ways,
> but my mind is so accustomed to seclusion
> that the palace feels like a house in flames.

ŚĀRADVATA: I've felt the same way ever since we entered the city.

> As if I were freshly bathed, seeing a filthy man,
> pure while he's defiled, awake while he's asleep,
> as if I were a free man watching a prisoner,
> I watch this city mired in pleasures.

ŚAKUNTALĀ: [*Indicating she feels an omen.*] Why is my right eye twitching?

GAUTAMĪ: Child, your husband's family gods turn bad fortune into blessings! [*They walk around.*]

PRIEST: [*Indicating the* KING.] Ascetics, the guardian of sacred order has left the seat of justice and awaits you now. Behold him!

ŚĀRṄGARAVA: Great priest, he seems praiseworthy, but we expect no less.

> Boughs bend, heavy with ripened fruit,
> clouds descend with fresh rain,
> noble men are gracious with wealth—
> this is the nature of bountiful things.

DOORKEEPER: King, their faces look calm. I'm sure that the sages have confidence in what they're doing.

KING: [*Seeing* ŚAKUNTALĀ.]

> Who is she? Carefully veiled
> to barely reveal her body's beauty,
> surrounded by the ascetics
> like a bud among withered leaves.

DOORKEEPER: King, I feel curious and puzzled too. Surely her form deserves closer inspection.

KING: Let her be! One should not stare at another man's wife!

ŚAKUNTALĀ: [*Placing her hand on her chest, she speaks to herself.*] My heart, why are you quivering? Be quiet while I learn my noble husband's feelings.

PRIEST: [*Going forward.*] These ascetics have been honored with due
ceremony. They have a message from their teacher. The king   125
should hear them!

KING: I am paying attention.

SAGES: [*Raising their hands in a gesture of greeting.*] May you be victorious, king!

KING: I salute you all!   130

SAGES: May your desires be fulfilled!

KING: Do the sages perform austerities unhampered?

SAGES:

> Who would dare obstruct the rites
> of holy men whom you protect—
> how can darkness descend   135
> when the sun's rays shine?

KING: My title "king" is more meaningful now. Is the world blessed by
Father Kaṇva's health?

SAGES: Saints control their own health. He asks about your welfare and
sends this message   140

KING: What does he command?

ŚĀRṄGARAVA: At the time you secretly met and married my daughter,
affection made me pardon you both.

> We remember you to be a prince of honor;
> Śakuntalā is virtue incarnate—   145
> the creator cannot be condemned
> for mating the perfect bride and groom.

And now that she is pregnant, receive her and perform your sacred
duty together.

GAUTAMĪ: Sir, I have something to say, though I wasn't appointed to   150
speak:

> She ignored her elders
> and you failed to ask her kinsmen—
> since you acted on your own,
> what can I say to you now?   155

ŚAKUNTALĀ: What does my noble husband say?

KING: What has been proposed?

ŚAKUNTALĀ: [*To herself.*] The proposal is as clear as fire.

ŚĀRṄGARAVA: What's this? Your Majesty certainly knows the ways of
the world!   160

> People suspect a married woman who stays
> with her kinsmen, even if she is chaste—
> a young wife should live with her husband,
> no matter how he despises her.

KING: Did I ever marry you?   165

ŚAKUNTALĀ: [*Visibly dejected, speaking to herself.*] Now your fears are
real, my heart!

ŚĀRṄGARAVA:

> Does one turn away from duty in contempt
> because his own actions repulse him?

KING: Why ask this insulting question?   170

ŚĀRṄGARAVA:

> Such transformations take shape
> when men are drunk with power.

KING: This censure is clearly directed at me.

GAUTAMĪ: Child, this is no time to be modest. I'll remove your veil.
Then your husband will recognize you.   175
[*She does so.*]

KING: [*Staring at* ŚAKUNTALĀ.]

> Must I judge whether I ever married
> the flawless beauty they offer me now?
> I cannot love her or leave her, like a bee
> near a jasmine filled with frost at dawn.

[*He shows hesitation.*]

DOORKEEPER: Our king has a strong sense of justice. Who else would   180
hesitate when beauty like this is handed to him?

ŚĀRṄGARAVA: King, why do you remain silent?

KING: Ascetics, even though I'm searching my mind, I don't remember
marrying this lady. How can I accept a woman who is visibly preg-
nant when I doubt that I am the cause?   185

ŚAKUNTALĀ: [*In a stage whisper.*] My lord casts doubt on our marriage.
Why were my hopes so high?

ŚĀRṄGARAVA: It can't be!

> Are you going to insult the sage
> who pardons the girl you seduced   190
> and bids you keep his stolen wealth,
> treating a thief like you with honor?

ŚĀRADVATA: Śārṅgarava, stop now! Śakuntalā, we have delivered our
message and the king has responded. He must be shown some proof.

ŚAKUNTALĀ: [*In a stage whisper.*] When passion can turn to this, what's   195
the use of reminding him? But, it's up to me to prove my honor now.
[*Aloud.*] My noble husband . . . [*She breaks off when this is half-
spoken.*] Since our marriage is in doubt, this is no way to address
him. Puru king, you do wrong to reject a simple-hearted person
with such words after you deceived her in the hermitage.   200

KING: [*Covering his ears.*] Stop this shameful talk!

> Are you trying to stain my name
> and drag me to ruin—
> like a river eroding her own banks,
> soiling water and uprooting trees?   205

ŚAKUNTALĀ: Very well! If it's really true that fear of taking another man's wife turns you away, then this ring will revive your memory and remove your doubt.

KING: An excellent idea!

ŚAKUNTALĀ: [*Touching the place where the ring had been.*] I'm lost! The   210
ring is gone from my finger. [*She looks despairingly at* GAUTAMĪ.]

GAUTAMĪ: The ring must have fallen off while you were bathing in the holy waters at the shrine of the goddess near Indra's grove.

KING: [*Smiling.*] And so they say the female sex is cunning.

ŚAKUNTALĀ: Fate has shown its power. Yet, I will tell you something   215
else.

KING: I am still obliged to listen.

ŚAKUNTALĀ: One day, in a jasmine bower, you held a lotus-leaf cup full of water in your hand.

KING: We hear you.   220

ŚAKUNTALĀ: At that moment the buck I treated as my son approached. You coaxed it with the water, saying that it should drink first. But he didn't trust you and wouldn't drink from your hand. When I took the water, his trust returned. Then you jested, "Every creature trusts what its senses know. You both belong to the forest."   225

KING: Thus do women further their own ends by attracting eager men with the honey of false words.

GAUTAMĪ: Great king, you are wrong to speak this way. This child raised in an ascetics' grove doesn't know deceit.

KING: Old woman,   230

> When naive female beasts show cunning,
> what can we expect of women who reason?
> Don't cuckoos let other birds nurture
> their eggs and teach the chicks to fly?

ŚAKUNTALĀ: [*Angrily.*] Evil man! you see everything distorted by your   235
own ignoble heart. Who would want to imitate you now, hiding behind your show of justice, like a well overgrown with weeds?

KING: [*To himself.*] Her anger does not seem feigned; it makes me doubt myself.

> When the absence of love's memory   240
> made me deny a secret affair with her,
> this fire-eyed beauty bent her angry brows
> and seemed to break the bow of love.[7]

---

7. Of the love god Kāma.

[*Aloud.*] Lady, Duṣyanta's conduct is renowned, so what you say is
groundless.   245

ŚAKUNTALĀ: All right! I may be a self-willed wanton woman! But it was
faith in the Puru dynasty that brought me into the power of a man
with honey in his words and poison in his heart. [*She covers her face
at the end of the speech and weeps.*]

ŚĀRṄGARAVA: A willful act unchecked always causes pain.

> One should be cautious   250
> in forming a secret union—
> unless a lover's heart is clear,
> affection turns to poison.

KING: But sir, why do you demean me with such warnings? Do you
trust the lady?   255

ŚĀRṄGARAVA: [*Scornfully.*] You have learned everything backwards.

> If you suspect the word of one
> whose nature knows no guile,
> then you can only trust
> people who practice deception.   260

KING: I presume you speak the truth. Let us assume so. But what
could I gain by deceiving this woman?

ŚĀRṄGARAVA: Ruin.

KING: Ruin? A Puru king has no reason to want his own ruin!

ŚĀRADVATA: Śārṅgarava, this talk is pointless. We have delivered our   265
master's message and should return.

> Since you married her, abandon her or take her—
> absolute is the power a husband has over his wife.

GAUTAMĪ: You go ahead.
[*They start to go.*]

ŚAKUNTALĀ: What? Am I deceived by this cruel man and then   270
abandoned by you? [*She tries to follow them.*]

GAUTAMĪ: [*Stopping.*] Śārṅgarava, my son, Śakuntalā is following us,
crying pitifully. What will my child do now that her husband has
refused her?

ŚĀRṄGARAVA: [*Turning back angrily.*] Bold woman, do you still insist   275
on having your way?
[ŚAKUNTALĀ *trembles in fear.*]

> If you are what the king says you are,
> you don't belong in Father Kaṇva's family—
> if you know that your marriage vow is pure,
> you can bear slavery in your husband's house.   280

Stay! We must go on!

KING: Ascetic, why do you disappoint the lady too?

> The moon only makes lotuses open,
> the sun's light awakens lilies—
> a king's discipline forbids him   285
> to touch another man's wife.

ŚĀRṄGARAVA: If you forget a past affair because of some present attachment, why do you fear injustice now?

KING: [To the PRIEST.] Sir, I ask you to weigh the alternatives:

> Since it's unclear whether I'm deluded   290
> or she is speaking falsely—
> should I risk abandoning a wife
> or being tainted by another man's?

PRIEST: [Deliberating.] I recommend this . . .

KING: Instruct me! I'll do as you say.   295

PRIEST: Then let the lady stay in our house until her child is born. If you ask why: the wise men predict that your first son will be born with the marks of a king who turns the wheel of empire.[8] If the child of the sage's daughter bears the marks, congratulate her and welcome her into your palace chambers. Otherwise, send her back to   300 her father.

KING: Whatever the elders desire.

PRIEST: Child, follow me!

ŚAKUNTALĀ: Mother earth, open to receive me!
[Weeping, ŚAKUNTALĀ exits with the PRIEST and the hermits. The KING, his memory lost through the curse, thinks about her.]

VOICE OFFSTAGE: Amazing! Amazing!   305

KING: [Listening.] What could this be?

PRIEST: [Reentering, amazed.] King, something marvelous has occurred!

KING: What?

PRIEST: When Kaṇva's pupils had departed,   310

> The girl threw up her arms and wept,
> lamenting her misfortune . . . then . . .

KING: Then what?

PRIEST:

> Near the nymph's shrine a ray of light
> in the shape of a woman carried her away.   315

[All mime amazement.]

8. See p. 880, n. 9.

KING: We've already settled the matter. Why discuss it further?
PRIEST: [*Observing the* KING.] May you be victorious! [*He exits.*]
KING: Vetravatī, I am bewildered. Lead the way to my chamber!
DOORKEEPER: Come this way, my lord! [*She walks forward.*]
KING:

> I cannot remember marrying 320
> the sage's abandoned daughter,
> but the pain my heart feels
> makes me suspect that I did.

[*All exit.*]

Act VI

[*The* KING's *wife's brother, who is city* MAGISTRATE, *enters with two policemen leading a* MAN *whose hands are tied behind his back.*]
BOTH POLICEMEN: [*Beating the* MAN.] Speak, thief! Where'd you steal this handsome ring with the king's name engraved in the jewel?
MAN: [*Showing fear.*] Peace, sirs! I wouldn't do a thing like that.
FIRST POLICEMAN: Don't tell us the king thought you were some famous priest and gave it to you as a gift! 5
MAN: Listen, I'm a humble fisherman who lives near Indra's grove.
SECOND POLICEMAN: Thief, did we ask you about your caste?
MAGISTRATE: Sūcaka, let him tell it all in order! Don't interrupt him!
BOTH POLICEMEN: Whatever you command, chief!
MAN: I feed my family by catching fish with nets and hooks. 10
MAGISTRATE: [*Mocking.*] What a pure profession![9]
MAN:

> The work I do
> may be vile
> but I won't deny
> my birthright— 15
> a priest
> doing his holy rites
> pities the animals
> he kills.

MAGISTRATE: Go on! 20
MAN: One day as I was cutting up a red carp, I saw the shining stone of this ring in its belly. When I tried to sell it, you grabbed me. Kill me or let me go! That's how I got it!
MAGISTRATE: Jānuka, I'm sure this ugly butcher's a fisherman by his stinking smell. We must investigate how he got the ring. We'll go 25 straight to the palace.

---

9. Because their profession involves taking animal life, fishermen rank low in the caste system.

BOTH POLICEMEN: Okay. Go in front, you pickpocket!
[*All walk around.*]

MAGISTRATE: Sūcaka, guard this villain at the palace gate! I'll report to the king how we found the ring, get his orders, and come back.

BOTH POLICEMEN: Chief, good luck with the king!   30
[*The* MAGISTRATE *exits.*]

FIRST POLICEMAN: Jānuka, the chief's been gone a long time.

SECOND POLICEMAN: Well, there are fixed times for seeing kings.

FIRST POLICEMAN: Jānuka, my hands are itching to tie on his execution garland.[1] [*He points to the* MAN.]

MAN: You shouldn't think about killing a man for no reason.   35

SECOND POLICEMAN: [*Looking.*] I see our chief coming with a letter in his hand. It's probably an order from the king. You'll be thrown to the vultures or you'll see the face of death's dog[2] again . . .

MAGISTRATE: [*Entering.*] Sūcaka, release this fisherman! I'll tell you how he got the ring.   40

FIRST POLICEMAN: Whatever you say, chief!

SECOND POLICEMAN: The villain entered the house of death and came out again. [*He unties the prisoner.*]

MAN: [*Bowing to the* MAGISTRATE.] Master, how will I make my living now?   45

MAGISTRATE: The king sends you a sum equal to the ring. [*He gives the money to the* MAN.]

MAN: [*Bowing as he grabs it.*] The king honors me.

FIRST POLICEMAN: This fellow's certainly honored. He was lowered from the execution stake and raised up on a royal elephant's back.

SECOND POLICEMAN: Chief, the reward tells me this ring was special   50
to the king.

MAGISTRATE: I don't think the king valued the stone, but when he caught sight of the ring, he suddenly seemed to remember someone he loved, and he became deeply disturbed.

FIRST POLICEMAN: You served him well, chief!   55

SECOND POLICEMAN: I think you better served this king of fish.
[*Looking at the fisherman with jealousy.*]

MAN: My lords, half of this is yours for your good will.

FIRST POLICEMAN: It's only fair!

MAGISTRATE: Fisherman, now that you are my greatest and dearest friend, we should pledge our love over kadamba-blossom wine. Let's   60
go to the wine shop!
[*They all exit together; the interlude ends. Then a nymph named* SĀNUMATĪ *enters by the skyway.*]

SĀNUMATĪ: Now that I've performed my assigned duties at the nymph's shrine, I'll slip away to spy on King Duṣyanta while the worshipers are bathing. My friendship with Menakā makes me feel a bond with Śakuntalā. Besides, Menakā asked me to help her daughter.   65

---

1. Condemned prisoners were taken to their executions dressed in robes and garlands, in the manner of sacrificial victims.

2. In Hindu myth two four-eyed dogs guard the path of the dead.

[*Looking around.*] Why don't I see preparations for the spring festival in the king's palace? I can learn everything by using my mental powers, but I must respect my friend's request. So be it! I'll make myself invisible and spy on these two girls who are guarding the pleasure garden.   70

[SĀNUMATĪ *mimes descending and stands waiting. Then a* MAID *servant named Parabhṛtikā, "Little Cuckoo," enters, looking at a mango bud. A* SECOND MAID, *named Madhukarikā "Little Bee," is following her.*]

FIRST MAID:

> Your pale green stem
> tinged with pink
> is a true sign
> that spring has come—
> I see you,   75
> mango-blossom bud,
> and I pray
> for a season of joy.

SECOND MAID: What are you muttering to yourself?

FIRST MAID: A cuckoo goes mad when she sees a mango bud.   80

SECOND MAID: [*Joyfully rushing over.*] Has the sweet month of spring come?

FIRST MAID: Now's the time to sing your songs of love.

SECOND MAID: Hold me while I pluck a mango bud and worship the god of love.   85

FIRST MAID: Only if you'll give me half the fruit of your worship.

SECOND MAID: That goes without saying . . . our bodies may be separate, but our lives are one . . . . [*Leaning on her friend, she stands and plucks a mango bud.*] The mango flower is still closed, but this broken stem is fragrant. [*She makes the dove gesture with her hands.*]   90

> Mango-blossom bud,
> I offer you to Love
> as he lifts
> his bow of passion.
> Be the first   95
> of his flower arrows
> aimed at lonely girls
> with lovers far away!

[*She throws the mango bud.*]

CHAMBERLAIN: [*Angrily throwing aside the curtain and entering.*] Not now, stupid girl! When the king has banned the festival of spring,   100
how dare you pluck a mango bud!

BOTH MAIDS: [*Frightened.*] Please forgive us, sir. We don't know what you mean.

CHAMBERLAIN: Did you not hear that even the spring trees and the
nesting birds obey the king's order?   105

> The mango flowers bloom without spreading pollen,
> the red amaranth buds, but will not bloom;
> cries of cuckoo cocks freeze though frost is past,
> and out of fear, Love holds his arrow half-drawn.

BOTH MAIDS: There is no doubt about the king's great power!   110
FIRST MAID: Sir, several days ago we were sent to wait on the queen by
Mitrāvasu, the king's brother-in-law. We were assigned to guard the
pleasure garden. Since we're newcomers, we've heard no news.
CHAMBERLAIN: Let it be! But don't do it again!
BOTH MAIDS: Sir, we're curious. May we ask why the spring festival   115
was banned?
SĀNUMATĪ: Mortals are fond of festivals. The reason must be serious.
CHAMBERLAIN: It is public knowledge. Why should I not tell them?
Has the scandal of Śakuntalā's rejection not reached your ears?
BOTH MAIDS: We only heard from the king's brother-in-law that the   120
ring was found.
CHAMBERLAIN: [To himself.] There is little more to tell. [Aloud.] When
he saw the ring, the king remembered that he had married Śakuntalā
in secret and had rejected her in his delusion. Since then the king has
been tortured by remorse.   125

> Despising what he once enjoyed,
> he shuns his ministers every day
> and spends long sleepless nights
> tossing at the edge of his bed—
> when courtesy demands that   130
> he converse with palace women,
> he stumbles over their names,
> and then retreats in shame.

SĀNUMATĪ: This news delights me.
CHAMBERLAIN: The festival is banned because of the king's melancholy.   135
BOTH MAIDS: It's only right.
VOICE OFFSTAGE: This way, sir!
CHAMBERLAIN: [Listening.] The king is coming. Go about your business!
BOTH MAIDS: As you say.
        [Both maids exit. Then the KING enters, costumed to show his
        grief, accompanied by the BUFFOON and the DOORKEEPER.]
CHAMBERLAIN: [Observing the KING.] Extraordinary beauty is   140
appealing under all conditions. Even in his lovesick state, the king is
wonderful to see.

> Rejecting his regal jewels,
> he wears one golden bangle
> above his left wrist;   145
> his lips are pale with sighs,

> his eyes wan from brooding at night—
> like a gemstone ground in polishing,
> the fiery beauty of his body
> makes his wasted form seem strong.   150

SĀNUMATĪ: [*Seeing the* KING.] I see why Śakuntalā pines for him
though he rejected and disgraced her.

KING: [*Walking around slowly, deep in thought.*]

> This cursed heart slept
> when my love came to wake it,
> and now it stays awake   155
> to suffer the pain of remorse.

SĀNUMATĪ: The girl shares his fate.

BUFFOON: [*In a stage whisper.*] He's having another attack of his
Śakuntalā disease. I doubt if there's any cure for that.

CHAMBERLAIN: [*Approaching.*] Victory to the king! I have inspected   160
the grounds of the pleasure garden. Let the king visit his favorite
spots and divert himself.

KING: Vetravatī, deliver a message to my noble minister Piśuna: "After
being awake all night, we cannot sit on the seat of justice today. Set
in writing what your judgment tells you the citizens require and send   165
it to us!"

DOORKEEPER: Whatever you command! [*She exits.*]

KING: Vātāyana, attend to the rest of your business!

CHAMBERLAIN: As the king commands! [*He exits.*]

BUFFOON: You've cleared out the flies. Now you can rest in some   170
pretty spot. The garden is pleasant now in this break between
morning cold and noonday heat.

KING: Dear friend, the saying "Misfortunes rush through any crack" is
absolutely right:

> Barely freed by the dark force   175
> that made me forget Kaṇva's daughter,
> my mind is threatened by an arrow
> of mango buds fixed on Love's bow.

BUFFOON: Wait, I'll destroy the love god's arrow with my wooden
stick.[3] [*Raising his staff, he tries to strike a mango bud.*]   180

KING: [*Smiling.*] Let it be! I see the majesty of brahman bravery.
Friend, where may I sit to divert my eyes with vines that remind me
of my love?

BUFFOON: Didn't you tell your maid Caturikā, "I'll pass the time in the
jasmine bower. Bring me the drawing board on which I painted a   185
picture of Śakuntalā with my own hand!"

---

3. It is clear in the original that the buffoon's staff parodies Indra's rod (a symbol of virility) and
the phallic arrows of the god of love.

KING: Such a place may soothe my heart. Show me the way!

BUFFOON: Come this way!

[*Both walk around; the nymph* SĀNUMATĪ *follows.*]

The marble seat and flower offerings in this jasmine bower are certainly trying to make us feel welcome. Come in and sit down!   190

[*Both enter the bower and sit.*]

SĀNUMATĪ: I'll hide behind these creepers to see the picture he's drawn of my friend. Then I'll report how great her husband's passion is. [*She does as she says and stands waiting.*]

KING: Friend, now I remember everything. I told you about my first meeting with Śakuntalā. You weren't with me when I rejected her, but why didn't you say anything about her before? Did you suffer a   195 loss of memory too?

BUFFOON: I didn't forget. You did tell me all about it once, but then you said, "It's all a joke without any truth." My wit is like a lump of clay, so I took you at your word . . . or it could be that fate is powerful . . .   200

SĀNUMATĪ: It is!

KING: Friend, help me!

BUFFOON: What's this? It doesn't become you! Noblemen never take grief to heart. Even in storms, mountains don't tremble.

KING: Dear friend, I'm defenseless when I remember the pain of my   205 love's bewilderment when I rejected her.

> When I cast her away, she followed her kinsmen,
> but Kaṇva's disciple harshly shouted, "Stay!"
> The tearful look my cruelty provoked
> burns me like an arrow tipped with poison.   210

SĀNUMATĪ: The way he rehearses his actions makes me delight in his pain.

BUFFOON: Sir, I guess that the lady was carried off by some celestial creature or other.

KING: Who else would dare to touch a woman who worshiped her   215 husband? I was told that Menakā is her mother. My heart suspects that her mother's companions carried her off.

SĀNUMATĪ: His delusion puzzled me, but not his reawakening.

BUFFOON: If that's the case, you'll meet her again in good time.

KING: How?   220

BUFFOON: No mother or father can bear to see a daughter parted from her husband.

KING:

> Was it dream or illusion or mental confusion,
> or the last meager fruit of my former good deeds?
> It is gone now, and my heart's desires are   225
> like riverbanks crumbling of their own weight.

BUFFOON: Stop this! Isn't the ring evidence that an unexpected meeting is destined to take place?

KING: [*Looking at the ring.*] I only pity it for falling from such a place.

> Ring, your punishment is proof   230
> that your face is as flawed as mine—
> you were placed in her lovely fingers,
> glowing with crimson nails, and you fell.

SĀNUMATĪ: The real pity would have been if it had fallen into some
other hand.   235

BUFFOON: What prompted you to put the signet ring on her hand?

SĀNUMATĪ: I'm curious too.

KING: I did it when I left for the city. My love broke into tears and
asked. "How long will it be before my noble husband sends news to
me?"   240

BUFFOON: Then? What then?

KING: Then I placed the ring on her finger with this promise:

> One by one, day after day,
> count each syllable of my name!
> At the end, a messenger will come   245
> to bring you to my palace.

But in my cruel delusion, I never kept my word.

SĀNUMATĪ: Fate broke their charming agreement!

BUFFOON: How did it get into the belly of the carp the fisherman was
cutting up?   250

KING: While she was worshiping at the shrine of Indra's wife, it fell
from her hand into the Gaṅgā.[4]

BUFFOON: It's obvious now!

SĀNUMATĪ: And the king, doubtful of his marriage to Śakuntalā, a
female ascetic, was afraid to commit an act of injustice. But why   255
should such passionate love need a ring to be remembered?

KING: I must reproach the ring for what it's done.

BUFFOON: [*To himself.*] He's gone the way of all madmen . . .

KING:

> Why did you leave her delicate finger
> and sink into the deep river?   260

Of course . . .

> A mindless ring can't recognize virtue,
> but why did I reject my love?

BUFFOON: [*To himself again.*] Why am I consumed by a craving for
food?   265

---

4. The Ganges River.

KING: Oh ring! Have pity on a man whose heart is tormented because
he abandoned his love without cause! Let him see her again!
[*Throwing the curtain aside, the maid* CATURIKĀ *enters, with the
drawing board in her hand.*]

CATURIKĀ: Here's the picture you painted of the lady. [*She shows the
drawing board.*]

BUFFOON: Dear friend, how well you've painted your feelings in this
sweet scene! My eyes almost stumble over the hollows and hills.   270

SĀNUMATĪ: What skill the king has! I feel as if my friend were before me.

KING:

> The picture's imperfections are not hers,
> but this drawing does hint at her beauty.

SĀNUMATĪ: Such words reveal that suffering has increased his modesty
as much as his love.   275

BUFFOON: Sir, I see three ladies now and they're all lovely to look at.
Which is your Śakuntalā?

SĀNUMATĪ: Only a dim-witted fool like this wouldn't know such beauty!

KING: You guess which one!

BUFFOON: I guess Śakuntalā is the one you've drawn with flowers falling   280
from her loosened locks of hair, with drops of sweat on her face, with
her arms hanging limp and tired as she stands at the side of a mango
tree whose tender shoots are gleaming with the fresh water she
poured. The other two are her friends.

KING: You are clever! Look at these signs of my passion!   285

> Smudges from my sweating fingers
> stain the edges of the picture
> and a tear fallen from my cheek
> has raised a wrinkle in the paint.

Caturikā, the scenery is only half-drawn. Go and bring my paints!   290

CATURIKĀ: Noble Māḍhavya, hold the drawing board until I come back!

KING: I'll hold it myself. [*He takes it, the maid exits.*]

> I rejected my love when she came to me,
> and how I worship her in a painted image—
> having passed by a river full of water,   295
> I'm longing now for an empty mirage.

BUFFOON: [*To himself.*] He's too far gone for a river now! He's looking
for a mirage! [*Aloud.*] Sir, what else do you plan to draw here?

SĀNUMATĪ: He'll want to draw every place my friend loved.

KING:

> I'll draw the river Mālinī   300
> flowing through Himālaya's foothills
> where pairs of wild geese nest in the sand

and deer recline on both riverbanks,
where a doe is rubbing her left eye
on the horn of a black buck antelope   305
under a tree whose branches
have bark dresses hanging to dry.

BUFFOON: [*To himself.*] Next he'll fill the drawing board with mobs of
ascetics wearing long grassy beards.
KING: Dear friend, I've forgotten to draw an ornament that Śakuntalā   310
wore.
BUFFOON: What is it?
SĀNUMATĪ: It will suit her forest life and her tender beauty.
KING:

I haven't drawn the mimosa flower on her ear,
its filaments resting on her cheek,
or the necklace of tender lotus stalks,   315
lying on her breasts like autumn moonbeams.

BUFFOON: But why does the lady cover her face with her red lotus-bud
fingertips and stand trembling in fear? [*Looking closely.*] That son-of-
a-bee who steals nectar from flowers is attacking her face.   320
KING: Drive the impudent rogue away!
BUFFOON: You have the power to punish criminals. You drive him off!
KING: All right! Bee, favored guest of the flowering vines, why do you
frustrate yourself by flying here?[5]

A female bee waits on a flower,   325
thirsting for your love—
she refuses to drink
the sweet nectar without you.

SĀNUMATĪ: How gallantly he's driving him away!
BUFFOON: When you try to drive it away, this creature becomes   330
vicious.
KING: Why don't you stop when I command you?

Bee, if you touch the lips of my love
that lure you like a young tree's virgin buds,
lips I gently kissed in festivals of love,   335
I'll hold you captive in a lotus flower cage.

BUFFOON: Why isn't he afraid of your harsh punishment? [*Laughing,
he speaks to himself.*] He's gone crazy and I'll be the same if I go on
talking like this. [*Aloud.*] But, sir, it's just a picture!
KING: A picture? How can that be?   340

---

5. The king's preoccupation with the bee recalls the events of Act I.

SĀNUMATĪ: When I couldn't tell whether it was painted, how could he realize he was looking at a picture?

KING: Dear friend, are you envious of me?

> My heart's affection made me feel
> the joy of seeing her—   345
> but you reminded me again
> that my love is only a picture.

[*He wipes away a tear.*]

SĀNUMATĪ: The effects of her absence make him quarrelsome.

KING: Dear friend, why do I suffer this endless pain?

> Sleepless nights prevent our meeting in dreams;   350
> her image in a picture is ruined by my tears.

SĀNUMATĪ: You have clearly atoned for the suffering your rejection caused Śakuntalā.

CATURIKĀ: [*Entering.*] Victory, my lord! I found the paint box and started back right away . . . but I met Queen Vasumatī with her maid   355
Taralikā on the path and she grabbed the box from my hand, saying, "I'll bring it to the noble lord myself!"

BUFFOON: You were lucky to get away!

CATURIKĀ: The queen's shawl got caught on a tree. While Taralikā was freeing it, I made my escape.   360

KING: Dear friend, the queen's pride can quickly turn to anger. Save this picture!

BUFFOON: You should say, "Save yourself!" [*Taking the picture, he stands up.*] If you escape the woman's deadly poison, then send word to me in the Palace of the Clouds. [*He exits hastily.*]   365

SĀNUMATĪ: Even though another woman has taken his heart and he feels indifferent to the queen, he treats her with respect.[6]

DOORKEEPER: [*Entering with a letter in her hand.*] Victory, king!

KING: Vetravatī, did you meet the queen on the way?

DOORKEEPER: I did, but when she saw the letter in my hand, she   370
turned back.

KING: She knows that this is official and would not interrupt my work.

DOORKEEPER: King, the minister requests that you examine the contents of this letter. He said that the enormous job of reckoning the revenue in this one citizen's case had taken all his time.   375

KING: Show me the letter! [*The girl hands it to him and he reads barely aloud.*] What is this? "A wealthy merchant sea captain named Dhanamitra has been lost in a shipwreck and the laws say that since the brave man was childless, his accumulated wealth all goes to the king." It's terrible to be childless! A man of such wealth probably had   380
several wives. We must find out if any one of his wives is pregnant!

DOORKEEPER: King, it's said that one of his wives, the daughter of a

---

6. Royal polygamy called for elaborate courtesies.

merchant of Ayodhyā, has performed the rite to ensure the birth of a son.[7]

KING: The child in her womb surely deserves his parental wealth. Go!   385
Report this to my minister!

DOORKEEPER: As the king commands! [*She starts to go.*]

KING: Come here a moment!

DOORKEEPER: I am here.

KING: Is it his offspring or not?   390

> When his subjects lose a kinsman,
> Duṣyanta will preserve the estates—
> unless there is some crime.
> Let this be proclaimed.

DOORKEEPER: It shall be proclaimed loudly. [*She exits; reenters.*] The   395
king's order will be as welcome as rain in the right season.

KING: [*Sighing long and deeply.*] Families without offspring whose
lines of succession are cut off lose their wealth to strangers when the
last male heir dies. When I die, this will happen to the wealth of the
Puru dynasty.   400

DOORKEEPER: Heaven forbid such a fate!

KING: I curse myself for despising the treasure I was offered.

SĀNUMATĪ: He surely has my friend in mind when he blames himself.

KING:

> I abandoned my lawful wife, the holy ground
> where I myself planted my family's glory,   405
> like earth sown with seed at the right time,
> ready to bear rich fruit in season.

SĀNUMATĪ: But your family's line will not be broken.

CATURIKĀ: [*In a stage whisper.*] The king is upset by the story of the
merchant. Go and bring noble Mādhavya from the Palace of the   410
Clouds to console him!

DOORKEEPER: A good idea! [*She exits.*]

KING: Duṣyanta's ancestors are imperiled.

> Our fathers drink the yearly libation
> mixed with my childless tears,   415
> knowing that there is no other son
> to offer the sacred funeral waters.

[*He falls into a faint.*]

CATURIKĀ: [*Looking at the bewildered* KING.] Calm yourself, my lord!

SĀNUMATĪ: Though a light shines, his separation from Śakuntalā keeps
him in a state of dark depression. I could make him happy now, but   420
I've heard Indra's consort consoling Śakuntalā with the news that the
gods are hungry for their share of the ancestral oblations and will

---

7. This rite (*puṃsavana*) is performed in the third month of pregnancy.

soon conspire to have her husband welcome his lawful wife. I'll have
to wait for the auspicious time, but meanwhile I'll cheer my friend by
reporting his condition. [*She exits, flying into the air.*]   425

VOICE OFFSTAGE: Help! Brahman-murder![8]

KING: [*Regaining consciousness, listening.*] Is it Mādhavya's cry of pain?
Who's there?

DOORKEEPER: King, your friend is in danger. Help him!

KING: Who dares to threaten him?   430

DOORKEEPER: Some invisible spirit seized him and dragged him to the
roof of the Palace of the Clouds.

KING: [*Getting up.*] Not this! Even my house is haunted by spirits.

> When I don't even recognize
> the blunders I commit every day,   435
> how can I keep track
> of where my subjects stray?

VOICE OFFSTAGE: Dear friend! Help! Help!

KING: [*Breaking into a run.*] Friend, don't be afraid! I'm coming!

VOICE OFFSTAGE: [*Repeating the call for help.*] Why shouldn't I be   440
afraid? Someone is trying to split my neck in three, like a stalk of
sugar cane.

KING: [*Casting a glance.*] Quickly, my bow!

BOW-BEARER: [*Entering with a bow in hand.*] Here are your bow and
quiver.   445

[*The KING takes his bow and arrows.*]

VOICE OFFSTAGE:

> I'll kill you as a tiger kills struggling prey!
> I'll drink fresh blood from your tender neck!
> Take refuge now in the bow Duṣyanta lifts
> to calm the fears of the oppressed!

KING: [*Angrily.*] How dare you abuse my name? Stop, carrion-eater!   450
Or you will not live! [*He strings his bow.*] Vetravatī, lead the way to
the stairs!

DOORKEEPER: This way, king.

[*All move forward in haste.*]

KING: [*Searching around.*] There is no one here!

VOICE OFFSTAGE: Help! Help! I see you. Don't you see me? I'm like a   455
mouse caught by a cat! My life is hopeless!

KING: Don't count on your powers of invisibility! My magical arrows
will find you. I aim this arrow:

> It will strike its doomed target
> and spare the brahman it must save—   460

---

8. Murder of a *brāhmaṇa* is among the most heinous sins.

a wild goose can extract the milk
and leave the water untouched.[9]

[*He aims the arrow. Then Indra's charioteer* MĀTALI *enters, having released the* BUFFOON.]

MĀTALI: King!

> Indra sets demons as your targets:
> draw your bow against them!   465
> Send friends gracious glances
> rather than deadly arrows!

KING: [*Withdrawing his arrow.*] Mātali, welcome to great Indra's charioteer!

BUFFOON: [*Entering.*] He tried to slaughter me like a sacrificial beast   470
and this king is greeting him with honors!

MĀTALI: [*Smiling.*] Your Majesty, hear why Indra has sent me to you!

KING: I am all attention.

MĀTALI: There is an army of demons descended from one-hundred-headed Kālanemi, known to be invincible . . .   475

KING: I have already heard it from Nārada, the gods' messenger.

MĀTALI:

> He is invulnerable to your friend Indra,
> so you are appointed to lead the charge—
> the moon dispels the darkness of night
> since the sun cannot drive it out.   480

Take your weapon, mount Indra's chariot, and prepare for victory!

KING: Indra favors me with this honor. But why did you attack Mādhavya?

MĀTALI: I'll tell you! From the signs of anguish Your Majesty showed,
I knew that you were despondent. I attacked him to arouse your anger.   485

> A fire blazes when fuel is added;
> a cobra provoked raises its hood—
> men can regain lost courage
> if their emotions are aroused.

KING: [*In a stage whisper.*] Dear friend. I cannot disobey a command   490
from the lord of heaven. Inform my minister Piśuna of this and tell
him this for me:

> Concentrate your mind on guarding my subjects!
> My bow is strung to accomplish other work.

BUFFOON: Whatever you command!   495
[*He exits.*]

9. The *hamsa*: in Sanskrit poetry this bird is said to have the ability to separate milk from the water with which it has been diluted.

MĀTALI: Mount the chariot, Your Majesty!
[*The* KING *mimes mounting the chariot; all exit.*]

Act VII

[*The* KING *enters with* MĀTALI *by the skyway, mounted on a chariot.*]

KING: Mātali, though I carried out his command, I feel unworthy of
the honors Indra gave me.

MĀTALI: [*Smiling.*] Your Majesty, neither of you seems satisfied.

> You belittle the aid you gave Indra
> in face of the honors he conferred,   5
> and he, amazed by your heroic acts,
> deems his hospitality too slight.

KING: No, not so! When I was taking leave, he honored me beyond my
heart's desire and shared his throne with me in the presence of the
gods: 10

> Indra gave me a garland of coral flowers[1]
> tinged with sandalpowder from his chest,
> while he smiled at his son Jayanta,
> who stood there barely hiding his envy.

MĀTALI: Don't you deserve whatever you want from Indra?   15

> Indra's heaven of pleasures has twice
> been saved by rooting out thorny demons—
> your smooth-jointed arrows have now done
> what Viṣṇu once did with his lion claws.[2]

KING: Here too Indra's might deserves the praise.   20

> When servants succeed in great tasks,
> they act in hope of their master's praise—
> would dawn scatter the darkness
> if he were not the sun's own charioteer?

MĀTALI: This attitude suits you well! [*He moves a little distance.*] Look   25
over there, Your Majesty! See how your own glorious fame has
reached the vault of heaven!

> Celestial artists are drawing your exploits
> on leaves of the wish-granting creeper[3]
> with colors of the nymphs' cosmetic paints,   30
> and bards are moved to sing of you in ballads.

---

1. The coral trees of heaven bear never-fading
flowers.
2. In his incarnation as half man, half lion,
the god Viṣṇu slew a demon.
3. The *kalpalatā* vine that grows in Indra's
heaven.

KING: Mātali, in my desire to do battle with the demons, I did not
notice the path we took to heaven as we climbed through the sky
yesterday. Which course of the winds are we traveling?

MĀTALI:

> They call this path of the wind Parivaha— 35
> freed from darkness by Viṣṇu's second stride,
> it bears the Gaṅgā's three celestial streams[4]
> and turns stars in orbit, dividing their rays.

KING: Mātali, this is why my soul, my senses, and my heart feel calm.
[*He looks at the chariot wheels.*] We've descended to the level of the 40
clouds.

MĀTALI: How do you know?

KING:

> Crested cuckoos fly between the spokes,
> lightning flashes glint off the horses' coats,
> and a fine mist wets your chariot's wheels— 45
> all signs that we go over rain-filled clouds.

MĀTALI: In a moment you'll be back in your own domain, Your Majesty.

KING: [*Looking down.*] Our speeding chariot makes the mortal world
appear fantastic. Look!

> Mountain peaks emerge as the earth descends, 50
> branches spread up from a sea of leaves,
> fine lines become great rivers to behold—
> the world seems to hurtle toward me.

MĀTALI: You observe well! [*He looks with great reverence.*] The beauty
of earth is sublime. 55

KING: Mātali, what mountain do I see stretching into the eastern and
western seas, rippled with streams of liquid gold, like a gateway of
twilight clouds?

MĀTALI: Your Majesty, it is called the "Golden Peak," the mountain of
the demigods, a place where austerities are practiced to perfection. 60

> Mārīca, the descendant of Brahmā,
> a father of both demons and gods,
> lives the life of an ascetic here
> in the company of Aditi, his wife.

KING: One must not ignore good fortune! I shall perform the rite of 65
circumambulating the sage.

MĀTALI: An excellent idea!
[*The two mime descending.*]

---

4. In heaven the Ganges flows with three streams before descending to earth. As the cosmic
strider, Viṣṇu scattered the darkness from heaven.

KING: [*Smiling.*]

> The chariot wheels make no sound,
> they raise no clouds of dust,
> they touch the ground unhindered—   70
> nothing marks the chariot's descent.

MĀTALI: It is because of the extraordinary power that you and Indra both possess.
KING: Mātali, where is Mārīca's hermitage?
MĀTALI: [*Pointing with his hand.*]

> Where the sage stands staring at the sun,   75
> as immobile as the trunk of a tree,
> his body half-buried in an ant hill,
> with a snake skin on his chest,
> his throat pricked by a necklace
> of withered thorny vines,   80
> wearing a coil of long matted hair
> filled with nests of śakunta birds.

KING: I do homage to the sage for his severe austerity.
MĀTALI: [*Pulling hard on the chariot reins.*] Great king, let us enter Mārīca's hermitage, where Aditi nurtures the celestial coral trees.   85
KING: This tranquil place surpasses heaven. I feel as if I'm bathing in a lake of nectar.
MĀTALI: [*Stopping the chariot.*] Dismount, Your Majesty!
KING: [*Dismounting.*] Mātali, what about you?
MĀTALI: I have stopped the chariot. I'll dismount too. [*He does so.*]   90
This way, Your Majesty! [*He walks around.*] You can see the grounds of the ascetics' grove ahead.
KING: I am amazed!

> In this forest of wish-fulfilling trees
> ascetics live on only the air they breathe   95
> and perform their ritual ablutions
> in water colored by golden lotus pollen.
> They sit in trance on jeweled marble slabs
> and stay chaste among celestial nymphs,
> practicing austerities in the place   100
> that others seek to win by penances.

MĀTALI: Great men always aspire to rare heights! [*He walks around, calling aloud.*] O venerable Śākalya, what is the sage Mārīca doing now? What do you say? In response to Aditi's question about the duties of a devoted wife, he is talking in a gathering of great sages' wives.[5]   105

---

5. In Gupta society, the sages were teachers of *dharma* and of the norms of behavior for women of the upper classes.

KING: [*Listening.*] We must wait our turn.

MĀTALI: [*Looking at the* KING.] Your Majesty, rest at the foot of this aśoka tree. Meanwhile, I'll look for a chance to announce you to Indra's father.

KING: As you advise . . . [*He stops.*]   110

MĀTALI: Your Majesty, I'll attend to this. [*He exits.*]

KING: [*Indicating he feels an omen.*]

> I have no hope for my desire.
> Why does my arm throb in vain?
> Once good fortune is lost,
> it becomes constant pain.   115

VOICE OFFSTAGE: Don't be so wild! Why is his nature so stubborn?

KING: [*Listening.*] Unruly conduct is out of place here. Whom are they reprimanding? [*Looking toward the sound, surprised.*] Who is this child guarded by two female ascetics? A boy who acts more like a man.

> He has dragged this lion cub   120
> from its mother's half-full teat
> to play with it, and with his hand
> he violently tugs its mane.

[*The* BOY *enters as described, with two female ascetics.*]

BOY: Open your mouth, lion! I want to count your teeth!

FIRST ASCETIC: Nasty boy, why do you torture creatures we love like   125
our children? You're getting too headstrong! The sages gave you
the right name when they called you "Sarvadamana, Tamer-of-
everything."

KING: Why is my heart drawn to this child, as if he were my own flesh?
I don't have a son. That is why I feel tender toward him . . .   130

SECOND ASCETIC: The lioness will maul you if you don't let go of her
cub!

BOY: [*Smiling.*] Oh, I'm scared to death! [*Pouting.*]

KING:

> This child appears to be
> the seed of hidden glory,   135
> like a spark of fire
> awaiting fuel to burn.

FIRST ASCETIC: Child, let go of the lion cub and I'll give you another
toy!

BOY: Where is it? Give it to me! [*He reaches out his hand.*]   140

KING: Why does he bear the mark of a king who turns the wheel of
empire?

> A hand with fine webs connecting the fingers
> opens as he reaches for the object greedily,

like a single lotus with faint inner petals   145
spread open in the red glow of early dawn.

SECOND ASCETIC: Suvratā, you can't stop him with words! The sage
Mārkaṇḍeya's son left a brightly painted clay bird in my hut. Get it
for him!

FIRST ASCETIC: I will! [*She exits.*]   150

BOY: But until it comes I'll play with this cub.

KING: I am attracted to this pampered boy . . .

Lucky are fathers whose laps give refuge
to the muddy limbs of adoring little sons
when childish smiles show budding teeth   155
and jumbled sounds make charming words.

SECOND ASCETIC: Well, he ignores me. [*She looks back.*] Is one of the
sage's sons here? [*Looking at the* KING.] Sir, please come here! Make
him loosen his grip and let go of the lion cub! He's tormenting it in
his cruel child's play.   160

KING: [*Approaching the* BOY, *smiling.*] Stop! You're a great sage's son!

When self-control is your duty by birth,
why do you violate the sanctuary laws
and ruin the animals' peaceful life,
like a young black snake in a sandal tree?   165

SECOND ASCETIC: Sir, he's not a sage's son.

KING: His actions and his looks confirm it. I based my false assumption on his presence in this place. [*He does what she asked; responding
to the* BOY'*s touch, he speaks to himself.*]

Even my limbs feel delighted
from the touch of a stranger's son—   170
the father at whose side he grew
must feel pure joy in his heart.

SECOND ASCETIC: [*Examining them both.*] It's amazing! Amazing!

KING: What is it, madam?

SECOND ASCETIC: This boy looks surprisingly like you. He doesn't even   175
know you, and he's acting naturally.

KING: [*Fondling the child.*] If he's not the son of an ascetic, what lineage does he belong to?

SECOND ASCETIC: The family of Puru.

KING: [*To himself.*] What? His ancestry is the same as mine . . . so this   180
lady thinks he resembles me. The family vow of Puru's descendants
is to spend their last days in the forest.

As world protectors they first choose
palaces filled with sensuous pleasures,

but later, their homes are under trees   185
and one wife shares the ascetic vows.

[*Aloud.*] But mortals cannot enter this realm on their own.

SECOND ASCETIC: You're right, sir. His mother is a nymph's child. She
gave birth to him here in the hermitage of Mārīca.

KING: [*In a stage whisper.*] Here is a second ground for hope! [*Aloud.*]   190
What famed royal sage claims her as his wife?

SECOND ASCETIC: Who would even think of speaking the name of a
man who rejected his lawful wife?

KING: [*To himself.*] Perhaps this story points to me. What if I ask the
name of the boy's mother? No, it is wrong to ask about another man's   195
wife.

FIRST ASCETIC: [*Returning with a clay bird in her hand.*] Look, Sarvadamana, a śakunta! Look! Isn't it lovely?

BOY: Where's my mother?

BOTH ASCETICS: He's tricked by the similarity of names.[6] He wants his   200
mother.

SECOND ASCETIC: Child, she told you to look at the lovely clay śakunta
bird.

KING: [*To himself.*] What? Is his mother's name Śakuntalā? But names
can be the same. Even a name is a mirage . . . a false hope to herald   205
despair.

BOY: I like this bird! [*He picks up the toy.*]

FIRST ASCETIC: [*Looking frantically.*] Oh, I don't see the amulet-box on
his wrist!

KING: Don't be alarmed! It broke off while he was tussling with the   210
lion cub. [*He goes to pick it up.*]

BOTH ASCETICS: Don't touch it! Oh, he's already picked it up! [*With
their hands on their chests, they stare at each other in amazement.*]

KING: Why did you warn me against it?

FIRST ASCETIC: It contains the magical herb called Aparājitā,[7] honored
sir. Mārīca gave it to him at his birth ceremony. He said that if it fell   215
to the ground no one but his parents or himself could pick it up.

KING: And if someone else does pick it up?

FIRST ASCETIC: Then it turns into a snake and strikes.

KING: Have you two seen it so transformed?

BOTH ASCETICS: Many times.   220

KING: [*To himself, joyfully.*] Why not rejoice in the fulfillment of my
heart's desire? [*He embraces the child.*]

SECOND ASCETIC: Suvratā, come, let's tell Śakuntalā that her penances
are over.

[*Both ascetics exit.*]

---

6. *Śakunta*, one of the Sanskrit and Prakrit
words for "bird," is etymologically related to
Śakuntalā (Woman of the Birds), who was so
named because she was found in the forest in
the company of birds. Now her son, Bharata,
mistakes *śakunta* for *śakuntalā*. Like the
women, the child speaks Prakrit, the "natural"
language, but once he has entered the social
world of men he must speak Sanskrit.

7. Meaning "invincible" or "unvanquished."

BOY: Let me go! I want my mother!   225
KING: Son, you will greet your mother with me.
BOY: My father is Duṣyanta, not you!
KING: This contradiction confirms the truth.

[ŚAKUNTALĀ *enters, wearing the single braid of a woman in mourning.*]

ŚAKUNTALĀ: Even though Sarvadamana's amulet kept its natural form
   instead of changing into a snake, I can't hope that my destiny will be   230
   fulfilled. But maybe what my friend Sānumatī reports is right.

KING: [*Looking at* ŚAKUNTALĀ.] It is Śakuntalā!

> Wearing dusty gray garments,
> her face gaunt from penances,
> her bare braid[8] hanging down—   235
> she bears with perfect virtue
> the trial of long separation
> my cruelty forced on her.

ŚAKUNTALĀ: [*Seeing the* KING *pale with suffering.*] He doesn't resemble
   my noble husband. Whose touch defiles my son when the amulet is   240
   protecting him?

BOY: [*Going to his mother.*] Mother, who is this stranger who calls me
   "son"?

KING: My dear, I see that you recognize me now. Even my cruelty to
   you is transformed by your grace.   245

ŚAKUNTALĀ: [*To herself.*] Heart, be consoled! My cruel fate has finally
   taken pity on me. It is my noble husband!

KING:

> Memory chanced to break my dark delusion
> and you stand before me in beauty,
> like the moon's wife Rohiṇī   250
> as she rejoins her lord after an eclipse.

ŚAKUNTALĀ: Victory to my noble husband![9] Vic . . . [*She stops when the
   word is half-spoken, her throat choked with tears.*]

KING: Beautiful Śakuntalā,

> Even choked by your tears,
> the word "victory" is my triumph   255
> on your bare pouting lips,
> pale-red flowers of your face.

BOY: Mother, who is he?
ŚAKUNTALĀ: Child, ask the powers of fate!

---

8. A woman separated from her lover
neglected her looks and wore her hair in a
single braid.

9. The traditional formula for greeting a royal
husband.

KING: [*Falling at* ŚAKUNTALĀ's *feet.*][1]

> May the pain of my rejection   260
> vanish from your heart;
> delusion clouded my weak mind
> and darkness obscured good fortune—
> a blind man tears off a garland,
> fearing the bite of a snake.   265

ŚAKUNTALĀ: Noble husband, rise! Some crime I had committed in a former life surely came to fruit and made my kind husband indifferent to me.
[*The* KING *rises.*]
But how did my noble husband come to remember this woman who was doomed to pain?   270
KING: I shall tell you after I have removed the last barb of sorrow.

> In my delusion I once ignored
> a teardrop burning your lip—
> let me dry the tear on your lash
> to end the pain of remorse!   275

[*He does so.*]
ŚAKUNTALĀ: [*Seeing the signet ring.*] My noble husband, this is the ring!
KING: I regained my memory when the ring was recovered.
ŚAKUNTALĀ: When it was lost, I tried in vain to convince my noble husband who I was.
KING: Let the vine take back this flower as a sign of her union with   280
spring.
ŚAKUNTALĀ: I don't trust it. Let my noble husband wear it!
[MĀTALI *enters.*]
MĀTALI: Good fortune! This meeting with your lawful wife and the sight of your son's face are reasons to rejoice.
KING: The sweet fruit of my desire! Mātali, didn't Indra know about   285
all this?
MĀTALI: What is unknown to the gods? Come, Your Majesty! The sage Mārīca grants you an audience.
KING: Śakuntalā, hold our son's hand! We shall go to see Mārīca together.   290
ŚAKUNTALĀ: I feel shy about appearing before my elders in my husband's company.
KING: But it is customary at a joyous time like this. Come! Come!
[*They all walk around. Then* MĀRĪCA *enters with* ADITI: *they sit.*]
MĀRĪCA: [*Looking at the* KING.]

> Aditi, this is king Duṣyanta,
> who leads Indra's armies in battle;   295

---

1. In Sanskrit poetry, the repentant lover, regardless of his rank, must fall at the feet of his beloved, expressing his remorse and asking for her forgiveness.

his bow lets your son's thunderbolt
lie ready with its tip unblunted.

ADITI: He bears himself with dignity.
MĀTALI: Your Majesty, the parents of the gods look at you with affec-
tion reserved for a son. Approach them! 300
KING: Mātali, the sages so describe this pair.

> Source of the sun's twelve potent forms,
> parents of Indra, who rules the triple world,
> birthplace of Viṣṇu's primordial form,
> sired by Brahmā's sons,[2] Marīci and Dakṣa. 305

MĀTALI: Correct!
KING: [Bowing.] Indra's servant, Duṣyanta, bows to you both.
MĀRĪCA: My son, live long and protect the earth!
ADITI: My son, be an invincible warrior!
ŚAKUNTALĀ: I worship at your feet with my son. 310
MĀRĪCA:

> Child, with a husband like Indra
> and a son like his son Jayanta,
> you need no other blessing.
> Be like Indra's wife Paulomī!

ADITI: Child, may your husband honor you and may your child live 315
long to give both families joy! Be seated!
[All sit near MĀRĪCA.]
MĀRĪCA: [Pointing to each one.]

> By the turn of fortune,
> virtuous Śakuntalā, her noble son,
> and the king are reunited—
> faith and wealth with order. 320

KING: Sir, first came the success of my hopes, then the sight of you.
Your kindness is unparalleled.

> First flowers appear, then fruits,
> first clouds rise, then rain falls,
> but here the chain of events is reversed— 325
> first came success, then your blessing.

MĀTALI: This is the way the creator gods give blessings.
KING: Sir, I married your charge by secret marriage rites. When her
relatives brought her to me after some time, my memory failed and I

2. These references establish Aditi and Mārīca's status as primordial parents of the universe and
of the gods themselves.

sinned against the sage Kaṇva, your kinsman. When I saw the ring, I   330
remembered that I had married his daughter. This is all so strange!

> Like one who doubts the existence
> of an elephant who walks in front of him
> but feels convinced by seeing footprints,
> my mind has taken strange turns.   335

MĀRĪCA: My son, you need not take the blame. Even your delusion has
another cause. Listen!

KING: I am attentive.

MĀRĪCA: When Menakā took her bewildered daughter from the steps
of the nymph's shrine and brought her to my wife, I knew through   340
meditation that you had rejected this girl as your lawful wife because
of Durvāsas' curse, and that the curse would end when you saw the
ring.

KING: [Sighing.] So I am freed of blame.

ŚAKUNTALĀ: [To herself.] And I am happy to learn that I wasn't rejected   345
by my husband without cause. But I don't remember being cursed.
Maybe the empty heart of love's separation made me deaf to
the curse . . . my friends did warn me to show the ring to my
husband . . .

MĀRĪCA: My child, I have told you the truth. Don't be angry with your   350
husband!

> You were rejected when the curse
> that clouded memory made him cruel,
> but now darkness is lifted
> and your power is restored—   355
> a shadow has no shape
> in a badly tarnished mirror,
> but when the surface is clean
> it can easily be seen.

KING: Sir, here is the glory of my family! [He takes the child by the hand.]   360

MĀRĪCA: Know that he is destined to turn the wheel of your empire!

> His chariot will smoothly cross
> the ocean's rough waves
> and as a mighty warrior
> he will conquer the seven continents.   365
> Here he is called Sarvadamana,
> Tamer-of-everything;
> later when his burden is the world,
> men will call him Bharata, Sustainer.[3]

---

3. Bharata is to become the emperor after whom ancient India (Bhāratavarṣa) is named. "Seven continents": those of the Hindu universe.

KING: Since you performed his birth ceremonies, we can hope for all 370
this.

ADITI: Sir, let Kaṇva be told that his daughter's hopes have been
fulfilled. Menakā, who loves her daughter, is here in attendance.

ŚAKUNTALĀ: [To herself.] The lady expresses my own desire.

MĀRĪCA: He knows everything already through the power of his 375
austerity.

KING: This is why the sage was not angry at me.

MĀRĪCA: Still, I want to hear his response to this joyful reunion.
Who is there?

DISCIPLE: [Entering.] Sir, it is I. 380

MĀRĪCA: Gālava, fly through the sky and report the joyous reunion to
Kaṇva in my own words: "The curse is ended. Śakuntalā and her son
are embraced by Duṣyanta now that his memory is restored."

DISCIPLE: As you command, sir! [He exits.]

MĀRĪCA: My son, mount your friend Indra's chariot with your wife 385
and son and return to your royal capital!

KING: As you command, sir!

MĀRĪCA: My son, what other joy can I give you?

KING: There is no greater joy, but if you will:

> May the king serve nature's good! 390
> May priests honor the goddess of speech!
> And may Śiva's dazzling power
> destroy my cycle of rebirths![4]

[All exit.]

4. All Sanskrit plays end with a traditional verse called *bharatavākvya* (the utterance of [the sage] Bharata), in which the play's pro- tagonist invokes the blessings of the gods on himself and the universal order.

THE CLASSICAL SANSKRIT LYRIC

A short Sanskrit poem is like a snapshot—a vivid picture of a passing moment, created not in pixels but in words, seeking to forever capture an intensely emotional experience. Yet the numerous lyric poems preserved in classical Sanskrit also follow literary and social conventions that are quite different from those of lyric poetry in the European languages. One vital difference is that the Western lyric—from **Sappho** and **Catullus** to **Shakespeare** and Baudelaire—often allows a poet to speak in his or her individual voice, either directly or through a distinctive persona, to express unique personal feelings and private experiences. In contrast, the Sanskrit lyric usually requires a poet to represent even the most subjective emotions in an imaginative, impersonal, and universal form, at a remove from his or her actual personality and biography. This contrast is the result not of different values placed on the individual (as is often mistakenly assumed) but of very different conceptions of the nature and function of poetry.

The ten poets included in this cluster have long been recognized as "masters" of miniature poetry, and they all belong to the classical period of Sanskrit literature (the fourth to the eleventh century). They brought a wide range of personalities, life experiences, and social backgrounds to their writing in varying historical circumstances. But each of them, including the three women poets—a rare and elusive category—display exceptional skill and imagination in the multifarious genre of short or lyric poetry.

The Sanskrit version of lyric poetry is called *subhāṣita*, something "beautifully expressed in language" within the limits of a single verse or condensed passage. There are two main types: poetry composed as a complete text in a short form, such as an epigram, a vignette, a eulogy, or a riddle, and poetry extracted from a longer work that can stand on its own, such as a description, a dramatic situation, a moment of epiphany, or even a piece of dialogue from a play. The most important criteria for recognizing a poem as a *subhāṣita* are that it be short (no longer than a verse or two or a few lines), self-contained (a complete thought, situation, or event), and well-crafted (the best and fewest words and images in the best order). At the same time, such a poem should capture a particular feeling, mood, or emotional state, using the power of suggestion to convey something larger than its literal meaning.

Since the middle of the first millennium, poets and scholars in Sanskrit have compiled large anthologies of brief poems and passages fitting this definition, drawing sometimes from a single author but more often from many authors. The chosen pieces may be composed in many different meters, genres, and styles; they usually cover a large variety of themes; and they capture different emotions and moods and their many nuances. A short poem in Sanskrit, however, cannot represent the full essence of an emotional state. According to the classical Indian tradition, a fundamental emotional experience, like that of love or compassion or anger, is too large and complex to be conveyed in a single verse or passage; it can be properly expressed only when a work has enough room to spell out all its facets and stages. A lyric can do no more than give us a glimpse of a *rasa*, the state's essence, most often by creating a mood, suggesting a situation, or offering a single scene in an instant flash.

The lyric poems below represent many features of Sanskrit *subhāṣita* poetry on a miniature scale. Bhartṛhari's seven poems are drawn from a collection of his work, whereas the short poems by the other nine poets in this selection are all taken from a large multiauthor anthology—the *Subhā-ṣitaratnakośa* (*A Treasury of the Gems of Beautifully Crafted Verse*), compiled by the Buddhist monk Vidyākara just before 1100, probably at a monastery near today's India–Nepal border. A connoisseur of Sanskrit lyric in all its diversity, Vidyākara gathered 1,738

pieces by more than 200 poets, most of whom had lived during the preceding four centuries.

All the poems in our selection use indirect suggestion (*dhvani*) rather than mere description to create a mood or delineate a theme. The lyric poets of classical Sanskrit achieve their effects by focusing on the sensuous details of everyday experience, constructing verbal images that fully engage all the senses. For instance, **Bāṇa's "The Horse Rises"** creates such an effective montage that we practically see a horse moving right before our eyes. The lyric poets also speak to us with wit and humor, combining precise observation—of the human and the natural worlds—with imaginative twists of language as well as thought or figuration (*alaṃkāra*). Their style is therefore realistic in its effects, even as it highlights the pleasures of perception, recognition, and remembrance.

BHARTṚHARI

B hartṛhari (fifth century) was a court poet whose skill in composing short poems in various genres made him a model for subsequent generations. Collected soon after his lifetime, his poetry is preserved in the *Śatakatryam* (*The Three Centuries*, or *Three Hundred Poems*); it is celebrated most for its chiseled images, its melancholy tone, and its biting criticism of the ways of the world. The poems, complete in themselves (rather than excerpts from longer works), are grouped into three thematic sections or "centuries." In the original book, the poems in the first section deal with

ethical and moral issues that arise in worldly affairs, those in the second focus on love and desire, while those in the third express disillusionment with the world and explore the complexities of renunciation. "I haven't been the cloud," for example, gives us unprecedented insight into a child's moral debt to its mother. "When she is out of sight" paints a small but exact picture of sexual attraction. And "For a moment he's a child" contemplates life's stages with the detachment of old age— foreshadowing **Shakespeare's** image of "the seven ages of man" more than a thousand years later.

[I haven't been the cloud][1]

I haven't been the cloud
    that brings a rain of riches
to fields parched by lack of money;

I haven't been the powerful storm
    that devastates
a mountain-range of enemies;   5

I haven't even been the bee
    that buzzes around the lotus-faces
of sweet-eyed young women—

I've only been the axe   10
    that cut my mother's youth in two.

[When she's out of sight]

When she's out of sight,
    we desire to see her;
when we behold her,
    we want to hold her in a sweet embrace;
when this long-eyed beauty   5
    is in our arms,
we wish our separate bodies
    to be one at once—
without difference.

[When I knew little]

When I knew little,
I was like an elephant, blind in rut—
I know everything, I said,
    and proudly thought my mind was omniscient.

But when I kept the company   5
of wise people, little by little
I learned that *I'm a fool*—
    and the madness left me, like a fever.

To His Patron

You're the master of wealth,
of infinite means.
    I'm a master, too—
    of words and their infinite meanings.

1. Translated by Vinay Dharwadker. The poems are drawn from Bhartṛhari's *Śatakatryam*.

You're a great warrior—   5
    I'm a debater
    with limitless skill in the art
    of crushing my opponents' pride.
Those who serve you
are blinded by riches—   10
    but they also wish to hear me,
    to purify their minds.
You disregard me,
so I disregard you more—
    I'm gone, O king,   15
and greater than your presence at court
    is my absence from it.

[A human being]

A human being
is allotted a span
    of a hundred years.
Half of it
passes at night;   5
half of the other half
is consumed by childhood,
    old age;
the rest is spent
in serving others—   10
with illness, separation, grief
    for companions.
What's happiness, then,
for living things,
in a life that's like   15
    the bubbles in the froth
    on ocean waves?

[As the sun rises and sets]

As the sun rises and sets,
comes and goes,
life is whittled away
    day by day.
Engrossed in business,   5
weighed down by many tasks,
we don't know
    how time passes.
We witness birth, old age,
misfortune, death—   10

but they leave us
    unshaken.
The world has taken leave of its senses,
drunk on the heady wine
of worldliness   15
    and the gratification
    of the senses.

[For a moment he's a child]

For a moment he's a child—
for a moment, too, a youth—
a connoisseur of love and desire.

For a moment he's a beggar—
and—also for a moment—   5
a master of all wealth, all luxury.

At the end of his active life,
a man—his limbs wizened by age—
like an actor—his face painted with wrinkles—

retires behind the curtain of death.   10

THREE WOMEN POETS

VIKAṬANITAMBĀ

As is the case for the other women poets in classical Sanskrit and ancient Indian literature, we know practically nothing about Vikaṭanitambā beyond what we can infer from the few poetic pieces attributed to her. Her name indicates that she may have belonged to southern India; brief references by later poets and scholars provide evidence that she lived some-time between the fifth and seventh centuries. She treats erotic themes candidly, skillfully using images to show rather than tell and preferring the technique of suggestion over graphic description. In "As he came to bed," for example, she heightens the moment of passion by hinting at the act of love rather than providing distracting details.

572[1]

As he came to bed the knot fell open of itself,
the dress held only somehow to my hips
by the strands of the loosened girdle.
So much I know, my dear;
but when within his arms, I can't remember who he was   5
or who I was, or what we did or how.

1. Translated by D. H. H. Ingalls. The number refers to the poem's position in Vidyākara's
Subhāṣitaratnakośa.

BHĀVAKADEVĪ

Like Vikaṭanitambā, Bhāvakadevī probably belonged to the middle of the classical period of Sanskrit poetry, but we can surmise even less about her life or personality. Her literary name indicates that she was prized by her contemporaries and successors for her emotional sensitivity. In "At first our bodies knew," Bhāvakadevī memorably evokes her bitterness in marriage by referring only indirectly to its source in her husband's unfaithfulness.

646[2]

At first our bodies knew a perfect oneness,
but then grew two with you as lover
and I, unhappy I, the loved.
Now you are husband, I the wife,
what's left except of this my life,   5
too hard to break, to reap the bitter fruit,
your broken faith.

2. Translated by D. H. H. Ingalls. The number refers to the poem's position in Vidyākara's
Subhāṣitaratnakośa.

VIDYĀ

Like Vikaṭanitambā and Bhāvakadevī, Vidyā is among the most frequently quoted women poets in classical Sanskrit, but only a few fragments of her poetry have survived. It is likely that she, too, lived between the fifth and the seventh centuries, but later than the other two women. Also like them, she is celebrated for her finely crafted love poems; they are explicitly set in the countryside, suggesting that she was more familiar with village life than with life at a royal court in a city. Her poem here is very oblique in its use of the technique of *dhvani*, or suggestion: a village housewife requests a neighbor to keep an eye on her hut while she goes out, ostensibly to fetch water from the river; but her expectation that she will return with visible scratches on her body indicates that she is really headed for a tryst with a lover on the riverbank.

807[3]

Good neighbor wife, I beg you
keep your eye upon my house a moment;
the baby's father hates to drink
the tasteless water from the well.
Better I go then, though alone, to the river bank   5
dark with *tamāla* trees and thick with canes,[4]
which with their sharp and broken stems
may scratch my breast.

3. Translated by D. H. H. Ingalls. The number refers to the poem's position in Vidyākara's *Subhāṣitaratnakośa*.
4. Vegetation characteristic of central India. In classical Sanskrit and later Indian lyric poetry, the riverbank—with shade and ground cover, not far from a village—is the favorite site for lovers' trysts, both before and after marriage.

BĀNA

Bāṇa was a *brāhmaṇa* scholar and writer who served as the court poet of King Harsavardhana, the principal ruler in northern India (at Kannauj, near Delhi) during the first half of the seventh century. Bāṇa composed two works that were major turning points in Sanskrit literature: *Harṣacarita*, about his royal patron, the first full-length account of an Indian ruler by a contemporaneous biographer, and *Kādambarī*, the first work of novelistic fiction in an Indian language, written in poetic prose. Bāṇa's short poems are excerpted from longer works; they are noted for their careful craftsmanship, complicated figuration, and psychological realism.

1166[1]

The horse rises, stretches his hind legs,
lengthens his body by lowering his spine,
then arches his neck down, his head bent to his chest,
and shakes the dust from his mane;
his nostrils quiver under the muzzle, sniffing for grass;   5
he whinnies softly as he scrapes the ground with his hoof.

1174[2]

The puff of smoke from the forest fire,
black as the shoulder of a young buffalo,
curls slightly, spreads, is broken for a moment, falls;
then gathers its power gracefully, and rising thick,
it slowly lays upon the sky   5
its transient ornaments.

1305[3]

At evening having warmed himself to heart's content
before the public fire nor minded how he scorched his rags,
he then lies down to sleep on straw within the village shrine.
But the wind blows wet with sleet. His shivering
soon wakes him, for his half a cloak   5
is old and cold and full of holes. He moans,
huddling from one corner to the next.

---

1. The numbers assigned to Bāṇa's poems
refer to their position in Vidyākara's *Subhā-*
ṣitaratnakośa. This poem is translated by Vinay

Dharwadker.
2. Translated by D. H. H. Ingalls.
3. Translated by D. H. H. Ingalls.

DHARMAKĪRTI

The poet Dharmakīrti (early seventh
century) was a Buddhist; probably
a monk in a monastery sponsored by a
royal patron, he may have been the
same person as the famous logician

and philosopher of that name and time.
His lyric pieces, which express specifically Buddhist values, stand out for
their uncompromising wit, epigram-
matic quality, and philosophical depth.

"Never to ask the wicked," for instance, is a perfect poetic expression of Buddhism's principles of moral firmness, mindfulness, and pursuit of the Middle Way, a path that avoids all extremes. But whether Hindu or Buddhist, the poet in classical India uses a short poem to create a specific mood, an aesthetic representation of a heightened emotional state. Thus, Dharmakīrti's "Your union with your lover" projects the mood of someone falling in love, highlighting the state of infatuation that occurs early in the process.

477[4]

Your union with your lover will be very brief,
like a dream or a magical illusion,
    and it will end in distaste:

I reflect on these truths a hundred times,
but my heart can't forget that girl   5
    with the eyes of a gazelle.

1213

Never to ask the wicked
for favors;
never to borrow
from a friend of meager means;

to be kind and loving in disposition,   5
just in action;
not to play foul
even at the hour of death;
to stand upright
in misfortune;   10
to follow in the footsteps
of the great:[5]

it's hard to do this—
as hard as it is to walk
on a sword's edge—   15

but good folks
don't need a sermon
about it.

4. Translated by Vinay Dharwadker. The numbers assigned to Dharmakīrti's poems refer to their position in Vidyākara's Subhā-ṣitaratnakośa.
5. Several core principles of Buddhism.

1729

There's no one riding ahead of me,[6]
there's no one behind me,
there are no fresh prints on this path:
    am I alone?

I see that the road
the ancients opened up long ago
is overgrown today:
    and I've definitely abandoned

that other—wide and easy—thoroughfare.

6. On the Buddhist monk's spiritual journey.

BHAVABHŪTĪ

Bhavabhūtī, a Hindu *brāhmaṇa*, was the best-known dramatist of the classical period after **Kālidāsa**. Most of the lyric verse with which he is represented in Sanskrit anthologies is taken from his two major poetic plays, *Mālatīmādhava* (*Mālatī and Mādhava*) and *Uttararāmacarita* (*King Rāma's Final Act*). He is celebrated for his individualism and experimentalism, for pushing his verse techniques and themes to an extreme, but he is especially renowned for his love poetry. "My love is married to me," which translates a single verse in Sanskrit, is a perfect example of Bhavabhūtī's originality and technical virtuosity: it projects the emotional state of a lover in a torrent of words and images resembling a modernist-style interior monologue, even as its content reminds us of a central theme in **Shakespeare**'s sonnets—a lover's desire for a complete and enduring "marriage of true minds" with his beloved. In thematic contrast, "The people in this world who scorn me" (one of the most frequently quoted lyrics in all of Sanskrit literature) gives us a unique image of a poet alienated from his own time and place who dreams of finding his ideal reader in posterity—a dream that this verse makes a reality for Bhavabhūtī himself. Many classical readers consider his "And as we talked together softly, secretly" to be the single most beautiful verse about love in Sanskrit poetry.

598[7]

And as we talked together softly, secretly,
cheek closely pressed to cheek
while our arms were busied in their tight embrace,
the night was gone without our knowing
the hours as they passed.   5

753[8]

A flood of tears blurs my vision time and again,
my limbs, numb from imagining her, are paralyzed,
my hand here breaks into a sweat, my fingers tremble,
as I try to paint my love:
                        tell me, how am I to do it?   5

783[9]

My love is married to me
as though she had melted into my mind

or was reflected in it or painted on it or sculpted in it
or set in it like a gem or cemented to it or engraved upon it

or as if she were nailed to it
by the five arrows of the god of love   5

or finely woven into the threads
of the very fabric of its thought

1731[1]

The people in this world who scorn me
no doubt have a special wisdom,
so I don't write for them:

instead, I write with the thought
that since the world is wide and time is endless,   5
one day someone will be born

whose nature is the same as mine.

---

7. The numbers assigned to Bhavabhūti's
poems refer to their positions in Vidyākara's
Subhāṣitaratnakośa. This poem is translated by
D. H. H. Ingalls.

8. Translated by Vinay Dharwadker.
9. Translated by Vinay Dharwadker.
1. Translated by Vinay Dharwadker.

YOGEŚVARA

Yogeśvara (ninth century) was a poet patronized by a king in eastern India in the late classical period. Probably from Bengal, he became the most celebrated lyric poet of "village and field"—of all aspects of country life—in Sanskrit. He captures the intangible qualities of village life and the countryside in several poems through a series of descriptions; but even when he seems to merely depict physical scenes in human and natural landscapes from a bird's-eye view, he succeeds in evoking powerful moods and emotions. Yogeśvara's range of emotions and situations is wider than we might expect: in "Now may one prize the peasant houses," we experience the sheer joy of harvest time; in "The warmth of their straw borne off by icy winds" we shiver with the peasants in the cold of incoming winter after threshing time; and in "When the rain pours down on the decrepit house" we feel deeply for the harried village wife struggling to survive in poverty.

257[2]

Now the great cloud cat,
darting out his lightning tongue,
licks the creamy moonlight
from the saucepan of the sky.

291

The days are sweet with ripening of sugar cane;
the autumn rice is high;
and brahmins, being overfed at feasts
to which the leading families invite them,
find that the heat grows hard to bear.[3]   5

314

Now may one prize the peasant houses
happy in the first harvest of the winter rice
and sweet with perfume from the jars of new-stored grain;
where the farmgirls take the pounder,
raise and shake and smoothly drop it,   5
their bracelets jingling as they raise their arms.

2. Translated by D. H. H. Ingalls. The numbers assigned to Yogeśvara's poems refer to their position in Vidyākara's *Subhāṣitaratnakośa*.

3. A satirical representation of the "parasitical" priestly caste. The poet is more sympathetic to the poor peasants in the countryside.

315

The fields where sesamum[4] has ripened
and now lies dry delight the doves;
the mustard turns to brown,
its flowers giving way to fruit;
the wind scatters the hemp   5
and makes the body shiver with its drops of sleet;
travelers, quarreling in empty argument,
huddle about the public fire.

318

The warmth of their straw borne off by icy winds,
time and again the peasants wake the fire
whose flame dies ever back, stirring with their sticks.
From the smoking bank of mustard chaff,
noisy with the crackling of the husks,   5
a penetrating odor spreads
to every corner of the threshing floor.

1163

The cat has humped her back;
mouth raised and tail curling,
she keeps one eye in fear upon the inside of the house;
her ears are motionless.
The dog, his mouthful of great teeth wide open   5
to the back of his spittle-covered jaws,
swells at the neck with held-in breath
until he jumps her.

1312

When the rain pours down on the decrepit house
she dries the flooded barley grits
and quiets the yelling children;
she bails out water with a potsherd
and saves the bedding straw.   5
With a broken winnowing basket on her head
the poor man's wife is busy everywhere.

4. Sesame.

MURĀRĪ

Like **Yogeśvara** before him, Murārī (mid-ninth century) was also a poet patronized by a king in eastern India. He may have belonged to Odisha or Orissa (the coastal region south of Bengal); without question he was a learned *brāhmaṇa* courtier, often praised for his highly elegant language, intricate craftsmanship, and wide-ranging literary allusions. His only surviving play is a dramatization of the *Rāmāyaṇa*, but his lyric poetry has also been preserved in quotations by later writers. Murārī's verses are dense and compact, full of surprising images and metaphors: in his two poems on moonlight, for example, he refers to "a group of carpenters" polishing "the tree of heaven," and to the power of a magnet to attract iron filings; in "My limbs are frail," he conjures up the idea that an aging man is "an actor in a farce," who is forced to wear "white hair / for makeup."

913[5]

Is the moonlight
   nothing but the powder
of the cleansing nut
   with which this sea of darkness
has been scrubbed bright,   5
   and its residue
precipitated to the bottom
   as shadows?
Or could the moon's rays
   be a group of carpenters   10
who polish the tree of heaven
   by planing it clean,
leaving its fallen bark
   for shadows?

958

As the moon ages,
   darkness covers the sky,
as if it were the smoke
   of opals about to burst into flames;
and though the sun   5

5. Translated by Vinay Dharwadker. The numbers assigned to Murārī's poems refer to their position in Vidyākara's *Subhāṣitaratnakośa*.

hasn't released its light as yet,
it draws out the bees
   imprisoned in the lotuses[6]
as a magnet attracts
   iron filings.   10

1019

O pearl free of flaws,
publish yourself—
   go furnish a house
or a king's necklace
   with your splendor,   5
bring your own virtues
   to fruit.
Why waste your life
   shut up in an oyster shell?
The ocean is enormous—   10
   who in this hole
can even calculate
   your worth?

1526

My limbs are frail,
my voice is weak,
   I suck up to the powerful—
I've been reduced
   to an actor in a farce.   5
I don't know
   in what new play
old age will cast me
   to play my part—
with this white hair   10
   for makeup.

1585

I remember this mountain,
I remember it well:
   here the jewels shine
so brightly at night

6. The lotus is photosensitive: its petals open at sunrise and close at sunset. The suggestion here is that if a bee happens to be feeding on a lotus at sundown, it may be "imprisoned" in the flower overnight when its petals close.

that the ravens gather 5
as if it were dawn,
and their cawing scares the owls
into the darkness of the caves;

here, when I took off
the wrap around your breasts, 10
you were so upset
that you tried to dress yourself
in the overhanging leaves,
and the forest-nymphs
amused themselves 15
by raising the branches
beyond your reach.

RĀJAŚEKHARA

Rājaśekhara (late ninth–early tenth century) was probably the son of a powerful court official in the Gurjara-Pratihara kingdom of north-central India. He was a poet and playwright composing in Sanskrit and in literary Prakrits, a theorist of literature, and a much-loved patron and friend of poets. He is especially famous because he publicly acknowledged his wife, Avantisundarī, as his equal in learning and taste, crediting her for his own literary success (the first Indian author to do so); he wrote his most famous play to please her, and she most likely hosted its first performance at their home. Rājaśekhara's short poems are verses taken from his plays; the best of them give us memorable images of the beauty of women and of the joys and intricacies of love. In "When people see her face," he pushes the technique of suggestion to an extreme with a clever inversion: he hints at a girl's extraordinary beauty by enumerating things to which her face, skin, eyes, eyebrows, and smile cannot be compared.

457[7]

When people see her face
    they stop talking about the moon;
when they see her skin,
    there's no more talk of gold.

7. The numbers assigned to Rājaśekhara's poems refer to their position in Vidyākara's *Subhā-ṣitaratnakośa*. This poem is translated by Vinay Dharwadker.

Waterlilies lose the contest   5
    against her eyes;
what's the nectar of moonlight
    when compared to her smile?
And the love god's bow is nothing
    when held up to her eyebrows.   10
But why say more—
    the truth is too well known,
that in the order of Creation
    the Creator shuns repetition.

336[8]

Youthfulness inscribes all her parts,
but is especially skillful in her eye's maturity,

for her gaze gathers all the expressions
of whichever man she chooses to look at,

and then conveys back to him   5
all that he feels as the one who looks at her,

whom she has found worthy of her gaze.

525[9]

The damsel of arched eyebrows,
gracefully circling as she whirls the yo-yo,
constructs three parasols:
with her skirt of southern silk,
with her beautiful pearl necklace,   5
and with her whirling braid of hair.

8. Translated by Vinay Dharwadker.   9. Translated by D. H. H. Ingalls.

SOMADEVA

eleventh century

How many different stories—truly different stories—have human beings invented? If we could read every story in the world and strip it down to its bare bones, how many distinct narrative cores would we find? Somadeva, a master storyteller from eleventh-century India, suggests that stories flow out of their tellers in streams and that all the streams, broadening into rivers, flow into an ocean of narrative that is potentially infinite.

LIFE

Somadeva was a brāhmaṇa scholar and courtier whose patron was Queen Sūryamati of Kashmir, an unusual woman with a strong interest in learning and the arts. In his prologue, he tells us that he compiled and composed the *Kathāsaritsāgara* to entertain the queen "when her mind had been wearied by the continuous study of the sciences." Trained in the traditional Indian disciplines of grammar, poetics and rhetoric, and philosophy (considered essential for any writer), he was exceptionally skilled in the crafts of both versification and narrative in the genre and style of Sanskrit *kāvya*.

Somadeva lived toward the end of the classical period of Indian literature, which stretched from about the fourth to the eleventh century. This period began with the establishment of the Gupta empire (320–550 C.E.) in northern India, and smaller imperial formations and kingdoms then emerged elsewhere on the subcontinent. The expansion of agriculture, mining and metallurgy, textile and handicraft production, and especially trade and commerce under the Gupta dynasty led to the rise of a wealthy and powerful merchant class and inaugurated several centuries of prosperity. Merchants became prominent citizens in busy port towns and cosmopolitan inland cities, investing in architecture and shipping; they crisscrossed the land on business and traveled widely overseas. Although they patronized pilgrimage sites and endowed temples and monasteries, their values were often secular and materialistic, focused on the acquisition and uses of wealth.

WORK

The large body of stories that Somadeva gathered in his *Kathāsaritsāgara* in the eleventh century reflected these developments. In contrast to earlier literature, which mostly emphasized frugality and otherworldliness in poorer economic conditions, the popular new tales of the classical period depicted a crowded world of traders, bankers, shopkeepers, con men, and thieves. Although the heroes and villains of these narratives are colorful characters, and their intrigues and wild schemes are often crooked, the stories themselves are concerned with more than the crass pursuit of wealth. Their recurrent concerns include the ancient Hindu themes of karma and rebirth, the memory of past lives and the power of curses, and *mokṣa*, the quest for liberation from worldly attachments. They also celebrate love and beauty in all their aspects, as well as the art of storytelling itself.

Somadeva brought together about 350 well-known stories, most of them transmitted from an earlier collection called *The Great Story* by Guṇāḍhya, which by the seventh century had been lost. Somadeva retold the tales in elegant Sanskrit couplets, in a heightened and distinctive style of verse narrative. The title, *Kathāsaritsāgara*, identifies the book as "the ocean into which the streams of narrative flow"; the work is thus intended to be, and has been received by generations of readers as, a large repository of all kinds of memorable stories. All the tales in the work are contained inside a main frame story, which recounts the adventures of Prince Naravāhanadatta, who becomes the king of the Vidyādharas (aerial spirits); the dominant themes of this narrative are the prince's acquisition of wealth and magical powers and his amorous relationships with several princesses and other beautiful women—including his great love, a courtesan he idealized. The nested short tales are told by various characters in the outer frame to amuse their friends, lovers, and spouses, in imitation of the stories that the great god Śiva is believed to tell his consort, Pārvatī, for her entertainment.

"The Red Lotus of Chastity," the story selected here, is a lively and entertaining example of the stories typically found in Somadeva's work and in classical literature in Sanskrit, as distinct from that language's earlier epic and religious narrative traditions. Though written much later, the story is set in the Gupta period of Indian history (probably in the fifth century); many of its characters belong to the wealthy merchant class of that time, and its action takes place in mainland India and on the islands of Indonesia. Its central theme is the value of fidelity in a marriage based on love, as it details the lengths to which a husband and a wife can go in order to remain faithful to each other.

The setup of the plot is unusual. A rich merchant of Bengal sails with his marriageable son to Indonesia to find a suitable bride for the young man in the community of wealthy Indian traders settled there. When they find a good match, however, the girl's father demurs because he does not want his beloved daughter to live far away, in India. But the girl has fallen completely in love and decides to marry the young man against her parents' wishes. Years later, after inheriting his father's trade in precious stones, the young husband decides to travel to another island in Indonesia; his wife, however, fears that he will be unfaithful to her during his long business trip abroad. To resolve their mutual anxieties, the couple appeals to the god Śiva, who gives them each a magical red lotus; if either of them commits adultery, then the lotus in the other's possession will wilt immediately.

What follows from this initial situation is a rollicking comedy of romantic love, sexual intrigue, and crafty worldliness. We encounter vivid characters—among them, the spoiled sons of a rich merchant, a corrupt Buddhist nun and her equally amoral protégée, and a wise and just king in a foreign land. The atmosphere is like that of a fairy tale, in which extraordinary events transform the destinies of ordinary people. But the characters themselves are realistically delineated and belong to social types that became standard figures both in India and abroad: Yogakaraṇḍikā and Siddhīkarī in "The Red Lotus of Chastity" are forerunners of the errant monks and nuns in later writing (such as **Chaucer's** *Canterbury Tales*), and Yogakaraṇḍikā, who makes a career of procuring women for men, also foreshadows the bawd in European Renaissance literature. The story's heroine, Devasmitā, bravely disguises herself as a man and undertakes a perilous journey overseas to foil an evil plot, to prove her own fidelity, and to test the love of her husband, Guhasena. She reminds us of many other cross-dressing women in both Indian and Western literature.

Like the earlier Buddhist *Jātaka* tales and Hindu animal fables of the *Pañcatantra*, the more secular and entertaining stories of the *Kathāsaritsā-gara* migrated from India to the Middle East and later to Europe. Besides the examples mentioned above, characters, situations, and plots from Somadeva's narratives turn up in works ranging from **Boccaccio**'s **Decameron** in the fifteenth century and **Shakespeare** at the end of the sixteenth century to Salman Rushdie's *Haroun and the Sea of Stories* (1990), which explicitly acknowledges its debt to the original "ocean of stories." Somadeva's eleventh-century work is especially famous as a model for *The Thousand and One Nights*.

From Kathāsaritsāgara[1]

The Red Lotus of Chastity

In this world is a famous port, Tāmraliptī,[2] and there lived a rich merchant whose name was Dhanadatta. He had no sons, so he assembled many brahmins, prostrated himself before them, and requested: "See to it that I get a son!"

"That is not at all difficult," said the priests, "for the brahmins can bring about everything on earth by means of the scriptural sacrifices.[3]

"For example," they continued, "long ago there was a king who had no sons, though he had one hundred and five women in his seraglio. He caused a special sacrifice for a son to be performed, and a son was born to him. The boy's name was Jantu, and in the eyes of all the king's wives he was the rising new moon. Once when he was crawling about on all fours, an ant bit him on the thigh, and the frightened child cried out. The incident caused a terrific disturbance in the seraglio, and the king himself lamented—'My son! O my son!'—like a commoner. After a while, when the ant had been removed and the child comforted, the king blamed his own anxiety on the fact that he had only one son.

" 'There must be a way to have more sons,' he thought, and in his grief he consulted the brahmins. They replied: 'Indeed, Your Majesty, there is one way by which you can have more sons. Kill the son you have and sacrifice all his flesh in the sacred fire. When the royal wives smell the burning flesh, they will all bear sons.' The king had everything done as they said and got as many sons as he had wives.

"Thus with the help of a sacrifice," concluded the brahmins, "we can bring you, too, a son."

So at the advice of the brahmins, merchant Dhanadatta settled on a stipend for their sacerdotal services, and the priests performed the sacrifice for him. Subsequently a son was born to the merchant. The boy, who was given the name Guhasena, grew up in due time, and his father Dhanadatta was seeking a wife for him. And the merchant voyaged with his son to the Archipelago[4] to find a bride, though he pretended that it was just a business expedition. In the Archipelago he asked the daughter of a prominent merchant, Dharmagupta, a girl named

---

1. Translated by J. A. B. van Buitenen.
2. During the Gupta era, an important port on the Bay of Bengal, a center for north India's trade with south India and Southeast Asia.
3. That is, those described in the Vedas.
4. Islands of Southeast Asia and Indonesia.

Devasmitā, On-Whom-the-Gods-Have-Smiled, in marriage for his son Guhasena. Dharmagupta, however, did not favor the alliance, for he loved his daughter very much and thought that Tāmraliptī was too far away. But Devasmitā herself, as soon as she had set eyes on Guhasena, was so carried away by his qualities that she decided to desert her parents. Through a companion of hers she arranged a meeting with the man she loved and sailed off from the island at night with him and his father. On their arrival in Tāmraliptī they were married; and the hearts of husband and wife were caught in the noose of love.

Then father Dhanadatta died, and, urged by his relatives to continue his father's business, Guhasena made plans for a voyage to the island of Cathay.[5] Devasmitā, however, did not approve of his going, for she was a jealous wife and naturally suspected that he would love another woman. So with his relatives urging him on and his wife opposing, Guhasena was caught in the middle and could not get on with his business.

Thereupon he went to a temple and took a vow of fasting. "Let God in this temple show me a way out," he thought. Devasmitā came along, and she took the same vow. God Śiva[6] appeared to both of them in a dream. He gave them two red lotuses and spoke: "Each of you must keep this lotus in his hand. If one of you commits adultery while the other is far away, the lotus in the other's hand will wither away. So be it!" The couple woke up, and each saw in the other's hand the red lotus which was an image of the lover's heart.

So, carrying his lotus, Guhasena departed, and Devasmitā stayed home watching hers. Presently Guhasena reached Cathay and went about his business, trading in precious stones. But the lotus he carried around in his hands aroused the curiosity of four merchant's sons who noticed that the flower never seemed to fade. They tricked him into accompanying them home and gave him quantities of mead to drink: when he was drunk, they asked him about the lotus, and he told them. Calculating that the merchant's trade in precious stones would take a long time to be completed, the mischievous merchant's sons plotted together, and, their curiosity aroused, all four set sail at once for Tāmraliptī, without telling anybody, to see if they could not undo the chastity of Guhasena's wife. Reconnoitering in Tāmraliptī, they sought out a wandering nun,[7] Yogakaraṇḍikā, who lived in a Buddhist monastery. They ingratiated themselves with her and proposed, "Reverend Madam, if you can bring about what we wish, we shall reward you richly."

"Of course, you boys want some girl in town," said the nun. "Tell me. I shall see to it. I have no desire for money, because I have a clever pupil named Siddhīkarī,[8] and thanks to her I have amassed a great fortune."

"How is that? You have acquired great wealth through the favor of your pupil?" the merchant's sons asked.

"If you are curious to hear the story, my sons," said the nun, "I shall tell you. Listen.

"Some time ago a merchant came to town from the North. While he was staying here, my pupil, in disguise, contrived to get herself employed in his house as

---

5. Not China but an island in Southeast Asia or Indonesia.
6. The destroyer god (Śiva), one of the two great gods of Hinduism.
7. Buddhist monks and nuns must have no possessions and are required to live on alms, which they collect by wandering.
8. She Who Can Accomplish What One Desires.

a maid of all work; and as soon as the merchant had come to trust her, she stole all the gold he had in his house and sneaked away at dawn. A drummer[9] saw her leave town and, his suspicions aroused by her fast pace, started with his drum in his hand to pursue and rob her in turn. Siddhīkarī had reached the foot of a banyan tree when she saw the drummer approach, and the cunning girl called out to him in a miserable voice: 'I have quarreled with my husband, and now I have run away from home to kill myself. Could you fasten the noose for me, my friend?'

" 'If she is going to hang herself, then why should I kill the woman?' thought the drummer, and he tied a noose to the tree. He stepped on his drum, put his head through the noose, and said. 'This is the way to do it.' The same instant Siddhīkarī kicked the drum to pieces—and the drummer himself perished in the noose. But at that moment the merchant came looking for her, and from a distance he discerned the maid who had stolen his entire fortune. She saw him come, however, and immediately climbed up the tree and hid among the leaves. When the merchant came to the tree with his servants, he saw only the drummer dangling from the tree, for Siddhīkarī was nowhere in sight.

" 'Can she have climbed up the tree?' the merchant questioned, and immediately one of the servants went up.

" 'I have always loved you, and here you are, with me in a tree!' whispered Siddhīkarī. 'Darling, all the money is yours. Take me!' And she embraced him and kissed him on the mouth and bit the fool's tongue off with her teeth. Overcome with pain the servant tumbled out of the tree, spitting blood, and cried something unintelligible that sounded like 'la-la-la.' When he saw him, the merchant thought that the man was possessed by a ghost, and in terror he fled home with his servants. No less terrified, Siddhīkarī, my pupil, climbed down from the top of the tree and went home with all the money."

The nun's pupil entered just as her mistress finished, and the nun presented her to the merchant's sons.

"But now tell me the truth," resumed the nun, "which woman do you want? I shall prepare her for you at once!"

"Her name is Devasmitā," they replied, "Guhasena's wife. Bring her to bed with us!" The nun promised to do so and gave the young men lodging in her house.

The wandering nun ingratiated herself with the servants at Guhasena's house by giving them delicacies and so on, and thus she gained entrance to the house with her pupil. But when she came to the door of Devasmitā's chambers, a dog which was kept on a chain at the door barked at her, though never before had the bitch been known to bark. Then Devasmitā saw her, and wondering who the woman was that had come, she sent a servant girl to inquire and then herself conducted the nun into her chamber. When she was inside, the nun gave Devasmitā her blessing, and after courteous amenities for which she found a pretext, the wicked woman said to the chaste wife: "I have always had a desire to see you, and today I saw you in a dream.[1] That is why I have come to visit you. I see that you are separated from your husband, and my heart suffers for you; if youth and beauty are deprived of love's pleasures, they are fruitless."

---

9. A *domba*, an executioner or low-caste functionary in cemeteries.

1. Holy persons are thought to have super-

natural gifts, such as the ability to dream true events and interpret them.

With such talk the nun gained Devasmitā's confidence, and after having chatted awhile she returned to her own home. The next day the nun took a piece of meat covered with sneezing powder and went to Devasmitā's house. She gave the meat to the dog at the door, and the animal at once swallowed it. The sneezing powder caused the dog's eyes to run, and the animal sneezed incessantly. Then the nun entered Devasmitā's apartment, and once she had settled down to her hostess' hospitality, the shrew began to weep. Pressed by Devasmitā she said, as if with great reluctance; "Oh, my daughter, go and look outside at your dog; she is crying. Just now she recognized me from a former life[2] when we knew each other, and she burst out in tears. Pity moved me to weep with her."

Devasmitā looked outside the door and saw the dog which seemed to be weeping. "What miracle is this?" she wondered for the space of a moment. Then the nun said: "Daughter, in a former life both she and I were the wives of a brahmin. Our husband had to travel everywhere at the king's orders as his envoy, and while he was gone, I carried on with other men as I pleased, to avoid frustrating the senses and the element. Our highest duty, you know, is to yield to the demands of sense and element. That is why I in this present life have the privilege of remembering past existences. But she in her ignorance guarded her chastity, and so she has been reborn a bitch, though she does remember her other life."

"What kind of moral duty is that?" thought Devasmitā, who was clever enough. "This nun has some crooked scheme afoot!" Then she said: "Reverend Madam, how long I have been ignorant of my real duty! You must introduce me to some handsome man!"

"There are some merchant's sons from the Archipelago who are staying in town," said the nun. "I shall bring them to you if you want."

Overjoyed the nun went home. And Devasmitā said secretly to her servant girls: "I am sure that some merchant's sons have seen the never-fading lotus which my husband carries in his hand, and out of curiosity they have asked him about it when he was drinking. Now the scoundrels have come here from their island to seduce me and have engaged that depraved nun as their go-between. Fetch me immediately some liquor loaded with Datura[3] drug and go and have a dog's-paw branding iron made." The maids did as their mistress told them, and one of them, at Devasmitā's instructions, dressed up as her mistress.

Meanwhile the nun selected one of the four merchant's sons, who each commanded to be taken first, and brought him, disguised as her own pupil, to Devasmitā's house. There she bade him go inside and went away unobserved. The maid who posed as Devasmitā gave the young merchant with all due courtesies the drugged liquor to drink, and the drink (as though it were his own depravity) robbed him of his senses. Then the girls stripped him of everything he wore and robed him monastically in air.[4] Thereupon they branded the dog's-paw iron on his forehead, dragged him outside, and threw him in a cesspool. In the last hours of night he came to his senses and found himself sunk in the cesspool—the very image of the Avīci hell[5] which his own wickedness had brought on! He got up, bathed, and, fingering the mark on his forehead, he returned naked to the nun's house.

---

2. The memory of past lives is a gift, enabling the rememberer to make amends for evil deeds of such lives.
3. A narcotic plant.

4. The Digambaras ("clad in air"), a major sect of Jaina monks, wander naked.
5. One of the many hells described in Hindu and Buddhist mythology.

"I won't be the only ridiculous one!" he thought, and so he told his brothers in the morning that he had been robbed on his way back. Pretending a headache from his long night and deep drinking, he kept his marked forehead wrapped in a turban's cloth.

The second merchant's son who went to Devasmitā's house that night was manhandled in the same way. He too came home naked and said that, despite leaving his jewelry at home, he had been stripped by robbers as he came back. And the next morning he too kept his head bandaged, supposedly because of a headache, to conceal the brand on his forehead. All four of them, though they dissimulated everything, were castigated, branded, plundered, and put to shame in the same fashion. Without disclosing to the nun how they had been maltreated ("Let the same thing happen to her!"), they departed.

The next day the nun, who thought that her plan had succeeded, went with her pupil to Devasmitā's house. With a show of gratitude Devasmitā courteously poured them drinks with Datura, and when the nun and her pupil had passed out, the chaste wife cut off their noses and ears[6] and tossed them outside in a sewage pit.

But then Devasmitā began to worry. "Might those merchant's sons now kill my husband in revenge?" She went to her mother-in-law and told her everything that had happened.

"Daughter," said her mother-in-law, "you have done well. But something bad may now happen to my son."

"Then I shall save him as Śaktimatī once saved her husband with her presence of mind!"

"And how did she save her husband?" asked her mother-in-law. "Tell me, my daughter."

"In my country," Devasmitā began, "we have a great Yakṣa[7] who is famous under the name of Maṇibhadra. He is very powerful, and our ancestors have built him a temple in our town. My countrymen come to this temple, each with his own presents, to offer them to Maṇibhadra in order to gain whatever it is they wish. There is a custom that any man who is found in this temple at night with another man's wife is kept with the woman in the sanctum of Maṇibhadra for the rest of the night, and the next morning they are brought to court, where they will confess to their behavior and be thrown in jail.

"One night a merchant named Samudradatta was caught in the act with another man's wife by one of the temple guards. The guard led the merchant away with the woman and threw them into the sanctum of the temple where they were securely chained. After a while the merchant's faithful wife, Śaktimatī, who was very ingenious, got to know what had happened. Immediately she took an offering for pūjā worship[8] and, disguised, went out into the night to the temple, full of self-confidence and chaperoned by her confidantes. When she came to the temple, the pūjā priest, greedy for the stipend she offered him, opened the gates for her, after informing the captain of the guard. Inside the temple she found her husband who was caught with the woman. She dressed the woman up to pass for

---

6. In Hindu law a punishment for women who commit adultery.
7. A type of demigod common to Hindu, Bud-
dhist, and Jaina mythologies.
8. The rite of worshipping holy or noble persons, guests, and images of gods and goddesses.

herself and told her to get out. The woman went out into the night in her disguise, and Śaktimatī herself stayed in the sanctum with her husband. When in the morning the king's magistrates came to examine them, they all saw that the merchant had only his wife with him. The king, on learning the fact, punished the captain of the guard and released the merchant from the temple as from the yawning mouth of death.

"So did Śaktimatī save her husband that time with her wits," concluded Devasmitā, and the virtuous wife added in confidence to her mother-in-law, "I shall go and save my husband with a trick, as she did."

Then Devasmitā and her maids disguised themselves as merchants,[9] boarded a ship on the pretext of business, and departed for Cathay where her husband was staying. And on her arrival she saw her husband Guhasena—reassurance incarnate!—in the midst of traders. Guhasena saw her too, from a distance, and drank deep of the male image of his beloved wife. He wondered what such a delicate person could have to do with the merchant's profession.

Devasmitā went to the local king and announced: "I have a message. Assemble all your people." Curious, the king summoned all citizens and asked Devasmitā, who still wore her merchant's disguise, "What is your message?"

"Among these people here," said Devasmitā, "are four runaway slaves of mine. May it please Your Majesty to surrender them."

"All the people of this town are assembled here," replied the king. "Look them over, and when you recognize your slaves, take them back."

Thereupon she arrested on their own threshold the four merchant's sons, whom she had manhandled before. They still wore her mark on their foreheads.

"But these are the sons of a caravan trader," protested the merchants who were present. "How can they be your slaves?"

"If you do not believe me," she retorted, "have a look at their foreheads. I have branded them with a dog's paw."

"So we shall," they said. They unwound the turbans of the four men, and they all saw the dog's paw on their foreheads. The merchants' guild was ashamed, and the king surprised.

"What is behind this?" the king asked, questioning Devasmitā in person, and she told the story, and they all burst out laughing.

"By rights they are your slaves, my lady," said the king, whereupon the other merchants paid the king a fine and the virtuous woman a large ransom to free the four from bondage. Honored by all upright people, Devasmitā, with the ransom she had received and the husband she had rejoined, returned to their city Tāmraliptī and never again was she separated from the husband she loved.

9. The motif of a woman disguising herself as a man, especially to perform a daring feat, is common in folk literature. Devasmitā bears a striking resemblance to more than one of Shakespeare's heroines.

III

Medieval Chinese Literature

The "Middle" in the European "Middle Ages" signifies the time between the Roman Empire and the Renaissance, a transitional period that has often been seen as a time of relative intellectual and cultural stagnation. In the case of China the situation is quite the reverse. If we use Western period terms, the *middle* of a Chinese "Middle Age" would mean "central." It is a period when Chinese thought and literature reached what many regard as their highest forms. During the medieval Period of Disunion (third through sixth centuries), a notoriously tumultuous age of political division, Buddhism, which had spread from India to China, took deep root in Chinese society, stimulating renewed interest in Daoist philosophy and the rise of religious Daoism. During the following two great medieval Chinese dynasties, the Tang and the Song (seventh through thirteenth centuries), classical Chinese poetry and prose reached an unprecedented height to which later ages would look back with awe and a sense that the achievements of its greatest writers could never be matched.

A Southern Song Dynasty hand scroll, "Streams and Mountains Under Fresh Snow," attributed to Liu Songnian, twelfth century.

CHINA'S PERIOD OF DISUNION (220–589)

In the second century the Han Empire (206 B.C.E.–220 C.E.) was crumbling. Natural disasters, bad labor conditions, and political intrigues in the central government all helped weaken it. In 184 C.E. the leader of a Daoist religious cult called "Way of Great Peace" staged a major insurrection, gathering hundreds of thousands of followers who attacked local government offices throughout the country. Although the rebellion was suppressed by local armies initially encouraged by the Han government, it ultimately fostered the rise of warlords, often former Han generals, and eventually led to the division of China into three kingdoms: Shu in the west, Wu in the south, and Wei in the northern heartland under the Cao family. The battles of the "Three Kingdoms Period" (220–280) caught the Chinese imagination, and their heroes have lived on in poetry, prose romances, and, recently, epic film series. The empire was briefly reunified by the short-lived Western Jin Dynasty, but in 316 non-Chinese invaders raided the north and the great aristocratic clans fled to the area around Nanjing, where a new government was set up by a prince of the royal house. For the first time in Chinese history non-Chinese rulers took control of China's traditional northern heartland—around the old capitals of Chang'an and Luoyang—forcing the Chinese court aristocracy to flee to the southeastern hinterland. The émigrés from the north, which had been the center of Chinese civilization for more than fifteen hundred years, found themselves suddenly in the rustic southeastern provinces, while their ancestral graves and estates were taken over by northern "barbarians." In exile of sorts, the Chinese aristocracy developed a strong cultural pride and sense of "Chineseness." Cultural legitimacy came to be defined not by the occupation of a place (the North China plain) but by the possession of a portable tradition. Although the northern ruling houses were "barbarian" in the eyes of the former Chinese aristocracy, they were no wild nomads. Their subjects were a largely Chinese population and some, like the Northern Wei Dynasty (386–534) of the Xianbei people, very astutely mixed tribal traditions with Chinese customs. China remained divided partly under foreign rule for centuries: China's north was split among various non-Chinese states and dynasties, while the south was ruled by a succession of short-lived Chinese dynasties.

NEW RELIGIONS OF SALVATION

The non-Chinese rulers of the north also understood that they needed a political tool to legitimate their governance over an ethnically mixed populace and to create harmony among peoples of various social and ethnic backgrounds—a tool that, ideally, was foreign like them: Buddhism. Buddhism originated in India around 500 B.C.E. when a prince of the Shakya clan in a small state in what today is south Nepal turned away in disgust from his privileged palace life, subjected himself to ascetic hardships, and eventually gained enlightenment. For the rest of his life he wandered and spread his teachings. In his first sermon he preached the "Four Noble Truths," central to all of the numerous schools of Buddhism that developed over time. He claimed that (1) pain, suffering, and anxiety are inevitable parts of human life; (2) they are caused by human desires and attachments; (3) it is possible for humans to overcome these attachments; and (4) humans can triumph over them by following the simple trajectory of the

"Eightfold Path," a regime of psychological and physical self-control that enables individuals to leave the cycle of constant rebirths and reach "buddhahood," the passing into nirvana (nothingness), like the historical Buddha himself.

The extraordinary success of Buddhism in China and, spreading from there, throughout East Asia is one of the great surprises of Asian history. China became Buddhist even though there were no forced conversions imposed by missionaries and traditional Chinese Confucian values and Buddhist practices were often at odds. Becoming a Buddhist monk meant betraying on the personal and political levels the duties of Confucian filial piety: you gave up the chances to continue the family line, and by shaving your head you mutilated the body that you had received from your parents and that you needed to return to your ancestors unharmed when leaving the world; even worse, as a follower of the Buddha you could claim to be no longer subordinate to state power, the paternal authority of the political world.

Buddhism radically altered the face of China. Brought by merchants active in the east–west trade along the so-called Silk Road, Buddhism was a religion for the masses. Like Christianity, which was gaining believers around the same time at the other end of Eurasia, it promised personal salvation and escape from a world of suffering, and its soothing ethics of compassion and mercy included people of all social classes, men and women alike. Chinese cities became home to large temple complexes that hosted religious services and addressed the needs of education and charity; the countryside was suddenly dotted with monasteries and colossal Buddha statues carved in stone (images of deities in human form had not existed in China, and the Chinese found the innovation so strange that

The Giant Wild Goose Pagoda in a Buddhist temple complex in Chang'an (modern-day Xi'an), China, was built during the Tang Dynasty. This is where the Chinese monk Xuanzang, whose adventure-filled trip to India is described in the novel *Journey to the West* (included in Vol. D), deposited the Buddhist scriptures he had acquired in the homeland of Buddhism.

they called the new religion "the teaching of icons"). Buddhism mobilized people as pilgrims set out on travels in search of holy places of Buddhism, scriptures, devotional objects, and wise teachers in China and even India. The new faith was welcomed by the people and patronized by rulers. Monasteries were not taxed, and monks and nuns were not required to perform labor service or military duty.

While Buddhism clashed with Confucian values, it resonated with Daoism in its promise of personal salvation from a corrupt world. Daoism was indigenous to China and took various forms before the arrival of Buddhism. Its intellectual foundations rested on two early Chinese

"Master Texts," *Laozi* and *Zhuangzi*. But Daoism also included a variety of practices, such as methods to promote longevity, certain breathing and sexual techniques, gymnastics, herbal medicine, and alchemy; and the leaders of some popular movements mobilized the underprivileged and poor for their own purposes under the banner of Daoist prophecies. The arrival of Buddhism in China transformed Daoism from an amorphous phenomenon into an organized religion and institution. Daoism now acquired a set of canonical texts (recorded from revelations), temples and monasteries with a celibate clergy, and a vast pantheon of Daoist gods, all on the model of the Buddhist canon of scriptures, the Buddhist monasteries, and the large pantheon of bodhisattvas (Buddhas who returned to the human world in order to help others attain buddhahood). Buddhism and Daoism were in fierce competition over patronage and audiences in part because their teachings were so similar. The closeness of Buddhist and Daoist ideas and teachings is evident from the frequency with which the earliest Chinese translations of Buddhist sutras—sermons of the Buddha recorded in Sanskrit and other Indian languages—used Daoist terminology to express new Buddhist concepts. This appropriation of Buddhism as a form of Daoism took a sudden turn in the fourth century when the brilliant Buddhist scholar and monk Kumārajīva (350–413), born of an Indian father and a Central Asian mother, was abducted by a Chinese ruler and set to work on translating Buddhist texts into Chinese; his abduction marked the beginning of large state-sponsored workshops that translated countless scriptures into Chinese. Kumārajīva rejected the earlier Daoist terminology, creating new words for the foreign Buddhist concepts out of transcriptions of the Sanskrit words into Chinese. Buddhism had become an independent cultural force in China.

The arrival of Buddhism and the emergence of the Daoist church led to a veneration of the ideal of the "recluse." Some recluses were true hermits, living far away from civilization; others, like the "**Seven Sages of the Bamboo Grove**," cultivated a form of libertine resistance to social norms; still others, such as the poet-recluse **Tao Qian**, decided to live on his family farm and not serve in government. The Period of Disunion was a time when authors became more self-reflexive and self-conscious of their place in literary history, resulting in a "literature about literature" by writers such as **Cao Pi**, **Lu Ji**, and **Wang Xizhi**.

THE NEW COSMOPOLITAN EMPIRES OF THE SUI AND TANG (589–907)

In the long run it was a northern dynasty, the Sui (589–618), that reunified China; these rulers were quickly supplanted by another northern dynasty, the Tang (618–907). The two dynasties forged a new culture that combined northern and southern traditions. The Sui emperors razed the old southern capital near Nanjing and forced the southern aristocracy to relocate to the old northern capital of Chang'an. Between the Yangzi and the Yellow River they built a canal that became a crucial means to transport goods and people between the north and south, reconnecting territory that had been divided for more than three centuries. But its attempt to recover the possessions of the Han Empire, in particular repeated unsuccessful campaigns against Korea, brought down the dynasty. The Sui Dynasty was overthrown by a provincial governor who founded his own dynasty, the Tang.

The long Tang Dynasty was an age of cultural confidence and, initially, of expansion, as Tang armies pushed outward at every frontier. Particularly important was the expansion to the northwest and control of the trade routes to the west. Chang'an, an old capital now clothed in new splendor, mirrored the cosmopolitan empire it controlled. It was laid out on a grid pattern, with a mighty walled palace city at its north and two bustling markets to the south. The city teemed with foreigners, who came to the Chinese capital by the Central Asian land routes or the South Asian maritime trade routes as merchants, diplomatic envoys, pilgrims, monks, or adventurers. Nestorian Christians, Zoroastrians, Jews, and Arab merchants mingled with Japanese monks and Persian doctors. The people of Chang'an quickly adopted new hairstyles, new games such as polo, and new musical instruments, importing exotic melodies and dances from China's Central Asian "west."

The Tang was an age of innovation. Tea became a major commercial crop, and its consumption spread from China to East Asia via monks who used it to stay awake during long hours of meditation and sutra recitation. New Buddhist schools appeared, such as Chan (better known in its Japanese form, "Zen"), an iconoclastic form of Buddhism that espoused mind-to-mind transmission of truth, claiming that the study of scriptures was of no use. Poetry by one elusive recluse named **Hanshan ("Cold Mountain")**, whose very existence is shrouded in mystery, exemplified this new trend.

The most influential invention during the Tang Dynasty was printing. A printed copy of the Buddhist Diamond Sutra, dated 868, is considered the world's oldest printed book. Sealed in a cave in remote Dunhuang, a Silk Road oasis in northwest China some 1100 miles from Chang'an, it was discovered by archaeologists in the early twentieth century.

The Tang period is most famous for its poetry. The civil service examination used by the Tang in recruiting its elites for government service came to require the composition of poetry, and it also became an integral part of social life—a medium of social exchange. In few other places in the world has lyric poetry ever enjoyed such centrality, and a number of major poets emerged whose works have made them renowned in China to this day. A great poem might deal with large philosophical issues, but it was just as likely to describe a meeting with an old friend.

A copy of the Diamond Sūtra, printed in 868 C.E. It is considered the world's oldest printed book.

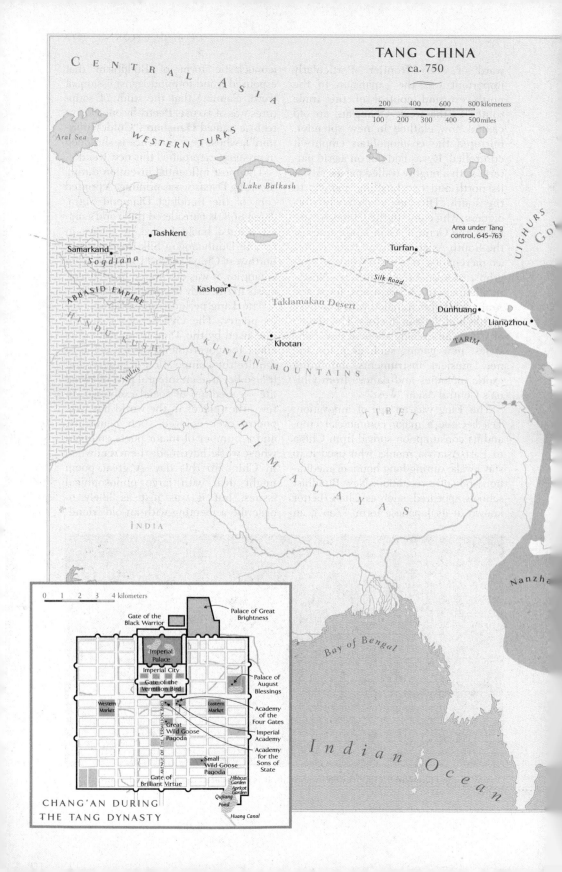

TANG CHINA
ca. 750

| 200 | 400 | 600 | 800 kilometers |
| 100 | 200 | 300 | 400 | 500 miles |

CENTRAL ASIA

WESTERN TURKS

Aral Sea

Lake Balkash

Tashkent

Samarkand

Sogdiana

ABBASID EMPIRE

HINDU KUSH

Kashgar

Taklamakan Desert

Khotan

KUNLUN MOUNTAINS

Indus

HIMALAYAS

INDIA

TIBET

Area under Tang control, 645–763

UIGHURS

Go

Turfan

Silk Road

Dunhuang

Liangzhou

TARIM

Nanzha

Bay of Bengal

Indian Ocean

CHANG'AN DURING THE TANG DYNASTY

| 0 | 1 | 2 | 3 | 4 kilometers |

Gate of the Black Warrior

Palace of Great Brightness

Imperial Palace

Imperial City

Gate of the Vermilion Bird

Western Market

AVENUE OF THE VERMILION BIRD

Great Wild Goose Pagoda

Small Wild Goose Pagoda

Gate of Brilliant Virtue

Eastern Market

Palace of August Blessings

Academy of the Four Gates

Imperial Academy

Academy for the Sons of State

Hibiscus Garden

Apricot Garden

Qujiang Pond

Huang Canal

Lake Baikal

MONGOLIA

Desert

Chinese cultural region
outside of the imperial borders

KHITAN

BOHAI

Sea of Japan

EMISHI
EZO

KOREA
Silla

JAPAN

Nara

Beijing

Po Hai

Dengzhou

Grand Canal

Ordos Desert

Jiaozhou

Weizhou

Yellow Sea

Lanzhou

subject of
detail map
at left

Yellow R.

Bianzhou
(Kaifeng)

Wei

Chang'an (Xi'an)

Luoyang

ZHONGNAN MTS.

Huai

Han

Yangzhou

Nanjing

East China Sea

Kuizhou

Chengdu

Yangtze

Hangzhou

Shaoxing

Pengze

Lake Poyang

TIANTAI MTS.

Xiang

Fuzhou

Quanzhou

Chaozhou

Guangzhou
(Canton)

Hainan

Pacific Ocean

VIETNAM

South China Sea

Poetry was seen as a way to record both an individual's personality and a country's historic moments. The writings of **Wang Wei, Li Bo**, and **Du Fu** came to exemplify poetic perfection, in different styles. The Tang was also the first period to witness the flowering of prose tales, such as **Yuan Zhen**'s "**The Story of Yingying**," which became a fertile source for later Chinese stories and drama.

In the 750s, the confidence of the Tang Dynasty was broken during the reign of one its most splendid emperors, Xuanzong. Xuanzong gave military governors in frontier regions great powers, hoping thereby to strengthen the defense of the empire. An able administrator, patron of the arts, and even scholar in his own right—he wrote a commentary on *Laozi* and set up a school for examinations in Daoist scriptures—Xuanzong was greatly devoted to a concubine of lower status, Yang Guifei (or "Prized Consort Yang"), whose family increasingly began to occupy strategic official positions. An Lushan, an associate of Yang's kinsmen, rebelled in 755, took Chang'an, and put the emperor to flight. Threatened by his own armies, Xuanzong was forced to witness the execution of his beloved concubine. Although the rebellion was soon put down, the dynasty never quite regained its former authority. Later writers looked back with melancholy to Xuanzong's long and prosperous reign, and the tragic love of Xuanzong and Yang Guifei lived on in later literature such as **Bo Juyi**'s "**Song of Lasting Regret.**"

A NEW DOMESTIC AGE: THE SONG DYNASTY (960–1279)

The Song Dynasty was a time of major social and intellectual changes. The old aristocratic families that had dominated the Tang Dynasty lost their power, and the government was opened up to social groups that had previously been largely excluded from political participation. Their inclusion was made possible by the heightened importance of civil service examinations, which during the Tang had merely supplemented hereditary privilege as a channel to official appointment. The lower Yangzi River region gained in importance, and southeasterners began their long prominence in Chinese intellectual life. In 1127 the Jin, a non-Chinese people on the northeastern frontier, conquered North China, and the Song court had to seek refuge in the south, establishing a new capital in Hangzhou. The so-called Southern Song Dynasty lasted until 1279, when the Mongols conquered China and established a foreign dynasty on Chinese soil.

Although printing emerged during the Tang, the technology did not revolutionize Chinese society until the Song. The rapid development of commercial printing during the eleventh century enabled literary works and scholarship to reach a far wider audience than ever before. As in Europe, the dissemination of learning through the printed book had a significant impact on all aspects of culture. A reexamination of the Confucian classics gave rise to a movement known as Neo-Confucianism, which came to dominate intellectual life by harking back to Tang Dynasty writers such as **Han Yu** and **Liu Zongyuan**, who had themselves spearheaded a visionary effort to recapture the moral and rhetorical force of the writings of antiquity. But whereas Han Yu and Liu Zongyuan sometimes leavened their strong intellectual stances with a good portion of satirical wit and a joy in cerebral mischief, the Neo-Confucian movement was for the most part a serious and ceremonious affair.

Meanwhile, Song Dynasty classical literature continued the forms of the Tang period, but with a difference—a less intense, more reflective and introverted tone that for later ages seemed to embody the personality of the dynasty. In the urban centers of the south a new form of poetry developed; these "song lyrics" treated lighter, more domestic themes. **Li Qingzhao**, a female poet, excelled in this new mode; she was also a scholar and connoisseur obsessed with collecting ancient objects—not unlike scholars during the Renaissance in Europe. Her riveting account of how she unsuccessfully tried to salvage her family collection of antiquities when fleeing south from the Jin in 1127, included below, testifies to the antiquarian and scholarly tastes of Song literati.

The medieval period, more than any other, shaped traditional China. Between the third and the thirteenth centuries China became a thoroughly Buddhist empire, with a powerful Daoist church and a political system predicated on the recruitment of bureaucrats through the Confucian civil service examinations. Tang poetry defined the standards for the later Chinese literary tradition. Chinese institutions, law codes, religions, literature, art, architecture, and material culture spread throughout East Asia, as younger emerging cultures on the Korean Peninsula and the Japanese archipelago were eager to adapt the newest technologies, ideologies, and art forms of Chinese civilization to their own domestic purposes. China's medieval period was thus the defining moment when East Asia emerged as a cultural sphere under Chinese influence.

HERMITS, BUDDHISTS, AND DAOISTS

Confucianism, the traditional ideology since the Han Dynasty (206 B.C.E.–220 C.E.), had emphasized the individual's responsibility toward society. But when Buddhism and religious Daoism rose to prominence during the medieval period, they endorsed the opposite: a life removed from society, whether as a solitary recluse or in the religious community of a monastery. The new value placed on retreat from worldly entanglements even led to a reevaluation of the legacy of Confucius (551–479 B.C.E.). With his famous saying "Shine in a world that follows the Way, hide when the world loses the Way!" Confucius sometimes even urged his disciples to retreat from the world in times of political turmoil, and he himself was intrigued by eccentric hermits who had chosen to do so. Together, these developments turned the hermit into one of the most important figures of medieval China.

Hermits, or followers of eremitism (from the Greek word erēmitēs, "desert dweller"), retreated from society because they disdained wealth, power, and fame, desired to preserve their inner nature and integrity, or wished to pursue spiritual and artistic aims. Their life was defined by the idea of a conscious choice of hermit life over other lifestyles, a sudden moment of revelation that convinces a person to make a radical life choice; the value of renunciation and deprivation from the comforts of society; and the idea that life in seclusion is ultimately more "natural" than life in society—a return to rather than a departure from one's inner nature.

In East Asia, hermits and recluses often did not live in total seclusion; instead, they were surrounded by family members, disciples, servants, or other like-minded people, and sometimes even chose to participate in social events. Still, the ideals of eremitism seriously challenge the values of life in society, and hermits and recluses have therefore often appeared as eccentrics and madmen, prophets and quacks, outcasts and dropouts. Eremitism influenced Chinese society for centuries; Western travelers of the early twentieth century reported chance encounters with these curious and exotic figures in remote areas.

Some of the earliest hermits we know of date to the earliest era of Chinese literature, including **Bo Yi** and **Shu Qi**, whose biography can be found in the *Historical Records* of the historian **Sima Qian** (included in Volume A). When the Zhou people conquered the Shang Dynasty in 1045 B.C.E., they refused to serve the conquerors, and retreated into the mountains to starve themselves to death. They became the prototype for virtuous officials who abandoned their positions to preserve their loyalty and moral integrity, a form of eremitism that would reemerge each time China fell under the rule of a foreign dynasty.

During the medieval period eremitism entered a new phase. After the Han Dynasty (206 B.C.E.–220 C.E.), civil wars broke out; the subsequent Period of Disunion lasted for more than three centuries (220–589). Warlords established their own kingdoms, non-Chinese invaders took over the traditional heartland

A tenth-century silk painting showing a mendicant monk, weighed down by the Buddhist texts he is carrying, and accompanied by a tiger.

of China in the north, and ill-fated dynasties rose and fell in quick succession. Making a life as a public official, as elites during the Han Dynasty had aspired to do, was not just difficult but often lethal. The number of gifted writers and intellectuals who died young on the execution block because of volatile factional politics was remarkably high during this period, encouraging fresh waves of eremitism.

But political turmoil was not the only reason for retreat. Equally important was the rise of Buddhism and religious Daoism, which valued retreat from society and the pursuit of goals beyond this world: personal salvation and immortality. Initiated around 500 B.C.E. by an Indian prince later known as "the Enlightened One" (Buddha), Buddhism took root in China during the Period of Disunion. The Buddha promised to people of all social classes that they could escape suffering in this world by eliminating their false desires and attachments to it. Although some schools of Buddhism taught that the liberation from attachments could be achieved in society, eremitic and monastic life certainly offered more favorable conditions for it. During the same period Daoist religious sects grew in strength, building temples and monasteries in the mountains and encouraging the search for immortality through alchemy, elixirs, diet, and certain bodily and sexual practices. The figure of the wild Daoist recluse, living untrammeled by outside expectations and in blissful violation of social rules, became a prominent trope in later Chinese literature and painting.

THE SEVEN SAGES OF THE BAMBOO GROVE

Rambunctious, impertinent, and self-indulgent, the "Seven Sages of the Bamboo Grove" represent the earliest incarnation of a Daoist-inspired intellectual libertinage that would mesmerize later writers. These wise men lived during the Wei Kingdom (220–265), a successor state to the Han Dynasty founded by the famous general Cao Cao and his son **Cao Pi**. Gifted poets themselves (Cao Pi's "**A Discourse on Literature**" is included in this volume), the Caos were the first ruling family to gather poets at their court and host a literary salon. The image of the Seven Sages came to symbolize a spirit of freedom and friendship—a liberating indulgence in poetry, drinking, music, and the art of social affront.

Two of the Seven Sages were particularly close friends: Ruan Ji (210–263) and Xi Kang (223–262). Ruan Ji's father was a poet, but the family was left in poverty after his early death. Ruan Ji seemed to have served in minor positions, without taking an active part in political life. He is known for an exceptional cycle of eighty-two poems titled "Songs of My Cares," three of which are included here. The tormenting contradictions that ripped through Ruan Ji's mind and life are best captured in the closing couplet of one of his poems: "All my life I have walked upon thin ice, / and none understand how this heart seethes."

Xi Kang was not just a writer but also a famous lute player and alchemist. He wrote a long poem on the supreme importance of lute playing for one's intellectual cultivation. On the eve of his execution—he was one of those intellectuals who fell victim to factional politics—we see him play his lute one last time.

The Seven Sages quickly became cultural icons, and Liu Yiqing (403–444), a prince of one of the sophisticated southern dynasties during the Period of Disunion, included many examples of their outrageous wit in his large collection of anecdotes, *A New Account of Tales of the World*. That work, with more than six hundred protagonists, fully captures the rarified atmosphere in the intellectual salons during the end of the Han and the Period of Disunion, when a new form of Daoist philosophical speculation called the "Study of the Mysterious" thrived. The anecdotes about Ruan Ji and Xi Kang included here give a taste of their acts of provocation: stripping naked in public, showing the white of one's eyes to one's superiors, and drinking with pigs have become no more acceptable over the centuries.

RUAN JI
210–263

Songs of My Cares I[1]

In the night I could not sleep,
restless I rose and plucked the harp.
Thin curtains mirrored the bright moon,
cool breeze blew into gown-folds.
A lone swan screeched out on the moors,   5
in the north woods birds flew singing.
I wavered then, what would I see?—
troubled thoughts injure a heart all alone.

Songs of My Cares XXXIII

One more day, then one more evening,
one more evening, one more dawn.
Complexion changed from what it was,
by itself the spirit wastes away.
I hold fire and boiling water in my breast,   5
all things in change are calling to me.
Thousands of problems that have no end,
more than deftest schemes can comprehend.
I fear only that in an instant
my soul will be whirled away by wind.   10
All my life I have walked upon thin ice,
and none understand how this heart seethes.

Songs of My Cares LXVIII

I looked out north on the Gorge of Dry Dark,
then westward I went to visit Shaoren.
I peered round to Sky's Ford in the distance,
a rashness uncurbed was my heart's delight.

1. All selections translated by Stephen Owen.

A shimmering wisp was Life and Death's gate,   5
roam there once and you will not seek it again.
Then I happened to meet with the dawn-wind hawk
and rode it in flight to the southern groves.
In the Pole-Star's incandescent floods
I sped instantly, indulging my most wanton will.   10
I repose at a feast in the Pure Citadel—
who now can stop me from leaving the world?[2]

2. The fantastic geography of the cosmos described in this heavenly journey has Daoist undertones.

LIU YIQING
403–444

From A New Account of Tales of the World[1]

When Ruan Ji whistled,[2] he could be heard several hundred paces away. In the Sumen Mountains (Henan) there appeared from nowhere a Realized Man about whom the woodcutters were all relaying tales. Ruan Ji went to see for himself and spied the man squatting with clasped knees by the edge of a cliff. Ji climbed the ridge to approach him and then squatted opposite him. Ji rehearsed for him briefly matters from antiquity to the present, beginning with the exposition of the Way of the Mystical Quiescence of the Yellow Emperor and Shen Nong,[3] and ending with an investigation of the excellence of the Supreme Virtue of the Three Ages (Xia, Shang, and Zhou).[4] But when Ji asked his opinion about it he remained aloof and made no reply. Ji then went on to expound that which lies beyond Activism, and the techniques of Resting the Spirit and Conducting the Vital Force.[5] But when Ji looked toward him for a reply, he was still, exactly as before, fixedly staring without turning. Ji therefore turned toward him and made a long whistling sound. After a long while the man finally laughed and said, "Do it again." Ji whistled a second time, but as his interest now was exhausted, he withdrew. He had returned about halfway down the ridge when he heard above him a shrillness like an orchestra of many instruments, while forests and valleys reechoed with the sound. Turning back to look, he discovered it was the whistling of the man he had just visited.

* * *

1. Translated by Richard B. Mather.
2. A Daoist breathing practice that enabled Daoist adepts to commune with spirits and enhance their longevity.
3. Two legendary rulers associated with the invention of Chinese herbal medicine and health practices. "The Way of Mystical Quies-

cence": a Daoist longevity technique.
4. The three dynasties that succeeded the age of legendary emperors: the Xia (ca. 2070–ca. 1500 B.C.E.), Shang (ca. 1500–1045 B.C.E.), and Zhou (ca. 1045–256 B.C.E.) dynasties.
5. Two Daoist longevity techniques.

When Ruan Ji was in mourning, Xi Xi went to pay him a visit of condolence. Now Ruan Ji was able to look with the whites of his eyes, and he used the whites of his eyes when greeting worldly gentlemen. When Xi Xi arrived, Ruan Ji did not perform the customary weeping. Observing his white eyes, Xi Xi withdrew in dismay.

Later, when Xi Xi's brother, Kang, learned of it, he took a gift of wine, and, tucking his zither under his arm, went to visit Ruan Ji, after which they became good friends.

* * *

On many occasions Liu Ling, under the influence of wine, would be completely free and uninhibited, sometimes taking off his clothes and sitting naked in his room. Once when some persons saw him and chided him for it, Ling retorted, "I take heaven and earth for my pillars and roof, and the rooms of my house for my pants and coat. What are you gentlemen doing in my pants?"

* * *

Ruan Xian and Ruan Ji lived on the south side of the street, and all the other Ruans lived on the north (sunny) side. The northern Ruans were all wealthy, while the southern Ruans were poor. On the seventh day of the seventh month the northern Ruans put on a grand sunning of their wardrobes, which all consisted of silk gauzes and colored and plain brocades, while Ruan Xian, using a bamboo pole, hung out a large pair of plain cloth calf-nose underpants in his central courtyard. When someone remarked about this, he replied, "I'm not yet able to be completely free of worldly matters, so I just do this, that's all!"

* * *

The Ruans were all great drinkers. When Ruan Xian arrived at the home of any of the clan for a gathering, they no longer used ordinary wine cups for drinking toasts. Instead they would use a large earthenware vat filled with wine, and sitting facing each other all around it, would take large drafts. One time a herd of pigs came to drink and went directly up to the vat, whereupon pigs and men all proceeded to drink together.

* * *

Xi Kang's body was seven feet, eight inches tall, and his manner and appearance conspicuously outstanding. Some who saw him sighed, saying, "Serene and sedate, fresh and transparent, pure and exalted!" Others would say, "Soughing like the wind beneath the pines, high and gently blowing."

Shan Tao said, "As a person Xi Kang is majestically towering, like a solitary pine tree standing alone. But when he's drunk he leans crazily like a jade mountain about to collapse."

* * *

While Xi Kang was wandering among the mountains of Ji Commandery (Henan), he met the Daoist adept, Sun Deng, and thereafter continued his wanderings in his company. As Kang was on the eve of departing, Deng said, "As far as your ability is concerned, it's high enough, but your way of preserving your own life is inadequate."

* * *

On the eve of Xi Kang's execution in the Eastern Marketplace of Luoyang (in 262), his spirit and manner showed no change. Taking out his seven-stringed zither, he plucked the strings and played the "Melody of Guangling." When the song was ended, he said, Yuan Jun once asked to learn this melody, but I remained firm in my stubbornness, and never gave it to him. From now on the 'Melody of Guangling' is no more!"

Three thousand scholars of the Grand Academy sent up a petition requesting Xi's release to become their teacher, but it was not granted. Sima Zhao (who had ordered the execution) himself later repented of it.

HANSHAN (COLD MOUNTAIN)
ca. 600–800

The Buddhist monk Hanshan may or may not have been a real person. The account included in the preface to his collected poems seems to be a sketch of a typical eccentric rather than the story of any individual. The Buddhist biographies tell us little about his life; instead, they feature Hanshan's extravagant conversations with his friend Shide and their master. Hanshan (literally, "Cold Mountain") is a mountain in the Tiantai mountain range in southeast China where a famous temple is located, but here it serves as a name around which a corpus of Buddhist poems gradually accumulated throughout the Tang period. The Hanshan poems were largely overlooked in China until modern times, when they were also admired in Japan and in the West thanks to the attention they received in the 1950s from the Beat poets, a group of American writers who experimented with drugs, unconventional forms of communal life and sexuality, and various Eastern religions.

The three hundred–odd poems that make up the Hanshan corpus are of very uneven quality. The best are among the finest expressions of Chan (Zen) Buddhism, a school of Buddhism that came to the fore during the Tang Dynasty and emphasizes paradox, madness, and austere meditation as means to enlightenment. The voice in the poems addresses outsiders, telling them about enlightenment. At times it seems to transcend all things human, but scriptures, books, or other people appear now and then. Since enlightenment cannot be put into words, the speaker can only point toward it in a series of figures; Cold Mountain becomes a landscape of the mind.

[Whoever reads my poems][1]

Whoever reads my poems
Must protect the purity in his mind.

1. Translated by Robert Hendricks.

Stinginess and greed must change into honesty day after day;
Flattery and deceit must *right now* become the upright!

Expel and banish, wipe out your bad karma;   5
Return to rely on, accept your true nature.

Today! You must attain the Buddha-body;[2]
Quickly! Quickly! Treat this just like it's imperial law![3]

[A thatched hut][4]

A thatched hut is home for a country man;
Horse or carriage seldom pass my gate:
Forests so still all the birds come to roost,
Broad valley streams always full of fish.
I pick wild fruit in hand with my child,   5
Till the hillside fields with my wife.
And in my house what do I have?
Only a bed piled high with books.

[A curtain of pearls][5]

A curtain of pearls hangs before the hall of jade
And within is a lovely lady,
Fairer in form than the gods and immortals,
Her face like a blossom of peach or plum.
Spring mists will cover the eastern mansion,   5
Autumn winds blow from the western lodge,
And after thirty years have passed,
She will look like a piece of pressed sugar cane.

[Here we languish][6]

Here we languish, a bunch of poor scholars,
Battered by extremes of hunger and cold.
Out of work, our only joy is poetry:
Scribble, scribble, we wear out our brains.
Who will read the works of such men?   5
On that point you can save your sighs.
We could inscribe our poems on biscuits
And the homeless dogs wouldn't deign to nibble.

[In my first thirty years][7]

In my first thirty years of life
I roamed hundreds and thousands of miles.
Walked by rivers through deep green grass

2. That is, gain enlightenment and become a Buddha.
3. A stock phrase used to conclude performances of ritual chants addressed to spirits or demons.
4. Translated by Burton Watson.
5. Translated by Burton Watson.
6. Translated by Burton Watson.
7. Translated by Gary Snyder, who was associated with the Beat Movement.

Entered cities of boiling red dust.
Tried drugs, but couldn't make Immortal;   5
Read books and wrote poems on history.
Today I'm back at Cold Mountain:
I'll sleep by the creek and purify my ears.

[Wonderful, this road to Cold Mountain][8]

Wonderful, this road to Cold Mountain—
Yet there's no sign of horse or carriage.
In winding valleys too tortuous to trace,
On crags piled who knows how high,
A thousand different grasses weep with dew   5
And pines hum together in the wind.
Now it is that, straying from the path,
You ask your shadow, "What way from here?"

[When people see the man of Cold Mountain][9]

When people see the man of Cold Mountain
They all say, "There's a crackpot!
Hardly a face to make one look twice,
His body wrapped in nothing but rags ...
The things we say he doesn't understand;   5
The things he says we wouldn't utter!"
A word to those of you passing by—
Try coming to Cold Mountain sometime!

[High, high from the summit of the peak][1]

High, high from the summit of the peak,
Whatever way I look, no limit in sight!
No one knows I am sitting here alone.
A solitary moon shines in the cold spring.
Here in the spring—this is not the moon.   5
The moon is where it always is—in the sky above.
And though I sing this one little song,
In the song there is no Zen.

[I longed to visit the eastern cliff][2]

I longed to visit the eastern cliff
countless years until today
I finally grabbed a vine and climbed
but halfway there met mist and wind
the trail was too narrow for clothes   5
the moss too slick for shoes
I stopped beneath this cinnamon tree
and slept with a cloud for a pillow

---

8. Translated by Burton Watson.
9. Translated by Burton Watson.
1. Translated by Burton Watson.
2. Translated by Red Pine.

[On Cold Mountain there's a naked bug]³

On Cold Mountain there's naked bug
its body is white its head is black
its hands hold two scrolls
in one is the Way in the other is Virtue
at home it makes no fire   5
for the road it packs no clothes
but always it carries the sword of wisdom
ready to strike troublesome foes

[Men ask the way to Cold Mountain]⁴

Men ask the way to Cold Mountain
Cold Mountain: there's no through trail.
In summer, ice doesn't melt
The rising sun blurs in swirling fog.
How did I make it?   5
My heart's not the same as yours.
If your heart was like mine
You'd get it and be right here.

[My mind is like the autumn moon]⁵

My mind is like the autumn moon
Shining clean and clear in the green pool
No, that's not a good comparison.
Tell me, how shall I explain?

[So Hanshan writes you these words]⁶

So Hanshan writes you these words,
These words which no one will believe.
Honey is sweet; men love the taste.
Medicine is bitter and hard to swallow.
What soothes the feelings brings contentment,   5
What opposes the will calls forth anger.
Yet I ask you to look at the wooden puppets,
Worn out by their moment of play on stage!

[Do you have the poems of Hanshan in your house?]⁷

Do you have the poems of Hanshan in your house?
They're better for you than sutra-reading!
Write them out and paste them on a screen
Where you can glance them over from time to time.

3. Translated by Red Pine.
4. Translated by Gary Snyder.
5. Translated by Burton Watson.
6. Translated by Burton Watson.
7. Translated by Burton Watson.

LITERATURE ABOUT LITERATURE

Ideas about the nature of literature and its social implications developed in China alongside literature itself, as they have in every civilization that has produced a long-standing literary culture. Debates among Chinese intellectuals about the social aspects of literature often revolved around the notion of influence: at their best, so the argument went, literary works could stir their readers to virtuous acts. At their worst, they might seduce readers into worlds of depraved fantasies and induce behavior that would bring disorder to society.

During the last half of the first millennium B.C.E. these questions about the power of words and hence the necessity to control them appeared frequently in Chinese discussions of political philosophy as well as in commentaries and prefaces to literary works themselves, such as the "Great Preface" (ca. first century C.E.) to the *Classic of Poetry* (ca. 600 B.C.E.) (included in Vol. A). By the third century C.E., this "literature about literature" had become a genre in its own right, as authors began writing freestanding treatises on the subject and explored new themes such as literary style, individual talent and technical craft, and literary reputation and personal vanity. The three texts included here are examples of the extraordinary explosion of literature about literature during the medieval period, which laid the foundations for many aspects of Chinese literary culture. **Cao Pi's "Discourse on Literature"** (ca. 218) is the first surviving treatise devoted to literature proper; **Lu Ji's "Poetic Exposition on Literature"** simulates the act of literary creation, while expounding on the art of literary creation; and **Wang Xizhi's "Preface to the *Orchid Pavilion Poems"*** (353) is the classical statement on the art of poetic partying—the social practice of composing poetry during drinking banquets with friends and colleagues, which became popular in the medieval period and remained so until modern times.

The notions that a poet has a lyric voice and individual style and that poetry is a fundamental art of social, political, and cosmic significance, open to anybody, took shape right at the time when these texts were written. Also, poetry in the five- and seven-syllable meter, the classical form of Chinese poetry until the twentieth century, became the predominant medium of personal poetic expression, displacing the venerable and more rigid four-syllable meter of the *Classic of Poetry*, which had dominated the preceding millennium.

As in premodern Europe, the concept of literature in traditional China encompassed much more than fiction. It included practical genres of the imperial bureaucracy, such as petitions to the emperor or examination essays, and also texts of a ritual nature, such as grave inscriptions or prayer texts. It had both a more pragmatic and a more cosmic scope than what we tend to associate with poetry: *wen*, the traditional term for literature, originally referred to the beautiful "pattern" of animal fur, but by extension it came to mean "written characters," "literature," and "civilization." The breadth of this concept is echoed in the high hopes pinned on literature in

"Wang Xizhi Watching Geese," a hand scroll by Qian Xuan, ca. 1295.

China. Literature was expected to be not only a means of personal artistic expression but also a vehicle for teaching moral lessons and for giving voice to political criticism, showing rulers the right path. In this view, *wen* is the particular "pattern" that is uniquely characteristic of humans and a manifestation of nothing less than the cosmic forces of the Dao, the natural Way.

The massive influx of Western literatures into China over the past century and a half has profoundly changed China's literary landscape. The modern Chinese term for literature, *wenxue*, is an invention of the nineteenth century, when translators of Western literatures

into Chinese needed a new term to refer to European fiction. And revolutionary literary movements in the twentieth century blamed the classical language and literature, among other parts of the tradition such as Confucianism, for China's national crisis and its inability to resist the humiliating encroachments of Western imperialism on Chinese territory. Yet literature maintained its traditional status. Indeed, the very fact that twentieth-century Chinese intellectuals saw their new revolutionary literary experiments as a way to restore national dignity provides still another example of the profound, undiminished significance of literature in Chinese culture.

CAO PI

Cao Pi (187–226) reigned briefly as Emperor Wen of the Wei Dynasty (220–265). His father, Cao Cao (155–220), a supreme general and poet, had served the faltering Han Dynasty (206 B.C.E.–220 C.E.). Gradually assuming imperial prerogatives, he ultimately persuaded the Han emperor to abdicate in favor of his son. Cao Pi competed with two other warlords over former Han territory, which gave the period the name of "Three Kingdoms Period" (220–280). In this climate of contested authority Cao Pi was wary of potential threats to his power, most notably his brother Cao Zhi (192–232), whom he envied for his poetic talent.

"A Discourse on Literature" (ca. 218) was part of his *Authoritative Discourses*, which he probably composed when appointed Crown Prince. "Discourse on

Literature" is the only surviving chapter. Cao Pi's claim that "literary works are the greatest accomplishment in the workings of a state" echoes earlier notions of the political function of literature, and also became influential at the imperial court of Japan. Cao Pi introduces many novel topics; most notably, he addresses the question of poetic talent, defined by an individual's unique "vital force" (*qi*), the fear of mortality, professional envy among poets, and the impossibility of perfection. Cao Pi's vision of literature says much about how he wanted to see himself: as an emperor who has control over the literary works of his close contemporaries—all of whom are dead by the time the treatise was written—but also as an emperor who stands at the center of his republic of letters, seeking glory for himself and his state.

From A Discourse on Literature[1]

Literary men have always insulted one another. Fu Yi and Ban Gu[2] were virtually brothers, but Ban Gu made fun of Fu Yi in a letter to his elder brother Ban Zhao, "Fu Yi got to be Imperial Librarian because he had a 'facility' in writing—that is, whenever he put his writing brush to paper, he couldn't stop himself."

Everyone is good at putting himself forward; but since literature is not restricted to one particular norm, few people can be good at everything. Therefore each person makes light of those things in which he is weakest by the criteria of his strengths. As the saying in the villages has it, "A worn-out broom is worth a thousand pieces of gold, so long as it belongs to me." This is a failure due to lack of self-awareness.

The great literary men of the day are Kong Rong, Chen Lin, Wang Can, Xu Gan, Ruan Yu, Ying Chang, and Liu Zhen.[3] These seven masters have a full store of learning and their language does not simply borrow the colors of their predecessors. Yet they have found it hard to gallop head to head on their mighty steeds a thousand leagues, thus to pay one another the respect due.

A superior person looks to himself when taking the measure of others and in this way avoids such entanglements of envy. Thus I have written this discourse on literature.

Wang Can excels in poetic expositions. Even though Xu Gan sometimes shows a certain languor of energy, he remains Wang Can's match. Even the great Han writers such as Zhang Heng and Cai Yong have not done better than works like Wang Can's "Beginning of the Journey," "Climbing High in a Building," "The Locust Tree," or "Thoughts on Travel," or works like Xu Gan's "The Black Gibbon," "The Syphon," "The Circular Fan," or "The Orange Tree." Their other writings are not on a par with these. In memorials, letters, and records, Chen Lin and Ruan Yu are preeminent.

Ying Chang's style is agreeable but lacks vigor. Liu Zhen's style is vigorous, but entirely on the surface with nothing held in reserve. Kong Rong's mastery of form and the quality of energy in his work is lofty and subtle, with something about it that surpasses everyone else. But he cannot sustain an argument, and the presentation of natural principle in his work is weaker than his command of diction—to the point that he sometimes includes playful spoofing. But at his best he rivals the Han writers Yang Xiong and Ban Gu.

Most people value what is far from them and treat what is close at hand with contempt. They respect reputation but disregard real substance. They also suffer all the hazards of a failure of self-awareness in claiming to be men of great worth.

On a basic level all literature is the same, but it acquires differences as it unfolds in its various branches. Generally speaking, memorials to the throne and disquisitions should have dignity; letters and discourses should be based on natural principles; inscriptions and eulogies should respect the facts; poems and poetic expositions should be beautiful. Each of these four categories is

---

1. Translated by Stephen Owen.
2. Two great writers of the Eastern Han Dynasty (the two centuries preceding Cao Pi).
3. The so-called Seven Masters of the Jian'an period (196–220); eminent writers in Cao Pi's day, all were probably dead when this treatise was written.

different, and a writer's abilities will lead him to favor some over others. Only a comprehensive talent can master all these forms.

Qi, "vital force" or "breath," is the most important factor in literature. *Qi* has its own norms, either clear or murky. And it is not something that can be brought about by force. As "breath," we may compare it to flute music. Two performers may be equal in knowing the melody and following the rules of the rhythm; but when there is an inequality in drawing on a reserve of *qi* or breath, we can tell a skillful player from a clumsy one. A father cannot pass this on to his son, and an elder brother cannot pass it on to his younger brother.

Literary works are the greatest accomplishment in the workings of a state, a splendor that never decays. Glory and pleasure go no further than this mortal body. To extend both of these to all time, nothing can compare with the unending permanence of a work of literature.

It was for this reason that writers of ancient times gave their lives to the ink and the brush and revealed what they thought in their writings. Without recourse to a good historian or dependence on a powerful patron, their reputations have been passed on to posterity on their own force.

When King Wen of Zhou was in prison, he wrote additions to the *Classic of Changes*; even in his glory the Duke of Zhou made the prescriptions that are the *Rites*.[4] The former did not forsake writing even in hardship; the latter was not distracted by health and pleasure. We can see from this that the ancients cared nothing for those great jade disks that were marks of wealth, but instead treasured the moment, fearful lest time pass them by.

Yet people tend not to exert themselves in this way. In poverty and low position, they fear hunger and cold; when they are rich and honored, they let themselves drift in the distractions of pleasure. They occupy themselves with immediate demands and neglect an accomplishment that will last a thousand years. The days and months pass overhead; here below the face and body waste away. We will pass suddenly into change with all the things of this world—and this causes great pain to a man with high aspirations. Kong Rong and the others have all passed away, and only the discourses composed by Xu Gan represent a truly individual accomplishment.

4. King Wen of Zhou and the Duke of Zhou, exemplary founding figures of the Zhou Dynasty (ca. 1045–256 B.C.E.), were tradition- ally credited with the authorship of two Confucian classics, the *Classic of Changes* and the *Rites*.

LU JI

Lu Ji (261–303) gained early fame for his writing, but his life was cut short when he was falsely charged with treason and executed. While **Cao Pi's "Discourse on Literature,"** written about two generations earlier, is an idiosyncratic and impressionistic essay symptomatic of a new literary culture, Lu Ji's "Poetic Exposition on Literature" is a systematic reflection on the workings of the poetic mind and the psychology of writing. Lu Ji dwells on the various steps of the writing process, familiar to writers of any age and place: the choice of topic, the first insecure draft, the painful work of polishing, the danger of conscious or unconscious plagiarism, the misery of writer's block, and the art of producing a compelling plot. Lu Ji's genre is congenial to his topic: the *fu*, variously translated as "poetic exposition," "rhapsody," or "rhyme-prose," had thrived since the Han Dynasty and encouraged lush verbiage and baroque exaggeration. Both his choice of genre and his interest in Neo-Daoist ideas of the mind compelled Lu Ji to sketch the poet as a figure of cosmic proportions, crafting words from the dark center of the universe as if experiencing the dawn of the world. Lu Ji's "Poetic Exposition," breathlessly grandiose, is a gem in the rich Chinese tradition of literature about literature.

The Poetic Exposition on Literature[1]

Whenever I consider what has been written by persons of talent, I find that I can somehow grasp their strenuous efforts, how they used their minds. Many indeed are the variations in the ways they brought forth their words and phrases, yet we can still understand and explain what is beautiful and valuable in them.

Whenever I myself compose a literary work, I can see quite well their states of mind. Yet I constantly fear failure because my own conceptions are unequal to the things of the world, or because my writing is unequal to my conceptions. I suppose it is not that understanding is difficult, but rather that the difficulty lies in being able to do it well.

For this reason I have written "The Poetic Exposition on Literature": first to pass on the splendid complexity of craft that we find in earlier writers, and second, to consider how success and failure come about in writing. I hope that someday this will be recognized as having treated all the fine points of the subject in detail.

When it comes to taking an ax in hand to chop an ax handle, the model is not far from you; however, it is hard indeed for language to follow the variations of motion in that hand. What can be put into words is all here.

1. Translated by Stephen Owen.

He stands in the very center and scans the darkness,
Fosters feelings and aims in classics of old.
He moves with four seasons and sighs at their passing,
Views all the world's things, broods on their fullness;
He grieves for leaves falling in harsh autumn,   5
He delights in sweet spring's supple branches;
His mind shivers as he takes frost to heart;
His aims are remote, they look down upon clouds.
He sings glorious achievements, inherited by our age,
Chants of pure fragrance, left from those before;   10
He roams in the groves and treasuries of literary works,
And admires the perfect balance in their well-wrought craft.
With strong feeling he puts book aside and takes his writing brush
To make it appear in literature.

This is how it begins: 15
    retraction of vision, inversion of listening,
    absorbed in thought and seeking all around,
    essence galloping to the world's eight ends,
    the mind roaming thousands of yards, high and low.
And when it is attained: 20
    light gathers about moods and they grow in brightness,
    things become luminous and draw each other forward;
He then quaffs the word-hoard's spray of droplets,
And rolls in his mouth the sweet moisture of classics;
He drifts between Heaven and the abyss, at rest in the current,   25
He bathes in falling streams, immersed in their waters.
Then, phrases from depths emerge struggling
    as when swimming fish, hooks in their mouths,
        emerge from the bottom of deepest pools;
and drifting intricacies of craft flutter down,   30
    as when winging birds, caught by stringed shafts,
        plummet from the high-tiered clouds.
He reaps what was unwritten by a hundred generations,
And picks rhymes neglected for a thousand years;
For it falls away—dawn's glorious bloom, unfurled already;   35
There opens instead the unblown bud of evening.
He sees past and present in a single instant,
Touches all this world in the blink of an eye.

Only then
    he selects ideas, sets out their kinds,   40
    tests his phrases, puts them in ranks,
    he strikes open all that contains the light,
    he plucks everything that holds sound within.
He may trust to branches to shake the leaves,
    Or trace waves upstream to find their source;   45
He may track what is hidden and reach the apparent,
    Or seek the simple and obtain the difficult.
The tiger shows its stripes, beasts are thrown to confusion,
    The dragon appears, birds fly off in waves.

It may be steady and sure, and simply enacted,   50
　Or tortuously hard, no ease in it.
He empties his unblurred mind, he concentrates thought,
Unites all concerns and brings forth words.
Earth and Heaven he cages within fixed shape;
All things he crushes beneath brush tip.   55
At first it hesitates upon his dry lips,
But finally flows freely through the moist pen.
Nature's laws bear the substance, they are a tree's trunk;
Patterns hang as the branches, a lavish lacework.
Truly mood and manner never fail to match: 60
Each variation is there upon the face.
When thought moves in joy, there will surely be laughter;
When we tell of lament, sighs have already come.
He may have grasped the tablet and dashed it off lightly,
Or held brush in lips, mind far in the distance.   65

Yet in this event there is truly a joy,
Held in firm honor by good man and Sage:
This trial of void and nothing to demand of it being,
A knock upon silence, seeking its sound.
He contains far expanses on writing's silk sheet,   70
He emits boundless torrents from the speck that is mind.
Language gives breadth, it is ever-expanding;
Thought pursues, growing deeper and deeper.
It spreads the rich scent of drooping blossoms,
Brings the dense darkness of green twigs: 75
Sparkling breeze flies, whirling gusts start;
Swelling clouds rise from writing brush groves.

There are tens of thousands of different forms,
The things of the world have no single measure:
Jumbled and jostling, they go fleeting past,   80
And shapes they have are hard to describe.
Diction shows talents in contests of craft;
Concept controls, it serves as the craftsman.
And there he strives between being and nothing,
In the deep or the shallows, not giving up.   85
Though he strays from the ruled circle and square,
He hopes to reach limits of features and shape.
Thus to make a brave display for eyes, prize extravagance;
But for the mind's content, honor the apposite.
That the words run out is no impediment;   90
Discourse attains its ends only in broadening.

Poems follow from feeling, they are sensuous, fine;
Poetic expositions give forms of things, clear and bright;
Stele inscriptions unfurl patterns to match substance;
Lamentations swell with pent-up sorrow;   95
Inscriptions are broad and concise, warm and gentle;
Admonitions repress, being forceful and sharp;

Odes move with grand ease, being opulent;
Essays treat essence, expansive and lucid;
Statements to the throne are even, incisive, dignified, calm;   100
Persuasions are flashy, deluding, entrancing.
Though fine distinctions are made in these,
They forbid deviation, restrain rash impulse.
Ask that words attain their ends, that principle come forth;
Have nothing to do with long-winded excess.   105

In things there are many stances,
In forms there are frequent shiftings.
When shaping conceptions, value deft craft,
In delivering words, honor allure.
When it comes to the alternation of sounds,   110
They are like the five colors, each sets off the other:
Though there is no law in their passing or halting—
A rocky path, one that we cannot make easy—
Still, if one grasps variation and knows succession,
It is like opening channels to draw in a stream.   115
If you miss your chance, draw together too slowly,
Your beginnings will always be following ends.
Errors in orientation of Earth and of Heaven
Bring mere muddiness and no vividness.

Sometimes you may transgress against previous sections,   120
Or trespass ahead to some later part.
Sometimes diction is faulty, yet principle right.
Or language is smooth, but the idea is blocked.
Avoid both failings and beauty is doubled;
If the two occur jointly, twice then the harm.   125
Judge relative merit by tiniest measures;
Choose to keep or discard by the breadth of a hair:
If what has been trimmed to most accurate measures
Follows truly straight lines, then it must be just right.

Perhaps pattern is lush and the principle rich,   130
But in terms of concept, it has no point.
It reaches its limit, no further significance;
It is used up entirely, it cannot increase.
Set a pregnant phrase in some essential spot,
And it will be a riding crop for the whole piece: 135
Though the word-hoard may follow the rules,
One must have this to strive for great merit.
The achievement large, the obstacles few,
Choose what is enough and do not change it.

Perhaps complex thoughts cohere, patterned finely,   140
They have lucid loveliness, splendidly bright,
They shimmer like brocades of many colors,
Move deeply, like a concert of strings.
But suppose you find what you aimed at lacks distinction—

Your work matches unwittingly some piece long ago.   145
Though the shuttle and loom were in my own feelings,
I must dread lest others have gone here before;
If it injures integrity, transgresses right,
Though I begrudge the doing, I must cast it away.

Perhaps blossom comes forth, a grain spike stands straight,   150
Removed from the crowd, detached from the sense:
A shape is here that no shadow can follow,
A sound to which no echo can join.
It stands there looming, inert and alone,
Not woven together with constant tones.   155
Mind in desolate zones where nothing answers;
Ideas circle aimlessly, unable to leave.
The mountains shimmer when jade lies in stone,
Streams have charm when their waters bear pearls;
Thornbush and underbrush need not be cut—   160
They too can have splendor when kingfishers roost.
If we link the art song to a popular tune,
We may enhance what made it rare.

Suppose words are put in rhymes too short;
They come to dead ends, the heart stirred all alone.   165
They look down to bleak stillness, lacking companion;
They look up to vast spaces and continue nothing.
Compare this to a string of limited range, strung alone—
Within it lies clear song, but nothing responds.

Suppose you trust your lines to dreary tones: 170
Words with aimless languor and wanting in splendor;
Forms compounded of lovely and ugly mixed,
Good substance encumbered by blemishes.
Like pipes in the hall too shrilly played—
Though there is response, it lacks harmony.   175

Suppose you neglect nature's laws, keep what is strange,
Pointless quest for the empty, pursuit of the subtle:
The words will want feeling, be short on love,
Your lines will drift randomly to no end.
As when strings are too thin and the bridges too tight,   180
There may be harmony, but no strong feeling.

But suppose you let yourself rush into choral unisons,
Lost in beauty bewitching, an orgy of sound:
You please the eye pointlessly, match common tastes,
The sound may be loud, but the tune will be low.   185
Be aware of songs like Fanglu and Sangjian—
Though strong feeling is there, it may lack dignity.

Suppose chaste indifference and graceful restraint,
Always pruning complexities, excising excess:

It will lack that "flavor withheld" of ritual broth,   190
Like the too pristine tones of a temple harp.
Though several join in with the one who sings,
Dignity you may have, but still lack allure.

In the degree it is cut, terse or elaborate,
In its forms, either sinking or ascending: 195
One enters variations by what then seems proper,
Fine turns will convey the most subtle moods.
Sometimes language is artless, but the lesson is artful;
Sometimes principle is plain, and the diction light;
Sometimes pursuit of the old yields something new;   200
Sometimes moving with murkiness restores clarity;
Sometimes glancing overviews give requisite insight;
Sometimes essence comes after toilsome honing.
Like the dancer who flings her sleeves to the rhythm,
Or a singer, sending voice in response to the strings.   205
This Wheelwright Pian could not put into words,[2]
Nor can glittering discourse catch the quintessence.

The overall laws of phrasing and writing's rules
Are things to which my heart has submitted:
I have a fine sense of this age's consistent flaws,   210
And recognize what is pure in good men before:
Though something comes from deep in the craftsman's mind,
It may still be mocked in the eyes of fools.
Such agate flourishes and filigree of jade
Are as common as wild beans on the central plain.   215
Never exhausted, like the Great Bellows,[3]
All nurtured together with Heaven and Earth.
Yet however abundant they are in these times,
I sigh that they do not fill my own open hands.
I am cursed by small capacity, too often empty,   220
It is hard to continue the past's apt words.
So I limp along in rhymes too short,
Bring forth commonplace tones to conclude my songs.
And some regret always remains at the end—
Never is my heart full, never am I satisfied.   225
I fear this vessel will be tested, lying in dust,
It will surely be mocked by the ringing jade.

At the conjunction of stirring and response,
At the boundary between blockage and passage,
What comes there can never be halted,   230

---

2. In an anecdote from *Zhuangzi* included in the "Speech, Writing, and Poetry" cluster in Volume A, the humble Wheelwright Pian teaches a duke the uselessness of books for transmitting true knowledge: he claims that he cannot convey in words the knowledge of his craft, which he has gained intuitively through practice.
3. Daoist image for the constant generative processes of the cosmos.

What goes off cannot be stopped.
When it hides, it resembles the shadow vanishing,
When it moves, it resembles the echoes that rise.
When Heaven's impulses move swiftly along the best course,
What confusion exists that cannot reach order?   235
Then winds of thought rise within the breast,
Word-streams go flowing through lips and teeth,
Bubbling forth in tumultuous succession,
Something only silk and writing brush can catch.
The writing gleams and overflows eyes;   240
The tones splash on, filling the ears.

But when the emotions are stalled and hampered,
Mind strains toward something, but spirit is unmoved,
I am left as inert as a bare, leafless tree,
Or a gaping void like a dried-up stream.   245
I draw the soul to search secret recesses,
Gather vital forces to seek from myself;
Nature's laws are hidden and sink away farther,
Thought strives to emerge, as if tugged along.
Sometimes I wear out my heart, and much is regretted;   250
Sometimes I follow thoughts' bent with few failings.
Although this thing does lie in the self,
It is not in the scope of my concentrated force.
I may ponder heart's void and turn against self,
That I do not know how to open this blockage.   255

Coda

The functioning of literature lies in its being
The means for all principles of nature.
It spreads thousands of miles and nothing can bar it;
It passes millions of years, is a ford across.
Ahead it grants models to ages coming,   260
Retrospectively contemplates images of old.
It succors the old kings' Way, on the verge of collapse;
It makes reputation known, does not let it be lost.
No path lies so far it cannot be included;
No principle so subtle it cannot be woven in.   265
Peer of clouds and rain with its nurturing moisture,
Divinity's semblance in its transformations.
When it covers metal and stone, virtue is spread;
Through strings and flutes flowing, it is daily made new.

WANG XIZHI

Wang Xizhi (ca. 303–361) has been the sublime model for aspiring calligraphers in East Asia for the past thirteen hundred years. He is known for developing "running script," the semicursive calligraphic style in which he drafted the "Preface to the *Orchid Pavilion Poems*." During China's medieval period poetry became a social pastime, to be written in a courtly salon or at feasts with friends. The most famous party in Chinese literary history was arguably a gathering at the "Orchid Pavilion" in Shaoxing, near Hangzhou in modern-day Zhejiang Province. In 353 forty-two friends met, composing poems and drinking, as they celebrated the spring purification ceremony. Their collected poems have largely been forgotten, but the preface and its scribe achieved immortal fame.

The preface combines the circumstantial with the philosophical. Descriptions of landscape turn into speculations about the immensity of the universe, the infinite variety of nature, and the awareness of inescapable death. Yet the gorgeous landscape assures Wang Xizhi that there is something that connects people through the ages: the ability to be touched by the world's beauty. Wang had lived through the cataclysmic events of the year 316, when northern invaders conquered the capital of the Jin Dynasty and the court fled southeast and set up a new capital. This expulsion from the traditional heartland of China to a remote southern province was a cultural shock. But it also afforded unexpected pleasures, such as the exotic landscape that Wang Xizhi and his company enjoyed and that stirred him to grand thoughts about their place in history.

Preface to the *Orchid Pavilion Poems*[1]

In the year 353, the ninth year of the Yonghe Reign, early in the last month of spring, there was a gathering at the Orchid Pavilion on the northern slopes of the Kuaiji Mountains;[2] our purpose, to carry out the spring ceremonies of purification. Many a good man came, the young and old alike. The place was one of mighty mountains and towering ridges covered with lush forests and tall bamboo, where a clear stream with swirling eddies cast back a sparkling light upon both shores. From this we cut a winding channel in which to float our winecups, and around this everyone took their appointed seats. True, we did not have the harps and flutes of a great feast, but a cup of wine and a song served well enough to free our most hidden feelings.

The sky that day was luminous, and the air was clear; gentle breezes blew softly around us. Above us we looked on the immensity of the universe; then, lowering our eyes, we saw nature's infinite variety. And as we let our eyes roam

1. Translated by Stephen Owen.

2. A favorite scenic spot even today, not far from Hangzhou.

and our hearts speed from thought to thought, we could experience the greatest delights of ear and eye—this was true happiness.

The times that human beings may be together occur within the fleeting glance of a lifetime: some find them in emotions spoken openly, face to face, in a single room; others invest their feelings in something external as they roam free, beyond the body's world. Our inclinations and aversions have a million different forms; the active man and the contemplative man are unlike; but still, when joy comes with a chance encounter, there is a brief moment of satisfaction, a cheerful self-containment with never a thought of old age coming on. Then, as we weary of the direction in which we are going, our mood shifts with life's events, and depression inevitably follows. In the blink of an eye the joy that has been becomes an experience past—yet still we cannot help having our feelings stirred by it. Even more there are our lives, whether long or short, changing and transforming, but ultimately bound to an end. As was said long ago, "Life and death are the greatest concerns." No escaping the pain in this.

Each time I examine the causes that brought emotion to men in the past, it is as though I have found there the mirror image of my own feelings. Never have I looked upon such writings without a brooding sigh, nor can I find words adequate to explain to myself why. But this I have learned: the belief that life and death are the same is a grand deception; to say that Ancestor Peng's[3] centuries are no more than the lifespan of an infant who died untimely—this is delusion, a forced conceit. Those in later times will look on today as we today look on the past—there is the sadness! For this reason I have written out the list of those present at that time and copied their compositions. Though ages change and experiences differ, all may share what stirs deep feelings. And those who read this in later times will also be moved by what is in this writing.

3. A legendary figure of fantastic longevity.

TAO QIAN
365–427

"Whenever I have been involved in official life I was mortgaging myself to my mouth and belly." Thus Tao Qian (also known as Tao Yuanming) explains his decision to leave public office and return to his family farm. No Chinese poet before or after him captures with more immediate emotion the simple pleasures of country life, the value of being true to one's inner nature, and the necessity to make and unmake choices in life. He is one of the most beloved figures in the Chinese poetic tradition. Generations of readers have been enticed by Tao Qian's candor and his pursuit of personal integrity. Yet his poetry gains its depth and appeal from its roots in the tensions of his humble circumstances, reflecting the fear of failure and mortality.

Although Tao Qian talks much about himself in his poems and became the stuff of legend in later ages, very little is known about his life. His great-grandfather was a noted official and general, and initially Tao Qian followed in his footsteps, serving for thirteen years in several undistinguished official posts. But in 405, when he was magistrate of Pengze, a county seat some thirty miles from his hometown, he suddenly resigned. He had occupied the position for only about eighty days. Instead of living off the grain paid to government officials as their salary, he returned to his family farm to produce his own; self-sufficiency became the principle that would allow him to pursue his true inclinations and live out the last two decades of his life in peace and tranquillity.

Tao Qian lived during the so-called Period of Disunion, the four hundred years between two great empires, the Han (206 B.C.E.–220 C.E.) and the Tang (618–907). This was a time of unprecedented uncertainty, when a series of dynasties followed each other in quick succession. In 316, half a century before Tao Qian was born, non-Chinese tribes invaded northern China. In the ensuing turmoil many of the great aristocratic families and their retainers emigrated to the region south of the Yangzi River. For the first time in Chinese history, "China" no longer meant the territory of the traditional northern heartland; it was now a shared cultural heritage held dear and claimed by the émigrés in the new south. For Tao Qian's generation, the climate, food, and landscape of the south must still have been novelties, enticing people to seek the simple life in the countryside and capture it in poetry.

Also, during the Period of Disunion Buddhism spread to all classes of Chinese society, and the Daoist church (an institution whose founders based their claims to religious leadership on earlier Daoist philosophical texts) gained many supporters. Both Buddhism and Daoism sanctioned the retreat from public life; Confucianism, in contrast, valued active service in the state bureaucracy above all else and accepted withdrawal only in times of incompetent government. Even though Tao Qian described his decision to leave public life as a personal choice, he lived in an age in which political turmoil and new religions encouraged that choice.

Tao Qian's poetry celebrates the pleasures of wine, friendship, and gardening; the joys of composing poetry, reading books, and playing the zither; and the desire for liberation from social strictures to pursue one's own inclinations. Poverty, hunger, and destitution do not call into doubt but rather throw into relief Tao Qian's decision to renounce public office. One grand theme of his poetry is the return to one's natural self, but it is unclear quite how far Tao Qian is willing to push this idea. To be sure, he renounces the pursuit of fame and official recognition and enjoys instead his wine and his garden. But he is also proud of his family line and seems deeply disappointed with his sons' lack of accomplishment. By the same token, writing and reading poetry was an exclusive domain of the educated elite, but the peasants in Tao Qian's poetry, his new neighbors, are apparently literate and he portrays them as sharing his literary interests.

Tao Qian despised worldly ambition, but no poet before him wrote so much about himself. "Substance, Shadow, and Spirit" dramatizes some of his inner tensions by staging a mock debate between three characters, each of whom proposes a different solution to how best to live life: to enjoy wine and forget mortality, as suggested by Substance; to strive to do good and precisely not to forget oneself, as endorsed by Shadow; or, as suggested by the conciliatory Spirit, to forget about both bodily pleasures and moral achievements and simply give oneself over "to the waves of the Great Change." "Biography of Master Five Willows" has been read as a self-portrait of Tao Qian, although he makes no direct reference to himself. In "Elegy" he seems to be coming back from the grave to imagine the scene of his own death and burial, an unprecedented use of a genre reserved for addressing the dead. Even "Peach Blossom Spring" is an autobiography of sorts, a tale about escape from oppressive rule (here from the First Emperor of the Qin Dynasty [221–206 B.C.E.], known in history for his extraordinary cruelty) to a land of self-sufficient happiness. It is also a parable of the impossibility of simply willing things to happen: the fisherman, an ambivalent figure who lives both in tune with nature and in contact with society, stumbles by chance upon the hidden cave while idly exploring an impressive grove of peach trees. After returning, the fisherman reports to the magistrate his spectacular discovery of a cave inhabited by a utopian society that managed to escape the vicissitudes of political turmoil. But to the official who sets out under orders to find the cave, the blissful cave of Peach Blossom Spring is forever beyond reach.

At first Tao Qian was admired as a recluse and man of principle, not as a poet. His straightforward style and simple diction contrast with the ornate imagery and sophisticated allusions in the poetry of his contemporaries. But a renewed interest in simplicity of expression during the Tang Dynasty propelled him to literary fame and has secured him a prominent position in the canon of Chinese poetry ever since. A sixth-century editor of Tao Qian's poetry praises him thus: "An extraordinary person rising above the crowd, Tao Qian followed his natural impulses and was content with his choices." An icon of self-fulfillment, whose poetry convinced people that reaching a state of contentment of sorts is possible, Tao Qian has timeless appeal.

The Peach Blossom Spring[1]

During the Taiyuan period of the Jin dynasty[2] a fisherman of Wuling once rowed upstream, unmindful of the distance he had gone, when he suddenly came to a grove of peach trees in bloom. For several hundred paces on both banks of the stream there was no other kind of tree. The wild flowers growing under them were fresh and lovely, and fallen petals covered the ground—it made a great impression on the fisherman. He went on for a way with the idea of finding out how far the grove extended. It came to an end at the foot of a mountain whence issued the spring that supplied the stream. There was a small opening in the mountain and it seemed as though light was coming through it. The fisherman left his boat and entered the cave, which at first was extremely narrow, barely admitting his body; after a few dozen steps it suddenly opened out onto a broad and level plain where well-built houses were surrounded by rich fields and pretty ponds. Mulberry, bamboo and other trees and plants grew there, and criss-cross paths skirted the fields. The sounds of cocks crowing and dogs barking could be heard from one courtyard to the next. Men and women were coming and going about their work in the fields. The clothes they wore were like those of ordinary people. Old men and boys were carefree and happy.

1. All selections translated by James Robert Hightower except "Biography of Master Five Willows."

2. From 376 to 396 C.E.

When they caught sight of the fisherman, they asked in surprise how he had got there. The fisherman told the whole story, and was invited to go to their house, where he was served wine while they killed a chicken for a feast. When the other villagers heard about the fisherman's arrival they all came to pay him a visit. They told him that their ancestors had fled the disorders of Qin times[3] and, having taken refuge here with wives and children and neighbors, had never ventured out again; consequently they had lost all contact with the outside world. They asked what the present ruling dynasty was, for they had never heard of the Han, let alone the Wei and the Jin.[4] They sighed unhappily as the fisherman enumerated the dynasties one by one and recounted the vicissitudes of each. The visitors all asked him to come to their houses in turn, and at every house he had wine and food. He stayed several days. As he was about to go away, the people said, "There's no need to mention our existence to outsiders."

After the fisherman had gone out and recovered his boat, he carefully marked the route. On reaching the city, he reported what he had found to the magistrate, who at once sent a man to follow him back to the place. They proceeded according to the marks he had made, but went astray and were unable to find the cave again.

A high-minded gentleman of Nanyang named Lui Ziji heard the story and happily made preparations to go there, but before he could leave he fell sick and died. Since then there has been no one interested in trying to find such a place.

> The Ying clan[5] disrupted Heaven's ordinance
> And good men withdrew from such a world.
> Huang and Qi[6] went off to Shang Mountain
> And these people too fled into hiding.
> Little by little their tracks were obliterated   5
> The paths they followed overgrown at last.
> By agreement they set about farming the land
> When the sun went down each rested from his toil.
> Bamboo and mulberry provided shade enough.
> They planted beans and millet, each in season.   10
> From spring silkworms came the long silk thread
> On the fall harvest no king's tax was paid.
> No sign of traffic on overgrown roads,
> Cockcrow and dogsbark within each other's earshot.
> Their ritual vessels were of old design,   15
> And no new fashions in the clothes they wore.
> Children wandered about singing songs,
> Graybeards went paying one another calls.
> When grass grew thick they saw the time was mild,
> As trees went bare they knew the wind was sharp.   20

---

3. During the first short-lived Chinese imperial dynasty (221–206 B.C.E.); the First Emperor was known for his megalomania and cruelty.
4. The dynasties that followed the Qin. The inhabitants did not know about anything that happened in the outside world between the third

century B.C.E. up to the fourth century C.E.
5. That is, the clan of the First Emperor of Qin.
6. Virtuous men who went into reclusion in the mountains to protest the tyranny of the Qin emperor.

Although they had no calendar to tell,
The four seasons still filled out a year.
Joyous in their ample happiness
They had no need of clever contrivance.
Five hundred years this rare deed stayed hid,   25
Then one fine day the fay retreat was found.
The pure and the shallow belong to separate worlds:
In a little while they were hidden again.
Let me ask you who are convention-bound,
Can you fathom those outside the dirt and noise?   30
I want to tread upon the thin thin air
And rise up high to find my own kind.

The Return

I was poor, and what I got from farming was not enough to support my family. The house was full of children, the rice-jar was empty, and I could not see any way to supply the necessities of life. Friends and relatives kept urging me to become a magistrate, and I had at last come to think I should do it, but there was no way for me to get such a position. At the time I happened to have business abroad and made a good impression on the grandees as a conciliatory and humane sort of person. Because of my poverty an uncle offered me a job in a small town, but the region was still unquiet and I trembled at the thought of going away from home. However, Pengze was only thirty miles from my native place, and the yield of the fields assigned the magistrate was sufficient to keep me in wine, so I applied for the office. Before many days had passed, I longed to give it up and go back home. Why, you may ask. Because my instinct is all for freedom, and will not brook discipline or restraint. Hunger and cold may be sharp, but this going against myself really sickens me. Whenever I have been involved in official life I was mortgaging myself to my mouth and belly, and the realization of this greatly upset me. I was deeply ashamed that I had so compromised my principles, but I was still going to wait out the year, after which I might pack up my clothes and slip away at night. Then my sister who had married into the Cheng family died in Wuchang, and my only desire was to go there as quickly as possible. I gave up my office and left of my own accord. From mid-autumn to winter I was altogether some eighty days in office, when events made it possible for me to do what I wished. I have entitled my piece 'The Return'; my preface is dated the eleventh moon of the year *yisi*.[1]

To get out of this and go back home!
My fields and garden will be overgrown with weeds—I must go back.
It was my own doing that made my mind my body's slave
Why should I go on in melancholy and lonely grief?
I realize that there's no remedying the past   5
But I know that there's hope in the future.
After all I have not gone far on the wrong road

1. A year in the Chinese sixty-year cycle; eleventh month in this lunar calendar corresponds approximately to December.

And I am aware that what I do today is right, yesterday wrong.
My boat rocks in the gentle breeze
Flap, flap, the wind blows my gown;   10
I ask a passerby about the road ahead,
Grudging the dimness of the light at dawn.
Then I catch sight of my cottage—
   Filled with joy I run.
The servant boy comes to welcome me   15
   My little son waits at the door.
The three paths are almost obliterated
   But pines and chrysanthemums are still here.
Leading the children by the hand I enter my house
   Where there is a bottle filled with wine.   20
I draw the bottle to me and pour myself a cup;
Seeing the trees in the courtyard brings joy to my face.
I lean on the south window and let my pride expand,
I consider how easy it is to be content with a little space.
Every day I stroll in the garden for pleasure,   25
There is a gate there, but it is always shut.
Cane in hand I walk and rest
Occasionally raising my head to gaze into the distance.
The clouds aimlessly rise from the peaks,
The birds, weary of flying, know it is time to come home.   30
As the sun's rays grow dim and disappear from view
I walk around a lonely pine tree, stroking it.

Back home again!
May my friendships be broken off and my wanderings come to an end.
The world and I shall have nothing more to do with one another.   35
If I were again to go abroad, what should I seek?
Here I enjoy honest conversation with my family
And take pleasure in books and zither to dispel my worries.
The farmers tell me that now spring is here
There will be work to do in the west fields.   40
Sometimes I call for a covered cart
Sometimes I row a lonely boat
Following a deep gully through the still water
Or crossing the hill on a rugged path.
The trees put forth luxuriant foliage,   45
The spring begins to flow in a trickle.
I admire the seasonableness of nature
And am moved to think that my life will come to its close.
   It is all over—
So little time are we granted human form in the world!   50
Let us then follow the inclinations of the heart:
Where would we go that we are so agitated?
I have no desire for riches
And no expectation of Heaven.
Rather on some fine morning to walk alone   55
Now planting my staff to take up a hoe,
Or climbing the east hill and whistling long

Or composing verses beside the clear stream:
So I manage to accept my lot until the ultimate homecoming.
Rejoicing in Heaven's command, what is there to doubt?   60

Biography of Master Five Willows[1]

We don't know what age the master lived in, and we aren't certain about his
real name. Beside his cottage were five willow trees, so he took his name from
them. He lived in perfect peace, a man of few words, with no desire for glory or
gain. He liked to read but didn't try too hard to understand. Yet whenever there
was something that caught his fancy, he would be so happy he would forget to
eat. He had a wine-loving nature, but his household was so poor he couldn't
always obtain wine. His friends, knowing how he was, would invite him to
drink. And whenever he drank, he finished what he had right away, hoping to
get very drunk. When drunk, he would withdraw, not really caring whether he
went or stayed. His dwelling was a shambles, providing no protection against
wind and sun. His coarse clothes were full of holes and patches; his plate and
pitcher always empty; he was at peace. He forgot all about gain and loss and in
this way lived out his life.

Qianlou's[2] wife once said, "Feel no anxiety about loss or low station; don't be
too eager for wealth and honor." When we reflect on her words, we suspect that
Five Willows may have been such a man—swigging wine and writing poems to
satisfy his inclinations. Was he a person of the age of Lord No-Cares? Was he a
person of the age of Getian?[3]

Substance, Shadow, and Spirit

Noble or base, wise or stupid, none but cling tenaciously to life. This is a great
delusion. I have put in the strongest terms the complaints of Substance and
Shadow and then, to resolve the matter, have made Spirit the spokesman for
naturalness. Those who share my tastes will all get what I am driving at.

I

Substance to Shadow

Earth and heaven endure forever,
Streams and mountains never change.
Plants observe a constant rhythm,
Withered by frost, by dew restored.
But man, most sentient being of all,   5
In this is not their equal.

---

1. Translated by Stephen Owen. "Master Five Willows" is Tao Qian's playful name for himself.
2. A figure of antiquity who preferred a life of poverty to serving in office.
3. Two legendary rulers of a golden age, before there were troubles in the world.

He is present here in the world today,
Then leaves abruptly, to return no more.
No one marks there's one man less—
Not even friends and family think of him;   10
The things that he once used are all that's left
To catch their eye and move them to grief.
I have no way to transcend change,
That it must be, I no longer doubt.
I hope you will take my advice: 15
When wine is offered, don't refuse.

II

Shadow to Substance

No use discussing immortality
When just to keep alive is hard enough.
Of course I want to roam in paradise,
But it's a long way there and the road is lost.
In all the time since I met up with you   5
We never differed in our grief and joy.
In shade we may have parted for a time,
But sunshine always brings us close again.
Still this union cannot last forever—
Together we will vanish into darkness.   10
The body goes; that fame should also end
Is a thought that makes me burn inside.
Do good, and your love will outlive you;
Surely this is worth your every effort.
While it is true, wine may dissolve care   15
That is not so good a way as this.

III

Spirit's Solution

The Great Potter[1] cannot intervene—
All creation thrives of itself.
That Man ranks with Earth and Heaven
Is it not because of me?
Though we belong to different orders,   5
Being alive, I am joined to you.
Bound together for good or ill
I cannot refuse to tell you what I know:
The Three August Ones[2] were great saints
But where are they living today?   10
Though Pengzu[3] lasted a long time
He still had to go before he was ready.

1. The personified force of creation and change in the cosmos.
2. Sage kings of antiquity, believed to have lived to a fabulous old age.
3. A legendary figure who supposedly lived eight hundred years.

Die old or die young, the death is the same,
Wise or stupid, there is no difference.
Drunk every day you may forget,   15
But won't it shorten your life span?
Doing good is always a joyous thing
But no one has to praise you for it.
Too much thinking harms my life;
Just surrender to the cycle of things,   20
Give yourself to the waves of the Great Change
Neither happy nor yet afraid.
And when it is time to go, then simply go
Without any unnecessary fuss.

Returning to the Farm to Dwell

I

From early days I have been at odds with the world;
My instinctive love is hills and mountains.
By mischance I fell into the dusty net
And was thirteen years away from home.
The migrant bird longs for its native grove.   5
The fish in the pond recalls the former depths.
Now I have cleared some land to the south of town,
Simplicity intact, I have returned to farm.
The land I own amounts to a couple of acres
The thatched-roof house has four or five rooms.   10
Elms and willows shade the eaves in back,
Peach and plum stretch out before the hall.
Distant villages are lost in haze,
Above the houses smoke hangs in the air.
A dog is barking somewhere in a hidden lane,   15
A cock crows from the top of a mulberry tree.
My home remains unsoiled by worldly dust
Within bare rooms I have my peace of mind.
For long I was a prisoner in a cage
And now I have my freedom back again.   20

II

Here in the country human contacts are few
On this narrow lane carriages seldom come.
In broad daylight I keep my rustic gate closed,
From the bare rooms all dusty thoughts are banned.
From time to time through the tall grass   5
Like me, village farmers come and go;
When we meet we talk of nothing else
Than how the hemp and mulberry are growing.
Hemp and mulberry grow longer every day
Every day the fields I have plowed are wider;   10

My constant worry is that frost may come
And my crops will wither with the weeds.

Begging for Food

Hunger came and drove me out
To go I had no notion where.
I walked until I reached this town,
Knocked at a door and fumbled for words
The owner guessed what I was after   5
And gave it, but not just the gift alone.
We talked together all day long,
And drained our cups as the bottle passed.
Happy in our new acquaintance
We sang old songs and wrote new poems.   10
You are as kind as the washerwoman,
But to my shame I lack Han's talent.[1]
I have no way to show my thanks
And must repay you from the grave.[2]

On Moving House

I

For long I yearned to live in Southtown—
Not that a diviner told me to—
Where many simple-hearted people live
With whom I would rejoice to pass my days.
This I have had in mind for several years   5
And now at last have carried out my plan.
A modest cottage does not need be large
To give us shelter where we sit and sleep.
From time to time my neighbors come
And we discuss affairs of long ago.   10
A good poem excites our admiration
Together we expound the doubtful points.

II

In spring and fall are many perfect days
For climbing high to write new poetry.
As we pass the doors, we hail each other,
And anyone with wine will pour us some.

1. Han Xin, eventually a general of Liu Bang, the founder of the Han Dynasty (206 B.C.E.– 220 C.E.), was able to repay the kindness he received from the washerwoman who had given him food when he was a poor youth. 2. An allusion to the story of a ghost who repaid a debt of gratitude to Lord Huan of Wei by tripping his enemy.

When the farm work is done, we all go home
And then have time to think of one another—
So thinking, we at once throw on a coat
And visit, never tired of talk and jokes.
There is no better way of life than this,
No need to be in a hurry to go away.
Since food and clothing have to be provided,
If I do the plowing, it will not cheat me.

In the Sixth Month of 408, Fire

I built my thatched hut in a narrow lane,
Glad to renounce the carriages of the great.
In midsummer, while the wind blew long and sharp,
Of a sudden grove and house caught fire and burned.
In all the place not a roof was left to us
And we took shelter in the boat by the gate.

Space is vast this early autumn evening,
The moon, nearly full, rides high above.
The vegetables begin to grow again
But the frightened birds still have not returned.
Tonight I stand a long time lost in thought;
A glance encompasses the Nine Heavens.[1]
Since youth I've held my solitary course
Until all at once forty years have passed.
My outward form follows the way of change
But my heart remains untrammelled still.
Firm and true, it keeps its constant nature,
No jadestone is as strong, adamantine.
I think back to the time when East-Gate[2] ruled
When there was grain left out in the fields
And people, free of care, drummed full bellies,
Rising mornings and coming home to sleep.
Since I was not born in such a time,
Let me just go on watering my garden.

From Twenty Poems After Drinking Wine

Preface

Living in retirement here I have few pleasures, and now the nights are growing
longer; so, as I happen to have some excellent wine, not an evening passes
without a drink. All alone with my shadow I empty a bottle until suddenly I find

---

1. That is, the entire sky; heaven was imagined as having nine layers.

2. A legendary ruler in the golden age, a time
of such plenty that no one bothered to steal.

myself drunk. And once I am drunk I write a few verses for my own amusement. In the course of time the pages have multiplied, but there is no particular sequence in what I have written. I have had a friend make a copy, with no more in mind than to provide a diversion.

V

I built my hut beside a traveled road
Yet here no noise of passing carts and horses.
You would like to know how it is done?
With the mind detached, one's place becomes remote.
Picking chrysanthemums by the eastern hedge   5
I catch sight of the distant southern hills:
The mountain air is lovely as the sun sets
And flocks of flying birds return together.
In these things is a fundamental truth
I would like to tell, but lack the words.   10

IX

I heard a knock this morning at my door
In haste I pulled my gown on wrongside out
And went to ask the caller, Who is there?
It was a well-intentioned farmer, come
With a jug of wine to pay a distant call.   5
Suspecting me to be at odds with the times:
'Dressed in rags beneath a roof of thatch
Is not the way a gentleman should live.
All the world agrees on what to do—
I hope that you will join the muddy game.'   10
'My sincere thanks for your advice, old man.
It's my nature keeps me out of tune.
Though one can learn of course to pull the reins,
To go against oneself is a real mistake.
So let's just have a drink of this together—   15
There's no turning back my carriage now.'[1]

X

Once I made a distant trip
Right to the shore of the Eastern Sea
The road I went was long and far,
The way beset by wind and waves.
Who was it made me take this trip?   5
It seems that I was forced by hunger.
I gave my all to eat my fill
When just a bit was more than enough.
Since this was not a famous plan
I stopped my cart and came back home.   10

---

1. That is, he has decided on the course of his life.

Finding Fault with My Sons

Over my temples the white hair hangs,
My wrinkled skin is past filling out.
Although five sons belong to me
Not one is fond of brush and paper.
Already Shu is twice times eight—   5
For laziness he has no match.
At Axuan's age one should study,
But love of letters is not in him.
Both Yong and Duan count thirteen years
And cannot add up six and seven.   10
Tongzi is getting on toward nine
And all he wants are pears and chestnuts.
If this is the way it is fated to be,
Just let me reach for the Thing in the Cup.[1]

From On Reading the *Seas and Mountains Classic*[1]

I

In early summer when the grasses grow
And trees surround my house with greenery,
The birds rejoice to have a refuge there
And I too love my home.
The fields are plowed and the new seed planted   5
And now is time again to read my books.
This out-of-the-way lane has no deep-worn ruts
And tends to turn my friends' carts away.
With happy face I pour the spring-brewed wine
And in the garden pick some greens to cook.   10
A gentle shower approaches from the east
Accompanied by a temperate breeze.
I skim through the *Story of King Mu*[2]
And view the pictures in the *Seas and Mountains Classic*.
A glance encompasses the ends of the universe—   15
Where is there any joy, if not in these?

Elegy

The year is *dingmao* of the cycle, the season that of the tone *wuyi*,[1] when days are cold and the nights long, when the wind blows mournfully as the wild fowl migrate, and leaves turn yellow and fall. Master Tao is about to depart from

---

1. That is, wine.
1. An ancient book that provides a fabulous geography, describing the countries surrounding China as inhabited by fantastic creatures and strange-looking human beings.
2. The travel narrative of an early king of the

Zhou Dynasty (ca. 1045–256 B.C.E.) who supposedly visited fantastic places outside of China.
1. Winter. "*Dingmao*": a cyclical date name (427 C.E.).

this lodging house to return for all time to his own home. Old friends are grieved and mourn for him: this evening they give him a farewell banquet, offering a sacrificial food, pouring libations of clear wine. They look, and his face is dim; listening, they no longer hear the sound of his voice.

Alas, alas, this vast clod, earth, that illimitable high firmament, together produce all things, even me who am a man. But from the time I attained human estate, my lot has been poverty. Rice-bin and wine-gourd have often been empty, and I have faced winters in thin clothes. Still I have gone happily to draw water from the brook and have sung as I walked under a load of firewood, going about my daily affairs in the obscurity of my cottage. As springs gave way to autumn, I have busied myself in my garden, hoeing, cultivating, planting or tending. I have rejoiced in my books and have been soothed by my zither. Winters I have warmed myself in the sun, summers I have bathed in the brook. There was little enough reward for my labor, but my mind enjoyed a constant leisure. Content with Heaven and accepting my lot, I have lived out the years of my life.

Men fear to waste their lives, concerned that they may fail to succeed. They cling to the days and lament passing time. During their life they are honored by the world, and after their death they still are mourned. But I have gone my own way, which is not their way. I take no glory in their esteem, nor do I feel defamed by their slander. I have lived alone in my poor house, drinking wine and writing poetry.

Aware of my destined end, of which one cannot be ignorant, I find no cause for regret in this present transformation. I have lived out my lifespan, and all my life I have desired quiet retirement. Now that I am dying, an old man, what have I left to wish for?

Hot and cold hasten on, one after the other.[2] The dead have nothing in common with the survivors. Relatives come in the morning, friends arrive in the evening, to bury me in the meadow and give comfort to my soul. Dark is my journey, desolate the grave. It is shameful to be buried extravagantly as was Huan Tui (whose stone coffin was three years a-making), and ridiculous to be parsimonious like Yang Wangsun (who was buried naked), for after death there is nothing. Raise me no mound, plant me no grove; time will pass with the revolving sun and moon. I never cared for praise in my lifetime, and it matters not at all what eulogies are sung after my death. Man's life is hard enough in truth; and death is not to be avoided.

---

2. That is, the seasons pass.

TANG POETRY

The poetry of the Tang Dynasty (618–907) is generally considered the high point of China's three-millennia-old history of poetry. Much compelling verse was written after the period, not least because the poetic giants of the Tang inspired later poets to write with self-conscious sophistication and skill. But later poets generally agreed that **Du Fu**, **Li Bo**, and their contemporaries had set a standard that could not be surpassed. For many centuries the elegant urgency and technical virtuosity with which these poets captured the world, as well as the scope of their poetic visions and themes, formed the basis for later poetic training and inspiration. The primacy of Tang poetry in the Chinese poetic canon continued until the early twentieth century, when Chinese intellectuals launched a revolutionary movement to replace the classical written idiom with vernacular spoken language. Today traditional poetry is popular once again, and the accomplishments of the Tang poets remain the high-water mark of what poetry can do.

POETRY AND TANG SOCIETY

Every educated Chinese during the Tang Dynasty was expected to be able to spontaneously dash off a poem with grace, or at least technical competence. Poetry was a form of social communication, not an arcane and highbrow art. The sheer mass of Tang poems still extant—close to 50,000, by some 2,200 authors—clearly indicates how common poetry was in everyday life. Many of those whose poems survived spent their lives in some official government position, after taking the civil service examination that qualified them for office. Whenever these scholar-officials were sent to a new post in the vast territory of the Tang Empire they would take leave from their colleagues and friends with a "farewell" poem and expect a poetic gift in return. In their new province, they would make friends by going on pleasure excursions or visiting temples and invariably writing poems about their journeys. They could also write poems to praise the imperial court or to criticize its policies. Poetry thus was a cultural custom, a craft that taught people how to pay attention to and share the significant moments in their lives—to find something lovely in a scene; to convey feelings about separation and friendship, painful and pleasurable events; to thank a host for a splendid evening party; or simply to express what would otherwise be awkward or impossible to say. Though the practice of writing poetry was general, only some thirty or forty truly talented poets achieved renown as artists of the highest caliber. Yet some otherwise undistinguished writers produced a remarkable number of fine poems that would be read and memorized for the next thousand years.

THE ORIGIN OF TANG POETRY

Chinese literature began with the folk songs and ritual ballads about historical events preserved in the *Classic of Poetry* (ca. 600 B.C.E.). Most of the poems in that collection have stanzas of four to six lines containing four to six characters each, with end rhymes for every couplet. During the Han Dynasty (206 B.C.E.– 220 C.E.), about half a millennium after the compilation of the *Classic of Poetry*, a new genre of poetry emerged. Written in lines of five or seven characters and displaying a much more melodious and flexible rhythm, it became the basis for Tang poetry. During the century preceding the Tang Dynasty, poets began to experiment with introducing tonal patterns into their poems. Although variations in tone are common in many languages, including English, they are usually associated with sentence patterns. Chinese differs in attaching tones to individual syllables. Poets started to arrange the tones of each syllable of the poem—in modern Mandarin Chinese, a syllable can be pronounced in one of four different tones—in symmetrical patterns. This innovation led to the birth of so-called regulated poetry, a verse form that requires syllables to alternate "level" and "deflected" tones and demands training to master. The spread of Buddhism in the first half of the first millennium may have helped spark the development of regulated poetry. Chinese monks translating Sanskrit texts into Chinese must have been struck by the absence of tones in Sanskrit, and this new awareness of a defining feature of their own language perhaps inspired the introduction of rules mandating the alternation of tones in poetry. Whatever the reason, the emergence of regulated poetry (also called "recent-style" poetry, as earlier poetic forms such as those used by **Tao Qian** came to be called "old-style" poetry) radically changed the reading and writing of poetry. By imposing more rules on the game of poetry, it enabled readers to judge poetic craftsmanship more objectively.

Both the prominent place of poetry in social communication and everyday life and these new technical demands gave poetry an unprecedented status in Tang society. Poetry was introduced into the prestigious civil service examination; successful aspirants were awarded the "presented scholar" degree (*jinshi*), a prerequisite for a career as a government official. Although there were debates about whether the inclusion of poetry composition was appropriate for such exams, and was later abolished, the tight formal requirements of the regulated poem made it easier to judge and compare the candidates' relative worth. Also, the candidates were forced to learn how to compose succinctly and eloquently. This skill would be useful in their later careers in government service, as they drafted many complex official documents.

REGULATED POETRY OF THE TANG

The two basic forms of regulated poetry are in four lines (*jueju*) and eight lines (*lüshi*), although longer poems composed of several stanzas were also common. Regulated poetry placed a new emphasis on the couplet, a unit of two lines. For the ambitious Tang poet, couplets provided an opportunity to display virtuosity, as they provided a showcase for the parallelism required of the regulated poem. Consider **Du Fu's** "**Spring Prospect**," which describes the fall of the Tang capital to rebels in 755 and the destruction of the great Tang Empire against the backdrop of innocent spring:

> The nation shattered, mountains and rivers remain;
> city in spring, grass and trees burgeoning.
> Feeling the times, blossoms draw tears;
> hating separation, birds alarm the heart.
> Beacon fires three months in succession,

a letter from home worth ten thousand in gold.
White hairs, fewer for the scratching,
soon too few to hold a hairpin up.

Let us examine how this five-syllable regulated poem reads in classical Chinese. Some of the rhymes and tones are hardly recognizable in the modern Mandarin pronunciation of the characters given here, but they did rhyme and tonally harmonize during the Tang Dynasty. "Level tones" are marked with a hyphen (–); "deflected tones," with a straight line (|):

FIRST COUPLET

國	破	山	河	在	(Chinese characters)
guó	pò	shān	hé	zài	(modern Mandarin pronunciation)
|	|	–	–	|	(tonal pattern)
nation	shattered	mountain	river	remain	(word-for-word translation)

城	春	草	木	深	
chéng	chūn	cǎo	mù	shēn	(rhyme word)
–	–	|	|	–	
city	spring	grass	tree	grow thick	

SECOND COUPLET

感	時	花	濺	淚	
gǎn	shí	huā	jiàn	lèi	
(|)	–	–	|	|	
feel	time	blossom	shed	tear	

恨	別	鳥	驚	心	
hèn	bié	niǎo	jīng	xīn	(rhyme word)
|	|	|	–	–	
hate	separation	bird	alarm	heart	

THIRD COUPLET

烽	火	連	三	月	
fēng	huǒ	lián	sān	yuè	
(–)	|	–	–	|	
beacon	fire	in succession	3	months	

家　書　抵　萬　金

jiā　shū　dǐ　wàn　jīn[(rhyme word)]

－　－　|　|　－

home　letter　worth　10,000　gold

白　頭　搔　更　短　**FOURTH COUPLET**

bái　tóu　sāo　gèng　duǎn

(|)　－　－　|　|

white　head　scratch　even　shorter

渾　欲　不　勝　簪

hùn　yù　bú　shèng　zān[(rhyme word)]

|　|　|　|　(－)

simply　want　not　hold　hairpin

The poem consistently relies on parallelism as it poignantly contrasts the stability of the natural cycle with the abrupt changes brought about by the rebellion. In the first couplet the capital Chang'an is taken by rebel forces, the emperor has fled to Sichuan Province and abdicated, and the "nation is shattered," yet, perversely, we see the "city in spring," untouched by the disaster of historic proportion. In the second couplet, even blossoms and birds appear startled by the human tragedy. The third couplet shows the economic costs of the rebellion: the rebels have cordoned off the capital so tightly that letters have become almost priceless, smuggled in and out only at risk of one's life. The last couplet lacks precise parallelisms but ends with thematic resonances and shows the poet in despair: the hairpin no longer secures his official cap to his head, because he has become too old and the dynasty he wanted to serve has fallen on hard times.

Parallelism in Tang poetry functioned on many levels beyond the grammatical, including thematic parallelism and contrast between lines or in the poem as a whole. Thus Tang writings on poetry distinguish many types. The parallel couplet was the central device of regulated poetry, and during the Tang people would write out their favorite couplets in lavish calligraphy on little hanging scrolls, which they could carry when traveling. Indeed, Tang poets compiled entire anthologies containing only beautiful couplets excerpted from famous poems. The emphasis on fashioning beautiful couplets created a huge market for practical manuals that explained how to avoid violating the tonal rules and how to come up with an impressive parallel. This approach later drew criticism from poets who saw artistic ambition and inspiration, rather than craft and training, as the keys to good poetry. But the attraction of Tang poetry lies precisely in the felicitous match of craft with inspiration. It was solid training in the rules of regulated poetry that enabled Tang poets to capture their experience of the world in memorable words. The ultimate art of Tang poetry is that it often hides its artfulness under the serene surface of natural imagery.

WANG WEI

ca. 699–761

One of the most prominent poets of his time, Wang Wei was also a well-respected painter and musician. He confesses in one poem that he was a poet only "by mistake" and that he must have been a painter in an earlier life.

Wang Wei was born into an aristocratic family and passed the civil service examination at the age of twenty. He rose steadily in the ranks of the official bureaucracy but his career was interrupted in 755, when the frontier general An Lushan rebelled against the Tang—leading to the siege that occasioned Du Fu's "Spring Prospect." Although the emperor and his immediate entourage fled, many officials were captured by the rebels and forced to work for An Lushan's military government. When the revolt was put down, Wang Wei escaped charges of collaboration only thanks to the intervention of his brother, a high-ranking government official. Once rehabilitated, he served in office until his death.

The An Lushan Rebellion was the most catastrophic event in three centuries of Tang Dynasty rule (618–907). That a simple frontier general of Central Asian origin could bring down an empire that was at the time the largest and most efficiently administered in the world came as a profound shock to the Chinese and their East Asian neighbors; and it became a defining moment for Wang Wei's generation. Yet unlike many of his contemporaries, such as Du Fu, Wang Wei wrote almost nothing about it. The poem "While I Was Imprisoned in Puti Monastery" is unusual in this regard. Written when Wang Wei was held captive by An Lushan's rebels, it describes efforts of the former Tang court musicians to resist the rebel government's request to perform at its victory banquet. The poem was circulated after the rebellion as proof of Wang Wei's resistance to the rebel government, thereby aiding his rehabilitation.

Although he could write in an ornate style on public court occasions, Wang Wei is known mainly for his ability to evoke tranquil scenes of rural retreat and convey a sense of dispassionate detachment from the world. His vignettes of reclusive life combine simplicity and deliberate craft. He bought a retreat in the Zhongnan Mountains and later the "Wang River" estate outside the capital, which he and his friend Pei Di celebrated in a series of poems.

Wang Wei also painted the various scenic spots he mentions in his poetry. None of his original paintings are preserved, but the survival of many imitations suggests that they were very popular. Wang Wei is considered a pioneer of Chinese landscape art, known particularly for his monochrome painting, which uses black ink-wash on white paper; this technique allows the painter to depict landscapes dominated by white. His interest in snow scenes is also evident in "White Rock Rapids," in which he paints—in poetry—families washing white silk under bright moonlight, with white rocks and dark rushes implicit in the background.

Wang Wei's poetry echoes his friendship with Buddhist monks and recluses and his commitment to Buddhism. Whereas other poets celebrated the landscape as it appears to the senses, Wang Wei often represents an insubstantiality that corresponds to the notion of the "emptiness" of things—the fundamental Buddhist conviction that all we perceive is illusion.

Zhongnan Retreat[1]

In middle years I am rather fond of the Tao;
My late home is at the foot of Southern Mountain.
When the feeling comes, each time I go there alone.
That splendid things are empty, of course, I know.
I walk to the place where the water ends   5
And sit and watch the time when clouds rise.
Meeting by chance an old man of the forest,
I chat and laugh without a date to return.

In Response to Vice-Magistrate Zhang

In late years I care for tranquility alone—
A myriad affairs do not concern my heart.
A glance at myself: there are no long-range plans.
I only know to return to the old forest.
Pine winds blow, loosening my belt;   5
The mountain moon shines as I pluck my zither.
You ask about reasons for success and failure:
A fisherman's song enters the shore's deeps.

From Wang River Collection

Preface: My retreat is in the Wang River mountain valley. The places to walk
to include: Meng Wall Cove, Huazi Hill, Grained Apricot Lodge, Clear Bamboo
Range, Deer Enclosure, Magnolia Enclosure, Dogwood Bank, Sophora Path,
Lakeside Pavilion, Southern Hillock, Lake Yi, Willow Waves, Luan Family Shallows, Gold Powder Spring, White Rock Rapids, Northern Hillock, Bamboo Lodge,
Magnolia Bank, Lacquer Tree Garden, and Pepper Tree Garden. When Pei Di[2]
and I were at leisure, we each composed the following quatrains.

* * *

Deer Enclosure

Empty mountain, no man is seen.
Only heard are echoes of men's talk.
Reflected light enters the deep wood
And shines again on blue-green moss.

Lake Yi

Blowing flutes cross to the distant shore.
At day's dusk I bid farewell to you.
On the lake with one turn of the head:
Mountain green rolls into white clouds.

1. All selections translated by and with notes   2. A fellow poet and minor official (b. 716),
adapted from Pauline Yu.   one of Wang Wei's closest friends.

Gold Powder Spring

Drink each day at Gold Powder Spring
And you should have a thousand years or more:
To soar on an azure phoenix with striped dragons,
And with plumes and tassels attend the Jade Emperor's
court.[3]

White Rock Rapids

Clear and shallow, White Rock Rapids.
Green rushes once could be grasped.
Families live east and west of the water,
Washing silk beneath the bright moon.

Written on Crossing the Yellow River to Quinghe

A boat sailing on the great river—
The gathered waters reach to the end of the sky.
Sky and waves suddenly split asunder:
A commandery city—a thousand, ten thousand homes.
Farther on I see a city market again;   5
There seems to be some mulberry and hemp.
Looking back at my old home country:
The water's expanse joins the clouds and mist.

While I Was Imprisoned in Puti Monastery, Pei Di Came to See Me. He Spoke of How the Rebels Ordered Music Played at Frozen Emerald Pond; after the Court Musicians Began to Play, Their Tears Fell. I Secretly Recited and Presented This to Pei Di[4]

From ten thousand homes of grieving hearts arises wild smoke.
The hundred officials—when will they again attend court?
Autumn sophora leaves fall within the empty palace.
Next to Frozen Emerald Pond, music from pipes and strings.

---

3. Daoists often engaged in alchemical experiments, believing that gold could confer immortality. Both the Queen Mother of the West, who rode on a phoenix chariot pulled by striped dragons, and the Jade Emperor, supreme deity in the Daoist pantheon, are associated with immortality.

4. Probably Wang Wei's only expression of political protest, written when he was imprisoned during the An Lushan rebellion in 756. After An Lushan and his soldiers entered the capital Chang'an, they forced members of the imperial conservatory to perform at a victory banquet for the rebels.

Farewell

Dismounting I give you wine to drink,
And inquire where you are going.
You say you did not achieve your wishes
And return to rest at the foot of Southern Mountain.
But go—do not ask again: 5
White clouds have no ending time.

LI BO
701–762

Although Li Bo (also known as Li Po and Li Bai) was raised in Sichuan in western China, speculations about his Turkic family background have enhanced his image as an exotic eccentric. Li Bo never attempted to take the civil service examination, which was the primary but not sole venue for advancement. Thanks to his connection with an influential Daoist at court, Li Bo gained a post at the eminent Hanlin Academy, an institution founded by Emperor Xuanzong to support unconventional intellectuals and literary talents. But Li Bo's drinking habits and unusual personality led to his dismissal only two years later. During the An Lushan Rebellion he joined the cause of a prince who attempted to establish an independent regime in southeast China, and after the rebellion was suppressed he was arrested for treason. Sentenced to exile, he was pardoned before he reached his remote destination; he died a few years later.

There are many legends about Li Bo's life, encouraged by the nonchalant poses projected in his poetry: according to one such legend, he drowned while trying to embrace the moon's reflection on the water. For someone who claimed in his poetry to converse and drink with the moon such an end was not implausible, though overindulgence in alcohol and Daoist longevity elixirs, which often contained mercury, might have played a role.

Much Tang poetry tends to treat the world at hand; Li Bo supplies an additional dimension by describing Daoist worlds beyond the world, evoking moments of history and legend, and even transforming everyday occasions into something miraculous. Because of his flair and capacity to see the world with fresh eyes, his contemporaries called him "the banished immortal"—an ethereal heaven-dwelling being exiled for a lifetime in the world of mortals as punishment for some extravagant misdemeanor.

Li Bo cultivated this reputation by writing poems that tell of encounters with immortals and of cloud-climbing excursions through the heavens.

Of the thousand-some poems by Li Bo that survive, many are written in the old verse form popular before the rise of regulated poetry during the Tang. Li Bo particularly liked to imitate folk songs and infuse his poetry with colloquial and bold language. In this way he could sometimes give voice to the common people's hardships: in "South of the Walls We Fought," for example, he echoes an older anonymous lament of soldiers fallen in battle, turning it into bitter criticism of the constant warfare of his time on the northern and northwestern frontier of Tang China against peoples such as the Tibetans.

Li Bo and **Du Fu** are considered the most important Tang poets, and readers and critics over the past millennium have devoted considerable effort to debating their relative merits and shortcomings. Quite apart from the greatness of their poetry, they made a particularly fitting couple, because they embody the two poles of poetic creativity that have been of greatest concern in the Chinese literary tradition: while Du Fu became the poet who captured, chronicled, and criticized reality within its limits, Li Bo came to stand for the poet who dedicated himself to breaking free from social convention and from the limits imposed by reality.

The Sun Rises and Sets[1]

The sun comes up from its nook in the east,
Seems to rise from beneath the earth,
Passes on through Heaven,
    sets once again in the western sea,
And where, oh, where, can its team of six dragons   5
    ever find any rest?
Its daily beginnings and endings,
    since ancient times never resting.
And man is not made of its Primal Stuff—
    how can he linger beside it long?   10
Plants feel no thanks for their flowering in spring's wind,
Nor do trees hate losing their leaves
    under autumn skies:
Who wields the whip that drives along
    four seasons of changes—   15
The rise and the ending of all things
    is just the way things are.

Xihe! Xihe![2]
Why must you always drown yourself
    in those wild and reckless waves?   20
What power had Luyang[3]

1. Translated by Stephen Owen.
2. Goddess who drove the sun's carriage.
3. According to legend, the lord of Luyang stopped the sun so that he could continue to fight in combat.

That he halted your course by shaking his spear?
This perverts the Path of things,
   errs from Heaven's will—
So many lies and deceits!   25
I'll wrap this Mighty Mudball of a world
   all up in a bag
And be wild and free like Chaos itself!

South of the Walls We Fought[4]

We fought last year at the Sanggan's source,
this year we fight on the Cong River road.
We washed weapons in the surf of Tiaozhi,
grazed horses on grass in Sky Mountain's snow.[5]
Thousands of miles ever marching and fighting: 5
until all the Grand Army grows frail and old.

The Xiongnu[6] treat slaughter as farmers treat plowing;
since bygone days only white bones are seen
   in their fields of yellow sand.
The House of Qin built the wall   10
   to guard against the Turk;
for the House of Han the beacon fires
   were blazing still.

Beacon fires blaze without ceasing,
the marching and battle never end.   15
They died in fighting on the steppes,
their vanquished horses neigh,
   mourning to the sky.
Kites and ravens peck men's guts,
fly with them dangling from their beaks   20
   and hang them high
      on boughs of barren trees.
The troops lie mud-smeared in grasses,
and the general acted all in vain.
Now I truly see that weapons   25
   are evil's tools:
the Sage will use them only
   when he cannot do otherwise.

---

4. Translated by Stephen Owen.
5. Four locations of Tang campaigns in the north and northwest.

6. Formidable enemies of the Han Empire (206 B.C.E.–220 C.E.).

Bring in the Wine[7]

Look there!
  The waters of the Yellow River,
    coming down from Heaven,
    rush in their flow to the sea,
    never turn back again   5
Look there!
  Bright in the mirrors of mighty halls
    a grieving for white hair,
    this morning blue-black strands of silk,
    now turned to snow with evening.   10
For satisfaction in this life
    taste pleasure to the limit,
And never let a goblet of gold
    face the bright moon empty.
Heaven bred in me talents,   15
    and they must be put to use.
I toss away a thousand in gold,
    it comes right back to me.
So boil a sheep,
    butcher an ox,   20
      make merry for a while,
And when you sit yourself to drink, always
    down three hundred cups.
    Hey, Master Cen,
    Ho, Danqiu,[8]   25
    Bring in the wine!
    Keep the cups coming!
And I, I'll sing you a song,
You bend me your ears and listen—
The bells and the drums, the tastiest morsels,   30
    it's not these that I love—
All I want is to stay dead drunk
    and never sober up.
The sages and worthies of ancient days
    now lie silent forever,   35
And only the greatest drinkers
    have a fame that lingers on!
Once long ago
    the prince of Chen
      held a party at Pingle Lodge.[9]   40
A gallon of wine cost ten thousand cash,
    all the joy and laughter they pleased.
    So you, my host,
How can you tell me you're short on cash?
Go right out!   45

7. Translated by Stephen Owen.
8. Two friends of Li Bo.
9. The scene of merry parties described by the

poet Cao Zhi (192–232), the brother of Cao Pi,
the author of "A Discourse on Literature."

Buy us some wine!
    And I'll do the pouring for you!
Then take my dappled horse,
    Take my furs worth a fortune,
Just call the boy to get them,   50
    and trade them for lovely wine,
And here together we'll melt the sorrows
    of all eternity!

Question and Answer in the Mountains[1]

They ask me why I live in the green mountains.
I smile and don't reply; my heart's at ease.
Peach blossoms flow downstream, leaving no trace—
And there are other earths and skies than these.

Summer Day in the Mountains[2]

Lazily waving a fan of white feathers,
Stripped naked here in the green woods,
I take off my headband, hang it on a cliff,
My bare head splattered by wind through pines.

Drinking Alone with the Moon[3]

A pot of wine among the flowers.
I drink alone, no friend with me.
I raise my cup to invite the moon.
He and my shadow and I make three.

The moon does not know how to drink;   5
My shadow mimes my capering;
But I'll make merry with them both—
And soon enough it will be Spring.

I sing—the moon moves to and fro.
I dance—my shadow leaps and sways.   10
Still sober, we exchange our joys.
Drunk—and we'll go our separate ways.

Let's pledge—beyond human ties—to be friends,
And meet where the Silver River ends.

1. Translated by Vikram Seth.   3. Translated by Vikram Seth.
2. Translated by Stephen Owen.

The Hardships of Traveling the Road I[4]

Clear wine in golden goblets, at ten thousand a peck:
Prized delicacies on jade plates, worth a myriad cash.
But I stopped the cup, threw down the chopsticks, was unable to eat:
I took out my sword, stared all around, my heart was blindly lost.
I wanted to cross the Yellow River, but ice blocked the waterway: 5
Was about to climb the Taihang range, but snow darkened the sky.
At my ease I let fall a line, sitting by the side of a stream;
Longed to be aboard ship again and dreamt of the realm of the sun.

    The hardships of traveling the road—hardships of traveling the road:
    So many branching roads!—and where now am I?   10
The long wind will smite the waves, and surely will come a time,
To hang straight the cloudy sail and cross the gray-blue sea!

Seeing Off Meng Haoran at Yellow Crane Tower,
on His Way to Guangling[5]

My old friend bids farewell in the west at Yellow Crane Tower.[6]
Amid misty blossoms of the third month goes down to Yangzhou.
His lone sail's far shadow vanishes in the deep-blue void.
Now I see only the Long River flowing to the edge of the sky.

In the Quiet Night[7]

The floor before my bed is bright:
Moonlight—like hoarfrost—in my room.
I lift my head and watch the moon.
I drop my head and think of home.

Sitting Alone by Jingting Mountain[8]

The flocks of birds have flown high and away,
A solitary cloud goes off calmly alone.
We look at each other and never get bored—
Just me and Jingting Mountain.

---

4. Translated by Paul Kroll.
5. Translated by Paul Kroll.
6. A famous scenic spot in the southeastern city of Hangzhou.
7. Translated by Vikram Seth.
8. Translated by Stephen Owen.

A Song on Visiting Heaven's Crone
Mountain in a Dream: On Parting[9]

Seafarers speak of that isle of Ying[1]—
but in blurred expanses of breakers and mist
   it is hard indeed to find.

Yue men tell of Heaven's Crone,[2]
appearing, then gone, it may be seen   5
   in the clouds and colored wisps.

Heaven's Crone reaches to sky
   and sideways runs to the sky,
its force stands over the Five Great Peaks,
   it casts Redwall in the shade.   10
Mount Tiantai[3] is forty and eight
   thousand yards high,
yet facing this it seems to tip,
   sagging southeastwardly.

And I, wishing to reach that place,   15
   once dreamed of Wu and Yue,
I spent a whole night flying across
   the moon in Mirror Lake.

The lake moon caught my reflection,
and went with me on to Shan Creek.   20
The place where Lord Xie spent the night
   is still to be found there now,
where green waters are ruffled in ripples,
   and the gibbon's wail is clear.

I put on the clogs of Lord Xie,[4]   25
and scaled that ladder into blue clouds.
Halfway up cliffside I saw sun in sea,
and heard in the air the Heaven-Cock crow.

A thousand peaks and ten thousand turns,
   my path was uncertain;   30
I was lost among flowers and rested on rock,
   when suddenly all grew black.

Bears roared and dragons groaned,
   making the cliff-streams quake,
the deep forests were shivering,—tiered ridges shook,   35

9. Translated by Stephen Owen.
1. One of the islands of immortals.
2. A mountain near the ancient southern
state of Yue.
3. A sacred Buddhist mountain in southeast-

ern China (modern Zhejiang Province).
4. A 5th-century poet renowned for his landscape poetry he was also famous for supposedly inventing special mountain-climbing
shoes.

clouds hung blue,—portending rain,
troubled waters rolled,—giving off mists.

Thunder-rumbling in Lightning Cracks,
hill ridges split and fell;
then the stone doors of Caves to Heaven   40
swung open with a crash.
A billowing vast blue blackness
    whose bottom could not be seen,
where sun and moon were gleaming
    on terraces silver and gold.   45

Their coats were of rainbow,—winds were their steeds,
the lords of the clouds—came down in their hosts.
Tigers struck harps, phoenixes drew coaches in circles,
those who are the Undying—stood in ranks like hemp.
All at once my soul was struck,—and my spirit shuddered,   50
I leapt up in dazed alarm,—and gave a long sigh.
I was aware only—of this moment's pillow and mat,
I had lost those mists and bright wisps—that had been here just
    before.

All pleasures in our mortal world   55
    are also just like this,
whatever has happened since ancient times
    is the water flowing east.

When I leave you now, you go,—when will you ever return?
just set a white deer out to graze   60
    upon green mountainsides,
and when I must go, I'll ride it
    to visit mountains of fame.

How can I pucker my brows and break my waist
    serving power and prestige?—   65
it makes me incapable
    of relaxing heart or face.

DU FU
712–770

Du Fu failed in his political ambitions, and his poetry was not widely read during his lifetime. But during the Song Dynasty (960–1279) he rose to the top of the poetic canon because of his versatility and ability to capture the dramatic historical events and spirit of his age. Ever since that time, Du Fu, together with **Li Bo,** has maintained the reputation as the greatest of Chinese poets.

Du Fu was the grandson of a prominent court poet. Although he dreamed of an official career, that dream was dashed after he twice failed the civil service examination. When An Lushan rebelled in 755, the imperial court escaped but Du Fu was left behind in the capital. Eventually he slipped through the enemy lines and made his way to the court of the new emperor in exile. There he briefly held one of the court positions he had so much desired; but following the recapture of the capital, he was exiled to a minor provincial post. He soon quit in disgust and embarked on a lifetime of travels. He first went to seek the help of relatives in northwest China, and then took up residence in Chengdu in Sichuan Province. In his later years Du Fu moved to Kuizhou, where he produced his most admired poetry sequence, the "Autumn Meditations."

Du Fu is considered the "poet-historian" of Chinese literature, carrying out the Confucian duty to chronicle and criticize the events of his time. Prophetically, he grasped that the An Lushan Rebellion was an event of major historical proportions. But it was his ability to capture the rebellion's impact on his life and on the lives of the people around him that gave depth to his voice. In "Moonlight Night" Du Fu imagines his wife, whom he had managed to send to safety while he remained trapped in the occupied capital, watching the moon and worrying about him; "Qiang Village" conveys the riveting scene of reunion, after Du Fu has finally escaped from the capital and is reunited with his family. But the effects of the rebellion linger on even after it is quashed: a decade later, he devotes "Ballad of the Firewood Vendors" to the local working women in his new home in Kuizhou who despair that the loss of life has destroyed the marriage prospects of an entire generation.

The greatness of Du Fu's poetry lies in its extraordinary range of themes, styles, and observations. His poetic mastery is particularly visible in his preferred verse form, the regulated poem, in which he can be not just witty but also prophetic and visionary. Even when he is sober and humble, his everyday observations can reach cosmic proportions and take the unsuspecting reader by surprise.

Painted Hawk[1]

Wind-blown frost rises from plain white silk,
a gray falcon—paintwork's wonder.

Body strains, its thoughts on the cunning hare,
its eyes turn sidelong like a Turk in despair.

You could pinch the rays glinting on tie-ring,   5
its stance, to be called to the column's rail.

When will it strike the common birds?—
bloody feathers strewing the weed-covered plain.

Moonlight Night[2]

From her room in Fuzhou tonight,
all alone she watches the moon.

Far away, I grieve that her children
can't understand why she thinks of Chang'an.

Fragrant mist in her cloud hair damp,   5
clear lucence on her jade arms cold—

when will we lean by chamber curtains
and let it light the two of us, our tear stains dried?

Spring Prospect[3]

The nation shattered, mountains and rivers remain;
city in spring, grass and trees burgeoning.

Feeling the times, blossoms draw tears;
hating separation, birds alarm the heart.

Beacon fires three months in succession,   5
a letter from home worth ten thousand in gold.

White hairs, fewer for the scratching,
soon too few to hold a hairpin up.[4]

1. Translated by Stephen Owen.
2. Translated by Burton Watson. This poem was written in 756, when Du Fu was held captive in the fallen capital of Chang'an during the An Lushan Rebellion and his wife and family had fled to safety in Fuzhou in the north.
3. Translated by Burton Watson. This poem was written when Du Fu was still a captive in Chang'an.
4. Officials used hairpins to keep their caps in place.

Qiang Village I[5]

Lofted and lifted, west of the clouds of red,
The trek of the sun descends to the level earth.
By the brushwood gate songbirds and sparrows chaffer,
And the homebound stranger from a thousand *li*[6] arrives.
Wife and children marvel that I am here: 5
When the shock wears off, still they wipe away tears.
In the disorders of the age was I tossed and flung;
That I return alive is a happening of chance.
Neighbors swarm up to the tops of the walls,
Touched and sighing, even they sob and weep.   10
The night wastes on, and still we hold the candle,
Across from another, as if . . .

My Thatched Roof Is Ruined by the Autumn Wind[7]

In the high autumn skies of September
    the wind cried out in rage,
Tearing off in whirls from my rooftop
    three plies of thatch.
The thatch flew across the river,   5
    was strewn on the floodplain,
The high stalks tangled in tips
    of tall forest trees,
The low ones swirled in gusts across ground
    and sank into mud puddles.   10
The children from the village to the south
    made a fool of me, impotent with age,
Without compunction plundered what was mine
    before my very eyes,
Brazenly took armfuls of thatch,   15
    ran off into the bamboo,
And I screamed lips dry and throat raw,
    but no use.
Then I made my way home, leaning on staff,
    sighing to myself.   20
A moment later the wind calmed down,
    clouds turned dark as ink,
The autumn sky rolling and overcast,
    blacker towards sunset,
And our cotton quilts were years old   25
    and cold as iron,
My little boy slept poorly,
    kicked rips in them.
Above the bed the roof leaked,
    no place was dry,   30

5. Translated by Paul Kroll. This poem was
written in 757, when Du Fu finally rejoined
his family after their separation during the turmoil of the An Lushan Rebellion.
6. About 250 miles.
7. Translated by Stephen Owen.

And the raindrops ran down like strings,
  without a break.
I have lived through upheavals and ruin
  and have seldom slept very well,
But have no idea how I shall pass   35
  this night of soaking.
Oh, to own a mighty mansion
  of a hundred thousand rooms,
A great roof for the poorest gentlemen
  of all this world,   40
  a place to make them smile,
A building unshaken by wind or rain,
  as solid as a mountain,
Oh, when shall I see before my eyes
  a towering roof such as this?   45
Then I'd accept the ruin of my own little hut
  and death by freezing.

I Stand Alone[8]

A single bird of prey beyond the sky,
a pair of white gulls between riverbanks.

Hovering wind-tossed, ready to strike;
the pair, at their ease, roaming to and fro.

And the dew is also full on the grasses,   5
spiders' filaments still not drawn in.

Instigations in nature approach men's affairs—
I stand alone in thousands of sources of worry.

Spending the Night in a Tower by the River[9]

A visible darkness grows up mountain paths,
I lodge by river gate high in a study,

Frail cloud on cliff edge passing the night,
The lonely moon topples amid the waves.

Steady, one after another, a line of cranes in flight;   5
Howling over the kill, wild dogs and wolves.

No sleep for me. I worry over battles.
I have no strength to right the universe.

8. Translated by Stephen Owen.   9. Translated by Stephen Owen.

Thoughts while Travelling at Night[1]

Light breeze on the fine grass.
I stand alone at the mast.

Stars lean on the vast wild plain.
Moon bobs in the Great River's spate.

Letters have brought no fame.   5
Office? Too old to obtain.

Drifting, what am I like?
A gull between earth and sky.

Ballad of the Firewood Vendors[2]

Kuizhou women, hair half gray,
forty, fifty, and still no husbands;
since the ravages of rebellion, harder than ever
    to marry—
a whole life steeped in bitterness and long sighs.   5
Local custom decrees that men sit, women stand;
men mind the house door, women go out and work,
at eighteen, nineteen, off peddling firewood,
with money they get from firewood, making
    ends meet.   10
Till they're old, hair in two buns dangling to the neck,
stuck with wild flowers, a mountain leaf, a silver pin,
they struggle up the steep paths, flock to the market gate,
risk their lives for extra gain by dipping from salt wells. 15
Faces powdered, heads adorned, sometimes a trace
    of tears,
cramped fields, thin clothing, the weariness of
    stony slopes—
But if you say all are ugly as the women of Witch's   20
    Mountain,
how to account for Zhaojun,[3] born in a village to
    the north?

---

1. Translated by Vikram Seth.
2. Translated by Burton Watson. This poem, written in 766, describes local customs in Kuizhou, set on steep hillsides along the Yangzi River, where Du Fu had settled.
3. Wang Zhaojun, a stunningly beautiful court lady of the Han Dynasty (206 B.C.E.–220 C.E.) who embodied the suffering of exile, because she was married off to a tribal chief of the fierce Xiongnu tribes as part of Han diplomacy on the unruly northern frontier. "Witch's Mountain": Wushan, near Kuizhou.

Autumn Meditations IV[4]

I've heard them say, Chang'an's like a chessboard;
sad beyond bearing, the happenings of these
    hundred years!
Mansions of peers and princes, all with new
    owners now;   5
in civil or martial cap and garb, not the same as before.
Over mountain passes, due north, gongs and
    drums resound;
wagons and horses pressing west speed the
    feather-decked dispatches.[5]   10
Fish and dragons sunk in sleep, autumn rivers cold;
old homeland, those peaceful times, forever in
    my thoughts!

4. Translated by Burton Watson. This poem comes from Du Fu's most famous poetic cycle, "Autumn Meditations."
5. Feathers attached to military dispatches marked the message as urgent; Uighurs were threatening from the north and Tibetans from the west.

BO JUYI
772–846

With more than 2,800 poems, Bo Juyi (or Bai Juyi) stands out as the most prolific Tang poet. In "Last Poem" we see him on his deathbed, still busy scribbling poems to send back to his friends. Like no writer before him Bo Juyi recorded his daily life in poetry, considering such matters as his taste for fresh bamboo shoots, prices on the flower market, or the purchase of his beloved estate outside the capital. Seeking to write poetry as autobiography, he was also a highly self-conscious poet: in "On My Portrait" he laughs at himself, "some mountain man," and reads in his own face signs portending ruin rather than success.

Bo Juyi came from a modest scholar-official family, passed the civil service examination in his late twenties, and then embarked on a succession of government appointments, interrupted by several years in exile after he incurred the emperor's displeasure. While serving in powerful positions in the provinces away from the capital he became increasingly drawn to Buddhism and the joys of reclusive life.

Bo Juyi wrote in many styles and guises, but his "New Music Bureau Poetry," which drew attention to corrupt political practices and social abuses, was especially important to him. During the earlier Han Dynasty (206 B.C.E.–220 C.E.) the imperial Music Bureau was founded to collect songs from the people and provide musical performances. Its mission reflected the Confucian conviction that rulers should adjust their policies to the needs of their subjects and that song and poetry were particularly effective means of communicating the complaints of the people to the emperor and the ruling class. Bo Juyi revived this method of conveying grievances. The poem "Salt Merchant's Wife," for example, attacks the luxurious life that the imperial monopoly on iron and salt afforded salt merchants, who collected the imperial tax on iron and salt trading and often pocketed large profits.

Though Bo Juyi sternly castigated the abuse of power for private gains, he sympathized with a different kind of abuse of power that would have fatal consequences: the infatuation of Emperor Xuanzong (685–762) with "Prized Consort Yang" (Yang Guifei). The emperor's love for the consort enabled her clan to advance into positions of power at court on the eve of the An Lushan Rebellion. Although their connection with the rebellion is unclear, people held her and her clan responsible; and when the capital was overrun by rebels and Emperor Xuanzong tried to escape, the military demanded Yang Guifei's execution—so she was strangled before the emperor's eyes. Yang's taste for luxury and the exclusive attention the emperor lavished on her both fascinated and repelled people. This tale of fateful conflict between duty and love inspired many later poems, novels, and plays, but Bo Juyi's "Song of

Lasting Regret," composed half a century after the rebellion, became its most influential early treatment; his friend Chen Hong added a prose account to it. Though Bo Juyi and Chen Hong treat the same set of events, they differ markedly in how they structure the story, what significant details they choose to dramatize it, and how they judge the lovers. These differences go beyond a personal disagreement of opinion between two friends, also showing that poetry and prose had its distinct narrative logic and moral values regarding love affairs.

Bo Juyi achieved great fame during his lifetime. Copies of his poetry collection spread outside China to other East Asian countries, including Japan, where he became one of the most popular Chinese poets. His poetry was included in Japanese anthologies, his "New Music Bureau Poetry" became a basic primer for male and female students alike, and his song about the tragic love of Emperor Xuanzong and Yang Guifei was taken as the archetypal expression of impossible and tragic love; as such, it was frequently alluded to in the central masterpiece of Japanese literature, the eleventh-century *Tale of Genji* by the court lady **Murasaki Shikibu**.

The Song of Lasting Regret[1]

Monarch of Han, he doted on beauty, yearned for a bewitching temptress;
Through the dominions of his sway, for many years he sought but did
    not find her.
There was in the family of Yang a maiden just then reaching fullness,[2]
Raised in the women's quarters protected, unacquainted yet with others.   4
Heaven had given her a ravishing form, impossible for her to hide,
And one morning she was chosen for placement at the side of the
    sovereign king.
When she glanced behind with a single smile, a hundred seductions
    were quickened;
All the powdered and painted ones in the Six Palaces[3] now seemed   8
    without beauty of face.

1. Translated by and with notes adapted from Paul Kroll. The asterisks in this selection mark divisions, not excerptions.

2. The future Yang Guifei, the Emperor Xuanzong's "prized consort."

3. Residences of the imperial concubines.

In the coolness of springtime, she was permitted to bathe in the
    Huaqing pools,[4]
Where the slickening waters of the hot springs washed over her firm flesh.
Supported as she rose by a waiting-maid, she was so delicate, listless:
This was the moment when first she acceded to His favor   12
    and beneficence.

Cloud-swept tresses, flowery features, quivering hair-pendants of gold,
And behind the warmth of lotus-bloom drapings, they passed the
    springtime nights—
Springtime nights so grievously brief, as the sun rose again high!
From this time onward the sovereign king no longer held early court.   16

Taken with pleasure, she attended on the feasts, continuing without let;
Springtime followed springtime outing, evening after evening
    she controlled.

Of the comely beauties of the rear palace,[5] there were three thousand
    persons,
And preferments and affection for all three thousand were placed on   20
    her alone.
In her golden room, with makeup perfect, the Delicate One serves for
    the night;
In a tower of jade, with the feast concluded, drunkenness befits love in
    spring.

Her sisters and brothers, older or younger, all were enfeoffed[6] with land;
The most enviable brilliance and glory quickened their doorways and   24
    gates.
Then it came to pass, throughout the empire, that the hearts of fathers
    and mothers
No longer valued the birth of a son but valued the birth of daughters.

The high sites of Mount Li's palace reached into clouds in the blue,
And transcendent music, wafted on the wind, was heard there   28
    everywhere.

Measured songs, languorous dancing merged with sound of strings and
    bamboo,
As the sovereign king looked on all day long, never getting enough . . .
Until, out of Yuyang, horse-borne war-drums came, shaking the earth,
To dismay and smash the melody of "Rainbow Skirts and Feathered   32
    Vestments."[7]

*   *   *

4. Famous hot springs some fifteen miles outside of the Tang capital of Chang'an.
5. The women's quarters.
6. Deeded.
7. An exotic Central Asian dance melody;

Emperor Xuanzong rescored it, and Lady Yang
danced to it costumed as a moon maiden.
"Yuyang": the headquarters of the rebel An
Lushan, east of modern Beijing.

By the nine-layered walls and watchtowers, dust and smoke arose,
And a thousand chariots, ten thousand riders moved off to the southwest.[8]

The halcyon-plumed banners jounced and joggled along, moving and
    stopping again,
As they went forth westward from the metropolis' gates, something   36
    more than a hundred miles.
And then the Six Armies would go no farther—there was no other recourse,
But the fluently curved moth-eyebrows[9] must die before the horses.

Floriform filigrees were strewn on the ground, to be retrieved by no one,
Halcyon tailfeathers, an aigrette of gold, and hairpins made of jade.   40
The sovereign king covered his face—he could not save her;
When he looked back, it was with tears of blood that mingled in
    their flow.

                    *   *   *

Yellowish grit spreads and scatters, as the wind blows drear and doleful;
Cloudy walkways turn and twist, climbing Saber Gallery's[1] heights.   44
Below Mount Emei there are very few men who pass by;
Lightless now are the pennons and flags in the sun's dimmer aura.

Waters of Shu's[2] streams deepest blue, the mountains of Shu are green—
For the Paragon, the Ruler, dawn to dawn, night upon night, his   48
    feelings:
Seeing the moon from his transient palace—a sight that tears at his heart;
Hearing small bells in the evening rain—a sound that stabs his insides.

                    *   *   *

Heaven revolves, the days roll on, and the dragon carriage was turned
    around;[3]
Having reached the spot, faltering he halted, unable to leave it again.   52
But amidst that muddy earth, below Mawei Slope,[4]
Her jade countenance was not to be seen—just a place of empty death.

Sovereign and servants beheld each other, cloaks wet from weeping;
And, looking east, to the metropolis' gates, let their horses take them   56
    homeward.

                    *   *   *

Returned home now, and the ponds, the pools, all were as before—
The lotuses of Grand Ichor Pool, the willows by the Night-is-Young Palace.

The lotus blossoms resemble her face, the willow branches her eyebrows;
Confronted with this, would it be possible that his tears should not fall?   60

---

8. The emperor and his retinue, fleeing from
An Lushan's rebel army.
9. That is, Lady Yang.
1. A sacred mountain in the southwestern
province of Sichuan.

2. An ancient name for the region.
3. That is, the emperor returned to the capital.
4. The site of Lady Yang's execution.

From the day that peach and plum flowers open, in the springtime breezes,
Until the leaves of the "we-together"[5] tree are shed in the autumn rain. . . .

The West Palace and the Southern Interior were rife with autumn grasses,
And fallen leaves covered the steps, their red not swept away.   64
The artistes, once young, of the Pear Garden have hair gone newly white;
The Pepper Room attendants and their budding nymphs are become
  aged now.

Fireflies flit through the hall-room at dusk, as he yearns in desolation;
When all the wick of his lone lamp is used, sleep still fails to come.   68
Ever later, more dilatory, sound the watch-drum and bell in the
  lengthening nights;
Fitfully sparkling, the River of Stars[6] streams onward to the dawn-
  flushed sky.

The roof-tiles, paired as love-ducks, grow chilled, and flowers of frost
  grow thick;
The halcyon-plumed coverlet is cold—whom would he share it with?   72
Dim-distanced, far-faded, are the living from the dead, parted more
  than a year ago;
Neither her soul nor her spirit have ever yet come into his dreams.

* * *

A Daoist adept from Linqiong, a visitor to the Hongdu Gate,[7]
Could use the perfection of his essential being to contact souls and   76
  spirits.
Because of his broodings the sovereign king, tossing and turning,
  still yearned;
So he set to task this adept of formulas, to search for her sedulously.

Cleaving the clouds, driving the ethers, fleeting as a lightning-flash,
Ascending the heavens, entering into the earth, he sought her out   80
  everywhere.
On high he traversed the sky's cyan drop-off, and below to the Yellow Springs;[8]
In both places, to the limits of vision, she was nowhere to be seen.

Of a sudden he heard rumor then of a transcendent mountain in the sea,
A mountain resting in void and nullity, amidst the vaporous seemings.   84

High buildings and galleries shimmer there brightly, and five-colored
  clouds mount up;
In the midst of this, relaxed and unhurried, were hosts of tender sylphs.
And in *their* midst was one, known as Greatest Perfection,[9]

5. A tree whose name sounds like the phrase
"we together." The falling of the leaves reminds
the emperor of his lost love.
6. The Milky Way.
7. An ancient name for the capital's gates.
8. A traditional name for the Chinese underworld. "Sky's cyan drop-off": the sky's blue
reaches; also a Daoist technical term for a specific region in the "Heaven of Nascent Azure."
9. The religious name (Taizhen) adopted by
Lady Yang when she briefly took orders as a
Daoist priestess, before receiving a title as the
emperor's consort.

Whose snow-white skin and flower-like features appeared to resemble   88
   hers.

In the western wing of the gatehouse of gold, he knocked at the jade bolting,
In turn setting in motion Little Jade who made report to Doubly Completed.[1]
When word was told of the Son of Heaven's envoy, from the House of Han,
Then, within the nine-flowered drapings, her dreaming spirit startled.   92

She searched for her cloak, pushed pillow aside, arose, walked forth
   distractedly;
Door-screens of pearl, partitions of silver, she opened out one after another.
With her cloud-chignon half-mussed to one side, newly awakened from sleep,
With flowered cap set awry, down she came to the ceremonial hall.   96

Her sylphine sleeves, puffed by a breeze, were lifted, flared and fluttering,
Just the same as in the dance of "Rainbow Skirts and Feathered Vestments."
But her jade countenance looked bleak, forlorn, crisscrossed with tears—
A single branch of pear blossom, in springtime laden with rain.   100

Restraining her feelings, focusing her gaze, she asked her sovereign king's
   indulgence:
"Once we were parted, both voice and face were lost to limitless vagueness.
There, within Zhaoyang Basilica, affection and favor were cut short,
While here in Penglai's[2] palaces, the days and months have   104
   lengthened.

"Turning my head and looking down to the sites of the mortal sphere,
I can no longer see Chang'an,[3] what I see is dust and fog.
Let me take up these familiar old objects to attest to my deep love:
The filigree case, the two-pronged hairpin of gold, I entrust to you to   108
   take back.

"Of the hairpin but one leg remains, and one leaf-fold of the case;
The hairpin is broken in its yellow gold, and the case's filigree halved.
But if only his heart is as enduring as the filigree and the gold,
Above in heaven, or amidst men, we shall surely see each other."   112

As the envoy was to depart, she entrusted poignantly to him words as well,
Words in which there was a vow that only two hearts would know:
"On the seventh day of the seventh month,[4] in the Hall of Protracted Life,
At the night's mid-point, when we spoke alone, with no one else around—   116

---

1. Two of Lady Yang's servants. "Doubly Completed" was the servant of a central Daoist goddess, the "Queen Mother of the West."
2. A Daoist island of the immortals in the eastern ocean (during Bo Juyi's time, sometimes associated with Japan).
3. The Tang capital.

4. According to popular legend, the only day when the constellation the Oxherd could cross the Milky Way to meet with his lover, the Weaver Maid; Lady Yang and the emperor had exchanged a love oath on that auspicious night. The festival is still celebrated today in East Asia as a Valentine's Day of sorts.

'In heaven, would that we might become birds of coupled wings!
On earth, would that we might be trees of intertwining limbs! . . .'"
Heaven is lasting, earth long-standing, but there is a season for their end;
This regret stretches on and farther, with no ending time.　　　　120

Chen Hong, *An Account to Go with the "Song of Lasting Regret"*[5]

During the Kaiyuan Reign,[6] the omens of the Stair Stars showed a world at peace, and there were no problems throughout all the land within the four circling seas. Xuanzong, having been long on the throne, grew weary of having to dine late and dress while it was still dark for the dawn audience; and he began to turn over all questions of government, both large and small, to the Assistant Director of the Right, Li Linfu, while the Emperor himself tended either to stay deep in the palace or go out to banquets, finding his pleasure in all the sensual delights of ear and eye. Previously the Empress Yuanxian and the Consort Wuhui had both enjoyed His Majesty's favor, but each in turn had departed this world; and even though there were in the palace over a thousand daughters of good families, none of them really caught his fancy. His Majesty was fretful and displeased.

In those days every year in December the imperial entourage would journey to Huaqing Palace. The titled women, both from the inner palace and from without, would follow him like luminous shadows. And he would grant them baths in the warm waters there, in the very waves that had bathed the imperial sun. Holy fluids in a springlike breeze went rippling through those places. It was then that His Majesty's heart was smitten: for he had truly come upon the one woman, and all the fair flesh that surrounded him seemed to him like dirt. He summoned Gao Lishi to make a secret search for this woman in the palaces of the princes; and there, in the establishment of the Prince of Shou, he found the daughter of Yang Xuanyan. She had already become a mature woman. Her hair and tresses were glossy and well arranged; neither slender nor plump, she was exactly of the middle measure; and there was a sensuous allure in her every motion, just like the Lady Li of Emperor Wu of the Han. He ordered a special channel of the warm springs cut for her and commanded that it be offered to her gleaming fineness. When she came out of the water, her body seemed frail and her force spent, as if she could not even bear the weight of lace and gauze; yet she shed such radiance that it shone on all around her. His Majesty was most pleased. On the day he had her brought to meet him, he ordered the melody "Coats of Feathers, Rainbow Skirts" played to precede her. And on the eve when their love was consummated, he gave her, as proofs of his love, a golden hairpin and an inlaid box. He also commanded that she wear golden earrings and a hair-pick that swayed to her pace. The following year he had her officially listed as Guifei, Prized Consort, entitled to half the provision as an empress. From this point on she assumed a seductively coy manner and spoke wittily, suiting herself to His Majesty's wishes by thousands of fetching ways. And His Majesty came to dote on her ever more deeply.

---

5. Translated by Stephen Owen.
6. The golden years of Emperor Xuanzong's reign, from 713 to 741.

At this time the Emperor made a tour of his nine domains and offered the gold-sealed tablets in ceremonies on the Five Sacred Peaks. On Mount Li during snowy nights and in Shangyang Palace on spring mornings she would ride in the same palanquin as the Emperor and spend the night in the same apartments; she was the main figure of feasts and had his bedchambers all to herself when he retired. There were three Great Ladies, nine Royal Spouses, twenty-seven Brides of the Age, eighty-one Imperial Wives, Handmaidens of the Rear Palace, Women Performers of the Music Bureau—and on none of these was the Son of Heaven the least inclined to look. And from that time on, no one from the Six Palaces was ever again brought forward to the royal bed. This was not only because of her sensual allure and great physical charms, but also because she was clever and smart, artful at flattery and making herself agreeable, anticipating His Majesty's wishes—so much so that it cannot be described. Her father, her uncle, and her brothers were all given high honorary offices and were raised to ranks of Nobility Equal to the Royal House. Her sisters were enfeoffed as Ladies of Domains. Their wealth matched that of the royal house; and their carriages, clothes, and mansions were on a par with the Emperor's aunt, Princess Taichang. Yet in power and the benefits of imperial favor, they surpassed her. They went in and out of the royal palace unquestioned, and the senior officers of the capital would turn their eyes away from them. There were doggerel rhymes in those days that went:

> If you have a girl, don't feel sad;
> if you have a boy, don't feel glad.

and:

> The boy won't be a noble,
>   but the daughter may be queen;
>   so look on your daughters now
>   as the glory of the clan.

To such a degree were they envied by people.

At the end of the Tianbao Reign,[7] her uncle Yang Guozhong stole the position of Chancellor and abused the power he held. When An Lushan led his troops in an attack on the imperial palace, he used punishing Yang Guozhong as his pretext. Tong Pass was left undefended, and the Kingfisher Paraphernalia of the imperial entourage had to set out southward.[8] After leaving Xianyang, their path came to Mawei Pavilion. There the Grand Army hesitated, holding their pikes in battle positions and refusing to go forward. Attendant officers, gentlemen of the court, and underlings bowed down before His Majesty's horse and asked that this current Chao Cuo[9] be executed to appease the world. Yang Guozhong then received the yak-hair hat ribbons and the pan of water, by which a great officer of the court presents himself to the Emperor for punishment, and he died there by the edge of the road. Yet the will of those who were with the Emperor was still not satisfied. When His Majesty asked what the problem was, those who dared speak out asked that the Prized Consort also be sacrificed to

---

7. Emperor Xuanzong's last reign period, from 742 to 756, leading up to the An Lushan Rebellion.
8. That is, the emperor fled west to Sichuan.

9. A Han Dynasty official, executed in 155 B.C.E. because he was blamed for helping to incite a rebellion.

allay the wrath of the world. His Majesty knew that it could not be avoided, and yet he could not bear to see her die, so he turned his sleeve to cover his face as the envoys dragged her off. She struggled and threw herself back and forth in panic, but at last she came to death under the strangling cord.

Afterward, Xuanzong came to Chengdu on his Imperial Tour, and Suzong accepted the succession at Lingwu.[1] In the following year the Monster himself [An Lushan] forfeited his head, and the imperial carriage returned to the capital. Xuanzong was honored as His Former Majesty and given a separate establishment in the Southern Palace, then transferred to the western sector of the Imperial Compound. As time and events passed, all joy had gone from him and only sadness came. Every day of spring or night of winter, when the lotuses in the ponds opened in summer or when the palace ash trees shed their leaves in autumn, the performers of the Pear Garden Academy would produce notes on their jade flageolets; and if he heard one note of "Coats of Feathers, Rainbow Skirts," His Majesty's face would lose its cheer, and all those around him would sob and sigh. For three years there was this one thing on his mind, and his longing never subsided. His soul sought her out in dream, but she was so far away he could not reach her.

It happened then that a wizard came from Shu; and knowing that His Majesty was brooding so much on Yang the Prized Consort, he said that he possessed the skills of Li the Young Lord, the wizard who had summoned the soul of Lady Li for Emperor Wu of the Han. Xuanzong was very pleased, and ordered him to bring her spirit. The wizard then used all his skills to find her, but could not. He was also able to send his spirit on journeys by riding vapors; he went up into the precincts of Heaven and sank down into the vaults of the Earth looking for her; but he did not meet her. And then again he went to the margins and the encircling wastelands, high and low, to the easternmost extreme of Heaven and the Ocean, where he strode across Fanghu.

He saw there the highest of the mountains of the Undying, with many mansions and towers; at the end of the western verandah there was a deepest doorway facing east; the gate was shut, and there was written "The Garden of Taizhen, Jade Consort." The wizard pulled out a hatpin and rapped on the door, at which a young maiden with her hair done up in a double coil came out to answer the door. The wizard was so flustered he couldn't manage to get a word out, so the maiden went back in. In a moment another servant girl in a green dress came out and asked where he was from. The wizard then identified himself as an envoy of the Tang Son of Heaven and conveyed the command he had been given. The servant said, "The Jade Consort has just gone to bed; please wait a while for her." Thereupon he was swallowed up in a sea of clouds with the dawn sun breaking through them as down a tunnel to the heavens; then the jasper door closed again and all was still and without a sound.

The wizard held his breath and did not move his feet, waiting at the gate with folded hands. After a long time, the servant invited him to come in and said, "The Jade Consort is coming out." Then he saw a person with a bonnet of golden lotuses, wearing lavender chiffon, with pendants of red jade hanging from her sash and phoenix slippers, and seven or eight persons in attendance on her. She greeted the wizard and asked, "Is the Emperor well?" Then she

1. Emperor Xuanzong abdicated to his successor, Emperor Suzong.

asked what had happened since the fourteenth year of the Tianbao Reign. When he finished speaking, she grew wistful and gestured to her servant to get a golden hairpin and inlaid box, each of which she broke in parts. She gave one part of each to the envoy, saying, "Express my gratitude to the Emperor and present him these objects as mementos of our former love."

The wizard received her words and these objects of surety; he was ready to go, but one could see in his face that something was troubling him. The Jade Consort insisted that he tell her what was the matter. Then he knelt down before her and said, "Please tell me something that happened back then, something of which no one else knew, so that I can offer to His Majesty as proof. Otherwise I am afraid that with the inlaid box and the golden hairpin I will be accused of the same kind of trickery that Xin Yuanping practiced on Emperor Wen of the Han."[2] The Jade Consort drew back lost in thought, as if there were something she was recalling with fondness. Then very slowly she said, "Back in the tenth year of the Tianbao Reign, I was attending on His Majesty, who had gone to the palace on Mount Li to escape the heat. It was autumn, in the seventh month, the evening when the Oxherd and the Weaver Star meet.[3] It was the custom of the people of Qin on that night to spread out embroidery and brocade, to put out food and drink, to set up flowers and melons, and to burn incense in the yard—they call this 'begging for deftness.' Those of the inner palace hold this custom in particularly high regard. It was almost midnight; and the guards and attendants in the eastern and western cloisters had been dismissed. I was waiting on His Majesty alone. His Majesty stood there, leaning on his shoulder, then looked up at the heavens and was touched by the legend of the Oxherd and Weaver Star. We then made a secret vow to one another, a wish that we could be husband and wife in every lifetime. When we stopped speaking, we held hands, and each of us was sobbing. Only the Emperor knows of this."

Then she said sadly, "Because of this one thought so much in my mind, I will be able to live on here no longer. I will descend again to the world below and our future destiny will take shape. Whether in Heaven or in the world of mortal men, it is certain that we will meet again and form our bond of love as before." Then she said, "His Former Majesty will not be long in the world of men. I hope that he will find some peace of mind and not cause himself suffering."

The envoy returned and presented this to His Former Majesty, and the Emperor's heart was shaken and much afflicted with grief. For days on end he could find no cheer. In the summer of that year, in the fourth month, His Majesty passed on.

In winter of the first year of the Yuanhe Reign, the twelfth month (February 807), Bo Juyi of Taiyuan left his position as Diarist in the Imperial Library to be the sheriff of Chou County. I, Chen Hong, and Wang Zhifu of Langya had our homes in this town; and on our days off we would go together visiting sites of the Undying and Buddhist temples. Our discussion touched on this story, and

2. Xin Yuanping gained the favor of Emperor Wen of the Han Dynasty by producing fake omens, such as the miraculous appearance of a jade cup with an auspicious inscription. When his frauds were discovered, he was executed.
3. See p. 1040, n. 4.

we were all moved to sighs. Zhifu lifted his winecup to Bo Juyi and said, "Unless such an event finds an extraordinary talent who can adorn it with colors, even something so rare will fade away with time and no longer be known in the world. Bo Juyi is deeply familiar with poetry and has strong sentiments. Why doesn't he write a song on the topic." At this Bo Juyi made the "Song of Lasting Regret." It is my supposition that he was not only moved by the event, but he also wanted to offer warning about such creatures that can so enthrall a man, to block the phases by which troubles come, and to leave this for the future. When the song was finished, he had me write a prose account for it. Of those things not known to the general public, I, not being a survivor of the Kaiyuan, have no way to know. For those things known to the general public, the "Annals of the Reign of Xuanzong" are extant. This is merely an account for the "Song of Lasting Regret."

Salt Merchant's Wife (in hatred of profiteers)[1]

The salt merchant's wife[2]
has silk and gold aplenty,
but she does not work at farming,
    nor does she spin the silk.
From north to south to east to west   5
    she never leaves her home,
wind and waters, her native land,
    her lodging is the boat.
Once she came from Yangzhou,
    a humble family's child,   10
she married herself a merchant,
    a great one from Jiangxi.
Her glinting hair-coils have grown rich,
    there golden pins abound,
her gleaming wrists have gotten plump,   15
    her silver bracelets tight.

On one side she shouts to her servants,
    on the other, yells at her maids,
and I ask you, how does it happen
    that you come to live like this?   20
Her husband has been a salt merchant
    for fifteen years now,
attached to no county or province,
    attached to the Emperor.

1. Translated by Stephen Owen.
2. Salt merchants were an intermediary social class; under the direct jurisdiction of the emperor, they enforced the state monopoly on iron and salt and were paid a percentage of the taxes they collected. In Bo Juyi's time, the imperial government had great difficulty enforcing the collection of taxes and staying on a sound fiscal footing.

Every year when salt profits   25
    are to enter official hands,
the lesser part goes to officials,
    the greater part goes to himself.
Official profits are meager,
    private profits are rich,   30
the Secretary of Iron and Salt
    is far and does not know.

Better still, here on the river,
    where fish and rice are cheap,
with pink fillets and oranges   35
    and meals of fragrant rice.
Having eaten her fill, in thick make-up
    she leans by the cabin aft,
both of her rosy cheeks
    are buds about to bloom.   40
This salt merchant's wife
was lucky to marry a merchant:
All day long fine food to eat,
all year long good clothes.
But good clothes and fine food   45
    have to come from somewhere,
and she would be struck with shame
    before some Sang Hongyang.[3]
But Sang Hongyang
died many years ago;   50
this happened not in the Han alone,
    it happens also now.

On My Portrait[1]

I didn't even know my own face,
then Li Fang painted my portrait true.

Observe with dispassion the spirit and frame—
this has to be some mountain man!

Wood of willow and cane soon decay;   5
the heart of a deer is hard to tame;

Why then in the palace's red plazas
have I waited five years on His Majesty?

---

3. Sang Hongyang (152–80 B.C.E.) was an exemplary manager of the salt and iron monopoly during the Han Dynasty (206 B.C.E.–220 C.E.); he ensured that the revenue went into the imperial treasury rather than into merchants' pockets.
1. Translated by Stephen Owen.

And worse, my too stiff and inflexible nature,
cannot join the world and wallow in its dirt.   10

These features not only foretell no honors,
I fear in them cause that will bring my ruin.

Best resign and depart, the sooner the better,
withdraw this body fit for clouds and streams.

Last Poem[1]

They have put my bed beside the unpainted screen;
They have shifted my stove in front of the blue curtain.
I listen to my grandchildren reading me a book;
I watch the servants, heating up my soup.
With rapid pencil I answer the poems of friends,   5
I feel in my pockets and pull out medicine-money.
When this superintendence of trifling affairs is done,
I lie back on my pillows and sleep with my face to the South.

1. Translated by Arthur Waley.

HAN YU

768-824

Han Yu is considered one of the great masters of Chinese classical prose. He was an influential Confucian scholar-official who, together with his friend **Liu Zongyuan**, spearheaded a literary reform movement. Reacting against contemporary strictures that mandated convoluted and ornate parallel phrases, they promoted the composition of freer prose modeled on more straightforward styles of ancient Chinese literature. The movement for "old-style prose" was not just stylistic: Han Yu saw himself as the defender of Confucianism against the intrusions of religious Daoism and Buddhism in Chinese society, and he called for a new commitment to Confucian values in private and public life.

Because his father died early, Han Yu was raised in the family of his elder brother. After a few unsuccessful attempts, he passed the civil service examination and eventually rose to high-ranking government posts in the Tang bureaucracy. His outspoken criticism resulted in interruptions of his career, however, and he was exiled twice during his life.

When necessary, Han Yu could write a highly wrought praise poem for the emperor in the archaic style of the ancient **Classic of Poetry** and deliver strident moralistic attacks on his opponents. But he also had a witty side. "The Biography of Tipp O'Hair" shows Han Yu drawing on his comic mode to treat a serious subject. Using the venerable genre of "biographies" of memorable officials that had become part of the dynastic histories compiled at court since the first was written by Han Dynasty historian **Sima Qian** (ca. 145–85 B.C.E.), Han Yu writes a mock-biography of a bunny called "Mao (brush-hair) Ying," or, in our translation "Tipp O'Hair." Tipp O'Hair, both rabbit and the brush made of his hair, has all credentials needed for a meteoric government career: he has a pedigree, because his ancestor had already served the emperors of high antiquity; and he is deeply learned but also useful, because he contributes fur to the production of brush tips. Tipp writes erudite compendia about all conceivable scholarly subjects; and he is lucky, because he is captured by the First Emperor of the Qin Dynasty (221–206 B.C.E.) in a rabbit hunt and makes a career in government as a writing brush.

Han Yu's mock biography of Tipp is amusing and entertaining, but its ultimate message is elusive. Does Han Yu make fun of the dusty genre of official biography and of autocratic emperors by confronting both with a bunny-official? Does he use a rabbit to criticize the current government for failing to appreciate its officials? A later official history called Han Yu's mock-biography "his most misguided composition" and castigates it as "a joke that has nothing to do with principle." It is undoubtedly an erudite prank that shows Han Yu's versatile esprit.

This piece by Han Yu—together with the following selection, written by his close friend Liu Zongyuan—allows a glimpse into the lively intellectual world of early ninth-century China. They show the obsession with passionate argument and the experimentation with old and new literary forms favored by literary circles such as Han Yu's. Later ages tended to focus on the serious Confucian message in his work, oblivious to his eccentric and entertaining wit.

The Biography of Tipp O'Hair[1]

Tipp O'Hair was a native of Zhongshan. His ancestor, Perspicacity D. Cottontail, assisted Emperor Yu in governing the East[2] and was conspicuous for his role in providing sustenance to the ten-thousand creatures. In recognition of this he was enfeoffed with the House of Coney, and at his death, he became one of the Twelve Calendrical Divinities.[3] Perspicacity once said, "My children and grandchildren, as the descendants of a divinity, should not be like common creatures; let them therefore be born from the mouth."[4] And it was so.

---

1. Translated by and with notes adapted from Elling Eide.
2. In Chinese cosmology, the East was governed by the zodiacal sign of the Rabbit.
3. That is, the signs of the zodiac; the Rabbit is the fourth.
4. According to a traditional Chinese belief, rabbits gave birth by spitting their young from their mouths.

Eight generations removed from Perspicacity was a descendant named Leveret. Tradition holds that he lived at Zhongshan during the Shang dynasty and acquired the arts of the spirits and immortals so that he could obscure the light and have a mysterious effect on things. To spy on the moon princess, Ever Beautiful,[5] he rode away to the moon on the back of the Lunar Toad. Thereafter his descendants lived in retirement and did not serve. Some say, however, that there was a Wylie Hare living at Eastside, a clever fellow and an excellent runner, who once had a contest with the greyhound Lu from Han. When Lu lost, he was so angry that he plotted with Magpie, a dog from Song, and together they killed Wylie, making mincemeat of his family.

At the time of the First Emperor of the Qin, General Meng Tian[6] stopped at Zhongshan on his way south to attack Chu. Preparing for a great hunt to intimidate the people of Chu, he summoned his adjutants and his commanders of the left and right to conduct a divination with milfoil stalks according to the *Lianshan Manual*.[7] They got a configuration relating to the designs of Heaven and the affairs of Man, and the diviner congratulated the general saying, "Today's bag, neither tusked nor horned, shall be of those who are clothed in brown. With only eight of the body holes, with defective lip and whiskers long, it shall sit by squatting down.[8] Take only the hair of highest grade and for documents it shall be an aid. When the world has unified written words, shall Qin not unite the feudal lords?" Subsequently, when they went hunting, they surrounded the O'Hair clan. Plucking out the best O'Hair, they brought Tipp back and presented their captive at the Zhangtai Palace. They also assembled his clansmen who were bound and tied. Then the Qin emperor had Meng Tian give Tipp a ritual bath for his installation in Ferule City. Calling him the Viscount of Ferule City, the emperor daily favored him with responsibility.

Tipp, as a man, was quick witted and had a good memory. From the age when knotted cords were used for keeping accounts down to the affairs of the Qin, there was nothing that he did not record: works on Yin and Yang, divination, and physiognomizing; medical prescriptions, genealogies, orographies, and geographies; dictionaries, maps, and pictures; the writings of the geniuses of the Nine Sects and the Hundred Schools; even the doctrines of the Buddha, Laozi,[9] and the foreign lands—all were set down in complete detail. He was also thoroughly versed in contemporary affairs. For keeping the ledgers on the government bureaus or recording the transactions of the market, he was the one the emperor employed. From the Qin emperor himself to the heir-apparent Fusu and the second son Huhai, from Prime Minister Li Si to livery officer Zhao Gao, down even to the common people, there was none who did not love and respect him. He was, moreover, very good at carrying out people's wishes. Upright or devious, clever or stupid, he followed his man; and although he

---

5. In Chinese mythology the moon is inhabited by the goddess Chang E ("Ever Beautiful"), as well as by a rabbit and a toad.
6. The supposed inventor of the writing brush. The best rabbit hair for brushes came from the Zhongshan area.

7. Like the canonical *Classic of Changes*, this work was a divination manual.
8. A description of a rabbit.
9. Founding figure of Daoism and allegedly the author of the *Daodejing*, featured in Vol. A.

might later be cast aside, he would remain silent to the end, letting nothing leak out. It was only the military men that he did not serve gladly, but even then, when called upon, he would sometimes go along.

Through successive promotions, Tipp rose to the Directorship of the Secretariat and was on increasingly intimate terms with the emperor who addressed him as "Mr. Secretary." When the emperor was personally deciding affairs of state and had weighed out his daily quota of documents with a weighing stone, even the palace ladies were not allowed to stand around, but Tipp and the candle holder were always in attendance, staying until the emperor retired. Tipp was on the friendliest of terms with Mark Black of Jiang, Potter E. Poole of Hongnong, and Mr. Bond of Guiji,[1] and they supported one another, going out together wherever they went. Thus, when the emperor summoned Tipp, they would always respond as a group without awaiting further orders, and the emperor never thought it strange.

In later years, on an occasion in the imperial presence, the emperor was having him groomed for an important assignment, but when Tipp took off his cap to express his appreciation, the emperor could see that he was losing his hair and that his copy work would not be up to the imperial expectation. The emperor laughed jovially and said, "Mr. Secretary is old and bald and can no longer afford me service. I once called you 'Mr. Secretary,' but now you are Mr. Too-Sick-to-Tarry." Tipp replied, "I have, as they say, given my heart." Thereafter he was no longer summoned. He returned to his fiefdom and ended his days in Ferule City.

Tipp's descendants are very numerous and are scattered throughout the Middle Kingdom and the barbarian lands. They all trace their line back to Ferule City, but only those still living in Zhongshan are able to perpetuate the work of their ancestors.

The Lord High Astrologer[2] observes: The O'Hairs belong to two different clans. One group originally had the Ji surname of the Zhou royal family. These are the descendants of King Wen of the Zhou who were enfeoffed at Mao, as is mentioned in *Zuo's Commentary* where it speaks of the fiefs of Lu, Wei, Mao, and Dan. In the Warring States period there were O'Hairs of this clan known as Master Mao and Mao Sui.[3] It is not known where the Zhongshan clan originated, but its descendants are flourishing and abundant. They were pushed aside by Confucius when he laid down his brush upon completion of the *Spring and Autumn Annals*, but this was through no fault of theirs. After General Meng plucked out the best O'Hair at Zhongshan and the First Emperor enfeoffed him with Ferule City, they were famous in subsequent generations, but nothing more has been heard of the O'Hairs who had had the surname Ji.

---

1. Roughly, Mr. Inkstick, Mr. Inkstone, and Mr. Paper, each from a place-name famous for the respective products.
2. Or "Grand Historian." Court historians were also responsible for the calendar. This closure is typical of official biographies in the style of the great Han Dynasty historian Sima Qian.
3. Here the O'Hair clan of rabbits is provided a pedigree. King Wen was the founder of the venerable Zhou Dynasty (ca. 1045–256 B.C.E.). Han Yu humorously backs up his claim with a reference to *Zuo's Commentary* to the *Spring and Autumn Annals*, a canonical history supposedly written by Confucius. Master Mao (a sage recluse) and Mao Sui (a bold retainer) both appear as historical figures in Sima Qian's *Historical Records*.

Although Tipp O'Hair first appeared before the emperor as a prisoner, in the end he was honorably employed. Tipp played a role in the Qin conquest of the feudal lords, but his reward was not commensurate with his service. How lacking was the Qin in gratitude![4]

4. The Qin emperor was known for his megalomania and cruelty, and the Qin Dynasty (221–206 B.C.E.) is generally considered a dark period of harsh government.

LIU ZONGYUAN
773–819

Together with his friend **Han Yu**, Liu Zongyuan belonged to a group of intellectuals who revolutionized Tang literary culture. Concerned with the big issues of life and deeply interested in Buddhist doctrines, he explored questions of proper moral behavior and the ironies of human existence. He was one of the most celebrated poets and essayists of the Tang Dynasty.

Liu Zongyuan took the civil service examinations and went on to serve in the imperial government. Because of his association with high officials whose faction fell out of favor and was accused of conspiracy, he was exiled several times. He died in exile in 819.

Like "**The Biography of Tipp O'Hair**" by Han Yu, Liu Zongyuan's "Theory of Heaven" is both serious and humorous. It records a passionate dispute between the author and Han Yu about the place of humans in the cosmos. The character

Han Yu proudly introduces his friend to his new "theory" about heaven: humanity is like a parasite gnawing away at nature, and those who would rid heaven and Earth of this evil deserve praise. It is unclear whether this colorful piece is a gory joke, a desperate cry for help from a moral pessimist, or the bravura defense of a position that is deliberately shocking, distasteful, and ridiculous enough to make us laugh. The point of "Theory of Heaven" is ultimately elusive.

Like Han Yu, Liu Zongyuan cared about serious questions of human morality and had strong political and intellectual opinions. But both also appreciated making arguments simply for the sake of their beauty and for the joy of defending a challenging point. They thus can be seen as among the earliest Chinese "intellectuals" in our modern sense of the word.

A Theory of Heaven[1]

Han Yu addressed Master Liu, "Do you know my theory about Heaven? Well, I will tell you my theory. These days whenever someone suffers from the torment of disease or is worn down by humiliation or endures hunger and cold, he looks

1. Translated by Stephen Owen.

up and cries out to Heaven: 'Those who harm folk flourish; those who help folk perish!' Or they look up and cry out to Heaven: 'Why have you caused things to go so utterly wrong?' No one who behaves like this truly understands Heaven.

"When a piece of fruit or a melon has become too rotten to eat, insects grow in it. When the vitality of a man's blood fails and becomes sluggish, abscesses, swelling pustules, and hemorrhoids form; insects grow in these too. When wood rots, there are grubs within; when plants putrefy, fireflies come forth from them. These are obviously things that appear only after decay sets in. When something decays, insects are born out of it; and when the Primordial Force or Yin and Yang decayed, out of that human beings were born.

"When insects grow in that thing, it decays even further. Chewing at it, boring holes in it, the harm that the insects inflict on the thing increases greatly. If someone were able to get rid of them, such a person would have done a good deed on behalf of the thing; but whoever lets them multiply and gives comfort to them is the enemy of the thing. The incremental decay that human beings cause to the Primordial Force and to Yin and Yang has also increased greatly. Men plow meadows and fields; they cut down the mountain forests; they dig down to underground springs to find wells that provide them with drink; they excavate graves in which to put their dead. Moreover, they dig latrines; they pound hard earthen walls to surround their homes and their cities; they raise platforms of pounded earth on which to build pavilions and lodges for their excursions; they dig channels for rivers and canals, irrigation ditches, and ponds; they kindle wood for fires; they alter metals by smelting them; they mold pottery and grind and polish stone. Everything in the world looks the worse for wear and nothing can follow its own nature—human beings are responsible for this. Seething in their fury, constantly battering, they assault, destroy, ruin, and wreck; nor have they ever desisted. Is not the harm they inflict on the Primordial Force and upon Yin and Yang even worse than what insects do?

"In my opinion if one were able to cut away at humanity and make them dwindle over the days and years, then the harm inflicted on the Primordial Force and Yin and Yang would steadily diminish. Whoever could accomplish this would have done a good deed for Heaven and Earth. But whoever lets them multiply and gives comfort to them is the enemy of Heaven and Earth. These days no one understands Heaven, so they cry out to it in reproach. In my opinion, when Heaven hears their cries of reproach, then those who have done it a good deed will inevitably receive a rich reward; but those who have inflicted harm on it will inevitably receive grave punishment. What do you think of what I have said?"

Master Liu then said, "Was there something that got you truly worked up that you propose this? It is well argued indeed and beautifully put. But let me carry this theory to its conclusion. Human beings refer to what is dark, mysterious, and above us as Heaven; they refer to what is brown and beneath us as Earth. They refer to that vast, undifferentiated murkiness in between as the Primordial Force; and they refer to the cold and heat as Yin and Yang. However large these are, they are no different from fruits and melons, abscesses and pustules, or plants and trees.

"Let us suppose there were someone or something able to get rid of what bores holes in them—would there be any reward for such a creature? Or one that let them multiply and gave them comfort—would there be any anger against such? Heaven and Earth are a large fruit. The Primordial Force is a large pustule. Yin and Yang are a large tree. How could such things reward a good deed or punish harms inflicted? Those who do such good deeds, do so on their own; those who inflict harm, inflict it on their own. To expect either reward or punishment is great folly. Those who cry out in reproach, expecting Heaven will feel sorry for them and be kind to them, show even greater folly. As for you, you trust in your own sense of kindness and right and move freely within that, during your life and on until your death. Why attribute your preservation or destruction, your gains and your losses, to a piece of fruit, a pustule, or a tree?"

YUAN ZHEN
779–831

The most important development in prose literature during the Tang was the emergence of the genre of so-called "classical tales" (*chuanqi*, literally "records of marvels"). Long fiction emerged late in Chinese literature; before the Tang Dynasty short anecdotes and parables were common. As tales became more popular, writers crafted longer narratives telling unusual stories of love and heroism, which sometimes included supernatural elements. Yuan Zhen's "The Story of Yingying" is the most famous and most enthralling example of this new genre.

Yuan Zhen's official career was a series of official appointments, followed by periods of exile caused by party politics, but he eventually rose to high office at court. He was the closest friend of **Bo Juyi**, with whom he exchanged many poems and shared, among much else, a fascination with tragic love affairs.

"The Story of Yingying," Yuan Zhen's only tale, may have been written while he was taking the civil service examination. It was intended as a "warming scroll"—a piece of writing that candidates circu-

lated informally in the hope of getting the attention of potential patrons. It sets out as a typical "talented scholar meets beautiful woman" tale, a popular theme. "The Story of Yingying" describes the seduction and rejection of the heroine Yingying by her distant cousin, an aspiring exam candidate. In this scenario, marriage would have been the obvious outcome. Yet the lovers, each in their own way, thwart the possibility of legitimate marriage and instead contribute to a story of heartbreak. One might see this as a thinly disguised account of the author's personal experiences. If it is indeed autobiographical, he is portraying himself in a most unflattering light. Is Yuan Zhen trying to justify the outrageous behavior of the faithless scholar? Might he have tried to absolve his guilt over a shabby deed by writing a confessionary tale about it? Does he bitterly mock the naiveté of the formulaic plot popular during his time, attempting to show that happy endings are rare in real life?

Not least because of its uncertain intent, "The Story of Yingying" became very popular, and it went through some drastic transformations in subsequent adaptations. The most famous later version was the thirteenth-century play *Romance of the Western Chamber*. Here all the troubling aspects of the work are smoothed over. The remarkably willful and cultivated Yingying is transformed into an ordinary, docile heroine, and the lovers are ultimately reunited to live happily ever after.

The Story of Yingying[1]

During the Zhenyuan period[2] there lived a young man named Zhang. He was agreeable and refined, and good looking, but firm and self-contained, and capable of no improper act. When his companions included him in one of their parties, the others could all be brawling as though they would never get enough, but Zhang would just watch tolerantly without ever taking part. In this way he had gotten to be twenty-three years old without ever having had relations with a woman. When asked by his friends, he explained, "Deng Tuzi[3] was no lover, but a lecher. I am the true lover—I just never happened to meet the right girl. How do I know that? It's because things of outstanding beauty never fail to make a permanent impression on me. That shows I am not without feelings." His friends took note of what he said.

Not long afterward Zhang was traveling in Pu,[4] where he lodged some ten *li*[5] east of the city in a monastery called the Temple of Universal Salvation. It happened that a widowed Mrs. Cui had also stopped there on her way back to Chang'an. She had been born a Zheng; Zhang's mother had been a Zheng, and when they worked out their common ancestry, this Mrs. Cui turned out to be a rather distant cousin once removed on his mother's side.

This year Hun Zhen[6] died in Pu, and the eunuch Ding Wenya proved unpopular with the troops, who took advantage of the mourning period to mutiny. They plundered the citizens of Pu, and Mrs. Cui, in a strange place with all her wealth and servants, was terrified, having no one to turn to. Before the mutiny Zhang had made friends with some of the officers in Pu, and now he requested a detachment of soldiers to protect the Cui family. As a result all escaped harm. In about ten days the imperial commissioner of inquiry, Du Que, came with full power from the throne and restored order among the troops.

Out of gratitude to Zhang for the favor he had done them, Mrs. Cui invited him to a banquet in the central hall. She addressed him: "Your widowed aunt with her helpless children would never have been able to escape alive from these rioting soldiers. It is no ordinary favor you have done us; it is rather as though you had given my son and daughter their lives, and I want to introduce them to you as their elder brother so that they can express their thanks." She summoned her son Huanlang, a very attractive child of ten or so. Then she called her daughter: "Come out and pay your respects to your brother, who

1. Translated by and with notes adapted from James Robert Hightower.
2. From 785 to 804.
3. An archetypal lecher.

4. Puzhou, a province northeast of Chang'an.
5. About 2½ miles.
6. The regional commander of Jiangzhou; he died in 799.

saved your life." There was a delay; then word was brought that she was indisposed and asked to be excused. Her mother exclaimed in anger, "Your brother Zhang saved your life. You would have been abducted if it were not for him—how can you give yourself airs?"

After a while she appeared, wearing an everyday dress and no makeup on her smooth face, except for a remaining spot of rouge. Her hair coils straggled down to touch her eyebrows. Her beauty was extraordinary, so radiant it took the breath away. Startled, Zhang made her a deep bow as she sat down beside her mother. Because she had been forced to come out against her will, she looked angrily straight ahead, as though unable to endure the company. Zhang asked her age. Mrs. Cui said, "From the seventh month of the fifth year of the reigning emperor to the present twenty-first year, it is just seventeen years."

Zhang tried to make conversation with her, but she would not respond, and he had to leave after the meal was over. From this time on Zhang was infatuated but had no way to make his feelings known to her. She had a maid named Hongniang with whom Zhang had managed to exchange greetings several times, and finally he took the occasion to tell her how he felt. Not surprisingly, the maid was alarmed and fled in embarrassment. Zhang was sorry he had said anything, and when she returned the next day he made shamefaced apologies without repeating his request. The maid said, "Sir, what you said is something I would not dare repeat to my mistress or let anyone else know about. But you know very well who Miss Cui's relatives are; why don't you ask for her hand in marriage, as you are entitled to do because of the favor you did them?"

"From my earliest years I have never been one to make any improper connections," Zhang said. "Whenever I have found myself in the company of young women, I would not even look at them, and it never occurred to me that I would be trapped in any such way. But the other day at the dinner I was hardly able to control myself, and in the days since, I walk without knowing where I am going and eat without hunger—I am afraid I cannot last another day. If I were to go through a regular matchmaker, taking three months and more for the exchange of betrothal presents and names and birthdates[7]—you might just as well look for me among the dried fish in the shop.[8] Can't you tell me what to do?"

"Miss Cui is so very strict that not even her elders could suggest anything improper to her," the maid replied. "It would be hard for someone in my position to say such a thing. But I have noticed she writes a lot. She is always reciting poetry to herself and is moved by it for a long time after. You might see if you can seduce her with a love poem. That is the only way I can think of."

Zhang was delighted and on the spot composed two stanzas of spring verses which he handed over to her. That evening Hongniang came back with a note on colored paper for him, saying, "By Miss Cui's instructions."

The title of her poem was "Bright Moon on the Night of the Fifteenth":

7. In order to determine an auspicious date for a wedding.
8. An allusion to the parable of help that comes too late, found in the early Chinese master text *Zhuangzi*.

> *I await the moon in the western chamber*
> *Where the breeze comes through the half-opened door.*
> *Sweeping the wall the flower shadows move:*
> *I imagine it is my lover who comes.*

Zhang understood the message: that day was the fourteenth of the second month, and an apricot tree was next to the wall east of the Cuis' courtyard. It would be possible to climb it.

On the night of the fifteenth Zhang used the tree as a ladder to get over the wall. When he came to the western chamber, the door was ajar. Inside, Hongniang was asleep on a bed. He awakened her, and she asked, frightened, "How did you get here?"

"Miss Cui's letter told me to come," he said, not quite accurately. "You go tell her I am here."

In a minute Hongniang was back. "She's coming! She's coming!"

Zhang was both happy and nervous, convinced that success was his. Then Miss Cui appeared in formal dress, with a serious face, and began to upbraid him: "You did us a great kindness when you saved our lives, and that is why my mother entrusted my young brother and myself to you. Why then did you get my silly maid to bring me that filthy poem? You began by doing a good deed in preserving me from the hands of ravishers, and you end by seeking to ravish me. You substitute seduction for rape—is there any great difference? My first impulse was to keep quiet about it, but that would have been to condone your wrongdoing, and not right. If I told my mother, it would amount to ingratitude, and the consequences would be unfortunate. I thought of having a servant convey my disapproval, but feared she would not get it right. Then I thought of writing a short message to state my case, but was afraid it would only put you on your guard. So finally I composed those vulgar lines to make sure you would come here. It was an improper thing to do, and of course I feel ashamed. But I hope that you will keep within the bounds of decency and commit no outrage."

As she finished speaking, she turned on her heel and left him. For some time Zhang stood, dumbfounded. Then he went back over the wall to his quarters, all hope gone.

A few nights later Zhang was sleeping alone by the veranda when someone shook him awake. Startled, he rose up, to see Hongniang standing there, a coverlet and pillow in her arms. She patted him and said, "She is coming! She is coming! Why are you sleeping?" And she spread the quilt and put the pillow beside his. As she left, Zhang sat up straight and rubbed his eyes. For some time it seemed as though he were still dreaming, but nonetheless he waited dutifully. Then there was Hongniang again, with Miss Cui leaning on her arm. She was shy and yielding, and appeared almost not to have the strength to move her limbs. The contrast with her stiff formality at their last encounter was complete.

This evening was the night of the eighteenth, and the slanting rays of the moon cast a soft light over half the bed. Zhang felt a kind of floating lightness and wondered whether this was an immortal who visited him, not someone from the world of men. After a while the temple bell sounded. Daybreak was near. As Hongniang urged her to leave, she wept softly and clung to him. Hongniang helped her up, and they left. The whole time she had not spoken a single word. With the first light of dawn Zhang got up, wondering, was it a dream? But the perfume still lingered, and as it got lighter he could see on his arm traces of her makeup and the teardrops sparkling still on the mat.

For some ten days afterward there was no word from her. Zhang composed a poem of sixty lines on "An Encounter with an Immortal" which he had not yet completed when Hongniang happened by, and he gave it to her for her mistress. After that she let him see her again, and for nearly a month he would join her in what her poem called the "western chamber," slipping out at dawn and returning stealthily at night. Zhang once asked what her mother thought about the situation. She said, "She knows there is nothing she can do about it, and so she hopes you will regularize things."

Before long Zhang was about to go to Chang'an, and he let her know his intentions in a poem. Miss Cui made no objections at all, but the look of pain on her face was very touching. On the eve of his departure he was unable to see her again. Then Zhang went off to the west. A few months later he again made a trip to Pu and stayed several months with Miss Cui.

She was a very good calligrapher and wrote poetry, but for all that he kept begging to see her work, she would never show it. Zhang wrote poems for her, challenging her to match them, but she paid them little attention. The thing that made her unusual was that, while she excelled in the arts, she always acted as though she were ignorant, and although she was quick and clever in speaking, she would seldom indulge in repartee. She loved Zhang very much, but would never say so in words. At the time she was subject to moods of profound melancholy, but she never let on. She seldom showed on her face the emotions she felt. On one occasion she was playing her zither alone at night. She did not know Zhang was listening, and the music was full of sadness. As soon as he spoke, she stopped and would play no more. This made him all the more infatuated with her.

Some time later Zhang had to go west again for the scheduled examinations. It was the eve of his departure, and though he had said nothing about what it involved, he sat sighing unhappily at her side. Miss Cui had guessed that he was going to leave for good. Her manner was respectful, but she spoke deliberately and in a low voice. "To seduce someone and then abandon her is perfectly natural, and it would be presumptuous of me to resent it. It would be an act of charity on your part if, having first seduced me, you were to go through with it and fulfill your oath of lifelong devotion. But in either case, what is there to be so upset about in this trip? However, I see you are not happy and I have no way to cheer you up. You have praised my zither playing, and in the past I have been embarrassed to play for you. Now that you are going away, I shall do what you so often requested."

She had them prepare her zither and started to play the prelude to the "Rainbow Robe and Feather Skirt."[9] After a few notes, her playing grew wild with grief until the piece was no longer recognizable. Everyone was reduced to tears, and Miss Cui abruptly stopped playing, put down the zither, and ran back to her mother's room with tears streaming down her face. She did not come back.

9. An exotic Central Asian dance melody mentioned in Bo Juyi's famous "Song of Lasting Regret" (see p. 1037, n. 7).

The next morning Zhang went away. The following year he stayed on in the capital, having failed the examinations. He wrote a letter to Miss Cui to reassure her, and her reply read roughly as follows:

I have read your letter with its message of consolation, and it filled my childish heart with mingled grief and joy. In addition you sent me a box of ornaments to adorn my hair and a stick of pomade to make my lips smooth. It was most kind of you; but for whom am I to make myself attractive? As I look at these presents my breast is filled with sorrow.

Your letter said that you will stay on in the capital to pursue your studies, and of course you need quiet and the facilities there to make progress. Still it is hard on the person left alone in this far-off place. But such is my fate, and I should not complain. Since last fall I have been listless and without hope. In company I can force myself to talk and smile, but come evening I always shed tears in the solitude of my own room. Even in my sleep I often sob, yearning for the absent one. Or I am in your arms for a moment as it used to be, but before the secret meeting is done I am awake and heartbroken. The bed seems still warm beside me, but the one I love is far away.

Since you said good-bye the new year has come. Chang'an is a city of pleasure with chances for love everywhere. I am truly fortunate that you have not forgotten me and that your affection is not worn out. Loving you as I do, I have no way of repaying you, except to be true to our vow of lifelong fidelity.

Our first meeting was at the banquet, as cousins. Then you persuaded my maid to inform me of your love; and I was unable to keep my childish heart firm. You made advances, like that other poet, Sima Xiangru.[1] I failed to repulse them as the girl did who threw her shuttle.[2] When I offered myself in your bed, you treated me with the greatest kindness, and I supposed, in my innocence, that I could always depend on you. How could I have foreseen that our encounter could not possibly lead to something definite, that having disgraced myself by coming to you, there was no further chance of serving you openly as a wife? To the end of my days this will be a lasting regret—I must hide my sighs and be silent. If you, out of kindness, would condescend to fulfill my selfish wish, though it came on my dying day it would seem to be a new lease on life. But if, as a man of the world, you curtail your feelings, sacrificing the lesser to the more important, and look on this connection as shameful, so that your solemn vow can be dispensed with, still my true love will not vanish though my bones decay and my frame dissolve; in wind and dew it will seek out the ground you walk on. My love in life and death is told in this. I weep as I write, for feelings I cannot express. Take care of yourself; a thousand times over, take care of your dear self.

This bracelet of jade is something I wore as a child; I send it to serve as a gentleman's belt pendant. Like jade may you be invariably firm and tender; like a bracelet may there be no break between what came before and what is to follow. Here are also a skein of multicolored thread and a tea roller of mottled bamboo. These things have no intrinsic value, but they are to signify

---

1. A bohemian poet (179–117 B.C.E.) who with his zither playing enticed the young widow Zhuo Wenjun to elope.

2. A neighbor girl repulsed the advances of Xie Kun (280–322) by throwing her shuttle in his face, knocking out two of his teeth.

that I want you to be true as jade, and your love to endure unbroken as a bracelet. The spots on the bamboo are like the marks of my tears,[3] and my unhappy thoughts are as tangled as the thread: these objects are symbols of my feelings and tokens for all time of my love. Our hearts are close, though our bodies are far apart and there is no time I can expect to see you. But where the hidden desires are strong enough, there will be a meeting of spirits. Take care of yourself, a thousand times over. The springtime wind is often chill; eat well for your health's sake. Be circumspect and careful, and do not think too often of my unworthy person.

Zhang showed her letter to his friends, and in this way word of the affair got around. One of them, Yang Juyuan, a skillful poet, wrote a quatrain on "Young Miss Cui":

For clear purity jade cannot equal his complexion;
On the iris in the inner court snow begins to melt.
A romantic young man filled with thoughts of love.
A letter from the Xiao girl,[4] brokenhearted.

Yuan Zhen[5] of Henan wrote a continuation of Zhang's poem "Encounter with an Immortal," also in thirty couplets:

Faint moonbeams pierce the curtained window;
Fireflies glimmer across the blue sky.
The far horizon begins now to pale;
Dwarf trees gradually turn darker green.
A dragon song crosses the court bamboo;   5
A phoenix air brushes the wellside tree.
The silken robe trails through the thin mist;
The pendant circles tinkle in the light breeze.
The accredited envoy accompanies Xi wangmu;[6]
From the cloud's center comes Jade Boy.[7]   10
Late at night everyone is quiet;
At daybreak the rain drizzles.
Pearl radiance shines on her decorated sandals;
Flower glow shows off the embroidered skirt.
Jasper hairpin: a walking colored phoenix;   15
Gauze shawl: embracing vermilion rainbow.
She says she comes from Jasper Flower Bank
And is going to pay court at Green Jade Palace.
On an outing north of Luoyang's[8] wall,

---

3. An allusion to the legend of the two wives of the sage ruler Shun, who stained the bamboo with their tears when he died.
4. A term for any young woman (here, Yingying).
5. That is, the author.
6. The Queen Mother of the West, a central goddess in the Daoist pantheon; she dwells in the Kunlun Mountains in China's far west, in

a huge palace inhabited by other immortals. Within its precincts grow the magic peach trees that bear the fruits of immortality once every three thousand years. This might be an allusion to Yingying's mother.
7. Perhaps an allusion to Yingying's brother.
8. Possibly a reference to the goddess of the Luo River, near the eastern capital of Luoyang.

By chance he came to the house east of Song Yu.[9] 20
His dalliance she rejects a bit at first,
But her yielding love already is disclosed.
Lowered locks put in motion cicada shadows;
Returning steps raise jade dust.
Her face turns to let flow flower snow 25
As she climbs into bed, silk covers in her arms.
Love birds in a neck-entwining dance;
Kingfishers in a conjugal cage.
Eyebrows, out of shyness, contracted;
Lip rouge, from the warmth, melted. 30
Her breath is pure: fragrance of orchid buds;
Her skin is smooth: richness of jade flesh.
No strength, too limp to lift a wrist;
Many charms, she likes to draw herself together.
Sweat runs: pearls drop by drop; 35
Hair in disorder: black luxuriance.
Just as they rejoice in the meeting of a lifetime
They suddenly hear the night is over.
There is no time for lingering;
It is hard to give up the wish to embrace. 40
Her comely face shows the sorrow she feels;
With fragrant words they swear eternal love.
She gives him a bracelet to plight their troth;
He ties a lovers' knot as sign their hearts are one.
Tear-borne powder runs before the clear mirror; 45
Around the flickering lamp are nighttime insects.
Moonlight is still softly shining
As the rising sun gradually dawns.
Riding on a wild goose she returns to the Luo River.
Blowing a flute he ascends Mount Song. 50
His clothes are fragrant still with musk perfume;
The pillow is slippery yet with red traces.
Thick, thick, the grass grows on the dyke;
Floating, floating, the tumbleweed yearns for the isle.
Her plain zither plays the "Resentful Crane Song"; 55
In the clear Milky Way she looks for the returning wild goose.[1]
The sea is broad and truly hard to cross;
The sky is high and not easy to traverse.
The moving cloud is nowhere to be found—
Xiao Shi[2] stays in his chamber. 60

All of Zhang's friends who heard of the affair marveled at it, but Zhang had determined on his own course of action. Yuan Zhen was especially close to him and so was in a position to ask him for an explanation. Zhang said, "It is a general

---

9. In "The Lechery of Deng Tuzi," the courtier Song Yu tells of the beautiful girl next door who climbed up on the wall to flirt with him.

1. A goose might be carrying a message.
2. A well-known legendary flute player of early China.

rule that those women endowed by Heaven with great beauty invariably either destroy themselves or destroy someone else. If this Cui woman were to meet someone with wealth and position, she would use the favor her charms gain her to be cloud and rain or dragon or monster—I can't imagine what she might turn into. Of old, King Xin of the Shang and King You of the Zhou[3] were brought low by women, in spite of the size of their kingdoms and the extent of their power; their armies were scattered, their persons butchered, and down to the present day their names are objects of ridicule. I have no inner strength to withstand this evil influence. That is why I have resolutely suppressed my love."

At this statement everyone present sighed deeply.

Over a year later Cui was married, and Zhang for his part had taken a wife. Happening to pass through the town where she was living, he asked permission of her husband to see her, as a cousin. The husband spoke to her, but Cui refused to appear. Zhang's feelings of hurt showed on his face, and she was told about it. She secretly sent him a poem:

> Emaciated, I have lost my looks,
> Tossing and turning, too weary to leave my bed.
> It's not because of others I am ashamed to rise;
> For you I am haggard and before you ashamed.

She never did appear. Some days later when Zhang was about to leave, she sent another poem of farewell.

> Cast off and abandoned, what can I say now,
> Whom you loved so briefly long ago?
> Any love you had then for me
> Will do for the one you have now.

After this he never heard any more about her. His contemporaries for the most part conceded that Zhang had done well to rectify his mistake. I have often mentioned this among friends so that, forewarned, they might avoid doing such a thing, or if they did, that they might not be led astray by it. In the ninth month of a year in the Zhenyuan period, when an official, Li Gongchui, was passing the night in my house at the Pacification Quarter, the conversation touched on the subject. He found it most extraordinary and composed a "Song of Yingying" to commemorate the affair. Cui's child-name was Yingying, and Gongchui used it for his poem.

---

3. Two ancient rulers whose infatuation with wicked concubines supposedly led to the end of their dynasties.

LI QINGZHAO

1084–ca. 1151

Li Qingzhao is one of the finest writers of Chinese song lyric (*ci*) and one of the most celebrated women poets of traditional China. Song lyric, a new poetic form that came to the fore during the Song Dynasty (960–1279), had begun as songs performed in the pleasure quarters of the bustling urban centers, but the genre eventually developed into a refined literary vehicle for delicately sketching mood and emotion. Li Qingzhao used the form with great virtuosity to capture her states of mind, displaying an effortless freshness that belies the precision of her poetic craftsmanship and her poems' emotional depth. She was also a true connoisseur of painting and antiquities in an age when the literary elite, like their European counterparts during the Renaissance, started to collect ancient artwork with great enthusiasm.

Born in northeastern China, in what is now Shandong Province, Li Qingzhao came from a distinguished literary family. Her father belonged to the literary circle of Su Shi, one of the greatest writers of the Song Dynasty, and after his appointment to the national academy in the capital, the family moved to Kaifeng. Her mother was also a poet, and Li Qingzhao was recognized as a promising poetic talent when still in her teens. In 1101, at age seventeen, she was married to Zhao Mingcheng, a student at the prestigious Hanlin Academy and son of a powerful official. Sharing an obsessive passion for books and learning, they began to amass a large collection of books, paintings, rubbings, and antiquities.

But the life they knew abruptly ended as the Song Dynasty lost its capital, the northern territories, and its emperor (himself an avid collector) to the invading Jin Tartars in 1126 and 1127. Li Qingzhao and her husband hastily fled south with part of their collection, but the pieces were gradually scattered and lost. Her husband left her due to an imperial summons and he soon fell ill and died. Li Qingzhao was now without a place of refuge and in constant flight from local rebellions. Finally she and the court settled in Hangzhou in the south in 1132. There has been much speculation as to whether Li Qingzhao married a second time in her late forties, then filed for divorce within a hundred days; a letter survives that accuses her second husband of greed and corruption, but many scholars deny its authenticity. Not much is known about her subsequent life, and even her year of death—1151 at the latest—is uncertain.

There is no better introduction to Li Qingzhao's remarkable world than her "Afterword" to her husband's study of early inscriptions, *Records on Metal and Stone*, a collection (now lost) of two thousand inscriptions from the second millennium B.C.E. to the tenth century C.E. Most prefaces and afterwords were stylized, scholarly, and relatively impersonal, but Li Qingzhao used the form to show the relationship between a work of scholarship and two lives. According to the "Afterword," the fate of Li Qingzhao and Zhao Mingcheng as a couple was mirrored in the fate of their collection of books and antiques: begun for their joint pleasure in the idyllic early years of their marriage, it increasingly grew into an obsession that dominated her husband's life, until at last both the collection and her husband's scholarly work reflected the differences between them. As she loses one piece after another of their shared possessions during her escape from the north, Li Qingzhao has to let go of her previous life and hopes. The residue of the collection represented many things to her. At one point it seemed to offer a way to purchase her husband's honor after a posthumous false accusation of treason; the books were also her companions as she ceaselessly fled from place to place, and the few pieces that ultimately remained became cherished mementos of the happier beginnings of her life. Throughout this short work Li Qingzhao returns again and again to the connection between people and their possessions, to the role of possessions in human relationships, and to the way in which such objects gain value and meaning.

The relatively few surviving song lyrics by Li Qingzhao, some of which are included here, are among the finest examples of the form. The ties between poetry and song in traditional China were old and complex. The works of poets were often set to music and were sometimes modified to answer musical needs. During the Tang period, however, an entirely new kind of music became popular: stanza-like melodies with musical lines of unequal length. In a language in which the pitch of a word (or "tone") is essential to understanding its meaning, Chinese song lyrics had to pay careful attention to the requirements of a particular melody—to be comprehensible, the pitch of the word had to match the pitch of the music. Tang poets began the practice of com-

posing lyrics for these popular irregular melodies, and this new poetic form came to be known as *ci*. These "song lyrics," which often concerned love, were frequently performed in the entertainment quarters of the great cities and at parties. By the early Song Dynasty the song lyric had evolved into a verse form whose character differed markedly from that of classical poetry. Primarily associated with delicate sensibility, it sought to evoke the passing mood.

In the lyrics to the melody "Note After Note" Li Qingzhao takes up the essential concerns of the form and one of the oldest questions in the Chinese tradition: the adequacy of language to express what occurs in the mind and heart. The lyric, which attempts to capture the essence of a particular moment, closes by wondering how the complex emotion she has evoked can be named by the simple word *sorrow*. Li Qingzhao had a genius for presenting scenes that could evoke feeling, as in the lyrics to "Southern Song," in which she describes changing from light summer clothes to a warmer autumn dress, decorated with scenes of a lotus pond. But the dress is old and its gilt lotus leaves are flaking off, giving the appearance of dying vegetation—a change she takes as both physical evidence and symbol of her own aging. It is at such moments that she answers in her own way the ancient question of how words can express the feeling of the moment, showing herself a true master not just of a particular poetic form but of verbal art generally.

From Records on Metal and Stone[1]

Afterword

What are the preceding chapters of *Records on Metal and Stone*?—the work of the governor, Zhao Defu.[2] In it he took inscriptions on bells, tripods, steamers, kettles, washbasins, ladles, goblets, and bowls from the Three Dynasties of high

---

1. All selections translated by Stephen Owen.
2. Sobriquet of Li Qingzhao's husband, Zhao Mingcheng.

antiquity all the way down to the Five Dynasties (immediately preceding our Song); here also he took the surviving traces of acts by eminent men and obscure scholars inscribed on large steles and stone disks. In all there were two thousand sections of what appeared on metal and stone. Through all these inscriptions, one might be able to correct historical errors, make historical judgements, and mete out praise and blame. It contains things which, on the highest level, correspond to the Way of the Sages, and on a lower level, supplement the omissions of historians. It is a great amount indeed. Yet catastrophe fell on Wang Ya and Yuan Zai alike: what did it matter that the one hoarded books and paintings while the other merely hoarded pepper? Changyou and Yuankai both had a disease—it made no difference that the disease of one was a passion for money, and of the other, a passion for transmission of knowledge and commentary. Although their reputations differed, they were the same in being deluded.

In 1101, in the first year of the Jianzhong Reign, I came as a bride to the Zhao household. At that time my father was a division head in the Ministry of Rites, and my father-in-law, later Grand Councilor, was an executive in the Ministry of Personnel. My husband was then twenty-one and a student in the Imperial Academy. In those days both families, the Zhaos and the Lis, were not well-to-do and were always frugal. On the first and fifteenth day of every month, my husband would get a short vacation from the Academy: he would "pawn some clothes"[3] for five hundred cash and go to the market at Xiangguo Temple, where he would buy fruit and rubbings of inscriptions. When he brought these home, we would sit facing one another, rolling them out before us, examining and munching. And we thought ourselves persons of the age of Getian.[4]

When, two years later, he went to take up a post, we lived on rice and vegetables, dressed in common cloth; but he would search out the most remote spots and out-of-the-way places to fulfill his interest in the world's most ancient writings and unusual characters. When his father, the Grand Councilor, was in office, various friends and relations held positions in the Imperial Libraries; there one might find many ancient poems omitted from the *Book of Songs,* unofficial histories, and writings never before seen, works hidden in walls and recovered from tombs. He would work hard at copying such things, drawing ever more pleasure from the activity, until he was unable to stop himself. Later, if he happened to see a work of painting or calligraphy by some person of ancient or modern times, or unusual vessels of the Three Dynasties of high antiquity, he would still pawn our clothes to buy them. I recall that in the Chongning Reign[5] a man came with a painting of peonies by Xu Xi and asked twenty thousand cash for it. In those days twenty thousand cash was a hard sum to raise, even for children of nobility. We kept it with us a few days, and having thought of no plan by which we could purchase it, we returned it. For several days afterward husband and wife faced one another in deep depression.

Later we lived privately at home for ten years, gathering what we could here and there to have enough for food and clothing. Afterward, my husband governed two provinces in succession, and he used up all his salary on "lead and wooden tablets" [for scholarly work].[6] Whenever he got a book, we would col-

---

3. All students at the Imperial Academy received an allowance of clothing.
4. A legendary emperor of the earliest times, when the world was still at peace.

5. From 1102 to 1106.
6. Throughout, the material in brackets is the translator's.

late it with other editions and make corrections together, repair it, and label it with the correct title. When he got hold of a piece of calligraphy, a painting, a goblet, or a tripod, we would go over it at our leisure, pointing out faults and flaws, setting for our nightly limit the time it took one candle to burn down. Thus our collection came to surpass all others in fineness of paper and the perfection of the characters.

I happen to have an excellent memory, and every evening after we finished eating, we would sit in the hall called "Return Home" and make tea. Pointing to the heaps of books and histories, we would guess on which line of which page in which chapter of which book a certain passage could be found. Success in guessing determined who got to drink his or her tea first. Whenever I got it right, I would raise the teacup, laughing so hard that the tea would spill in my lap, and I would get up, not having been able to drink anything at all. I would have been glad to grow old in such a world. Thus, even though we were living in anxiety, hardship, and poverty, our wills were not broken.

When the book collection was complete, we set up a library in "Return Home" hall, with huge bookcases where the books were catalogued in sequence. There we put the books. Whenever I wanted to read, I would ask for the key, make a note in the ledger, then take out the books. If one of them was a bit damaged or soiled, it would be our responsibility to repair the spot and copy it out in a neat hand. There was no longer the same ease and casualness as before. This was an attempt to gain convenience which led instead to nervousness and anxiety. I couldn't bear it. And I began to plan how to do away with more than one meat in our meals, how to do away with all finery in my dress; for my hair there were no ornaments of bright pearls or kingfisher feathers; the household had no implements for gilding or embroidery. Whenever we would come upon a history or the work of a major writer, if there was nothing wrong with the printing and no errors in the edition, we would buy it on the spot to have as a second copy. His family had always specialized in *The Book of Changes* and the *Zuozhuan*,[7] so the collection of works in those two traditions was most perfect and complete. Books lay ranged on tables and desks, scattered on top of one another on pillows and bedding. This was what took our fancy and what occupied our minds, what drew our eyes and what our spirits inclined to; and our joy was greater than the pleasure others had in dancing girls, dogs, and horses.

In 1126, the first year of the Jingkang Reign, my husband was governing Zechuan when we heard that the Jin Tartars were moving against the capital. He was in a daze, realizing that all those full trunks and overflowing chests, which he regarded so lovingly and mournfully, would surely soon be his possessions no longer. In the third month of spring in 1127, the first year of the Jianyan Reign, we hurried south for the funeral of his mother. Since we could not take the overabundance of our possessions with us, we first gave up the bulky printed volumes, the albums of paintings, and the most cumbersome of the vessels. Thus we reduced the size of the collection several times, and still we had fifteen cartloads of books. When we reached Donghai, it took a string of boats to ferry them all across the Huai, and again across the Yangzi to Jiankang. In our old mansion in Qingzhou we still had more than ten rooms of

---

7. Two works of the Confucian canon: a divination manual and the commentary to the *Spring and Autumn Annals*.

books and various items locked away, and we planned to have them all brought by boat the next year. But in the twelfth month Jin forces sacked Qingzhou, and those ten or so rooms I spoke of were all reduced to ashes.

The next autumn, the ninth month of 1128, my husband took charge of Jiankang Prefecture but relinquished the position in the spring of the following year. Again we put everything in boats and went up to Wuhu and Gushu intending to take up lodging on the River Gan. That summer in the fifth month we had reached Chiyang. At that point an imperial decree arrived, ordering my husband to take charge of Huzhou, and before he assumed that office, to proceed to an audience with the Emperor. Therefore he had the household stop at Chiyang from which he would go off alone to answer the summons. On the thirteenth day of the sixth month he set off to carry out his duty. He had the boats pulled up onto the shore, and he sat there on the bank, in summer clothes with his headband set high on his forehead, his spirit like a tiger's, his eyes gleaming as though they would shoot into a person, while he gazed toward the boats and took his leave. I was in a terrible state of mind. I shouted to him, "If I hear the city is in danger, what should I do?" He answered from afar, his hands on his hips: "Follow the crowd. If you can't do otherwise, abandon the household goods first, then the clothes, then the books and scrolls, then the old bronzes— but carry the sacrificial vessels for the ancestral temple yourself; live or die with them; don't give *them* up." With this he galloped off on his horse.

As he was hurrying on his journey, he suffered sunstroke from the intense heat, and by the time he reached imperial headquarters, he had contracted a malarial fever. At the end of the seventh month I received a letter that he was lying sick. I was much alarmed, considering my husband's excitable nature and how nothing had been able to prevent the illness deteriorating into fever; his temperature might rise even higher, and in that case he would have to take chilled medicines; then the sickness would really be something to be worried about. Thereupon I set out by boat and in one day and night traveled three hundred leagues. At the point when I arrived he was taking large doses of *chaihu* and yellow *qin*;[8] he had a recurring fever with dysentery, and the illness appeared terminal. I was weeping, and in such a desperate situation I could not bring myself to ask him what was to be done after his death. On the eighteenth day of the eighth month he could no longer get up; he took his brush and wrote a poem; when he finished, he passed away, with no thought at all for the future provision of his family.

When the funeral was over I had nowhere to go. His Majesty had already sent the palace ladies elsewhere, and I heard that crossings of the Yangzi were to be prohibited. At the time I still had twenty thousand *juan* of books, two thousand copies of inscriptions on metal and stone with colophons,[9] table service and mats enough to entertain a hundred guests, along with other possessions equaling those already mentioned. I also grew very sick, to the point that my only vital

8. Chinese herbal medicine.
9. Short essays containing the essential scholarly information on the inscriptions. These were Zhao Mingcheng's copies and rubbings of early inscriptions. "*Juan*": analogous to a book chapter, and used to measure the size of books or libraries.

sign was a rasping breath. The situation was getting more serious every day. I thought of my husband's brother-in-law, an executive in the Ministry of War on garrison duty in Hongzhou, and I dispatched two former employees of my husband to go ahead to my brother-in-law, taking the baggage. That winter in the twelfth month Jin invaders sacked Hongzhou and all was lost. Those books which, as I said, took a string of boats to ferry across the Yangzi were scattered into clouds of smoke. What remained were a few light scrolls and calligraphy pieces; manuscript copies of the collections of Li Bo, Du Fu, Han Yu, and Liu Zongyuan;[1] a copy of *A New Account of Tales of the World*;[2] a copy of *Discourses on Salt and Iron*; a few dozen rubbings of stone inscriptions from the Han and Tang; ten or so ancient tripods and cauldrons, a few boxes of Southern Tang manuscript editions—all of which I happened to have had removed to my chambers to pass the time during my illness—now a solitary pile of leftovers.

Since I could no longer go upriver, and since the movements of the invaders were unfathomable, I went to stay with my younger brother Li Hang, a reviser of edicts. By the time I reached Taizhou, the governor of the place had already fled. Proceeding on to Shan through Muzhou, we left the clothing and linen behind. Hurrying to Yellow Cliff, we hired a boat to take us toward the sea, following the fleeing court. The court halted a while in Chang'an, then we followed the imperial barge on the sea route to Wenzhou and Yuezhou.[3] In the twelfth month of the fourth year of the Jianyan Reign, early in 1131, all the officials of the government were released from their posts. We went to Quzhou, and then in the third month of spring, now the first year of the Shaoxing Reign (1131), we returned to Yuezhou, and in 1132, back again to Hangzhou.

When my husband had been gravely ill, a certain academician, Zhang Feiqing, had visited him with a jade pot—actually it wasn't really jade but *min*, a stone like jade. I have no idea who started the story, but there was a false rumor that they had been discussing presenting it to the Jin as a tribute gift. I also learned that someone had made formal charges in the matter. I was terrified and dared say nothing, but I took all the bronze vessels and such things in the household and was about to turn them over to the imperial court. But by the time I reached Yuezhou, the court had already gone on to Siming. I didn't dare keep these things in the household any longer, so I sent them along with the manuscript books to Shan. Later, when the imperial army was rounding up defeated enemy troops, I heard that these had all been taken into the household of General Li. That "solitary pile of leftovers" of which I spoke had now been reduced by about fifty or sixty percent. All that remained were six or so baskets of books, painting, ink, and inkstones that I hadn't been able to part with. I always kept these under my bed and opened them only with my own hands.

At Kuaiji I chose lodging in a cottage belonging to a local named Zhong. Suddenly one night someone made off with five of the baskets through a hole

---

1. Four famous Tang Dynasty (617–907) writers of poetry and prose; see selections above.
2. A 5th-century book of anecdotes, some of which are included above in the "Hermits, Buddhists, and Daoists" grouping.

3. This itinerary follows the general route of the northerners to the southeast toward the sea, as they fled the threat of an invasion of South China by the Jin Tartars.

in the wall. I was terribly upset and offered a substantial reward to get them back. Two days later Zhong Fuhao next door produced eighteen of the scrolls and asked for a reward. By that I knew the thief was not far away.[4] I tried every means I could, but I still couldn't get hold of the rest. I have now found out that they were all purchased at a low price by the Circuit Fiscal Supervisor, Wu Yue. Now seventy or eighty percent of that "solitary pile of leftovers" is gone. I still have a few volumes from three or so sets, none complete, and some very ordinary pieces of calligraphy, but I still treasure them as if I were protecting my own head—how foolish I am!

Nowadays, when I chance to look over these books, it's like meeting old friends. And I recall when my husband was in the hall called "Calm Governance" in Laizhou: he had first finished binding the volumes, making title slips of rue leaves to keep out insects and tie-ribbons of pale blue silk, binding ten *juan* into one volume. Every day in the evening when the office clerks would go home, he would do editorial collations on two *juan* and write a colophon for one inscription. Of those two thousand items, colophons were written on five hundred and two. It is so sad—today the ink of his writing seems still fresh, yet the trees by his grave have grown to an armspan in girth.

Long ago when the city of Jiangling fell, Xiao Yi, Emperor Yuan of the Liang, did not regret the fall of his kingdom, yet destroyed his books and printings [unwilling to see them fall into the hands of his conquerors]. When his capital Jiangdu was sacked, Yang Guang, Emperor Yang of the Sui, wasn't concerned with his own death, only with recovering his books [his spirit overturning the boat in which they were being transported so that he could have his library in the land of the dead]. It must be that the passions of human nature cannot be forgotten, even standing between life and death. Or maybe it is Heaven's will that beings as insignificant as ourselves are not fit to enjoy these superb things. Or it might be that the dead too have consciousness, and they still treasure such things, give them their devoted attention, unwilling to leave them in the world of the living. How hard they are to obtain and how easy to lose!

From the time I was eighteen until now at the age of fifty-two—a span of thirty years—how much calamity, how much gain and loss I have witnessed! When there is possession, there must be lack of possession; when there is a gathering together, there must be a dissolution—that is the constant principle of things. Someone loses a bow; someone else happens to find a bow—what's worth noticing in that? The reason why I have so minutely recorded this story from beginning to end is to serve as a warning for scholars and collectors in later generations.

Written this second year of the Shaoxing Reign (1132), the eighth month, first day.

Li Qingzhao

---

4. That is, she knew that her landlord, Zhong Fuhao, was involved in the theft.

Song Lyrics

To "Southern Song"

Up in heaven the star-river turns,
    in man's world below
        curtains are drawn.
A chill comes to pallet and pillow,
    damp with tracks of tears.   5
I rise to take off my gossamer dress
and just happen to ask, "How late is it now?"

The tiny lotus pods,
    kingfisher feathers sewn on;
as the gilt flecks away   10
    the lotus leaves grow few.
Same weather as in times before,
    the same old dress —
only the feelings in the heart
are not as they were before.   15

To "Free-Spirited Fisherman"

Billowing clouds touch sky and reach
    the early morning fog,
the river of stars is ready to set,
    a thousand sails dance.
My dreaming soul moves in a daze   5
    to where the high god dwells—
I hear Heaven speak,
asking me with urgent concern
    where I am going now.

And I reply that my road is long,   10
    and, alas, twilight draws on;
I worked at my poems and for nothing have
    bold lines that cause surprise.
Into strong winds ninety thousand miles
    upward the Peng[1] now flies.   15
Let that wind never stop,
let it blow this tiny boat away
    to the Three Immortal Isles.[2]

1. A huge mythical bird described in the ancient Masters Text *Zhuangzi* (see Vol. A). Here it appears as a figure of greatness that smaller creatures cannot comprehend.   2. In the eastern sea, believed to be inhabited by immortals.

To "Like a Dream"

I will always recall that day at dusk,
   the pavilion by the creek,
and I was so drunk I couldn't tell
   the way home. My mood left me,
it was late when I turned back in my boat   5
and I strayed deep among lotuses—
how to get through?
how to get through?
and I startled to flight a whole shoal
   of egrets and gulls.   10

To "Drunk in the Shadow of Flowering Trees"

Pale fog, then dense clouds—
   gloomy all day long;
in the animal-shaped censer
   incense burns away.
Once again it is that autumn holiday: 5
to my jade pillow behind the gauze screen
at midnight the cold first comes.

By the eastern hedge I took wine in hand
   after twilight fell.
A fragrance filled my sleeves unseen.   10
Don't tell me this does not break your heart—
the west wind blowing up the curtains
and the person,
   as gaunt as the chrysanthemums.

To "Spring in Wuling"

The wind dies down, the fragrance in dirt,
   the flowers now are gone;
late afternoon, too weary to comb my hair.
Everything in the world is right; I am wrong;
   all that will happen is done;   5
before I can say it, tears come.

Yet I've heard it said that at Double Creek
   the spring is lovely still,
and I think I'll go boating there.
But then I fear   10
   those little boats of Double Creek
won't budge if they are made to bear
   this much melancholy.

To "Note After Note"

Searching and searching, seeking and seeking,
so chill, so clear,
dreary,
  and dismal,
    and forlorn.   5
That time of year
  when it's suddenly warm,
    then cold again,
now it's hardest of all to take care.
Two or three cups of weak wine—   10
how can they resist the biting wind
  that comes with evening?
The wild geese pass by—
that's what hurts the most—
and yet they're old acquaintances.   15

In piles chrysanthemums fill the ground,
looking all wasted, damaged—
who could pick them, as they are now?
I stay by the window,
how can I wait alone until blackness comes?   20
The beech tree,
  on top of that
    the fine rain,
on until dusk,
the dripping drop after drop.   25
In a situation like this
how can that one word "sorrow" grasp it?

IV

Japan's Classical Age

Although Japan consists of the four main islands of Hokkaidō, Honshū, Shikoku, and Kyūshū and about a thousand smaller islets, its contacts with the continent have always been close. In fact, much of what makes Japanese culture distinctive stems from the creative ways in which the Japanese adapted Chinese and Korean culture to their own circumstances. For example, the Japanese imported the Chinese writing system, but used it to produce their own distinct literature. They produced literature in two literary languages, one vernacular and the other Chinese-style, which differed strikingly in themes, rhetoric, and the gender of their authors. Some of the greatest works of Japanese literature were written by women in the vernacular language.

Much like the Romans confronting the older and more established civilization of the Greeks, early Japanese writers faced the challenging task of building their own literature on the sophisticated precedents of their mother culture while asserting their own originality. In addition to literature, Japan adopted crucial institutions and cultural practices from

Illustrated Biography of Prince Shōtoku, painted in 1069 by Hata no Chitei. This is part of a series of ten panels that depict the life of Prince Shōtoku (574–622), founder of Buddhism in Japan and considered the first author in Japanese history.

China, such as the concept of a state headed by a divine monarch, a government system based on administrative statutes and laws, Buddhism used as a state religion protecting the people's welfare, city planning, temple architecture, sacred sculpture, religious rituals, court music and elegant dances, imperial excursions, medicine, the culture of painting, calligraphy, and tea. But whereas Rome had conquered Greece and had its young elite educated by Greek slaves, early Japanese had relatively little actual contact with China and knew it mostly from books, thus feeling less self-conscious about their cultural identity. They believed in the numinous power of their language and their gods and were proud of the pristine simplicity of their earliest literature. Unlike parts of Korea and Vietnam, which at certain points in their history were conquered by China, Japan was never directly colonized by China; its inhabitants could admire their old neighbor at a safe distance.

CONTINENTAL CULTURE AND BI-LITERACY

The cultural dialogue with China resulted in one of the world's most complex literary traditions. Writing was invented in China some eighteen centuries before the Japanese learned how to read and write. Unlike Koreans and Vietnamese, who exclusively used Chinese-style writing for centuries, the Japanese used the Chinese writing system to produce texts in two literary languages: vernacular Japanese and Chinese-style writing (also called "Sino-Japanese," *kanbun*, or simply "Literary Chinese"). Chinese-style writing was transnational, enabling the Japanese court to participate in the diplomatic and cultural exchange with China and other states in the Chinese sphere of influence such as Korea and Vietnam;

playing a role similar to that of Latin in medieval Europe, it became the official language of the imperial administration and the Buddhist clergy, and was thus associated with high status, serious purpose, and male authorship. Although vernacular literature, in particular poetry, could serve similarly prestigious purposes at court, it became the preferred medium for emotional intimacy, romance, psychological sophistication, and fiction, all of which were associated with female sensibility.

Because the Chinese and Japanese languages belong to radically different language families, adopting Chinese characters to write Japanese required complex adjustments. Chinese is a noninflected language, with a "subject–predicate–object" word order; and literary Chinese is largely monosyllabic, meaning that most words consist of one or at most two syllables. Japanese, in contrast, is agglutinative, meaning that it strings short semantic elements together into long, complex words. It has highly inflected verbs and adjectives, which can carry a number of suffixes; these qualify such things as the mood, probability, or duration of an action or the social status of an agent. Moreover, Japanese has a "subject–object–predicate" word order and is polysyllabic—indeed, one word can sometimes fill an entire line of poetry. Chinese-style writing was written according to the Chinese word order and used the Chinese characters "logographically" for their meaning, each character representing a word. When Chinese-style writing was read out loud, the Japanese reader would perform a translation of sorts, adjusting the Chinese-style phrase to Japanese word order and adding inflections as needed. In contrast, vernacular Japanese writing mixed characters used for meaning with characters used "phonographically," for their sound value only. These characters functioned basically like a syllabic alphabet. As a result, in phonographic writing one word could require many Chinese characters.

Despite this complexity, Japan was not a bilingual culture; very few people learned spoken Chinese in addition to their native tongue. Japanese readers voiced Chinese texts in Japanese pronunciation. Their East Asian neighbors would be able to read the same text but would pronounce it in their languages and dialects. This led to a fascinating communicative paradox that can occur only in cultures with nonalphabetic writing systems. The Japanese ambassadors who visited China in order to present tribute gifts and bring home the newest law codes, Buddhist texts, musical instruments, and poetry collections could usually not ask for directions or the simplest things. Yet they could write sophisticated Chinese-style poetry for their Chinese hosts and communicate through so-called "brush talk": conversations through written messages in the shared Chinese script.

THE LITERATURE OF THE NARA COURT (710–784)

In early Chinese histories, the Japanese islands appear as a fabled realm of multiple polities, one of which—the Yamato clan—was ruled by a female monarch. During the fourth and fifth centuries the chieftains of the Yamato clan, based in western Japan south of modern-day Kyoto, managed to assert their local power over a broader territory. They sent tribute missions to China, benefiting in turn from the authority they gained from the titles and gifts that the Chinese emperors bestowed on them. By the eighth century the Yamato clan had established hegemony over most of Japan in the Nara Basin south of modern-day Kyoto. With the help of scribal specialists who

had previously emigrated from Korea, the Yamato clan turned the medium of writing into a political tool that helped them enforce central control over an increasingly large territory. Rulers also realized that legitimate political authority required historical precedent. The two earliest longer texts produced in Japan were therefore historical chronicles that traced Yamato rule back to the age of the gods and their creation of the Japanese islands. *Records of Ancient Matters* (712), written in the vernacular, connected the Yamato clan to Amaterasu, the sun goddess, who is still worshipped today in the shrines at Ise as the ancestor of the reigning emperor. *Chronicles of Japan* (720), written in Chinese-style, also used Chinese yin-yang cosmology to explain the emergence of the Japanese archipelago.

In the process of state formation, Japan's early rulers relied on the beliefs and practices of the "Way of the Gods," the Buddhist law, and Confucian political ethics. The Way of the Gods, called Shintō in Japanese, is rooted in early Japanese folk religion and is concerned with the veneration of sacred sites in nature (such as mountains and rivers), the exorcism of evil-doing spirits, and the purification from polluting forces such as illness and death; it found expression in *Records of Ancient Matters* and thus also legitimated the rule of Amaterasu's descendants over Japan. Buddhism, which originated in India with the teachings of Buddha Shakyamuni and reached Japan via China and Korea, was adopted by Yamato rulers in the sixth century C.E. as a means to promote the welfare of the state. Buddhism promised above all the salvation of human beings from the suffering that comes with desires and attachments to the impermanent things of this world. But already in China it had turned into an instrument of statecraft, through which a sovereign could claim universal legitimacy and ask for protection of his or her realm. Buddhism also provided an important cultural link to Korea and China, as Japanese monks went to study the most recent Buddhist debates and schools on the continent. Confucianism, too, had broad appeal for the individual and the state. Confucius had propagated an ethics of benevolent behavior and self-cultivation. He emphasized the importance of social hierarchies and the value of filial devotion toward one's parents, a value that also applied to the head of state. Early Japanese rulers adopted the Chinese model of elite education and founded a state academy for the study of the Confucian Classics. Although in Japan the examination system was never used as a tool for government recruitment as in China, Japanese education until the modern period was based on the canonical Chinese texts. They have left their traces in the entire corpus of Japanese literature up until the twentieth century.

State building on the Chinese model and increasing literacy resulted in the first great period of Japanese literature during the late seventh and the eighth centuries. In 710 Nara became the first stable capital. Previously, capitals had often moved for each new reign, because people feared that the death of the ruler polluted the site. Nara was a radiant city, modeled on Chinese capitals with their quadrangular grid of large avenues and streets, a large palace complex to the north, and markets of various kinds. Its rulers commissioned the compilation of the earliest chronicles and of local gazettes. The Chinese-style poetry of Japan's earliest extant poetry anthology, *Florilegium of Cherished Airs* (751), describes imperial excursions, poetry banquets, and receptions for foreign diplomats who were entertained in the proud new capital and celebrated in verse. Slightly later, the earliest vernacular poetry anthology, **The Man'yōshū (Collection of Myriad Leaves)**, was compiled. Its prominent poets, including **Kakinomoto no Hitomaro, Ōtomo no Tabito,** and **Yamanoue no Okura**, developed a stunning breadth of themes and styles, ranging from ritual evocations of the

The Tōdaiji Temple complex in Nara, Japan, was built in the eighth century and has been frequently repaired and reconstructed over the centuries. The building here, the "Great Buddha Hall," is today one of the largest wooden buildings in the world.

divine imperial lineage to shattering death laments, from lighthearted praises of the powers of wine to desperate calls of support for the poor and oppressed. The literature of the Nara Period pulses with excitement over the new possibilities of technologies, such as writing and literature, and of active participation in the larger world of East Asia. Japan's new profile as an emerging state that had outgrown its tribal past did not go unnoticed among its neighbors. In the early eighth century it gained the new name "Nippon" ("at sun's root"), which signaled that Japan had been accepted as the eastern border of the Chinese sphere of influence.

HEIAN COURT CULTURE (794–1185)

As the result of struggles between the imperial court and the Buddhist clergy, the court moved to a new capital in 794: Heian-kyō ("the Capital of Peace"), modern-day Kyoto. Despite centuries of warrior rule and occasional civil wars, Kyoto would remain the seat of the imperial court until 1868. The four centuries of the Heian Period, when Kyoto was the sole political and cultural center of Japan, became in retrospect a golden age, viewed by subsequent ages as the pinnacle of culture. The literature produced by Kyoto's court aristocracy defined all later standards of taste and embodied a refinement of sensibilities that had timeless appeal.

Heian literature was mostly produced by and for the capital elite. There are descriptions of travel in the provinces, such as **Ki no Tsurayuki**'s *Tosa Diary*, but Heian aristocrats found the countryside at best rustic and charming, at worst embarrassing and primitive. The capital was the center of all ambitions and hopes: aristocrats eagerly awaited the promotion ceremonies that could secure them a higher rank and better post in the extensive court bureaucracy. In their court diaries, written in Chinese-style, they meticulously recorded the daily court routine. These diaries show mostly the official side of Heian life. For a picture of Heian after nightfall, we need to look at vernacular tales and women's diaries. Here we learn that men often had several wives and carried on several romantic affairs at once. They visited their lovers in the women's homes, plying them with allusive poetry or the tasteful calligraphy of a "morning-after note," written on a paper of just the right shade and adorned with just the right twig or blossom in season.

We get a remarkable close-up of the everyday lives, pleasures, and anxieties of Heian aristocratic women from works such as **Murasaki Shikibu**'s *The Tale of Genji* and **Sei Shōnagon**'s *The Pillow Book*. Heian women were dressed in a dozen layers of clothing whose shades carefully matched the season and occasion. They were hidden from view, spending their days in the dimly lit interiors of their residences waiting for welcome distractions: the banter of servants, an occasional outside caller with whom to exchange the latest gossip (if it was a man, the lady hid behind a screen as they talked), a love letter, or, even better, festivals or pilgrimages to nearby temples that broke the daily routine. Aristocratic women usually received a thorough education in *waka* poetry (classical Japanese verse composed in the set pattern of 5-7-5-7-7 syllables). They were also trained in music, dance, and often even the Chinese Classics, although Chinese scholarship was traditionally a male domain. Heian elite women had ample time to read and write and developed a subtle sense of propriety and distinction in social relations, clothing decorum, the delicate psychology of romantic affairs, and poetry exchanges.

By the tenth century, *waka* poetry was enshrined as the canonical court genre. *Waka* was both a way to parade one's literary sophistication and a simple

This detail from a twelfth-century illustrated hand scroll of Lady Murasaki's diary gives us a glimpse of the dress and domestic situation of women at the Heian court.

form of everyday communication between men and women, who spent most of their time apart. A century earlier, two emperors with particularly Sinophile tastes had commissioned the compilation of Chinese-style poetry anthologies, which celebrated the cultural achievements of the court and its poets. But by the late ninth century the short and intimate *waka* form became popular: *waka* contests entertained the aristocracy and poets wrote *waka* on screen paintings in the imperial palace. Emperor Daigo's sponsorship of the first imperial *waka* anthology, **The Kokinshū** (**Collection of Ancient and Modern Poems**), in 905, first established the high status of *waka* at court. Between the tenth and fifteenth centuries Japanese emperors commissioned a total of twenty-one *waka* anthologies. Having one's name included in one of these anthologies was the highest aspiration for generations of poets.

Waka relied heavily on a vast, but well-defined, vocabulary of seasonal

phenomena and romantic love. Poets used this metaphorical and allusive imagery on public occasions in order to commemorate court events, praise the emperor, or participate in poetry contests. But they also used *waka* for more intimate purposes— to rekindle a love affair, to convey travel experiences, or to express feelings of longing, loneliness, or existential frustration with the impermanence of the world. Ki no Tsurayuki, the author of the "**Japanese Preface**" (or **Kana Preface**) to *The Kokinshū*, boldly claimed that *waka* originated in the age of the gods out of the universal human impulse to burst out in "song" in response to the outside world. Tsurayuki's preface became the foundational statement on the nature, history, and function of poetry and had a profound impact not just on literature but also on other traditional arts.

In addition to the establishment of *waka* at court, the ninth century saw the invention of the kana syllabary, which profoundly changed Japanese literature. Although the invention of the kana syllabary did not fundamentally alter how Japanese wrote, it introduced a script that became specifically associated with women: it was called "women's hand." Before the tenth century, both Chinese-style and vernacular texts were written in Chinese characters. In the new kana system, the characters used phonographically, for sound value, were replaced with a letter standing for a syllable: the curvier *hiragana* script was used for inflections and grammatical particles, while the square-shaped *katakana* script transcribed foreign loanwords such as Sanskrit terms and Buddhist vocabulary (and Western-language words in the modern period). The invention of these two kana scripts expanded Japan's rich vernacular prose literature, adding to the literary spectrum fictional tales, autobiographical diaries, and other genres that were associated with female sensibility, if not outright female authorship.

Of the world's prominent premodern literary traditions, Japan's is the only one in which women dominated certain areas. An important element in the flourishing of women's literature was the rise of the Fujiwara clan. The Fujiwara managed to gain a position of great influence by inserting themselves as regents between the emperor and the court administration. Fujiwara regents married their daughters into the imperial family, hoping that their grandsons would become future emperors. To that end, Fujiwara regents often lavished attention on their daughters, securing for them an education of the highest distinction and providing them with the most talented ladies-in-waiting. Because the emperor usually had several consorts and other lower-ranking women at his disposal, such polish was a way to attract the emperor's attention and gain a competitive advantage over rivals. Some of the greatest works of Japanese literature

were written by prestigious ladies-in-waiting: Murasaki Shikibu and Sei Shōnagon served in the rival households of two Fujiwara daughters, empresses to Emperor Ichijō. The ambitions of the Fujiwara family to dominate the court and the imperial lineage created an environment in which female literary talent was instrumental in the success of the male members of the clan.

The political power of the Fujiwara clan also touched other aristocratic clans. **Sugawara no Michizane**, Japan's most celebrated Chinese-style poet, came from a prominent family of academy scholars. When he quickly rose in the ranks to one of the most prestigious court positions, a Fujiwara rival managed to have him demoted and exiled to distant Kyūshū, where he died in bitterness and misery. Despite these political maneuverings, the Heian Period was later considered a high point of cultural confidence and imperial rule.

MEDIEVAL JAPAN AND WARRIOR RULE

In the latter half of the twelfth century, the Heian world fell apart. The trigger was a protracted civil war between two warrior clans—the Heike and the Genji—vying for control over court and capital, a war that ultimately resulted in the establishment of a military government in Kamakura, southeast of today's Tokyo. Although the clans and the cities from where they ruled kept changing and a number of emperors attempted to reassert their imperial authority, Japan was dominated by military clans until 1868. Whereas the emperor—a symbolic figure of authority, often enjoying little actual power—remained in Kyoto with his court, military rulers, the so-called shoguns, in fact ruled the country through a feudal system of domain lords and their samurai. The civil war, which ushered

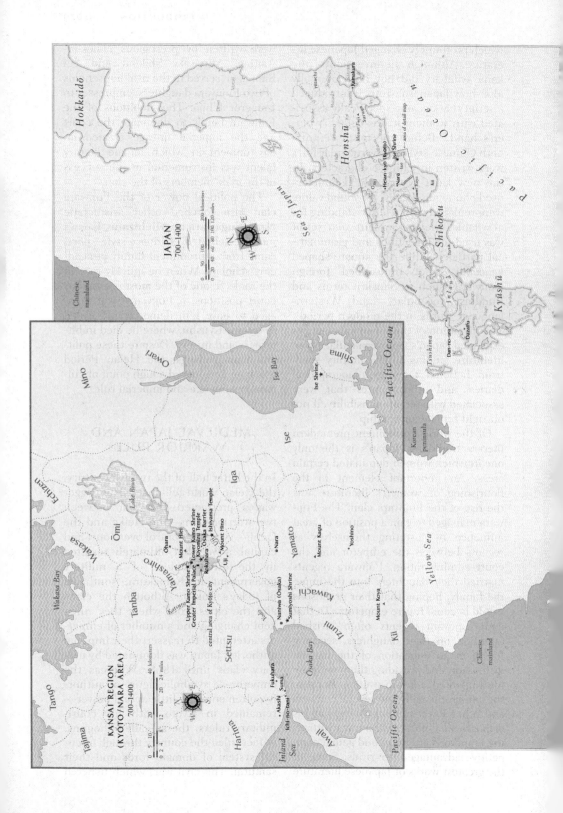

JAPAN
700–1400

0 50 100   200 kilometers
0 20 40 60 80 100 120 miles

Chinese
mainland

Hokkaidō

Homshū

Sea of Japan

Heian-kyō (Kyōto)
Ōtsu
Nara
Iga
Ise Shrine
Ise
Mount Kōya
Kii

Kamakura
Mount Fuji
Suruga

Shikoku

Tsushima

Dan-no-ura

Dazaifu

Kyūshū

Korean
peninsula

Yellow Sea

Chinese
mainland

Pacific Ocean

— area of detail map

KANSAI REGION
(KYŌTO/NARA AREA)
700–1400

0 5 10   20   40 kilometers
0 2 4 8 12 16 20 24 miles

Tango

Tajima

Tanba

Wakasa

Echizen

Wakasa Bay

Ōmi

Lake Biwa

Ōhara
Mount Hiei
Kamo
Upper Kamo Shrine
Greater Imperial Palace
Lower Kamo Shrine
Kiyomizu Temple
Rokuhara
Ōsaka Barrier
Ishiyama Temple
Katsura
central area of Kyōto city

Yamashiro

Uji
Mount Hino
Ōtsu

Mino

Owari

Ise Bay

Ise

Shima

Ise Shrine

Iga

Nara
Mount Kagu
Mount Hino
Yamato
Yoshino

Kawachi

Izumi

Settsu

Naniwa (Ōsaka)
Sumiyoshi Shrine

Mount Kōya

Kii

Ōsaka Bay

Harima

Fukuhara
Suma
Akashi
Ichi-no-tani

Awaji

Inland
Sea

Pacific Ocean

Pacific Ocean

This is traditionally considered a portrait of Minamoto no Yorito (twelfth century), the founder of the Kamakura shogunate, although some scholars have argued that it represents the fourteenth-century shogun Ashikaga Tadayoshi.

in the medieval age in Japan, was so cataclysmic that Buddhist minstrels sang of the valiant deeds of the refined and courtly Heike—the eventual losers—and their wild and uncouth opponents from the east: the victorious Genji. Their chants were subsequently recorded in *The Tales of the Heike*. They infused what in reality had been a series of bloody wars with the Buddhist message that all power, splendor, and pride of this world must eventually fall before the law of impermanence. They endowed the Heike warriors with the elegance of the bygone Heian court to which medieval Japanese now looked back with nostalgia.

The medieval world was startlingly different from its Heian predecessor. Local shoguns, perhaps seeking their own cultural validation, became gener- ous patrons of the arts, enabling cultural and literary production to flourish in new sites beyond the imperial court. They sponsored Zen monasteries, which became centers of Chinese scholarship and a new type of Chinese-style poetry. The shoguns also patronized theater performances and Noh playwrights, including **Zeami Motokiyo**, the most important Noh dramatist, who wrote pieces that appealed to the warrior class such as *Atsumori*, a play based on the tragic death of a Heike noble.

Warrior rule also brought significant shifts in education and public values. Compared to the aristocratic Heian Period, now more people had access to basic education, and the austere war- rior ethic valued honor, self-sacrifice, prowess, and loyalty to one's lord. Rather than depending largely on hereditary status within the adminis- tration of the imperial court, active involvement in government was now more haphazard and uncertain. Some responded by retreating from public life: they took Buddhist vows and settled outside the cities. **Kamo no Chōmei's "An Account of a Ten-Square-Foot Hut"** and **Yoshida Kenkō's** *Essays in Idleness* suggest that Buddhist faith or artistic pursuits can address the uncertainties of life and the desire for salvation.

Although the medieval world remained attached to the values encapsulated in the works of the Heian Period, it pro- duced a literature more strongly influ- enced by the warrior ethos and the needs of a broader spectrum of society. Despite the profound differences between these two periods, both classical and medieval Japan created works that laid the foun- dation for the Japanese literary tradition and can thus together be considered the formative age of Japanese culture.

THE MAN'YŌSHŪ
(COLLECTION OF MYRIAD LEAVES)
ca. 759

As one of Japan's two oldest extant poetry anthologies, *The Man'yōshū* stands at the beginning of Japan's literary tradition. So influential on later traditions was this collection that its title was adopted as a name for Japan's earliest period of cultural flourishing during the late seventh and eighth centuries: the "Man'yō Age." Containing more than 4,500 poems, *The Man'yōshū* is a monumental compendium of poetic knowledge. Many of its poems give expression to the most elemental human experiences: love, separation, and mourning. Others celebrate public occasions at court and are designed to inspire and entertain. Some poems describe the political order and praise the gods and the imperial institution, while others deplore the injustices of the world. The poems frequently refer to myths and legends about the origin of names, human institutions, and customs, but they also include an encyclopedic array of plant and animal names and references to the natural world. Because Japan adopted the Chinese writing system and imported the rich store of Chinese literature, the earliest Japanese poets also rested on the shoulders of some nineteen centuries of China's literate tradition. But part of the fascination of *The Man'yōshū* lies in its having taken shape during a time of bold experimentation, when Chinese and native traditions were blended—a time that also saw the first flowering of Chinese-style poetry composition.

THE MAN'YŌ AGE

During the two centuries preceding the compilation of *The Man'yōshū*, the Japanese archipelago underwent changes more profound than any others it would experience before the modern period. Within this brief span, a loose confederation of competing clans, whose wealth was drawn from the cultivation of rice and whose principal cultural accomplishment was the erection of enormous burial mounds, had remade itself into a society with a national identity, a ruling imperial family, an elaborate government administration, a complex system of religious beliefs, and a command of letters and literature. The introduction of Buddhism from Korea in the mid-sixth century changed the face of Japan, bringing along with it a culture of writing and literature, temple architecture, sophisticated art and religious sculpture, and a religious model for the protection of the state based on the imperial patronage of Buddhism. By the mid-seventh century, the future Emperor Tenji (626–671) enhanced the power of the Yamato rulers by doing away with powerful rival lineages and instituting an incisive set of reforms designed to centralize power. Tenji is said to have established a state academy for Chinese learning; the earliest Chinese-style poetry was composed during banquets at his court.

Literature depended on court culture, and until the eighth century the location of the court changed with each sovereign to avoid the pollution believed to be caused by the previous ruler's death. Tenji attempted to move away from the heartland of Yamato, where earlier capitals had been, to the north, near Lake Biwa. But after only four years the new capital of Ōmi was abandoned by his brother and successor Emperor Tenmu, who moved his court back to Yamato. Empress Jitō (r. 687–96), his wife and successor, had court poets like the *Man'yōshū* poet Kakinomoto no Hitomaro sing her praises, and she built the first Chinese-style capital, with a spacious gridlock pattern centered on the palace complex—the residence of the newly important "heavenly sovereign" (*tennō*), as the former Yamato tribal chieftain was now called.

How could Japan catch up so swiftly with contemporary developments in China? From the seventh through ninth centuries, Japan sent about twenty diplomatic missions to the Chinese court. From the Chinese perspective, Japan was paying homage and tribute to China, like many other states in the Chinese influence sphere. On its part, the young and fledgling state of Japan looked to the venerable civilization of China with great admiration. The envoys and monks who had visited China came home with a rich harvest of experience—and a treasure trove of texts. They made recommendations to the Japanese emperor on how to adapt the most recent Chinese law codes, ritual manuals, Buddhist scriptures, medicinal literature, or poetry collections to the political, religious, and aesthetic needs of the Japanese court. During this period Kyūshū, the southernmost of the four main Japanese islands, served as the gateway to China and Korea. Despite its peripheral location, the flourishing government quarters at Dazaifu frequently hosted embassies going back and forth between Japan, Korea, and China, and it was therefore nicknamed "the distant capital." The officials who served in Dazaifu were in particularly close contact with new developments, and some of the greatest *Man'yōshū* poets owed their inspiration to mix indigenous and Chinese traditions to the time they spent there.

THE ANTHOLOGY

The Man'yōshū was slowly aggregated over the course of the eighth century. It is an anthology of anthologies, made up of parts of earlier poetry collections that have not survived. Portions of the first twenty volumes were already completed in the early eighth century, and its last poem dates from 759, but the entire collection probably reached its current form only in 785, when its final compiler, Ōtomo no Yakamochi, died. Most poems were composed between the mid-seventh and mid-eighth centuries. The poems are divided into three topical categories: "miscellaneous poems," composed during imperial excursions or on seasonal topics; "exchange poetry," songs exchanged between lovers, relatives, or friends; and "mourning poems" performed at the burial sites of sovereigns and princes or composed more generally on the subject of death, a particularly prominent topic in early Japanese poetry.

The Man'yōshū was compiled during the period when the new technology of writing was for the first time being used to produce longer texts. The anthology shows the ingenuity of early Japanese scribes in adapting the Chinese writing system to record the Japanese language. In the writing of the poems in *The Man'yōshū*, Chinese characters were used in three different ways: for their meaning, for their sound when read in Chinese, and for their sound when read in Japanese. The Chinese graph denoting "person," for instance, could naturally be used for its semantic value when the poet wanted to write the word "person." But it could also be used to approximate the sound of its Chinese pronunciation, which Japanese rendered *jin*, or *nin* (in modern Mandarin it is read *ren*). Or it could be used to represent the Japanese sound of its meaning: *hito*, the Japanese word for "person." For example, Hitomaro, the name of the first of the poets in the selections printed here, came to be written with the "person" character standing for the phonetic element "Hito." This system, which relied on thousands of Chinese characters working on three different levels, is daunting to master. But it allowed for a playfulness that still charms readers today and that is impossible in any language that, like English, relies solely on a phonetic alphabet.

The Man'yōshū also shows the variety of Japanese verse forms. In fact, it laid the groundwork for all later forms of poetry until haiku poetry, which came to the fore in the seventeenth century. Whereas the artistry of Chinese poetry is rooted in the dexterous use of rhyme and the tonal qualities of each syllable, the Japanese language has neither tones nor significant rhymes. Because the sound system of Japanese employs no stress accent, each syllable is pronounced with virtually equal emphasis; as a result the forms of meter based on stress that are familiar in English poetry are nonexistent in Japanese poetry. Moreover, because most Japanese syllables consist of a single vowel or consonants followed by a vowel, with only five vowel sounds, rhymes are so ubiquitous that they become meaningless to the ear. Instead, Japanese poetry depends on the rhythm created by alternating phrases of long and short syllable counts. Japan's most archaic songs employ this pattern, which originally varied from combinations of phrases with four syllables paired with those of six to alternations of five- and three-syllable phrases. By the mid-seventh century the accepted pattern became an alternation of five and seven syllables, establishing a rhythm that would prevail in Japanese poetry up to the present.

There are two main forms. The chōka, or long poem, consists of an indeterminate number of lines of alternating five- and seven-syllable phrases, culminating in a couplet of two seven-syllable phrases. The tanka, or short poem, is identical in form to the last five lines of a chōka: that is, it is a thirty-one-syllable poem arranged in lines whose syllable counts are 5, 7, 5, 7, 7. Approximately 4,200 of the 4,516 poems in the collection are tanka. Even most of the chōka have satellite tanka known as "envoys" that serve to sum up or expand on the theme of the original chōka. Although many of the chōka are the most memorable poems in the anthology, the form largely disappeared after the age of The Man'yōshū in favor of the thirty-one-syllable short verse, which became the dominant form of classical Japanese poetry.

The Man'yōshū was compiled at the imperial court and its prominent poets were literate and erudite, yet this earliest Japanese poetry anthology contains the voices of many people far from court, including simple peasants, soldiers guarding the eastern frontier against hostile tribes, and mothers seeing off their sons as they embark on dangerous missions to China. The collection transmits oral song traditions that were recorded owing to the new technology of writing, and almost two thousand poems of the collection are anonymous.

SELECTED POETS OF
THE MAN'YŌSHŪ

Attributed to Emperor Jomei (r. 629–41), a sovereign who ruled over a still largely preliterary realm, the second poem of the anthology (and the first poem included below) gives a vivid sense of the power of language that many poems in The Man'yōshū celebrate. The emperor gazes in satisfaction over his land, possibly performing the ritual of "land viewing," in which emperors would grace their territory symbolically with an imperial blessing while also asserting imperial control over it. The act of gazing draws its power from the act of naming parts of the divine landscape that the emperor sees from Mount Kagu, one of the three mountains of Yamato.

The poem by Princess Nukata (ca. 638–690s) leads us into the increasingly more literate world of Emperor Tenji's court. We know little about Nukata beyond her royal descent; she was one of those highly educated women in early Japan who distinguished themselves as poets, was at some point involved with the later Emperor Tenmu (r. 672–86), but then served his brother Emperor Tenji (r. 668–71). The occasion for the poem is courtly—an elegant competition to frame the better argument for the rival beauties of spring and autumn. Presenting a strong opinion on the topic, the poem is a famous example of the Chinese rhetoric of parallel couplets being put to new use in a Japanese vernacular poem.

Kakinomoto no Hitmaro (flourished ca. 680 700) is considered the foremost poet in *The Man'yōshū.* By the tenth century he was referred to as the "sage of poetry" and became a figure of religious veneration. He served Empress Jitō (r. 687–96), whom he accompanied on imperial excursions. He is the earliest poet whose poems have been preserved in large numbers on a wide range of topics. We know that there was a "Hitomaro poetry collection," which is now lost. Hitomaro could employ potent language of monumental simplicity: the *chōka* written at Yoshino, a numinous place situated in the mountains east of Yamato that since earliest times was associated with imperial visits, celebrates the power of the empress by comparing her to the pristine landscape. How he dealt with more ambivalent and risky topics can be seen in his poem on the ruins of Ōmi. Around 689 Hitomaro was in the retinue of Empress Jitō when passing the capital where

Emperor Tenji had ruled three decades earlier. Because Emperor Tenmu, Jitō's predecessor and husband, had violently deposed Tenji's son from his rule at Ōmi, the site was problematic for the Jitō court. In this poem the constancy of the place stands in ironic contrast to the disappearance of the ancient capital. The place-names express Hitomaro's ambivalence through the rhetorical device of poetic epithets (*makura kotoba*; literally, "pillow words"). These formulaic epithets, a feature of the Japanese poetic tradition, were attached to numinous place-names or the names of palaces and gods: Yamato, for example, is "sky-seen," while Tenji's cursed Ōmi is "far from heaven." Hitomaro's poetry expresses loss and transience with unique and poignant imagery. This power is especially evident in Hitomaro's many poems on death, represented in our selections by poems on the death of one of his wives and the death of a stranger, as well as Hitomaro's own deathbed poem.

The poetry of Ōtomo no Tabito (665–731) and Yamanoue no Okura (ca. 660–733) brings us into yet another world, when missions to the Chinese court had resumed after a hiatus of three decades, bringing a new wave of Chinese culture to Japan. Tabito held an official post in Dazaifu, on the southernmost island of Kyūshū, and his "Thirteen poems in praise of wine" pay homage to famous Chinese drinkers such as the bohemian "**Seven Sages of the Bamboo Grove**" and the recluse poet **Tao Qian**. The ironical verve with which the poet argues for the blessings of drunkenness is a poetic mode that was entirely new in Japanese poetry. Okura, possibly of Korean descent, spent several years in China as a member of a diplomatic mission. He infuses his poetry with novel themes such as reflections on moral and religious questions. A declaration of love to his children is couched as a playful jibe at the Buddha and his teaching that one should give up all worldly attachments. Using poetry to unmask injustices and failings in society was a tradition that ultimately went back to the Chinese *Classic of Poetry* (ca. 600 B.C.E.), and in his "Dialogue on Poverty" Okura puts this tradition to startling use: a plaint of a poor man is followed by one from a much poorer man, and in the end, although this "destitute man" has nothing left in his unused rice pot but spiderwebs, the village chief, whip in hand, appears to recruit him for forced government labor. The critical thrust of this poem—which might even be self-critical, given that Okura was himself a government official—is unique in early Japanese poetry.

As often happens to periods that bear the weight of representing the origins of a culture, the Man'yō Age came to be associated with notions of emotional immediacy and sincerity—with innocence, vigor, and a seeming artlessness that stood in marked contrast to the controlled, more self-conscious polish that would define Japanese poetry throughout the subsequent classical era. And yet, a careful reading of *The Man'yōshū* reveals a work of great variety and considerable complexity, in which new confidence in the artistic effects of language and the new technology of writing take the place of preliterate beliefs in the incantatory power of words.

FROM THE MAN'YŌSHŪ[1] (COLLECTION OF MYRIAD LEAVES)

Emperor Jomei

A poem composed by the Emperor when he ascended Mount Kagu and viewed the land

> In Yamato
> There are crowds of mountains,
> But our rampart
> Is Heavenly Mount Kagu:[2]
> When I climb it   5
> And look out across the land,
> Over the land-plain
> Smoke rises and rises;
> Over the sea-plain
> Seagulls rise and rise.   10
> A fair land it is,
> Dragonfly Island,
> The land of Yamato.

1. All selections translated by Edwin Cranston, with the exception of "Poem written by Kakinomoto Hitomaro when he parted from his wife in the land of Iwami," "Poem Written by Kakinomoto no Hitomaro upon seeing a dead man lying among the rocks on the island of Samine in Sanuki," and Ōtomo Tabito's "Thirteen poems in praise of wine."

2. Mount Kagu was said to have descended from Heaven and settled among the hills in Yamato Province, the location of Jomei's court near the later capital of Nara. Yamato, like "Dragonfly Island," was also an ancient name for Japan.

Princess Nukata

When the Emperor [Tenji] commanded the Palace Minister, Fujiwara no Kama-
tari, to match the radiance of the myriad blossoms of the spring mountains
against the colors of the thousand leaves of the autumn mountains, Princess
Nukata decided the question with this poem:

When spring comes forth
That lay in hiding all the winter through,
  The birds that did not sing
Come back and sing to us once more;
  The flowers that did not bloom   5
Have blossomed everywhere again.
  Yet so rife the hills
We cannot make our way to pick,
  And so deep the grass
We cannot pluck the flowers to see.   10
  But when on autumn hills
We gaze upon the leaves of trees,
  It is the yellow ones
We pluck and marvel for sheer joy.
  And the ones still green,   15
Sighing, leave upon the boughs—
Those are the ones I hate to lose.
For me, it is the autumn hills.

Kakinomoto no Hitomaro

A poem composed by Kakinomoto no Hitomaro on passing the ruined capital of
Ōmi

From that hallowed age
When the monarch Suzerain of the Sun
  Reigned at Kashihara
By Unebi, called the Jewel-sash Mount,[1]
  Each and every god   5
Made manifest in the world of men,
  One by one in evergreen
Succession like a line of hemlock trees,
  Ruled under heaven
All this realm with uncontested sway:[2]   10
  Yet from sky-seen
Yamato did one depart—

1. One of the Three Mountains of Yamato (Mount Kagu, mentioned in Jomei's poem above, is another). "Jewel-sash": a pillow word (formulaic epithet), literally ceremonial attire for worship.
2. Jimmu, the legendary first emperor of Japan and descendant of the sun goddess, ruled from Kashihara Palace in Yamato Province, the location of the courts of all subsequent emperors, gods "made manifest in the world of men."

Whatever may have been
The secret of his sage intent—
And passed across   15
The slopes of blue-earth Nara Mountain
To a land, remote
Beyond the distant heaven,
    The land of Ōmi
Where water dashes on the rocks,   20
    To the palace of Ōtsu
In Sasanami of the gently lapping waves;[3]
    And there, as it is said,
He[4] ruled this realm beneath the sky:
    That sovereign god,   25
August ancestral deity—
    His great palace stood
Upon this spot, as I have heard;
    Its mighty halls
Rose here, so all men say;   30
    Where now spring grasses
Choke the earth in their rife growth,
    And mists rise up
To hide the dazzling springtime sun;
    Now I view this site   35
Where once the mighty palace stood,
And it is sad to see.

ENVOYS

Still Cape Kara[5] stands
In Shiga of the gently lapping waves,
    Changeless from of old;   40
But it will wait in vain to see
The courtiers' boats row back.

    Broad the waters stand
By Shiga of the gently lapping waves;
    The lake is still;   45
But how can it ever meet again
The men of long ago?

3. In 668 Emperor Tenji moved the capital north from Yamato to Ōtsu Palace in Ōmi, near Japan's largest lake (Lake Biwa). After his death in 671, his successor shifted the capital again to Yamato.
4. Emperor Tenji.
5. A scenic spot in Shiga Prefecture, which surrounds Lake Biwa.

Poem composed by Kakinomoto no Hitomaro when the Sovereign went on an excursion to the palace at Yoshino[1]

> Where our Sovereign reigns,
> Ruling the earth in all tranquility,
>   Under the heaven
> Of this realm she holds in sway,
>   Many are the lands,   5
> But of their multitude,
>   Seeing the clear pools
> That form along this mountain stream,
>   She gave her heart
> To the fair land of Yoshino,   10
>   And where blossoms fall
> Forever on the fields of Akizu
>   She planted firm
> The mighty pillars of her palace halls
>   Now the courtiers,   15
> Men of the palace of the hundred stones,
>   Line up their boats
> To row across the morning stream,
>   Vie in their boats
> To race upon the evening stream;   20
>   And like the stream
> This place shall last forever,
>   Like these mountains
> Ever loftier shall rise
>   Beside the plunging waters   25
> Of the torrent her august abode:
> Long though I gaze, my eyes will never tire.

ENVOY

> Long though I gaze,
> Never shall I tire of Yoshino,
>   Within whose stream   30
> The water-moss grows smooth forever,
> As I shall come to view these sights anew.

Poem written by Kakinomoto no Hitomaro when he parted from his wife in the land of Iwami and came up to the capital[1]

> At Cape Kara
> on the Sea of Iwami,
> where the vines
>   crawl on the rocks,
> rockweed of the deep   5
> grows on the reefs
> and sleek seaweed

---

1. A famous mountainous area that was known for its pristine and sacred beauty. Empress Jitō had a palace there, not far from the Yamato capitals, and Hitomaro visited it several times in her retinue.

1. Translated by Ian Hideo Levy.

grows on the desolate shore.
As deeply do I
think of my wife   10
who swayed toward me in sleep
　　like the lithe seaweed.
Yet few were the nights
we had slept together
before we were parted   15
like crawling vines uncurled.
And so I look back,
still thinking of her
with painful heart,
this clench of inner flesh,   20
but in the storm
of fallen scarlet leaves
on Mount Watari,[2]
crossed as on
　　a great ship,   25
I cannot make out the sleeves
she waves in farewell.
For she, alas,
is slowly hidden
like the moon   30
　　in its crossing
　　　　between the clouds
over Yagami Mountain
just as the evening sun
coursing through the heavens   35
has begun to glow,
　　　　and even I
who thought I was a brave man
find the sleeves
of my well-woven robe   40
drenched with tears.

ENVOYS

The quick gallop
of my dapple-blue steed
races me to the clouds,
passing far away   45
from where my wife dwells.

O scarlet leaves
falling on the autumn mountainside:
stop, for a while, the storm
your strewing makes, that I might glimpse   50
the place where my wife dwells.

---

2. *Watari* means "crossing"; thus the leaves fall at the very spot where the poet might have caught one last glimpse of his wife.

Poem composed by Kakinomoto no Hitomaro, sorely grieving with tears of blood, after his wife died

On the Karu Road,
Karu of the wing-filled sky,
Was the village
Where she lived, my own dear wife,
And to look at her   5
Was all I wanted in my heart:
But had I always gone,
There were many eyes of men;
Had I gone frequently
Others surely would have known.   10
So, like branching vines,
After parting we would meet again,
I thought, as confident
As one who rides in a great ship,
And though ever yearning,   15
Kept our love secret, deep and still
As a pool walled round with rock,
Gleaming softly like a glinting gem.
But as the coursing sun
Goes down the sky to darkness,   20
Or the radiant moon
Is lost to view within the clouds,
So she who lay with me
As yielding as the seaweed to the wave
Passed and was gone,   25
As leaves of autumn pass and are no more:
It was a messenger,
Azusa-wood staff in hand, who brought the news.
His words buzzed in my ears
Like a distant sound of *azusa*-wood bows:[1]   30
Wordless, helpless,
Ignorant of all device,
I could not bear to stand
Listening to the mere bruit of it,
And so, imagining   35
Even the thousandth portion
Of my longing
Might somehow be assuaged,
I went where she
Had always gone to look about,   40
To the market of Karu,
And there I lingered listening.
On the hilltop
Of Unebi, called the Jewel-sash Mount,
The birds were singing,   45
But I could not hear the voice I knew;

1. The twanging of these bows was believed to summon spirits from the world beyond. Also, messengers were said to carry staffs of *azusa* (catalpa) wood.

Nor were there any
Passing on the jewel-spear road,
    Not even one,
Resembling her, of those that traveled there: 50
    In my helplessness
Crying my beloved's name,
I waved my useless sleeves.[2]

TWO TANKA

On the autumn hills
The trees are dense with yellow leaves—
    She has lost her way,   55
And I must go and search for her,
But do not know the mountain path.

Now that yellow leaves
Are scattering from the boughs,   60
    I see the messenger
With his *azusa*-wood staff,
And days with her return to mind.

Poem written by Kakinomoto no Hitomaro upon seeing a dead man lying among the rocks on the island of Samine in Sanuki[1]

The land of Sanuki,
    fine in sleek seaweed:
is it for the beauty of the land
that we do not tire
    to gaze upon it?   5
Is it for its divinity
that we deem it most noble?
Eternally flourishing,
    with the heavens
        and the earth,   10
    with the sun
        and the moon,
the very face of a god—
so it has come down
        through the ages.   15

Casting off
from Naka harbor,
we came rowing.
Then tide winds

---

2. The waving of sleeves was associated with rituals to call back the spirits of the dead.
1. Translated by Ian Hideo Levy. In Japan's creation myth, Sanuki (part of Shikoku, one of Japan's four main islands) was one of the first places born from the union of the creator couple, the gods Izanagi and Izanami.

blew through the clouds;   20
on the offing
we saw the rustled waves,
on the strand
we saw the roaring crests.
Fearing the whale-hunted seas,   25
our ship plunged through—
we bent those oars!
Many were the islands
near and far,
but we beached on Samine—   30
        beautiful its name—
and built a shelter
        on the rugged shore.

Looking around,
        we saw you   35
lying there
on a jagged bed of stones,
the beach
        for your finely woven pillow,
by the breakers' roar.   40
        If I knew your home,
I would go and tell them.
If your wife knew,
she would come and seek you out.
But she does not even know the road,   45
        straight as a jade spear.
Does she not wait for you,
        worrying and longing,
your beloved wife?

ENVOYS

If your wife were here,   50
she would gather and feed you
the starwort that grows
on the Sami hillsides,
but is its season not past?

Making a finely woven pillow   55
of the rocky shore
        where waves from the offing
                draw near,
        you, who sleep there!

A poem composed by Kakinomoto no Hitomaro sorrowing over himself as he lay at the point of death in Iwami Province[1]

> On Kamo Mountain
> Embedded among boulders
> Here I rest my head—
> Unknowing, my beloved wife
> Must even now be waiting.   5

Two poems composed by his wife,[1] *a maiden of the Yosami, when Kakinomoto no Hitomaro died*

> You for whom I wait
> Day after day, do they not
> Say you lie mingled
> With the shells, my love,
> In the bed of Pebble River?   5

> To meet face to face—
> We shall not meet so any more;
> Rise up, O clouds,
> Stand along Pebble River—
> I would gaze and remember.   10

Ōtomo no Tabito[1]

Thirteen poems in praise of wine by Lord Ōtomo Tabito, the Commander of the Dazaifu[2]

> Rather than engaging
> in useless worries,
> it's better to down a cup
> of raw wine.

> Great sages of the past   5
> gave the name of "sage"[3] to wine.
> How well they spoke!

> What the Seven Wise Men[4]
> of ancient times
> wanted, it seems,   10
> was wine.

1. Hitomaro's deathbed poem. Iwami was a remote area on the western coast of Japan.
1. Probably the woman addressed in the previous poem.
1. Translated by Ian Hideo Levy.
2. Government headquarters in Kyūshū, southernmost of the main islands of Japan, an important outpost for regulating contacts with China and Korea. In Tabito's time the city was nicknamed "the distant capital."

3. So called by those who drank it secretly during a short period of prohibition in China.
4. The so-called Seven Sages of the Bamboo Grove, Daoist-inspired intellectuals in 3rd-century China who stayed aloof from the unstable political establishment by writing poetry, drinking, philosophizing, and offending common taste. Some of their poems are included in the "Hermits, Buddhists, and Daoists" cluster in this volume.

Rather than making pronouncements
    with an air of wisdom,
it's better to down the wine   15
and sob drunken tears.

What is most noble,
  beyond all words
    and beyond all deeds,
is wine.

Rather than be half-heartedly human,   20
I wish I could be a jug of wine
and be soaked in it!

How ugly!
  those men who,
    with airs of wisdom,   25
      refuse to drink wine.
Take a good look,
and they resemble apes.

How could even
a priceless treasure   30
be better than a cup
    of raw wine?

How could even a gem
that glitters in the night
be as good as drinking wine   35
and cleansing the heart?

Here in this life,
on these roads of pleasure,
it is fun to sob drunken tears.

As long as I have fun   40
    in this life,
let me be an insect or a bird
    in the next.[5]

Since all who live
must finally die,   45
let's have fun
while we're still alive.

Smug and silent airs of wisdom
are still not as good
as downing a cup of wine   50
and sobbing drunken tears.

---

5. According to Buddhism, bad actions in this life can result in rebirth into a lower state in the next.

Yamanoue no Okura

Dialogue on Poverty

(THE POOR MAN)

On sodden nights
When rain comes gusting on the wind,
  On freezing nights
When snow falls mingled with the rain,
  Shivering helplessly   5
In the all-pervading cold,
  I take a lump
Of hardened salt and nibble on it
  While I sip diluted
Lees of *sake* from my cup.   10
  Clearing my throat,
Sniffling as my nose begins to run,
  Stroking the few hairs
Of my meager, scraggly beard,
  I puff myself up: 15
"What do people matter anyway,
  Aside from me?"
But still I'm cold, and so I take
  My hempen quilt
And pull it up around my shoulders.   20
  I put on every
Sleeveless homespun frock I own,
  Layer upon layer,
But the night is cold. And he,
  The man more destitute   25
Than even I, on such a night
  His father and mother
Must be starving, bodies chill and numb;
  His wife and children
Moaning softly in the dark: 30
  Yes, you—at times like these
How do you manage to go on,
How do you get through your life?

(THE DESTITUTE MAN)

Although men say
That heaven and earth are vast,   35
  Have they not dwindled
To a narrow frame for me?
  Although men say
That the sun and moon are bright,
  Have they not refused   40
To grant their shining unto me?
  Are all men thus,
Or am I alone deprived?

Though by rare chance
I was born into the world of men,   45
    And as any man
I toil to make my living on the land,
    Yet must I throw rags
About my shoulders, mere rotten
    Shreds of a sleeveless   50
Frock, hemp with no padding,
    Dangling like branches
Of sea pine over my bones;
    And in this crazy hut,
This flimsy, tumbling hovel,   55
    Flat on the ground
I spread my bedding of loose straw.
    By my pillowside
My father and my mother crouch,
    And at my feet   60
My wife and children; thus am I
    Surrounded by grief
And hungry, piteous cries.
    But on the hearth
No kettle sends up clouds of steam,   65
    And in our pot
A spider spins its web.
    We have forgotten
The very way of cooking rice;
    Then where we huddle,   70
Faintly whimpering like *nue* birds,[1]
    Deliberately,
As the saying goes, to cut
    The end of what
Was short enough before,   75
    There comes the voice
Of the village chief with his whip,
    Standing, shouting for me,
There outside the place we sleep.
    Does it come to this—   80
Is it such a helpless thing,
The path of man in this world?

    Though we may think
Our lives are mean and frustrate
    In this world of men,   85
We cannot fly into the air,
It being so we are not birds.

Respectfully presented with deep obeisance by Yamanoue no Okura

---

1. Ominous birds associated with loneliness and melancholy.

A poem of longing for his children; with preface

Shaka Nyorai preached truly with his golden mouth that he had equal compassion for all beings, even as for Rāhula.[1] He also preached that there is no love surpassing that for a child. The greatest sage still had the feeling of love for his child. Who then of the green grass of the world would not love his children?

> When I eat melons
> My children come to my mind;
> When I eat chestnuts
> The longing is even worse.
> Where do they come from,   5
> Flickering before my eyes,
> Making me helpless
> Incessantly night after night,
> Not letting me sleep in peace?

ENVOY

> What are they to me,   10
> Silver, or gold, or jewels?
> How could they ever
> Equal the greater treasure
> That is a child?

---

1. Shaka Nyorai is the Japanese name for the Buddha; Rāhula was the son he fathered while still an Indian prince, before becoming an ascetic and gaining enlightenment. Parental love is generally considered an attachment that prevents us from gaining enlightenment.

POETRY OF THE HEIAN COURT

Japan has the world's oldest living tradition of court poetry. For more than 1,300 years, Japanese sovereigns have called on courtier-poets to compose praise poems and demonstrate their poetic sophistication; over about half of that time span, poetry collections representing the best and brightest courtier-poets of the realm were compiled at imperial command. The poetry of the Heian court constitutes the defining moment in this long tradition, and the selections that follow showcase the two genres that dominated at the Heian court: Chinese-style poetry, represented here by Sugawara no Michizane, Japan's foremost Chinese-style poet, and the thirty-one-syllable *waka* poem, which was enshrined as the main form of vernacular Japanese court poetry by *The Kokinshū* (*Collection of Ancient and Modern Poems*), the first imperial *waka* collection. Although today the composition of poetry for events at the imperial court has been reduced to ritual formality, it continues a once proud tradition of refined entertainment that linked the writing of poetry to imperial power.

Court poetry is radically different from poetry as we know it today. First, it is panegyric, addressed to the sovereign and the political system that he

(in early Japan also she) embodies: its primary purpose is to celebrate that sovereign. It is performative: poets do not labor over their lines in isolation but recite their poetry publicly at court events. It is also "occasional" poetry, composed for specific social occasions including the large events of life and its passing pleasures. Lastly, court poetry is topic bound, composed on themes with fitting seasonal associations. Whether writing on simple topics such as "Cherry Blossoms" or creating visual vignettes such as "Fireflies Flutter among White Dew," the poet-courtiers had to come up with witty, fresh treatments of well-worn topics in order to impress the audience and build their reputation as both poets and courtiers.

Poetic mastery in the courtly tradition required astute variation, technical virtuosity, and poetic erudition. Poetry was so important in Heian Japan that to return from an outing when the cherries bloomed without having penned a suitable memento would quickly consign a courtier to social oblivion. A handsome, wellborn man who was inarticulate was no better than a boor. His career as a bureaucrat would stagnate, and his prospects for an interesting love life were nil.

SUGAWARA NO MICHIZANE

845–903

The courtier, poet, and scholar Sugawara no Michizane is considered the most outstanding Japanese poet of Chinese-style poetry. He used this traditional genre for trenchant observations and personal plaint as had no other poet before him.

Michizane came from a family of remarkable scholars, who had served as professors at the State Academy devoted to Chinese studies. Although the Sugawara clan was renowned for Chinese scholarship and Chinese-style poetry, its members had never held the highest offices at court. Alone in his family, Michizane eventually rose from the academy to the second-highest position in the state. Yet the spectacular series of promotions during the reign of Emperor Uda (r. 887–97), who favored Michizane, would eventually exact a heavy price. The powerful Northern branch of the Fujiwara clan regarded his career as a threat. In 886 a purge initiated by the Fujiwara sent Michizane off to a dreary governor post in the provinces, a demotion he deeply resented. But the most damaging hit came in 901, only two weeks after he had received yet another illustrious promotion in rank: on trumped-up charges, Michizane was suddenly banished to a minor post in faraway Kyūshū, the southernmost island of Japan. He died after two sorrowful years in exile, a broken man.

But the passing of the man Michizane was the birth of the god Tenjin. Some twenty years after his death, natural disasters and other inauspicious events at court were attributed to the wrath of his revengeful spirit. His reputation was rehabilitated and shrines to him in the guise of Tenjin were built to pacify the exiled poet's spirit. Today, he is revered at thousands of shrines throughout Japan as the god of scholarship (and a divine helping hand to students praying for academic success in the challenging university entrance exams).

Michizane identified strongly with the scholarly tradition of his family, as is evident in the selections in this anthology. Like the Chinese poet **Bo Juyi**, whom he admired greatly, he compiled his own literary collection, and he offered it to the emperor, together with the literary collections of his father and grandfather.

Plum blossoms, Michizane's emblem and the origin of many legends that grew around him, frame his poetic work. His first poem, "On Looking at the Plum Blossoms on a Moonlit Night," composed when he was eleven, shows his early training in writing on set topics and crafting parallel couplets, a distinctive feature of Chinese-style poetry. His last poem, "In Exile, Spring Snow," which also dwells on plum blossoms, shows that Michizane never lost hope of being recalled from exile. To the end he awaited liberation, pointing to famous examples of freed captives in classical Chinese literature, the books that had defined his life and identity.

On "Looking at Plum Blossoms on a Moonlit Night"[1]

Written when I was in my eleventh year. My father had Scholar Shimada test me. That's when I composed my first Chinese-style poem. Thus I include it as the beginning of my collection.[2]

Moon glistens like snow under brightened skies.
Plum blossoms seem like radiant stars.
Just lovely—this golden mirror turning
And in the courtyard the perfume of their jade calyces.

I Stop Practicing the Zither

No doubt: playing zither and reading books is an asset for a true scholar:
Under the window of my study rests my seven-stringed zither.[1]
Intense concentration shows no effect, in vain do I go over the score.
My finger technique is full of mistakes and I have to ask my teacher again
    and again.
In my "Deep Gorges"—no flow of an autumn torrent.   5
And my "Winter Crows"[2] never conveyed the desolation of cries at night.
The friends, who "know my tone,"[3] all say that I'm wasting my time for
    nothing.
Well, isn't my family tradition more in poetry composition?

The Hardships of Professors

My family is not one of generals,
With Confucian studies we make our living.
My venerable grandfather reached the third court rank
And my dear father served as high court noble.
They understood the power of studying the past   5
And bequeathed it for their descendants' glory.
The day I was promoted to the status of "advanced student"[1]
I eagerly wished to establish myself in our family trade.
The year I became professor at the state academy

---

1. All selections translated by Wiebke Denecke.
2. In 900, shortly before his exile, the aging Michizane compiled his own poetry collection and offered it up to the reigning Emperor Daigo, together with the collections of his father and grandfather, who had also been prominent scholar-officials and poets. This childhood poem was on a topic assigned for poetry practice by his tutor, Shimada.
1. In China this instrument had been associated with refinement and scholars.
2. Like "Deep Gorges," a musical piece from the zither repertoire.
3. "The one who knows the tone" became a stock expression for "a close friend." In a well-known anecdote, the brilliant zither player Bo Ya enjoys playing for his friend Zhong Ziqi, who is the only one who understands his playing and "knows his tone." After Zhong Ziqi's death Bo Ya never played his zither again.
1. The title of a student selected to prepare for the civil service examination, given to Michizane at the age of 23 (unusually young).

Luckily our lecture hall was rebuilt.   10
Everybody rushed to extend their congratulations
Only my father was startled.
Why was he so startled?
"Unfortunately you are our only child!
Certainly, the official rank of a professor[2] is not bad   15
And a scholar's salary is decent.
But I once also held this post
And learnt to be cautious, afraid of human emotions."
When I first heard his kind advice
I felt as if stepping on ice, unsure how to proceed.   20
In my fourth year the council decided
To have me teach all students.[3]
Hardly had I been at the lectern for three days
When slanderous rumors reached my ears.
This year, when recommending students for advancement,   25
The criteria for pass and fail were real clear.
But the first talentless student who failed
Badmouthed me and filed a complaint, demanding unearned promotion.
In my teaching there are no shortcomings
And in my selection for advancement I was fair.   30
How true! My father's advice
When he warned me before all this happened.

Note on My Library

There is a house in Senpū Ward in the eastern sector of the capital, a corridor in the southwest corner of the house, and a room at the southernmost end of the corridor. The room is hardly more than ten feet square: when setting foot there those entering or leaving have to squeeze past each other and those getting up and sitting down end up on tightly lined mats. Yet out of this room have emerged about a hundred men who passed the "advanced student" and "presented scholar" examinations. That's why scholars regard this room as a "Dragon Gate" of sorts.[1] It goes also by the name of "Mountain Shade Pavilion," because it lies west of a small hill. Near the entrance there is a plum tree and a few steps to the east there are clumps of bamboo. Each time the plum tree is in bloom and the bamboo is touched by the wind it heightens and brightens one's spirits and nourishes one's mind.

When I passed the "advanced student" examination my father said, "This room has a famous reputation. Why not move in here, while you are studying hard for the coming exams?" So I tidied up the room, shifting the blinds and mats around, and moved my books to a safe place. But, oh my, when space conditions are

2. Sixth rank.
3. During Michizane's first three years as a professor, the lectures were given by his senior colleague, whose death gave Michizane the opportunity to lecture.
1. "To climb the Dragon Gate" was a Chinese

expression for passing the civil service examinations; Michizane here is describing the private academy run by his father. "Presented scholar" was the highest degree in the State Academy in Kyoto; "advanced student," a step toward it, was itself a title rarely bestowed.

cramped, people get edgy and distressed. Among my friends there are some I feel close to and some I don't know well. Some put on a friendly face, although they have no interest to connect on a deeper level, while others are annoying like some lowborn people but we are on familiar terms. Some claim to seek enlightenment, when they pry among my private books and notes, while others pretend to pay a courtesy call, only to barge in right when I am trying to rest.

Another thing: a brush and a scraper are implements for writing texts and erasing mistakes. But as for that flock of crows which descends on me, they have no idea what these things are used for. They wield the scraper, scratching and damaging the desks, and fiddle around with the brush until they have soiled and spoiled my books. Yet another thing: the foundation for proper study is excerpting and excerpting implies the production of notes. I am by nature not very organized and systematic, so I can't help sometimes stopping my brush (in the middle of study) and leave slips of paper strewn about with excerpted notes. That's when people sneak into my library—hard to know what they are really up to—and the clever ones, when they see the notes, fold them up and tuck them away into their gown, but the stupid ones simply snatch them up, tear them in two and throw them away! These kinds of things annoy me to the extreme, and there are countless other petty annoyances I could go on about.

One more thing. Sometimes a friend comes for some compelling reason on important business and enters the library, whereupon those sneaky intruders, not bothering to find out whether the person who is with me has important business, walk straight in with unimportant trifles. That's what makes me despair! Really, it makes me despair. That Dong Zhongshu let down his curtain and Master Xue[2] climbed over the wall was not only because they wanted to focus on their studies, they also wanted some peace of mind. When writing this piece today I don't mean it to be a treatise on how to break off relations. I simply want to pour out my worries in writing. I am especially ashamed that I did not establish a private academy that would attract talented men, but instead need to establish some rules for unwanted intruders of my library. This is for those who do not understand me, and those who do understand me number about three or so people. I hope that with the small net designed to keep out swallows and sparrows I don't end up driving phoenixes away.

Written in trepidation on the first day of the seventh month of 893.

Seeing the Plum Blossoms When Sentenced to Exile[1]

When the East Wind blows,
send me your fragrance
you plum blossoms!
With your master gone,
don't forget about spring.

2. Figures known for hiding from the throng of followers they attracted. Dong Zhongshu (ca. 179–104 B.C.E.), a leading Confucian thinker during the Han Dynasty, was said to lower the curtains of his room and lecture only to a select group of advanced students, letting them pass their lecture notes on to the beginners.

1. Michizane's most famous vernacular poem. Legend has it that the tree in his garden in Kyoto was so touched by this poem that it flew to be with him in Dazaifu, his place of exile in the south.

In Exile, Spring Snow

They fill the town, overwhelm the district: so many plum blossoms!
Just like blossoms early in the year, rustled by wind in the sunlight.
What I see sticking to the feet of the geese might be letters on cloth
And that, there, the white dots on the head of the crows, makes me
  hopeful that I will return home.[1]

1. Two Chinese allusions that express Michizane's hopes of returning from exile. A certain Su Wu, long held by northern tribes, was rescued when a Han emperor happened to shoot the goose to whose leg he had attached a message; and a prince of the state of Yan, held hostage by the king of Qin, was told he could return home when crows' heads turned white and horses grew horns—improbable events that came to pass, leading to his freedom. This was Michizane's last poem.

THE KOKINSHŪ

ca. 905

The age of *The Kokinshū*, the period around 900, was a turning point in Japanese history. Vernacular poetry gained public stature, and vernacular prose genres such as tales and diaries, which would culminate in **The Tale of Genji** and **The Pillow Book**, started to emerge. The flourishing of vernacular literature went hand in hand with the development of a new script—the kana syllabic alphabet, also called "women's hand"—which complemented the hitherto exclusive use of Chinese characters in writing Japanese. Politically, members of the Fujiwara family, which would dominate the court for the rest of the Heian Period, increasingly inserted themselves as powerful regents to the emperor, marrying their daughters into the imperial family.

Japan's earliest imperial poetry anthologies date from the early ninth century, when Emperor Saga, who was thoroughly trained in Chinese Classics and an avid poet himself, commissioned three anthologies of Chinese-style poetry. Following this tradition, Emperor Daigo commissioned *The Kokinshū* (a short form of *Kokinwakashū*, "Collection of Ancient and Modern Waka Poems"), the first anthology of vernacular *waka* poetry. The success of this collection helped enshrine the thirty-one-syllable *waka* poem (composed in a 5-7-5-7-7 pattern) as the dominant form, intended to represent the splendor of the reigning court.

Compiled by a team headed by **Ki no Tsurayuki** (ca. 868–945), a leading figure of the emerging vernacular literature (for his biography and his other pioneering work, see his **Tosa Diary**, excerpted in this volume), *The Kokinshū* contains more than one thousand poems, complete with a vernacular Japanese and a Chinese-style preface, and is arranged by topical categories in twenty books. The books on the four seasons and on "love" dominate the collection, but there are also books on topics such as "parting," "travel," "mourning," and "puns and wordplay."

The anthology and its books are arranged according to principles of association and progression into an overarching narrative that far exceeds the meaning of the individual poems. Sequences of poems with subtle variations on the same topic are the building blocks that make the anthology into a coherent text of its own. For example, the books on the seasons and on love lend themselves to a natural cycle of beginning, high point, and end or the familiar pattern of first glimpse of the beloved, courtship, passion, marriage (or liaison), disillusion, separation, loneliness, and despair. The compilers' ability to fashion a narrative out of poems composed by many different authors on different occasions is often stunning and would be much imitated. Though the principles of association and progression invented by the compilers of The Kokinshū would become increasingly sophisticated in later poetry anthologies, these structural devices are already fully realized in the first imperial anthology, demonstrating that one of the world's most compressed genres can transcend the apparent limitations of its form.

In contrast to collections such as The Man'yōshū—Japan's earliest poetry anthology, with its tones of archaic grandeur and simplicity best exemplified by Hitomaro's writings—The Kokinshū values poetic elegance, intellectual twists, and erudite refinement. The contradiction between empirical evidence and conventional knowledge generates many of the clever conceits of Kokinshū poetry: a typical strategy is "elegant confusion," as when early plum blossoms at the beginning of spring are mistakenly interpreted as late snowflakes, or vice versa, and the discovery

of the error—or the uncertainty about the real nature of white stuff on plum tree branches—becomes the main point of the poem. In addition to daring visual metaphor, the waka poetry in The Kokinshū relies on a variety of rhetorical figures that drastically condense poetic expression: "poetic pillows" (utamakura) are poetically evocative place-names, which in the space of a few syllables summon up a host of associations. An entire poetic geography of the Japanese archipelago developed that was based on these resonant names. "Pivot words" (kakekotoba) are phonetic puns, in which a sequence of syllables has two different meanings. Aided by the new phonetic kana syllabary, plays on double meaning apparently increased greatly during the Kokinshū age, showing a heightened awareness of the disjunction between phonetic sound and written character.

At least as influential as its poetry was Ki no Tsurayuki's "Japanese Preface" to The Kokinshū (also called "Kana Preface," because it used the vernacular syllabary). It is the canonical statement on the principles of waka poetry, grounding it in a universal instinct for song. Although Ki no Tsurayuki's vision of poetry ultimately relied on the Chinese *Classic of Poetry* and its *"Great Preface"* (included in Vol. A), he argued against the traditions of arduous training and sophisticated craftsmanship that characterized traditional Chinese-style poetry, favoring instead a spontaneous expression of human imagination. Originally conceived fairly narrowly as a polemic against the high status of Chinese-style poetry and an attempt to elevate vernacular waka poetry to a courtly art, Tsurayuki's statement became so influential in Japanese culture that it came to inform broad assumptions about how humans are moved to create works of art.

The Kokinshū

From The Japanese Preface[1]

by Ki no Tsurayuki

The seeds of Japanese poetry lie in the human heart and grow into leaves of ten thousand words. Many things happen to the people of this world, and all that they think and feel is given expression in description of things they see and hear. When we hear the warbling of the mountain thrush in the blossoms or the voice of the frog in the water, we know every living being has its song.

It is poetry which, without effort, moves heaven and earth, stirs the feelings of the invisible gods and spirits, smooths the relations of men and women, and calms the hearts of fierce warriors.

Such songs came into being when heaven and earth first appeared. However, legend has it that in the broad heavens they began with Princess Shitateru, and on earth with the song of Susano-o no mikoto.[2]

In the age of the awesome gods, songs did not have a fixed number of syllables and were difficult to understand because the poets expressed themselves directly, without polish. By the time of the age of humans, beginning with Susano-o no mikoto, poems of thirty-one syllables were composed.[3] Since then many poems have been composed when people were attracted by the blossoms or admired the birds, when they were moved by the haze or regretted the swift passage of the dew, and both inspiration and forms of expression have become diverse. As a long journey to distant places begins with one step and is completed after many months and years, and as a high mountain is created by the accumulation of dust and mire at its skirts and gradually reaches the trailing clouds of the heavens, so too has poetry been.

* * *

Nowadays because people are concerned with gorgeous appearances and their hearts admire ostentation, insipid poems, short-lived poems have appeared. Poetry has become a sunken log submerged unknown to others in the homes of lovers. Poems are not things to bring out in public places as openly as the opening blossoms of the pampas grass.

Japanese poetry ought not to be thus. Consider its origins: Whenever there were blossoms at dawn in spring or moonlit autumn nights, the generations of sovereigns of old summoned their attendants to compose poetry inspired by these beauties. Sometimes the poet wandered through untraveled places to use the image of the blossoms; sometimes he went to dark unknown wilderness lands to write of the moon. The sovereigns surely read these and distinguished the wise from the foolish.

* * *

1. Translated by Laurel Rasplica Rodd.
2. The naughty younger brother of Amaterasu, the sun goddess who is the ancestor of the Japanese emperors. "Princess Shitateru": an earthly deity who composed a dirge after her husband was killed.

3. The earliest historical chronicles of Japan credit the god Susano-o with the composition of the first *waka* poem ("poems of thirty-one syllables"), in praise of a new palace he had constructed for his wife.

This poetry has been handed down since days of old, but it is especially since the Nara period that it has spread far and wide. In that era the sovereign must truly have appreciated poetry, and during his reign Kakinomoto no Hitomaro of the Senior Third Rank was a sage of poetry.[4] Thus ruler and subjects must have been one.

On an autumn evening the crimson leaves floating on the Tatsuta River looked like brocade to the sovereign, and on a spring morning the cherry blossoms on Yoshino Mountain reminded Hitomaro of clouds.[5] There was also a man named Yamabe no Akahito. He was an outstanding and superior poet. Hitomaro cannot be ranked above Akahito, nor Akahito ranked below Hitomaro.

Aside from these, other great poets were heard, as generations succeeded each other like the segments of the black bamboo in a line unbroken as a twisted thread. Earlier poems were gathered in a collection called the *Man'yōshū*.

After that there were one or two poets who knew the ancient songs and understood the heart of poetry. However, each had strengths and weaknesses. Since that time more than one hundred years and ten generations have gone by. Of those who composed during this century, few have known the ancient songs and understood poetry. I would like to give some examples, but I will exclude those of poets of high rank and office, whom I cannot criticize lightly.

Among the others, one of the best known of recent times[6] was Archbishop Henjō, whose style is good but who lacks sincerity. His poetry is like a painting of a woman which stirs one's heart in vain.

> along slender threads
> of delicate twisted green
> translucent dewdrops
> strung as small fragile jewels—
> new willow webs in spring

* * *

Ariwara no Narihira has too much feeling, too few words. His poems are like withered flowers, faded but with a lingering fragrance.

> is this not that moon—
> is this spring not that spring we
> shared so long ago—
> it seems that I alone am
> unaltered from what was then

* * *

Fun'ya no Yashuhide used words skillfully but the expression does not suit the contents. His poetry is like a tradesman attired in elegant robes.

4. Hitomaro (flourished ca. 680–700) is one of the most famous poets in *The Man'yōshū (Collection of Myriad Leaves)*, an 8th-century compilation of this earliest flourishing of poetry.

5. The Tatsuta River was associated in poetry with colorful autumn foliage; Yoshino was famous for its scenic beauty and its cherry blossoms.

6. This section offers judgments of the so-called Six Poetry Immortals, six famous poets who lived closer to Ki no Tsurayuki's time.

> as soon as the gales
> begin to rage   the trees and
> field grass bend before
> them   no wonder they call this
> wind from the mountains Tempest

* * *

The poetry of Priest Kisen of Mount Uji is vague, and the logic does not run smoothly from beginning to end. Reading his poems is like looking at the autumn moon only to have it obscured by the clouds of dawn. Since few of his poems are known, we cannot make comparisons and come to understand them.

> this is how I live
> in my retreat southwest of
> the capital   though
> men call Uji Mountain[7] a
> reminder of worldly sorrow

Ono no Komachi is a modern Princess Sotōri.[8] She is full of sentiment but weak. Her poetry is like a noble lady who is suffering from a sickness, but the weakness is natural to a woman's poetry.

* * *

> I have sunk to the
> bottom   and like the rootless
> shifting water weeds
> should the currents summon me
> I too would drift away

* * *

Ōtomo no Kuronushi's songs are rustic in form; they are like a mountaineer with a bundle of firewood on his back resting in the shade of the blossoms.

* * *

> well now   I'll go to
> Mirror Mountain   gaze upon
> it and then travel
> on   for I wonder if I've
> aged in all these years I've lived

There are others as well who are known, as numerous as the leaves of the trees of the forest, as widespread as the ivy which crawls in the fields, but they think anything they compose is poetry and do not know what poems are.

In the reign of the present sovereign[9] the four seasons have unfolded nine times. The boundless waves of his benevolence flow beyond the boundaries of the Eight Islands;[1] his broad compassion provides a deeper shade than Mount

---

7. The name puns on "grief"; the mountain is generally associated with gloom.
8. The consort of a 5th-century emperor. Ono no Komachi is the best woman poet in *The*

Kokinshū.
9. Emperor Daigo (r. 897–930).
1. The major islands of Japan.

Tsukuba. During his moments of leisure from the multifarious affairs of state, he does not neglect other matters: mindful of the past and desiring to revive the ancient ways, he wishes to examine them and to pass them on to future generations. On the eighteenth day of the Fourth Month of Engi 5 (905), he commanded Ki no Tomonori, Senior Secretary of the Ministry of Private Affairs, Ki no Tsurayuki, Chief of the Documents Division, Ōshikōchi no Mitsune, Former Junior Clerk of Kai Province, and Mibu no Tadamine, functionary in the Headquarters of the Palace Guards, Right Division, to present to him old poems not included in the *Man'yōshū* as well as our own. We have chosen poems on wearing garlands of plum blossoms, poems on hearing the nightingale, on breaking off branches of autumn leaves, on seeing the snow.[2] We have also chosen poems on wishing one's lord the lifespan of the crane and tortoise, on congratulating someone, on yearning for one's wife when one sees the autumn bush clover or the grasses of summer, on offering prayer strips on Ōsaka Hill, on seeing someone off on a journey, and on miscellaneous topics that cannot be categorized by season. These thousand poems in twenty books are called the *Kokinwakashū*. These collected poems will last as long as the waters flowing at the foot of the mountains; they are numerous as the grains of sand on the shore. There will be no complaints that they are like the shallows of the Asuka River;[3] they will give pleasure until the pebbles grow into boulders.

Now then, our poems have not the fragrance of spring blossoms, but a vain reputation lingers, long as the endless autumn night. Thus we fear the ear of the world and lack confidence in the heart of our poetry, but, whether going or staying like the trailing clouds, whether sleeping or rising like the belling deer, we rejoice that we were born in this generation and that we were able to live in the era when this event occurred.

Hitomaro is dead, but poetry is still with us. Times may change, joy and sorrow come and go, but the words of these poems are eternal, endless as the green willow threads, unchanging as the needles of the pine, long as the trailing vines, permanent as birds' tracks.[4] Those who know poetry and who understand the heart of things will look up to the old and admire the new as they look up to and admire the moon in the broad sky.

From Book 1. Spring

1[1]

Composed on a day when spring arrived within the old year

Spring has come
before the year's turning:
should I speak now

---

2. The preface here alludes to the different books of *The Kokinshū*, starting with the books on the four seasons.

3. A river famous for its shallowness (often used as an image of shallow love).

4. Or "handwriting," referring to the physical manuscript of *The Kokinshū*.

1. Poems 1–259 and 635–640 are translated by Lewis Cook; poems 495–500 and 553–658 are translated by Edwin Cranston.

of the old year
or call this the new year?[2]

Ariwara no Motokata

2

Composed on "the first day of spring"

Waters I cupped my
hands to drink, wetting
my sleeves, still frozen:
might this first day of
spring's wind thaw them?

Ki no Tsurayuki

3

Topic unknown

Where are the promised
mists of spring?
In Yoshino,[3] fair hills
of Yoshino, snow
falling still.

Anonymous

23

Topic unknown

Spring's robe of mist
is frail indeed—
its weft is sure
to be frayed by
the mountain winds

Ariwara no Yukihira

2. This poem, which opens *The Kokinshū* and
its six books of poetry on the seasons (two
books each for spring and autumn, one book
each for summer and winter), plays on the
discrepancy between the official lunar and the
unofficial solar calendars. According to the
solar calendar, the first day of spring always
occurs in early February; in the lunar calendar, the new year begins in January or February. Thus the (lunar) first day of spring
sometimes preceded (solar) New Year's Day.

Some commentators see this poem as alluding
to the "old and new" poetry announced in the
title of *The Kokinshū*.
3. A poetic place-name (*utamakura*), which by
the time of *The Kokinshū* had become associated with heavy snowfall, cherry blossoms, and
reclusion. Hitomaro, the leading *Man'yōshū*
poet, had praised its beauties and imperial
landscape when visiting in the retinue of an
empress (see p. 1089).

24

Presented at the Empress's poetry match in the reign of Kanpyō

Even the greens
of the evergreen pine
are refreshed
by the coming
of spring

Minamoto no Muneyuki

25

Composed in response to imperial command

My loved one's robes
stretched out to dry
Each shower of spring[4]
deepens the greens
of the meadows

Ki no Tsurayuki

26

Composed in response to imperial command

Green threads
of the willows
spun by spring's wind
their tangled flowers
burst into bloom

Ki no Tsurayuki

27

On willow trees near the Great Western Temple

Their pale green threads
spun by the wind and
laced with gems
of white dew—
willows in spring

Archbishop Henjō

4. There is a pun on two meanings of the word *haru*, which can mean "to stretch" or the season "spring."

From Book 2. Spring

69

Topic unknown

On hills where mists of spring
trail, glowing faintly,
do the flowers' fading
colors foretell
their fall?[5]

Anonymous

70

Topic unknown

If saying "stay!"
would stop their
falling, could I hold
these blossoms
more dear?

Anonymous

71

Topic unknown

It's their falling without regret
I admire—
Cherry blossoms:
a world of sadness
if they'd stayed.

Anonymous

72

Topic unknown

I seem bound to sleep
in this village tonight:
led astray by falling
blossoms, I've forgotten
my way home.

Anonymous

---

5. This poem opens the second book of spring, marking the middle of the season. It is the first of a sequence of twenty-one poems on the topic "falling cherry blossoms."

73

Topic unknown

Are they not like
this fleeting world?[6]
Cherry blossoms:
no sooner do they flower
than they fall.

Anonymous

From Book 6. Autumn

256

On seeing autumn leaves on Otowa Mountain while visiting Ishiyama

From that first day
the winds of autumn sounded,
the tips of trees on
Otowa Mountain's[7] peak
were turning color.

Ki no Tsurayuki

257

Composed for a poetry contest at the house of Prince Koresada

White dew
all of a single color:
how then does it dye
the leaves of autumn
a thousand different shades?[8]

Fujiwara no Toshiyuki

258

Composed for a poetry contest at the house of Prince Koresada

As the dew of autumn's night
settles in place,
will the falling tears
of wild geese
dye the fields yet deeper?

Mibu no Tadamine

---

6. Literally, "world of a cicada's discarded shell."

7. A pun on *oto*, "sound," exemplifying the rhetorical device of "pivot words" (*kakekotoba*), or puns, which abound in *The Kokinshū*. The following four poems are from a 19-poem sequence on "autumn leaves."

8. The assumption here and in 258 and 259 is that dew causes the leaves to change color.

259

Topic unknown

Surely the autumn dew
must have its varied ways
to turn the mountain's leaves
so many shades
of color.

Anonymous

From Book 11. Love

495

Topic unknown

Memories revive
As on evergreen mountains
Wild azalea flares:
Unspoken love burns stronger
For the silence where it dwells.

Anonymous

496

Topic unknown

Loving secretly
Is too hard for me to bear:
I shall let my heart
Reveal to him its color,
The blush of the safflower.

Anonymous

497

Topic unknown

On the autumn fields,
Mingled with the plumegrass,
Blossoming flowers—
Colors flaunted openly, I'll love;
If not, there is no way to meet.

Anonymous

498

Topic unknown

The warbler[9] singing
On the very topmost branch
Of my garden plum:
Even such a cry as that
Will break forth from my yearning!

Anonymous

499

Topic unknown

Can the young cuckoo[1]
Singing in the footsore hills
Be as sad as I,
Yearning for you all night long,
Unable to sleep a wink?

Anonymous

500

Topic unknown

The mosquito flares,[2]
Sputtering, fill the house with smoke,
Now that summer's here—
How long must they still smolder on,
These fires in my stifled heart?

Anonymous

553

Topic unknown

Once I fell asleep
In a momentary doze, and saw
Him for whom I long,
Since when I have begun to place
My trust in the things called dreams.

Ono no Komachi

9. A spring bird.
1. A bird associated with early summer.
2. One of the few annoying items of everyday

life accepted in the refined vocabulary of the
courtly *waka* tradition.

554

Topic unknown

When pressed with longing
Fiercely through desire's hour
In the bead-black dark,
I slip off the robe of night
To lie with it inside out.[3]

Ono no Komachi

From Book 13. Love

635

Topic unknown

Autumn nights, long
only in name:
let's meet, we say,
yet dawn comes to part us
before we've begun.

Ono no Komachi

636

Topic unknown

For me, not long
enough at all:
autumn nights have always
taken their measure
from the depths of one's love.

Ōshikōchi no Mitsune

637

Topic unknown

Just as the morning sky
is brightening to dawn,
how sad that we must
sort our robes
and part.[4]

Anonymous

3. Wearing nightclothes inside out was believed to bring a desired dream. "Bead-black": a poetic epithet (*makurakotoba*) for night.
4. This and the following poems are from a sequence on "parting at dawn." With the arrival of dawn, marked by the crowing of a rooster, the lover must depart to avoid being seen.

638

Topic unknown

Dawn has come—
I resign myself to parting:
why then must thoughts
I can't find words for
cling to my heart?

Fujiwara no Kunitsune

639

From the empress's poetry contest in the Kanpyō era

Dawn has come—
on the path home from love
I am drenched:
rainfall swelling
my falling tears.

Fujiwara no Toshiyuki

640

Topic unknown

I begin to cry
regret for our parting
even before the rooster
crows the break
of dawn.

Utsuku

657

Topic unknown

Driven straight along
By a longing without bound,
    I'll come by night,
For surely none will rebuke me
For trespass on the path of dreams.

Ono no Komachi

658

Topic unknown

Though on paths of dreams
With no resting for my feet
I run to and fro,
Such rendezvous are nothing
To one glimpse of you that's real.

Ono no Komachi

KI NO TSURAYUKI
ca. 868–945

Ki no Tsurayuki is a pioneering figure in the history of Japanese vernacular writing, which before him was reserved for poetry—almost all prose was composed in the official Chinese-style language. Already renowned as a prominent courtier-poet and as one of the four compilers of the first imperial anthology of Japanese poetry, **The Kokinshū** (*Collection of Ancient and Modern Poems*), Tsurayuki produced near the end of his life a prose work that captured what was distinctive about Japanese vernacular poetry and transplanted its innovations into a new form: the first prose diary in Japanese, *Tosa Diary*. Part memoir, based on his own travel experiences, and part imaginative fiction, Tsurayuki adopted the voice of a gentlewoman and used the new *kana* script (a syllabic alphabet associated with women's writing) to craft an extraordinary work.

Although Ki no Tsurayuki came from a relatively humble family, he obtained some minor government posts and began to gain renown as a court poet during staged poetry contests, a pastime that was just becoming popular in the 890s. These public competitions between two parties who composed and recited poems on set topics such as love or the four seasons

were a sign that vernacular Japanese poetry was slowly gaining official recognition at court. During the ninth century, emperors had sponsored Chinese-style poetry, a genre of much higher status, and vernacular poetry had functioned mostly as a medium for expressing private sentiment and love. A crucial breakthrough for vernacular *waka* poetry (poetry of thirty-one syllables in a 5-7-5-7-7 pattern) came in 905, when the ruling emperor, Daigo, ordered Tsurayuki and three other leading poets to compile the first imperial anthology of Japanese poetry. Tsurayuki's preface to the anthology, the so-called "**Kana Preface**," laid the foundations for the principles of later *waka* poetry and helped enshrine *waka* as the leading courtly genre. Later, from 930 to 935, Tsurayuki received a middle-rank appointment as provincial governor of Tosa, a province on Shikoku, one of the four main islands of Japan. A decade later he died an official of undistinguished rank, but a poet renowned for his technical virtuosity and moving lyricism.

Tosa Diary, written around 935, is a day-by-day record of the travels of an unnamed governor of Tosa returning back to the capital after the conclusion of his appointment in the provinces. The diary, partially based on Tsurayuki's own experiences as the governor of Tosa, is written in the voice of a female attendant in the governor's retinue. This ironic distance between the author and the narrator is highlighted as the diary opens: "I wrote this wondering what it would be like for a woman to try her hand at one of those diaries that men are said to keep." There are many theories about why Tsurayuki assumed a female voice. Perhaps he wanted to break free from the constraints of male official diary writing, whose focus on court protocol and administrative matters left little space for poetry and the expression of moods and emotions. Adopting this fictional persona allowed him to say things that could be said only from a woman's perspective.

Poetry is central to the short diary, which features fifty-seven poems by the fictional lady, her travel companions, and locals on the scene. The company is stirred to poetry by the beauties of the scenery, by famous old poems, or by feelings of grief over events that have happened since their departure from the capital five years before—one woman, for example, had lost her child.

The contrast between the governor's retinue and the rustic locals they meet along the way is a source of humor and irony. Country bumpkins, who lack the education and refinement of the capital company, appear in embarrassing situations, but Tsurayuki also casts an ironic glance at the spoiled urbanites, who, for example, get frightened by rough weather at sea and are calmed only by the unperturbed sailors' songs—a more popular and far earthier type of verse than the elegant courtly *waka*.

Tsurayuki's *Tosa Diary* is a bold experiment in the expressive potential of vernacular Japanese prose, the literary contours of the female voice, and the power of *waka* poetry to capture and communicate the deepest human emotions. The tone of the diary, with its nostalgic yearning for the capital—the home of courtly tastes and lifestyles—echoes that of the "travel poems" in *The Kokinshū,* and in some ways the diary acts out the theoretical claims Tsurayuki had made in the "Kana Preface," thirty years earlier, about the nature of *waka*. But his *Tosa Diary* leads the reader into new territory, where song and poetry emerge from a much broader spectrum of society and where prose records memorable encounters between the sensibilities of courtier and commoner in Heian Japan's rustic countryside.

From Tosa Diary[1]

I wrote this wondering what it would be like for a woman to try her hand at one of those diaries that men are said to keep. One year, around eight in the evening of the twenty-first day of the Twelfth Month, I embarked on a journey. What follows are notes on some of the things that took place.

A certain person[2] had just received official clearance to return to the capital upon completing the usual term of four or five years in his provincial posting. We set out from the governor's mansion to the place where we were to board our boat, and people we knew and some we didn't came to see us off. Those who had come to know us well over the past few years were loath to see us go, and we spent the whole day, well into the night, in confusion, getting ready to depart. . . .

1. Translated by and with footnotes adapted from Gustav Heldt. All ellipses, marking omissions from the original, are Heldt's, as are bracketed additions.
2. Ki no Tsurayuki himself.

It is now the seventh [of the First Month], and we still are in the same harbor of Ōminato. I recall, in vain, that today the New Year's Presentation of White Horses[3] is held at court. The only white we can see here is that of the waves.

During the day, long chests were delivered to us from the home of someone who lives in a place called "Pond." Despite the name, there were no carp in them, but they were filled with many other foods, including perch and numerous other fish from both river and sea. The fresh greens reminded us of the New Year's plucking of shoots at home in the capital. The gifts came with this poem:

> A wild moor
> thick with weeds
> but no water:
> such is the "Pond" where I
> gathered these herbs.

How charming. The "Pond" of the poem is the name of the place. The poem was by a woman of rank who came to live with her husband in the provinces. The chests' contents were shared with everyone, including the children. When all had eaten their fill, the sailors drummed on their taut bellies. The sound was enough to startle even the sea god. No doubt we are in for waves.

Much else happened during the day. Someone came bringing lunch boxes. I'm sure his name will come back to me in a moment. It was clear that his heart was set on making a verse for the occasion. After talking about this and that for a while, he sighed mournfully and remarked, "Alas, the waves are rising," and then recited his poem:[4]

> Louder than the roar of the
> white-crested waves
> rising in your path
> will my cries resound
> when you depart.

He must have some voice. How could this poem compare with the things he had brought? We made a show of being impressed, but no one offered a poem in reply. Even though there was someone among them who was more than capable of replying, all we did was praise his poem and continue eating until nightfall.

Finally the man said, "Excuse me," and got up to leave. Just then, a child sitting in the back of our group whispered, "I'll offer a reply." Those of us near enough to hear were surprised and started to speak among ourselves, saying how charming this would be, and that if the girl was really going to compose something, she ought to do so at once. Hoping he might wait for the poem, we looked around for our erstwhile guest. But he had already left, no doubt because night had fallen.

3. The announcement of promotions and new appointments to official posts.
4. To offer departing travelers a poem predicting rough seas was inauspicious. The narrator pretends to have forgotten the versifier's name so that she can frankly report the embarrassing scene.

We still were curious. Someone asked the child to tell us what she had composed. She was shy and said nothing until pressed, then recited this poem:

> The sleeves of those who leave
> and those who stay
> are drenched in a stream of tears,
> swelling to soak them
> ever more.

What a fine verse—was it because the poet was so pretty that this seemed such a pleasant surprise? Still, what were we to do with a child's verse? An aunt or an uncle might put their signature on it. Not the right thing to do, perhaps. Someone suggested sending the verse to our visitor, but nothing was done, after all. . . .

The morning of the ninth [of the First Month]. We rowed out from Ōminato hoping to reach the harbor at Naha. Since we were leaving the bounds of the province, a great many people came to see us off. Fujiwara no Tokizane, Tachibana no Suehira, and Hasebe no Yukimasa in particular had been following us since the day we left the governor's mansion. These are truly men of feeling, their consideration as deep as the ocean before us.

We were about to leave the harbor and row into the offing, and these people had come to see us off. As we rowed out to sea, those who remained ashore receded into the distance, and those on the boat faded from their sight. Those on the shore must have had things left unsaid, and those of us on the boat felt the same, but there was no help for it. Nonetheless, I spoke this verse to myself before giving up such thoughts:

> I would send my feelings
> across the sea,
> but feelings not being words
> how could they know
> my thoughts?

We passed by the Uda Pines. Both the number of trees and the years they have grown there are beyond counting. The waves washed up near each root, and cranes flew above each branch. Unable to remain silent, someone on the boat composed this verse:

> I gaze across at the pines:
> the cranes that roost
> on every branch
> must take these evergreens
> for age-old companions.

The poem could hardly rival the sight itself. I watched the mountains and sea as we rowed into the gathering dusk. In the dark of night, I couldn't tell east from west, and we could only leave it to the captain to judge the weather. Even the men on board, not used to traveling at sea, were worried. As for the women, lying with their heads against the bilge, they could only weep aloud.

Feeling sorry for them, and not at all worried themselves, the crew and captain
began singing boatmen's songs:

> In the fields in spring
> I weep aloud,
> my hands are cut
> by sharp blades of grass,
> the greens that I gather
> will be grabbed by his father,
> devoured by his mother.
> How I long to go home![5]

> Where's that girl
> who just last night
> begged for my money
> telling sweet lies
> buying on credit
> bringing no payment
> not even bringing herself?[6]

There were many others that I won't write down. They made us laugh, and
though the sea was rough, our hearts were eased a bit. . . .

At daybreak on the thirteenth a little rain fell, then it stopped after a while.
Several of the women got off the boat and went looking for a suitable place to
bathe. Looking out at the sea, I composed this verse:

> All of the clouds
> look so like waves
> I wish for a diver,
> a girl I could ask
> "Which is the sea?"

Since it is past the tenth of the month, the moon in the dawn sky is charming.
From the day we boarded the boat, the women have not once worn fine robes of
red silk, fearful of catching the sea god's attention. Now, barely hidden by the
cover of a few scant reeds, they have hitched up their skirts past their knees,
carelessly showing the abalones and clams that go so well with sea squirts.[7] . . .

The twentieth. The weather is still unfavorable, and our boat stays in port.
Everyone is complaining. Frustrated and anxious, I wonder how many days
have passed since we set out. Has it been twenty? Thirty? Just counting them
would hurt one's fingers. How dreary.

I stay awake all night. The moon of the twentieth rises in the sky, not from
the rim of a mountain peak but straight from the sea. Was it a sight like this
that was seen, in the distant past, by the man known as Abe no Nakamaro, who

---

5. The song supposedly expresses the plight
of a young woman married to a farmer's son.
6. A comic song in the voice of a merchant
deceived by a girl.

7. That is, male genitals; "abalones and clams"
are female genitals. The sea god was believed
to be ever-lustful.

had journeyed to the land of the Tang?[8] When he was readying to board a boat to return home, the people of that realm, reluctant to see him go, held a farewell party. They composed Chinese verses and, hesitating to part, lingered until the moon of the twentieth rose in the night sky. At the sight of the moon, Master Nakamaro said, "In my country, verses such as this were sung by the gods in their sacred age and, even today, are composed by people of all ranks— high, middle, and low—when they feel the regret of parting, or in celebration or in sadness," and he composed this:

> I look out
> across the wide blue sea
> and see the same moon
> that once rose over Mount Mikasa
> in distant Kasuga.[9]

Aware that the people of that country would be unable to understand the verse as recited, he sketched its meaning in Chinese characters[1] and explained it to someone there who had learned our language. They must have been able to understand his feelings, since they expressed immoderate praise for his poem. The speech of China and that of our country may differ, but the light of the moon is the same everywhere, and so it must be with the human heart.

Inspired by this story from the past, someone composed the following verse:

> The same moon I saw
> in the capital
> over the mountain rim
> now rises from the ocean's waves
> and sets there, too.

The fourth [of the Second Month]. The captain told us, "The weather looks very bad today," so we ended up staying in port. And in spite of that, there was not a single wind-tossed wave all day. Our captain is useless when it comes to predicting the weather.

The beach where we docked was covered with a variety of lovely shells and pebbles. Seeing them, someone on our boat who had lost a daughter composed this verse:

> Let the incoming waves
> bring to shore
> "forgetting shells"
> that I might gather
> to ease my longing for her.

---

8. Abe no Nakamaro (697–770) was 19 when he accompanied one of the regular diplomatic missions from Japan to China; he studied, passed the civil service examination, and served there in the Chinese government until his death. 9. Near Nara, which served as capital of Japan from 710 to 784. When Nakamaro left for China, the members of his embassy were seen off with prayers at the Kasuga shrine. 1. Literally, "men's letters"; using Chinese characters was a male prerogative, in contrast to the vernacular kana script associated with female writing.

Hearing this, someone else felt compelled to compose this to dispel the gloom
of those on board:

> I'll not gather shells
> of forgetfulness—
> I'd rather keep
> my longing
> for that bright gem.[2]

The parent has been made weak as a child on account of her daughter. Someone may well ask, "Was she really as pretty as a gem?" Still, they say, "a dead
child has a pretty face." . . .

The ninth [of the Second Month]. We were filled with impatience as our
boat was towed upriver before daybreak, but since there isn't enough water in
the river, we are reduced to a crawling pace. Eventually we came to a fork in
the river called Wada no Tomari. Here, people begged for rice and fish and
some was handed out.

As the boat was towed upstream, a place called Nagisa Villa came into view.
Looking at it and thinking of its past, we realized that it was indeed a charming
place. In the hills behind were pine trees, and inside the courtyard, plum trees
were in bloom. People started talking. Long ago this was a famous place. This
is where the middle captain, Ariwara no Narihira, in attendance on Prince
Koretaka, composed that poem,

> If in this world
> no cherry flowers bloomed
> then would our hearts
> be at ease
> in springtime?

Then someone with us here and now composed a verse evoking the setting and
its past:

> Though a thousand years
> may have passed,
> the chill in the sound
> of these pines
> hasn't changed.

And yet another person composed this:

> Longing for their lord,
> the plum blossoms
> of his ancient dwelling
> are as fragrant now
> as they were in the past.

---

2. That is, the child. The previous poem contains a play on "forgetting" (*wasure*) her by hurrying
to the shore and gathering *wasuregai* clams.

And so we continued upstream, rejoicing as we drew nearer to the capital. Several of my fellow travelers were accompanied by children they had not had when they went down this same river, children born during their stay in the province of Tosa. Whenever the boat stopped, they would carry their children with them as they went ashore. Seeing this, the mother whose child had died was unable to contain her grief and sobbed as she composed this:

> Those who had none
> now return with theirs:
> others' children
> bring sorrow to one who
> has lost her own.

What must the father have felt as he heard this? Such overwhelming emotions, and the poems they provoke, are hardly matters of self-indulgence. It is said in China and here as well that poetry is an action one resorts to when feelings cannot be silenced. . . .

The sixteenth. This evening we made our way to the capital. . . .

We waited for night before entering the city,[3] and as we were taking our time, the moon came into view. We crossed the Katsura River under its brilliant light. Some of our party commented on how different this river was from the Asuka, notorious for varying between depths and shallows without warning. In response, someone composed this poem:

> The light of the moon
> on this river's waters
> remains as unchanged as
> its evergreen namesake,
> the moon's *katsura* tree.[4]

Someone responded with this:

> Once as distant
> as heaven's clouds,
> the Katsura River
> now soaks my sleeves
> as I cross.

Yet another person composed this verse:

> Though the Katsura River
> does not run through
> my heart,
> the depths
> of both must be the same.

So much joy on returning to the capital, hence so many poems.

---

3. Kyoto.
4. According to Chinese legends, the katsura laurel, an evergreen, grows on the moon.

As the night deepened, we could not tell one place from another. We are glad to be back in the capital! When we reached our residence and passed through the gate, we saw very clearly in the bright moonlight how things were. The house was far more dilapidated than we had been warned while away. The same must be true of the sensibilities of those we left in charge of the house. Though a fence divided our houses, we were as one family, and our neighbors offered to look after our place. To think that we had sent gifts every time we sent a message. Still, we did not raise our voices in complaint tonight. Unpleasant as it may be, we will have to offer a token of gratitude.

On the grounds of our residence, there is a depression filled with water, like a pond. It was surrounded by pine trees. During the past five or six years (it feels like a thousand), half of them have died, though some saplings have begun to grow among the surviving trees. Everything else was in ruin, and many sighs were heard. I recalled everything that had happened, and among the most painful were memories of the girl who, though born in this house, had not come back with us. Those who had traveled with us on the boat were playing noisily with their own children. There was one still unable to overcome her grief, and someone who understood quietly composed this:

> Even as a child born here
> does not return,
> how sad to see
> these pine saplings
> growing by our house.[5]

As though this were not enough, he composed another:

> If only I could have seen her
> for as long as the
> pine's thousand years
> and not known the sorrow
> of that distant parting.

I have much else to regret, much that is difficult to forget, but there is no end to writing such things. I should throw this away and be done with it.

---

5. The young trees are a reminder of the irreplaceability of the dead child.

SEI SHŌNAGON

ca. 966–1017

The gifted coterie of women writers who served as ladies-in-waiting to the Japanese imperial consorts of the late tenth and early eleventh centuries produced a number of superlative literary works that today stand at the center of the canon of Japanese literature. Next to **Murasaki Shikibu**'s *The Tale of Genji* is *The Pillow Book* by Sei Shōnagon, who earned no kind words from Shikibu. In her diary she grumbled that Shōnagon was "dreadfully conceited" and "thought herself so clever, littering her writings with Chinese characters, but if one examined them closely, they left much to be desired." Shikibu was annoyed by Shōnagon's pretensions to break into the domain of Chinese learning, reserved at the time for male aristocrats. As ladies-in-waiting to two imperial consorts who maintained competing literary salons, Shikibu and Shōnagon were themselves engaged in an intense rivalry that spurred them to produce works to which later generations would look up with nostalgic awe. In design, form, and purpose, the two books are polar opposites. *The Tale of Genji* is an extensive, intricate, patient work of fiction. *The Pillow Book* is a slender catchall of personal observation, impressionistic and highly opinionated. Shōnagon has a sharp tongue, a keen eye, and a brush that moves masterfully between capturing lyrical moods and making pithy points. That she is both a supreme embodiment and a critical arbiter of Heian courtly tastes gives *The Pillow Book* a delightful depth.

SEI SHŌNAGON AND THE HEIAN COURT

Sei Shōnagon, whose actual name was probably Kiyohara Nagiko, was the daughter of a provincial governor noted for his poetry (in Heian Japan names were context-dependent, and a gentlewoman was usually named after the court title of a male relative). Although Shōnagon's father was a middle-ranking courtier with an appointment in the provinces, she seems to have spent all her life in the capital, the seat of the imperial court. Between 993 and 1000 she served Empress Teishi (977–1000), one of the consorts of Emperor Ichijō (980–1011). What we know about Shōnagon's life is mostly contained in *The Pillow Book*, which does not mention a husband or children, but other sources of the period suggest that she was briefly married to an undistinguished man named Tachibana no Norimitsu and had at least one child. In the *Pillow Book* Sei Shōnagon repeatedly mocks Norimitsu as a hopeless boor who lacks poetic sensibility, and the marriage apparently did not last long.

Shōnagon lived during the middle of the Heian Period, which was named after its capital, Heian-kyō, the "Capital of Peace and Tranquility" (present-day Kyoto). The Heian court, centered on the symbolic figure of the emperor, followed a complex aristocratic system. The large bureaucratic apparatus of ministries and offices reflected a strict hierarchy based on rank as well as an educational system whose focus was the study of the Chinese Classics. Although aristocratic women like Shōnagon received an excellent training in Chinese literature, they produced literature written only in vernacular Japanese; Chinese-style genres, which stood at the top of the literary hierarchy, were largely the domain of male aristocrats. Shōnagon particularly relished the moments when she succeeded in using her Chinese learning to outdo a man, even if she was bound to use vernacular Japanese and the vernacular *kana* script (called "woman's hand") in her sophisticated responses to his letters.

In the Heian court, where men and women were strictly segregated, letters exchanged between lovers, relatives, or friends played a crucial role in social relations. Although they spent their days participating in an extensive array of court ceremonies, receiving visitors and engaging in witty conversation, the women were generally hidden away, secured in their residences in spaces behind paper doors and screens through which they would usually speak with their visitors unseen. Writing provided an outlet, enabling them both to dispel their boredom and to express private sentiments that transcended or critiqued the swirl of rumors, whispers, and intrigue that defined their lives.

Aristocratic men enjoyed considerably more freedom. Men usually lived in or near the living quarters of their wives' parents, but they often pursued romantic interests elsewhere; they took several wives and installed them in separate residences, visited at their whim. Marriage arrangements were loose. Marriages could be established by a man's frequent visits; a cessation in visiting was equivalent to a divorce. If his visits became increasingly sporadic as he was drawn to romantic adventures elsewhere, the woman was left waiting and worrying about the future of their relationship.

Daughters were crucial pawns in the marriage politics of the Heian imperial court. Beginning in the latter half of the tenth century, the northern branch of the powerful Fujiwara clan controlled the imperial succession through the so-called regent system. It became customary for a Fujiwara regent to rule on behalf of a child emperor and to marry his daughters into the imperial family. Thus, the Fujiwara regents became uncles and grandfathers of future emperors and were often more powerful than those emperors. Shōnagon lived during one of the most successful regencies of the Heian Period, that of Fujiwara no Michinaga (966–1027). Michinaga had his eldest daughter Shōshi appointed consort of Emperor Ichijō, to whom she bore two later emperors. While Murasaki Shikibu served in Shōshi's lively entourage, which featured several other prominent women writers, Shōnagon was lady-in-waiting to Shōshi's cousin, Teishi. Teishi was the daughter of Fujiwara no Michitaka, an elder brother and rival of Michinaga, who became regent in 990. After Michitaka unexpectedly died in an epidemic in 995 and, in the following year, Teishi's brother Korechika was sent into exile on the urging of their increasingly powerful uncle, Teishi lost her footing at court. Michinaga's daughter Sōshi advanced to the position of highest consort, and Teishi had to leave the palace. Although Shōnagon continued to serve Teishi until the young empress died in childbirth in 1000, these last few years must have been painful and humiliating, in stark contrast to the earlier, happier times at court that *The Pillow Book* evokes so vividly.

THE PILLOW BOOK AND HEIAN LITERATURE

The Pillow Book chronicles with wit and humor the moments of glamour and ennui, the obsessions and trivia, of Heian court life. It centers on questions of aristocratic taste, the paramount importance of learning and education, and the pleasures of experiencing the world through the refined languages of literature, art, and music. Over the course of *The Pillow Book*, as Shōnagon expounds on why some kinds of carriages should move faster than others, why priests should be handsome, or how a lover should make his good-byes, she emerges as an impatient and imperious figure. She is every inch the aristocrat, whose fastidious standards brook no slipshod behavior. So deft is she at homing in on human foibles and skewering the offender that the effect of her sharp sallies can be shattering. We chuckle at her delicious wit, but we are glad we are not the objects of her scrutiny. *The Pillow Book* is written in a compact and forceful style, which favors brevity and compression and produces surprising effects by means of unusual juxtapositions. Shōnagon's literary persona favors witty repartee, sly self-promotion, and occasional cutting insults. Her candor in admitting her hypercritical nature, and her display of ruthless honesty toward others and herself, gives her an irrepressible, magnetic voice. She is a presence.

The exact date of composition and the title of *The Pillow Book* have been subjects of much debate. It was probably finished around 1005, after Empress Teishi's death. Writing *The Pillow Book* in memory of her late patroness, Shōnagon focused exclusively on those happy years when Teishi's standing at court was at its height. That she was painfully aware, as she was composing the book, of the tragic fall that lay in store for Teishi and herself makes the work all the more poignant.

In the last section of our selections Shōnagon wants us to know that even the paper on which she wrote her original *Pillow Book* came from that happy period, before Teishi lost her place at court. Paper was a rare commodity and Teishi's brother Korechika, before his ignominious exile, had brought the empress a stack from the supply being used in the palace for copying the *His-*

torical Records by the Chinese historian **Sima Qian** (included in Vol. A). We can be sure that this connection to China's canonical history—written eleven centuries earlier—certainly pleased her. Just as Sima Qian had chronicled the history of China up until his own time, the Han Dynasty, so Shōnagon understood herself as a chronicler of Heian court life.

Even more contested than *The Pillow Book*'s date and title is its original format. The more than three hundred separate sections can be grouped into three basic types: diary-style entries describing datable events at court, catalogues of objects or attributes, and essayistic jottings on general topics. This mélange is unusual. Some moments in *The Pillow Book* exhibit the intimacy of a typical Heian women's diary, others evoke scenes that look as if they were taken from a Heian romantic tale such as *The Tale of Genji*, and yet other parts resemble the philosophical musings of the later essay genre (such as **Yoshida Kenkō**'s *Essays in Idleness*). That *The Pillow Book* contains such variety in one book, sometimes even within a single section, makes it unique. It is also a uniquely jumbled text: the earliest surviving copy of *The Pillow Book* dates to several hundred years after Shōnagon's time, and the text has come down to the present in four manuscript lineages that differ both in content and in the arrangement of individual sections. Two versions group the entries by type, while the version now considered more authentic and canonical (represented in the selection here) freely mixes the diary entries, catalogues, and essayistic sections.

Shōnagon's brush follows the rhythms of Heian court life with its cycle of annual festivals—occasions for sumptuous display for men and women alike—and its keen awareness of questions of rank and propriety. Section 2, "Times of Year," takes us through some of the annual highlights. In section 6,

"The Emperor's Cat," a cat receives court rank and the poor dog Okinamaro receives a beating, is expelled, and returns in humiliation. This story is often read as an allegory for Korechika's exile, throwing a critical light on the cruel workings of court politics and intrigue. The story in section 20 about an imperial consort who knew the entire *Kokinshū (Collection of Ancient and Modern Poems)* by heart shows the pleasures and pressures of court life: the ability to recite a famous poem, to render it in beguiling calligraphy, or to adapt it to a new occasion when poetry composition was a key aspect of living at court and to maintaining one's reputation. Shōnagon enjoys reporting the occasions when she succeeded in coming up with a witty solution to an unexpected challenge, though she often emphasized how badly things could have turned out without the stroke of her genius at the right moment. There can be no doubt that Shōnagon liked to emerge triumphant: in section 82, her overconfident claim that a snow mountain they had built in the garden of the palace would survive for an impossibly long time forces her to take hilarious measures in seeking to win her dispute with the Empress.

To receive favorable judgment and to pass astute judgment were highly desirable in the Heian court. Therefore, the vocabulary of judgment and taste is particularly central to *The Pillow Book*. The most important term is *okashi*, which can mean anything from "delightful," "intriguing," or "charming" to "engaging" or just "interesting" and occurs more than four hundred times in *The Pillow Book*. The word is so pervasive that the translator of our selections renders it nearly thirty different ways. In the book's famous opening section alone—"In spring, the dawn— when the slowly paling mountain rim is tinged with red, and wisps of faintly crimson-purple cloud float in the sky"—it appears three times. Shōnagon's frequent outcries of *okashi* are much more than an indulgence in superficial pleasure or beauty. There is a delicacy in *The Pillow Book* that helps us see, hear, and feel the world around us with superior nuance. Whether representing changes in robes to match the cherry blossom season, a cuckoo's cry so faint that the hearer wonders whether it is actually heard or only imagined, or the thoughts piqued by various insects, the details in *The Pillow Book* capture the sensuous variety of life. *The Pillow Book* seems to prescribe a restrained cultivation of feeling—a responsiveness to the emotional environment—along with physical grace and a genuine appreciation of shape, proportion, color, and tone: an appreciation that includes the power to make subtle distinctions.

This cultivated aestheticism isn't always focused on things that are beautiful. In a world that values the matching of tastes, Shōnagon is quick to pinpoint moments when they clash. Ugly and repellent details—fleas dancing under ladies' skirts, houseflies alighting with their "damp little feet," silver tweezers that can pull out unsightly hair, or a slovenly looking woman making out in broad daylight with a "scrawny man with hair sprouting from his face"—also make occasional appearances in *The Pillow Book*. These mismatches appear not just in the list of "dispiriting" and "distressing things," or in "things that cannot be compared," but also in the diary section: Shōnagon's tale about the argument over the snow mountain is suggestively intertwined with the story of a bawdy begging nun who occasionally intrudes and scandalizes the company. In the midst of her sublime expressions of courtly taste and beauty, Shōnagon is also attracted to the grotesque, even as she castigates it.

Unlike other Heian classics such as *The Kokinshū, The Tales of Ise,* and *The Tale of Genji, The Pillow Book* did not become a canonical text in the medieval period. Its relative neglect is attributable in part to its containing far less poetry—the main focus of those studying these texts—than the other three works. In the early modern period it became the subject of parodies. *The Mongrel Pillow Book* of 1606 apes *The Pillow Book*'s aesthetics of lists: "Things that have ones hair stand on end . . . Putting on armor in winter without underclothes . . . Malaria. The prospect of an evening spent in conversation with one's boy favorite."

Shōnagon continues to fascinate readers, and its large number of translations and adaptations have made *The Pillow Book* into a favored work of world literature. Today Shōnagon's strong female voice inspires in her readers a kind of empathy with the world of an eleventh-century Japanese gentlewoman that she herself could never have dreamed of.

From The Pillow Book[1]

1 *In spring, the dawn*—when the slowly paling mountain rim is tinged with red, and wisps of faintly crimson-purple cloud float in the sky.

In summer, the night—moonlit nights, of course, but also at the dark of the moon, it's beautiful when fireflies are dancing everywhere in a mazy flight. And it's delightful too to see just one or two fly through the darkness, glowing softly. Rain falling on a summer night is also lovely.

In autumn, the evening—the blazing sun has sunk very close to the mountain rim, and now even the crows, in threes and fours or twos and threes, hurrying to their roost, are a moving sight. Still more enchanting is the sight of a string of wild geese in the distant sky, very tiny. And oh how inexpressible, when the sun has sunk, to hear in the growing darkness the wind, and the song of autumn insects.

In winter, the early morning—if snow is falling, of course, it's unutterably delightful, but it's perfect too if there's a pure white frost, or even just when it's very cold, and they hasten to build up the fires in the braziers and carry in fresh charcoal. But it's unpleasant, as the day draws on and the air grows warmer, how the brazier fire dies down to white ash.

2 *Times of year*—The first month; the third, fourth and fifth months; the seventh, eighth and ninth; the eleventh and twelfth—in fact every month according to its season, the year round, is delightful.

On the first day of the year, the sky is gloriously fresh and spring mists hang in the air. It's quite special and delightful the way people everywhere have taken particular care over their clothing and makeup, and go about exchanging New Year felicitations.

On the seventh day, people pluck the new shoots of herbs that have sprung up in the patches of bare earth amidst the snow[2]—they're wonderfully green and fresh, and it's charming just what a fuss is made over these herbs, which

---

1. Translated by and with notes adapted from Meredith McKinney.
2. In this passage Shōnagon describes some of the court festivals of the first four months of the year. The seventh day of the First Month is the Festival of Young Herbs, when various herbs are made into a gruel that is supposed to ward off evil spirits and to protect one's health throughout the year.

normally aren't to be seen at such close quarters. Those of good family who live outside the palace brighten up their carriages and set off to see the Parading of the Blue Roans. It's fun how, when the carriages are pulled over the big ground beam of the central palace gate, all the ladies' heads are jolted together so that your hair combs tumble out and can easily break if you aren't careful, and everybody laughs. I remember seeing a large group of senior courtiers and others standing about near the Left Gate Watch guardhouse, gaily snatching the attendants' bows and twanging them to startle the horses—also, peeping through the carriage blinds and delightedly glimpsing groundswomen and other serving ladies coming and going near one of the lattice fences further in. Witnessing such a scene, of course you sigh and wonder just what sort of people they must be, to manage to be so at ease in the 'nine-fold palace.' But when I actually saw them at such close quarters at the palace, the attendants' faces were all dark and blotchy where their white powder hadn't covered the skin properly, precisely like black patches of earth showing through where snow has half melted—a truly horrible sight. The horses' rearing and lunging was quite terrifying, so I retreated to the depths of the carriage, where I could no longer really see.

On the eighth day, there's a special thrill in the noise of all the carriages hurtling about as everyone who's received a promotion does the rounds to exchange felicitations.

On the fifteenth day, the day of the full moon, a delightful scene always takes place in the houses of the nobility after the festival food is served. Both the senior and junior gentlewomen of the house go about looking for a chance to strike each other with gruel sticks,[3] constantly glancing behind them to make sure they aren't hit themselves. It's marvellous fun when someone manages somehow to get in a strike, and everyone bursts into delighted peals of laughter— though you can certainly see why the poor victim herself feels upset.

A young man has recently begun to call on his new wife.[4] Now it's time for him to set off for the palace, and lurking in the background peeping out is one of her gentlewomen, gleefully self-important and struggling to contain herself till he leaves. The gentlewomen who are sitting gathered around the girl all smile, realizing perfectly well what's going on, but she secretly motions them to stay quiet. Meanwhile, the girl sits there innocently, seeming to have noticed nothing. Then up comes the gentlewoman, with some excuse such as 'I'll just pick this up,' darts over and strikes her and runs off, while everyone collapses in laughter. The young man doesn't take it amiss but smiles amiably, and as for the girl, it's quite charming to see that though she doesn't seem particularly surprised, she is nevertheless blushing slightly.

The gentlewomen strike each other too, and I gather men even get struck sometimes. It's also amusing to witness someone for some reason lose her temper and burst into tears, and roundly abuse whoever has struck her. Even the more exalted people in the palace join in the day's fun.

There's a charming scene in the palace at the time of the Spring Appointments List.[5] It's snowing and everything's icy, and men of the fourth and fifth

3. To mark the first full moon of the year, a special gruel that averted evil influences was served. It was believed that a woman whose loins were struck by sticks retrieved from the fire used to cook that gruel would soon give birth to a son.

4. It was common at the time for a young husband to be adopted into his wife's family and visit her at her parents' home, rather than move with her to a separate residence.
5. The time when court officials receive new appointments and promotions.

ranks are walking about holding their letters requesting promotion. The youthful, high-spirited ones inspire you with confidence in them, but there are also old white-haired fellows who go around confiding in people, in hopes that this will improve their chances. They approach some gentlewoman and obliviously set about singing their own praises to her, and they can have no idea that some of the younger gentlewomen are busy imitating them and laughing behind their back. 'Do please mention me favourably to the Emperor or Empress,' they implore us—and it's a fine thing if they actually gain the post they want, but really most pathetic when they fail.

The third day of the third month is full of the soft sunshine of spring. Now is the time when the peach trees begin to bloom, and of course the willows too are particularly lovely at this time. It's charming to see the buds still cocooned in their sheaths like silkworms—but on the other hand, once the leaves have opened they're rather unpleasant.

If you break off a branch of splendidly flowering cherry and arrange it in a large flower vase, the effect is delightful. And it's particularly charming if a gentleman, be it one of Her Majesty's brothers or a normal guest, is seated nearby engaged in conversation, wearing a cloak in the cherry-blossom combination with undersleeves displayed.

And how delightful it all is at the time of the Festival in the fourth month![6] The court nobles and senior courtiers in the festival procession are only distinguishable by the different degrees of colour of their formal cloaks, and the robes beneath are all of a uniform white, which produces a lovely effect of coolness. The leaves of the trees have not yet reached their full summer abundance but are still a fresh young green, and the sky's clarity, untouched by either the mists of spring or autumn's fogs, fills you with inexplicable pleasure. And when it clouds a little in the evening or at night, how unbearably lovely then to hear from far in the distance the muted call of a *hototogisu*,[7] sounding so faint you almost doubt your ears.

It's delightful, as the day of the Festival approaches, to see the attendants going to and fro carrying tight rolls of dark leaf-green or lavender fabric,[8] wrapped lightly in just a touch of paper. Patterning effects such as graded dye and dapple dye strike you as unusually beautiful at this time.

The little girls who will be in the procession are also enchanting. They've already washed their hair and done it nicely, but they may still be wearing their everyday threadbare and rumpled clothes, and they trot around full of excited anticipation, crying 'Rethread my high clogs for me!' or 'Sew up the soles of my shoes!' But for all their boisterous posturing and prancing, once they're dressed up in their festival finery they suddenly begin parading about with great solemnity, like self-important priests at the head of some dignified procession, no doubt starting to feel thoroughly nervous. It's also touching to see, in the festival procession, a parent or aunt or perhaps an older sister accompanying the little girls and carefully tending their clothing as they walk.

When you see a man who's set his heart on becoming Chamberlain, but who's in no position to achieve his goal just yet, dressed specially in the Chamberlain's

6. The Kamo Festival, still one of the most important festivals of Kyoto; it includes a large procession through the city from and back to the Kamo Shrines.

7. A kind of cuckoo whose call is much praised by Japanese poets.

8. Used to make up the robes worn at the festival.

green formal cloak[9] for the day of the Festival, you wish for his sake he didn't have to take it off again. It's a pity that it isn't damask like the real one, however.

4 *It breaks my heart to think* of parents sending a beloved son into the priesthood. Poor priests, they're not the unfeeling lumps of wood that people take them for. They're despised for eating that dreadful monastic food, and their sleeping arrangements are no better. A young priest must naturally be full of curiosity, and how could he resist the forbidden urge to peep into a room, especially if there's a woman in there? But this is criticized as disgraceful too.

Exorcist priests have an even harder life.[1] If they ever nod off, exhausted from their long labours, people complain that they do nothing but sleep. How constrained and miserable this must make them feel!

Well, this is how things used to be, anyway. These days, in fact, priests lead a much easier life.

* * *

6 *The Emperor's cat* had received the fifth rank, and was given the appropriate title-name 'Myōbu.' It was a charming creature, and the Emperor was quite devoted to it.

One day its carer, Muma no Myōbu,[2] found it lying basking on the veranda. 'How vulgar!' she scolded. 'Back you come inside.' But the cat continued to lie there asleep in the sun, so she decided to give it a fright. 'Okinamaro!' she cried to the dog. 'Here, boy! Come and get Myōbu!' The foolish dog couldn't believe its ears, and came rushing over, whereupon the terrified cat fled inside through the blind.

The Emperor was at that time in the Breakfast Room, and he witnessed this event with astonishment. He tucked the cat into the bosom of his robe, and summoned his men. When the Chamberlains Tadataka and Narinaka appeared, the Emperor ordered them, 'Give Okinamaro a thorough beating and banish him to Dog Island! Be quick about it!'

Everyone gathered and a noisy hunt ensued. The Emperor went on to chastise Muma no Myōbu, declaring that he would replace her as Myōbu's carer as she was completely untrustworthy, and thenceforth she no longer appeared in his presence. Meanwhile, they rounded up the dog, and had the guards drive it out.

We all pitied the poor thing. 'Oh dear,' we said, 'and to think how he used to swagger about the place as if he owned it.'

'Remember how on the third of the third month the Secretary Controller decked him out with a garland of willow and a peach-flower comb, and tied a branch of cherry blossom on his back? Who'd have guessed then that he'd meet with such a fate?'

'And the way he always attended Her Majesty at meal times. How we'll miss him!'

---

9. Usually only the Chamberlain could wear the color green, which was permitted to members of his office of lesser rank on this occasion.
1. Exorcizing a tenacious possession required that incantations and spells be performed for

many hours.
2. A title for a gentlewoman of fifth rank. It was also applied to cats, and only cats of fourth and fifth rank were permitted in the emperor's palace.

Then around noon three or four days later, we heard a dog howling dreadfully. What dog could be howling on and on like this? we wondered, and as we listened dogs gathered from everywhere to see what was afoot. One of the cleaning women came running in. 'Oh, it's dreadful! Two of the Chamberlains are beating the dog! It's bound to die! His Majesty banished it, but apparently it came back, so they're teaching it a lesson.'

Alas, poor creature! It was Okinamaro. 'It's Tadataka and Sanefusa doing it,' someone said.

We sent someone to stop them, but at that point the dog finally ceased its howling. 'It's dead,' came the report, 'so they've thrown it outside the guardhouse.'

That evening as we were sorrowing over poor Okinamaro, up staggered a miserable trembling creature, terribly swollen and looking quite wretched. Can it be Okinamaro? we wondered. What other dog could be wandering around at this hour in such a state?

We called his name, but he didn't respond. 'It's him,' some of us declared, while others maintained that it wasn't, till Her Majesty said, 'Send for Ukon. She would recognize him.' We duly did so, and when she came Her Majesty showed her the dog and asked if it was indeed Okinamaro.

'There's certainly a likeness,' replied Ukon, 'but this dog looks simply revolting. And you only have to say his name and Okinamaro bounds happily up, but this dog doesn't respond at all. It must be a different dog. And they did say they'd killed him and thrown out the corpse, didn't they? How could he have survived after two men had beaten him like that?' This moved Her Majesty to fresh sorrow.

It grew dark. We gave the dog some food, but it didn't eat it, so we decided that it was indeed a different dog and left it at that.

The next morning, Her Majesty had performed her ablutions and had her hair combed, and I was holding the mirror for her to check that all was in order when I spied the dog, still there, crouching at the foot of a pillar. Seeing it I said aloud to myself, 'Oh poor Okinamaro, what a terrible beating he got yesterday! It's so sad to think he must be dead. I wonder what he'll be reborn as next time. How dreadful he must have felt!'

At this the dog began to tremble, and tears simply poured from its eyes. How extraordinary! I realized it was indeed Okinamaro! It was pitiful to recall how he'd avoided revealing himself the night before, but at the same time the whole thing struck me as quite marvellous. I set down the mirror and said, 'So you're Okinamaro, are you?' and he threw himself on the ground, whimpering and weeping.

Her Majesty laughed with relief, and sent for Ukon and told her the story. There was a great deal of laughter over it all, and the Emperor heard and came in to see what was happening. He laughed too, and observed, 'Isn't it odd to think a dog would have such fine feelings.' His gentlewomen also heard of it and gathered round, and this time when we called the dog he got up and came.

'His poor face is all swollen!' I cried. 'I do wish I could do something for it.'

'Now you're wearing your heart on your sleeve,' everyone teased me.

Tadataka heard from the Table Room, and sent saying, 'Is it really him? I must come and have a look.'

'Oh dear no, how awful!' I declared. 'Tell him it's not Okinamaro at all!'

'He's bound to be found out sooner or later,' came Tadataka's reply. 'You can't go on hiding him forever.'

Well, in due course Okinamaro was pardoned, and everything returned to normal. Now has there ever been such a delightful and moving moment as when Okinamaro began to tremble and weep at those pitying words of mine? Humans may cry when someone speaks to them sympathetically—but a dog?

* * *

20 *The sliding panels that close off the north-east corner* of the Seiryōden, at the northern end of the aisle, are painted with scenes of rough seas, and terrifying creatures with long arms and legs.[3] We have a fine time complaining about how we hate coming face to face with them whenever we open the door from the Empress's room.

On this particular day, a large green porcelain vase had been placed at the foot of the nearby veranda railing, with a mass of absolutely gorgeous branches of flowering cherry, five feet long or more, arranged in it with the flowers spilling out over the railing. His Excellency Korechika,[4] the Grand Counsellor, arrived around noon. He was wearing a rather soft and supple cloak in the cherry-blossom combination, over deep violet gathered trousers of heavy brocade and white under-robes, and he had arranged the sleeves of his wonderfully glowing deep scarlet-purple damask cloak for display. The Emperor was present, so His Excellency placed himself on the narrow veranda outside the door to converse.

Inside the blinds, we gentlewomen sat with our cherry-blossom combination Chinese jackets worn draped loosely back from the shoulders. Our robes were a fine blend of wisteria and kerria-yellow and other seasonal combinations, the sleeves all spilling out on display below the blinds that hung from the little half-panel shutters.

Suddenly, from the direction of the Imperial Day Chamber came the loud pounding of the attendants' feet as they arrived to deliver His Majesty's meal. The sound of the cry 'Make way!' reverberating through the scene of this gloriously serene spring day was utterly delightful. Then the Chamberlain arrived to report that he had delivered the last tray and the meal was in place, and His Majesty departed by the central door.

Korechika saw His Majesty on his way along the corridor, then returned to seat himself by the vase of blossoms once more. Her Majesty now moved aside her standing curtain and came out to the edge of the threshold near him to talk, and all those present were simply overcome with the sheer splendour of the scene. At this point Korechika languidly intoned the lines from the old poem:

> 'The months and years may pass,
> but let this remain unchanging
> as Mount Mimoro . . .'[5]

3. The frightening scenes from Chinese legends painted on the panels in the emperor's private residence, the Seiryōden, served as a protective device, required because the north-east was considered unlucky in geomancy.
4. The brother of Empress Teishi, whom Shōnagon served.
5. Part of a poem from *The Man'yōshū*. Mount Mimoro, the site of an ancient Shinto shrine associated with the imperial line, figures here as an auspicious image of continuity.

—and most enchanting it was, for seeing her splendour we did indeed long for Her Majesty to continue just like this for a thousand years.

No sooner had those in charge of serving the Emperor's meal called the men to remove the trays than His Majesty returned.

Her Majesty now turned to me and asked me to grind some ink, but I was so agog at the scene before me that I could barely manage to keep the inkstick steady in its holder. Then Her Majesty proceeded to fold a piece of white paper, and said to us, 'Now I want each of you to write here the first ancient poem that springs to mind.'

I turned for help to the Grand Counsellor, who was sitting just outside. 'What on earth can I write?' I begged him, but he only pushed the paper back to me, saying, 'Quick, write something down yourself for Her Majesty. It's not a man's place to give advice here.'

Her Majesty provided us with the inkstone. 'Come on, come on,' she scolded, 'don't waste time racking your brains. Just quickly jot down any ancient poem that comes to you on the spur of the moment. Even something hackneyed will do.' I've no idea why we should have felt so daunted by the task, but we all found ourselves blushing deeply, and our minds went quite blank. Despite their protestations, some of the senior gentlewomen managed to produce two or three poems on spring themes such as blossoms and so forth, and then my turn came. I wrote down the poem:

> With the passing years
> My years grow old upon me
> yet when I see
> this lovely flower of spring
> I forget age and time.[6]

but I changed 'flower of spring' to 'your face, my lady.'

Her Majesty ran her eye over the poems, remarking, 'I just wanted to discover what was in your hearts.'

'In the time of Retired Emperor Enyū,'[7] she went on, 'His Majesty ordered the senior courtiers each to write a poem in a bound notebook, but it proved fearfully difficult, and some of them begged to be excused from the task. The Emperor reassured them that it didn't matter whether their calligraphy was skilful or otherwise, nor whether the poem was appropriate to the occasion, and finally after a great deal of trouble they all managed to produce something. Our present Regent,[8] who was Captain Third Rank at the time, wrote the following poem:

> "As the tide that swells
> in Izumo's Always Bay
> so always and always

6. Shōnagon cleverly adapts an old poem to the situation at hand. The original poem was written by an admiring father to his daughter; Shōnagon makes it into a compliment to the empress.

7. The father of the present emperor, Teishi's husband.
8. Michitaka, the father of Teishi and Korechika.

oh how my heart swells and fills
deep with love to think of you."

but he changed the last line to read "deep with trust in you, my lord," and His Majesty was full of praise for him.'

When I heard this, I felt a sudden sweat break out all over me. I do think, though, that that poem of mine isn't the sort of thing a young person could have come up with. Even people who can usually turn out a fine poem found themselves for some reason at a loss that day, and several made mistakes in their writing.

There was also the occasion when Her Majesty placed a bound book of *Kokinshū* poems in front of her, and proceeded to read out the opening lines of various poems and ask us to complete them. Why on earth did we keep stumbling over the answers, even for poems we'd engraved on our memories day in and day out? Saisho only managed about ten. Others could produce only five or six, and really, you'd think they could simply have admitted that they couldn't recall them. But no, they kept agonizing over the task. 'But we can't be so rude as to refuse point-blank to answer,' they wailed, 'when Her Majesty has been so good as to put the question to us,' which I found rather amusing.

Her Majesty then read out the complete poem for each of those that nobody had been able to answer, marking them with a bookmark, and everyone groaned, 'Oh of course I knew that one! Why am I being so stupid today?' Some of us had copied out the *Kokinshū* many times, and should really have known it all by heart.

'As I'm sure you are all aware,' Her Majesty began, 'the lady known as the Senyōden Consort, High Consort in the reign of Emperor Murakami,[9] was the daughter of the Minister of the Left, of the Smaller Palace of the First Ward. When she was still a girl, her father gave her the following advice: "First, you must study calligraphy. Next, you must determine to outshine everyone in your skill on the seven-stringed *kin*.[1] And you must also make it your study to commit to memory all the poems in the twenty volumes of the *Kokinshū*."

'Now the Emperor had learned of this, so one day, when he was kept from his usual duties by an abstinence,[2] he took a copy of the *Kokinshū* to the High Consort's quarters, and set up a standing curtain between them. She found this unusual behaviour rather odd, and when he opened a book and began asking her to recite the poem that so-and-so had written on such-and-such a date and occasion, she was intrigued to realize what he was up to—though on the other hand, she would also have been dreadfully nervous that there might be some which she would forget or misquote. He called in two or three of his gentlewomen who were well-versed in poetry, and had them extract the answers from her, and keep count of her mistakes with *go* counters. It must have been a wonderful scene to witness. I do envy them all, even the people who were merely serving on this occasion.

---

9. That is, 946–61; this story serves as an example of how admirable people were "in the old days."
1. A zitherlike instrument of the koto family,
particularly difficult to play; by Shōnagon's time it was somewhat old-fashioned.
2. A period of forced seclusion, prescribed by divination, to avoid evil influences.

'Well, he pressed her to go on answering, and she went through them making not a single mistake, though she cleverly gave just enough of each poem to show she knew it, and didn't try to complete them. His Majesty decided he would call a halt just as soon as she made a mistake, and as she went on and on he even began to get rather irritated, but they reached the tenth volume and still she hadn't made a single slip. "This has been quite futile," he finally declared, and he put a marker in the book and retired to another room to sleep. All very wonderful it was.

'When he awoke many hours later, he decided that it would never do to leave the matter hanging, and moreover it had better be done that day, since she might refresh her memory with another copy of the work if he left it till tomorrow. So he produced the remaining ten volumes, had the lamps lit and proceeded to work his way through the rest of the poems until long into the night. But she never made a single mistake.

'Meanwhile, word was sent to her father that the Emperor had returned to her quarters and that the test was continuing. The Minister flew into a panic with worry that she might fail the test; he ordered numerous sutras to be said for her,[3] while he placed himself facing the direction of the palace and spent the entire night in heartfelt prayer. Altogether a fascinating and moving story,' Her Majesty remarked in conclusion.

His Majesty too heard the tale with admiration. 'I wouldn't be able to manage more than three or four volumes myself,' he remarked.

'In the old days, even the most inconsequential people were impressive. You don't hear such stories these days, do you,' everyone agreed, and all the Empress's gentlewomen, and those who served the Emperor and were permitted to visit the Empress's quarters, gathered round and began talking. It was indeed a scene to fill the heart with ease and delight.

* * *

22   *Dispiriting things*—A dog howling in the middle of the day. The sight in spring of a trap for catching winter fish. Robes in the plum-pink combination, when it's now the third or fourth month. An ox keeper whose ox has died. A birthing hut where the baby has died. A square brazier or a hearth with no fire lit in it. A scholar whose wife has a string of daughters.[4]

A household that doesn't treat you hospitably, though you're there because of a directional taboo[5]—this is particularly dispiriting if it happens to be at one of the season changes.

A letter from the provinces that arrives without any accompanying gift. You might say the same for a letter sent from inside the capital, but this would contain plenty of things you wanted to hear about and interesting news, which makes it a very fine thing to receive in fact.

You've taken special care to send off a beautiful, carefully written letter, and you're eagerly awaiting the reply—time passes, it seems awfully long in coming,

3. That is, chanted by a priest to ensure her success.
4. Daughters would interrupt the continuous line in the family profession of scholarship, a male domain. "The plum-pink combination": the season for these colors lasted from the eleventh to the second month.
5. A ban on movement in a particular direction to avoid disturbing gods (whose movements were charted by divination), thereby temporarily halting the progress of a traveler.

and then finally your own elegantly folded or knotted letter is brought back, now horribly soiled and crumpled and with no sign remaining of the brush stroke that sealed it. 'There was no one in,' you're told, or 'They couldn't accept it on account of an abstinence.' This is dreadfully dispiriting.

A carriage is sent off to fetch someone you're sure is going to come. You wait, and finally there's the sound of the carriage returning. 'It must be her,' you think, and everyone in the house goes out to see—but the driver is already dragging the carriage back into its shed. He drops the shafts with a noisy clatter. 'What happened?' you ask. 'She's going somewhere else today, so she won't be coming,' he replies offhandedly, then he hauls out the harness and off he goes.

It's also very dispiriting when a man stops coming to visit his wife at her home. It's a great shame if he's gone off with a lady of good family who serves at court, and the wife sits moping at home, feeling ashamed and humiliated.

A little child's nurse has gone out, promising that she won't be long. You do your best to keep the child entertained and comforted, but when you send word saying 'please hurry,' back comes a message to the effect that she won't be able to return this evening. This is not just dispiriting, it's downright hateful.

It's even more dispiriting for a man when a woman fails to visit him.[6] And when the night has grown late at his house and suddenly he hears a subdued knock at the gate, and with beating heart he sends to find out who it is, only to have the servant return and announce the name of some other, boring person, well the word 'dispiriting' doesn't begin to cover it.

An exorcist priest comes to quell a spirit that has possessed a member of the household. With a confident air he hands the medium the rosary and the other paraphernalia to induce possession, and sets about his incantations in a high, strained, cicada-like chant. But there's no sign of the spirit shifting, and the medium fails to be possessed by the Guardian Deity.[7] Everyone who's gathered to pray, men and women both, begins to find this rather odd. The exorcist chants on until the change of watch two hours later, when he finally stops, exhausted. 'Get up,' he says to the medium as he retrieves the rosary. 'The spirit just won't budge,' and running his hand back from his forehead over his bald head he declares, 'Oh dear, the exorcism was quite futile.' Whereupon he lets out a yawn, leans back against some nearby object and falls asleep. It's truly awful for him when someone not especially important comes over to him, though he's feeling dreadfully sleepy, and prods him awake and forces him into a conversation.

Then there's the house of a man who has failed to receive a post in the recent Appointments List. Word had it that he was certain to get one this year, and all his former retainers, who have scattered far and wide or are now living off in the country-side somewhere, have gathered at his house in anticipation. His courtyard is crammed with the coming and going of their carriages and the tangle of their shafts; if he sets off on an excursion they all jostle to accompany him; and they eat, drink and clamour their way through the days as they wait[8]—but as the last day dawns, there's still no knock at the gate. 'How odd,'

6. It was usual for men to visit women, who would be hidden away, waiting in their residences. Only under special circumstances could the roles be reversed.

7. The help of a Guardian Deity is required to transfer the spirit that is causing the illness.
8. The appointments were announced over a three-day period.

they think, and as they sit straining to catch the sound, they hear the cries of the outriders as the court nobles emerge from the palace at the close of the Appointments ceremonies. The underlings who have spent a chilly night shivering outside the palace waiting to hear the news come trudging back dejectedly, and no one can even bring himself to ask them what happened. When some outsider inquires, 'What appointment did your master receive?' they always reply evasively, 'Oh, he's the former Governor of So-and-so.'

All those who really rely on him feel quite devastated. As morning comes, a few among the people who've been packed in together waiting begin to creep stealthily away. Those who've been many years in his service, however, can't bring themselves to leave his side so lightly. It's terribly touching to see them weaving solemnly about as they pace the room, hopefully counting on their fingers the Provincial Governorships due to come to the end of their term the following year.

There are also those times when you send someone a poem you're rather pleased with, and fail to receive one in reply. Of course there's no more to be done about it if it's to a man you care for.[9] Even so, you do lose respect for someone who doesn't produce any response to your tasteful seasonal references. It also dampens the spirit when you're leading a heady life in the swim of things and you receive some boring little old-fashioned poem that reeks of the longueurs of the writer, whose time hangs heavy on her hands.

You have a particularly fine fan intended for some ceremonial event, and you hand this precious thing to a person who you trust will treat it well, but when the day arrives it comes back to you with something quite unforeseen painted on it.

A messenger delivers a congratulatory birth gift or a farewell present, and isn't given any gift in repayment. Messengers should always be given something, such as decorative herbal balls or New Year hare-mallets,[1] even if they're only delivering some object of no permanent use. If he receives something when he's not expecting to, he will feel thoroughly pleased that he made the delivery. However, it's particularly dispiriting when he's come feeling sure he'll receive something for this errand, and his excited hopes are dashed.

A house where four or five years have passed since they brought in a husband but there's still been no joyous birth celebration is most depressing.

A couple has already produced numerous children, all now adult, and indeed of an age at which there could even be grandchildren crawling about, yet the two parents are indulging in a 'daytime nap.'[2] It's dispiriting for the children who witness this, with nowhere to turn while their parents are off behind closed doors.

The purificatory hot bath that you have to get up to take on New Year's Eve is not merely dispiriting, it's downright irritating.

Rain all day on New Year's Eve. Perhaps this is what's meant by the expression 'a single day of purificatory abstinence.'

* * *

9. Failure to respond to a love poem with a poem in reply signified rejection.
1. Protective charms given on the first hare day (day 4 of the 12-day cycle) of the year.
2. That is, daytime sex.

30 *A priest who gives a sermon should be handsome.* After all, you're most aware of the profundity of his teaching if you're gazing at his face as he speaks. If your eyes drift elsewhere you tend to forget what you've just heard, so an unattractive face has the effect of making you feel quite sinful. But I'll write no further on this subject. I may have written glibly enough about sinful matters of this sort in my younger days, but at my age the idea of sin has become quite frightening.

I must say, however, from my own sinful point of view, it seems quite uncalled-for to go around as some do, vaunting their religious piety and rushing to be the first to be seated wherever a sermon is being preached.

An ex-Chamberlain never used to take up the vanguard of imperial processions, and once he retired from the post you'd no longer see him about the palace. These days things are apparently different. The so-called 'Chamberlain fifth-ranker' is actually kept in reasonably busy service, but privately he must nevertheless miss the prestige of his former post and feel at a loss how to fill his days, so once he tries going to these places and hears a few sermons he'll no doubt develop a taste for it and start to go along on a regular basis.

You'll find him turning up there with his summer under-robe prominently displayed beneath his cloak even in baking summer weather, and the hems of his pale lavender or blue-grey gathered trousers loose and trodden. He has an abstinence tag[3] attached to his lacquered cap, and he no doubt intends to draw attention to the fact that although it's an abstinence day and he shouldn't leave the house, this doesn't apply to him since his outing is of a pious nature. He chats with the officiating priest, even goes so far as to help oversee the positioning of the ladies' carriages, and is generally completely at home in the situation. When some old crony of his whom he hasn't seen recently turns up, he's consumed with curiosity. Over he goes, and they settle down together and proceed to talk and nod and launch into interesting stories, spreading out their fans and putting them to their mouths when they laugh, groping at their ornately decorated rosaries and fiddling with them as they talk, craning to look here and there, praising and criticizing the carriages, discussing how other priests did things this way or that in other Lotus Discourses[4] and sutra dedication services they've been to, and so on and so forth—and not listening to a word of the actual sermon they're attending. Indeed they would have heard it all so often before that they'd gain nothing from it anyway.

And then there's another type. The preacher has already seated himself when after a while up rolls a carriage, accompanied by only a couple of outriders. It draws to a halt, and the passengers step out—three or four slender young men, dressed perhaps in hunting costume or in cloaks more delicately gauzy than a cicada's wing, gathered trousers and gossamer silk shifts, and accompanied by a similar number of attendants. Those already seated move themselves along a little to make way for them when they enter. They seat themselves by a pillar near the preacher's dais and set about softly rubbing their rosaries as they listen to the sermon, and the preacher, who no doubt feels rather honoured to have them there, throws himself with fresh vigour into the task of putting his message

---

3. A label attached to the hat to signify that the wearer is under abstinence taboo (see p. 1138, n. 2).

4. Formal debates by priests on the Lotus Sutra, held on special ceremonial occasions.

across. The young men, however, far from casting themselves extravagantly to the floor as they listen, instead decide to leave after a decent amount of time has passed, and as they go they throw glances in the direction of the women's carriages and comment to each other, and you'd love to know what it was they were saying. It's funny how you find yourself watching them as they depart, interestedly identifying the ones you know, and speculating on the identity of those you don't.

Some people really take things to extremes, though. If someone mentions having been to a Lotus Discourse or other such event, another will say, 'And was so and so there?' and the reply is always, 'Of course. How could he not be?' Mind you, I'm not saying one should never show up at these places. After all, even women of low standing will apparently listen to sermons with great concentration. Actually, when I first started attending sermons, I never saw women going about here and there on foot to them. Occasionally you would find women in travelling attire, elegantly made up, but they were out as part of another excursion to some temple or shrine. You didn't often hear of women attending sermons and the like in this costume, though. If the ladies who went to sermons in those days had lived long enough to see the way things are today, I can just imagine how they would have criticized and condemned.

* * *

39 *Refined and elegant things*—A girl's over-robe of white on white over pale violet-grey. The eggs of the spot-billed duck. Shaved ice with a sweet syrup, served in a shiny new metal bowl. A crystal rosary. Wisteria flowers. Snow on plum blossoms. An adorable little child eating strawberries.

40 *Insects*—The bell cricket. The cicada. Butterflies. Crickets. Grasshoppers. Water-weed shrimps. Mayflies. Fireflies.

The bagworm[5] is a very touching creature. It's a demon's child, and the mother fears it must have the same terrible nature as its parent, so she dresses it in ragged clothes and tells it to wait until she returns for it when the autumn wind blows. The poor little thing doesn't realize that its mother has deserted it, and when it hears the autumn winds begin in the eighth month, it sets up a pitiable little tremulous cry for her.

The snap-beetle is also touching. Though it's a mere insect, it has apparently dedicated itself to the Buddhist Way, for it continually touches its forehead to the ground in prayer as it walks along. It's fascinating the way you find it wandering about in astonishingly dark places, making that clicking sound.

Nothing is more unlovely than a fly, and it properly belongs in the list of infuriating things. Flies aren't big enough to make them worth bothering to hate, but just the way they settle all over everything in autumn, and their damp little feet when they land on your face . . . And I hate the way the word is used in people's names.[6]

Summer insects[7] are quite enchanting things. I love the way they'll fly round above a book when you've drawn the lamp up close to look at some tale. Ants

---

5. A small insect thought to resemble a demon and to utter cries of despair.
6. Sometimes "fly" (*hae*) was used in the names of people of the lower classes.
7. Insects such as moths or mayflies that are attracted to flames.

are rather horrible, but they're wonderfully light creatures, and it's intriguing to see one running about over the surface of the water.

* * *

68 *Things that can't be compared*—Summer and winter. Night and day. Rainy days and sunny days. Laughter and anger. Old age and youth. White and black. People you love and those you hate. The man you love and the same man once you've lost all feeling for him seem like two completely different people. Fire and water. Fat people and thin people. People with long hair and those with short hair.

The noisy commotion when crows roosting together are suddenly disturbed by something during the night. The way they tumble off their perches, and flap awkwardly about from branch to branch, squawking sleepily, makes them seem utterly different from daytime crows.

* * *

71 *Rare things*—A son-in-law who's praised by his wife's father. Likewise, a wife who's loved by her mother-in-law.

A pair of silver tweezers that can actually pull out hairs properly.

A retainer who doesn't speak ill of his master.

A person who is without a single quirk. Someone who's superior in both appearance and character, and who's remained utterly blameless throughout his long dealings with the world.

* * *

82 *Once when Her Majesty was in residence* in the Office of the Empress's Household, a Continuous Sutra Reading[8] took place in the western aisle. A scroll of the Buddha's image was set up, and of course the monks were seated as usual.

Two days into the ceremony, we heard below the veranda a queer voice saying, 'Would there be any distribution of the offerings[9] for me?' and a monk was heard to reply, 'Come come, what can you be thinking? The ceremony's not over yet.'

Wondering who this person was, I went over to have a look, and discovered the voice belonged to a nun well past her prime, dressed in horribly grimy clothes and looking like a little monkey.

'What is it she wants?' I asked.

At this, she replied herself in a carefully affected tone, 'I am a disciple of the Buddha, come to ask for the altar offerings, and these monks are refusing to give them to me.'

Her voice was remarkably bright and elegant for a beggar. What a pity someone like her should have sunk to this, I thought, yet at the same time I couldn't help feeling there was something unpleasantly pretentious and flamboyant about her, given her circumstances.

'So altar offerings are the only thing you'll eat, are they? This is wonderfully pious of you,' I remarked.

---

8. A ritual recitation that would continue through several days and nights.

9. Offerings of food on Buddhist altars were generally handed out after the ceremony.

She was reading me carefully. 'No one's saying I won't eat other things,' she said slyly. 'It's because there's nothing else that I'm asking for offerings.'

I put together some snacks and rice cakes and gave the bundle to her, whereupon she became extremely friendly, and began to chatter about all manner of things.

Some young gentlewomen then came out, and all set about questioning the woman about where she lived, and whether she had a man, and children. She produced such entertaining replies, elaborating them with jokes and suchlike, that everyone kept drawing her out with endless questions, such as whether she sang and danced, until she set about singing,

> 'Who oh who shall I sleep with tonight?
> I think I'll sleep with "Hitachi no Suke"
> for I love the silk touch of her skin in bed . . .'

with much more besides. She also sang,

> 'The peak of Man Mountain[1] stands proud in fame.
> Its scarlet tip has quite a name!'

waving her head about as she sang in a manner that was utterly grotesque. The ladies all laughed in disgust and cried, 'Away with you! Away with you!'

'Poor thing,' I said. 'What shall we give her?'

At this point Her Majesty intervened. 'You've been making the woman act in a way that I've really found very difficult to have to overhear. I simply had to block my ears. Give her this gown[2] and send her on her way immediately.'

'Here's a generous gift from Her Majesty. Your own gown's filthy, so make yourself nice and clean with this one,' we said, and tossed the gown to her. She abased herself in thanks, and then lo and behold she proceeded to drape the gown over her shoulder and perform a dance! She really was disgusting, so we all withdrew inside again and left her to it.

This apparently gave her a taste for visiting, because after this she was often to be seen wandering about drawing attention to herself. We took to calling her 'Hitachi no Suke,' after her song. Far from wearing the nice clean gown, she still went about in her filthy one, which made us wonder with considerable annoyance what she'd done with the one we gave her.

One day Ukon paid us a visit, and Her Majesty told her about the woman. 'They have tamed her and more or less installed her. She's always coming around now,' she said, and she had Kohyōe take up the tale and give an imitation of Hitachi no Suke.

'I'd love to see her,' said Ukon, laughing. 'Do show her to me. You all seem to be great fans of hers. I promise I won't entice her away from you.'

A little later, another much more refined beggar nun turned up at the palace. We called her over and questioned her in the same way, and were touched by how shamefaced and piteous she was. Her Majesty gave her a gown, and she

---

1. A mountain outside the capital, famous for its autumn colors. The "peak" here refers both to the mountain and to the tip of a penis.

2. Payments or gifts were usually made in clothing.

abased herself in thanks and retreated, overcome with tears of joy. This was all very well, but Hitachi no Suke happened to come along and catch sight of her as she was leaving. After that, Hitachi no Suke didn't show up again for a long time, and none of us would have given her a second thought I'm sure.

Towards the middle of the twelfth month there was a great fall of snow. The maids collected a large mound of it on the veranda, so then we ladies decided we should have a real snow mountain built out in the garden. We summoned the servants and set them all to work under Her Majesty's orders. The grounds-men who had come in to clean got involved as well, and together they all set about creating an absolutely towering snow mountain. Some of the senior offi-cials from the Empress's Office also gathered to give advice and enjoy the scene. The original three or four groundsmen had soon swelled to around twenty. Her Majesty even sent to ask the servants who were at home to come and help, informing them that everyone involved would receive three days extra pay, and the same amount would be deducted from all those who didn't come; some who heard this came running hastily to join in, though the message couldn't reach those whose homes were more distant.

When the construction was finally completed, the officials from the Empress's Office were summoned and each was given two large bundles of silk rolls. These they spread out on the veranda, and everyone in turn came and took a roll, bowed and tucked it into his belt, and retired. The senior courtiers, who were dressed in informal hunting costume for the job instead of their usual formal cloaks, remained behind.

'How long do you think it will last?' Her Majesty asked everyone. One guessed ten days, another suggested a little longer. Everyone gave opinions ranging over a week or two.

'What do you think?' Her Majesty then asked me.

'I think it will stay there until beyond the tenth day of the first month,' I replied.

Even Her Majesty thought this highly unlikely, and all the ladies were unan-imous in declaring that it couldn't last beyond the end of the year at the very latest.

'Oh dear,' I thought privately, 'I've probably overestimated. I suppose it can't really last as long as that. I should have said something like the first day of the new year instead'—but I decided that even if I turned out to be wrong, I should stand by what I said, and I stubbornly continued to argue my case.

On the twentieth day it rained, but there was no sign of the snow mountain melting away. All that happened was that it lost a little of its height. I was beside myself with fervent prayers to the Kannon of White Mountain[3] to pre-serve it from melting.

On the day when the snow mountain was made, the Aide of Ceremonial Tadataka came to call. I put out a cushion for him, and during our talk he remarked, 'You know, there's not a place in the palace that hasn't built a snow mountain today. His Majesty has ordered one made in his garden, and they're

3. A sacred mountain famous for its perpetual snow. On its summit was an important shrine to Kannon, the Bodhisattva of Mercy who hears people in need.

busy making them in the Crown Prince's residence and in the Kōkiden and Kyōgokudono[4] as well.'

I then had someone nearby convey to him the following poem.

> Our singular snow mountain
> we thought was so uniquely ours
> has multiplied abroad
> and become merely commonplace
> as the common snow that falls.

He sat tilting his head admiringly over it for a while, then he finally said, 'It would be merely flippant of me to attempt to sully this marvellous poem with one in response. I shall simply tell the tale of it to everyone when we're gathered before His Majesty,' and he rose and departed. I must say this diffidence struck me as rather odd, in someone with his reputation for being a great poetry-lover.

When I told Her Majesty, she remarked, 'He must certainly have been deeply impressed with it.'

As the month drew to a close, the snow mountain seemed to have shrunk a little, but it still remained very high. One day around midday we'd gone out to sit on the veranda, when Hitachi no Suke suddenly appeared again.

'Why are you back?' we asked. 'We haven't seen you here for ages.'

'Well, the fact is I met with a misfortune,' she replied.

'What was it?' we asked.

'I shall tell you my thoughts at the time in question,' she said, and then she proceeded to recite, in ponderously drawn-out tones,

> 'Alas I am awash
> with envy at the gifts whose burden
> weights her till she limps—
> who is that "deep-sea fisher girl"
> to whom so many things are given?'

and with that she gave a nasty laugh. When no one deigned to look in her direction, she clambered on to the snow mountain and walked about for some time before she finally left.

After she had gone we sent word to Ukon telling her what had happened, and she made us laugh all over again when she replied, 'Why didn't you get someone to accompany her and bring her over here? What a shame! She must have climbed the snow mountain and walked round like that because you were ignoring her.'

The year ended without any change to our snow mountain. On the night of the first day of the new year, there was a great fall of snow.

Excellent! I thought. There'll be a fresh pile of snow for the mountain—but then Her Majesty decided that this wasn't fair. 'We must brush off the new snow and leave the original heap as it was,' she declared.

4. The home of Teishi's rival Shōshi, another wife of Emperor Ichijō; one of her ladies-in-waiting was Murasaki Shikibu, the author of *The Tale of Genji*.

Next morning when I went to my room very early, the chief retainer of the Office of the Empress's Household arrived, shivering with cold. On the sleeve of his night-watch cloak, which was a deep, almost cirron-leaf green, he held something wrapped in green paper, attached to a sprig of pine needles.

'Who is this from?' I inquired, and when he replied that it came from the Kamo High Priestess, I was filled with sudden delighted awe, and took it and carried it straight back to Her Majesty.

Her Majesty was still asleep when I arrived, and in order to get in I tugged a go-board table over to the lattice shutter facing her curtained dais, and stood on it while I struggled to raise the shutter. It was extremely heavy, and because I was only lifting one end of it, it grated against the next one, which woke Her Majesty.

'Why on earth are you doing that?' she inquired.

'A message from the Kamo High Priestess has arrived,' I replied. 'I simply had to get the shutter open so you would have it as early as possible.'

'Well, this certainly is early,' she said, getting up. She opened the package, and found two hare-mallets, the heads wrapped in imitation of hare-wands, decorated prettily with sprigs of mountain orange, creeping fern and mountain sedge. But there was no letter.

'I can't believe there would be no message,' said Her Majesty, searching, and then she discovered on one of the little pieces of paper that wrapped the mallet heads the following poem.

> When I went searching
> the mountain for the echoing ring
> of the woodsman's axe
> I found the tree he cut was for
> the festive hare-wands of this day.[5]

A delightful poem, and delightful too was the scene of Her Majesty composing her reply. In all her letters and replies to the High Priestess, you could see just how much trouble she took from the number of problems she had with her writing. To the man who had brought the message she gave a white-weave shift, and another of maroon which was I think in the plum combination, and it was lovely to see him making his way back through the snowy landscape with the robes over his shoulder. It's only a pity that I never discovered what Her Majesty wrote in reply.

As for the snow mountain, it showed no sign of melting away but continued to stand there, just as if it really was Koshi's famous snowy mountain. It now looked quite black with dirt, and was not a sight to please the eye, but I nevertheless felt elated at the thought of being proved right, and prayed that it could somehow be made to survive until the middle of the month. Everyone declared that it couldn't last beyond the end of the first week, and we were all waiting anxiously to witness the final outcome, when it was suddenly decided on the third day that Her Majesty would return to the imperial palace. I was terribly disappointed at the thought that I'd have to leave without ever knowing the moment of my mountain's final end, and others also said it was a great shame to

---

5. The first hare day of the year, when decorated sticks and poles were presented to members of the court and hung in rooms to ward off evil spirits.

have to leave now. Her Majesty agreed, and indeed I'd very much wanted her to witness that my guess had been right. But we had to leave and that was that.

There was great upheaval for the move, with Her Majesty's effects and all the other things being carried out, and in the midst of this I managed to call over to the veranda one of the gardeners who was living under a lean-to roof he had set up against the garden wall, and have a confidential word with him. 'You must take great care of this snow mountain, and make sure no children climb on it and destroy it. Keep a firm watch on it until the fifteenth. If it lasts till then, Her Majesty intends to reward you with a special gift, and you'll get high praise from me personally as well,' I said, and to persuade him further I heaped on him various leftovers, fruit and so on, though this would have enraged the kitchen maids and servants, who disliked him.

All this made him beam with pleasure. 'That's very easily done,' he assured me. 'I'll guard it carefully. The children will be sure to try and climb it.'

'You must forbid it,' I warned him, 'and if there's anyone who won't obey then let me know.'

I accompanied Her Majesty on her move to the palace, and stayed there until the seventh day, when I went home.

I was so anxious about my snow mountain while I was at the palace that I was constantly sending servants of various sorts, from the toilet cleaner to the head housekeeper, to keep the gardener up to the mark. On the seventh day I even sent along some of the leftovers from the Festival of Young Herbs feast, and everyone laughed at the tale of how reverently he'd received them.

Once I was back home the snow mountain continued to obsess me, and the first thing I did every morning was send someone over, just to keep him reminded of how very important it was. On the tenth day I was delighted to hear that enough still remained to last until the fifteenth. Day and night my constant stream of messengers continued, but then on the night of the thirteenth there was a terrific downpour of rain. I was beside myself, convinced that this would finally finish off my mountain. All that night I stayed up, lamenting that it couldn't possibly last another day or two. Those around me laughed and declared that I really had lost my mind. When one of our party left I leapt up and tried to rouse the servants, and flew into a rage when they refused to get up, but finally one emerged and I sent her off to bring a report.

'It's down to the size of a round cushion,' she reported. 'The gardener has looked after it most assiduously, and he hasn't let the children near it. He says it should last till tomorrow morning, and he's looking forward to his reward.' I was absolutely thrilled. I could hardly wait till the next day, when I decided I would compose a suitable poem and send it to Her Majesty with a container full of the snow. The anticipation was becoming quite unbearable.

The next morning I got up while it was still dark. I gave one of the servants a box and sent her off with the order to choose the whitest of the snow to put in it, and be careful to scrape away any that was dirty. But she was no sooner gone than back she came, dangling the empty container, to report that the last of the snow mountain had already disappeared. I was devastated. The clever poem that I had laboured and groaned over, and that I'd looked forward to being on everyone's lips, was to my horror suddenly quite worthless.

'How on earth could this have happened?' I said miserably. 'There was all that snow still there yesterday, and it's disappeared overnight!'

'The gardener was wringing his hands in despair,' replied the maid. 'He said that it was there until late last night, and he'd been so looking forward to getting his reward.'

In the midst of all the fuss, word arrived from Her Majesty, inquiring whether there was any snow left today. Thoroughly mortified, I replied, 'Please tell Her Majesty that I consider it a great victory that it was still there until yesterday evening, despite the fact that everyone predicted it couldn't last beyond the end of the year. But after all, my prediction would have been altogether too impressive if the snow had remained until the very day I guessed. During the night some spiteful person must have destroyed the last of it.'

This was the first subject I raised in Her Majesty's presence when I went back to the palace on the twentieth. I related to her how appalled I'd been to see the maid return with the empty container dangling from her hand—like the wandering performer's act with the empty lid, when he came on announcing 'the Buddha's thrown his body off Snow Mountain and all that's left is his hat'[6]—and I went on to explain how I'd planned to make a miniature snow mountain in the lid and send a poem with it, written exquisitely on white paper. Her Majesty laughed a great deal at my story, as did everyone else present.

'I fear I've committed a grave sin by destroying something you had so set your heart on,' Her Majesty then told me. 'To tell the truth, on the night of the fourteenth I sent some retainers there to remove it. When I read your message, I thought you were wonderfully clever to have guessed something like this had happened.'

The fellow apparently emerged wringing his hands and pleading, but he was told that it was an order from the Empress, and was forbidden to tell anyone from my place about it, on pain of having his house destroyed. They threw all the snow away near the south wall of the Left Palace Guards Office, and I gather they reported that it was packed down very hard, and there was a great deal of it. Her Majesty admitted that it would actually have lasted through even as far as the twentieth, and would no doubt have received some added snow from the first snowfall of the spring, too. Then she went on to relate that His Majesty had also heard about it, and had remarked to the senior courtiers that a great deal of thought had obviously gone into this contest of ours. 'Well then,' she said in conclusion, 'tell us the poem you'd prepared. After all, I've made my confession, and as you can see, you actually won your bet.'

The ladies added their voices to Her Majesty's request, but I replied sulkily, 'I don't see why I should be expected to turn around and tell you my poem, after the depressing things I've just heard'—and in truth I was by this time feeling thoroughly miserable.

At this point His Majesty arrived, and he said to me teasingly, 'I've always believed you were a favourite with Her Majesty, but I must say this has made me wonder.' This only served to depress me even more deeply, and by now I was close to tears.

'Oh dear, oh dear,' I moaned, 'life's so hard! And to think how overjoyed I was, too, about the snow that fell after we'd built the mountain, and then Her Majesty decided it shouldn't count, and ordered it removed.'

---

6. A comic image of absence, apparently referring to an act based on the well-known story that the Buddha threw himself off Snow Mountain in exchange for enlightenment.

Then His Majesty smiled and remarked, 'I suppose she just didn't want to see you win.'

* * *

104 *Things that are distressing to see*—Someone wearing a robe with the back seam hitched over to one side, or with the collar falling back to reveal the nape of the neck.

A woman who emerges with a child slung on her back to greet a special visitor.

A priest acting as Yin-Yang master, who conducts his purification ceremony with that little white paper cap[7] stuck on his forehead.

I do hate the sight of some swarthy, slovenly-looking woman with a hairpiece, lying about in broad daylight with a scrawny man with hair sprouting from his face. What kind of a picture do they think they make, lounging there for all to see? Of course this is not to say they should stay sitting upright all night for fear people will find them disgusting—no one can see them when it's dark, and besides, everyone else indulges in the same thing at night. The decent thing to do is to get up early once it's morning. No doubt it doesn't look quite as bad for people of high station to take daytime naps in summer, but anyone less than attractive will emerge from a nap with a face all greasy and bloated with sleep, and sometimes even a squashed cheek. How dreary for two such people to have to look each other in the face when they get up!

It's most distressing to see someone thin and swarthy dressed in a see-through gossamer-silk shift.

* * *

144 *Endearingly lovely things*—A baby's face painted on a gourd. A sparrow coming fluttering down to the nest when her babies are cheeping for her.

A little child of two or three is crawling rapidly along when his keen eye suddenly notices some tiny worthless thing lying nearby. He picks it up in his pretty little fingers, and shows it to the adults. This is very endearing to see. It's also endearing when a child with a shoulder-length 'nun's cut' hairstyle[8] that's falling into her eyes doesn't brush it away but instead tilts her head to tip it aside as she examines something.

A very young son of a noble family walking about dressed up in ceremonial costume. An enchanting little child who falls asleep in your arms while you're holding and playing with it is terribly endearing.

Things children use in doll play. A tiny lotus leaf that's been picked from a pond. A tiny *aoi*[9] leaf. In fact, absolutely anything that's tiny is endearing.

A very white, plump child of around two, who comes crawling out wearing a lavender silk-gauze robe with the sleeves hitched back, or a child walking about in a short robe that looks more long sleeves than robe. All these are endearing. And it's very endearing when a boy of eight or ten reads something aloud in his childish voice.

It's also enchanting to see a pretty little white chick, its lanky legs looking like legs poking out from under a short robe, cheeping loudly as it runs and pauses

7. A Buddhist priest should not wear the white paper cap of a Yin-Yang diviner in a Shintō ceremony.

8. That is, with long bangs, resembling the hair of women who shaved the crown of their head in a tonsure.

9. A plant used in Japanese heraldry.

here and there around someone's feet. Likewise, all scenes of chicks running about with the mother hen. The eggs of a spot-billed duck. A green-glass pot.

* * *

257 *Things that give you pleasure*—You've read the first volume of a tale you hadn't come across before, and are longing to go on with it—then you find the other volume. The rest of it can sometimes turn out to be disappointing, however.

Piecing back together a letter that someone has torn up and thrown away, and finding that you can read line after line of it.

It's extremely pleasing when you've had a puzzling dream which fills you with fear at what it may portend, and then you have it interpreted and it turns out to be quite harmless.

It's also wonderfully pleasing when you're in a large company of people in the presence of someone great, and she's talking, either about something in the past or on a matter she's only just heard about, some topic of the moment, and as she speaks it's you she singles out to look at.

Then there's the pleasing moment when you've heard that someone who matters a lot to you and who's far from you—perhaps in some distant place, or even simply elsewhere in the capital—has been taken ill, and you're worrying and wringing your hands over the uncertainty, when news arrives that the illness has taken a turn for the better.

Someone you love is praised by others, and some high-ranking person comments that his talents are 'not inconsiderable.'

When a poem that you've composed for some event, or in an exchange of poems, is talked of by everyone and noted down when they hear it. This hasn't yet happened to me personally, but I can imagine how it would feel.

It's very pleasing when someone you don't know well mentions an old poem or story that you haven't heard of, and then it comes up again in conversation with someone else. If you come across it later in something you're reading, there's the delightful moment when you cry, 'Oh is *that* where it comes from!', and you enjoy recalling the person's mention of it.

Managing to lay hands on some Michinoku or any good quality paper.

You feel very pleased with yourself when a person who rather overawes you asks you to supply the beginning or end of some bit of poem they quote, and you suddenly recall it. It so often happens that as soon as anyone asks you, even something you know perfectly well goes clean out of your head.

Finding something you need in a hurry.

How could you fail to feel pleased when you win at a matching game,[1] or some other kind of competition?

Managing to get the better of someone who's full of themselves and overconfident. This is even more pleasing if it's a man, rather than one of your own circle of gentlewomen. It's fun to be constantly on your guard because you're expecting him to try to get even with you, and it's also fun to have been fooled into relaxing your guard over time, as he continues to act quite unconcerned and pretend nothing's happened.

When someone you don't like meets with some misfortune, you're pleased even though you know this is wicked of you.

---

1. A popular diversion in which participants competed in matching objects such as shells, flowers, or paintings.

You've sent out your robes to be freshly glossed[2] for some event, and are holding your breath to see how they come out, when they're delivered looking absolutely beautiful. A comb that's come up delightfully with polishing is also pleasing. There are a lot of other things of this sort too.

It's very pleasing when you've finally recovered from a nasty illness that's plagued you day in, day out for months. This is even more the case when it's not your own illness but that of someone you love.

And it's wonderfully pleasing when a crowd of people are packed into the room in Her Majesty's presence, and she suddenly spies someone who's only just arrived at court, sitting rather withdrawn by a distant pillar, and beckons her over, whereupon everyone makes way and the girl is brought up and ensconced very close to Her Majesty.

* * *

529 *I have written in this book* things I have seen and thought, in the long idle hours spent at home, without ever dreaming that others would see it. Fearing that some of my foolish remarks could well strike others as excessive and objectionable, I did my best to keep it secret, but despite all my intentions I'm afraid it has come to light.

Palace Minister Korechika one day presented to the Empress a bundle of paper. 'What do you think we could write on this?' Her Majesty inquired. 'They are copying *Records of the Historian*[3] over at His Majesty's court.'

'This should be a "pillow,"[4] then,' I suggested.

'Very well, it's yours,' declared Her Majesty, and she handed it over to me.

I set to work with this boundless pile of paper to fill it to the last sheet with all manner of odd things, so no doubt there's much in these pages that makes no sense.

Overall, I have chosen to write about the things that delight, or that people find impressive, including poems as well as things such as trees, plants, birds, insects and so forth, and for this reason people may criticize it for not living up to expectations and only going to prove the limits of my own sensibility. But after all, I merely wrote for my personal amusement things that I myself have thought and felt, and I never intended that it should be placed alongside other books and judged on a par with them. I'm utterly perplexed to hear that people who've read my work have said it makes them feel humble in the face of it. Well, there you are, you can judge just how unimpressive someone is if they dislike things that most people like, and praise things that others condemn. Anyway, it does upset me that people have seen these pages.

When Captain of the Left Tsunefusa was still Governor of Ise, he came to visit me while I was back at home, and my book disconcertingly happened to be on the mat from the nearby corner that was put out for him. I scrambled to try and retrieve it, but he carried it off with him, and kept it for a very long time before returning it.

That seems to have been the moment when this book first became known—or so it is written.

2. Silk was made shiny by being beaten on special blocks.
3. The *Historical Records* by Sima Qian.
4. This concluding section explains the ori-

gins of *The Pillow Book* and of its title. A "pillow" might simply be a notebook for daily jottings kept at hand in some private place.

MURASAKI SHIKIBU

ca. 978–ca. 1014

The Tale of Genji is the undisputed masterpiece of Japanese prose and often considered the first great novel in the history of world literature. That it was written by an eleventh-century court lady is even more extraordinary. Virginia Woolf, who reviewed its first complete English translation—the masterful rendering by Arthur Waley—in 1925, responded to Murasaki Shikibu with the lonely empathy of an early twentieth-century woman author: "There was Sappho and a little group of women all writing poetry on a Greek island six hundred years before the birth of Christ. They fall silent. Then about the year 1000 we find a certain court lady, the Lady Murasaki, writing a very long and beautiful novel in Japan." Although originally written for a narrow circle of court aristocrats in Kyoto, *The Tale of Genji* had unparalleled success in engaging generations of passionate readers and it is now uniquely representative of Japanese literature. Vast in scale and peopled by hundreds of characters, this thousand-page tale depicts the lives and loves of a former prince—Genji—who dies two-thirds through the book, and the lives and loves of his descendants. On a deeper level, *The Tale of Genji* is about the human ability to be touched by other people and by the outside world, about the tantalizing line between love and lust, and about the vulnerability of women in a male-dominated world. It celebrates the power of poetry, music, and dance to shape society and give depth to human life. Revered for its psychological insight, it captures a world that, however remote from our own, has always retained the sharp authenticity of real life. At its most basic, it chronicles the struggle with the most fundamental of human experiences: love, art, and death.

LIFE AND TIMES

The actual name of the author of *The Tale of Genji* is unknown. It was common at the time to name women after the office held by a male relative. "Shikibu" refers to the appointment her father held at the "Ministry of Ceremonial." The nickname "Murasaki" ("lavender," "purple") is based either on the heroine Murasaki in *The Tale of Genji* or on the color of wisteria, the emblematic flower of her clan. Murasaki Shikibu's ancestors had belonged to a branch of the Fujiwara ("wisteria fields") clan, which had managed since the tenth century to dominate the throne by ruling as regents on behalf of young emperors and marrying their daughters into the imperial family. Despite Murasaki's distinguished ancestry, her family eventually declined to the level of provincial governors. Her father had a mediocre career in the court administration, although he was known as a poet and scholar of Chinese literature. Through him Murasaki got a glimpse of life outside the Heian capital of Kyoto, when in her teens she accompanied him for a couple of years on one of his appointments in the provinces. After returning to the capital, Murasaki was briefly married to the much older Fujiwara no Nobutaka, a middle-ranking aristocrat. When he died in 1001, Murasaki was in her early twenties, now a widow with a two-year-old daughter. Murasaki probably started writing *The Tale of Genji* after the death of her husband. These early chapters won her a growing reputation and led to an invitation from Empress Shōshi around 1006 to serve as lady-in-waiting at the imperial court, where she remained until her death around 1014.

The flourishing of female literature during this time was in no small part a result of the efforts of the Fujiwara regents to fill the ranks of their daughters' entourage with the most talented and educated women. Shōshi was one of the consorts of Emperor Ichijō, and she was far more successful than her rival, Empress Teishi, whom **Sei Shōnagon**, the author of *The Pillow Book*, served. She bore Ichijō two emperors and her fortunes reflected the power of her father, the regent Fujiwara no Michinaga. Employment as ladies-in-waiting gave Heian women writers the financial support and leisure to produce literature that commanded the attention of society in the capital.

Murasaki had broad learning in vernacular literature—*waka* poetry, women's diaries, and tales—but also acquired a profound understanding of the Chinese Classics and Chinese poetry. While aristocratic women at the time were often knowledgeable in Chinese literature, they did not produce Chinese-style texts in the authoritative idiom of the male court bureaucracy and the Buddhist clergy, writing instead in the vernacular language. In her diary Murasaki confesses:

> When my brother, the Secretary at the Ministry of Ceremonial, was young and studied the Chinese classics, I used to listen to him and became unusually good at understanding those passages which he found too difficult to grasp. My father, a most learned man, was always lamenting this fact: "Just my luck!" he would say. "What a pity that she was not born a man!"

A father's admiration for his daughter's academic brilliance cannot conceal the fact that in Heian society, Chinese learning was truly valuable only for men.

In Heian Japan men and women were strictly segregated and women's lives were extremely circumscribed. The role of a lady was to marry and bear children; and if she came from a suitably good family, she was apt to find herself a pawn in the marriage politics of the imperial court. A noblewoman's days were spent behind curtains and screens, hidden from the world (or from the male world). A man's first marriage often took place when he was still a boy of twelve or thirteen; women were even a year or two younger. Because of the ages of the spouses and the likelihood of the first marriage in particular being a political and economic arrangement, both husband and wife tended eventually to seek love elsewhere, although only men could have multiple marriage partners. The purpose of marriage was procreation, continuation of the family line, and the creation of advantageous alliances with other families. Ordinarily a man's several wives lived in different establishments. His first wife would typically remain in her parents' house. Initially, the young husband might take up residence there or merely visit. Sometimes her parents would furnish the newlyweds with a house of their own, though doing so was less common when the couple married at a young age and the maternal grandparents would be expected to assume many of the child-rearing duties. If in time a man took a second or third wife, he would usually live with his first (and main) wife and commute between the separate residences. It was in this world of gender asymmetries that Heian women's literature thrived. At the same time, Heian women used the status they had as female authors to voice how women suffered from their dependence on their husbands, lovers, and patrons.

An early sixteenth-century illustrated calligraphic excerpt from chapter 17, "The picture contest," of *The Tale of Genji*. The artwork is attributed to Reizei Tamehiro.

THE TALE OF GENJI

Although Genji's women play an important role in the tale, it is named after its male protagonist. He is the son of the reigning emperor and his beloved but low-ranking consort, Kiritsubo ("Paulownia Pavilion"). Her favor with the emperor makes her a target of vicious rivalry among the emperor's higher-ranking women, such as the Kokiden Consort, his principal wife. Genji's mother dies in despair when he is in his third year, and his father is eventually forced to remove him from the imperial line to protect him from the ill will of his other consorts. He makes the boy a commoner, bestowing the family name "Genji" on him. As Genji grows up his brilliance elicits sighs of admiration wherever he appears, and he is soon being called "the Radiant Prince." The emperor dotes on his remarkable son, who reminds him all the more painfully of his former favorite consort. He eventually finds solace in the young Fujitsubo, daughter of a previous emperor, who resembles Kiritsubo but is of highest rank.

With even more determination than his father, Genji embarks on a search for women who can replace the mother he barely remembers. His fatal attraction to Fujitsubo leads to one of his greatest transgressions. Fujitsubo gives birth to a son who later becomes emperor and whom everybody believes to be the son of Genji's father. Later, Fujitsubo's niece Murasaki becomes Genji's great love. Sometimes Genji's escapades with women of very high rank lead to disaster: after his affair with Oborozukiyo, who is the younger sister of his father's principal wife, the Kokiden consort (and thus his mortal enemy), he is forced into exile to the rustic countryside. Sometimes lack of attention, rather than sexual transgression, brings about disaster: Genji's failure to respond to the jealous passion of the lady at Rokujō, widow of a former crown prince, leads inexorably to the death of some of the most important women in his life.

Genji is charismatic, irresistible, and tantalizingly flawed. Charming and handsome, brilliant and ardent, rakish but faithful in his own way (unlike other men, he never abandons any woman he has loved), he is an extraordinary literary figure. Readers may hate Genji or adore him, but we can hardly deny that his creator has fashioned a character who is both larger than life and believably human.

The fifty-four-chapter tale falls broadly into three parts. The first thirty-three chapters describe Genji's career from his birth through his exile and his eventual glorious return to the capital. They focus on the various women with whom he becomes involved in his younger years. Chapters 34 through 41 treat the darker years of Genji's life, concluding with the death of Murasaki and Genji's own death. The remaining thirteen chapters, not featured here, move away from the elegant capital to the countryside. Lacking the radiance of Genji's presence, the world is populated with compromised protagonists and darker entanglements with life's sufferings.

Though *The Tale of Genji* is a coherent whole, it can also be appreciated as a collection of interrelated episodes revolving around Genji, his women, and their descendants, in part because of how the work was composed. Since Murasaki wrote it over a span of a dozen years, probably starting with what eventually became chapter 5 ("Little Purple Gromwell," included here), the tale developed in thematic sequences. It first circulated in various shorter installments—single chapters or sequences—among Kyoto's court aristocracy. The sequences show how Murasaki's protagonists, interests, and narrative techniques evolved over time. The "Broom Cypress Sequence," for

example, which includes chapters 2, 4, 6, and sequels in chapters 15 and 16, was apparently inserted later. Whereas the core chapters of the tale's first part show Genji dangerously in love with high-ranking women who were close to the emperor, in the "Broom Cypress Sequence" he pursues women of the middle and lower aristocracy. The key prelude to Genji's later conquests occurs in chapter 2 ("Broom Cypress," included here), when the seventeen-year-old Genji and his friends while away a rainy night in his quarters at the palace debating what makes the perfect woman. In the process, the young men trade stories of their experiences with women. Although Genji dozes off now and then, he takes away the lessons from that night and applies them to his pursuit of women in the following chapters of the sequence.

In *The Tale of Genji* Murasaki sometimes relied on conventions from earlier tales, so-called *monogatari*. A typical plot element was an illustrious aristocrat's discovery of a heroine in humble circumstances. This describes the situation of Genji's mother, and also many of Genji's exploits. Liaisons between high-ranking men and humble women were far more popular in literary romances than in Heian reality. A real-life Genji would probably never have married somebody like the character Murasaki, orphaned and without appropriate family background. But in romantic tales, the total infatuation of an aristocrat with a lower-ranking woman was an expression of passion and emotional depth; for female readers it perhaps even inspired hope that they might find salvation and social mobility through the power of romantic love. Because of the social gap between Genji and his lovers, the tale's low-ranking heroines spend considerable energy agonizing about their lowly position and trying to cope with social marginalization. Another typical plot element of earlier tales is the pursuit of love in unexpected or forbidden places. There is no lack of such episodes in Genji's career; he strongly resembles the real-life Ariwara no Narihira (825–880), the epitome of a romantic lover and hero of the earlier *monogatari The Tales of Ise.*

The Tale of Genji displays the remarkable blend of Murasaki's talents. She was a gifted poet, inserting several hundred poems in the tale. Where modern readers might expect Genji and his lovers to exchange love letters in prose, Murasaki has them communicate through elaborate poems. Indeed, most of the protagonists are named after imagery from those poems, and until the early modern period readers studied *The Tale of Genji* to enhance their skills in poetry composition. Also, Murasaki was a perceptive reader of women's confessional diaries and a masterful prose stylist, relying on the nuanced expression of interiority developed by women diarists before her for the intimate psychological portrayal of *The Tale of Genji*'s fictional protagonists. Lastly, her expertise in Chinese literature inspired her to enrich recurring motifs with resonant references to Chinese poetry. In the first chapter she evokes "**The Song of Lasting Regret**" by the Tang poet **Bo Juyi**, which tells of the tragic love between a Chinese emperor and a low-ranking concubine, as a poignant analogy to the fate of Genji's mother; like a motif in music, Bo Juyi's gripping ballad keeps reappearing throughout the novel in various guises.

In its day *The Tale of Genji* was just another vernacular tale that, in the estimation of the learned elite, stood far below the Chinese-style writing by Heian men. Chinese learning—a cov-

eted quality for a male aristocrat—was a dubious asset for a court lady. In her diary Murasaki tells how angry she was when somebody teased her for her Chinese learning and gave her the nickname "Our Lady of the Chronicles." But in truth this title should have pleased her: in "Fireflies" (chapter 25, included here) Genji discusses the worth of romantic tales with Tamakazura, his best friend's daughter, and she inspires him to argue that fiction is in some way more truthful than official Chinese-style histories such as the venerable *Chronicles of Japan*: vernacular tales tell the real stories that are left out of the Chinese-style histories.

Whether meant as a playful jibe or a serious polemical claim, Murasaki's bold comparison of popular vernacular tales to canonical Chinese-style histories facilitated the canonization of *The Tale of Genji* in later ages. *The Tale of Genji* became the subject of erudite scholastic commentaries; it inspired screen paintings and illustrated hand scrolls, Noh and puppet plays, poetry handbooks, parodies, and, more recently, woodblock prints, films, and manga (comic book) versions. This "Genji cult" is in part a result of the late nineteenth-century promotion of *The Tale of Genji* from the status of a brilliant masterpiece to that of a modern national classic said to encapsulate Japanese sensibility. But leaving politics aside, one of the many reasons for *The Tale of Genji*'s timeless appeal is that it is a grand meditation on the emotional and psychological dynamics of love. It seduces the reader with its extensive depictions of courtship and passion, but its ultimate theme is the deeper longing to find a common language through which to connect with another person.

MAIN CHARACTERS IN *THE TALE OF GENJI*

AKASHI LADY, *daughter of the Akashi Novice; meets Genji during his exile and bears him a daughter who eventually becomes empress*

AKASHI NOVITIATE, *former governor of Harima, father of the Akashi Lady*

ASSISTANT HANDMAID, *Genji's aged and coquettish admirer*

BISHOP, *Murasaki's great-uncle, a distinguished Buddhist cleric*

EMPEROR SUZAKU, *Genji's elder half brother, son of the Kokiden Consort; succeeds the Kiritsubo Emperor on the throne*

EMPEROR REIZEI, *son of Genji and Fujitsubo, but believed to be the son of Genji's father; succeeds Suzaku as emperor*

FUJITSUBO, *daughter of an earlier emperor; Genji's father's empress with whom Genji has a son, the later Emperor Reizei*

GENJI'S WIFE, *daughter of the Minister of the Left; marries Genji at age 16, when Genji is 12*

KIRITSUBO EMPEROR, *Genji's father*

KOKIDEN CONSORT, *daughter of the Minister of the Right; mother of Emperor Suzaku and archenemy of Genji*

KOREMITSU, *Genji's foster brother and confidant*

LADY AT ROKUJŌ, *daughter of a Minister and widow of a deceased Heir Apparent; Genji's neglect of her has fatal consequences*

MINISTER OF THE LEFT, *father of Genji's wife and of Tō no Chūjō, Genji's friend*

MINISTER OF THE RIGHT, *father of the Kokiden Consort and Oborozukiyo*

MURASAKI, *unrecognized daughter of Prince Hyōbu and niece of Fujitsubo; raised by Genji, who later marries her*

OBOROZUKIYO, *daughter of the Minister of the Right and younger sister of Kokiden; enters the service of Suzaku; Genji's affair with her leads to his exile*

PRINCE HYŌBU, *Fujitsubo's elder brother, Murasaki's father*

TAMAKAZURA, *daughter of Tō no Chūjō by a low-ranking mistress; discovered by Genji, who installs her into his mansion and passes her off as his own daughter*

TŌ NO CHŪJŌ, *son of the Minister of the Left and brother of Aoi; his name is the title of a post he occupies*

From The Tale of Genji[1]

FROM CHAPTER I

Kiritsubo

The Lady of the Paulownia-Courtyard Chambers

In whose reign was it that a woman of rather undistinguished lineage captured the heart of the Emperor and enjoyed his favor above all the other imperial wives and concubines? From the very moment she began serving His Majesty certain ladies at the court whose high noble status gave them a sense of vain entitlement despised and reviled her as an unworthy upstart. The situation was

1. Translated by Dennis Washburn. Except as indicated, all notes are his. Murasaki Shikibu often alludes directly to works of poetry (both Chinese and Japanese), fiction, history, and court records. Most of these allusions are to Japanese poems compiled in imperial anthologies during the 10th and early 11th centuries. Notes throughout this selection cite the source of only some of these allusions.

even more vexing for ladies of lower rank, since they knew His Majesty would never bestow such affectionate attention on them. As a result, the mere presence of the woman at morning rites or evening ceremonies seemed to provoke hostile reactions among her rivals; and the anxiety she suffered as a consequence of these ever-increasing displays of jealousy was such a heavy burden that gradually her health began to fail.

His Majesty could see how forlorn she was, how often she returned to her family home. He felt sorry for her and wanted to help; and though he could scarcely afford to ignore the admonitions of his advisers, his behavior eventually became the subject of palace gossip. Ranking courtiers and attendants found it difficult to stand by and observe the troubling situation, which they viewed as deplorable. They were fully aware that a similarly ill-fated romance had thrown the Chinese state into chaos.[2] Feelings of concern and consternation gradually spread through the court, since it appeared that nothing could be done. Many considered the relationship scandalous, so much so that some openly referred to the example of the Prized Consort Yang. The only thing that made it possible for the woman to continue to serve was the Emperor's gracious devotion.

The woman's father had risen to the third rank as a Major Counselor before he died. Her mother, the principal wife of her father, was a woman of old-fashioned upbringing and character who was well trained in the customs and rituals of the court. Thus, the reputation of her family was in no way inferior and did not suffer by comparison with the brilliance of the highest nobility. Unfortunately, her family had no patrons who could provide political support, and after her father's death she had no one she could trust. She thus found herself at the mercy of events and with uncertain prospects.

Was she not, then, bound to the Emperor by some deep love from a previous life? For in spite of her travails, she eventually bore him a prince—a pure radiant gem like nothing of this world. Following the child's birth His Majesty had to wait impatiently, wondering when he would finally be allowed to see the boy. As soon as it could be ritually sanctioned, he had the infant brought from the home of the woman's mother, where the birth had taken place,[3] and the instant he gazed on the child's countenance he recognized a rare beauty.

Now as it so happened the Crown Prince[4] had been born three years earlier to the Kokiden Consort, who was the daughter of the Minister of the Right. As the unquestioned heir to the throne the boy had many supporters and the courtiers all treated him with the utmost respect and deference. He was, however, no match for the radiant beauty of the newborn prince; and even though the Emperor was bound to acknowledge the higher status of his older son and to favor him in public, in private he could not resist treating the younger prince as his favorite and lavishing attention upon him.

2. The courtiers are referring to "Song of Lasting Regret" by the Tang Dynasty poet Bai [Bo] Juyi (772–846). The poem recounts the infatuation of the Emperor Xuanzong (685–762) with Yang Guifei, which caused him to neglect affairs of state. Due to a rebellion he was forced to execute his lover.

3. It was customary for births to take place outside the palace in order to avoid defilement. A period of confinement for ritual purification usually followed a birth, which is why the Emperor has to wait to see his son.

4. Genji's half brother Suzaku [editors' note].

The mother of the newborn prince did not come from a family of the highest rank, but neither was she of such low status that she should have been constantly by the Emperor's side like a common servant. Certainly her reputation was flawless, and she comported herself with noble dignity; but because His Majesty obsessively kept her near him, willfully demanding that they not be separated, she had to be in attendance at all formal court performances or elegant entertainments. There were times when she would spend the night with him, and then be obliged to continue in service the following day. Consequently, as one might expect, other courtiers came to look down on her not only as a person of no significance, but also as a woman who lacked any sense of propriety. Moreover, because the Emperor treated her with special regard following the birth of his second son, the Kokiden Consort and her supporters grew anxious; they worried about the effect of such an infatuation on the prospects of the Crown Prince and wondered if the younger prince might not surpass his half brother in favor and usurp his position. The Kokiden Consort had been the Emperor's first wife. She had arrived at the palace before all the other women, and so His Majesty's feelings of affection for her were in no way ordinary. He considered her protests troubling, but he also had to acknowledge that she was deserving of sympathy, since she had given him two imperial princesses in addition to the Crown Prince.

Even though the mother of the newborn prince relied on the Emperor's benevolence for protection, many of the ladies at court scorned her. She grew physically weak, and because she felt powerless and had no one to turn to for help, she suffered greatly because of his love.

Her chambers at the palace were in the Kiritsubo—named for its courtyard, which was graced with paulownia trees. Because the Kiritsubo was in the northeast corner of the palace, and thus separated from the Emperor's quarters in the Seiryōden, he would have to pass by the chambers of many of the other court ladies on his frequent visits to her. Their resentment of these displays was not at all unreasonable, and so it was decided that the woman herself would have to go more often to the Seiryōden. The more she went, however, the more her rivals would strew the covered passageways connecting the various parts of the palace with filth. It was an absolutely intolerable situation, for the hems of the robes of the accompanying attendants would be soiled. On other occasions, when the woman could not avoid taking the interior hallways, her rivals would arrange for the doors at both ends to be closed off so that she could neither proceed forward nor turn back, trapping her inside and making her feel utterly wretched. As the number of these cruel incidents mounted, His Majesty felt sorry that his beloved should have to suffer so and ordered that she be installed in the chambers of the Kōrōden, a hall next to the Seiryōden. To do so, however, he had to move the lady who had resided there from the very beginning of her service at court to other quarters, causing her to nurse a deep resentment that proved impossible to placate.

When the young prince turned three, the court observed the ceremony of the donning of his first trousers. Employing all the treasures from the Imperial Storehouse and the Treasury, the event was every bit as lavish as the ceremony for the Crown Prince. Numerous objections were raised as a consequence of this ostentatious display, and everyone censured the ceremony as a breach of protocol. Fortunately, as the young prince grew his graceful appearance and matchless temperament became a source of wonder to all, and it was impossible for anyone to entirely resent him. Discerning courtiers who possessed the most refined sensibility could only gaze in amazement that such a child should have been born into this world.

During the summer of the year when the young prince turned three, his mother's health began to fail. She asked for permission to leave the court and return to her family home, but the Emperor would not hear of it and refused to let her go. She had been sickly and frail for some time, and so His Majesty had grown accustomed to seeing her in such a condition. "Wait a little while," he simply told her, "and let's see how you feel later." Whereupon, over the course of the next five or six days, she became seriously ill. The woman made a tearful entreaty, and at last she received permission to leave the palace. Even under these dire circumstances she was very careful to avoid any behavior that could be criticized as untoward or inappropriate. She decided to retire from the court in secret, leaving her young son behind.

Resigned to the fact that the life of his true love was approaching its end, and mindful of the taboo against defiling the palace with death, His Majesty was nonetheless grief-stricken beyond words that the dictates of protocol prevented him from seeing her off. The woman's face, with its lambent beauty conveying that air of grace so precious to him, was now thin and wasted. She had tasted the sorrows of the world to the full, but as she slipped in and out of consciousness, she could not convey to him even those feelings that might have been put into words. The Emperor, who now realized that his beloved was on the verge of death, lost control and made all sorts of tearful vows to her, no longer able to distinguish past from future. She, however, could not respond to him. The expression of weariness in her eyes made her all the more alluringly vulnerable as she lay there in a semiconscious state. The Emperor was beside himself and had no idea what he should do. He had granted her the honor of leaving in a carriage drawn by servants, but when he returned to her chambers again, he simply could not bring himself to let her go.

"Didn't we swear an oath to journey together on the road to death? No matter what, I cannot let you abandon me," he said.

She was deeply moved by his display of sorrowful devotion. Though breathing with great difficulty, she still managed to compose a verse for him.

> Now in deepest sorrow as I contemplate
> Our diverging roads, this fork where we must part
> How I long to walk the path of the living

"Had I known that things would turn out like this . . . " She evidently wanted to say more to him, but her breathing was labored. She was so weak and in such pain the Emperor longed to keep her at the palace and see it through to the end, come what may. But when he received an urgent message informing him that the most skilled of priests had been called to her family home to chant the requisite prayers of healing for her that evening, His Majesty at last agreed that his beloved should leave the palace, unbearable as it was for him to make that decision.

His heart was full and he could not sleep as he impatiently waited for the short summer night to end. Even though his messenger had barely had time to get to the woman's home and return with news of her condition, a dark foreboding assailed him. As it turned out, when the messenger arrived at the woman's residence, he had found the family distraught and weeping. "She passed away after midnight," they informed him. The messenger returned to the palace in a state of shock. The Emperor, stunned and shaken by the news, was so upset that he shut himself away from the rest of the court.

His Majesty desperately wanted to see the young prince his beloved had left behind at the palace, but there was no precedent for permitting anyone to serve at court while having to wear robes of mourning. So it was decided that the boy should be sent from the palace to his mother's residence. Too young to fully comprehend what was going on, he knew from the way people around him were behaving, and from the Emperor's ceaseless tears, that something was terribly wrong. The death of loved ones is always a source of grief, but the little boy's puzzled expression only added to the unspeakable sadness of it all.

᭞ ᭞ ᭞

The days passed in a meaningless blur for the Emperor, who dutifully observed each of the seven-day ceremonies leading up to the forty-ninth day after the funeral. Despite the passage of time, His Majesty was so lost in grief he could find no comfort. He was indifferent to the consorts and ladies-in-waiting who attended him in the evenings and instead passed his days and nights distracted and disconsolate. For all who observed his grief it was truly an autumn drenched by a dew of tears.

Over in the chambers of the Kokiden the mother of the Crown Prince and her faction remained implacably unforgiving. "Is he still so in love with her," she complained, "that even after her death he doesn't consider the feelings of others?" And indeed it was true that whenever the Emperor looked at the Crown Prince, his thoughts would inevitably drift in yearning to the younger prince, and he would then dispatch his most trusted ladies-in-waiting or nurses to the family home of his late beloved to inquire after the boy.

* * *

The soughing of the wind, the chirring of insects . . . these brought only sadness to him. The quarters of the Kokiden Consort were close by on the north side of his private chambers in the Seiryōden. It had been a long time since she last came to serve him here, and on this particular evening, with the moon in full splendor, he could hear her indulging in musical entertainment to pass the night. The Emperor was appalled and found it quite unpleasant. The courtiers and ladies-in-waiting who observed his countenance at that moment listened uneasily as well. The Kokiden Consort was a proud and haughty woman who behaved as though she couldn't care less about His Majesty's grief.

* * *

The days and months passed, and the young prince finally came back to the palace. He had grown even more splendid and handsome—to the point where he did not seem to belong to this mortal world. His worried father, knowing that the beautiful die young, took the boy's good looks as an unlucky omen.

In the spring of the following year the time came for the Emperor to formally designate the heir apparent. He was seized by a desire to pass over the presumed Crown Prince, his son by the Kokiden Consort, and appoint his favored younger son instead, but he knew that the little prince had no supporters and that the court would never accept such a move, which might prove dangerous to the boy. So in the end he went against his personal wishes and confirmed the Crown Prince as his heir apparent—all the while keeping his true feelings concealed. The courtiers remarked among themselves that no matter how much His Majesty preferred the younger son, he knew there were limits to his affection. When the Kokiden Consort caught wind of these rumors, she felt both relief and satisfaction.

The grandmother of the young prince had long been sunk in a deep depression and, finding no means to console herself, she finally passed away. Was her death the answer to her prayers to be allowed to go to her daughter? The Emperor was once more plunged into grief beyond the measure of ordinary mortals. By this time the young prince was almost six and was old enough now to understand what was happening. Deeply attached to his grandmother, he wept inconsolably. As she neared her death, she recognized how accustomed her grandson had grown to being with her through the years, and she repeated over and over how sad she was to leave him alone in the world.

With both his mother and grandmother gone, the young prince moved back to the palace for good. When he turned seven he underwent the ceremony of the First Reading, which initiated him into the study of the Chinese classics. The court had never known a child so precociously intelligent, and His Majesty, knowing how others felt and believing that talent and beauty die young, could not help but view such abilities with alarm. "How could anyone possibly resent him now," the Emperor declared. "Because he has lost his mother, I want him treated with affection." Eventually even the Kokiden Consort and her attendants were won over, and whenever the young prince accompanied his father to the Kokiden chambers, he would be permitted entry behind the curtains where the ladies-in-waiting were serving His Majesty. The fiercest warriors and most implacable enemies would have smiled had they seen him, and the ladies of the court were reluctant to let him out of their sight. The Kokiden Consort had given the Emperor two princesses as well, but neither of them could compare in beauty to this boy. The other consorts and ladies felt no inhibitions around him—indeed, they allowed him to catch glimpses of their faces—and his own appearance was so elegant that they would experience an embarrassed excitement whenever they saw him. All the courtiers considered him exceptionally splendid, a playmate to be treated with special deference.

His formal training included instruction on the koto and flute, and word of his talents echoed throughout the palace—though if I were to go into all the details about his abilities my account would seem exaggerated and he would come across as too good to be true.

The Emperor learned that among the members of a mission from the Korean kingdom of Koryō was a diviner skilled at the art of physiognomy. An old edict by the Emperor Uda had forbidden the presence of foreigners within the palace, so His Majesty discreetly arranged to have the young prince meet with this man at the Kōrōkan, the residence provided for foreign missions. The Major Controller of the Right assumed the role of guardian and accompanied the boy to the mission under the pretense that he was the father of the child. The diviner was both puzzled and astounded. Tilting his head back and forth in disbelief that this child could really be the Major Controller's son, he said,

"The young man's features tell me he is destined to be ruler of this country, perhaps even attaining the supreme position of emperor. Yet if that is what fate has in store for him, I foresee chaos and great sorrow for the court. On the other hand, if his destiny is to ascend to a position such as Chancellor and act as a guardian of imperial rule, then it appears he will be a great benefactor to the state. Still, I must say that judging by his features alone the path leading to the Chancellorship seems less likely."

The Major Controller was himself a scholar of considerable learning and discernment, and his conversations with the men of the Korean mission were deeply engaging. The party composed and exchanged verses in Chinese; and because the mission planned to leave for home in a day or two, one of the diviner's poems expressed the joy at having met such a remarkable boy face-to-face and the sorrow of having to part from him so soon. In response to the heartfelt expression of this poem the young prince composed an accomplished verse of his own. The diviner praised his effort as auspicious and bestowed lavish gifts on him. In return, the diviner received splendid presents from the imperial household. Naturally, news of this encounter spread through the court. His Majesty did not let on that he knew anything about it, but the grandfather of the Crown Prince, who happened to be the Minister of the Right, caught wind of the gossip and, not knowing quite what to make of it, grew suspicious.

The Emperor in his wisdom had earlier sought out the opinion of a Japanese diviner, whose reading of the boy's physiognomy accorded with his own thinking at the time. His Majesty had been holding back on installing the young prince in the line of succession, and was thus impressed by the perspicacity of the Korean diviner, who recognized the boy's imperial lineage. Even so, he could not be sure how long his own reign would last, and he hesitated to appoint his son prince-without-rank. He anxiously wondered whether the boy, who lacked support from his mother's family, would not end up precariously adrift once he was no longer in the line of succession. For that reason he determined that the boy's prospects might be better if he were made to serve as a loyal subject of the imperial court, and so he had his son tutored accordingly in the arts and in various fields of learning. The boy was so exceptionally bright it seemed a shame to demote him to commoner status, but the Emperor knew that if he made the boy a prince of the blood his son would suffer the calumny and scorn of the court. He consulted yet another diviner who was wise in the ways of Indic astrology; and when this reading proved to be in line with the others and with His Majesty's own thoughts on the matter, it was decided to confer on the boy the clan name of Minamoto—Genji[5]—thereby making him a commoner.

Months and years passed, but there was never a moment when the Emperor forgot his love for the lady who had resided in the chambers looking out on the paulownia courtyard. Thinking he might find someone who could assuage his grief, he had women of appropriate breeding and talents brought before him. But it was all in vain, for where in the world could he expect to find her equal? Just when he had reached the point where he found everything tiresome and was contemplating retiring from the world, an Assistant Handmaid informed him of a young woman, the fourth princess of the previous emperor, whose beauty was matchless, whose reputation at court was beyond reproof, and

5. The name "Genji" is the reading of the characters for Minamoto (*gen*) and "family name" (*ji*).

whose mother had raised her with extraordinary care and devotion. Since this Assistant Handmaid had once served at the court of the previous emperor, she was familiar with the mother of this young woman and accustomed to waiting on her. In the course of her service she had been able to observe the fourth princess as she grew from childhood, and even now would occasionally see her. "I have served at court for three successive reigns," she told the Emperor, "and I have never before seen anyone who even closely resembles the late lady of the Kiritsubo. The daughter of the former empress, however, definitely puts me in mind of her. She is a woman of exquisite refinement and beauty." *Could this really be true?* His Majesty, who could barely contain himself, began to make some discreet inquiries.

The mother of the fourth princess warned her daughter about the situation at the palace. "The Kokiden Consort is a vindictive woman. Just look at the unfortunate example of the lady in the Kiritsubo. The treatment she suffered was truly appalling." She was still struggling with the Emperor's request, unable to decide if she should allow her daughter to go to him, when she passed away. Thinking that the princess was now helpless and alone, His Majesty again approached her, saying "I will think of you as an equal to my own daughters." Her ladies-in-waiting, her supporters from her mother's family, and her older brother, Prince Hyōbu, who served in the Ministry of War, were all of the opinion that attending the Emperor would bring solace to her and would be preferable to living in her current wretched condition. So it was that she was sent to the palace and installed in the Higyōsha, which was also called the Fujitsubo because its chambers looked out onto a courtyard graced with wisteria. The young woman was thereafter referred to as Fujitsubo, and truly in face and figure she bore an uncanny resemblance to the deceased lady of the Kiritsubo. Fujitsubo, however, was of undeniably higher birth, and that status protected her from criticism, since the courtiers were predisposed to judge her a superior woman. Since she lacked no qualifications, the Emperor did not feel constrained in his relationship with her. The court had never accepted His Majesty's love for the lady of the Kiritsubo, and so his affection for her was viewed as inappropriate and inopportune. The Emperor never wavered in his undying love for the lady of the paulownia-courtyard chambers, but it is a poignant fact of human nature that feelings change over time. Inevitably his attention shifted toward Fujitsubo, who, it seems, brought comfort to his heart.

Because the young Genji was always at his father's side, he was constantly in the presence of the women who attended His Majesty most frequently. These women grew familiar with the boy and gradually came to feel that they did not have to be reserved around him. Of course, none of the consorts considered herself inferior to the others, but even though each one was very attractive in her own individual way, there was no denying that they all had passed, or were on the verge of passing, the peak of their charms . . . all but Fujitsubo, that is. She still possessed the loveliness of youthful beauty, and try as she might to keep herself hidden away behind her screens, Genji, who was always nearby, would catch glimpses of her figure. He had no memory of his mother, and when he heard the head of the imperial household staff say that Fujitsubo looked just like her, his young heart ached with wistful longing—if only he could always be close to his father's new consort!

Genji and Fujitsubo were the two most precious people to the Emperor. "Do not be shy around the boy," His Majesty told Fujitsubo. "It may seem strange and curious, but I feel as though it is fitting for him to think of you as his mother. Do not think him discourteous, but cherish him for my sake. His face and expressions are so like his mother's—and since you resemble her, you can't blame him for thinking of you the way he does." After the Emperor made his request, Genji, in his boyish emotions, would try everything, even references to the transient blossoms of spring or the blazing leaves of autumn, to get Fujitsubo to recognize his yearning affection for her. When the Kokiden Consort learned of the unprecedented favoritism His Majesty was displaying toward these two, she once more grew cold and distant toward Fujitsubo and her retinue. Moreover, her earlier ominous dislike of Genji and his mother flared up again, and she found the boy repellent. Her son, the Crown Prince, was considered flawlessly handsome, and his reputation was above reproach. Nonetheless, he was no match for the lustrous beauty of Genji, who possessed an aura that prompted the courtiers to call him the Radiant Prince. Because Fujitsubo was his equal in looks and in the affections of the Emperor, she came to be referred to as the Princess of the Radiant Sun.

It pained the Emperor that his son would eventually grow out of his youthful good looks, but when Genji turned twelve preparations were made for the coming-of-age ceremony in which his hair would be done up and his clothes and cap worn in the style of an adult. His Majesty personally tended to every little detail of the ceremony, adding touches that went beyond custom and set a new standard. The ceremony that had initiated the Crown Prince into manhood had been a spectacular affair held in the Shishinden, the great ceremonial hall of the palace. The Emperor wanted Genji's ceremony to be just as majestic and proper. He had various offices, including the Treasury and the Imperial Granaries, make formal preparations for the many banquets and celebrations that would follow the ceremony, and he left special instructions that no expense should be spared and that his directives should be carried out so as to make the occasion one of utmost splendor.

His Majesty was seated facing east under the eastern eaves of his residence in the Seiryōden, and the seats for Genji and the minister who would bestow the cap were located in front of him. Genji appeared before the Emperor at around four in the afternoon, during the Hour of the Monkey.[6] The lambent glow of his face, which was still framed on either side by the twin loops of his boyish hairdo, made his father feel all the more regretful about the change in appearance that was about to take place. The honor of trimming back Genji's hair fell to the Minister of the Treasury, whose face betrayed the pain he felt the moment he cut Genji's beautiful locks. The Emperor had a hard time keeping his emotions in check. *If only his mother were here to see this ceremony*, he thought, struggling to maintain his composure.

The capping ritual followed, and when that was finished, Genji withdrew to an antechamber to rest and change into the formal attire of an adult—an outer

6. In premodern Japan the hours of the day, like the months, were designated by the signs of the Chinese zodiac. The Hour of the Monkey was ca. 3–5 P.M. [editors' note].

robe with the underarm vents sewn up. Stepping down into the garden east of the Seiryōden, he faced his father and performed obeisance, placing his ceremonial wand on the ground, rising and bowing left, right and left again, then sitting and repeating his actions to show his gratitude. He cut such a magnificent figure that all in attendance were moved to tears. As might be expected, the Emperor found it harder than the others to hide his feelings. At that moment the sad events of the past, which he normally kept himself from dwelling on, came flooding back. Since Genji was still at a tender age, His Majesty had fretted that cutting his locks and putting his hair up in the style of an adult man would spoil his looks. To his amazement the ceremony only added to Genji's aura of masculine beauty.

The Minister of the Left, who performed the capping ritual, had taken the younger sister of the Emperor as his principal wife. She gave him a daughter, whom he doted upon, raising her with the utmost care. The Minister was troubled when he learned that the Crown Prince evidently desired his daughter, because he was secretly planning to arrange a match for her with Genji. And so in the days leading up to the ceremony, he approached the Emperor with his proposal. His Majesty replied, "I see. Well . . . given that the boy seems to have no patrons for his coming-of-age ceremony, and since we have to select an aristocratic young woman to sleep with him on the night of his initiation, let's choose your daughter." Thus encouraged, the Minister followed through with his plans.

After the ceremony, Genji withdrew into the attendant's antechamber. As the party was making a celebratory toast in his honor, the Emperor gave permission for Genji, who had no rank, to sit at a place below the imperial princes, but above the ministers. The Minister of the Left, who was seated next to him, casually dropped a few hints about his daughter, but Genji, who was still at an age when he felt diffident and embarrassed about such matters, did not respond.

An attendant from the imperial household staff brought a message from the Emperor to the Minister, requesting his presence. The Minister went to the imperial quarters where a senior lady-in-waiting presented him with the appropriate gifts that custom demanded—a white oversized woman's robe made especially for this presentation, along with a set of three robes. His Majesty vented his pent-up emotions, presenting a cup of rice wine to the Minister and reminding him of his responsibilities toward Genji.

> When you with purple cords first bound his hair
> Did you not also bind your heart and swear
> Eternal vows to give him your daughter

The Minister composed this reply.

> So long as the deep purple cords that bind our hearts
> As firmly as they bind this youth's hair never fade
> So our mutual vow will retain its deep hue

He stepped down from the long bridge that connected the imperial residence in the Seiryōden and the Ceremonial Court in the Shishinden, and performed obeisance in the east garden. There he received a horse from the Left Division of the imperial stables and a falcon caged in a mew from the Office of the Chamberlain. Princes and nobles lined up along the foot of the stairs leading down from the Seiryōden into the east garden and each received gifts appropriate to their rank.

Decorative boxes of thin cypress wood filled with delicacies and baskets of fruit were among the items prepared for the Emperor that day. The Major Controller of the Right, who had acted earlier as Genji's guardian, had been put in charge of the presentations. The garden overflowed with trays stacked with rice cakes flavored with various fillings, and with four-legged chests of Chinese-style lacquer stuffed with presents for the lower ranking attendants— so many that their numbers surpassed even the presentations made at the coming-of-age ceremony held for the Crown Prince. Indeed, it was an incomparably magnificent affair.

That evening Genji departed for the residence of the Minister of the Left, which was located on Sanjō avenue. The ceremony welcoming Genji as groom and solemnizing his wedding was conducted with unprecedented attention to proper form. Feeling a touch of dread, the Minister was captivated by the masculine beauty of Genji, who still looked quite boyish. In contrast his daughter, who at sixteen was four years older than her new husband, was put off by Genji's youthfulness and considered their match inappropriate.

The Minister enjoyed the full confidence of the Emperor. After all, his principal wife, the mother of the bride, was His Majesty's full sister. Thus, the bride came from a distinguished line on both sides of her family. Moreover, the addition of Genji to the Minister's family diminished the prestige of his rival the Minister of the Right, who as grandfather of the Crown Prince would eventually assume power as Chancellor. The Minister of the Left had numerous children by several wives. His principal wife had given him, in addition to Genji's bride, a son who was now Middle Captain in the Inner Palace Guard. This young man, Tō no Chūjō,[7] was exceptionally handsome, and the Minister of the Right could hardly ignore such a promising prospect, even though he was not on good terms with the Minister of the Left, his main rival for power. He therefore arranged to marry the young Tō no Chūjō to his fourth daughter, who was his greatest treasure in the world. His regard for his son-in-law was every bit as strong as that given to Genji by the Minister of the Left. For their part, the two young men forged an ideal friendship.

Because the Emperor was always summoning him, Genji found it difficult to live at his wife's residence.[8] In his heart, he was obsessed with the matchless beauty of the Fujitsubo Consort, who seemed to be exactly the kind of woman he wanted to take as his wife. *Was there no one else like her*, he wondered. He found his bride to be a woman of great charm and proper training, but he was not really attracted to her. He had been drawn to Fujitsubo when he was a child, and the torment caused by his feelings for her was excruciating. Now that he was an adult, he was no longer permitted behind the curtains of the

7. I am following custom and using this name for Genji's close friend, brother-in-law, and rival. The name "Tō no Chūjō" refers to his positions as Middle Captain in the Inner Palace Guard (Chūjō) and in the Office of the Chamberlain. Like most of the male characters, he is identified by his position at court throughout the narrative, but since his positions and ranks change over time, it is easier to refer to him throughout by this initial appellation.

8. Uxorilocal marriage arrangements were widespread in the Heian period, and thus it was common for a young nobleman to make his father-in-law's residence his primary abode [editors' note].

consorts. Whenever there was a musical entertainment, he would play the flute in accompaniment to Fujitsubo's koto, his notes subtly conveying his true feelings for her. The sound of her soft voice was a comfort to him, and the only times he felt happy was when he was at the palace. He would serve there for five or six days in succession, occasionally spending a mere two or three days at his wife's residence. His father-in-law attributed Genji's behavior to his youth and did not fault him for it, but continued to do all he could to offer support at court. He chose only the most exceptional ladies-in-waiting to serve his son-in-law and daughter, and he went out of his way to put on the musical entertainments that Genji so enjoyed and to show him every favor.

When Genji stayed at the palace he took up residence in the Kiritsubo. The women who had once served his mother had not been dismissed and scattered, and so they were now assigned to wait on him. Orders were sent down to the Office of Palace Repairs and to the Bureau of Skilled Artisans to rebuild and expand the former residence of Genji's mother, a villa on Nijō avenue. The project was to be carried out so splendidly that there would be no other villa like it. The setting of the surrounding woods and hills was already unparalleled; and when the garden pond was enlarged the result was so eye-catching that it created a stir. Genji thought wistfully that such a villa would be the perfect residence for a wife who had all the qualities of his ideal woman, Fujitsubo.

It is said that it was the Korean diviner who, in his admiration, first bestowed on Genji the sobriquet, Radiant Prince.

FROM CHAPTER II

Hahakigi

Broom Cypress

The Radiant Prince—a splendid, if somewhat bombastic, title. In fact, his failings were so numerous that such a lofty sobriquet was perhaps misleading. He engaged in all sorts of flings and dalliances, but he sought to keep them secret out of fear he would end up as fodder for those gossips who delighted in passing along stories about him and thereby leave behind for later generations a reputation as a careless, frivolous man. Genji was keen to avoid the censure of the court, and, thus constrained, went about with a serious and sincere demeanor for a time, abstaining from all elegantly seductive or charming affairs. No doubt the Lieutenant of Katano, that legendary lover, would have been amused.[9]

Genji was serving as Middle Captain in the Palace Guard at the time, and in fact he preferred being stationed there. Consequently, his visits to his wife, who resided at the estate of her father, the Minister of the Left, all but ceased. Although people expressed their suspicions about him, wondering if his heart wasn't in wild turmoil over a secret lover, Genji was not the sort who carried on common affairs impulsively or brazenly. There were rare occasions, however, when he strayed from his professed path of moderation; and he had the unfortunate tendency to become obsessed with relationships that brought him stress and pain, giving himself over entirely to behavior that could hardly be called proper.

9. The tale of the amorous Lieutenant of Katano referred to here has not survived.

During a stretch in the rainy season when there was no break in the clouds, a directional taboo[1] forced Genji to stay on and attend the Emperor for a longer than normal period. The members of the household of the Minister of the Left grew anxious and resentful at Genji's neglect of his wife, but they continued to arrange every detail of his wardrobe so that he would cut a remarkable figure at court. Moreover, the sons of the Minister, Genji's brothers-in-law, would spend all their free time in Genji's palace quarters when they happened to be in service. One of these sons, Tō no Chūjō, was a Middle Captain who also served in the Office of the Chamberlain. He was a full sibling to Genji's wife—he and his sister had both been born to Princess Ōmiya—and of all the Minister's children he was closest to Genji and could behave in a more intimate and relaxed manner in his friend's presence at entertainments and amusements. Tō no Chūjō preferred the company of Genji because the residence that his own father-in-law, the Minister of the Right, had painstakingly provided and maintained for him was a dreary, uninspiring place. It must be added that he was fond of having affairs with other women.

Tō no Chūjō also had dazzlingly furnished quarters at his father's residence at Sanjō, but he was always accompanying Genji on his comings and goings. They were constantly together, day and night, pursuing the same interests and diversions, and he in no way lagged behind the Radiant Prince in his accomplishments. Because they were inseparable, it was natural that they did not stand on ceremony with one another. They never kept their innermost feelings hidden, but displayed an easygoing harmony whenever they spoke.

They had spent a particularly tedious day doing nothing at all on account of the interminable rain; and because there was hardly a sign of anyone in the palace during the tedious hours of the early evening, Genji's quarters there took on a more relaxed atmosphere than usual. Drawing an oil lamp beside him, Genji perused some Chinese classics. Tō no Chūjō pulled out some letters written on paper of various hues from a small cabinet near him and was seized by the desire to read them. Genji would not allow that, but he did say, "I'll let you look at a few of the more appropriate ones . . . there are several I'd be ashamed for you to read." Tō no Chūjō protested, feeling a little resentful. "But it's just those letters you don't feel free to share with me that I'm most curious about. I've exchanged many letters of the most common variety with ladies of all ranks, and at the time we were corresponding I couldn't wait to read them. Yet when I go back over them, the only ones really worth looking at were written when the women were being petulant or impatient from waiting." Tō no Chūjō knew, of course, that Genji would never keep letters from high-ranking ladies—letters he had to keep absolutely secret—lying scattered about in a commonplace cabinet like this where anyone could see them. Genji would certainly hide his most intriguing letters in a secret location, and would be comfortable sharing only those from easygoing ladies of decidedly second-rate backgrounds. "Well, you certainly have a lot of them, don't you," said Tō no

1. A directional taboo, or prohibition, required a person to avoid traveling in a certain direction so as not to disturb gods whose movements over time were predictable (based on Chinese zodiacal and calendrical practices) and could be charted by the Bureau of Divination. Such prohibitions were often used as a convenient excuse for a gentleman to avoid meeting his wife or lover [editors' note].

Chūjō, who went on to interrogate Genji about the author of each of the missives. He found it amusing that his suppositions and guesses about the letters were sometimes right on the money, and other times wildly off the mark. Still, Genji gave very little away, and, by leading his friend on, he managed to disguise the identities of the letter writers.

"You must have a great number of letters at your place," said Genji. "I'd really like to take a peek at them. If you let me, I'll gladly open this cabinet to you." Tō no Chūjō answered, "I have very few worth looking at. You see, I've come to the realization that as far as women are concerned there aren't many who are flawless enough to make you think *she's the one*. I've come across many who have passable skills in the arts, who can write flowing characters that create an impression of a superficial elegance, who show a kind of facile understanding of how to respond in verse on certain occasions . . . and yet even if you choose a woman on the basis of such accomplishments, she almost always fails to live up to the expectations created by her talents and disappoints in the end. She'll swell with pride, going on and on about her own accomplishments, looking down on others and, all in all, behaving rather foolishly. Her parents are always waiting on her, spoiling her with affection and lavishing attention, keeping their precious little princess hidden away in the recesses of their estates until some man hears about her extraordinary gifts and gets all worked up. Beautiful, young, and carefree, with little to distract her, she'll follow the lead of others, dedicate herself to some trivial diversion, and as a result acquire and perfect some skill. Naturally those who look after her keep silent about her flaws, keeping up appearances and spreading plausible-sounding rumors that make her seem better than she really is. Since such rumors are all a man has to go on, can he really afford to assume the worst about her without actually meeting her? So a man goes about, wondering if she's the genuine article, and when they finally meet . . . well, it's rare that a woman actually lives up to her reputation."

Listening to Tō no Chūjō's lament, which gave the impression of a world-weary man who had experienced the shame of such disappointments, Genji smiled wryly. Although he knew that his friend's account of women was hardly the whole of the matter, he had had a few affairs that matched Tō no Chūjō's experiences. "Can there really be women," Genji asked, "who lack even the most trivial merits?"

"I'm not saying that," Tō no Chūjō responded. "Who would be foolish enough to be drawn to a woman with absolutely no talent? A woman who has nothing to recommend her is as rare as one who is perfect in every way. My point is that a woman who is born into the nobility is raised with the greatest care, which includes concealing her many faults. So of course she's going to look superior to other women. A woman born into a family of middling rank will reveal her sensibility and habits of mind with a style and personality all her own, and so you would expect to discover various things that distinguish her from others. As for women of the lowest class . . . well, I'm not especially interested in learning anything about them."

Genji's curiosity was piqued by the worldly posture his friend had assumed. "I wonder about your standards. Can you really classify all women on the basis of just three levels? How do you discriminate between a woman born of a noble family . . . say rank three or above . . . whose social position has been ruined and whose rank has fallen so that it is indistinguishable from others, and a woman of less distinguished background . . . say rank four or lower . . . whose family has so prospered at court that they can now lavishly furnish her residence and adopt a smug attitude that proclaims their daughter inferior to no one?" Just as Genji posed his question, the Warden of the Left Mounted Guard and the Junior Secretary from the Ministry of Rites showed up, explaining that directional prohibitions for that day were keeping them confined to the palace. They both had reputations as elegant lovers, and since they were also eloquent speakers—fluent, logical, and precise—Tō no Chūjō was eager to detain them and get their opinions on his idea of classifying women according to three levels. Their subsequent conversation touched upon topics of a highly questionable and even slightly disreputable nature.

The Warden addressed the matter straight away. "A woman who is a parvenu will likely be judged by court society as inferior despite her rise in status, especially if her pedigree is not appropriate to her rank. On the other hand, a woman who may have a distinguished pedigree, but who lacks the means to make her way at court will see her fortunes and position diminish over time, and her prospects and reputation crumble away until she cannot maintain her status in spite of her pride. Events will then conspire to make her situation more and more untenable. Looking at each of these types of women, I'm afraid we have to relegate them both to your middle category. Provincial governors toil away, tied up with petty people and affairs; but even among that lot, consigned to a middling station in life, there are various gradations that distinguish them. We live in an age when we sometimes find governors who are really not at all inferior, even though they come from the middle ranks. Actually, there are some of the fourth rank who are qualified to serve as a counselor, who have unsullied reputations and comfortable fortunes and prospects, and who are easier to take than some inexperienced or immature nobility of higher rank. There are many instances of such men who maintain splendid households where their daughters are nurtured with the utmost care. Nothing is lacking, nothing held back, no expense spared to raise them in the most dazzling manner . . . and as a result they grow into excellent young ladies who are beyond reproach. These women go into court service and many of them find unexpected good fortune, marrying above their station."

Genji smiled at that. "I guess that when all is said and done, the key is finding a girl from a rich family."

Tō no Chūjō responded petulantly. "Now you're talking nonsense. Such a remark is not worthy of you."

The Warden continued his disquisition. "The highborn lady who brings together both pedigree and public reputation, yet who in private lacks personal breeding and manners, is eccentric and not worth discussing. She's the type who makes you wonder in disappointment how she could have been brought up like that. Of course, it strikes one as perfectly natural when a woman's pedigree and reputation are in harmony and her character is flawless. So you assume that's the way things ought to be and aren't surprised by her, even though such a woman is a rarity. But perhaps I should set aside any discussion of the highest-ranking ladies, for someone as lowly as I could never be on their level. Beyond these types, you sometimes unexpectedly come across an adorable, defenseless girl whose existence is unknown to court society. She lives in a lonely, sublimely dilapidated residence shut away from the world behind a gate overgrown with weeds, and so of course you think of her as an exceptionally rare find. You're mysteriously drawn to her, your imagination stimulated by the things that make her different, and you wonder how she could have ended up in a place like that. Her father is likely to be some pathetic, overweight old man, her brothers probably all have unpleasant faces, and there in the women's quarters in the inner recesses of the residence . . . which, no matter how you try to imagine it, is nothing out of the ordinary . . . is a fiercely proud lady with all the refined demeanor of one who has somehow managed to acquire some accomplishments, even if she is not of the first rank and thus not all that much to talk about. And yet because you would never expect to find a woman like that in such a place, how could you not find her alluring? Of course, you can't compare the discovery of a woman like that to opting for a flawless woman of superior rank, but by the same token it is difficult to simply toss her aside."

The Warden here glanced knowingly at the Junior Secretary, who, interpreting the expression as a subtle reference to the flawless reputation of his own sister, kept his counsel on the matter. Genji seemed lost in thought: *I wonder about all this. Are there really women like that out in the world? After all, when I consider my wife, there don't seem to be any perfect women among the highest classes.* Genji was dressed in an intentionally casual manner in an informal robe, minus trousers, over soft white under robes. He had neglected to tie up the cords of his outer robes, and as he half-reclined amidst his books and papers in the dim shadows cast by the lamp, he cut such an attractive figure that the other men felt a desire to see him as a woman. He was so beautiful that pairing him with the very finest of the ladies at the court would fail to do him justice.

During the course of the young men's discussion of various types of women, the Warden remarked, "There are women who are flawless enough for a commonplace affair, but when the time comes to take a wife, you find it impossible to decide even if you have a large number of women to choose from. The same is true of men who serve at court and are expected to be rock-solid pillars of society. It proves quite difficult to produce a man of true worth and ability, and so no matter how gifted or clever he may be, in the end there will never be more than one or two who are fit to govern. That's why superior people command their inferiors, and inferiors follow their superiors, mutually accommodating each other to carry out public affairs. Now then, just consider the person who is to take charge of the private affairs of your household. It wouldn't do at all if she doesn't have the proper qualifications. That being the case, a man is naturally going to look around because he knows that a woman may possess some good qualities while lacking others. After all, it is rare to find one who, though maybe not perfect, is at least acceptable . . . and even a man who is not inclined to compare the appearance of this woman to that one is going to take great care in making his decision, since the one he chooses will be his mate for life. All things being equal, he will take someone whose tastes match his own and who does not have the kind of flaws he must spend all his time correcting and setting in order. Well, this is all very hard, and a woman is not necessarily going to fulfill all a man's expectations. That's why a man who does not allow his affections to stray, who focuses his attention on one woman and does not discard the karmic bonds of his first marriage vows, will always be seen as sincere, honest and loyal. And a woman who is able to keep her husband from straying is the one we take to be refined and attractive.

"Given all that . . . how should I put this . . . having observed all sorts of relationships in society, I can't help having doubts as to whether there is any woman who is perfectly elegant, or who can live up to the ideals in a man's heart. In the case of your lordships, what kind of woman could ever be worthy enough to meet your exalted standards? No doubt she would have to be young and beautiful and beyond reproach in every way. She would be well versed in composition, but her choice of words would be modest and her brushstrokes light and delicate, leaving you a little agitated and longing for a more revealing response. You are forced to wait, feeling unbearably impatient until that moment when you can get close enough to her to make your advances and exchange a few words. But she will say very little, speaking under her breath in a faint voice that shows how adept she is at concealing her flaws. Just when you think she is most pliant and feminine, she starts to fret about whether or not you really love her. And then when you humor her, she becomes flirtatious. This has to be the worst fault in women.

"Above all, a wife must never neglect her duty to assist her husband. A husband can get along well enough if a woman is not too emotionally demanding, does not make a big fuss over niceties, and doesn't give herself over to fashion. Of course, a man doesn't want a wife who is too serious, who busies herself with supporting her husband and managing the household to the extent that she keeps her hair swept back all the time, exposing her ears and making herself unattractive. A man who goes to work in the morning and returns home in the evening doesn't want to have to go to the trouble of talking with a stranger about the odd behavior of people he has encountered in public and private, or about the good and bad things he has seen and heard. If he has a wife who is close to him and will listen to his stories and understand him, then doesn't he assume he should be able to discuss such matters with her? Maybe he suddenly recalls something and smiles, or perhaps tears come to his eyes, or maybe he relives some feeling of righteous indignation at something that occurred to someone. Or he might have feelings that he just cannot keep to himself, and thinks he might share them with her and ask her opinion. But if she is unattractive or too preoccupied to understand, he ends up turning away in disillusionment. Remembering something he has kept inside, a thought that makes him laugh or let out an audible sigh, he will mention it, almost as if speaking to himself, and all she will do is look up with a blank expression and reply, 'Did you just say something?' What man wouldn't regret marrying someone like that?

"When all is said and done, we men really should consider picking a completely childlike, compliant woman . . . a woman we can mold into an acceptable and flawless wife. Even when she gives you some cause for concern, you still have the feeling that there is some value in disciplining her. When you are with such a woman face-to-face, she is truly vulnerable and precious to you, and you are compelled to view her faults through forgiving eyes. Even so, there will be occasions when you have to be apart, and you tell her about something important that must be done, or give her some task, trivial or practical, that must be carried out to the letter. It will turn out that she cannot act on her own and is unable to do things as you instructed. This is really quite annoying and her unreliability will cause you no end of trouble. Why does it always seem that it's the cold, distant, slightly unpleasant woman who, depending on the occasion, is able to perform well in front of others and bring honor to your house?" The Warden had tried to cover all aspects of the subject, but was unable to come to any firm conclusions. Instead, he finished his analysis by heaving a great sigh.

"Considering all of this," the Warden continued, "you can't choose a wife solely on the basis of her family background, and certainly not on the basis of her looks alone. If you can find a woman who is not so strange or demure as to make you regret your choice, if she is serious through and through and has a quiet personality, then you ought to consider her dependable. Should she have any talents beyond these basic qualifications, or be sweet-tempered, you should count yourself lucky. Even if she is deficient in certain respects, you shouldn't make unreasonable demands for her to improve. So long as she is morally upright and not fretful or jealous, then she will over time acquire an outward grace. Her comportment will be modest, she will protect her honor, and she will endure things she has a right to complain about, hiding her resentment behind feigned ignorance or pretending to be nonchalant. Unfortunately, there are cases where a woman can no longer suppress the emotions that have been building up inside her heart, and she will leave behind some fierce words that chill your soul, or compose a moving poem to which she has attached a memento that will remind you of her, then hide herself away in some village deep in the mountains or on a deserted strand along the shore. When I was a child I would hear stories like that, which the ladies-in-waiting would read aloud, and I found them so touching I was moved to tears. Now, when I think back on it, their tales seem frivolous and overly dramatic. A woman who casts aside a man who has deep feelings for her and runs off to hide in utter disregard of the husband's feelings, even when she has just cause for being upset, will stir anxieties that last a lifetime. The whole affair is extremely tiresome. Some people will praise her actions, saying how exquisitely profound her emotions are; and as a result her feelings of sad regret will accumulate to the point where she decides to become a nun. Having made up her mind, her heart seems pure and serene and she can no longer even consider returning to her former life. Her acquaintances come to call on her, telling her how melancholy it is that things should have come to this. When her husband hears of this he weeps, and the messenger and older ladies-in-waiting tell her what a shame it is and how sad that her husband has such deep feelings. The woman, who still has lingering affection for him, will then realize she had no reason to throw away his love. She will gather together the hair she had clipped from her forehead when she took vows as a nun and, feeling forlorn and helpless now that there is no turning back, will break down and cry. Though she had kept her emotions in check up to that moment, once she gives in to her feelings she is no longer able to hold back her tears whenever she considers her situation. Because she now seems to have so many regrets, the Buddha himself must look at her as one whose heart is tainted by base attachments. Half-hearted devotion to the Buddha is an even more certain path to Hell than being mired in the five evils of earthly existence.[2] Even if the marital bond was deep enough

2. In Buddhism the five evils are lust, wrath, greed, worldly attachment, and pride (ego).

that the husband takes her back before she renounces the world, is there any couple that would not harbor at least some resentment upon recalling such an incident? For better or worse they live together as husband and wife, and their relationship is based on a deep karmic bond and shared emotions that can weather almost anything that might happen. Yet whenever a wife runs away, can any couple ever completely put aside their feelings of mutual reproach?

"It is folly for a wife to resent her husband, display her anger, and quarrel obsessively over some little affair he has had on the side. A man's affections may stray, but so long as he is still capable of the kind of feelings he had for her when they were first married, then she has good reason to think that their relationship has strong emotional bonds. If she makes a big fuss over his dalliances, however, those bonds may be cut for good.

"In general, then, a woman should be modest in all things. She should give a gentle hint when she knows something is going on that justifies her resentment. Or she should imply, without being spiteful, that there have been some occasions that have bothered her. If she behaves in such a way, her husband's regard for her will surely increase. Most of the time a man's wandering heart can be calmed by the guidance of his wife. A woman who is too lenient and turns a blind eye to her husband's behavior may in contrast seem easygoing and lovable, but in the end will be dismissed as frivolous. As Bai Juyi put it, 'Who can tell where an unmoored ship will drift?'[3] Isn't that the truth?"

Tō no Chūjō nodded and replied, "Staying on the same subject, it's a serious matter when a person you like for her charm and sensitivity gives you cause to wonder if they can be trusted. Although people may choose to put up with their partner's wayward behavior and even fool themselves into believing they see some improvement, that doesn't mean that the wayward partner has reformed. In any case, when an indiscretion brings discord to a marriage, there is probably no better recourse than to calmly ignore it." His remarks described perfectly the situation of his own sister, which was no doubt his intention, and so it irritated him that her husband, Genji, was not joining in the discussion, but was pretending to nod off instead.

The Warden, who now found himself regarded as the expert on such matters, whinnied on and on. Tō no Chūjō, who wanted to hear what he had to say, assumed the role of disciple and listened eagerly.

"Compare women to artisans, if you will," the Warden continued. "For example, a woodworker may indulge his imagination and create all sorts of items . . . toys meant for a moment's diversion, objects not based on any model or pattern. These things look fashionable and amaze you with the cleverness of their construction, and insofar as they are new and different and in keeping with the times, they attract attention as modern and up-to-date, and so have a certain charm. Yet to have something of true beauty made properly . . . formal furnishings, say, or some decorative object for your residence that has a conventional form . . . the distinction between a maker of novelties and a master craftsman is plain for all to see. To take another example, there are many skilled painters at the palace, but when you have to pick one to do basic sketching for a work, it is hard to tell at a glance which ones are the truly skilled artists. Paintings that present startling scenes of the mountains on the isle of

---

3. A reference to a poem on marriage included in the collected writings of [Bo] Juyi.

Hōrai where the immortals dwell, or that show the stern visages of beasts from exotic lands or the faces of demons no man has ever seen all give play to the imagination and astonish our eyes, since they bear no resemblance to the real world. Such works are fine, given what they are, and any painter will do. But when it comes to realistically depicting scenes in the everyday world . . . mountain vistas, flowing streams, the familiar look of our dwellings . . . the attention to detail and the technical execution of the master painter in serenely presenting familiar objects or in depicting the steep, rugged landscape of the mountains or in piling layer upon layer of thick foliage to create the impression that one is far removed from society or in placing a garden enclosed by a bamboo fence in the foreground . . . all require a special power and grace that are far beyond the skills of an ordinary artist.

"Or take calligraphy. Even a person with no real knowledge of the art can add a flourish here and there to create the impression . . . at least at a cursory glance . . . that he has great talent, while a person who can in fact write with true skill and care may appear to lack the ability of a master. But when you compare the works of such people side by side, you can see that the latter is closer to the genuine thing. So it is with all trivial matters of art and pleasure. I know that when it comes to human emotions it is even more the case that you cannot trust the affected elegance a woman puts on as a show for a particular occasion. Shall I tell you how I came by this knowledge, though I may have to speak indiscreetly about an affair?" He shifted a little closer, and Genji woke up. Tō no Chūjō was sitting across from him, his chin cupped in his hands, listening in earnest anticipation. It made for a charming tableau, resembling a scene in which a learned priest expounds on the ways of the world. It was the kind of moment, however, when young men find it hard to keep their relationships secret.

"Some time ago," the Warden resumed, "when I was still a very low-ranking official, I was quite taken with a young woman. But, as I presumed to mention to your highnesses earlier, she was not exceptionally beautiful, and so I decided in my youthful, fickle heart that I would not take her as my main wife. Though I thought of her as someone I could always turn to and rely on, there was something lacking, and I was sure I could do better. So I played around and cheated on her, and when she became distressingly jealous she lost favor with me. I kept hoping that she would not be like that, and wanted her to be a little less sensitive. While I found it irksome that she was so unforgiving and suspicious, I was also puzzled that she had lost patience with a man of such a low rank as I. At the same time, I couldn't understand why she still had feelings for me. I often felt sorry for her, and so I eventually brought my tendency to stray under control.

"Her temperament was such that somehow or another she contrived to do her best for me, even in matters for which she had no innate ability. She prodded herself, ashamed of faults she didn't want others to see, and she earnestly supported me in every way, trying her best never to go against my wishes in even the slightest matter. At the beginning I had thought of her as a strong-willed woman, but in the end she was yielding and accommodating. She worried that she might put me off if she did not make herself attractive, and whenever she allowed herself to be seen by someone not close to her, she would fret about it, feeling that perhaps she had shamed her husband. She did her utmost to maintain her wifely virtue, and as we grew accustomed to living as husband and wife, I was not at all ill disposed toward her except for that one detestable flaw . . . her jealousy, which she could not control.

"At the time she seemed so absurdly obedient and fearful, and I thought I should teach her a lesson . . . you know, shake her up a little so she would stop being jealous and mend her ways. So I pretended I was truly fed up and that we should break off our relationship. Since she had previously shown only a submissive attitude to me, I thought for sure I could teach her a lesson, and intentionally treated her with wretched callousness. When, as usual, she got angry, I told her that if she were going to be so willful and disagreeable, then I would put an end to our marriage and not meet her again despite the deep bond we shared as husband and wife. I said, 'If you really want us to separate, just keep harboring your baseless suspicions. But if you want us to have a long future together, then you have to accept that there will be hardships and try to not let things bother you. Rid yourself of your twisted disposition, and I will find you endearing. As soon as I work my way up at court and achieve respectable status, no other woman will ever compete with you for my devotion.' I thought I was being so clever in straightening her out with such assertive words, but she just smiled vaguely and replied, 'It doesn't bother or worry me that you are in a period in your life when you have neither status nor distinction, nor am I waiting impatiently for you to achieve success. But I find it painfully unbearable to have to always hide my feeling of wretchedness and rely on the uncertain hope that as the months and years go by the day will finally arrive when you reform your behavior. So the time has come when we must go our separate ways.' Her spiteful words made me very angry and I said a number of hateful things to her. At that point the woman, unable to control her passions, grabbed my hand and bit one of my fingers. I put on a show of outrage and, holding out my crooked finger, stalked out. 'Now that you've disfigured me like this,' I threatened, 'how can I possibly show myself at court? You yourself said I'm of no consequence, so now that you've done this how do you expect me to get ahead? If this is how things are, then it looks like we really are through from now on.' I composed a poem.

> As I bend my wounded fingers counting
> The times I called on you, your flaws it seems
> Are not confined to jealousy alone

'You won't have me to resent anymore,' I said, and as expected she burst into tears and shot back.

> Having counted in my heart the times
> I showed restraint at your behavior
> Now I have to take my hand from yours

She challenged me in this manner, and even though I did not believe our relationship would really change, I drifted about seeing women here and there and let many days pass without once communicating with her. Then one night, near the end of the eleventh month, I was detained at the palace in order to rehearse music and dance for the Rinji festival at the Kamo Shrine. A miserable sleet was falling that night, and as I was saying good-bye to my companions, who were going their separate ways, it occurred to me that I had no other place to go but hers. Sleeping at the palace seemed a dreary prospect, and the thought of visiting some woman who puts on an air of refined elegance chilled me to the bone. And so, all the while wondering what she thought about me, I went to peek in on her and see how she was faring. As I brushed the snow off myself, I felt constrained by feelings of embarrassment; and yet I hoped that perhaps tonight her icy resentment had thawed. The lamps had been dimmed and turned toward the walls, and softly padded robes had been plumped up and hung over a large filigree basket to be warmed and perfumed. The blinds were raised just as they were supposed to be, and the room gave the appearance that she had been waiting for me to return that very evening. Since everything was prepared just to my liking, I felt a swelling pride until I noticed she was nowhere to be found. Only the women who served her were there, as I had expected, and they told me she had gone to her parents' residence for the evening. She had left no elegant poem to rouse my interest, no word at all that she was anxious to see me. She had simply left and locked herself away, showing no consideration for me. I was quite let down and couldn't help wondering if her unyielding spitefulness wasn't implicitly signaling to me that I should go ahead and hate her if I wanted. The rooms gave no indication she was having an affair . . . was her aim to make me angry and suspicious of her? Yet the hues and stitching of the robes she had laid out for me were prepared with more than normal care, just as I would have wished. Clearly she was taking care to look after me even though she now assumed I had abandoned her.

"Things being the way they were, I figured she would never cut me off completely, and so I tried to downplay our spat and make up with her. And though she did not defy me by hiding herself away and making me run around looking for her, or by replying in a way that would cause me embarrassment, still she told me, 'I cannot continue putting up with you the way you are now. If you reform and develop a more steady disposition, then maybe we can see each other.' Even though she spoke to me like that, I was convinced she could never leave me, and so I thought I'd let her stew a while longer to punish her. 'All right, then, let's do as you suggest,' I told her, showing her just how stubborn I could be. She suffered so much during that time that at last she died. I knew then that I should never have made light of her, and I can't help thinking now that it's good enough for a man if his wife is someone who is wholly dependable. It was always worthwhile talking to her, regardless of whether we were discussing some trivial, passing matter or an important issue. She was so skilled at dyeing cloth that it's no exaggeration to compare her to the goddess of fall foliage, Princess Tatsuta herself. And when it came to weaving, she was as skillful as the Celestial Weaver Maid we celebrate at Tanabata.[4] Gifted in such ways, she was an exceptional wife." The Warden felt a keen sorrow at the memory. Tō no Chūjō tried to console him, saying "Her weaving may have been unsurpassed, but her real virtue was following the example of the Celestial Weaver Maid, who faithfully keeps her vow of love with the Celestial Oxherd. The fact is, you cannot expect to find someone again whose weaving

---

4. Tanabata is a festival on the seventh day of the seventh lunar month that celebrates the annual meeting of the young lovers Orihime (the celestial weaver maid, i.e., the star Vega) and Hikoboshi (the celestial oxherd, i.e., the star Altair). Because their love distracted them from their heavenly responsibilities, they were separated by the Milky Way and are allowed to meet only once a year, crossing on a bridge formed by the wings of a flock of magpies. Princess Tatsuta (Tatsuta-hime) is the goddess of fall who weaves the brocade of autumn foliage on Mount Tatsuta. She is thus the patron goddess of weaving and dyeing.

compares with that of Princess Tatsuta. When the passing flowers or autumn foliage are not in harmony with the hues of the season, they do not stand out as brightly, and their beauty dissipates. Women are just like that . . . their beauty passing out of season. That's why it's so difficult in this hard life to decide upon a wife." His words were an encouragement to continue talking.

The Warden once more resumed his discussion. "After she died, I started calling on a woman whose family lineage was peerless and who seemed to have an exquisitely refined temperament. She wrote poetry in a flowing hand, was well trained in the plucking style of the koto, and sang like a master. I couldn't find any flaws in anything I saw or heard of her. She was also passably good-looking, and so even while I continued to be on familiar terms with the woman who bit my finger, I was also secretly visiting this other woman, and eventually grew very attracted to her. After the death of my wife, while I was grieving and wondering what I should do, I came to the realization that nothing could be done for those who have died and started visiting the other woman more frequently. After I became familiar with her, I began to notice that she was somewhat ostentatious . . . and flirtatious. Since she did not seem to be the sort of woman I could trust, I began to keep my distance a little, and when I did so she started meeting another man in secret.

"It was an autumn evening during the tenth month. The moon was bright and seductive, and as I set out from the palace I encountered a certain high-ranking courtier. We got into my carriage together, and though I was intending to stay the night at the home of my father, who was a Major Counselor at the time, this courtier told me he was quite eager to stop by a certain place where a woman was waiting for him. Because the house he mentioned happened to be on the way to my father's house, I caught a glimpse of its garden through the fence and saw the moon shimmering on the surface of the pond. Finding it hard to pass by a dwelling where even the moon seemed to have taken up residence, I dismounted the carriage with the man. He apparently had had this sort of rendezvous before, and seemed very excited when he sat down on the widely spaced boards of an open veranda near the inner gate. He struck a dashing pose as he gazed up at the moon. Chrysanthemums, their colors faded by the autumn frost, were arrayed gorgeously, and the scarlet profusion of scattered maple leaves rustling in the breeze looked magnificent. The man took out a flute from the breast fold of his robe and began to play various popular *saibara* such as "The shade is good."[5] He also sang a few verses: "Let us tarry awhile at the well of Asuka, the shade is good, the waters cool, the grasses inviting . . . " The woman inside accompanied him skillfully, having apparently readied her six-string koto. Her instrument reverberated clearly, and she played it flawlessly, softly, having tuned it to a folksy minor key, and the sound that wafted from the other side of the bamboo blinds seemed quite fashionably modern, a perfect accompaniment to the pure autumn moon. The man was charmed and impressed, and moved closer to the blind. Alluding to a poem about visiting the abode of a beautiful woman, he tried to get a response from her, saying 'I see no trace of anyone having disturbed the fallen leaves in your garden.' He picked some chrysanthemums and composed a poem.

5. The genre of music referred to here, the *saibara*, was a popular form in which the lyrics of folk songs (usually) were set to Chinese music. Lines from various *saibara* appear throughout the narrative.

> How lovely are the peerless moon
> And music here . . . yet do they draw
> Aught but coldhearted men to you

'I hear you have spoken ill of me. But never mind. Let me have one more song. When a person you want to encourage to listen is present, you should put all your skills on display.' The woman replied to his brazen bantering, affecting a disinterested voice.

> A leaf can never hope to stay the autumn breeze
> Any more than words or music could make tarry
> This flutist who accompanies the bitter wind

She responded seductively, unaware that I was witness to her distasteful forwardness. She then switched to a larger thirteen-string koto tuned to the *banshiki* mode,[6] darker in tone and thus appropriate for the season. Her style of plucking was lively and contemporary, and yet, even though her playing sparkled, listening to her left me feeling unsettled and embarrassed. When a lady you are seeing intimately from time to time goes out of her way to be fashionably elegant, she is certainly very alluring, at least on those infrequent occasions when you actually meet. But if on one of your rare visits a woman you are considering as a possible mate behaves too voluptuously, then you begin to grow wary and worry she might not be reliable after all. On the basis of what I observed that evening, I decided to end my affair with that lady.

"Though I was young and inexperienced at the time, when I look back and compare those two women, their capriciousness made them seem inscrutable and unreliable to me. And from now on I will likely be even more inclined to feel that way about women. Your lordships may take delight only in the pleasures of those fragile and fleeting charms of a young lady who poets would liken to the dew on bush clover that scatters when you pluck the flower, or to sleet on leaves of dwarf bamboo that melts away at your touch. But though you may feel that way now, just wait another seven years, and when you reach my age you will think the same way I do. Please take my poor, humble advice and be careful with women who lead you on. They'll cheat on you and make you look foolish in the eyes of others." And so he advised them.

Tō no Chūjō continued nodding. Genji smiled faintly, apparently agreeing with the Warden, and remarked, "It seems in both cases your romantic escapades were awkward and unlucky." They all had a good laugh.

Tō no Chūjō spoke up next. "I'd like to tell you about a foolish woman I knew. I started seeing her in secret, and because it looked as though I would have to keep seeing her on the sly, I didn't think our affair would last. But as we grew intimate I came to have deeper feelings for her, and even though I could not meet her very often, I simply couldn't get her out of my mind. Eventually our relationship reached the stage where I could see she trusted me; and many times I honestly thought if she depends on me so much, then there must be things I do that upset her. If there were, however, she never let on about them. Even when I did not visit her for long stretches, she did not jealously resent me or think me inconsiderate. Instead, she kept up appearances morn-

---

6. A musical mode particularly suitable for winter [editors' note].

ing and night, as if she expected me every day. She was so meek and docile that I was moved to pity and assured her that she could always rely on me.

"She had no parents and was quite lonely and helpless. That's why I found it touching that she apparently thought of me as her provider. She was so quiet and unassuming that I was unconcerned and let my guard down . . . but then, during one of those long stretches when I did not call on her, she received some rather deplorable messages from my wife's household . . . messages that implied threats against her. Unfortunately I heard about that only much later.

"I was unaware there had been such unpleasantness, and even though I had not forgotten her, we went so long without exchanging a word that she grew despondent. She was so wretched worrying over the baby girl I had fathered by her that she sent me a wild pink, suggesting, I suppose, that the child was like the flower, hidden from sight and easy to overlook." Tears welled up in Tō no Chūjō's eyes.

"And the letter that accompanied the flower?" asked Genji.

"Nothing special, really," he replied. "She sent this poem.

> The hedge around the hut of the mountain peasant
> Grows untended now . . . let fall your tender mercy
> Let it fall like dew and settle on this wild pink[7]

"With her verse fresh in my mind, I went to see her. She was as faithful and uncomplaining as ever, but her face was worn with care. It was autumn, and as she gazed out from her dilapidated house at the overgrown garden drenched in dew, her tearful expression seemed to vie in sadness with the melancholy chirring of the bell crickets. I felt as though I were in some old romance.

> I cannot judge which of these flowers is fairest
> Their colors mingling in never-ending summer
> But there is none dearer than my little wild pink

"I turned my attention from the child and comforted the lady by reminding her of the old poem in which a lover promises to visit always, so that dust never settles on their bed.[8] She replied with this.

> Autumn arrives and rough winds shake
> Dew from wild pinks and tears from sleeves
> That wipe dust from my lonely bed

---

7. The word translated as "wild pink" is *nadeshiko*. In the two poems that follow immediately below, the word for "wild pink" is *tokonatsu*. Although the two names refer to the same flower, Murasaki Shikibu uses both in this sequence of poems to distinguish between mother and child. In the first poem, *nadeshiko* refers to Tō no Chūjō's child by his lover, while in the second and third poems *tokonatsu* refers to the woman. Both *nadeshiko* and *tokonatsu* may be identified as other flowers (e.g., a carnation or a gillyflower), but both are generic names for "pinks." I have chosen to use the name "wild pink" to suggest the well-worn theme in the tradition of Japanese literature that Murasaki Shikibu drew on of a beautiful lover who is discovered by a man in an out-of-

the-way place, like a wild flower growing in a hidden spot. The two poems below also play on the word *tokonatsu*, which is a homophone for "never-ending summer," and which has an element, *toko*, that is a homophone for "bed." [The mother appears in chapter 4 (*Yūgao*) as Genji's lover, the lady of the Evening Faces. The little girl is the future Tamakazura, who will later be taken in by Genji. In chapter 25, included in the selections below, she discusses with Genji the virtue and vices of romantic tales—editors' note.]

8. Poem from *The Kokinshū* by Ōshikōchi no Mitsune: "I long to stop even a mote of dust from settling on this bed of pinks that have come into bloom since first you and I lay on our bed."

"She spoke casually, giving no hint that she harbored any serious resentment. Even when she wept, she seemed ashamed and awkward and tried to hide her face from me. It was painful to her that I might see she felt I had been cruel, and so I was reassured about our relationship and did not visit her again for a long time. During that interval she ran off somewhere, disappearing without a trace.

"She may still be alive somewhere, but her situation must be precarious and uncertain. If only she had given some indication of how strongly attached to me she was at that moment when I was so moved by her plight, then she would never have had to run away like that. I would never have neglected her as I did, but would have treated her properly, just like any other woman I called on, and looked after her forever. I cherished that little wild pink, and so assumed I would always be able to visit her. But now I am unable to track her whereabouts. Certainly this woman belongs to the category of the unreliable type you mentioned earlier. She appeared so unruffled, never letting on that she found my treatment of her cruel, but in the end my feelings for her, which had never waned, turned out to be nothing more than a futile, one-sided love. Now, even as I'm slowly getting her out of my heart, I sometimes think about her, imagining that she has not forgotten me altogether . . . that there are evenings when she realizes she cannot blame anyone else for her predicament and her heart smolders with regret. She is certainly the type of woman you cannot rely on or hold to for very long.

"Although a difficult woman is memorable, and thus hard to get out of your mind, when things do not go well and you find it troublesome to continue seeing her . . . as you found with the woman who bit your finger . . . you tire of the relationship. And a talented woman like your koto player is almost certain to be burdened by the sin of infidelity. As for the woman I spoke of, she was so utterly lacking in character that I have doubts about her as well. So I have reached the point where I find it impossible to choose which type of woman is best. It has proven difficult to compare each respective relationship between men and women in this manner. Where is the woman who could combine the virtues of the three women we discussed without inevitably bringing with her all their unmanageable flaws? Set your sights on the beautiful goddess of fortune, Kichijōten,[9] and not only will her holiness bore you stiff, but you'll end up reeking of incense to boot!" The young men all laughed at that.

"But come now," Tō no Chūjō prodded the Junior Secretary from the Ministry of Rites, "there must be a few unusual affairs going on around your place. Tell us a little about them."

"Do you honestly think anything worth discussing happens in a place as lowly as mine?" the young man said. But Tō no Chūjō pressed him, insisting that he was waiting for a response, and so the Junior Secretary wracked his brain to come up with some tale.

"When I was still a student of letters at the academy in the Ministry of Ceremonials,[1] I happened to be calling on a clever young woman. Like the woman

9. Images of Kichijōten were common in Buddhist temples, and it was said that monks often fell in love with her [editors' note].
1. This official academy or university was loosely based on Chinese bureaucratic models and used to train young men for positions in the govern-

ment. The course of study largely emphasized the Confucian Canon and focused on the fields of Chinese Classics, law, ethics, and letters (primarily history and poetry). It also provided instruction in practical fields such as mathematics and yin-yang studies [i.e., divination].

the Warden mentioned, she was a good companion. I could discuss official matters with her, and she was also deeply prudent when it came to the conduct of household affairs. Her brilliance would put an unprepared scholar to shame, and so it was hard to hold my own with her in any conversation we had.

"I began to attend an academy to study Chinese with a certain scholar who just happened to have many daughters. As things turned out, I became intimate with one of them, and when her father found out he brought out some ceremonial sake cups and spoke to me in an overly suggestive tone, reciting a line from Bai Juyi's poem in praise of marriage: 'Listen while I recite a poem about the two paths of life.' You know the poem . . . the one that extols the virtues of a wife who comes from an impoverished home and urges the husband to cherish her. I hadn't actually fallen head over heels for the woman or anything like that, but I was mindful of her father's feelings. In any case I was beholden to him, and she was a kind and considerate support to me. Even during our pillow talk she would impart her knowledge of Chinese, teaching many crucial things I would need for my official position. Her own writing was clear, almost mannish. She employed a precise, rational diction and never mixed the more feminine kana script with her Chinese characters. Naturally I couldn't break off the relationship, because with her as my teacher I was able to learn how to write halting verses in Chinese. Even now I can't forget the debt I owe her . . . but then again for a man like me who has no intellectual talents at all to have to rely on a woman I was intimate with and have her witness my pathetic performances . . . well, it was too shameful. Your lordships, of course, would never need such an efficient and rigorous helpmate. As for me, even though our relationship strikes me as trivial and regrettable now, at the same time she was someone I was drawn to, perhaps as a result of a karmic bond from a former life. It seems that men are really the feckless ones." The moment he finished, both Genji and Tō no Chūjō cajoled him, saying "Well, well, a most intriguing lady indeed" in order to get him to finish up his story. Knowing he was being led on, the Junior Secretary feigned distaste, a comical sneer crinkling his nose as he continued.

"Now then, I did not go to see her for the longest time, and when I finally dropped in on some errand, she was not at all the relaxed, familiar woman she had once been, but instead stayed behind a bothersome screen when we met. It seemed to me she was being peevish, which was foolish behavior, and so I thought this might be the perfect opportunity to break up with her. Yet I knew that such an intelligent woman would never hold a grudge for a frivolous reason. She understood the ways of the world and would not be resentful. She spoke in a voice that sounded rushed and breathy. 'These past few months I have been indisposed by a severe malady and prescribed a regimen of herbal tonic concocted mainly of garlic. This has rendered me extremely malodorous and incapable of meeting you tête-à-tête. Though we cannot meet directly, I would be pleased to undertake any miscellaneous tasks you might request of me.' Her words were so admirably learned, and so . . . manly. When I got up to leave she was perhaps feeling anxious and restless, for she added in a screechy voice, 'Please do come by when this odor has dissipated!' I felt very sorry to leave without responding to her, but there was no reason to hang around and, to tell the truth, the odor was getting to me. So I had no choice but to cast an imploring look at her as if to excuse myself. I sent this poem.

On an evening when a spider's busy spinning
Announces I will soon be here, why should I be told
To wait until the smell of garlic passes from you

"'What sort of excuse are you giving me,' I asked. The words had barely left my lips, and I was on the verge of making my escape, when her reply came chasing me down.

If my love could bring you every night,
Why then should the daytime be so blinding
Or this smell of garlic so offensive[2]

"You have to admit that she was certainly quick." He spoke so calmly that the young nobles found the whole account implausibly sordid. "A complete fabrication," they said, laughing. "Where could anyone ever find a woman like that? You might just as easily have gone off to meet a demon. The whole thing is creepy and weird." Flicking their thumbs with the nail of their index finger to show their disapproval, they chided the Junior Secretary and pressured him to tell them something better than that. But the young man just sat there and replied, "How can I serve you up anything stranger that that?"

The Warden interceded. "Generally speaking, it is really pathetic how people of no importance, men or women, think they have to show off every last little thing they have learned. A woman who acquires knowledge of Chinese and has read the Three Histories or the Five Classics lacks all feminine charm . . . but then again, why should we assume that a woman, just because she is a woman, would go through life without acquiring any knowledge at all of public and private affairs? Though she may not receive any formal education, a woman who has even a modicum of intelligence will retain many things she sees and hears. Through such knowledge she may learn to write cursive Chinese characters, and the next thing you know she's sending stiffly written letters half-filled with Chinese script to other ladies who don't have a clue what to do with them. When you see such a woman you're filled with chagrin, wondering why she couldn't be a bit more soft-spoken and ladylike. She may not have intended to show off her learning in the letter, but of course as it is being read aloud in a halting, strained voice the whole thing seems calculated. There are many examples of this sort of behavior among the upper ranks of court ladies.

"A woman with aspirations to being a poet will become so obsessed with the art of composition that she'll insert allusions to felicitous old phrases even in the opening lines of her correspondence. She'll send off a poem at the most inopportune moments, which can be quite off-putting. If the man doesn't reply, he's inconsiderate, and if he can't come up with an equally learned allusion, he looks ridiculous. For instance, at some seasonal festival, when a man is really busy . . . let's say on the morning of the Sweet Flag Festival in the fifth month when you don't have a moment to think calmly about anything . . . she whips out a poem with some fabulous allusion playing on the words 'sweet flag' and 'sweet eyes,' or some such nonsense. Or maybe it's the Chrysanthemum Festival, when you have no time at all to wrack your brains to come up with

---

2. The poem plays on the word *hiru,* meaning either "daytime" or "garlic." This wordplay explains the Junior Secretary's admiration of her quick wit.

some difficult poem in Chinese as the occasion demands, and here she is sending you a lamentation that strains to play on the words 'chrysanthemum' and 'dew.'[3] The poem is not only unsuitable to the time and place, but also a downright nuisance. What otherwise might have seemed a charming or moving poem at a subsequent reading ends up being totally inappropriate and not worth a second glance because of the manner in which it was sent. Composing a poem with no forethought is not very tactful.

"It is far easier to deal with a woman who has no talent for discerning the proper moment or season to compose, who does not put on airs and try to act refined in a way that leaves you wondering why she did what she did. In all cases a woman should pretend to be ignorant, even if she has a little learning. And when she has something to say, she should just focus on a couple of points and skip the rest."

While the Warden was droning on Genji was preoccupied with thoughts of one woman in particular . . . Fujitsubo. Comparing her to the women he had heard about this evening, he was moved to an even greater admiration, since she seemed to be that rare type who was neither extravagant nor lacking in any way.

There was no conclusion to their discussion; and in the end as daybreak neared their ramblings came to include some rather queer and disreputable stories.

* * *

FROM CHAPTER V

Wakamurasaki

Little Purple Gromwell

* * *

With no one to talk to, and with idle time to kill after the healing rites were completed, Genji stepped out under cover of the heavy evening mist and set out toward the fence he had seen earlier. He had already sent his attendants back to their homes and was peeking through the fence with Koremitsu. In a nearby room, which was facing west toward Amida's Pure Land,[4] they saw a nun performing religious devotions before her own personal image of Amida Buddha. The blinds were raised a little, and she was apparently making an offering of flowers. Leaning against one of the central pillars, she had placed a sutra scroll on top of an armrest and was struggling to read the scripture—but she did not look like an ordinary woman. She was probably over forty, her complexion quite fair and graceful, and though she was thin, her cheeks were plump, and the strands of her hair, which had been cut attractively to neatly

---

3. The Sweet Flag Festival, which fell on the fifth day of the Fifth Month, was celebrated at the court with equestrian and archery competitions. The Chrysanthemum Festival was observed on the ninth of the Ninth Month; chrysanthemums were thought to possess properties that ensured a long life, and so on that day, the flowers were wrapped in thin cot- ton cloths that, once dampened with dew, were rubbed over the body to take advantage of chrysanthemums' supposed life-prolonging properties [editors' note].

4. Devotees of Pure Land Buddhism believe that they will be reborn in the "Western Paradise" of the Buddha Amitabha [editors' note].

frame the area around her eyes, struck Genji as more distinctively fashionable than the long hair that was the common style. Watching her, he was touched by her appearance.

Two pretty adult attendants, also neatly turned out, were with her, and some young girls were playing there, running in and out of the room. One of them, who must have been about ten years old, was wearing a white singlet under a soft, crinkled outer robe dyed the rich yellow of mountain rose and lined with a yellow fabric. She didn't look like the other girls at all; her features were so attractive that Genji could tell at once that she would grow up to be a woman of surpassing beauty. Her hair flowed out behind her, spreading open in the shape of a fan as she stood there, her face red from brushing tears away.

"What happened?" the nun asked her. "Did you get into a quarrel with the other girls?" When the nun looked up to speak, Genji could see the resemblance in their faces and assumed that they must be mother and daughter.

"Inuki let my baby sparrow out of the cage and it flew away." The girl was pouting.

One of the young women sitting there said, "Careless as usual. Inuki's in for a real scolding this time. What a nuisance she is! So where did the sparrow go? It's such a darling little thing, it would be horrid if the crows get to it." She stood up and went out, her hair quite long and luxuriant. She was quite easy on the eyes, Genji thought. Apparently her name was Shōnagon, and she was the nurse who looked after the little girl.

"How childish!" the nun said. "Really, this whole thing is just too petty. You pay no heed to me, even though I could pass away any day now, and instead go running about chasing after sparrows. How many times have I told you it's a sin in the sight of Buddha to capture living creatures. It's deplorable. Come over here!"

The girl knelt down beside her. Her face was remarkably sweet, her unplucked eyebrows had the most charming air about them, and the cut of her hair and the look of her forehead, with those bangs swept up so innocently, were unbearably cute. Genji couldn't stop gazing at her. *I'd really love to see her when she's grown up.* It occurred to him that his desire to see her grown up was kindled by her uncanny resemblance to Fujitsubo, the woman to whom his heart was eternally devoted. It was thus natural that his gaze would be drawn to the girl, and tears came to his eyes.

Stroking the child's hair, the nun told her, "You may not be fond of combing your hair, but it's so lovely. You are such a silly girl, and your childishness weighs heavily on my mind. Other children your age don't act like this. Even though your mother was only ten when her father passed away, she still understood everything going on around her. It won't be long before I die and you'll be left completely alone in the world. How will you ever manage to get by?"

Seeing the nun weep so bitterly, Genji felt a pang of sympathetic sorrow. The girl, with her childish emotions, stared at her grandmother, then hung her head and stared at the floor. Her hair came cascading down around her face. It was splendidly lustrous.

Just then the nun composed a verse.

> The evanescent dewdrop tarries, reluctant
> To disappear into the sky and abandon
> The tender shoot of grass to its uncertain fate

The other young woman, who was still sitting in the room, was now crying. "How true!" she said, and composed this reply.

> How could the dewdrop disappear
> Without knowing the destiny
> Of the shoot of grass it clings to

Just then the bishop entered. "What are you doing? You're clearly visible from the outside. Why, today of all days, are you out on the veranda? I just found out from the ascetic who lives up the mountain that his lordship, Captain Genji, has arrived to receive treatment for his fever. He arrived in such secrecy that I knew nothing about it. I've been here all this time and didn't pay my respects to him."

"How awful," the nun said, lowering the blinds. "Has anyone seen us like this? We're not at all presentable."

"Don't you want to take this opportunity," asked the bishop, "to catch a glimpse of the Radiant Genji? After all, he has such a noble reputation at the court. His looks are enough to make even the heart of a monk who has renounced society forget the sorrows of life and desire to live on in this world. I shall send him a letter."

Upon hearing the bishop stand up to leave, Genji also retired, delighted at the thought that he had discovered such a gorgeous child under these circumstances. His amorous companions were always going out, and so they were skilled at finding the kind of unusual woman that one rarely meets at court. Genji, however, could only go out occasionally, and so he was even more delighted to have the unexpected good fortune to stumble across a girl like this. She was certainly lovely, but her beauty made him curious. Who was she? She resembled Fujitsubo so closely that he was completely taken with the notion that he might be able to make her a replacement for the woman he loved, keeping the girl by him mornings and evenings as a comfort to his heart.

Genji had withdrawn and was lying down and resting when a disciple of the bishop called out for Koremitsu. They were close by, so Genji could hear everything they said. The disciple was apparently reading the bishop's message: "I just now learned that his lordship has passed by my residence, and though I was caught by surprise, I still should have called on you. However, as you know, I have secluded myself in this temple, and so I regret that you have traveled here in secret, for I could have made my abode, rough and humble though it is, ready for you. I feel this is truly unfortunate, for it was in no way my intention to slight you."

Genji sent back a reply: "Starting around the tenth of this month I began suffering repeated bouts of ague. The attacks were so frequent I found them hard to bear, and so on the advice of others I came discreetly to see the ascetic here. I chose to keep my journey a strict secret, because if the ascetic's spells were ineffective for me, it would certainly damage his reputation. It would be a much greater pity if such a venerable ascetic were to fail than it would be if the healer were some ordinary priest, and so I wanted to exercise some caution. I shall go to your residence presently."

The bishop himself appeared soon after. Even though he was a priest, he had a reputation at court as a man of flawless breeding and dignity, and his bearing was enough to put people to shame. Genji, who was dressed in humble fashion, felt awkward before him. The bishop spoke of the time he had spent in seclusion here, and then insisted repeatedly that Genji pay him a visit. "My house is a rustic hut, not much different from this abode here, but you can at least get a view of a cool stream there." Genji felt embarrassed as he recalled the fawning manner in which the bishop had described his radiant looks to the women, who had never seen him. Still, he was eager to learn more about the lovely little girl, and so he went with the bishop.

Just as the bishop said, the garden at his residence exuded an air of elegance. The trees and grasses, which were familiar varieties, had been cultivated with special care. Because it was the night of the new moon, cressets had been set along the banks of the stream, the light from their fires reflecting in the water, and oil lamps were hung beneath the eaves. The room facing south at the front of the house had been cleaned and neatly prepared. The refined scent of incense wafted out from the interior and mingled with the scent of the ritual incense offered to the Buddha, suffusing the entire area around the residence. Genji's perfumed robes carried their own special scent, which the people in the house could not help but notice.

The reverend bishop instructed Genji on the evanescence of this world and on the worlds to come. Genji, with some trepidation, was forced to acknowledge to himself the gravity of his sin of loving Fujitsubo, and it was torment knowing he could do nothing about the one thing preoccupying his heart. It seemed that he was doomed to suffer obsessively on account of his sin for the rest of this life; and what made it worse for him was always imagining the kinds of terrible retribution that awaited him in future lives. He thought he would like to leave the base temptations of this world and retreat to a humble abode like this . . . but then he found it hard to concentrate on the bishop's lesson, since the alluring vision of that young girl he had spied on during the day lingered in his heart alongside the image of the woman, Fujitsubo, the girl so resembled.

"Who lives here?" Genji asked. "On arriving today, I was reminded of a dream I wanted to ask you about."

The bishop smiled. "So you want to suddenly change the subject to your dreams, do you? Well, you can ask, but I'm afraid I'll disappoint you. You probably didn't know the former Major Counselor, since he passed away some time ago, but his primary wife was my younger sister. After he died she took religious vows and left her household to become a nun. She has been suffering from a variety of ailments recently, and since I no longer go back to the capital she decided to seclude herself by taking my residence for her haven."

Genji said, "I've heard that the Major Counselor had a daughter. My motive in asking about her, by the way, is quite sincere. It is not frivolous curiosity."

"He did indeed. One daughter. Let's see . . . it's been more than ten years now since she died. The late Counselor intended to send her into service at the court, and so he raised her with the greatest care. When he passed away before he could realize his hopes and dreams, my sister ended up raising her daughter by herself. When the girl reached womanhood Prince Hyōbu, who was Minister of War at the time,[5] was able to conduct a clandestine affair with her, using one of her scheming ladies-in-waiting as his go-between. Prince Hyōbu's pri-

---

5. The name Prince Hyōbu is taken from the Ministry of War (Hyōbushō). Since this prince is identified by his position, I continue to use this name as a matter of convenience.

mary wife, however, was a woman of impeccable birth, and as a result my niece suffered various insults that brought worry and grief. She grew increasingly despondent day by day, until at last she died. I have witnessed with my own eyes how sick from worry a person can get."

Genji gathered from the bishop's story that the little girl he had seen was the granddaughter of the nun. The prince in question was the older brother of Fujitsubo, which explained the resemblance between the woman Genji loved and the little girl. Now he felt an even stronger desire to see the girl and make the child his own. She was possessed of both a noble lineage and extraordinary beauty, but she also had an obedient temperament, and was not impudent or forward. He wanted to get close to her, raise and train her in accordance with his own desires and tastes, and then make her his wife.

"A sad tale, indeed," Genji remarked. "Did your niece leave any children behind to remember her by?" He wanted to find out for sure what had become of the little girl he had seen earlier.

The bishop told him, "A child was born just before my niece died . . . a girl. The child is the cause of terrible worry for my sister, who as death approaches fears she will leave her granddaughter in an unsettled situation."

So she's the one I was looking at.

"I know this will sound like a bizarre request, but would you do me the kindness of asking the girl's grandmother to consider allowing me to take charge of the child? I have good reasons for this request. I do call upon my primary wife from time to time, but we really don't get along so well, and I live alone for the most part. You may not consider her the proper age for such an arrangement, and you may think I am motivated by some common, base desire. But if you do, you are being unkind and dishonoring my intentions."

"Such a proposition would normally be met with great joy, but the girl is still so innocent it would be difficult, would it not, to take her as a wife . . . even if the whole thing was done in jest? A woman becomes an adult when a husband looks after her, and so it is not my place to deal with the details concerning such a matter. If I may, I will consult with her grandmother and try to obtain an answer for you."

The bishop was so forbiddingly sincere and stiffly formal in his manner of speech that it made Genji's youthful spirit feel small, and he was unable to come up with a clever response.

"It's time," continued the bishop, "to perform my devotions before the shrine of Amida Buddha in the prayer hall. I have not finished early evening services yet, but I will call on you again when they are over."

The bishop left and Genji was feeling ill. It had started to rain, bringing a cooling breeze. To top it off, the water in the pool of a nearby waterfall had risen with the spring runoff, and the roar was clearly audible. He could just barely make out the sound of sleepy voices reciting sutras, a sound that sent chills through him. The atmosphere of the place would have affected even the most insensitive of people, and, coupled with his preoccupation with both Fujitsubo and the girl, it prevented him from getting any sleep at all. The bishop had told him that he was off to early evening devotions, but it was already late at night. Genji could clearly sense that the women who resided in the interior of the house were not asleep, and though they were trying to be quiet he could make out the clicking of rosary beads rubbing against an armrest and the elegant, inviting rustle of robes. Because they were near him, he slid open ever so slightly the center panels of the screens that had been set up outside his room and lightly tapped the palm of his hand with a fan in order to draw their attention. Apparently they thought it unlikely that anyone would be there, but at the same time they couldn't very well ignore his summons, and so he heard one of the women moving over toward him. Confused, she then retreated a bit and said, "That's odd. I thought I heard something. I must be deluded."

Genji spoke up. "They say the guiding voice of the Buddha will never delude you or lead you astray, even in the darkest places." The voice was so youthful and aristocratic that her own voice sounded hesitant and embarrassed when she asked, "Guiding to where? I'm not sure I understand you."

"You probably think something is amiss, which is reasonable, since I called out so suddenly. Please present the following to your mistress."

> Glimpsing that sweet child, so like a shoot of spring grass,
> The sleeves of my traveling robes never dry out
> Damp as they are from dew and my own endless tears

The woman responded, "You surely know there is no one here who would accept that kind of message. To whom should I give it?"

"It so happens," Genji explained, "that I have reasons for my request, and so I ask for your understanding."

The woman retreated back into the interior of the house and spoke with the nun, who was confused by the request. It was, after all, shocking in so many respects.

"Really, these young people and their modern ways!" she grumbled. "Apparently this lord is under the misapprehension that the girl is old enough to understand the relationship between men and women. And how did he come to hear about our poems that referred to her as 'young grass'?"

She was confused, but realized she was being rude by taking such an inordinately long time to respond. So she sent the following.

> Are you comparing the dew-soaked pillow
> Of a single night's journey to these sleeves
> Covered by the moss of ancient mountains

"My robes, it seems, will never dry."

"I'm not very experienced at communicating this way through a messenger," Genji answered. "Please forgive me, but I would be grateful if you would allow me a moment to speak with you about a serious matter."

The nun turned to her attendants. "I'm afraid he's mistakenly heard that the girl is older than she is. He seems to be such a high-ranking lord, I feel humbled before him. How should I respond?"

"You must answer him," one of her women advised. "It would be a pity if you made him feel awkward."

"Yes, I suppose you're right," the nun relented. "But if I were still a young woman, I'd find it rather improper to meet him. His words are so earnest they make me feel unworthy." She rose and moved nearer to him.

"I realize that this is all quite sudden for you, and under these circumstances you must think my request rash and immoderate. But I assure you, I have no base desires in my heart, and swear to you that the Amida Buddha himself understands the depths of my feelings, which you seem to find incomprehensible." Genji spoke in a very respectful manner, since he was himself feeling awkward about raising the subject so directly in the presence of her quiet dignity.

"I must admit I never imagined that we would meet," the nun responded, "but that doesn't mean I consider the karmic bond between us to be shallow. Why should I, since we are speaking to one another like this?"

"I was moved when I heard about the painful struggles the girl has endured," Genji continued, "and wondered if you would consider me a substitute for the mother who has passed away. I was at a very tender age myself when I lost my mother and grandmother, the ones who should have cared most closely for me. As the months and years have passed I feel I have been living in a peculiar, drifting state. The girl's situation is so similar to my own that I sincerely ask permission to be her companion. Because I am concerned about how you will interpret my request, I feel constrained in bringing this up to you. However, I will have very few opportunities to approach you."

"I know I should be overjoyed by your request, but I am very reluctant to grant it. I don't know what you've heard about the girl, but isn't it possible that you are misinformed about how old she is? Insignificant though I am, the girl who lives here is completely dependent on me for support, and she's so young, I couldn't possibly agree to your request."

"I know all about her." Genji pressed his case. "If you will just consider the depths of my feelings, which are anything but common, you will put your reservations aside."

In spite of his insistent pleadings, the nun was convinced Genji was unaware of the inappropriateness of the request and would not give her assent. When the bishop returned, Genji at once closed up the folding screen. *Well, at least I've made the request. At least I can feel relieved about that.*

With the arrival of dawn the sound of monks confessing their sins in the hall where they devotedly chanted the Lotus Sutra came drifting down the mountainside. Their voices mingled nobly with the roar of the waterfall.

Genji sent a verse to the bishop.

> Voices of atonement waft down the mountain . . .
> As I awake from dreams and earthly desires
> The sound of falling waters calls forth my tears

The bishop replied.

> Purified in these mountain waters
> My own heart is unmoved by the sound
> Calling forth the tears that soak your sleeves

"I wonder if my ears have grown accustomed to the falling waters?"

The sky brightened to reveal an overcast day. The continuous crying of mountain birds mingled together, so that Genji could not tell from which direction they were coming. The various blossoms on the trees and grasses, whose names he did not know, were scattering in wild profusion, making it look as though someone had spread a brocade cloth over the landscape. He looked on in wonder at the deer ambling about, pausing here and there as they moved along. The scene was a diversion from his illness.

Normally, the old healer wasn't able to get out and about very easily, but somehow he managed to make his way to the bishop's residence and performed a protective spell. His voice was hoarse, and he was missing so many teeth his pronunciation was a little off, but he read the *dharani*[6] in a voice that possessed the august quality appropriate to a priest of great distinction and merit.

The party that would escort Genji back to the capital arrived and, after offering their congratulations on his cure, presented him with a message conveying best wishes from the Emperor. The bishop busily prepared delicacies not normally served at court, offering unusual types of fruits and nuts that had been harvested from various places, including the deep valley below.

"I have made a solemn vow to remain here for the year," the bishop told Genji, offering him some rice wine, "and so I will not be able to see you off. Ironically, my vow is now making me regret having to part with you."

"The waters of this mountain will remain in my heart. I have been undeservedly blessed by a gracious message from His Majesty, who is anxiously awaiting my return. However, I shall return here again before the season of spring blossoms has passed."

> Returning to court, I shall tell them
> You must go see the mountain cherries
> Before the breeze scatters their petals

Genji's manner of speaking and the tenor of his voice were dazzling. The bishop replied.

> The udumbara blooms once in three thousand years
> When a perfect lord appears[7] . . . having looked on you
> I no longer have eyes for those mountain cherries

Genji smiled and sagely remarked, "The Lotus Sutra teaches that the flower of the udumbara blooms only once and in its proper time, which is quite rare. You flatter me."

The healer received the wine cup and looked at Genji in tearful reverence.

> The pine door waiting deep in the mountains
> Has now been opened so that I can see
> The face of a flower ne'er glimpsed before

As a memento of their meeting, he presented Genji a *tokko*.[8] The metal rod, with its diamond-shaped points at both ends, was one of the implements he used in his esoteric rituals to symbolize the strength and wisdom needed to break free of earthly desires.

The bishop also presented several appropriate gifts. One was a rosary made of embossed seeds from the fruit of the bodhi tree that the famed Prince Shōtoku had acquired from the Korean kingdom of Paekche. The rosary had been placed in a Chinese style box that was wrapped up in a gauze pouch and attached to a

---

6. Dharani are spells or incantations used for meditation, healing or protection. They consist of a phrase or line originally in Sanskrit that encapsulates a central teaching of a sacred text in Buddhism. Dharani were used as an aid in meditation and, in this case, as a protective spell.

7. A Buddhist belief (the udumbara is a variety of fig) [editors' note].

8. This is an abbreviation of *tokkosho* (Sanskrit, *vajra*), a Buddhist ritual implement [editors' note].

branch of five-needle pine. Another gift was a set of medicine jars made of lapis lazuli, which were filled with medicines and attached to branches of wisteria and cherry.

Genji had arranged to have gifts and offerings brought from the capital for the healer and for the monks who had chanted sutras for him. He presented the required gifts to everyone there, even the woodcutters who lived in the vicinity, and after making an offering for continued sutra readings, he prepared to leave.

The bishop went inside with Genji's message and conveyed it directly to the nun. She replied to him, "No matter what he says, I couldn't possibly give him an answer now. If his heart is really set on the girl, then maybe we can consider it in four or five years."

The bishop agreed with her and told Genji how matters stood. Genji was deeply dissatisfied that the nun had thwarted his desires and responded by having one of the pages serving at the bishop's residence take a note to her.

> Making my way back through morning mists
> Having seen the flower's hues at dusk
> How painful to have to leave them now

Though the nun dashed off her reply, the brushstrokes were elegant and her characters truly graceful.

> It may be hard for the mist to leave the flower
> But gazing at the sky obscured by morning haze
> I can judge neither what it portends . . . nor your aims

Just as Genji was about to board his carriage, a crowd of people, including his brothers-in-law, arrived from the palace to greet him.

"You left without bothering to tell any of us where you were going!" Tō no Chūjō and his brothers had wanted to follow Genji, and so they vented their grievances to him. "We would have loved to join you on your excursion here, but you heedlessly abandoned us. It would be a shame to return to the capital without resting for a while in the shade of these stunningly beautiful blossoms."

They all sat down on the moss in the shade of some craggy outcroppings and passed around the wine cups. The cascading waterfall behind them made an elegant backdrop.

Tō no Chūjō pulled a flute from the breastfold of his robe and began to play clear, dulcet notes. Sachūben kept time by tapping a fan on the palm of his left hand and sang the line "West of the temple at Toyora" from the *saibara* "Kazuraki." The men in the party were all extraordinarily handsome, but Genji, still listless from his fever and leaning against a boulder, was incomparable. His looks were so awesomely superior that no one could take their eyes off him. Tō no Chūjō was gifted at playing the flute, so he had made certain to bring with him attendants who could accompany him on the double-reed *hichiriki* and the seventeen-pipe *sho*.[9] The bishop brought out his own seven-string koto and insisted that Genji play it. "Please, just one song for us. I'd like to give the birds in the mountains a surprise."

---

9. The *hichiriki* is a type of flageolet. The *sho* is a mouth organ, similar to panpipes, made of bamboo.

Genji demurred. "I'm still not feeling all that strong," he said. But then before they all set off he managed to pluck out a not uncharming tune.

Even the humblest monks and pages wept in regret that Genji was leaving so soon. Within the bishop's residence some of the older nuns, having never before seen a man of such extraordinary appearance, remarked, "He surely cannot be a person of this world." The bishop wiped away a tear and said, "Ahh, I am so deeply saddened when I consider what karmic bond should have determined that a man so impressively handsome would be born during the final period of the Dharma in this troubled realm of the rising sun."[1]

To the little girl's innocent heart, Genji seemed a paragon of beauty. "He is even more splendid than my father, the Captain of the Guards."

"If that's how you feel," said one of the female attendants, "then why don't you become his child?"

The girl nodded, thinking how wonderful it would be if only she could. Subsequently, whenever she played with her Hina dolls[2] or drew pictures of the court, she pretended that the lord was the Radiant Genji, and she would dress him in the finest attire and treat him most solicitously.

Genji first went straight to the palace to inform his father of all that had happened in recent days. The Emperor thought his son looked thin and haggard, and he was worried that it might be something serious. He asked Genji about the effectiveness of the venerable healer, and, on hearing the details, remarked graciously, "We must promote him to a more senior rank as a priest. He has apparently accumulated much merit through years of austerities, so why have we never heard of him before?"

The Minister of the Left arrived at the palace as well and spoke to his son-in-law. "I thought about coming to meet you, but since you had gone off in secret I hesitated, not knowing what you were doing. Why don't you come and spend a leisurely day or two at my residence? I can escort you there right away."

Genji did not feel much like going with him, and left the palace reluctantly. The Minister had his own carriage brought around, and then humbled himself by getting in second. His deferential gesture was a polite way of showing the care and solicitude with which he was treating his son-in-law, but it made Genji feel uncomfortable.

Once they arrived at the Minister's residence Genji could see that they had made preparations for his visit. It had been a long time since they had last seen him, and in the interim they had refurbished everything, adding decorations so that the place shone like a burnished jewel. As usual, Genji's wife stayed in her quarters and did not come out to meet him. She finally appeared only after her father had coaxed her repeatedly. Genji watched as she sat there stiffly, not moving a muscle, so prim and proper, arranged like some fairy-tale princess in a painting. *I doubt if it would do any good to tell her what's in my heart or to speak about my trip to the mountains, but it would be wonderful if she would just respond to me in a pleasant manner. Still, the plain truth is that she remains cold and remote in my presence, and we're becoming increasingly distant and estranged as the years go by.* He found the whole situation unfair and intolerable.

---

1. This is a reference to the doctrine of *mappō*, the last of the Three Ages of Buddhism, when the Law or Dharma is corrupted. This doctrine was extremely influential during the Heian Period in Japan.

2. Dolls dressed as highborn men and women [editors' note].

"Just once in a while I'd like to see you acting like a normal wife. I've been quite ill recently, but you couldn't be bothered to even ask how I was. I know that such callous behavior isn't rare for you, but I resent it all the same."

She paused for a moment, then responded, "Yes, I know how you feel. As the poet put it, 'How hurtful it is to be ignored.'" She cast a sidelong glance at him—an expression that gave her face an air of extreme reticence and an affect of grace and beauty.

"You so rarely speak to me," Genji shot back, "so why is it that when you do, you have to say such strange and unpleasant things? You cite the line 'How hurtful it is to be ignored,' but that poem referred to lovers having an affair, not to married couples. What a deplorable thing to say! You're always doing things to put me off, to make me feel awkward. And all the while I've tried various things hoping that the time will come when your attitude toward me changes. But now I see that you have grown even more distant. All right then, perhaps some day, in some life to come . . ."

He withdrew to their bedchamber for the night, but she did not follow after him. He couldn't bring himself to call for her, and so he sighed and lay down. He pretended to fall asleep, even though he was thoroughly disgruntled, his mind troubled by all the difficulties that may arise in relationships between men and women.

He couldn't get the girl out of his mind, and he was curious to see what that little shoot of grass would look like when she was fully grown. The nun, acting as the girl's grandmother, had not been at all unreasonable thinking that the child was not an appropriate age for him. It would thus be difficult to make any hurried advances at this stage. So how could he contrive to bring her with him and always have her as a comfort and joy? The girl's father, Prince Hyōbu, was certainly a refined and graceful man, but his looks did not possess her lambent sheen. So how could it be that the girl bore such a striking family resemblance to Fujitsubo? Was it because the girl's father and aunt were both born to the same imperial consort? Mulling over these points, the family connections made him feel closer to her, and somehow his desires became more urgent.

The day after returning from his mountain retreat, Genji sent letters to the house in Kitayama. His letter to the bishop merely implied what his intentions were. In the letter to the nun he wrote: "Awed and constrained by your august countenance, I was unable to express my thoughts clearly and openly to you. I would be overjoyed if you could at least understand that my decision to address you in this manner is evidence of the depth of my feelings and the sincerity of my motives." He enclosed a letter to the girl as well, which he had folded up in a knot.

> The vision of the mountain cherry
> Continues lingering inside me
> Though I left my feelings there with you

"As Prince Motoyoshi put it, 'I fear the wind that blows in the night.' I too worry that the wind might scatter the blossoms so that I may no longer view them."[3]

---

3. See the following *waka* poem: "Anxious that the wind during the night may have scattered the blossoms of plum, I rise early to view them."

The handwriting was of course magnificent, and even though the letter had been wrapped casually, to the eyes of the older people there it was startlingly beautiful. They were troubled about how to respond, perplexed by the situation.

The nun sent a reply. "I did not give your proposition any serious consideration after you left, and now, even though you have so graciously written to us, I have no idea how to respond. She is not even capable of writing the *Naniwazu*[4] in kana yet, and so even though she now has your letter, it really does no good.

> You left your heart just before
> The mountain blossoms scatter
> Short-lived, like your devotion

"I am now all the more concerned."

The bishop's reply was essentially the same, and Genji was frustrated. After a few days he sent Koremitsu off as a messenger. "There should be a person there, a nurse named Shōnagon. Meet her and find out what you can." *It's his nature I suppose*, Koremitsu thought. *He can never let anything go.* Koremitsu had caught only the briefest glimpse of the girl—and thought she looked very young—but it was pleasant to recall the moment he had seen her.

Receiving yet another letter of proposal from Genji, the bishop thanked Koremitsu, who then met with Shōnagon and conveyed Genji's wishes. He spoke in detail about Genji's feelings and told her about his status and circumstances. He was a smooth, glib talker, and was able to put together quite a convincing case for his lord. For all that, the girl was absurdly young to be married off, and everyone there felt that the request was somehow ominous, even distasteful, and they wondered what Genji had in mind.

Genji had poured his soul into his letter, which was written with deep sincerity, and as he had done before, he included a folded note for the little girl: "I long to see those unconnected characters as you practice writing 'My love for you is not shallow like the reflection of Mount Asaka you see when you peek into the mountain spring.'"[5]

> What does shallow Mount Asaka have to do
> With these deep feelings . . . why is the reflection
> Of your face in the mountain spring so distant

The nun replied for the girl.

> They say one feels regret after drawing water
> From a mountain spring . . . so how could you see the face
> Of a lover in a spring as shallow as this

Koremitsu carried the general sense of her rejection back to Genji. The nurse, Shōnagon, had told him, "Once we have spent some time here and my

---

4. The *Naniwazu* refers to a poem in the Kana Preface to *The Kokinshū* included in this volume that children in particular used, along with the poem on Mount Asaka that appears below, as a text to practice writing the kana syllabary: "The flowers blooming on the trees in Naniwazu tell us winter is over, the spring is here. Flowers blooming on the trees!"

5. The place-name Asaka plays on the homophone *asa*, meaning shallow. The poem Genji cites that the girl would have practiced writing is from the *Man'yōshū*. The poems that follow make variations on similar lines in the *Kokin rokujō*, a *waka* anthology.

young lady's grandmother is feeling better, we will travel to the capital and definitely be in touch with you then." Genji was irritated and dissatisfied.

Fujitsubo was ill and had withdrawn from the palace to her home. Genji could see his father's anxious, grieving expression, which aroused great feelings of pity. Yet he also considered it an opportunity, and was soon lost in a reverie, as if his spirit had drifted out of his body. He stopped calling on his various women and instead idled away the days at the palace or at his own villa, dreamily gazing out until evening, when he would then pester one of Fujitsubo's ladies-in-waiting, Ōmyōbu, to intercede on his behalf. It is not clear how she managed to arrange a tryst, but after some truly outrageous and exhausting machinations she pulled it off and Genji was able at last to be with the woman he considered perfect. His meetings with her were so brief, however, they merely intensified the pain of his lonely yearnings. Were these trysts real, or were they a dream? He could no longer tell.

Her Highness was in a state of constant distraction, for she was all too aware that her unimaginable affair with Genji was genuinely shocking. She was determined to put an end to their relationship, since she found the prospect of continuing to meet him extremely unpleasant and depressing, and her appearance betrayed just how difficult it was for her to cope with the situation. Still, she somehow managed to maintain a sweet and familiar attitude toward Genji, and her dignified demeanor and discretion put him to shame. Her behavior only made him realize that there was no one like her in the world, that he could find no flaws in her—and that realization gave rise to a wistful anguish as he was left to wonder why it was that the woman who turned out to be his ideal was forbidden to him.

How could he possibly tell her all the things he wanted to say? He wished he might reside in obscurity in the perpetual darkness of the Kurabu Mountains. Unfortunately, his nights were short, and brought him nothing but sorrow and pain.

> Though I am with you here and now
> So rare are nights like this I long
> To lose myself inside this dream

He was sobbing now. Feeling pity for him, she replied.

> Will we not be forever the stuff of gossip . . .
> No one has ever suffered the anguish I feel
> Trapped in a dream from which I never awaken

Fujitsubo's turmoil was understandable, and he felt ashamed before her. Ōmyōbu gathered up his robes and brought them to him.

Genji returned to his residence and spent a tearful day in bed. When he was told that Fujitsubo would no longer accept his messages, even though he knew she had always refused to read them anyway, he was hurt and could not focus his thoughts. He did not appear at court, but locked himself away for two or three days. His Majesty was worried by his son's absence and wondered if something was wrong, if he had fallen ill again. In the face of what Genji had done with Fujitsubo, he was terrified by his father's concern.

Fujitsubo was distressed by her plight, and her illness, which had prompted her to withdraw from the palace in the first place, worsened. Messengers arrived one after another urging her to return to the palace, but she refused. There could be no doubt that she was not feeling normal, but no one knew what was wrong with her. As it turned out, she had already secretly surmised her condition, and the shock of realizing that she was expecting a child upset her. She was now panicked and confused. *What will become of me?* More and more, as the summer progressed, she refused to get up. She was now in her third month, and her condition was obvious. Her ladies-in-waiting observed this and grew worried and suspicious. She lamented that she should have to suffer such a strange and unhappy fate.

Because no one guessed what had actually happened, Fujitsubo's attendants were surprised to learn that their lady had said nothing to His Majesty until now. Only Fujitsubo knew, in her heart of hearts, what had happened. Her closest attendants, Ōmyōbu and Ben, the daughter of Fujitsubo's nurse, tended to her intimately in the bath, and so they had clearly seen her condition and recognized what was happening. They were troubled, because they knew they did not dare discuss the situation between themselves. Ōmyōbu in particular felt sad that her lady's inescapable karmic destiny had brought her to this pass. In order to explain the delay in reporting the pregnancy, they had no choice but to tell the Emperor that they had been beguiled by a spirit and had not recognized their mistress's condition right away. The women who served Fujitsubo all assumed that that was indeed the case, and the Emperor, overwhelmed with even more feelings of pity and concern, was constantly sending messengers to ask how she was doing. Their visits, however, only kept her in a constant state of dread and depression.

Genji had a weird and terrifying dream. He summoned a diviner to interpret it and was told it signified that he would be the father of an emperor. This was shocking and unthinkable. The diviner added, "Your dream also means that your fortunes are crossed and that you must exercise caution and good behavior."

Genji felt awkward, and so he told the diviner, "This isn't my dream. I have merely relayed to you what someone of very high rank told me. So until the dream actually comes true, don't say anything to anyone about it." Genji was trying to make sense of things in his own mind, but when he heard that Fujitsubo was pregnant he realized that her child might be what his dream portended. He sent increasingly desperate messages to Fujitsubo, but Ōmyōbu was now having second thoughts. Communicating like this was extremely risky and difficult, and she found she could no longer act as a go-between for Genji. Even her brief one-line replies, which had always been infrequent at best, stopped altogether.

Fujitsubo returned to the palace in the seventh month. Because he had not seen her for so long, His Majesty's desire had only grown stronger, and he lavished his gracious affection on her. She was now a little plump, and her face had grown thin and careworn, but her appearance was truly, incomparably lovely. As he had done before, the Emperor would spend the whole day in her chambers. The early autumn sky told them it was the appropriate season for musical diversions, and so His Majesty was constantly calling for Genji, who had a talent for performance, to come and play various pieces on the koto or the flute. Genji had to struggle to keep his emotions in check on these occasions, though there were moments when his expression betrayed the feelings he found so hard to suppress. For her part, Fujitsubo would obsess over things she wished had turned out differently.

The health of the nun who had been staying at the mountain temple in Kitayama improved, and she finally returned to her residence in the capital. Genji inquired after her and sent her letters from time to time. It did not surprise him that in her replies she continued to refuse his proposition, but it didn't bother him that much because he was preoccupied by his concern with Fujitsubo and had little time to think much about other matters.

By the ninth month, as the end of autumn was approaching, Genji was lonely and depressed. A gorgeous moonlit evening inspired him at last to go to the place of a woman he had been secretly visiting. But then the weather changed—it turned stormy and a chill evening rain began to fall. The lady lived in the vicinity of Rokujō and Kyōgoku, and as he left the palace her place began to seem a little far off to him. On the way he saw a weather-beaten house standing in the gloomy shade of an ancient grove of trees.

Koremitsu was accompanying Genji as usual. "That used to be the house of the late Major Counselor. I guess you should know that I visited it recently and learned that the nun has taken a turn for the worse. They have no idea what to do for her."

"What a pity," Genji replied. "I must pay her a visit. Why didn't you tell me about this earlier? Have a message taken to her."

Koremitsu sent one of the attendants in with instructions to say that Genji had arrived with the express purpose of calling on the nun. The messenger entered and announced his lord's visit. The women were caught off guard, and one of them said, "This is most awkward. Our lady has been feeling much worse these last few days and couldn't possibly meet your lord." Still, it would have been rude and uncouth to send him away, so they prepared a space on the veranda under the eaves on the south side of the house and invited Genji in.

"Frightfully untidy, I'm afraid," one of the women said to him, "but my lady wanted to show some gratitude for your visit. Your arrival was so unexpected, however, that you caught us unprepared. So please forgive the dark and gloomy atmosphere of this chamber."

The place did strike Genji as quite odd, but he answered, "I have been meaning to visit you all this time, but I refrained from doing so because I have been treated in such a way as to make me believe nothing would come of it. I am anxious about you, having just learned that your illness has taken a turn for the worse."

"My ailments are no worse than usual, though I do sense now that I am nearing my end," the nun told him. "You have been gracious enough to call on me, but I'm not able to greet you directly. With regards to your proposal, the girl is still at an innocent age and lacks judgment, but once she is a little more mature, by all means think of her as you would any other woman and take her as one of your own. I'm so worried about leaving her behind in this world, isolated and helpless, that my anxiety creates a burden of attachment for me that will surely be a hindrance on the path to the salvation I pray for."

Because she was in a room close by, Genji could catch fragments of her weary voice. "We are not worthy of this, and should be grateful for his attentions," he heard her continue. "If only the girl were old enough to be able to thank him properly."

Genji was keenly moved. "If my feelings for the girl were truly shallow, then why would I embarrass myself by coming here and possibly looking lecherous?

The moment I recognized there was some kind of karmic bond between us, I was deeply attracted to the girl and convinced to an almost mystical degree that our bond was not something that belonged to this world." He turned to one of the attendants and continued. "My visit here may have been in vain, but may I ask for a word with the girl herself?"

"Oh, I don't know about that," one of the nun's attendants interjected. "She has been kept in the dark about all of this, and is now fast asleep." Just as the woman said these words, the girl's voice could be heard inside. "Grandmama, Lord Genji is here . . . you know, the man who visited us at the temple? So why haven't you gone out to meet him?" The women were all mortified and tried to hush the girl. But she protested, "But didn't Grandmama say that the sight of him was always a comfort to her?" She spoke as if she were informing them of something that would benefit her grandmother. Genji was utterly charmed, but he had to be considerate of the bruised feelings of the flustered women there, and so he pretended he hadn't heard a thing. After politely bidding farewell and leaving his best wishes for them, he made his way home. *She may be a little girl*, he thought, *but I can't wait to see her after she's been properly trained.*

The next day Genji sent a most solicitous letter inquiring after the health of the nun. As always, he included a small folded letter for the girl.

> Hearing a young crane cry I long to go to it
> But my boat tangled among the reeds is hindered
> And I cannot leave this inlet to tend its needs

"As the poet put it, 'I always yearn to go back to the same person.'"[6] Genji deliberately composed his note in a childish hand that was so delightful the women told the girl to imitate it in her copybook.

Shōnagon replied, "Our lady may not make it through the day, and we are preparing to take her back to the temple in Kitayama. She may not be able to express in this world her gratitude for your visit and your expressions of concern." Genji felt very sad when he heard this.

One autumn evening, when he was more preoccupied than ever with his longing for Fujitsubo, the woman who constantly tormented his heart, he felt his seemingly perverse desire to possess her little niece growing even stronger. He remembered a line from the nun's poem—"The evanescent dewdrop tarries, reluctant to disappear into the sky"—and thought lovingly of the girl. At the same time he was anxious and unsure, thinking that she might not live up to his expectations. The image of a *murasaki*[7]—a little purple gromwell—popped into his head.

---

6. *Kokinshū* 732 (Anonymous): "I always yearn to go back to the same person, like a little boat that has made its way through the channel and comes rowing home."

7. The Japanese species of gromwell is a small plant that produces white flowers in the summer. Its purple roots were used to make dye for clothing. As in other cultures, purple was associated with royalty, and so I have translated *murasaki* as "purple gromwell" to indicate both the rustic image of the word and its imperial associations. The Japanese name for wisteria is *fuji*, alluding to the girl's aunt, Fujitsubo, and suggesting through the color purple shared by the two plants the nature of their relationship. Since *murasaki* (or *wakamurasaki*) is the smaller, more rustic plant, Genji's poem acknowledges a difference in their relative status. His poem alludes to *Kokinshū* 867 (Anonymous): "Because of this one purple gromwell, I look on all the grasses in Musashino with tender feelings."

> How I yearn to quickly pluck up and make my own
> That little purple gromwell sprouting in the wild
> With roots that share their color with wisteria

During the tenth month His Majesty decided to plan a visit to the Suzaku Palace. The dancers for the day of departure were to be selected from among sons of aristocratic families, high-ranking officials, and courtiers who had talents suitable for the occasion. From princes and ministers on down, each and everyone practiced their skills. It was a hectic, busy time.

Because of all the preparations, it occurred to Genji that he had not contacted the nun in her mountain temple for some time. When at last he sent a messenger there, he received the following reply from the bishop: "I am sorry to report that she passed away on the twentieth of last month. I know it is the reality of this world that we must all die, but still I cannot help mourning her."

After reading this, Genji experienced the poignant sorrow of the evanescent world and wondered what would become of the girl who had been the source of such worry for the nun. The girl was so young, she must be yearning for her grandmother. Genji had vague memories of being left behind by his own mother, and so he sent his deepest condolences. Shōnagon composed a sympathetic reply.

Genji learned that after the twenty-day period of mourning and confinement was over, the girl came back to the capital and was now at the late nun's residence. He waited until a seemly period of time passed, then went to call on her one evening when he had some free time. The place was run-down and desolate and there were few people about—the kind of place that would surely frighten a child. Genji was shown to the same space on the south side of the residence that they had used on his previous visit. He was moved to tears by Shōnagon's heartbreaking account of her mistress's final days.

"There is talk that the girl's father would have her come to his villa," Shōnagon told him. "But the nun was quite concerned about that prospect. After all, her own daughter, this child's late mother, found the place unbearably cruel and depressing. The girl is now at that in-between stage, no longer a child, but not old enough to really understand the motives of other people. And with all the other children at her father's residence, she is not likely to be welcomed with open arms, but will instead be belittled and treated as a stepchild. With so many indications that the girl will be badly served there, we are grateful for your passing words of kind consideration. Still, we cannot fathom your future intentions, and even though we should feel happy on occasions like this when you visit us, we remain extremely hesitant about your proposal . . . after all, the girl is simply not appropriate for you. Her character is immature and undeveloped, even for someone her age."

"Why do you continue to waver when I have repeatedly opened up to you like this? I know in my heart that my feelings of longing and pity, which her innocence stirs in me, are signs of a special bond between us from a former life. If I may, I would like to speak with her directly and tell her how I feel."

> Seeing the young tangled seaweed struggle to grow
> Amid reeds in the bay of Wakanoura
> Can the wave, once it has drawn near, recede again

"It would be too hateful for the wave to have to withdraw now," Genji concluded.

Shōnagon answered, "You are truly gracious, my lord, but . . . "

> If the algae at Wakanoura yielded
> Without knowing the true intentions of the wave
> Would it not be set adrift upon the shallows[8]

"It just isn't reasonable." The polished manner of her verse made it almost possible for Genji to forgive her refusal. He murmured, "Why does the day when we may finally meet never come?"[9] The younger women in the house shivered in delight and admiration.

The little girl had been lying down, crying and grieving for her grandmother, but then her playmates told her, "A lord dressed in court robes has arrived. Perhaps it is the prince, your father!" She got up and went out to see for herself.

"Shōnagon!" she called out. "Where is the nobleman in court robes? Is my father here?" Her voice sounded achingly sweet as she approached.

"I'm not your father," said Genji, "but that doesn't mean you should treat me as a stranger. Come over here."

The girl immediately recognized his voice and realized this was the splendid lord who had called on them before, and she was embarrassed that she had spoken improperly. She went over to her nurse and said, "I want to go now. I'm sleepy."

"Why do you want to hide from me? Please come over here and rest at my knees. Please, come closer."

"As you can see," said Shōnagon, pushing the girl toward him, "she really knows very little about the world."

The girl sat innocently on the other side of the blinds from Genji, who put his hand through to search around for her. Her lustrous hair was draped over soft, rumpled robes, and even though he did not have a clear view of her, when he touched the rich thickness of the strands he imagined how attractive she must really be. When he tried to hold her hand she was put off that a stranger should have come so close to her and pulled away in fright. "I told you I was sleepy," she said to Shōnagon. At that moment Genji slipped inside the curtains and told her, "You must think of me now as the one you will rely upon. So please don't be distant or afraid."

His actions were upsetting to Shōnagon. "What are you thinking, my lord?" she exclaimed. "Impetuously barging in here like this during a period of mourning . . . it's outrageous. You can talk to her all you like, but it won't do you any good. She's just too young to understand."

"You may be right," Genji answered, "but just what do you think I'm going to do with someone so young? Carefully observe the sincerity of my feelings, the purity of my heart, and you will realize that they are peerless, that you will find nothing like them in this world."

The wind was blowing violently and hail began to fall. It was a lonely, terrifying night. "Why," Genji asked, tears in his eyes, "should she have to spend any more time in this isolated, deserted house?" He couldn't stand the idea of

---

8. Both poems play on the homophone *waka*, meaning "youthful."
9. Compare this *waka* poem by Fujiwara no Koremasa: "Though I keep my impatience a secret, as the years go by, why is it so hard to pass beyond the barrier gate of Ōsaka, the slope where we may finally meet?"

going home and abandoning them here. "Lower the shutters. It looks like it will be a frightful evening," he ordered. "I shall stand guard for you tonight. Please, everyone, gather closer to me."

With a remarkable air of familiarity about him, he went inside the curtained area where the girl slept. The women found his behavior shockingly abnormal, but they did not know what to do and did not even try to move from where they were sitting. Shōnagon couldn't stand it. She was beside herself, but she couldn't very well offer vehement objections, or make a scene; and so she stayed put as well, sighing in lament.

The girl, not knowing what was going on, was truly scared and trembling. Genji felt sorry for her, thinking that her beautiful figure was shivering because of the cold, and he had a singlet brought in and wrapped around her. Genji knew perfectly well that his behavior was not normal, and so he spoke sensitively to the girl.

"You really must come with me. There are many gorgeous paintings at my residence . . . and Hina court dolls to play with." His manner was kind and intimate as he spoke of things he was sure would appeal to her childish heart and allay her fears. Nonetheless, she still found it hard to sleep, and spent the night tossing and turning.

As the night wore on the wind continued to gust and the women whispered among themselves. "How forlorn we would have been had he not come here. If only they were a little closer in age, it would be so wonderful." Shōnagon, worried about her charge, hovered just outside the curtains the whole time. When the wind began to die down a little, Genji got ready to go home. It was still dark, and he had a knowing look on his face, as if he were leaving some romantic tryst.

"Now that I've witnessed her circumstances with my own eyes," Genji said, "it seems too pathetic and I will now, more than ever, be anxious about her. She should be moved to my residence, where I spend my days and nights in solitary reverie. How can she remain here like this? It's a wonder she isn't in a constant state of terror."

Shōnagan replied, "Prince Hyōbu has hinted that he would come for her, but that won't happen until after the forty-nine-day period of purification is complete."

"He *is* the one who really ought to look after her," Genji agreed, "but they have grown accustomed to living apart and the girl most likely regards him as much a stranger to her as I am. I may have only just met her today, but my feelings and motives are not shallow . . . indeed, they are far more worthy than her father's." Genji stroked the girl's hair, then glanced back repeatedly at her as he made his way out.

*　*　*

Genji experienced a swirl of conflicting emotions. There would be gossip about what was going on,[1] and he would undoubtedly gain a reputation as a lecher. If the girl were of an age when she could understand these matters and consent to the relationship, then people would understand and it would all seem normal. But she was not of that age, and if her father were to come

1. That is, Genji's intentions to take away the girl [editors' note].

searching for her, then Genji's own actions would be seen as wild and rash. Yet in spite of all this, if he were to let this opportunity slip away, he would have bitter regrets. And so he left while it was still dark. His wife remained her usual sullen and distant self. "I just remembered some pressing matters I have to attend to," Genji told her. "I shall return shortly." After going to his own quarters in the house at Sanjō and changing his robes, he set off alone with Koremitsu, who was riding alongside the carriage on his horse. He left before the women attendants even realized he was gone.

He knocked on the gate and someone who had been apprised of the situation opened it. Genji had his carriage drawn inside quietly. Koremitsu tapped at the double doors in the corner of the main hall, then coughed as a signal. On hearing this, Shōnagon knew who was there and came out. "My lord has arrived," Koremitsu announced.

"The girl is resting inside," Shōnagon told him. "Why have you come out so late at night?" She assumed they were stopping by on the way back from their previous rendezvous at the palace.

Genji spoke up. "I have something I must tell her before she is moved to her father's residence."

"Whatever would that be? And how could she possibly give you a clear answer?" Shōnagon laughed and began to withdraw.

Genji suddenly barged in, and Shōnagon was completely taken aback. "The older women are in there . . . they are absolutely unpresentable!"

"She's not awake yet, is she?" Genji said. "Well, then, I suppose I shall have to get her up. How can she remain asleep, oblivious to this lovely morning mist?" He went straight on in to the girl's sleeping quarters. Shōnagon was so flabbergasted that neither she nor her women could utter a peep in protest.

Genji picked up the girl, who was sleeping innocently, and woke her in his arms. She was still half asleep, and so she thought her father had come for her. Stroking her tangled hair, Genji said to her, "Come with me. I'm acting as a messenger for your father."

When she saw that it wasn't her father holding her, she was startled and fearful. "Come now, is that any way to act? I am just the same as your father." As he was carrying the girl out, Koremitsu, Shōnagon and the others all asked him what was happening.

"I told you I was worried about not being able to come here very often, and so I want to move her to my residence, which is much safer and more comfortable. If cruelly she were moved to her father's villa, it would be that much more difficult for me to communicate with her. One of you may accompany me if you wish."

Shōnagon, who was now frantic, replied, "But today is the worst possible time you could have chosen. What should I say when her father comes for her? If it is, as you say, truly fated for her to be your wife, then surely that is how things will turn out later on. As it is now, she is just too young, and you have given us no time to think about things, which is putting all of the attendants in an awkward position."

"Very well, then," Genji responded, "some of you may follow her later." He had his carriage brought around, and everyone there was stunned and at a loss what to do. The girl, not knowing what was happening, was frightened and started to cry.

With no way to stop him, Shōnagon brought out the clothes she had been sewing the previous night and, changing into a not altogether unattractive robe herself, got into the carriage with him.

Genji's residence in Nijō was close by, and so they arrived before the first light. The carriage was drawn up to the west hall and Genji alighted. He easily swept the girl up in his arms and brought her out. Shōnagon wavered. "This is all like a dream. What should I be doing?"

"That's entirely up to you. Now that I've brought the young lady here you may return if you wish. I'll be happy to have someone escort you back." Shōnagon smiled bitterly at his words, for she had no choice but to resign herself to the situation. She got out of the carriage. This had all been so sudden and outrageous that nothing could be done about it. She could not calm her heart. *What will her father say? And what about my young mistress? What will become of her? To have been left behind by all the people who loved her . . . it's just too much to bear . . .* She could hardly hold back her tears, but she knew that this was a momentous occasion and that to shed tears now would be an omen of bad luck. So she restrained herself.

The west hall was not usually inhabited, and there were no curtains or furnishings. Genji summoned Koremitsu and ordered him to have curtains, screens, and the like placed here and there where he indicated. He had the silk blinds hanging between the pillars around the inner chamber removed, and he had his attendants straighten up the room. When they were finished, he sent for robes and bedding from the east hall, then went in to rest. The girl now found the scene genuinely creepy, and, uncertain about Genji's intentions, she began to tremble. Still, she managed not to cry out loud.

"I want to sleep with Shōnagon," she whimpered in a girlish voice.

"You must no longer sleep with her," Genji instructed, whereupon the girl fell prostrate, weeping and feeling completely forlorn. Her nurse couldn't sleep either and stayed up all night lost in her thoughts.

As the dawn broke they looked around. The residence and furnishings gave off a resplendent air—even the sand in the garden looked as though someone had scattered jewels all around them. Shōnagon remained hesitant, but it appeared that there were no other women serving in this hall. It was a pavilion where Genji would receive less intimate guests who called infrequently. There were male servants just outside the bamboo blinds, and one of the men, who had heard that his lord had brought a woman here, was whispering to the others. "I wonder who she is? She must be someone extraordinary."

Cooked rice and water for washing up were brought in, and the sun was already high when they finally got up. Genji said, "This won't do at all . . . we have no one in service here. Choose those women at your former residence you would like to have as attendants for your young lady and I will send for them this evening." Genji next summoned some page girls from the east hall, then told his servants, "Have these pages select several younger girls to serve over here." Presently four captivating little girls appeared. The young lady was still asleep, her robes wrapped around her. Genji made her get up.

"This pouting and cold behavior will not do!" Genji scolded. "Would a man who is wild at heart have done all this for you? A woman must be kindhearted and obedient." And with those words, from that moment, her training began.

Her features were even more beautiful than when he had seen her from a distance. He spoke warmly to her, telling her stories and showing her all sorts of delightful pictures and playthings, which he had brought in for her, and did everything he could to soothe her feelings. Eventually she got up and inspected her quarters. She was wearing her dark mourning robes, soft and rumpled, and looked so adorable as she sat there with her innocent smile that Genji couldn't help smiling himself as he watched her.

Genji left for the east hall, and the young lady went over to the edge of the veranda and peeked out at the pond and the trees in the garden. She was fascinated by the grasses, which had been withered by the frost so that they looked like something out of a painting. A crowd of male courtiers of the fourth or fifth rank, none of whom she knew, bustled in and out, making her feel that she had come to some splendid place. She examined the captivating pictures on the folding screens and door panels, and with her childish disposition she was able to quickly comfort herself.

Genji did not go to the palace for two or three days so that he could spend time talking with the girl and making her feel at ease in her new surroundings. He wrote poems and drew pictures, presenting them to her with the thought that they might serve as a model for her own practice. He put them together to make a very charming collection. One of the poems, which he copied on purple-colored paper, was taken from *Kokin rokujō*.

> I've never been there, but lament my fate
> Each time I hear the name "Musashino"...
> The place where little *murasaki* grows

The girl took up the sheet of paper and studied the unusual, exquisite brush-strokes. In smaller characters Genji had added his own verse.

> Unable to cross the dewy plains of Musashino
> I have yet to see the purple roots of the gromwell there...
> How I long for you little kin of the wisteria

"Why don't you try writing something?" Genji encouraged her... though Fujitsubo was still obviously on his mind.

"But I can't write well," she protested, looking up at him. She was so lovely he couldn't help but smile.

"Even if you can't write well, you must at least try. You won't get better if you don't write anything. Let me show you."

He found it charming the way she held her brush and how she turned away from him when she wrote... and he thought it strange that he should have such feelings. "I've made a mistake," she said, trying to keep him from seeing what she wrote. But he made her show it to him anyway.

> I worry, unsure why you grieve...
> Tell me again which plant is it
> The one I am related to

Her writing was quite immature, but he could see at once that she had the talent to be accomplished in composition. The lines of her brush strokes were rich and gentle, and they resembled the hand of her late grandmother. If she practiced more modern models, he knew that she would be able to write very well.

He had court dolls and dollhouses made especially for her, and as they passed the time together he was able to distract himself from his painful longing for Fujitsubo.

The women who had remained behind at the girl's former residence were flustered and embarrassed when Prince Hyōbu came back and asked for his daughter, for they did not know what they should say to him. Genji had told them not to let anyone know what had happened . . . at least not for a while. Because Shōnagon was in agreement and told them it was best to keep quiet, all they could tell the father was "Shōnagon took your daughter into hiding, but she didn't tell us where." Prince Hyōbu assumed nothing could be done and resigned himself to the situation. *Her grandmother was opposed to sending the girl to my residence, and so Shōnagon was moved to carry out her wishes, even if it meant going to this extreme. But why couldn't she just gently tell me that it would be too unbearable to move the girl, rather than willfully spiriting her away?*

When he left the house he said tearfully, "Let me know if you hear any news of her." This troubled the women.

He sent an inquiry to the bishop as well, but the bishop had no clue as to her whereabouts. Prince Hyōbu suffered feelings of longing and regret about the child's beauty, which would now go to waste. The enmity his primary wife had harbored toward the girl's mother had abated, and even she regretted that she would not be able to raise the girl as she had hoped.

Gradually her attendants arrived and gathered in her quarters. Genji and the girl, whom he called his little Murasaki, possessed a rare, modern look as a couple. The youngest attendants and the little girls who were her playmates passed the time together without a care. Although there were lonely evenings when Genji was away and she cried out of yearning for her grandmother, she gave no thought at all to her father. From the beginning she had grown accustomed to not having him around, and she was now exceedingly close to the man who was her new father. Whenever he returned, she would be the first to go out to greet him. They would talk together lovingly, and she never felt distant or embarrassed when he held her to his bosom. Insofar as they looked like a father and a daughter, their behavior was quite endearing.

If a woman has a calculating heart and a troublesome disposition that makes an issue of everything, then a man has to take care that he not allow her emotions to lead her astray and keep her from fulfilling his desires. She will tend to be jealous and resentful, and difficulties he never imagined, such as a separation, will naturally arise. Murasaki, however, was an absolutely captivating companion for Genji. A real daughter, when she had reached this age, would not have been able to behave so intimately, to have gone to sleep or risen in such close proximity to him. Genji came to feel that his young Murasaki was a rare hidden treasure, his precious plaything.

* * *

FROM **CHAPTER VII**

Momiji no ga

An Imperial Celebration of Autumn Foliage

The procession to the Suzaku Palace was set to take place sometime after the tenth day of the tenth month. Because it promised to be an unusually lavish event, the imperial consorts and ladies, who were not permitted to leave the palace, complained bitterly that they would not be able to see it. His Majesty was also disappointed that Fujitsubo would not be able to view the procession, and so he had the musicians and dancers perform a dress rehearsal in front of his living quarters in the Seiryōden.

Genji, a Captain in the Palace Guard, performed a dance titled "Waves of the Blue Sea." His partner was Tō no Chūjō, who, as son of the Minister of the Left, was unquestionably superior to other men in terms of his looks and training. Performing next to Genji, however, he seemed like some nondescript tree deep in the mountains growing beside a cherry in full bloom. As the bright slanting rays of the setting sun shone down on them, the music swelled and the performance reached its climax. Genji was carefully following the prescribed form of the dance, but his movements and expressiveness were without peer. The music paused and he recited the accompanying verse in Chinese by Ono no Takamura in a voice as sweet and ethereal as the cry of the Buddha's heavenly Kalavínka bird.[2] The Emperor was so moved by the performance that he brushed away a tear, while all the upper-ranking courtiers and princes were weeping. At the conclusion of Genji's recitation the lively music, which had paused for him, started up again. Genji had twirled the sleeves of his robe around his arms at the very end of the verse, and he was now readjusting them, his face flushed, looking even more radiant than usual.

As auspiciously splendid as Genji's dance had been, the Kokiden Consort found it strangely disturbing and remarked, "His looks are enough to captivate the gods in the heavens. It seems weirdly unpleasant." The younger women deplored her unkind words.

Fujitsubo might have enjoyed viewing the dance more had it not been for the terrible guilt she felt at having received the Emperor's gracious gift of ordering this rehearsal for her benefit. To make matters worse, she had to watch a dance performed by the very man with whom she had conducted her outrageous affair. The whole thing seemed like a dream to her. That evening she was in service to the Emperor in his chambers.

"Waves of the Blue Sea" had swept everything before it at the rehearsal that day. "What did you think of it?" His Majesty asked Fujitsubo. She struggled to answer, but managed to stammer out, "It was certainly a special performance."

"Genji's partner did not look bad either," the Emperor continued. "When it comes to form and gesture, good breeding will out. Professional dancers, those who have some reputation, are no doubt skillful, but they cannot display the same natural, unaffected beauty and grace that we saw today. They performed so magnificently, I have to admit I'm worried that when they dance under the

---

2. A bird mentioned in Buddhist sutras for its surpassingly beautiful voice, to which the Buddha's voice is often compared [editors' note].

autumn foliage on the day of the procession, it might be a bit of a letdown. But never mind . . . I so wanted you to see the performance that I had them prepare for it."

The following morning Genji sent a note to Fujitsubo. "How did I look yesterday? As I danced, my heart was being torn apart by an unrequited love such as the world has never known."

> I should never have danced in your presence
> With thoughts so troubled . . . did you understand
> When in wild abandon I twirled my sleeves

"I feel uncertain before your grace."

Unable to shake the captivating sight of his face and elegant dancing figure, Fujitsubo could not very well pretend she had not seen his note, and so she replied.

> Chinese dancers conceived the "Waves of the Blue Sea"
> Twirling their sleeves so long ago and far away
> But your every gesture touched me here and now

"My heart is overflowing."

Genji had not expected a reply, and so he was ecstatic. Smiling, he thought that her words, which displayed knowledge of ancient dance and foreign courts, showed she had already acquired the dignity expected of a future empress. He unrolled the letter and pored over it as if it were some treasured sutra.

On the day of the procession the princes of the blood and all members of the court participated. Genji's older half brother, the Crown Prince, accompanied the Emperor, and as was customary two boats were rowed around the lake at the site of the performance. One boat, adorned with the head of a dragon, held performers playing Chinese court music, while the other boat, adorned with the head of a blue heron,[3] carried performers playing Korean court music. There were many varieties of Chinese and Korean dance, and the sound of musical instruments and drums reverberated in all directions. Genji had looked so spectacular at the rehearsal the previous evening that the Emperor's old fears that his son might be fated to die young were revived, and he had sutras read for Genji at various temples here and there to ward off evil. Members of the court who heard about this were sympathetic and thought it a reasonable precaution, but the Kokiden Consort, mother of the Crown Prince, spitefully remarked, "Isn't this really taking things a bit too far?"

The Emperor had gathered and selected the most distinguished players from among courtiers of both high and low rank to serve as the flutists and drummers who would accompany "Waves of the Blue Sea." He had the performers divided into sides—those playing Chinese music on the left, those playing Korean music on the right. He then chose two Consultants from the Council of State, men who also served as the directors of the Left and Right Gate Guards, to conduct the Chinese and Korean music respectively. Prior to this performance each aristocratic house had sought out the most skilled dance instructors and secluded themselves away to practice under their tutelage.

3. The term for these boats is *ryōtōgekisu* (dragon head, blue heron head). In China it referred to a single boat with a carving of a dragon's head at the prow and one of a blue heron's head at the stern, but in Japan it referred to a pair of boats.

The intermittent soughing of the wind in the pines mingled with the indescribably polished sound of forty musicians playing in the shade of tall trees in autumn foliage. Truly it sounded like a breeze blowing down from the deepest mountains, and amidst the multihued leaves that had fallen all around, the dazzling performance of "Waves of the Blue Sea" was sublime. The autumn leaves that had adorned Genji's headdress at the outset had dropped off as the dance proceeded. Having lost a little of its luster, the headdress was now suffering in comparison with Genji's lambent face. So the Consultant who was conducting the musicians of the Left plucked some of the chrysanthemums that had been placed in front of the Emperor and inserted them into the headdress. As the day drew to a close, a chill evening drizzle began to fall, as if the scene had moved the very sky itself. The color of the chrysanthemums now adorning Genji's spectacular figure had faded slightly with the frost, and their beauty was beyond the power of words to describe. Genji himself was putting all his skill into his performance, dancing in a way that would never be equaled again. As he executed the final movements, retracing his steps just before he exited with a flourish, it seemed that an unearthly chill coursed through all of the spectators. Lower-class people were also watching from beneath the trees, or from the shade of craggy rocks, or from beneath the fallen leaves of the mountain trees, and though one would hardly have imagined that they had the sensitivity to appreciate the performance, they were able to dimly recognize the sadness of transient beauty and wept accordingly.

The fourth prince, the Emperor's son by the Shōkyōden Consort, was still a boy. Nonetheless, his performance of "Dance of the Autumn Wind" proved to be the most spectacular event after Genji's dance. Because those two performances were so dazzling, everything that followed seemed bland by comparison, which put a damper on the whole affair.

That evening both Genji and Tō no Chūjō were promoted—Genji to the senior third rank, which was rather an extraordinary rise given his previous status; Tō no Chūjō to the lower division of the senior fourth rank, which was also an unusual rise. Other high-ranking courtiers had reason to rejoice as well, since those who deserved promotions received them. Since they had all benefited from Genji's success—his own rise having helped pull everyone up with him—it makes one curious to know just what virtue from a previous life now endowed him with the qualities that drew everyone's admiring eyes and caused hearts to be joyful.

At around the time of the procession Fujitsubo left the court and withdrew to her own residence. As always, Genji sought out every opportunity to see her, and consequently, complaints from the Minister of the Left's household to the effect that he was never around reached his ears. Moreover, he learned that his wife was more distressed than usual, because one of her attendants had reported to her that Genji had plucked a certain "wild grass"—meaning Murasaki—and that "he was keeping her in his villa at Nijō." *It's natural she would feel upset*, Genji thought, *since she knows nothing at all about the situation or how young Murasaki is. Even so, why can't she just tell me how she feels and vent her resentments like a normal woman. I could then speak without reserve, tell her all the things I feel in my heart and put her mind at ease. But no, she has to be so damnably suspicious all the time. It's no wonder I find myself conducting these illicit affairs*. Still, he had to admit that there were no flaws in his wife's appearance or manners that made him feel dissatisfied. And even though she did not understand his feelings for her, she was the first woman he had known, and so he could not help but regard her with special tenderness. He was sure that over time her attitude toward him would change and she would come to understand. After all, he had faith that, given her gentle and serious nature, she would naturally come around to him. The feelings he had for her were special and different from those he had for other women.

Murasaki was now comfortable with Genji. Possessed of both a virtuous character and attractive looks, she would innocently follow after Genji, clinging to him. For the moment, he was inclined not to give the people in his residence too much information about her, and he kept her in a separate wing of the villa, which he had done up in a lavish manner. He would visit her mornings and evenings, instructing her in all manner of things, copying out books for her to emulate in her writing practice. It made him feel as though he had taken in a daughter from some aristocratic household. He gave special care to setting up the household office and choosing the staff to serve her, so that she would never have cause for worry or complaint. Apart from Koremitsu, Genji kept everyone else in the dark about this woman he was treating so solicitously. Her father, Prince Hyōbu, had been unable to discover what had happened to her. Murasaki would often reflect on the past, and she missed her grandmother terribly. For that reason Genji would try to divert her whenever he was at Nijō, and he even spent the night with her on occasion. Yet he was busy going here and there, visiting his many other women and going out during the evening, and so there were times when she would call after him and tell him how she ached to be with him. He found her unbearably sweet at those moments. Whenever he returned from two or three days of service at the palace, or from a visit with his wife at Sanjō, she would always look depressed. He found this distressing, and because he sometimes felt as though he were caring for a motherless child, he was no longer comfortable going out on his nighttime escapades. Upon hearing how well Genji was caring for the girl, the bishop at Kitayama was relieved and happy, even though he still considered the arrangement abnormal. Each time he conducted a memorial service for his sister, the late nun, Genji never failed to provide solemn, elaborate offerings.

Genji very much wanted to find out how Fujitsubo was doing. She had withdrawn to her own villa on Sanjō avenue, and so he called on her there. He was met by several of her ladies-in-waiting—Ōmyōbu, Chūnagon, and Nakatsukasa— and it bothered him that they acted so formally, clearly treating him as if he were a stranger. He stayed calm, keeping his feelings to himself as he exchanged pleasantries and court gossip with the women. Just then the Minister of War, Prince Hyōbu, arrived. When he learned that Genji was there as well, he granted him an audience. The Prince's elegant looks and bearing bespoke of his high breeding, and Genji found his softly erotic, seductive manner so appealing that he imagined that the Prince would be a very alluring partner were he a woman. What's more, because the Prince was the older brother of Fujitsubo and the father of Murasaki, Genji felt a surge of intimacy with the man, speaking to him in a relaxed, warmly familiar way. Noticing that Genji was kindly opening up to him more than usual, the Prince found him quite enchanting. Unaware that Genji was now his son-in-law, he had a similar erotic fantasy, imagining what Genji would be like as a woman.

Being Fujitsubo's older brother, he had the right to go in behind her curtains to speak to her when evening came. Genji was jealous of him, recalling the times when, as a little boy, he would be permitted to accompany his father behind Fujitsubo's curtains and address her face-to-face with no intermediaries. When he thought of the pain their separation caused him, he could hardly stand it.

"Though I should visit you more often," Genji said, "I normally don't have any reason to come here, so naturally I have neglected to stay in touch. Still, it would make me happy if you would send word should you ever need me to take care of something." His manner was serious and he made no pretense of showing the usual charming warmth as he left Fujitsubo's residence. Ōmyōbu had been useless to Genji in arranging a meeting with Fujitsubo, and it was clear that Fujitsubo now regretted more than ever the karmic destiny that had brought them together. In the face of her mistress's coldhearted attitude, Ōmyōbu felt so ashamed, so at a loss, that as the days went by she found she was no longer able to help Genji in any way. Mutually lost in their unending torment, Fujitsubo and Genji realized how evanescent their bond had been.

Murasaki's nurse, Shōnagon, observed the wonderful though completely unexpected rapport that had developed between Genji and her young mistress and was convinced that their relationship was a blessing from the Buddha, to whom the old nun had constantly prayed and made hopeful offerings. Yet Shōnagon continued to be assailed with doubts about Murasaki's future. *Genji's wife is a woman of unquestionably high status and breeding, and he is involved with a number of other women as well. Surely when the girl came of age someone would cause problems for her, would they not?* It was only because Genji seemed so devoted to Murasaki that Shōnagon felt she could trust him.

Murasaki was told that three months was an appropriately long period to wear robes of mourning for her grandmother, and so she put them away at the end of the twelfth month, just in time for the New Year. Having known no parent other than her grandmother, she was influenced by the old nun's tastes and continued to wear modest robes of plain crimson, purple, or yellow. In spite of these preferences, she was lovely, and even cut a rather modern, fashionable figure.

On the morning of the first day of the New Year, Genji peeked in on Murasaki's quarters on his way to court to attend the ceremony offering congratulations to the Emperor.

"Your change of attire makes you look more grown up than usual," he laughed, exuding a dazzlingly gentle and affectionate appeal. Before he knew it, Murasaki was absorbed in arranging her Hina court dolls, setting out various accessories on a series of three-foot-long shelves and spreading the little dollhouses that had been made for her all around the room until it was overflowing with her playthings.

"That Inuki!" Murasaki grumbled. "Last night during the demon-purification ritual, she was following the exorcist and got so excited by his mask and lance that she broke this. I've been trying to fix it." Clearly she regarded this as a major crisis.

"She really is inconsiderate, isn't she?" Genji responded. "I'll have it repaired for you. You just remember that there is no crying or pouting today . . . it would bring bad luck."

His dashing looks, together with the grand size of his retinue, made his departure for court seem so ceremonious that the women attendants at his residence came out onto the veranda to see him off. Murasaki also stepped outside to watch him leave, then went back inside and dressed up her Genji doll to match the attire he was wearing to the palace.

"I hope you'll start acting a little more mature this year," Shōnagon scolded her charge. "Here you are, already past your tenth birthday and you're still playing with these dolls. It just won't do. You have a husband now, and you really must start behaving more like a proper wife, and looking more like a lady for him. You still can't stand for me to fix up your hair."

Shōnagon scolded Murasaki in order to shame the girl for always being so absorbed in her playthings. But the effect of her admonition was to make Murasaki finally understand her circumstances for the first time. *So he's my husband, is he? The attendants here all have husbands . . . but they're really ugly. Mine, on the other hand, is a dashing, handsome young man.* It may have been true that she was still attached to her playthings, but her newfound awareness of her relationship with Genji signaled that she was now a year older. The people who served at Genji's mansion had found her childish behavior, which could be quite pronounced at times, awkward and inappropriate; and yet they had no idea that she was in fact a wife in name only, for Genji had not had sex with her even though they slept together.

Following the ceremony at the palace, Genji went to the Minister of the Left's residence on Sanjō. His wife, as always, presented an icy, beautiful perfection that emitted not the slightest hint of demure attitude or endearing warmth. He felt uncomfortable in her presence. "How happy it would make me if this year at least you could exhibit a new attitude so that we might have a little more normal relationship as husband and wife." She, however, was in no mood for reconciliation. Having heard that he had set up another woman at his villa and that he was giving her special attention as someone of great value to him, she could not help feeling depressed and awkward around him. She struggled to act nonchalant, pretending that she knew nothing about what was going on; and she found it hard, whenever he was intimate and unreserved, to remain stubborn and refuse to open up to him. Indeed, the gentle way she always responded was a special quality that set her apart from other women. Four years older than her husband, she was, at the age of twenty-two, now in her prime; and this was a problem for Genji because her flawless beauty and manners made him lose confidence when he was in her presence. There was nothing lacking in her, no flaws that he could detect anyway, and when he reflected on his own behavior he had to admit that her resentment was justifiable, since it was caused by those inexcusable affairs his fickle heart led him to pursue. After all, she was the only daughter of the Minister of the Left—a man who of all the nobles of similar rank had the weightiest reputation at court— and Princess Ōmiya, who was the younger sister of the Emperor. The greatest care had been lavished on his wife's upbringing, which meant that her sense of pride was exceptionally strong and that she would take even the most trivial slight or indiscretion as a serious and unpleasant injustice. This in turn made Genji resentful, wondering why it was that he was the one who always had to humor her pride. And so their hearts remained distant and unreconciled.

The Minister of the Left was disturbed by his son-in-law's fickleness, and yet whenever he saw Genji he would always forget his resentments, treat him deferentially, and do everything in his power to look after him. The following morning, as Genji was dressing and preparing to leave for court, the Minister dropped by to look in on him. Now that Genji had been promoted to the third rank, his father-in-law had ordered the servants to bring in a famous obi made of lacquered leather studded with gemstones that would show at the back of his robe and indicate his new status. He also had his servants straighten up the back of Genji's robes, and was so particular about the choice of shoes it was almost as if he were putting them on Genji's feet himself. His solicitous behavior was somehow both touching and a little pathetic.

"Should I wear this on official occasions?" Genji asked. "The privy banquet will be held soon, on the Day of the Rat . . . is it the 21st or the 23rd this year? Either way, I have to practice my Chinese verse for the event."

"I have better obi for events like that," the Minister sniffed. "This one just struck me as rather unusual looking. That's all." He pressed Genji to put it on, being almost religiously devoted to looking after him any way he could. Genji's appearances at Sanjō were certainly infrequent, but just to see this remarkable young man coming and going from his residence was a source of great joy and pride for the Minister.

Genji set off to make his New Year's round of visits. He did not have all that many places to call on—he paid his respects to the Emperor, to the Crown Prince, and to Fujitsubo's father, the former emperor. He also dropped by Fujitsubo's villa on Sanjō.

"He looks even more remarkable today. It makes one shudder to think that he just gets better looking the older he is." Fujitsubo's women were praising him up and down, and so she could not resist peeking through the gaps between her curtains to steal a glimpse. Immediately she was lost in her own troubled thoughts.

Her pregnancy was a source of considerable anxiety. Would she survive it? She was supposed to have given birth during the twelfth month, but here it was, the New Year already. Her attendants were in a state of anticipation, thinking that surely their mistress would give birth sometime this month. Even His Majesty was having preparations made at court. But the first month passed with no indication that the birth was imminent, and rumors were now flying around court society. Was this delay the fault of some malign spirit? Such gossip made Fujitsubo feel even more miserable, for just as she was frightened by the possibility that she might die in childbirth, she was just as deathly afraid that the secret of her affair with Genji would be exposed. Her mental anguish eventually made her physically ill.

It was now increasingly clear to Genji that he was the father, and so to ward off evil spirits he discreetly ordered esoteric rites to be performed at various temples around the capital. He fully understood the evanescent nature of the world, but he could not help torturing himself with the thought that his relationship with Fujitsubo would end too soon and come to naught. Then, sometime after the tenth of the second month, Fujitsubo gave birth to a prince. The Emperor and all the people at Fujitsubo's residence in Sanjō were relieved and excited by this auspicious event, even if Genji and Fujitsubo were not. His Majesty had been praying for her to live a long life, yet now the thought of a long life was a burden to Fujitsubo, given all her cares. When rumors reached her that the Kokiden Consort had tried to curse her by praying for an unlucky birth, she realized that news of her death would have served as a source of amusement to some at the court. She drew strength and determination from that thought, and gradually her health and spirits improved.

The Emperor's desire to see the child as quickly as possible was boundless. Genji, who was keeping his feelings to himself, was also extremely anxious to see the child . . . to confirm whether or not he was the father. Choosing a time when he knew there would be no one else around, he paid a visit to Fujitsubo.

"My father is eagerly waiting to see the child," Genji told her. "I thought I might take a look at the baby and then report to the Emperor."

"That's out of the question . . . the baby was just born and is not presentable in his present condition." Fujitsubo quite reasonably refused, for there was no denying that the baby bore a shocking, almost otherwordly resemblance to Genji—a living reproduction. Suffering from the demon of guilty conscience, Fujitsubo was convinced that anyone who saw the baby would instantly understand the sin she had committed with Genji. Since sanctimonious people were always eager to discover and condemn even the most minor of faults, what would they say about this . . . what would happen to her reputation? Dwelling on such possibilities, Fujitsubo was deeply distressed, body and soul.

Genji would meet with Ōmyōbu once in a while, doing his utmost through her to plead his case with Fujitsubo. Not surprisingly, his pleas fell on deaf ears. He continually pestered her about the young prince until finally Ōmyōbu told him, "Why must you insist on seeing him? You'll have your chance in due time." Even though she tried to reassure him, she seemed as troubled at heart as he.

Constrained by his surroundings, Genji could not speak frankly with Ōmyōbu. "Will there ever be a time or conditions when I can speak directly to Fujitsubo, without having to rely on an intermediary?" It was heartbreaking to see him on the verge of tears.

> What bond from a previous life
> Should have joined us, then determined
> That now we must be kept apart

"I cannot understand these things," he lamented.

Having witnessed the torments her lady was experiencing, Ōmyōbu found it impossible, in the face of Genji's sadness, to curtly refuse him. She recalled the poem by Fujiwara no Kanesuke that evoked the "hearts of parents lost in darkness," and replied.

> One looks upon the child and suffers regret
> One cannot see the child and suffers in grief
> Through such darkness do parents wander this world

"How sad that the birth of this child should keep your hearts from finding peace," she murmured. With no means of communicating with Fujitsubo, Genji returned to his residence. Troubled by the possibility of idle chatter at the court, Fujitsubo told Ōmyōbu that she could no longer tolerate her leading Genji here . . . that was how she really felt. Wary that Ōmyōbu might bring Genji to her, she was no longer able to trust her lady-in-waiting as she had in the past, and stopped treating her as a confidante. She continued to treat

Ōmyōbu kindly, so that no one would suspect anything was amiss, but there were times now when she appeared displeased by Ōmyōbu's conduct. Aware that she was estranged from Fujitsubo, Ōmyōbu felt sad that things had not turned out as she had expected.

The baby was taken to the palace during the fourth month. Larger than usual for a baby that age, the boy was already able to turn himself over. His face bore a striking resemblance to Genji's, but it never occured to the Emperor that Genji might be the child's true father. Rather, he assumed that people who shared unparalleled good looks would naturally resemble one another. His affection and care for the baby were boundless. His affection for Genji also knew no limits, but the lack of recognition and support for Genji among the high-ranking courtiers had made it impossible for him to install Genji in the line of succession. He constantly regretted his decision, and it was a source of pain for him to now look on his son's mature bearing and features and have to think what a waste it was to have removed Genji from the imperial line. It was thus a source of consolation for him that Fujitsubo, the fourth daughter of the previous emperor, and thus a woman of unimpeachable status, had given him a son who possessed the same radiant beauty as Genji. He considered the child a flawless jewel and lavished the greatest care on him—attention that, for Fujitsubo, merely added to the guilt and anxiety filling her heart.

One day, when Genji decided, as was his wont, to pass the time performing music in Fujitsubo's quarters at the palace, His Majesty joined them. He was carrying the infant prince in his arms. "I have many, many children," he remarked to Genji, "but you were the only one I was able to be with all day from the time you were this one's age. Maybe it's because this little one brings those days back to me that I think he looks so much like you. I wonder if all children look the same when they are very young?" It was obvious that the Emperor found the child adorable.

Genji felt himself blanch. Fear, shame, elation, pity . . . all these emotions overwhelmed him to the point that he felt he was going to cry. The baby prattled and smiled, and looked almost preternaturally cute. Was it all that unreasonable or vain of Genji to think—assuming he really did resemble this child during his own infancy—that he himself must indeed have been incredibly precious. Fujitsubo could hardly stand to be there—she was so mortified that she began to perspire. At the same time Genji, who had been so eager to see the child, was unnerved in his presence, and the turmoil in his heart forced him to withdraw from Fujitsubo's quarters.

Genji returned to his Nijō villa and, after resting for a while to calm his nerves, he decided that he should pay a visit to his wife. Pinks were brightly blooming amidst the vibrant green of the plantings that seemed to cover the entire front garden, so he had one of them picked and sent to Ōmyōbu. There were so many things he had to write to Fujitsubo.

> Though I see you in him, the one so like this little pink,
> Because I cannot tell you so, my heart knows no comfort
> My tears heavier than the dew on this flower's petals

"No matter how much I long to see the little one bloom, because our relationship was not meant to last in this vain world . . ."

His note must have been delivered at an opportune moment. Ōmyōbu showed it to Fujitsubo and encouraged her lady to write back: "You really should answer him, even if, as Ōshikōchi no Mitsune put it, your response in no more than a mote of dust on the petal of a pink."[4] Fujitsubo was deeply moved and sent back a simple poem written in the faintest of hands. Her characters looked as though she had pulled the brush away before finishing each stroke.

> Though I may consider it the source
> Of the heavy dew that soaks my sleeves
> How could I discard this precious pink

Ōmyōbu was overjoyed that her lady had responded, and she promptly delivered the poem to Genji. At that moment Genji was lying languidly, absently lost in pensive thoughts, sure that his poem had been in vain and that no reply would be coming back to him. But as soon as he saw Ōmyōbu, his heart beat wildly and he was so happy he wept.

Feeling that it was not good for him to just lie around and mope, absorbed in his cares, he decided he should go to the west hall to see the one person who was his solace. His hair was mussed, he had carelessly tossed on a loose robe, and he was playing a sweetly nostalgic air on his flute when he looked in on Murasaki. She was reclining on an armrest, her elegant appearance calling to mind the image of pinks drenched in dew · perfectly lovely and cute. As enchanting as she looked, it turned out that she was nursing a new grudge against Genji. This was unusual for her, but there she was, sitting with her back toward him, annoyed that he had not come to see her sooner even though he had been in his quarters for some time. Genji moved over to the veranda at the edge of the room and knelt there.

"Come over here," Genji coaxed her, but she ignored him and continued to sulk. She expressed her resentment toward him by murmuring lines from the *Man'yōshū*: "Is he like seaweed on the shore at high tide, which I long for so much, but see so seldom?" She covered her mouth with the sleeve of her robe, apparently embarrassed at her own precociousness. It made her all the more sweetly charming.

"Ahh, that's unfortunate . . . you've already learned how to complain just like an adult. Well, then, let me remind you of this poem: "Were I to see you morning and night, just as often as the divers at Ise see the seaweed, would I not grow weary of you?"[5]

He summoned a servant and had her bring in a thirteen-string koto for Murasaki to play. "This instrument is difficult because the second string closest to you is thin and easily broken," Genji told her. He then tuned the instrument to a lower key to reduce the tension on the strings. He played a few short songs to test the tuning, and then pushed the koto over in front of her. Murasaki found it impossible to continue sulking, and she played beautifully. She was still so small that she had to raise herself up and stretch to reach the strings, but he found the movements of her left hand, as she pressed the strings to make the instrument reverberate, delightfully refined. He instructed her by accompanying her on the flute. She had a quick memory and could pick up even the difficult keys in just one try. Clever, possessed of a charming disposition . . . she was everything he had long hoped for in a woman. The court song "Hosoroguseri" may have had a peculiar sounding title, but as Genji focused on playing it in his

---

4. Poem from *The Kokinshū* (see p. 1183, n. 8).   **5.** Anonymous poem from *The Kokinshū*.

fascinating style, Murasaki accompanied him, skillfully keeping time to the rhythm even though she was so young.

Oil lamps were brought in and they looked at paintings together. He had mentioned earlier to his retinue that he intended to go out, and so a member of his escort began to cough to signal it was time to go. "It looks like it might rain . . ." one of his guards remarked, and Murasaki at once became sullen and depressed, as she always did when Genji was about to leave. She stopped looking at the paintings and lay face down. Genji found her so endearing that he began to stroke her hair, which was spilling abundantly over her shoulders. "I suppose you miss me when I'm away?" he asked her. She nodded.

"I hate going even a single day without seeing you." Genji was trying to comfort her. "But since you are still a child, I have to ask you to be patient a little while longer and to not worry so. I have such fond feelings for you, but I must also consider the feelings of others and not offend those who may be jealous and resentful. Those women are troublesome, and that's why, for the present at least, I have to visit them as I do. When you are grown up I won't have to go out anymore, but for now I want to avoid the harm that might arise as a result of the jealousy of other women so that we might live a long life and be together as much as we desire."

Murasaki felt embarrassed to hear Genji speak about their relationship in such detail, and so she did not answer him. She drew herself up onto Genji's lap and went to sleep. Genji felt terribly sorry for her and told his attendants, "I'll not be going out this evening." They all rose and withdrew, and he had his dinner, which he normally ate in his own rooms, brought to her quarters instead. He woke Murasaki and told her, "I'm not going out after all." Her mood at once improved and she got up. They ate together, but Murasaki was still anxious about his plans and merely picked at her food. "If you're not going out," she suggested, "then why not sleep here tonight?" *If it is so difficult for us to part at a moment like this*, Genji mused, *then how much more difficult will it be when we have to part on the inevitable road of death?*

* * *

FROM **CHAPTER IX**

Aoi

Leaves of Wild Ginger

The court changed when the Emperor abdicated and the Crown Prince took the throne as Emperor Suzaku. The Kokiden faction, headed by the Minister of the Right, was now in ascendance, and Genji began to feel that everything was more difficult for him. Just before His Majesty stepped down he had promoted his favored son to Major Captain of the Right—a rise in status that required the Radiant Prince, in keeping with the dignity of his new position, to begin showing more restraint in pursuing his frivolous nightly adventures. The result was that his many lovers began to complain more and more of his heartlessness. Was it in retribution for causing all these lamentations that Genji suffered from what he saw as the unending cruelty of Fujitsubo, who kept her distance from him? Now, more than ever, she served at the side of the Retired Emperor—almost as if she were some low-ranking attendant. This did not sit well with the Kokiden Consort, but she was now Imperial Mother and had to serve exclusively at the palace—an arrangement that was a source of considerable relief to Fujitsubo.

Depending on the occasion, the Retired Emperor would sponsor musical entertainments so lavish and spectacular they became the talk of court society. He seemed more content now than when he had held power. The only thing lacking for him was Fujitsubo's little son, the new Crown Prince. He yearned to see the boy, who could not be by his side. Having long worried that Fujitsubo's son had no supporters at court, he asked Genji to look after the boy's affairs—a request that was of course awkward for Genji, but one that also made him happy.

At this point I must bring up another, entirely separate matter. At the time Emperor Suzaku ascended the throne, an imperial princess was appointed as the new High Priestess for the Imperial Shrine at Ise. The mother of this princess was the lady at Rokujō—the woman Genji had long been visiting discreetly—while the father was an imperial prince who had actually been ahead of Suzaku in the line of succession, but who had died before he could take the throne. Because the princess was appointed High Priestess under these circumstances, the lady at Rokujō, who no longer had any confidence in the reliability of Genji's feelings, was greatly worried about her daughter's future. The girl was, after all, only thirteen and would be alone in Ise. Thus, the lady at Rokujō had for some time been giving serious consideration to leaving the capital herself and accompanying her daughter to the Imperial Shrine. When the Retired Emperor heard about her plans to leave, he was extremely upset and spoke sharply to Genji about the matter.

"Do I need to remind you," he scolded, "that she was the first wife of my late brother, and would have been an Imperial Consort? He had special affection for her, but now I hear rumors about how carelessly you treat her, as if she were some ordinary woman. It's pathetic. I look on her daughter, the High Priestess, as one of my own, and so you must put an end to this frivolous behavior . . . not just for her sake, but for mine as well. If you persist in playing these irresponsible little games, then don't be surprised when your reputation is in ruins."

Genji could not deny that his father was speaking the truth. Thoroughly chastened, he refrained from answering, whereupon the Retired Emperor added, his tone a little softer, "Never do anything to dishonor or shame a woman. Treat them all gently and give them no cause to resent you." With that admonition ringing in his ears, Genji humbly withdrew from his father's presence terrified at the thought that a day might come when his father learned the truth about Genji's wildly reckless affair with Fujitsubo.

If his father was lecturing him about it, it was obvious gossip about his affair with the lady at Rokujō had spread through the court, and that his promiscuity had damaged her honor and his reputation. He could just imagine how terribly she must be suffering, but there was simply no way he could formally acknowledge their relationship. For one thing, the lady herself was embarrassed that at the age of twenty-nine she was having an affair with a man seven years younger. Moreover, she always tried to appear distant and aloof, and so Genji had grown more reserved with her. Now, however, everyone at court, even the Retired Emperor, knew what was going on, and she lamented that Genji's feelings for her were so shallow.

Genji had long been pursuing the daughter of Prince Shikibu—a lady he knew as Asagao, Princess of the Bellflowers. His efforts had so far proven futile, however, and when Princess Asagao heard rumors of his affair, she resolved never to end up like the lady at Rokujō and refused to give even the most perfunctory of replies to his vain entreaties. Even so, she showed a proper attitude and conducted herself in a way that would give no offense to Genji, and so he continued to consider her a woman of superior qualities.

Needless to say, the household of the Minister of the Left was not amused by Genji's restless disposition; but then again, since he showed no qualms about carrying on so openly, it would have been useless to have complained to him about it. His wife, for one, did not harbor any deep resentment toward him, not least because she was now pregnant and suffering most pitifully not only from morning sickness, but also from anxiety over the dangers posed by the coming birth. Genji thought the pregnancy remarkable, and for the first time felt sympathy for his wife. Because everyone was so overjoyed for her, there was a concern that such happiness could invite bad fortune, and so various prayers and rituals of abstinence[6] were commissioned in order to ensure safe delivery for mother and child. With all these things going on, Genji had less and less time to even consider the feelings of his other women. He was especially mindful of the feelings of the lady at Rokujō, but despite his best intentions not to neglect her, his visits practically ceased altogether.

The High Priestess of the Kamo Shrine stepped down at about that time, and her successor was the third daughter of the Retired Emperor by the Kokiden Consort. This girl was a special favorite of both parents, and it bothered them that unlike her siblings she would have to live isolated from court life. Unfortunately, there were no other princesses appropriate for the position. Although the rituals of investiture were austere, as was customary with Shinto shrines, they would nonetheless be solemn and grand. The Festival of the Kamo Shrine, which was held in the fourth month, was always a major event in the capital; those who accompanied the High Priestess's procession would decorate their carriages and headdresses with heart-shaped leaves of wild ginger.[7] Because this year marked the new Priestess's inaugural procession, many attractions would be added to the public events already scheduled, and the Festival, in keeping with the special status of the High Priestess, would be an especially glorious one.

A few days before the start of the Kamo Festival twelve high-ranking officials were required to attend the Priestess during the procession to her ritual of purification, which took place on the banks of the Kamo River. Given the auspicious nature of the event, only men with honorable prospects and good looks were chosen for this task, and every detail of their appearance was carefully considered—from the color of the trains on their robes and the pattern of their trousers, to the choice of horses and saddles. By special order of Emperor Suzaku, Genji was chosen to participate, and when those who planned to view

6. That is, periods of seclusion [editors' note].

7. *Aoi*, the Japanese word for "wild ginger," is also a homophone for the words *au hi*, which mean "the day we will meet." The combination of the heart-shaped leaves of the plant, which is an evergreen, and the romantic implications of its name is played on later in this chapter in an exchange of poems between Genji and an older lady, Naishi, who appears earlier in the tale. Because much of this chapter centers on Genji's wife, she has been identified traditionally as Aoi.

the procession heard about this decision, they gave extra thought in advance to preparing and positioning their carriages along the route.

The thoroughfare of Ichijō was crammed with carriages and bustling with people. Viewing platforms had been erected at various sites and decorated with great care. Those decorations, together with the sleeves of the court ladies' robes, which trailed out from beneath the blinds set up on the platforms, created their own splendid spectacle.

Genji's wife rarely left her father's residence to go view events like this. Moreover, she had given no thought at all of going to view this particular procession, since she was feeling ill and nervous. Her younger attendants, however, all complained to her.

"What is my lady thinking? How could we ever hope to enjoy the beauty of the procession if we have to sneak off just to take a peak?"

"Ordinary folk, even the lowest woodcutters and hunters who have no connection with anyone in the procession, will be there to take in the sights. They'll especially want to catch a glimpse of your husband."

"People from distant provinces will bring their wives and children to take a look. So it's just not fair that we have to miss it!"

Princess Ōmiya, who, as the younger sister of the Retired Emperor, truly understood the importance of such matters, heard these complaints and urged her daughter to go. "You've been feeling better recently, and your attendants will feel left out and dissatisfied if you don't." And with that, all the women were suddenly informed, to their joy, that their lady would be going out after all.

Because the sun was already well up, they left without formally preparing the carriages in a manner befitting the status of the Minister's household. By the time they arrived, Ichijō avenue was already packed with carriages lining both sides of the street, and it was difficult finding a place to park the imposing and dignified vehicles, unhitch the oxen, and set the shafts on their supports. Many noblewomen already had their carriages positioned there, and the male guards escorting Genji's wife decided to clear a space by pushing aside those that had no guardsmen protecting them.

Among the carriages that had been lined up in that space, two of them exuded a special air of refinement—informal in style, with roofs and blinds made of *hinoki*[8] wicker, slightly worn, but adorned with silk curtains. The women inside had obviously intended to remain inconspicuous. The fresh, vibrant colors of the cuffs of their sleeves, the hems of their skirts, and the ends of their singlets all peeked out coyly from beneath the blinds. The guards escorting Genji's wife were explicitly told not to touch these two carriages and warned, "This is not a carriage you can just push aside as you wish!" Unfortunately, the young men in both parties had been drinking too much, and in the end there was no way to prevent the situation from getting out of control. The older retainers from the Minister's household commanded the young men to desist, but they were unable to stop a fight from breaking out.

The lady at Rokujō, whose daughter would soon go off to serve as the Ise Priestess, had been thinking she might find relief from her tormented feelings about Genji by coming discreetly to view the procession for the Purification Ritual. Her attendants, aware of her desire to remain incognito, did not reveal

8. A Japanese evergreen used for various building purposes [editors' note].

her identity, but it was obvious to the men accompanying Genji's wife whose carriages they were moving.

"Don't let them talk to us like that," several of the men shouted. "They must think they can still rely on Lord Genji!"

Several of Genji's attendants had been assigned to accompany his wife's party. They all regarded this incident as most regrettable, but it would have been extremely awkward for them to intervene, and so they looked the other way. In the end, the carriages of Genji's wife and her attendants were positioned in the spaces that had been cleared away, and the carriages of the lady at Rokujō had been relegated to a place behind them, where she could neither see nor be seen. She was in an agony of anger and indignation; and now that her identity had been revealed, after having gone to such great lengths to conceal it out of concern that her shameful feelings for Genji might be exposed, there was no limit to the feelings of chagrin and remorse she suffered. Because the stands for her carriage shafts had been broken in the melee, they had to be propped up on the wheel hubs of some unknown carriages next to hers. It must have looked unsightly, and she was mortified, wondering vainly why she had ever decided to come here.

She no longer wanted to view the procession and wished instead to go home, but there was no space to move her carriage. Just then cries rang out from the crowd, "They're on their way!" Her resolve weakened, and now she wanted to wait until her cruel lover had passed. She recalled an ancient poem in which the Goddess of Ise asks a man to stop his horse at Sasanokuma to let it drink from the Hinokuma River—all so that she might have the chance to gaze upon him.[9] Anxious, she wondered if Genji would stop to acknowledge her . . . but no, he continued on, coldly passing by without so much as a glance in her direction. The turmoil in her heart was greater than ever. Genji feigned disinterest in the many carriages that lined the way, even though they were more splendidly decorated than usual, with the hems of robes spilling out from beneath the blinds as though the occupants were in competition with one another. Still, he did occasionally smile and give a sly, sidelong glance at certain carriages, and when he recognized the carriages of his father-in-law, he assumed a solemn expression as he passed. The men in his escort silently bowed to show their deep respect for Genji's wife. The Rokujō lady, overwhelmed by this display, which clearly demonstrated the inferiority of her status, could not have felt more wretched.

> How cruel this river of purification . . . it grants
> The merest glimpse of your reflection in its chill waters
> Reminding me all the more of how wretched my fate is

She knew it would be disgraceful to weep in front of her women, so she comforted herself with the thought that she would have regretted passing up the opportunity to witness the radiance of his appearance and the beauty of his countenance on such a dazzling occasion.

The high-ranking nobles who accompanied the Kamo Priestess on the procession were superbly decked out, each in keeping with his status at court, and attended by magnificent-looking escorts. The appearance of those of the high-

---

9. A sacred song for the Sun Goddess from *The Kokinshū*.

est rank was especially breathtaking; and yet, as remarkable as they were, they seemed to pale in comparison with Genji's radiance. One of the eight men in his retinue, which had been assembled just for this event, was a man of the sixth rank, a lieutenant in the Right Imperial Guard. It was most unusual to assign someone of his status to this kind of duty, but he was so remarkably good-looking that he was chosen anyway. The other men in Genji's escort were also dazzlingly resplendent; and Genji's appearance, which was always esteemed by the court, was so awe-inspiring that the very trees and grasses seemed to bow before him. Normally, it would be considered improper and unsightly for ladies of rank who, for the sake of modesty, wore veils beneath their deep-brimmed hats, or for nuns who had renounced the world to literally fall over one another in an effort to catch a glimpse of him. Today, however, was different, and no one reproved them. Women of the lower classes—their mouths drawn in where they were missing teeth, their hair tucked modestly inside their robes—jostled each other and made fools of themselves, clasping their hands to their foreheads in supplication to Genji. Vulgar men were grinning stupidly from ear to ear, unaware of how ridiculous their faces looked. Daughters of minor provincial officials, who Genji would never so much as glance at, had arrived in their lavishly decorated carriages, hopelessly preening and posturing because they knew Genji would be passing by. So many amusing things to observe—including the many women who, having been favored by a covert visit from Genji, were now lamenting to themselves that they no longer belonged among the blessed few he favored.

Prince Shikibu, the Minister of Ceremonials, was viewing the procession from one of the platforms, and when he saw Genji, ominous thoughts came to him. *He has matured so, and his appearance is truly spectacular. Surely he will attract the attention of gods and demons.* His daughter, Princess Asagao, had exchanged many letters with Genji over several years and so she knew his sensibilities were anything but ordinary. Now that she was seeing his beauty for the first time, her heart was deeply moved. *A woman can be touched by a man's sincerity, even if he is rather ordinary looking. How much more appealing, then, is the sincerity of a man whose looks are as stunning as his?* Despite these sentiments, she was not inclined to allow her relationship with Genji to become any more familiar or intimate. Her younger attendants were all praising him so much they sounded uncouth, and she found it irritating to listen to them.

When the Kamo Festival proper was held a few days later, no one from the Minister of the Left's residence came out to view it. Genji had been informed of the quarrel between the carriages, and he felt sorry for the lady at Rokujō. He was also offended by his wife's conduct. "It's a shame," he remarked, "that such a dignified person should show so little sympathy or kindness toward others. She probably never intended for such a thing to happen, and yet her temperament prevents her from even considering the possibility that women who share the kind of relationship she and the lady do should be mutually affectionate and supportive. No wonder her subordinates, who lack judgment and status, acted as outrageously as they did. As for the lady who suffered this insult, she has such a superior upbringing and is so sensitive to any slight that the whole sordid incident must have been terribly unpleasant for her."

Genji felt such pity that he went to Rokujō to visit the lady. She, however, was reluctant to see him. Her daughter, after all, was still living in the residence while undergoing the rites of purification that would prepare her to serve as the High Priestess at Ise. Branches of the sacred *sakaki* tree[1] had been placed at all the corners and gates, and thus the lady did not feel comfortable letting Genji in to see her, since that would run the risk of defilement. Genji thought her precaution perfectly reasonable, but he still muttered to himself, "Why must things always be like this? Why do women have to flash their horns and quarrel?"

Genji retreated to his own residence at Nijō. On the day of the Kamo Festival he went with Murasaki to view the festivities. After ordering Koremitsu to prepare their carriages, he went over to the west hall.

"Will all your little ladies be going as well?" he teasingly asked, referring to Murasaki's playmates. Observing her outfit and makeup, which exuded an exceptionally graceful air, he couldn't help smiling. "Very well, then, shall we be going? Let's view the festival together." He stroked her hair, which looked even more lustrous than usual, and added, "It's been a while since you've had the ends trimmed. Today would be an auspicious time to do it." He summoned a scholar from the Bureau of Divination and asked him which hours that day would be lucky or unlucky for trimming hair. He then told Murasaki, "Have your little ladies come forth." He looked them over and found their childish figures delightfully charming. Their hair had been trimmed gorgeously and hung down in sharp relief over the outer trousers of their festive robes . . . altogether adorable. "I'll cut your hair," Genji said to Murasaki. "It's really thick, isn't it? What would become of it if you just let it grow out." He found trimming her hair a little difficult. "Ladies with very long hair tend to cut the side locks that frame their foreheads a little shorter than the rest. I don't think you would look as attractive without short locks." When he finished with the trimming, Genji offered the obligatory benediction, expressing the hope that her hair might grow "a thousand fathoms."

Murasaki's nurse, Shōnagon, had been watching them, her heart filled with gratitude. Genji composed and recited a verse.

> I shall protect you, watching your hair grow
> Like strands of rippling seaweed stretching up
> From the thousand-fathomed depths of the sea

Murasaki chose to write out her reply.

> You claim your love is as deep as the thousand-fathomed sea
> Yet how am I to know that's true, since you wander so much
> Coming in and going out like uncertain, restless tides

Such clever wit, and such youthful beauty. She's perfect, Genji thought.

So many sightseeing carriages had arrived for the Kamo Festival that there were no spaces anywhere this day as well. They had trouble finding a place to stop and pulled up near the parade grounds and pavilion where the Mounted Guard held their archery competition during the fifth month of each year. "So many high-ranking officials have brought their carriages here, the area is really

---

1. *Sakaki* is a flowering evergreen tree native to Japan. It is sacred in the Shinto religion and branches of *sakaki*, decorated with slips or streamers of paper, are used for ritual offerings and purifications.

bustling," Genji said, sounding a little confounded and irritable. He had his carriage pause for a moment next to a lady's carriage that was not at all inelegant. The lady's carriage was filled with occupants, and a fan was thrust out beckoning him over to them. "Would you like to set your carriage here?" a woman asked. "We could make some space for you." Genji was somewhat taken aback, wondering what kind of woman could be so coquettish. This spot, however, was an excellent place from which to view the Festival parade, and so he decided to accept the invitation. "How did you manage to come by this space?" he asked. "It's good enough to make people resent you, so I'll take you up on your offer." The lady in the carriage then broke off a section of her stylish folding fan and wrote out the following.

> The wild ginger, with its heart-shaped leaves, adorns another
> Though its name, *aoi*, promises the day when we'll meet . . .
> In vain I waited for the Kamo god to bless this day

"I cannot pass beyond the ropes marking off that sacred space."

Genji recognized the handwriting. It was the old Assistant Handmaid, Naishi no Suke. He found it shocking that someone her age should be flirting like a young woman. He was genuinely displeased and sent back a curt reply.

> The feelings of one adorned with those heart-shaped leaves
> Are certainly fickle, since she can "meet this day"
> Any man she wants from among the eighty clans

Naishi was filled with bitter thoughts at Genji's cruelty.

> A bitter adornment, this wild ginger
> With its empty promise of meeting you . . .
> Mere leaves signifying vain and false hopes

Many women, not just Naishi, experienced pangs of jealousy as they tried to guess the identity of the lady riding with Genji. They resented that for her sake he chose to keep his blinds down, because it denied them an opportunity to catch a glimpse of him. The women gossiped among themselves.

"He was so splendid-looking the day of the procession."

"Yes, but today he's going about rather informally, don't you think?"

"Who is that riding with him, I wonder? She must be a special woman."

Genji remained disgruntled. *What a complete waste of time, exchanging verses that play on a subject like leaves of wild ginger.* Anyone not as impudent as Naishi would certainly have refrained from sending a note out of respect for the lady riding with him.

For her part, the lady at Rokujō had never in all her life experienced the kind of torment brought on recently by her dark, obsessive thoughts. She had, it is true, resigned herself to Genji's cruel neglect, but the thought of leaving him behind in order to go with her daughter to Ise brought an agonizing sense of loneliness. She was also fully aware that she would be an object of derision at the court. Whenever she thought, wistfully, that perhaps she ought to stay behind in the capital, she would become anxious, for she knew that if she stayed she would expose herself to even more extreme levels of ridicule. Her days and nights were so filled with troubled thoughts that she couldn't help but recall the *Kokinshū* poem: "Am I a float on the line of the fisherman of Ise that my heart should be adrift like this, bobbing on the waves?"[2] Finding no relief from her obsessive, insecure state of mind, she fell ill.

Genji wasn't in the least concerned about her stated desire to accompany her daughter to Ise, and he never once tried to dissuade her by telling her that it was out of the question. Instead he remarked, rather sarcastically, "I understand. It's perfectly reasonable for you to find repugnant the prospect of continuing a relationship with a man as worthless as I. Yet no matter how unpleasant it may be for you now, if you were to stay with me to the end, that would indicate you're a woman of no shallow sensibility, would it not?" On hearing such hateful words, the lady withdrew even deeper into her dark thoughts. Distressed and depressed, she had decided to go see the procession only because she had wanted some relief from her insecurity and indecisiveness. And then, when she did go, she found herself buffeted about, as if she were adrift on the violent rapids of the river of lustration.

While all of this was taking place, a malignant spirit was causing concern for everyone at the Minister of the Left's Sanjō residence. Genji's wife was suffering terribly, and under the circumstances it was not appropriate for him to be going around visiting his other women. Indeed, during this period he only rarely went to his own residence in Nijō. True, he had never warmed to his wife much, but he did consider her someone of special importance to him. He was wracked with grief that she should now be suffering so much as a consequence of her remarkable pregnancy, and he had prayers and rites performed for her in his own quarters at his father-in-law's residence.

Many souls of the deceased and spirits of living persons were exorcised and forced to reveal their names. One particular spirit, however, resisted all attempts to move it into the body of a medium and persisted in clinging fast to Genji's wife. It did no real harm, but it would not leave her body, even for a few moments. The deeply obsessive nature of this spirit, which would not obey even the holiest of exorcists, made it clear that this was no commonplace possession. The attendants considered the various women Genji called on and whispered among themselves, "Only the ladies at Rokujō and Nijō have a special place in his heart . . . perhaps their resentment is especially strong." Diviners were brought in to confirm these suspicions, but they failed to do so. Whenever they questioned the spirits they learned nothing that would suggest any of them was driven by revenge or hatred. There was the spirit of a former nurse and spirits that had haunted the families of the Minister and Princess Ōmiya for generations; but these had appeared simply because their daughter was in a fragile condition. None of them were really malicious, but seemed to have shown up at random. Why, then, was Genji's wife constantly shouting out and weeping? She was always nauseous or had choking sensations, and she would writhe around as if in unbearable agony. Genji and her parents were frightened and upset, wondering how this would all turn out and worrying that she might die.

Because the Retired Emperor repeatedly sent messages of concern and graciously ordered prayers and rituals, her death would be all the more lamentable. Upon hearing that everyone at the court was worried, the lady at Rokujō was afflicted with the troubling thought that she was being diminished as sympathy for her rival grew. She had always had a jealous, competitive streak, but until

2. Anonymous poem from *The Kokinshū*.

that absurd quarrel over the carriages had unsettled her heart, it had never been as pronounced as it was now, and she felt a degree of resentment that no one at the Minister's household could have ever imagined.

The lady knew, as a result of her confused emotions, that her condition was not normal, and so she decided to undergo esoteric Buddhist healing rites. However, she had to move out of her residence and have the rites performed elsewhere in order to avoid defiling her daughter, who was still preparing to be the High Priestess of Ise. Genji heard about her plans and, moved to pity as he wondered how she was feeling, went to call on her. Because she was not at her usual residence in Rokujō, he had to be exceptionally discreet when he visited. He repeatedly asked her to overlook the way he had neglected her recently, pointing out that it was due to circumstances beyond his control. He even tried to elicit her sympathy by describing the terrible suffering of his wife.

"I'm not all that concerned about her myself," he said, "but I do feel sorry for her parents, who are upset and making rather too much of a fuss about it. So while she is in this condition, I really should stay close by her. If you could take all of these things into account, I would be very grateful." Genji pleaded with her, but he could see from the expression on her face that she was suffering even more than usual, and he felt terribly sorry for her.

The lady had been moody and withdrawn that night, but when, in the welter of her yearnings and resentments, she saw how ravishing he looked as he prepared to leave at the crack of dawn, she was tempted to reconsider her decision to leave the capital with her daughter. At the same time, she was realistic enough to know that Genji, who already held his wife in high esteem, would feel even greater affection and lavish his attentions solely on *that woman* once the child was born. And when that happened, *she* would be left waiting, fretting impatiently over whether Genji would ever show up and knowing that whenever he did come to see her, it would be out of some lukewarm sense of duty or pity. Her tangled emotions opened her eyes afresh to the reality of her situation. After waiting all day for his "morning-after" letter, it finally arrived that evening—a short, curt note with no poem attached: "Her condition had been improving recently, but now she has suffered a relapse, and I really must stay here."

She read the note and thought it was just another of his typical excuses. Even so, she sent a response.

> Intimate with the path of love, where dew has soaked my sleeves,
> My sad fate is to have followed that path too far and end
> With robes soaked in mud, like a peasant cultivating fields

"Perhaps it is fitting to remind you of the old poem about the water of the mountain well. The poet, having tried to draw water from a well so shallow, regrets that she too gets nothing but damp sleeves."[3]

Genji pored over her response, marveling at the beauty of her script, which was so superior to everyone else's, and wondered why the world had to be so damnably complicated. He felt painfully torn—on the one hand, he couldn't simply abandon a woman of her sensibility and looks, and, on the other, there was no way he could settle on just one woman. He sent his reply well after dark.

---

3. Anonymous poem from an earlier *waka* anthology, the *Kokin waka rokujō*.

"What do you mean that only your sleeves are damp? Your feelings for me must not be very deep."

> How shallow the path of love you follow
> That you merely dampen your sleeves with dew
> While I drench myself where the mud is deep

He added, among other things, "Do you imagine that my feelings for you are insincere, that I would not reply to you in person were my wife's condition not truly serious?"

At the Minister's residence the obsessive spirit was appearing more persistently and causing Genji's wife great distress. The lady at Rokujō then heard gossip to the effect that it was either her own living spirit or that of her late father. She gave the rumors careful consideration. Even though she had never wished ill fortune to befall others, she had often lamented her own bad luck, and she was aware that the living spirit of a person who is preoccupied with personal desires and attachments might wander from the body. She had lived for so many years convinced that she had suffered as much grief and anxiety as it was possible for one person to suffer, and now it was as if her soul had been torn asunder. That day when the foolish incident with the carriages occurred, she had been treated disdainfully, and *that woman*, Genji's wife, had in effect ignored her as though she were beneath contempt. After the procession to the Purification Ritual was over, her heart and mind lost their moorings and drifted, all on account of that one incident, and she found it truly difficult to calm her nerves.

Lately, whenever she dozed off, she began having a recurring dream. She would find herself in the beautifully appointed, luxurious quarters of some woman—Genji's wife, she assumed—and would then watch in horror as her living spirit, so completely different from her waking self, would move around the woman, pulling and tugging at her, and then, driven by menacingly obsessive emotions, violently striking and shaking her. Because of this recurring dream, the lady had many moments when she believed she was losing her grip on reality. *Ah, how horrible this is! What they say is true after all. A person's living spirit really can leave the body and wander about.*[4] *And even if it isn't true in my case, people at the court prefer to speak ill of others, and this situation will provide fodder to those who relish spreading malicious gossip.* Fearing that she would be notorious, the lady made a resolution to herself. *They say it's common for people to leave behind their obsessive attachments and resentments when they die. I've always considered such a thing deeply sinful and ominous, even when it has happened to people with whom I have no connections. But now there are rumors that it's my living spirit that's acting in such a grotesque, unearthly way. It must be retribution for the sins of a former life. I must never give another thought to that cruel man.* She resolved over and over to put him out of her mind, but, resolve as she might, to so resolve was just another way to think about *him*.

As part of a series of purification rites in preparation for her departure for Ise, the daughter of the lady at Rokujō was to have moved during the previous year into a detached residence at the palace called the Shosai-in, which served

---

4. Poem from *The Kokinshū* by Ōshikōchi Mitsune: "It must have wandered off, abandoning my body . . . this heart of mine that goes its own way, doing things I do not intend."

as the pavilion of the First Lustration. However, there had been a number of complications, and so it was decided that she would not move into the pavilion until the autumn. Thereafter, in the ninth month, the Ise Priestess would move again, undergoing the Second Lustration at a temporary shrine built for this purpose on the plains of Sagano, famous for its lovely autumn vistas. The attendants in the residence at Rokujō thus had to make preparations for two purification rites, one right after the other. Their mistress, alas, was distracted and depressed and lying prone in her suffering, unable to rouse herself. This was no trivial matter for the ladies-in-waiting to the Priestess, since her mother's illness could be defiling; and so they commissioned prayers and rites. In truth, the lady didn't really seem all that sick, and as the days and months passed no one was sure exactly what was wrong or how serious it was. Genji was constantly inquiring after the lady's health, but because his wife, who was far more important to him, was suffering so much, he was burdened with seemingly endless concerns.

Because they assumed it was not yet time for Genji's wife to give birth, every-one at the Sanjō residence was caught off guard when she went into labor and appeared to be on the verge of delivering the child. More and more malignant spirits were drawn to her as the moment of the birth neared, and the number and intensity of the prayers and rites meant to assure a safe childbirth increased. Still, that one stubborn, obsessive spirit remained more intransigent than ever. Even the most venerable of the priests found this spirit abnormal, and they were unable to exorcise it. As they tried to make the spirit show itself, their prayers finally forced it to speak to them through Genji's wife. The spirit, in a weeping voice wracked with pain, pleaded with the priests. "Please stop for a moment. I have something I must say to Lord Genji." The attendants at once whispered among themselves, "Just as we thought . . . there's some reason for this after all."

Genji was shown in where his wife was lying behind her curtains. Because she seemed to be near death, her parents withdrew a short distance away in case their daughter had some last words for her husband. The priests ceased their prayers and lowered their voices as they chanted the Kannon chapter of the Lotus Sutra. Their murmuring created an atmosphere at once uncanny and sublime. Genji lifted the curtains and looked in on his wife. There was something alluringly attractive about her as she lay there, her belly large and distended. Even someone with whom she had no connection at all would have been distracted gazing at her, so it was natural for Genji to feel overwhelmed with regret and sorrow. Her long, luxuriant black hair, which had been pulled back and tied up, stood out in a vivid contrast to the white of her maternity robes. She was always so prim and proper that Genji had never found her special elegance all that attractive. Now, for the first time, as she lay there in her vulnerable, helpless condition, she struck him as not just precious, but voluptuous.

He took her hand. "How terrible this is. Must you cause me to grieve so?" He began to cry and could speak no further. She weakly raised her head and gazed at him with that expression that had hitherto always made him feel uncertain and inadequate in her presence. Tears filled her eyes, and when he gazed back at her—a woman who now seemed so accessible to him—how could he not be deeply touched?

Because she was crying so intensely, Genji assumed she was thinking of her poor, anxious parents and, on seeing him here like this, regretting that they would soon part.

"You mustn't brood so much about everything," Genji comforted her. "You don't feel well now, but you'll get better. And even if death should separate us, remember that husbands and wives are destined to meet in the next world. You have a deep bond with your father and mother, and no matter how many times you are reborn, that bond is never-ending. I am sure there will be a time when you will see them again."

"No, no, that's not why I'm crying. I'm crying because the exorcists' prayers hurt me so. I asked for you to come here so that I might have a moment of relief from them. I never imagined that I would come here in this form, but now I know the truth. The spirit of a person lost in obsessive longing will actually wander from the body." The voice that came from his wife's lips had a gentle, seductive familiarity. "Just as they did in ancient times . . ."

> Bind the hems of my robes
> To keep my grieving soul
> From wandering the skies

As he was listening to the voice, his wife's appearance changed and she no longer looked like herself. Genji was trying to comprehend this inexplicable, eerie phenomenon when he suddenly realized he was gazing on the countenance of the lady at Rokujō. He was horrified. He had dismissed out of hand the rumors claiming the spirit possessing his wife was the lady's, considering them nothing more than the idle gossip of vulgar, insensitive people. But he was witnessing the possession with his own eyes and understood now that such things did happen in this world. It was uncanny. *How wretched*, he thought, and then answered her, saying, "You sound like someone I know, but I'm not certain. Tell me who you are." The spirit replied in a way that left no doubt it was *she*. To say that he was shocked would not do justice to the sense of horror he experienced. At the same time, the presence of the attendants made him feel awkward and embarrassed, since they might recognize that the spirit was the lady's.

When the voice grew a little more subdued, Genji's mother-in-law, thinking that her daughter was feeling more comfortable, brought in a hot medicinal infusion. The attendants raised his wife from behind and supported her in a squatting posture, and she gave birth to a boy. The joy everyone felt was boundless, though the malign spirits that had been forced into mediums raised a tremendous fuss, since they resented the safe delivery. There was still the afterbirth to worry about, but thanks to the numerous prayers and supplications to the Buddha, it was a normal birth. The abbot of the Enryakuji temple on Mt. Hiei and the other distinguished priests quickly withdrew, wiping the sweat from their proud, satisfied faces. All the women in the household were finally able to relax a little after so many days of worry and devoted service. They were sure that the worst was over; and even though new prayers and rites for the mother were ordered, for the moment the baby became the center of attention. Everyone let their guard down as they were absorbed in helping out with the remarkable child. The Retired Emperor, princes of the blood, and the highest ranking officials all attended, without fail, the traditional banquets held on the third, fifth, seventh and ninth nights following the birth to joyously celebrate. They brought with them exquisite and remarkable gifts of food and clothing, and because the child was a boy, the celebrations were all the more lively and auspicious.

When the lady at Rokujō learned about all of this, she grew agitated. She had heard that Genji's wife had been in a precarious state, but now, apparently, everything was fine, and she felt both jealous and disappointed. She continued to feel weird, as though she were not herself, and her robes reeked of the smell of poppy seeds exorcists burn to drive out a lingering spirit. Strangely, the smell would not dissipate, but continued to permeate her body no matter how often she tried washing her hair and changing her robes. She was disgusted at herself, and worried what others might say or think. She couldn't very well discuss this with anyone, so she was forced to suffer in isolation, which only made her emotional turmoil worse. Genji was feeling somewhat calmer, but whenever he recalled the unpleasant moment when the lady's spirit had addressed him unbidden in that weird and shocking manner, he was reminded of the pain she was experiencing because he had not called on her in such a long time. He vacillated, thinking that perhaps he should visit her in person. But then every time he considered the idea of a visit, he couldn't help worrying that he might be appalled, wondering how she could have fallen to such a state. After considering all the options, he decided it would be best for her if he just sent a message.

Everyone was worried about the prognosis for Genji's wife, who had suffered so grievously, and kept a vigilant watch over her. Naturally, Genji stopped going out on his nightly amorous excursions, even though his wife was still quite sick and unable to see her husband in the customary manner. The baby boy was exceptionally handsome, and because there were worries that his looks might attract the resentful attention of malignant spirits, every effort was made from the moment of his birth to protect him and bring him up with the greatest care. Genji's father-in-law was tremendously pleased, since things had worked out as he had hoped; and though he continued to show concern over his daughter, who had not yet fully recovered, he assumed that her condition was simply the aftereffect of having been so ill, and that there was no reason to be unduly alarmed.

On seeing the beauty of the eyes and features of the baby, who bore a striking resemblance to Fujitsubo's child, Genji thought lovingly of his other, unacknowledged son, the new Crown Prince, and was seized with an unbearable desire to go to the palace to visit him.

"I've not been to the palace for some time, and that concerns me. Since my confinement ends today, I had better go there." He then added, with some resentment, "I wonder if I might speak to my wife directly, without a curtain between us? Why do we always have to be so formal with one another, especially now?"

"As you wish, my lord," one of the women responded. "Your relationship with my lady need not be so formal and distant. Though she is terribly weakened by her ordeal, there is no need to separate the two of you with screens or curtains."

The attendants brought in a cushion for him and placed it close to where his wife was lying. He went in, sat down, and began speaking to her. She answered from time to time, but she still seemed very weak. He remembered the state she had been in at the time he was certain she was about to die, and now felt as if it had all been a dream. He spoke of the period when she had been in mortal danger, and it made his heart ache to think that she had been on the point of death, and to recall how she had stopped breathing, but then recovered and spoke to him so urgently.

"There is so much I want to tell you, but they say you are too weak and not up to it, so I'll let it go for now," he said. He reminded her to drink her medicine, and showed her consideration in other ways as well. Her attendants were deeply impressed by his ministrations, amazed that he had learned such things.

Her appearance as she lay there was heartbreakingly adorable, so weak and pale that he could hardly tell if she were dead or alive. Her abundant hair was properly done up, and the strands that were lying across the pillow were incomparably elegant. He gazed possessively at her, feeling strange that in all this time he should ever have found her deficient in any way.

"I must go visit my father, but I shall return quickly," Genji told her. "How happy it would make me if I could always gaze on you as I am doing now. But your mother is constantly nearby, and so out of deference to her I have refrained from seeing you directly, lest I be considered rash. You must do all you can to get well, then move back to your own chambers. One reason you are not improving may be that you have become too childishly dependent on others."

With these words he took his leave, put on splendid robes and went out. In the past she rarely saw him off, but this time she lay there watching him in rapt attention.

The Autumn Ceremonial for Court Promotions was scheduled for that evening, and because the Minister of the Left had to preside over the event, he too left his daughter at his Sanjō residence and headed for the palace. Each of his sons was hoping to receive a promotion, and since they didn't want to be separated from their father on this particular day, they all left with him.

As a result, there were very few people at the Minister's residence that evening, and while the villa was deserted a malignant spirit suddenly assaulted Genji's wife. The choking sensation she experienced made breathing difficult, and she was in great distress. She stopped breathing before there was time to inform those who had gone to the ceremony. On hearing the news, everyone was stunned, and they left the palace not knowing where their feet were taking them. Though it was the evening of the Autumn Ceremonial, in the face of such a tragedy it would not have been appropriate to continue the event. The crisis had arisen in the middle of the night, and so they were unable to call for the abbot at Mt. Hiei, or even for a distinguished priest. They had all relaxed and let their guard down, assuming that the worst was over, and because her death was so unexpected, the attendants at the Minister's residence were in a panic—confused, stumbling about, bumping into things. Messengers bearing condolences from various noble houses crowded into the residence at Sanjō, but there was no one to take their messages, and the whole house was shaking from the uproar. It was frightening to see how upset everyone was. Because so many malignant spirits had possessed her, they followed prescribed custom and left her body lying there. They didn't disturb her or move the position of her pillow, lest her soul fail to find its way back should it try to return. They kept watch over her for two or three days, but when her appearance began to change, they realized they had reached the end, that she was indeed gone, and were overwhelmed by grief.

With his wife's tragic death coming on the heels of his shocking encounter with the living spirit of the lady at Rokujō, Genji was preoccupied with thoughts of the tiresome nature of this world, and as a result he felt put off by the words of condolences he received from people—even from women with whom he had a special relationship. Genji's father-in-law, the Minister of the Left, was deeply honored to receive condolences directly from the Retired Emperor. It was an honor that brought a moment of relief to his unremitting sorrow, and it left him crying tears of both joy and grief. On the advice of others, the Minister spared no expense or effort in commissioning mystery rites intended to revive his daughter; and though it was evident for all to see that her body was decaying away, in his distracted state he vainly persisted until there was nothing more to be done. When at last they took his daughter's body to be cremated on the plains of Toribeno, many heartrending moments occurred along the way.

* * *

At the Nijō villa his men and women were preparing for his arrival, cleaning and polishing. The senior attendants all appeared before him, and they vied to outdo one another in the splendor of their clothing and makeup. Genji couldn't help but be touched by the lively scene before him, which contrasted so starkly with the lonely, melancholy scene he had left behind at the Sanjō residence. He changed out of his mourning robes and went over to Murasaki's quarters in the west hall. The clothing and furnishings there had been changed with the advent of winter, and the rooms had a bright, fresh look to them. The outfits of the pretty women and girls there were pleasing to his eyes, and Murasaki's nurse, Shōnagon, had made sure that all the preparations had been carried out to his complete satisfaction. Indeed, everything looked wonderful to him.

Murasaki was sweetly done up . . . really lovely. "It's been a long time," Genji began. "You've become quite the young lady." He raised the lower half of the curtains to peek in on her, and when he did so she shyly turned away from him. Even so, he could see that her beauty was perfection itself. Glimpsing her profile in the lamplight, he could tell from her eyes and face that she looked exactly like Fujitsubo, the woman who had so possessed his heart, and he was overjoyed. He moved closer to her and spoke of all the things that had happened, and of how anxious he had been, wondering how she had fared during his period of mourning. "I want to talk to you at leisure, tell you stories of all that took place while I was away. For the time being, however, I'll sleep in the east hall. Having just come out of mourning, it might be bad luck for me to stay here just now. But soon we will have all the time in the world to be together . . . so much so that you may come to regard me as a nuisance."

Shōnagon, who was listening in on them, was delighted by his words, but then she immediately began having anxious thoughts about the precarious position of her young charge. After all, there were many highborn ladies Genji visited discreetly; and it was also possible that he would be drawn to some new lady who might appear on the scene and take the place of his late wife. Shōnagon's suspicious nature was an unattractive trait, but her doubts were understandable, since her primary responsibility was to look after Murasaki.

Genji returned to his own chambers. One of his female attendants, Chūjō no kimi, massaged his legs, and he was finally able to relax and fall asleep. The next morning he sent a letter to his little son at Sanjō. The melancholy reply, obviously written for him by the boy's grandmother, filled him with inexhaustible grief.

With little to occupy him, Genji would lose himself in reveries of longing. Yet because he was reluctant to wander about on some random nocturnal adventure, he could not rouse himself to go out. His little Murasaki was now grown up and ideal in all respects. She looked spectacular, and he felt that now was the appropriate time to consummate their relationship. From time to time he would casually drop hints about their marriage, but she seemed to have no idea what he was talking about.

They whiled away the hours, relieving their tedium by playing Go or word games like *hentsugi*, writing down radicals or parts of a Chinese character and trying to guess which one it was. Murasaki had a clever and engaging personality, and she would demonstrate endearing talents in even the most trivial of pastimes. For several years he had driven all thoughts of taking her as a wife out of his mind, dismissing her talents as nothing more than the accomplishments of a precocious child. Now he could no longer control his passion—though he did feel pangs of guilt, since he was painfully aware of how innocent she was.

Her attendants assumed he would consummate their relationship at some point, but because he had always slept with her, there was simply no way for them to know when that moment would come. One morning Genji rose early, but Murasaki refused to get up. Her behavior worried her attendants. "What's wrong?" they whispered. "She seems unusually out of sorts today." Right before Genji returned to his own quarters, he placed just inside her curtains a box filled with inkstones, brushes, and paper, which she was to use for the customary morning-after letter.[5] When there was no one else around, Murasaki finally lifted her head and found his betrothal note folded in a love knot at her pillow. Still in a daze, she opened the letter.

> How strange that we have stayed apart so long
> Though we slept together night after night
> With only the robes we wore between us

The poem was written in a playful, spontaneous manner, as if he had allowed his emotions to carry him along. It had never crossed her mind that he might be the kind of man who harbored such thoughts about her, and she burned with shame when she recalled their sordid first night. *How could I have been so naïve? How could I have ever trusted a man with such base intentions?*

Genji returned to her quarters at midday, peeking in through her curtains. "Something seems to be bothering you . . . are you not well? It would be quite tedious for me if we weren't able to play Go today." Murasaki was still lying face down. She pulled the bedding up over her face so that she would not have to look at him. When her attendants withdrew, Genji went over to her. "Why are you acting so despondent? Are you displeased with me? I never imagined that you could be so cold. Your women must think this is all very queer." He tugged her bedding away. She was bathed in perspiration, and tears had soaked the hair framing her forehead. "Now this won't do at all!" Genji was put out.

---

5. After a couple's first night together the man was supposed to leave the woman a poem, to which she should respond [editors' note].

"Tears on the first day of your marriage? It's ominous . . . very inauspicious." He tried all sorts of things to cheer her up, but she thought him truly horrid and refused to speak. "All right, then, have it your way," he told her spitefully. "I won't come here anymore if you insist on putting me to shame!" He opened the box with the writing implements and checked inside. There was no reply note. *She's still a child after all*, he thought ruefully. He now felt sorry for her and decided to stay with her inside the curtains for the rest of the day. He passed the whole time trying to comfort her, but this proved difficult. Her refusal to warm up to him, however, merely made her look all the more precious to him.

It was the First Day of the Boar in the tenth month, when the moon rose in the north-northwest. The custom was to serve cakes made of pounded rice on this day, so as evening wore on and they reached the hour of the Boar a little after 9:00, Genji had rice cakes shaped to look like baby pigs brought in to him and Murasaki. The Boar was a symbol of fertility, but the First Day of the Boar was not an auspicious time for marriage. Moreover, Genji was still in mourning, and so he made sure their celebration was subdued, serving the rice cakes in Murasaki's quarters only. Looking at the various colors of the rice cakes, which were flavored with beans, or chestnuts, or poppy, among other things, and nestled in cypress boxes, Genji remembered that he had to have white rice cakes prepared for tomorrow evening, the Third Night of their marriage. He stepped out and summoned Koremitsu. "Have rice cakes brought here tomorrow," he ordered, "though not as many as today. This was not an auspicious day for rice cakes."

Seeing Genji's wry smile, Koremitsu caught on immediately. He did not press his lord on the matter, but simply replied with a perfectly serious expression on his face. "Of course, my lord. It is most reasonable of you to choose an auspicious day to serve rice cakes." He then added, rather drolly, "Let's see . . . tomorrow is the Day of the Rat. Shall I tell them you're having rice cakes in the shape of baby mice to celebrate the event? And just how many will you need?"

"I suppose a third as many as we had today . . . that should be enough," Genji told him. And with that Koremitsu, who knew just what to do, withdrew. *He's certainly an experienced hand*, thought Genji. Koremitsu spoke of this to no one else, and had the rice cakes prepared at his own residence, without telling anyone why he needed them. He was so discreet, in fact, it was almost as if he had made them himself.

Genji was finding it so difficult to comfort Murasaki that he was at a loss. At the same time he was delighted when it occurred to him that, for the first time in her life, she must have felt like a stolen bride. With that realization came another. *She has been precious to me for many years, but my feelings for her during all that time were nothing compared to what I feel for her now. The heart is a peculiar thing. Now I find it impossible to be apart from her, even for a single night.*

Koremitsu stealthily brought a box filled with the rice cakes Genji had ordered late the previous night. Deeply considerate and sensitive to the situation, Koremitsu thought it might be embarrassing for Murasaki if he asked her nurse, Shōnagon, to take the box into her chambers. So instead he summoned Shōnagon's daughter, Ben. "Take this to your young mistress, and don't let anyone see you." He handed her an incense jar, inside of which he had hidden the box of rice cakes. "Now listen to me. This is a gift to celebrate an auspicious event, so you must set it beside her pillow. Be very careful. You must carry out my instructions to the letter." Ben thought that this request was suspicious, but she took the jar anyway. "I have never," she insisted, "been unfaithful in serving my lady." He cut her short. "Don't use the word *unfaithful*. The very uttering of it on an occasion like this is bad luck." Ben considered the whole affair very odd, but she was young and really had no idea what Koremitsu was talking about. She placed the jar inside her lady's curtains next to her pillow. Genji, as he always did, explained the significance of the rice cakes to Murasaki.

Murasaki's attendants had known nothing about this. It wasn't until the next morning, when Genji had the box of rice cakes taken away, that they finally realized their lord had formally taken their young mistress as his wife. When could all of the dishes have been brought in? The stands on which the plates rested looked fabulous, their legs intricately carved in the shape of flowers. Various kinds of rice cakes had been specially prepared, and everything used for the Third Night celebration—the silver plates, silver chopsticks, silver chopstick rests—had been exquisitely arranged. Shōnagon wondered, *Has he actually gone so far as to recognize her as his wife?* And when she saw it was true, she was profoundly grateful and wept at this proof of Genji's honorable intentions. The other women were disappointed that they had not been let in on the secret, and they grumbled among themselves. "Of course it's wonderful that things have turned out like this, but why did our lord have to keep it secret? And that Koremitsu . . . whatever could he have been thinking?"

Following his marriage to Murasaki, Genji would feel so anxious about her whenever he went to the palace or called on the Retired Emperor, even for a short visit, that a vision of her would come to him and he would see her face. He found his own attraction to her mysterious. He received resentful letters from his other women enticing him to visit, and their notes did make him feel bad for them. But the very thought that such visits would be hard on his new bride troubled him. He recalled a line from an old *Man'yōshū* poem: "How can I endure a single night apart from you?"[6] He simply could not bring himself to go out on his nocturnal forays, but instead pretended he wasn't feeling well and was indisposed. He passed the time sending replies to his ladies along the lines of "I've been preoccupied of late with thoughts of the sad evanescence of this world. Once this mood of mine has passed, we shall, I assure you, meet again."

Oborozukiyo, the lady Genji associated with that evening of the misty moon, could not get him out of her mind. Her older sister, the Kokiden Consort, who was now the Imperial Mother, was extremely displeased to learn about this infatuation, and was further annoyed when her own father, the Minister of the Right, dismissed her concerns. "Why should I be bothered about this?" he said. "If she realizes her heart's desire and becomes one of Genji's wives, I won't complain. After all, the woman who was most significant to him has apparently died." The Kokiden Consort replied, "And what's wrong with her entering service in the Women's Quarters?" She seemed to have her heart firmly set on sending her younger sister to court to serve her son, Emperor Suzaku.

6. Poem from *The Man'yōshū*: "Now that we are betrothed, sharing a pillow of new grasses, how can I endure a single night apart from you?"

For his part, Genji did not consider Oborozukiyo just another woman, and he thought it a shame that she should be sent into service at the palace. At the present moment, however, he was not inclined to divide his attention among his women. He wanted to focus on Murasaki alone. *I'd better let it be,* he thought. *Murasaki is good enough. Life is brief, and so I should just settle down with her. I must never again stir resentment in a woman.*

This train of thought brought back the incident with the lady at Rokujō. He had learned a fearful lesson. He was sorry for her, but now he could never feel comfortable recognizing her formally as a wife. If she could be satisfied with continuing to meet as they had over the years, if she could go on being his companion, a woman who could talk with him on those occasions when it was natural and proper to do so, if they could just be a comfort to one another . . . as he mulled over their relationship he knew that no matter how difficult it was, she was a woman he could not easily abandon.

*   *   *

FROM CHAPTER XII

Suma

Exile to Suma

*   *   *

Oborozukiyo[7] returned to court service in the seventh month. Suzaku had a strong lingering affection for her, and so he kept her near him as he had always done, acting as though he knew nothing of the imprecations directed at her by certain courtiers. He would on occasion reproach her for one reason or another while also offering tender vows of love. In both looks and bearing Suzaku possessed a youthful grace and elegance, and Oborozukiyo was certainly grateful for, and embarrassed by, his show of noblesse oblige. Yet her heart had room only for her memories of Genji. On one occasion, during a musical performance, Suzaku remarked, "It's at times like this that I miss Genji the most. I venture to say that there are many here who miss him even more than I. It seems as if the light has gone out of everything." He then added, "I have acted contrary to my father's wishes. I shall come to regret my sin." Tears welled up in his eyes, and at that moment Oborozukiyo could no longer restrain her own. "I have learned from experience that the world is a tiresome place," he continued, "and no longer feel that I want to remain in it much longer. If I were no longer here, how would you feel about it? It makes me bitter to think that my death would not affect you nearly as much as the absence of one who still lives nearby. The poet who wrote the line 'while I am in this world'[8] did not express noble sentiments." His manner was so gentle, and his words suffused with such profound emotion, that tears began to stream down Oborozukiyo's cheeks. "For whom do you weep?" Suzaku asked. "It makes me sad that you have yet to give me a child . . . it's as if something were missing in my life. I have considered

7. Genji's affair with her, described in pages not included here, forced him to leave the capital and go into exile to rustic Suma [editors' note].

8. *Waka* poem by Ōtomo no Momoyo: "What

good would it do to die of longing? I want to be with my love for those days I am alive." The line *ikeru hi* ("those days I am alive") is misquoted in the text as *ikeru yo* (literally, "the world I live in").

adopting the Crown Prince as my father instructed me, but given the enmity between my mother and the Fujitsubo Consort it would cause too much trouble to do so." Certain people were conducting affairs of state in a manner contrary to his wishes, but he was too young and weak-willed to resist, even though he was disappointed and bothered by many things, including Genji's exile, that had been carried out in his name.

At Suma the winds of autumn, the "season of anxious grief,"[9] were intensifying; and though his villa was some distance from the shore, each night the waves, which Middle Counselor Yukihira observed were stirred by winds blowing through the barrier pass,[1] sounded as if they were breaking quite close. Genji had never experienced anything as affecting as the autumn in this place.

He had only a few attendants with him, and because they were all asleep he was lying awake by himself, his head propped up on his pillow, listening to the winds howling from every direction. Feeling as though the waves were crashing near his residence, tears welled up instinctively . . . so many that it seemed his pillow might float away. He tried playing his seven-string koto a little, but the music just made him feel even more frightened and alone, and so he abruptly stopped and murmured the following poem.

> Does the wind blow from where my loved ones mourn
> For I seem to hear in the sound of waves
> Voices crying in pain from loneliness

Hearing his poem, his attendants were startled awake. Seeing how splendid Genji looked, they were overcome by emotion, and as they arose unsteadily they were quietly wiping their noses to disguise their tears. Genji wondered, *How must my attendants feel? For my sake alone they have come wandering with me to this sorry existence, having left behind their comfortable, familiar homes and parted with parents and siblings from whom even the briefest absence would be hard to bear.* Such musings made him miserable, but then he realized that it must make his attendants feel forlorn to see him so downhearted like this. And so, during the days that followed, he diverted them with playful banter, and in moments of idle leisure he would make scrolls by gluing together pieces of paper of various hues and practice writing poems. He also drew remarkable-looking sketches and paintings on rare Chinese silk of patterned weave and used them to decorate the front panels of folding screens. Before he came to Suma he had heard about the views of the sea and mountains here, and he had imagined from afar what they looked like. Now that they were right before his own eyes, he depicted those rocky shores, whose incomparable beauty truly surpassed anything he had imagined, in charcoal sketches of unrivalled skill. A member of his escort remarked with impatient frustration, "If only we could summon the great masters Chieda and Tsunenori[2] and have them color in your sketches . . ." Genji's gentle, familiar behavior and splendid bearing helped his

9. Anonymous poem from *The Kokinshū*: "Looking upon the light of the moon filtering through the trees, I see that autumn, season of anxious grief, has arrived."
1. Poem from *The Kokinshū* by Ariwara no Yukihira: "How mournful, the winds that blow through the barrier pass onto the strands at

Suma to chill a traveler's sleeves." The allusion here is not a perfect match, and Murasaki Shikibu may have cited the wrong poem.
2. Tsunenori flourished during the reign of Emperor Murakami (r. 946–67). Not much is known about Chieda.

attendants forget the cares of the world. Four or five were in constant attendance, and they were overjoyed to be able to serve him so intimately.

One pleasant evening, when the garden flowers near the veranda were a riot of colors, Genji stepped out into a passageway that framed a view of the sea. As he stood there motionless for a few moments, he didn't look like an earthly being, given the odd juxtaposition of his beauty and the setting, and so the divine splendor of his appearance was eerily unsettling. His loose purple trousers, cinched at the ankles, were lined with a pale green; his robe was a soft white silk twill. His dark blue cloak was loosely tied, giving him a casual air as he began reciting in hushed tones the opening lines of his ritual devotions: "I, a disciple of Shakyamuni Buddha . . ." He slowly chanted a sutra in a voice so sonorous that it too seemed like nothing of this world. From boats in the offing came voices of fishermen singing as they rowed over the waves. Viewed from a distance, the vague outlines of the boats resembled little birds floating on the sea, creating a lonesome effect. Just then a line of migrating geese flew overhead, their cries like the creaking of the oars, and Genji gazed out at the scene in rapt silence, his hands, white and lambent in contrast to the dark beads of his rosary, moving slightly to brush away the tears running down his cheeks. His magnificent appearance gave comfort to his retainers, all of whom were yearning for their loved ones back home. Genji composed a verse.

> Is it because these wild geese, the first of autumn
> Were with the loved ones I miss in the capital
> That their cries echo mournfully across the skies

Yoshikiyo responded.

> Though not companions of mine from the past
> These geese crying out still stir memories
> One after another of my old life

Koremitsu also responded.

> Am I to consider these geese as companions
> On my exile when they willfully chose to leave
> Familiar homes for distant realms beyond the clouds

The Lesser Captain of the Right Palace Guard—the young man whose loyalty cost him a promising career—composed yet another poem.

> Even wild geese who leave familiar homes
> To migrate through distant skies find comfort
> So long as they are with their companions

"What would become of me if I were to lose sight of my companions?" Although the Lesser Captain's father, who had once been Vice Governor of Iyo, had recently been appointed Vice Governor of Hitachi, the young man had decided not to accompany him, but went into exile with Genji instead. The choice must have caused him great distress, but he put on a brave front and pretended that nothing bothered him.

The full moon rose vivid and bright, bringing back memories to Genji. "That's right . . . tonight is the fifteenth." Staring up at the face of the moon, he lovingly imagined the music that would be playing on a night like this at the palace, with all the ladies gazing out at the night sky. When he murmured a line from Bai

Juyi—"Feelings for acquaintances of old, now two thousand leagues distant"[3]—
his attendants could not restrain their tears. With indescribable yearning he
recalled the poem Fujitsubo sent him complaining about how the "ninefold
mists" kept her from the palace. As memories of this and other moments came
to him, he wept aloud. He heard someone say "The hour is late." However, he
could not bring himself to retire.

> As I gaze at the moon I am at peace
> Even if only briefly, for it shines
> On the distant palace I long to see

He had warm recollections of a certain night when he had talked intimately
with Emperor Suzaku about times past. *How closely he resembles our late
father!* Genji whispered a line from a poem in Chinese by the exiled Sugawara
no Michizane: "The robe bestowed on me by the emperor is now with me
here."[4] Truly the robe never left his sight, but was always near him.

> My sleeves both right and left are wet with tears
> Tears of bitter resentment on the one
> Tears of longing for you on the other

* * *

As the days and months passed there were many occasions back in the capital when the courtiers, Emperor Suzaku first among them, experienced pangs
of wistful longing for Genji. The Crown Prince in particular constantly shed
tears whenever he thought of him, so that his nurses, especially Myōbu, looked
on with pity.

Fujitsubo, who had always been fearful about her son's position, was beside
herself with anxiety now that Genji was not there to look after his interests. At
the beginning of his exile the princes who were his half brothers and other high-
ranking noblemen who had been close to him would send sympathetic notes
inquiring how he was faring. Many at the court deemed these exchanges of
heartfelt correspondence, which included poetry in Chinese, extraordinarily
felicitous. When the Kokiden Consort learned about these letters, however, she
harshly disparaged them. "One might expect a man who has incurred official
censure to find it a daily struggle just to savor the taste of food as he would
like . . . but not Genji. He resides in an attractive villa, writing letters critical of
the court, and like that traitorous official in the Qin Dynasty, gets his syco-
phants to go along with everything he says. Why, they'd call a deer a horse if he
told them to!"[5] When word spread of what she said and the asperity with which
she spoke, people at the court were afraid, and no one wrote to Genji anymore.

The passage of time brought no comfort to Murasaki. When the women
who had been serving Genji in the east hall moved to her quarters in the west
hall, they had been skeptical of her, wondering why their lord would have
brought such a young lady to his villa. But after they got to know her—her
charming, endearing looks, her steady, sincere personality, her kindness and

3. The poem by [Bo] Juyi from which this line
is taken was written on the moon festival in
autumn.
4. A line from a Chinese-style poem which
Sugawara no Michizane wrote in exile when
he looked at a robe he had received from the
emperor while still at court. The poetry of
famous Chinese and Japanese exiles, such as
[Bo] Juyi and Michizane, keeps Genji company
during his own time in exile [editors' note].
5. This anecdote is related in Sima Qian's *Historical Records*, included in Vol. A [editor's note].

deep sensitivity—not one of them chose to leave. Those ladies-in-waiting of higher status and greater discernment were able once in a while to catch a glimpse of her behind her screens, and when they did they saw that their lord's preference for her over his other ladies was perfectly justified.

The longer Genji stayed at Suma, the more living apart from Murasaki became intolerable for him. Despite his torment, he rejected the idea of having her come to live with him in a place completely unsuitable for her. *How could I have her live in a place I myself consider retribution for past sins?* Everything in this province was so different from the capital. He had never before been exposed to the sight of lower class people, who had no inkling of who he was, and they were a shock to his sensibilities—naturally he found them uncouth and beneath him. From time to time smoke would rise quite near his villa, and at first he imagined it was from the fires the fishermen used to extract salt. Later he learned it was smoke from smoldering brush that had been cleared on the mountain behind the villa. It was all such a marvel to him that he composed a poem.

> Like brush burning at the huts of rustics
> My heart smolders with my constant yearnings
> For tidings from my loved one back at home

* * *

Just when life was feeling most tiresome, Tō no Chūjō suddenly paid a visit. He may have been the son of the Minister of the Left, but he was also the husband of the younger sister of the Kokiden Consort and so his career had not suffered. He was a man of sterling character and, having been promoted to Consultant at the third rank, he now possessed an impeccable reputation. Despite his good fortune, however, the palace was a dreary place for him with Genji gone, and at every event he found himself longing for his old friend. It finally reached the point where he no longer cared that he might become the subject of malicious gossip and censure, and he decided to venture to Suma. The moment he laid eyes on Genji he experienced a joy, mingled with a few tears, he had not savored in a long time.

In Tō no Chūjō's eyes the villa at Suma had a vaguely Chinese style about it. The setting was like something out of a painting, and the effect created by the fence of bamboo wattle, the stone steps, the pine pillars, all as rustic and simple as Bai Juyi's hut, was peculiarly charming.[6] Eschewing royal colors, Genji was dressed without ostentation, wearing dark bluish gray hunting cloak and trousers, cinched at the ankles, over a humble light red robe, creating the impression that he was a mountain peasant. Though Genji was intentionally dressed like a provincial, his looks were so dazzling that Tō no Chūjō couldn't help smiling. The personal effects he kept close at hand were simple and humble-looking, and his sitting room was completely exposed to view from the outside. The boards for Go and backgammon, the furnishings, and the pieces used for playing *tagi*[7] had all been fashioned intentionally to have an appropriately countrified look to them, while the implements used for the Buddhist

6. This resembles the description of the hut [Bo] Juyi gives in one of his poems.
7. A game that is similar to tiddlywinks, except

that the object is to flip stones onto a board instead of into a cup.

rituals he practiced showed signs of his wholehearted devotion. Even the meal provided was prepared in an intriguing way in harmony with the setting.

Tō no Chūjō, spotting some fishermen carrying shellfish they had just harvested, summoned them over and asked them what it was like to live for so many years on these shores. They told him about the various hardships and worries they had experienced, and though their babbling speech was in a rough dialect he found hard to follow, he was nonetheless moved as he observed them, since they made him realize that all people, no matter what their status, experienced similar emotions and were not that different. As a reward for the shellfish, he adorned them with robes and other gifts, and the honor he bestowed on them made them think, if only for a moment, that the world was their oyster.

Genji's horses were stabled close by, and Tō no Chūjō watched in amazement as someone brought rice stalks from a strange-looking storehouse in the distance—apparently some kind of granary—to feed them. The scene reminded him of a line from the *saibara* "Asukai," and he sang the words "the grasses are inviting."[8] He then told Genji all that had happened during the months he had been away, alternately crying and laughing. "My father," he said, "is always fretting over your son, and it makes him feel sad that the little one should be so innocent about what is happening in the world." Genji could hardly bear to think about the boy. There is no way for me to record all that was said between them, and I can't even do justice to a small part of their conversation. They did not sleep that night, but passed the time composing Chinese poetry until dawn. Still, even Tō no Chūjō had to be mindful of the consequences of rumors at the court, and so he hurried back to the capital at daybreak. Such haste made his departure all the harder for Genji to take. They took up their cups of wine and toasted one another, reciting together a line of verse composed by Bai Juyi to bid farewell to his friend, Yuan Zhen, who had visited the poet in exile: "Into the wine cup in spring, Pour tears of drunken sorrow." All their companions wept with them, apparently in bitter regret that the two friends should have to part after so short a time together.

A formation of wild geese flew across the dimly lit sky. Genji composed the following.

> In what spring will I be allowed at last
> To go and view the capital again . . .
> How I envy these geese returning home

Tō no Chūjō could hardly bring himself to leave.

> Will not the wild geese that leave unsated
> From this enchanting abode lose their way
> On the road to the capital in bloom

The gifts from the capital were elegant and in good taste. In seeing off his guests, Genji showed his appreciation for them by making a present of a black horse. "You may think it inauspicious to receive a memento from someone in exile," he said, "but like me, this horse misses home, for he tends to neigh whenever he feels a breeze coming from the direction of the capital."[9] It was an exceptionally fine-looking steed.

8. "Let us tarry awhile at the well of Asuka, the shade is good, the waters cool, the grasses inviting . . ."

9. Allusion to a Chinese poem.

"Keep these in remembrance of us," Tō no Chūjō replied, presenting Genji with several items, including a remarkable flute that had a reputation at court for its fine tonal qualities. All the same, he was careful not to give presents that might invite censure. By now the sun was rising, and because it was already late to be starting off, he hurried away, flustered, glancing back over and over. How forlorn Genji looked as he saw the party off. "When will I see you again? Surely this exile won't last much longer."

Genji replied with a poem.

> Oh crane, you who can soar so near the clouds
> Above the palace . . . look on one whose life
> Is pure and spotless as a day in spring

"While I fully expect to return, it is difficult for people who suffer the misfortune of exile, even the wisest sages of the past, to mingle again successfully in court society, and so . . . well, I don't feel as though I want to see the capital again."

Tō no Chūjō answered with a verse of his own.

> Longing for the companion who flew beside him
> Wing-to-wing, the solitary crane, with no guide
> To help cries out among the clouds . . . and the palace

"Your absence is so painful, I now regret the good fortune of being your close friend." They had not had time to converse at their leisure, and his departure left such a void that Genji spent the rest of the day sunk in melancholy reverie.

On the Day of the Serpent, which fell during the first ten days of the third month, one of Genji's attendants, a person who took pride in his knowledge of such things, told him, "This is a day when a person who has the sort of cares that trouble you should perform rites of purification." And so Genji, who had wanted to go view the shore in any case, headed down to the sea. He had some simple soft blinds erected to create a temporary enclosure for himself, then summoned a diviner, a master of the way of yin-yang who traveled back and forth between the capital and this province. As part of the purification ritual, a large doll to which all defilements and malign spirits had been transferred was placed in a boat and set adrift on the waves. Watching it float away, Genji was reminded of his own fate.

> Like a ritual doll drifting out
> Into an unknown expanse of sea
> I am overwhelmed by my sorrow

Sitting in the midst of a bright, cheerful setting, he looked indescribably handsome. The surface of the sea was serenely calm and gave no sign which way the currents were flowing, but as he pondered the flow of his own life, his past and his future, he composed another poem.

> Surely the myriad deities
> Must take pity on me . . . after all
> Is what I have done truly a crime

The wind suddenly picked up and the skies darkened. People began bustling to get ready to leave, even though the purification ritual was not finished. Rain fell suddenly and violently, and his attendants were so flustered they were unable to raise the parasols as they made their way back to the residence. The party had not prepared for this kind of storm; the wind, unlike anything they had seen before, blew away everything around them, and the waves broke with terrifying power, forcing everyone to flee before their fury. With each flash of lightning and crash of thunder, the surface of the sea shimmered like a silk quilt spread out before them. While the party struggled, barely managing to make it back, they feared they might be struck by lightning at any moment.

"I've never gone through anything like this!" said one of the attendants.

"Usually you see some signs that the wind is going to pick up. This is a shockingly rare occurrence," replied another.

Even as they spoke, stunned and dismayed, the thunder continued unabated, and the torrential rain fell so hard it seemed as though it would pierce through whatever it struck. *Is the world coming to an end*, they all wondered, feeling forlorn and confounded. All the while Genji was calmly reciting a sutra. The thunder lessened somewhat when darkness fell, but the wind howled on throughout the night.

When it seemed that the storm was subsiding, one of the attendants remarked, "Surely this is a sign of the power of all the prayers I've been offering."

"If it had gone on much longer," his companion added, "we would have been swallowed up by the waves for sure."

"I've heard that a tsunami can kill a person in an instant," someone else chimed in, "but I never knew anything like this could happen."

When dawn approached everyone was finally able to fall asleep. Genji was also able to rest a little, but as he dozed off, someone—a person whose features he could not make out very clearly—approached him in a dream. "You have been summoned to the palace," the figure demanded, "so why have you not made an appearance?" The figure was walking about, apparently searching for him. Seeing this, Genji was startled awake. The Dragon King in the sea was known to be a connoisseur of genuine beauty, and so Genji realized he must have caught the deity's eye. The dream gave him such a horrifying, uncanny sensation that he could no longer stand residing in this abode by the sea.

FROM **CHAPTER XIII**

Akashi

The Lady at Akashi

Several days passed, but the rain and wind did not let up, and the thunder did not abate. These endless hardships made Genji increasingly lonely and miserable, and under such circumstances, facing a dark past and bleak future, he could no longer put on a brave front. *What should I do?* he asked himself as he pondered his situation. *If this storm drives me back to the capital before I receive a pardon, I'll be a laughingstock. Perhaps it would be best to leave here and seek out some abode deep in the mountains, leaving no trace of myself in the world.* But then he had second thoughts. *Even if I were to leave for the mountains, people would still gossip about me, saying that I retreated in a panic, driven off by the wind and waves. Later generations would consider me utterly contemptible.* These thoughts weren't the only thing troubling him. The dream he had a few nights earlier, during which he had seen that foreboding figure, kept recurring.

Day after day went by without a break in the clouds, and he grew increasingly anxious, fretting about what was happening in the capital and thinking abjectly that if things continued like this he would be cast utterly adrift. Yet because it was too stormy to even poke one's head outside, no one arrived from the capital to see him.

At last a messenger arrived from his Nijō villa. The man, who had rashly braved the weather, was soaked to the point of looking weird and unearthly. He was also of very humble station—had Genji passed such a person on the road at an earlier point in his life, he would not have recognized him as human, and would have had his servants brush him aside. The fact that Genji now felt a deep kinship with such a man brought home just how far he had come down in the world and how much his self-esteem had collapsed.

The man carried a letter from Murasaki: "This terrible, tedious storm goes on without end, making me feel as though the skies were closing me off from you even more than before, for now I cannot even gaze in your direction."

> How fiercely must the winds blow across those strands
> During this time when endless waves drench the sleeves
> Of one who is longing for you from afar

The account she gave of her anguish affected him greatly, and after opening her letter his mood turned to dark despair and he felt like the poet whose river of tears "overflowed its banks."[1]

"Even in the capital," the messenger informed him, "people are viewing this storm as an eerie omen, and I've heard they plan to hold a ritual congregation of the Sutra for Benevolent Rulers to protect against a disaster.[2] High-ranking officials who usually attend the palace to conduct affairs of state cannot do so because the roads are all blocked." The messenger's manner of talking was stiff and unclear, but because Genji was curious about court matters, he was eager to learn more. He summoned the man to appear before him and questioned him further.

"Day after day the rain falls with no let up and the winds continue to gust," the messenger said. "Everyone is alarmed and amazed by this extraordinary weather. Of course, we haven't seen anything like what you've had here at Suma, what with hail falling so hard it drills into the ground and with this constant rumbling of thunder." The expression on the man's face, which told of his surprise and fear of the terrible conditions at Suma, sharpened all the more the sense of isolation felt by Genji's attendants.

As the storm raged on and on, Genji began to wonder if this might not be the end of the world . . . but then, the following morning, the wind picked up with even greater intensity, the tide surged, and waves broke violently on the shore, looking as if they might sweep away even the rocky crags and hills. No words could describe the booming thunder or the flashing lightning, which seemed to be crashing down right on top of them. Everyone was frightened out of his wits.

---

1. Poem from Ki no Tsurayuki's *Tosa Diary,* included in this volume: "The river of tears has overflowed its banks and further dampens the sleeves of both the one who goes and the one who stays behind."

2. This congregation, called Ninnōe, was held in the palace in the fall and spring, or in times of emergency, to protect the realm.

"What misdeed did we commit," bemoaned one attendant, "that we should suffer this tragic destiny? Must we die without seeing our parents again, without looking on the beloved faces of our wives and children?"

Genji regained his composure, resolute in the conviction that having committed no great crime his life would not end on these shores. Still, his attendants were in such a state of panic that he had an offering of multicolored strips of cloth made to the gods of the sea. He also made numerous supplications. "Oh deity of Sumiyoshi,"[3] he intoned, "you who calm and protect these nearby shores, if truly you are the manifestation of the Buddha taken form as the guardian divinity of this region, then deliver us from harm!" His attendants were deeply distressed by the prospect that not only they themselves but their lord as well would be swept into the sea and perish in this unheard-of fashion. A few of them gathered their courage as best they could and, regaining a sense of propriety, joined their voices in praying to the Buddha and the gods, each offering his own life in exchange for the safety of their lord. Turning in the direction of the Sumiyoshi Shrine, they made their supplications.

"Our lord reared in the bosom of the Emperor's palace, and had every sort of pleasure lavished upon him. Yet has not his profound compassion spread throughout this great realm of eight islands, lifting up and saving many who were mired in sin and impiety? What crime has he committed that he must now suffer retribution by drowning here amidst these foul, unjust waves and wind? You gods of heaven and of earth, show us clearly that you discern right from wrong! Though guiltless, he has been charged with crimes, stripped of office and rank, separated from home, driven into exile. Grieving anxiously morning and night, he has suffered this tragic fate . . . is he about to lose his life as well because of some sin in a former life, or some crime committed in this one? Gods and Buddha, if you are just, then put an end to our lordship's suffering!"

Genji once more offered prayers to the Dragon King and to the myriad gods of the sea, but the thunder only crashed all the more loudly, and lightning struck the gallery connecting Genji's quarters to the rest of the villa. Flames leapt up and the passageway caught on fire, throwing everyone into a state of panic. No one had enough wits about him to be able to deal with the situation, and so they had their lord move to the rear of the residence, to a room that, from the looks of it, must have been the kitchen. Everyone, irrespective of rank, crowded into the space, and the thunder could barely be heard above the tumultuous din of the crying and shouting there. As the day ended, the sky was black as an ink stone.

Finally the winds gradually subsided, the rain tapered off, and sparkling stars were visible. Genji's attendants felt embarrassed for their lord, thinking it was an affront to his dignity to remain in a place as strange and disreputable as this, and so they wanted to try to move him back to the main hall. They hesitated, however, discussing what they should do. One of them declared, "Even the quarters that escaped the fire have an ominous air about them. The people over there are in a state of shock, noisily stomping about, and the blinds have all been blown away." Another attendant replied, "In that case, let's wait until morning."

All the while Genji was meditating and softly invoking the name of the Buddha. Feeling unsettled and restless, he mulled over all that had happened.

---

3. A Shinto shrine near Osaka [editors' note].

After the moon rose he could make out clearly just how close to the villa the tide had surged. Pushing open a door of rough wattle and glancing outside, he gazed off toward the shore at the roiling surf left in the wake of the storm. No one in the immediate vicinity possessed the qualifications—sensitivity, proper judgment, ability to divine past and future—needed to make sense of all this and reliably sort things out. Instead, the only people to make their way to the villa were those strange, lowly fisher folk, who gathered at a residence where they had heard a nobleman resides, babbling away in an unfamiliar dialect; but even though Genji considered them exceedingly bizarre, he couldn't very well have them chased away. One of his attendants remarked, "If the wind hadn't subsided for a while, the high tide would have left nothing behind. The mercy of the gods is boundless!" Feeling forlorn, he composed a verse.

> Had the gods of the sea shown no mercy
> Then the tide surging from all directions
> Would surely have swept me into the deep

Genji had maintained his composure throughout the tumult of the storm, but it had been terribly nerve-wracking and exhausting and he began to doze off in spite of himself. The room he was using as a temporary shelter was so crude and rough that he could not lie down, so he slept while propping himself up against a pillar. As he did so, his late father came to him in a dream and stood before him, looking just as he did when he was alive. "Why do you remain in such a strange, unseemly place as this?" His father took his hand and, pulling Genji to his feet, exhorted him. "Hurry now! Board a boat and leave these shores, following wherever the deity of Sumiyoshi may lead you!"

Genji felt overjoyed. "From the moment I was separated from your august presence," he said, "I have been beset with all manner of sorrows, so that now I feel I ought to end my life on this shore."

"Such rash thoughts simply will not do! All these trials are a mere trifle . . . retribution for some minor misdeeds. Though I committed no serious breach of conduct during my reign, I was unknowingly guilty of some misdeeds and have spent all my time after death atoning for them[4] without once giving any thought to matters of this world. But then I saw how deeply mired you are in your troubles here, and I could not bear it. I entered the sea and rose up to these shoals; and though I am now utterly exhausted, I must take this opportunity and hurry on to the capital, where I will speak to Suzaku on your behalf." With that he rose to leave.

Genji was upset his father was going away so soon, and because he wanted to accompany him, he began to weep. He looked up, but there was no one there—only the shining face of the moon. It had all felt so real, it hadn't felt like a dream at all. The lingering presence of his father remained, so palpable that Genji was profoundly moved by the sight of the wispy lines of clouds trailing across the night sky like traces of his father's ghostly presence. He had not seen his father's figure for many years, not even in his dreams; and now, even though he had glimpsed for only a few fleeting moments the face he had been longing so impatiently to see, the image continued to linger, hovering before

---

4. This statement by Genji's father is an apparent reference to a vision by the monk Nichizō, who saw the historical Emperor Daigo suffering the torments of hell.

his mind's eye. The poignant sense of gratitude he felt toward his father, who had flown to aid him when his life had reached its nadir and he was in despair and contemplating the end of his life, also made him look at the storm in a different, more positive light. The after-effect of his dream was a boundless sense of happiness and relief that someone was looking out for him. His heart was full of conflicting emotions, and even though he had seen his father only in a dream, the turmoil in his heart distracted him from the sorrows of the waking world. He wanted to go back to sleep in hopes of seeing his father again, but the irritation he felt at himself for not responding to his father in more detail kept him from being able to close his eyes, and he stayed awake until dawn.

A small boat approached the shore and several men came toward the exile's abode. When one of Genji's retainers asked them to identify themselves, they answered, "The former governor of Harima province, a novitiate who has recently taken his vows, had this boat readied and we journeyed here from the bay at Akashi. If Yoshikiyo, the Minamoto Lesser Counselor, is here, our lord would like to meet and discuss some matters at length."

Yoshikiyo was startled by their arrival and seemed not to know what to make of it. "I was familiar with the man before he was a novitiate and still governor of Harima, and had opportunities to converse with him over the course of several years. However, we had a mutual falling out over some trifling matter, so it has been a long time since we exchanged any correspondence of a particularly personal nature. What business would bring him here over such rough seas?"

Genji's dream, especially his father's exhortation, was still vivid in his mind, and he told Yoshikiyo to hurry up and meet with the novitiate. So Yoshikiyo went down to the boat, scarcely believing that it had set out during the storm amidst such violent waves and wind.

"Earlier this month," the novitiate explained, "a remarkable-looking figure came to me in a dream and told me something incredible. 'On the thirteenth of this month,' he announced, 'I will give you a clear sign, so have a boat prepared and no matter what happens, make for Suma when the wind and waves subside.' Because he had informed me in advance, I did as instructed and had a boat ready. Then I waited as long as I could, until the ferocity of the rain and wind and thunder alarmed me and made me worry for the safety of your lord. Then it hit me that there have been many examples, even in other lands, where a person who acted on his belief in a dream saved the state. Though your lord may have no use for my message, I could not let the appointed day spoken of in my dream pass without reporting these tidings to him. So I set out in the boat, and a miraculously favorable wind blew it along until we arrived at this strand. Truly this can only be a sign of divine favor. Is it possible that some sign was given to your lord here as well? If so, then please convey my words to him, ashamed though I am to beg your indulgence."

Yoshikiyo discreetly reported what he had heard. Genji mulled over the information, turning over in his mind all things past and future—disturbing things he had seen in both his dreams and his waking life—that might be taken as signs from the gods. *If I hesitate out of fear that gossips will ruin my reputation by criticizing me for following after some eccentric novitiate, I could end up rejecting what might be genuine divine assistance. If that happened, I'd be an even greater laughingstock. It is hard enough to turn away from the advice of men . . . how much harder, then, to defy the gods. It's proper that I should be deferential, even in minor matters, and yield to the views of those higher in rank who are older, respected and trustworthy. A sage of old once advised that 'One cannot be censured for following.' In truth, I failed to heed those words, and as a result I've had to undergo many bitter, unprecedented hardships, including this life-threatening storm. In the face of all that, salvaging my reputation for posterity no longer seems so important. What's more, my father did admonish me in my dream, so why should I have any doubts about the novitiate's story?*

After deliberating in this way, Genji sent his reply: "Though I have encountered unheard-of difficulties in this unfamiliar province, no one from the capital has inquired after me. I have gazed after the sun and moon coursing through the sky to who knows where, and thought of them as my only companions from home . . . but now to my great joy a fisherman's boat arrives.[5] Is there a retreat on the shores of Akashi, some place where I might withdraw in peace?" The novitiate's delight knew no bounds, and he expressed his deep gratitude. "This is all fine and well," said a member of Genji's escort, "but our lord should go aboard before dawn so that he will not be seen."

Genji boarded the boat accompanied by the usual retinue of four or five of his most trusted attendants. The miraculous breeze that had brought the boat here picked up again, and they arrived at Akashi so quickly it was as if they had flown there. The shores of Suma and Akashi were separated by only a few miles, and so the journey would have been short in any case. Even so, the willfulness of the breeze seemed uncanny all the same.

What Yoshikiyo had told him years earlier was true—the scenery on the shores of Akashi was truly spectacular. For Genji, who was hoping for a peaceful sanctuary, the only thing that detracted from the place was the large number of people bustling about. The novitiate's estate extended from the waterfront up into the recesses of the hills, and he had brought together on his land all sorts of attractive buildings constructed with an eye to how well they suited the seasons and the topography—a thatched-roof cottage near the shore that would intensify the pleasures of viewing the four seasons, a magnificent meditation hall standing beside a stream flowing down out of the hills on a site perfect for performing ritual devotions and focusing one's thoughts on the next world, a row of granaries, built to provide for the needs of this world and filled with the bountiful harvests of autumn in order to sustain the novitiate throughout his remaining years of life. Fearful of the recent tidal surges, the novitiate had moved his daughter and her entourage to a residence at the foot of the hills, allowing Genji to occupy comfortably the villa near the sea.

The sun was gradually rising just as Genji was moving from the boat to a carriage. As soon as the novitiate caught a glimpse of him in the dim early morning light, he immediately forgot about his own advancing years and felt as though his life had been extended. Beaming with a joyous smile, he at once offered a prayer to the deity of Sumiyoshi. It seemed to him that he had been allowed to grasp the light of the sun and the moon in his hands, and so it seemed perfectly natural that he should busy himself tending to Genji's needs.

To capture the scene in a painting—not just the beauty of the setting, which goes without saying, but also the elegance of the buildings, the indescribable

---

5. Poem by Ki no Tsurayuki: "To my great joy a fisherman's boat arrives, borne by a breeze that blows on one who has been soaked by waves."

appearance of the grove of trees surrounding them, the rocks and plants in the gardens, the waters of the inlet—seemed impossible for anyone but the most inspired of artists. The residence here was much brighter and more cheerful than the villa at Suma Genji had occupied these many months, and the utterly charming furnishings brought back fond memories. The novitiate's lifestyle was, as Yoshikiyo had reported, no different from that enjoyed at the most distinguished aristocratic houses in the capital; indeed, the blinding brilliance of his lifestyle appeared, if anything, to be superior.

* * *

It was now the fourth month, and with the change of the seasons Genji was provided with superb new robes and silk curtains to hang around the dais in his sleeping quarters. He found the tendency of his host, the novitiate, to obsess over every last detail when serving him somewhat pathetic and overdone, but at the same time he observed that the old man's proud dignity revealed a nobility of character, and so he allowed the novitiate to have his way in such matters.

Murasaki continued to send messages as frequently as ever. One quiet, calm moonlit evening, when a cloudless sky spread far into the distance over the sea, the scene brought to mind the water in the garden pond at his Nijō villa, and he was filled with an ineffable yearning—a yearning for what or for whom he could not articulate. Before his eyes, off in the distance, was the island of Awaji. "Ah, how far away it seemed . . ."[6] he murmured.

> This moon illuminates the poignant beauty
> Of Awaji island . . . ah, how far it seems
> Bringing painful longings for my distant home

He took his seven-string koto from its cover and plucked a few notes. He had not touched it for some time, and the sight of him aroused restless emotions in his attendants, who found their lord troublingly sad and beautiful.

Genji performed a tune titled "Kōryō,"[7] utilizing all his skills to produce an immaculate rendition. The music mingled with the rustling of the pines and the rippling sound of the waves and wafted toward the lady's residence at the foot of the hill, sending shivers of delight through the refined young ladies-in-waiting there. The rustic denizens of that shore, who certainly were unable to recognize the song, walked along the beach exhilarated, even though they ran the risk of catching cold in the sea breeze. Unable to restrain himself, the novitiate relaxed his devotions and hurried over to Genji's residence.

"It would seem I am still driven by memories to return to the world I supposedly left behind when I took my vows," he said, tears welling up. "The atmosphere conjured by your music, which draws me here this evening, is surely a harbinger of the Pure Land paradise I pray for in the coming life."

Memories came flooding back to Genji's heart as well—the musical entertainments to celebrate the various seasons at court, with this person on koto, that person on the flute, the sound of voices singing in chorus, the way people so often praised him lavishly for his skills, how it felt to be honored and

6. Poem by Ōshikōchi no Mitsune: "Ah, how far away it seemed . . . the moon I viewed at Awaji. Is it the special atmosphere of the setting here this evening that makes it look so near?"

7. A "secret" song composed by the legendary musician Linglin for the Yellow Emperor, China's fabled first emperor.

respected by everyone from the Emperor on down, not to mention the circumstances of those he loved and his own status back then. He felt like he was in a dream, and the overtones his koto produced as he played in that trancelike state conveyed an unearthly, frightening loneliness.

The novitiate could not help feeling maudlin, and he sent for a *biwa* lute[8] and a thirteen-string koto from the villa at the base of the hill. Playing the role of an itinerant priest performing on the lute, he played a couple of very charming, unusual tunes. He presented the thirteen-string koto to Genji, who played a little on the instrument. The novitiate marveled at how brilliantly talented he was in a variety of arts. Even an instrument that does not produce an especially distinct timbre may, depending on the occasion, sound quite superior. As the music drifted across the waters stretching interminably into the distance, the stirring cry of a water rail, so like the rapping of some paramour at the gate of his beloved, rang out amidst the shadows of trees in rampant foliage more vivid and fresh than even the blossoms of spring or the leaves of autumn at their peak.

Genji was impressed by the novitiate's koto, which produced such unique tones, and by his host's own sweetly charming skills. "The thirteen-string koto is most delightful when played in a relaxed, informal style by a woman who exudes a gentle and intimate grace." Genji was referring to women in general, but the old novitiate, misinterpreting his intent, smiled and replied, "I'm not sure that any woman, no matter how gentle or graceful, could play better than my lord. I myself learned to play under the tutelage of a disciple of the Engi-period emperor, Daigo,[9] but as you can see I'm not especially gifted, and so I've cast aside the things of this world. Still, whenever I was depressed I would play a little, and as a result there is someone here who learned the instrument by imitating me, and so her style naturally resembles Emperor Daigo's. Of course, I am just a humble mountain rustic, hard of hearing, and it may be that I am so used to the sound of the wind rustling in the pines that I can no longer tell the difference between it and the sound of the koto. Even so, would you permit me to arrange for you to hear her in private?" His voice was tremulous, and he seemed to be on the verge of breaking down in tears.

"I should have known that in a place such as this, where people are accustomed to the superior music of nature, my performance would not sound like a koto. All very regrettable . . ." Genji pushed the instrument away. "It's odd, really, but since ancient times the thirteen-string koto has been considered a woman's instrument. Emperor Saga[1] passed down the techniques, and it is said that his daughter, the fifth princess, was the most skillful virtuoso of her age, though no one remains in her lineage to pass along that style of performance. Nowadays, for the most part, those who have achieved a reputation as master of the koto choose to approach this instrument superficially, as a pleasant diversion and no more. Thus it is fascinating that an older style of performance should have survived, hidden away in a place like this. How will I manage to hear this person you spoke of?"

"There is nothing to prevent you from listening to her," the novitiate said. "You could even summon her. After all, if I may point to the story handed

8. A four-stringed pear-shaped Japanese lute [editors' note].

9. Daigo (885–930) ruled from 897 to 930 C.E.;

the Engi period was 901–23 [editors' note].

1. Ruled 809–23 C.E. [editors' note].

down by Bai Juyi, there was a woman, the wife of a merchant, who won praise for her talent with the lute . . . and what you said of the koto is true of the lute as well. In ancient times there were very few people who could calmly strum that instrument and reveal its true nature, but the lady I mentioned can play it exceptionally well, with a gentle charm and few hesitations. I'm not sure how she managed to learn the lute as well, but when I hear her music mingling with the sound of the waves it sometimes brings on feelings of melancholy, and other times provides a respite from my accumulating sorrows."

Delighted that the old man was a true connoisseur, Genji swapped instruments with him, exchanging the thirteen-string koto for the lute. As expected, the novitiate's skill on the koto was well above average. He played tunes in a style no longer heard in the modern world. His spectacular fingering showed a touch of continental flair, and the vibrato he produced with his left hand was deep and clear. Though they were not at Ise, Genji had one of his men, who had a fine voice, sing the line "Shall we pick up shells along the pristine shore?" from the *saibara* "The Sea at Ise," while he himself kept rhythm by using flat wooden clappers. From time to time he joined in the singing, and the novitiate would often pause to praise him. As the night wore on the old man had unusual delicacies brought out and pressed wine upon everyone so that they would naturally forget the cares of the world.

The late night breeze off the shore was chilly and the light of the setting moon seemed intensely clear. As the world grew quiet the novitiate opened up to Genji, telling him, through one small anecdote after another, all that had happened in his life—the burdens he had when he first moved to Akashi, and how he had devoted himself single-mindedly to his religious practice with the next life in mind. He even brought up, without prompting, his daughter's situation. Genji was amused by this show of paternal devotion, but at the same time he was also touched by the young lady's predicament.

"I hesitate to mention it," the old man continued, "but I wonder if your move to a strange province such as this, temporary though it may be, isn't the work of the gods and the Buddha who, by troubling your heart for a brief period, are showing kindness and pity toward an old priest like me who has prayed to them for so long. I say this because it has been eighteen years since I first placed my faith in the deity of Sumiyoshi. From the time my daughter was a little girl I had ambitions for her, and so each spring and autumn, without fail, I go to pray at the Sumiyoshi Shrine. I practice my devotions day and night at each of the six prescribed times, but rather than concentrating my prayers on the wish to be reborn on a lotus in the Pure Land, I ask that my ambitions for my daughter be fulfilled and that she be granted a noble position at court. Regrettably, sins from a previous life have brought me misfortune in this one, and I have become the miserable mountain peasant you see before you. My father was able to rise in status as a minister of state, but I have ended up a rustic provincial. It grieves me to imagine what might become of my descendants, how low they might sink should my family's decline continue; and that is why from the moment my daughter was born, I have invested all my hopes and expectations in her. As a consequence of my deep resolve to present her by any means possible to a high-ranking nobleman in the capital, I have rejected many suitors who wished to take her as a wife. Some of those suitors were men whose status was higher than mine, and I have suffered harsh treatment on account of their resentment of me. However, I don't consider that a hardship, and I admonish my daughter by reminding her that as long as I'm alive I'll look after her, even though, as you can see from the narrow cut of my sleeves, I don't have much wealth to give her. And I've told her that if I die while she is still young and unmarried, she should throw herself into the sea." He broke down sobbing. He said so many other things besides, it is impossible to relate them all here. Genji was listening to all this during a period in his own life when he had been beset constantly with various problems, and so the old man's story invited tears of sympathy.

"Accused without basis and cast adrift in an unfamiliar land," Genji responded, "I have wracked my brain trying vainly to identify the misdeed I supposedly committed. But now, on hearing your tale this evening and reconsidering the matter, I am deeply moved by the realization that we truly share a bond from a previous life that is anything but shallow. Why did you not tell me earlier that you knew all this? Once I had departed the capital I lost my attachments and came to find the fickleness of the world insipid and tiresome; and while passing the days and months pursuing only religious austerities, I grew disconsolate and melancholy. I heard faint reports about your daughter, but because it seemed likely that you would reject as inauspicious the suit of an exile without status, I had no confidence to even try. Now it appears that you are beckoning me to her quarters. To have her share my lonely bed would be a comfort."

The young lady's father was thrilled beyond measure at these words.

> Do you know as well what it means to sleep alone . . .
> Then perhaps you understand the boredom she feels
> Waiting for the dawn on Akashi's lonely strand

"You may well appreciate," he added, "how much greater my own sense of melancholy has been, wearied as I am from years of concern over her." Now that he had finally spoken of his daughter, his body was trembling in agitation—though he did not lose his air of refinement and dignity.

"That may be," Genji replied, "but those who are accustomed to living on this bay may not appreciate how lonely it is for someone like me . . ."

> In lonely travel robes, on a pillow of grass
> I wait in sleepless grief for dawn at Akashi
> Unable to weave a dream and join my lover[2]

Genji was in dishabille, and there is simply no way to describe how charming he looked at that moment.

The novitiate talked on and on at length about all sorts of things, but it would be annoying to record them all here. However, because I have not written down

---

2. This poem, like the one it answers, plays primarily on the word *akashi*—referring to the place-name and to dawn breaking. Lovers would share robes as part of their bedding, and it was believed this act ensured that they would meet in their dreams. Travel robes convey an image of sleeping alone, thus making it impossible to meet one's lover in a dream and intensifying the sense of loneliness.

everything exactly as it happened or was spoken, I may have accentuated some of the man's more eccentric and stubborn characteristics.

With things going more or less as he had hoped, the novitiate felt as though a burden had been lifted from him. At around noon the following day Genji sent a letter to the lady's residence at the base of the hill. He had given careful attention to the letter, thinking that the lady seemed on the one hand like someone of dauntingly superior talent who would be hard to approach, and, on the other, like an unexpected find hidden away in this obscure location. He prepared the letter with exquisite care, writing on light brown Korean paper.

> Gazing sadly at the sky, is it near or far . . .
> How I want to pay a visit to those treetops
> At the abode obscured by mist and faint rumor

"My longing for you has overwhelmed my secret love."[3] Was that the full extent of his letter?

The novitiate had already arrived at his daughter's residence and was waiting with secret anticipation. Things were working out as expected, and by the time the letter arrived he had already arranged for refreshments for the messenger, plying him with wine until the man was embarrassingly drunk.

The lady took a long time to compose her reply. Her father entered her quarters and pressed her to answer, but she refused to listen to him. Intimidated by the brilliant wit of Genji's letter, she felt inadequate and ashamed to set her own hand to paper, which would expose the truth about her. Comparing his status to hers, it was obvious that the gulf separating them was enormous. She withdrew to lie down, telling her father that she wasn't feeling well. Unable to persuade his daughter, and his patience now exhausted, the novitiate wrote the reply for her: "For a woman whose sleeves have about them the rustic air of the provinces, your graciousness brings a surfeit of happiness that is too much for her to bear. She is too overwhelmed even to read your letter, but observing her . . ."

> Lost in lonely thoughts, gazing sadly
> At the same sky you are viewing now
> Are not her feelings the same as yours

"Is my view of her perhaps too romantic?" The note was written on Michinokuni paper, which lent it an old-fashioned aura, but Genji was a little surprised, shocked even, at the seductive allure of the calligraphy, which was embellished with refined flourishes. The novitiate had presented Genji's messenger with, among other things, an exceptionally fine set of women's robes.

The following day Genji sent another note: "I've never seen a letter by proxy before."[4]

> How wretched my uncertain heart
> Knowing there is no one who asks
> "Do tell me, how are things with you"

---

3. Anonymous poem from *The Kokinshū*: "Though I never wanted to let the colors of my love show, my longing for you has overwhelmed my secret."

4. The word Genji uses, *senjigaki*, refers to a letter dictated by the emperor or by an aristocrat.

"The difficulty of speaking of my feelings to one I have not yet seen . . ." This time he used an extremely soft, thin paper, and his calligraphy was exquisite. Only a young lady who was excessively shy and introverted would have failed to appreciate it, and indeed when the Akashi lady saw it she was amazed. Still, she remained convinced that the immeasurable difference in status between them made any relationship hopelessly unsustainable, and it made her cry to know he was courting her even though she was of such inferior rank. She remained outwardly impassive, but this time she did as she was told and replied to him. Writing on heavily perfumed paper of light purple hue, her brush-strokes were thick and bold in some places, thin and wispy in others—a technique she employed to disguise any flaws in her hand.

> How could you ever declare such feelings
> To me, a person you have never met . . .
> Can rumors really trouble you so much

Her calligraphy and phrasing had an aristocratic flair not at all inferior to those of the most distinguished ladies.

Remembering all the exchanges he had engaged in with women back in the capital, Genji regarded the lady's letter with delight. Of course, he was mindful of prying eyes and of the censure he would surely suffer if he wrote too often, so he would let two or three days lapse between letters, and even then he corresponded only when he guessed that she might be experiencing emotions similar to his own— on an early evening passed in the quiet diversion of solitary idleness, for example, or a dawn that provided a scene of poignant beauty. Her replies on these occasions were always appropriate, and after thinking about her responses he concluded that she was a lady of discretion and noble character, and thus someone he very much wanted to meet. He asked Yoshikiyo to describe her and reacted with some distaste at the look on the young man's face as he did so—a look that seemed to say *she belongs to me*—and he felt a twinge of pity that his retainer's aspirations to win the lady for himself, which he had harbored for many years, would be thwarted right before his eyes. Genji believed, however, that he could justify his actions so long as the lady encouraged him to pursue a relationship. The problem was that she was proving even more aloof and proud than most highborn women. Genji found this kind of behavior damnably irritating, and so as time passed they began to engage in a contest of wills.

After crossing the barrier pass at Suma his anxiety about Murasaki back in the capital only grew worse, and many times his resolve weakened as he wondered what to do—after all, being apart made it difficult to "bear this foolish game."[5] Should he have her come in secret to Akashi? Each time he asked himself this question, he ended up thinking better of it. No matter what happened, he believed that he would not spend many more years like this in exile, and so if he brought her here now, he would be criticized.

That same year the court witnessed many uncanny omens and disturbing incidents. On the evening of the thirteenth day of the third month—that is, the very day of the storm at Suma—thunder and lightning crashed and wind and

---

5. Anonymous poem from *The Kokinshū*: "When I try to stay away and not meet you, just to see what will happen, my yearning is so great I can no longer bear this foolish game."

rain raged at the palace as well. During the night Emperor Suzaku dreamed that his father, the late Emperor, appeared below the steps leading out to the garden on the east side of the imperial quarters in the Seiryōden. His father was glaring at him, obviously in a foul mood, and so Suzaku sat up in a formal posture to show his respect. His father told him many things, and so must have said something about Genji. Suzaku was extremely frightened, but he was also moved to pity at the realization that his father's spirit had not yet been reborn in the Pure Land. Later, when he discussed his dream with his mother, the Kokiden Consort, she told him, "On nights when it rains and storms it's natural for you to dream of things that preoccupy your mind. A sovereign mustn't allow such trivial matters to upset him."

For some reason—perhaps because he had looked directly into his father's furious gaze—Suzaku began to have trouble with his eyes. His suffering was beyond endurance, and purification rites and exorcisms were performed constantly at both the palace and the residence of the Kokiden Consort.

Other incidents also brought grief to the palace. Suzaku's grandfather, the Minister of the Right who served as his Chancellor, suddenly died. Being advanced in years, his death was not unexpected or strange, but it was still a shock all the same, coming as it did after everything else that had happened. Then, on top of all this, the Kokiden Consort began to suffer from an unknown malady, and she grew weaker over time.

Occasionally Suzaku would give voice to his concerns, telling his mother, "If Genji has been exiled without just cause, then there is no escaping the conclusion that all these problems are the result of karmic retribution. I think the time has come to restore him to his former rank."

The Kokiden Consort brushed aside his concerns and strongly admonished her son. "If you do that you'll be criticized for lacking substance and lose respect. If you permit a man who has been expelled from the capital to return after less than three years, what will people say?" Her words made Suzaku waver, but as the days and months continued to go by, the afflictions he and his mother suffered grew ever more severe.

With the coming of autumn to Akashi the sea breezes began to blow, stirring melancholy thoughts that were especially poignant. Genji was still sleeping in his solitary bed, but his loneliness was unbearable. He often spoke to the novitiate, telling the old man, "One way or another you will have to devise some pretext to have your daughter come here." Genji was convinced that it would be improper for him to go to her, and in any case the lady had shown no indication that she was inclined to meet him. *Only a provincial woman whose circumstances were utterly wretched,* she thought, *would frivolously exchange vows as my father has encouraged me to do on the basis of some flimsy, seductive flattery from a man of the capital who has come here for a brief stay. He would never respect me or consider me one of his wives, and if I were to yield to him it would only add to my misery and woe, would it not? During this period of my life, while I remain a young, unmarried woman, my parents, who harbor these unattainable ambitions for me, seem to have placed their extravagant expectations for the future on very uncertain supports. And even if he did take me as a wife, wouldn't that merely add to their worries? So long as Genji remains at Akashi the happiness I feel just exchanging letters with him is fortune enough for me. For many years I heard reports about him, and now I'm able to catch brief, indirect signs of his presence at a place where I never imagined I might meet such a man. I was told that his skill on the koto was peerless, and when I hear the notes from his instrument wafting to me on the breeze, I can guess what he is doing during the day. Now he has gone so far as to recognize my existence by courting me like this, and that is too great an honor, much more than someone like me, someone whose circumstances have been reduced to the status of the fisher folk here, could ever deserve.* As these thoughts raced through her mind, she felt more and more ashamed, and could not bring herself to even contemplate the possibility that she might have an intimate relationship with Genji.

Although the lady's parents were confident that the prayers they had offered over so many years would surely be answered, they also began to have ominous misgivings as they imagined how much sorrow they would experience if, having thoughtlessly rushed to give their daughter to Genji, there came a time when he no longer cared for her or counted her among his wives. They had heard how great and magnanimous he was, and yet how bitter would be their misery were he to abandon her! Relying upon the unseen Buddha and gods with no sign or proof of their blessing, knowing nothing of Genji's intentions or of their own daughter's karmic destiny, they tortured themselves with their obsessive worrying.

Genji was constantly pressing the novitiate. "If only I could hear the sound of her koto mingling with the sound of the autumn waves . . . what a waste, not to be able to listen to her play in this perfect season."

The novitiate ignored his wife's concerns and, without a word to his servants, secretly chose a propitious day to arrange a tryst. He went about busily sprucing up his daughter's quarters so that her rooms looked resplendent, and then, on the thirteenth day of the eighth month, with a nearly full moon shining gloriously, he sent a message to Genji that consisted of nothing more than a single line of verse: "On an evening too precious to waste."[6] Though Genji considered the wily old man a rather elegant pander, that didn't stop him from donning an informal cloak and setting out very late that night. A stylish carriage had been provided for him, but he thought it was too ostentatious for an occasion such as this and set out on horseback instead. His escort, which included only Koremitsu and a few attendants, was modest. He realized for the first time that the villa at the foot of the hill was farther away than he thought. From the road he could see all around the shore, and the moonlight reflecting off the inlets brought to mind an old verse describing such a scene as one to be viewed with "dear companions."[7] The words "dear companions" at once brought his beloved Murasaki to mind, and he immediately felt the urge to ride on past the villa and continue on to the capital. Instinctively, he muttered a poem to himself.

> Take flight, my stallion, with autumn moon reflecting
> Off your lustrous coat . . . carry me through cloudy skies
> So I may meet my love, if but for a moment

The villa of the Akashi lady, a stylish structure with many admirable touches, was set deep in a grove of trees. Whereas the residence near the shore that

6. Poem by Minamoto no Saneakira: "On an evening too precious to waste, if only I could show the moon and the blossoms to one who understands, as I do, true beauty."

7. The source is not clear. An early commentary cites the following poem: "Shall we go to view it, dear companions, the moon's visage in the depths of the inlets at Tamatsushima?"

Genji was using was grand and attractive, the villa here was the kind of place where a person would lead a forlorn, solitary existence. Genji experienced a sweet, sublime sorrow at the thought that living here would allow him to contemplate to the full the sadness of life. The novitiate's handbell sounded a note of profound melancholy as it reverberated faintly from the meditation hall nearby and mingled with the soughing of the pines. The roots of the pine trees growing on the craggy rocks created a tasteful backdrop, and the chirruping of insects filled the garden. Genji glanced about, surveying the scene. The lady's quarters had been burnished with special care, and the door, made of exceptional wood, had been left open a crack so that the moonlight could stream in.

Genji stood uncertainly, hesitating before finally saying a few words of courtship. The lady, however, had been determined not to allow her relationship with him to become as intimate as this, and so she grew sullen and depressed, displaying a cold disposition that signaled she would not permit him to have his way.

She's getting above herself with these superior airs. Genji was irritated and resentful. *When a courtship has gone as far as ours, it is customary for the woman, even one whose high status makes her difficult to approach, to set aside her stubborn willfulness and yield. Could it be that she is belittling me for my loss of status? It would hardly be appropriate under the circumstances to force myself on her, but to lose a battle of wills with her would make me look pathetic.* If only his handsome figure, confused and resentful, could have been displayed to a woman who was truly sensitive to beauty!

A curtain close by rustled and one of the silk streamers decorating it brushed lightly across the strings of a koto. The faint notes conjured in Genji's mind a pleasant image of the lady plucking the instrument, looking relaxed and unguarded. "Is this the koto I've heard so much about?" He asked her this and many other things besides, all trying to persuade her to play.

> If there were someone I could talk to
> Intimately, would I awaken
> From the dream that is this world of woe

She replied.

> Wandering just as I am, lost in the darkness
> Of a night without end, how could I speak to you
> Not knowing what is dream, what is reality

The dignified bearing of her figure, which he could barely make out in the dim light, put him very much in mind of the lady at Rokujō, who was now in Ise with her daughter.

Apparently the Akashi lady had not been prepared for his visit and, unaware of her father's machinations, had been caught off guard. It had never occurred to her that he might make such outrageous advances like this, and so she was quite flustered and upset. Moving into a room just off her private chambers, she somehow managed to securely latch the sliding door from the inside. Genji had no intention, it seemed, of trying to force the door open, but then again, how could he simply leave things as they were? The lady was aristocratic and tall, and her sense of propriety and dignity made Genji feel embarrassed and uncertain. Thinking about how their relationship had been destined by these strange circumstances, he was moved by the depth of the bond ordained by their karma. Surely his love for her would grow stronger the more intimate they became with one another.

He had come to loathe the long nights of autumn, which dragged on tediously for him in his solitary bed; but this night seemed to be rushing toward dawn, and so, mindful as ever that prying eyes might catch sight of his visit, he hurriedly left her, murmuring sweetly gentle words to her.

He very discreetly dispatched the customary morning-after letter. His secrecy makes one wonder, was he bothered by a guilty conscience? The Akashi lady, worried about gossip, was equally careful to keep their affair secret, even from the others at her villa at the foot of the hill, and so she did not show the messenger bearing Genji's letter any special treatment or give him any lavish gifts. Her father deplored her aloof behavior.

Following this initial tryst, Genji would from time to time call on the lady in strictest secrecy. Their residences were separated by some distance, and there were nights when he was reluctant to venture out, concerned that he might encounter some of the local fishermen, who were by nature loquacious and prone to gossip. On those nights when he did not visit, the lady would be upset, taking his absence as proof that just as she had imagined all along his feelings for her were not sincere. Her father, seeing his daughter suffer and knowing she had good reason for feeling the way she did, worried about how it would all turn out. He forgot about his devotions and his prayers for rebirth in paradise, unable to focus on anything besides waiting and listening for indications that Genji was calling on his daughter. It was truly pathetic that the heart of a man who had ostensibly taken vows could be so troubled by worldly affairs.

* * *

FROM CHAPTER XXV

Hotaru

Fireflies

* * *

The rainy season continued for longer than usual this year, and the women at Rokujō were bored and had no way to brighten either the skies or their mood. So they passed the days and nights amusing themselves with illustrated tales. The Akashi lady prepared some stylish and interesting works of that type and sent them over to the quarters of her daughter, the Akashi Princess.

Meanwhile, the lady in the west hall, Tamakazura, was more intrigued than the others by these stories, which she found fascinating and strange, perhaps because she had come from the provinces. Whatever the reason, she was utterly absorbed in reading them day and night. Quite a few of the young women who had been assigned to her quarters were proficient at reading and copying, and so she was able to collect quite a few texts, many of which described the personal circumstances of a variety of remarkable characters. She couldn't tell if those stories were true or mere fiction, and, moreover, she couldn't find a single character whose circumstances were similar to her own. It appeared as though the heroine princess in *The Tale of Sumiyoshi*[8] experienced many remarkable incidents considered unusual not only in her own day,

8. A well-known tale in the author's time [editors' note].

but also in the present generation; and she compared the heroine's narrow escape from a forced marriage to the Chief Auditor to her own experience with the loathsome Taifu no Gen.

Genji couldn't avoid seeing these illustrated tales, which were left scattered all around Tamakazura's quarters. "Ahh . . . how tedious," he chided. "Women are by nature blithely content to allow others to deceive them. You know full well these tales have only the slightest connection to reality, yet you let your heart be moved by trivial words and get so caught up in the plots that you copy them out without giving a thought to the tangled mess your hair has become in this humid weather."

Genji smiled. "Of course, if we didn't have these old tales to read," he continued, "we'd have nothing to divert us in our idle hours. What's more, we can find even among this mass of falsehoods some stories that are properly written and exhibit enough sensitivity that we are moved to imagine that perhaps the events they relate really took place. On the one hand, we may know that it's all silly, but we're still fascinated and affected by the fiction. When we read about some lovely princess lost in troubled thoughts, we are drawn to her story . . . . or when we encounter a tale that makes us wonder uncertainly if what it describes is really plausible or proper, we are nonetheless surprised and amazed that it can be told with such marvelous exaggeration. Of course later on, when we come back to the same tale again in a calmer state of mind, we might dislike it or think it inappropriate . . . yet even then there may be aspects of the story that seem as charming to us as when we first read it. Recently, whenever I overhear one of the ladies-in-waiting reading to my little daughter,[9] I have been struck by the realization that there are without doubt skilled storytellers in this world . . . that such tales must come from the mouths of people accustomed to spinning lies . . . but perhaps that is not the case?"

As soon as he spoke those words, Tamakazura shot back, "There is certainly no doubt that someone practiced at lying would be inclined to draw such a conclusion . . . for all sorts of reasons. I remain convinced, however, that these stories are quite truthful." She pushed her inkstone away, and when she did Genji responded, "Have I been speaking rudely of your stories? Tales have provided a record of events in the world since the age of the gods, but histories of Japan like the *Nihongi*[1] give only partial accounts of the facts. The type of tales you are reading provides detailed descriptions that make more sense and follow the way of history."

Genji smiled again before continuing. "A story may not relate things exactly as they happened out of consideration for the circumstances of its characters. Yet at those moments when one wants to pass on to later generations the appearance and condition of people living in the present . . . both the good and the bad, which are the things you never tire of reading about no matter how many times you've heard them . . . it is difficult to keep them shut away in your heart. And so you begin to tell stories about them. If you want to be upright and proper, then you will select only the good details to relate. Or if you want to play to people's baser interests, then you will compile the strange and won-

9. His daughter by the Akashi lady; she is being raised by Tamakazura [editors' note].
1. *Chronicles of Japan.* One of the two 8th-century chronicles of Japan, written in Sino-

Japanese and modeled on the Chinese official histories, that told the history of the Japanese islands from the Age of the Gods to recent times [editors' note].

drous details of bad behavior. But in either case you will always be speaking about things of this world. Styles of storytelling may differ in other lands, and even in Japan tales from the past certainly differ from those of the present . . . and of course there are distinctions between deep and shallow topics and themes. For that reason the narrow-minded conclusion that all tales are false-hoods misses the heart of the matter. Even the Dharma, which was explicated for us through Sakyamuni's[2] splendidly pure heart, contains *hōben*, those parables he told to illustrate the truth of the Law. There are many contradictory parts in the sutras that raise doubts in the mind of an unenlightened person. However, if you carefully consider the matter, you realize that all the sutras have a single aim. The distinction between enlightenment and suffering is really no different from the distinction between the good and the bad in tales such as these. In the end the correct view of the matter is that nothing is worthless." Genji was now claiming that tales were beneficial.

"So tell me," he concluded, "have you found any stories of piously foolish men like me among all your old scrolls? There couldn't possibly be any fictional princesses in this world who are as extremely aloof and coldly heartless as you . . . who pretend not to notice anything. So how about it . . . shall we make a story unlike any other that has ever been told and pass it on to later generations?"

Genji sidled over next to her. Tamakazura turned away from him, hiding her face in her collar, and said "Even if we don't make a story together, the relationship we do have is so bizarre and unbelievable it will likely never become the subject of court gossip."

"You think it's bizarre? Truly there has never been a daughter as cruel as you." He had moved close to her and was being much too forward.

> Having a surfeit of cares and longings
> I seek answers for them in tales of old
> But find there no child as unfilial

"Even the teachings of Buddha admonish unfilial children," he added. When she refused to show her face, he began stroking her hair. As he did so, her resentment led her to reply.

> Though I have searched through all these ancient tales
> Truly I find no models in this world
> For parental feelings resembling yours[3]

He felt ashamed when he heard her poem, and so went no farther than stroking her hair. Given her situation, whatever would become of her?

Murasaki was also reading illustrated tales, under the pretext that the Akashi Princess had requested them, and was finding it hard to put them down. Looking at an illustration from *Tales of Kumano*,[4] she remarked, "This is quite skillfully rendered." She gazed at the little girl, who was innocently taking a nap, and remembered when she was that age.

Genji studied the illustration. "How precocious children were back then. I was quite reserved by comparison when I was their age . . . a model of behavior,

2. The Buddha (lit., "Sage of the Sakyas") [editors' note].
3. Genji has taken Tamakazura in as his daughter, but is also attracted to her. His ear-

lier advances have been a constant source of pain and consternation for Tamakazura [editors' note].
4. This tale has been lost.

really." In truth, he was fond of being the model for all sorts of unheard-of behavior.

"You shouldn't be reading love stories in front of her," he continued. "She may not be all that intrigued by some young girl holding a secret love in her heart, but she is destined to be empress, and it would be most unfortunate if she grew to accept the idea that it was normal for such affairs to actually take place." Had Tamakazura heard what he just said, she certainly would have taken umbrage at the difference in the way he treated his daughter and the way he treated her.

"People with shallow minds may imitate the behavior they read about in these stories, but they look rather pathetic when they do," Murasaki replied. "In the *Tale of the Hollow Tree* the young Fujiwara princess, Atemiya, is a dignified woman of probity, and she never goes astray, but because her manner is so stiff and unyielding she lacks feminine grace, and her story ends up being just as bad an influence."

"People in real life seem to be the same," Genji said. "Everyone has their own way of doing things, but it is hard to strike a proper balance. A woman who has been brought up with the greatest care by parents who are not without breeding may grow up to be innocent and childlike, but the fact that she may also have many flaws will, sad to say, lead people to wonder what her parents were up to and how they went about raising their daughter. On the other hand, when you see a young woman who in appearance and behavior is exactly what she should be for someone of her status, clearly her parents' efforts have paid off and she brings honor to their house. If a young lady's nurses or attendants praise her to an absurd degree, then when her actions or words don't match her puffed-up reputation she will not seem as attractive. Parents should never let people who lack taste and judgment go about praising their daughters." He was determined to do everything in his power to ensure his own daughter would avoid criticism.

Many of the tales depicted mean, vindictive stepmothers. He worried that the Akashi Princess might get the idea that all stepmothers were like those she read about, so he took extra precaution in the selection of stories, and had clean copies and illustrations made for her.

* * *

FROM CHAPTER XL

Minori

The Rites

* * *

The following day Murasaki was in pain and unable to get up, perhaps because she had overexerted herself by staying up throughout the dedication ceremony. At every event like this she had ever attended over the years, she would always wonder if *this day* would be the last time she would see the faces and figures of those who had gathered, the last time she would see them display their various talents or hear them play the koto or the flute. On such occasions she would be moved even by the sight of faces normally beneath her notice. Her feelings were of course even stronger whenever she observed the other ladies at

Rokujō—women with whom she naturally shared a gentle rivalry, especially when they appeared together at some concert or diversion held in the summer or winter, and a mutual affection. Although no one can expect to remain for very long in this world, the thought that she would soon leave the other ladies behind, going forth all alone to an unknown destination, brought home to Murasaki the poignant sorrow of the evanescence of life.

When the dedication ceremony ended and each of the guests had begun to make his or her way home, she felt a twinge of regret that this would likely be the last time she saw any of them. She sent a poem to Hanachirusato.[5]

> While my life, like these rites, must soon come to an end
> We may rely on the truth of the sacred law
> That karma will bind us through all the worlds to come[6]

Hanachirusato replied.

> Even had these rites not been this magnificent,
> They would still have forged a lasting bond between us . . .
> Undeserving though I am, with little time left

Immediately after the dedication ceremony, other solemn rites such as the continuous reading of the Lotus Sutra and the ritual of confession and penance were attentively performed. Because the esoteric healing rites that had been carried out every day over a long period showed no signs of helping Murasaki recover, Genji commissioned additional services at various holy sites and temples known for the efficaciousness of their prayers.

When summer arrived, Murasaki's fainting spells increased even though the weather was no hotter than usual. There were no alarming symptoms that one could point to as the source of her malaise. She was simply growing weaker, without ever suffering the sort of pain that caused others distress. Worried about what was to become of their mistress if she continued to weaken, her attendants observed her condition with regret and sorrow, and fell into dark despair.

Because Murasaki's health was slowly failing, the Akashi Empress[7] withdrew from the palace and went to the Nijō villa. She was to take up residence in the east hall, and so Murasaki waited there to receive her. The ceremony greeting Her Majesty's arrival was nothing out of the ordinary, but Murasaki found everything about it moving, since she knew she would never witness it again. She listened attentively as the name of each nobleman who had escorted the Akashi Empress—a very large group of senior officials indeed—was read out.

Since the two women had not seen each other for a long time, they seized this moment as a rare opportunity to speak intimately and at length. Genji arrived. "I feel like a bird evicted from its own nest. It's obvious that I'm of absolutely no use this evening, so I'll take my leave and retire for the night." He

---

5. One of Genji's ladies, also living in his Rokujō mansion [editors' note].
6. This poetic exchange gives the chapter its title. The word *minori*, which clearly means "rites" here, also refers to the Law (the Dharma), that is, the Buddha's teachings.

7. Genji's daughter, the Akashi Princess who becomes the Kiritsubo Consort, has been elevated to the title of empress. From this point on I will identify Genji's daughter as the Akashi Empress.

went back to his quarters feeling quite happy to see Murasaki up and about—it was, however, only a brief moment of comfort for him.

"Since we will be staying in separate quarters," Murasaki said, "I would be deeply honored to have Your Majesty come to see me in the west hall. I know it is presumptuous of me to make such a request, but it is a considerable strain on me to leave my residence to visit you here." Murasaki said. She stayed a while longer, and when the Akashi lady joined them they continued their quiet, heartfelt conversation.

Murasaki had many things on her mind, but wisely she did not broach the subject of what would happen after her death. She calmly made a few passing references to the ephemeral nature of life, but the serious manner in which she talked made it clearer than any words she might have spoken just how sad and forlorn she felt. When she saw all the children of the Akashi Empress, tears welled up[8] and her face blushed with a most lovely glow. "I had so wanted to see each of them grow up . . . it would seem my heart regrets having so little time left."

Her Majesty wept as well and wondered why Murasaki had to be so fixated on death? The subject of their conversation shifted, providing Murasaki the chance to speak about the ladies-in-waiting who had served her closely over the years. She did her best to avoid saying anything inauspicious, as if she were making last requests, but she felt sorry for her attendants, who would have nowhere else to turn once she was gone. "When I am no longer around," she remarked, "please remember to look after them." Because a sutra reading[9] was about to begin, Murasaki retired to her own quarters in the west hall.

Niou, the Third Prince, had the most charming appearance of all Her Majesty's many children as he walked around the villa. During those intervals when Murasaki was feeling a little better, she would have him sit next to her and, when no one was around, ask him, "Would you remember me if I were not here?"

"I would miss you very much, Grandmama. You are much more important to me than father or mother! If you weren't here, I'd feel awful!" The way he rubbed his eyes to hide his tears was so adorable she had to smile despite her sadness.

"When you are all grown up, you are to live here, and when the red plum and the cherry tree that grow in front of the west hall are in bloom in their respective seasons you must not forget to view and enjoy them. And at the appropriate times you must make offerings of their branches to the Buddha in my memory."

The little boy nodded solemnly, then stared into Murasaki's face. Just as he was about to cry, he stood up and scampered off. She had raised him and the Third Princess with special consideration, and it filled her with pity and regret to know she would not be able to help raise them to adulthood.

The heat of summer was so oppressive she couldn't wait for autumn to arrive; and when it did, and the weather turned cooler, her spirits revived a

8. Because Murasaki had raised the Akashi Empress, she has a close connection to these children [editors' note].
9. This reading may be the *Sutra of Great Wisdom* (Daihannyakyō), which an empress would normally have performed during the

second and eighth months (though the reading could be held on special occasions as well). However, the timing does not seem right here, and it is likely that the sutra reading is part of the healing rites for Murasaki.

little. Still, this was but a temporary respite, for even though the chill autumn winds were not yet blowing—winds that cut through one, bringing only sorrows[1]—she was already spending her days in dewy tears.

The Akashi Empress was preparing to return to the palace. Murasaki wanted to ask her to stay on a little longer, even though such a request would overstep the bounds of propriety. It would also have been awkward, since His Majesty was now sending one messenger after another urging her to return. In the end she didn't ask, and because she was so weak, she was unable to go to the east hall to see Her Majesty off. That was when the Empress took the extraordinary step of calling on her in the west hall. Murasaki was humbled and shamed that the Empress would deign to visit her, but she thought it would have been truly senseless not to meet, and so she had special seating and furnishings prepared to receive her exalted guest.

Despite the fact that she was terribly emaciated, Murasaki still looked remarkable; the loss of weight had, if anything, distilled her beauty, which now possessed a boundless nobility and grace. Once, in the glorious flowering of her prime, her looks exuded to an almost excessive degree a lambent glow like the bright fragrance of blossoms. Now her infinitely cherished appearance, which brought to mind the transient nature of the mortal world, possessed a deeper loveliness, one that evoked incomparable feelings of compassion and sweet sorrow.

At dusk, as a terrible, chilling wind began to blow, she propped herself up on an armrest thinking she would gaze out at her garden when she saw Genji arrive.

"How good that you're able to get up today! Her Majesty's visit has apparently cheered you, has it not?"

She felt bad for him—he looked so happy whenever she was briefly feeling better that it moved her to imagine how devastated he would be when the end came.

> How brief the moment when you see me sitting up . . .
> As brief as the time that dew clings to bush clover
> Before being blown off and scattered by the wind[2]

It was an apt comparison, for the dew clung precariously to the stems of bush clover in her garden that bent and sprang back with each gust of wind. Genji gazed out at the scene, and the feelings of melancholy desolation that accompanied this season were unbearable.

> Our lives are like fragile dewdrops vying
> To disappear . . . would that no time elapse
> Between the first one to go and the last

He could not brush all the tears from his eyes.

The Akashi Empress replied.

> Who can look at this world, so like the dewdrops
> That cannot resist the blasts of autumn winds
> And think only the drops on the top leaves fade

1. Poem by Izumi Shikibu: "What sort of wind is it, this wind that blows in autumn . . . how it cuts through one, bringing only sorrow."

2. Murasaki's poem plays on two senses of the word *oku*—"to be up/sit up" and "to settle."

As they exchanged poems, Genji treasured the sight of these two women, ideal beauties both; and though he wished he could go on gazing at them like this for a thousand years, he knew that such a dream could never be fulfilled, and his heart ached, for he had no way to keep his beloved from dying.

"You should leave now. I'm feeling very ill," Murasaki said. "It's terribly rude of me to say I'm too ill to do anything for you." She pulled a standing curtain over and lay down so that they would not have to see her suffering. This time it did not appear she would recover.

"What's wrong?" The Akashi Empress took Murasaki's hand and watched her tearfully. She really did look every bit like a dewdrop fading away, and so they hurriedly sent off countless messengers to commission more sutra readings. There had been episodes like this in the past, and she had always recovered, but Genji suspected that the malignant spirit of the Rokujō lady might still be at work, and so he did everything he could to protect Murasaki, ordering prayers and services to be held throughout the night. His efforts were in vain, however, for just as dawn approached, she passed away.

The Akashi Empress thought it a sign of the boundless karmic bond she shared with her surrogate mother that she had not returned to the palace and was with Murasaki until the very end. Neither she nor Genji could accept that her death was part of the natural order of things, that such partings were common to all. To them her death was singular and overwhelming, and so of course they felt as if they were wandering lost in the sort of dream one has in that twilight time between night and the dawn. No one there could make a rational judgment about anything. The attendants and other servants were completely stunned.

Genji suffered the most, and because he was upset and not thinking clearly, he summoned his son,[3] who was in attendance nearby, and had him move over in front of Murasaki's curtain. "It appears this is the end," he said. "It would be a great shame to go against her wishes at this point and not carry out what she had desired for so many years. The holy men who performed the healing rites and the priests reading scripture have all gone silent and have probably left, but some of them may still be here, so tell one of them to cut her hair like a nun's. It won't do any good for her in this life, but if she shows a mark of her devotion to the Buddha, then at least she may rely on his mercy to comfort her on the dark path she is to follow. Is there some priest suitable for the task?" From the expression he wore as he spoke, it seemed that Genji was trying to be strong, but the color had drained from his face and, unable to bear his loss, he could not stop his tears. His son looked on in sympathy, thinking his father's grief was perfectly understandable.

"Sometimes a malignant spirit will do this kind of thing just to torment the bereaved ones . . . what I mean is, the spirit may be making it appear that she is not breathing . . . that may be what's happening here. If that's the case," Genji's son offered, "then it would be best to do what she wanted in any case, since according to the Contemplation Sutra,[4] making vows to uphold the pre-

---

3. Genji's oldest child from his first marriage. Long ago this son once caught an enthralling glimpse of his stepmother Murasaki, but has had no chance since to satisfy his yearning to see her again [editors' note].

4. One of the three major scriptures of Pure Land Buddhism along with the *Sutra of Infinite Life*, which is also known as the *Larger Pure Land Sutra*, and the *Amida Sutra*.

cepts for even one day and night will lead to rebirth in Amida's Pure Land. Of course, if she *is* dead, simply cutting her hair at this point would have little benefit . . . it won't provide a light to guide her in the next world, and would make the grief of those who look at her even worse. So I wonder if it's for the best?" He wanted to do all he could to make arrangements for the funeral and period of confinement, and so he summoned several priests from among those who had not yet withdrawn and were willing to serve during the weeks ahead. He also saw to all other necessary preparations.

Although he had longed for Murasaki for years after catching a glimpse of her on the morning after the autumn tempest, Genji's son had never harbored any improper or presumptuous fantasies about her. *In what world to come will I ever see her again as I did on that morning long ago? I never did hear her speak . . . not even a faint whisper.* Not a day had gone by since when she hadn't been on his mind. *As it turns out, I will never hear her voice . . . and if I'm ever to satisfy my hope of seeing her again, the only time to do so is right now, even if it means gazing at her lifeless form.* He had been trying to control himself, since it would look odd if he exhibited excessive grief, but these thoughts brought him to tears. The attendants were loudly weeping and wailing, and Genji's son, in an effort to control his own emotions, scolded them. "Really now, be still for a while!" As he spoke, he lifted one of the panels of Murasaki's standing curtain and peered inside. Because it was still difficult to make things out in the dim light of early dawn, Genji had placed a lamp near Murasaki's bed and was gazing at her. He so regretted that such a lovely face would soon be no more—a face infinitely dear to him, one possessing such noble grace   it seemed he no longer had the will to even try to hide his beloved from the gaze of his son, who was peeking in on this scene.

"Here she is, her face looking the same as ever . . . and yet it's clear she's no longer with us." Genji covered his face with his sleeves. His son, blinded by tears, could not see very well. To clear his vision he closed his eyes tight and then opened them so he could look at her, and when he did he was overcome by a feeling of sadness unlike anything he had ever known. He feared he would lose his composure completely. Her hair was stretched out beside her, left just as it was when she died, incomparably lustrous and beautiful with not one strand of those thick, cascading tresses out of place. In the bright glare of the lamplight her complexion had an alabaster glow, and as she lay there passively, no longer concerned that she was exposed to his gaze, her face, needless to say, looked more pure and spotless than when she was alive, since she had always avoided being seen and concealed her real appearance under makeup. Gazing on her unique, extraordinary beauty, he wished her soul, which had already departed, would soon return to her body—though he knew such a wish was unreasonable.

The women who had been her closest attendants were too overcome by grief to be able to think clearly, and so Genji forced himself to calm down, regain his composure, and set about making arrangements for the funeral. Although he had witnessed many sorrowful events in the past, he had no experience handling such matters directly himself. Undertaking this sad responsibility was like nothing else he had ever done in the past or would do in the future.

* * *

KAMO NO CHŌMEI

ca. 1155–1216

Retreating from civilization in times of crisis has a long history in East Asia. Since antiquity, there have been legends of extraordinary individuals who became recluses to stay true to themselves, or to their dynasties and lords. It was in the spirit of this tradition and in pursuit of Buddhism that Kamo no Chōmei decided to retreat into a mountain hut outside the capital, devoting himself to "An Account of a Ten-Foot-Square Hut." In this most poignant of Japanese essays on life in reclusion he evokes visions of disturbing destruction in the capital and of furtive pleasures in his mountain hut, attempting to come to terms with the impermanence of the world and the futility of people's attempts to find illusory stability in their houses, in their possessions, or in other people.

Chōmei came from the venerable Kamo family, a lineage of Shinto priests serving the Kamo Shrine north of Kyoto. Although he lost his father in his teens he received an extensive education in poetry and music. This earned him in 1201 a prestigious invitation from the retired Emperor GoToba to serve in the Imperial Poetry Office, the bureau that compiled imperial poetry anthologies in the tradition of *The Kokinshū*. Some of the poems he wrote at the time prefigure his later life of contemplation. In one composed for a poetry contest at court, which the emperor singled out for particular praise, Chōmei said:

All night long,
Alone in the deep mountains.
But then: though clouded in sight,
Shining through the needles of a
    black pine,
There is the moon of dawn.

In 1204, at around the age of fifty, Chōmei took Buddhist vows and retreated into the mountains. He had failed to receive a position at the Kamo Shrine, on which he had long pinned his hopes, and even the emperor's hasty creation of an alternative post at the shrine could not keep him in the capital. After a few years in Ōhara, northeast of Kyoto, he built a hut near Hino Mountain, southeast of Kyoto, where in 1212 he wrote "An Account of a Ten-Foot-Square Hut." In his time Chōmei was famous as a poet and the author of a manual of poetic lore, which contained his reflections on the poetic value of "mysterious depth" (*yūgen*). This notion later became a cardinal concept in the aesthetics of Zen, Noh theater, tea ceremony, linked verse, and haiku. Chōmei also compiled *Tales of Awakening*, a collection of Buddhist tales designed to guide people toward deeper understanding and salvation. But the work that has made him memorable for readers through the ages is undoubtedly the account of his life in reclusion.

Chōmei lived through the tumultuous decades of transition from the splendid aristocratic world of the Heian court in Kyoto (794–1185) to the austere medieval world of warrior rule, when shoguns—military rulers—took control over the disempowered imperial court and ruled the country from Kamakura near modern-day Tokyo. Experiencing this watershed moment of Japanese history was disorienting enough, but Chōmei and his contemporaries were convinced that they lived in the "Latter Day of the Law" (mappō)—the third and most degraded era of Buddhism. According to the cyclical cosmology developed in Tang China (618–907), evil and disaster would prevail during this last period and the teachings of the historical Buddha (fifth century B.C.E.) would lose their power. Sensing such an age approaching, many aristocrats retreated to the countryside, took holy vows, and devoted themselves exclusively to holy practices or a contemplative life spent on literary and artistic pursuits.

Like **Yoshida Kenkō**'s *Essays in Idleness*, which was written a good century later, Chōmei's "An Account of a Ten-Foot-Square Hut" belongs to the "recluse literature" produced by medieval writers who, when confronted with the chaos of life, took solace in Buddhism, poetry, and other artistic pursuits. The "Account" is written in an elegant mixture of Japanese and Chinese-style diction and rhetoric. It weds flamboyant poetic imagery to scholastic parallel phrasings, which are a hallmark of Buddhist literature. This hybrid style is emblematic of the nuanced tensions in Chōmei's life and work. He is an anxious victim, but also an ironic witness of his time. In moments of ironic distance he derides humans for their deluded efforts to build houses and amass possessions, offering us darkly beautiful images of destruction: fires unfolding like gorgeous fans, house shingles whirling through the air like alluring winter leaves. Beautiful images also enable

Chōmei to capture futility in less disturbing, more transcendental terms. You will never look at rivers quite in the same way once you have grasped the essay's memorable opening metaphors for impermanence: rivers, foam, dew, morning glories. But the attachments to the hut that Chōmei proudly calls his own, to the leather trunks that hold his books of poetry and music, to his musical instruments, and ultimately even to the idea of tranquillity in his recluse life seem to cause him equal amounts of pleasure and guilt. Although he counts out loud for his readers how he gradually downsized his livelihood from his family's large house to the mere ten squares of his recluse hut, the very sin of attachment to things remains. Does his recitation of the name of Amida Buddha, who promises rebirth in a western paradise, the "Pure Land," relieve him of his existential worries? Can writing, poetry, or music be a saving grace, although they too belong to the world of attachments that ultimately create suffering?

Written by an evocative recluse poet who had made a radical life choice during a tumultuous, transitional period, "An Account of a Ten-Foot-Square Hut" offers us shocking and pleasurable insights into the "ephemeral, locust-shell world" of Japan's Middle Ages.

An Account of a Ten-Foot-Square Hut[1]

The current of the flowing river does not cease, and yet the water is not the same water as before. The foam that floats on stagnant pools, now vanishing, now forming, never stays the same for long. So, too, it is with the people and dwellings of the world. In the capital, lovely as if paved with jewels, houses of the high and low, their ridges aligned and roof tiles contending, never disappear however many ages pass, and yet if we examine whether this is true, we will rarely find a house remaining as it used to be. Perhaps it burned down last year and has been rebuilt. Perhaps a large house has crumbled and become a small one. The people living inside the houses are no different. The place may be the same capital and the people numerous, but only one or two in twenty or

1. Translated by and with footnotes adapted from Anthony H. Chambers, who has supplied the bracketed material in the text.

thirty is someone I knew in the past. One will die in the morning and another will be born in the evening: such is the way of the world, and in this we are like the foam on the water. I know neither whence the newborn come nor whither go the dead. For whose sake do we trouble our minds over these temporary dwellings, and why do they delight our eyes? This, too, I do not understand. In competing for impermanence, dweller and dwelling are no different from the morning glory and the dew. Perhaps the dew will fall and the blossom linger. But even though it lingers, it will wither in the morning sun. Perhaps the blossom will wilt and the dew remain. But even though it remains, it will not wait for evening.

In the more than forty springs and autumns that have passed since I began to understand the nature of the world, I have seen many unexpected things. I think it was on the twenty-eighth of the Fourth Month of Angen 3 [1177]. Around eight o'clock on a windy, noisy night, a fire broke out in the southeastern part of the capital and spread to the northwest. Finally it reached Suzaku Gate, the Great Hall of State, the university, and the Popular Affairs Ministry, and in the space of a night they all turned to dust and ash. The source of the fire is said to have been the intersection of Higuchi and Tominokōji, in makeshift housing occupied by *bugaku* dancers.[2] Carried here and there in the violent wind, the fire spread outward like a fan unfolding. Distant houses choked on smoke; nearby, wind drove the flames against the ground. In the sky, ashes blown up by the wind reflected the light of the fire, while wind-scattered flames spread through the overarching red in leaps of one and two blocks. Those who were caught in the fire must have been frantic. Some choked on the smoke and collapsed; some were overtaken by the flames and died instantly. Some barely escaped with their lives but could not carry out their possessions. The Seven Rarities and ten thousand treasures[3] all were reduced to ashes. How great the losses must have been. At that time, the houses of sixteen high nobles burned, not to mention countless lesser homes. Altogether, it is said that fire engulfed one-third of the capital. Thousands of men and women died, and more horses, oxen, and the like than one can tell. All human endeavors are foolish, but among them, spending one's fortune and troubling one's mind to build a house in such a dangerous capital is particularly vain.

Then, in the Fourth Month of Jishō 4 [1180], a great whirlwind arose near the intersection of Nakanomikado and Kyōgoku and raged as far as the Rokujō District. Because it blew savagely for three or four blocks, not a single house within them, large or small, escaped destruction. Some were flattened; some were reduced to nothing more than posts and beams. Blowing gates away, the wind carried them four or five blocks and set them down; blowing fences away, it joined neighboring properties into one. Naturally, all the possessions inside these houses were lifted into the sky, while cypress bark, boards, and other roofing materials mingled in the wind like winter leaves. The whirlwind blew up dust as thick as smoke so that nothing could be seen, and in its dreadful roar no voices could be heard. One felt that even the winds of retribution in hell could be no worse than this. Not only were houses damaged or lost, but

2. Performers of a stately dance introduced from China.
3. Things of immense value. The "Seven Rari-

ties" named in Buddhist texts were precious substances (variously identified in different translations at different times).

countless men were injured or crippled in rebuilding them. As it moved toward the south-southwest, the wind was a cause of grief to many people. Whirlwinds often blow, but are they ever like this? It was something extraordinary. One feared that it might be a portent.

Then, in the Sixth Month of the same year, the capital was abruptly moved.[4] The relocation was completely unexpected. According to what I have heard, Kyoto was established as the capital more than four hundred years ago, during the reign of the Saga emperor. The relocation of the capital is not something that can be undertaken easily, for no special reason, and so it is only natural that the people were uneasy with this move and lamented together about it. Objections having no effect, however, the emperor, the ministers, and all the other high nobles moved. Of those who served at court, who would stay behind in the old capital? Those who vested their hopes in government appointments or in rank, or depended on the favor of their masters, wasted not a day in moving, while those who had missed their chance, who had been left behind by the world, and who had nothing to look forward to, stayed sorrowfully where they were. Dwellings, their eaves contending, went to ruin with the passing days. Houses were disassembled and floated down the Yodo River as the land turned into fields before one's eyes. Men's hearts changed; now they valued only horses and saddles. No one used oxen and carriages any more. People coveted property in the southwest and scorned manors in the northeast. At that time I had occasion to go to the new capital, in the province of Tsu. I saw that there was insufficient room to lay out a grid of streets and avenues, the area being small. To the north, the city pressed against the mountains and, to the south, dropped off toward the sea. The roar of waves never slackened; a violent wind blew in off the saltwater. The palace stood in the mountains. Did that hall of logs[5] look like this? It was novel and, in its way, elegant. Where did they erect the houses they had torn down day by day and brought downstream, constricting the river's flow? Open land was still plentiful, houses few. Even though the old capital had become a wasteland, the new capital was yet unfinished. Everyone felt like the drifting clouds. Those who had lived here before complained about losing their land. Those who had newly moved here bemoaned the pains of construction. In the streets, I saw that those who should have used carriages rode on horses, and most of those who should have dressed in court robes and headgear wore simple robes instead. The ways of the capital had changed abruptly; now they were no different from the ways of rustic samurai. I heard that these developments were portents of disorder in the land, and it turned out to be so: day by day the world grew more unsettled and the people more uneasy, and their fears proved to be well founded, so that in the winter of the same year the court returned to this capital.[6] But what became of all the houses that had been torn down? Not all of them were rebuilt as they had stood before.

4. Kiyomori, the overbearing leader of the Taira clan, had the capital temporarily moved from Kyoto to Fukuhara, near today's Kobe, in 1180. This was an unprecedented show of power by a warrior (samurai) clan against the imperial court. Events surrounding the rise and fall of the Taira (also called Heike) are told in the warrior epic *The Tales of the Heike*.

5. A primitive temporary palace of logs built by a 7th-century empress.

6. The court quickly returned from Fukuhara to Kyoto, and within a few years the Taira clan was exterminated.

I have heard that in venerable reigns of ancient times, emperors governed the nation with compassion: roofing his palace with thatch, Yao of China refrained from even trimming the eaves; seeing how thin the smoke that rose from the people's hearths, Nintoku of Japan[7] forgave even the lowest taxes. They did so because they took pity on the people and tried to help them. By measuring it against the past, we can know the state of the present.

Then, was it in the Yōwa era [1181–1182]?—long ago, and so I do not remember well, the world suffered a two-year famine, and dreadful things occurred. Droughts in spring and summer, typhoons and floods in fall—adversities followed one after another, and none of the five grains ripened. In vain the soil was turned in the spring and crops planted in the summer, but lost was the excitement of autumn harvests and of the winter laying-in. Consequently, people in the provinces abandoned their lands and wandered to other regions, or forgot their houses and went to live in the mountains. Various royal prayers were initiated and extraordinary Esoteric Buddhist rites were performed, to no effect whatever. It was the habit of the capital to depend on the countryside for everything, but nothing was making its way to the capital now. How long could the residents maintain their equanimity? As their endurance wore down, they tried to dispose of their valuables as if throwing them away, but no one showed any interest. The few who did engage in barter despised gold and cherished millet. Beggars lined the streets, their pleas and lamentations filling one's ears. In this way, the first year struggled to a close. Surely the new year would bring improvement, one thought, but on top of the famine came an epidemic, and conditions only got worse. The metaphor of fish in a shrinking pool fit the situation well, as people running out of food grew more desperate by the day. In the end, well-dressed men wearing lacquered sedge hats, their skirts wrapped around their legs, went intently begging house to house. One would see them walking, exhausted and confused, then collapse, their faces to the ground. The corpses of people who had starved to death lay along the earthen walls, and in the streets, their numbers were beyond reckoning. A stench filled the world, as no one knew how to dispose of so many corpses, and often one could not bear to look at the decomposing faces and bodies. There was not even room for horses and carriages to pass on the Kamo riverbed. As lowly peasants and woodcutters exhausted their strength, firewood, too, came to be in short supply, and so people with no other resources tore apart their own houses and carried off the lumber to sell at market. I heard that the value of what one man could carry was not enough to sustain him for a single day. Strangely, mixed in among the firewood were sticks bearing traces here and there of red lacquer, or of gold and silver leaf, because people with nowhere else to turn had stolen Buddhist images from old temples and ripped out temple furnishings, which they broke into pieces. I saw such cruel sights because I was born into this impure, evil age.[8] There were many pathetic sights as well. Of those who had wives or husbands from whom they could not part, the ones whose love was stronger always died first. The reason is that putting themselves second and pitying the others, they gave their mates what little food they found. So it was that when parents

7. An early Chinese and an early Japanese emperor; both are known for benevolent rule and compassion toward the people.
8. The last of the three periods in Buddhist cosmology: the age of the "degenerated Law," when the teachings of the Buddha still survived but were no longer put into practice.

and children lived together, the parents invariably died first. I also saw a small child who, not knowing that his mother was dead, lay beside her, sucking at her breast.

The eminent priest Ryūgyō of Ninna Temple,[9] grieving over these countless deaths, wrote the first letter of the Sanskrit alphabet on the foreheads of all the dead he saw, thereby linking them to the Buddha. Wanting to know how many had died, he counted the bodies he found during the Fourth and Fifth Months. Within the capital, between Ichijō on the north and Kujō on the south, between Kyōgoku on the east and Suzaku on the west, more than 42,300 corpses lay in the streets. Of course, many others died before and after this period, and if we include those on the Kamo riverbed, in Shirakawa, in the western half of the capital, and in the countryside beyond, their numbers would be limitless. How vast the numbers must have been, then, in all the provinces along the Seven Highways. I have heard that something of the sort occurred in the Chōjō era [1134], during the reign of Emperor Sutoku, but I do not know how things were then. What I saw before my own eyes was extraordinary.

Then—was it at about the same time?—a dreadful earthquake shook the land. The effects were remarkable. Mountains crumbled and dammed the rivers; the sea tilted and inundated the land. The earth split open and water gushed forth; boulders broke off and tumbled into valleys. Boats rowing near the shore were carried off on the waves; horses on the road knew not where to place their hooves. Around the capital, not a single shrine or temple survived intact. Some fell apart; others toppled over. Dust and ash rose like billows of smoke. The sound of the earth's movement and of houses collapsing was no different from thunder. People who were inside their houses might be crushed in a moment. Those who ran outside found the earth splitting asunder. Lacking wings, one could not fly into the sky. If one were a dragon, one would ride the clouds. I knew then that earthquakes were the most terrible of all the many terrifying things. The dreadful shaking stopped after a time, but the aftershocks continued. Not a day passed without twenty or thirty quakes strong enough to startle one under ordinary circumstances. As ten and twenty days elapsed, gradually the intervals grew longer—four or five a day, then two or three, one every other day, one in two or three days—but the aftershocks went on for perhaps three months. Of the four great elements, water, fire, and wind constantly bring disaster, but for its part, earth normally brings no calamity. In ancient times—was it during the Saikō era [855]?—there was a great earthquake and many terrible things occurred, such as the head falling from the Buddha at Tōdai Temple,[1] but, they say, even that was not as bad as this. Everyone spoke of futility, and the delusion in their hearts seemed to diminish a little at the time; but after days and months piled up and years went by, no one gave voice to such thoughts any longer.

All in all, life in this world is difficult; the fragility and transience of our bodies and dwellings are indeed as I have said. We cannot reckon the many ways in which we trouble our hearts according to where we live and in obedience to our status. He who is of trifling rank but lives near the gates of power cannot rejoice with abandon, however deep his happiness may be, and when his sorrow is

9. A temple in Kyoto with close ties to the imperial family.
1. One of the great temples in Nara, the ancient capital before Kyoto was founded. The famous monumental Buddha statue in this temple is now known as the "Great Buddha." See the illustration on p. 1076.

keen, he does not wail aloud. Anxious about his every move, trembling with fear no matter what he does, he is like a sparrow near a hawk's nest. One who is poor yet lives beside a wealthy house will grovel in and out, morning and evening, ashamed of his wretched figure. When he sees the envy that his wife, children, and servants feel for the neighbors, when he hears the rich family's disdain for him, his mind will be unsettled and never find peace. He who lives in a crowded place cannot escape damage from a fire nearby. He who lives outside the city contends with many difficulties as he goes back and forth and often suffers at the hands of robbers. The powerful man is consumed by greed; he who stands alone is mocked. Wealth brings many fears; poverty brings cruel hardship. Look to another for help and you will belong to him. Take someone under your wing, and your heart will be shackled by affection. Bend to the ways of the world and you will suffer. Bend not and you will look demented. Where can one live, and how can one behave to shelter this body briefly and to ease the heart for a moment?

I inherited my paternal grandmother's house and occupied it for some time. Then I lost my backing,[2] came down in the world, and even though the house was full of fond memories, I finally could live there no longer, and so I, past the age of thirty, resolved to build a hut. It was only one-tenth the size of my previous residence. Unable to construct a proper estate, I erected a house only for myself. I managed to build an earthen wall but lacked the means to raise a gate. Using bamboo posts, I sheltered my carriage. The place was not without its dangers whenever snow fell or the wind blew. Because the house was located near the riverbed, the threat of water damage was deep and the fear of robbers never ebbed. Altogether, I troubled my mind and endured life in this difficult world for more than thirty years. The disappointments I suffered during that time awakened me to my unfortunate lot.[3] Accordingly, when I greeted my fiftieth spring, I left my house and turned away from the world. I had no wife or children, and so there were no relatives whom it would have been difficult to leave behind. As I had neither office nor stipend, what was there for me to cling to? Vainly, I spent five springs and autumns living in seclusion among the clouds on Mount Ōhara.[4]

Reaching the age of sixty, when I seemed about to fade away like the dew, I constructed a new shelter for the remaining leaves of my life. I was like a traveler who builds a lodging for one night only or like an aged silkworm spinning its cocoon. The result was less than a hundredth the size of the residence of my middle age. In the course of things, years have piled up and my residences have steadily shrunk. This one is like no ordinary house. In area it is only ten feet square; in height, less than seven feet. Because I do not choose a particular place to live, I do not acquire land on which to build. I lay a foundation, put up a simple, makeshift roof, and secure each joint with a latch. This is so that I can easily move the building if anything dissatisfies me. How much bother can it be to reconstruct it? It fills only two carts, and there is no expense beyond payment for the porters.

---

2. Probably a reference to the death of his father.
3. Chōmei came from a family of Shinto priests at the Kamo Shrine in Kyoto. He was greatly disappointed when he failed to secure a position at the shrine.
4. Northeast of the capital.

Now, having hidden my tracks and gone into seclusion in the depths of Mount Hino,[5] I extended the eaves more than three feet to the east, making a convenient place to break and burn brushwood. On the south I made a bamboo veranda, on the west of which I built a water-shelf for offerings to the Buddha, and to the north, behind a screen, I installed a painting of Amida Buddha, next to it hung Fugen,[6] and before it placed the Lotus Sutra. Along the east side I spread soft ferns, making a bed for the night. In the southwest, I constructed hanging shelves of bamboo and placed there three black leather trunks. In them I keep selected writings on Japanese poetry and music, and the *Essentials of Salvation*. A koto and a biwa[7] stand to one side. They are what are called a folding koto and a joined lute. Such is the state of my temporary hut. As for the location: to the south is a raised bamboo pipe. Piling up stones, I let water collect there. Because the woods are near, kindling is easy to gather. The name of the place is Toyama. Vines cover all tracks. Although the ravines are overgrown, the view is open to the west. The conditions are not unfavorable for contemplating the Pure Land of the West. In spring I see waves of wisteria. They glow in the west like lavender clouds. In summer I hear the cuckoo. Whenever I converse with him, he promises to guide me across the mountain path of death. In autumn the voices of twilight cicadas fill my ears. They sound as though they are mourning this ephemeral, locust-shell world. In winter I look with deep emotion upon the snow. Accumulating and melting, it can be compared to the effects of bad karma. When I tire of reciting the Buddha's name or lose interest in reading the sutras aloud, I rest as I please, I dawdle as I like. There is no one to stop me, no one before whom to feel ashamed. Although I have taken no vow of silence, I live alone and so surely can avoid committing transgressions of speech. Although I do not go out of my way to observe the rules that an ascetic must obey, what could lead me to break them, there being no distractions here? In the morning, I might gaze at the ships sailing to and from Okanoya, comparing myself to the whitecaps behind them, and compose verses in the elegant style of the novice-priest Manzei;[8] in the evening, when the wind rustles the leaves of the *katsura* trees, I might turn my thoughts to the Xunyang River and play my biwa in the way of Gen Totoku.[9] If my enthusiasm continues unabated, I might accompany the sound of the pines with "Autumn Winds" or play "Flowing Spring" to the sound of the water. Although I have no skill in these arts, I do not seek to please the ears of others. Playing to myself, singing to myself, I simply nourish my own mind.

At the foot of the mountain is another brushwood hut, the home of the caretaker of this mountain. A small child lives there. Now and then he comes to

---

5. Southeast of the capital, where Chōmei wrote this account.
6. A bodhisattva (enlightened being), widely worshipped by Japanese Buddhists; he is often shown seated on an elephant, symbolizing the slow and steady progress toward enlightenment. Amida Buddha presided over the Pure Land paradise, where anyone who appealed to him by reciting his name—as Chōmei does in the end of this account—could be reborn.
7. A pear-shaped four-stringed lute.

8. An 8th-century poet who took Buddhist vows and thus a model for Chōmei, who alludes here to Manzei's best-known poem: "To what shall I compare the world? Whitecaps behind a ship that rows out at dawn." (Only a few of Chōmei's many allusions to Japanese and Chinese poems are cited in these notes.)
9. The founder (1016–1097) of a particular Japanese school of biwa playing. Xunyang River is where the Chinese poet Bo Juyi (772–846) wrote his famous "Ballad of the Lute."

visit. When I have nothing else to do, I take a walk with him as my companion. He is ten years old; I am sixty. Despite the great difference in our ages, our pleasure is the same. Sometimes we pluck edible reed-flowers, pick pearberries, break off yam bulbils, or gather parsley. Sometimes we go to the paddies at the foot of the mountain, collect fallen ears of rice, and tie them into sheaves. If the weather is fair, we climb to the peak and gaze at the distant sky above my former home, or look at Mount Kohata, the villages of Fushimi, Toba, and Hatsukashi. Because a fine view has no master,[1] nothing interferes with our pleasure. When walking is no problem and we feel like going somewhere far, we follow the ridges from here, crossing Mount Sumi, passing Kasatori, and visit the temple at Iwama or worship at the Ishiyama temple. Then again, we might make our way across Awazu Plain and go to see the site where Semimaru lived, or cross the Tanakami River and visit the grave of Sarumaru Dayū.[2] On our return, depending on the season, we break off branches of blossoming cherry, seek out autumn foliage, pick ferns, or gather fruit. Some we offer to the Buddha, and some we bring home to remind us of our outing. When the night is quiet, I look at the moon at the window and think fondly of my old friends; I hear the cries of the monkey and wet my sleeve with tears.[3] Fireflies in the grass might be taken for fishing flares at distant Maki Island; the rain at dawn sounds like a gale blowing the leaves of the trees. When I hear the pheasant's song I wonder whether it might not be the voice of my father or mother; when the deer from the ridge draws tamely near I know how far I have withdrawn from the world. Sometimes I dig up embers to keep me company when, as old men do, I waken in the night. This is not a fearful mountain, and so I listen closely to the owl's call. Thus from season to season the charms of mountain scenery are never exhausted. Of course one who thinks and understands more deeply than I would not be limited to these.

When I came to live in this place, I thought that I would stay for only a short time, but already five years have passed. Gradually my temporary hut has come to feel like home as dead leaves lie deep on the eaves and moss grows on the foundation. When news of the capital happens to reach me, I learn that many of high rank have passed away since I secluded myself on this mountain. There is no way to know how many of lower rank have died. How many houses have been lost in the frequent fires? Only a temporary hut is peaceful and free of worry. It may be small, but it has a bed on which to lie at night and a place in which to sit by day. Nothing is lacking to shelter one person. The hermit crab prefers a small shell. This is because he knows himself. The osprey lives on rugged shores. The reason is that he fears people. I am like them. Knowing myself and knowing the world, I have no ambitions, I do not strive. I simply seek tranquillity and enjoy the absence of care. It is common practice in the world that people do not always build dwellings for themselves. Some might build for their wives and children, their relations and followers, some for their intimates and friends. Some might build for their masters or teachers, even for valuables, oxen, and horses. I now have built a hut for myself. I do not build for

1. From a couplet by Bo Juyi: "A fine view has no particular master. Mountains belong to those who love mountains."
2. Semimaru and Sarumaru were earlier Heian poets to whom many legends became attached.
3. In Chinese poetry, monkey cries are considered sad.

others. The reason is that given the state of the world now and my own circumstances, there is neither anyone I should live with and look after, nor any dependable servant. Even if I had built a large place, whom would I shelter, whom would I have live in it?

When it comes to friends, people respect the wealthy and prefer the suave. They do not always love the warmhearted or the upright. Surely it is best simply to make friends with strings and woodwinds, blossoms and the moon. When it comes to servants, they value a large bonus and generous favors. They do not seek to be nurtured and loved, to work quietly and at ease. It is best simply to make my body my servant. How? If there is something to be done, I use my own body. This can be a nuisance, but it is easier than employing and looking after someone else. If I have to go out, I walk. This can be painful, but it is not as bad as troubling my mind over the horse, the saddle, the ox, the carriage. Now I divide my single body and use it in two ways. My hands are my servants, my legs my conveyance, and they do just as I wish. Because my mind understands my body's distress, I rest my body when it feels distressed, use it when it feels strong. [And] though I use it, I do not overwork it. When my body does not want to work, my mind is not annoyed. Needless to say, walking regularly and working regularly must promote good health. How can I idle the time away doing nothing? To trouble others is bad karma. Why should I borrow the strength of another? It is the same for clothing and food. Using what comes to hand, I cover my skin with clothing woven from the bark of wisteria vines and with a hempen quilt, and sustain my life with asters of the field and fruits of the trees on the peak. Because I do not mingle with others, I am not embarrassed by my appearance. Because food is scarce, my crude rewards taste good. My description of these pleasures is not directed at the wealthy. I am comparing my own past only with my present.

The Three Worlds exist only in the one mind.[4] If the mind is not at peace, elephants, horses, and the Seven Rarities will be worthless; palaces and pavilions will have no appeal. My present dwelling is a lonely, one-room hut, but I love it. When I happen to venture into the capital, I feel ashamed of my beggarly appearance, but when I come back and stay here, I pity those others who rush about in the worldly dust. Should anyone doubt what I am saying, I would ask them to look at the fishes and birds. A fish never tires of water. One who is not a fish cannot know a fish's mind. Birds prefer the forest. One who is not a bird cannot know a bird's mind. The savor of life in seclusion is the same. Who can understand it without living it?

Well, now, the moon of my life span is sinking in the sky; the time remaining to me nears the mountaintops. Soon I shall set out for the darkness of the Three Paths.[5] About what should I complain at this late date? The essence of the Buddha's teachings is that we should cling to nothing. Loving my grass hut is wrong. Attachment to my quiet, solitary way of life, too, must interfere with my enlightenment. Why then do I go on spending precious time relating useless pleasures?

4. It is a basic Buddhist belief that the phenomena in the world are constructs of our minds, without objective existence. The "Three Worlds," in order of the level of enlightenment of their inhabitants, are the world of desire, the world of form, and the world of formlessness.
5. Human beings who had committed wrongs were believed to be reborn into one of three lesser "paths": as hell creatures, animals, or hungry ghosts.

Pondering this truth on a tranquil morning, just before dawn, I ask my mind: one leaves the world and enters the forest to cultivate the mind and practice the Way of the Buddha. In your case, however, although your appearance is that of a monk, your mind is clouded with desire. You have presumed to model your dwelling after none other than that of Vimalakirti, but your adherence to the discipline fails even to approach the efforts of Suddhipanthaka.[6] Is this because poverty, a karmic retribution, torments your mind, or is it that a deluded mind had deranged you? At that time, my mind had no reply. I simply set my tongue to work halfheartedly reciting the name of the compassionate Amida Buddha two or three times, and that is all.

The monk Ren'in[7] wrote this late in the Third Month of Kenryaku 2 [1212], at his hut on Toyama.

---

6. The most foolish of the Buddha's disciples, who nevertheless ultimately achieved enlightenment. "Vimalakirti": a wealthy man who achieved enlightenment even without becoming a monk.

7. Chōmei's religious name.

YOSHIDA KENKŌ

ca. 1283–1352

"Phenomenon and essence are fundamentally one." Yoshida Kenkō, who moved with ease between a life in reclusion and a life at court, expressed this bold insight and many others in his *Essays in Idleness*. Some of the aesthetic principles he formulated there went back to the time of *The Man'yōshū*, Murasaki Shikibu's *The Tale of Genji*, Sei Shōnagon's *The Pillow Book*, and *The Tales of the Heike*. But he created his own distinct approach by focusing his attention on everyday things, which he considered the best way to capture the mysterious impermanence of life.

Kenkō came from a prominent family of Shinto priests, the Urabe, but did not continue his family's profession. Instead, in his younger years he served Emperor GoNijō (reigned 1301–08) as personal secretary and archivist, before shaving his head and becoming a Buddhist monk around the age of thirty. Like **Kamo no Chōmei**—Buddhist recluse and author of **"An Account of a Ten-Foot-Square Hut"**—Kenkō was a well-known poet who compiled his own personal collection of *waka* poetry, the classical Japanese verse form in thirty-one-syllables. Indeed, he was hailed as one of the "four kings of *waka* poetry" of his time and continued to participate in poetry contests and cultural events in the capital even after taking his religious vows.

Kenkō lived through a period of intense instability: the chaotic transition between two medieval military governments, the Kamakura shogunate (1185–1333) and the Muromachi or Ashikaga shogunate (1336–1573), which controlled affairs from the Muromachi clan quarters of Kyoto. In the latter part of his life Kenkō became closely associated with the new Ashikaga shoguns and contributed to the lively mingling of scholars, poets, and samurai at their court.

Kenkō's fame rests on his *Essays in Idleness,* a book in 243 sections that offer personal musings, observations, and random jottings, each ranging in length from one sentence to several pages. He might have started his *Essays* right after leaving court life, when in his early thirties. This first part, sections 1 to 30, is full of nostalgia for Heian aristocratic culture couched in language reminiscent of *The Tale of Genji* and *The Pillow Book.* Kenkō penned the rest of his *Essays* between 1329 and 1333, when he was in his late forties. This second part reveals a new preoccupation with renunciation, death, Chinese literature, and Daoism.

Both the physical and spiritual environment impressed on Kenkō the evanescence of earthly life. Time itself became an obsession. The embrace of impermanence, which had long been a main tenet of Buddhist beliefs, took on new urgency for people living through a period of political chaos. Kenkō might have responded with despair, denial, or self-indulgence, but he displayed an intellectual attitude; transience, he decided, was more than the source of beauty or sorrow, it was the defining quality of life. To appreciate this fact in all its aspects—spring giving way to summer, youth yielding to age—was to understand life. "If a man were never to fade away like the dews of Adashino," he writes, "never to vanish like the smoke over Toribeyama, but lingered forever in the world, how things would lose their power to move us! The most precious thing in life is its uncertainty."

In the modern period Kenkō's *Essays* were placed into a lineage of "essay literature," which also included *The Pillow Book* and "An Account of a Ten-Square-Foot Hut." Kenkō's brief entries proclaim themselves to be written in an informal mode for his own enjoyment. Full of personal statements and declarations of private taste, the essays lack a unifying theme and instead combine reminiscences, anecdotes, narrative fragments, meditations, aesthetic pronouncements, witty notes, evocative descriptions, and pithy aphorisms. But Kenkō was also a monk and wrote in the mode of reclusion literature, although he never abandoned the court altogether. In fact he was not worried about his afterlife: it was this life that he enjoyed, with all its riveting tensions, imperfections, and moments of melancholy.

Thirst for introspection, nostalgic longing for things past, and an acute sense of the incompleteness of human experience, as well as of the presence of decay and death, are salient features of Kenkō's attitude toward life. In his *Essays in Idleness* he expressed these elements in memorable phrases and anecdotes mixing everyday trivialities with the unspeakable and philosophical, urging us on to confront the challenges of the human condition in our own place and time.

From Essays in Idleness[1]

What a strange, demented feeling it gives me when I realize I have spent whole days before this inkstone, with nothing better to do,[2] jotting down at random whatever nonsensical thoughts have entered my head.

1. Translated by Donald Keene.
2. "Idleness" in the work's title is taken from this expression, "with nothing better to do."

4

It is admirable when a man keeps his thoughts constantly on the future life and is not remiss in his devotions to the Way of the Buddha.

10

A house, I know, is but a temporary abode, but how delightful it is to find one that has harmonious proportions and a pleasant atmosphere. One feels somehow that even moonlight, when it shines into the quiet domicile of a person of taste, is more affecting than elsewhere. A house, though it may not be in the current fashion or elaborately decorated, will appeal to us by its unassuming beauty—a grove of trees with an indefinably ancient look; a garden where plants, growing of their own accord, have a special charm; a verandah and an open-work wooden fence of interesting construction; and a few personal effects left carelessly lying about, giving the place an air of having been lived in. A house which multitudes of workmen have polished with every care, where strange and rare Chinese and Japanese furnishings are displayed, and even the grasses and trees of the garden have been trained unnaturally, is ugly to look at and most depressing. How could anyone live for long in such a place? The most casual glance will suggest how likely such a house is, to turn in a moment to smoke.

A man's character, as a rule, may be known from the place where he lives. The Gotokudaiji minister stretched a rope across his roof to keep the kites from roosting. Saigyō,[3] seeing the rope, asked, "Why should it bother him if kites perch there? That shows you the kind of man this prince is." I have heard that Saigyō never visited him again. I remembered this story not long ago when I noticed a rope stretched over the roof of the Kosaka palace, where Prince Ayanokōji lives. Someone told me that, as a matter of fact, it distressed the prince to see how crows clustering on the roof would swoop down to seize frogs in the pond. The story impressed me,[4] and made me wonder if Sanesada may not also have had some such reason.

29

When I sit down in quiet meditation, the one emotion hardest to fight against is a longing in all things for the past. After the others have gone to bed, I pass the time on a long autumn's night by putting in order whatever belongings are at hand. As I tear up scraps of old correspondence I should prefer not to leave behind, I sometimes find among them samples of the calligraphy of a friend who has died, or pictures he drew for his own amusement, and I feel exactly as I did at the time. Even with letters written by friends who are still alive I try, when it has been long since we met, to remember the circumstances, the year. What a moving experience that is! It is sad to think that a man's familiar possessions, indifferent to his death, should remain unaltered long after he is gone.

---

3. One of Japan's most influential *waka* poets (1118–1190). The minister, later called by his name, Sanesada, was a poet.

4. It illustrates the prince's commitment to living by Buddhist principles, as he saved sentient beings—the frogs—from their predators.

74

They flock together like ants, hurry east and west, run north and south. Some are mighty, some humble. Some are aged, some young. They have places to go, houses to return to. At night they sleep, in the morning get up. But what does all this activity mean? There is no ending to their greed for long life, their grasping for profit. What expectations have they that they take such good care of themselves? All that awaits them in the end is old age and death, whose coming is swift and does not falter for one instant. What joy can there be while waiting for this end? The man who is deluded by fame and profit does not fear the approach of old age and death because he is so intoxicated by worldly cravings that he never stops to consider how near he is to his destination. The foolish man, for his part, grieves because he desires everlasting life and is ignorant of the law of universal change.

82

Somebody once remarked that thin silk was not satisfactory as a scroll wrapping because it was so easily torn. Ton'a[5] replied, "It is only after the silk wrapper has frayed at top and bottom, and the mother-of-pearl has fallen from the roller that a scroll looks beautiful." This opinion demonstrated the excellent taste of the man. People often say that a set of books looks ugly if all volumes are not in the same format, but I was impressed to hear the Abbot Kōyū say, "It is typical of the unintelligent man to insist on assembling complete sets of everything. Imperfect sets are better."

In everything, no matter what it may be, uniformity is undesirable. Leaving something incomplete makes it interesting, and gives one the feeling that there is room for growth. Someone once told me, "Even when building the imperial palace, they always leave one place unfinished." In both Buddhist and Confucian writings of the philosophers of former times, there are also many missing chapters.

97

There are innumerable instances of things which attach themselves to something else, then waste and destroy it. The body has lice; a house has mice; a country has robbers; inferior men have riches; superior men have benevolence and righteousness; priests have the Buddhist law.

157

If we pick up a brush, we feel like writing; if we hold a musical instrument in our hands, we wish to play music. Lifting a wine cup makes us crave saké; taking up dice, we should like to play backgammon. The mind invariably reacts in this way to any stimulus. That is why we should not indulge even casually in improper amusements.

Even a perfunctory glance at one verse of some holy writing will somehow make us notice also the text that precedes and follows: it may happen then, quite suddenly, that we mend our errors of many years. Supposing we had not at that moment opened the sacred text, would we have realized our mistakes?

5. Distinguished poet (1289–1372) and close associate of Kenkō.

This is a case of accidental contact producing a beneficial result. Though our hearts may not be in the least impelled by faith, if we sit before the Buddha, rosary in hand, and take up a sutra, we may (even in our indolence) be accumulating merit through the act itself; though our mind may be inattentive, if we sit in meditation on a rope seat, we may enter a state of calm and concentration, without even being aware of it.

Phenomenon and essence are fundamentally one. If the outward form is not at variance with the truth, an inward realization is certain to develop. We should not deny that this is true faith; we should respect and honor a conformity to truth.

THE TALES OF THE HEIKE
fourteenth century

No other work in Japanese literature can match *The Tales of the Heike* in its appeal to the popular imagination. Besides helping to create the samurai ideal, it has offered its Japanese readers practically everything: heroic spirit, dramatic energy, vivid description, musical language, humor, and pathos. The tale re-creates events of the late twelfth century, which brought vast changes to Japanese political life, including the eclipse of the aristocracy and the rise and fall of great military clans. The tale's pitch-perfect rendering of the theme of evanescence—the notion that all who flourish are destined to fail and humankind is but dust before the wind—touches a chord that resonates throughout Japanese culture. As a result, *The Tales of the Heike* has influenced more writers in more subsequent genres, from medieval Noh plays to modern television dramas, than any other work of Japanese literature.

THE GENPEI WARS (1180–85)

The Tales of the Heike enshrined the memory of the Genpei Wars, fought between the Minamoto clan (whose Sino-Japanese designation was *Genji*) and the Taira clan (or *Heike* in Sino-Japanese). These wars marked the transition from the court-centered ancient period to the medieval period, which came to be dominated by military clans. At the beginning of the twelfth century the power of the court nobility was slowly declining, as the central bureaucracy and its local branches atrophied. A power vacuum began to form in the provinces, and the governors and their agents who had been deputized to maintain law and order gradually emerged as a warrior class. By the middle of the century the court administration was in paralysis. Retired emperors ruled behind the throne while the Fujiwara, which had been the most prominent clan of the courtly civil aristocracy, clung to a mere shred of its previous authority. The explosion that eventually ignited civil war was a dispute over imperial succession in 1156. The winner enlisted the support of the two most powerful military clans, but in so doing set in motion their rise as independent political forces within the capital. In a predictable sequence of events, the two clans began to quarrel, and the defeated house withdrew to the eastern provinces. This was the Minamoto, or Genji. The ascendant clan of the Taira, or Heike, remained in the capital, where it enjoyed twenty years of arrogant splendor before the Genji finally took revenge. Fighting began in 1180 and raged on for five years. When it was over, the Heike had been annihilated, and the Genji established a military dictatorship based in the northeastern city of Kamakura that would rule Japan for two centuries.

ORIGIN AND VERSIONS OF THE TALES

Most likely, The Tales of the Heike originated as a collection of stories written down by priests associated with Buddhist temples from the oral performances by minstrels, who were often blind. These minstrels traveled the countryside reciting the daring feats and tender passions of the famous warriors of the Genpei Wars, accompanying their recitation on the biwa (a pear-shaped lute). These chanters recreated their narrative with every performance. As a text meant for oral performance The Tales of the Heike came to be preserved in many versions, which differ considerably in content and style and sometimes reflect adaptation to local audiences. Eventually more than a hundred variants came into being, but the one that has become standard and is translated here is the version set down by a man named Kakuichi, himself a biwa minstrel, in 1371. He shaped the disparate materials into a unified text of literary merit, framed by Buddhist moral sentiments. The seductive blend of oral qualities and elegant literary craft in Kakuichi's version accounts for some of the most striking features of The Tales of the Heike: formulaic language and imagery, the use of repetition and variation, structural contrast in the sequence of episodes and in the portrayal of protagonists, stress on action, exaggeration, lists of names or precedents, and the use of parables and analogies from Chinese and Japanese history to lend weight and antique flair to particular plot twists or character depictions.

BUDDHIST FRAMEWORK

The Tales of the Heike is not only a chronicle of the struggles between the Heike and Genji clans. It is also a profound reflection on the Buddhist law of retribution, which was at work in the spectacular rise and utter defeat of the Heike clan and its leader, Taira no Kiyomori. His arrogance and selfish caprice set in motion the events leading up to the Genpei Wars, and his horrible death, marked by violent convulsions and ominous fevers accompanied by insatiable thirst, prefigures the punishment that awaits him in hell as retribution for his actions in life. Although he dies in 1181, four years before the final defeat of his clan, Kiyomori's bad karma reaches beyond his grave, enables the Genji military successes, and induces the Heike's retreat from the capital and their final defeat in western Japan. Buddhist beliefs shape the broad narrative arch of The Tales of the Heike and the motivations of its protagonists. The awareness of the impermanence of all things, of the inevitability of disillusionment in life, and of the possibilities of awakening to the truth through Buddhist faith is the baseline of The Tales from its first to its final lines. Pure Land Buddhism, still today one of the most popular of the many schools of Buddhism, is particularly prominent in The Tales of the Heike. It promises its believers rebirth in a western paradise presided over by the Amida Buddha, the "Buddha of Infinite Light." Again and again characters in The Tales of the Heike will face west, inspired by the hope for rebirth into the Pure Land, and invoke the name of this Buddha in their last moments before execution, death in battle, or suicide. And women, servants, and samurai will wish to stay alive only so that they can continue to pray for their dead husbands' and masters' favorable rebirth in the Pure Land.

STRUCTURE AND PLOT

Divided into twelve books and a concluding "Initiates' Book," *The Tales of the Heike* unfolds in three parts. The first part, books 1 through 6 (sometimes called "chapters"), focuses on the flamboyant character of Kiyomori, the head of the Heike clan, and portrays his conflicts with Retired Emperor GoShirakawa and various members of the Genji clan. After Kiyomori's miserable death in book 6, attention turns in the second part (books 7 through 12) to the Genji clan and three of their leaders: Yoritomo, who commands the Genji in the northeast and will establish Japan's first shogunate in Kamakura after the defeat of the Heike in 1185; his cousin, the brutish Yoshinaka, who for a time holds the capital and is eliminated by Yoritomo in 1184, when his ambitions get out of hand; and Yoritomo's youthful and brilliant half brother Yoshitsune, who deals a crippling blow to the Heike in the surprise attack at Ichi-no-tani in 1184 (book 9) and masterminds their final rout—the naval battle at Dan-no-ura in 1185 (book 11). In this battle Kiyomori's widow, Emperor Antoku (Kiyomori's grandson by his daughter Kenreimon'in), and virtually all the men of the clan are sent to their deaths at sea. Yet, although the second part of *The Tales of the Heike* depicts the resurgence and triumphal victory of the Genji, the main focus of the narrative is on a series of Heike figures whose various deaths result from their forefather Kiyomori's evil deeds. The third part, the "Initiates' Book," is considered a text containing secret knowledge in certain schools of Heike performance. A self-contained tale, it takes us into the calm aftermath of the Genpei Wars, to the mountain temple north of Kyoto. There Kiyomori's daughter Kenreimon'in, now a nun, spends her life praying for the repose of the souls of her son, Emperor Antoku, and of the other dead Heike. The former empress's loneliness and nostalgia for the past is evoked in richly lyrical passages and dramatic poetic imagery. *The Tales of the Heike* ends with her death.

Although *The Tales of the Heike* unfolds its sprawling narrative in twelve books with numerous chapters, subplots and digressions, and a parade of hundreds of protagonists, many of whom figure only a few times and disappear without further trace, the work has a powerful unity due to its Buddhist framework. It starts with the sound of the bells of the world's first Buddhist monastery in India, which echo the "impermanence of all things" and the universal lesson that "the proud do not prevail for long but vanish like a spring night's dream." And it finds its proper closure on a reconciliatory note with the "Initiates' Book," when the nun, the only survivor of the slain Heike, performs pious service for the clan. In the end she finds peace with Retired Emperor GoShirakawa, who comes to visit her in the wilderness and for whom she recapitulates in tears her fate and the demise of her clan in Buddhist terms. *The Tales of the Heike* can thus be seen as an offering to the dead Heike—a narrative prayer for the peaceful repose of their souls. In a world where the dead were considered powerful forces who could wreak havoc and misfortune (and whose vengeance in such forms as natural disasters, epidemics, and catastrophes caused entire capitals to be abandoned in early Japan), such a pious offering was not just meaningful but necessary.

The Tales of the Heike belongs to the genre of "warrior tales." This genre flourished in the medieval period, when the military houses came to prominence, after the court-centered aristocratic world of the Heian Period (794–1185) had come to an end with the Genpei Wars. It includes anything from dry chronicles documenting particular uprisings or wars to highly lyrical warrior romances aimed at exploring the emotional experiences of the protagonists. Some of these tales were written from the perspective of the victors; others, like The Tales of the Heike, empathized with the tragedy of the defeated. Many of the warrior tales took shape over time at the hands of several compilers and include episodes that circulated separately in collections of anecdotes. While the fact-oriented warrior chronicles were largely written in the official idiom of Chinese-style prose, the psychological warrior romances used a mixed Chinese–Japanese style. This hybrid stood between the language of Heian romantic tales such as The Tale of Genji, filled with poetry and lyrical imagery, and Chinese-style official prose, as evoked by the inclusion of highly formal imperial edicts, letters and petitions, prayers, Buddhist homilies, and a large array of allusions to Chinese Classics and official histories. In this way the Heike warriors appear in more than one dimension, both as romantic protagonists, with complex psychology and touching entourages of women, children, and servants, and as displaced court officials fallen from grace and power.

The cultivation of the courtly arts of poetry and music is particularly central in The Tales of the Heike. Its battles display carnage but relatively little brutality. Tadanori, Kiyomori's brother, risks his life when he briefly returns to the capital, which the Heike had already left in haste, just to ask the famous poet Shunzei to include some of his poems in the imperial anthology that Shunzei had been commissioned to compile (book 7.16).

The Genji who later kills Tadanori identifies him from a signed poem fastened to the dead man's quiver, and that death brings tears to friends and foes alike—a sign of how highly all regarded courtly refinement (book 9.14).

Still, The Tales of the Heike brims with military action. A common convention in the depiction of battle scenes is to parade the warriors in their splendid outfits before the audience's eyes. Each warrior's robe, sword, arrows, horse, and saddle are described in loving detail; red brocade was reserved for heroes of highest social status, while black or dark colors indicated that the warrior belonged to a lesser order. Before engaging a foe in battle a warrior would announce his name in a thundering voice: there was a direct relation between the enemy's social status and the glory that his killing would bring. The winner would take the head of the defeated to prove his valor and success in battle. The head trophy was a symbol of victory, but it also served to identify the defeated. Grueling recognition scenes, in which relatives or former lovers must identify a slain head, are an important plot element in The Tales of the Heike, heightening the audience's emotional empathy. Warriors are the work's main subject, yet its point of view is closer to that of the courtiers—as if, despite the loss of the aristocracy's political and economic viability, this was the only group considered capable of appreciating the sad implications of the tale. As the loser in history's upheaval, it could be counted on to identify with the fate of the Heike. But the story had a far broader appeal, as courtly values were becoming common currency. Earlier, the thought that life's glory is as brief as a spring night's dream could have been expressed only in court poetry or the prose of a noblewoman. Now it became a message for the illiterate masses, who listened to the minstrels' lute performances.

The Tales of the Heike are chanted to the plucking of the pear-shaped biwa, a four-stringed instrument with frets. The performance schools that survive today use an eighteenth-century musical score that fixed the music, rather than relying on the improvisational skills of the individual performer. The three basic performance styles are simple declamation, intoned recitation, and a more elaborate aria-like mode of exposition. Some of the recurrent melodic formulas correspond to the content of the passage: there is a formula for prayers or religious scenes, a formula for battle scenes, a specific formula for the performance of poems, and a formula for passages radiating elegance and dignity.

The popularity of *Heike* performances reached its peak in the fourteenth and early fifteenth centuries, when this previously humble form became an upper-class performance art; many of the blind minstrels traveled to perform before regional feudal lords and samurai, in addition to performing in services at Buddhist temples and at poetry and tea gatherings in the residences of the nobility in Kyoto. With the rise of Noh theater in the fourteenth century, Heike heroes found their way into the repertoire of warrior dramas. And they inspired plays of the Kabuki theater and puppet theater, new urban forms of entertainment that developed in the seventeenth century. As new media such as film, television, and manga appeared in the twentieth century, *The Tales of the Heike* has continued to be a fertile source of inspiration—and it will undoubtedly be drawn on in still-to-be-invented art forms of the future.

CHARACTERS IN *THE TALES OF THE HEIKE*

Imperial Family

GOSHIRAKAWA (1127–1192; reigned 1155–58), *Retired Emperor and head of the imperial clan*

TAKAKURA (1161–1181; reigned 1168–80), *Emperor and son of Retired Emperor GoShirakawa; father of Antoku*

ANTOKU (1178–1185; reigned 1180–85), *son of Emperor Takakura and Kenreimon'in; a child emperor, he is held by the Heike and drowns in the final battle at Dan-no-ura at age 7*

NUN OF THE SECOND RANK (ca. 1185), *Principal wife of Taira no Kiyomori and mother of Munemori, Shigehira, and Kenreimon'in; drowns in the final battle at Dan-no-ura*

The Taira Clan (Heike)

KIYOMORI (1118–1181), *Taira clan head*

SHIGEMORI (1138–1179), *eldest son of Kiyomori; until Kiyomori's early death a restraining influence on Kiyomori*

MUNEMORI (1147–1185), *son of Kiyomori and Nun of the Second Rank; Taira clan head after his father's death in 1181*

ATSUMORI (1169–1184), *nephew of Kiyomori; killed in the battle at Ichinotani*

TADANORI (1144–1184), *younger brother of Kiyomori; pupil of the famous poet Fujiwara no Shunzei; dies in the battle at Ichi-no-tani*

The Minamoto Clan (Genji)

YORITOMO (1147–1199), *leader of the Minamoto in eastern Japan and founder of the Kamakura shogunate*

YOSHITSUNE (1159–1189), *younger half brother of Yoritomo and one of the chief Minamoto commanders; defeats the Heike in the final battle at Dan-no-ura*

From The Tales of the Heike[1]

FROM *BOOK ONE*

The Bells of Gion Monastery (1.1)

The bells of the Gion monastery in India echo with the warning that all things are impermanent. The blossoms of the sala trees teach us through their hues that what flourishes must fade.[2] The proud do not prevail for long but vanish like a spring night's dream. In time the mighty, too, succumb: all are dust before the wind.

Long ago in a different land, Zhao Gao of the Qin dynasty in China, Wang Mang of the Han, Zhu Yi of the Liang, and An Lushan of the Tang all refused to be governed by former sovereigns. Pursuing every pleasure, deaf to admonitions, unaware of the chaos overtaking the realm, ignorant of the sufferings of the common people, before long they all alike met their downfall.

More recently in our own country there have been men like Masakado, Sumitomo, Gishin, and Nobuyori, each of them proud and fierce to the extreme. The tales told of the most recent of such men, Taira no Kiyomori, the lay priest of Rokuhara and at one time the prime minister, are beyond the power of words to describe or the mind to imagine.

Kiyomori was the oldest son and heir of Taira no Tadamori, the minister of punishments, and the grandson of Masamori, the governor of Sanuki. Masamori was a ninth-generation descendant of Prince Kazurahara, a first-rank prince and the minister of ceremonies, the fifth son of Emperor Kanmu.

FROM *BOOK SIX*

Summary The selection from Book 6 takes us halfway into the tale, which to this point has largely been an account of the Heike (or Taira) clan's ascendancy. The clan controls half the provinces in Japan and enjoys sufficient military might to impose its will on the capital. As head of the clan, Kiyomori has attained the pinnacle of worldly success, been named Chancellor of the Realm, and been appointed to the most exalted of court ranks. His sons have also fared handsomely, and the clan possesses innumerable private estates and agricultural fields.

Yet Kiyomori abuses his power with such brutality that even his own son is repulsed. Shigemori, the hope of the future, confronts his father, urging restraint, but his voice goes unheard; after praying that either his father's heart be softened or his own life be cut short, he dies. Shigemori's untimely death is only one sign of the gods' apparent displeasure. The country is wracked with a series of natural disasters. Fires, tornadoes, and earthquakes are all interpreted as portents that Kiyomori is steering Japan toward some horrendous calamity. And indeed the remainder of Kiyomori's allotted time is beset with plot and counterplot, treachery and betrayal. He has lost the support of the powerful retired emperor and the bulk of the imperial family. Members of the aristocracy, who once saw Kiyomori as a protector, now revile him. The Buddhist temples stop their squabbling and unite their private armies against the hated despot. And

1. Translated by and with notes adapted from Burton Watson.
2. According to Buddhist legend, the Gion monastery, which was built by a rich merchant in a famous garden in India, was the first Bud- dhist monastery. The temple complex included a building known as Impermanence Hall. The Buddha died under the yellow blossoms of sala trees, which turned white to express their grief.

worst of all, Kiyomori's depredations have driven each of these former allies to embrace his most serious rival, the potent warrior house of the Minamoto, or Genji.

Yoritomo, head of the Genji clan, cuts a deal with the retired emperor. GoShirakawa agrees to pardon him for past offenses; in return, Yoritomo will lead his men against the Heike. Battle is joined in 1180. The war between the Heike and the Genji has begun, and rages inconclusively for a full year before the onset of Kiyomori's final illness.

The Death of Kiyomori (6.7)

After this, all the warriors of the island of Shikoku went over to the side of Kōno no Michinobu.[3] Reports also came that Tanzō, the superintendent of the Kumano Shrine,[4] had shifted his sympathies to the Genji side, despite the many kindnesses shown him by the Heike. All the provinces in the north and the east were thus rebelling against the Taira, and in the regions to the west and southwest of the capital the situation was the same. Report after report of uprisings in the outlying areas came to startle the ears of the Heike, and word repeatedly reached them of additional impending acts of rebellion. It seemed as though the "barbarian tribes to the east and west"[5] had suddenly risen up against them. The members of the Taira clan were not alone in thinking that the end of the world was close at hand. No truly thoughtful person could fail to dread the ominous turn of events.

On the twenty-third day of the Second Month, a council of the senior Taira nobles was convened. At that time Lord Munemori,[6] a former general of the right, spoke as follows: "We earlier tried to put down the rebels in the east, but the results were not all that we might have desired. This time I would like to be appointed commander in chief to move against them."

"What a splendid idea!" the other nobles exclaimed in obsequious assent. A directive was accordingly handed down from the retired emperor[7] appointing Lord Munemori commander in chief of an expedition against the traitorous elements in the eastern and northern provinces.[8] All the high ministers and courtiers who held military posts or were experienced in the use of arms were ordered to follow him.

3. A Genji supporter. His father has just been killed by a Heike partisan, and Michinobu's revenge rallies the warriors of Shikoku (one of the four main islands of Japan) to the side of the Genji. This is a serious setback for the Heike, because Shikoku lies in the southwestern portion of the country, where the clan has traditionally been strong.
4. One of the most important shrines in Japan, in an area that had long been under the sway of the Heike.
5. A Chinese phrase used to refer to all directions.
6. Kiyomori's son, successor to Shigemori.
7. Emperor GoShirakawa reigned only from 1155 to 1158, but until his death in 1192 he

had a considerably greater say in the government than the series of reigning emperors who succeeded him. Following the convention of the period he had abdicated early and assumed the status of "retired emperor," probably to gain more room for political maneuvers. At this point in the tale, GoShirakawa is nominally allied with the Heike, but only because he is in effect Kiyomori's hostage. On the surface, then, he does the Heike's bidding, when in fact he is in league with the Genji. The retired emperor is so duplicitous that, in the turmoil, it is hard at any given moment to tell whose side he is really on.
8. That is, against the Genji.

When word had already gotten abroad that Lord Munemori would set out on his mission to put down the Genji forces in the eastern provinces on the twenty-seventh day of the same month, his departure was canceled because of reports that Kiyomori, the lay priest and prime minister, was not in his customary good health.

On the following day, the twenty-eighth, it became known that Kiyomori was seriously ill, and people throughout the capital and at Rokuhara[9] whispered to one another, "This is just what we were afraid of!"

From the first day that Kiyomori took sick, he was unable to swallow anything, not even water. His body was as hot as though there were a fire burning inside it: those who attended him could scarcely come within twenty-five or thirty feet of him so great was the heat. All he could do was cry out, "I'm burning! I'm burning!" His affliction seemed quite unlike any ordinary illness.

Water from the Well of the Thousand-Arm Kannon on Mount Hiei[1] was brought to the capital and poured into a stone bathtub, and Kiyomori's body was lowered into it in hopes of cooling him. But the water began to bubble and boil furiously and, in a moment, had all gone up in steam. In another attempt to bring him some relief, wooden pipes were rigged in order to pour streams of water down on his body, but the water sizzled and sputtered as though it were landing on fiery rocks or metal, and virtually none of it reached his body. The little that did so burst into flames and burned, filling the room with black smoke and sending flames whirling upward.

Long ago, the eminent Buddhist priest Hōzō was said to have been invited by Enma, the king of hell, to visit the infernal regions. At that time he asked if he might see the place where his deceased mother had been reborn. Admiring his filial concern, Enma directed the hell wardens to conduct him to the Hell of Scorching Heat,[2] where Hōzō's mother was undergoing punishment. When Hōzō entered the iron gates of the hell, he saw flames leaping up like shooting stars, ascending hundreds of yojanas[3] into the air. The sight must have been much like what those attending Kiyomori in his sickness now witnessed.

Kiyomori's wife, the Nun of the Second Rank,[4] had a most fearful dream. It seemed that a carriage enveloped in raging flames had entered the gate of the mansion. Stationed at the front and rear of the carriage were creatures, some with the head of a horse, others with the head of an ox. To the front of the carriage was fastened an iron plaque inscribed with the single word *mu*, "never."

In her dream the Nun of the Second Rank asked, "Where has this carriage come from?"

9. An eastern district of the capital, where the Heike had their headquarters.
1. A source of holy water offerings for a nearby image of Thousand-Armed Kannon, a Buddhist deity known for compassion.
2. The hottest of the eight hells, reserved for punishing particularly egregious offenses, including murder, theft, lust, cruelty, and deceit.
3. A Hindu unit of distance (equivalent to

several miles).
4. It was not unusual for members of the aristocratic and military classes to retire into religious life, often without fully renouncing their emotional attachments and worldly ambitions. Kiyomori himself took Buddhist vows in 1168, with no discernible difference in his conduct; and his wife, now a nun, has obviously not forsaken her husband.

"From the tribunal of King Enma," was the reply. "It has come to fetch His Lordship, the lay priest and prime minister of the Taira clan."

"And what does the plaque mean?" she asked.

"It means that because of the crime of burning the one-hundred-and-sixty-foot gilt-bronze image of the Buddha Vairochana in the realm of human beings,[5] King Enma's tribunal has decreed that the perpetrator shall fall into the depths of the Hell of Never-Ceasing Torment. The 'Never' of Never-Ceasing is written on it; the 'Ceasing' remains to be written."

The Nun of the Second Rank woke from her dream in alarm, her body bathed in perspiration, and when she told others of her dream, their hair stood on end just hearing about it. She made offerings of gold, silver, and the seven precious objects[6] to all the temples and shrines reputed to have power in such matters, even adding such items as horses, saddles, armor, helmets, bows, arrows, long swords, and short swords. But no matter how much she added as accompaniment to her supplications, they were wholly without effect. Kiyomori's sons and daughters gathered by his pillow and bedside, inquiring in anguish if there were something that could be done, but all their cries were in vain.

On the second day of the second intercalary month, the Nun of the Second Rank, braving the formidable heat, approached her husband's pillow and spoke through her tears. "With each day that passes, it seems to me, there is less hope for your recovery. If you have anything you wish to say before you depart this world, it would be good to speak now while your mind is still clear."

In earlier days the prime minister had always been brusque and forceful in manner, but now, tormented by pain, he had barely breath enough to utter these words. "Ever since the Hōgen and Heiji uprisings,[7] I have on numerous occasions put down those who showed themselves enemies of the throne, and I have received rewards and acclaim far surpassing what I deserve. I have had the honor to become the grandfather of a reigning emperor and to hold the office of prime minister, and the bounties showered on me extend to my sons and grandsons. There is nothing more whatsoever that I could wish for in this life. Only one regret remains to me—that I have yet to behold the severed head of that exile to the province of Izu, Minamoto no Yoritomo! When I have ceased to be, erect no temples or pagodas in my honor, conduct no memorial rites for me! But dispatch forces at once to strike at Yoritomo, cut off his head,

5. The Buddhist monasteries had already earned Kiyomori's ire by siding with the Genji. When the monks then mocked him in effigy, trampling a big wooden ball dubbed "Kiyomori's head," Kiyomori dispatched his troops. By the time the fighting was over, the two great temples of Nara, Kōfukuji and Tōdaiji, had been burned to the ground and an immense 53-foot bronze statue of the Buddha, known in Sanskrit as Vairocana and prized since its erection in the 8th century, had been completely destroyed. *The Tales of the Heike* describes Kiyomori as delighted with the results, but others at court are aghast at the level of destruction.
6. Precious substances mentioned in Bud-

dhist texts (variously identified in different translations at different times).
7. The Hōgen Disturbance (1156) was a succession dispute in which the Heike and the Genji joined forces to support the then-reigning emperor, GoShirakawa. The Heiji Disturbance (1160) was a clash that arose between the two military clans when Retired Emperor GoShirakawa encountered a second challenge, this time from a faction that included the Genji. Under Kiyomori's command the Heike defeated the Genji; but Kiyomori made the tactical mistake of sparing the life of his enemy's 14-year-old son, Yoritomo, around whom the Genji would later rally to ultimately crush the Heike.

and hang it before my grave—that is all the ceremony that I ask!" Such were the deeply sinful words that he spoke!

On the fourth day of the same month, the illness continuing to torment him, Kiyomori's attendants thought to provide some slight relief by pouring water over a board and laying him on it, but this appeared to do no good whatsoever. Moaning in desperation, he fell to the floor and there suffered his final agonies. The sound of horses and carriages rushing about seemed to echo to the heavens and to make the very earth tremble. Even if the sovereign of the realm himself, the lord of ten thousand chariots, had passed away, there could not have been a greater commotion.

Kiyomori had turned sixty-four this year. He thus was not particularly advanced in age. But the life span decreed him by his actions in previous existences had abruptly come to an end. Hence the large-scale ceremonies and secret ceremonies performed on his behalf by the Buddhist priests failed to have any effect; the gods and the Three Treasures of Buddhism[8] ceased to shed their light on him; and the benevolent deities withdrew their guardianship.

And if even divine help was beyond his reach, how little could mere human beings do! Although tens of thousands of loyal troops stationed themselves inside his mansion and in the grounds around it, all eager to sacrifice themselves and to die in his place, they could not, even for an instant, hold at bay the deadly devil of impermanence, whose form is invisible to the eye and whose power is invincible. Kiyomori went all alone to the Shide Mountains of death, from which there is no return; alone he faced the sky on his journey over the River of Three Crossings to the land of the Yellow Springs.[9] And when he arrived there, only the evil deeds he had committed in past days, transformed now into hell wardens, were there to greet him. All in all, it was a pitiful business.

Since further action could not be postponed, on the seventh day of the same month Kiyomori's remains were cremated at Otagi in the capital. The Buddhist priest Enjitsu placed the ashes in a bag hung around his neck and journeyed with them down to the province of Settsu, where he deposited them in a grave on Sutra Island.

Kiyomori's name had been known throughout the land of Japan, and his might had set men trembling. But in the end his body was no more than a puff of smoke ascending in the sky above the capital, and his remains, after tarrying a little while, in time mingled with the sands of the shore where they were buried, dwindling at last into empty dust.

FROM *BOOK SEVEN*

Summary With Kiyomori dead (1181), the Heike must depend for leader-ship on his feckless son Munemori. But cowardice and poor judgment are Munemori's most notable qualities, and the Heike position rapidly deteriorates. In the two years between the death of Kiyomori

---

8. That is, the Buddha, the Dharma (the Law or teachings of the Buddha), and the Sangha (the Buddhist spiritual community).
9. The Chinese underworld. The Shide Mountains were a range crossed by spirits of the dead on their way to Enma's court of judgment. The River of Three Crossings had to be forded by human spirits on the seventh day after death, and the worst sinners were required to use the deepest, most difficult crossing.

and the events of Book 7, the Heike troops fall back before the Genji on both northern and eastern fronts. When Heike troops attempt a last stand in the mountains of the north, they are taken by surprise and sent into a disastrous, headlong rout. The Genji leader Yoshinaka crushes a large Heike force and heads for the capital. He enlists the help of the powerful monks at Mount Hiei, northeast of Kyoto, who turns down the Heike's request for support. The Heike are forced to flee west with Emperor Antoku, still a child, and the imperial regalia. Retired Emperor GoShirakawa openly defects to the Genji and flees from the city in a different direction. Kiyomori's brother Tadanori, a refined man and gifted poet, has to leave the capital together with the doomed Heike. Knowing that he will soon meet his death, he returns once more to the capital in haste, to convey a final wish to his former poetry teacher.

Tadanori Leaves the Capital (7.16)

Taira no Tadanori, the governor of Satsuma, returned once more to the capital, although where he had been in the meantime is uncertain. Accompanied by five mounted warriors and a page, a party of seven horsemen in all, he rode along Gojō Avenue to the residence of Fujiwara no Shunzei.[1] The gate of Shunzei's mansion was closed and showed little sign of opening.

When Tadanori announced his name, there was a bustle inside the gate, and voices called out, "Those men who fled from the city have come back!" Tadanori dismounted from his horse and spoke in a loud voice. "There is no cause for alarm. I have come back merely because I have something I would like to say to His Lordship. You need not open the gate—if you could just have him come here a moment. . . ."

"I was expecting this," said Shunzei. "I'm sure he won't make any trouble—let him in."

The gate was opened and Shunzei confronted his caller, whose whole bearing conveyed an air of melancholy.

"You have been good enough to give me instruction for some years," said Tadanori, "and I hope I have not been entirely unworthy of your kindness. But the disturbances in the capital in the last two or three years and the uprisings in the provinces have deeply affected all the members of my clan. Although I have not intended in any way to neglect my poetry studies, I fear I have not been as attentive to you as I should have been.

"The emperor has already left the capital, and the fortunes of my family appear to have run out. I heard some time ago that you were going to compile an anthology of poetry at the request of the retired emperor.[2] I had hoped that, if you would be so kind as to give your assent, I might have perhaps one poem included in it in fulfillment of my lifelong hopes. But then these disorders descended on the world and the matter of the anthology had to be put aside, a fact that grieves me deeply.

1. A prominent poet and scholar (1114–1204), with whom Tadanori had studied poetry.
2. In 1183 Retired Emperor GoShirakawa had appointed Shunzei as chief compiler of the seventh imperial poetry anthology. These anthologies were the most prestigious venue for poets to gain reputation. (For selections from the first imperial poetry anthology, The Kokinshū, see above.)

"Should the state of the world become somewhat more settled, perhaps work on the anthology can be begun. I have here a scroll of poems. If in your kindness you could find even one of them to be worthy of inclusion, I will continue to rejoice long after I have gone to my grave and will forever be your guardian in the world beyond."

Reaching through the opening in his armor, Tadanori took out a scroll of poems and presented it to Lord Shunzei. From among the poems he had composed in recent years, he had selected some hundred or so that he thought were of superior quality and had brought them with him now that he was about to take final leave of the capital.

As Shunzei opened the scroll and looked at it, he said, "Since you see fit to leave me with this precious memento of your work, you may rest assured that I will not treat it lightly. Please have no doubts on that score. And that you should present it to me now, as a token of your deep concern for the art of poetry, makes the gesture more moving than ever—so much so that I can scarcely hold back the tears!"

Overjoyed at this response, Tadanori replied, "Perhaps I will find rest beneath the waves of the western ocean; perhaps my bones will be left to bleach on the mountain plain. Whatever may come, I can now take leave of this uncertain world without the least regret. And so I say good-bye!"

With these words he mounted his horse, knotted the cords of his helmet, and rode off toward the west. Shunzei stood gazing after until the figure had receded far into the distance. And then it seemed that he could hear Tadanori reciting in a voice loud enough to be heard from afar:

> Long is the journey before me—my thoughts race
> with the evening clouds over Wild Goose Mountain.

Deeply grieved at the parting, Shunzei wiped back the tears as he turned to reenter his house.

Later, after peace had been restored and Shunzei had begun compiling the anthology known as the *Senzaishū* [*The Collection of a Thousand Years*],[3] he recalled with deep emotion his farewell meeting with Tadanori and the words that the latter had spoken on that occasion. Among the poems that Tadanori had left behind were several that might have been included in the anthology. But since the anthology was being compiled by imperial command, Shunzei did not feel that he could refer to Tadanori by name. Instead, he selected one poem entitled "Blossoms in the Old Capital" and included it with the notation "author unknown." The poem read:

> In ruins now, the old capital of Shiga by the waves,
> yet the wild cherries of Nagara still bloom as before.[4]

Because Tadanori was among those branded as enemies of the sovereign, perhaps less might have been said about him. And yet there is great pathos in his story.

---

3. This imperial poetry collection was completed in 1188, after the fall of the Heike.
4. The poem refers to Ōmi, where Emperor Tenji had briefly built a capital and reigned from 668 to 671. For the earliest poem lamenting the fall of this ephemeral capital, and on the evanescence of things in general, see Kakinomoto no Hitomaro's poem, p. 1087 (from *The Man'yōshū*).

The Flight from Fukuhara (7.20)

Palace Minister Munemori and the other Heike leaders, with the exception of Lord Koremori, took their wives and children with them when they left the capital. But for persons of less exalted station, such a course of action was impossible. They had to leave behind all their loved ones, never knowing when they might meet again. Even when the time of reunion is fixed, when promises have been made to return on such-and-such a day, at such-and-such an hour, how long is the interval of waiting! How much harder was it, then, for these people, this day their last together, the hour of parting even now at hand—little wonder that those departing and those left behind alike should wet their sleeves with tears.

Some followed the Heike leaders because they recalled how for generations their families had served under them, others because they could not forget great kindnesses bestowed in more recent years or days. But whether young or old, now they had nothing but backward glances, barely able to tear themselves away. Some would go to spend their days on distant sea paths or sleep by wave-lapped beaches, others to journey far afield over steep mountain passes, whipping their horses onward, manning the rudders of their boats, each with his own thoughts, his own memories as he made his way in flight.

When Palace Minister Munemori arrived at Fukuhara,[5] the site of the former capital, he summoned the more important samurai who served under him, several hundred men both young and old, and addressed them as follows: "Blessings imparted to us through good deeds piled up in the past have now run out; misfortunes born of accumulated evil press down on us. And so the gods have turned against us, and the retired emperor has cast us aside. We have left the imperial city and now are travelers on the highway, with nowhere to turn.

"But they say that even those who lodge for one night beneath the same tree are bound by karma from a former existence and that those who dip water from the same stream do so because of deep ties from other lifetimes. And how much deeper are the ties in our case! You are no mere one-day sojourners at our gate but retainers who have served our family for generation after generation. Ties of kinship link some of us, making us anything but strangers; generations of service in other cases have forged profound bonds between us. The prosperity of our clan in past times brought wave after wave of bounty to you, enabling you to fulfill your personal needs. Now, should you not consider how best to repay that debt of gratitude? The emperor, who gained his throne through observance of the Ten Good Precepts[6] in a previous existence, has departed from the capital, taking with him the three imperial regalia.[7] Wherever he may venture, to what-

---

5. The present city of Kōbe. It served briefly as a capital during late 1180, when Kiyomori, who had an estate there, insisted on removing the government from Kyoto. The move met with strong opposition, including from some members of his own clan; this resistance, combined with the aggression of the Genji in the east, forced Kiyomori to return the capital to its traditional location.
6. The avoidance of killing, stealing, adultery, lying, duplicitous language, slandering, equivocating, coveting, anger, and false views.

7. Objects viewed as symbols of the emperor's legitimacy and authority: a strand of jewels, a mirror, and a sword. In the Japanese creation myth, the sun goddess is said to have conferred the three regalia on her grandson as he was about to descend to the Japanese islands, establishing the imperial line. Here, the young emperor carries with him the sword and the jewels. The mirror is at Ise, the Shinto shrine honoring the ancestral gods of the imperial family (where it is said to remain to this day).

ever faraway wilderness, to whatever remote mountain recess, should we not wait for and attend him?"

The warriors, young and old alike in tears, replied, "Even lowly birds and beasts know how to repay a debt of kindness and show gratitude to those who have favored them. Why, then, should we, who are human beings, not be aware of what duty demands? For twenty years and more you have looked after our wives and children and tended to the wants of your followers—we owe everything to our lord's beneficence. Moreover, we are fighting men, bearers of arms, trained to life in the saddle—would we not count it a disgrace to be double-hearted? Therefore, wherever the ruler may go, be it beyond Japan to the lands of Silla or Paekche, Koguryo, or Pohai,[8] to the end of the clouds or the end of the sea, we will never cease to attend him!"

In different voices but speaking with one intent, they made their declaration, and all the Heike lords seemed heartened by their response.

The Heike spent one night at Fukuhara, their former home. It was the beginning of autumn and the moon was a waning crescent. In the late hours of the night, when the moon had set, all was quiet, and in the travelers' beds, mere makeshifts of grass, tears mingled with the dew, for everything around them moved them to sadness.

Not knowing when they might return here again, they gazed about them at the various spots where the late prime minister Kiyomori had built his capital.

For spring there had been the Flower-Viewing Knoll, for autumn, the Moon-Viewing Strand. The Hall of the Bubbling Spring, the Pine-Shaded Hall, the Riding Ground Hall, the two-story Viewing Stand Hall, the Snow-Viewing Palace, the Reed-Thatched Palace, the mansions of the nobles, the Temporary Imperial Palace built on orders from Lord Kunitsuna[9]—their roof tiles in the shape of mandarin ducks, their terraces of precious stone—all had in the course of three years fallen into ruin. Old moss covered the pathways, autumn grasses blocked the gates. Pine seedlings sprouted from the roof tiles, vines had overgrown the walls. Tall buildings leaned to one side, encrusted with moss; only pine winds passed there now. Window blinds had rotted away, leaving the sleeping rooms exposed to view, but only the moon looked in.

When dawn came, the Heike set fire to the imperial palace at Fukuhara, and Emperor Antoku and those accompanying him all took to the boats. Even though their departure was perhaps not as painful as that when they left the capital, it nevertheless filled them with regret.

The evening smoke rising up from the seaweed fires of the fisherfolk, the dawn cries of deer on the hillcrest, the sound of the waves washing ashore in cove after cove, the moon reflected in the tears on their sleeves, the crickets chirping in a thousand autumn grasses—all that they saw, all that they heard seemed to overwhelm them with feeling, leaving nothing that did not wound their spirits.

The more than one hundred thousand horsemen who only yesterday had set out bridle to bridle from the foot of Ōsaka Barrier today were a mere seven thousand souls casting off their mooring lines amid the waves of the western

8. Various parts of the Korean Peninsula and northeastern China.
9. Fujiwara Kunitsuna, a close supporter of the Taira, whose son Kiyokuni was adopted by Kiyomori. He was a member of the emperor's cabinet, or the council of state, ranking just below the three ministers of state.

ocean. The cloud-strewn sea was calm and still now, the bright day drawing to a close. The lone islands were veiled in evening mist, and the moon's rays floated on the water.

Cleaving the waves of distant inlets, drawn on by sea tides as they sped forward, the boats seemed to mount the clouds in mid-sky. By now the capital was even farther away than the clouds, so many were the mountains and rivers that had come between. "What a long way we've journeyed!" they thought, and there was no end to their tears.

Spying a flock of white birds resting on the waves, they exclaimed, "Ah yes! Ariwara no Narihira saw birds like these on the Sumida River and asked what they were called." They were called "capital birds,"[1] a name to stir sad memories in all who heard it.

The Heike departed from the capital on the twenty-fifth day of the Seventh Month, in the second year of the Juei era [1183].[2]

FROM BOOK NINE

Summary   In the capital, a new emperor has acceded to the throne to replace the child sovereign Antoku, whom the Heike took along. And Yoritomo, for his part, has gained both increased power and a certain legitimacy; Retired Emperor GoShirakawa has conferred on him the title of shogun (short for sei-i-tai shōgun, "barbarian-subduing commander").

Meanwhile, the Heike have regrouped along the Inland Sea, back in an area they have controlled for a century and flush with confidence. With the panic of the retreat behind them, they throw up defenses along the coast, secure control of the entrances to the Inland Sea, recruit supporters, and prepare to retake the capital.

The Attack from the Cliff (9.12)

After this, the other Genji warriors charged into the fray, the Chichibu, the Ashikaga, the Miura, the Kamakura, and the Inomata, Kodama, Noiyo, Yokoyama, Nishitō, Tsuzukitō, and Shinotō leagues, until all the Genji and Heike forces had closed in combat. The two sides repeatedly dashed into each other's ranks, calling out their names back and forth, shouting and clamoring until the hills resounded with their cries, the din of their charging horses echoing like thunder. The arrows whizzing back and forth resembled nothing so

---

1. A reference to a poem in *The Kokinshū* by Ariwara no Narihira (825–880), a famous poet and lover (and later a model for Prince Genji in *The Tale of Genji*), which came to embody the courtier's nostalgia for the capital. The poem is accompanied by the following headnote: "When they reached the bank of the Sumida River, which flows between the provinces of Musashi and Shimōsa, they were miserably homesick for the capital. They dismounted and stood for a time on the bank, thinking, 'How very far we have come!' The ferryman interrupted their laments. 'Come aboard quickly; it's getting late.' They got into the boat and prepared to cross, all in wretched spirits, for there was not one among them who had not left someone dear to him in the city. A white bird with a red bill and red legs chanced to be frolicking near the river. Since it was a species unknown in the capital, none of them could identify it. 'What kind of bird is that?' they asked the ferryman. 'A capital-bird, of course,' he replied with an air of surprise. Then Narihira recited this poem. "If you are in truth / what your name seems to make you, / I will put to you, / capital-bird, this question: / do things go well with my love?"
2. The short reign of the child emperor Antoku.

much as torrents of rain. Some warriors, a wounded comrade on their backs, struggled to make their way toward the rear; others, despite being wounded, continued to fight while the mortally wounded fell dead where they were. Men rode side by side, grappling together and slashing at each other until one delivered a fatal stab to the other. Some held their foe down while they cut off his head; others, pinned down, had their heads lopped off in a like manner. Neither side revealed any weakness that its attackers could turn to advantage, and the Genji forces through their frontal attack alone did not seem to be able to gain victory.

Meanwhile, Yoshitsune had circled around to the rear and by dawn of the seventh day had climbed up to the region of Hiyodori Pass, preparing to swoop down on the Heike position at Ichi-no-tani. Just then, two stags and a doe, perhaps startled by the Genji horsemen, fled downhill in the direction of the Heike stronghold at Ichi-no-tani.

Catching sight of them, the Heike soldiers in the fort below exclaimed excitedly, "All the deer around here must have been so frightened of us that they fled far off into the mountains. That these deer would deliberately come toward a large force like ours seems highly peculiar! It must mean that the Genji are getting ready to charge down on us from above!"

Takechi Kiyonori, a man from Iyo Province, came forward. "Whatever it means," he said, "if they come from the direction of the enemy, we shouldn't let them by!" and he proceeded to fell the two stags with his bow and arrows, though he let the doe get away.

"What's the good of your shooting at deer!" objected Moritoshi of Etchū. "With just one of those arrows, you could have held off ten of the enemy. Killing is a sin to begin with, and then you waste arrows!" he grumbled.

Yoshitsune looked down over the Heike stronghold in the distance. "Try sending some of the horses down," he ordered. A few of the saddled horses were accordingly sent galloping down the slope. Some broke their legs and fell along the way, but others managed to reach the bottom without mishap. Three of them pulled up near the roof of Etchū Moritoshi's encampment and stood there trembling with fright.

Observing this, Yoshitsune announced, "If the riders are careful enough, the horses can get down without injury. Look lively, now—I'll show you how it's done!" Leading a force of thirty horsemen, he plummeted down the slope. The rest of the force followed, the incline so steep that the stirrups of the men in the rear clattered against the armor and helmets of those ahead of them. The ground was sandy, with scatterings of small rocks and stones, so that the riders fairly slid down for a distance of some seven hundred feet until they reached a shelflike stretch that halted their fall.

Peering down below, they could see only huge moss-shrouded rocks, a sheer drop of some hundred and forty or fifty feet. No way to go back where they had come from, no way to go forward that they could see, the men were utterly baffled, exclaiming, "This is the end!"

Just then, Sawara Yoshitsura came forward. "In Miura where I come from, we think nothing of galloping day and night over places like this just to get at a bird on the wing. This is a Miura-style racecourse!" he declared and led the way by plunging down the slope. The rest of the men followed. "Ei! Ei!" they cried in muffled voices, encouraging their horses on, the descent so terrifying that they kept their eyes closed as they went down. It seemed a feat impossible for mere human beings to accomplish, instead a performance by devils or spirits.

Halfway down, they began calling out their battle cries, and as the voices of the three thousand horsemen[3] came echoing back from the surrounding hills, they sounded like the shouts of one hundred thousand.

The men under Murakami Yasukuni began setting fires and before long had burned down all the Heike barracks and makeshift buildings. By chance, a strong wind was blowing and black smoke billowed through the air, throwing the Heike soldiers into such panic that they scrambled toward the beaches fronting the encampment, certain that in that direction lay their only hope for escape.

A number of boats were drawn up in readiness along the shore, but the fleeing troops were in such haste to board them that at times four or five hundred or even a thousand men, all fully armed, struggled to get into a single boat, impossible as that was. After advancing no more than three hundred and fifty yards from shore, three large vessels sank before the eyes of the onlookers.

Thereafter, the order went out: "Persons of rank are to be allowed aboard, underlings are not!" and swords and halberds were used to enforce it. But even after the order became known, men continued to cling to the boats that refused to take them, trying to climb aboard. As a result, a hand was cut off here, an arm severed at the elbow there, until the waters along the Ichi-no-tani shore turned crimson and the bodies floated side by side.

The Heike warrior Noritsune, the governor of Noto, had fought many battles and had never once been defeated, but what must have been his thoughts now? Mounted on his steed Usuguro, Gray Black, he fled westward. At the Akashi shore in Harima he boarded a boat and made his way across the straits to Yashima in Sanuki.[4]

The Death of Tadanori (9.14)

Taira no Tadanori, the governor of Satsuma, served as commanding general of the western flank at the battle of Ichi-no-tani. Dressed in a battle robe of dark blue brocade and armor laced with black silk, he rode a sturdy black horse fitted with a lacquer saddle flecked with gold. Surrounded by some hundred horsemen under his command, he was retiring from the engagement in a calm and unhurried manner, halting his horse now and then to parry with one of the enemy.

Okabe no Rokuyata, a member of the Inomata group of Genji warriors, spotted Tadanori and galloped after him in pursuit, urging his horse forward with spurs and whip and shouting, "Who goes there? Declare your name!"

"I'm a friend!" replied Tadanori, but as he turned to speak, he revealed enough of his face to make it apparent that his teeth were blackened.[5]

"Ha!" thought Rokuyata. "No one on our side looks like that! This must be one of the Taira lords." Overtaking Tadanori, he began to grapple with him. On

3. A good example of how the tale exaggerates for dramatic effect. Historical evidence suggests that Yoshitsune had about 100 men with him.

4. On the island of Shikoku, across the Inland Sea from Ichi-no-tani.

5. Identifying Tadanori as a noble and one of the Heike.

seeing this, the hundred horsemen under Tadanori, fighting men recruited from other provinces, fled as fast as they could, not one of them coming to his aid.

"Wretch!" exclaimed Tadanori. "You should have believed me when I said I was a friend!" Brought up in Kumano, a powerful man trained to act with lightning speed, Tadanori drew his sword and struck three blows at Rokuyata, two while the latter was still seated in the saddle and a third after he had unhorsed him. The first two glanced off Rokuyata's armor and did no harm. The third pierced his face, though not with sufficient force to kill him.

Tadanori pinned his attacker to the ground and was about to cut off his head when Rokuyata's page, rushing up from behind, drew his long sword and with one blow cut off Tadanori's arm at the elbow.

Tadanori realized this was the end. "Give me time enough for ten invocations of the Buddha!" he said. Gripping Rokuyata, he flung him a bow's length to the side. Then he faced west and, in a loud voice, recited these words: "His bright light illumines the worlds in the ten directions. Without fail He gathers up all living beings who recite His name!" He had scarcely concluded his recitation when Rokuyata approached from behind and struck off his head.

Rokuyata felt that the man had died like a true commanding general, but he still did not know his name. He found a slip of paper fastened to Tadanori's quiver, however, on which was written a poem entitled "On a Journey, Lodging Beneath the Blossoms." It read:

> Evening drawing on, I'll take lodging in the shade of this tree,
> and make its blossoms my host for the night.

The poem was signed "Tadanori."

Having thus learned who his opponent was, Rokuyata impaled the head on the tip of his long sword and, lifting it high up, declared in a loud voice, "You have heard much these days of this Taira lord, the governor of Satsuma—I, Okabe no Rokuyata Tadazumi, have killed him!"

When they heard Tadanori's name, the Taira and Genji warriors alike exclaimed, "What a pity! A man skilled both in arms and the practice of poetry, a true commanding general!" And there were none who did not wet their sleeve with tears.

The Death of Atsumori (9.16)

The Heike had lost the battle. "Those Taira lords will be heading for the shore in hopes of making their getaway by boat!" thought Kumagae Naozane to himself. "Fine! I'll go look for one of their generals to grapple with!" and he turned his horse in the direction of the beach.

As he did so, he spotted a lone warrior riding into the sea, making for the boats in the offing. He was wearing a battle robe of finely woven silk embroidered in a crane design, armor of light green lacing, and a horned helmet. He carried a sword with gilt fittings and a quiver whose arrows were fledged with black and white eagle feathers and held a rattan-wound bow in his hand. He was seated in a gold-rimmed saddle, astride a gray horse with white markings.

The lone warrior's horse had swum out about two hundred feet from the shore when Kumagae, waving with his fan, called out, "Ho there, General! I see you. Don't shame yourself by showing your back to an enemy. Come back!"

The rider, acknowledging the call, turned toward the beach. As he was about to ride up out of the waves, Kumagae drew alongside and grappled with him, dragging him from his horse. Pinning him down so as to cut off his head, Kumagae pushed aside his helmet. The face he saw was that of a young man of sixteen or seventeen, lightly powdered and with blackened teeth.

Gazing at the boy's handsome face, Kumagae realized that he was just the age of his own son Kojirō, and he could not bring himself to use his sword. "Who are you? Tell me your name and I'll let you go!" he said.

"Who are you?" asked the young man.

"No one of great importance—Kumagae Naozane of the province of Musashi."

"Then there's no need for me to tell you my name," the young man replied. "I'm worthy enough to be your opponent. When you take my head, ask someone who I am—they will know all right!"

"Spoken like a true general!" thought Kumagae. "But simply killing this one man can't change defeat into victory or victory into defeat. When my son Kojirō has even a slight injury, how much I worry about him! Just think how this boy's father will grieve when he hears that he's been killed! If only I could spare him."

But as he glanced quickly behind him, he saw some fifty Genji horsemen under Toi and Kajiwara coming toward him. Fighting back the tears, he said, "I'd like to let you go, but our forces are everywhere in sight—you could never get away. Rather than fall into someone else's hands, it's better that I kill you. I'll see that prayers are said for your salvation in the life to come."

"Just take my head and be quick about it!" the boy said.

Kumagae was so overcome with pity that he did not know where to strike. His eyes seemed to dim, his wits to desert him, and for a moment he hardly knew where he was. But then he realized that, for all his tears, no choice was left him, and he struck off the boy's head.

"We men who bear arms—how wretched is our lot!" he said. "If I had not been born of a warrior family, would I ever have faced a task like this? What a terrible thing I have done!" Again and again, he repeated the words as he raised his sleeve to brush the tears from his face.

After some time, aware that he must get on with the business, he removed the boy's armor and battle robe and wrapped the head in them. As he was doing so, he noticed a brocade bag with a flute in it that had been fastened to the boy's waist. "Ah, how pitiful!" he said. "Those people I heard at dawn this morning playing music in the enemy stronghold—he must have been one of them! Among all the ten thousand troops from the eastern provinces fighting on our side, is there anyone who carries a flute with him into battle? These highborn people—how gentle and refined they are!"

Later, when Kumagae's battle trophies were presented to Yoshitsune for inspection, there were none among the company who did not weep at the sight.

It was subsequently learned that the young man slain by Kumagae was Atsumori, the seventeen-year-old son of the master of the Palace Repair Office, Taira no Tsunemori. From that time onward, Kumagae's desire to become a Buddhist monk grew even stronger. The flute in question had been presented by Retired Emperor Toba to Atsumori's grandfather, Tadamori, who was a skilled player. From him it had been passed down to the son, Tsunemori, and in turn had been given to Atsumori because of his marked aptitude for the instrument. It was known by the name Saeda, Little Branch.

It is moving to think that for all their exaggerated phrases and flowery embellishments, even music and the arts can in the end lead a man to praise the Buddha way.

FROM BOOK ELEVEN

Summary The final battle comes in 1185. The bulk of the Heike have gone no farther than several miles across the Inland Sea, to the island of Shikoku, when Yoshitsune strikes, and once again takes the Heike by surprise. With a mere hundred men in a few small boats and a storm brewing windward, the tactical genius braves the gale, making the daring calculation that it will carry them across before the enemy notices. The move is inspired, for the Heike expect an attack in fair weather. And the foul weather enables the Genji to make record time; what is normally a three-day crossing is over in six hours. Yoshitsune and his men hit land on the eastern side of the island. The enemy camp is above them, to the north. The small force rides through the night, again in record time, and surprises the Heike at daybreak. Yoshitsune lights fires to suggest a much larger expedition. Seeing the hills ablaze to their rear and the enemy approaching, the Heike, awaiting a frontal attack from the sea, assume they are outnumbered, and rush to their ships and abandon the island. On board the ships are Kiyomori's hapless son, Munemori; Kiyomori's widow, the Nun of Second Rank; their daughter, Kenreimon'in; and their grandson, the child emperor Antoku.

The Drowning of the Former Emperor (11.9)

By this time the Genji warriors had succeeded in boarding the Heike boats, shooting dead the sailors and helmsmen with their arrows or cutting them down with their swords. The bodies lay heaped in the bottom of the boats, and there was no longer anyone to keep the boats on course.

Taira no Tomomori boarded a small craft and made his way to the vessel in which the former emperor was riding. "This is what the world has come to!" he exclaimed. "Have all these unsightly things thrown into the sea!" Then he began racing from prow to stern, sweeping, mopping, dusting, and attempting with his own hands to put the boat into proper order.

"How goes the battle, Lord Tomomori?" asked the emperor's ladies-in-waiting, pressing him with questions.

"You'll have a chance to see some splendid gentlemen from the eastern region!" he replied with a cackling laugh.

"How can you joke at a time like this!" they protested, their voices joined in a chorus of shrieks and wails.

Observing the situation and evidently having been prepared for some time for such an eventuality, the Nun of the Second Rank, the emperor's grandmother, slipped a two-layer nun's robe over her head and tied her glossed silk trousers high at the waist. She placed the sacred jewel, one of the three imperial regalia, under her arm, thrust the sacred sword in her sash, and took the child emperor in her arms. "I may be a mere woman, but I have no intention of falling into the hands of the enemy! I will accompany my lord. All those of you who are resolved to fulfill your duty by doing likewise, quickly follow me!" So saying, she strode to the side of the boat.

The emperor had barely turned eight but had the bearing of someone much older than that. The beauty of his face and form seemed to radiate all around him. His shimmering black hair fell down the length of his back.

Startled and confused, he asked, "Grandma, where are you going to take me?"

Gazing at his innocent face and struggling to hold back her tears, the nun replied, "Don't you understand? In your previous life you were careful to observe the ten good rules of conduct,[6] and for that reason you were reborn in this life as a ruler of ten thousand chariots. But now evil entanglements have you in their power, and your days of good fortune have come to an end.

"First," she told him tearfully, "you must face east and bid farewell to the goddess of the Grand Shrine at Ise.[7] Then you must turn west and trust in Amida Buddha to come with his hosts to greet you and lead you to his Pure Land. Come now, turn your face to the west and recite the invocation of the Buddha's name.[8] This far-off land of ours is no bigger than a millet seed, a realm of sorrow and adversity. Let us leave it now and go together to a place of rejoicing, the paradise of the Pure Land!"

Dressed in a dove gray robe, his hair now done in boyish loops on either side of his head, the child, his face bathed in tears, pressed his small hands together, knelt down, and bowed first toward the east, taking his leave of the deity of the Ise Shrine. Then he turned toward the west and began chanting the *nenbutsu*, the invocation of Amida's name. The nun then took him in her arms. Comforting him, she said, "There's another capital down there beneath the waves!" So they plunged to the bottom of the thousand-fathom sea.

How pitiful that the spring winds of impermanence should so abruptly scatter the beauty of the blossoms; how heartless that the rough waves of reincarnation should engulf this tender body! Long Life is the name they give to the imperial palace, signaling that one should reside there for years unending; its gates are dubbed Ageless, a term that speaks of a reign forever young. Yet before he had reached the age of ten, this ruler ended as refuse on the ocean floor.

Ten past virtues rewarded with a throne, yet how fleeting was that prize! He who once was a dragon among the clouds now had become a fish in the depths of the sea. Dwelling once on terraces lofty as those of the god Brahma, in palaces like the Joyful Sight Citadel of the god Indra,[9] surrounded by great lords and ministers of state, a throng of kin and clansmen in his following, now in an instant ended his life beneath this boat, under these billows—sad, sad indeed!

---

6. That is, the ten commandments of Buddhism (see p. 1296, n. 6). The reward for adhering to these precepts is, rebirth in one of the Buddhist heavens or, for those whose fidelity is less than complete, rebirth in the human realm.
7. Where the ancestral gods of the imperial family are enshrined.

8. The Amida Buddha is revered as the ruler of the Pure Land, or Western Paradise, into which those who believe in him and recite his name are reborn.
9. A Buddhist deity who dwells on a lofty peak towering at the center of every world and battles pugnacious demons living by the sea. "Brahma": a Hindu god of creation.

The Imperial Lady Becomes a Nun (1)

Kenreimon'in took up residence in the Yoshida area, at the foot of the eastern hills, in a small hermitage belonging to a Buddhist monk of Nara named Kyōe. No one had lived there for many years, and the hut had fallen into disrepair. The garden was buried in weeds, and wild ferns sprouted by the eaves. The blinds had rotted away, leaving the sleeping room exposed to view and offering little shelter from the wind or rain. Although blossoms of one kind and another opened in season, no occupant was present to admire them; and although the moonlight streamed in night after night, no one sat up until dawn delighting in it.

In earlier times, Kenreimon'in had rested on a jeweled dais, brocade hangings surrounding her, but now, parted from all those who had meant anything to her, she resided in this shabby, half-decayed retreat. One can only surmise how forlorn her thoughts must have been. She was like a fish stranded on land, a bird that has been torn from its nest. Such was her present life that she recalled with longing those earlier days when her home had been no more than a boat tossing on the waves. Her thoughts, journeying far away over blue-billowed waters, rested once again on the distant clouds of the western sea. In her reed-thatched hut deep in moss, she wept to see the moonlight fill her garden by the eastern hills. Truly, no words can convey her sadness.

On the first day of the Fifth Month in the first year of the Bunji era [1185], Imperial Lady Kenreimon'in took the tonsure and became a nun.[1] The priest who administered the precepts to her was the Reverend Insei of Chōrakuji. In return she made an offering to him of an informal robe that had belonged to her son, the late emperor Antoku. He had worn the robe until his final days, and it still retained the fragrance of his body. She had brought it all the way with her when she returned to the capital from the western region, regarding it as a last memento of her child, and had supposed that whatever might come, she would never part with it. But since she had nothing else to serve as a gift, she offered it with a profusion of tears, hopeful that at the same time it might help her son attain buddhahood.

The Reverend Insei could find no words with which to acknowledge the offering but, wetting the black sleeves of his clerical robe, made his way from the room in tears. It is said that he had the robe remade into a holy banner to hang in front of the Buddha of Chōrakuji.

By imperial order when she was fifteen, Kenreimon'in had been appointed to serve in the palace, and when she was sixteen, she advanced to the position of imperial consort, attending at the emperor's side. At dawn she urged him to look to the official business of the court; when evening came she was his sole companion for the night. At the age of twenty-two she bore him a son, who was designated as the heir apparent, and when he ascended the throne she was honored with the palace appellation of Kenreimon'in.

Because she was not only the daughter of the lay priest and prime minister Kiyomori but the mother of the nation's ruler as well, she was held in the highest

---

1. The events of Kenreimon'in's last years, which constitute "The Initiates' Book," overlap with those of the preceding books.

respect by everyone in the realm. At the time of which we are speaking, she had reached the age of twenty-nine. Her complexion retained the freshness of peach or damson petals; her face had not lost its lotuslike beauty. But hair ornaments of kingfisher feathers were no longer of any use to her, for her hair had been shorn; her whole figure had suffered a change.

Despairing of this fickle world, Kenreimon'in had entered the true path of religion, but this had by no means brought an end to her sighs. While she could still recall how those she loved had sunk beneath the waves, the figure of her son, the late emperor, and her mother, the Nun of the Second Rank, remained to haunt her memory. She wondered why her own dewdrop existence had continued for so long, why she had lived on only to see such painful sights, and her tears flowed without end. Short as the Fifth Month nights were, she found them almost too long to endure, and since sleep was, by the nature of things, denied her, she could not hope to recapture the past even in her dreams. The lamp, its back to the wall, gave only a flicker of dying light, yet all night she lay awake listening to the mournful pelting of rain at the dark window.[2] The Shang-yang lady, imprisoned in Shangyang Palace, had endured similarly mournful nights, but her grief could hardly have been greater than Kenreimon'in's.

Perhaps to remind himself of the past, the previous owner of the retreat had planted an orange tree by the eaves,[3] and its blossoms now wafted their poignant fragrance on the breeze, while a cuckoo from the hills, lighting there, sang out two or three notes. Kenreimon'in, remembering an old poem, wrote the words on the lid of her inkstone box:

> Cuckoo, you come singing, tracing the orange tree's scent—
> is it because you yearn for someone now gone?

The ladies-in-waiting who had once attended her, but lacked the strength of character needed to drown themselves on the sea bottom as had the Nun of the Second Rank or the Third-Rank Lady of Echizen,[4] had been taken prisoner by the rough hands of the Genji warriors. Returned now to the capital where they had once lived, young and old alike had become nuns, their aspect wholly changed, their purpose in life utterly vanished. In remote valleys, among rocky cliffs, sites they had never even dreamed of in the past, they passed their days. The houses where they had dwelled before all had disappeared with the smoke of battle; mere traces of them remained, little by little overgrown with grasses of the field. No familiar figures came there anymore. They must have felt as desolate as those men in the Chinese tale who, having spent what they thought

---

2. A paraphrase from the poem "The White-Haired Lady of Shangyang" by Bo Juyi (772–846), a Chinese poet among the most popular in Japan. In "The Song of Lasting Regret," included in this volume, Bo Juyi tells the story of the tragic love between the Tang Emperor Xuanzong and his most beloved consort, Prized Consort Yang, who was executed before his eyes during a rebellion; the poem alluded to here focuses on one of the many ladies in the imperial harem who were forced to retire to the Shangyang Palace when Prized Consort Yang began to monopolize Emperor Xuanzong's affections.

3. An allusion to a poem in *The Kokinshū*: "Scenting the fragrance / of orange blossoms that await / the Fifth Month's coming, / I recall a perfumed sleeve / worn by someone long ago."

4. Who committed suicide after hearing of the death of her husband Michimori, Kiyo-mori's nephew.

was a mere half day in the realm of the immortals, returned to their old home to confront their seventh-generation descendants.[5]

And then, on the ninth day of the Seventh Month,[6] a severe earthquake toppled the tile-capped mud wall and rendered Kenreimon'in's dwelling, already dilapidated, even more ruinous and unsound, so that it was hardly fit for habitation. Worse off than the lady of Shangyang Palace, Kenreimon'in had no green-robed guard to stand at her gate. The hedges, now left untended, were laden with more dew than the lush meadow grasses, and insects, making themselves at home there, had already begun crying out their doleful chorus of complaints. As the fall nights grew longer, Kenreimon'in found herself more wakeful than ever, the hours passing with intolerable slowness. To the endless memories that haunted her were now added the sorrows of the autumn season, until it was almost more than she could bear. Since her whole world had undergone such drastic change, no one was left who might offer her so much as a passing word of consolation, no one to whom she might look for support.

The Move to Ōhara (2)

Although such was the case, the wives of the Reizei senior counselor, Takafusa, and of Lord Nobutaka, Kenreimon'in's younger sisters, while shunning public notice, managed to call on her in private. "In the old days I would never have dreamed that I might sometime be beholden to them for support!" exclaimed the imperial lady, moved to tears by their visit, and all the ladies in attendance shed tears as well.

The place where Kenreimon'in was living was not far from the capital, and the bustling road leading past it was full of prying eyes. She could not help feeling that fragile as her existence might be, mere dew before the wind, she might better live it out in some more remote mountain setting where distressing news of worldly affairs was less likely to reach her. She had been unable to find a suitable location, however, when a certain lady who had called on her mentioned that the Buddhist retreat known as Jakkō-in in the mountains of Ōhara was a very quiet spot.

A mountain village may be lonely, she thought to herself, recalling an old poem on the subject, but it is a better place to dwell than among the world's troubles and sorrows.[7] Having thus determined to move, she found that her sister, the wife of Lord Takafusa, could probably arrange for a palanquin and other necessities. Accordingly, in the first year of the Bunji era, as the Ninth Month was drawing to a close, she set off for the Jakkō-in in Ōhara.

As Kenreimon'in passed along the road, observing the hues of the autumn leaves on the trees all around her, she soon found the day coming to a close, perhaps all the sooner because she was entering the shade of the mountains.

5. In this legend, a traveler who spent half a year in the enchanted cottage of a mountain nymph returns home to find that his sons are dead and six generations have passed.
6. About six months after the Heike are defeated. Since spirits of the dead were held capable of returning to wreak havoc on the liv-

ing, it is widely assumed that this great earthquake is the Heike's revenge.
7. With a slight alteration, she quotes a poem in The Kokinshū: "It is true enough / that a mountain hermitage / offers small comfort, / yet life is far better there / than in the vexatious world."

The tolling of the evening bell from a temple in the fields sounded its somber note, and dew from the grasses along the way made her sleeves, already damp with tears, wetter than ever. A stormy wind began to blow, tumbling the leaves from the trees; the sky clouded over; and autumn showers began to fall. She could just catch the faint sad belling of a deer, and the half-audible lamentations of the insects. Everything contrived to fill her with a sense of desolation difficult to describe in words. Even in those earlier days, when her life had been a precarious journey from one cove or one island to another, she reflected sadly, she had never had such a feeling of hopelessness.

The retreat was in a lonely spot of moss-covered crags, the sort of place, she felt, where she could live out her days. As she looked about her, she noted that the bush clover in the dew-filled garden had been stripped of its leaves by frost, that the chrysanthemums by the hedge, past their prime, were faded and dry—all reflecting, it seemed, her own condition. Making her way to where the statue of the Buddha was enshrined, she said a prayer: "May the spirit of the late emperor attain perfect enlightenment; may he quickly gain the wisdom of the buddhas!" But even as she did so, the image of her dead son seemed to appear before her, and she wondered in what future existence she might be able to forget him.[8]

Next to the Jakkō-in she had a small building erected, ten feet square in size, with one room to sleep in and the other to house the image of the Buddha. Morning and evening, day and night, she performed her devotions in front of the image, ceaselessly intoning the Buddha's name over the long hours. In this way, always diligent, she passed the months and days.

On the fifteenth day of the Tenth Month, as evening was approaching, Kenreimon'in heard the sound of footsteps on the dried oak leaves that littered the garden. "Who could be coming to call at a place so far removed from the world as this?" she said, addressing her woman companion. "Go see who it is. If it is someone I should not see, I must hurry to take cover!" But when the woman went to look, she found that it was only a stag that had happened to pass by.

"Who was it?" asked Kenreimon'in, to which her companion, Lady Dainagon no Suke,[9] struggling to hold back her tears, replied with this poem:

> Who would tread a path to this rocky lair?
> It was a deer whose passing rustled the leaves of the oak.

Struck by the pathos of the situation, Kenreimon'in carefully inscribed the poem on the small sliding panel by her window.

During her drab and uneventful life, bitter as it was, she found many things that provided food for thought. The trees ranged before the eaves of her retreat suggested to her the seven rows of jewel-laden trees that are said to grow in the Western Paradise, and the water pooled in a crevice in the rocks brought to mind the wonderful water of eight blessings[1] to be found there. Spring blossoms, so easily scattered with the breeze, taught her a lesson in impermanence:

---

8. These two paragraphs in effect offer a digest of the conventional autumn imagery in classical Japanese poetry.
9. One of Emperor Antoku's nurses and a lady-in-waiting to Kenreimon'in.
1. According to one of the Buddhist sutras, a pond in the Pure Land has waters that possess eight virtues: purity, coolness, sweetness, softness, luster, peace, healing, and growth. The sutra also notes that paradise, or the Pure Land, is ringed with seven rows of trees having gold roots, copper-gilt trunks, white-gold branches, agate twigs, coral leaves, moonstone blossoms, and pearl fruit.

the autumn moon, so quickly hidden by its companion clouds, spoke of the transience of life. Those court ladies in the Zhaoyang Hall in China who admired the blossoms at dawn soon saw their petals blown away by the wind; those in the Changqiu Palace[2] who gazed at the evening moon had its brightness stolen from them by clouds. Once in the past, this lady too had lived in similar splendor, reclining on brocade bedclothes in chambers of gold and jade, and now in a hut of mere brushwood and woven vines—even strangers must weep for her.

Summary   After Kenreimon'in has lived in her hermitage for about half a year, Retired Emperor GoShirakawa decides to visit her. The journey to the mountain recesses of the little temple known as Jakkō-in proves arduous. The royal entourage, modestly limited to some dozen nobles, makes its way through the thick summer wilderness. When they come on the humble cottage, where the only visitors have been monkeys swinging in the trees, the retired emperor is astonished; and when Kenreimon'in descends from the mountain, where she has gone to pick wildflowers, GoShirakawa at first does not even recognize her. Tearfully, they reminisce, as the thoughts of better days rush in upon them. And then, in an incredible passage of just a few paragraphs, Kenreimon'in relives all the horrid experiences of her clan, which the tale has spent hundreds of pages chronicling. Neither Kenreimon'in nor the retired emperor can quite believe how the world has changed, how the fortunate have fallen. When she finishes, it is time for the ex-emperor to leave.

The Death of the Imperial Lady (5)

While they were speaking, the bell of the Jakkō-in sounded, signaling the close of the day, and the sun sank beyond the western hills. The retired emperor, reluctant though he was to leave, wiped away his tears and prepared to begin the journey back.

All her memories of the past brought back to her once more, Kenreimon'in could scarcely stem the flood of tears with her sleeve. She stood watching as the imperial entourage set out for the capital, watching until it was far in the distance. Then she turned to the image of the Buddha and, speaking through her tears, uttered this prayer: "May the spirit of the late emperor and the souls of all my clanspeople who perished attain complete and perfect enlightenment: may they quickly gain the wisdom of the Buddhas!"

In the past she had faced eastward with this petition: "Great Deity of the Grand Shrine of Ise and Great Bodhisattva Hachiman, may the Son of Heaven be blessed with most wonderful longevity, may he live a thousand autumns, ten thousand years!" But now she changed direction and, facing west with palms pressed together, in sorrow spoke these words: "May the souls of all those who have perished find their way to Amida's Pure Land!"

On the sliding panel of her sleeping room she had inscribed the following poems:

> When did my heart learn such ways?
> Of late I think so longingly of palace companions I once knew!

2. Two residences where the Chinese emperor's consorts lived during the Han Dynasty (206 B.C.E.–220 C.E.); the Chinese names impart a faded grandeur, and the characters with which they are written—the Brilliant Sun Pavilion (Zhaoyang Hall) and the Palace of Long Autumn [Nights] (Changqiu Palace)—enhance the poetic touch of the sentence.

> The past, too, has vanished like a dream—
> my days by this brushwood door cannot be long in number!

The following poem is reported to have been inscribed on a pillar of Kenreimon'in's retreat by Minister of the Left Sanesada, one of the officials who accompanied the retired emperor on his visit:

> You who in past times were likened to the moon—
> dwelling now deep in these faraway mountains, a light no longer
>   shining—

Once, when Kenreimon'in was bathed in tears, overwhelmed by memories of the past and thoughts of the future, she heard the cry of a mountain cuckoo and wrote this poem:

> Come then, cuckoo, let us compare tears–
> I too do nothing but cry out in a world of pain

The Taira warriors who survived the Dan-no-ura hostilities and were taken prisoner were paraded through the main streets of the capital and then either beheaded or sent into exile far from their wives and children. With the exception of Taira no Yorimori,[3] not one escaped execution or was permitted to remain in the capital.

With regard to the forty or more Taira wives, no special punitive measures were taken—they were left to join their relatives or to seek aid from persons they had known in the past. But even those fortunate enough to find themselves seated within sumptuous hangings were not spared the winds of uncertainty, and those who ended in humble brushwood dwellings could not live free of dust and turmoil. Husbands and wives who had slept pillow to pillow now found themselves at the far ends of the sky. Parents and children who had nourished each other no longer even knew each other's whereabouts. Although their loving thoughts never for a moment ceased, lament as they might, they had somehow to endure these things.

And all of this came about because the lay priest and prime minister Taira no Kiyomori, holding the entire realm within the four seas in the palm of his hand, showed no respect for the ruler above or the slightest concern for the masses of common people below. He dealt out sentences of death or exile in any fashion that suited him, took no heed of how the world or those in it might view his actions—and this is what happened! There can be no room for doubt—it was the evil deeds of the father, the patriarch, that caused the heirs and offspring to suffer this retribution!

After some time had gone by, Kenreimon'in fell ill. Grasping the five-color cord[4] attached to the hand of Amida Buddha, the central figure in the sacred triad, she repeatedly invoked his name: "Hail to the Thus Come One Amida, lord of teachings of the Western Paradise—may you guide me there without fail!" The nuns Dainagon-no-suke and Awa-no-naishi attended her on her left and right, their voices raised in unrestrained weeping, for they sensed in their

---

3. Who abandoned his clan. Yorimori is richly rewarded by the Genji, both because he defected when the Heike fled the capital and because his mother was the one who per- suaded the Heike to spare Yoritomo's life. He becomes a member of the emperor's cabinet.
4. At the hour of death, the cord would lead the faithful to the Pure Land.

grief that her end was now at hand. As the sound of the dying woman's recitations grew fainter and fainter, a purple cloud appeared from the west, the room became filled with a strange fragrance, and the strains of music could be heard in the sky. Human life has its limits, and that of the imperial lady ended in the middle days of the Second Month in the second year of the Kenkyū era [1191].

Her two female attendants, who from the time she became imperial consort had never once been parted from her, were beside themselves with grief at her passing, helpless though they were to avert it. The support on which they had depended from times past had now been snatched from them, and they were left destitute, yet even in that pitiable state they managed to hold memorial services each year on the anniversary of her death. And in due time they, too, we are told, imitating the example of the dragon king's daughter in her attainment of enlightenment and following in the footsteps of Queen Vaidehi,⁵ fulfilled their long-cherished hopes for rebirth in the Pure Land.

5. The wife of an Indian king who embraced Buddhism. She is said to have entered the Pure Land after listening to the preaching of Prince Siddhārtha, the historical Buddha and founder of Buddhism. The Nāga king was a Buddhist deity in dragon form and protector of the faith; his daughter grasped the Buddhist doctrines and attained enlightenment at the remarkable age of seven.

Selected Bibliographies

I. Circling the Mediterranean: Europe and the Islamic World

On the idea of the Mediterranean, see the classic 1949 study by Fernand Braudel, *The Mediterranean and the Mediterranean World in the Age of Philip II*, trans. Siân Reynolds (1972–1973; rpt., 1996), as well as the increasingly influential work of Peregrine Horden and Nicholas Purcell, *The Corrupting Sea: A Study of Mediterranean History* (2000). On late antiquity and the early Middle Ages, see Peter Brown, *The World of Late Antiquity: From Marcus Aurelius to Muhammad* (1989), and Averil Cameron, *The Mediterranean World in Late Antiquity*, A.D. 395–600 (1993).

For an overview of medieval Islamic history, see John Esposito, *Oxford History of Islam* (2000); Albert Hourani, *A History of the Arab Peoples* (2002); Seyyed Hossein Nasr, *Islam: Religion, History and Civilization* (2003). Information on almost any subject can be found in P. J. Bearman et al., eds., *Encyclopaedia of Islam*, 12 vols. (2nd ed., 1960–2005). A useful account of Persian poetics is offered by Julie Scott Meisami, *Medieval Persian Court Poetry* (1987).

For a survey of Europe's history from the fall of Rome to the beginnings of the Renaissance, three classic and still valuable studies are R. W. Southern, *The Making of the Middle Ages* (1953); Charles Homer Haskins, *The Renaissance of the Twelfth Century* (1927); and J. W. Huizinga, *The Autumn of the Middle Ages* (1919), trans. Rodney J. Payton and Ulrich Mammitzsch (1996). For information on almost any topic pertaining to medieval Europe, see *The Dictionary of the Middle Ages*, gen. ed. Joseph Strayer, 13 vols. (1989), with *Supplement 1*, ed. William Chester Jordan (2003).

Classic overviews of medieval European literary history and its place within the discipline of world literature can be found in Ernst Robert Curtius, *European Literature and the Latin Middle Ages* (1948), trans. Willard Trask (1953), and Erich Auerbach, *Mimesis: The Representation of Reality in Western Literature* (1946), trans. Willard Trask (1953; rpt., 2003). On the literary interactions of the Islamic world and medieval Europe, see María Rosa Menocal, *The Arabic Role in Medieval Literary History* (1987), and the reappraisal of Menocal's work in *A Sea of Languages: Literature and Culture in the Pre-modern Mediterranean*, ed. Suzanne Conklin Akbari and Karla Mallette (2011).

Petrus Alfonsi
A full translation of the *Disciplina Clericalis* by Joseph Ramon Jones and John Esten Keller appears as *The Scholar's Guide* (1969). See the insightful biography by John Tolan, *Petrus Alfonsi and His Medieval Readers* (1993). For a reading of the *Disciplina Clericalis* that places it in the context of other medieval frame-tale narratives, see David A. Wacks, *Framing Iberia: "Maqāmāt" and Frametales in Medieval Spain* (2007).

Apuleius
Two accessible English translations of Apuleius's work include helpful introduction and notes: see

Apuleius, *The Golden Ass*, trans. P. G. Walsh (1994), and Apuleius, *The Golden Ass or Metamorphoses*, trans. E. J. Kenney (1998). For an overview of Apuleius's other works, see *Apuleius: Rhetorical Works*, ed. Stephen J. Harrison, John L. Hilton, and Vincent J. C. Hunink (2001), and for a biography of the writer in his social and intellectual context, see Stephen J. Harrison, *Apuleius: A Latin Sophist* (2000 [the 2004 paperback edition has an updated bibliography]). Offering a perspective more rooted in comparative literary history is John J. Winkler, *Auctor and Actor: A Narratological Reading of Apuleius's "The Golden Ass"* (1985; rev. ed., 1991).

Farid ud-Din Attar
For a full version of the poem, see Farid ud-Din Attar, *The Conference of the Birds*, trans. Afkham Darbandi and Dick Davis (1984); for thematic studies of the *Conference*, see Dick Davis, "The Journey as Paradigm: Literal and Metaphorical Travel in Attar's *Mantiq al-Tayr*," *Edebiyât*, n.s. 4.2 (1993); Dick Davis, "Sufism and Poetry: A Marriage of Convenience?" *Edebiyât*, n.s. 10.2 (1999); and Jerome W. Clinton, "The Downward Path to Wisdom: Gender and Archetype in the Story of Sheikh Sam'an," in *A Pearl in Wine: Essays on the Life, Music, and Sufism of Hazrat Inayat Khan*, ed. Pir Zia Inayat Khan (2001). For a biographical overview, see Benedikt Reinert, "Attar," in *Encyclopaedia Iranica*, ed. Ehsan Yarshater, vol. 3 (1989). On Attar's *Biographies of the Saints*, see Paul E. Losensky, "Words and Deeds: Message and Structure in 'Attar's *Tadhkirat al-awliya*'," in *'Attar and the Persian Sufi Tradition: The Art of Spiritual Flight*, ed. Leonard Lewisohn and Christopher Shackle (2006).

Augustine
A wonderful introduction and detailed notes can be found in the translation by Henry Chadwick (1991) and also the 3-volume edition and commentary by James J. O'Donnell (1992), both titled *Confessions*. O'Donnell's text is available online from the Stoa Consortium in cooperation with the Perseus Project at www.stoa.org/hippo/. For an account of Augustine's life by the foremost historian of early Christianity in the Roman Empire, see Peter Brown, *Augustine of Hippo: A Biography* (1967; 2nd ed., 2000). A provocative and engaging life of the bishop and saint appears in James J. O'Donnell, *Augustine: A New Biography* (2005). On Augustine's own reading practices and the reading communities that formed in

his wake, see Brian Stock, *Augustine the Reader: Meditation, Self-Knowledge and the Ethics of Interpretation* (1996).

Avicenna
For a full translation of the *Mi'raj-nameh*, together with a detailed commentary, see Peter Heath, *Allegory and Philosophy in Avicenna (Ibn Sina) with a Translation of the Book of the Prophet Muhammad's Ascent to Heaven* (1992). Christiane J. Gruber and Frederick S. Colby have edited a collection of essays on the literature and pictorial art associated with the mi'raj tradition, *The Prophet's Ascension: Cross-Cultural Encounters with the Islamic Mi'raj Tales* (2009). For a brief overview of Avicenna's life and works, see Muhsin Mahdi and Dimitri Gutas et al., "Avicenna," in *Encyclopaedia Iranica*, ed. Ehsan Yarshater, vol. 3 (1989).

Beowulf
See the invaluable guide to the poem by Andy Orchard, *A Critical Companion to 'Beowulf'* (2003). A useful collection of essays is Robert Bjork and John Niles, eds., *A Beowulf Handbook* (1997). For a broad view of Anglo-Saxon literature and culture, see Malcolm Godden and Michael Lapidge, eds., *The Cambridge Companion to Old English Literature* (1991).

The Christian Bible
A full text with useful notes can be found in *The New Oxford Annotated Bible: New Revised Standard Version*, ed. Michael D. Coogan, Marc Z. Brettler, Carol Newsom, and Pheme Perkins (4th ed., 2010). For a brief overview of the historical background of the Bible and the diverse reading communities that have made it their own, see John Riches, *The Bible: A Very Short Introduction* (2000). The poetic and artistic qualities of scripture are on view in *The Literary Guide to the Bible*, ed. Robert Alter and Frank Kermode (1987). A more idiosyncratic reading of the Bible, rooted in a deep knowledge of history but with the profound inquisitiveness of a science fiction writer, appears in Isaac Asimov, *Asimov's Guide to the Bible: The Old and New Testaments* (1981; rpt., 1988). An intriguing interpretation of the Bible as graphic novel is Siku's *The Manga Bible: From Genesis to Revelation* (2008).

Giovanni Boccaccio
The standard biography is Vittore Branca, *Boccaccio: The Man and His Works*, trans. Richard Monges and Dennis J. McAuliffe (1976). Useful

guides to the *Decameron* include Giuseppe Mazzotta, *The World at Play in Boccaccio's "Decameron"* (1986); David Wallace, *Giovanni Boccaccio: "Decameron"* (1991); and Millicent Marcus, *An Allegory of Form: Literary Self-consciousness in the "Decameron"* (1979).

Geoffrey Chaucer
The most complete edition of Chaucer's poetry, with authoritative notes and commentary, is *The Riverside Chaucer*, ed. Larry D. Benson (3rd ed., 1987). An engaging portrait of Chaucer and his times can be found in Donald R. Howard, *Chaucer: His Life, His Works, His World* (1987). On the manuscript history of the *Canterbury Tales* in historical context, see Derek Pearsall, *The Canterbury Tales* (1985), and for an art-historical perspective focused on the poem's interlocking structure, see V. A. Kolve, *Chaucer and the Imagery of Narrative: The First Five Canterbury Tales* (1984). On Chaucer's role in the premodern invention of the subject, see Lee Patterson, *Chaucer and the Subject of History* (1991). On sexuality and gender, including influential readings of the Wife of Bath and the Pardoner, see Carolyn Dinshaw, *Chaucer's Sexual Poetics* (1989).

Christine de Pizan
A full translation of Christine de Pizan's *City of Ladies* appears in Rosalind Brown-Grant, trans., *The Book of the City of Ladies* (1999); another popular translation of the same title is by Earl Jeffrey Richards (1982). *Christine de Pizan: Her Life and Works* (1984), by Charity Cannon Willard, is a highly readable biography of the author by a scholar who played a crucial role in reawakening modern readers' interest in Christine's writings. Well-chosen excerpts from Christine's numerous works of prose and poetry, accompanied by influential critical essays, appear in Renate Blumenfeld-Kosinski and Kevin Brownlee, ed. and trans., *The Selected Writings of Christine de Pizan* (1997). For an insightful study of the interrelation of the text and illuminated miniatures in Christine's manuscripts, see Sandra Hindman, *Christine de Pizan's "Epistre Othéa": Painting and Politics at the Court of Charles VI* (1986). A study of Christine de Pizan's *City of Ladies* in the light of premodern feminism is Maureen Quilligan's *The Allegory of Female Authority: Christine de Pizan's "Cité des Dames"* (1991).

Dante Alighieri
Charles Singleton's annotated translation of Dante's *Divine Comedy*, with facing-page Italian text, is unsurpassed (6 vols., 1970–1975; rpt., 1990–1991). See also Singleton's groundbreaking and still stimulating short studies *Commedia: Elements of Structure* (1954) and *Journey to Beatrice* (1958). Short articles on a range of topics appear in *The Dante Encyclopedia*, gen. ed. Richard Lansing (2000), and a synoptic view of the encyclopedic quality of the *Comedy* is given in Giuseppe Mazzotta, *Dante's Vision and the Circle of Knowledge* (1993). The influence of Singleton remains strong in recent generations of Dante scholarship. Robert Pogue Harrison responds to Singleton's *Journey* in his *Body of Beatrice* (1988), while Teodolinda Barolini pushes back against the theologizing impulse of Singleton's work in *The Undivine Comedy: Detheologizing Dante* (1992). On Dante's relationship to his poetic forebears, from Virgil to the Occitan troubadours, see Teodolinda Barolini, *Dante's Poets: Textuality and Truth in the "Comedy"* (1984).

Abolqasem Ferdowsi
A complete version of the *Shahnameh* with an excellent introduction can be found in Abolqasem Ferdowsi, *Shahnameh: The Persian Book of Kings*, trans. Dick Davis (2006); for a fuller analysis of how the epic poem fits into Persian political history, see Davis, *Epic and Sedition: The Case of Ferdowsi's "Shahnameh"* (1992). A summary of Ferdowsi's life appears in Djalal Khaleghi-Motlagh, "Ferdowsi, Abu'l-Qasem: i. Life," in *Encyclopaedia Iranica*, ed. Ehsan Yarshater, vol. 9 (1999). For a broad overview of the place of Ferdowsi's epic in the traditions of oral poetry, see Olga Davidson, *Poet and Hero in the Persian Book of Kings* (1994), and Kumiko Yamamoto, *The Oral Background of Persian Epics: Storytelling and Poetry* (2003). On the interrelation of poetry and history writing in medieval Persia, viewed comparatively against medieval European literature, see Julie Scott Meisami, *Medieval Persian Court Poetry* (1987). See also Meisami, *Persian Historiography to the End of the Twelfth Century* (1999), especially her discussion of the *Shahnameh* itself; more generally, she provides a very useful framework for understanding the practice of writing history in medieval Persia.

Ibn Ishaq
A full version of the text can be found in Alfred Guillaume, ed. and trans., *Ibn Ishaq: The Life of Muhammad* (1955; rpt., 2003). Guillaume's translation, which appears in this anthology, is

a composite text drawn from the versions of at-Tabari and Ibn Hisham. A scholarly account of the evolution of Ibn Ishaq's text appears in Wim Raven, "Sira and the Qur'an: Ibn Ishaq and his Editors," in *The Encyclopaedia of the Qur'an*, ed. Jane Dammen McAuliffe, vol. 5 (2006). A sensitive account of the adaptation of Ibn Ishaq by later generations of Muslim writers can be found in W. Montgomery Watt's "Translator's Foreword," in Abu Ja'far Muhammad ben Jarir al-Tabarī, *Muhammad at Mecca*, trans. W. Montgomery Watt and M. V. McDonald, vol. 6 of *The History of al-Ṭabarī*, (1988). Two good modern biographies of Muhammad are Karen Armstrong, *Muhammad: A Biography of the Prophet* (1991; rev. ed., 1993), and W. Montgomery Watt, *Muhammad: Prophet and Statesman* (1961; rpt., 1974).

Kebra Nagast

An excellent account of the continuities of Jewish and Islamic traditions within Ethiopian Christian culture can be found in Wendy Laura Belcher, "African Rewritings of the Jewish and Islamic Solomonic Tradition: The Triumph of the Queen of Sheba in the Ethiopian Fourteenth-Century Text *Kəbrä Nägäst*," in *Sacred Tropes: Tanakh, New Testament, and Qur'an as Literature and Culture*, ed. Roberta Sterman Sabbath (2009). For a short overview of the *Kebra Nagast*, see Paolo Marrassini, "*Kebra Nagast*," in *Encyclopaedia Aethiopica*, gen. ed. Siegbert Uhlig, vol. 3 (2007). A wide-ranging perspective on the sources of the *Kebra Nagast* appears in Stuart C. Munro-Hay, *Quest for the Ark of the Covenant: The True History of the Tablets of Moses* (2005). On the intersection of Ethiopian literary history with pictorial art, focused specifically on the *Kebra Nagast*, see Denis Nosnitsin, "Ethiopian Literature in Ge'ez," in the richly illustrated *Arise and Go Toward the South: 2000 Years of Christianity in Ethiopia*, ed. Annegret Marx et al. (2007).

Marie de France

A full collection of Marie's lais appears in Robert Hanning and Joan Ferrante, trans., *The Lais of Marie de France* (1978; reprint, 1995). A still useful overview of her work is Emanuel J. Mickel, Jr., *Marie de France* (1974); for an insightful reading of Marie within the framework of medieval gender categories, see R. Howard Bloch, *The Anonymous Marie de France* (2003).

Medieval Lyrics

On the Latin and vernacular lyrics of medieval Europe, see Peter Dronke, *The Medieval Lyric* (1968; 3rd ed., 1996). On Dante and other lyric poets of medieval Italy, see Robert Pogue Harrison, *The Body of Beatrice* (1988). On the Jewish poets of medieval Spain, see the wonderful study and sensitive translations to be found in Peter Cole, *The Dream of the Poem: Hebrew Poetry from Muslim and Christian Spain, 950–1492* (2007). On the Arabic poetry of Spain in its cultural context, see Jerrilynn D. Dodds, María Rosa Menocal, and Abigail Krasner Balbale, *The Arts of Intimacy: Christians, Jews, and Muslims in the Making of Castilian Culture* (2008). For translations of Persian lyric poetry, see Dick Davis, *Borrowed Ware: Medieval Persian Epigrams* (1996) and *The Faces of Love: Hafez and the Poets of Shiraz* (forthcoming [2012]). For a brilliant study of the resonance of medieval lyric with the poetics of modern popular music, see María Rosa Menocal, *Shards of Love: Exile and the Origins of the Lyric* (1994).

The Qur'an

An extraordinarily readable translation of the Qur'an with good annotations is M. A. S. Abdel Haleem, *The Qur'an: A New Translation* (2004). See also his *Understanding the Qur'an: Themes and Style* (1999). A scholarly collection of essays appears in Jane Dammen McAuliffe, ed., *The Cambridge Companion to the Qur'an* (2009); for detailed information on specific topics, see also McAuliffe, ed., *The Encyclopaedia of the Qur'an*, 5 vols. (2001–2006). A useful overview is W. Montgomery Watt and Richard Bell, *Introduction to the Qur'an* (rev. ed., 2001). To get a sense of the rhythm and musicality of Qur'anic recitation, see Michael Sells, "Sound, Spirit, and Gender in the Qur'an" (1991), reprinted as an appendix to his *Approaching the Qur'an: The Early Revelations* (2nd ed., 2007), which includes a CD.

Sir Gawain and the Green Knight

For the text of the poem in Middle English, with excellent notes and introduction, see *Sir Gawain and the Green Knight*, ed. J. R. R. Tolkien and E. V. Gordon (2nd ed., rev., Norman Davis, 1967); see also Simon Armitage, trans., *Sir Gawain and the Green Knight: A New Verse Translation* (2007). A useful collection of essays on the works of the author of *Sir Gawain and the Green Knight* is Derek Brewer and

Jonathan Gibson, eds., *A Companion to the Gawain-Poet* (1997). On the historical background, see John M. Bowers, *The Politics of Pearl: Court Poetry in the Age of Richard II* (2001). For an intriguing reading of the poem in the context of fourteenth-century philosophy, see Ross G. Arthur, *Medieval Sign Theory and Sir Gawain and the Green Knight* (1987).

Song of Roland

An edition of the poem with facing page English translation, plus a separate volume of commentary, can be found in Gerald J. Brault, *The Song of Roland: An Analytical Edition*, 2 vols. (1978). For a well-written introduction to the epic with emphasis on the role of narratology, see Eugene Vance, *Reading the Song of Roland* (1970). On the context of emergent French nationalism and feudal politics, see Peter Haidu, *The Subject of Violence: The "Song of Roland" and the Birth of the State* (1993). For a reading of the *Song of Roland* in terms of European views of Islam, with a special focus on gender, see Sharon Kinoshita, *Medieval Boundaries: Rethinking Difference in Old French Literature* (2006), especially chap. 4. On the interrelation of the genres of epic and romance, see the lively analysis of Sarah Kay, *The Chansons de geste in the Age of Romance* (1995).

The Thousand and One Nights

The best short overview of the history of the *Nights*' composition and translation is Dwight F. Reynolds, "A Thousand and One Nights: A History of the Text and Its Reception," in *Arabic Literature in the Post-classical Period*, ed. Roger Allen and D. S. Richards (2006). The novelist Robert Irwin has published a widely available (but not always consistently reliable) guide called *The Arabian Nights: A Companion* (1994; rpt., 2004). The two best collections on the *Nights* focus respectively on the formation of the work and on its reception. The first is *The Arabian Nights Reader*, ed. Ulrich Marzolph (2006), which includes many of the crucial, groundbreaking scholarly articles on the *Nights* by such authors as Muhsin Mahdi, the modern editor of the Arabic text, and Nabia Abbott, the discoverer of the ninth-century manuscript fragment that is the first evidence of the work; the second, which offers some very useful correctives to Irwin, is *The Arabian Nights in Historical Context: Between East and West*, ed. Saree Makdisi and Felicity Nussbaum (2008).

Fruitful literary analyses of the *Nights* include Sandra Naddaff, *Arabesque: Narrative Structure and the Aesthetics of Repetition in the 1001 Nights* (1991), which features a comparative and theoretical literary analysis of the Porter and the Three Ladies group of tales, and David Pinault, *Story-telling Techniques in the Arabian Nights* (1992), which offers an excellent comparative analysis of the Syria and Cairo compilations of the *Nights* and their historical contexts. Provocative food for thought on the *Nights'* role in modern fiction, especially in magical realism, can be found in Jorge Luis Borges, "The Translators of *The Thousand and One Nights*" (1934), trans. Esther Allen, in *Selected Non-fictions* (in paperback as *The Total Library: Non-fiction, 1922–86*), ed. Eliot Weinberger (1999), and in *The Translation Studies Reader*, ed. Lawrence Venuti (2nd ed., 2004). Finally, http://journalofthenights .blogspot.com/ provides an appropriately abundant and fertile overview of everything imaginable responding to the *Nights*—adaptations (music, opera, theatre, film, video games, toys, etc.), recently published studies and articles, new translations, political issues (especially censorship), et cetera.

Travel and Encounter

An engaging overview of the many facets of travel writing can be found in Felipe Fernandez-Armesto, *Pathfinders: A Global History* (2006). For a historian's view of the evidence for Marco Polo's travels and the importance of his work as a source widely read at the dawn of the Age of Exploration, see John Larner, *Marco Polo and the Discovery of the World* (1999). Essays on Marco Polo's original text and on modern literary and cinematic adaptations of his work are available in *Marco Polo and the Encounter of East and West*, ed. Suzanne Conklin Akbari and Amilcare Iannucci (2008). On Ibn Battuta, a useful introduction by H. A. R. Gibb accompanies his translation of selections in *Travels in Asia and Africa, 1325–1354* (1929, with many reprints). A more detailed overview of the writer and his travels is provided by Ross E. Dunn, *The Adventures of Ibn Battuta, a Muslim Traveler of the Fourteenth Century* (1986; rev. ed., 2005). A biography of the anonymous author of *The Book of John Mandeville* and an overview of the work can be found in M. C. Seymour, *Sir John Mandeville* (1993); see also the brilliant study of *The Book of John Mandeville* in its many vernacular versions by Iain Macleod Higgins, *Writing East: The "Travels" of Sir John Mandeville* (1997).

II. India's Classical Age

Daniel H. H. Ingalls's *An Anthology of Sanskrit Court Poetry* (1965) still offers the best critical introduction to the classical lyric tradition; it also contains a complete, annotated translation of Vidyākara's eleventh-century *Subhāṣitaratnakośa*. *Theater of Memory: The Plays of Kālidāsa*, ed. Barbara Stoler Miller, (1984), and J. A. B. van Buitenen's *Tales of Ancient India* (1959) provide similar overviews of the classical dramatic and narrative genres, with translations of representative texts. A. Berridale Keith's *A History of Sanskrit Literature* (1928) remains a useful source of information. Sheldon Pollock's *The Language of the Gods in the World of Men: Sanskrit, Culture, and Power in Premodern India* (2006), which is more advanced, is the most comprehensive, up-to-date, and stimulating account of the world of Sanskrit literature and culture. Edward Dimock et al., *The Literatures of India: An Introduction* (1974), and Sheldon Pollock, *Literary Cultures in History: Reconstructions from South Asia* (2003), include excellent discussions of the classical period in the context of other Indian literatures. General historical background is provided in Burton Stein, *A History of India* (1998), and Stanley Wolpert, *A New History of India* (8th ed., 2008); and a more detailed analysis appears in Upinder Singh, *A History of Ancient and Early Medieval India: From the Stone Age to the 12th Century* (2009).

Classical Sanskrit Lyric

Daniel H. H. Ingalls's *An Anthology of Sanskrit Court Poetry* (1965) provides the most balanced introduction to the classical Sanskrit lyric, containing a complete, annotated translation of Vidyākara's eleventh-century collection, *Subhāṣitaratnakośa*, and an excellent critical discussion. Barbara Stoler Miller's *Bhartṛhari: Poems* (1967) focuses on the multifaceted work of a single poet, translating 200 poems from his fifth-century *Satakatryam*. J. Moussaieff Masson and W. S. Merwin's *Sanskrit Love Poetry* (1977), an unusual collaboration between an American scholar of Sanskrit and an American poet, provides a more panoramic view, offering memorable examples from the second to the sixteenth century. Edward Dimock et al., *The Literatures of India: An Introduction* (1974), contains stimulating analyses by several scholars on the aesthetic, cultural, and historical dimensions of Sanskrit poetry. Martha Ann Selby, *Grow Long, Blessed Night: Love Poems from Classical India* (2000), compares the Sanskrit lyric to the lyric in early Prakrit and classical Tamil by presenting poems on a common theme.

Classical Tamil Lyric

A. K. Ramanujan's compilation, *Poems of Love and War: From the Eight Anthologies and the Ten Long Poems of Classical Tamil* (1985), is the most comprehensive literary and scholarly representation in English of classical Tamil poetry and poetics. His earlier collection, *The Interior Landscape: Love Poems from a Classical Tamil Anthology* (1967), offers a partial but more compact introduction to the subject. Two books by George L. Hart III, *The Poems of Ancient Tamil: Their Milieu and Their Sanskrit Counterparts* (1975) and *Poets of the Tamil Anthologies: Ancient Poems of Love and War* (1979), provide alternative translations and extended commentary in English. K. Kailasapathy's older work, *Tamil Heroic Poetry* (1968), offers a useful comparative perspective on classical Tamil poetry, as does Martha Ann Selby's more recent study, *Grow Long, Blessed Night: Love Poems from Classical India* (2000).

Kālidāsa

Theater of Memory: The Plays of Kālidāsa, ed. Barbara Stoler Miller, trans. Edwin Gerow, David Gitomer, and Barbara Stoler Miller (1984), provides the best translations of and commentary on Sanskrit drama and the classical Indian stage; it includes a detailed discussion of how the plays may have been performed. Other English versions of Kālidāsa's plays appear in Michael Coulson, *Three Sanskrit Plays* (1981), and Velcheru Narayana Rao and David Shulman, *How Úrvaśi Was Won* (2009). Translations of Kālidāsa's poetry include Leonard

Nathan, *The Transport of Love* (1976); Hank Heifetz, *The Origin of the Young God* (1985); and David Smith, *Birth of Kumāra* (2005).

Somadeva
C. H. Tawney's *The Kathá Sarit Ságara: or, Ocean of the Streams of Story*, 2 vols. (1880–1884), provides a complete translation, later edited with additional notes by N. M. Penzer (10 vols., 1924–1928; rpt., 1968). A selection of the stories, together with a critical discussion, is included in J. A. B. van Buitenen, *Tales of Ancient India* (1959). A new partial rendering, with an updated, contemporary perspective on Somadeva's classic, appears in Sir James Mallinson, *The Ocean of the Rivers of Story*, 2 vols. (2007–2009).

Viṣṇuśarman
Arthur W. Ryder's *The Pañchatantra* (1925; rpt., 1956) is a reliable rendering of the Sanskrit text, though its English style is now outdated. An alternative rendering, more recent but more uneven, is available in Chandra Rajan, *The Pañchatantra Viṣṇu Śarma* (1993). The history of the *Pañchatantra* and its transmission to the Middle East and Europe are discussed comprehensively in Joseph Jacobs, *History of the Aesopic Fable* (1889), and Maurice Winternitz, *A History of Indian Literature* (1963). Tales from the *Hitopadeśa*, another important ancient Indian source, are translated in *Animal Fables of India: Narayana's Hitopadesha, or, Friendly Counsel*, trans. Francis G. Hutchins (1985).

III. Medieval Chinese Literature

Two books by Mark Lewis, *China Between Empires: The Northern and Southern Dynasties* (2009) and *China's Cosmopolitan Empire: The Tang Dynasty* (2009), provide lively depictions of China's medieval world. Edward H. Schafer's *The Golden Peaches of Samarkand: A Study of T'ang Exotics* (1963) vividly evokes the multiethnic atmosphere of Tang culture.

For a general survey of medieval literature, see the relevant chapters in *The Cambridge History of Chinese Literature*, ed. Stephen Owen and Kang-i Sun Chang, 2 vols. (2010). On medieval poetry in particular, see Stephen Owen, *The Making of Early Chinese Classical Poetry* (2006); Kang-i Sun Chang, *Six Dynasties Poetry* (1986); and Kōjirō Yoshikawa, *An Introduction to Sung Poetry*, trans. Burton Watson (1967). Xiaofei Tian's *Beacon Fire and Shooting Star: The Literary Culture of the Liang (502–557)* (2008) is a compelling study of literary court culture in the South during the Period of Disunion.

Han Yu
Charles Hartman's *Han Yü and the T'ang Search for Unity* (1986) provides an intellectual biography of Han Yu. Stephen Owen, *The Poetry of Meng Chiao and Han Yü* (1975), is a fine study of Han Yu's poetry.

Hermits, Buddhists, and Daoists
Aat Vervoorn surveys early Chinese eremitism in *Men of the Cliffs and Caves: The Development of the Chinese Eremitic Tradition to the End of the Han Dynasty* (1990). Alan Y. Berkowitz discusses the medieval recluse tradition in *Patterns of Disengagement: The Practice and Portrayal of Reclusion in Early Medieval China* (2000). Donald Holzman's *Poetry and Politics: The Life and Works of Juan Chi, A.D. 210–263* (1976) is an extensive biography of Ruan Ji. Graham Hartill and Wu Fusheng's *Songs of My Heart: The Chinese Lyric Poetry of Ruan Ji* (1988) is a complete translation of Ruan Ji's poetry. Robert G. Henricks has translated Xi Kang's philosophical essays in *Philosophy and Argumentation in Third-Century China: The Essays of Hsi K'ang* (1983). For a complete translation of *New Accounts of Tales of the World*, see Richard B. Mather, *Shih-shuo Hsinyü: A New Account of Tales of the World* (1976; 2nd ed., 2002); and Nanxiu Qian, *Spirit and Self in Medieval China: The Shih-shuo Hsin-yü and Its Legacy* (2001), is a broad study of the world of this collection of anecdotes and its creative influence until modern times. Burton Watson, *Cold Mountain* (1962), contains lively translations of a selection of Hanshan's poetry. Excellent literary translations have been done by Gary Snyder, a poet associated with the Beat movement, in *Riprap and Cold Mountain Poems* (1965), and by Red Pine, *The Collected Songs of Cold Mountain* (1983; rev. ed., 2000).

There is also a complete annotated translation by Robert Henricks, *The Poetry of Han-shan* (1990), who emphasizes the Buddhist dimension of the poetry.

Li Qingzhao

Chapter 4 of *The Red Brush: Writing Women of Imperial China* (2004) by Idema Wilt and Beata Grant is devoted to Li Qingzhao's life and work. Pinqing Hu gives a portrait of her life in *Li Ch'ing-chao* (1966). A discussion of her "Afterword" can be found in Stephen Owen's *Remembrances: The Experience of the Past in Classical Chinese Literature* (1986). For a discussion of the development of the song lyric, see Kang-i Sun Chang's *The Evolution of Chinese Tz'u Poetry: From Late T'ang to Northern Sung* (1980). For more translations of Li Qingzhao's song lyrics, see James Cryer's *Plum Blossom: Poems of Li Ch'ing-chao* (1984), Sam Hamill's *The Lotus Lovers: Poems and Songs* (by Li Ye and Li Qingzhao) (1985), and Kenneth Rexroth and Ling Chung's *Li Ch'ing-chao: Complete Poems* (1979).

Literature about Literature

Stephen Owen's *Readings in Chinese Literary Thought* (1992) gives a captivating introduction to major works of Chinese literary thought and provides a bilingual translation of the original texts with detailed commentary. James Liu's *Chinese Theories of Literature* (1975) sketches major Chinese paradigms of the concept of literature. To explore literary thought in more recent times see *Modern Chinese Literary Thought: Writings on Literature, 1893–1945*, ed. Kirk Denton (1996). For scholarly essays on Chinese literary criticism in general see *Chinese Aesthetics and Literature: A Reader*, ed. Corinne H. Dale (2004). For a broader exploration of literary interpretation in Chinese and Western literatures, see Longxi Zhang's *The Tao and the Logos: Literary Hermeneutics, East and West* (1992).

Howard L. Goodman's *Ts'ao P'i Transcendent: The Political Culture of Dynasty-Founding in China at the End of the Han* (1998) traces Cao Pi's life as emperor and writer. For other translations of Lu Ji's rhapsody, see E. R. Hughes's *The Art of Letters: Lu Chi's "Wen fu,"* A.D. 302, *A Translation and Comparative Study*, with a forenote by I. A. Richards (1951), and Sam Hamill's *The Art of Writing: Lu Chi's Wen fu* (rev. ed., 1991).

Liu Zongyuan

Liu Tsung-yüan and Intellectual Change in T'ang China, 773–819 (1992) by Jo-shui Chen (Ruoshui Chen) situates Liu Zonghuan's work in the intellectual climate of the mid–Tang Dynasty.

Tang Poetry

Stephen Owen's *Traditional Chinese Poetry and Poetics: Omen of the World* (1985) provides a general introduction to Chinese poetry. For an anthology of guided readings in various genres of Chinese poetry, see Zongqi Cai's *How to Read Chinese Poetry: A Guided Anthology* (2008). To further explore the breadth and development of Tang poetry, see Stephen Owen's four magisterial studies: *The Poetry of the Early T'ang* (1977), *The Great Age of Chinese Poetry: The High T'ang* (1981), *The End of the Chinese 'Middle Ages': Essays in Mid-Tang Literary Culture* (1996), and *The Late Tang: Chinese Poetry of the Mid-Ninth Century (827–860)* (2006).

For translations of Wang Wei's poetry, see Pauline Yu's *The Poetry of Wang Wei: New Translations and Commentary* (1980), G. W. Robinson's *Poems of Wang Wei* (1973), and Vikram Seth's *Three Chinese Poets: Translations of Poems by Wang Wei, Li Bai, and Du Fu* (1992). For studies that explore Wang Wei's life, and his penchant for painting and Buddhism, see Marsha Wagner, *Wang Wei* (1981); Lewis Calvin and Dorothy Brush Walmsley, *Wang Wei, the Painter-Poet* (1968); and Jingqing Yang, *The Chan Interpretations of Wang Wei's Poetry: A Critical Review* (2007).

For translations of Li Bo's poetry, see Vikram Seth's *Three Chinese Poets: Translations of Poems by Wang Wei, Li Bai, and Du Fu* (1992). Paul Kroll's *Studies in Medieval Taoism and the Poetry of Li Po* (2009) and Paula Varsano's *Tracking the Banished Immortal: The Poetry of Li Bo and Its Critical Reception* (2003) are compelling studies of the poetry; Arthur Waley's *The Poetry and Career of Li Po, 701–762 A.D.* (1950) is a biography.

Among translations of Du Fu, David Hawkes's *A Little Primer of Tu Fu* (1967), an introductory bilingual edition of a few of the poems, is particularly recommended. See also Burton Watson's *The Selected Poems of Du Fu* (2002). For studies of Du Fu's life and legacy see David McCraw's *Du Fu's Laments from the South* (1992) and Eva Shan Chou's *Reconsidering Tu*

Fu: Literary Greatness and Cultural Context (1995).

For Bo Juyi's poetry, see Howard S. Levy's *Translations from Po Chü-i's Collected Works* (1978), David Hinton's *The Selected Poems of Po Chü-i* (1999), and Burton Watson's *Po Chü-i: Selected Poems* (2000). Arthur Waley's *The Life and Times of Po Chü-i* (1949) is a vivid evocation of Bo Juyi's life in his literary context.

Tao Qian
A. R. Davis's *T'ao Yüan-ming, A.D. 365–427, His Works and their Meaning*, 2 vols. (1984), and James Robert Hightower's *The Poetry of T'ao Ch'ien* (1970) provide complete translations of Tao Qian's poetry. Because his works circulated only in manuscript form for centuries before the advent of print, there are many different versions of his poems; Xiaofei Tian's *Tao Yuanming & Manuscript Culture: The Record of a Dusty Table* (2005) is a compelling study of how early editors adapted Tao Qian's

pieces, based on their own image of him. Robert Ashmore's *The Transport of Reading: Text and Understanding in the World of Tao Qian (365–427)* (2010) discusses cultures of reading and interpretation in Tao Qian's work and time. Wendy Swartz's *Reading Tao Yuanming: Shifting Paradigms of Historical Reception (427–1900)* (2008) traces the changing images of Tao Qian from his death up until the twentieth century.

Yuan Zhen
You can read more Tang tales in Yang Xianyi and Gladys Yang's *Tang Dynasty Stories* (1986) and William H. Nienhauser Jr.'s *Tang Dynasty Tales: A Guided Reader* (2010). Stephen Owen's *The End of the Chinese 'Middle Ages': Essays in Mid-Tang Literary Culture* (1996) contains an excellent chapter on "The Story of Yingying." For a translation of the *Romance of the Western Chamber*, see Stephen H. West and Wilt L. Idema, *The Story of the Western Wing* (1995).

IV. Japan's Classical Age

To further explore early and medieval Japanese history see Conrad Schirokauer, David Lurie, and Suzanne Gay's *A Brief History of Japanese Civilization* (2nd ed., 2006) For a shorter treatment of Japanese history in the context of East Asia, Patricia Bückley Ebrey, Anne Walthall, and James B. Palais, *East Asia: A Cultural, Social, and Political History* (2nd ed., 2009), is recommended.

Traditional Japanese Literature: An Anthology, Beginnings to 1600, ed. Haruo Shirane (2007), and Donald Keene's *Anthology of Japanese Literature: From the Earliest Era to the Mid-Nineteenth Century* (1955) are great treasure troves of original early and medieval Japanese texts in English translation; see also *Traditional Japanese Poetry: An Anthology*, trans. Steven D. Carter (1991), and *Classical Japanese Prose: An Anthology*, ed. Helen Craig McCullough (1990). Lovers of travel literature will appreciate Donald Keene's *Travelers of a Hundred Ages: The Japanese As Revealed Through 1,000 Years of Diaries* (rev. ed., 1999). Keene presents a sweeping history of premodern Japanese literature in *Seeds in the Heart: Japanese Literature from Earliest Times to the Late Sixteenth Century* (1993).

Earl Miner, Hiroko Odagiri, and Robert E. Morrell's *The Princeton Companion to Classical Japanese Literature* (1985) is a reliable reference work to the world of Japanese literature. Groundbreaking studies of the interplay between Chinese and Japanese cultural traditions in Japanese literature include David Pollack, *The Fracture of Meaning: Japan's Synthesis of China from the Eighth Through the Eighteenth Centuries* (1986); Thomas LaMarre, *Uncovering Heian Japan: An Archaeology of Sensation and Inscription* (2000); and Atsuko Sakaki, *Obsessions with the Sino-Japanese Polarity in Japanese Literature* (2005). Tomiko Yoda's *Gender and National Literature: Heian Texts in the Constructions of Japanese Modernity* (2004) is a compelling study of how Heian texts have influenced modern Japanese identity and self-understanding.

An Account of a Ten-Foot-Square Hut

Other translations include Donald Keene's "An Account of My Hut," in *Anthology of Japanese Literature: From the Earliest Era to the Mid-Nineteenth Century* (1955) and Yasuhiko Moriguchi and David Jenkins's *Hōjōki: Visions of a Torn World* (1996). Burton Watson's *Four Huts: Asian Writings on the Simple Life* (1994) presents Chōmei's essay together with three other famous texts by Chinese and Japanese poets on life in reclusion. Michele Marra compares Chōmei's and Kenkō's understanding of impermanence in "Semi-Recluses (*tonseisha*) and Impermanence (*mujō*): Kamo no Chōmei and Urabe Kenkō," *Japanese Journal of Religious Studies* (1984). For an exploration of Chōmei's work, see Thomas Blenman Hare's "Reading Kamo no Chōmei," *Harvard Journal of Asiatic Studies* (1989). Michele Marra's *The Aesthetics of Discontent: Politics and Reclusion in Medieval Japanese Literature* (1991) provides a broader view of Japanese medieval recluse literature.

Essays in Idleness

For a complete translation, with an introduction and annotation, see Donald Keene's *Essays in Idleness: The Tsurezuregusa of Kenkō* (1967). An interesting study of the connection between Buddhism and Japanese literature at this time is William R. LaFleur's *The Karma of Words: Buddhism and the Literary Arts in Medieval Japan* (1983). Linda H. Chance's *Formless in Form: Kenko, "Tsurezuregusa," and the Rhetoric of Japanese Fragmentary Prose* (1997) examines the *Essays in Idleness*, highlighting contrasts between Japanese and European prose writing. Michele Marra's *The Aesthetics of Discontent: Politics and Reclusion in Medieval Japanese Literature* (1991) is a compelling study of Japanese medieval recluse literature.

The Man'yōshū

Good partial translations include Nippon Gakujutsu Shinkōkai's *The Manyōshū*, ed. Donald Keene (1965), Ian Hideo Levy's *The Ten Thousand Leaves* (1981), and Edwin Cranston's evocative translations in *A Waka Anthology*, vol. 1, *The Gem-Glistening Cup* (1993). Levy has also produced a detailed study of one poet, *Hitomaro and the Birth of Japanese Lyricism* (1984). Robert H. Brower and Earl Miner's *Japanese Court Poetry* (1961) contains a general study of the anthology, and Gary L. Ebersole's *Ritual Poetry and the Politics of*

Death in Early Japan (1989) explores the religious and historical context of the anthology's poems on death and mourning.

Murasaki Shikibu

This anthology uses a new translation by Dennis Washburn; the three previous English translations of *The Tale of Genji* all have their partisans. The first English translation was published by Arthur Waley in installments between 1925 and 1933. Edward G. Seidensticker's *The Tale of Genji* (1976) is a beautiful translation, more faithful than Waley's. The translation by Royall Tyler (2001) is sparkling.

For a glimpse into the life of the author, see *Murasaki Shikibu: Her Diary and Poetic Memoirs*, trans. Richard Bowring (1982). Ivan Morris, *The World of the Shining Prince: Court Life in Ancient Japan*, with a new introduction by Barbara Ruch (1964; rpt., 1994), is a colorful account of the world that Murasaki and her characters inhabit.

The best brief introduction to the tale is Richard Bowring, *Murasaki Shikibu: "The Tale of Genji"* (1988). Two excellent longer studies are Norma Field, *The Splendor of Longing in the "Tale of Genji"* (1987), and Haruo Shirane, *The Bridge of Dreams: A Poetics of "The Tale of Genji"* (1987). *Envisioning "The Tale of Genji": Media, Gender, and Cultural Production* (2008), a collection of articles edited by Shirane, gives fascinating glimpses of how *The Tale of Genji* influenced later literature, art, and popular culture.

Poetry of the Heian Court

Robert Borgen's *Sugawara no Michizane and the Early Heian Court* (1986) is a detailed biography of Michizane and contains many translations from his poetry. For further translations of his poetry and of the Chinese-style imperial anthologies of the ninth century, see Judith N. Rabinovitch and Timothy R. Bradstock's *Dance of the Butterflies: Chinese Poetry from the Japanese Court Tradition* (2005) and Burton Watson's *Japanese Literature in Chinese*, 2 vols. (1975–1976).

Two complete translations of *The Kokinshū* are available in English: Helen Craig McCullough's *Kokin Wakashū: The First Imperial Anthology of Japanese Poetry, with "Tosa Nikki" and "Shinsen Waka"* (1985) and Laura Rasplica Rodd and Mary Catherine Henkenius's *Kokinshū: A Collection of Poems Ancient and Modern* (1984); Edwin A. Cranston's *A Waka Anthology*, vol. 2, *Grasses of Remembrance* (2006), contains selections from *The Kokinshū* with ample commentary. *Brocade by Night: "Kokin Wakashū" and the Court Style in Japanese Classical Poetry* (1985), McCullough's companion volume to her translation of the anthology, is a detailed study of the Chinese influences on Kokinshū poetry. On the interplay of poetry and politics at the Heian court, see Gustav Heldt's study *The Pursuit of Harmony: Poetry and Power in Early Heian Japan* (2008). Robert H. Brower and Earl Miner, *Japanese Court Poetry* (1961), is still the standard account of the development of the *waka* tradition in premodern Japan.

Sei Shōnagon
The selections printed in this anthology are taken from a complete translation by Meredith McKinney, *The Pillow Book* (2006). Other important translations include the pioneering translation of Arthur Waley, *The Pillow-Book of Sei Shōnagon* (1928); Ivan Morris, *The Pillow Book of Sei Shonagon*, 2 vols. (1967) (the second volume contains useful notes and appendices); and the sampling in Helen Craig McCullough, *Classical Japanese Prose: An Anthology* (1990). Ivan Morris's *The World of the Shining Prince: Court Life in Ancient Japan* (1964), a colorful portrayal of the Heian period, will be helpful to readers of both *The Pillow Book* and *The Tale of Genji*.

The Tales of the Heike
In addition to Burton Watson's partial translation (2006) used for the selections in this anthology, Helen Craig McCullough's complete translation, *The Tale of the Heike* (1988), is recommended; it contains much useful background material and introductions to the work and its literary status. Paul Varley offers a useful discussion of social issues in "Warriors as Courtiers: The Taira in *Heike monogatari*," in *Currents in Japanese Culture: Translations and Transformations*, ed. Amy Vladek Heinrich (1997). David T. Bialock's *Eccentric Spaces, Hidden Histories: Narrative, Ritual, and Royal Authority from "The Chronicles of Japan" to "The Tale of the Heike"* (2007) discusses *The Tales of the Heike* in its relation to Japanese and Chinese modes of history writing. Elizabeth Oyler's *Swords, Oaths, and Prophetic Visions: Authoring Warrior Rule in Medieval Japan* (2006), a compelling study of the relation between the rise of warrior rule and *The Tales of the Heike*, examines key protagonists and episodes from the text.

Ki No Tsurayuki
Complete translations of *Tosa Diary* include Helen Craig McCullough's *Kokin Wakashū: The First Imperial Anthology of Japanese Poetry, with "Tosa Nikki" and "Shinsen Waka"* (1985) and Earl Miner's *The Tosa Diary*, in his *Japanese Poetic Diaries* (1969).

McCullough's *Brocade by Night: "Kokin Wakashū" and the Court Style in Japanese Classical Poetry* (1985) focuses on *The Kokinshū* but also outlines the broader context of Tsurayuki's literary activities, and includes a discussion of *Tosa Diary*. Lynne Miyake, "The Tosa Diary: In the Interstices of Gender and Criticism," in *The Woman's Hand: Gender and Theory in Japanese Women's Writing*, ed. Paul Gordon Schalow and Janet A. Walker (1996), discusses Tsurayuki's diary in the context of gender.

Timeline

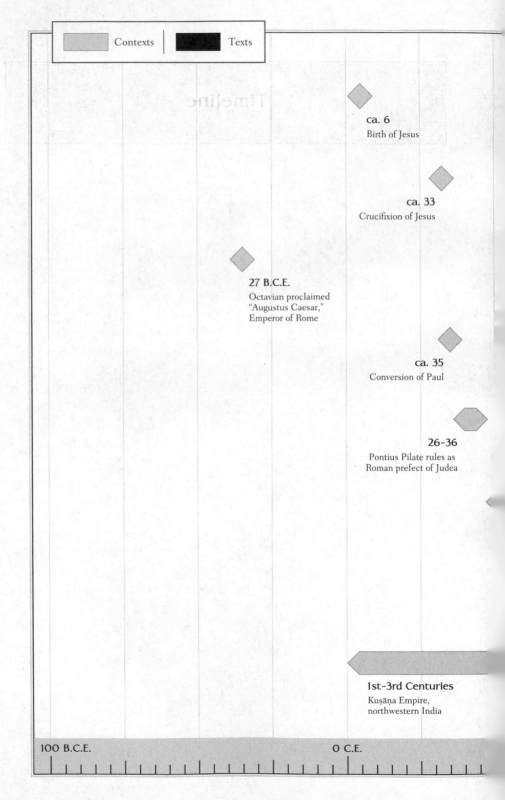

Contexts | Texts

ca. 6
Birth of Jesus

ca. 33
Crucifixion of Jesus

27 B.C.E.
Octavian proclaimed
"Augustus Caesar,"
Emperor of Rome

ca. 35
Conversion of Paul

26-36
Pontius Pilate rules as
Roman prefect of Judea

1st-3rd Centuries
Kuṣāṇa Empire,
northwestern India

100 B.C.E.   0 C.E.

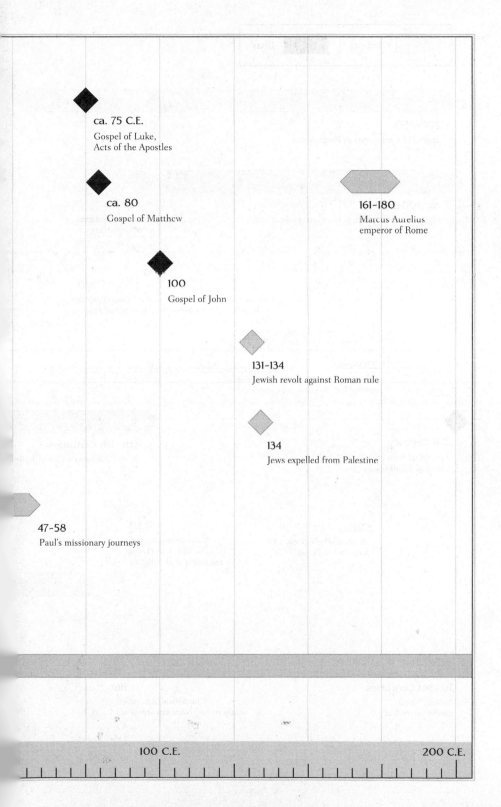

ca. 75 C.E.
Gospel of Luke,
Acts of the Apostles

ca. 80
Gospel of Matthew

161-180
Marcus Aurelius
emperor of Rome

100
Gospel of John

131-134
Jewish revolt against Roman rule

134
Jews expelled from Palestine

47-58
Paul's missionary journeys

100 C.E.

200 C.E.

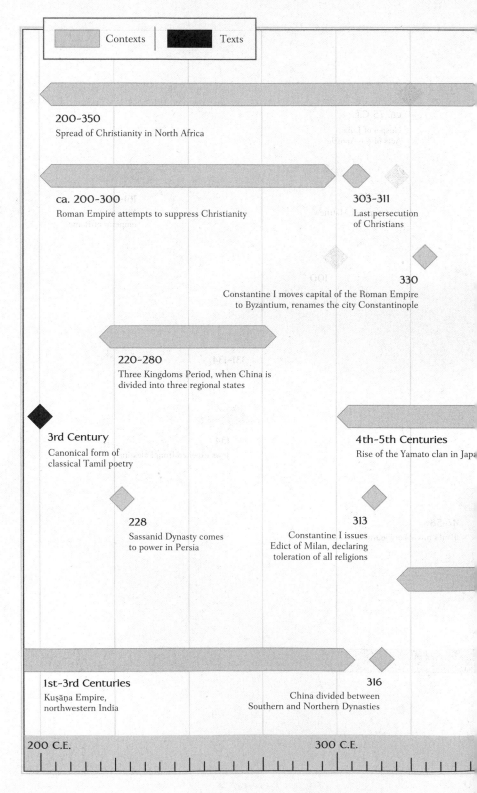

Contexts | Texts

200-350
Spread of Christianity in North Africa

ca. 200-300
Roman Empire attempts to suppress Christianity

303-311
Last persecution
of Christians

330
Constantine I moves capital of the Roman Empire
to Byzantium, renames the city Constantinople

220-280
Three Kingdoms Period, when China is
divided into three regional states

3rd Century
Canonical form of
classical Tamil poetry

4th-5th Centuries
Rise of the Yamato clan in Japan

228
Sassanid Dynasty comes
to power in Persia

313
Constantine I issues
Edict of Milan, declaring
toleration of all religions

1st-3rd Centuries
Kuṣāṇa Empire,
northwestern India

316
China divided between
Southern and Northern Dynasties

200 C.E.   300 C.E.

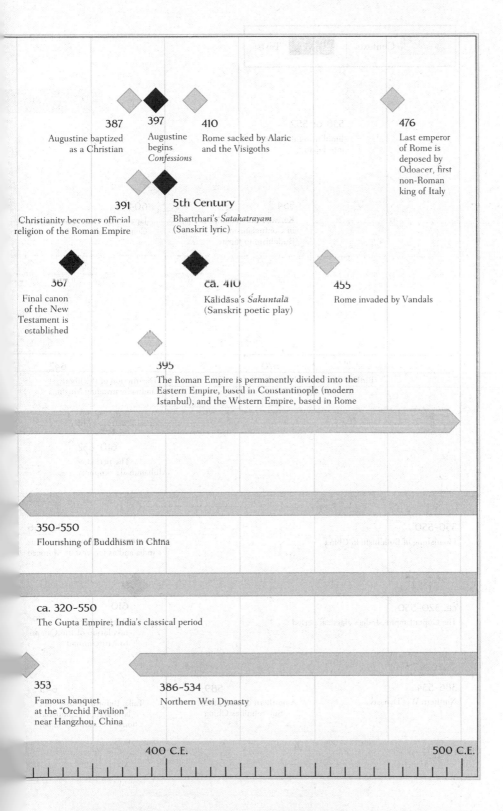

387

Augustine baptized
as a Christian

397

Augustine
begins
Confessions

410

Rome sacked by Alaric
and the Visigoths

476

Last emperor
of Rome is
deposed by
Odoacer, first
non-Roman
king of Italy

391

Christianity becomes official
religion of the Roman Empire

5th Century

Bhartrhari's *Śatakatrayam*
(Sanskrit lyric)

367

Final canon
of the New
Testament is
established

ca. 410

Kālidāsa's *Śakuntalā*
(Sanskrit poetic play)

455

Rome invaded by Vandals

395

The Roman Empire is permanently divided into the
Eastern Empire, based in Constantinople (modern
Istanbul), and the Western Empire, based in Rome

350–550

Flourishing of Buddhism in China

ca. 320–550

The Gupta Empire; India's classical period

353

Famous banquet
at the "Orchid Pavilion"
near Hangzhou, China

386–534

Northern Wei Dynasty

400 C.E.

500 C.E.

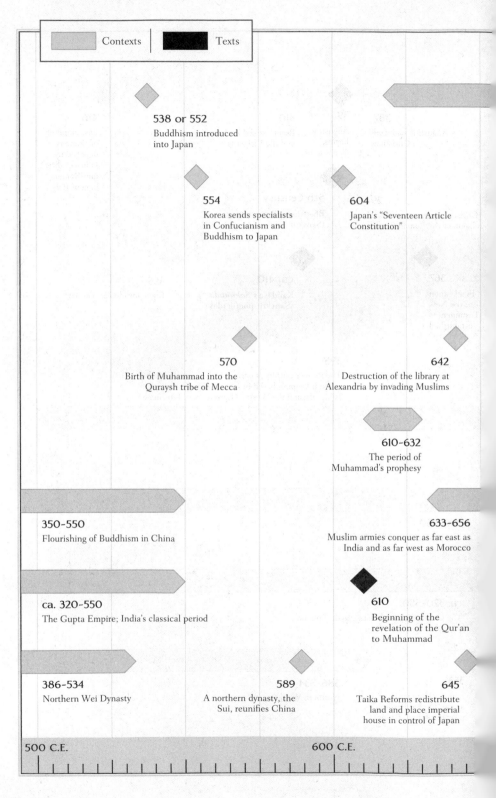

Contexts   Texts

538 or 552
Buddhism introduced
into Japan

554
Korea sends specialists
in Confucianism and
Buddhism to Japan

604
Japan's "Seventeen Article
Constitution"

570
Birth of Muhammad into the
Quraysh tribe of Mecca

642
Destruction of the library at
Alexandria by invading Muslims

610–632
The period of
Muhammad's prophesy

350–550
Flourishing of Buddhism in China

633–656
Muslim armies conquer as far east as
India and as far west as Morocco

ca. 320–550
The Gupta Empire; India's classical period

610
Beginning of the
revelation of the Qur'an
to Muhammad

386–534
Northern Wei Dynasty

589
A northern dynasty, the
Sui, reunifies China

645
Taika Reforms redistribute
land and place imperial
house in control of Japan

500 C.E.   600 C.E.

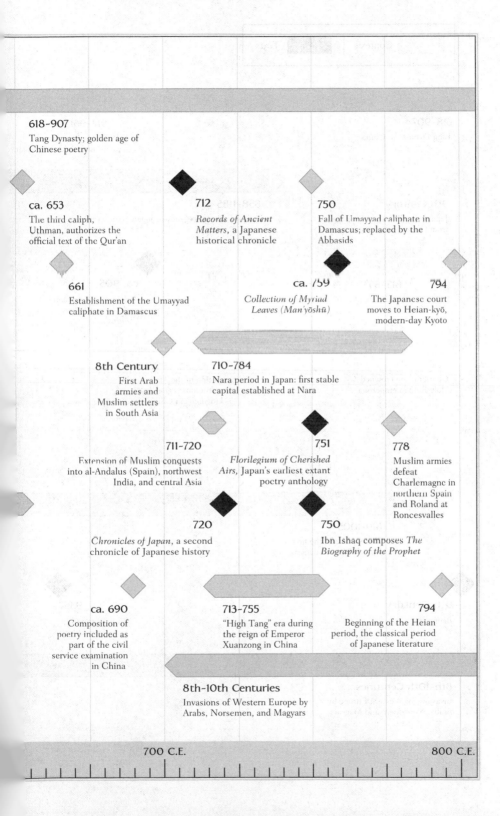

618–907
Tang Dynasty; golden age of Chinese poetry

ca. 653
The third caliph, Uthman, authorizes the official text of the Qur'an

712
Records of Ancient Matters, a Japanese historical chronicle

750
Fall of Umayyad caliphate in Damascus; replaced by the Abbasids

661
Establishment of the Umayyad caliphate in Damascus

ca. 759
Collection of Myriad Leaves (Man'yōshū)

794
The Japanese court moves to Heian-kyō, modern-day Kyoto

8th Century
First Arab armies and Muslim settlers in South Asia

710–784
Nara period in Japan: first stable capital established at Nara

711–720
Extension of Muslim conquests into al-Andalus (Spain), northwest India, and central Asia

751
Florilegium of Cherished Airs, Japan's earliest extant poetry anthology

778
Muslim armies defeat Charlemagne in northern Spain and Roland at Roncesvalles

720
Chronicles of Japan, a second chronicle of Japanese history

750
Ibn Ishaq composes *The Biography of the Prophet*

ca. 690
Composition of poetry included as part of the civil service examination in China

713–755
"High Tang" era during the reign of Emperor Xuanzong in China

794
Beginning of the Heian period, the classical period of Japanese literature

8th–10th Centuries
Invasions of Western Europe by Arabs, Norsemen, and Magyars

700 C.E.

800 C.E.

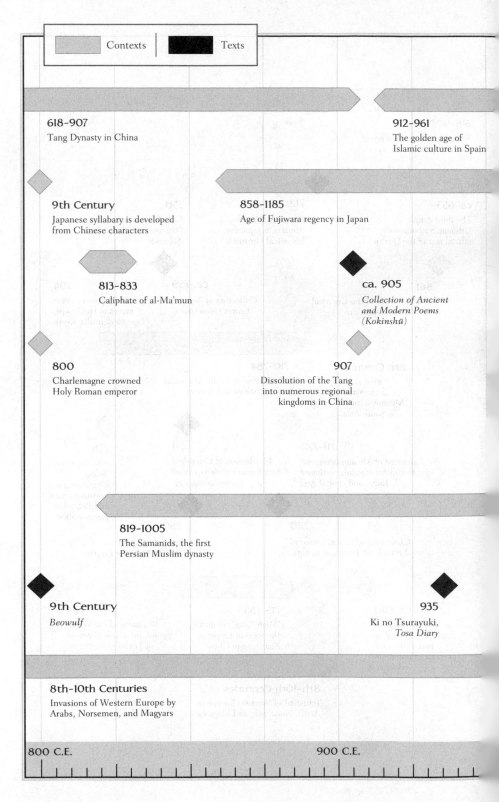

Contexts   Texts

618–907
Tang Dynasty in China

912–961
The golden age of
Islamic culture in Spain

9th Century
Japanese syllabary is developed
from Chinese characters

858–1185
Age of Fujiwara regency in Japan

813–833
Caliphate of al-Ma'mun

ca. 905
*Collection of Ancient
and Modern Poems
(Kokinshū)*

800
Charlemagne crowned
Holy Roman emperor

907
Dissolution of the Tang
into numerous regional
kingdoms in China

819–1005
The Samanids, the first
Persian Muslim dynasty

9th Century
Beowulf

935
Ki no Tsurayuki,
Tosa Diary

8th–10th Centuries
Invasions of Western Europe by
Arabs, Norsemen, and Magyars

800 C.E.   900 C.E.

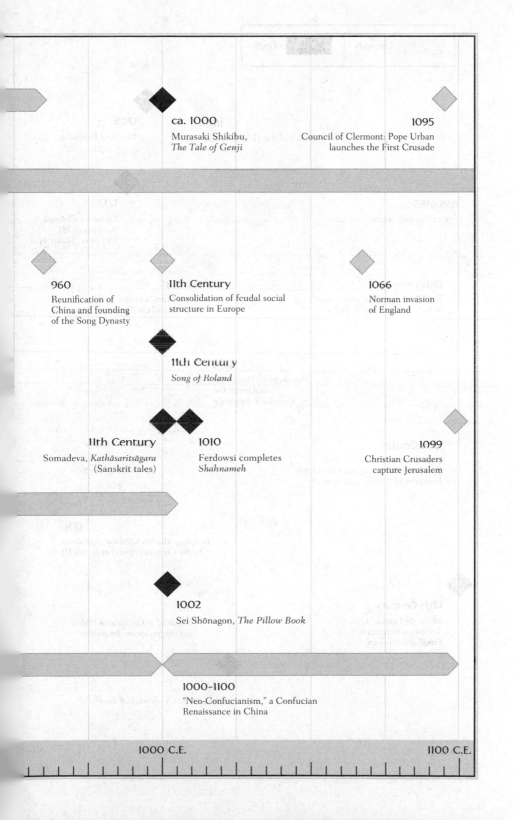

ca. 1000
Murasaki Shikibu,
The Tale of Genji

1095
Council of Clermont: Pope Urban
launches the First Crusade

960
Reunification of
China and founding
of the Song Dynasty

11th Century
Consolidation of feudal social
structure in Europe

1066
Norman invasion
of England

11th Century
Song of Roland

11th Century
Somadeva, *Kathāsaritsāgara*
(Sanskrit tales)

1010
Ferdowsi completes
Shahnameh

1099
Christian Crusaders
capture Jerusalem

1002
Sei Shōnagon, *The Pillow Book*

1000–1100
"Neo-Confucianism," a Confucian
Renaissance in China

1000 C.E.   1100 C.E.

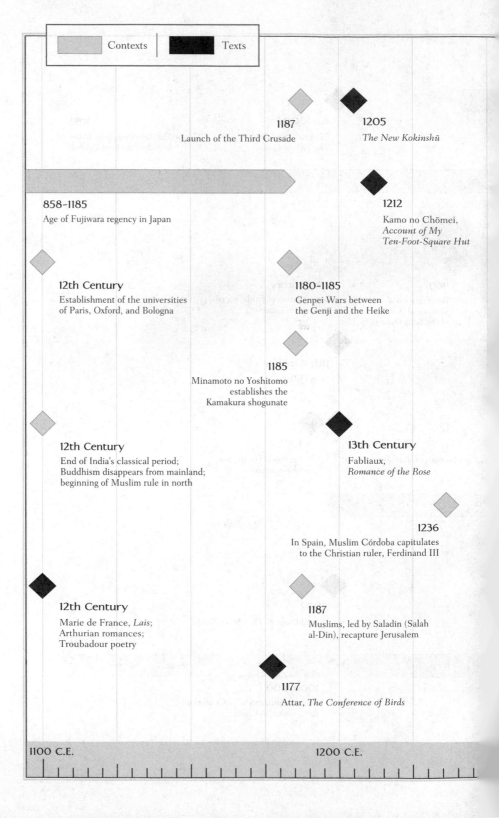

Contexts   Texts

1187
Launch of the Third Crusade

1205
The New Kokinshū

858-1185
Age of Fujiwara regency in Japan

1212
Kamo no Chōmei,
*Account of My
Ten-Foot-Square Hut*

12th Century
Establishment of the universities
of Paris, Oxford, and Bologna

1180-1185
Genpei Wars between
the Genji and the Heike

1185
Minamoto no Yoshitomo
establishes the
Kamakura shogunate

12th Century
End of India's classical period;
Buddhism disappears from mainland;
beginning of Muslim rule in north

13th Century
Fabliaux,
Romance of the Rose

1236
In Spain, Muslim Córdoba capitulates
to the Christian ruler, Ferdinand III

12th Century
Marie de France, *Lais*;
Arthurian romances;
Troubadour poetry

1187
Muslims, led by Saladin (Salah
al-Din), recapture Jerusalem

1177
Attar, *The Conference of Birds*

1100 C.E.   **1200 C.E.**

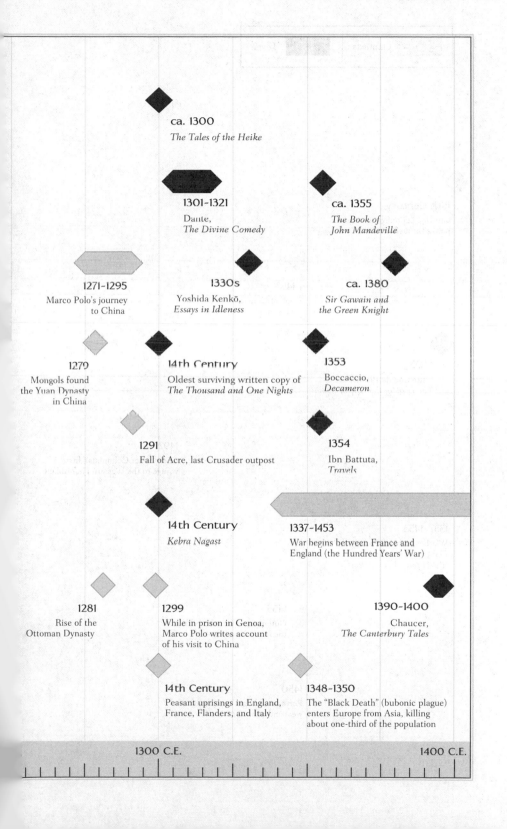

ca. 1300

The Tales of the Heike

1301–1321

Dante,
The Divine Comedy

ca. 1355

*The Book of
John Mandeville*

1271–1295

Marco Polo's journey
to China

1330s

Yoshida Kenkō,
Essays in Idleness

ca. 1380

*Sir Gawain and
the Green Knight*

1279

Mongols found
the Yuan Dynasty
in China

14th Century

Oldest surviving written copy of
The Thousand and One Nights

1353

Boccaccio,
Decameron

1291

Fall of Acre, last Crusader outpost

1354

Ibn Battuta,
Travels

14th Century

Kebra Nagast

1337–1453

War begins between France and
England (the Hundred Years' War)

1281

Rise of the
Ottoman Dynasty

1299

While in prison in Genoa,
Marco Polo writes account
of his visit to China

1390–1400

Chaucer,
The Canterbury Tales

14th Century

Peasant uprisings in England,
France, Flanders, and Italy

1348–1350

The "Black Death" (bubonic plague)
enters Europe from Asia, killing
about one-third of the population

1300 C.E.

1400 C.E.

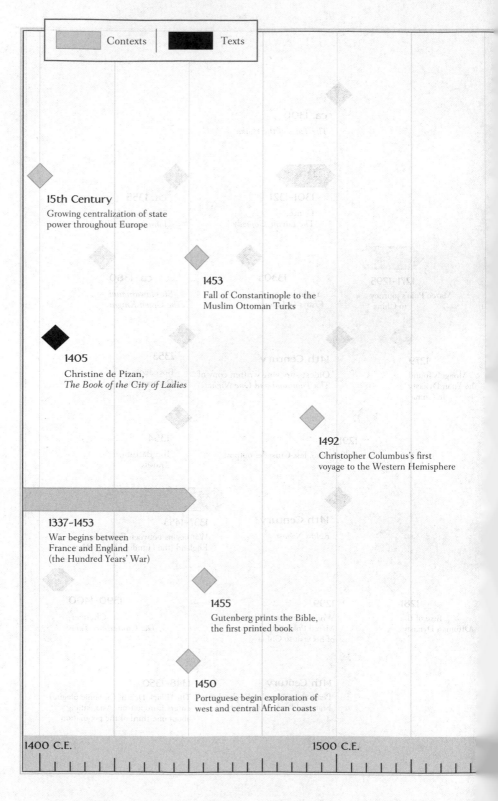

Contexts	Texts

15th Century
Growing centralization of state
power throughout Europe

1453
Fall of Constantinople to the
Muslim Ottoman Turks

1405
Christine de Pizan,
The Book of the City of Ladies

1492
Christopher Columbus's first
voyage to the Western Hemisphere

1337–1453
War begins between
France and England
(the Hundred Years' War)

1455
Gutenberg prints the Bible,
the first printed book

1450
Portuguese begin exploration of
west and central African coasts

1400 C.E.   1500 C.E.

1600 C.E.

1700 C.E.

Permissions Acknowledgments

Alexander the Wild: "Strawberry Picking," trans. by Peter Dronke from THE MEDIEVAL LYRIC, third ed., by Peter Dronke (1996). Reprinted by permission of the publisher, Boydell & Brewer Ltd.

Petrus Alfonsi: From THE SCHOLAR'S GUIDE: A TRANSLATION OF THE TWELFTH-CENTURY DISCIPLINA CLERICALIS of Pedro Alfonso, trans. by Joseph Ramon Jones and John Esten Keller. Copyright © 1969 by The Pontifical Institute of Mediaeval Studies, Toronto, Canada. Reprinted by permission of the publisher.

Alfonso X: "The Scorpions," trans. by Peter Dronke from THE MEDIEVAL LYRIC, third ed., by Peter Dronke (1996). Reprinted by permission of the publisher, Boydell & Brewer Ltd.

Apuleius: From THE GOLDEN ASS, trans. by P. G. Walsh (1999). By permission of Oxford University Press.

The Archpoet: "His Confession" from MEDIEVAL LATIN LYRICS by Helen Waddle (London: Constable, 1929). Reprinted by permission of Constable & Robinson Ltd.

Daniel Arnaut: "The Art of Love" from THE LYRICS OF THE TROUBADORS AND TROUVERES, trans. by Frederick Goldin, copyright © 1973 by Frederick Goldin. Used by permission of Doubleday, a division of Random House, Inc.

Fariddoddin Attar: From THE CONFERENCE OF BIRDS by Farid ud-din Attar, trans. with an introduction by Afkham Darbandi and Dick Davis (Penguin Classics 1984). Copyright © 1984 by Afkham Darbandi and Dick Davis. Reproduced by permission of Penguin Books Ltd.

Augustine: From CONFESSIONS, trans. F. J. Sheed. Copyright © 2006 by Hackett Publishing Company, Inc. Translation © 1942, 1943 by Sheed & Ward, Inc. Assigned to Hackett Publishing Company, Inc., in 1992. All rights reserved. Reprinted by permission of Hackett Publishing Company, Inc.

Avicenna: From ALLEGORY AND PHILOSPHY IN AVICENNA (IBN SINA) by Peter Heath. Copyright © 1992 by the University of Pennsylvania Press. Reprinted with permission of the University of Pennsylvania Press.

Avraham Ibn Ezra: "Elegy for a Son" from THE DREAM OF THE POEM: HEBREW POETRY FROM MUSLIM AND CHRISTIAN SPAIN, 950–1492, trans. and ed. by Peter Cole. Copyright © 2007 by Princeton University Press. Reprinted by permission of Princeton University Press.

Bana: Translations by Daniel H. Ingalls reprinted by permission of the publisher from AN ANTHOLOGY OF SANSKRIT COURT POETRY: VIDYAKARA'S SUBHSITARATNAKOSA (Harvard Oriental Series, 44). Cambridge, Mass.: Harvard University Press. Copyright © 1965 by the President and Fellows of Harvard College. Translation by Vinay Dharwadker from THE COLUMBIA BOOK OF SOUTH ASIAN POETRY to be published by Columbia University Press. Reprinted with permission of the publisher.

Beatrice of Dia: "A Lover's Prize," trans. by Peter Dronke from THE MEDIEVAL LYRIC, third ed., by Peter Dronke (1996). Reprinted by permission of the publisher Boydell & Brewer Ltd.

Beowulf: From BEOWULF, trans. by Seamus Heaney. Copyright © 2000 by Seamus Heaney. Used by permission of W. W. Norton & Company, Inc.

Bhartrhari: Translations by Vinay Dharwadker from THE COLUMBIA BOOK OF SOUTH ASIAN POETRY to be published by Columbia University Press. Reprinted with permission of the publisher.

Bhavabhūtī: Translation by Daniel H. Ingalls reprinted by permission of the publisher from AN ANTHOLOGY OF SANSKRIT COURT POETRY: VIDYAKARA'S SUBHSITARATNAKOSA (Harvard Oriental Series, 44). Cambridge, Mass.: Harvard University Press. Copyright © 1965 by the President and Fellows of Harvard College. Translations by Vinay Dharwadker from THE COLUMBIA BOOK OF SOUTH ASIAN POETRY to be published by Columbia University Press. Reprinted with permission of the publisher.

Bhāvakadevī: Reprinted by permission of the publisher from AN ANTHOLOGY OF SANSKRIT COURT POETRY: VIDYAKARA'S SUBHSITARATNAKOSA, trans. by Daniel H. Ingalls (Harvard Oriental Series, 44). Cambridge, Mass.: Harvard University Press. Copyright © 1965 by the President and Fellows of Harvard College.

Bo Juyi: "The Song of Lasting Regret," trans. by Paul W. Kroll from THE COLUMBIA ANTHOLOGY OF TRADITIONAL CHINESE LITERATURE, ed. Victor H. Mair. Copyright © 1994 Columbia University Press. Reprinted with permission of the publisher. "[Chen Hong, An Account to Go with the 'Song of Lasting Pain']," "Salt Merchant's Wife (in hatred of profiteers)" and "On My Portrait" from AN ANTHOLOGY OF CHINESE LITERATURE: BEGINNINGS TO 1911, ed. and trans. by

Guido Guinizzelli: "Love and Nobility," trans. by James J. Wilhelm from LYRICS OF THE MIDDLE AGES: AN ANTHOLOGY, ed. by James. J. Wilhelm. Copyright © 1990 by James J. Wilhelm. Reproduced by permission of Taylor and Francis Group, LLC, a division of Informa plc.

Hadewijch of Brabant: "The Cult of Love," trans. by Peter Dronke from THE MEDIEVAL LYRIC, third ed., by Peter Dronke (1996). Reprinted by permission of the publisher, Boydell & Brewer Ltd.

Hafez: Poems from THE FACES OF LOVE: HAFEZ AND THE POETS OF SHIRAZ by Dick Davis. Copyright © 2008–2012. Reprinted by permission of Mage Publishers, www.mage.com.

Yehuda Halevi: "To Ibn al-Mu'allim" and "Lord" from THE DREAM OF THE POEM: HEBREW POETRY FROM MUSLIM AND CHRISTIAN SPAIN 950–1492, trans. and ed. by Peter Cole. Copyright © 2007 by Princeton University Press. Reprinted by permission of Princeton University Press.

Han Shan: "In my first thirty years of life" and "Men ask the way to Cold Mountain" from RIPRAP AND COLD MOUNTAIN POEMS by Gary Snyder. Copyright © 1965 by Gary Snyder. Reprinted by permission of Counterpoint. "I longed to visit the eastern cliff" and "On Cold Mountain there's a naked bug," trans. by Red Pine from THE COLLECTED SONGS OF COLD MOUNTAIN, rev. and expanded. Copyright © 2000 by Bill Porter. Reprinted with the permission of Copper Canon Press, www.coppercanyonpress.org. "Whoever reads my poems" is reprinted by permission from THE POETRY OF HAN-SHAN, ed. by Robert G. Henricks, the State University of New York Press, © 1990, State University of New York. All rights reserved. Poems translated by Burton Watson from COLD MOUNTAIN: 100 POEMS BY THE T'ANG POET HAN-SHAN. Copyright © 1970 by Columbia University Press. Reprinted by permission of the publisher.

Han Yu: "The Biography of Tipp O'Hair," trans. by Elling Eide from T'ang Studies, 8–9 (1990–91): 108–11. Reprinted by permission of the T'ang Studies Society.

Hildegard of Bingen: "Responsory for the Virgin" from SYMPHONIA: A CRITICAL EDITION OF THE 'SYMPHONIA ARMONIE CELESTIUM REVELATIONUM,' second edition, with an introduction, translations, and commentary by Barbara Newman. Copyright © 1988, 1998 by Cornell University. Used by permission of the publisher, Cornell University Press.

Muhyiddin Ibn 'Arabi: "Gentle Now, Doves" from STATIONS OF DESIRE: LOVE ELEGIES FROM IBN 'ARABI AND NEW POEMS, trans. by Michael A. Sells, copyright © 2000 by Michael A. Sells. Reprinted by permission of the publisher, IBIS Editions.

Ibn Battuta: From TRAVELS IN ASIA AND AFRICA 1325–1354, trans. by H. A. R. Gibb. Copyright © 1929 George Routledge & Sons. Reproduced by permission of Taylor & Francis Books UK.

Ibn Ishaq: Excerpts from THE BIOGRAPHY OF THE PROPHET: THE LIFE OF MUHAMMAD with introduction and notes by A. Guillame. Reprinted by permission of Oxford University Press.

Ibn Zaydun: From "Al-Zahra" from ANDALUSIAN POEMS, trans. by Christopher Middleton and Leticia Garza-Falcon (David R. Godine, Publisher, Inc. 1993). Reprinted by permission of J. C. Middleton.

Jahan Khatun: "Heart, In His Beauty's Garden" from THE FACES OF LOVE: HAFEZ AND THE POETS OF SHIRAZ by Dick Davis. Copyright © 2008–2012. Reprinted by permission of Mage Publishers, www.mage.com.

Kālidāsa: "Śakuntala and the Ring of Recollection," trans. by Barbara Stoler Miller from THEATER OF MEMORY: THE PLAYS OF KĀLIDĀSA, ed. by Barbara Stoler Miller. Copyright © 1984 by Columbia University Press. Reprinted by permission of the publisher.

Kamo no Chōmei: "Account of My Ten-Foot-Square Hut," trans. by Anthony Chambers from TRADITIONAL JAPANESE LITERATURE: AN ANTHOLOGY, BEGINNINGS TO 1600. Copyright © 2006 by Columbia University Press. Reprinted by permission of the publisher.

Ki no Tsurayuki: "Kanajo," "The Japanese Preface" by Ki no Tsurayuki, trans. by Laurel Rasplica Rodd from KOKINSHU: A COLLECTION OF POEMS ANCIENT AND MODERN, trans. and annotated by Laurel Rasplica Rodd with Mary Catherine Henkenius, copyright © 1996 by Cheng & Tsui Company, Inc. Used by permission of Cheng & Tsui Company, Inc. "Tosa Diary," trans. by Gustav Heldt, from TRADITIONAL JAPANESE LITERATURE, ed. by Haruo Shirane. Copyright © 2007 by Columbia University Press. Reprinted by permission of the publisher.

Kokinshū: Poems 23–27 translated by Lewis Cook are reprinted by permission of the translator. Poems from A WAKA ANTHOLOGY: Vol. 2 THE GEM-GLISTENING CUP by Edwin Cranston. Copyright © 1993 by the Board of Poems from A WAKA ANTHOLOGY: GRASSES OF REMEMBRANCE by Edwin Cranston. Copyright © 2006 by the Board of Trustees of the Leland Stanford Jr. University. All rights reserved. Used with the permission of Stanford University Press, www.sup.org. Translation by Edwin Cranston of 118 first appeared in "The Dark Path: Images of Longing in Japanese Love Poetry" in the Harvard Journal of Asiatic Studies 35 (1975): 60–100. Poems from TRADITIONAL JAPANESE LITERATURE, trans. by Lewis Cook, ed. by Haruo Shirane, copyright © 2007 by Columbia University Press. Reprinted by permission of the publisher.

"Kshemendra," from Kavikanthabharana, trans. by W. S. Merwin. Copyright © 1998 by W. S. Merwin. Used by permission of the The Wylie Agency LLC.

Li Bo: "The Hardships of Traveling the Road, I" and "Seeing Off Meng Haoran at Yellow Crane Tower, on His Way to Guangling," trans. by Paul W. Kroll, reprinted by permission of Paul W. Kroll.

Jaloloddin Rumi: "Dissolver of Sugar," "The Question," and "An Empty Garlic" from OPEN SECRET: VERSIONS OF RUMI, trans. by John Moyne and Coleman Barks. Reprinted by permission of Coleman Barks. "Only Breath" from THE ESSENTIAL RUMI, trans. by Coleman Barks, with John Moyne. Copyright © by Coleman Barks. Reprinted by permission of Coleman Barks.

Shem Tov Ardutiel: From "The Battle of the Pen and Scissors" from THE DREAM OF THE POEM: HEBREW POETRY FROM MUSLIM AND CHRISTIAN SPAIN 950–1492, trans. and ed. by Peter Cole. Copyright © 2007 by Princeton University Press. Reprinted by permission of Princeton University Press.

Sei Shōnagon: From THE PILLOW BOOK, trans. by Meredith McKinney (Penguin Classics 2006). Copyright © 2006 by Meredith McKinney. Reproduced by permission of Penguin Books Ltd.

Sir Gawain and the Green Knight: Trans. by Simon Armitage. Copyright © 2007 by Simon Armitage. Used by permission of W. W. Norton & Company, Inc., and Faber & Faber Ltd.

Somadeva: "The Red Lotus of Chastity" from TALES OF ANCIENT INDIA, trans. by J. A. B. van Buitenen. Copyright © 1959 by the University of Chicago. Reprinted by permission of the University of Chicago Press.

Song of Roland: From THE SONG OF ROLAND, trans. by Frederick Goldin. Copyright © 1978 by W. W. Norton & Company, Inc. Used by permission of W. W. Norton & Company, Inc.

Song of Summer: From THE CAMBRIDGE SONGS ed. and trans. by Jan M. Ziolkowksi. Copyright © 1998 by Jan Ziolkowski. Reprinted by permission of Medieval Renaissance Text and Studies and the translator.

Tales of the Heike: From TALES OF THE HEIKE, trans. by Burton Watson, ed. by Haruo Shirane. Copyright © 2005 by Columbia University Press. Reprinted with permission of the publisher.

Tao Qian: "Biography of Master Five Willows" is reprinted by permission of the publisher from REMEMBRANCES: THE EXPERIENCE OF THE PAST IN CLASSICAL CHINESE LITERATURE by Stephen Owen. Cambridge, Mass.: Harvard University Press. Copyright © 1986 by the President and Fellows of Harvard College. Poems from THE POETRY OF T'AO CH'IEN, trans. by James Robert Hightower (1970) are reprinted by permission of Oxford University Press.

The Thousand and One Nights: From THE ARABIAN NIGHTS: THE THOUSAND AND ONE NIGHTS, trans. by Husain Haddawy. Copyright © 1990 by W. W. Norton & Company, Inc. Used by permission of W. W. Norton & Company, Inc. [The Third Old Man's Tale], trans. by Jerome W. Clinton, is reprinted by permission of the translator.

Vidyā: Reprinted by permission of the publisher from AN ANTHOLOGY OF SANSKRIT COURT POETRY: VIDYAKARA'S SUBHSITARATNAKOSA, trans. by Daniel H. Ingalls (Harvard Oriental Series, 44). Cambridge, Mass.: Harvard University Press. Copyright © 1965 by the President and Fellows of Harvard College.

Vikatanitamba: Reprinted by permission of the publisher from AN ANTHOLOGY OF SANSKRIT COURT POETRY: VIDYAKARA'S SUBHSITARATNAKOSA, trans. by Daniel H. Ingalls (Harvard Oriental Series, 44). Cambridge, Mass.: Harvard University Press. Copyright © 1965 by the President and Fellows of Harvard College.

Viṣṇuśarman: Selections from THE PAÑCATANTRA, trans. Arthur W. Ryder. Copyright © 1925 by the University of Chicago; renewed 1953 by Mary E. and Winifred Ryder. Reprinted by permission of the University of Chicago Press.

Walther von der Vogelweide: "Dancing Girl," trans. by Peter Dronke from THE MEDIEVAL LYRIC, third ed., by Peter Dronke (1996). Reprinted by permission of the publisher, Boydell & Brewer Ltd.

Heinrich von Morungen: "The Wound of Love," trans. by Peter Dronke from THE MEDIEVAL LYRIC, third ed., by Peter Dronke (1996). Reprinted by permission of the publisher, Boydell & Brewer Ltd.

Wang Wei: From THE POETRY OF WANG WEI, trans. by Pauline Yu. Copyright © 1980 by Pauline Ruth Yu. Reprinted with permission of Indiana University Press.

Wang Xizhi: "Preface to the Orchid Pavilion Poems" from AN ANTHOLOGY OF CHINESE LITERATURE: BEGINNINGS TO 1911, ed. and trans. by Stephen Owen. Copyright © 1996 by Stephen Owen and the Council for Cultural Planning and Development of the Executive Yuan of the Republic of China. Used by permission of W. W. Norton & Company, Inc.

Yogeśvara: Reprinted by permission of the publisher from AN ANTHOLOGY OF SANSKRIT COURT POETRY: VIDYAKARA'S SUBHSITARATNAKOSA, trans. by Daniel H. Ingalls (Harvard Oriental Series, 44). Cambridge, Mass.: Harvard University Press. Copyright © 1965 by the President and Fellows of Harvard College.

Yoshida Kenkō: From ESSAYS IN IDLENESS: THE TSUREZUREGUSA OF KENKŌ, trans. by Donald Keene. Preface copyright © 1998 by Donald Keene. Copyright © 1967 Columbia University Press. Reprinted by permission of the publisher.

Yuan Zhen: "The Story of Ying-ying," trans. by James R. Hightower, from TRADITIONAL CHINESE STORIES: THEMES AND VARIATIONS, edited by Y. W. Ma and Joseph S. M. Lau. Copyright © 1978 by Columbia University Press. Reprinted by permission of Joseph S. M. Lau.

IMAGES

2–3 bpk, Berlin / Bodleian Library, Oxford UK / Hermann Buresch. / Art Resource, NY; 4 Giraudon / Art Resource, NY; 5 Erich Lessing / Art Resource, NY; 10 SSPL/Science Museum / Art Resource, NY; 14 Wikimedia Commons; 15 HIP / Art Resource, NY; 314 Art Resource, NY; 836–37 Art Resource, NY; 841 Borromeo / Art Resource, NY; 844 © Rubin Museum of Art / Art Resource, NY; 696 © The Metropolitan Museum of Art / Art Resource, NY; 808 © 2011 The British Library; 971 Allen Lee Taylor / Getty Images; 973 HIP / Art Resource, NY; 978 Erich Lessing / Art Resource, NY; 988 © The Metropolitan Museum of Art / Art Resource, NY; 1073 © Corbis; 1076 Sakamoto Photo Research Laboratory / Corbis; 1078 Wikimedia Commons; 1081 Burstein Collection/Corbis; 1156 The Art Archive / Private Collection Paris / Gianni Dagli Orti.

COLOR INSERT

Ibe Ezra. Scala / Art Resource; Diamond Sutra. HIP / Art Resource; Koran fragment. bpk, Berlin / Art Resource, NY; Text from *Beowulf*. HIP / Art Resource, NY; Servants at Work. Burstein Collection / Corbis; Page from Gutenberg's Bible. Lebrecht Music & Arts / Corbis; The Printer's Workshop. The Trustees of the British Museum / Art Resource; Nushirvan Receives an Embassy. LACMA / Art Resource, NY.

Index